THE COMPLETE EVELYN MAYNARD TRILOGY

KAYDENCE SNOW

Cover design by Mila Book Covers
Editing by Kirstin Andrews
kaydencesnow.com
Formatted by AB Formatting & Design

VARIANT LOST

THE EVELYN MAYNARD TRILOGY
PART ONE

BY KAYDENCE SNOW

ONE

I looked down at my watch: two minutes past midnight. It was officially my seventeenth birthday.

In the uncomfortable plastic seat next to me, my mother, Joyce, saw me checking the time. She kept her voice low as she reached for my arm. "Happy birthday, Evie."

"Don't," I grumbled and pulled my arm out of her reach.

She sighed and sat up straighter. To the casual observer she looked completely calm, sitting in the departures lounge at gate twelve at Melbourne Airport, her hands folded gently in her lap. It was a well-practiced mask—she was on high alert. We were sitting in seats with a wall at our backs as she scanned the airport every few seconds. Her oversized handbag was still slung over her shoulder, just like mine, in case we needed to move fast.

I bit down on my tongue to stop myself from crying. I was trying to be as alert as she was, but I kept thinking about the reason *why* we were at the airport, waiting to board a flight to Los Angeles with tickets purchased only hours before and new counterfeit passports tucked into our bags. I had committed a cardinal sin in my mother's eyes: I had made friends and got myself a boyfriend.

Naturally, we had to change our names and leave the country.

Ever since I could remember, my mother and I had been running, never staying in one place for longer than a few months, never getting close to other people. I was used to this routine, but this time I was more than just frustrated with having to start at another new school and memorize another new name. This time, for the first time, I was actually leaving something behind.

A flash of movement caught my attention and my mother stiffened, but she relaxed when she realized it was just a Variant, rushing through the airport at superhuman speed. The man in a suit had a panicked look on his face as he used his ability to get to his gate on time.

He was one of the approximately 18 percent of the world's population lucky enough to have Variant DNA, but his ability was a common one. I was just a boring human, a fact my mother was eternally grateful for, as it made it easier for us to blend in.

A painfully polite female voice came through the speakers: "Ladies and gentlemen, Qantas flight QF83 to Los Angeles will begin boarding shortly."

I tuned her out. I had taken more flights in my seventeen years than most people did their entire lives. I knew the boarding procedures better than half the ground staff.

I knew many things your average teenager didn't.

Instead of explaining the reasons behind our nomadic lifestyle, my mother had taught me how to be invisible. I knew to place myself near an exit in every building. I knew how to spot a person or vehicle that was following me and how to lose them. I knew how to completely wipe the memory of any electronic device. I knew how to forge official documents.

I knew everything except what I actually wanted to know—*why?*

I *didn't* know why my mother chose the places we went to over the years, zigzagging from one continent to the next. Until now, whenever I'd suggested America, she'd shut me down with a firm "no," but all of a sudden we were on our way to LA, and from there to Nampa, Idaho—a very specific location that I suspected was chosen very randomly.

Whatever the reason Joyce had chosen Nampa, the first leg of our journey was about to begin. Boarding had started.

With another surreptitious look around the airport, my mother placed herself behind me as we joined the line, shielding me from some unspoken potential threat. I rolled my eyes at her and faced the front as her dark blue eyes narrowed in exasperation.

 I had the same eyes—dark blue—and just like her, you could see the blue in them only in natural light. I had her thick chocolate-brown hair too, but hers was cut short, and mine reached the middle of my back, falling in soft waves.

I was also just as stubborn. In a display of this trait, I crossed my arms over my chest and stared at my feet, concentrating on the swirls of little double helixes that littered my DNA socks. The machine ahead beeped rhythmically as the attendants scanned boarding passes, and I shuffled forward, wondering how such a great day had managed to turn to absolute shit in a matter of hours.

We had lived in Fitzroy, one of the most hipster suburbs of Melbourne, Australia, for almost eight months. Our moves hadn't been quite as frequent for the past few years. I was a teenager—moody, hormonal, and antisocial—which made it easier for my mother to prevent me from getting too close to anyone.

It's so much easier to make a friend at six than it is at sixteen. *Want to be my friend? OK!*—done deal. By the time you're in your teens, people have established friendships and years of shared experiences, and you're more aware of what others think of you. No one wants to disturb the delicate balance of their already angst-ridden existence by befriending the new girl.

Also, I had given up. With our next move always around the corner, I'd learned to make superficial conversation, seem friendly with a few people, but never truly get to know anyone.

Imagine my surprise when I not only made friends in Fitzroy but also got a boyfriend.

Somehow, Harvey Blackburn and his sister managed to weave their way into my solitary life. It happened slowly, over many weeks—sitting together in class, then at lunch, then chatting online. Then, somehow, Harvey and I were "a thing." I'd been on a few secret dates before, but none had gotten as close as Harvey. Harvey was the first of many things for me.

But even with the very first friends I'd ever made, I never spoke about our strange lifestyle in any detail, and I changed the topic when asked directly. I never invited them over. I rarely met with them outside of school, and then only when I was sure my mother was at work. I had to be careful. I burned to tell my mom about my first boyfriend, but I kept my mouth shut.

I'd been good at keeping my two lives separate, until earlier today.

Harvey, knowing he wouldn't be seeing me on my actual birthday, had pulled me around the corner of the English classroom and presented me with a small gift box, his warm chocolate eyes sparkling with excitement. Inside was a charm bracelet with a heart charm attached.

I had never been given a gift from anyone but my mother. I was elated, and I slipped.

I forgot to take the bracelet off and hide it before going home. As if she was looking for evidence of my treachery, my mother spotted it as soon as I walked into the house. She came out of the kitchen, her eyes homing in on the offending jewelry.

I replayed the scene in my mind—my mother wiping her hands on a tea towel, her greeting catching in her throat as the smile fell from her face, the cold look in her eyes, the fear in her voice as she quietly asked, "What have you done, Evelyn?"

"*Miss?*"

We'd reached the front of the line. The attendant was looking at me expectantly, her palm outstretched. My mom nudged me.

I shook her hand off my shoulder and darted forward, passport and boarding pass in hand. "Sorry," I muttered.

The lady gave me a tight smile, scanned the boarding pass, and checked my fake passport with the efficiency of an often-repeated task. She didn't even hesitate before handing them back, and my heart sank yet again. A big part of me had hoped she would notice it was a fake and we would be forced to stay. The forgery was very good though; she had no idea. No one ever did.

I didn't return her smile as I moved past. Pausing as she repeated the process with my mother, I looked longingly back in the direction of the exit. I imagined myself pushing past the remaining passengers waiting to board and making a run for it, catching a taxi straight to Harvey's house.

It was a stupid fantasy.

With a shuddering breath, I followed my mother as she took the lead up the narrow corridor toward the aircraft. There was no going back for us—we never returned to any place we had previously lived in.

When I was younger, I used to cry and ask why I didn't have friends and why I didn't have a dad. As I got older, my questions became more specific. I asked why we couldn't stay anywhere for longer than a few months, why we couldn't use our real names, what or who we were running from in the first place.

My mother did her best to explain things to me without actually giving me any answers. It always came back to her fervent declarations that everything she ever did was for me. Her vague explanations just weren't enough for me anymore.

We trudged up the narrow aisle of the plane to our seats. I settled into the window seat, buckled my seatbelt, and turned away as my mother lowered herself into the seat beside me.

She sighed deeply and leaned over me, but she didn't touch me. "I'm so sorry, Evie . . ."

At least, for once, she wasn't making excuses. I glued my attention to the people in safety vests bustling about on the ground below. She had said those same words, but with a decidedly less gentle tone, only hours before.

We had spent the evening fighting, crying, and packing. As she'd yanked open drawers and shoved clothes into a bag, my mother had admonished me again. "How could you be so careless, Evelyn?"

"Careless?" I was sitting in the middle of the bed, refusing to participate in the packing. "I made some friends and got a boyfriend. And I didn't tell them anything!" I almost screeched in frustration, angry tears rolling down my red cheeks.

"I'm sorry, but that's just not good enough," she spat, not sounding sorry at all. She held her hands out, a bundle of clothing in each one, before letting them flop to her sides. "It would only be a matter of time before you slipped. That's what getting close to people does—it makes you let your guard down, and you tell them things about yourself. Deep, important things."

"What things?" I yelled as she resumed stuffing our belongings haphazardly into bags. "How could I tell them anything when I don't *know* anything?"

"We do not have time to have this argument again. We're leaving in twenty minutes. Anything you don't pack will be left behind."

We stared each other down, both of us breathing hard, both of us stubborn in our silence.

Finally, her shoulders slumped. "Please, Evie," she said quietly. Her wide eyes were pleading, and her hands had begun to shake. She was no longer mad at me; now she was just scared.

I was still mad at *her*, but I caved in and reluctantly got ready to leave. Again.

I didn't even get to say goodbye to my friends, to hug them tightly and say I'd never forget them. I'd tried to send a quick message to Harvey before my mother had burst into the room and confiscated my phone, wiping it clean and destroying the sim card.

The pilot's voice coming through the intercom as we taxied snapped me back into the present. "Welcome aboard flight QF83. My name is Bob Wheeler, and I'll be your captain today. Sitting next to me is Andy Cox, your copilot. Andy is a Variant with an ability to control the weather, so I'm pleased to let you know that we can guarantee a turbulence-free flight tonight."

He continued to deliver the usual speech introducing the flight crew, but my mind was momentarily distracted, even from my ire at my mom. I had never met a Variant with an ability to control the weather, and I itched to research the science behind how it was possible, the impact it might have on weather patterns, the physics behind it all.

Science still didn't fully understand the Light—the energy that fueled Variant abilities and made it possible for people to control the weather, run faster than a Maserati, or read minds. It was a fascinating area of study. All sense of social propriety went out the window whenever I realized I was speaking to a Variant, and I would start firing all kinds of inappropriate and intrusive questions, my curiosity getting the better of me. I burned to ask the copilot how his ability worked, but I was strapped into an economy seat and had no way of making that happen. My mind returned to my previous miserable thoughts, and I slumped back with a sigh.

"That's an interesting Variant ability," Joyce piped up beside me.

I grunted and went back to looking out the window. She was making an effort, but I wasn't ready to let go of my resentment.

The plane took off, and everyone settled into the routine of a long-haul flight. My mother attempted to make conversation with me a few more times before finally giving up with a frustrated huff. I was determined to maintain my simmering outrage at how she had ruined my life, and I sulked, staring out at the pitch-black sky, forty thousand feet above the ground.

We were halfway across the Pacific Ocean when the plane crashed.

There was no warning—no time for anyone to wonder what was happening, get scared, hold each other. One minute we were gliding through the air, the next there was a loud *bang*, the plane lurched sideways, and we were plummeting.

I reached for my mother at the same time she reached for me, and we grasped each other's hands as our eyes met, wide with fear. There was no opportunity to say anything. No time to tell her the two simple things that actually needed to be said—*I'm sorry. I love you.*

A terrible metallic sound scraped against my ears, and then her hand was violently ripped out of mine, her mouth forming an O as she disappeared into darkness. The back of the plane had completely separated from the rest of it, as if a giant had torn it apart like a loaf of bread.

I stared at the emptiness next to my seat. There was the floor of the plane, there was my foot in my DNA sock (the shoe was gone), and there was the jagged line where the metal and wires and fabric had come apart, right between her seat and mine.

Beyond that there was nothing. Darkness.

We were still falling. People were screaming over the deafening whistle of rushing air as various items flew by me and out of the gaping hole through which my mother had disappeared. I focused on the jagged, torn edge of the plane, a piece of the carpet flapping furiously in the wind. My mother, my only family, was gone—probably dead. My mind couldn't process it, so instead, it helpfully supplied relevant statistics.

Statistically speaking, flying is the safest mode of transport.

The odds of a plane crashing are one in 1.2 million.

The odds of actually dying in a plane crash are closer to one in eleven million.

By comparison, the odds of dying in a car accident are about one in five thousand.

Just my luck that I would be on that one in 1.2 million flights.

As we plunged through the dark, I considered another number—2,130. The last time I had checked the in-flight information screen, that's about how many miles we were from Hawaii. I had calculated the distance, as it was the nearest land with things like hospitals and emergency response teams. Assuming the pilot had sent a distress call, it would be hours before anyone could get to us—if I even survived the crash in the first place.

I don't remember hitting the water. I remember the flapping piece of carpet by my feet, and I remember that useless information running through my head, but I have no recollection of the impact. After that is just disjointed flashes of memory.

The water was freezing cold. It felt like spikes of ice, all piercing my skin at the same time in a million different spots. People were shouting. Not many—nowhere near as many as were on the plane. I wore a life jacket. When had I put that on? Something was burning furious and bright nearby. I wanted to go closer to the heat, but I couldn't move. I couldn't do anything but shiver.

The fire was still there, but it had calmed down significantly. Like the embers of a campfire. No one was shouting anymore. The water rippled gently in front of me, calm and black like tar—impenetrable. I couldn't see even an inch past its surface. I couldn't feel my arms or my legs.

A light. Was it the fire? No, that had gone out a long time ago. It tinged the darkness. Violet. Dawn was coming. But that wasn't right either. This light was sharp, focused, and moving. There was a sound too—a loud whooshing from above. The water in front of my face rippled from the wind created by the helicopter blades. Helicopter! I had to look up, shout, wave, do something so they didn't leave.

I was being lifted into the light, but I was still cold and wet and I still couldn't feel my legs. The light wasn't warm and welcoming. It was harsh and bright, and the loud whooshing overwhelmed me. Someone lifted me from behind. An arm wrapped around my middle, holding me steady. The water seemed really far away now.

It was loud inside the helicopter. I was being jostled where I lay, tied down with something over my chest and hips. I couldn't see. My eyes were closed, and I didn't know how to open them. Voices shouted over the helicopter engine, only snippets of conversation.

". . . only survivors? Are you positive?"

"Yes." A firm "yes." His voice was clear, close. Strong and masculine, but smooth like warm honey. "We searched the whole area. Only her and the copilot. I don't know how she even survived. She was in the water so long."

Then a sliding sound and a third voice, farther away. ". . . in touch with her people . . . never got on the flight . . . last minute change of schedule . . . good intel, but can't predict . . ."

A hand landed on my calf. The man with the honey voice. I knew it belonged to him, but I didn't know how. It was good that I could feel my legs again.

~

When I woke up in the hospital, I had been asleep for nearly two days, but I didn't know it at the time. They told me all of it later. Nurses and doctors piled into my room, marveling at the lack of permanent injury and my fast recovery. Variants were more resilient against injury and faster to recover, but I, as someone who was only human, was lucky to have survived, or so the doctors kept saying. I didn't feel lucky.

No. When I first woke up, it was only for a few moments. The sounds came first: the soft thrum of machines, a quiet beeping, muffled voices. Then I felt the soft blankets and pillows under me.

I managed to lift my heavy eyelids and found myself looking up at those corkboard squares that make up the ceilings of hospitals and office buildings. The fluorescent light was off, but it was still very bright in the room. It must have been morning.

I angled my head down and scanned the space. There was a door on my left and a window on my right, a hospital tray on wheels under it. In the corner, next to the window, was a chair. A man was sitting in it.

I could tell it was a man by the broad set of his shoulders, the muscles in his tattooed forearms. His elbows rested on his knees, and his head was in his hands. He had dark hair and a buzz cut. His fingers were digging into his scalp; I had a feeling that if he had more hair, he would be pulling at it. He was dressed in black: black boots planted firmly on the floor, black pants, and a black T-shirt.

I tried to speak, but all I managed was a straggled inhale. It was enough to get his attention anyway. His head snapped up. He looked young, maybe in his twenties, but the look in his intense eyes gave me the impression that he had lived a thousand lifetimes while he'd sat in that ugly hospital chair. He had a five o'clock shadow covering his strong jaw and shocking ice-blue eyes. They pierced me, as the frigid water had pierced me.

"You're awake." I don't think he meant to say it out loud. It just came out on a breath. And then he was on his feet and next to my bed, leaning over me.

He reached a hand out as if to touch me and then pulled it back sharply. "I'll get a doctor." It was the man with the honey voice.

I was asleep again before he'd even left the room. The ice in his eyes was making me remember, and I couldn't handle it yet.

~

The next time I woke up, it didn't take me as long to gain consciousness.

I opened my eyes and lifted myself into a more comfortable position. I felt so much stronger than the first time, as if I didn't need to be in the hospital at all. It was dusk, the window on the right still letting in the fading light.

My eyes immediately went to the chair in the corner, but the room was empty, and for a second I wondered if I had hallucinated the man with the ice-blue eyes. Then I heard the tap turn on in the bathroom, and a moment later he walked out of it. He was still dressed in all black, but this time he wore a long-sleeved T-shirt, fitted enough to hint at the strong torso underneath. He was tall, his head nearly reaching the top of the doorframe.

As he turned, closing the door behind him, our eyes met. He paused for a second and then stepped up to the foot of my bed, resting one hand on the railing. He watched me with a neutral expression on his face. I watched him back, not feeling at all awkward about maintaining eye contact with a complete stranger for so long. A scar cut through the middle of his right eyebrow, and a black-and-gray tattoo was peeking out of the black fabric at his neck.

"How you feeling?" His voice was firm, forceful, but it still felt like honey washing over me.

My own voice was groggy, though clear enough in the silent room. "You pulled me out of the water." I didn't bother answering his question. It wasn't important at that moment.

"No. My colleague did. I pulled you into the chopper."

He wasn't going to insist I focus on my health, on getting better, on getting my strength up—all those empty things people insisted when they were trying to avoid speaking about the difficult things. The important things. *Good.*

"You sat with me. I could hear your voice. Even over the engine."

"Yes . . ." He looked away briefly before meeting my gaze again, letting the word trail off. As if he was going to add more but decided not to.

"Only the copilot and I made it. There were no other survivors?" I had to be sure. I had to hear someone say it.

"No." His answer was definitive, but his eyes narrowed slightly, wondering whom I was asking about. Whom I had lost.

I screwed my eyes shut, fisting the hospital sheets in my weak fingers.

My mother . . .

My mother was on the plane with me.

There were no other survivors.

She was not a survivor. She was . . . she . . .

"My mother." I opened my eyes as I said it.

His face fell when the two words left my mouth. He lifted his other hand to the railing of my bed and leaned heavily on the utilitarian gray plastic, hanging his head. He swore under his breath and started breathing hard.

Why was he so upset?

I had so many questions. *What happened? Why did the plane crash? How did no one else survive? Why did I make it? Why not her? How did you know where to search? Where am I? What's going to happen now? Who are you? Why are you still here? Why do you care?*

But I couldn't find it in me to care about the answers.

No. That one little word had confirmed what I had suspected since I'd first woken up, with a stranger sitting in the chair at my bedside instead of my mother.

I'd felt strong when I'd woken up a few moments earlier, but now I felt weak again. An awful pressure built in my chest, and a lump formed in my throat.

She was gone. Forever. I would never see my mother again. Never speak to her, hug her, argue with her. *Argue.* That was the last thing we'd done. She died thinking I was mad at her.

I was alone in the world. I was motherless. An orphan. I had felt lonely for much of my life, but whatever my mother's reasons were for keeping us distant from other people, she had always been there for me. She was the one constant in my life, the one person I could always rely on.

Yes, I had felt lonely in the past, but lying in that hospital bed with a stranger at my bedside, I truly knew what it meant to feel *alone.*

I'm alone.

Fat tears finally overflowed, and I wrapped my arms around my torso. I began to sob as I rolled onto my side toward the window, every muscle in my body taut with despair.

Boots squeaked across the linoleum, and then the thin hospital blanket was pulled over my shoulder. The bed behind me dipped, and his body pressed into mine from behind, his arm snaking around my front. He held me tight and I heard his voice, close to my ear.

"You are not alone."

I must have said that out loud. His declaration made me cry harder—ugly, unrestrained tears. Sobs wracked my body as I curled into a ball.

He held on to me through it all. We didn't touch, nowhere did our skin make contact, but he held me tight until my crying calmed down to soft sobs. He held me tight as the sobs gave way to silent tears pooling on the pillow. He held me tight as I drifted off into blissful unconsciousness again.

When I woke up the next morning, there was a nurse at the foot of my bed, writing something on a clipboard, and the stranger really was gone.

TWO

On the morning of my eighteenth birthday, I woke up half an hour before my alarm in a bed that didn't feel like mine. In a room that belonged to me but held none of my personality. In the life I had been living for the past year but still didn't fit into.

I didn't have that moment of bliss, those hazy few seconds when you don't know what day it is or what's going on. I opened my eyes and immediately knew it was my birthday; it had been exactly one year since my mother died.

I lay on my back and stared at the ceiling.

Swallowing hard around the thick lump in my throat, I just managed to stop myself from falling apart first thing in the morning. I had to keep going, be strong. It's what my mom would have wanted.

I tried to concentrate on something else, running through what my day looked like, but other than a chemistry quiz, there wasn't much noteworthy. My thoughts kept turning back to the moment my world had come crashing down as hard as the plane we were on. I rolled onto my side. Instead of getting lost in the memory of when I'd realized I was alone in the world, I forced myself to focus on what had happened *after*.

When the hospital in Hawaii released me, social services had decided it was best to send me on to the destination my mother had chosen for us. They couldn't have known she had randomly opened a map and pointed.

After a long boat ride and several trains and buses—because I refused to get on a plane—it was the Idaho social services who placed me in Nampa with Martha and Barry, or Marty and Baz, as they liked to be called. They were a nice enough couple in their fifties, semiretired and a little bored. Why not get a foster kid to spice things up a little? Unfortunately, I wasn't that exciting.

I had my own room, and as much as they encouraged me to make it mine, I couldn't bring myself to do it. I looked around at the twin bed, desk, and mostly empty wardrobe as I pulled the blanket tighter around my shoulders. I was still stuck in my old ways—not getting too comfortable, the next move always around the corner.

Marty and Baz made an effort to get to know me, to make me feel like part of the family. It wasn't their fault I didn't know how to be part of a family.

The alarm I hadn't needed went off, filling the impersonal room with a high-pitched beeping. I reached for my smartphone and turned it off. Sitting on the edge of my bed, I scratched at the tingling sensation at my wrists, willing my body to catch up with my mind and get moving.

I had bought the smartphone myself after selling some fake IDs, feeling too awkward to accept anything other than the basics—food and clothing—from my would-be parental figures. Marty and Baz had repeatedly offered to buy me more clothes, books, makeup, and other "normal teenage girl stuff." I refused, but one indulgence I did allow them to provide was journal subscriptions. I devoured scientific literature the way most teenage girls went through fashion magazines. I was top of my class in all my science and most of my math classes at school. I had subscriptions to *The American Statistician*, *Advances in Physics*, *New Scientist*, and a few others.

I got up from the bed only to sit back down at my desk, pushing an old issue of *New Scientist* out of the way. I turned on the ancient computer running Windows XP and waited impatiently for it to wake up. We both struggled a little to get going in the mornings.

While I waited for the geriatric tech to boot up, I stood and reached into the half-empty closet for an outfit. My eye caught on my mother's sundress with the big poppy flower print, and the lump in my throat reappeared.

If all it took to push me over the edge today was a glimpse of fabric, maybe I needed to skip school.

Not much had survived the plane crash. The crash investigation team had managed to recover some luggage, and the only salvageable items were a few photos and some clothes, including my mother's favorite summer dress. None of our documents were found. My mother's body, along with more than two hundred others, was also never found.

I got dressed in jeans and a loose sweater, consciously training my mind on how the cotton-poly blend aggravated the persistent itch at my wrists. The lump had receded, and I planted myself in front of the computer once again, giving my mind another distraction.

There were only two constants in my life now—science and my bordering-on-obsessive search for the honey-voiced stranger who had saved me in more ways than I could articulate.

I opened Tor—I only ever used the secure browser—and logged in to some of the forums I frequented, as well as checked a few non-mainstream sites for any news.

I hadn't even learned his name before he'd disappeared. I had tried asking the nurses and doctors when I woke up, but they couldn't give me any information on his identity. They just said he was part of the Melior Group rescue team who had brought me in. He had not spoken much to anyone but had been very interested in my progress and test results, ensuring I had the best care possible.

I didn't know much about the Melior Group at the time. I had heard of them, of course—the elite private security firm that employed Variants with rare abilities almost exclusively, had ties to Variant communities as well as mainstream law enforcement, and operated all over the world. Every high-profile Variant had a Melior Group bodyguard on the payroll, and governments often employed them to aid in peacekeeping, rescue missions, and other shadier things, I was sure. Things with words like *intelligence* and *dark ops* involved.

When the air crash investigators interviewed me, I did my best to get them to shed light on my stranger's identity. They wouldn't elaborate on why a Melior Group team had been sent out on a simple rescue mission for a civilian plane crash. The word *classified* was thrown around more than once.

I tried contacting Melior Group directly once I was settled in Nampa, but I hit a brick wall and more *classified*s. That's when I'd powered up the ancient computer and put my research skills to use. Unfortunately that wasn't getting me anywhere either. I was really getting sick of the word *classified*.

I was no closer to finding him now than I had been that first day in the hospital, but it had become a bit of an obsession. At some point I turned to shadier corners of the Internet, posting to forums, detailing my experience, and chatting to other people who'd had run-ins with Melior Group special teams. I was trying to find any link, no matter how tenuous, to someone else who may have crossed paths with him.

As with a complex mathematical problem or opaque scientific theory, the harder it was to puzzle out, the more determined I became to solve it.

But it wasn't just the challenge of it. The fact that the word *classified* had come up so often told me there was more than just a simple engine failure to blame for my mother's death. I had made it my mission to find out *why* my mom had lost her life. The stranger was my closest link to that information.

On a more emotional level, I *needed* to find him. The strength of my inexplicable pull to this man who had held me in my darkest hour frightened me a little. His team had saved me—they had pulled me out of the icy water and provided first aid—but my honey-voiced stranger had saved me on a much deeper level. He had stayed with me, cared for me, held me as I completely fell apart. Had I been alone when I woke up in that hospital, I don't think I would have had the strength to get better, to keep living my empty life. I was too emotionally wrecked to realize it at the time, but his presence had given me a tiny scrap to hold on to—a glimmer of hope that maybe I didn't have to be alone in the world.

Yes, I wanted to find the answers to all my questions surrounding my mom's death, but I also needed to look into his ice-blue eyes one more time and thank him for saving me.

The itching, which was spreading up my forearms, reminded me I needed to get to school, so I logged out and headed into the kitchen.

Marty was bustling about near the stove, her gray hair perfectly combed into a "fashionable" bob.

"Good morning!" She beamed at me over her shoulder, rushing to turn knobs and juggle pans. "You're up a little early, but it's good timing."

Marty was a morning person, always full of positive energy. I was not a morning person. Coffee would have helped, but even after living in the States for a whole year, I still couldn't get used to the filtered crap they drank.

I rubbed my temple and went to extract the milk from the fridge, trying to decide if Cap'n Crunch or Wheaties was a more anniversary-of-mother's-death kind of breakfast cereal. Marty stepped in front of me and smiled, holding a plate of pancakes in front of her.

"Happy birthday, kiddo," she said, much softer than I was used to hearing her speak. "I know this day is bittersweet for you, but hopefully this will help to make it just a little sweeter."

"Oh." I hadn't realized we were on birthday pancakes terms. "Thank you." My own voice was soft and, I hoped, genuine.

She gave me a little squeeze just above my elbow. Marty and Baz were not huggers, and for that at least, I was grateful.

I sat at the breakfast bar and ate my pancakes, Marty next to me with a large mug of American pond sludge coffee. They were delicious—Marty was a great cook—but they weren't my mom's.

Once again, grief threatened to pull me under. I choked down a mouthful of pancakes, eyes stinging as I stared down at the countertop.

Marty chatted about pointless things while I ate and tried really hard to stop myself from crying, then she left for work. Once I was alone, I took a few deep breaths, unable to finish the food.

I put the dishes in the dishwasher, slung my bag over my shoulder, and walked to school. It was the same route I had taken every day for the last year. The same boring suburban streets, the same cars, the same trees.

It took me a lazy twenty minutes to walk to Nampa High School. Students were milling about, trying to squeeze in every last second of free time before the first class. As I approached the low brick building, a brown-haired boy wearing a bomber jacket jogged over the grass to me.

"Hey, Eve!" He smiled. I had a feeling he was on the football team, but I couldn't remember his name. "Happy birthday."

How did he know? I wasn't exactly friends with anyone.

I didn't reply to his birthday wish. I simply stood there with a confused look on my face, so he filled the silence with his own voice. "Can I take you out for your birthday tonight? Or maybe tomorrow? Whenever you're free, really. I have the game next week, but other than that . . ." He looked at me expectantly.

Nameless football guy didn't actually want to take me out. He just wanted to get lucky.

When I'd first arrived in Nampa, I went through a brief promiscuous phase. I was doing whatever I could to ignore that my mother had died, so I fully embraced everything about high school life I couldn't have embraced with her around. I dated a lot, no one exclusively, and gained a bit of a reputation. On top of that, I could make *really* good fake IDs, and I suddenly had a whole crowd of people to distract myself with.

My sudden popularity didn't last long. Just as I couldn't settle into my new "home," I also couldn't find it in me to try to make friends. I had attempted to embrace my new freedom, but that was just it—this so-called freedom existed because my mother wasn't around anymore. I couldn't make myself give a shit about any of the trivial things I'd so desperately cared about before she died. Who cares about making friends when you've lost the only family you ever had?

I became a loner and only made time for my science and my mysterious stranger. Every once in a while, one of the boys would try to ask me out on another date. I always said no.

Football guy was still waiting for my response, but thinking about my rebellious months made me think about how my mother would have lost her shit if she'd known how careless I'd been. I didn't know what was more distracting or unwanted—the unbidden emotion or the persistent itchiness on my arms. I needed to get away from the linebacker before I had a very public emotional meltdown.

"My mother died one year ago today," I deadpanned.

I hadn't intended to say that, but the boy's reaction was proving enough of a distraction. He looked equal parts horrified and uncomfortable. As he opened his mouth to say something, I blinked once and walked past him into the school building. I preferred to let him think I was rude and odd than to have him see me cry.

The rest of the day passed without incident. With my mother's face constantly at the forefront of my mind, the sensation of her hand sliding out of mine achingly present on my skin, I went through the motions. I went to classes, ate lunch, aced the chemistry quiz, and did my best to avoid the other students. Word of my strange declaration to football guy spread, and before second period was over, I started getting weird looks. Thankfully, everyone gave me a wide berth.

By the end of the day, I was sick of all the passive attention, tired from constantly being on the lookout for the overwhelming grief that was becoming impossible to ignore. I just wanted to get back to Marty and Baz's and lose myself in an article or a school assignment.

The day had turned out to be beautiful, the afternoon sun warm enough that I could take my sweater off and walk home in just a tank top, but my foul mood wouldn't allow me to appreciate it. The itchy, tingly sensation had spread up my arms to my chest and was making itself infuriatingly known nearly all the way up my legs too. With a grunt of frustration, I picked up my pace and scratched at my arms, hoping I could stop myself from ripping the tank top off or sticking my hand down my pants in public.

This new development—bursts of itching—had started not long after I was settled with Marty and Baz, and it came with insane amounts of energy. Every week or two I would have more physical energy and more mental energy for study and reading. Occasionally I would stay awake all night, not feeling tired at all the next day. I took up running to try to manage it, pushing myself until I struggled to breathe. It was never painful, more like a persistent hum. A harmless kind of vibration throughout my body that made me insanely itchy and feel as if I were on cocaine. No biggie.

It always started out faint, as it had that morning—a tickle at my wrists and ankles—but if I ignored it for too long, the infuriating itchiness all over my body would have me removing layers of clothing, which would begin to feel like burlap.

I never mentioned this to Marty or Baz. I didn't want further inconvenience them, and I really couldn't complain about the extra study time. I read up on the symptoms, learning many new, very long words, and did my best to self-diagnose, monitoring my symptoms and vital signs closely. My extensive research suggested the extra energy was neither a symptom nor a cause of anything of concern.

Across the street, a girl in jogging gear was walking her Labradoodle, her face in her phone, reminding me that I was outside where anyone could see me scratching like a maniac. I extracted my hand from the waistband of my pants, where it was dangerously close to reaching a particularly itchy spot on my ass, and picked up my pace.

It made sense that the odd humming energy would rear its unpleasant head today. It wasn't as if anything good ever happened on my birthdays.

I used to think birthdays were special. Like any child, I used to look forward to the presents, the fuss, the cake. My mom had done her best to make it special, even if it was just the two of us celebrating. No matter what day of the week it fell on, she would call in sick for both of us, and we would spend the morning in bed watching TV and eating birthday pancakes. In the afternoon, we always went out and did something fun.

We used to pick up and move just before or after my birthdays too.

When I turned eight, we had just moved to Tokyo. We were in high spirits that afternoon. It was a new place, new streets to explore, exciting new food to try.

As we wandered around Shibuya intersection, the world exploded into chaos. People screaming and running, a loud *boom,* the smell of burning—something acrid with a harsh chemical smell to it. Mostly I remember the shared terror of everyone out on the street that day, so clear it was almost palpable.

Many people died. It made the news all over the world. My mother and I got away unscathed, but we left Tokyo that same afternoon. We didn't leave the country, but we went to another part of Japan—a smaller, quieter part. News of the tragedy in Tokyo made it there before we did.

That must have been the record. We were in Tokyo for five days before my mother decided it was time to leave. On my birthday.

That was one of the worst birthday incidents, last year notwithstanding, but there were other things.

Like the flood two days before my ninth birthday, when we were living in Vietnam, destroying most of our possessions. Or my mother getting mugged on the way to her night shift on my twelfth birthday, when we were living in Turkey. Or when we were living on the coast of Croatia and my mother woke me in the middle of the night, three days after my fourteenth birthday, whispering frantically to me that "they found us," sending a jolt of terror down my spine and spurring me into action.

It was after that birthday that I started paying more attention to the things she'd been teaching me, like digital footprints and falsifying documents.

I managed to make it to Marty and Baz's without scratching too much out in public, but I knew I was in for a sleepless night. When I walked into the house and shut the door, I breathed a big sigh of relief, scratching indulgently at my forearms, but I stopped quickly at the sound of movement in the living room. I'd been hoping to head straight to my room so I could change and go for a run, but I'd forgotten that Baz would be home.

"Hey, kiddo!" he boomed as I came around the corner. I didn't know why they both liked calling me "kiddo." It was as if they'd huddled together, deciding that a nickname would bring us closer, and chose "kiddo."

My real full name was Evelyn Maynard. That much, at least, my mother made sure I always knew. But I couldn't use that name. What would be the point of disappearing constantly if you kept popping up with the exact same name? Every time we had moved, we'd created documentation with new names. The last name would be completely new, but my first name was always some variation of a name beginning with E—Emma, Elle, Ebony, sometimes even Evelyn. That way, I could just tell kids my nickname was E, and it would be less confusing for me, easier to remember.

While living in Melbourne, we had created some new identification (we always had fresh identities ready to go), and I'd given myself the name Eve Blackburn. Harvey and I hadn't started dating yet, but I had a pretty big crush on him, so I created an identity with his last name.

It was the name I boarded the plane with, the name that was on the passenger manifest, the name that everyone in Nampa knew me by. It was the name that had followed me into my current life. That was Eve Blackburn's bed, Eve's room, Eve's house, her school and her life. No wonder Evelyn Maynard felt out of place there.

"Hey, Baz." I tried to smile at him, but even I could feel that it didn't reach my eyes.

"Happy birthday." Baz's smile was genuine, unlike mine, as he got out of his favorite chair. Baz was as gray as Marty and had sported an impressive handlebar mustache the entire time I'd known him.

"Thank you," I said to his back as he made his way into the kitchen.

"Want a snack?"

"No thanks. I'm just going to go for a run."

"Okie dokie."

I'd made it past the kitchen and into the hallway, dying to have another scratch, when he called out again. "Oh, by the way, you got a letter. Left it on your bed. Looks fancy." He smiled at me before his head disappeared behind the fridge door.

"OK. Thanks," I mumbled, confused. I never got mail. Who would be sending me letters? Who would be sending me *fancy* letters?

I softly closed the bedroom door. I couldn't help but be suspicious as I stared at the envelope. The fact that it had arrived on my birthday was enough to make me wary. Was this it? Was this the awful thing that would happen this year? What horrible news was within? Maybe there was anthrax inside?

I lowered myself to my knees, facing the bed, and dragged the envelope to the edge of the mattress, pinching one corner. It was A4 size, and the pale gray paper was thick under my fingers. It felt expensive. My current name, Eve Blackburn, and the address were printed in the middle, and there was a logo in the top corner, *BHI* in a distinctive font. I flipped it, but there was no return address.

Having gleaned all I could from examining the outside, I had no choice but to open it. Taking the Band-Aid approach, I tore it open as fast as I could. Inside were several booklets printed on glossy paper, and on top a letter addressed to me. The letterhead had the same logo and an elaboration of what the letters stood for—Bradford Hills Institute.

I read through the letter twice, reading slowly the second time to make sure I didn't miss anything or misconstrue the meaning. Bradford Hills Institute—the most exclusive educational facility in the country—was offering me a full scholarship to study any scientific field of my choosing at a tertiary level. The school year was not finished yet—I still had a few months of high school to go—but because of their unique approach to learning, they weren't concerned with a high school diploma and wanted me to start classes as soon as possible. A spot had recently opened up, and they were offering it to me.

Apparently they had been keeping an eye on me and were impressed with my grades and my approach to study. I had no idea they had even been speaking to my teachers.

I sat on the floor and stared at the letter for several minutes. Less than half an hour ago, I'd been walking back from school thinking about how awful things always happened around my birthday, yet there I was—holding in my hands something that made me so excited I almost forgot what day it was. It was an opportunity to start yet another new life. In New York, no less!

Maybe it was my own morbid curiosity, a need to see what the universe had in store for my birthday this year, or maybe I'd simply gotten used to moving, and some subconscious, impatient part of me was nudging me to move on, but I knew I wanted to go.

After the shock wore off, I called the number at the bottom of the letter and said yes to Bradford Hills.

I spoke for about an hour to Stacey from admissions, and she explained how it would all work, answered the few questions my frazzled mind remembered to ask, and told me she could book my plane ticket the very next day if I was ready. I said yes. I was saying yes to everything, and it had my heart hammering a million miles an hour.

Marty got home from water aerobics as I was finishing my phone call, and I sat her and Baz down to tell them the news. They were both very excited for me and very impressed. Bradford Hills Institute was exclusive, but it was well-known. Apart from being an educational institute, they did research in many fields, especially around Variants, and they specialized in teaching young Variants to control and manage their abilities. As a result, Bradford Hills had a higher population of students with Variant DNA. For a human to be accepted, their academic performance had to be exceptional. I had no idea what they had seen in me, but I wasn't about to question them on it.

After an intense run, I spent the rest of the night packing and researching Bradford Hills on the Internet. I barely noticed the itchiness as I crawled into bed around three in the morning, hoping the excitement had allowed me to expel enough energy to get a few hours' sleep before my flight.

What I didn't count on was the overwhelming wave of emotions I'd been avoiding all day hitting me as soon as I turned the light out. The grief and pain I had worked so hard to push down finally washed over me as I lay in the bed that, come tomorrow, I would no longer need to pretend was mine.

Nothing could remind me of my mother as much as packing up and starting over. There were no fake passports or rushed dashes to the airport, but I was moving on nonetheless. I was about to do something we had been doing together my whole life, and for the first time, I would be doing it without her.

Tears rushed down my cheeks and into my hair as I struggled to take a breath against the crushing pressure on my chest. With a broken sob, I rolled onto my side and buried my face in the pillow, letting the emotion course through me as violently as it had that day in the hospital. Only this time, I didn't have a mysterious stranger with intense eyes to curl around me and comfort me.

I didn't have my mother by my side as I prepared to start yet another new life, and I didn't have *him* to comfort me through the knowledge that I didn't have *her*.

I was all alone. Again.

THREE

I checked my seatbelt one last time as the distinctively mechanical clicks and hums started up beneath my seat. While the pretty flight attendant delivered her practiced instructions, I swallowed around the lump in my throat and murmured along.

My mom and I had taken so many flights that we didn't even bother listening to the safety information. While most of the other passengers learned how to inflate the life jacket, my mom would be absorbed in some novel as I devoured a journal article. Sometimes we would whisper along with them, reciting the instructions word for word, making each other giggle like schoolgirls.

Halfway through, I gave up and stared out the window, watching Nampa, Idaho, disappear below me. I knew I would never go back. My meager possessions were stuffed into a duffel bag in the overhead compartment, not even enough to fill a bag that needed to be checked.

Bradford Hills Institute paid for my ticket to New York. Within two hours of my phone call with Stacey from admissions, I'd received an email with a ridiculous number of attachments, flight details.

It was the first flight I'd taken since the one that literally crashed and burned. I should have been scared, traumatized, upset.

I wasn't.

I had cried it all into my pillow the night before, and the statistics hadn't changed. A car accident was still more likely.

When I landed at LaGuardia, Bradford Hills had a car waiting for me, complete with a smartly dressed driver holding a sign with my name on it.

I was driven past Manhattan into Upstate New York, the concrete and steel giving way to tall trees and wide roads. The Institute was in the town of Bradford Hills and took up half its surface area. Its reputation as a hub of Variant research, education, and training preceded it. Bradford Hills Institute was to Variant studies what Harvard was to law—internationally renowned and notoriously exclusive.

I tried not to dwell on it too much as I took in the campus. We drove through the main gates and up a wide, curving, tree-lined avenue. Signs posted at regular intervals had arrows pointing in various directions, toward this building or that. We seemed to be following the ones that said "Administration and Reception

Vast green lawns, dotted with people strolling around or sitting in groups, rolled out beyond the trees. The layout and buildings were not designed to be utilitarian—not harshly jutting out of the earth or bunched together. Rather, buildings throughout the massive campus blended seamlessly into their natural surroundings, hugging the gentle slopes of the hills and nestling between ancient oak trees, some of them covered in vines, none of them obnoxiously tall. They were old red-and-black brick structures, with ornate windows and wide doorways, oozing history and tradition.

The administration building was in the middle of it all. As we pulled up, it was plain to see this structure was not old and historic like the others, but the contrast to its elderly companions wasn't jarring.

I was too busy staring at the perfectly manicured grounds to notice my driver had exited the car, and I was a little startled when he opened my door for me. He stood back and waited for me to exit.

I timidly crawled out of the spacious back seat and just stood there, unsure what to do.

He saved me from having to figure out what to say. "Shall I have your bag delivered to your residence hall, miss?"

"Oh, no, thank you." Bag. Singular. Overhead compartment compliant. "I'll just hold on to it. Thank you." I spoke too fast as I dragged the item in question from its spot on the back seat. I was out of my element. There is no scientific journal dedicated to the social nuances of interaction with posh, rich people—and their drivers.

There was a pause. Neither one of us quite knew how to proceed. "Thank you for picking me up from the airport . . . and driving me here. Um . . . am I supposed to check in with someone, or . . . ?"

"You are most welcome, miss." Was that a hint of a smile on his serious face? "Please make your way to the main reception area, and they will take care of you from there."

"Great! Thank you." That was the third time I'd thanked the man in less than five minutes, and I internally rolled my eyes at my own awkwardness.

He inclined his head in that subtle way posh people have, walked around to the driver's side, and left me there.

I took a deep breath and walked up the stairs and through the front door.

The cavernous reception area was so spacious I was confident Marty and Baz's three-bedroom house could fit into it three times over. Warm natural light flooded in through the floor-to-ceiling windows that made up three of the walls, and a long reception desk with several people behind it was situated straight ahead. My sneakers squeaked obnoxiously on the polished gray concrete floor as I made my way up to it.

I counted five receptionists, three women and two men, all in matching navy-blue collared shirts, all perched on high office chairs, and all on the phone. They spoke in quiet, efficient voices, their posture as impeccable as their clean-cut appearance.

I stopped in front of the desk and stood awkwardly, trying to tuck back some of the loose strands of hair that had fallen out of my messy bun. When was the last time I'd washed it? Two days ago? Three?

"You're welcome, ma'am. Have a nice day." The receptionist closest to me, a young woman with blonde hair pulled into a tight bun, ended a call. As I opened my mouth to say who I was, she pressed a series of buttons on the phone in front of her and continued speaking into her headset, not even acknowledging my presence.

"Bradford Hills Institute. Please hold the line," she said politely to three callers in a row before finally looking up at me expectantly, a perfectly pleasant smile on her face. I guess it was my turn to speak.

"Hi. I'm Eve Blackburn." I gave myself a silent pat on the back for not accidentally saying Evelyn Maynard. Even after living as Eve for a whole year, I still tripped up on the last name. "Um, I was told to come in here. To report to someone, or . . ." Stacey from admissions hadn't actually told me what to do when I got here, despite the pages and pages of information she had sent in her email.

"OK." The receptionist kept the smile plastered on her face as she ticked away at her computer for a few seconds. "Ah, here we are." She turned back to me. "New student. Welcome to Bradford Hills. You're scheduled to meet with someone from admissions at ten, but you're a little early. Please take a seat and I'll let him know you're here." She gestured to one of two seating areas I had walked past on my trek from the front doors. The seating areas were mirror images of each other, settled on either side of the reception desk and consisting of low leather couches around low glass tables.

I smiled politely and squeaked over to the nearest couch, dropping my duffel bag on the floor and sitting in a spot with a clear view of the elevators. There were two on either side of the reception desk. Everything in this building was very symmetrical.

Once again, Bradford Hills had planned everything perfectly. Had I needed to collect checked luggage, I would have arrived at the exact scheduled time. They couldn't have known I owned next to nothing and would be out of the airport so fast—and therefore early for the appointment I hadn't known had been made for me.

After a few minutes of trying to breathe quietly so I wouldn't disturb the receptionists, I looked around for a distraction from how awkward I felt in this world of full scholarships, personal drivers, and neat buns. From the pile of magazines in front of me, I grabbed the latest edition of *Modern Variant*—a glossy monthly publication that printed human interest stories about high-profile Variants and goings-on in Variant society. It wasn't exactly the kind of thing I usually picked up. I loved learning about Variant abilities and the scientific explanations behind them, but I had little interest in the social and political drama of a world I had never dreamed I would get near. Still, since I was about to be thrust into a school where most of the staff and students were Variant, it couldn't hurt to read up on current affairs.

On the front cover was a photo of a smiling brunette, her hair pulled back into a tasteful style, her perfect teeth gleaming. She looked to be in her late forties or early fifties, the laugh lines around her eyes prominent. The headline read "Senator Christine Anderson on her Crusade to Bring Variant Issues to the Forefront of Political Debate."

I had seen this woman pop up in the news lately, giving passionate speeches about equality between humans and Variants and legislating for equal rights. I got a sense she was making a roundabout argument that Variants were hard-done-by or disadvantaged. I guess you could argue that, to a point—humans made up the majority of the population, and majority usually rules. If you asked me, Variants had all kinds of advantages when you considered the supernatural abilities and stronger resistance to injury or illness. But what did I know?

I skimmed the main article about the senator, but I soon lost interest and closed the magazine, returning it to the pile.

Just as I dropped it down on the massive coffee table with a *flap*, the elevators pinged and opened. A man wearing dress pants and a dark blue shirt stepped out slowly. His clothing was immaculate—pleats in correct places, and tailored perfectly—but he wore no tie, and his shirtsleeves were rolled up to the elbow. He was tapping very fast at his phone, and his messy brown hair, cut short at the sides, had fallen over his face, in defiance of the neat and ironed look of his clothing.

When he finished typing his message, he slid the phone into his left pocket and reached up to swipe his hair back, his rolled-up shirtsleeve tightening around his defined forearm as he did so. He turned and looked straight at me with a polite smile.

His eyes were gray. For a second I thought they were blue, but that was just the color of his shirt and the reflection of the bright blue sky through the window he was facing.

"Eve." He didn't say it like a question: *Are you Eve?* He said it like a statement. He knew who I was.

Despite his defiant hair, his effortlessly polished look left me feeling self-conscious. I was in jeans, ripped at the right knee, and a plain white T-shirt with an oversized black cardigan over the top. I should have made more of an effort. For the third time that day, I felt as if I had no business being there.

I rose from my seat slowly, pulling the cardigan sleeves over my hands. "Yes. Hi." Eloquent. It was the best I could manage at the time.

"I'm Tyler Gabriel. I work in administration. Stacey, who you spoke with yesterday, has updated me on your file. You've been assigned to me for orientation. Let's go to my office and have a chat. Get you settled in." He had put his hands in his pockets and almost imperceptibly relaxed his stance. Was he trying to make me more comfortable with his body language? I liked him already.

"OK. Great. I actually have a lot of questions. This happened so fast." I reached down for my duffel bag while slipping my satchel over my shoulder.

He swiped my duffel off the floor before I could and straightened, chuckling. "Of course. You wouldn't have been admitted here if you didn't have a curious mind. I hope I can answer them all."

I followed him to the elevators, my eyes level with the collar of his shirt. As he reached over to press the button, the muscles in his back tightened beneath the dark blue fabric, and I realized I'd been staring. *Crap! Don't get a crush on the fancy school's fancy admissions guy.*

I stepped to the side so I wouldn't be standing behind him like a creep and averted my eyes, letting them roll over to the reception desk again. All three of the perfectly coiffed women were looking at Tyler Gabriel with secretive smiles and shy looks.

The elevator pinged, and we stepped inside.

"How was your flight, Eve? You've come from Idaho somewhere, yes?"

"Yes, Idaho. The flight was fine. Uneventful." Which was a nice change from the last one I'd taken. I pushed that thought to the back of my mind, swallowing the lump in my throat, and tried to focus on the present moment.

In the reflection of the mirrored doors, Mr. Gabriel was staring at me intently, concern written all over his face. He took a breath as though to say something, but then the elevator lurched to a stop and the doors opened. He cleared his throat and stepped out, turning left.

We were on the fifth floor, the top of the building. Voices and the occasional phone ringing hummed through the air as we walked past rows of offices. We stopped at a door halfway down the corridor, "Mr. T. Gabriel" written in neat gold print on the panel next to it. He stepped in and held the door open for me.

Inside, directly opposite the door, a large desk housed a computer monitor and various other items, including several newspapers stacked haphazardly on top of one another. Two tub chairs were positioned invitingly in front of the desk. To my right, a large window spanning the width of the wall looked out onto the avenue I'd been driven up earlier and, in the distance, the front gates. On the left, a shelf stacked with books, folders, and a few knickknacks was making its best attempt—but failing—to be as neat and proper as the institution it was in.

I could relate to that shelf.

"Please have a seat." He gestured to the tub chairs as he lowered my duffel to the floor.

As I walked farther into the room, four wall-mounted TVs across from the desk—all on different channels, all muted—blinked off. I recognized CNN and CSpan before the screens went black.

I turned back to the desk to see Mr. Gabriel pointing a remote.

"Sorry. Forgot to turn them off." He shrugged and dropped the remote on top of the newspapers. As if it was normal to have four televisions in your office.

"Why do you have four televisions in your office?" I sat down in the chair closest to the window. *Shit! That was inappropriate and nosy!* I was too relaxed with this man, his casual shirtsleeves and carefully relaxed posture had put me at ease better than I'd thought. He was that coveted thing that all school administrators, counselors, and teachers strove for—*approachable.*

Before I could cringe and apologize, he answered, "I like to keep an eye on what's happening in the world."

"Oh . . . OK." *Why though?* I really wanted to prod further, but I kept my mouth shut.

He sat in the chair next to me instead of behind his big desk, crossed his legs, and angled his body toward mine. *We're on the same side, you can talk to me*, his posture was saying.

"Welcome to Bradford Hills." He looked me right in the eyes with a relaxed kind of intensity, as if he was studying me. That I could understand—the need to study something, to know it in order to understand it.

"Thank you, Mr. Gabriel."

"Please, call me Tyler, or if you prefer, Gabe—that's what some of the other students and staff like to call me. We are not strict with titles and labels here. We like to create a more relaxed, fluid learning environment. For example, my role sits somewhere between admissions counselor and academic advisor—among other things."

So the relaxed vibe was intentional. I nodded, not sure what to say to that. I wasn't expecting a place as exclusive and old as Bradford Hills to have such a relaxed approach.

"Before we go any further, I am obliged to tell you something about myself." His tone didn't suggest that he resented this rule; it was the same as it had been thus far—relaxed and easy.

"OK." I sat up a little straighter.

"As you probably know, many of the staff and students here are Variants, myself included. I have an uncommon ability, and I find that most people are more at ease if they know what it is and how it works."

I leaned toward him a little, intrigued. The few Variants I'd met before mostly had common abilities—a woman with enhanced strength carrying four bulky suitcases through the airport, a kid with enhanced speed flying past me in the corridor on his way to class. Enhanced strength, speed, hearing, and sight were the most common.

"I have the ability to tell when someone is lying to me. Don't worry, I can't read your mind or anything so invasive as that. It's more like a mental alarm system that alerts me when someone is being untruthful."

"Really?" I could feel the smile spreading over my face, my eyes widening, while he carefully monitored my expression. My mind raced with a million questions about whether his DNA differed from that of Variants with more physical manifestations of power. "That is so cool!"

His eyebrows raised in surprise, but he reined it in quickly, arranging his features into a neutral expression. He did smile though, a pleasant, easy smile. "I have to say, I was not expecting that response. Most people are uneasy when I first tell them. They immediately start worrying about what they might've lied about recently, paranoid that I'm about to expose their deepest secrets."

"Yes, I suppose that would be worrying . . . now that I think about it. Should I be worried?" I still wasn't really freaked out by his ability—I had nothing to hide. I'm fairly certain my mother did, but I had no idea what it was, so there was no way for me to be evasive about it. I was more concerned that my response was abnormal.

His smile spread wider, the gray in his eyes becoming lighter. "Not at all. And don't stress that you didn't react how most others do. It's a good thing. It tells me you're more concerned with matters that are of far greater importance than my ability."

He had leaned toward me too at some point, and his compliment made me suddenly aware of how close we were sitting, our elbows on the arms of our chairs, heads bent toward each other. Like two friends having an intimate conversation, rather than a student and administrator who had just met. He must have realized the same thing, because we looked away and straightened up in our chairs at the same time.

He cleared his throat. "Right. Now, you'll need to fill out these forms and return them to reception." He grabbed an envelope off his desk and handed it to me. "And it's standard protocol for all our students to have a blood test to screen for the Variant genetic markers."

"Oh, that won't be necessary." A particular protein was present in the blood of Variants—it was the most accurate indicator there was Variant DNA present. I had been put through all kinds of tests in the hospital after the crash, and nothing had come up then. "I had a battery of tests about a year ago, and they didn't find anything."

"I'm afraid we insist on running our own tests." He smiled politely, a little apologetic. "It's a requirement for all students. Do you understand why?"

"Yeah." I nodded. A big part of the work Bradford Hills did was helping young Variants learn how to manage their abilities; knowing which students may present with an ability at any moment would be incredibly useful.

Tyler (I had, without thinking about it, decided to call him Tyler—Gabe was too casual somehow) gave me a satisfied nod, and I remembered his ability. He knew I was telling the truth when I said I understood.

"The information is all in the envelope. Just go down to the clinic on campus, and I'll call you in for a meeting when the results come through."

He spent the next half hour patiently explaining how Bradford Hills Institute operates and answering all my questions. He helped me choose my subjects, steering me toward some specialized Variant studies units.

"Correct me if I'm wrong, but I think you have a keen interest in Variant abilities." He had worked me out pretty quickly, but I guess that was his job. "Some of these introductory Variant units, combined with your other science studies, will give you a good foundation for delving further into that area of research if you decide you like it. Plus, it gives you an excuse to be as curious and nosy about people's abilities as you want."

He had *really* worked me out. I laughed out loud, and he grinned, a mischievous look in his eyes.

He sent me on my way with the fat envelope, my class schedule, my residence hall assignment, and a *giant* map of the campus. The thing was seriously like one of those folding maps you get at truck stops—the ones that are bigger than a newspaper when spread out completely.

I stuffed all the papers except the map into my handbag, jostling my duffel on my other shoulder as I rode the elevator back down.

In the lobby, the reception lady I had spoken to was on the phone and didn't notice my polite smile—which lingered as I thought about the last hour. It was clear why all the reception girls had googly eyes for Tyler. He was smart, easy to talk to, made you feel comfortable in his presence—and he was gorgeous. Those searching gray eyes and the messy hair that kept falling over his forehead . . .

Crap! I'd told myself not to get a crush on him, and there I was, not even an hour later, having failed miserably.

FOUR

Outside, I stopped at the top of the stairs and unfolded the giant map, the sun pleasant on my face. The weather was warming up; T-shirts-and-shorts season couldn't come too soon.

The admin building was near the edge of the curving maze of lines and markers; Res Hall K was much farther in. I took off, the strap of my duffel bag digging into my shoulder.

After a few minutes of walking down the curved, tree-lined paths, I reached a neat three-story building. About a dozen stairs led up to double doors, which opened into a cool foyer. I made my way over to a small elevator on the left and pressed the button. My every step echoed up past the stairs twisting through the center of the building, reaching all the way to the third floor.

The elevator was quiet and smooth—it must have been a recent addition to the obviously older building. I double-checked my messy scrawl at the top of the map—*room 308*—before following the signs to the right.

I paused when I reached the door, key in hand. I was sharing the room with two other girls—a Zara Adams and a Beth Knox—and I didn't want to just barge in on them. After a few moments of awkward indecision, I knocked.

A moment later, a girl with brown eyes and short, silky red hair cracked open the door. "What?"

She obviously wasn't in the mood for visitors, but I wasn't a visitor, so I couldn't just go away. I shuffled my feet. "Uh . . . hi . . . um . . . I'm Eve. I live here?" It came out as a question.

"*What?*" This time there was confusion mixed in with the annoyance. Shuffling and other voices came from inside the room. Someone was crying softly.

I took a deep breath and forced myself to speak clearly. "Sorry. I just arrived today. I've been assigned to this room. Are you Beth? Or Zara?"

She sighed and rolled her eyes. "Right. Of course. Your timing is fucking great." The sarcasm rolling off her was almost visible. "You might as well come in." She opened the door wide.

Gripping the strap of my duffel tighter in some desperate attempt to have something to hold on to, I stepped inside.

Red—she still hadn't told me her name—closed the door just a little too forcefully and turned her back to me, walking over to a couch where two other girls were sitting.

The room was small but comfortable looking. Most of it was taken up by the three-seater couch pushed up against the wall to my left. A TV stand with a flat screen on top of it, a coffee table littered with tissues, and a round dining table surrounded by three mismatched chairs filled the rest of the space. A door to the right led into the bathroom—I could just make out the edge of the sink through the crack—and on the opposite wall were three evenly spaced doors: the bedrooms.

As I opened my mouth to ask which room was mine, I realized no one was speaking. I looked over to the couch and met three sets of eyes staring at me.

The redhead was sitting on the arm of the couch. In the middle was a blonde girl, her long platinum locks unbrushed and her eyes red and puffy. On her other side was another redhead. Her hair was lighter, longer, and had more orange in it than the first girl's, and freckles sprinkled her nose and cheeks. She was the only one with a small smile on her face.

"Hi. I'm Beth. That's Zara." The freckled redhead pointed to the girl who had answered the door.

So I would be sharing with two redheads. What were the statistical probabilities of that? Only 2 percent of people had red hair. Were they related? I dismissed the thought immediately. Their features were too different despite the color of their hair—also two very different shades of red.

I half raised my hand in a little wave and was about to introduce myself, but the blonde on the couch cut across me.

"So you're my replacement then." It wasn't a question. It was a statement, delivered with bitterness and anger. I had no idea why this girl thought I was replacing her, but I didn't want to be on the other end of her death stare.

"Umm . . ."

"Oh, forget it. It's got nothing to do with you anyway." The end of her sentence morphed into a wail, and she started sobbing again, dropping her head into her hands, which were clutching a bunch of tissues. "I can't believe they're actually kicking me out. 3.8! 3.8 GPA because of that one stupid paper, and I'm out. My parents are fuming! They spent all this money to send me here, and now I'll have to go to Yale or something. Ugh!" A disgusted look crossed her features, as if the word *Yale* personally offended her.

"Holy shit. They're that strict?" The words were out of my mouth before I could stop them. If they were throwing out people who were paying tuition, they definitely wouldn't hesitate to get rid of someone on a scholarship. I had better keep my grades up. *No pressure.*

All three sets of eyes flew back to me. Beth was rubbing soothing circles over her friend's back, while Zara sat with her arms crossed over her black T-shirt.

"You're still here?" Zara gave me a flat look and then rolled her eyes. "Yes. And it's not like a 'three strikes and you're out' thing. You don't get a warning. As soon as you slip, they throw you out on your ass. And it's not just grades either. Since this isn't just a college and not everyone is just a student, there are other factors. Like if you're spending some of your time studying and some working for one of the departments, you have to show that you're continuing to be an asset to the Institute."

She got up and grabbed the strap of my duffel, yanking it unceremoniously off my shoulder. "Anna has been attending here since she was sixteen, and now she's out. As you can imagine, it's a stressful situation." She made her way to the middle door and tossed my bag in without looking where it landed. "This used to be her room. Guess it's yours now. Mind giving us a minute?"

The last bit was delivered with less sarcasm, and I could appreciate that I was intruding on a private situation.

Even though I didn't mean to. Even though this was technically my home now.

I nodded and walked into my new room. Zara nodded back as I passed—a quick nod that seemed to say "thanks"—and I gave her a small smile in return.

I closed the door softly and took a look around. Directly opposite the door was a window with a wide sill and thick timber frame, typical of these older buildings. A desk and chair, nightstand, and stripped twin bed composed the room's only furniture. It was small and basic, but it was also clean and light and cozy. It already felt more *mine* than my bedroom in Nampa ever had.

Most importantly it was private. I wouldn't have to share sleeping quarters with anyone. After a lifetime of never getting past superficial friendship, I preferred to be alone.

It took me twenty minutes to unpack my clothing, a few notebooks, and the one framed picture I had of my mother. I left my toiletries sitting on the desk, as I didn't want to walk through the common area while Anna was still out there.

After I'd carefully refolded my T-shirts and arranged the hangers in color-coded order, I flopped down on the bed, no idea what to do with myself. It was around midday, and using my trusty campus map to go in search of the cafeteria seemed like an excellent idea. But I was trapped by the crying blonde on the other side of the door.

Instead I spent five minutes making a list of all the things I needed to buy with my fancy new scholarship allowance money—like sheets for the bare bed I was lying on, towels, shampoo, and conditioner. Everything study related, such as textbooks, pens, and notebooks, would be provided by the Institute. I was expecting a package by the end of the day.

An hour later, my new roommates knocked on my door and let themselves in. They found me lying across my bed, legs up on the wall, head hanging off the edge.

"Hi. Eve, right?" Beth's simple blue skirt swished around her knees as she came in, a more reluctant Zara following behind.

I scrambled up into a sitting position and tried to look casual. "Yes. Hi. Nice to meet you properly, Beth. Is your friend going to be OK?"

"Oh, yeah. She'll be fine. She tends to be a little dramatic, and it all happened so fast. Her parents picked her up. Sorry you walked right into the middle of that."

"That's OK." I wasn't sure what else to say.

"So, Zara and I were just heading to the caf for some lunch. You wanna come with? It would be nice to get to know you."

Zara was picking at her nails in the doorway. She looked up at me, her expression completely blank.

I was just about to decline—Beth seemed nice enough, but I wasn't going to spend time with someone who clearly wanted nothing to do with me—when Zara straightened up, dropping her arms to her sides.

"It's fine. You can come. Whatever."

"Well, gee, with an invitation like that, how could I possibly refuse?" Two could play at the sarcasm game.

She stared me down for a moment, then smiled wide. "Well, all right then. I guess we'll get along just fine. Let's go, ladies."

I followed the Reds—as I had taken to calling them in my head—out of the building and through the grounds, listening to their chatter but not contributing much. Honestly, I would have preferred to go to lunch on my own, but since these girls were going to be my roommates, possibly for the next few years, a good relationship with them was probably worth a little effort.

A few years.

The concept of staying anywhere longer than a year was foreign to me, but I could do this—embrace it, buckle down, study hard. I might even make some friends. Might as well start with my roomies.

The cafeteria was an *entire building*. It was a flat, one-story structure, one of the smallest on campus, but it stretched wide. Picnic tables were scattered across the lawn, stretching toward the front doors and a paved, covered area with café tables. Clusters of people were eating outside, taking advantage of the sunshine.

As we made our way toward the entrance, a brightness to my right caught my eye. A group of people were milling around a picnic table, on top of which sat a boy, his feet on the bench.

Boy was probably the wrong word. He was . . . big. Big arms, big chest, big tall body, big booming laugh. A white T-shirt stretched over his defined chest. The only reason I hadn't mistaken him for a hulking man was his face—too youthful and carefree to belong to anyone much past my own age.

The brightness was coming from his big hands. Which were on fire. I stopped, fascinated. This was the second uncommon and very impressive Variant ability I had encountered since getting here, and it had only been a few hours.

The Reds must have noticed I'd stopped walking. They'd doubled back to stand beside me.

"That's Kid," Beth said.

I watched the guy in question lazily wave his hand in front of his torso, the flame coming off his fingers dancing languorously along with his movements.

"He has a fire ability, as you can see, and he's fond of showing it off. Not that anyone minds. It's pretty cool. Or . . . hot, I guess. In more ways than one." A smile had crept into Beth's voice.

"Kid?" I asked without taking my eyes off him. "What kind of name is that?"

"His name is actually Ethan Paul. Everyone just calls him Kid. I don't actually know why."

As if he could hear us talking, he looked up from his spot on the bench, and our eyes met. He held my gaze as he curled his fingers and threw a ball of fire the size of a baseball right at me. I gasped in surprised delight, a smile pulling at my lips, but before it even got halfway, it fizzled out into a puff of smoke.

A wide grin spread over Kid's face, and he leaned back onto the table, his hands behind him.

Zara chuckled. "That's one of his favorite tricks, but his fire isn't really dangerous. I mean, he could start a fire if he sparked up while holding a piece of wood or something but not, like, remotely. He doesn't have a Vital, so there are limits to what he can do. They keep a pretty close eye on him though, because if he were to meet his Vital, he could be seriously dangerous."

About 10 percent of Variants were Vitals, people who didn't have abilities themselves but had direct access to the Light and the capability to channel it. I had never met a Vital, and Zara's mention of them made we wonder how many there were at Bradford Hills. Their direct link to the Light—the energy that made abilities possible in the first place—fascinated me. Vitals were a kind of conduit; they could draw Light into themselves and pass it on to Variants through skin-on-skin contact, basically giving the Variant a power boost.

All Vitals eventually found a Variant, or two or three, that was meant for them—if they didn't already know each other. They were drawn together. The Light flowed through a Vital into their Bonded Variant easier than water through a sieve. Science was still working on understanding Variant abilities, and one of the least understood aspects of it was the Light and how Vitals accessed it.

If someone like Kid found his Vital, he would have access to unlimited power. Theoretically, he could raze entire towns, even cities, to the ground. No wonder Bradford Hills Institute was watching him closely.

Kid was still looking at me, but the grin had fallen away, replaced by a more serious face. My own expression must have been curious. I was studying him.

I had to stop doing that—looking at people like puzzles to solve or experiments to complete. It would not help my chances of making friends.

I turned away to resume our walk. My heart was racing, but not from fear. I had been surprised, sure, and a little excited to see another cool ability close up, but at no point had I felt fear. That wasn't normal. Any normal person with functioning survival instincts would have been scared of a ball of fire flying at their face, right?

I was probably overthinking it. As we entered the cafeteria, I focused back on the Reds.

"He's obviously noticed you, so here's your first piece of Bradford Hills insider advice: stay the hell away from Ethan Paul. His power may be harmless, but he is dangerous to the female student population." Zara delivered this in what I was quickly learning was her default voice—flat and slightly disinterested. As if she had explained this a million times and was over it.

"He's actually kind of a nice guy if you speak to him for longer than a few minutes . . . and don't mind the whole throwing balls of fire at your face thing." Beth moved toward a very long buffet display at the back of the room. At least I wouldn't have to worry about where my meals were coming from—once again, part of the full scholarship.

"So is he going to roofie me, or is he a nice guy?" I asked.

Zara snorted as she helped herself to some pasta.

Beth giggled. "She didn't mean it like that. It's more like . . . he's a distraction. I mean, he's hot, a natural at most sports, and throws these amazing parties at his uncle's house where he lives, just up the road from here, but he's never had a girlfriend. He seems to fixate on a girl and then get bored with her quickly. Meanwhile, the girls get distracted from their study or work, and their contribution slips. Sometimes that can get them kicked out. It's partly what happened with Anna. She was seeing Kid a lot the last few weeks, and she wasn't spending enough time focusing on her studies."

Zara carried our trays to a free table near a window. "Yeah, and the thing is, because he's Variant, they're more lenient. You hardly ever see Variant kids getting kicked out."

"What do you mean?" One minute they were telling me the school was really strict, no second chances, and now they were telling me it was lenient.

Zara rolled her eyes and started eating her pasta while Beth elaborated: "There are no second chances if you're a human. But because this is one of only a few schools in the country that specializes in helping Variants learn how to control their—sometimes dangerous—abilities, they tend to be more forgiving. They can't have someone like Kid never learning how to properly control his power out in the world. It could be disastrous."

"You mean it would be bad press. Especially with these Variant Valor dickheads spouting their superior race bullshit lately. They can't afford to look bad or dangerous right now. So yeah, the Variants pretty much get away with everything, while we Dimes have to bust our asses." Zara slapped her fork down on her tray and pushed it away, her pasta half-eaten, and stared out the window.

I cringed at her casual use of the word *Dimes*—a derogatory slang term for humans. There were simply more of us—we were a dime a dozen. *Dimes* for short.

The extremist group Variant Valor was rather fond of the term. They saw all humans as Dimes—common, unremarkable, inferior. Those nuts believed that Variants were superior in every way and should therefore rule the humans. They were completely unhinged, staging protests, posting elitist propaganda all over the Internet, and occasionally causing violent incidents. They were shit-stirrers of the worst kind—dogmatic.

"So I'm guessing you're both human then?" I hedged, unsure how safe this topic was but curious nonetheless.

"Yes," Beth answered for both of them. Zara was still looking out the window. "My blood tests returned a clear human result. Zara's tested positive for Variant DNA, but—"

"But I'm defective," Zara cut across her, leaning forward on the table. "I've never manifested an ability or made a connection with a Variant who has one, so I'm not a Vital either."

"Oh. OK." Not all people who tested positive for Variant DNA had abilities—the gene could be dormant. Some people went their whole lives without knowing they had it. Why did Zara resent it so much?

Beth cleared her throat. "So, Eve, where are you from?"

It was a common enough question that I was prepared for. I gave them a vague answer about moving around a lot, and they both commented on how that explained my indistinct accent. Then I put the focus back on them. It was easy. If you asked people enough questions, they wouldn't notice you weren't sharing much about yourself.

We spent the rest of the hour chatting. Beth was from Atlanta and studying literature and journalism. Zara was from Anaheim and studying political science and Variant studies. They had both been attending and sharing the same dorm in Bradford Hills since they were sixteen. The Institute wasn't concerned with age—any given class could have kids as young as twelve along with adults studying for their third degree. They told me more about how the Institute worked; we discussed movies and favorite foods.

For a while, I actually felt normal.

By the time we left, full on pasta, I was beginning to feel more comfortable with the Reds. Beth was lovely and friendly; Zara clearly had a chip on her shoulder, but her sarcasm and ire were not directed at me. I didn't know what her beef with the world was, but I could understand it. I had my own beef with the world. Being less than impressed with what life had thrown at us so far was one thing we had in common.

When we got back to our res hall, three boxes were waiting for me at our door. Two had the Bradford Hills logo on the side, and one was just a plain box with a note taped to the top:

Eve,

These are the supplies BHI provides to all its full scholarship students. The last box is a care package from me. I noticed you arrived without certain essentials that BHI does not provide, so I took the liberty of arranging them for you. I hope you don't mind. Have a good first day of classes tomorrow, and again, please don't hesitate to come see me if you need to.

Best,

Tyler Gabriel

It was handwritten on a piece of notebook paper. Had he delivered these himself? How thoughtful.

"You got Gabe as your admin?" Zara was reading over my shoulder. "Nice."

"Very nice!" Beth leaned over my other shoulder to get a look herself. "He's scrumptious. Never dates students though."

I was beginning to think Beth was a little boy obsessed. "Um . . . wouldn't that be illegal or whatever?"

"Between students and anyone on the teaching staff, yeah. But Gabe doesn't teach. It's frowned on, but there aren't any rules against it exactly. The student body varies in age so much, plus many of the older students work for the Institute in some capacity too, so the lines are kind of blurred. It's a moot point anyway. Many have tried and failed."

She sighed as she picked up one of the boxes and carried it into my room, and I had a sneaking suspicion she was speaking from experience. Zara grabbed one too, and I picked up the last one, kicking the door shut behind us.

"Thanks guys." I couldn't decide if it felt nice to have them helping or intrusive to have them touching my stuff.

Thankfully, they left me alone to unpack and set up my room. After unpacking the extra box Tyler had sent, I scrunched up the list of things I needed to buy and threw it away. He had thought of everything, down to new sheets.

When I came out later in the evening, the Reds suggested we order a pizza, sparking a brief argument about whether to get pineapple as a topping—Zara was pro, but Beth was firmly against. They turned to me.

"You're the decider, Eve." Beth smiled, and Zara raised her eyebrows expectantly.

I didn't want to get on either of their bad sides this early on, but I had to make a stand. I gave Zara an apologetic look. "I love pineapple, but it does *not* belong on pizza."

Zara huffed, and Beth did a fist pump before picking up the phone to order. "Anna loved it too, and I could never get those two to let me order a good, pineapple-free pizza. Looks like the tables have turned."

"Whatever." Zara tried to keep the annoyed look on her face but couldn't contain her laughter in the end.

I laughed along with them, wishing I had these kinds of silly memories with lifelong friends.

As the Reds continued to reminisce, I did my best to push out the longing for what I'd never had. What mattered was what was *ahead* of me. Soon, Zara and Beth and I would make our own memories together.

I had a feeling they would be good friends to have.

FIVE

After doing a little research on fire abilities during one of my sleepless nights, I didn't see the guy who'd thrown a ball of fire at me as a welcome to Bradford Hills for a while. Then on my third day of classes, I had the same lecture as Zara in Variant Abilities 101, and there he was.

He was chatting with a guy with dirty blond hair who was impeccably dressed in chinos and a gray shirt. When Kid saw us come in, he slapped his friend on the shoulder and came right over.

Zara immediately rolled her eyes and crossed her hands over her chest.

"Hey, Zee." He grinned, looking between us and smiling widely. I was mesmerized by his light amber eyes, a sharp contrast to his coal-black hair, cut short at the sides. "Are you going to introduce me to your new friend?"

"Don't call me that, *Kid*," she spat. "And no, I'm not. She just got here. I'd like her not to get expelled."

"What?" He chuckled, looking at her as if she were a little batty. "Who got expelled?"

"Anna, you dick. Her parents picked her up three days ago."

"Shit. Are you serious?" His playful demeanor dropped and he focused all his attention on Zara, giving me a chance to study him further. He was built like an athlete. Even standing one step below us in the aisle of the lecture theater, he was a little taller than me, and his V-neck T-shirt, pulled tight over his chest, accentuated his broad shoulders. A tattoo peaked out from under his left sleeve, but I was a little distracted by the curves of his defined biceps and didn't get a good look at it.

The lecturer walked in, and we all had to get to our seats.

Even though I hadn't said a word to Kid, I couldn't help but be intrigued, but my new friend's warning to stay away from him was hard to ignore. If anything, my instant attraction was warning enough to keep my distance. I didn't need any distractions here. I couldn't afford to get sidetracked by a beautiful, very muscly, annoyingly confident boy.

Over the next week and a half, Kid tried to get close to me at every opportunity. Once, he came into class late and spent an inappropriate amount of time looking around the half-full lecture theater before zeroing in on me and sitting in the seat right next to mine. Even though half the row was empty.

I focused hard on the lecture and my notes and made a conscious effort not to look in his direction, but about halfway through, a flash of light caught my attention. I looked over to see several tiny scraps of paper on fire and floating above his desk. I watched, transfixed, as the little flickers danced around, my note taking frozen in midsentence.

Just as they were getting too big to go unnoticed by other people, he made a subtle motion with his hand, and they spluttered out, little bits of ash floating down to the table and the floor.

I smiled despite myself and looked up at him. He was watching the front of the room intently, as though none of it had happened. Then one side of his mouth lifted into a smirk.

Self-satisfied show-off. He knew he had my attention, and that was apparently enough.

Another time he saw me come into the cafeteria. He took a step toward me, but a girl with shiny auburn hair sidled up to him and pressed herself against his side, whispering something in his ear.

I shook my head and headed toward the food, ignoring him once again.

Every other time he'd tried to approach me, he'd been thwarted either by Zara's sarcastic quips and raised brows or my own evasion tactics.

I didn't think I was likely to run into him on the other side of campus though, so when it finally came time to get the Variant DNA test Tyler had insisted on, it was a relief to stop worrying about dodging Kid for a while.

After putting the test off for two weeks, sure it would come back negative, I'd received a stern text message from Tyler (*Why are your blood test results not on my desk yet?*), caved, and made an appointment. On my way, I'd also caved by stepping foot inside a Starbucks for the first time in months. This one was on campus, conveniently located near the medical buildings, where my appointment would take place.

My first two weeks at Bradford Hills had allowed me to start falling into a routine, which consisted mostly of classes, study, and hanging out with the Reds. I hadn't had a chance to explore much past the confines of the campus—the campus itself was so huge that I still hadn't seen it all, sticking to the buildings that contained my classes, my food, and my bed. Unfortunately, that meant I hadn't had a chance to find a coffee shop with a decent latte. Starbucks would never compare to the amazing Melbourne coffee that had been my introduction to the black gold, but at least it provided something other than that American filtered crap.

I was relieved to find the Starbucks mostly empty. Only five or six people were milling about, waiting on orders and seated at tables. Just to be safe, I checked the time before ordering. Still twenty minutes until my appointment with the campus nurse.

Stepping up to the counter, I ordered my latte in the smallest size possible, moved along, and took my phone from my back pocket. I was dressed casually, as usual. Sticking to campus didn't really require anything dressier than jeans, flats, and a warm sweater. Even though the sun was out, there was still a chill on the breeze.

I scrolled through my schedule and to-do list as I waited. The massive campus was still a pain to navigate, but at least catching up in the coursework was proving relatively easy. Tyler had not exaggerated when he said that Bradford had a different approach to education. It really wasn't a problem that I was joining classes so late in the year. They worked at a different pace and with a different structure.

Even so, the amount of reading that piled up after my first meetings with all my professors had been overwhelming, but once again, my weird spurts of energy had saved me. An episode a few days after arriving— three nights without sleep—gave me plenty of extra time to read up on the study materials and even do some extra research, in between several vigorous workouts. It had been a productive few days.

I was on top of everything. The only reason I was checking my schedule was to fill time while I waited for my latte. After all, it wasn't as if I had any friends to message.

As I put my phone away, I sensed someone behind me, standing a little too close. I turned my head to find Kid craning over my shoulder. So much for not running into him on the other side of campus.

"Damn." He leaned away to a more comfortable distance and grinned at me. "I was hoping to see who you were texting. So I could tell him to back off."

"That's a bit presumptuous." I faced the counter again, giving him my back. "You don't even know my name."

"You're right." He chuckled, stepping up next to me and reaching his hand out as if to shake mine. "I'm Ethan Paul, and you are . . ." He raised his brows expectantly, his amber eyes shining with mirth.

"On my way to an appointment and don't have time for this," I deadpanned, forcing myself to look away from those eyes.

He laughed. "Oh, come on. You won't even tell me your name? What have I done to deserve such suspicion?"

I sighed and rolled my eyes, willing the barista to hurry with my latte. When the young guy behind the counter finally pushed the beverage toward me, I realized the flaw in my getaway plan.

"Tall latte for Eve," the barista announced before turning away to make the next coffee.

"Shit," I muttered under my breath, taking a sideways glance at Kid.

He was looking right at me, grinning. Deep dimples gave him a very innocent look, which the sparkle in his eyes elevated to an infectious kind of glee. It was a stark contrast to his large, intimidating frame. He towered over me, once again dressed in jeans and a tight white T-shirt. How was he not cold? Despite a string of cool spring days, I hadn't seen him in a jacket or sweater once.

With another eye-roll (my new roommate was rubbing off on me—Zara was a pro eye-roller), I jammed a lid on my latte and rushed toward the exit as the barista called out behind me, "Venti dark roast for Ethan."

Of course his order only took seconds to fill. All they had to do was pour the stale filtered excuse for coffee into a giant cup and hand it over.

"Hey, *Eve*!" he called after me, emphasizing my name, as I stepped outside. "Wait!"

I didn't slow down, but he caught up to me anyway.

"Hey, come on. All I'm trying to do is introduce myself. You're new around here. You could use some friends."

I pulled up short and faced him. "I have plenty of friends, thank you very much," I lied, crossing my arms over my chest. He had hit a sore spot.

He loudly gulped his sip of coffee before lowering the cup, the easy expression on his face gone. "Of course. I didn't mean anything by it."

Realizing I may have overreacted a little, I made a conscious effort to relax my stance and tried giving him a small smile. "I really do have to go."

"Wait." The sudden seriousness of his tone made me stop. "Look, I don't know what Zara has told you about me, but all I'm saying is maybe you could get to know me a little before making up your own mind."

Dammit. He had a point. His cocky and boisterous behavior had been in line with Zara and Beth's description of his womanizing ways and careless attitude toward school, but Beth *had* defended him a few times. I hadn't seen him be mean or intentionally rude to anyone since he'd thrown the fireball at me on my first day.

Now he was standing right in front of me, and I wasn't entirely sure I still wanted to avoid him.

"So, can we start again?" He rubbed the back of his neck, and I tried not to stare at the way his arm muscles popped out in that position.

"Yes. OK." I nodded, extending my hand. "My name is Eve."

He wrapped his hand around mine firmly but gently. "Hi, Eve. I'm Ethan, but my friends call me Kid." He flashed me his brilliant smile with a side of dimples, and I did my best to focus on the word *friend*. That's all we would be—friends. I could handle that.

But even as I was trying to convince myself I wasn't attracted to him, I was noticing how warm his hand felt wrapped around mine, which looked tiny by comparison. Neither one of us was pulling away, which left us standing there, holding each other's hands and staring at each other. I wondered if his palm felt tingly too.

I pulled my hand out of his and stepped back, taking a sip of my mediocre latte. He glanced down at his palm, looking bewildered for a second, before shoving it into his pocket.

"So, *Eve*." He smiled widely, obviously still happy to finally know my name. "Where are you off to?"

"I have an appointment with the campus nurse. Apparently it's school policy to run a full blood workup on new students. Seems a little intrusive if you ask me, but my admissions guy, Tyler, is insisting."

"Oh, Gabe is your admin guy? Sweet!"

"You know him?" I guess it wasn't much of stretch. The Variant community here seemed tight-knit and well established.

"Yeah. We live together."

"Oh!" I fixed him with a very surprised look. Maybe Zara had read him *way* wrong.

He tossed his head back and laughed loudly. "Not like that, *Eve*. We grew up together."

"Oh. Sorry. So you're related?"

"Nah, not really."

My curiosity was piqued, but I was making an effort to curb that in social situations, so I didn't ask for more information. Realizing we had been talking for some time, I checked my phone and saw I only had five minutes to find the correct building, then the correct room, for my appointment.

Cursing, I started walking in what I hoped was the right direction. "I'm going to be late for my appointment. Nice to meet you, Kid. Bye!"

He grabbed me by the back of my sweater, stopping me in my tracks, and chuckled. When I looked over my shoulder, he pointed at a low ivy-covered building next to the one that housed the Starbucks. "You want to go there."

"Right," I breathed, embarrassed. "Of course. Thanks. See ya!" I took off in my new direction.

"You're welcome, *Eve*!" he yelled after me. "Nice to meet you, *Eve*! See you later, *Eve*!"

I couldn't contain my smile as I lifted my hand over my head to wave, rushing to my appointment.

Twenty minutes later, I walked back out, my coffee long gone, my right elbow bandaged where the nurse had inserted the needle. After I'd signed some paperwork, the young nurse had taken several vials of my blood with gentle fingers and practiced movements and told me the results would be ready in two weeks.

Emerging into the fresh air, I paused. I wasn't due to meet the Reds for lunch for another hour, and I had nothing to do until then. Was trying to explore this end of campus worth the risk of getting completely lost? I had stupidly left my trusty giant map behind in my room. I may have had the table of elements memorized, but my sense of direction was seriously awful.

As I looked around this quieter part of campus—the buildings just as old and impressive as all the others, the oak trees swaying in the light spring breeze—I spotted someone familiar.

My new friend was hard to miss, his big frame towering over everyone else in the vicinity. Kid was standing near the entrance to the Starbucks, talking to the blond, well-dressed boy I had seen him with several times. They were standing close, their heads bent together, their faces serious.

I knew I shouldn't be staring—I had vowed to treat people like people, not puzzles—but my indecision about what to do with my free hour was completely forgotten. All I could do was watch and wonder what Kid and his friend were discussing so intently.

As he replied to something Kid had said with a wave of his hand, the blond looked in my direction. Our eyes met, his gaze rooting me to the spot. Kid soon turned to look at me too, and I finally snapped myself out of it and glanced around the square, struggling to remember which direction I had come from to get there. I headed for the main path, hoping to find one of those signposts with the arrows.

Eyes downcast, embarrassed for getting caught staring, I nearly barreled into Kid when he stepped into my path.

"Oh shit." I jumped, my heart flying into my throat, my hand clutching at my chest.

"Hey, Eve." He sounded relaxed. "How was the blood test?"

"Um." I looked up at him. He was just standing there casually, his hands in his pockets, his face as relaxed as his voice sounded. I looked back toward the Starbucks, but his friend had disappeared. "It was fine. Didn't hurt at all."

"That's good. What are you up to now?"

"Did you wait for me?" I was relieved he didn't seem worried about my awkward staring, but it had suddenly occurred to me that his behavior was beginning to border on stalkerish.

"What?" He chuckled, flashing his dimples. "I bumped into my friend and we got talking. I think you saw me standing with him . . ." There was a hint of humor in his voice—so, he'd noticed me staring after all.

"Right. Sorry. Um, I'm meeting some friends for lunch soon, so . . ." I was ready to be away from this whole awkward encounter.

"OK, OK." He chuckled again but stepped out of my path. "I won't keep you from your super early lunch. I just wanted to invite you to my party. It's next weekend."

"I don't know . . ." I hadn't been to a party since my wild streak in Nampa. Considering I was here on a scholarship, my focus should probably be on my studies, not getting drunk with frat boys. Not that there were any fraternities or sororities at Bradford Hills Institute.

"It's just a party at my place, and it will mostly just be Bradford students. You can bring your friends too, if you want." He pulled his phone out of his pocket and handed it to me, my fingers closing around the sleek black rectangle reflexively. "Put your number in there, and I'll send you the details."

I watched him for a moment, standing there with his mischievous eyes and his big arms and his confident personality. I quickly put my number in his phone, muttering as I typed, "I'll think about it."

"Sweet!" He put the phone back in his pocket and beamed at me. "See you there."

"I said I'd think about it, Kid." I laughed despite myself.

"What? Can't hear you!" He started to walk away in the opposite direction. Apparently he had somewhere to be, now that he'd completed his mission of inserting himself into my life. "I'll see you at my party! Bye!"

I caught one more glimpse of his brilliant smile before turning away, shaking my head.

I decided to risk getting lost after all and took a walk around campus, sending a message to Tyler to let him know I had done the blood test. His reply was almost instant.

Finally! That was slower than a reaction between covalent compounds.

I snorted at the lame joke before replying.

Chemistry humor. Really?

Be thankful it wasn't a pun.

Haha! Good point.

I'll let you know when the results arrive and we can set a meeting to discuss.

It would be a boring meeting with *nothing* to discuss, but I wasn't going to pass up an opportunity to spend some time with Tyler Gabriel. I put my phone away and headed to the cafeteria.

Halfway through our tacos, as Zara and Beth were chatting about their morning classes, my phone went off. Before I could wipe the salsa off my fingers, Beth unashamedly leaned over to read what the message said.

"Party next Sat at 1175 Oakwood Cres. Bring your friends! Hope to . . . Hey! I was reading that." Beth sounded outraged as I swiped the phone away, but there was a big smile on her face.

"God, you two have no boundaries." They really didn't. They were constantly walking into my room without knocking, barging into the bathroom to ask me things while I was in the shower, reading my messages, borrowing my things, and just generally getting all up in my business. They acted the same way with each other. I guess it was nice that they were treating me like one of their own, but it was taking some getting used to.

"Who needs boundaries when you have friends like us?" Beth tried to grab the phone, but I held it out at arm's length. Of course, that put it in Zara's range, and she yanked it right out of my hand.

"Hope to see you there." She picked up where Beth had left off, tucking her sleek red hair behind her ear. "Winky face." Her face scrunched up in disgust as I flopped back in my chair, giving up.

"Who's inviting you to a party?" Beth asked at the same time Zara demanded in much growlier voice, "Why is Ethan Paul inviting you to a party?"

"Kid invited you to his party?" Beth bounced in her seat, but this time I was the one who spoke over her. "How do you know it's from him?"

Zara rolled her eyes, crossing her arms over her chest. "I know his address. We're not going."

"Oh my god, can we please go?" Beth pleaded, hanging off my arm and leaning into me. "Zara never wants to go to these things, and I never get invited. Please!"

"Look, I only just met him properly this morning, and he invited me. I haven't decided if I'm going yet."

"These elitist things are just another excuse for that crowd to reinforce their own inflated sense of importance. Beth never gets invited because she's a Dime. I *always* get invited because technically I have Variant DNA and my parents run in these god-awful Variant society circles. You're invited because they're not sure what you are yet, and they want to keep you on their side in case your blood test comes back positive."

Beth groaned as Zara completed her diatribe, and I stared at her, stunned. Here I was thinking it was just a party.

"Or maybe I don't get invited because I don't know Kid or his friends, and Eve got invited because he likes her?" Beth was clearly trying to sound firm, but she always seemed to come across as gentle and polite. "Please, Eve, can we go?"

She gave me her puppy dog eyes, the freckles on her nose only adding to the innocent act. I rolled my eyes, and before I could even voice my agreement, she was thanking me and hugging me from the side.

"I've lost my appetite. I'll see you guys later." Zara didn't wait for a response before scraping her chair back and hurrying out of the building.

Beth and I shared a look, and then she leaned forward. "Bradford Hills Institute and other Variant-affiliated organizations hold regular events. Things like luncheons, fundraising balls, and socials. The goal is to facilitate as many Variant introductions as possible in the hopes of finding a Variant-Vital match. Zara grew up going to these things, and she used to enjoy them, but as time went on and her ability never manifested, she felt more and more pressure from her parents, and she started to resent even being invited anymore. She's just over it."

Beth really cared deeply for Zara. She sighed before continuing. "Most abilities manifest by age thirteen. Zara's nineteen and still nothing. It's likely she has the dormant gene and her parents are real assholes about it. They make her feel like a disappointment over something she has no control over."

"OK. I can understand that. But what does it have to do with Kid's party? It's not like it's an official Bradford Hills event."

"Yeah, it is, but a lot of younger people use parties—especially Kid's parties, because they're legendary—as an informal way of doing the same thing, trying to find a Vital. All it really means is that people there are more likely to talk to someone they don't know than they are at a regular party, but for Zara it just turns the knife—reminds her that she's a failure in her parents' eyes."

"Well, if it means so much to her, we don't have to go. I'm not huge on parties anyway."

"Oh, *we are going to this party*. You already agreed. It's happening!" The excited smile was back. "Don't worry about Zara. She just needs to cool off. She'll be fine."

I reluctantly agreed, figuring Beth knew Zara better than I did, and allowed myself to get a little excited about the prospect of a party. Plus it was making Beth ridiculously happy.

True to Beth's word, when we all got back to our res hall after classes, Zara apologized for how she'd reacted at lunch and seemed to be in a much better mood. I breathed a sigh of relief as Beth pulled me into a lengthy conversation about what to wear, while Zara rolled her eyes at us and shut herself in her bedroom.

SIX

People streamed past me in every direction as I stood in front of the admin building, looking up and down between my trusty map and what felt like an infinite number of possible paths to take. Several lanes wide enough to accommodate two cars, as well branching veins of narrower walkways, wound away from me on all sides.

My destination was the Variant History Museum on the other side of campus, but I had seriously underestimated my bad sense of direction. While most of the lecture halls and study rooms were grouped at the east end of campus, near the residential buildings, the rest of campus was an unfamiliar maze of various office buildings, research labs, and three separate libraries. Three!

I took a deep breath of fresh air, fighting back frustration.

My only lecture had been canceled, and I had the morning off. With nowhere to be until lunch with the Reds, I'd ventured out into the sunshine in nothing more than leggings and a long T-shirt, loose around my hips, hoping to explore my new home a little bit.

The enormous campus was just one of a million things I still needed to figure out in this crazy elite world. Still, there were many things I was enjoying.

The Reds topped the list. Yes, Zara had her moments, but she was the most honest and open person I had ever met. Beth was the perfect counterbalance, always giving people the benefit of the doubt, effortlessly caring and thoughtful, though never hesitating to call Zara out on her shit. Those two had clearly been friends for a long time, and although that should have left me feeling left out, it didn't. I was already beginning to feel as if I belonged with them.

It was an odd feeling—*belonging*. Even when I'd made friends with Harvey and his sister in Australia, it hadn't happened this fast or this effortlessly.

I was really enjoying my classes too. Chemistry was my favorite by far, and I was even considering applying for a lab assistant position with the research lab on campus. It would allow me to earn some extra cash, and I would be making even more of a contribution to Bradford Hills, cementing my place here.

I was turning my map every which way, trying to figure out which path was correct, when Tyler stepped into my field of vision.

"Lost?" he asked with a soft smile on his face. He was dressed similarly to when I'd first met him—gray pants and a navy shirt, sleeves rolled up to the elbows. He slung his messenger bag over his shoulder, then had to swipe his messy hair out of his eyes.

So adorable!

"Nope! I'm all good." I didn't want to admit I couldn't read a simple campus map, so I tucked the offending piece of paper into my bag.

"Liar." He chuckled and then raised his eyebrows, waiting for something.

How could I have forgotten his ability?

"Right. Human lie detector." I wasn't sure if I was more embarrassed about being lost or lying to him about it. "That's really not fair, you know. I'm so embarrassed. Give me a partial differential equation and I'm all over it. Ask me to read a map . . . Well, just don't ask me to read maps, OK?"

"Fairness is subjective, and I can't turn my ability off, so that's a moot point. But don't be embarrassed about being lost. This campus is massive, and it can be confusing. Where are you going?"

I was grateful he didn't tease me and glad to have someone point me in the right direction. I was doubly glad it was Tyler. This was only the second time I'd met him. The first time he'd encouraged my curiosity, and now he was quickly dispelling my embarrassment over not being able to do a simple task. Trying to resist liking this guy was beginning to feel futile.

"I was trying to get to the Variant Museum."

His face brightened and he smiled wider. "Great! I can guide you there myself. I'm heading that way."

He gestured to a path leading in the complete opposite direction I was going to take and took off at a leisurely pace.

"Right. This is the way I was going to go too." I stepped up next to him, matching his slow pace.

"Liar!" This time he did laugh, but it wasn't mocking—more amused and lighthearted.

"Dammit!" I laughed too, letting the ease of his presence and the warm sun melt my embarrassment away.

The occasional tree provided shade as we walked down the narrow, fern-lined path, chatting easily. He asked about how I was settling in, and I thanked him profusely for his care package. He waved it off as nothing and asked about my classes; I was loving them all. He seemed pleased to hear that and began recommending articles I might find interesting.

"It was written in the mid-nineties, but it's still widely regarded as the beginning of serious Variant genetics research. It's a good starting point for the basics if you want to know more."

Tyler was telling me about an old research paper when we emerged into another bustling square. It was nowhere near as busy as the area around the admin building, but there were plenty of people milling about—albeit more suits and high heels than T-shirts and backpacks. Three low buildings edged the sides of the square, and at the base of the one directly opposite us was a café, outdoor seating scattered around its doors.

Standing near the café, facing us, was a man dressed in all black—long-sleeved top, pants, and boots. He was with a short girl with long black hair and a tall boy with short black hair.

I watched him closely as we emerged from the path.

Tyler pulled up short. "Oh, whoops. We've actually gone past where you need to turn off for the museum, but if you just—"

"Holy shit!" I cut him off midsentence as realization hit me. I couldn't believe my widening eyes.

I knew that man. I had been looking for that man for over a year.

That was my honey-voiced stranger.

"Eve?" I could feel Tyler watching me, concern leaking into his voice, but I had no attention to spare for him. I couldn't take my eyes off the stranger. Maybe he wasn't really there, and if I looked away, he would disappear again. Just as he'd done in the hospital.

He looked up, his eyes landing on Tyler first, his hand raising in greeting. Then his focus shifted to me, and a look of pure shock crossed his face.

He was real!

I launched myself across the square and straight for him. His eyes widened, the shock replaced by horror.

I didn't stop to contemplate his reaction, or the alarm in Tyler's voice as he called my name again, or all the people who were no doubt giving me strange looks as I barreled through their quiet day.

I pulled up right in front of him, staring into his face to make sure it was really him. Ice-blue eyes stared back. There was the strong jaw, the scar through the right eyebrow, the closely cropped hair.

"Holy shit, it's really you!" I declared at an inappropriate volume as I wrapped my arms around his middle, pressing my cheek to his firm chest.

He froze, holding his arms out and going stiff. Several people gasped, and the level of background noise considerably lessened. Was that me drowning out the noise, completely in the moment, overjoyed at finally finding my stranger? Or had everything really gone silent?

"Eve." This time there was a hint of panic in Tyler's voice when he said my name. He placed a firm hand on my shoulder, and I let him pull me backward. The stranger was not returning my hug. I looked around slowly at the silent onlookers' faces—at the looks of shock, worry, or amazement.

My stranger just looked pissed off.

Did they frown on hugging here? I could have sworn I had seen people hug.

"I can't believe you're really here," I said at a more normal volume.

The stranger spoke at the same time, his hushed tone discernible only to our weird little group. "How the hell did you find me? I've been blocking your annoyingly persistent attempts for over a year."

Life was resuming its regular rhythm around us—general chitchat, footsteps, chairs scraping on concrete. Whatever the crowd had poised itself to witness hadn't happened, and they were all moving on with their day.

"Wait. What? You knew I was looking for you?"

"Looking" was an understatement. I had called Melior Group repeatedly, even though they never gave me any new information. I had trawled the Internet, read through pages and pages of redacted documents released under the Freedom of Information Act, sifted through paranoid conspiracy theories on forums, frequented some of the darkest corners online. I had done all I could think to do for a whole year to find any scrap of information that would lead me to him.

And there he stood, telling me he knew I'd been looking for him and had actively blocked me.

He pressed his lips together and crossed his arms over his chest, taking a step back. "It's kind of my job to know things."

"What?" None of this was making sense. "Why? I just wanted to thank you." To begin with. I wanted to thank him profusely, and then I wanted to ask a million questions. Perhaps I had been naive to think someone who worked for Melior Group would be willing to answer them.

The two people he had been standing with, who looked like brother and sister, started laughing softly. As if it were absurd that anyone would want to thank him for anything.

"Do you two *know* each other?" Tyler cut into our conversation, sounding incredulous, but we both ignored him.

"There's no need to thank me. I was just doing my job."

"That's not your decision to make. Whether or not I *need* something is my business." I matched his stance, crossing my arms over my chest in defiance. I had been overjoyed when I first saw him standing across the square, but that had quickly turned to frustration. What was his problem?

"Answer the question. How did you find me?" We were standing off against each other, him determined to get answers to his paranoid question, me getting more and more angry as he ruined a moment I'd been thinking about for more than a year.

"Self-absorbed much?" This meeting had gone so wrong so fast. "I was offered a scholarship, and I took it. Nothing to do with you and your snarky ass. I've been so preoccupied with this move for the last month I haven't even looked for you."

He turned his attention to Tyler, ignoring me completely. "You know this . . . girl? Has she asked you about me?"

Before Tyler had a chance to answer, I jumped in. "Hey! Asshole! *The girl* is standing right here." Fists clenched, I stepped back into his personal space. I had just as much right to be here as he did. "What the hell is your problem?"

He didn't flinch, but his breathing became labored as I got in his face. He looked as angry as I felt.

Before our bizarre standoff could escalate any further, three distinct groans came from behind me. I turned to see Tyler and the brother and sister clutching their heads in pain.

"Man. Rein it in, would you?" Tyler spoke directly to the stranger, visibly making an effort not to double over.

Confused, I looked back at the stranger to see a horrified expression on his face. He met my eyes, his features hardening into anger, before he turned on his heel and stalked away.

I wanted to run after him—after all that, I still hadn't actually thanked him—but I found myself rooted to the spot.

What the hell had just happened?

I turned around, the question on my lips, to see my three companions all staring at me, no longer holding their heads.

Tyler was the first to spring into action, throwing me one last perplexed glance before hurrying off after the stranger. "Dot, interference please," he yelled over his shoulder as he broke into a run.

"I got this, Gabe," the black-haired girl yelled after him. She turned to face me fully, a wide smile spread over her face as she looked me up and down. "I don't know who you are, girlie, but you've got some serious balls, accosting the 'Master of Pain' like that. I'm Dot. That's my brother, Charlie"—the boy behind her lifted his hand in a lazy wave—"and I can't wait to hear *this* story. Charles, coffee."

Charlie rolled his eyes and walked off in the direction of the café while Dot linked her arm through mine, guiding me toward one of the alfresco tables.

Up close, I could see her heavily made-up eyes were green, like moss, and her long black hair was perfectly straight. She was wearing a blouse, buttoned to the neck, and wide skirt that gave off the vibe of a fifties housewife, but she'd paired them with a studded leather jacket and hazardous-looking six-inch heels that only just put her at eye level with me. Her outfit seemed to say, "Yeah, I'm short—I dare you to point it out to me."

I wasn't about to point it out to her. It was an adorably deadly ensemble. Or maybe it was dangerously cute.

We sat down, but as soon as my butt hit the seat, I was up again. I had come *this close* to finally being able to get some answers, and now, once more, he had disappeared. I should have been chasing after him, like Tyler. I should never have let him walk away in the first place.

I didn't get very far. Dot grabbed my wrist and, with surprising strength, pulled me back down into my seat.

"Let go! I have to go after them." There may have been a hint of hysteria in my voice.

"Yeah, no. That's a bad idea, cowboy."

"Cowboy? Who . . . What? Please let go! I have to find him and . . ."

"Thank him," she finished for me.

"Yes." I met her eyes, the fight draining out of me.

She smiled back reassuringly and released my wrist. "Why is that exactly? What did he do to have you searching for him for a whole year for a simple thank you?"

"He saved my life." It was so much more complicated than that, but it was the truth.

Charlie returned just in time to hear my response. He joined his sister in regarding me with confusion.

"Huh," he muttered as he sat down between us, lowering a tray with three giant cups and assorted muffins onto the table. He was much taller than Dot, but they had the same dark green eyes and black hair, his cut short and a little messy. In complete contrast with the outrageous outfit his sister was sporting, he was dressed in simple dark clothing.

"And how did he save your life?" Dot asked as they both lifted their giant cups to their lips and took a sip.

Stalling, I reached for my own cup and had a taste. Scrunching my face up in disgust at the pure American pond sludge within, I placed it back on the table and pushed it away.

These two seemed to know both the stranger and Tyler. They had to have at least some of the answers I needed. Whether or not I could trust them was a whole other question. I would have to take a gamble—give something to get something back.

"Just over a year ago, I was on a plane that crashed over the Atlantic. That . . ." Asshole? Jerk? Angel? ". . . *man* saved me. He was part of the team that pulled me out of the freezing water, performed first aid, and got me to a hospital. The copilot and I were the only survivors. Two hundred and twenty-eight people died, and I lived. I'm pretty sure it was because of him."

I reached for a blueberry muffin to mask the foul taste in my mouth. I'd left out the fact that my mother had died and the fact that my stranger had been there for me at the lowest point in my life. I hadn't talked about those two things with anyone; I wasn't about to start with these two.

"Heavy." Charlie leaned back in his seat, sipping his coffee.

"And you've been trying to find him to thank him?" Dot asked.

"Yeah." It wasn't a lie. I really did want to thank him. They didn't need to know that I also wanted to grill him with questions—such as why a special ops team was sent out to a civilian crash site, or how they even knew where to search, or even what brought the plane down. I was so close to being able to ask those questions. I had to be careful.

"Look, I don't really know you guys, but I'm happy to tell you more about it if you answer some of my questions. Quid pro quo."

"Deal." Dot leaned forward on the table, all business. "Did you know he was Variant?"

"Hey, you already got two. It's my turn. What's his name?"

"Alec Zacarias. Did you know he was Variant?"

"Not on the night of the crash. After, when I woke up in the hospital and was told I was rescued by a Melior Group team, I put two and two together. What's his ability?"

"Pain."

Pain? The sudden headaches that had come over them earlier made more sense now, as did the crowd's bated breath when I'd caused a scene. He was dangerous. Or at least, the people of Bradford Hills thought he was dangerous.

"Pain? Elaborate."

She didn't argue that it was her turn to ask the question. "He can cause pain by skin-on-skin contact. He's very good at controlling it—he has to be—but sometimes, when he's highly emotional, it kind of bleeds out of him and can give people around him headaches, or sometimes it makes them feel sick. He's spent a lot of time learning to manage his ability, but it doesn't make any difference to people who don't know him. They avoid him like the plague because they think getting anywhere near him could hurt them."

"That's why you were so surprised that I was touching him so easily."

"Yes. And now that you know . . ." A sad, resigned look fell over her face.

"Now that I know, it changes nothing. He still saved my life. And if what you say about his control of his ability is true, then I'm not afraid of him. I've given him no reason to want to harm me."

She looked a little surprised, but a small smile had wiped the sad look off her face. "Well, all right then."

That acceptance sounded loaded—as if it was for more than just my previous statements. She had observed me, questioned me, and now was accepting me in some way.

"All right indeed." Charlie was a man of few words, but his emphatic agreement with his sister made me feel as if something had been decided. "But you should still be careful."

"Yeah." Dot elaborated, "Alec is mostly just . . . misunderstood, but he can still be dangerous, and he doesn't know you, so proceed with caution. OK?"

"Noted." I gave them a firm nod. I wasn't an idiot. Someone with an ability to cause excruciating pain was dangerous; I just wasn't scared of him. Kind of like I wasn't scared of Kid when he threw that ball of fire at my head. Maybe I was turning into some kind of adrenaline junkie. "So, how do you two know Alec then? And how does Tyler fit into it?"

"Charlie and I are cousins with Alec. And Tyler . . . they've known each other since a very early age, and they went through some difficult things together some years back. They're family too, if not technically related by blood. They live together with . . . It's kind of complicated."

They lived with Kid? Kid had told me himself just a week ago that he lived with Tyler. Dot was being as cagey about the situation as Kid had been, and my curiosity was piqued, but I could only focus on one mystery at a time.

Dot waved her hand dismissively. "I'm sure you'll meet them all eventually anyway, now that we're friends."

"Friends?" I raised my eyebrows but couldn't help the smile pulling at my lips.

"Of course! What's your name, by the way?"

I laughed, amused at how she could be so sure of our friendship without even knowing my name. "Eve Blackburn."

Even though the circumstances of our meeting had been a bit strange, I genuinely liked Dot and Charlie and wanted to get to know them more. If they could help me pin Alec down, that was a bonus.

"Listen, thank you for explaining some things to me, and thank you for the coffee and muffin, but I'm serious about delivering this thanks. Can you point me in his direction? Please?"

"Oh, Eve, honey, no." It was Dot's turn to laugh, and Charlie joined her. "We'll help, I promise, but not today. When he's that pissed off, Tyler is just about the only person he'll allow in the same room as him. And anyway, I have no idea where he went. When he doesn't want to be found, you won't find him."

"Don't I know it." I had been *not finding* him for a year.

"Another day. I promise. He has to stick around for the next few weeks anyway—official Melior Group business." She gave me an exaggerated wink. Charlie shook his head at her, but he was smiling too.

Dot kept firing questions at me and sharing about herself and her brother. I found out Dot was the same age as me, and Charlie was only a year older. The conversation flowed so seamlessly that my plan to visit the museum was completely abandoned, and my mission to track down Alec almost forgotten. Almost.

Charlie mostly just watched us with his intelligent eyes, only occasionally throwing in a word or two. When he formed another complete sentence, it took me a little by surprise.

"Are you Variant, Eve?"

Dot and I both looked at him as he casually finished off his coffee, waiting for me to answer.

I found my voice. "No. I mean, I'm still waiting for my blood test results, but I've had tests before, and they came back negative, so . . . Um, are you guys?"

In answer, they shared a look, and a small gray blur came darting out of nowhere—startling me—climbed up Dot's voluminous skirt, and perched itself on her shoulder. Once it stopped moving, I could see it was a ferret.

"This is Squiggles." Dot scratched it under the neck and smiled wide at me. "My ability allows me to communicate with animals. It's referred to as 'control' of animals, but it's not a master-subject kind of dynamic. I simply ask them to do things, and they're almost always happy to oblige."

"Wow! That's amazing!"

All of a sudden, I was the one firing questions. During my interrogation, I found out we were in some of the same classes. Dot was taking some science units in preparation for a career as a vet.

"Naturally, I'll already know what's wrong with the animals—I can just ask them—but I need to learn how to actually heal them."

When she casually mentioned that Charlie was her Vital, the intensity of my interest and the speed at which I was firing questions doubled. Charlie was the first Vital I had ever met, and I wanted to know everything.

They were more than happy to explain things to me patiently. I knew that Bonds could form between any connected people—siblings, lovers, friends—but friendship Bonds were rare. There was a direct correlation between the strength of the Bond and the strength of the relationship between Variant and Vital, so the Bond sometimes pulled people who were not related by blood closer together, turning friendships into something more.

I had started reading an article about it the other night. The only relationship that never presented Variant-

Vital Bonds was parent-child, and often the people in the Bond were close in age. Research had yet to determine why this was exactly.

He was only a year older, but Charlie had the protective big brother thing down pat. Apparently being Dot's Vital only heightened the dynamic, bringing a supernatural element into his instinct to protect his sister. She said it could be overbearing at times, but they were so close it was hard to stay mad at each other.

"I'm sorry, Eve," Charlie cut me off midsentence as I was trying to ask another question, "but I have to get to my Variant Abilities lecture."

"Oh, of course. Sorry." I checked the time on my phone, swearing under my breath. I had to get to the same lecture. We had been talking for hours, and I'd completely missed lunch with the Reds. "I'm in that class too actually."

I laughed nervously, worried that I had bored them with my overbearing questions, but they both smiled, the resemblance clear in the curve of their mouths.

"I'll see you soon." Dot hugged me goodbye and turned in the opposite direction. "Give our new friend our numbers, Charles," she called over her shoulder, her big skirt swishing around her calves as the sharp black heels clicked on the concrete. Squiggles settled in around her neck like a live scarf.

"Have a good afternoon, Dorothy!" he called after her, and she made a gagging sound.

"Neither of us likes our full name much. So naturally we use them all the time." Charlie chuckled. As we walked to class together, he followed his sister's instructions, putting both their numbers in my phone.

Zara walked up to the lecture theater at the same moment we did. "What happened to you at lunch?"

I was relieved she didn't sound upset I'd stood them up. Before I had a chance to answer, she spotted Charlie next to me. Her sarcastic mask fell over her face, and she crossed her arms over her chest.

"Charles," she deadpanned, arching one eyebrow in a decidedly hostile way. I had no idea eyebrows *could* be hostile.

"Zara." He smiled, unaffected by the dangerous eyebrow or her use of his full name. "See you later, Eve." He gave me a friendly wave and went in search of a seat.

"What was that about?" I asked as we made our way to our own seats.

"You should be careful with that one. He's his sister's Vital, and she gets a little protective. If you're not careful, you could get your eyes gouged out. By a bear."

I laughed, a little too loudly, my voice carrying through the massive lecture hall. "You mean a ferret? I met Dot this morning. She seems really nice actually."

"What is it with you and that family?" Zara grumbled, pulling her books out of her bag.

"What?"

"Dot and Charlie are Kid's cousins."

"Wait, does that mean that Kid and Alec Zacarias are brothers?" If Dot and Charlie were cousins with both Alec and Kid, it made sense. I just wasn't sure how Tyler fit into it.

"No, they're cousins too. It's a big family. Wait"—her voice rose in pitch—"how do you know *Alec*?"

"I met him this morning too."

"What do you mean *met him*?" She turned on me, her eyes wide. "One does not simply *meet* the 'Master of Pain.'"

I rolled my eyes at what was obviously a common yet twisted nickname. "We'll talk about it later," I whispered back to her. The lecturer had arrived, and the rest of the room was falling into silence.

I ignored her huff of frustration. Her problem with Dot and Charlie probably had to do with her aversion to all things related to the Variant community in New York. I felt a little sad for her—she had so much anger about her situation—but at the same time, I just couldn't feel bad about having made more friends.

Plus, I had finally, *finally* found my stranger. Even though I hadn't been able to speak to him properly, at least now I knew his name. I knew who he was. Not only that, but Dot had promised to help me deliver my thanks.

I did my best to focus on the lesson, but I kept smiling to myself, practically giddy. The scholarship letter that had brought me to Bradford Hills had also delivered me to something I had been chasing for a whole year; it had thrown me directly into the path of Alec Zacarias.

Maybe my bad birthday luck was finally running out.

SEVEN

Beth's cute red heels clicked on the smooth footpath as we walked past the grand front gates of Bradford Hills Institute. It was a mild spring evening, and Zara, Beth, and I were on our way to Ethan Paul's party.

Beth was beside herself with excitement, her freshly curled hair bouncing around her shoulders. Zara had illustrated her lack of enthusiasm by waiting until the last minute to get ready and putting in almost no effort, although she still looked fierce in her black jeans and gray jacket, her short silky red hair and simple black eyeliner completing the look.

I'd opted for jeans too, paired with a long-sleeved black top I'd borrowed from Beth. It was cut low in the front, showing more cleavage than I was used to, but she'd gotten so much joy from getting ready together that I couldn't be mad about it.

Kid's house was just off campus on a wide, leafy street. Half the walk there seemed to be devoted to reaching the end of his ridiculous driveway—clearly, his family had money.

We'd passed the intimidating iron gates and were making our way up the tree-lined gravel drive when my curious mind popped up again. Maybe the Reds knew more about why Kid, Alec, and Tyler all lived together. "So, how many people actually live here?"

"Including the army of servants?"

I had a feeling Zara's sarcasm was going to be in overdrive tonight. Beth just laughed lightly. Nothing was going to ruin *her* good mood.

"I'm just curious about . . ." I wasn't sure how to finish that without sounding really nosy.

"About why Kid doesn't live with his parents?" Zara finished for me.

"Something like that," I mumbled.

"It's because they're dead."

I stopped in my tracks and turned to look at her.

"Zara!" Beth had pulled up too, her lacy skirt swinging around her knees. She fixed Zara with a stern look and looped her arm through mine in an explicit show of solidarity. I had told the Reds about never knowing my father and losing my mother. It had come up one night while we were sitting around in our pajamas, watching episodes of *Cosmos*—it had been my turn to pick the TV show.

Realization crossed Zara's face, wiping the sarcastic mask away.

"It's OK." I gave them both a smile. "I just wasn't expecting that."

"I didn't mean to be an insensitive douche." Zara was defensive most of the time, so it was easy to see when she was being sincere.

"Guys, I'm fine. Really." I extracted my arm from Beth's death grip. "What happened to Kid's parents?"

Beth gave me a weak smile and shrugged her delicate shoulders, but Zara tried to explain.

"I don't know the full story. It happened before I started at Bradford, so I've only heard what other people have told me. Basically, when he was little, Kid's parents were on some trip overseas, and they died in this massive accident. Alec's, Tyler's, and Josh's parents were all there too."

"Who's Josh?"

"Oh, he lives here too. He's Kid's friend."

Josh had to be the preppy blond guy I had seen Kid with.

"Anyway, this is Ethan and Alec's uncle's house. He took them in after . . . you know. He's high up in Melior Group management, so he's never around. Those guys basically raised themselves. I'm not sure why the other two ended up here as well. I guess traumatic shit tends to make people close."

"Right." I didn't really know what to say to that. I was taking Zara's account with a grain of salt—it had mostly been pieced together from gossip. I was curious about the truth, of course, but mostly I just felt sad for Kid. And Tyler, even though I didn't know him that well. And Alec, even though he had been a jerk to me. And the Josh guy too, even though I hadn't even met him.

I knew what it was like to lose a parent.

"OK. Enough depressing shit." Beth waved her hands between us maniacally. "We have a party to get to."

As if to illustrate her point, the low thud of music reverberated from the house, beckoning us to finish our trek up the obscenely long driveway.

As we continued our walk, I tried to put the new information out of my mind. A party was no place to be asking a guy I'd only met a few times about how his parents died.

The house had *presence*. As we rounded the curved driveway and it came into view past the oak trees, I slowed a little to take it in. It was huge but not obnoxiously hulking—classy—and screamed sophisticated opulence.

A few people were milling about the front, chatting on the stairs leading up to the front door.

"What do we do?" Beth asked, a tremble in her voice.

"What do you mean? It's a party. We go inside, have a drink, make meaningless chitchat." Why was she so confused?

"No, as in, should we be checking in with someone? What if you need an invitation to go in?"

"We have an invitation. Kid invited us."

"No, like a proper physical one."

"What?" I laughed a little.

Zara just stood there with an amused smirk on her face, not helping at all as I tried to talk sense into Beth.

"I'm going in. You two can stand around and"—I waved a hand in their general direction—"do whatever this is, or you can come with."

I turned and walked toward the front door, exchanging polite smiles with the half-drunk people on the stairs. Behind me, two sets of heels crunched along the gravel. They caught up to me as I reached the door.

What we found inside was just like any other house party. Just bigger. Much, much bigger and more over-the-top.

The foyer was massive, immediately dragging your eye up to what felt like an abyss but was actually three floors of staircases with an extravagant chandelier at the top. We headed toward the music, which was coming from the back of the house.

After walking down a cavernous hallway, we emerged into a large open-planned area with floor-to-ceiling windows along the back wall. Giant speakers in the back corner of the room looked as if they belonged onstage at a rock concert, and a DJ with a professional setup was whipping the crowd into a frenzy. At least a hundred people were writhing and contorting in a drunken dance in front of the speakers, where I guess the living room furniture usually was.

In an enormous kitchen on the right, plastic cups and liquor bottles littered the surfaces of stone benchtops. On the left, a dining table, which looked as if it could seat twenty, hosted a group of guys playing an intense-looking card game; a bunch of drunk people were playing a much rowdier drinking game at the table's other end.

In the five short minutes we'd been there, at least three people in various states of drunkenness had come up to Zara to say "hi." She'd tolerated the first, ignored the second, and flat out told the third to "fuck off." She seemed to know a lot of people here, and even Beth waved to a few friendly faces. I knew no one, so when I saw Dot marching in my direction, a big smile plastered on her face, I returned it enthusiastically.

She closed the distance between us and wrapped me up in a big hug. "You made it!" she half yelled before turning to Zara. "Hey, Zee!"

Zara's face scrunched up, but before she had a chance to tell my new friend to fuck off, Dot turned to Beth. "Hi, I'm Dot. You must be Beth. Love your skirt!"

Beth returned her greeting and gushed about Dot's unique outfit: a bright pink skintight dress with rips in the fabric—strategically placed so they weren't revealing anything outrageous—black fishnets, pink Mary Jane heels, and an actual candy necklace.

Dot and Beth chatted as our little group made its way through the crowd toward the back of the room. Half of the window wall was opened onto the outdoor area.

As we passed the threshold into the backyard, Charlie appeared, heading in the opposite direction. He was dressed simply in black jeans and a blue T-shirt, and he had a guy with brown hair pulled into a bun on his arm. When he spotted me, he made his way over with a big smile and dropped a kiss on my cheek.

"Hey Eve." He spoke close to my ear. "I'll catch up with you later. I'm a little busy right now." He winked and gave me a cheeky grin.

I hadn't seen Dot much in the few days since we first met, but Charlie and I had gotten into a few lengthy, nerdy conversations after our Variant studies lectures. We'd really clicked, and I soon realized Zara's warning to stay away from him was moot—he wasn't interested in me. He wasn't interested in anyone with boobs.

I laughed and nudged him in the direction of his date. "Have fun. I'll see you later."

The two of them disappeared into the throng inside as I turned to join the girls.

People in various stages of undress were milling about the pool—the clear centerpiece of the sprawling backyard—drinking, dancing, and jumping into the water. A girl with a water ability was sitting in a lounger by the pool, waving her hands in lazy, elegant movements that alternated between creating elaborate, fountain-like shapes and crashing water down on her swimming friends, all of them laughing uncontrollably.

A more chilled out crowd was chatting around a fire pit surrounded by comfy-looking chairs—maybe a little *too* chilled out, judging by the heady scent of weed wafting from that direction.

A canopy of string lights provided the only illumination and, if it weren't for all the drunken idiots, would have actually set a charming mood over the whole setting. They extended as far as the tables and chairs on the other side of the pool. The rest of the yard—and I had a feeling there was quite a bit more of it—was cast into darkness.

To the left was a fully stocked bar complete with stools and four frantic waiters serving all manner of drinks. One of them had super speed and was mixing cocktails so fast that the cocktail shaker in his hands turned to a blur.

"Uh, how are they getting away with that?" I gestured to the bar, frowning, surprised to see alcohol being served so freely to people under twenty-one.

"Oh, thank god!" Instead of answering me, Zara headed toward the bar without waiting to see if we were following.

"Ooh! Great idea! Let's have cocktails." Dot grabbed me with one hand and Beth with the other, answering my question as she walked. "The staff are paid very well to not check IDs."

Beth bounced rather than walked beside her. "This is the best party I've ever been to!"

I smiled, glad she was having fun and glad I'd somehow made that possible. I knew Zara didn't want to be here, but I was touched she'd come along with the sole intention of protecting me and Beth from whatever exaggerated threat she thought the Variants of Bradford Hills posed. She was a hard-ass, but with a gooey center.

The fire pit had reminded me of Kid's ability and the persistent guy it belonged to. I still hadn't seen him. I let Dot order our drinks as I leaned back on the bar and looked around.

The reflection of the string lights on the pool's surface were keeping me mesmerized when Dot pushed a bright green concoction in a tall glass into my face.

I gave her a worried look. "Do I want to know what's in this?"

"Probably not!" She grinned at me as the Reds joined us, and we all clinked glasses and took a sip. The drink was fruity but potent—definitely not something I should drink too fast.

As I took my second sip, Beth lost her footing and bumped into me, both of us spilling some of our drinks in the process. I steadied her, then my spine went rigid as I realized what had caused her to stumble.

A girl in a white one-piece bathing suit, her wet hair still plastered to her head, had shoved my new friend as she walked past with two other bikini-clad girls.

"Hey, watch it," I called out, letting a little bit of ire enter my tone.

The girl completely ignored me, speaking to her friends in a voice that was intentionally loud. "Who invited the Dimes?"

Every muscle in Zara's body stiffened, and she slammed her drink down on the bar, turning her blazing eyes on the mean girl. Dot stepped into her path, preventing her from going after the bitch, and I briefly considered going after her myself—*who the fuck did she think she was?*

"She's not worth it, Zara." Dot kept her hands on Zara's shoulders.

"She's right," Beth piped in, and Zara started to relax. "It's no worse than the hateful things humans say about Variants—calling you guys freaks of nature and a danger to society. She's just showing off to her friends."

"Doesn't make it right," I grumbled, passing Zara her drink so she would have something else to focus on.

"No, it doesn't, but I'm not letting this ruin my night!" Beth took a sip of her drink and smiled.

I took her lead and tried to steer the conversation onto other topics. After a while, even Zara joined in.

After a few minutes of chatting, Dot suddenly turned to me. "Oh, by the way, you're not gonna believe this! Alec is here."

I laughed. "Doesn't he live here?"

"Yes, but he never comes to these things. He's either away or he hides up in his room, glaring at the crowd from his window." She gestured to a spot high up on the house behind us, and we all turned to look. All the windows on the two top floors were dark.

"Maybe you could thank him tonight," Beth interjected.

After I'd mentioned to Zara in class that I'd met him, she'd demanded to know everything, so I'd told the Reds that evening about Alec saving my life. It was a bit of a relief to finally tell someone the full story. I'd gone a year without even mentioning my mother's death, and after only knowing them for a few weeks, the Reds had made me feel comfortable enough to want to spill it all—all except how Alec had been there for me in the hospital. I didn't want to tell anyone about that; it felt too private. I just wasn't sure if it was my privacy or his that I was protecting.

Dot agreed with Beth. "I promised I would help you pin him down, and tonight might be a good opportunity. He must be in one hell of a good mood to be down here with all these people."

"Right." I squared my shoulders and slammed the rest of my drink back, abandoning the empty glass on the bar behind me. "Where is he?"

All three of them laughed.

After her giggles subsided, Dot held up one finger and closed her eyes, taking a deep breath. Then she opened them again and just stood there, smiling at me serenely. Beth and I exchanged a confused look, but Zara had a small, knowing smile on her face.

Just as I was about to ask what the hell we were doing, Squiggles climbed up Zara's leg and perched on her shoulder. I was expecting Zara to make a derisive comment about "vermin" and throw the little ferret into the pool, but she surprised me by smiling wider and giving it a scratch on the head.

"I missed you too, girl." Her voice was so low I almost hadn't heard.

Zara and Dot clearly had more history than I'd thought, but that was a conversation for another day. I had a moody man to find.

Dot smiled at her furry friend and turned to me. "Squiggles says he's in the living room, by the dining table." Apparently, Squiggles had a knack for reconnaissance.

I turned around and headed back inside.

He was leaning on the wall near the card-game end of the table, dressed in all black again—jeans and a T-shirt. Everyone was giving him a wide berth, shrinking away and staying well out of Alec's reach if they had to walk past.

As he lifted his beer to his mouth, he spotted me. I smiled, going for a friendly approach, but he looked away as he finished the last few drops of his drink, ignoring me. He leaned over a girl with dreadlocks to set his empty bottle on the table, and she visibly jumped in her seat.

He was unaffected by it, returning to his spot against the wall and crossing his arms over his chest.

I waded through the crowd until I was right in front of him, looking him square in his ice-blue eyes. He just stood there, silent. The black-and-gray tattoos completely covering his right arm and peeking out of the left sleeve of his T-shirt did nothing to make him seem more approachable. The small frown line that had appeared on his forehead wasn't helping either.

Refusing to wither under his stare, I made myself speak: "Look, I know we got off on the wrong foot the other day, and I'm sorry about the part I played in that, so can we start again? Please?"

His frown only deepened.

I extended my hand and forged on. "I'm Eve. It's nice to finally meet you properly."

A few people laughed, and some others gasped in shock. He chose to side with the amused group, chuckling softly, a cruel smirk on his face. I was trying really hard not to let his mocking attitude get to me, but the tension in my shoulders was building.

When it became clear he wasn't going to shake my hand, I dropped it and stepped a little closer to him, trying to make this conversation as private as possible.

"I just want to thank you, OK?" I kept my voice low, despite the blaring music. "Can I have five minutes of—"

"Not this shit again." He uncrossed his arms and pushed off the wall, standing at his full, intimidating height. "I already told you. I was just doing my job. Leave me alone."

"Yes, well, speaking of your job"—if he wouldn't let me thank him for saving my life, at least I could try getting some answers—"maybe you could explain to me exactly what made the plane crash? Or how you guys knew where—"

"Shut the fuck up," he growled, stepping farther into my personal space while still being careful not to touch me. "We can't talk about this here."

I'd spoken as quietly as I could in a room full of partying people, and his growly response had been even quieter, so I doubted anyone had heard our exchange. Still, it was clear he wasn't willing to speak to me about any of it. Not in a room full of people. Considering the secretive nature of his job, it made sense, but would he ever allow me to say my piece or give me any answers?

I had been nothing but nice, but he was being downright hostile. It meant a lot to me that I say these things to him, that I ask some questions, but the asshole couldn't take five minutes out of his busy scowling-and-intimidation schedule.

"What the fuck is your—"

"Go away."

This time a woman had interrupted me. She'd appeared next to Alec, handing him another beer and taking a sip of her own, watching me with narrowed eyes. Her blonde hair was pulled back into a messy bun, and she was wearing skintight jeans and a top that was little more than a scrap of fabric. She oozed a confidence I'd only ever come close to in a chemistry lab.

Pressing her amazing body up against Alec, she draped one elegant hand over his shoulder, then smiled widely at me and fluttered her lashes.

"What the fuck is *your* problem?" *Who just walks up to a person and tells them to "go away"?*

The smile fell from her face, replaced by something much more malevolent, and I suddenly regretted my outburst.

Before the situation could escalate, Alec wrapped his arm around her middle and pulled her in close, stepping between us and giving me his back—a wordless dismissal after he'd barely acknowledged my presence.

My blood boiled.

Zara appeared at my side, slinging an arm over my shoulder and turning me in the opposite direction. "That went well," she mumbled, bugging her eyes out at me as Dot pushed a drink into my hand with a commiserating look.

"Maybe we could try to forget all the drama and go have a dance?" Beth was trying to salvage the night again, and I couldn't blame her.

"Stellar idea, Beth!" Dot led the way to the dance floor.

The girls—and the cocktail in my hands—slowly coaxed me out of my shitty mood. We danced and joked together, jumping around to pop music until we were panting and sweaty, but my eyes kept wandering over to where Alec was still standing with the snide girl. I couldn't help it; the situation felt so unresolved. Plus I was curious about this woman who could touch Alec so casually when everyone else avoided him like the plague. Zara was dancing closest to me, so I asked her.

"Ah, yeah, that's Dana. Her ability is to block other abilities."

"That's interesting." I hadn't heard of that one before, and I wondered how it worked. Did it have something to do with blocking access to the Light? It made sense, though, why she was unafraid to touch Alec. His ability couldn't hurt her.

"Yeah, it's unique." Zara followed my gaze, so we both ended up watching Dana push Alec up against the wall and kiss him, his hands gripping her hips, as we talked. "But it makes her as much of a pariah as him."

"Why?"

"Variants love their abilities. Having a connection to the Light, even a small one without a Vital to amplify it, is revered. Would you want to be around someone whose mere presence takes away what's special about you?"

Of course. No one would want their ability stripped away. Except Alec. Alec seemed happy to be rid of his ability. He was embracing being powerless as enthusiastically as he was embracing Dana.

I felt a little voyeuristic watching them as they shared such an intimate moment, but they were the ones making out in the middle of a party. My gaze felt locked on his hand as it trailed lower, gripping her firmly by the ass.

As if he could feel my eyes on him, he opened his and looked directly at me. I should have looked away, but I couldn't, and he held my stare as he continued to kiss the girl in his arms.

I was so focused on my stare-off with Alec that I didn't notice someone coming up behind me until a warm, sweaty body pressed against my back.

"You like to watch, huh?" The guy's breath reeked of beer as it washed over my cheek. "Do you like to *be watched* too? I can help you put on a show."

His hand landed on my hip, and my face scrunched up in disgust. "Eew! No chance in hell!" I spoke loudly, getting the attention of my friends, and the relaxed smiles fell from their faces.

I tried to step out of his grasp, but his grip on my hip tightened, and his other arm wrapped around my shoulders. My instinct was to elbow him in the stomach—all the paranoid advice my mother had given me about avoiding abduction flashing through my mind—but before I had the chance, Zara and Dot stepped up, each taking a sweaty arm, and shoved the drunk away from me.

"She said *no*, asshole!" Dot yelled as Zara stared daggers.

Beth gently wrapped her hand around mine and tugged me backward, and I turned around to get a good look at the guy. Between Zara and Dot's defensive stances, I glimpsed him swaying just a little where he stood, eyes glazed. He was a little older than us, wearing jeans, a tank top, and a backward baseball cap.

"Why don't you crawl back into whatever hole you came out of, Franklyn, and leave our friend alone?" Dot was doing all the talking while Zara just stood there, looking intimidating.

The guy laughed, as if it were all a big joke, and walked off, waving his hands in the universal "yeah, yeah" gesture.

My new friends surrounded me.

"Are you OK, Eve?" Beth put a hand on my shoulder.

"I'm . . ." My eyes were flying about the room, my brain trying to take in as much information as possible in its heightened state. Once again, my attention snagged on Alec. Dana was still pressed up against him, but she was in a conversation with some other girl. Alec was staring right at me. His expression was completely blank, but his eyes held a perplexing intensity that was evident even from across the room.

I couldn't stand the scrutiny and looked away, giving my friends a smile. "I'm fine, guys. Really."

They looked skeptical.

"I might get some water or something." I really was OK. My brain had processed the fact that the immediate danger had passed, but the oppressive crowd and loud music had become a little overwhelming. My friends all offered to go with me, but I insisted they stay. I didn't want to ruin their night any further, and honestly, a moment alone was exactly what I needed.

I managed to squeeze my way off the dance floor and picked up my pace as soon as I was free of the throng. As I passed the kitchen, focused on the foyer ahead, I barreled into someone.

The guy had come from around the huge kitchen island, shouting to someone behind him and not looking where he was going. As we crashed into each other, the beer he'd been holding, filling two red cups to the brim, ended up all over his very neat outfit. Only a few drops had landed on my sleeve, but his pale green Oxford shirt and beige chinos were dripping.

I stepped back, my hands out in front of me, eyes going wide in shock. His perfectly smooth dirty blond hair fell over his forehead as he surveyed the mess down his front. He looked vaguely familiar, and my brain got stuck on trying to place him, completely forgetting that I should be apologizing.

"Shit," he muttered. He glanced at me, then dropped his arms by his sides, resigned, before turning around and disappearing toward the front of the house.

As he walked away, I finally realized who he was: Kid's friend—the one I'd seen him hanging out with around campus and the one the Reds had said lived here. I couldn't remember his name though.

I stood there stunned for all of three seconds before another familiar guy stepped into my field of vision. The drunk from the dance floor was back.

"Hey! There you are!" He spoke as if we were old friends, not as if he had accosted me on the dance floor.

He started moving toward me, arms wide as if to give me a hug. I held both hands in front of me and started backing away.

Naturally, I ended up bumping into another person.

Big, warm hands landed on my shoulders, steadying me, followed by Kid's booming voice. "Franklyn, leave the lady alone." There wasn't an ounce of humor in his tone. It was serious and firm, but the drunk guy laughed anyway and started slurring about what a great party this was.

I half turned to look at Kid, craning my neck to meet his eyes.

"Thanks." Just having his strength at my back made me feel calmer. We smiled at each other, but the moment didn't last long. I still wanted to get out of there, and he still had a drunk dickhead to deal with.

"Anytime. Excuse me while I . . ." He gestured to our "friend."

I nodded and walked toward the foyer, immediately missing the steadying weight of Kid's hands on my shoulders.

EIGHT

I speed-walked toward the front of the house, trying to look casual, but the whole thing had shaken me up. I wanted nothing more to do with that drunk guy. Thank god Kid had been around to step in.

When I got to the giant staircase at the front of the house, I sprinted up it, desperate for a moment away from the party and the craziness of it all. I was out of breath by the time I reached the landing, my heart beating fast inside my chest—whether from residual fright or from the run up the million-step staircase, I wasn't sure. I needed to sit, calm myself, but I couldn't just plonk down in the middle of the corridor.

Voices drifted up from below, and I groaned—I hadn't gotten far enough away.

The drunk guy slurred something unintelligible while laughing boisterously. Kid's booming voice, talking over the top of him, carried up the stairs.

"Dude! Not cool. You need to leave."

It didn't sound as if drunk guy was going to go without a fight, and I didn't envy Kid his task of trying to get a wasted person to do—well, pretty much anything.

Not wanting to get caught between them again, I rounded the corner and made my way, much more slowly and quietly, up the second flight of stairs. Convinced no one would be up in this part of the house, I walked to the first door on my left and let myself in, turning immediately and pressing my ear to the wood.

Nothing. Even the booming music from the giant speakers was muffled to a distant rhythmic thud. I relaxed my shoulders and turned to check out where I was, only to find myself staring into a pair of amused green eyes.

I jumped, startled by the guy standing in the middle of the room. He was taller than me, not by much but enough that I needed to angle my head up to look him in the eye. He wasn't as tall as Kid and nowhere near as wide—no one was quite as big as Kid—but he had presence

"Jeez!" My hand flew up to my throat, trying to calm my panic. "You scared the crap out of me! What the hell, man?"

He chuckled, crossing his arms over his chest loosely. "You're the one that barged into *my* bedroom without knocking, *and* you made me spill beer all over myself."

It was the guy I'd run into downstairs. He'd changed out of his beer-soaked shirt and into a grungy Metallica T-shirt. Combined with his now mussed hair, it was such a contrast to the polished look of his original outfit that he almost looked like a new person.

His eyes were the same though. A rich green, almost emerald, muted in the dim light of his bedroom.

"Right. Fair point. Sorry about that. I didn't know there was anyone in here. And sorry about before . . ." I made a waving gesture at his chest, indicating where the beer had soaked him. He had the build of a soccer player, lithe and defined, his biceps not bulging out of the T-shirt sleeves but still making themselves known. ". . . with the beer and all that."

As I spoke, I took in the room. The tall ceilings, wood paneling, and heavy drapes over the window were in line with the opulence of the home, as was the sheer size of the space—yet the room was filled with personality. Opposite the neatly made king-size bed, a leather couch faced a large fireplace in the left-hand wall. Surrounding the fireplace and curving around the two adjoining walls were floor-to-ceiling bookshelves bursting with books, records, CDs, and even tapes. In one section of the shelf sat an impressive-looking stereo system.

"I didn't like that shirt anyway." His voice dragged my gaze away from the bookshelf and back to him. "Hiding from someone?"

"Ah, yeah. Some drunk guy—Freddy? Frankie? Something."

His face got serious. "Franklyn? Are you all right?" He took a step toward me, his eyes running over me from head to toe. "You need me to go take care of it?"

"No! No, it's fine. Kid's already kicking him out, I think." The last thing I wanted was more drama, and Kid seemed as though he had it under control.

"Right. OK." He visibly relaxed. "I'm Josh Mason, by the way."

I made a mental note to remember his name. Zara had mentioned it in the driveway earlier, but I'd forgotten it.

"I'm Eve Blackburn. I'm kind of new here." The shelf was drawing my attention again, and I found myself drifting toward it. "So, you're not related to Ethan and Alec, are you? You don't look alike." I couldn't help digging for some information—something to confirm or deny the facts of the tragic story Zara had told.

"No. I just live with them. We grew up together." He didn't seem inclined to elaborate.

I was wary of being too nosy, and besides, the bookshelf now had me thoroughly distracted. "You must read a lot."

Obvious, but I was so occupied with scanning the sea of titles that I wasn't really paying attention to what I was saying. Some familiar ones jumped out at me. He had the classics—Dickens, Bronte, Austen, Tolstoy—but also some modern literature and, in among those, some nonfiction too—philosophy, history, and a bit of politics.

His chuckle came from close behind me. He had followed me over, his movements completely silent on the soft carpet. "Yeah, I like to read. Do you read?"

"Yes. More like *devour* the words."

He laughed, a soft, contained sound.

"Although I don't read as much fiction as you," I continued. "I don't mind philosophy and politics, but there's still too much subjectivity. Give me an edition of *New Scientist* any day. Even textbooks . . ." I trailed off—I was sounding like a total nerd and maybe a bit of a show-off. *I, an intellectual, read scientific journals and textbooks for fun.* I groaned internally, afraid to look at him. Maybe it was time to slowly back out of the room and leave the gorgeous boy with the full lips and kind eyes alone.

He stepped up next to me and leaned one shoulder on the shelf to my right. "As interesting as I find science,

I struggle with the journals. Too much jargon."

We were looking at each other now, him casually leaning on the shelf, arms crossed, me with my arm still resting on the spine of the book I'd been looking at, my mouth slightly parted in shock. He wasn't freaked out or put off.

Then I remembered where I was. Of course everyone here would be intelligent and well-read. Bradford Hills Institute was the most exclusive school in the country.

"You must be studying some science subjects then?" he asked. "Are you taking any of the Variant studies units?"

I quickly did my best to cover my astonishment and tried to act naturally, pushing my sleeves up to my elbows to give my hands something to do. *Natural*, however, was becoming increasingly difficult to pull off; I was speaking to a guy that was not only ridiculously good looking and intelligent but also actually interested in speaking to *me*.

We chatted briefly about which classes we were both taking. He was twenty, a bit older than me, but due to Bradford Hills' unique way of structuring classes, we had a few in common. When I made an intentionally cheesy joke about how organic chemistry is difficult because those who study it have "alkynes" of trouble, Josh laughed and leaned forward, lightly touching my forearm where it rested on the shelf. His warm hand felt soft on my bare skin.

A tingling warmth at the point of contact reminded me of when Kid and I first shook hands. We both stopped laughing, and the air became heavier around us. I looked down at where we were connected, marveling at the sensation. He must have mistaken it for discomfort, because he withdrew his hand and rubbed the back of his neck, looking a bit uncomfortable.

"So . . ." My voice sounded shaky even to myself. That buzzing energy was starting up again. It had been nearly a week since my last stretch of sleeplessness, and it was choosing this particular moment to rear its head. *Great.* "What kind of music do you like? By the look of your shelves . . . all of it." I laughed lightly. There were easily just as many records, CDs, and tapes jammed onto the shelves as there were books.

He laughed and looked at me with a sparkle in his green eyes, the awkwardness gone. "I don't mind most music, but what I really love is rock."

"So all these are . . ."

"Yep. Everything from AC/DC to ZZ Top. From Foo Fighters to Linkin Park to Marilyn Manson to . . . well, you get the idea. There's such a variety in sound and style and so many subgenres. So much to listen to, and real artistry in the way the music is made. These guys really play their instruments, you know?"

His enthusiasm was downright adorable, and I smiled wide, equally amused at his excitement and impressed with his knowledge.

He returned my smile and crouched down, flipping through some records stacked along the bottom shelf. "You wanna hear something?"

"Sure." I could watch Josh geek out over rock music for the rest of the evening. I didn't even need to go back to the party. What party?

He plucked out a record and walked over to the stereo system, lifted the flap, extracted the record from its sleeve, and placed it gently on the turntable.

As a slow, moody guitar filled the space, he walked back over to me, eyes never leaving mine. "This is Led

Zeppelin. It's one of their less well-known songs, but I love it. Rock doesn't have to be all high energy and loud banging. There's real emotion in music like this."

He stopped right in front of me.

The itching, as hard as I tried to ignore it, was burning at my wrists. It was torture not to reach up and scratch my arms, but Josh's eyes had pinned me to my spot.

He gently laid his hand on my waist, and I reacted instantly, placing my hand on his bicep. We leaned into each other slowly, keeping eye contact until our faces were so close that I could see how dilated his pupils were, the green around them almost pulsing.

Our lips met softly at first, in a gentle kiss that felt like a sigh. I'd only met him twenty minutes ago, but kissing him felt like a much-anticipated reunion after a long absence, as if I'd been waiting for him for years. We moved into each other simultaneously. His arms wrapped around my middle, pressing me into his chest as I lifted my own arms around his neck, one hand twisting into his hair.

The kiss was soft, but also intense and warm. Comforting and firm. Our breathing deepened as our lips moved against each other. It felt so natural. It felt like home.

That warm tingly feeling was back but so much *stronger*. It was everywhere, bleeding in and out of me. His touch felt like liquid gold. The sensation was present wherever our skin touched, but my whole body felt connected to him. I was acutely aware of his every movement, every twitch of his fingers against my spine, every breath that pressed his chest impossibly closer to mine.

When he pulled away, the lights seemed to dim. I leaned forward, moving with him, a snake leaning toward the snake charmer. He had broken the kiss but didn't let me go. We stood there, holding each other, looking into each other's eyes as a look of shock spread over his face.

The kiss had been nothing short of spectacular—I'd never been kissed like that before. Judging by his speechlessness and the way his hands were flexing against my back, bunching the fabric of my shirt, I had a feeling he'd liked it too.

So why had he broken it?

As if coming out of a fog, the details of our surroundings drifted back into focus, and movement to my right caught my attention. I immediately tensed up, assuming someone was in the room with us. Then the whole picture became clear, and shock and a hint of fear rushed down my spine.

A book was floating in midair above the couch. And it wasn't the only one. Books, records, CDs, clothes, and other various inanimate objects were floating all around the room. Even the heavy drapes were lifting off the ground, as if they were the softest sheer curtains caught in a breeze.

I glanced back into Josh's face, and his expression matched mine, his gaze trained behind me. We still held each other, frozen to the spot, both of us trying to process what we were seeing.

Had I done this? Would my blood test come back positive? Was I somehow a Variant? *Oh my Stephen Hawking!* How was I supposed to make it stop? I had no idea how I'd even done it. What if all this crap came tumbling down and knocked us both out?

Before I could descend into full-blown panic, Josh spoke distractedly. "Did I mention I'm a Variant?" He looked back at me, the shock on his face mixing with wonder. "Telekinetic ability."

His last word trailed off as his shell-shocked expression morphed into a wide, almost manic smile. He was looking at me like a kid who'd woken up on Christmas morning to find a puppy under the tree.

A frown pulled at my brows. This was getting weird. The fact that Josh had such a unique power came as a surprise, and part of me wanted to ask a million questions, but his strange behavior was putting me off. Add to that the fear that I might die under a stampede of inanimate objects, and the whole situation was getting pretty overwhelming.

He seemed to realize the oddity of it then, and a horrified expression melted the smile off his face.

"Holy shit!" He dropped his arms and stepped away from me lightning fast. Immediately, all the crap floating eerily about the room thudded to the ground.

I shrieked and covered my head with my hands while lifting one knee up and huddling against the bookshelf. Miraculously, nothing hit me. Not a single item even grazed me on its way down.

"It's OK. You're safe." There was a tinge of panic in his voice as his hand landed gently on my shoulder. "It could never hurt you . . . I would never . . . that is to say . . . it's impossible for my ability . . . Shit!"

As I straightened, he snapped his hand back.

I finally found my voice. "What the hell is happening?"

"How is this possible?" he was mumbling to himself. "I thought Kid . . ." He swallowed audibly and looked at me again, eyes wide, a mixture of incomprehensible emotions written all over his face. After a moment, he managed to pull a coldly neutral expression down over it all.

"You need to leave." He spoke evenly, but with hardness to his tone.

"What? Why?" Was he somehow blaming me for this? And why did he mention Kid? I had maybe met the guy two times—it wasn't as if we were dating. Josh and I had just shared an incredible kiss, and now he was throwing me out? Although he hadn't said it in so many words, I was 60 percent sure Josh had enjoyed the kiss too. *Right?* Shit.

"It's complicated. I can't really explain . . . Look, you just need to go before someone sees . . . Please." His mask of calm was slipping, and a hint of frantic energy was coming through in his voice and posture. He raised a hand, palm upturned, and gestured toward the door.

I hung my head, unable to look at him. Refusing to let him see me upset, I turned and forced myself to walk at a steady pace to the door, letting my features crumble into a pained expression now that he couldn't see my face.

Kid chose that moment to swing the door open, without knocking, two meters in front of me, sweeping aside all the debris that had fallen to the ground.

"Dude! Where have you been? I can't find . . ." His booming voice stopped midsentence when he saw my face, his brow creasing in confusion. Or maybe it was concern. I couldn't be sure. My ability to read what people were feeling through simple body language was obviously on the fritz.

"Hey, Eve." His voice was much softer now. "You OK?" Then his eyes scanned the room, taking in the chaos. "Whoa! What the hell happened in here?"

I was done. I was *so* done with this party and this house and these people. Maybe Zara had been right about avoiding them. Once again something wonderful was being ripped away from me.

Anger settled in the pit of my stomach. That was good. I could use anger to propel me out of this room, out of this house, and away from this whole messed-up situation.

"Whatever," I ground out between gritted teeth, squaring my shoulders and pushing past Kid and out the door. To be fair, I didn't push past Kid—no one could really push past Kid if he didn't want them to—but he stepped out of my way as I pretended I was pushing past him, and for that one small concession, I was glad.

I stormed down the corridor and flew down the two flights of stairs. At the bottom, I nearly barreled into the Reds, who were just coming around the corner.

"Oh my, Eve, are you OK?" Beth had concern written all over her face.

"Would everyone stop asking me that?" I snapped at her.

Sweet, lovely Beth didn't deserve that. I was being a jerk. As much of a jerk as Josh had been. The anger drained out of me. "I'm sorry. I didn't mean that."

"That's OK. What happened?" My rude outburst was already forgotten. That's just the kind of person Beth was.

"Nothing. I'm all right. Really." I forced a smile in response to the skepticism on both their faces. "I'm just over this party. Going to head home. Can you tell Dot and Charlie goodbye for me?"

I was already on the move again before I'd finished speaking.

"Want us to go with you?" Zara asked.

I was touched by their concern, but it only added to the emotional turmoil already whipping around inside of me. Tears pricked at my eyes as I kept going. "No, no. All good. You guys have fun. I'm fine. Promise!" I managed to make my voice sound even. Just.

Despite the fact that I had shared some of my deeply personal history with them already, my instinct in my current emotional state was still to run away from the Reds. I wanted someone to comfort me. To help me make sense of what had just happened. But I hadn't been that close to anyone since my mother died. Maybe I just didn't *know* how to get close to someone. Maybe the distance my mother had devoted herself to establishing between us and the rest of the world was permanent.

Maybe I would never have true friends that I could talk to. Maybe I would never have a boyfriend to share my life with. Maybe that's what Josh had picked up on in his bedroom when he'd shut off from me—that it was impossible to get close to me. He was Variant, after all; maybe his superhuman senses allowed him to sense these things.

The tears spilled over in earnest as I reached the end of the long driveway. Thankfully, there was no one around to see. At the gates, I broke into a run and I didn't stop until I reached the front door of our residence hall.

I was so focused on the pit of negative emotions writhing inside me I didn't even register that the tingling, itching sensation had completely left my wrists.

NINE

I pulled my knee-length jacket tighter over my chest as I walked to class, regretting my decision to wear flats instead of boots. The warm weekend had given way to a chilly Monday morning. The sun was hidden behind fat clouds threatening to burst with rain.

I had gone straight to bed after the party, welcoming the oblivion of sleep, and spent all of Sunday holed up in my room, reading and studying, trying to distract myself from the feelings of rejection and self-consciousness. When the Reds had invited me to lunch, I told them I just wanted to read. Later, Beth had come in on her own, brow creased with worry. I'd been so close to telling her the whole story, but I hadn't wanted to relive it all, so I'd convinced her I was just tired, and she left me alone.

As I approached the building where my first lecture was due to start soon, I was hunching my shoulders against the cold, my gaze turned down.

I didn't see them until it was too late.

"Eve." Ethan's booming voice was unmistakable.

I looked up, my steps faltering. He was standing with Josh at the door to the building, students streaming past them. Ethan was in his usual white T-shirt and jeans, apparently not bothered by the cold at all, and Josh was back to his preppy, polished look, the collar of a neat shirt peeking out underneath a cashmere sweater.

I did *not* want to see them. I was mostly over what had happened at the party on Saturday. Mostly. But I wanted nothing more to do with them. I was heeding the Reds' warning about Kid and extending it to Josh.

Squaring my shoulders and narrowing my eyes, I marched past them and into the building.

"I need to speak to you," Josh said from behind me. They were following me.

"That's funny," I threw over my shoulder as I kept walking. "You had nothing to say to me on Saturday night. Couldn't wait to get me out of your room, as I recall." OK, so maybe I wasn't as over it as I'd thought.

"Yes, I was a jerk. Will you please stop so I can explain?" He was keeping his voice low. The corridor was teeming with people. I couldn't decide if I was grateful no one would overhear us talking about my embarrassing encounter or if I was further insulted he didn't want anyone to hear us speaking to each other.

"Just leave me alone." Frustration leaked into my voice as I sped up.

"Where are you going?" Ethan chuckled.

I stopped—I had no idea. I'd been so busy trying to get away from them that I hadn't paid any attention to where I was going. Unfamiliar rooms lined up on either side of the unfamiliar hallway. We appeared to be at the back of the building somewhere, standing next to a narrow stairway.

"Shit!" I turned around, figuring it was best to get this out of the way so I could get to class. "What do you want?"

In perfect synchronicity, they each looked down an opposite length of hallway, checking for prying eyes. Their movements made me acutely aware there was no one else around in this part of the building. I was alone with two guys I didn't really know, and not only were they bigger and stronger than me, they also had rare and dangerous Variant abilities.

They stepped closer, and I retreated instinctively, my back pressing against the railing of the staircase.

Josh leaned forward, his voice low. "Look, I just need to know if you told anyone about the . . . what happened at the party."

He wanted to make sure I would keep my mouth shut?

"Oh my god!" My voice was much louder than his, echoing up the stairs behind me. "Do you have a girlfriend? You're an even bigger asshole than I thought."

"Shh!" Ethan craned his neck around the corner.

Josh's lips pursed in annoyance. "What? No, I don't have a girlfriend. That's not what this is about."

"What then?" I refused to lower my voice, raising it a notch just to spite them. "You don't want anyone to know that you got it on with the new girl, who's here on scholarship and is probably a Dime? Don't want to damage your reputation? You only date Variant bitches, is that it?"

"Variant bitches! Hah!" Ethan laughed, trying hard to do it quietly and mostly failing. Ethan didn't do anything quietly.

Josh just looked even more irritated. "Would you please lower your voice?" he whisper-yelled at me, stepping even farther into my personal space. "This has nothing to do with any other girls or anything as petty as reputation. Look, I know you're new here and you still don't understand how the Variant world works, but if anyone knew what happened the other night, we could all be in danger. Including you."

His words sent a chill down my spine, making me acutely aware of how close he was to my vital organs. I swallowed audibly and looked away from his intense stare.

"Are you threatening me?" I meant for it to sound outraged, as though I wouldn't stand for this, but it came out sounding weak and quiet.

Immediately Josh stepped away, and the amusement disappeared from Ethan's face.

"No! I am so sorry." His green eyes looked sincere. "We didn't mean to . . . I'm not trying to scare you."

He sighed and flopped down onto the stairs. "Maybe I should just—"

"No," Ethan cut him off midsentence. "It's safer this way. You know it." He crossed his arms over his chest and leaned on the wall opposite the stairs.

The path down the corridor was clear again, but I stayed put. Even though they'd been a little intense, they hadn't actually threatened me—and they were being just cryptic enough that my stupid curiosity was piqued.

"Why am I in danger?" It seemed like the most pertinent question to ask.

Josh looked up at me from his spot on the stairs, his intense green eyes reminding me of the way those eyes had taken me in just before we'd kissed. I looked away quickly. I didn't want to be reminded of that. Mostly because

I wanted it to happen again. Why did he have to be so damn hot and mysterious?

"It's a dangerous time to be a . . . Variant. The government is tightening regulation on the use of our abilities—all you need to do is pick up a newspaper to know that. People like Ethan and I are closely monitored. We're left alone for now mostly because our abilities haven't grown too far past what they were when they manifested. When we . . . when you were over the other night, I realized that my ability is much stronger than I originally thought because—"

Ethan cleared his throat and threw Josh a pointed look.

". . . because of . . . reasons," he finished lamely, looking away from me, and I rolled my eyes. "I'm sorry. The less you know the safer it is. If anyone found out about how strong my ability was and it got back to certain people, . . . it just wouldn't be good for me, OK? And anyone close to me, like Ethan, would immediately fall under suspicion, and it wouldn't be good for them either. You were right in the thick of it when it happened. So that's not good for *you*."

"Right." I looked from one to the other, barely containing my skepticism. "So for reasons that you can't explain, your powers are suddenly stronger, and for more vague reasons, that puts you in danger, and I happened to stumble into this mess, so now I'm up shit creek too? That about cover it?"

Josh pulled himself back into a standing position. "Yes?" It came out as a question.

"OK. Well, I have no interest in sharing that particular embarrassment with anyone anyway, so your secret is safe with me. Now can we just pretend like none of this ever happened and go to class?"

Both of them sighed in relief and nodded. I gave a single nod and took off in what I hoped was the direction of my lecture hall.

I wasn't entirely buying their "we're all in danger" spiel, but pretending the incident with Josh never happened was fine by me. My ego and confidence were bruised enough.

The next day was even colder, made worse by the steady rain that had started overnight and seemed to intensify as I got ready for the day. Staying in bed and listening to the rain was tempting, but there was no way I was going to miss chemistry lab.

I trudged to the science building, already getting excited about which experiments we might be running. Not one to make the same mistake twice, I wore the boots I had wished for the previous day and a jacket with a hood pulled low. Luckily, the science building was one of the closer ones to my res hall, and it only took me five minutes to walk there.

Head down, I ran the last few meters—just as a particularly nasty gust of wind sent the rain flying sideways—and came to a stop under the cover of the front of the building. Lifting my head and pulling the hood off, I came face to face with the intense blue-eyed stare of Alec Zacarias.

I stood there, stunned, as other students filed into the building, desperate to get out of the rain.

Alec had his hands stuffed into the pockets of his black coat, the collar turned up against the wind, as he alternated watching me and scanning the area around us. When the last student entered the building, he took a step in my direction.

"I know those two spoke to you yesterday"—his voice was low, muffled by the sound of the rain, but loud enough that I could hear him clearly—"but I need to make sure you understand the gravity of the situation."

"Well, hello to you too," I huffed. Who accosts someone in the morning—before they've even had their coffee—and starts talking *at* them without even saying hello? "Wait . . ." His words registered, and my skin prickled with embarrassment. "They told you about that?"

I averted my gaze, the embarrassment giving way to a spike of outrage. So I was supposed to keep it a secret, and they could tell whomever they wanted?

"They trust me. And they were right to keep it quiet. No one can know what happened, do you understand? This is not something you gossip with your girlfriends about before you have a pillow fight. When we say tell no one, we mean tell *no one*."

"Pillow fight?" I chuckled—this had to be one of the strangest conversations I'd ever had. And my mother and I'd had some doozies. "You don't spend much time with women, do you?"

He leaned down so our faces were closer together, his shoulders hunching, the hard set of his features laced with frustration.

"I don't spend a lot of time with anyone, *precious*." He spat the last word out like an insult. "Now, start taking this seriously. Those two dickheads are my family, and I will do whatever it takes to protect them. They can't . . . they're too young to get dragged into . . ."

The frustration in his eyes had melted into a desperate kind of pleading, the eyebrow scar becoming more pronounced as he raised both brows slightly. He couldn't seem to bring himself to speak the words, to actually plead with me, but it was written all over his face. "And *you* . . . you definitely shouldn't be anywhere near *any* . . . "

His shoulders sagged—his voice had turned to honey.

It was the first time I'd heard that voice since the hospital, and it broke something inside me. My insides twisted into a knot under my warm coat. I knew I was seeing the real Alec for the first time since that night.

Without thinking about it, I reached out and placed my hand on his shoulder gently. I spoke as quietly as he had, injecting as much sincerity into my voice as I could muster. "I won't say anything. I promise."

The muscles under my touch relaxed a little, and he gave me a nod as he straightened, squaring his shoulders, making my hand fall away.

Encouraged by the calmer, more approachable Alec, I figured I had nothing to lose by trying to bring up the crash and the hospital again. "About the night of the plane crash . . ."

His attention had caught on something behind me, but his eyes flicked back to mine, the frown back in place.

"I don't have time for this." The honey was gone from his voice again. "Make sure you keep your promise."

He adjusted the collar of his coat and rushed into the rain. I turned to watch as he crossed paths with Dot, who was jogging toward the chemistry building.

"Hey, Alec." She greeted him with a little surprise in her voice, her steps faltering.

"Hey, Dot. Get to class. You're late." He didn't slow down at all and soon disappeared around a corner.

Dot joined me under the cover of the entranceway. "What's going on? You OK?"

"Yeah." I tried to give her a smile, but it fell flat. "Um, I just tried to thank him again, and he got all weird about it. Again." It wasn't the whole truth. As much as I wanted to confide in my friend, there was something in me that didn't want to break Alec's confidence. All three of them had been very serious about me keeping my kiss with Josh a secret.

"Damn. Why was he here though? He rarely ventures far from the admin building when he's on campus."

"Beats me." I had become a pretty good liar living with my mother. I shrugged my shoulders and tried to change the topic. "Do you have a class here too?"

"Oh shit! I am so late for my biology lab!"

It worked like a charm. She rushed inside the building and I followed, matching her pace. I was late for my chemistry lab too.

That evening, the itching at my wrists returned again. It briefly reminded me how the beginnings of an episode had come on right before I'd kissed Josh at the party, only to perplexingly disappear. Most likely that had been a milder surge of energy, which my body had expelled immediately as I ran from the Zacarias mansion back to my res hall.

This surge of energy was *not* mild.

The itching spread up my arms and legs quicker than ever before, and I declined the Reds' invitation to watch a movie over hot chocolate—perfect rainy weather activities, according to Beth—so that I could hide in my room, tear my clothing off, and spend the night scratching unashamedly. I alternated doing sit-ups and push-ups with long stretches of study and reading, trying to exhaust my body and my mind.

I had four sleepless nights—more than any episode so far—which worried me a little. But at least it allowed me to get way ahead on all my coursework and read every scientific article on Variant DNA Tyler had recommended. But eventually the tingling, nervous energy left my body.

I spent the week trying to focus on my studies and ignore all the things I was worried about but powerless to deal with. Of course, this turned out to be impossible.

The intensity and length of my latest itchy energy—along with the fact that it had come right after I'd kissed a Variant—was disconcerting. Of course, several previous tests had confirmed my human status, but how could I reconcile that with the odd things I was experiencing? I was suddenly glad Tyler had insisted on the blood test—I need to confirm I was normal, that it was all in my head. Until then, I was doing my best to pretend this problem didn't exist.

The fact that I didn't have the full story behind why Ethan, Josh, and Alec were being so secretive about Josh's ability and our kiss was also driving me insane. But I couldn't pretend *they* didn't exist. In fact, I couldn't seem to get away from them.

It was a classic case of the Baader-Meinhof phenomenon—now that I knew who Ethan and Josh were, I was seeing them everywhere. When I was having coffee with Dot and Charlie or chatting to the Reds after class, one or both of them would join us. They acted perfectly naturally, making conversation and joining in whatever the group was doing, not giving me any more attention than anyone else but not ignoring me either.

They were basically pretending nothing had happened. It was infuriating.

They never spoke to me or approached me when I was alone, never giving me a chance to ask for answers. Not that they weren't around when I was by myself.

When I went for my early morning runs, trying to expel the crazy energy, I would spot Josh sitting under a tree and reading a book or Ethan throwing a football with some friends. One or both of them were in half of my classes, but they never sat next to me. As I walked out of Starbucks, mediocre latte in hand, there was Ethan walking in, giving me a friendly smile and a "hey, Eve" but hurrying past before I could stop him. As I walked into the library to do some research for an assignment, there was Josh, coming in a few minutes after and settling into a chair with a book.

They even crashed a girls' night. The Reds had suggested we go see a movie in Bradford Hills, since I hadn't had a chance to explore the town. We made a night of it, deciding to go for dinner as well. As we reached the gates of the Institute on our way out, Ethan and Josh appeared. They engaged the Reds in conversation, Ethan's easygoing personality putting even Zara at ease after a few minutes, and ended up spending the whole evening with us. Neither of them sat next to me at dinner or in the theater, and they walked us all the way back to our res hall, even though it meant they would have to double back to get home.

I'd seen Alec around as well. Unlike the other two, he made it clear he was watching me. His hard stare would be unashamedly fixed on me, his mere presence reminding me to keep my mouth shut—which I'm sure was his intention. If I stared back at him too long or if I tried to approach him, he would turn around and stalk off.

Even Tyler was popping up where I didn't expect him. Although, to be fair, he did work at Bradford Hills. For all I knew, it was normal for him to be talking to my physics professor as I walked in for class, or to be passing by me in hallways and on the leafy lanes of campus more and more. He would always give me a friendly smile, but he never seemed to have time to stop and chat. I had no idea if Ethan and Josh had told him about the kiss, and I was not about to ask.

I knew they weren't actually stalking me, that it was just the curious state of my mind noticing them more than before. Still, it was getting a little weird how one of them was always around.

But their constant presence and my increasingly suspicious mind were not even remotely as alarming as what happened in the middle of the night, one week after I'd been sworn to secrecy about what I'd seen in the Zacarias mansion.

Nothing was as perplexing as why I found myself racing back there, feeling as if my chest were being torn open.

TEN

When I woke up, it was instant. One second I was asleep, and the next I was sitting up in bed, eyes wide, all senses on alert.

Something was wrong. *Really* wrong.

For a second I wondered if I was in pain. What had woken me? Was I in danger? But even before the worry had a chance to take root in my mind, I knew that wasn't it. I was fine. I was warm and safe in my bed.

Yet I *knew* that something was wrong. I could feel it with every fiber of my being. It took only another second of confusion before I threw the sheets off and jumped out of bed. I had to do something. I had to stop it.

Somewhere in the depths of my mind, I knew this wasn't logical. I just had to *go*.

I slipped my feet into flats and grabbed a cardigan off the back of my chair on my way through the door, slipping it over my shoulders as I rushed through the living space.

"What?" Beth shot up into a sitting position on the couch. Zara was out on a date, but Beth had stayed in, binge-watching something. "Where are you going? It's the middle—"

But I was already through the door and running. Halfway down the corridor, I heard the door slam behind me.

My heart was beating frantically against my ribcage. I was running out of time. I was too far away.

What if I don't get there in time? A cry tore itself free from my mouth as I sprinted down the three flights of stairs. I couldn't wait for the elevator.

Beth caught up to me as I burst out of the front doors and flew down the front steps, the cool night air doing nothing to snap me out of my frenzy.

"Wait!" She grabbed my elbow.

I wrenched it out of her grasp and broke into a sprint, darting over the lawns in the most direct path toward the front gates.

Beth managed to keep up with my frantic pace. "Eve, what's going on? You're freaking me out."

"Don't!" I sounded distraught, even to my own ears. "Don't try to stop me. I have to hurry. Before it's too late to save him."

The words had sprung out of my mouth without thought, but they rang true. *I have to save him.*

"Save who? Is someone in trouble?"

I didn't answer. I had no idea who "him" was or where my frantic feet were taking me, only that they were following some inexplicable pull, running on pure instinct and adrenaline.

I passed Bradford Hills Institute's massive front entrance and turned sharply to the left, Beth hot on my heels. Something in my voice, my expression, my frenzied behavior must have convinced her this was serious, and she was sticking to my side like the good friend she was.

My breath was becoming labored and my legs burned, but I was nearly there. I could feel it. The pull was easing the closer I got, yet also somehow becoming more urgent. My heart beat wildly for reasons that had nothing to do with the punishing pace I'd set.

He was fading away. I had to get to him *now* or I would be too late.

I turned right at the next street, dashing across the road, barely checking for cars.

Just a little farther. I grabbed the iron gate of the Zacarias mansion and used my momentum to propel myself around the corner.

My feet crunched on the gravel of their ridiculously long driveway. *Nearly there.* I could feel him even more now, but it was . . . *less*. He was getting weaker.

Beth had begun to fire questions at me again. Questions I had no answers to. "Oh my god, Eve. Why are we here? What the hell is going on?"

At the end of the driveway, where the trees ended, a charred mess resembling a vehicle was sending coils of acrid black smoke into the night sky.

The shock of seeing something so unexpected in the perfectly manicured front yard, combined with my own exhaustion, finally brought me to a stuttering stop. I leaned over, resting my hands on my shaking knees, and struggled to draw oxygen into my lungs, but the terror slamming into me from somewhere deep within wouldn't allow me to pause for long.

This is where it happened.

"Holy shit!" Just as spent as me, Beth continued to ask questions between gasping breaths. "What happened here? Eve, you have to start talking! Please, just . . ."

I ignored her, springing back into action, the urgency of my single-minded task impossibly doubling again. I ran up the front stairs and pushed through the front door, which was already ajar. No hesitation. No wondering where to go, which room to search for. I didn't even think to call out. I just bolted straight through the house, past the kitchen, and out another half-open door.

I *needed* to get to him.

I ran as fast as I could around the pool and to the right, finally sprinting into the pool house.

Josh was pacing the main area inside, barefoot and wearing only a David Bowie T-shirt and boxers, his hands in his hair. Bowie's painted face seemed somehow out of place in a life-and-death situation.

". . . to get him warm. It's the only chance we have." Tyler's voice was coming from the back of the building, along with another deep male voice swearing profusely.

Josh's hands dropped from his hair, a shocked expression falling across his features as I flew past him. "Eve? What . . . ?"

Both he and Beth following me down the short hallway and into a tiled bathroom area. On the left was a wooden door with a small square window—a sauna. On the right, the glass wall of a steam room, steam billowing out of the wide-open door and past the three people huddled around the entrance.

Held between Tyler and Alec, Kid was unconscious, his head lolling to one side, his big body completely limp. He was dressed in only his underwear.

Tyler saw me first, barely sparing me a frown before focusing on his task. He had his hands under Kid's arms and was half carrying, half dragging him into the steam room. Alec had his legs, the muscles in his shoulders bunching with the strain.

As soon as I laid eyes on him I knew. This was why I was here.

He was dying.

I bent over as a sob broke past my lips and fat tears spilled over, running down my cheeks. It felt as if a piece of my soul was being torn away from me, making it hard to will my limbs into moving.

But the tearing pull in my chest was impossible to ignore.

In the moment it had taken me to absorb the scene and fall apart completely, Tyler and Alec had carried Kid into the steam room and lowered him onto the wide bench, his head and shoulders propped up on the adjoining tile wall. They were all speaking over me—frantic, confused voices—but none of it registered. My mind and body had homed in on the reason I'd woken up in a panic and sprinted here like a crazed person.

There was no doubt in my mind that if I could just touch him, everything would be OK.

I stumbled into the steam room, pushing past Alec as he tried to close the door, and fell to my knees next to the bench. At last, my hand reached out to press against Kid's chest.

I took a deep breath. For the first time that night, the sense of hopelessness, the feeling that he was slipping away, ceased. Everyone else in the room had gone quiet. The only sounds were my own breathing, still a bit erratic, and the soft whistle of steam being pumped into the room.

The agonizing pull in my chest had eased, replaced with the instinctual knowledge of what he needed next. I became acutely aware of—and more than a little annoyed by—the wide-open glass door letting all the heat out.

He was too cold.

"Close the door. I . . . I can't . . . I won't be able to . . . He needs to be warm!" My last statement came out as a panicked shout.

It broke the stupefied spell everyone was under, and they all sprang into action. Several voices spoke over one another in the background, becoming muted as someone finally closed the door to the steam room.

He was getting warmer, but he needed . . . *more.*

Urgency not unlike the itchy hyper-energy I'd been experiencing over the last year spread through me. But this felt heavier somehow. *That* feeling was all about me and the need to expel it—whatever *it* was. *This* feeling was about Kid. He needed this. His life depended on it.

I took a deep breath and lifted my hand from his chest. The panic slammed back into me immediately, demanding that I resume contact, but I managed to ignore it for the few seconds it took me to undress.

I kicked my shoes off as I ripped the cardigan away from my body and pulled my oversized T-shirt up and over my head. Feet shuffled and throats cleared behind me, and the realization darted through my mind that I was now standing in nothing more than my underwear and a tank top in a room full of people I barely knew. But I didn't have time to be embarrassed or self-conscious.

The frantic pull toward the fragile boy on the bench had become almost painful yet again. Without further thought, I swung a leg over his slumped form and lifted myself onto the tiled bench over him, my knees pressing into his sides. I swept my messy, tangled hair out of the way before lowering my whole body onto his, my belly and chest resting on his torso as I gently dropped my head onto his chest.

Eyes closed, I gave in to whatever it was that had brought me to his side so swiftly and decidedly. Every point where our skin made contact hummed—a warm, pleasant sensation. Slowly, my breathing began to even out.

After some time—*minutes? hours?*—his chest rose under my cheek in a deep sigh. I slowly lifted my head to look into his face as his eyes cracked open. He shifted under me, and his big hands landed softly on my back as we stared at each other.

After only a moment, his eyelids drooped closed again and his head lolled to the side against the tiles.

I dropped my cheek back down to his chest. His heartbeat was stronger, and his breathing steadier. My skin was still humming wherever it touched his. Gradually, the furious energy of the evening's events drained out of me.

At some point, I passed out.

~

When I woke up, I was warm, the pleasant humming feeling still flitting over my skin. I opened my eyes slowly, lazily. It must have been around dawn; the dark room had a soft blue tinge to it—the first light of day creeping in. I was bundled into a bed with the softest sheets my skin had ever touched.

My head was resting on his shoulder, my arms tucked in front of me between our chests. He had one arm under my neck and the other slung gently over my waist, his fingers resting on the sliver of exposed skin between my underwear and the bottom of my tank top.

I should have been freaked out. There should have been a million questions going through my mind. Instead, I was still half-asleep and still in the daze that had brought me to him in a panic, only the panic was gone. It just felt right. I was *supposed* to be here in this bed in the arms of Ethan Paul at dawn, hours after he had nearly died. This was where I belonged.

Nothing existed outside the pleasant humming of our touch. Nothing existed past the edge of the bed.

Everything felt sluggish: my mind, my body, the light with its lazy blue hues beckoning me back to sleep. But I needed to check on him. I knew he was alive—I could feel his chest expanding with strong steady breaths, hear his heart beating under my cheek—but I had to look into his face to convince myself.

As I shifted gently in his arms, angling my head to get a better look at him, his body responded immediately. The hand on my waist pressed down ever so slightly—as though to keep me in place but unsure if demanding this halting of movement was permitted.

I dragged my eyes slowly up his chest, over the curve of his neck, past the angle of his jaw, to look into his face.

His eyes opened. They looked as sluggish and relaxed as I felt.

An inexplicable warmth flooded my chest at the sight of him conscious and well, if still a little out of it. I sighed with pleasure, and the corners of my mouth curved up infinitesimally in a lazy smile. He responded with a soft smile of his own.

For a few moments we just stared at each other, as if to make sure the other person was real. I'd never looked someone in the eye for so long before. With anyone else, in any other setting, it would have been too weird, too intimate. One of us would have turned away, cracking a silly joke to dispel the intensity.

Yet staring into Ethan's eyes as we held each other felt perfectly normal and comfortable. It didn't matter that I hardly knew the guy, that we had met only a handful of times. In that moment, I knew *him*. I knew who he was underneath all the bullshit and the secrecy and the big boisterous personality that matched his big boisterous physique.

It felt right to have his hand on my waist—his fingers now flexing just slightly on my bare skin. It felt natural when we both leaned in.

We were on opposite ends of an invisible tether, being tugged toward each other.

It was not a desperate and frenzied embrace—it was slow with inevitability. Our lips met halfway and pressed together softly. Once again moving in tandem, my arm traced his shoulder and landed behind his neck while his hand snaked up from my waist, underneath my tank top, toward the middle of my back.

We pulled each other closer at the same time.

Our chests pressed together as the kiss deepened, still slow and gentle but steadily increasing in intensity.

As naturally as it had started, the kiss came to an end with slow pecks against swollen lips. Our foreheads met, and our noses rubbed gently together.

He extracted his hand from the back of my tank top, and his fingers tangled into my hair, beginning a gentle massage on my scalp.

"Thank you." He whispered it so softly that if my face hadn't been pressed into his, I wouldn't have heard him. I wasn't sure what he was thanking me for, and I couldn't find the energy to think about it. Unconsciousness was tugging at me again.

He rolled onto his back and took me with him, gently cradling my head and settling it into his shoulder. The arm under me curved around, his hand finding the sliver of exposed skin once more. It seemed we both still craved skin contact.

I settled into his side, and we both went back to sleep.

~

When I woke up the second time, it was broad daylight, made painfully obvious by the sun streaming in through the window in front of my face, blinding me even through my closed lids.

I groaned softly and shifted, intending to roll over and away from the offensive light, but I froze. There was an arm slung over my middle and a warm chest pressed into my back.

Why was someone in my bed?

Even as the thought floated through my mind, I realized it was inaccurate. I couldn't have been in *my* bed. There was no window directly opposite my bed and therefore no way sunlight could be shining on my face.

I was in someone else's bed. With . . . someone?

I was now wide awake, all senses on alert, my heart hammering in my chest.

Forcing myself to take a deep, calming breath, I tried to pinpoint the last thing I could remember, but my train of thought was immediately interrupted by the person behind me, who had responded to my deep breath with a breath of their own and a tightening of their arm around my waist. He—I didn't know any women with arms that wide—snuggled in closer to my back, nuzzling his face into the back of my head.

Did he just smell my hair?

I needed to extract myself from this person and try to figure out where I was.

As slowly as I could, I wrapped my fingers around the wrist resting on top of me and lifted it gingerly, then awkwardly shimmied toward the edge of the bed.

Behind me, the mystery person froze. He cleared his throat and gently extracted his arm from my grip, and the mattress dipped as he shifted farther away from me.

I turned my head to finally find out who had kidnapped me and . . .

"Ethan?" He was propped up on his elbows, mirroring my position, shirtless, the blanket pooling around his hips. He had a wary, slightly shocked look on his face—as if he too was trying to figure out what was going on.

"Uh . . . hey?" His eyes flicked down my body and flew back up to my face.

I looked down at myself—I was wearing only my tank top. The left strap had slipped off my shoulder, pulling the front down to almost reveal my left nipple. I gasped and immediately pulled it back up, suddenly very aware of how *naked* Ethan was in the bed next to me.

My mind warred between dragging the blanket up to cover myself and throwing it off to see exactly how nude we were under it.

I needed all the facts before I could form a conclusion, so, sitting up fully, I lifted the blanket off my lap and peered down. At the sight of my fluro pink underwear, still securely in place, I breathed a sigh of relief.

Ethan chuckled. I turned my head sharply in his direction and glared at him. He was still leaning back on his elbows, his coal-black hair sleep tousled and looking . . . sexy. Dammit! He looked sexy, OK?

But I wasn't going to let his shirtlessness and messy hair distract me from my fact-finding mission. I whipped my hand over to grab the blanket at the base of his stomach, yanking it away so I could look under it.

Ethan chuckled again and asked, "Like what you see?" in his gritty, sexy morning voice just as the door to the room burst open. Josh, Alec, and Tyler spilled inside.

As if the situation weren't ridiculous enough, apparently it was time to throw in the boy I'd recently kissed who'd then rejected me, the man who had saved my life and then actively avoided me for a year, and a staff member at the educational institute I currently attended whom I'd begun to develop a crush on. This was turning into a bad improv comedy show.

We all froze. Me with a handful of blanket held over Kid's crotch, Josh gripping a steaming mug of coffee in each hand, Tyler similarly holding two plates of food, and Alec just watching everything with narrowed eyes.

Ethan was the one to break the silence. He burst out with his booming signature guffaw and flopped back onto the pillows. This snapped us all out of the awkward spell we were under. While Ethan continued to laugh on the bed beside me, Josh and Tyler began to speak over each other, setting the mugs and plates down on the desk near the door.

Alec just crossed his arms over his chest and leaned in the doorway, the slight frown on his face unchanged and directed at me.

I grabbed the blanket and dragged it up to my chin, scooting back until I hit the headboard. The pressure of held-back tears was making my face ache. I pulled my knees up to my chest, unable to look away from Alec's stare, its intensity pinning me there, his eyes accusing.

I had no idea what was going on or how to get myself out of this situation. I was in a room with four other people, but I felt so alone.

I was still meeting Alec's glare when the tears welled over and my breath started coming in broken pants.

Alec's expression shifted to something incomprehensible—but unnervingly intense. He dropped his arms and took a step into the room before changing his mind, turning on his heel, and stalking out, slamming the door behind him.

That's when the others realized I was crying.

The room fell silent as tears began trailing down my cheeks. I dropped my eyes to focus intently on the blanket covering my knees, tracing the swirly pattern in the fabric. I was hoping everyone would just go away so I could think.

Tyler cursed softly. Next to me, Ethan had begun to fidget, unsure of what to do with the crying girl in his bed.

After the longest and most awkward few moments of my life, Tyler finally decided to take charge.

"Eve." He was using his serious, adult-in-charge voice. "What's wrong?"

Despite how confused and scared I was, I looked up at him—his authoritative tone made me feel as though I had to. My gaze wandered from his neutral, serious expression to Josh's intense, confused eyes and then finally over to Ethan, who looked . . . as if he was in pain?

Something about that seemed familiar. I felt so lost, and I had no idea how to explain it to them.

It must have showed on my face, because Josh explained it for me, his voice quiet but confident. "Oh my god. She doesn't remember."

Ethan's pained expression turned into one of shock, and he stared at me, eyes wide.

It must have dawned on him then what this scenario must look like from my perspective—the girl who found herself half-naked in his bed without any memory of how she got there.

I looked around at them again; they all wore matching horrified expressions.

"No!" Ethan reached for me, then thought better of it and snapped his hand back, completely getting out of the bed.

But that only made it worse. Now he was standing there in nothing but his underwear, and looking at his almost naked body somehow felt *more* intimate than having him lying next to me.

"This is *so* not what it looks like, Eve. Oh god! Why doesn't she remember?" The last bit was aimed at Tyler.

"I'm not sure. This isn't how the connection usually forms. It was a traumatic experience for both of you. Maybe her mind just can't . . ."

As Tyler spoke, Ethan grabbed a T-shirt from a chair by the bed and pulled it over his head. "So, what do we do? Eve, what can we do?"

"I don't know." My voice was shaking. "I need to know . . . I just . . . why am I here? Did we . . . ?"

Tyler attempted to answer my disjointed questions. "You came here last night because Kid was in trouble and you wanted to help. Nothing untoward happened." He looked uncomfortable.

Ethan, his hands in fists, leaned on the bed, putting himself at eye level with me but not getting any closer. "You saved my life." He said it with such intensity, such conviction, that I couldn't suspect he was lying or being dramatic.

I stopped crying and released the death grip I had on my knees, straightening up as the sensation at the back of my mind nudged at me again.

I brought my hand up to my chest, rubbing lightly just below my neck. Lingering remnants of the urgency, the pain I'd felt last night tugged at my memory. I glanced around the room and my eyes caught on Josh. The bright colors of his David Bowie T-shirt served as the anchor my mind needed to put it all together.

It came rushing back—the sudden way I woke up, the overwhelming desperation that had me sprinting all the way here, the pain at seeing Ethan unconscious and vulnerable, the crushing worry that he might die, the unexplainable urge to touch him.

I sprang to my feet, and Ethan straightened. He was so tall that my standing on the bed put me only half a head above him.

"I have a feeling she's remembering it." A tentative smile spread across his face, bringing his dimples out.

He almost died.

The urge to be sure he was all right slammed back into me, and I bounced across the mattress and launched myself at him. He caught me, wrapping his arms around my waist as mine wrapped tightly around his shoulders.

I breathed a sigh of relief and smiled wide as I felt the strength in his grip. He was OK. He had made it.

Our embrace only lasted a moment before two sets of strong hands yanked me back onto the bed. As soon as I was away from Ethan, Tyler and Josh released me and stepped back, though they remained standing close.

"Probably best if we keep the physical contact to a minimum now that you're back to full strength. We wouldn't want to burn down the pool house." Tyler sounded as if he was explaining their weird behavior, but I only had more questions.

"OK, someone better start explaining. Preferably with visual aids. Because I'm no longer worried that you're a bunch of creeps who drugged me and had your way with me, but I am still really confused." I must have looked like a crazed person sitting in the middle of the bed in my underwear, my face tear-streaked but smiling—*because Ethan was OK.*

Instead of answering me, Ethan made a beeline for the plates on the desk and started shoveling food into his mouth. "Man, I'm starving!"

"OK. Fair enough." It was Tyler, once again, who was attempting to answer my questions. "But you both need to eat and . . . ah . . . get dressed. Why don't we give you some privacy, and then we can talk out in the living room?"

Now that he mentioned it, I *was* pretty hungry. And now that he mentioned it, I *was* sitting in a bed in my underwear. I'd spent a little bit of time with Josh and Ethan, but Tyler was still firmly in the category of "official Bradford Hills representative" in my mind. All my interactions with him had been strictly related to Institute business, despite his laid-back approach. Even though I knew he lived here, it was still a little odd for me to be seeing him off campus. *In my underwear.*

I slowly lifted the blanket back over myself, feeling self-conscious again, and nodded. Tyler grabbed the other plate and walked out of the room, herding Ethan through in front of him.

Josh didn't follow them straight away. He walked around to my side of the bed, a small smile playing at his lips. He leaned down in front of me, just like Ethan had moments earlier, and looked at me with those intense green eyes.

"You're amazing." He raised one hand and brushed my cheek with his knuckles. Instinctively I leaned into the touch, and that tingling feeling spread like warm butter where our skin met. It felt amazing. It felt like . . . when I'd touched Ethan last night.

As I grasped at half-understood facts, beginning to *maybe* connect them into a half-comprehensible theory, Josh straightened and walked toward the hall. Grabbing the mugs off the table, he exited the room and turned, smiled at me again, and flicked his eyes to the door. It swung slowly closed at his command.

ELEVEN

As soon as I was alone in the room, I didn't want to be.

I needed answers and knew they had them, but I also just wanted to be around them. The pull I had toward these two guys I hardly knew was beyond anything I could explain. I didn't *feel* as if I hardly knew them. I felt as if we were family who just hadn't seen each other in a really long time. As if there was an established connection regardless of what I knew about their favorite foods and music preferences.

I was relieved to find a bathroom connected to the room I was in and a spare toothbrush left on the counter for me. After a quick freshen up, I got dressed. It felt warm, so I opted not to put the oversized T-shirt or cardigan back on, but I couldn't go out there in just my underwear. I rifled through the items on the chair and decided to borrow the shorts that were obviously intended for Ethan.

By this point, I was so hungry that my stomach was in a constant state of grumbles. I followed the intoxicating smell of bacon down the short hallway.

". . . both of you. It's a delicate situation, to say the least."

"What's a delicate situation?" I wasn't eavesdropping; I'd simply walked in while Tyler was speaking. It was odd seeing him outside the confines of Bradford Hills, but at least it wasn't as awkward as him piling into the little bedroom with the other boys when I was half-naked.

I had run through the pool house so fast the previous night that I had no memory of what it actually looked like. Now, walking out from the back of the structure, I saw an open-planned living area. Directly opposite me, a wall of windows looked out onto the yard, the double doors in the middle flung open, letting the breeze in. Alec was leaning in the doorway, looking out at the pool, his back to us all.

To my right was a small kitchen area; on my left, couches and a TV. The whole space was decorated in the Hamptons style—lots of whites and blues with touches of light timber.

Ethan sat at a round dining table under the window facing me, already finishing his first plate of food and loading up his second. Tyler and Josh were situated on either side of him.

All three of them looked up and smiled. "We'll get to that," Tyler assured me. "Have something to eat."

He didn't have to tell me twice. I marched over to the table and sat across from them, snatching up a plate heaped with food. As the bacon and eggs landed on my tongue, I moaned, and my eyes rolled back into my head. I felt as if I hadn't had a meal in days. All my focus was on my plate, until the smell of coffee hit me.

I reached for the steaming mug in front of me but paused with it halfway to my mouth. *American coffee*. I set it back down, a disgusted look on my face. "I don't know how you guys drink this swamp water. I need to find somewhere that does a decent latte around here or I'm going to go nuts. And don't say Starbucks! Don't get me started—" I looked up. They were all staring at me. "—on Starbucks."

Even Alec had turned around to look at me, an *almost* smile on his face. I didn't have a chance to wonder about this sudden improvement in his mood though. Without so much as a "goodbye" to anyone, he turned around and walked out.

I returned my attention to the three people still present, beginning to feel a bit self-conscious. "What?"

Ethan just chuckled and took a sip of his swamp water.

It was Josh who answered me, leaning on the back of his chair. "We've just never seen someone eat as much as Ethan."

"Oh." I shrugged. I was not about to apologize for a healthy appetite. Although, looking down at my plate, I had eaten a lot more than I usually did. Double the amount of bacon I could normally stomach, and there must have been at least five eggs on the plate, plus the toast, mushrooms, and avocado.

Tyler must have recognized the confused expression on my face, because he leaned forward. "It's natural to be hungry after something like last night."

"Right." It was time for answers. "And what exactly was that?"

Tyler sat up straight. Falling back into more familiar conversation territory for us—facts and information—felt reassuring.

"Eve, you're not human. If there was any doubt over your blood work, it was eliminated last night."

"What?" I spoke around another mouthful of food as I attempted to digest the bombshell Tyler had just dropped. "When did my blood work come back? Are you saying I'm Variant? Do I have a healing power? Wait, but how would I have known that Ethan was in trouble?" My mind was racing with the possibilities.

"Slow down." Tyler chuckled. "Your blood work came in on Friday—a little early. Since you had not presented any powers and I knew you were being truthful when you said you didn't believe you were Variant, I was waiting until Monday to set a meeting. But we've suspected . . ." He threw a meaningful look in Josh's direction.

Josh casually sipped on his own pond sludge, looking completely unfazed by the situation. "Since the night of the party. When we kissed," he finished, his green eyes trained on me the whole time.

I lifted my chin and crossed my arms defiantly, refusing to be embarrassed. He was the one who had made it weird by throwing me out and then practically stalking me.

Ethan had stopped eating too. I shifted my gaze in his direction to find him grinning at me.

And then the memory slammed into my consciousness.

We kissed!

I gasped, my hand shooting to my mouth, my eyes going wide.

"Remembering more from last night?" His grin was mischievous, despite the adorable dimples in his cheeks.

Was he teasing me? I resumed my defiant posture and stared at him.

Tyler was thoroughly confused. "What the hell?"

Again, Josh saved me from having to answer. "They kissed. Last night, or rather early this morning, in bed."

"What?" Tyler and I spoke at the same time. Apparently he didn't know this piece of the story either. How the hell did *Josh* know that?

"I was there. One of us was in the room with you right up until an hour before you woke up. We had to monitor you and make sure you were both OK." A serious expression passed over Josh's face. "Ethan, you came so close . . . and Eve, you passed out and we couldn't wake you. It was scary."

He was worried about us. Both of us. Ethan slapped a big hand on his friend's shoulder and squeezed.

"It's all good bro. I made it. Eve's fine. Everything's totally copacetic." He grinned and went back to eating. Josh rolled his eyes at him, but I caught the affectionate smile on the end of it.

Tyler cleared his throat, ready to steer the conversation back toward a more productive topic. "Well I guess that's natural under the circumstances. But let's focus. We have a lot to cover."

"Right. What exactly are those circumstances?" Even though my brain had begun to piece it together, the logic and evidence undeniable, I still needed to hear it. It didn't feel real.

"You are not only Variant, Eve." Tyler leaned forward, fixing me with his serious look. "You're a Vital. And it would seem you've already found your Bond in Ethan and Josh."

My mind went blank for a moment, struggling to process this information and reconcile it with the fact that I'd grown up believing I was human. I blinked slowly and looked at the three guys sitting across from me, one by one. Tyler's eyes were cautious, assessing my reaction. Next to him, Ethan and Josh were watching me with matching tender looks on their faces. Soft smiles just for me.

I'm a Vital. I tried the label on for size in my mind.

I had unbridled access to limitless power. Two people with some of the rarest and most fascinating abilities I had ever seen were in my Bond.

I have a Bond.

A Bond—a group consisting of at least one Vital and one Variant. A tight, unbreakable connection defined by the Light shared between the people in it, tethering them to each other for the rest of their lives.

I took a deep breath, pushing aside my contradicting feelings of apprehension and excitement, and chose to focus on the more immediate questions.

"So that's why I knew Ethan was hurt? The Light was instinctively drawn to saving him. I couldn't have stopped myself from sprinting here like a maniac if I'd tried. And Josh, when we kissed, that's why all that stuff started flying around the room. It was you doing it, with your ability. But it was me too because I was feeding you more Light."

Now they were all smiling. Tyler looked relieved, probably because I was allowing my curious mind to connect the dots rather than freaking out. I should have been more floored, more surprised. But as soon as the initial shock wore off, it all made perfect sense.

I hate unanswered questions more than anything, and this revelation was allowing so many pieces to fall into place. I felt strangely calm about it. If anything, I was becoming excited. Hungry to learn more about my Light access, about my connection to the boys, my mind had sprung into full curiosity mode.

But before I had a chance to start firing my million questions, Alec walked back into the room. He marched right up to us and set a takeaway coffee cup on the table in front of me. Resting one hand on the back of my chair, he leaned down, careful not to touch me, his intense eyes level with mine.

"Thank you for saving my cousin's life. I don't have a lot of family left. I'm glad we've found . . . their Vital. Ethan and Josh's Vital. You." He frowned at the end, looking a little unsure of what he was saying.

"I couldn't have stayed away if I tried. There's no need to thank me." I bit my lip. I'd unintentionally thrown his words back in his face. After trying to thank him for saving my life several times and being repeatedly dismissed, here I was, doing the same. "You're welcome," I hastened to add, injecting as much sincerity into the words as I could and giving him a smile—despite the fact that he'd been a massive asshole to me.

He nodded once and straightened, walking back to his spot in the doorway, facing us.

"Love you too, bro!" Ethan piped in.

Alec smiled briefly but ignored him otherwise. "The latte is from a café nearby. Best non-American pond sludge coffee in town."

Stunned, I looked down at the little cup in front of me. He'd gone out to get me coffee? How . . . thoughtful. I'd known the kind, gentle stranger who had been there for me in the hospital was in there somewhere. I just wished it hadn't taken someone nearly dying to bring it out of him.

My first tentative sip of the latte got me way more excited than what could be considered normal. It was good. Really good! So good that it made me think of Melbourne—the city that had made me such a coffee snob in the first place.

"What did I miss?" Alec asked.

"Eve and Kid kissed," Josh threw in before anyone else could speak, leaning back, hands crossed behind his head, a teasing smile on his lips. He seemed to be getting an unusual amount of pleasure from sharing that little fact.

Alec looked from me to Ethan and then sighed heavily, pinching the bridge of his nose. "I leave for five minutes . . . This is getting out of hand." He turned to Tyler, speaking to him directly. "The connection is too strong now. Avoidance is futile. We're going to have to start teaching them to control it, or the three of them are screwed and we won't be able to do much to protect them."

His words were heavy with frustration, and I understood why. Josh's power could be incredibly destructive unchecked—as evidenced by the sheer volume of stuff floating around his room after our brief kiss—and Ethan's was even more dangerous.

I sat bolt upright, a new question occurring to me, and I blurted it out without thinking. "How come we didn't light the bed on fire?"

Alec pinched the bridge of his nose again, sighing deeply; Tyler looked up to the ceiling, his expression decidedly uncomfortable; Josh choked on his sip of coffee; and Ethan laughed, loud and from deep in his chest.

"We still can, if that's what you want," he said on the end of his laugh, leaning his elbows on the table and giving me a devilish grin.

I was momentarily embarrassed at my choice of words, not to mention distracted by Ethan's obvious flirting, but I pushed it all aside and rolled my eyes. "You know what I mean. If brief contact with Josh had all his worldly possessions floating around like we were in a scene from *Carrie*, why didn't Ethan's fire ability go haywire when we . . . touched?"

Tyler was quick to explain. "You were both weakened. He had nearly died, and you had completely drained yourself feeding him the power he needed to survive. At that point, almost all the Light was being used to sustain you, Eve, as your levels recovered. Although I suspect that even as your levels of Light rose slowly, you were still channeling small doses into Ethan.

"As soon as we put you two in the bed, you both immediately gravitated to each other, seeking out contact, despite being passed out. Eve, you began to cry in your sleep when we lifted you off Ethan—once we were sure he wouldn't die, of course.

"Ethan wouldn't have been able to muster even a matchstick-sized flame in his state, and you had no energy to spare for his ability. It was all being used to keep you both alive. That's why you were so hungry this morning— your body is craving energy, from all sources. You don't realize you're even doing it, Eve, but right now you're building up your stores, drawing Light into yourself, ready for when it might be needed next."

"So last night we were simply too weak for it to be dangerous. But this morning when I hugged him, that's why you pulled me off?"

"Yes." Tyler nodded, and Josh answered simultaneously with a vague "More or less. Sure. That's why."

Tempting as it was to delve into why the boy who had kissed me had pulled me out of a hug with another boy who had kissed me, I had more pressing concerns. Such as why Ethan had been dying in the first place.

"What exactly happened to Ethan last night? Why didn't you just call an ambulance?"

This time no one jumped in to answer. Silence filled the room as all the boys turned to Tyler.

When Tyler answered, I knew I wouldn't get the full story.

"Basically he used too much of his ability. There was an incident, and he used his fire to . . . help someone. He used too much. We don't have direct access to the Light like you do, Eve. We can use our abilities without a connection to a Vital, but it's limited. If we push it too far, it starts feeding on our life force."

I watched Ethan as Tyler spoke. His face was serious again, piercing me with his amber eyes.

"A hospital wouldn't have been able to help him?"

"There is nothing that modern medicine can do when we overuse our abilities. There have been studies. I'll send you links to some research. When we deplete ourselves like that, our body temperature plummets, like we're going into hypothermia. The hypothesis is that the ability uses every bit of energy available to it—it drains the very life from our veins, the very heat from our flesh. The only chance we have is to warm the body up and hope it can heal itself. It happens so fast that even waiting for an ambulance would have taken too long."

"Of course, having a Vital helps," Josh added. "As you saw last night. If it wasn't for you, Eve, Ethan probably wouldn't have . . . made it."

The room fell silent, everyone looking down at their hands, their mugs, the table.

I began to understand how close these four were. Even though only Alec and Ethan were actually related, it was clear they were all family. The kind that runs deeper than blood.

"The burned-out car." The charred remains of the vehicle I'd encountered on my mad dash here had to connect with what they were telling me. Sort of telling me. Kind of alluding to without *actually* telling me anything.

I looked from one to the other, waiting for confirmation. Ethan and Josh avoided my eyes, and Tyler was staring into space, lost in thought. The only one who returned my gaze was Alec, his blue eyes unwavering. I raised my eyebrows and gave him a "start talking" look.

"Ty?" He surprised me by turning to Tyler, who recovered from his distracted stare and gave Alec a slight nod.

"Yes. That was Ethan," Alec finally confirmed.

"Holy shit! What happened?"

"We can't tell you that. It's classified," Tyler cut in.

"I am so sick of that word." I rolled my eyes, flopping back in my seat. The fact that Tyler had even used that word told me this had something to do with Melior Group and Alec's secretive, dangerous job, but Alec's deferring to Tyler spoke volumes too. "Wait, do you work for Melior Group?" I fired the question at Tyler before he could give me any more evasive talk.

"You're too observant for your own good." He sighed, but it was said with affection, and warmth sparked in my chest at his praising of my intellect. "Yes. I work for Melior Group *and* for Bradford Hills. They're two of the biggest Variant associated institutions in the country—they need to have a collaborative relationship. I act as a sort of liaison. My position isn't a secret, but it's not exactly advertised either." He fixed me with a meaningful look, and I nodded.

"Yeah, and that technically puts Tyler's rank above Alec's, even though Alec is older by two years." Josh lifted his mug up to his mouth, barely covering a cheeky grin. I was starting to think Josh was a bit of a shit-stirrer. I knew I probably shouldn't encourage him, but the corners of my mouth twitched up involuntarily.

"Man, it's not even funny." The humor in Ethan's voice contradicted his statement. "Ever since he became Alec's boss, he's been even bossier in all other areas of our lives."

"I am not bossy!" Tyler sounded downright outraged.

"And Tyler is not my boss. He just happens to outrank me," Alec finally piped in. "Can we please get this conversation back on track?"

"Look," Tyler said to me. "There are some things happening—things we can't really tell you about yet—but it's a dangerous time to be a Variant. Especially one with an intimidating ability like Ethan's. Things happened last night, and if it wasn't for Ethan, people might have lost their lives."

"Oh my god! Someone tried to kill you guys?"

"Eve, please! We can't tell you more. And you can't tell anyone what happened here. It would put you in danger too. Do you understand?" His gray eyes were fixing me with an intense look.

"Fine." I meant for it to sound sarcastic, but it came out soft and meek.

My brain was running a million miles an hour.

The Reds had said that without his Vital, Ethan's ability was limited to small fire-setting and visually impressive tricks. It would have taken an incredible amount of Light to destroy a car and fight off a bunch of super assassins (OK, so I was filling in some of the blanks with my own version of what happened). Ethan didn't have that kind of power. Not without me around to feed it to him. He had endangered his own life.

Tension filled my muscles as worry and frustration bubbled up within me.

I stood up and leaned my hands on the table, fixing my eyes on the big idiot sitting across from me. Surprised and wary, he leaned away, looking to Tyler and Josh on either side for backup.

"Ethan . . ." *Dammit.* "What's his middle name?" I stage-whispered to Alec.

"Terrence." He smirked.

"Ethan Terrence Paul." I said with as much force in my voice as I could muster. "What you did last night was reckless and irresponsible. Don't you dare ever do that again. Don't you push your ability past its limits. Don't push it *at all* unless I'm there to give you more juice than you possess in your . . . admittedly . . . very large body.

"But that's not the point." The energy drained out of me, and my shoulders slumped. "You could have died. And I felt like I was dying right along with you. Don't ever do that to me again."

I fixed him with one last meaningful look before grabbing my delicious latte and walking out of the pool house. With nowhere else to go, I wandered to the edge of the pool, watching the bright sun glistening on the blue surface of the water, taking a few cleansing breaths before finishing the last drops of my coffee.

After a few moments, Ethan came to stand at my elbow.

"I heard you, Eve. I get it. This is going to be an adjustment for all three of us, but I promise I will never willfully do anything that might hurt you ever again. It's impossible now that I know you're my Vital, now that my ability has recognized your Light. I'm sorry last night was such a mess. I'm OK now."

I released a heavy breath and looked up at him. There was nothing but sincerity in his eyes.

I nodded, giving him a small smile. There really wasn't much else he could say or I could ask for. This was new territory for all of us, and we would just have to do our best to navigate it together.

I was rewarded with one of his big, infectious grins.

We moved toward each other, naturally wanting to hug it out, but we never got the chance. Three frantic voices of protest piped up behind us, and we snapped away from each other, sticking our arms to our sides like naughty children caught in the act of trying to steal a cookie out of the jar.

"No hugging!" Alec shouted, stalking toward us and emphatically cutting through the air with both arms. "For fuck's sake! No touching at all. Eve has no idea how to control the amount of Light she releases, and Ethan has never had practice controlling higher levels of his ability."

He was right. We had no idea how dangerous it could be. We could end up lighting all of Bradford Hills on fire.

And yet I *wanted* to see what Ethan could do with the extra power from me. My brain was itching to learn everything about our connection, to explore it hands-on. Instead of looking appropriately chastised, I couldn't contain the excited smile pulling at the corners of my mouth.

There was nothing I loved more than a good experiment, and here was a big, muscly, dimpled one standing right in front of me.

TWELVE

When I was living a quiet, pretend life in Nampa, if someone had told me I was a Vital and would one day be standing by a massive pool on the grounds of a mansion in Bradford Hills, about to test the limits of my power, I would have suggested they get psychiatric help. But there I was, the calm blue water glistening in the bright sunshine as I stood next to *my* Bonded Variant with a rare and powerful fire ability, getting excited to see what we could do together.

Ethan had the same look on his face as I assumed I did, just as enthusiastic to find out what this connection really meant. He was even bouncing a little on his feet.

"No. Don't even think about it. What did I *just* say?" Alec's voice was beginning to sound more like a growl.

"We really must be cautious with this. It would be best to explore your connection in a safe, *controlled* environment." Tyler looked all kinds of wary.

Josh was standing back slightly from our tense group, looking amused, his hands in his pockets. I could tell the exact moment when the idea hit him: his eyebrows raised, and his head tilted slowly, eyes drifting to the water. "We do have a—"

"Pool!" I shouted over the top of him, unable to contain my excitement. He laughed, a little surprised at my outburst.

I spun to face Alec and Tyler, who were standing shoulder to shoulder, both with their arms crossed, both wearing disapproving expressions.

"It's a perfect controlled environment," I reasoned, hoping to appeal to Tyler's academic curiosity. "What could contain fire better than a large pool of water? Plus this is probably the best time to try this safely. We're both still kind of weak from last night, so neither one of us will be firing on all cylinders. Right? Pleeease!" I pressed my hands together in supplication.

Tyler dropped his arms, his resolve wavering.

Behind me, a giant splash spattered my calves. At Tyler's first sign of weakness, Ethan had jumped in the pool.

Alec was still glaring at everyone. "This is a bad idea."

"Maybe." Tyler sounded wary again. "But we have to try it sometime. And she does make some good points. Might as well get it over with while there's no one home." He looked down at his watch, checking the time.

"Yes!" I fist-pumped and spun around, running toward the water before he could change his mind.

I dropped the borrowed shorts from my hips and stepped into the pool, opting to take the steps instead of jumping in. Ethan was standing in the middle, water dripping off his wet hair and down his broad chest. The water only reached a few inches below his sternum, which was moving up and down rhythmically as he breathed, slightly winded from his dive. His eyes were trained on the spot where the water met my body, following it up as I waded farther in.

While he watched my progress, I took in his tattoo. I'd noticed the little match on his left arm peeking out from under his T-shirt a few times, and I'd been vaguely aware last night—and when I'd seen him shirtless in the bedroom—that the ink covered a much larger area, but my full focus had been elsewhere. Now, I was paying attention. Coming off the little wooden match was a massive flame, the fire licking up Ethan's arm and over his shoulder in vivid reds and oranges that seamlessly blended into one another. It was beautiful and suited him perfectly.

Behind me, everyone else had gone silent too. The sudden hush gave me a twinge of nervousness. As Alec had pointed out, I had no idea what I was doing.

Thankfully, Ethan took the lead.

"Come here." He held a hand out, beckoning me forward.

"The Light transfer is triggered most easily if her emotions are running high—a physiological reaction will stir it naturally." I knew Josh was thinking about our kiss as he spoke. I was too.

"Perhaps that's not the best way to go forward though." Tyler sounded a little uncomfortable. "Maybe we should try a more controlled transference, a smaller dose, if you will."

Alec sighed loudly. He was not on board with this, but he was clearly outnumbered, and outranked by Tyler.

"All right. Let's start slow then." Ethan held out his other arm in invitation. "See if you can feel the Light and push it through your hands. OK?"

I nodded as I closed the distance between us. The water was just below my shoulders as I stood in front of Ethan and reached my hands out, placing them in his. We watched each other, curiosity mixing with excitement, and prepared ourselves.

Except I had no idea what I was supposed to be feeling.

Obviously I had channeled the Light before. Obviously I had access to it. I had pushed enough of it to both Ethan and Josh to know that it was there, coursing through our connection. But I hadn't done those things on purpose. They'd just happened. *How was I supposed to replicate that now?*

That familiar soft, tingling feeling flitted over my skin where our hands met. Was that what it was? Should I be trying to increase that somehow? And where did the Light come from? Should I try to . . . get more of it from somewhere?

I was no longer meeting Ethan's eyes. I was staring at our joined hands, my view of them distorted by the water, a frown of concentration on my face. Why was this so difficult? It had come easily the last few times.

I looked to the side of the pool, searching for guidance from the person who always seemed to be ready with knowledge.

Tyler stood with his hands in his pockets, a thoughtful expression on his face. Next to him, Alec was crouching down, his face level with mine and his disapproval written all over it. His body was poised to jump into action, as if he was expecting the worst.

"She's overthinking it," Josh said from behind me. He didn't sound worried or frustrated. He was just stating the fact—as he had when I couldn't remember what I was doing in bed with Ethan.

I didn't have a chance to ponder how he'd figured me out so quickly, because Ethan was apparently in agreement with him.

"Stop overthinking it." He tugged on my hands and pulled me closer.

For the millionth time in the past twenty-four hours, I found myself in Ethan Paul's arms. His right arm banded around the middle of my back, pulling me up and firmly against him, my feet leaving the bottom of the pool. My hands instinctively went to his shoulders, and our proximity demanded that I meet his eyes again. They still held excitement, the amber almost dancing, the sun reflected off the water making them light and free.

He lifted his right hand out of the water, and his fingers gently caressed the back of my neck, making their way up into my hair. He leaned his head forward as though to kiss me, and—though I briefly considered the fact that we had an audience—my body reacted immediately. My breathing shallowed, my heart pattered inside my chest. I felt lost in his eyes and found in his arms. My lips had parted of their own volition, my brain remembering the last kiss we'd shared.

I wanted more.

But he didn't kiss me. He lowered his head until our foreheads were touching, and then he told me what I needed to hear.

"You can do this, Eve." He whispered it so softly that I don't think the others even heard, but I felt it inside of me as surely as I felt his breath on my face.

That's when I felt the Light.

I didn't have a name for it before, but now that I knew what it was, I was *sure* that was the unbridled power I was feeling. Every spot on my body where we touched—my hands, my forearms, the front of my thighs, my forehead—was tingling pleasantly, as it always had when we'd made contact, but now it was so much more than a tingle. The energy was almost audible, like a *buzz*.

I could *feel* the power coursing through me and flowing into him, and it felt *incredible*!

Ethan's eyes went wide. He pulled his head away and looked at me in astonishment. He'd never felt it before. The last time I'd pushed any Light at him, he'd been passed out, nearly dead. Neither one of us had known or been able to really appreciate what had been happening.

But he was feeling it now, and by the look of pure serenity on his face, it felt just as good to be on the other side. He lifted his head toward the sky and closed his eyes.

That pure look on his face tugged on some invisible string within me. Even though we were pressed against each other, I wanted to be closer. I needed more of him. It was easy to lift my legs in the water and wrap them around his middle. I used my hands to pull myself higher, wrapping my arms around his neck.

That's when things got really hot. Literally.

Ethan's arm around my waist stiffened, and his eyes snapped open. There was heat in his stare now, a new intensity.

Our moment was interrupted by panicked shouting and a lot of obscene language coming from outside the pool. The water was on fire.

The water was on fire!

All around us were flames, flicking twelve, thirteen feet into the air, blocking the other guys from view. I couldn't see the bottom of the pool. I couldn't see the water at all.

I shrieked and pulled myself impossibly closer to Ethan, lifting my body even higher onto his and burying my head in his shoulder.

He chuckled and playfully squeezed my sides. "It can't hurt you, Eve."

Now that he mentioned it, it wasn't actually hurting me. It looked mean and scary, but I was not being burned alive in the pool.

I slowly extracted my face from the safety of Ethan's neck and looked around. The flames were dying down already. Ethan was reeling them back in, a focused expression on his face.

As the flames disappeared completely, Tyler and Alec came back into view. Both were crouching by the edge of the pool, wearing matching horrified expressions.

Josh stood behind them, grinning. "Told you she was fine. It can't hurt her. It can't hurt me either, now that we're both in her Bond," he drawled, rolling his eyes.

"Why can't it hurt me?" I directed the question to the fire fiend between my legs. I wasn't quite ready to let go.

"It's a self-preservation thing. I'm able to do what I do because of the power you provide. We're connected now. Your Light and my ability know each other. They recognize each other. My fire couldn't hurt its power source if it wanted to. Same goes for Josh's telekinesis. We can't harm each other with our abilities anymore because that would cause you pain."

"Cool!" I'd have to delve into the theory of that later. Right now I had the practical application in front of me, and I wasn't about to waste this opportunity. "Show me."

I adjusted my grip so I was more on the side of Ethan's body, my right arm slung around his neck. I lifted my left arm in front of our faces, wiggling my fingers in a demonstration of what I wanted him to do.

He flashed me his brilliant grin and lifted his hand up beside mine. Just as I'd seen him do when showing off for his friends, he formed his hand into a loose claw, then flexed his fingers, opening his palm flat. But what emerged this time was *not* a little magic trick fireball.

It was a flamethrower. The fire whooshed from his hand and climbed into the air, fast and intense, the center of the blaze a dangerous blue.

"Whoa!" Ethan's look of surprise morphed into a focused expression once again as he reined in the inferno.

When the giant flamethrower had shrunk to a moderate-sized flamethrower, I tentatively reached my hand out. Logically speaking, sticking your hand into a raging fire was a reckless thing to do, but there was no longer any apprehension in me. In fact, I felt a strange kind of affection for that fire.

The complete lack of any sensation as the flames engulfed my hand was mind-blowing. There wasn't even any heat as I touched my palm to Ethan's, pressing each of my fingers against his much bigger ones.

I have no idea how long we were in that pool, both of us staring, transfixed, at our hands pressed together and enveloped in flames. But eventually I felt a gentle touch on my shoulder, and then someone was extracting me from Ethan's grip. For a second, Ethan's hold on me tightened possessively, but when we both realized it was Josh in the pool with us, he came back to himself and released me.

Josh pulled me back against his chest, both arms looped around my front, and dragged me through the water a few steps away from Ethan and the fire that was still flying off his fingers. He held me against him as we both watched Ethan slowly contain the flames.

Only then did Josh release a heavy breath and let me go. Apparently everyone had decided it was time to pull us apart before we lit something up that wasn't impervious to it as I was. Since Josh was immune to Ethan's ability too, the task of breaking us out of our trance had fallen to him. Although, as I turned around, I saw Alec had his shirt off and looked ready to jump into the water. I knew he would do anything to protect his cousin, but I questioned his self-preservation instincts, even as I took in the many tattoos covering his chest and arms.

Tyler was standing a bit farther back, but his posture was radiating tension as well. Our little fire show must have been as anxiety-inducing for them as it had been mesmerizing for us.

I cleared my throat, praying it didn't sound as awkward as I was suddenly feeling. "I'm going to go dry off."

Murmured agreements chorused around me as I moved to get out of the pool, avoiding eye contact with all of them. Alec cursed under his breath, pulling his shirt back on.

"You guys go ahead." Ethan's voice drew my eyes away from their intense examination of the pavers around the pool. "I need a minute."

I turned my head just in time to see him disappear under the water. Alec cursed again and stalked off toward the house.

I marched in my underwear and white tank top, which was definitely see-through by now, into the pool house in search of towels.

I found some in a bathroom and dried off, putting my remaining dry clothing back on. Testing my connection to Ethan had been exhilarating, but the events of the past few hours were beginning to catch up to me. A lot had happened, a lot of information had been dumped on me, yet there was so much I still didn't know. It couldn't have been more than an hour or two since I'd woken up in Ethan's arms, but I was exhausted.

I was ready for a break and some proper clothing; it was time to head back to my res hall and rejoin the real world.

I felt more than a little uncomfortable walking out of the pool house in just a cardigan and oversized T-shirt, pulling the hem down constantly because I'd decided not to keep my wet underwear on. Of course, the person I least wanted to see me naked in this scenario was the one waiting for me outside.

The others had disappeared and left Tyler to deal with me.

THIRTEEN

Tyler was sitting on the edge of one of the loungers, his head bent over his phone, typing rapidly. He must have changed at the same time I did, and he was now in jeans and a T-shirt. It was the first time I'd seen him dressed in anything other than slacks and a button-down.

He was easily one of the most intelligent people I'd ever met, and I genuinely looked forward to speaking to him whenever I had the chance. After last night, though, things were going to be different between us. How could they not be? I had just become permanently, supernaturally glued to two people he considered family, right after one of them nearly died. Those kinds of events forced a certain intimacy between people.

I didn't necessarily mind the idea of being closer to Tyler; I *had* been developing a serious crush on him since we first met. I just hoped it didn't ruin the relationship we already had.

On the other hand, I didn't even want to think about what it meant that I was still crushing on him despite having an attraction to both Ethan and Josh—an attraction that was more than just the Light-fueled connection between us. How did this work in Variant Bonds with more than one Variant involved? I would need to broaden my research to include Variant-specific sociology and psychology instead of just focusing on the hard science.

As I approached him tentatively, he looked up, swiping his messy hair out of his eyes, and gave me a wide and genuine smile.

"You did exceptionally well, Eve."

"Thank you." I ducked my head as I replied. I wasn't a blusher—my cutaneous blood vessels happened to be deeper in the skin, so when I got embarrassed, my cheeks didn't get red—but if I was, I would have been blushing. Why was his praise making me shy? He had praised me before, and I hadn't felt embarrassed.

"I was just texting the others to let them know I would drop you back at the Institute. I think we've all had enough excitement for the day. Plus, I don't want to risk Beth coming back here and making a scene. We need to keep a low profile." He stood, and we started walking back toward the house.

"Oh shit! Beth!" I had completely forgotten about my new friend and how she'd followed my crazy ass all the way here last night. She'd stuck with me, and I'd *completely forgotten* about her. I was a terrible friend!

"It's all right. We covered for you. We managed to convince her you were safe with us for the night, but she's going to have questions. That girl can be . . . forceful." He chuckled, as amused with Beth's strong protective instincts as I was touched by them.

As we spoke, Tyler led the way through a side door off the house's massive entrance hall, down some stairs, and into a cavernous garage with at least half a dozen cars.

"I'm sure she'll understand when I explain it all to her. She's one of the nicest people I've ever met."

"I'm glad you're making friends, but Eve, you can't tell her anything." He stopped and faced me fully, making sure I could see the seriousness on his face.

"I don't understand." Why would he want me to keep my newfound Vital status from my new friend—one of my only friends? "I thought this was a good thing. You were all so excited this morning. I've read up a little on American Variant history. I haven't come across anything that indicates it's bad to be a Vital."

"No. It's not a bad thing. And we *are* happy. I'm happy that Ethan and Josh have found you. You're incredible to have the Light necessary to sustain not one but *two* such strong abilities. But there are things at play here you don't understand."

He sighed and got into the driver's side of a black sedan that looked more expensive than the commercial plane I'd flown in to get here from Nampa. I followed suit and strapped myself into the passenger side, careful to pull the long T-shirt over my thighs and maintain some semblance of modesty.

It wasn't sitting well with me that he was being secretive. He had always encouraged my curiosity. "Don't do that. Don't be vague and evasive. That's Alec's thing."

"Please don't take Alec's behavior personally. He's had a lot of pain in his life. No pun intended." He laughed a little, but it was half-hearted. "We all have."

I didn't know what to say to that, but Tyler must have taken my silence as an invitation to continue, and I hung on every word.

"We all lost our parents at a young age. They were close, and as a result, we kids were too. They all died in a big accident . . . Ethan was only nine when it happened and Josh was ten. I was fifteen and Alec was seventeen. Alec and I thought we were grown up until, all of a sudden, we had no parents to turn to. But we grew up pretty fast after that—Ethan and Josh needed us to."

I swallowed around the lump in my throat, doing my best to keep my voice even. "I'm so sorry that happened to you."

He smiled weakly. "The point is, Alec is not always the best at expressing how he feels, but he's very protective of those two. Now that we know you're their Vital, he's going to be protective of you too. We both are. We're going to do all we can to guide you through this, Eve. To keep you all safe."

"And to make sure we don't burn Bradford Hills to the ground? Secretly though, because no one can know what I am, right?" I was trying to lighten the mood.

It worked, managing to get a smile out of him as he pulled out of the garage. "I'm not being intentionally evasive. There's just so much you don't know, and it only takes five minutes to drive back to the Institute. I can't possibly cover it all, but if I don't get you back there soon, it's going to raise even more questions."

"I don't understand." I looked out my window, watching the beautiful trees whiz past as we drove down their massive driveway.

"I know. I'm sorry. Look, the Vital power is revered in our community, yes, but it's also coveted, and that makes it dangerous for you. Haven't you noticed that every high-profile Vital you see in the news is surrounded by security? But it's not just that. This could be dangerous for Ethan and Josh too. There are things happening on a bigger level—bigger than all of us—that could make them targets if it became known they've found their Vital."

Ethan and Josh could be in danger. Now that he'd said that, I was no longer annoyed by his being vague. I just wanted to know who was trying to hurt my guys. I tried not to dwell on the fact that I was suddenly thinking of them as *my guys* as I tried to push the irrational murderous rage aside. "OK."

"OK?" There was a tiny hint of surprise in Tyler's voice. He hadn't been expecting me to cave in so easily. "I promise I'll explain everything. Just not today. I'm going to set it up so we're having regular one-on-one sessions—I'll say it's intensive tutoring to bring you up to speed with your Variant studies. Your test results will be enough of an explanation. There's no hiding those now. I will arm you with all the information you need to navigate this clusterfuck as best you can. I promise."

So much had happened that his cursing didn't even surprise me. I was beyond being fazed by language from an authority figure.

"I need you keep this to yourself. You can't even tell anyone about your test results. Not until after our next meeting, which is when I'm meant to officially tell you. Can you do that, Eve? Do you trust me?"

We were pulling into the main gates of the Institute, and his eyes were focused on the path ahead, but all his other senses were focused on my reaction.

"No. I hardly even know you. Why would I trust you?" I crossed my arms over my chest, staring straight ahead just as he was.

Out of the corner of my eye, I saw his lips twitch into an involuntary smile. "Liar."

"Dammit!" I dropped my arms and turned on him. Stupid lie detector ability. "No fair."

With some of the seriousness of the moment dispelled, I flopped back in my seat, unable to pretend I was still mistrustful and suspicious. Curious and a bit worried, yes, but nothing they'd done so far indicated they were shady in any way. I did trust them, and Tyler probably would have known it even without his ability.

"Great! Now that we've established that you trust me, can we establish an official meeting so I can pretend to tell you for the first time that your blood test came back positive for Variant DNA? I have a slot at 9 a.m. on Thursday."

"Fine. Thursday it is. I'll wait for my answers—many, many detailed answers. But what am I supposed to tell Beth? And Zara, come to think of it, because there is no way Beth didn't fill her in."

"Right. About that." We came to a stop near the back entrance of my residence hall, and he angled his body toward mine but didn't meet my eyes. "Obviously, we couldn't tell her what was really going on. There was no covering up the burned-out car, and she's a smart girl, so she knew it had something to do with Ethan's ability. We kept it as close to the truth as we could. We told her he had overused his ability, that he was in trouble . . ."

Taking a deep breath, he told me the rest in a rush. "We told her you and Ethan were secretly seeing each other and that's why you were so upset, and that we called you when he collapsed because we knew you would want to be there for him."

I blinked in astonishment, my eyebrows slowly rising as Tyler finally met my gaze. At least he had the decency to look sheepish about it.

"You what?!" How was I supposed to convince the Reds I was dating Ethan Paul—notorious womanizer and destroyer of scholarships—when I'd shown nothing more than a fascination with his ability and a passing interest in the guy wielding it?

"I know. I'm sorry, but it's done now. We panicked. We had no idea what was happening, and we had to do something to cover it up. When Josh blurted out that Ethan was your boyfriend, we all just ran with it."

"Unbelievable . . ." I muttered to myself, but the idea of being with Ethan *did* intrigue me. We had kissed, after all, and there was no denying we were drawn to each other. I just couldn't be sure how much of that was mutual attraction and how much was driven by the Light coursing through my body.

Once again, I didn't have the luxury of space and time to figure it out for myself. I would have to pretend to be in a relationship with a boy whom I'd only known a few weeks—and whom I now liked more than I cared to admit. Throwing the "boyfriend" label into the mix seemed like an unnecessary complication. *Ugh! What a mess!*

"Eve?" Tyler snapped me back to the present. "We can't keep sitting here. Someone will notice."

"Right. Fine. I'll pretend to have the hots for Ethan. How hard can it be?" Probably harder than I expected. I was an exceptional liar when it came to handing over a fake passport or using my fake name, but I didn't know if I could lie to the two girls who had fast become my friends. I didn't know if I wanted to.

I got out of the car, slamming the door just a little bit harder than necessary, and trudged into the building.

When I made it upstairs, I peeked my head in the room and, finding it completely silent, breathed a sigh of relief as I pushed inside.

My phone was still charging by my bed, where I'd left it in my rush to get to Ethan. I had a few missed calls from Zara and Beth, but they must have found my phone in my room and given up quickly. There were also a few messages in our group chat.

Zara: We're heading out to catch up with some friends but when we get back . . . questions. So many questions!

Beth: What she said. Hope you're OK. xo

I winced, not looking forward to that particular conversation. Then I smiled in spite of myself. It was nice having friends who cared enough about me to demand explanations for strange behavior.

It made me feel even worse that I would have to lie to them.

I typed out a quick response—*Home now and I'm fine. No need to rush back!*—and dropped my phone back on the nightstand.

I wanted to throw myself onto the bed next to it. I was wrecked; the heaviness of the situation, coupled with the fact that I'd helped Ethan set the damn pool on fire, was getting to me. However, I also smelled like chlorine, so I headed for the bathroom first.

I took a long, hot shower, using the time to think about what I would say to Zara and Beth when they got back, but my brain was too fried to get very far.

"It's just a casual sex thing. He's hot, and I'm not talking about his fire ability." I couldn't even get to the end of that one without cringing.

"We have a lot in common actually?" That came out as a question.

"It was an accident. I . . . tripped . . ." Ugh. I rolled my eyes at myself.

I gave up. Hopefully the right thing would just come to me.

I dried my hair as quickly as I could, leaving it a big, frizzy mess, and pulled on underwear and a tank top before climbing into bed and falling asleep at two in the afternoon.

I woke up an hour later to Zara jumping on me and yelling, "No sleeping during your interrogation!" at the top of her lungs.

I groaned and tried to push her off, but Beth had already jumped on my legs, and I was pinned down. I started laughing in spite of myself. They released me, Zara moving to perch on my desk chair while Beth just leaned on the wall at the foot of my bed.

"Spill," Zara demanded, and I immediately got super nervous.

I still had no idea what to say but decided sticking as close to the truth as possible was probably the best option.

"Look, I know you warned me off him, but he's not what I expected." That was true. Ethan had shown me a tender, vulnerable side I had a feeling few people ever saw. "Beth, you've said he can be a nice guy if you get to know him. I didn't tell you guys, because it's all so new, and, I mean, we've only kissed, so it's not even that serious."

Their frowns of confusion made me realize my mistake—if it wasn't that serious, why had I been a hysterical mess last night?

"That is to say"—I scrambled for an explanation—"it wasn't really that serious until last night. I don't know, I guess knowing he might be in danger kind of made me realize how much I care about him." Also true. I just left out that my intense interest in his well-being had more to do with our supernatural connection.

"So, you're saying that you haven't even slept with him?" Zara sounded incredulous.

Technically I had, but I knew she wasn't referring to the actual sleeping we had done. At least this was one thing I could be truthful about. "No. Yes. That is to say, you are correct—we have not had sex." I looked down at my hands clasped in my lap, a little embarrassed.

"Oh god, are you a virgin? This just gets better and better. Ethan Paul is not the guy you want to lose your V-card to."

"I don't know," Beth piped in from the foot of the bed. "Doing it with someone who's more experienced might be good. They know what to do and all that."

"Um, girls? Not a virgin. I had a boyfriend when I was living in Australia, and I dated a bit while I was living in Idaho."

"Ooh, the plot thickens." Zara awkwardly pulled herself over on the wheelie chair and rested her elbows on the bed beside me, dropping her chin into her hands. "Tell us about the Aussie."

"Wait, weren't you in the middle of interrogating me about Ethan?"

"Aww, it's 'Ethan' now. I guess 'Kid' is too casual a nickname for a beau," Beth cooed.

"Beau?" Zara and I both laughed.

"Who says *beau* anymore? It's not 1956, Mary Sue," Zara teased, then turned back to me. "Look, we were worried, but you seem to really like him, and honestly, I've never heard of him actually dating someone. Like putting actual time and effort into getting to know a girl. So that's promising. Just be careful and know that we're here if it ends in tears."

"What she said," added Beth, smiling warmly, "except the Mary Sue bit. That was just mean. I am a modern woman. Hear me roar!"

I leaned back against my pillow, relieved the conversation hadn't been as difficult as I thought it was going to be.

We spent the rest of the afternoon lounging around the living room, eating junk food and talking about exes. I didn't have too much to contribute after my Harvey story was relayed, but it felt so good to be doing normal girl things with people I could actually call my girlfriends.

An afternoon spent relaxing, followed by a good night's sleep, did wonders for my energy levels and outlook on the whole situation.

The Reds had promised—at my insistence—not to tell anyone about me and Ethan. Considering his reputation, they were happy to keep it to themselves.

The girls weren't upset with me, the boys would be glad our secret was safe, and I was excited. I had so much to learn about this world I was apparently a part of, and I couldn't wait.

~

The Reds and I walked toward the Variant studies building together, me with much more pep in my step than was normal for anyone on a Monday morning. Ethan and Josh were in my first lecture for the day—Variant History—and I was looking forward to seeing them.

As we approached the front of the building, I spotted my boys immediately, chatting together as people streamed past them through the front doors. They turned in my direction at the same time and smiled in greeting. I couldn't help the grin that spread across my face in response, my eyes flicking from one to the other.

Thankfully, we were far enough away that the girls thought I had eyes only for Ethan. Beth grabbed my arm and bounced up and down excitedly before remembering it was supposed to be a secret and making a visible effort to calm herself. Zara just rolled her eyes and walked off toward the humanities building, waving goodbye as she dragged Beth along with her.

Ethan laughed as I walked up to them, no idea how I was supposed to act. "Should I just ignore you? Should we pretend like . . ." I spoke quietly, unsure how to end that sentence. We were pretending so many things already.

"Good morning, Eve. Why, yes, I'm doing just fine, thanks." Ethan chuckled before slinging an arm over my shoulders and moving us off toward class.

I froze up, worried we were about to burn down the science building. "What are you doing?" I hissed in Ethan's ear.

"Chill," he stage-whispered back. "As long as we avoid skin contact, we should be fine. Only over clothes." He winked at me, managing to make the comment both informative and suggestive. I rolled my eyes at him but found myself fighting laughter.

Josh snickered, stepping up on my other side. He handed me a latte and smiled a secret smile.

He'd brought it from the only café in town that made a decent latte; I was touched. "Thanks."

Ethan chose seats near the back of the lecture hall, and I found myself seated between him and Josh. A few people stopped by to say hi to Ethan, but I kept my eyes glued to my notebook, pretending to revise my notes.

As Ethan chatted with a guy on the football team about some upcoming game, I felt Josh's hand land gently on my leg under the little foldout table—over the fabric of my tights and nowhere near any exposed skin. He squeezed gently and spoke very low, so only I could hear. "You're doing fine, Eve. Just try to relax. Everything will be OK."

And then he pulled away. When I glanced over at him, his head was buried in a book, and he looked so unassuming that I wondered if I'd imagined the entire moment.

Once again, Josh had picked up on what was going on inside my head and given me the encouragement I needed. I hadn't even realized how nervous I was until he reminded me to relax.

The rest of class passed by uneventfully, and the lecture managed to interest me enough that I forgot about the two boys on either side of me and all that sat between us—at least for one hour.

I had no more classes with the guys that morning, but at the end of my second class, I noticed Josh *happened* to be sitting on a bench outside and *happened* to leave just as I left, heading in the same direction.

As I emerged from my third class, with Zara, they were both there, chatting with Tyler. I didn't even need to look back to know they were following Zara and I as we headed to the cafeteria. I guess the stalking thing wasn't about to let up now that we knew we were in a Bond. If anything, I had a sneaking suspicion it was about to intensify.

Pretending to the world I was someone different was not new to me. I had been doing it my whole life. The new part was constantly having to resist the urge to go to them. Now that I knew who they were, *what* they were to me, all I wanted was to be close to them, talk to them, walk with them, touch them. It was infuriating to have to pretend we were nothing to each other.

By the end of the day, I was over being vigilant. As I finally collapsed into bed, looking forward to a good sleep and a break from it all, I realized I would be denied even that simple luxury.

My arms and legs were itchy in that now all too familiar way. I kicked the covers off—they suddenly felt as if they were made of raw wool.

Now that I thought about it, I had been scratching absentmindedly all day. I had been so distracted by Ethan and Josh and our situation I hadn't noticed the tickle beginning at my wrists and ankles.

With a sigh of frustration, I got out of bed, any semblance of fatigue gone, and prepared myself for another sleepless night.

FOURTEEN

The following three days were torture.

Ethan, Josh, and I were avoiding being seen together too much outside of class, but that meant we couldn't talk about our situation, and the longer I waited to get the full story, the more questions I had. It was driving me mental.

To make matters worse, my insane levels of energy were back. I hadn't slept at all the past three nights. As an upside, I was now ahead in all my coursework. In my extra time, I was devouring anything I could get my hands on to satiate my thirst for Variant-related knowledge, whether that was Variant studies journal articles or trashy tabloids about high-profile Variant people.

From a gossip website, I learned all about Senator Christine Anderson's Variant ability to understand and speak any language, her passion for purebred poodles, and her determination to have Variant interests represented on a national level. When I clicked through to an article about a Variant actress whose ability was to slightly alter her physical appearance, I drew the line and tried to read something from the business pages.

The name Zacarias caught my attention. It was an article about Alec and Ethan's mysterious uncle—Lucian Zacarias, head of Melior Group—and Davis Damari, another rich Variant who ran a pharmaceutical company. The two had struck some big deal to start a revolutionary new venture together. When it started talking about "mergers" and "dividends," I got bored and gave up.

There was very little about Lucian Zacarias on the Internet—the perks of being in charge of an international spy agency, I guess. There was, however, a lot on Davis Damari. Most interesting was that he hadn't manifested an ability until his thirties, unheard of in the Variant world, as most people presented with an ability by age twenty. His story had given many twenty-something Variants hope. I made a mental note to ask Tyler about it, then got sucked down another gossip website hole.

I had gone for 5 a.m. runs and done countless sit-ups and push-ups, but the energy was not abating. By the time Thursday came around, I was still bouncing off the walls, and the itchiness was coming and going more often. This worried me; the itchiness usually subsided as soon as I exhausted myself. The buzzing energy took a bit longer, but it usually went not long after.

Maybe it was something related to my Vital nature and Tyler would have some insight. I was glad our appointment was for first thing in the morning—I didn't think I could wait any longer.

I arrived twenty minutes early and paced the corridor outside Tyler's locked office, trying not to scratch, failing miserably, and garnering a few strange looks from other staff making their way to their offices.

At ten to nine, he arrived.

"Finally!" I groaned as he came around the corner.

He paused briefly in surprise before an amused look crossed his face.

"Sorry," I said. That was rude. "I didn't mean to jump down your throat. I'm just . . ."

"Eager?" he supplied, unlocking the door and stepping inside. "Enthusiastic? Frustrated? Slightly crazed?"

"Yes. All of the above." I laughed nervously, closing the door behind us and sitting down in one of his tub chairs.

He deposited his messenger bag on his desk and sat next to me, as he had on the first day. "OK. Let's dive right in then. Perhaps you might like to ask some questions?"

I nodded emphatically and opened my mouth to start firing them off, but . . . nothing came out. I had been thinking about this for three days straight. There were so many things vying for my attention—the Light, the Variant-Vital relationship, my blood tests—I couldn't get my mind to focus on just one.

What did come out surprised me, although it shouldn't have; it was the only thing I couldn't research. "Why do we have to keep this a secret?"

Tyler blew out a heavy breath. "Right to the hard stuff, huh?"

"I just don't understand." I looked down at my hands. "I know that being a Vital is a big deal—that they're a cherished and respected part of Variant culture. So why do Josh and Ethan not want anyone to know I'm theirs? Is it because it's . . . me? Because I wasn't raised Variant and I have no idea what I'm doing? I don't want to embarrass them, but—"

Tyler cut me off midsentence, placing a gentle hand on my arm. "Eve. No."

I hadn't realized I was feeling so insecure about my new Vital status and my connection to the boys, but now that I was saying it, I realized it had been in the back of my mind since Tyler dropped me off, imploring me to lie to my friends.

"It's not like that at all," Tyler said. "Ethan and Josh are ecstatic to have found you. When a Variant finds their Vital, it's like a piece of the puzzle they didn't know was missing falls into place. No one could ever resent that. They couldn't care less what anyone, human or Variant, thinks about your Bond."

"Then what is it?"

"This is such a precarious issue . . ." he muttered, almost to himself. Then he turned his eyes back to me with a determined expression. "OK. I promise this is all related."

I nodded and shifted in my seat to face him more fully. His hand slipped off my arm as he began to speak, and I immediately missed his comforting touch.

"Throughout history, the balance of power has shifted between Variants and humans. At times, Variants, thinking our abilities made us superior, have enslaved and demeaned the humans for our own gain. At other times, the humans, considering us too great a threat, have imprisoned and segregated us, treating us like mutants, abominations, and defective versions of themselves. It has swung back and forth throughout history and from region to region. Sometimes religion was used to justify the segregation, sometimes politics, and sometimes a simple survival need—more land for farming and crops available to *us* at the exclusion of *them*. It's all bullshit, of course."

He was obviously passionate about this. He'd begun to gesture with his hands, his voice rising.

"Two Variant parents are just as likely to produce a human child as two human parents. There is no discernible reason why some people are born with the Variant gene and others aren't. It's not hereditary and it's not contagious. We have isolated a protein that, when present, indicates the individual is Variant, but we have no idea what causes it. And even when it is present, that doesn't guarantee the child will ever present with abilities or Vital access to Light—they could just have a dormant gene. This hatred of one another has nothing to do with actual differences. It's a basic psychological phenomenon of self-identification; the 'us versus them' theory. We are better able to quantify to ourselves who we *are* by identifying who we're *not*. Are you following?"

"Yep. We've been slaughtering one another since the dawn of time, and we like to join clubs to give ourselves some illusion of belonging. Go on."

I knew all this. It was basic history and psychology. I needed to know how it related to my present situation.

Tyler smiled at me indulgently and continued. "In a nutshell, in the last fifty years or so, we have enjoyed relative peace between humans and Variants, at least in the Western world. We've worked hard to create unity, understanding, and equality. We have laws that prevent discrimination, we work side by side, and mixed marriages are no longer as taboo as they used to be, although those are only possible for Variants without a Vital. But that's a whole other thing I won't get into right now."

He was alluding to the fact that most Variant-Vital connections that weren't between blood relations resulted in romantic relationships. I'd done a little research into this during my sleepless nights, but when the journal articles that came up had headings like "Polyamorous Relationships in Variant Bonds and the Associated Social Implications for Wider Communities: A Longitudinal Study," I quickly moved on to other things. I was definitely attracted to both Ethan and Josh, and I was about 80 percent sure the feeling was mutual, but I wasn't ready to deal with the idea of dating them both. *At the same time.*

I avoided meeting Tyler's eye and waited for him to continue.

"Over the last few years, cracks have appeared in our current harmonious coexistence. There are radical groups on both sides arguing for the dominance and superiority of one group over another. Variant Valor are Variant elitists who think a genetic fluke makes them better than 'average' humans. These are the type of people who use the word *Dimes* proudly. The Human Empowerment Network are fearmongering nuts who think Variant abilities are an abomination and need to be controlled if not entirely purged. They are loud and outrageous, and at the moment they're seen mostly as radicals on the fringe, but they are gaining support at alarming rates. The Melior Group is keeping a very close eye on the situation while making considerable efforts to maintain positive relations with the mostly human government. It's one of the things Alec is involved in."

The information about Alec had me sitting up straighter. The kind gesture with the latte notwithstanding, he was still avoiding me like the plague, and I still hadn't managed to deliver my thanks to him, let alone question him about the night my mother died. Any insight was precious.

Tyler saw my enthusiasm and held up a hand. "I can't tell you much more than that, so don't even ask. The point is, the government and Variant organizations like Bradford Hills and Melior Group are on edge at the moment. The reason we wish to keep this secret is twofold."

He twisted to face me fully, and a weary expression crossed his face. "Firstly, if Melior Group found out Ethan and Josh had found their Vital, they would be recruited. Their abilities are rare and powerful, and in dangerous times, having power like that . . . well, let's just say they wouldn't have a choice. I don't want either of them being forced to fight, and they don't want it either."

Ethan was only one year older than me, and Josh was two. We were college kids—they couldn't go around waving guns and abilities, getting in life-threatening situations, any more than I could. My heart did a little jump in my chest at the thought of them in danger, but Tyler was still speaking, so I did my best to focus on him.

"Secondly, it's dangerous for you. We've managed to suppress this in the press to avoid panic in the Variant community, but there have been a series of abductions in the last six months all over the world. All of them Vitals, none of them found yet. If it became known you were a Vital, your very life could be in danger. We may not be able to contain this information much longer—Variants like to gossip more than a bunch of sixteen-year-old girls—but regardless, it's better that no one learns of your true nature."

I slumped back in my chair and stared off into space, scratching my left wrist absentmindedly. All three of us were in danger—the guys from being recruited into a life of violence, and me from potentially getting kidnapped by some lunatic terrorist organization.

Some of the guilt about lying to the Reds lessened. This was so much bigger than gossip-filled confidences between roomies.

How had my life changed this much in a few short weeks? What did we do now? Just avoid each other and hope that the connection went away? From my reading, I knew that was impossible. Once the Bond was formed, it was for life. But just as I was avoiding thinking about how being in a relationship with more than one guy would work, I was trying not to think about how *permanent* the Bond was.

This situation was overwhelming on every level—from the global-extremist-group one right down to the personal-relationship one.

"What do we do now?" I turned my slightly panicky question to the only person who had a chance at making me feel better about this situation.

"We train." Tyler declared with a firm nod.

"Right." I nodded too, much more spasmodically. "We train." I took my sweater off. The itch had spread to my elbows, and the sleeves had begun irritating my arms. But I couldn't focus on that. Tyler was speaking again, and he was the man with the plan.

"It's too late to suppress your blood test results now. The Institute will know you have Variant DNA, but we can use that to our advantage. It gives us an excuse for you to have more one-on-one sessions with me."

"Right. Good excuse." I stood up and paced, my energy levels refusing to be ignored any longer. I did my best to concentrate on what Tyler was saying as I gave in and started scratching my arms from wrist to shoulder.

"The official story will be that you're getting extra tutoring in your Variant studies, and you will, but we'll also use the time to teach you how to get a handle on your Light. With practice, you will be able to control how much you channel and how much of that you funnel into Ethan and Josh. Eventually you'll be able to touch them without Light transferring automatically, and you'll be able to choose to push larger amounts to them without having to get . . . ah . . . so close."

"Learn how to transfer Light without sucking face. Got it." My breathing had begun to speed up, and I moved on to scratching my neck.

Tyler laughed and then looked at me quizzically. "Eve, are you all right?"

"Yeah, yeah. Just a little jittery. Lots to consider. Lots to do. Is it hot in here?" I moved over to the window and yanked it up. "It feels hot in here."

"Oh . . . kay . . ."

"So what do I tell people when they ask about my new Variant status?"

"The truth. Your blood tests came back positive, but it's news to you. You've never had any hint of an ability. Leave it at that. It means you'll be forced to attend some Variant events that get put on from time to time to facilitate Variants meeting one another, but we can handle that. The guys and I have been going to those things since I can remember."

"Cool, cool. Keep it vague and go to some parties." I laughed nervously; the notion of going to some exclusive Variant dating event suddenly seemed hilarious. "I don't think I have anything to wear to a nice party. Oh man!"

The itching was becoming unbearable as it spread farther. I was alternating between scratching my arms and the top of my chest, right down into my cleavage.

Tyler stood up, eyebrows raised, his attention fixed on my hand down my top.

I couldn't worry about him though; my T-shirt was starting to feel like a cotton torture device. I grabbed the bottom of it with both hands, ready to yank it over my head.

"Eve! No!" Tyler took a step toward me, his right hand raised in a "stop" motion in front of my torso. "What the hell are you doing?"

Through the fog of insane energy and unbearable itchiness, I managed to stop myself from stripping in front of my new tutor, but I was still really uncomfortable. Why wasn't it going away? I had gone for a two hour run just that morning after staying up all night and studying. I felt as if I was going to explode!

I grunted through gritted teeth and shook my hands next to my sides while jumping up and down, trying to *literally* shake some of the intense energy out of my body. I looked at Tyler pleadingly. "I don't know what to do. It's *so* itchy. And it's everywhere, and I feel like I could run a marathon and still have extra . . . help me!" I didn't know what I expected him to do. I had no idea what to do myself, but I felt scared. It had never been this intense before.

Realization crossed his features, and he ran one hand through his messy brown hair, breathing out a curse. "This is happening sooner than anticipated," he said, more to himself.

Another growl of frustration from me and I had his full attention again.

"It's going to be OK, Eve," he said. "This is just an overflow of Light. It knows now that you have two very powerful abilities to feed, and it's flowing freely into you to get to them. It just needs to be released. And you're going to release it all into me."

He took another step toward me and held his hands out in invitation.

"What? How?" Was he saying he was going to kiss me?

"Transference comes much more instinctively with members of your Bond, but it is possible for a Vital to release Light to any Variant. It doesn't feel as natural or as good, but it can be done quite easily by most Vitals. And you're already worked up—your heart is beating like crazy, your breaths are shallow and erratic, and your emotions are all over the place. The floodgates are open. We just need to give it something to pour into."

He punctuated his statement with a flick of both wrists, emphasizing that he wanted me to take his hands.

So he wasn't going to kiss me after all.

Trusting that he knew what he was talking about, I stepped forward and placed my hands in his. As soon as our skin made contact, I could feel the excess energy draining out of me. The sense of relief was so intense that my eyes rolled back, and I may have made an embarrassing sound of pleasure.

My shoulders relaxed, the tension easing out of the taut muscles all over my body. My breathing evened out, and the itchiness disappeared, draining out of me right along with the Light.

Within minutes, I was calmer, more relaxed, more myself. I was surprised at how easily I was able to transfer the Light to Tyler after what he'd said about it being more unnatural with people who weren't in my Bond. I didn't know what it was supposed to feel like, but it felt good. *Exquisite*. As good as when it had happened with . . .

My eyes snapped open.

Tyler was staring, transfixed, at our joined hands, his mouth open slightly, his breathing heavy and deep.

He looked up and met my gaze. For a few moments we just stood there, holding hands and looking at each other, the realization that had dawned on us both hanging heavy in the air.

"That," he said softly, and swallowed hard, "felt fucking . . ."

"Amazing," I finished, my voice as soft and breathy as his, and my hands squeezed his reflexively.

He responded by gently tugging me toward himself. Our eyes were still locked on each other, and I could see the gray in his almost alive with movement. Just as Ethan's had been in the pool.

Inch by inch we drifted toward each other. It felt like that first day when we'd sat side by side in this very office, chatting and drawing closer without realizing it. Only it was way more intense, and now I knew why we were drifting.

Tyler, just like Ethan and Josh, was *mine*. He was in my Bond.

"How is this possible?" he whispered, echoing my train of thought.

"I don't . . . I . . . I'm . . ." I had no idea what I was trying to say. All I knew was that his lips were mere inches from mine, and I wanted to close the distance.

It didn't matter that he was about to be my tutor, that I'd been trying really hard to stop myself from developing a crush on him, that I knew this urge was driven by my Vital instincts—a Light-driven reaction, pushing me to solidify my connection to another member of my Bond. All I could think about was how his lips would feel on mine.

I flicked my eyes down to those very lips, but that's what seemed to break the spell for him. He stepped away from me and dropped my hands. The sudden movement startled me, and I couldn't mask the disappointment that fell over my face.

"Oh, Eve." The pity in his eyes made me feel foolish. Like another one of those females on campus harboring fantasies for the hot guy on the staff. Which is exactly what I was—a girl with a crush. Of course he wouldn't want this. I too would resent being stuck by an uncontrollable supernatural force to someone seven years my junior.

I went to turn away from him, to try to cover up my childish disappointment, but with a firm hand on my forearm, he stopped me. He pulled me toward him and enveloped me in a hug. It was not the kiss I was hoping for, but it was still contact, some semblance of the intimacy that the Light inside me was pacified by, even if my girlish emotions weren't.

I wrapped my arms around his middle and dropped my head on his shoulder.

"It's not that I don't . . . ." He sighed. I guess he was struggling with how to process this as well. "We're in such a delicate situation already. We can't have the ethics committee sticking their noses in too because it looks like I'm getting too close to one of the students. It's better if we keep it platonic."

He squeezed me a little bit tighter before releasing me.

I couldn't help feeling the sting of rejection. I knew he had a point about raising suspicion with the Bradford Hills staff, but I wondered if that was also a convenient excuse for not jumping at the chance to deepen our Bond as enthusiastically as Ethan and Josh had—or as romantically.

With some effort, I pushed away the self-conscious thoughts; we had bigger things to deal with. I'd hardly had a chance to figure out what was happening between me, Ethan, and Josh in the first place, and now a massive curveball had been thrown at us in the form of Tyler being part of my Bond.

I gave him my best "I'm OK" smile. He looked relieved, moving to sit behind his wide, heavy desk in a deliberate effort to put some distance between us.

It was probably best to get the conversation going again. We only had half an hour left of our session, and we had so much to cover. "Well, that was unexpected, but I guess it doesn't change much. I still need to train. Learn."

"Yes." He nodded definitively. "It certainly was unexpected. I never thought I would have a Vital. It's less common with passive abilities like mine. Active, physical abilities like Ethan and Josh's tend to need more Light to sustain them. And the fact that you have two people connected to your Light already . . . three is not unheard of, but it is rare."

We spent the remaining half an hour going over my vigorous new schedule. Some of my class commitments had been pulled back, including all my Variant studies. I would now be doing all Variant learning in daily sessions with Tyler. One of the things he wanted me to focus on was meditation. Apparently finding inner Zen was the key to fully controlling my Light. If I could control how much I took into myself, then I could avoid the itchy, sleepless ball of energy situation I'd found myself in the past few days. And if I could control how much I transferred, I wouldn't be slamming the guys with it every time we touched, making them dangerous to any living (or inanimate) thing in their general vicinity.

Tyler told me that all four of them had been practicing meditation from an early age. It wasn't as important for Tyler, considering the benign nature of his ability, but it was crucial for the other three. Apparently Alec had worked very hard for many years, doing daily mindfulness practice, to gain the kind of control he had. Ethan and Josh had some control over theirs already, but the amounts of Light I gave them access to put things on a whole other level. We all had work to do.

Until we were certain things wouldn't get out of control, I was to avoid skin contact with Ethan and Josh at all costs and come to Tyler if my Light became unbearable again. It was the only way to avoid suspicion and minimize the chances of a disaster. In the meantime, we would train at their house as often as possible. The privacy of their massive, secure, isolated estate made it the only safe place for me to transfer Light to Ethan and Josh.

Having the Reds think I was in a relationship with Ethan would help with that.

He handed me my new, far busier, schedule at the end of the hour and ushered me toward the door, where he asked me to keep another secret.

"If you see Ethan and Josh today, don't tell them about the . . . us," he finished uncertainly. "Let me tell them later, at home. I don't want to chance their reactions in public."

"Oh. OK." I wondered what kind of reaction he was worried about, but before I had a chance to ask, his phone rang, and he hustled me out the door before rushing to answer it.

Naturally, I bumped into Ethan and Josh as soon as I stepped foot outside the building.

FIFTEEN

"Hey, babe!" Ethan flashed me his dimpled grin while Josh waved from behind him. I froze. *Busted.* I hadn't had a chance to prepare for this. And what was with the pet name?

"Oh, h-hey, um, sweetie. What's up? What's going on? Why . . . uh. What, whatcha doin' here?" I ended that eloquent outburst with a stilted laugh and a shuffle of my feet, crossing my arms over my chest before immediately propping them on my hips. *Smooth.*

Why was it that lying to government officials about my identity was so easy, but trying to lie to Ethan and Josh was making me feel like the most awkward person on earth?

They exchanged a look, chuckling but confused.

"We just thought we would come and see how your meeting with Gabe went." Ethan said. "Maybe grab some coffee?"

"Are you OK?" Josh interjected. *Crap!* Not Josh. Josh knew things just by looking at me. Stupid, observant, sexy . . . no! *Focus, dammit!*

I couldn't look at him, so I addressed his shoulder. "Mmmhmm. Yep. Fine. How are you?"

"Fine." He cocked his head to the side, trying to make eye contact. I could practically see the curiosity wafting off him.

I needed to get things moving before they started asking questions.

"Sweet. So yeah, gotta get lunch! I'm starving." I marched off toward the cafeteria, hoping they wouldn't follow me or notice I had just suggested lunch at 10 a.m.

Of course they followed me. They had been following me around for the last several weeks; why would they stop now?

Josh caught up to me first and stepped up on my right. Ethan surprised me by coming up on my left and draping a strong arm over my shoulders. I jumped a little but managed to keep walking. After days of avoiding even speaking too much in public, we were suddenly at the casual touching stage?

"What are you doing?" I stage-whispered to him out of the corner of my mouth. "Aren't we supposed to be keeping things secret?" People were already throwing us curious glances, murmuring to one another.

"Yeah, but only about the Bond," he whispered into my ear. I could feel his warm breath in my hair. It made me lean into him a little more.

"Wh-what?" I had to shake my head to clear it. The Light inside me was practically singing at his close proximity. It was thoroughly enjoying being around my Variant guys, especially since I was still on a high from the intense Light transfer with Tyler only half an hour ago.

"We need to keep our connection a secret, but it's only a matter of time before everyone starts gossiping about why we're spending so much time together. This way we get to have some control over what the gossip is. Plus, it gives me an excuse to touch you in public." As he spoke the last sentence, his hand started to travel down my back toward my ass. I slapped it away and fixed him with a glare.

He laughed out loud, drawing even more attention to us, and returned his arm to my shoulders, dropping a quick kiss to the top of my head.

"This is so not fair," Josh muttered on my other side. His gaze was fixed straight ahead, and a tiny muscle was twitching in his jaw.

We'd made it to the square outside the cafeteria, but instead of heading toward the entrance, Ethan led me to another building. As if they had planned ahead, Josh opened the door so Ethan could hustle me inside.

"I thought we were going to lunch." We were inside what looked like another residence hall. It was deserted.

Neither of them answered me as they walked toward the back of the building. Josh opened another door under the stairway, standing next to it like a butler, and Ethan ushered me into what I now saw was a storage closet. Mops and brooms were stacked on one wall, a shelving unit with cleaning supplies on the other.

"What the hell? What are we doing here?"

Josh closed the door behind him, and Ethan reached up to pull the cord on a little light bulb swinging from the ceiling.

It was a small space, not intended for three people to stand inside. Definitely not intended for someone Ethan's size. We were cramped, and it should have been uncomfortable, but I found myself liking the proximity to both of them.

I was facing Ethan, his broad, white-cotton-clad chest just inches away. Josh stood directly behind me, blocking the door.

"Something is wrong, and you're trying to keep it from us." Ethan crossed his arms over his chest. "Spill." He had that serious look on his face, the one that disappeared the dimples.

"What are you talking about? I'm fine." *More than fine now that I'm alone in a confined space with the two of you.* The Light was apparently not as determined as I was to ignore the whole "getting involved with multiple people" thing. It churned inside me, chomping at the bit to flow into the guys crammed with me in the storage closet. It was making me confuse the supernatural urge for a more basic, physical one.

Or was it? How much of my attraction could be attributed to the Bond connection, and how much was just me?

Josh placed a gentle hand on my shoulder and pulled lightly, trying to get me to turn to him. I knew I should resist, that Josh's way of picking up on unspoken things was freakishly accurate, but I melted into his touch. Behind me, Ethan stepped in a little closer.

I was careful not to meet Josh's eyes. Like a child playing hide and seek, I was trying to convince myself that if I couldn't see him, then he couldn't see me and my secret.

"Eve." His voice was soft but firm. "What happened? We only want to help. It's all we ever want when it comes to you—to help and to protect. I know it has something to do with your session with Tyler this morning."

My eyes snapped up. "How . . . ?" and then I immediately realized my mistake. He smirked, satisfied. I had just confirmed his suspicion.

"No fair!" I half-heartedly slapped his chest, but instead of removing my hand, I left it resting just over his heart, feeling the soft fabric of his mint-green shirt and the warmth of his body under my palm.

"What did he tell you that freaked you out? I'm sure whatever it is, it's perfectly normal . . ."

I chuckled. "Oh, I know it's normal. Or as normal as a paranormal connection can be." My voice had dropped to a mutter, and Josh frowned.

Ethan grunted in frustration behind me, his chest bumping my back. He was having trouble figuring out what we were talking about, and I didn't blame him.

"Eve." Josh narrowed his eyes, but he didn't remove my hand from its position on his chest.

"Look, it's nothing bad. I don't think. Tyler is going to tell you tonight anyway. We really should get to class."

Unsurprisingly, my attempt at deflecting didn't work.

"So there *is* something to tell then," Josh said. "Come on, Eve. What is it?"

I shook my head and pressed my lips together.

"*Eve.*" I wished he would stop saying my name with increasing levels of disapproval in his voice.

"We're not leaving this dirty storage room until you tell us what's going on." Ethan stepped impossibly closer, pressing his body flush with my back.

My brain latched onto his use of the word *dirty*. Logically I knew he was referring to our current location, but coupled with his body heat radiating behind me and the feel of his hard chest pressed into my spine, I was considering all the other connotations of the word.

"Please . . ." I wasn't sure how I'd originally intended that sentence to end, but I collected my thoughts enough to say: "I promised I wouldn't say anything."

I immediately groaned in frustration. I'd given them another clue. I'd also given away the fact that their proximity was directly correlated to how much information I was giving away.

"It's something Tyler wants you to keep from us?" Josh's voice was considerably lower now, his intense green eyes trained on me. "Why?"

Again, I shook my head, refusing to answer. But it was too late. They had figured out my weakness.

Moving in tandem, Ethan placed his hands on my waist just as Josh stepped forward and grabbed my arm, lifting it from his chest to his shoulder. Instinctively I raised my other arm, and Josh grabbed it so he was holding both my wrists. He ran his hands slowly up my arms, stopping at my shoulders, at the very edge of my shirt's collar, careful not to actually touch my skin.

At least some of us had the presence of mind to avoid sudden and violent Light transfer. It certainly wasn't in the forefront of *my* mind.

"Eve." When he whispered my name again, it was more pleading than demanding. Ethan wasn't saying anything, but his chest pressed into my back with each heavy breath he took, the warm air tickling my scalp. His fingers dug into my sides, and I immediately arched into him, inadvertently pressing my chest against Josh, tight as we were against each other.

His sudden intake of breath told me I wasn't the only one affected by our current situation. The hardness pressing into both my backside and low on my belly confirmed it. Josh's hands left my shoulders and replaced Ethan's on my waist as Ethan's warm hands slid down over my T-shirt, stopping on my hips.

Ethan's forehead came to rest on the back of my head, and he cursed softly. "If she doesn't tell us what this is about soon, I'm going to break the 'no skin contact' rule. In a big way."

"Eve. Please." This time Josh actually did plead with me, punctuating it with a squeeze of his hands on my waist.

I was torn. My Light-driven instinct was to please the members of my Bond, to strengthen the connection. But what the hell was I supposed to do when I would end up disappointing one of them regardless? Plus I had no idea how to actually tell them. "This is so hard. You guys have put me in a really tight spot."

Ethan groaned, and they both chuckled. I realized what I had just said and laughed. At least some of the tension was dispelled.

"What I mean to say is, I don't want to disappoint you or let you down. It feels painful to think about. But I also don't want to disappoint Tyler or let him down. That's *just as painful.*"

I equally hoped that they would get the idea and that they would be more confused and drop it.

"Holy shit." Of course Josh got it right away.

"What?" Ethan was nuzzling his nose in my hair. I wasn't sure he'd even heard what I said.

"She's his Vital. Tyler is part of our Bond."

"What? Are you sure?"

"Yes." Josh and I answered at the same time.

"I don't know how to feel about this," Ethan said. Josh just stared at me, looking as if he wasn't sure what to make of it either.

And now I understood why Tyler had wanted to tell them himself. Would they be angry? Would they be disappointed in me?

Ethan must have suspected our connection when we first shook hands, and Josh had thought I was his for several weeks, even if I'd had no idea what was going on. A couple days ago they'd had to deal with the fact that they would be sharing me. Now they would be sharing me with Tyler too. Was there enough of me to go around? Could I handle that much Light coursing through me?

And what would this mean for *their* relationship? These guys were like family—in some ways more than family. I didn't want to be the thing that came between them. Josh was already bothered that Ethan had an excuse to touch me in public when he couldn't. That didn't sit well with me either; I wanted to give them equal attention, equal Light.

How would that work with Tyler in the mix? Considering our current position—the guys pressed up against me, all of us breathing hard, using every ounce of self-control to avoid the skin contact we knew was unsafe—it was clear they were interested in a romantic and physical relationship. And while I needed some time to get my head around being with more than one person, I wanted them too. How was I supposed to keep things even when Tyler had made it clear he wanted our relationship to be platonic?

The tight proximity of two warm bodies I'd craved moments ago suddenly felt stifling, and I swallowed hard and pushed on Josh's chest. He backed away immediately, and I saw he was staring at Ethan over my head. While I'd been having my quiet mental freak out, they'd been having a silent conversation. The look on his face was incomprehensible. How was he able to read me so clearly when I couldn't decipher his feelings at all? It wasn't fair.

"If there had to be another one . . ." Josh looked down at me as he spoke, but it was Ethan who finished the thought.

". . . better him than anyone else." I heard a smile in his voice as he said it.

Predictably, Josh saw the inner turmoil written on my face and gave a confident smile. "It's OK, Eve. I can see why Gabe might have been wary of our reaction, but we're OK with this."

"Really?" I stepped back into his arms, and he wrapped me up in a tight hug.

"Yes. It's going to be an adjustment, but hey, what else is new? And like Ethan said, better Gabe than some random."

"Yeah, don't go fusing any randoms to our Bond," Ethan piped up before stepping forward and encircling us both in his big arms. "Group hug!"

We all laughed, and the heavy weight in my chest lifted a little.

After checking that the coast was clear, we left our hidey-hole and walked off campus to the café where Alec had gotten my latte. We took the morning off, having amazing coffees and then lunch, chatting about lighter things, before heading back for afternoon classes.

As the three of us walked back to campus, I got a message from Dot asking where I was. I shot her a quick reply, telling her I was on my way back and would see her in our biology lecture, but as we came through the front gates of the Institute, she came marching up to us with an amused grin on her face.

She was wearing black-and-silver boots that looked as if they were part of a video game character's armor, and she'd paired them with a pinafore dress—with a massive matching bow in her hair—and a studded choker. She looked like a toddler assassin, and the look on my face was just as amused as hers. I was amused by her outfit; I had no idea why *she* was amused.

"So, suddenly you're a Variant and you're dating my cousin. Someone's been busy." She nudged Ethan out of the way and matched our pace as we kept walking to class.

"Dot, I'm sorry I didn't tell you. It's just . . ." I had no idea how to end the sentence.

"It's all good. Gabe told me he would be meeting with you this morning to give you your test results, so I knew before you did. He wanted me to keep an eye on you once the news was out." She giggled, and I laughed nervously along with her. It was better that she thought she found out before I did.

"This one, however"—she turned around to glare at Ethan, who managed to look sheepish and satisfied with himself at the same time—"failed to mention he was boning *my* new friend."

"Look, it's all kind of new and—wait. Boning? Um, that's not . . ."

Ethan's booming voice drowned me out. "*Your* new friend? I saw her first Dot."

"Technically, Gabe saw her first," Josh cut in.

"Gabe doesn't count, bro." Ethan laughed, and the two of them started bickering as Dot looped her arm through mine and spoke in a more serious tone.

"It's all good, Eve. Considering his reputation, I can understand why you weren't telling everyone you guys were seeing each other. And I can totally understand why you would want to go public with it now that the cat's out of the bag about your DNA test."

"Yeah . . . wait. What?" The stuff about Ethan's reputation made sense, but she'd lost me when she started sounding paranoid about my DNA test.

"Yeah, the next few days might be a little . . ." She waved her hand in the air and gave me a pitying look, making me even more worried. "Most students start here at the beginning of semester, and everyone's test results come out at once, resulting in a frenzy of information sharing and speculation, with no one person singled out. You arrived at the end of the year, so your results are going to be the talk of campus for a while. People are going to want to suss you out, so expect some extra attention. It's why Gabe told me your results ahead of time. He was hoping it wouldn't get out for a day or two, but he underestimated the power of gossip. Welcome to my world."

I groaned, hoping she was exaggerating, but even as we approached our lecture, I noticed more eyes on me than I'd ever been comfortable with. With a sinking feeling, it dawned on me that the people staring this morning when Ethan had tucked me under his arm weren't interested only in our relationship—they were interested in my newfound status. I was no longer a Dime, and the whole student population knew it.

That was *exactly* why Ethan had put on the affectionate boyfriend routine—to send the message I was already his. He had outed us before I'd even had a chance to express an opinion on the matter, without asking if I might have one. I was more than a little annoyed at him but decided to deal with one problem at a time. My sudden popularity was a more pressing issue.

By the time I walked out of my last class for the day, I was already over it. Several people I'd never met before had come up to talk to me. Some of them came right out and said they'd heard about my test results and proceeded to tell me about their own abilities or lack thereof. Some of them just acted extra friendly, inviting me to hang out with them and asking if I would be attending some gala happening soon.

All of them made a point of shaking my hand, and it didn't take me long to figure out why. They were making skin contact to check if I was their Vital or Variant—to see if we were connected.

The boys and Dot did their best to run interference, chatting to people who approached and trying to take some of the attention off me. I was grateful they were trying to shield me, but there was only so much they could do. Yes, these people had ulterior motives, but they weren't technically doing anything wrong.

Dot took it all in stride, but Ethan and Josh became more and more agitated as the afternoon wore on. Josh managed to cover it well, keeping a neutral, bored expression on his face, but the tick in his cheek was incessant. Ethan became visibly surly, his usually light and carefree demeanor disappearing behind a frown and crossed arms.

None of my protectors had been in my last class, and I'd had to deal with the vultures on my own. My own arms were crossed over my chest and my head was turned down as I exited the lecture hall. If I avoided eye contact, maybe no one would have an excuse to start a conversation.

I was wrong.

"Eve, right?"

The overly friendly male voice came from close by, and I groaned even as I looked up. Ethan, Josh, and Dot were standing together just a few feet away, but my view of them was blocked by a broad chest as a guy about my age stepped into my path.

"Yeah, hi." I wasn't even trying to hide the disinterest in my voice.

He chuckled. "Long day, huh?"

In answer I just stared at him, waiting for him to get it over with. He had honey-blond hair and looked friendly enough, but I was not in the mood.

"Look, I get it. I just want to introduce myself. I'm Rick, and this is my ability."

He held his hand out, just as I'd seen Ethan do many times, but instead of fire, what appeared between his fingers was electricity, sparking and darting around in a mesmerizing dance. My fatigue with all the unwanted attention warred with my fascination for unique abilities, and I couldn't help a small, amused smile pulling at my lips as I watched the blue bolts moving in jerky movements between his fingers.

My view of Rick's ability was interrupted by a bright ball of fire shooting between us. Rick laughed and dropped his hand, the electricity disappearing, as I jumped, startled.

Ethan stepped up behind me, wrapping a possessive arm over my front and pulling me against him.

"Hey, Rick." He sounded friendly, but I could hear a hint of tension in his voice. "I see you've met my *girlfriend*."

Josh and Dot joined us as Rick answered, still friendly and seemingly oblivious to Ethan's hostility. "Hey, Kid. Yeah, I was just introducing myself." He extended his hand.

I shook it as quickly as I could and pulled my hand back, shrinking into Ethan's warmth. I had been outraged he'd all but staked his claim on me this morning without discussing it with me, but after the afternoon I'd had, I was glad he'd done it. I shuddered to think how much worse my day would have been if I'd had to deal with things on my own.

Of course I felt nothing when I touched Rick's hand, and he wouldn't have either. But apparently he was in the mood to stir some shit.

"Hmm. That was quick. Not sure if I felt a little something or—"

Ethan tensed, but before he could react, before Rick had even finished his sentence, Zara barreled into our little group, Beth hot on her heels.

"Beat it. I need to talk to my friend." She looked kind of mad, speaking over her shoulder to Rick.

Beth kept throwing her furtive glances and only waved at me in hello. I waved back as Rick laughed.

"Excuse me," he said. "We were having a conversation."

"And now it's over. I said leave, you overgrown toaster."

Dot chuckled, and Ethan's big shoulders shook behind me as he tried to contain his own mirth.

"God," Rick said, "you're such a bitch, Zara."

"Thank you." She smiled at him; I was pretty sure she genuinely took it as a compliment.

"Whatever. I have to go anyway. See you around, Eve." Rick winked at me and walked off.

Zara turned on me. "Why didn't you tell us you were a Variant?"

"Zara," Beth soothed, "come on, I'm sure that—"

"She only just found out, you psycho," Dot interrupted. "She got her test results this morning."

Zara rounded on her. "Why are you even here, Dot? What, now that she's officially a Variant, you think she's yours? She might not even have an ability. Are you going to drop her as fast as you did me when you realize she's not special?"

"What? I didn't drop you. You're the one that stopped coming to things or answering my calls. Don't put your identity crisis shit on me. Or Eve for that matter."

They were beginning to raise their voices, and I really didn't want to give the Bradford Hills gossip mill more to talk about. In one day, I'd found out I had not two but *three* Variants in my Bond, been claimed by Ethan, and been accosted by half the student population. Now two of my three friends were about to have a public showdown over old grievances brought up by my current situation.

As someone who had spent her whole childhood pretty much alone, I was not used to this level of attention.

"Enough!" I yelled, stepping out of Ethan's arms to look at them all. "I can't handle this shit. I'm leaving. *Alone*. Can I get, like, two freaking seconds to process? I just . . . Dammit!"

They all stared at me, stunned.

Charlie chose that moment to walk up, oblivious to what was going on. "Hey. What have I missed?"

"Where the hell have you been?" It didn't seem fair that he'd managed to avoid all the drama of the day and was now standing there, casually unaffected by it all.

"I've been in the library all day working on my thesis. What's going on?"

"Eve's test results spread around campus like wildfire, and she's been swatting people away like flies all day. Dot and Zara are finally having it out about why they stopped being friends, and Ethan and Eve are officially a couple," Josh supplied helpfully, giving me an understanding look. I had no doubt he understood what I was feeling—he'd proven himself to be very good at it—and it must have been frustrating for him not to be able to do anything about it in public. Being reminded of another complication in my life only added to my foul mood.

Charlie whistled low, stuffing his hands in his pockets. "A bit then."

"I'm leaving." I didn't wait for a response from anyone. I just walked off toward my res hall, trying to forget the day for just a few minutes and focus on the swaying branches of the trees lining the walkway, and the sound of the rustling leaves.

Charlie caught up to me quickly, matching my pace in silence, giving me space. Which was exactly what I needed.

"How much did you already know?" I asked once I was feeling a bit calmer.

"I've known about your test results as long as Gabe. I do some work for Melior Group in their cyber division— it gives me access to certain . . . information."

He gave me a cheeky smile. The access he was talking about wasn't, I suspected, entirely legal. I shook my head at him but smiled a little despite myself.

"I suspected there was something between you and either Ethan or Josh, but that was only confirmed today."

"Yeah . . ." Ethan *or* Josh. I wanted so badly to tell him it was both, to have at least one thing off my chest, but I kept my mouth shut.

We reached the front of my building, and he turned to face me. "The attention will die down as the novelty does, and Ethan's overprotectiveness will go with it. Dot and Zara will sort their own shit out—that has nothing to do with you and has been a long time coming. And we'll get you through all this new Variant stuff. Everything will be OK, Eve."

"Thanks, Charlie." I gave him a hug. It was exactly what I needed—someone to cut through the shit and remind me that, as overwhelming as this felt now, it would pass.

We said goodbye, and I headed upstairs, locking myself in my room for some much needed alone time.

I went to bed feeling better about the situation but utterly exhausted and a little wary after the crazy day. I was not at all superstitious, putting all my faith in science, but a sense of foreboding still hung over my head as I lay on my bed, staring at nothing. My life at Bradford Hills was about to get more complicated.

So much for focusing on my studies and having a few quiet years while I got my degree.

SIXTEEN

Ethan's face was frozen in shock, his amber eyes wide, his hands out at his sides as if to steady himself. There wasn't much he could do about his current situation though, floating as he was, eight feet off the ground in Josh's bedroom.

"Shit shit shit," Josh muttered, his eyes as wide as Ethan's. He held his arms out toward him, keeping him elevated with his telekinetic ability.

I was standing off to the side with my lower back pressed against the couch, my hands over my mouth. I had done my part for this training session—I had identified the Light inside me, monitored the levels, and transferred a specific amount to Josh through our hands. All I could do now was stay out of the way.

Tyler stepped up to Josh with slow, deliberate movements, but his posture was relaxed and confident. "It's OK. You've got this, Josh."

"What?" Josh sounded much less calm. "It doesn't feel like I've got it, Gabe!"

"You do. You're holding him up. He's safe for now."

"What if I drop him?"

"You won't. You have enough Light, courtesy of our Vital." He flashed me an affectionate smile, and I just stared back, wide eyed. "If you were straining or overusing your ability, Eve would have noticed. She'd be feeling a pull to you. Are you feeling a pull, Eve?"

I dropped my hands to my throat to answer. "Nope! You're doing great, Josh."

"See, you're doing great." Tyler gave Josh an easy smile, and I could see some of the tension in his back release. "Now, take a deep breath and focus."

Tyler encouraged and guided Josh until he gently and precisely lowered Ethan to his bed, unharmed, and we all breathed a massive sigh of relief. Josh rested his hands on his knees and took several deep breaths.

Half my evenings and most of my weekends were now spent at the Zacarias mansion, training with Ethan and Josh. It was the safest place to do so without being discovered, but we still had to be careful. Dot and Charlie were close with the boys and spent a lot of time at the house, not to mention all the gardeners, cleaners, and other staff that were ever present.

Josh's ability appeared to be limited to items he could see, so we were able to close ourselves into a room and practice without fear of him accidentally floating one of the staff out of a window. It was a little more difficult to find time to train with Ethan. Tyler insisted we do it in the pool for safety reasons, but the only time there was no one around was at night. Luckily, he too was getting better at controlling his ability, and I was hoping Tyler would let us practice outside the pool soon. Some nights it was way too cold to be outside in a bikini.

I gave Josh a reassuring pat on the back as he straightened. The fabric of his Green Day T-shirt felt soft under my palm. He was in the comfort of his home, and I'd learned that meant he would be in one of his seemingly endless supply of band Ts.

"I'm so sorry, Kid." Josh still looked a little worried.

"It's all good, bro!" Ethan scooted to the edge of the bed. "But there are healthier ways to express your jealousy over the fact that *I'm* Eve's boyfriend and not you." He flashed us both a cheeky grin.

"You mean *pretend* boyfriend, right? You haven't actually asked me out yet," I reminded him.

"Uh huh. Sure thing, dumpling."

"Come here, dimples, you have a cobweb in your hair."

After Ethan's calling me "babe," the nickname thing had stuck around, and now we were in an ongoing game where we called each other by a different pet name every time. We hadn't run out yet, but they were starting to get more and more inventive.

Tyler told us to take a break while he made a few calls and headed downstairs. The three of us collapsed on Josh's couch and he put some music on while we chatted.

As the boys started bickering about something—it was both their favorite pastime *and* how they showed affection—I slipped out and made my way to the end of the hallway. To Alec's bedroom door.

I had been keeping my eyes open for an opportunity to approach him about the night of the crash again, but he'd started actively avoiding me, so I wasn't having much luck. Tyler had mentioned he was home. I just hoped he wasn't sleeping.

Wringing my hands, I mentally chastised myself for my own nervousness. This whole situation had turned into something way bigger than it ever needed to be. Part of that was his fault for making it so difficult, but part of it was mine for letting it get to me so much.

Steeling my shoulders, I knocked firmly on his door. My heart beat a little faster at the sound of movement on the other side, but I took a deep breath, determined to look calm and confident.

He opened the door in a towel. All the things I was going to say to him, all the words I had practiced for over a year, just flew out of my head, chased away by broad shoulders, corded muscles, countless tattoos, and that towel, slung dangerously low.

"Can I help you?" His voice was low but still devoid of that smooth sweetness I remembered from the night of the crash.

I snapped my eyes up to his face, feeling like an idiot for staring. The eyebrow with the scar quirked just a little in amusement, his lips pulled into a crooked smirk.

"Hey, um . . . sorry, I just . . . uh . . ." Words were eluding me, and now embarrassment was making it even more difficult to get my shit together.

Usually, by this stage, he would have closed the door in my face, but apparently he wanted to watch me squirm.

"Yes? What's up?" The cruel little smirk grew as he leaned one arm on the doorway and grabbed the edge of his towel with the other, pulling it up but then dragging it just a little lower and leaving his thumb tucked into it. Naturally, my eyes were drawn to the newly exposed sliver of skin, and he chuckled.

He was enjoying torturing me.

Just as the outrage was about to overpower my ridiculous stupor, Dana sidled up to him, wearing one of his black T-shirts, her blonde hair all messed up.

What had I been thinking, trying to force my thanks onto him by going to his bedroom?

Dana looked at me with raised eyebrows, as if asking "what?" but Alec's face had gone blank.

When I *still* didn't say anything, frozen to the spot by the shock of Alec's shirtlessness and the sheer awkwardness of the situation, she simply turned her face into his neck, completely ignoring me. Her hand reached for his where it was still holding the towel, and her elegant fingers inched their way under the fabric.

Alec used his free hand to slam the door closed, but it wasn't in my face; I had already turned to leave. The overtly sexual act was apparently all I'd needed to snap me out of it.

Instead of heading back to Josh's room, I went to the stairs, jogging halfway down the first flight and plonking myself down. I needed a moment.

With a low, frustrated growl, I banged the side of my head against the railing a few times. Alec had been a dick about the whole thing, purposely making me more uncomfortable, but Alec was always a dick about everything. And Dana's dismissive attitude had been downright rude, but maybe she just wasn't a morning person.

I had been the one to intrude. *I* was the one who had created the opportunity for the awkwardness and the rudeness.

I was still sitting there, berating myself, when unintelligible shouting came from above. Alec's voice boomed from behind a closed door, then the same door slammed, then footsteps hurried in my direction.

I shot up, not wanting to get caught on the stairs, but before I could make my getaway, Dana bounded past, taking the stairs at breakneck speed and not even slowing down to acknowledge me.

When I heard Ethan calling my name, I headed back to my guys.

~

A few days later, as I walked toward the front gates of Bradford Hills Institute, I caught another venomous look from a girl with short black hair and long, toned legs. I knew Ethan had a reputation, but the number of girls I was getting dirty looks from surprised me. I hadn't said anything to him, not eager for him to confirm exactly how many women he'd slept with.

According to Dot, Ethan had never stayed with a girl as long as he had with me, and they were wondering what made me so special. Sometimes out loud, as I walked past. If they only knew . . .

I ignored the black-haired girl, keeping my eyes trained ahead and focusing on the feel of the warm sun on my back. I was on my way to the Zacarias mansion to get ready for an exclusive gala dinner. Josh had offered to pick me up, but I had insisted on walking, wanting to enjoy the nice weather.

When I rounded the bend in the path, I saw him leaning on the massive gate. His yellow shirt was perfectly fitted, the sleeves rolled up to the elbows in a way that was unusually casual for him when in public. His dirty blond hair was perfectly set in a neat style, and his head was bent over a small paperback.

I slowed to take him in for a moment before he noticed me, a smile playing on my lips. Of course they would never let me walk to their house alone, unprotected, but I couldn't be mad about getting to catch Josh absorbed in a novel, looking like the promise of summer in his cheerful shirt and black sunglasses.

I walked right past him, keeping my pace steady and fighting the mirth bubbling up inside, threatening to spill over in a fit of giggles.

He caught up to me almost immediately, tucking the novel into his back pocket and flashing a brilliant smile.

"You couldn't wait until I finished the chapter?" He laughed, shoving his hands into his pockets. We still couldn't hold hands, as much as I wanted to.

"Oh, hey, Josh," I said with exaggerated surprise, and that time we both laughed.

We walked in companionable silence for a while and then started chatting about classes and books and what had been happening over the past few weeks.

"How are the Reds?" he asked. "Zara still giving you the cold shoulder"

"Nah, it's all sorted now." Zara had eventually apologized for dragging me into a fight that was between her and Dot. I quickly accepted her apology and told her it wasn't my intention to deceive her; it was a flat out lie and I felt bad about it, but now that I knew my guys could be in danger if our secret came out, my resolve to keep them safe was unwavering.

Once we cleared the air, we had a group hug—instigated by Beth. She could have thrown her hands up and avoided the whole situation—it had even less to do with her than it did with me—but she helped Zara work through her emotions and encouraged us to talk it out. She was a good friend.

Things went back to normal with my roomies, but Zara and Dot's relationship got decidedly more icy. They were both loud, strong, and stubborn, and even Beth couldn't get them to sit down and talk.

"Ethan still at baseball practice?" I asked Josh.

"Football," he corrected, chuckling. "He should be back any minute now, but he can take his time. I like having you to myself."

We shared a loaded look but didn't let it linger. Being this close and not being able to reach out and touch him was torture. Time alone with either of them was rare, but at least I could be affectionate with Ethan in public.

He had attempted to apologize for being an overprotective oaf that day, but I'd stopped him halfway through his awkward speech. His hulking presence had turned out to be a lifesaver, and I could understand why he'd done it.

Josh cleared his throat. "How are your sessions with Gabe going?"

"Yeah, really good. I'm actually starting to like meditating."

The meditation was just one part of my new routine. During the day I attended my science classes and went to my intensive tutoring sessions with Tyler. We were breezing through my Variant studies theory and spent half of each session working on my Light control. Tyler talked me through how to quiet my mind and focus on identifying that low thrum of the Light coursing through me.

It was pure energy, unadulterated power. Now that I knew what I was looking for, I realized it had always been there; it had always been part of me, under the surface, waiting to find the Variants with the abilities it was created to sustain.

I practiced transferring Light to him in controlled, deliberate amounts. It was always through our hands, and he would always pull away as soon as it was done, going to sit behind his desk.

"Do you think your control is improving?" I asked.

"Yeah, I guess. It'll take time."

"I think you're doing great. I mean, you haven't accidentally floated anyone up to the ceiling in days."

He grinned. "Oh, come on! That happened once."

It *had* only happened that one time with an actual person, but it had happened plenty of other times with inanimate objects. Tyler was always there to keep us calm and focused though.

It was fascinating to watch Tyler's natural leadership shine through and the others take his lead. Apparently, he also had serious clout with Bradford Hills Institute, because no one questioned his decision to pull me from half my classes and tutor me himself. Zara, however, did raise it one day over lunch, a suspicious look in her eyes. I shrugged and played it off as the Institute's decision—that because I'd had so little contact with Variants growing up, they wanted me to learn all I could in case my ability manifested.

She grumbled a bit about "Variants digging their claws into me" and "indoctrination," but thankfully, she dropped it.

Beth, on the other hand, was a hopeless romantic, had multiple crushes, and devoured romance novels like I did science journals. She jumped in, gushing about how I got to "spend hours every day locked in a room with Tyler Gabriel."

The conversation had then turned to which guys were single, descending into a gossip session, and I'd breathed an internal sigh of relief. Every time I had to actively lie to them, my heart would race, and I would have to work really hard to make sure I looked calm and casual. It was exhausting.

At least the gossip was no longer about me. Mostly. When it appeared I wasn't Bonded to anyone and there was no sign of me having an ability, the attention had slowly died down.

The current hot topic was tonight's exclusive Variant society event. Bradford Hills Institute, with sponsorship from the Melior Group, was hosting a gala in Manhattan. The black-tie event was a fundraiser for Senator Anderson's upcoming re-election campaign. The New York senator, the woman I had read about online, was one of the only Variants in the Senate and a Bradford Hills Institute alumnus.

As we started walking up their long, tree-lined driveway, Josh raised the event with a visible cringe. "You still dreading tonight?" He already knew the answer. I'd been complaining about it since realizing I would have to go.

Anyone who was anyone in American Variant society would be flashing their cash at this gala, and most Variants my age would be using it as one of those networking events Zara had spoken about with such derision. All my fellow Variant students were excited to meet other young Variants in the hope they might find a Bond.

I already had my Bond, so I had very little interest in the whole thing. Of course, no one knew that, so the guys were insisting I attend in order to avoid suspicion. I'd tried to argue, but Tyler had put his foot down, and since he was in charge of pretty much everything, I had to go.

"Oh, no! I can't wait!" I laid the sarcasm on thick, giving Josh a wide fake smile before rolling my eyes and deadpanning, "I would rather listen to a climate change debate." There was nothing left to debate—the science was solid and definitive.

"Wow. OK." Josh chuckled, "I know you don't want to go, but I'm looking forward to spending some extra time with you. And you'll finally meet Ethan and Alec's uncle."

I had yet to meet the elusive Lucian Zacarias. The boys had told me he would be at the event tonight but was flying in too late to make an appearance at home, instead staying at their apartment in the city—because of course they had an apartment in the city. On the Upper East Side. Where else?

"Yeah, it'll be good to meet him." I gave Josh a genuine smile as we climbed the stairs to the front door. All the guys had a lot of respect and affection for their absent father figure.

"Good." He smiled back, opening the door for me. "Now, can I keep you to myself a little longer before Dot disappears you? What takes all afternoon to get ready?"

I had no idea, but Dot had insisted. I dared not defy her for fear of having a bear carry me in its claws to her tiny, waiting feet.

I did hope, however, that she had a dress I could borrow. Even though Zara had flat out refused to go, she'd given me some details on what to expect. This particular event was one of the big ones. It was not a "jeans and nice top" kind of party.

I had exactly two dresses in my meager wardrobe. One was a T-shirt dress, which was too casual, and the other was my mother's summer dress. One of a few items that had been salvaged from the plane crash, it had big yellow and red poppies on a black background, and the full skirt fanned out if you twirled on the spot. I couldn't bring myself to wear it yet, and even if I could, this event was no more a "summer dress" event than a "jeans and nice top" event. I needed a gown.

"Beats me." I laughed. "But I'm happy to put it off a little longer."

"Come. I have something for you." Excitement sharpened his features as he took off his sunglasses.

"Oh?" My curiosity was piqued.

My sneakers squeaked softly on the polished marble of the entrance hall as I followed him into a room on the right.

It was a formal sitting room. On the opposite wall was a massive fireplace; in front of it, a wide glass coffee table and two velvet upholstered couches facing each other. After a quick glance to either side, Josh shut the doors behind us.

As soon as the doors were securely closed, he took two long strides and wrapped his arms around me. Dropping my bag to the floor, I returned the hug eagerly and pressed my cheek into his shoulder, taking a deep breath. His crisp white shirt smelled like clean laundry warmed by the sun.

In public, Ethan always had an arm slung over my shoulders as we walked, a hand on my knee as we sat together, a palm to my back as we passed through a door; Josh had to suppress his instinct to touch me or even look at me too long. But behind closed doors, it was Josh pulling me back to lean against him as we listened to Tyler explain the next exercise, hugging me tight after a long day, pulling me into his lap as we took a rare break to just hang out and listen to music. As we became closer, the Bond deepening naturally, it was getting more and more frustrating to have to keep a distance.

"I missed you," Josh mumbled into my hair.

"I saw you yesterday in class, you goof." I chuckled, but I knew what he meant. Having to sit side by side and be constantly wary that someone could be paying too much attention was torture. It was almost worse than not seeing each other at all. "I missed you too," I added, because I really had.

We stood like that for a few moments, just holding each other.

My relationship with my Bond was still undefined and confusing, but I couldn't deny that I craved each of their company. I needed Ethan's infectious positivity; Josh's observant, caring attention; Tyler's confident leadership and challenging conversation. The Light was pushing me toward my Variants, but I needed them in ways that had nothing to do with the Light.

With a soft kiss to the corner of my mouth, he released me and reached for a flat, rectangular box—big enough to fit two of my science textbooks—that had been sitting on the coffee table.

"What did you do? What is this?" I wasn't sure how I felt about impromptu gifts from my kind of, not really boyfriend, whom I was definitely attracted to.

"Open it." With the excitement in his face, you would think he was the one who'd just been presented with a surprise gift.

I undid the black silk bow and lifted the silver lid, placing it on the table. Tissue paper—held together by a little round sticker with "Dior" embossed on it—concealed the box's contents.

I hesitated. I may not have had a keen interest in fashion, but even I knew Dior. This was a very expensive gift, probably more than I could guess at. I wasn't sure I could accept something so extravagant.

"Stop." As usual, Josh knew what I was fretting about. "Please don't let something as petty as money ruin this moment. I got it not because it's expensive. I got it because it's beautiful, and I want to see you in it. And also because I figured you would need something to wear tonight. Let me do this for you."

I could have argued. I could have told him it was just too much; there are plenty of beautiful things that don't cost more than an average car. But I didn't want to ruin the moment, so I chose to accept it graciously. Once again, Josh had done something thoughtful for me.

I smiled at him and shook my head, tearing the tissue paper and lifting the dress out. It tumbled down between us in a cascade of soft fabric and delicate beading. It was easily the most beautiful thing I had ever held. The dress was a dark, gunmetal gray, the bottom of it covered in rich emerald-green beading, dense at the bottom and getting sparser toward the middle.

I launched myself at Josh, squishing the garment between us, and he dropped the box to return the hug. Wrapping my arms around his neck, I pressed my mouth to his enthusiastically, and as naturally as I'd initiated, he responded. His arms circled my middle, and he deepened the kiss, sighing with what could not be mistaken for anything other than satisfaction and relief.

It was the first time we'd kissed since the night of the party, but just as it had that night, it felt as if we'd been doing it for years. Our lips moved against each other in perfect rhythm, our bodies pressing together as though they were made to fit.

As I reveled in the moment, thoroughly enjoying the new level of intimacy, I vaguely registered the logical part of my brain reminding me why we hadn't been kissing all this time. The kiss had been spontaneous, and I hadn't made sure my Light flow was locked down.

As the kiss gained a new level of heated intensity, the alarm bells in my head got louder too. The Light was flowing freely and fast out of me and straight into Josh.

He grunted in frustration before pulling away and looking at me, the green in his eyes more vibrant than I'd ever seen it. "You can't go kissing me like that."

He had a point. The coffee table next to us was floating in midair. Josh focused his gaze on it, managing to lower it to the ground gently and without smashing the giant piece of glass that composed the top.

I grinned at him. "No harm done! See? You're getting better at that."

"Mmmhmm," he murmured, no longer listening. Instead he buried his face in my neck, running his lips feather soft up to my ear. "If that's the reaction I get, I'm buying you a dress every damn day."

"Don't you dare." I meant it to sound firm, but it came out on a whisper. Someone had to put a stop to this, or I really would run out of time to get ready. I took a deep breath and nudged his shoulder. "Hey, you're ruining my new dress, you brute."

I felt him smile against my neck, sending another shiver down my spine, and then he backed off.

Before he stepped away completely, I dropped one last chaste kiss on his cheek. "Thank you, Josh. I really do love it."

"You're welcome," he said before moving over to the double doors to make sure the coast was clear.

He took the box with him and disappeared into the back of the house as I gingerly carried my new dress up the stairs. I was smiling to myself, the feeling of Josh's soft lips still present on mine, so I didn't notice until I was halfway up that Dot was standing on the landing, hands on her hips and a deep frown on her face, her damp black hair falling in a mess around her shoulders.

My heart sank. How much had she seen? I was supposed to be Ethan's girlfriend, yet I had just come out of a room with Josh, and if he was having as much trouble containing his smile as I was, we were definitely busted.

SEVENTEEN

"Finally!" Dot huffed, throwing her arms up and letting them flop down at her sides. "Where have you been? We're behind schedule already."

"There's a schedule?"

"Come on. I need you to help me straighten my hair. Do you know what you're wearing?"

She took off, climbing the second set of stairs to the level where all the guys' bedrooms were. I followed, breathing a sigh of relief. Maybe she hadn't seen anything after all.

At the top of the stairs, in answer to her question, I held up my new dress, letting the delicate fabric tumble down between us.

She gasped and took it from me. "I love it! When did you have time to go shopping?"

I shrugged, hoping she wouldn't press me too much on it, and we headed toward one of the spare rooms—the one she used when she stayed the night.

Even though we were "behind schedule," instead of following her in, I found myself gravitating toward Ethan's room.

Josh's room seemed to be where everyone congregated during our rare moments of freedom, but Ethan's room was the same size and had almost as impressive a bookshelf. But where Josh's shelves were crammed with books and music, Ethan's were bursting with cookbooks.

I'd discovered Ethan's love of cooking one night when I came over for training. Ethan was at practice for one of his many sports, so the session had been between only me and Josh, with Tyler supervising. It was around dinnertime when we finished and headed downstairs, the smell of something incredible hitting me before I even entered the kitchen.

Ethan was at the stove, several steaming pots and pans in front of him as he expertly bustled between them, lifting the lid to peer into this one, stirring that one, adding something to a third. He looked completely in his element and was so engrossed he didn't even hear us come in.

"So, my 'boyfriend' cooks!" I used air quotes around the word *boyfriend*. "The plot thickens."

He looked up, flashing me a quick smile but keeping his attention on the food. "I don't think I could get any thicker, babe," he spoke over his shoulder as he grabbed something out of the fridge. "It would just be gratuitous to go any bigger. People would think I was on steroids."

I laughed and took a seat at the bench.

"Ooh, gratuitous! Someone learned a big new word," Josh teased, sitting next to me.

Ethan just flipped him off before dipping a spoon into one of the pots and bringing it to my lips. I let him spoon the sauce into my mouth, immediately closing my eyes and moaning at the taste. It was creamy and rich but not heavy, with an amazing earthy flavor.

I opened my eyes to find them both staring at me with amused smiles.

"Ethan, this is incredible," I declared, already wanting more.

The usually confident guy surprised me with his quiet and sheepish "Thanks."

"You'll stay for dinner then?" Josh asked, and I nodded enthusiastically. Ethan could feed me any damn time he wanted.

He may have been big and naturally talented at sports, but Ethan's real passion was food. I learned more about it over dinner, as he told me all about the dishes we were eating, what he wanted to try to cook next, and what his favorites were.

After dinner he took me to his room to show me all the cookbooks. I couldn't believe how many he had. He told me he had bought some but that most were his mother's. She was a chef before she died, and they used to cook together when he was little. My heart broke over the bittersweet look that came into his eyes, but he didn't speak about his parents very long, changing the conversation to something lighter. I understood that—I didn't like talking about my mother either. I was glad he'd felt comfortable enough to tell me a little bit about his.

I enjoyed learning about each of them as we spent more time together. I learned that Ethan could cook and that he had a sweet side under that bravado. I learned that Josh liked to read with music on—actually, Josh liked to do almost everything with music on. I learned that Tyler was a workaholic, but he loved his job, and that he was a bit of control freak.

The door to Ethan's room swung open just as I reached it, bringing me back into the present. He stood on the other side, barefoot and shirtless, in nothing but jeans, slung low on his hips.

"Hello, dearest." Another new pet name, delivered with a bright smile.

"Hey, sexy," I shot back without even thinking about it, my focus on his broad chest and the way his fire tattoo wrapped around his shoulder. I had seen him shirtless plenty of times, but there was something more intimate about it at the threshold of his bedroom.

At hearing my choice of nickname, his smile widened. "Damn. Now I can't use that one. I was saving it for a special occasion."

He turned, giving me a view of his back, the muscles rippling as he reached for a T-shirt on his bed. I followed him into the room.

"Were you? That's good to know." Even though we joked and flirted all the time, somehow it felt heavier in that moment, less lighthearted.

He took his time pulling the white T-shirt over his head. Then he turned to face me, and, just as with Josh, we seemed to gravitate toward each other.

He pulled me into his arms, and I had to lift up onto my toes to reach his shoulders and return the hug—which wasn't a simple hug for long. Within seconds, his lips were on mine.

I quickly forced myself to pull away, making a conscious effort to bring my Light flow back under control. I couldn't indulge in this kiss as I had with Josh. While Josh's ability could be destructive, Ethan's was downright dangerous.

He tightened his hold on my waist.

"Ethan." I gave him a warning look. I couldn't speak about the danger with Dot so close by.

He frowned, loosening his grip a little. "What's happening?" he whispered, his face still only inches from mine. "Why . . . ?"

He trailed off, but I knew what he was asking. Why were we so drawn to each other so suddenly?

"It might be because I kissed Josh just before," I whispered back. "The Light. It wants to deepen the Bond evenly. I . . ." *I want to deepen the Bond.*

"Did you?" The cheeky smile had returned. He wasn't jealous that I'd kissed his best friend; he was pleased by it. I smiled back, intrigued at his reaction. Maybe it had something to do with the Light fusing us *all* closer together and not just deepening my Bond to each of them individually?

That's how Dot found us—holding each other and whispering.

"For fuck's sake, Eve. Did I not say we were on a schedule? You can make out later."

She marched over, yanked me away from Ethan with a vicelike grip on my forearm, and dragged me into the next room.

Thankfully, instead of teasing me or asking question about our relationship, she just launched into talking about dresses and makeup and asking my opinion on which shoes she should wear.

We put some music on and took our time doing each other's hair and talking about pointless things. Squiggles was curled up on the bed, watching us with a contented look on her furry little face. From time to time Dot would look at her with concentration, and Squiggles would spring into action, retrieving a tissue from the bathroom or digging a tube of mascara out of a bag across the room. It was adorable and handy at the same time.

As I was halfway through straightening Dot's silky black hair, Charlie wandered past the room and stuck his head in.

"Charles!" Dot yelled before he'd even had a chance to say "hello." "Come!"

"Dorothy." He glared at her but walked toward us anyway. "What do you want?"

She glared back at him through the mirror as he gave me a kiss on the cheek in greeting. "Juice me up. I'm feeling a little drained, and I still need Squiggles to fetch things for me."

"You could just get off your lazy ass and fetch things yourself."

"And you could stop *being* an ass and fulfill your birth-given duty to be my living battery."

"Whatever." He slapped a hand half over Dot's face, and the half that I could see smiled a little at the pleasant sensation of the Light coursing into her.

"You're lucky I haven't started my makeup yet."

Charlie ignored her and turned to me. "How are you, Eve? Excited for tonight?"

My eyes were glued to his hand on his sister's face. I burned to ask him more about how the Vital-Variant connection worked between siblings, what it felt like to expel Light, how he managed to control the flow, if he too had experienced the crazy itching and energy that came with overflow. But they didn't know I was a Vital, so I had to keep my mouth shut and focus on the conversation. What was he asking about?

"Oh, I guess. Yeah?" I didn't sound convincing at all, and they both chuckled.

Charlie released his sister's face, and I went back to straightening her hair as he chatted with me about what to expect that evening, trying to give me all the facts so I wouldn't be so nervous.

Not that snooty social events were complicated, but he was—just like Tyler—really good at explaining complicated things in simple language. Charlie was writing his thesis in the Variant studies field, so he had joined a few of my study sessions with Tyler, helping to advance my knowledge where he could. I appreciated his insights and company, despite his presence meaning I couldn't transfer Light to Tyler or practice controlling my Light flow.

It was also a bit ironic that the knowledge I most craved was about the biggest thing we had in common.

"Just stick with one of us during the night and you'll be fine," he finished, and I nodded, hoping he hadn't noticed I'd barely heard a word. "Anyway I'll leave you girls to . . . whatever this is."

He waved a hand in our general direction, already walking backward toward the door.

"You're welcome to join us." I smiled at him.

"Thanks, but no thanks. I may be gay, but I'm still a man and won't need more than half an hour to get ready. I've got better things to do with my time."

He was teasing us, a wicked grin falling over his face as he turned and ran for the door. Dot grabbed the first thing her fingers found on the vanity, and so did I, the lipstick and comb landing lamely in the spot Charlie had just dashed away from.

His laughter echoed in the hall as he disappeared down the stairs, and Dot and I couldn't help the laughter that bubbled forth in his wake.

By the afternoon, my hair and makeup were done. All I had left to do was put on the amazing dress Josh had given me, but my stomach was grumbling, and I decided it would be safer to have a snack without it on.

I left Dot to finish her own makeup—she had been drawing on and repeatedly wiping away something she called a "dramatic brow"—and headed downstairs to the kitchen.

Some of the bread Ethan had baked *from scratch* the other day was still left over, wrapped up in the pantry. I did a fist pump; it was just enough for two thick slices with butter and jam—also homemade by Ethan.

I was just putting the jam back in the fridge when Alec stormed into the kitchen. He never just walked anywhere—he stormed in, radiating hostility, or stalked, unseen, startling you when you finally spotted him.

His features immediately hardened upon seeing me. I was having that effect on him a lot. The nice gesture with the latte after I'd saved Ethan's life was the first and last time he'd shown me any kindness since the plane crash. As the weeks wore on, he avoided me more and more.

I knew he was helping Ethan and Josh gain better control of their abilities, sharing all he had learned over years of striving to master his own. They talked about it often—Alec's tips on meditation, his patience when they messed up, the laughs they shared when some mishap inevitably happened.

Those conversations made me feel a little left out. While Tyler was being incredibly attentive with my own training, Alec was never around during our group sessions. I'd briefly mentioned this to Tyler once, and he'd said something about Alec not wanting to intrude when we were all together as a Bond. Then he'd quickly changed the subject. I caught how his brow furrowed though, making me suspect there was more to the story.

"Is that the last of Ethan's bread?" the man in question asked me in the kitchen.

"Yeah . . ." I was about to offer some to him, then realized there wasn't enough, and if I went back upstairs without food, I was pretty sure Dot would sic Squiggles on me. Or a bear.

He huffed, mumbled something about me "taking his brothers *and* his bread," and stormed back out of the kitchen. I rolled my eyes at his retreating form. His behavior was beginning to border on juvenile.

As I trudged back up the two flights of stairs, plate of delicious bread in hand, I tried to put Alec out of my mind. He was just so frustrating!

"Earth to Eve!" Dot snapped me out of it before I could start obsessing again. She grabbed one of the slices of bread off the plate.

"Sorry. How did it go with the brows?" I bit into the other slice, reveling in the deliciousness of homemade bread *and* jam.

In answer she wiggled the brows in question and smiled around her mouthful of bread. They were perfectly symmetrical and, I had to admit, dramatic.

I gave her an appreciative look and a thumbs-up.

"What's got you all distracted?"

"Nothing." I rolled my eyes. "Just Alec being . . . Alec."

"What's he done now?" She chuckled, pushing various clothes and bits of makeup off the bed so she could sit down. Squiggles scampered into her lap and intently watched her eat.

"I just don't know what his problem is. He can't even stand to be in the same room as me. What have I ever done to him?" I joined her on the bed, leaning back but being careful not to ruin my hair. Dot had expertly put it up into a smooth low bun.

"Don't stress. He's just worried you're going to take away his family since you're their Vital. He'll get over it once he realizes how awesome you are."

I sighed and nodded. I had figured the same thing. Those boys were really close, and Alec didn't seem to have many other people in his life due to his ability. Now all of a sudden here I was—Bonded to all three of them and changing the dynamics.

"Wait! What?" I snapped my head up, nearly choking on my last bite of bread. She grinned at me wickedly.

How did she know we were Bonded? I hadn't told a soul, and I was certain the boys hadn't either.

"Oh, come on, Eve." She rolled her eyes. "You three might be fooling everyone else, but I can see how attached Ethan is to you, and I can see the secret looks you share with Josh when you think no one is paying attention. Ethan doesn't get close to anyone outside his family, and he's telling you about his parents and his cooking after a few weeks? And Josh used to lock himself in his room for days on end, his head buried in books, but now he's constantly hanging out with you, noticing things even Ethan, your *boyfriend*, doesn't? It's kind of obvious, really."

"Well . . . shit." How could we be failing so badly at keeping our secret? At least she didn't seem to know about Tyler. Maybe that connection wasn't as obvious because he was keeping the kind of distance between us that Josh and Ethan wouldn't or couldn't.

"Is it really so obvious?" I asked on a desperate whisper, fighting the urge to track my guys down to make sure they were OK. If Dot knew, maybe everyone knew, and what if they were in danger?

"Chill." Dot chuckled.

I'd started to get up, and she grabbed my arm and pulled me back down to the bed. It reminded me of the first time we'd met and she'd done the same thing as I went to chase after Alec. Those were simpler times . . .

"It's not that obvious. I only know because I know *them* and I'm smart and I notice stuff. Also Squiggles saw you guys training in the pool one night, and she told me all about it. She is such a gossip!" She was talking about Squiggles as if she were a person and not a ferret, and for a second I questioned her sanity, but when I looked down at the elongated ball of fur, the look on her little face was *guilty*.

"You used your ability and your ferret to spy on us? Dot!" I was no longer paranoid about our safety, but I couldn't believe she'd done that.

"Spy is such a negative word. I . . . inquired . . . surreptitiously."

I gave her a look that made it clear I wasn't buying it. "Who else knows?"

"Charlie."

"Dammit, Dot!"

"I'm sorry! But he's my Vital, not just my brother. Could you keep anything from someone in your Bond?"

She had a point; I couldn't imagine lying to any of them. My time in the storage closet with Ethan and Josh had proven that—although I was pretty sure that wasn't how Dot and Charlie got information out of each other.

"He already suspected anyway, and I haven't told anyone else. Squiggles might be a gossip, but I'm not. You're lucky she can only talk to me."

"Dot, this is serious. You guys can't tell anyone."

"I know." She put her serious face on. "Charlie went on about the dangers of the situation for, like, an hour after I told him. We don't want to put any of you in danger. We just want to help."

I nodded, uneasy that the circle of people who knew of our secret was widening, but at this point, there was no option but to trust them.

"Come on. Time to get dressed." Dot pulled me off the bed and handed me the dress Josh had given me.

I allowed myself a smile as I caressed the soft fabric. At least now I wouldn't have to be evasive with her about where I got it. Maybe sharing this new part of my life with Dot would actually make things easier.

EIGHTEEN

As I stood in front of the mirror, it became clear how observant Josh truly was. The dress fit me perfectly, the bottom of it floating just above the ground.

It clung in all the right places, accentuating my figure and only slightly fanning out from about mid-thigh. There was no beading whatsoever at the top; the soft fabric was cut high in the front and glided over my breasts delicately. You could say it was conservative, except that the back was completely nonexistent, consisting of nothing more than two slim strips of fabric draping over my shoulders.

It was more out there than I would have chosen for myself, but neither my cleavage nor my legs were on display, and as a result, I felt comfortable. Sexy even. I wanted to let my hair down to cover my back a little, but Dot insisted on showing off the stunning lines of the dress and made me leave it up.

We kept my makeup understated—I would have felt uncomfortable in anything remotely as heavy as her everyday look—and she lent me a pair of actual emerald earrings, which matched the dress perfectly. I was paranoid about losing them and tried to refuse, but she insisted.

"I just need to get dressed and I'll be right down," she shouted over her shoulder as she walked into the bathroom.

I grabbed a small black clutch—also borrowed from Dot—and made my way downstairs. I kept my hand on the banister and went carefully, still getting used to walking in something so long, but the dress was surprisingly forgiving and nowhere near as constricting as it looked.

As I neared the bottom, I looked up and stopped in my tracks.

All three of my guys, plus Alec and Charlie, were standing near the front door, waiting for us.

Ethan and Josh were chatting quietly with Alec, who had his back to me, and Charlie was standing off to the side with Tyler, who had his face in his phone, as always.

Josh was following my descent down the stairs, and it was meeting his gaze that stopped me.

He was wearing a black suit with a white shirt and, in a subtle nod to the beading on my dress, a green bow tie. His blond hair was slicked back, and he was smiling at me with so much warmth in his face I almost forgot the others were there.

Ethan was in black pants, a white jacket, and a blood-red tie and matching pocket square, hinting at his fire ability. He looked up and stopped speaking, his eyes rapidly flying up and down my body to take in my sophisticated new look.

Tyler was the next to look up, at first distractedly, obviously in the middle of something important on his phone, but then with his full attention on me. He was in navy blue, and his gunmetal gray tie was almost as close a match to the top part of my dress as Josh's bow tie was to the bottom. I wondered briefly if he'd had a part in choosing the dress too, but judging by how his hand slowly lowered his phone and his lips parted slightly in shock, he had no idea.

He took a small step toward me, his free hand lifting as if to reach for me, but he pulled up short and looked away, brow furrowing. Did he feel as drawn to me as I did to him in that moment? My grip on the banister tightened as images of the kisses I'd shared with Josh and then Ethan earlier in the day flashed through my mind. What would it feel like to kiss Tyler too?

No one was speaking. Josh put his left hand in his pocket and lifted his right, drawing my attention to him. With his finger pointed to the ceiling, he twisted it in a circle, silently asking me to show him the back.

I looked down, slightly embarrassed, but the dress was making me feel confident, so I slowly pivoted on the spot until I could place both hands on the banister, giving them only a partial view of my exposed back and looking over my shoulder.

Alec turned just as I did. Because his back was to the others, I was the only one who could see his face.

He was in all black, as usual, his suit clearly tailor-made and hugging his tall form perfectly, but he wore no tie. "I have to go to your stupid event, but I refuse to wear a tie," it seemed to say. His outfit was grudging and uncompromising, just like its wearer.

Where Ethan's eyes had flown all over my body, not knowing where to look first, Alec took his time.

With a deliberate intensity I could scarcely understand, Alec drew his eyes over my face, down the curve of my neck, and over my shoulder, sliding them down the naked expanse of my back all the way to my ass, where they lingered.

I felt exposed. I could almost physically feel his stare caressing my body.

I should have felt uncomfortable, outraged even, that he was looking at me so . . . so *lasciviously*. He was Ethan's older cousin, he was dangerous, he was frustrating, and he clearly wanted nothing to do with me.

Yet there he stood, practically licking my body with his eyes. And there I stood, *enjoying it*.

Not taking his eyes off my ass, he spoke. "If you guys are done drooling, we should probably get going."

His voice didn't betray even a hint of the perplexing intensity in his stare. He dragged his eyes back up, stopping just before making eye contact with me, then turned and walked to the front door. He opened it and leaned on the frame.

"We have to wait for Dot." Josh stepped forward and extended his hand.

I descended the last few steps and placed my palm gently in his, making sure my Light was in check.

"You look stunning." He spoke low, but his voice carried through the marble foyer clearly. "As I knew you would. Thank you for wearing it."

"You look smokin'!" Ethan's voice boomed in comparison to Josh's, and everyone chuckled.

"I don't know what you two were doing in there for four hours, but you do look lovely, Eve." There was a hint of amusement in Charlie's voice as he walked past, going to stand by the door with Alec.

Apparently the guys had all forgotten he was there too.

Josh's eyes widened, and he dropped my hand. We'd been standing at the foot of the stairs hand in hand for way longer than was appropriate if I was supposed to be Ethan's girlfriend.

Charlie laughed at Josh's abrupt shift, and knowing he knew our secret, I couldn't help laughing too. The wide-eyed, worried looks on all three of my guys' faces only made me laugh harder.

"Oh, relax. We know." Dot came down the stairs in a pair of the very high, very dangerous-looking heels I had refused to wear. They were sparkling black, matching her perfectly straight, shiny black hair. In contrast, her full-skirted, calf-length dress was white with some kind of subtle, textured pattern. It was only when you got up close that you could see the pattern consisted of little skulls.

"What do you mean, you know?" Tyler was all business as he stepped forward, half blocking me from Dot with his body. *From Dot.* I'm not sure if he even realized how protective the move was, but it surprised me, finally quieting the giggles I was struggling to control.

"Oh, come on, Gabe, did you really think you could keep the fact that Ethan and Josh had found their Vital from me and Charlie?" Dot breezed past him, patting him on the shoulder as she went, not fazed at all.

"Car's here," Alec announced, walking out without waiting for anyone else.

Tyler pressed his lips together, as if biting something back, and glared at Dot as we all made our way outside.

The "car" was a sleek stretch limo with a driver who was on a first-name basis with all of them. We piled inside, careful not to ruffle our clean-cut appearance.

Even with the privacy screen up, Tyler wasn't willing to talk about my Vital status out loud. He opted to say whatever he had to say via text, having a heated conversation with Dot and Charlie, their fingers flying across their screens as they threw each other loaded glances and I looked on, amused.

"Gabe! We know. We've got their backs, man," Charlie finally said aloud, giving Tyler a pointed look and ending the conversation.

We arrived in Manhattan about an hour later, our limo pulling up outside a very fancy-looking hotel. There was even a red carpet leading to the entrance and a horde of people behind velvet ropes.

I groaned. "Can't we go through the back or something?" I hadn't even wanted to go to this thing, and now I had to deal with . . . *are those paparazzi?*

Alec surprised me by being the one to answer. "I think that's the first time you and I have agreed on anything." He gave me a small crooked smile, rendering me completely speechless.

"I'm a representative of Melior Group, and Alec and Ethan are nephews of the managing director. We have to be seen," Tyler explained.

"I don't have to be seen by anyone," Josh piped up. "I could take her through the back."

"No," Tyler, Ethan, and Alec replied immediately, surprising me once again.

Dot and Charlie were falling over each other laughing. I didn't think it was that funny, but then Josh groaned, dragging a hand down his face. "That's not—"

"You said it. It's out there now!" Dot cut him off, reaching for the door. "Come on, Charles, let's be seen."

Shaking his head, Charlie followed her out.

As the door clicked shut behind them, the double entendre of Josh's words dawned on me. I should have been mortified, but for some reason, my first reaction was to snort-laugh.

As if they'd been waiting for my reaction, the others laughed too. Hesitant chuckles gave way to unrestrained laughter and ended in full-bellied, uncontrolled guffaws. It was the first time I'd heard Alec laugh. I liked the sound. He seemed to be in a much better mood than usual.

As we finally calmed down, Tyler wiped the tears from the corners of his eyes. "Let's get this over with."

He straightened his tie and stepped out of the car. Immediately, the flashing lights intensified, and people started shouting. I could have sworn that some of the voices sounded angry and aggressive, but I couldn't dwell on it, because Ethan had stepped out too and was offering me his hand.

I checked my Light, making sure it was locked down, before placing my hand in his and letting him help me out. His fingers flexed around mine, and he quickly placed my hand in the crook of his elbow; I must not have done a very good job of stopping the Light from transferring.

As Josh appeared on my other side, Tyler set a brisk pace down the length of the red carpet. I glanced behind us and was almost startled by how close Alec was to my back. They had pretty much boxed me in, shielding me from the worst of the crowd.

As the grand doors closed behind us, one malicious voice rose over all the others.

"Fucking elitist pigs!"

I turned around, stunned. Alec was still close behind me, and my sudden stop caused him to pull up short, his hand landing on my shoulder just as a bright camera flash blinded me through the window.

Alec nudged me, dropping his hand quickly, and Ethan pulled me away from the entrance.

"What was that about?" I asked no one in particular.

"That was the Human Empowerment Network getting louder and more obnoxious," Tyler explained. "They've been kicking up a fuss for decades, but in the last few years, there are more and more of them. They show up with picket signs at Variant events, disrupt businesses owned by Variants, send hate mail to prominent Variant persons. I've never seen a crowd this large though."

He looked a little worried, his eyes on the tinted windows and the throng outside. Now that I knew what I was looking for, I could see at least a hundred people behind the photographers, shouting and waving handwritten signs.

They looked *so* angry. "Are they dangerous?"

"Don't worry, Eve." Tyler turned his attention back to me, fixing me with a relaxed smile. "You're safe."

I returned his smile, but I was still worried. *That wasn't what I'd asked.*

Tyler quickly excused himself to go stand in a corner of the room, where he was soon in conversation with a man wearing a simple black suit and a serious, commanding expression. Taking a look around, I noticed several other men dressed identically to the one Tyler was speaking to. They were positioned at the edges of the room, keeping a watchful eye on everything, the bulges under their jackets hinting at the weapons they carried. It didn't take a genius to figure out that Tyler was demanding information from his Melior Group minions and ordering them around appropriately.

"Don't worry, beautiful. I'll protect you." Ethan gave me one of his brilliant, dimpled smiles.

"My hero," I teased, rolling my eyes, but I was secretly thankful for the comforting feel of his strong arm under my hand.

I didn't get the chance to dwell on my worries for long. Alec had disappeared into the crowd, but Ethan and Josh guided me through the impressive, lavish lobby and into the ballroom.

To call the room opulent would have been an understatement. The ballroom was softly lit by chandeliers, expensive linen draping the tables at the edges of the room, thousands of candles and fresh flowers covering every flat surface.

"Wow," I breathed, and they both smiled at me.

"It's got nothing on you in that dress," Josh whispered close to my ear, and I couldn't stop the wide smile from pulling at my mouth.

Women in stunning dresses and men in perfectly tailored suits milled about, only adding to the extravagance, and the next hour was a blur of new faces and names as the boys introduced me to people. I met some of their friends who didn't go to Bradford Hills, some of Tyler's work colleagues, and a few "acquaintances" they told me they had to be nice to for the sake of Ethan's uncle and his business dealings.

"At least we don't have to deal with Davis," Josh muttered.

"Ugh!" A frown crossed Ethan's perfect face. "Thank god. I can't stand that guy."

I looked between them. "Who?"

Josh leaned in to answer. "Davis Damari. One of Uncle Lucian's business acquaintances. Can't put my finger on why, but he gives me the creeps."

Of course. I remembered reading about Damari on the Internet. As another couple approached us, I made a mental note to avoid him. If Josh had a bad feeling about Damari, there was almost certainly a reason for it.

Later in the evening, Dot introduced me to her parents. Both she and Charlie clearly took after their father, getting their black hair and green eyes from him. Their mother was a natural blonde, but I could see her delicate features and petite form reflected in Dot.

"So this is the infamous Eve my daughter keeps telling me about." Her mother smiled warmly and shook my hand. "I hope you know you won't be able to get rid of her now. You've got a friend for life in Dot."

Instead of getting embarrassed by her mother's comments, Dot just smiled and nodded.

"I certainly hope so." I chuckled. I'd only known Dot for a few weeks, but she'd claimed me as her friend from day one, and I wasn't complaining.

We chatted for a little while, and then they excused themselves to go speak to some of their friends.

Dot grabbed us two glasses of champagne from a tray as it floated past on a waiter's hand. No one even tried to stop her. Several people our age, or even younger, were sipping on alcoholic drinks. I guess legal drinking age didn't apply when you had this much money and influence.

The bubbly drink was delicious. It was better than any wine or champagne I'd ever tried, and I shuddered to think how much it must have cost to supply an event this large with champagne that good.

We helped ourselves to canapés as we chatted. The bite-sized morsels of pure deliciousness rivaled even Ethan's skill with food, and I smiled affectionately as he tasted each one, his face getting all serious while his mouth dissected the nuance of flavor in each piece.

As we stood around, my friends pointed out other people from the constant stream of glamorous attendees filtering through the room. There were many celebrities, which explained the paparazzi, as well as several high-profile billionaires (with a *b*!) and politicians.

Dot and Ethan were doing most of the talking, and it didn't take long for it to turn into a game. One of them would point out a person in the crowd, and the other would have to state their name; their ability, if they had one;

and an interesting fact about them.

As they went back and forth, forgetting that the point was to get me up to speed on who was who, I stopped paying attention. I only tuned back in when Dot pointed toward the grand entrance at a couple who had just arrived.

"Those are Zara's parents," Ethan answered immediately, his competitive streak shining bright, "Con and Francine Adams. Neither of them has a Vital, but interestingly, they both have the same ability—enhanced speed. Mrs. Adams used to head up research and development for one of our uncle's tech companies. She was fired, but that's not widely known." He looked at Dot with a satisfied smile, way too proud of himself.

I was beginning to understand why Zara hadn't wanted to come. Her parents looked harsh and unpleasant even from across the room, smiling even less than Alec. They weren't speaking to anyone, although they stood out in the crowd; they were both tall, and Mrs. Adams had Zara's bright red hair. Mr. Adams was surveying the room intently as he sipped on his champagne.

Someone stepped in front of me, obstructing my view. The man was wearing a black pinstripe suit and looked as though he was in his mid-forties. He was tall and broad in the shoulders, with dark hair and intense eyes—like Alec's, but not as bright blue, and surrounded by more laugh lines. When he smiled politely, I saw a hint of Ethan's dimples as well.

"Uncle Lucian!" Ethan confirmed my suspicion, stepping forward and giving his uncle a warm hug, complete with the enthusiastic, affectionate thumps on the back that men seemed to always inflict on one another. The more love between the men, the louder and more violent the thumps.

Lucian Zacarias greeted Josh, Dot, and Charlie just as warmly, and then his full attention was on me.

"Uncle, this is Eve Blackburn. My girlfriend," Ethan introduced me, his arm wrapping around my middle as he smiled widely. He had been introducing me to people as his "girlfriend" all evening, but those interactions had been tinged with the same lightheartedness that was always present when we were pretending we were an item.

When he introduced me to his uncle, his chest puffed out, his arm around me flexed possessively, his smile was genuine and warm. Ethan clearly cared for his uncle and craved his approval. Knowing that approval, in that moment, rested on what he thought of me made me a little nervous.

"Is she?" was Lucian's perplexing response. His face was still relaxed, a small smile playing on his lips, but he was studying me intently, eyes flying over my features, from my eyes to my lips to my hair.

His examination was making me feel self-conscious, so I looked down at his very shiny black shoes as I extended my hand, hoping he didn't notice the little shake in it. "It's a pleasure to meet you, sir."

I managed to look up and make eye contact again as he gently took my hand and shook it.

"The pleasure is all mine, I assure you." He sounded sincere, and some of my nerves melted away.

He released my hand just as the guest of honor arrived. We all turned to see Senator Christine Anderson, resplendent in a stunning gold gown, make her entrance. People crowded around her immediately.

She's much shorter than I expected, I thought as she disappeared, buried in a sea of suits, dresses, and jewels. *Not as short as Dot, but nearly.*

"Duty calls, I'm afraid. I'll catch up with you kids later. Enjoy your evening, Eve." Lucian gave me an amused smile, and I frowned—what did he find so amusing about me?—but he'd already turned away, pushing through the crowd toward the senator.

Before long we were sitting down to a six-course meal while a string quartet played onstage at the back of the room. Tyler was seated at the senator's table with Lucian, while the rest of us were on one of the many tables filled with young Variants eager to mingle. I'd caught only glimpses of Alec since we'd arrived, but I couldn't spot where he was sitting. I wondered if he was at a table with Dana—I had seen him speaking to her—but pushed the thought aside.

The organizers had arranged the seating plan so that no one would be next to someone they already knew, facilitating the process of finding the members of your Bond, if you had one. Ethan blatantly switched the name cards around so that I was seated between him and Josh.

The food was exquisite, and even getting to know the other people at our table wasn't too bad. The champagne continued to flow freely, and it wasn't long before I was busting for the toilet. Halfway through dessert, I excused myself and headed toward the bathrooms.

". . . Eve Blackburn. You certainly haven't mentioned her in your updates."

The sound of my name pulled me up just short of the corridor leading to the bathrooms. I pulled back and tried to look casual while straining to hear what was being said.

"Eve? Why would I mention her? Our calls would be unnecessarily long and boring if I briefed you on every one of Ethan's playthings."

Lucian Zacarias was the one who had spoken my name, and it was Alec's voice answering, reducing my connection with Ethan to something cheap and dirty. I swallowed hard, my brow furrowing. I knew he was just trying to throw his uncle off, protecting our secret, but it still hurt to be referred to as one of Ethan's "playthings."

There was a long pause, and I leaned in to hear better.

"Alec, you and I both know she's much more."

"Not here," Alec replied immediately, lowering his voice.

"No, certainly not."

It sounded as if the conversation was over before it had really begun; they would be coming around that corner any second. In a panic, I decided to beat them to it.

I rushed into the corridor, nearly barreling into Alec.

"Oh, hello!" I said a little too loudly. "Sorry, got to go. I'm busting! Too much champagne."

Laughing nervously, I speed-walked to the ladies room, hoping they would attribute my odd behavior to too much alcohol.

I was equally impressed and disturbed by how calm they'd both looked when I'd appeared, even though they had *just* been talking about me. I guess it came with the territory when you, respectively, ran and worked for an agency like the Melior Group.

In the bathroom, once my bladder was empty, I looked at myself in the mirror and practiced my neutral, polite face. Had something in my expression given our secret away? I knew Lucian Zacarias wasn't a mind reader, so it couldn't have been that. The boys had told me he was a shield—similar to Dana, but where her ability blocked all others from working around her, Lucian's blocked them from affecting *him* specifically. I wasn't sure how he'd figured out his nephews weren't presenting the whole truth about me, but I had a feeling I would need a better poker face with Variant high society.

As I walked back to our table, I scratched absentmindedly at my forearm, gradually becoming aware that my ankles were a little itchy too.

Shit.

I cursed myself for getting distracted by all the glitz and glamour, the cloak and dagger, and the politics and gossip of the evening—for letting my concentration slip. I had to get my Light under control.

Because there was no way we could explain me transferring Light to any one of my guys when I wasn't even supposed to be a Vital.

NINETEEN

With dinner over, people moved out of their seats, mingling about the room, going to the bar. Ethan and Josh got stuck talking to a dignified, elderly gentleman with a cane. As she dragged me away, Dot explained that he used to be the dean of Bradford Hills Institute and took every opportunity to talk the ears off current students, regaling them with stories that began with "when I was dean" or "back in the sixties."

Dot introduced me to a couple of her other girlfriends, and I promptly forgot their names—I had met so many people that night, my brain was refusing to retain any more information. Not that it mattered—I got separated from Dot soon after.

While the frenzy of people introducing themselves had died down on campus, there were plenty of people at the gala who were enthusiastic to meet me. I got swept up in a dizzying game of musical chairs, except I was the chair and everyone wanted to sit on me. One of the guys was always nearby, keeping an eye on me, but I had to make pleasant conversation with all the new Variants without them as buffer.

". . . noticed the increased security?" a young guy with glasses and platinum-blond hair continued, drawing my attention away from the itch at my elbow. "There's a Melior Group guard in every corner."

"It's because of the Dimes out front," his tall, skinny friend replied, rolling his eyes. "Not that they're any kind of threat against a room full of Variants."

They both laughed, their noses in the air. Were their derisive comments and casual use of slurs supposed to impress me?

I frowned at them, but my attention was pulled away again. The itchiness on my arms had spread, and now it was around my neck and chest. I took a sip of my champagne and tried, surreptitiously, to scratch my collarbone. Suddenly I was wishing the dress had a plunging neckline.

"I have to go," I rudely declared, cutting the blond off midsentence. I turned on my heel and walked away, scratching with my free arm as I finished off my champagne and scanned the room.

Looking for Ethan was probably the best bet; he was the tallest. Alec was nearly as tall, but not quite. But Alec wasn't relevant—why was I even thinking about him?

Ethan's booming laugh came from somewhere to my right, and I headed in that direction, depositing my empty champagne flute on a side table. I found him surrounded by a crowd of bimbos and had to push my way through to get to him.

The girl with short black hair who had glared at me as I left campus that morning had her hand on his bicep, laughing with her head thrown back. I wanted to tear her arm out of its socket, but I settled for shoving her out of the way and taking her place by Ethan's side.

"What's up, buttercup?" He smiled wide at me, all but ignoring his growing harem.

"Yeah, hi," I said hurriedly as I again tried to scratch my chest through the fabric of my dress. I was in no mood to play our nickname game. "I need your help."

He nodded.

"Um, excuse me." One of the chicks behind me was not happy to see me monopolizing Ethan's attention. "Ethan was in the middle of telling us a story."

I completely ignored her and leaned up to whisper in Ethan's ear, very careful not make skin contact. "I need you to help me scratch an itch."

I gave him a pointed look. He wasn't always the best with hints. My big guy was all about direct communication.

I could almost see his mind going into the gutter as his lips curved into a naughty grin, but he got there in the end, realization wiping the cheeky look off his face. "Oh. Right." And then louder, for the benefit of his audience. "Yes, we have to go speak to that guy. About that thing."

He barreled through the small crowd of disappointed girls, all of them giving me dirty looks as we passed.

"Real smooth," I said dryly, rubbing my arm against the beading on the side of my dress, trying to find relief.

"Haha! You put me on the spot. It was the best I could do. There's Josh." He pointed to a back corner near the bar, where Josh was speaking to some people I didn't recognize.

As we approached, he looked up, saw me writhing in my own skin, deduced the situation immediately, and extracted himself from the conversation before we even got to him.

"Ethan, stay here with her. I'll find Gabe."

Ethan nodded and somehow managed to usher me to the end of the bar without actually touching me.

The dress that had felt like smooth butter gliding over my skin just a few hours ago was beginning to feel like coarse wool. Tearing it off my body in strips seemed like a perfectly reasonable idea.

Thankfully, Josh and Tyler returned quickly, managing to look casual while still moving through the crowd as fast as they dared.

Tyler positioned himself next to me, our backs to the wall at the end of the bar, and Josh and Ethan stood facing us, blocking most of my body from view. Ethan had ordered drinks while we waited, and he handed them out, leaning one elbow on the bar counter. To any casual observer, we would have looked as if we were simply chatting.

I didn't know what to do next, terrified of making a scene, so I kept my eyes trained ahead of me, on a spot in the middle distance between Josh and Ethan's heads. The itching was becoming unbearable.

"Eve." Tyler spoke without looking directly at me. "Take a few deep breaths. Remember your meditation practice. You're going to have to do this discreetly."

"Here? In front of everyone?" Couldn't we go find a private room somewhere?

"My agents are under strict instructions to keep the three of you in sight, but even if I call them off, there are eyes and ears everywhere. It would look too suspicious for us to slink off into a bathroom stall together. Now, focus."

I wanted to argue, but we were running out of time. Instead I did as Tyler said, focusing on the cool air as I breathed in through my nose and the warm air as I breathed out. The amount of Light coursing through my veins, demanding to be released, made the mindfulness technique frustratingly difficult.

"Good girl. Now, place your hand in mine and try to release it slowly."

My hand found his, and our fingers laced together instinctively. I tried to release the Light gradually, but once it knew it had an outlet, it just rushed out.

Tyler grunted, and Josh covered the sound up by coughing. Ethan clapped him on the back animatedly, drawing away any unwanted attention.

I took a deep breath, sighing in relief as the nervous energy drained out of me along with the excess Light, the itchiness disappearing completely, my breathing returning to normal. Next to me, Tyler was taking slow, measured breaths.

He squeezed my hand in reassurance, and I squeezed back, whispering a sincere "Thank you."

He nodded, still not looking directly at me, and released my hand. We'd managed to pull it off without anyone noticing; that was what I needed to focus on—not the fact that I'd let it get to that stage in the first place. I'd have plenty of time for crippling self-doubt later.

At the other end of the room, on the stage, someone was trying to get the crowd's attention. The music had stopped, and people were halting their conversations to face the speaker.

"Good evening, ladies and gentlemen." The young woman at the lectern wore a simple black gown, her hands clasped around a clipboard. "Welcome to the Variant Party Fundraising Gala. It is my great pleasure to introduce to you the reason we are all here, the most influential Variant voice in politics, Senator Christine Anderson."

Ethan and Josh turned around but stayed in front of Tyler and me, shielding us from anyone who happened to turn our way. Not that it mattered anymore—we were out of the woods, and everyone's eyes were trained on the senator, her gold dress shimmering in the candlelight as she made her way onstage.

As she began to speak, Tyler's hand reached up behind me, the very tips of his fingers landing at the base of my neck. I gasped, my lips parting and eyes widening just a fraction. After weeks of him building up very clear boundaries, only touching me on the hands during Light transfer, the sudden physical contact was unexpected.

He tilted his head in my direction but kept his eyes forward, speaking very softly. "You look stunning tonight. I'm sorry I didn't get a chance to tell you sooner."

It was a simple compliment, but it was undoing all the hard work I'd put in to even out my breathing.

He didn't say anything else, but his fingers trailed a feather-soft path down the length of my spine, stopping where the fabric started. Then he placed his palm, firmly and confidently, just above the curve of my ass. It felt as if his hand were on fire—as if Ethan were touching me with his fire hands—but the delicate, deliberate movements were so Tyler.

My "thank you" died in my throat, and I swallowed hard, trying not to look affected. What was he doing? What if someone saw? Did I want him to stop? *No. I definitely didn't.*

After only a few moments of exquisite torture—the spot where his palm connected with my bare skin tingling in a way that had nothing to do with the Light—he removed his hand and took a step away.

Everyone was clapping; Senator Anderson had said something impressive. I guess I would never know what it was.

I didn't hear a word of the rest of the speech, focusing instead on controlling my breathing. There was something deeply intimate about the way Tyler had touched me.

I craved more.

What did this mean for the strictly platonic tutor-student approach he'd been adamant about maintaining?

When the speech finished, the music kicked back up, and the people in the room were on the move again— dancing, getting back into conversations, making their way to the bar for more drinks. I excused myself and said I had to find the bathroom. I didn't actually need to go, but I did need a moment to myself.

As I stepped out of the ballroom, I glimpsed Alec turning down the corridor to the bathrooms. I stopped, unsure about my next move.

The smart thing would be to continue into the ladies' room and avoid him altogether. But I needed a distraction from the confusing feelings Tyler had stirred up by keeping me at arm's length for weeks and then touching me *like that*.

And I still *needed* to say my piece to Alec. His dogged avoidance of me had turned my simple wish into a mission I refused to fail; the more he resisted, the more determined I became that he would hear it. Plus, I was convinced he knew more about how and why my mother died. I wasn't sure how much of it was "classified," but I had to at least ask those questions. I had to try.

I had never seen Alec in a better mood. People were more forthcoming with information when in a good mood. *Right?* The release of excess Light had made me calmer, and I may have been a little emboldened by the three glasses of champagne I'd had. So I waited.

He came out of the bathroom a few minutes later, pausing halfway up the corridor when he spotted me blocking his way.

"My, what a determined look you have on your face, Eve." He narrowed his eyes, but there was some humor in his smirk. For once it wasn't all menace. "You wouldn't be trying to ruin this perfectly lovely evening, now, would you?"

"Look." I held one hand out, pleading. "Just give me five minutes. I *need* to get this off my chest. You don't even have to speak, just listen. And then I promise I will never bother you again."

"Highly doubt that," he muttered before stalking forward slowly. "You know I can easily overpower you. You're not actually blocking my way."

"Yes. I am aware of your scary pain ability." I waved my hands in his general direction. "Everyone keeps reminding me. But I don't think you would actually use it on me."

He just watched me, but he wasn't making a run for it, so I drove my case home in the most pathetic way I knew how.

"Pleeease." I drew out the word as only someone who was slightly drunk could.

He rolled his eyes, and I knew I had him. "Fine."

"Oh my god." Excitedly I shook my hands in front of me, shifting from one foot to the other.

But before I had a chance to start, a group of girls came laughing and stumbling down the corridor. They jostled past me but quieted when they saw Alec, skirting the walls to avoid contact with him. In his usual unyielding fashion, he stared them down, not moving an inch to get out of their way.

Once they were gone, he stepped past me and I deflated, thinking he had changed his mind. But then I heard a door open, and he declared in an impatient tone: "I don't have all night."

I spun around, stunned, and didn't waste any time, walking through the door into what I realized was the cloakroom. There was no one inside and it was very dim, the only light coming from the serving window in the wall to my left. It was just enough to see by.

He followed me in, closing the door behind him, and stood in the middle of the small room, arms crossed, feet wide, surrounded by coats and furs. I took a deep breath and gathered my thoughts, moving in front of the door to block his exit.

Facing him fully, I looked straight in his ice-blue eyes and said what I had been waiting to say for over a year.

"I don't think you understand how much it meant to me what you did. And I'm not just talking about pulling me out of the water and getting me medical attention. I don't know what happened to you to make you think that you don't deserve thanks, but you do."

He tightened his arms across his chest but averted his eyes, looking uncomfortable.

I kept going, determined to get it all out before he bolted. "You saved my life by doing your job, and maybe it was just part of your job, but you and your team still deserve my gratitude for doing that. So, thank you."

I paused, wanting to make sure I got the next bit right. "But what you did in the hospital after—*that's* what meant the world to me. *That's* what had me trying to track you down for a year."

He finally looked at me again, his brow creasing.

"You were there for me in the lowest moment of my entire existence. I felt more alone and adrift when I woke up in that hospital bed than I ever did floating by myself in the middle of the Pacific. I don't know what made you stay with me, or what made you comfort me when I realized that my . . ." *mother died.* I still couldn't bring myself to say it. "What you did for me in the hospital is what truly saved me. I may have been too destroyed by grief at the time, but after, I realized you had given me hope—a hint of the idea that I didn't have to be alone in the world. And for that I am truly grateful."

His arms slowly dropped to his sides as I spoke, an incomprehensible expression falling over his face, so intense that I almost withered beneath it. Almost.

"Alec Zacarias, *thank you.*" Finally, I had said it. *Finally*, he had heard it.

"I had no idea . . ." His voice was softer than I'd heard it since I first saw him in the square months ago. That smooth honey quality—the one I lived to hear—was back. "If it really meant that much to you, I accept your thanks. You're more welcome than you know."

With a sigh of relief, I leaned back against the door and closed my eyes; he had taken me seriously, and he'd accepted my thanks. I'd been so focused on delivering it, I hadn't realized how much I'd been dreading his response.

I tried to focus on how to phrase my next question—how to bring up the night of the crash. I hoped the moment we'd just had would soften him up enough to give me the answers I needed.

But I never got a chance to say anything else.

I heard him step forward, and when I opened my eyes, he was right in front of me, his eyes searching my face. I was reminded of how he'd looked at me on the stairs at the start of the evening, and a warm shiver ran down my spine.

His eyes flicked down to my lips, making his intention very clear.

I had no idea how I'd found myself in this situation, but apparently I wasn't interested in getting out of it, because I didn't say anything or move away. Instead, I tilted my face up, and my lips parted of their own volition.

"Put your hands behind your back. Don't touch," he whispered.

His tone wasn't forceful or demanding, but my body obeyed immediately. Some small part of my functioning brain briefly registered that this was a bad idea, considering his ability to deliver excruciating pain regardless of whether I was touching him or not, but I didn't care. If anything, the potential danger made it more exciting.

He placed his hands on either side of my head, against the door, and leaned in, kissing me with all the demanding force that had been missing from his voice a moment ago. I moaned into his mouth, surprising myself. He didn't press his body into mine. Nowhere did we touch except our lips.

He pulled away after only a few dizzying seconds.

And for the first time since I'd met him, it was I who ran from him.

My head spinning, I turned around, yanked the door open, and ran to the ladies' room. I shut myself into a stall and took several deep breaths.

What the hell was I doing? Why had I been so willing to do as he asked? So eager for him to kiss me?

This was wrong. I knew it was wrong. *But it had felt so right.*

I was on the verge of panic. I felt as though I'd betrayed not only the three amazing guys I was connected to but also myself.

Yes, Tyler was reluctant and cautious, doing everything in his power to keep things between us platonic, but he was still a part of my Bond. Ethan and Josh clearly wanted to be with me, but we were forced to take it slow. My relationship with them was ambiguous and restrained, but I was their Vital, and they were my Variants. They were *mine*.

Even just being attracted to Alec made me feel awful. I had three, *three*, guys that I knew without a shadow of a doubt were mine in one way or another, and I still wasn't satisfied. *What the hell was wrong with me?*

A few women came into the bathroom, chatting, and I did my best to calm myself, straightening my dress and taking another breath before flushing the unused toilet and stepping out. Smiling at them politely, I washed my hands, checked my reflection, and went back outside.

Alec was nowhere to be seen.

I made my way back to the ballroom and hunted down a waiter, snagging a champagne from his tray and downing it in three big gulps. Because adding more alcohol to the mix after doing something stupid was always a good idea, right?

With the formal proceedings of the evening over, the lights were dimmed and the music turned up. Everyone appeared to relax. Both the dance floor and the bar became more and more crowded as the night wore on. I spent the rest of the gala avoiding the guys as much as I could and dancing with Dot, distracting myself as best I could from my own poor choices. She threw me a couple of questioning glances but thankfully didn't prod me for an explanation.

By the end of the evening, my hair had completely come loose from the bun, and I shuddered to think what my makeup looked like. As all the beautiful people in their shiny eveningwear streamed out of the ballroom, I realized I was drunk.

At least I wasn't the only one. Dot was a giggly mess, and Tyler's eyes had a distinct glassiness to them, although he held his liquor much better than I did. Ethan and Josh had had a few drinks, but neither of them was messy. I suppose they couldn't afford to really lose control with the kinds of abilities they had. Charlie was the only one who hadn't had anything to drink. He'd glued himself to Dot and me, declaring that "someone has to take care of your drunk asses."

I hadn't seen Alec since the . . . incident in the cloakroom. I was hoping he had done his disappearing act and I wouldn't have to see him again for a few days.

"Man, Alec is such a jerk." The alcohol in my system had significantly thinned the filter between my brain and my mouth, and everyone laughed as our group spilled onto the street. All the paparazzi were gone, as was the angry crowd with the signs, but I did notice a few of Tyler's men hovering close by.

Dot slung an arm over my shoulders. "Did"—she hiccupped—"did you try to thank him again, and he ran away again?"

"No." I leaned into her, overbalancing, but Josh was on my other side and pulled us up straight. "I mean, yes. I mean, I made him listen to . . . and it was a really good thanks, you know? Like, I put a lot of effort into how I was . . . how I worded it. And then he listened. He *listened*, Dot!" She nodded sagely. "And I was so happy. And then that . . . that jerk face, douche canoe ruined it."

Everyone else laughed at my choice of words, but Dot sounded outraged. "No!"

"Yep." I was still with it enough to stop myself from elaborating on *how* exactly he'd ruined it, which was a miracle, because it would have made the next five minutes even more awkward than they were.

We decided not to wait for the limo to be pulled around, walking up the street to where it was parked

"I've texted the driver. He's on his way," Tyler told us as he pulled open the door.

The limo's interior light came on, and the mystery of Alec's whereabouts was solved.

He was seated in the middle of the back seat, legs stretched out in front of him, his shirt unbuttoned and half off his shoulders. Straddling his lap was Dana, one of the straps of her dress hanging down. Their hands were all over each other.

For a beat everyone just stared, and then Dot shrieked, "EEW!" and covered her eyes with her hands.

Alec's head whipped up, and his eyes went straight to mine. They widened in pure horror just as Tyler slammed the door shut.

Bile rose in the back of my throat, and tears burned my eyes. I turned, shoving past Ethan and Josh, and managed to make it to some trashcans by an alleyway before I doubled over and vomited.

Dot was at my side in an instant, my messiness sobering her up. She expertly pulled back my hair while shouting at the boys, "Stay back, this is strictly a girlfriend job!"

I was so grateful to Dot in that moment. It was bad enough that I was vomiting Dom Perignon all over a dirty alley, getting it on the beautiful green beading at the bottom of my dress. I really didn't need my guys seeing this shit up close.

When my stomach was empty, Dot handed me a napkin, and someone produced a bottle of water. For once I wished I could blush, if only so they could all see how embarrassed I was without me having to speak.

"I'm so sorry," I said, my voice low and hoarse—just like my feelings. "That was so gross." I wasn't sure if I meant what we'd all witnessed in the limo or my vomiting. And I wasn't sure if the vomiting was due to the alcohol or the fact that Alec had kissed me and then promptly forgot about it, running straight to that . . . woman.

"It's OK, Eve," Tyler said as I avoided eye contact with everyone. "Let's get you home. Alec and Dana took a cab." He opened the door of the limo once again, but I cringed away.

"Nope!" I said a little too loudly. "I am not getting in that car. Nyet. Nein. Non. No way."

"She's got a point," Dot, my hero for the night, piped in. "I don't want to catch any diseases. We'll walk. It's only four blocks."

Charlie said he'd walk with us, and Ethan wrapped a comforting arm around my shoulders. "I'll go too. My cocoa puff could probably use a walk to sober up."

"Thanks, muffin." I tried to inject the usual playfulness into my voice, but it just came out flat. I was confused, tired, guilty, and still a little drunk; I smelled like vomit; my feet hurt; and I had been humiliated twice over. I was so ready for bed.

TWENTY

The next morning I woke up in an unfamiliar room, the light streaming through the window sending a searing jolt of pain through my skull. I really had to stop making this "waking up in strange beds" thing a habit.

Wherever I was looked like a high-end hotel room. The walls were a muted gray, the half-drawn curtains a rich teal color. I rolled away from the light to face the wardrobe, leaving plenty of room on either side of me on the king-sized bed.

At least this time there was no one in bed with me. I lifted the covers to check the situation anyway; I had on my underwear and a very large white T-shirt. A vague memory of comforting arms steadying me as I stumbled into a bathroom, said T-shirt in hand, drifted back to me.

Once one thing wormed its way into my fragile mind, so did the rest.

Like a disaster comedy played in reverse, I remembered the walk to Ethan's uncle's apartment, where we'd planned to stay, Ethan draping his jacket over my shoulders as I started to cry. He had asked me quietly what was wrong, and I'd snuggled into his side and refused to answer. He hadn't prodded me, instead just holding me close as we walked.

Before that had been the vomiting. As I remembered the rank smell of the trashcans and everyone's eyes on me, I groaned and lifted the soft sheet over my head.

Before that had been Alec and *her* in the limo.

Before that had been champagne and dancing.

And before that had been Alec. In the cloakroom. Kissing me.

As that particular memory assaulted me, I threw the covers off and sat bolt upright in bed.

Alec had kissed me!

I'd let him. I enjoyed it. I wanted more. *What the fuck was wrong with me?* My chest tightened, all the awful feelings from the previous night returning and riding another wave of nausea.

I was an awful, selfish, treacherous *harlot*.

And Alec was a man-whore. Who kisses a girl and then does *that* in the back of a car with another girl on the same night? Dirty car sex is dirty car sex—I don't care how fancy the car happens to be.

I couldn't think about any of this clearly; the pounding in my head wouldn't stop. And I was too guilty and angry and hurt. And just so damn confused.

I groaned and dropped my throbbing head into my hands.

The door opened, softly scraping the carpet under it.

"Look who's up!" Ethan was way too loud. "Hey, drunky."

The mirth in his voice made my stomach knot. Did he know what Alec and I had done in the cloakroom? Is that why he was enjoying seeing me in pain?

I snapped my eyes open to look at him, ignoring the stabbing in my head, but he didn't seem upset. He was smiling at me with his trademark dimpled smile, nothing but affection in his eyes.

It made me feel like shit.

"I feel like shit." Apparently the filter between my brain and my mouth was still flimsy.

"Yeah, I bet. Hopefully this will help." He lifted his arms, a paper bag in one hand and a tray with coffee in the other. He made his way over me, awkwardly stepping over something on the ground.

I leaned over the edge of the bed to see what it was; a pillow and blankets were lying there in a heap. "You slept on the floor?"

"Yeah." He sat down on the edge of the mattress and handed me the coffees. He was dressed in shorts and a tank top, a light sheen of sweat covering his forehead. He had been for a run. "Dot and Charlie might know our secret, but my uncle stayed here last night too. It would have been weird if we didn't sleep in the same room. But I wasn't going to take advantage of a crying drunk girl. Even if we are in a *pretend* relationship."

He fixed me with a rare serious look. The intensity of it surprised me.

"Pretend . . ." I let the word hang in the air. We may have been forced to pretend for the outside world, but we both knew there was something between us.

And I'd just ruined it by kissing his cousin!

To cover the guilty look on my face, I took a sip of the coffee. The latte was good, and a genuine smile of pleasure crossed my features. "Yum."

He beamed at me, opening the paper bag. The smell of bacon made me realize how desperate my empty stomach was for food. "Bacon and egg bagels. Dig in, my drunk little bagel."

I snatched the bagel out of his hand and ripped into it with a satisfied moan.

Ethan chuckled as he bit into his own. "God, I love feeding you."

I looked away, suddenly self-conscious. "Thanks?"

He ignored my awkwardness and finished his breakfast in three big bites. "I'm going to grab a shower. We're leaving in half an hour, so you might want to think about getting dressed." He casually leaned forward to wipe a stray crumb off my cheek, planted a kiss on the top of my head, and headed toward the door.

"Ethan."

At the sound of my voice, he stopped.

I took a deep breath. I still hadn't had a chance to unravel my thoughts and feelings, but there was no way I could keep the events of last night from any of them.

"About last night. I'm sorry . . ." I didn't know how to finish the sentence. I'm sorry I kissed your cousin? I'm sorry I'm such a mess? I'm sorry I'm a failure at being a Vital and a pretend, but not-really-pretend, girlfriend?

"Don't worry about it, bagel baby. It happens to the best of us. And you didn't do anything *that* embarrassing." He gave me a reassuring smile and walked out of the room.

I sighed and took another bite of the delicious bagel I didn't deserve. It was probably better to tell them all at once anyway.

Lucian had left for the airport by the time I dragged my aching body out of bed, so I didn't get to see him again. I had no memory of getting back to the apartment the night before, and I had almost no chance to check it out before we made our exit, so even as we pulled out of the parking garage, I still had no idea what it really looked like.

The seven of us were driven back to Bradford Hills in the same limo, and I made sure to sit as far away as I could from the end where we'd caught Alec mid-coitus the previous night. He was back to his brooding self, the glimpse of a relaxed nature from last night gone.

And he was back to ignoring me.

The drive back was subdued. I wasn't the only one with a hangover. Dot, Josh, and Tyler were all quiet and looked about as fresh as I felt. Tyler spent most of the ride tapping away at his phone, and Josh produced a book.

I chanced a look at Alec, not sure what I was even looking for. Some kind of acknowledgment of what we'd done? Some semblance of caring about the people we'd hurt?

He was staring out the window, sitting in the same spot where he'd had his encounter with Dana last night. The images of his hands all over her assaulted my mind again, and I couldn't help the disgusted expression that came over my face.

He looked up just in time to see it, our gazes locking across the car, and his eyes narrowed. Was he pissed off at *me*?

Then, before I could be sure I'd seen it, a hurt look crossed his features, and he turned away, back to the city zipping past.

Did he think I was disgusted by him? Was I? I guess I was, but only because of what he'd done in the limo. Did he think I was disgusted by our kiss? Wasn't I? If I was being honest with myself, I wasn't. I'd enjoyed it and wanted more.

Maybe I was just disgusted with myself. I had no idea about anything anymore. I'd hoped to use the ride back to clear my head, think about how I would broach the subject with the guys, but it was just getting more confusing.

I huffed and rolled my eyes at myself, and they landed on Josh. He was still holding his book in front of him, but his piercing green eyes were on me, his head tilted slightly to the side. He slowly turned his head to glance at Alec before turning back to me, fractionally lifting one eyebrow in a silent question.

Of course Josh had noticed. But this was not the time to get into it, all of us crammed into the limo and the driver within earshot. I shook my head almost imperceptibly. After another curious glance at Alec, Josh returned his attention to his book.

After dropping Dot and Charlie off at their house, we arrived back at the Zacarias mansion, and everyone piled out of the limo. Tyler said he would drive me back to my res hall and started to head toward their garage.

I stayed where I was, my overnight bag at my feet, my jeans and loose-fitting sweater feeling constrictive on my body, the bright sunshine bringing on another headache. "Actually, can I come inside?"

Alec was already at the front door, and as I spoke, he paused and turned around.

"I need to speak to the three of you. It can't wait."

"Of course." Tyler smiled gently at me and picked up my bag as he passed. "We can talk in my office."

"Everything OK, babe?" Ethan asked as he followed suit.

"Let's just get inside." There was a waver in my voice. My heart was hammering, and that pressure on my chest was back.

Josh looked between me and Alec and followed Ethan inside.

"You wouldn't," Alec whispered as I passed him.

I paused and looked him dead in the eye, injecting as much steel into my voice as I could. "Watch me."

I didn't wait for his reaction before I walked inside, but I heard him following close behind.

We deposited all our bags at the foot of the stairs and filed into Tyler's office. Tyler leaned on the front of his desk, his hands by his sides. Ethan took a seat next to him on top of the desk, and Josh stood on Tyler's other side, his arms crossed loosely over his chest.

I walked to the couch in the corner and sat down, wringing my hands in my lap. But that put me below their eye level, and having the three of them looking down on me made me even more uncomfortable, so I stood up. But then I thought, *Maybe they should be looking down on me. Maybe that's what I deserve.* So I sat back down. But then I realized that I had no idea how to start, so I stood up again and started pacing the room.

My three guys were all watching me with varying degrees of caution.

"Eve?" Tyler was the first to speak. "You're starting to worry me. What's the matter?"

"I'm sorry. I'm just trying to figure out how to tell you this."

"OK, now I'm getting worried too." Ethan had one of his rare intense looks on his face. "Nothing good ever came out of 'we need to talk.'"

Josh remained silent, his focus drifting between me and something by the door.

I turned slightly to see what he was looking at. Alec had followed us in. Almost. He was leaning against the doorframe, eyes narrowed and following my every movement. Why did he always stand in doorways? Was it his agency training, always putting himself in a spot where he could observe the whole room? Or was it just him, always needing to be in a place that allowed him to escape any situation easily? He was never fully in or out.

If his stare was meant to intimidate me, it failed; all it did was steel my resolve.

"Shut the door. This is a private conversation." I didn't tell him which side of the door I wanted him on—that was up to him—but he was either in this room, this conversation, or not. I refused to let him be half in and half out.

He stepped inside and kicked the door closed with one booted foot, then gestured for me to continue, eyebrows raised, a hint of a smirk on his face. He didn't think I would do it. *Arrogant asshat.*

I turned back to my guys, doing my best to ignore him.

"OK." I took a deep breath and focused on Tyler's crossed feet resting on the dark carpet. "I know we haven't exactly discussed the nature of our relationship yet—like, romantically—but I know enough about Variant Bonds to know where it's likely heading, and . . ." I blew out a big breath, choking on my words.

"What are you saying, Eve?" There was a slight tremor in Ethan's voice. Like a coward, I still couldn't look at him. "You don't want it to go there? Have we done something to make you feel uncomfortable? God, I knew I shouldn't have slept in the same room as you last night. Idiot! I swear to god, nothing happened." He was getting more and more upset as he spoke; it was breaking my heart.

I still couldn't look at him, but I shook my head, hot tears welling up in my eyes.

"It's not that, Kid." Josh—correct, as usual—spoke at last. He too was working at keeping his voice even. "Tell us what you have to tell us, Eve."

"It's not that I don't want you. This. It's that I've done something, and . . . it's that I don't think you'll want *me* . . ." My words cut out on a sob, and the room fell into silence.

"Eve. Whatever it is, just tell us, and we'll figure it out together." Tyler was the only one who still sounded calm. He had no idea what I was about to say, but his faith that we could work through it was unwavering. Another sob escaped me, and I had to fish a tissue out of my pocket to disgustingly blow my nose before speaking again.

None of them were moving to comfort me, and for that, at least, I was grateful. I wouldn't have been able to do this with them showing me any more of the kindness I no longer deserved.

I knew I had to look them in the eyes when I finally told them, so I lifted my head. Three sets of gorgeous, concerned, loving eyes looked back at me, and I nearly broke down again.

"Alec kissed me."

Three sets of eyes, now shocked and confused, flew to the man standing behind me.

"Last night at the party, he . . . that is to say, *we* kissed. I let it happen. I even . . ." *liked it*. I couldn't get the last two words out.

"What the fuck, man?" I'd never heard so much emotion in Tyler's voice. He pushed off his desk, fists clenched at his sides.

"Why would you do that to us?" Ethan had deflated in his spot on the desk, his shoulders sagging. He sounded so hurt. *Betrayed*.

Josh just glared.

All three of them were directing their hurt and anger at Alec, dismissing my part in it. They assumed I was the victim, the one that needed protecting.

I didn't deserve them.

"Stop!" I yelled, throwing my hands out. My breathing was coming in pants, and tears streamed down my face, unstoppable now that they had started. "We *both* did this. I deserve just as much of your anger as he does."

I wasn't defending him, but I deserved to have them yell at *me*, turn away from *me*, want nothing more to do with *me*. Coming between them was the last thing I wanted. They had been family since birth, and I'd been around for only a few months. Now they were at each other's throats.

Before I could say anything else, Josh held his arm out at his side and, with a motion that was now familiar to me from our training, flung it out. A book from the shelf behind him came hurtling out into the room. At first I thought he was aiming for me, but his gaze was still focused over my shoulder, and the book sailed right past me.

I spun around just in time to see it heading for Alec's face, but instead of whacking him in the nose as it should have, it came within an inch of his head, bounced away, and thudded to the ground. Alec didn't even flinch. He just stood there, arms crossed.

"What the fu—" Josh's confused utterance was interrupted by Ethan jumping into motion. He lifted his hand, fingers curled, and a ball of blue fire appeared. This was not the harmless magic trick he flicked around to impress his friends. This was angry fire, dangerous and lethal.

151

In the space of a heartbeat, he was hurling it at his older cousin, but just as the book had deflected away from him, the fire curved over Alec's shoulder and sputtered out into nothing, leaving him completely unharmed.

Ethan looked down at his hand as if it were a faulty gadget, his brow creasing.

Alec finally spoke, sounding resigned. "You can't hurt me."

"Holy shit," Tyler and Josh said in tandem from behind me.

My brain had begun to piece things together since the book had bounced off Alec harmlessly, just as all those items had bounced off me in Josh's room when we'd first met. Just as Ethan's fire had curved benignly over my skin in the pool.

I was reeling, but when Alec spoke those words, confirming what my brain was slow to articulate, a deep-seated rage from somewhere deep inside my chest began to fill me. It coiled around my insides, memories fueling it as it grew.

When I first saw him at Bradford Hills, naively hugging him, everyone around us had doubled over in pain, yet I felt nothing. When his hand landed on my bare shoulder as we entered the gala, it had felt pleasant, not painful. When he kissed me, he didn't tell me not to touch him to protect me from his ability; it was to protect himself. To keep me from finding out . . .

The room had gone completely still. The rage was spreading out to my limbs, filling me with explosive energy. This had nothing to do with the Light. This was purely emotional, and it was about to rain down on Alec's head.

"Wait, does this mean that she's *that* . . ." Tyler was struggling to finish a sentence. "I can't believe I didn't see it before . . ."

"Yeah. Look—" Alec began.

But I didn't give him the chance to try to explain himself or justify everything he had done—I cut across him.

"You knew!" The shriek that came out of me was like no other sound I'd ever heard myself make. It was guttural and feral, and it had the desired effect—he stopped talking and regarded me warily. "All this time you knew. From that night in the hospital, you knew we were connected, and you said nothing!"

"Hospital? What hospital?" Tyler asked, confused.

I hadn't told anyone Alec had stayed with me after the crash, but I couldn't stop to explain now. I barreled on.

"You knew I was completely alone in the world. I'd just lost my mother, and I thought I would never belong anywhere again for the rest of my life. And you knew I belonged with you, and you said nothing! Instead you actively avoided me, blocking my attempts to find you. For a whole fucking year! Why were you so determined to make me miserable? *What did I do to you?*"

The last question came out on a sob, but I didn't let him answer, a new wave of rage edging me on.

"The last few months, you haven't been staying away from me because you though I didn't need to thank you. You weren't avoiding touching me because of your pain ability. Your ability could never hurt me. You've been avoiding me like the bubonic fucking plague because you didn't want me to realize I'm your Vital. Because if I touched you, I would have known."

I was breathing hard, the words pouring out of me as fast as they were coming into my mind, frenzied and laced with hurt.

"And last night. It was perfectly natural for us to be attracted to each other. It was natural for me to want it, to like it. But I didn't know that. I thought I was an awful person for having those feelings for you, for going outside my Bond. I felt like the scum of the earth for what we did, when in reality, there was a reason it felt right. And *you knew*. You let me feel like shit about it when you knew, this whole time, that I was your Vital. You . . . you *fucking asshole!*"

I screamed the last part into his face, my fists tightly clenched, completely giving in to the rage.

He stared back at me with intense, stormy eyes, his own breathing getting faster, his shoulders tense under his shirt. He kept his mouth shut, but an all too familiar tension entered his stance.

I knew this look. I'd seen it over and over every time he'd bolted out of a room to avoid me. He was about to run. I was done letting him.

"NO!" I declared with more finality in my voice than I knew I was capable of. "You don't get to leave. You don't get to run away from me anymore. You don't get to avoid this clusterfuck you've created. I'm the one that's going to leave now, and you're going to stay here and sort this shit out with the three people who have been your closest family since day one. You owe them that much."

I took a deep breath and walked to the door. With one hand on the handle, I said in a much softer voice, "Don't any of you dare follow me."

And then I walked out, purposely slamming the door. As I started climbing the stairs, Tyler's office erupted into a frenzy of voices.

TWENTY-ONE

I pushed open the door to Josh's room, stepped inside quickly, and slammed it closed, leaning against it as I tried to catch my breath.

It felt good to slam doors.

I didn't know why I'd chosen Josh's room. Maybe because it was the first door at the top of the stairs. Maybe because this was where we'd been spending the most time together. Or maybe because this was where it had all started—with a kiss and a room full of floating books.

But that wasn't where it had started. Like so many other things, that was a lie. It had really started in the hospital with Alec.

Another wave of anger surged through me, and with a grunt of frustration, I pushed off the door and started pacing the room. I was feeling so many things, I had no idea where to start unpacking them. Anger seemed like the easiest one to latch on to. It was safe and defensive.

He had avoided me for a year. A whole fucking year!

And it wasn't just me he'd hurt. He had deceived the three people closest to him, and in a way, that was even worse. I had only known them for a few short months, but one thing was painfully obvious—they would do anything for one another. Did I factor into that equation now? Logically, considering our Bond, I must, but . . .

I paused to lean against the bookshelf by the fireplace, feeling drained. I had gone from crippling guilt and self-loathing over what I thought was a betrayal to searing rage over Alec's *actual* betrayal in under a minute. It was a lot to handle.

My thoughts started down a dark and twisted path—what exactly did this mean about my Bond, about our connection? If Alec could resist it so easily, that meant Tyler could too. Maybe Josh and Ethan weren't entirely thrilled about it either and were just being nice. After all, they were adamant about keeping it a secret. Maybe they resented my barging into their family, throwing their perfect lives into chaos. Maybe *none* of them really wanted me around.

Hot tears started pouring down my face again as doubt and worry overtook the anger. There was no denying I was already attached to them. Much of that had to do with our supernatural connection, yes, but I would be lying if I said I didn't like it. The Light coursing through me had tethered us together, and for the first time since my mother died, I didn't feel as if I was alone in the world.

But maybe that was an illusion too. If Alec could lie about it, hide it, and keep seeing other women, maybe the strength of our Bond was all in my head. Was I so afraid of being alone that I'd deluded myself into thinking our connection was stronger than it actually was?

I started sobbing, sinking to my knees, a horrible gaping wound opening in my chest. It was that same crushing feeling I'd had in the hospital. And it terrified me.

But something inside wasn't allowing me to fall apart this time. A surge of anger rose up again, and I growled in frustration and lashed out with both arms, knocking the contents of the shelf to the ground. Josh's books, CDs and other random items fell in a mess that closely resembled my current emotions: chaotic and haphazard.

The force of my own blow sent me swinging sideways, and I landed on my hands and knees in among the stuff I'd knocked to the ground. I was breathing hard, my vision blurry from the tears still flowing freely through my rage. I tried to take some deep, calming breaths for the millionth time that morning, wiping the tears from my eyes.

As the mess under me came into focus, my attention snagged on something right under my face. A photo album had fallen open, its pages half-covered by another book. I frowned and leaned my head closer, pushing the book aside.

Someone familiar looked out at me from one of the images—the chocolate hair, the dull blue eyes, the black dress with the yellow and red poppies. The very dress that was hanging in my closet; the one I couldn't bring myself to wear.

I was looking at a photo of my mother.

She was standing outside—smiling, bare feet in the lush grass—in the center of four other young women, their arms around one another's waists. She must have been around my age when this was taken, maybe a little older.

I pulled the photo out of its sleeve and brought it up to my face, absorbing every detail of my mother's youthful image as I sat back on my heels.

I missed her so much. Being reminded of her now, when I was already in such an emotional state, was like a punch in the guts. But my brain, always looking out for me with its logical thinking, reminded me how weird this was.

Why did Josh have a photo of my mother in his room? How did they know her? Or, more accurately, used to know her? Because I would have noticed if they'd been around growing up. That's not something I would have forgotten. *Right?*

Great, now I was questioning my own memory and possibly my sanity.

No. They had definitely not been around when I was growing up. No one had been around when I was growing up. My mother had made damn sure of that.

A sickening thought hit me, sending a chill of fear down my spine.

What if they were what my mother had been running from this whole time?

Obviously my mother had known something serious enough to keep us moving my entire childhood. How much of it had had to do with the four men downstairs—four powerful, dangerous men?

She looked happy in that photo. People don't leave happy lives for no good reason.

I stood up on shaky legs. There had to be an explanation.

I folded the photo and stuffed it into my back pocket, moving toward the door, determined to get some

155

answers. I would march down there, ask why they had a photo of my mother, and make them tell me everything. I was done with being kept in the dark by the people closest to me.

But halfway to the door, I stopped. Uncertainty wrapped around my throat like a vice, making it hard to move or breathe. If they had known who I really was this whole time, that meant they *all* had been lying to me.

My mother's face flashed through my mind. The sensation of her hand slipping out of mine as she disappeared into the darkness . . .

It had been a confusing, overwhelming day, but one thing I could be sure of without a shadow of a doubt? My mother had always had my best interests at heart. She may have kept a lot of secrets, but I never questioned her love for me. As much as I'd struggled with our nomadic lifestyle, I'd always trusted her.

I wasn't about to stop now.

If my mother had given up her life to keep me away from this place, possibly away from these people, then I needed to get out of here. Now.

The balcony was my best bet. I crossed the room, listening for approaching footsteps, and peered through the curtains by the balcony door. The coast was clear.

As quickly and quietly as possible, I made my way outside and over to the stairs leading into the grounds, then rushed down them. The stairs ended at the side of the house. Just around the corner was the winding driveway, the window to Tyler's office, and past that, the grand front doors.

I had to get across the open grass area to reach the cover of the trees lining the driveway. Anyone who happened to look out on that side of the house would see me. I hoped like hell they were all still in the office, too preoccupied with Alec's revelations to look out the window.

I took a deep breath and crossed the grass at a steady pace. If anyone in the house were to look out, it would seem suspicious if I was running like a maniac or sneaking like a cat burglar.

Those twenty seconds were the longest of my life. I didn't dare turn around. The adrenaline pumping through my body was demanding that I break into a run, but I managed to remain in control until I reached the trees.

Then I did break into a run. No one could see me now, and I needed to put as much distance as possible between me and the mansion.

I ran as fast as I could to the front gates, emerging onto the wide, tree-lined street. Once again I had to keep a normal pace. I couldn't chance drawing attention, but I didn't know how long it would be before they noticed I was missing. I settled on a light jog and hoped that if I kept a steady pace, I would just look as if I were out for a run.

Nothing to see here people; just burning some calories.

I made it to campus without incident, but my heart was hammering in my chest. I'd spent the entire time glancing back, expecting to see Tyler's black SUV pulling up behind me, the tinted windows hiding the men inside poised to grab me.

I had been so focused on getting out of the Zacarias mansion and away from the guys that I'd neglected to make any real plan. As I reached the front door of the room I shared with the Reds, I paused, realizing my potentially fatal mistake.

This is the first place they would come looking for me. What other place did I have to go? *Stupid!* How could I have been so predictable? What if they'd already noticed my absence and were on their way? What if they'd called

Zara and Beth, and my roomies unknowingly delayed my escape. Or, and here my stomach sank, what if Zara and Beth were in on it? Did they know too?

I was crippled with indecision, my hand poised over the door handle. *Go in or run for it again? Quick! Decide! Your life could depend on it!*

The memory of my mother's voice repeatedly telling me to "never trust anyone" had me pulling my hand back.

I looked up and down the corridor, no idea how much time I had. Doing my best to stop my hands from shaking, I quietly made my way back down the hallway, then ran down the stairs and out the door.

Pausing, I glanced around the corner. I only had a partial view of the lane winding up toward the front gate, but no black SUVs were coming toward me, so I hurried down the stairs.

The sun had retreated behind clouds and taken some of the heat with it. If I wasn't so flushed from the running and the panic, I would have been cold. I took the walking tracks through campus to a side entrance—the one closest to the center of town and the train station.

Memories of all the times my mom and I had packed up and disappeared kept flashing through my mind. Tears pricked my eyes as panic threatened to take over, but I knew I had to get out of town. *Fast.* It was what she would have done.

The adrenaline was not letting up, making it difficult for me to calm my breathing and formulate some kind of plan. As I walked through town toward the train station, I kept looking over my shoulder, fractured thoughts and half-baked strategies flying through my mind too fast to grasp.

Only one paranoid thought managed to stick—I needed to change my appearance. The image of my mother hacking mercilessly at her hair before dying it some awful yellow-blonde burst across my brain.

I gathered my hair into a ponytail, my eyes scanning the busy street in front of me. Without thinking about it too much, I snagged a hoodie that was slung over the back of a chair in front of a café, its owner probably inside paying their bill. Awkwardly juggling the two pieces of clothing as I hastened my steps, I pulled my loose sweater over my head and dropped it in the trash, pulling on the gray hoodie in its place. It was at least two sizes too big and smelled faintly of smoke.

I thought about getting a taxi into the city, but my mother and I had never taken taxis when we moved. Taxis had cameras and route logs and drivers who made small talk and remembered your face. The anonymity of public transport was a much better way to go.

I made it to the station only to find that the next train to New York wasn't due for another ten minutes. I had no choice. I had to wait. I picked a spot near the exit and pulled my hood low over my face.

Those ten minutes felt like hours. I was jumpy and constantly looking around, expecting them to burst onto the platform at any moment. I probably looked like a paranoid drug addict.

When the train finally pulled into the station, I all but sprinted into it, launched myself into a seat in the far back, then bounced my leg maniacally until the doors closed and we moved off. At last, I took a deep breath and leaned back.

I was so on edge that when my phone rang in my back pocket, it startled me so badly that I shot out of my seat, gaining me some strange looks, including one from a guy in a bright pink leotard and Santa hat. Even the weirdos on the train thought I was a weirdo.

The incoming call was from Tyler. I waited for it to ring out, then unlocked the screen. I had sixteen text messages and twelve missed calls. How had I not heard it going off before? I had been so focused on my surroundings, so worried I was about to get caught, that I'd forgotten it was even in my pocket.

The messages were from Ethan and Josh—text after text asking where I was and if I was OK, and saying that they wanted to talk. The last few said how worried they were.

There was one from Zara too:

You OK? Your boyfriend and his 3 pseudo brothers showed up here looking for you. What did you do? LOL

And then another one straight after.

What did THEY do? I don't care what kind of scary abilities they have, I will fuck them up.

Shit. They knew I was on the run.

It took an hour to get into the city, and I watched the doors with trepidation at every stop, waiting for one of them to step inside and haul me off. Past getting out of Bradford Hills, I had no plan whatsoever. Knowing they knew I was gone, I would have to find which train was leaving first and just go there. I would literally be getting on a train going anywhere, just like that stupid Journey song.

Which made me think of how Josh loved his music and how frantic Ethan's last text was and how Tyler had tried to call me *twelve* times. A little lump in my throat formed as I thought of them.

But I had to be strong. Something was not right here. This was exactly the kind of thing my mom had been warning me about my whole life. They had lured me in—these feelings were not real. It was the opposite of emotional blackmail. It was emotional entrapment. Was that a thing? I'd have to look it up in one of the psych books. If it wasn't a thing, I was making it thing. I gave myself props for coining a term while under duress and on the run.

It was a good distraction for about three seconds.

I turned my phone off and focused on not getting upset—my life depended on it. As soon as the train pulled into Grand Central, I would beeline for the ticket counter.

I was beginning to get hot and uncomfortable in the hoodie, so I took it off as the train pulled into the station. It was probably good to change my appearance again anyway. I was now in just jeans and a black tank top, the hoodie tied around my waist.

Stepping off the train and into the crowd, I looked around. The ticket counters would probably be in the main section, and following the crowd off the platform was my best bet for avoiding attention. Everyone was heading toward a staircase leading up, so I joined the flow of bodies and tried to keep pace.

At the bottom of the stairs, one hand on the railing, I looked up to see where I was going, and my eyes locked with a pair of ice-blue ones.

My stomach dropped.

Alec was standing with his legs apart and his arms crossed over his black-clad chest. He was staring right at me, eyes narrowed, but he was too far away for me to see his expression. Was it angry? Annoyed? Murderous?

None of the others were anywhere in sight, and I wasn't sure if that was a good or bad thing. Regardless, I was caught.

I had tried my best to do as my mother would have wanted, and I had failed.

TWENTY-TWO

Alec's intense stare pinned me to the spot. Panic rose inside me again, my palms getting sweaty and my breathing becoming erratic. He couldn't hurt me with his ability, but there was more than one way to inflict pain, and I had a feeling Alec was intimately acquainted with all of them.

I looked over my shoulder, searching for another way out. There was nothing other than the edge of the platform and the dark tunnel into which the train was disappearing. I briefly considered taking my chances with the tunnel, but I knew the limits of the human body and I had a better chance of surviving an altercation with Alec than I did with a moving train, so I turned back to him.

He flopped his arms by his sides and rolled his eyes. "Can we just talk?" His voice echoed off the concrete walls.

The platform had cleared. It was just me and him. He started down the stairs, and I immediately backed away, matching him step for step.

Halfway down, he slowed to a stop, his brow creasing as he watched me retreat. "Are you . . . *scared*? Evelyn, you know I can't hurt you with my ability. I would never do that, even if I could."

"How do you know my name?" I gritted out between clenched teeth. His use of my real name had confirmed my suspicions. I no longer believed he would give me the truth about anything, but I couldn't help asking the question.

"That's what we need to talk about. I handled this so badly . . . but when the boys went to look for you, you were gone, and . . ." He looked uncertain, his eyebrows drawn together in confusion, but he wasn't making any sense.

I had nothing left to lose. I reached into my back pocket and pulled out the photo from Josh's room.

"I know." I thrust the photo toward him, my voice shaky but loud in the cavernous space. "What . . . ? Why . . . ?" I wasn't sure what I was accusing him of. My mother had never actually told me why she kept us moving, but it *had* to have something to do with Bradford Hills. It was too much of a coincidence.

He finished his descent and stood before me, reaching for the photo. As soon as he grabbed it, I stepped back, putting more distance between us.

With a soft curse, he pulled his phone out of his pocket, tapped at it, then put it away again.

"I don't know what's going on in that head of yours, but you don't know the full story." He held the photo out so I could see it. "What do you think this proves? Obviously it has you spooked enough to run away." I didn't move to retrieve the photo—it felt like a trap.

Why did he sound as if he only now realized I was making a run for it? Wasn't that the whole reason he was here? To kidnap me back to Bradford Hills and . . . and . . .

It was becoming more difficult to think clearly. I let out a grunt of frustration, turning away from him and tugging at my hair.

When I spun back around, realizing I'd given my back to the enemy, he was in the exact same spot he was in before, arms crossed over his broad chest, watching me with those intense blue eyes.

When he'd raked his gaze over my body the night of the gala, it had felt exciting and sensual. Now his gaze just made my skin crawl.

"What are we waiting for?" I wanted him to make a move. Maybe if we got off this platform, I could try to get away from him. "Why aren't you gagging me and throwing me into the back of a van?"

He threw his head back and laughed, a hollow, humorless sound. "You are so far off the mark it's hilarious. And we're waiting for reinforcements."

So that's what he'd done on his phone. *Shit!* I might have been able to slip away from Alec in the crowd, but there was no way I could get away from an entire team of trained special agents. My shoulders sagged in defeat, and I wrapped my arms around myself, my nails digging into my sides.

Itchiness crept up my arms—maybe some of my fidgety energy had nothing to do with adrenaline.

Just as I'd realized my control of my Light had slipped in my mad escape attempt, the "reinforcements" came barreling down the stairs.

It was not a Melior Group Special Forces team, as I had imagined. It was Tyler, Josh, and Ethan, all wearing matching looks of concern. Taking two steps at a time, Ethan made it onto the platform first and headed straight for me.

A cold jolt of fear went straight through my body, and I backed away, arms raised. He stopped in his tracks, the concern on his face replaced with shock.

"Eve?" He looked so broken and vulnerable. His big shoulders sagged, one muscled arm stretched out to me, his fire tattoo peeking out from his T-shirt sleeve. It made me remember how good it felt to be held in those big arms, and I longed to step into them.

I scratched at my arms frantically, trying somehow to discern how much of my nervous energy could be attributed to the excess Light coursing through me and how much was due to my instincts.

Tyler and Josh took a more measured approach. Josh stepped up next to Ethan and placed a hand on his shoulder, watching me warily. Tyler, as usual, took charge of the situation. He moved forward slowly, his arms held up in front of him, as if he were approaching a wild animal. I suppose I might have looked like one, my wide eyes darting between them, still looking for an escape route, while my fingernails raked frenziedly at various parts of my body. The itching was getting worse.

Alec, true to form, was hanging back and leaning on the railing of the staircase, letting everyone else clean up the mess he'd made. Typical. He was always ready to run away. How dare he? I was supposed to be the one running away today. *Dick!*

As Tyler regarded me cautiously, Alec filled them in, his voice dripping mocking amusement. "She was actually trying to run away. She thinks we're here to kidnap her and stuff her into a—what was it? The back of a van? She thinks we've been keeping something from her."

"You *have* been keeping something from her. From all of us!" Ethan responded, eyes still locked on me.

I was getting confused. Why were they fighting among one another? It seemed like Ethan was even on my side. But he had been keeping things from me too. Hadn't he?

Unaffected by his younger cousin's reprimand, Alec handed the photo to Josh. The amusement had left his now hard voice. "She found a photo of Joyce with our moms. She's convinced herself that it's proof of something shady and underhanded."

Josh examined the photo before passing it to Ethan, the looks on their faces indecipherable.

Tyler, on the other hand, didn't take his eyes off me, but neither did he try to get closer. "Eve, I can understand how you might have come to some frightening conclusions, considering all that has happened over the last few weeks. But your Light is out of control, and it could get dangerous if you don't get a handle on it."

"Stay away from me!" I was scared he would try to grab me under the pretense of helping me expel the Light. At the same time, I was craving his contact just as much, the Light inside me begging to be released. My hands were now under my tank top, scratching at my belly; I was seriously considering ripping the thin fabric off.

"I'm not going to do anything until you say so. Neither are the others. Eve. Look at me."

I couldn't help myself; I looked into his face. He wore a neutral expression, but his gray eyes were overflowing with intensity. It was a little mesmerizing.

"Good. Now, just try to take some deep breaths." He took an exaggerated inhale, and I mimicked him, both of us exhaling together. Some of my mindfulness practice came back to me, and I focused on calming my breathing.

"Good." He was speaking in the gentle, encouraging voice he always used in our tutoring sessions. "That's good. OK, now, I know you're scared, so I'm not going to argue with you, but I am going to ask you to consider the facts." He was appealing to my natural affinity for learning, for logic, for the scientific process. "What are the facts, Eve? What is the observable truth? What is the simplest explanation? Ockham's Razor, Eve."

I continued to take deep breaths as I thought about it. What did I *know*?

I knew that that the unbridled power coursing through me was verging on unbearable. The Light was *demanding* to be released.

I knew I was connected to the four men standing on the platform with me. I'd learned enough about the nature of Variant Bonds and physiology to be able to recognize this for what it was.

I knew Tyler always encouraged me to ask questions and learn more, just as he was doing now. He had never been evasive with me.

I knew Josh was so observant and in tune with my body language and facial expressions that he sometimes knew what I was thinking before I did.

I knew Ethan had done all he could to make it clear I was his to all the other Variants at Bradford Hills, without actually giving away that we were connected.

I knew Alec was a total douche bag—but that wasn't really relevant at the moment.

I knew they were somehow connected to my mother—to my past before I had any memories of it. The photo I'd found, and that Alec had used my real name, was evidence of that.

I knew my mother had kept us running my whole life to keep us from something dangerous. But . . .

I never knew what that was exactly. I had no concrete evidence to suggest it had anything to do with my guys. My guys.

My Bond. The men that I was connected to by a tether stronger than anything on this physical plane.

I knew they couldn't harm me if they wanted to. I had stuck my hand in Ethan's fire enough times to know it was harmless to me. Josh's telekinesis had items bouncing off me as if I was surrounded by a force field, and Alec . . . Alec had hurt me badly but not with his ability.

As I puzzled these things out, I was trying, and failing, to get a handle on my Light, but at least my fear was subsiding. When I'd found that photo, I'd assumed the worst, my body going into fight or flight mode and choosing what I'd spent my entire childhood perfecting—flight. My suspicion wasn't completely gone, but perhaps my fear was unwarranted.

Someone was calling my name.

"Eve!" Alec's almost panicked voice crashed into my consciousness. "Evie!"

I snapped out of my thoughts and looked at him. He had used my childhood nickname, the name my mother used to call me. No one had called me that since before the plane crash.

But why was he so desperate to get my attention?

I looked over to the other three. They were all staring intently at my face. Ethan's eyes, almost of their own accord, flicked down to my body, then back up to my eyes.

The infuriating itch had spread to every part of my body, and I was frantically running my nails over my skin, from my arms to my shoulders to my belly to my legs. My bare legs . . . *Why wasn't I wearing pants?*

I looked down at myself. Without even being conscious of it, I had stripped down to my underwear, the Light raging through me so uncomfortable that I had removed the constrictive fabric. But that wasn't the most shocking thing.

I was glowing!

Every inch of my body had a soft white luminescence to it. Like a nightlight or a Christmas tree or *fucking plutonium*!

Any semblance of trying to get my Light under control went out the window, and I went into full panic mode.

"What the fuck?" I screeched, my eyes darting around the platform in a futile search for a solution.

"Eve, please let me help you." Tyler sounded desperate. He was breathing hard, his messy hair hanging loose over one side of his forehead, his eyes wide.

"Yes! Make it go away!"

He was in front of me before I even finished speaking, holding his hands out in the familiar way. I squeezed my eyes shut and grabbed him around the wrists, needing something to hold on to.

As soon as we made skin contact, the Light poured out of me. But unlike our usual transfer sessions, it didn't channel through my hands and into Tyler at the points where we touched. It burst out of me everywhere, as if every part of my body, every pore on my skin, was releasing Light as freely as any river.

It was a force of nature.

"Whoa! You feel that?" Ethan's voice came from somewhere behind Tyler, followed by the heavy thud of booted feet running up the concrete steps.

"Yeah . . ." Josh sounded unsure of his answer, which was odd for him.

"Back up, you two," Tyler said from right in front of me.

I was reveling in the relief from the frenetic energy, but I forced myself to open my eyes. Tyler was looked as shocked as he had been the first time we'd done this. He released my arms and placed one hand on my neck. The other he laid flat against the exposed skin on my back.

I could feel the Light transferring through the spots where Tyler was touching me. It was the first time I'd transferred Light through someplace other than my hands (unless you counted the times I'd done it while kissing), and if the fractured conversation I'd just heard was anything to go by, apparently I didn't even need the contact.

But that was impossible according to every bit of research I'd read about how Light transfer works. What the hell was wrong with me? Not only was I releasing Light without skin contact, I was *glowing*.

I reached out, still needing something to keep me grounded, and grabbed a fistful of Tyler's shirt in each hand. With my hands in front of my face, I was beyond relieved to see I was no longer glowing.

"Incredible." Tyler's breath washed over my face. He was holding me close. On a train platform. In one of the busiest terminals in the world. And I was in my underwear!

I looked around nervously. By some miracle, the platform was completely empty of people. Josh came up behind me and draped my discarded, stolen hoodie over my shoulders.

I pressed myself a little closer to Tyler and said, with as much conviction as I could, "Thank you."

He smiled in relief and gently kissed my forehead in place of a "you're welcome." Then he released me into Josh's arms.

Josh spun me around and pulled me into a bone-crushing hug, and I wrapped my arms around his waist and held on tight. I'd only been on the run for a few hours, but it felt so good to be back with them. How could I have ever felt unsafe with my guys?

With one final squeeze that expelled all the air from my lungs, Josh released me. He held the hoodie out so I could pull my arms into the sleeves, then darted his eyes around the platform before kissing me quickly on the lips.

I turned away from Josh to find Ethan still standing in the same spot, arms by his sides, his expression guarded. He'd looked so hurt and rejected when I'd moved away from him in fear, and it was killing me to see the uncertainty still in his eyes.

I rushed over and launched myself at him, wrapping my arms around his shoulders and my legs around his middle. He caught me effortlessly, holding me much more gently than Josh had, considering his size. I buried my head in his neck, and he mirrored me, breathing deeply. For a few moments, he rocked us side to side, then lifted his head.

Unlike Josh, he didn't bother to look around the platform before kissing me. He just mashed his lips to mine, pouring all his feelings into that fierce kiss. I returned it just as enthusiastically, knowing he needed the reassurance and comfort.

Just as our tongues met, the kiss deepening naturally, Tyler cleared his throat.

"We're running out of time. Alec is keeping the crowd off the platform, but there isn't much he can do about the train that's about to roll in."

As if to prove his point, the distinctive *whirr* and *clack* of an approaching train issued from the darkness of the tunnel. I pushed against Ethan's shoulders, and after a moment of reluctance, he released me. Once again, Josh was there with clothing, handing me my jeans and shoes.

I hurried to pull on the pants, and Josh zipped the hoodie up over my bra just as the train rolled into the platform. Tyler shoved my discarded tank top into his pocket and led our group to the stairs, Ethan with his fingers laced through mine and Josh close behind us.

I had tried and failed to do as my mother would have—to run. I hadn't even made it out of the state, but I had succeeded at something I'd never even seen her attempt.

I'd found someone to trust.

Ethan Paul, Joshua Mason, Tyler Gabriel, and even Alec Zacarias had—through the Light-fueled, supernaturally intense connection we shared—become a part of my life.

Despite the many complicated issues we had to work through, they were as much a part of me as I was of them. If I couldn't trust my Bond, whom could I trust?

TWENTY-THREE

Like a sentinel, Alec stood at the top of the stairs with his feet planted wide, his arms crossed. He had pulled the sleeves of his black top up to his elbows, and the tight muscles in his forearms were on full display. There was obvious tension in his shoulders.

In front of him, a disgruntled mob of New Yorkers was getting increasingly impatient. Many were muttering and throwing pissed-off sideways glances in Alec's direction. He wasn't using his ability—no one was doubled over in pain—so I had no idea how he'd managed to keep them all at bay, but none of them were even trying to get past.

Tyler reached the top first and whispered something to Alec before pushing through the crowd. Alec nodded once, and just as Ethan and I made it to the top, he dropped his arms by his sides. His hand landed right next to mine, and he wrapped his warm, calloused fingers around it.

When our hands connected, he didn't even turn his head to look at me. He just held on and took the lead, dragging me along behind him. The intense Light transfer I'd just experienced on the platform was keeping the energy satiated for the time being—I felt only a light tingling where we touched, a tiny amount of Light passing from me to him.

Still, the Light was pulling us toward each other like magnets. I'd just had an intense couple of days, punctuated by the most overwhelming Light overflow I'd experienced to date—I mean, I fucking glowed!—and the Light was demanding closeness to my Bond. I'd melted into my guys on the platform like chocolate left in the sun. Each of them, in their unique way, made me feel as if that was exactly where I belonged—in their arms.

Now the Light was pushing me to bring Alec into that fold too. At least, I was pretty sure I was experiencing an instinctual reaction to our connection. Why else would my traitor hand grab on to Alec's and hold on? I was still pretty pissed off at him, and the logical side of my mind was reminding me he was still a massive jerk.

But there we were, hand in hand, pushing through the grumbling crowd. With Ethan still holding firmly on to my other hand, we made a short human chain as we rushed toward the exit.

Tyler's black SUV came to a screeching halt in front of us just as we stepped out onto the street. Josh took shotgun, and I found myself squished into the middle between Alec and Ethan.

As soon as all the doors were shut, Tyler took off as if we were in a high-speed car chase. Ethan draped an arm over my shoulders and held me so tight I wasn't sure I even needed my seatbelt, but Alec made me put it on anyway, holding the clip out at my side silently while dialing a number on his phone.

He made several efficient calls, speaking softly but firmly and saying things like "contain the situation," "pacify the civilians," and "acquire CCTV footage." I tried to listen in, but the motion of the car and the softness of Ethan's embrace lulled me. Other than Alec's few phone calls, the car was silent.

A few minutes after his last call, Alec's hand landed on my thigh. I opened my eyes to look at him, but he had his face angled toward the window.

He took a deep breath and squeezed my leg firmly, his quiet voice carrying in the silent car. "Don't ever do that again, Evelyn."

Next to me, Ethan tensed. All of my sleepiness vanished, replaced by more of the rage that had coursed through me in Tyler's study. I sat up straight, shrugging Ethan's arm off.

"Do what?" I demanded through gritted teeth. "Lie? Evade? Keep secrets?"

He snapped his head around, and for the first time since I'd come face to face with him on the platform, I looked properly into his vibrant ice-blue eyes. Pain flickered across his face before that familiar emotionless mask fell into place.

Before he had a chance to reply, Tyler raised his voice from the front seat. "Enough! We will discuss this like adults, or we won't discuss it at all."

Alec clamped his mouth shut and glowered at me, but I wasn't willing to back down. I clenched my hands into fists.

"The hell we won't! I deserve answers!" Of course, taking my anger at Alec out on Tyler wasn't fair, but the frustration was growing fast.

"Yes, you do," Tyler answered in a level voice, fixing me with a look in the rearview mirror. "But can we try to do it without everyone getting so worked up? Or do you want to go another round of glow-in-the-dark, Eve?"

That sobered me up, and I checked in with my body. Sure enough, my elevated emotions had caused my control to slip again, and I was surprised to find Light coursing through me so soon after I'd expelled it into Tyler. I took a few deep breaths and slammed the mental door shut, preventing it from getting out of hand.

I had forgotten Alec's hand still resting on my leg, so I was startled when he suddenly whipped it away, pressing himself to the car door and as far away from me as possible. I looked over, giving him my best "what the fuck" look. His reaction was confusing, considering how drawn the other three were to my Light, their abilities pushing them to instinctively seek me out.

I didn't have time to dwell on it though. I had so many other questions.

"OK, fine," I said in a much calmer voice. "I'll behave. But can someone please start speaking?"

Surprisingly, it was Josh who answered, leaving Tyler to concentrate on the road. At the speed he was maintaining, we would be back in Bradford Hills in record time.

"The photo you found, of your mother—the other women in it are our mothers. They were all friends a long time ago. For the first five years of your life, Eve, we were like family. Our parents were close, and we spent almost every day together. Then one day, your mother and you just disappeared. I was only seven at the time, so I don't remember much, but I remember everyone being really upset about it. They refused to answer any of our questions. I think they knew more than they told us, but I guess now we'll never know."

He leaned his head on the window, seemingly lost in thought.

Ethan spoke next, but instead of picking up where Josh had left off, he knocked the breath out of me with his soft, insecure voice. "Why did you run?"

I took his big hand in both of mine and squeezed tightly, swallowing around the lump in my throat. I hated that I'd hurt him.

Before I had a chance to explain myself, Tyler did it for me. "She thought her mother had kept them on the run all those years because she was trying to keep her from us."

Shocked, I looked to the front of the car, but he didn't meet my eyes.

"She saw the photo of her mother, she was already in a highly emotional state, she panicked. She was reeling from Alec's revelation, and she wondered what else we could be keeping from her. She spent her childhood running from place to place, her mother keeping them constantly on the move to evade an unexplained threat. It came naturally to her to run."

The car descended into silence, all of us staring at him in astonishment.

"How . . . ?" I was positive I hadn't told Tyler anything about my mother keeping us on the run, not even how much I'd moved around as a child. I *knew* I hadn't told any of them how panicked I was when I found the photo, although I guess that would be a logical conclusion.

He cleared his throat and glanced at me in the mirror. "I've been noticing some . . . enhancements to my ability with all the extra Light I've been receiving. With a particularly large dose, like just now, not only can I tell when someone is being untruthful, I can tell what they are being untruthful about and what the basic truth behind the situation is."

After another beat of silence, the car erupted into animated noise, all of us shouting over one another. Ethan was asking if that would apply to all their abilities and what enhancements he might experience, Josh was outraged that Tyler had not told us all about this sooner, Alec was demanding to know what else Tyler "knew to be the truth," and I wanted to know more about how it worked. How much Light was needed to kick this into action? How long did it last?

Unfortunately, none of us got any answers. We pulled into the parking garage at the mansion, and Tyler shut off the engine. Turning in his seat, he silenced us all with a stern look.

"Look, this is pretty new, and I'm still figuring it out, but in the interest of transparency"—he looked pointedly at Alec—"I wanted to share it with you all. Going forward, I think we need to be more honest with one another, and I'm trying to lead by example. Now, I don't know about any of you, but it's nearly dinner time, and I haven't eaten since breakfast. I'm still hungover, and I need food."

Without waiting for a response, he got out of the car and went inside.

As soon as Tyler mentioned food, my stomach grumbled. I too hadn't eaten since my breakfast bagel. *Was that only this morning?* Not to mention that intense, unbridled Light transference had left me feeling depleted in every way, just as it had on the night Ethan nearly died.

An unspoken agreement settled between us, to put the heavy conversation on hold until our bellies were full. We sat in companionable silence around the big kitchen island, wolfing down leftovers.

Ethan situated himself next to me and ate one-handed, his other hand resting on my knee. He'd refused to leave my side since the train station. I hated seeing the larger-than-life, boisterous show-off acting so insecure. I hadn't seen a hint of the dimples since that morning.

Alec was the first to finish eating. Sitting at the head of the bench, he was resting his chin on his clasped hands and watching me intently.

Done with being intimidated by him, I returned his gaze. All our interactions over the last few months whirred through my brain, every conversation, every look falling under a new light. Knowing he was part of my Bond had made certain things click into place—his tenderness at the hospital and his willingness to help keep an eye on me once we found out I was connected to Josh and Ethan—but it raised more questions than it answered.

"Why did your ability hurt Tyler?" It was just one of a million questions that had been running through my head when I'd opened my mouth to speak.

At his confused look, I elaborated. "When I first saw you at Bradford Hills, remember? I ran up and hugged you, and everyone freaked out because they thought you would hurt me." I chuckled, knowing now how impossible that was, and the others laughed with me. Even Alec dropped his hands to the bench and smirked. "You got all worked up and lost control of your ability, and everyone got a headache. If Tyler is in my Bond, why was he affected?"

Tyler hummed thoughtfully around his last bite of stir-fry. "We weren't connected yet."

I gave him a questioning look. "I was under the impression that Bonds were a preordained kind of deal. You can't choose who you connect with—you just hope to find the people the Light has fused you to already."

"Well, yes. The connection is a force of nature we have little control over, but it still needs to be formed, strengthened, developed. When you first saw Alec in the square, our connection hadn't formed yet. We hadn't touched, you hadn't transferred Light to me. It was an inevitability now that we were in such close proximity, but it still wasn't an actuality at that point."

I nodded. The Light inside me had still needed to get to know him.

"Oh shit!" Josh laughed out loud from the end of the bench. "Finally, the field is leveled."

"Yes!" Tyler and Ethan exclaimed at the same time, turning to high-five him over my head.

"What am I missing here?" I grinned, totally lost but overjoyed at the reappearance of Ethan's dimples.

"Every year, at Thanksgiving, we play a game of football," Ethan explained, returning his possessive hand to my knee, "and every year Alec cheats by using his ability. Now he can't do it anymore!" He bounced a little in his seat as he finished.

Alec leaned back, his arms crossed loosely over his chest. He was staring daggers at the other three, but there was amusement in his face too. "I do no such thing. You know my ability leaks out when I get excited. It's a total accident."

A chorus of skeptical remarks and teasing was thrown his way.

"This is why I didn't tell any of you I was part of your stupid Bond! You're just going to use it against me!" He said it jokingly, but it had a sobering effect, and everyone fell quiet again.

"Wait a minute." Something wasn't making sense to me. Actually, a lot wasn't making sense to me; this just happened to pop into my mind first. "I was in the hospital. They did tests. How come they didn't pick up that I had Variant DNA?"

Everyone turned to Alec.

"Uh, yeah. I took care of that."

"Elaborate, please!"

"I had the tests intercepted and the results of the Variant screening falsified." No hint of remorse. Not even a scrap of sheepishness on his face.

Overlooking the disturbing fact that this had been easy for him to do, I asked the obvious question. "Why?"

It was a heavy, loaded "why," encompassing more than just the falsified records. It was the question I had been struggling with since the moment I realized we were connected and he had been lying for over a year.

He sighed and stood up, leaning on the counter. The posture put his head just under one of the pendant lights hanging over the island, and it cast his face into shadow.

"Look, the reasons why I did what I did are complicated, but I want you to know one thing, Evie. Your safety was always the primary concern. I suspected, from the moment I wrapped my arms around your frozen, soaking body, that you were mine. When I got a good look at your face, when I couldn't find it in me to leave your hospital bedside, I knew who you really were. I took the necessary measures to ensure that your status as a Variant—a Vital, no less—would remain secret. To keep you from this world, to keep you safe. I know you feel betrayed, and—"

I shot out of my seat. "You have no idea how I feel. How dare you presume to know what I'm thinking or feeling when you've kept me at arm's length for this long? You have no clue who I am as a person."

"I know you better than you might think!" The declaration was heavy with bitterness, and he'd raised his voice to match mine. "What I'm trying to say is, I stayed away from you for a year and I thwarted your attempts to find me, but I didn't abandon you. I kept tabs, I watched your grades, I vetted your foster parents, I had agents tail you when necessary. The only reason I didn't realize you had ended up back here was because the agents were only instructed to alert me of anything dangerous or suspicious. I would have stepped in without a second thought had you needed me."

A part of me was outraged and disturbed to know I'd been practically stalked for the past year, but a much bigger part of me latched on to his last statement: that he would have been there had I needed him. Hot tears welled up in my eyes.

"I needed you." It came out sounding weak and vulnerable. I was so sick of crying. I swatted away the tears on my cheeks in frustration.

I heard him walk over to me, but I couldn't look at him. All our conversations were ending in shouting or tears or both, and I just couldn't do it anymore. After a moment, he walked away, muttering about needing a shower.

As soon as things had become difficult, once again, Alec had run.

I dropped my hands and sighed in defeat. The others all stood from their seats, but it was Tyler who pulled me into a hug. I pressed my cheek against his chest and wrapped my arms around his middle. It was unnerving how comforting his touch was, especially considering he'd kept a careful boundary between us when it came to showing affection.

I felt better, safer, and more alive with one of them near me. I positively hummed when one of them touched me. No wonder I'd descended more and more into paranoid hysteria the farther I ran away from them; I needed them as much as they needed me.

He held me for a long time, and I listened to the boys cleaning up in the kitchen, putting containers back in the fridge, doing the dishes.

After a while, he nudged my chin up until I met his gaze. His gray eyes held warmth and tenderness, but they were tired and bloodshot. Another pang of guilt shot through me for putting them through this.

"I want you to feel safe with us," he stated firmly as his hand massaged the back of my neck, "and not just because your Light-driven instincts tell you that you belong with us. I want you to feel safe on every level, including the highly logical, questioning one you're so good at. I know that Alec's lies have tested your trust, but please believe me when I say we had no idea about any of this. So—"

"Wait," I cut him off, "I need to know. When you say you had no idea, what does that mean?" How much had they all lied to me?

"It means we didn't know you were really Evelyn Maynard." There was a hint of bewilderment in his eyes. "I was twelve when you and your mom disappeared, and it's not like I looked at pictures of her every day for the past decade. There was something familiar about you when we first met, but I couldn't put my finger on it. Later, when we found out we were Bonded, I put the feeling down to our connection and dismissed it. Ethan and Josh just thought they had found their Vital—it never even crossed any of our minds that you were anyone other than who you said you were."

"So you haven't been keeping it from me this whole time?" I needed to hear him say it again.

"Eve, no. I promise. It didn't fall into place until this afternoon, when Josh's book bounced off Alec and I realized he was in our Bond too. That's when I knew who you must be—because we always suspected you were his. He's been keeping this from us too. But no more secrets, OK? If you want to know something, ask. If something makes you uncomfortable or unsure or worried, just tell us. I'm never letting you out of my sight again, so let's make sure you're comfortable where you are, OK?"

He smiled—tired but genuine—and it was infectious, pulling my own lips up at the corners.

"Bunch of stalkers," I whispered and leaned in without thinking.

He closed the distance but, instead of kissing me, squeezed me to his chest one more time. His words had soothed my most pressing anxiety—I believed he hadn't been lying to me. I couldn't see him being very good at it anyway. He held truth above all else as a virtue.

"Stay the night," he said, letting me go and turning toward the door. "I have to go deal with the lying one before I crash."

No sooner had Tyler released me than Ethan stepped up and threaded his fingers through mine. "You'll stay, won't you?" he asked softly.

"Yes. I don't want to be anywhere else right now."

"You can take my room," Josh piped up from the sink, where he'd just finished with the dishes.

Ethan cleared his throat. "Is it OK if I sleep in there with you? I'll take the couch, of course. I just . . . I can't have you out of my sight right now."

"Of course, big guy." I punctuated that with a wide yawn.

Turning out the lights, Josh led the way to his room, and then they left me alone to get ready for bed.

I was wrecked. The day's events had taken a massive toll on my body. Glancing at the clock, I couldn't believe it was only eight. After rushing through my bedtime routine, I pulled my phone out and texted the Reds.

Staying at Ethan's tonight. See you guys tomorrow?

The reply was instant.

170

Zara: what? What was with them all showing up here earlier? You can't just not explain that.

Beth: you ok?

Me: *I'm fine. I promise! It was just a misunderstanding.*

Understatement of the century. How was I going to explain that one?

Zara: I smell a story . . .

Beth: you can tell us all about it tomorrow. Cant's wait to hear all about the party too! I guess it was good if it's still going ;)

Zara: Gross . . . But you better at least be getting some if you're ditching us again.

Me: *haha!*

Beth: They're having that Variant alumni event on campus tomorrow because of the senator being in town. Maybe we could crash that and try to score some free hors d'oeuvres?

Zara: You get free food at the cafeteria every day you fruit-loop!

Beth: So? This is fancy free food.

Me: *Sounds great! See you guys tomorrow. Xo*

Zara: xo

*Beth: *a series of sexually suggestive emojis.**

I had just snuggled in under the dark blue covers of Josh's ridiculously big bed when there was a quiet knock at the door.

"Come in."

Ethan walked inside, wearing nothing but boxers, with Josh hot on his heels in underwear and a tank top, both of them carrying bundles of bedding. I tried not to stare, but judging by Ethan's dimpled smirk, I failed.

"I hope you don't mind," Josh said as he came to stand by the bed, "but I'm going to sleep in here too. It is my room, after all. I'll take the floor. Can I borrow a pillow?"

Ethan was setting up on the couch by the fireplace. It occurred to me how silly it was for Josh to be asking to borrow one of his own pillows, and I laughed.

His green eyes sparkled. "So, that's a 'no' on the pillow? Harsh."

It was ridiculous for them both to sleep uncomfortably when the king-size bed could easily accommodate us all. We were all exhausted, and if I was being honest, I was craving their touch. I had expelled so much Light earlier and made such a concentrated effort to stem its flow afterward that there couldn't possibly be any danger of levitating the bed or setting it on fire.

"Actually, no, you can't take this pillow," I teased, flopping back onto the item in question. "But you can still use it," I finished quietly and flipped the corner of the blanket down in invitation.

Slowly his eyebrows rose in surprise. "You sure?"

"Yep. Get in here. I need cuddles."

His makeshift bedding forgotten on the floor, he climbed in on my left and gave me a brilliant smile.

I hadn't forgotten Ethan. Lifting myself up onto my elbows, I saw him standing by the couch, awkward and uncertain. One of his arms hung by his side, and he was rubbing it with the other, his eyes darting all about the room before finally meeting my gaze.

I gave him a big smile and lifted the other corner. That was all the invitation he needed. Sprinting across the room, he launched himself at the bed and landed half across me, his face buried in my hair.

After our giggles subsided, he gave me the softest kiss on the cheek, whispered "good night," and rolled off me. I turned onto my side, toward Josh, and Ethan draped his arm over my middle, snuggling into my back. He was asleep in minutes.

Josh turned the lamp off and lay back down. The only light was moonlight streaming in through the windows, and it took my eyes a few minutes to adjust. I brushed a stray lock of blond hair off his forehead, and he captured my hand, pressing a warm kiss to my palm before resting our joined hands on the bed between us.

"Do you think Ethan's going to be OK?" I whispered.

"Yeah." Josh whispered back, a sad smile playing on his lips. "He just has some . . . abandonment issues. He was only nine when our parents were killed. He puts on a cocky façade, but deep down, he's still that kid, crying for his parents. Finding you—and now, discovering who you are—it's like finding a family all over again. To have that in his hands and then for it to slip away so suddenly . . . it just brought a lot of memories back. He'll be fine once he wakes up and sees you're still here."

"I'm so sorry." I could tell by the end he wasn't talking only about Ethan. Josh had gone through the same things; he just wasn't as expressive about it.

"It's OK. I get it." He squeezed my hand for emphasis. Of course Josh got it. Josh got everything.

"I was scared and I panicked, but I know I hurt you all by running off like that. Well, maybe not Alec. I think Alec would have preferred for me to go away." I let that hang in the darkness between us.

Josh sighed. "He cares. Trust me. It might not seem like it, but what the four of us went through—we're closer than family. We have no secrets. The fact that he kept this from us for so long tells me that he puts your safety even above our friendship. I believe that in his own messed-up way, he was convinced he was doing the right thing. He couldn't have known you would be connected to all of us. We always suspected that you and Alec were, but not us. That's why we didn't realize who you were from the start."

"So why is he still being . . . him, now that it's all out in the open? He's still acting like he wants nothing to do with me."

"Eve, he chased you down to New York just like we did. He helped bring you back here, where you belong. He's just . . . We all have our issues. Alec is no exception."

He paused, pain written all over his face. I gave his hand a squeeze, just as he had mine, and he smiled sadly.

Storing the information on Alec away for another time, I leaned forward on the pillow and pressed my forehead to Josh's, running my fingers through his dirty blond hair.

"I never even got to say goodbye," he whispered so softly I almost didn't hear him.

I knew exactly how he felt. "I never got to say goodbye to my mother either."

It had been one hell of a rollercoaster of a day, and I just had no tears left. I pressed my lips to his gently, then hesitated. I didn't want him to think I was kissing him to shut him up. But he responded immediately, placing his hand on my hip and scooting forward to deepen the kiss. I leaned into him, but as soon as I moved, Ethan's grip on my waist tightened, pinning me to his chest.

I chuckled against Josh's lips. "I think someone's not quite ready to let me go."

He pressed another desperate kiss to my lips before pulling away. "I don't think he ever will be. I don't think any of us will. So don't bother trying to leave. We'll just keep coming after you."

I smiled and let sleep finally take me.

At some point in the dead of night, the door creaked open, and I pushed my face farther into the pillow to shield my eyes from the light. The brightness disappeared quickly, but in its place were two hushed voices, one firm and sure, the other smooth like honey. I could have sworn they were talking about me, but I was half-asleep and couldn't be sure I wasn't dreaming.

Josh snuggled in closer to my front, and Ethan sighed into my hair. I felt cocooned and safe, surrounded by my Bond, and my breathing evened out again, matching theirs.

TWENTY-FOUR

The next morning, I woke up when Ethan jostled me. I was pressed into his side, my head resting on his shoulder, with Josh spooning me. Ethan carefully eased himself out of bed, his movements slow and measured, but I was a light sleeper. I kept my eyes closed and pretended I was still asleep as he got up.

He dropped a kiss onto my head, shuffled around in the bathroom for a few minutes, and then left, probably to go for a run. That boy had more energy than I did when I had Light overflow.

As soon as the door closed, Josh nuzzled into me tighter. Apparently I wasn't the only one pretending to be asleep. A secret smile spread over my face, but I kept my eyes closed. That is until I felt him—all of him—pressing into my ass. I don't think he meant to do it, because he exhaled loudly and rolled away.

Biting my lip, I kept pretending to be asleep to avoid an awkward situation. With a deep sigh he got out of bed, kissed me in the same spot Ethan had, and left the room.

I stayed in bed a while longer, drifting in and out of sleep, until my two bedroom companions burst into the room.

"Morning, my little panini!" Ethan was carrying a plate containing not a panini but homemade French toast.

"Morning . . . coffee." My voice was still croaky from sleep, and whatever new nickname I'd been about to call him was forgotten as soon as I saw the little takeaway cup in Josh's hand.

They sat on the end of the bed, watching me enjoy my French toast and latte and nursing massive cups of their own. I didn't hold back on the moans and compliments. I was feeling spoiled. This was the second morning in a row I'd woken up to breakfast and good coffee, delivered by my boyfriend. Boyfriends? Bondmates? Ugh! It was too early to get into all that.

We didn't talk about the previous day, just enjoying a light and easy morning together. Before long it was time for me to head back to campus. Ethan said he would wait for me downstairs, and Josh said he had "a date with pain and a yoga mat" and left soon after.

On my way to the bathroom, I paused, noticing the bundles of bedding the boys had abandoned were now spread out on Josh's couch and the soft rug next to the fireplace. Had my hazy dream of someone talking last night been real after all?

I could understand Tyler coming in to check on us and deciding to sleep on the couch. I was still his Vital, and after what I had pulled, wanting to stay as close to me as possible was a natural reaction. But the second lot of bedding, the one that suggested Alec had stayed too, had me scratching my head.

Maybe what Josh had been hinting at during our whispered pillow talk wasn't so far from the truth. Maybe Alec really did care, but he was too messed up to know how to deal with it.

I wanted to hunt him down—I was pretty sure he would be doing yoga with Josh somewhere—and sort this mess out, but I knew better than most that when it came to running away from things, especially emotional things, explaining it, or even understanding it, was rarely easy. I'd spent my whole life running with my mother, and I still didn't know why.

Which was another thing I hoped the guys could shed some light on, considering they had known her. Us. I couldn't believe we had known one another when we were kids! I was having trouble imagining it. I had so many questions.

But first, I needed a shower, a change of clothes, and to check in with my roomies.

The plan was for Tyler to drive me back to campus, but Ethan volunteered to come along too, obviously not ready to be away from me.

It was a quiet ride, the pattering rain and rhythmic back and forth of the windshield wipers lulling me into a contemplative silence. We hadn't even made it out of the driveway when Ethan reached over from the back seat to caress the back of my neck, leaving his fingers there for the duration of the ride. After asking how I'd slept, Tyler didn't speak much, lost in his own thoughts. He looked as if he wasn't nearly as well rested as me.

What had he and Alec talked about last night?

Too soon, we were pulling up behind my building, and it was time to say goodbye.

Tyler grabbed my hand tenderly. "I'm glad you're back where you belong, and I hope we can gain your trust." The rain and his quiet tone made me feel cocooned in the car.

"You already have. It's just Alec . . ." He smiled warmly, waiting for me to finish, but I didn't know how. My feelings were all over the place. "I just don't know how I'm supposed to believe anything he says."

A heavy, thoughtful look fell over Tyler's features, and he turned to watch the rain hitting the windshield. "My ability is more passive than the others. It can't hurt them no matter how much I use it, so they're not ever going to be immune to it. I can't speak for the others, but *I* promise to always be truthful with you, Eve."

He gave me a meaningful look, his gray eyes serious. He hadn't said it in so many words, but I was pretty sure he was telling me that if I asked, he would share whatever his ability allowed him to learn.

I nodded, and he smiled again, looking back to the front. I was starting to realize the burden Tyler must carry—it couldn't be easy to know so many secrets and have no one to share them with. Maybe, eventually, I could be that for him. He could ease my worry, and I could share his burden—if he let some of his walls down, that is.

With one last squeeze of my hand and a satisfied nod, he released me.

Ethan jumped out of the back seat and opened the door for me, wrapping me up in a massive hug as soon as I got out. "I don't want to let you go, baby cakes," he muttered into my hair after we'd been standing in the rain for far too long.

I chuckled. The silly nicknames were back in full force, and the mood between us was getting lighter again. "Come on, you big teddy bear. I'll see you tomorrow. I'm getting soaked."

When he still didn't let go, I pulled away slightly, gently grabbing his face between my hands and forcing him to look at me. "I'm going inside to hang out with the Reds. I'm *not* leaving. I'll be right here, and you can check in with me on the phone anytime. OK? I'm not leaving. I promise."

He nodded and leaned down to kiss me. I wanted to deepen it, but the rain was making me pretty cold. Luckily, I didn't have to choose; Tyler barked at us to hurry up, and with matching wide smiles, we pulled apart, Ethan taking my place in the front seat and me running for the cover of the entrance.

I took the stairs instead of the elevator, needing the few extra minutes to set my thoughts straight. I would need to speak to the guys about letting the Reds in on the secret. Charlie and Dot already knew some of it, so why couldn't the Reds? I trusted them, and I really hated lying.

When I entered our little living area, they were both on the couch, mugs of coffee in their hands and some morning show on the TV.

"Well, well. Look who finally decided to grace us with her presence." Zara gave me a mocking grin.

"Hey, Eve. Want some coffee?" Beth did her best not to laugh while taking a sip of her own. They both knew very well how I felt about their "coffee." Beth had taken to amusing herself by offering me a cup every chance she got.

Scrunching up my nose in disgust, I shook my head. "How was your weekend?" I asked, dropping my bag and plonking myself on the couch between them. I wanted to get them talking and keep the attention off me. Naturally, it didn't work.

"Um, no." Zara poked me in the ribs. "How was *your* weekend?"

"Yes, I want to know all about the gala. And where did you get that dress? Dot posted a photo of you guys, and you looked freaking incredible." Beth started firing a litany of questions.

But before I had a chance to answer any of them, the door to our room burst open, startling us all and causing Beth to slosh a good portion of her coffee all over the place.

Tyler and Ethan barged in, slamming the door closed and locking it.

"Hey!" Zara jumped to her feet. "What the fu—"

"Get away from the windows!" Tyler's authoritative voice cut across her, and we all obeyed immediately, jumping up from the couch to go stand by Ethan, who was trying to make a call by the door.

Tyler took two long strides to the window and peered outside before drawing the curtains half-closed over it.

"They've jammed the signal." Ethan cursed under his breath, tucking the phone into his back pocket and reaching for me.

I let him pull me against his side, watching Tyler closely.

Zara tried again. "What the fuck is going on?"

"Someone is invading the campus," Tyler answered, keeping an eye on the window. "We saw vehicles and heavily armed people setting up positions at the east gate. It looks like the Human Empowerment Network, but that doesn't make sense . . ."

"Oh my god." Beth sounded panicked. Zara had her phone out, but she put it away quickly after confirming with a huff that Ethan was right about the cell service. The two of them held hands and looked to Tyler. He was the adult in the room, the person with authority, the Bradford Hills staff.

My breathing had become quick and shallow. Every horror story I'd seen on the news about American mass shootings and lax attitudes toward gun control came flooding back. Statistics assaulted my brain.

It is estimated that there are between 270 and 310 million guns in America—almost one for every person.

There were more than fifteen thousand gun-related deaths in America in 2017, and that was just *deaths*—it didn't even include the more than thirty-one thousand *injuries*.

I held on to Ethan a little tighter. The muscles under his damp T-shirt were taut with tension.

"I don't think the staff know what's happening yet." Tyler was still looking through the window. "They haven't advanced past the gates. I think they're securing the perimeter. It's too organized for a renegade group of humans. What the hell is this?"

He was trying to assess the situation, but he didn't have all the facts. I knew how incredibly frustrating that was.

Then it hit me—we had a way of getting more information without even leaving this room. He'd told us about it just last night in the car.

I straightened and gasped. Everyone turned to look at me.

"Ty, we need more info." I didn't wait for a response, extracting myself from Ethan's protective hold and walking over to him. As I placed my hand in his, understanding fell over his features, and he gave me one decisive nod.

I closed my eyes, took a deep breath, and dropped any attempt at stemming the flow of Light. He pivoted to face me and grabbed my other hand as the Light flowed freely into him. After only a few moments, I opened my eyes and gave him a questioning look.

"Let's find out," he murmured, dropping one of my hands to pull the curtain back slightly.

Ethan stepped up behind me and placed his hands on my shoulders, both of us waiting with bated breath to see if it would work.

"Oh my gosh!" Beth breathed at the same time Zara said, "Holy fuck!"

I turned to them in surprise, having almost forgotten they were in the room. I guess my secret was out.

"They're going after the alumni event. They're waiting until all the exits are blocked before moving in. But this isn't just the humans. Variant Valor is here too. Are they working together?" he asked in disbelief, speaking more to himself than any of us.

"No," he continued. "Variant Valor is just using the chaos to . . . it's unclear. The bulk of the force is going to come up through here." He pointed to the main avenue winding up from the east gate and toward the admin building, behind which the event was to be held. "At least a hundred Human Empowerment Network and a much smaller force of Variant Valor assailants. There are a lot of angry people down there. This is going to get violent very fast."

"We have to do something." I couldn't wrap my brain around why the human extremists were allowing themselves to be manipulated by the Variant extremists, or why the Variant extremists were trying to get Variants killed. Politics and strategy were not my strong suits, but even I knew people were about to die needlessly. "We might be the only people who know about this."

"We need a distraction," Ethan growled from behind me. "Something to take them off track. Buy us a little time. Maybe we could somehow alert . . . the authorities." He was talking about Melior Group. The local law enforcement would be severely out of their depth.

"If you can cause a distraction, I can make it down to the event and warn everyone," Beth said with determination, but when I spun around to face her, there was fear in her eyes.

Zara looked as shocked as I did. Then she rolled her eyes and put her hands on her hips. "Fuck! *We*. We can warn everyone."

"No." Tyler was using his adult voice. "It's too dangerous."

I couldn't let him talk us out of it. We *had* to do something.

"The chemistry lab!" I blurted, and they all looked at me as if the stress had broken my capacity for thought. "It's just south of here, and it's close enough to the avenue to draw them away from the admin building for at least a little while. I can think of six ways to cause a massive explosion just off the top of my head. That should be distracting enough, right?"

Tyler still looked skeptical. "Well, yeah, but . . ."

"We don't have time for this!" I got in his face. "I know you want to protect me, but people are going to die. We have to do something."

A resolute look crossed his features, and he dropped my hand, reaching behind his back. "Right. You two," he addressed the Reds, "come down to the ground floor and wait for the explosion. Then—*only* then—run for it. Raise the alarm and then hide. That's it. Don't go off script."

They both nodded emphatically, eyes wide.

He turned to me and pulled a gun out from behind his back, cocking it and holding it by his side. "Eve, juice him up." He nodded in Ethan's direction.

"Is that a gun?" It was a stupid question, but in my defense, I had never seen a gun before. All of a sudden, the gravity of the situation hit me. "Why do you have a gun? Oh my god!"

"He said juice me up, babe. No time for freak-outs over firearms." Ethan spun me around and planted his lips on mine.

It was what I needed to snap me out of it. I plastered myself to him and let the Light flow freely. Then, as quickly as he'd initiated the kiss, Ethan pulled away and dragged me toward the door, where Tyler was waiting with one hand on the knob.

"Stay close to me and do exactly as I say." Tyler didn't wait for a response. He cracked the door open and peered down the corridor, then made for the stairs. We all followed, much more noisily.

At the back door, he again checked that the coast was clear before nodding once to the Reds and darting outside.

I squeezed Zara's hand in goodbye and reached out to Beth, but Ethan was already pulling me through the door and my fingers only just scraped hers. She gave me a shooing motion before pulling the door closed.

My heart was hammering in my chest as I scrambled to keep up with Tyler, keeping my eyes peeled for danger.

We rushed over to the next building and huddled in its entranceway. The solid door was locked, and the chemistry building was on the other side, so we would have to go around.

Before we could keep moving, however, two people came around the corner. I was so startled I jumped on the spot, my heart leaping into my throat. Tyler raised his gun but lowered it immediately when he saw it was Dot and Charlie.

"Charlie!" he hissed in their direction.

Charlie looked over, registered the gun in Tyler's hand, and immediately grabbed Dot by the elbow, dragging her over to us.

"Hey! What . . ." She was slower to pick up on the situation, but once she saw us, her heavily lined eyes widened in panic.

Tyler gave them the rundown. "Campus surrounded. Comms down. At least thirty armed at east gate. More at other entry points, plus heavy vehicles. It's humans, but there is more at play here. They're going after the Variants at the event."

"Where do you want us?" A hard mask had fallen over Charlie's face.

"We're on our way to create a distraction and delay them, but we need backup."

"I can do that," Dot piped up. I'd never heard the confident girl sound so quiet and unsure. "Write a note on something."

Moving with the kind of ease that comes from having done something your entire life, Dot and Charlie held hands, and I could almost *smell* the Light Charlie was pushing to his sister. Before he was even done transferring, Dot's face tightened into a look of concentration. Next to me, Ethan pulled a scrap of paper out of his wallet and started scribbling a note on the back.

By the time he finished writing, Squiggles was scampering up Dot's leg and onto her shoulder. Tyler passed Dot the note, and no sooner had she handed it to the ferret than Squiggles was off again, the paper held gingerly in her teeth.

Tyler gave Dot a nod of thanks. "Stay out of sight. Go up to Eve's room and hide."

Dot's brow creased in defiance, but Tyler didn't give her a chance to argue. The boys were already on the move again.

TWENTY-FIVE

A few tense minutes later, we made it to the science building—which was locked.

"Dammit!" I cursed, but apparently Ethan had run out of patience for locked doors. He picked up a rock and smashed it through the glass by the old-fashioned doorknob, reaching through and unlocking it from the inside.

With Tyler in front, we scaled the two flights of stairs and ran down the corridor to the chemistry lab. As we came to a screeching halt at the door, it swung inward, a very surprised professor in a lab coat standing at the threshold.

"Gabe? What is this?" His eyes flicked down to the gun, and he stepped back.

"Peter, the school is being invaded by armed gunmen. We need access to the lab."

"What?" The older mad looked terrified. "Why?"

"There's no time for explanations." Tyler's tone brooked no arguments. "Go down to the basement level, lock yourself into a storage room, and stay there."

The man nodded and rushed past, heading for the stairs. We were lucky to have run into him. The labs had secure doors, and you needed a key card or a code to enter.

We burst into the room and Tyler ran to the window, yelling, "Do your thing!" over his shoulder. "We don't have much time."

I needed something that we could explode *fast*. I considered dragging the hydrogen tanks downstairs and having Tyler shoot them from a distance, but they were bulky and awkward, and it would take ages. Then I toyed with the idea of combining nitric acid with an organic solvent in a closed container of some sort, but I would need massive amounts of both for the kind of explosion we needed, and again, it would take time to set up. In the end, I decided the simplest solution was the most effective.

Running to the back corner of the room, I checked the gas tanks and started turning the knobs, letting the methane flow freely. Ethan didn't ask what I was doing, simply taking my lead and turning the other knobs until all five tanks were releasing the highly flammable gas into the air.

I did a quick calculation. The room was approximately seventy by fifty feet with seven-foot-high ceilings, meaning it had a volume capacity of 24,500 cubic feet. With all five tanks flowing, it wouldn't take longer than two minutes to fill the room with enough methane to cause a pretty big explosion.

"Close that window! Let's go!" I yelled. Tyler obeyed immediately, pulling the small window shut and leading the way out of the room.

The building was deserted, and I prayed that it stayed that way.

When we made it outside, I pointed to a building across the avenue.

Tyler shook his head. "Too exposed. We can't go running across their path."

"We need to be farther away when it goes boom," I explained. Without waiting for a response, I dashed across the wide avenue, forcing myself not to look toward the south gate, where I knew there were many people with loaded guns.

The guys were hot on my heels as we rounded the corner of the building opposite the chemistry lab. Tyler looked back to where we had come from, then whirled on me. "I said you do exactly as I say. What the hell were you thinking?"

Ignoring him, I reached out to give Ethan another quick zap of Light, then pointed up at a window on the second floor. "I need you to throw a fireball through that window. One of the blue ones."

"What?" His face twisted in panic. "This whole plan hinges on me? I've never thrown a fireball that far!"

"You've never had me. You can do this." I checked my watch. It had been four minutes. It was more than ready to go.

"They're on the move." Tyler cursed profusely. His ability was still coming in useful. "Ethan. Now!"

Narrowing his eyes and squaring his shoulders, my big guy stepped out from behind the corner and rolled his neck. After another moment of hesitation, he lifted his arm by his side, and an angry blue ball of fire appeared in his grasp. He leaned back, lifting his front leg, and pitched it like a baseball. It arched through the air magnificently and smashed, dead center, through the window I had pointed out.

There was a split second of silence and then a *BOOM*, louder than anything I'd ever heard. The burst of heat that followed was so intense it was hard to inhale. Ethan pivoted, shielding my body with his, as Tyler pulled me back behind the safety of the wall. A shard of glass still managed to make it to my face, slicing a fine line across my right cheek. It stung like a bitch but didn't feel too serious.

With the immediate danger over, Ethan backed away from me, and Tyler leaned in.

"You OK?" He raked his eyes over my face and body, looking for injuries more serious than the cut on my face.

"I'm good." I nodded as he ran his thumb under the cut gently, his brows furrowing. I pulled a tissue out of my pocket and pressed it to the cut, giving him a reassuring smile.

All three of us peered out from our hiding spot. One corner of the science building was on fire, flames licking the sides of the walls, and all the windows of the second-floor lab had been blown to pieces. The explosion had been visually impressive and probably loud enough to be heard miles away. If Squiggles hadn't made it to Alec, this would have gotten his attention.

It had certainly gotten the attention of the gun-wielding people, now inching toward the charred building.

"It worked." Tyler pulled us back behind the wall. "But it won't last long."

"What do we do now?" Ethan was breathing as hard as me, fire flickering down the length of his arms. With all the danger, coupled with the extra Light I had pushed into him, he was having trouble controlling his ability.

"You two do nothing. Find a way into this building and hide. Ethan, you fry anything that moves in your direction. I'm going to go check if Zara and Beth managed to warn the others."

"No!" Ethan and I protested at the same time.

I folded my arms. "We are not separating right now. I refuse."

"I agree. We should stick together." Ethan matched my stance, backing me.

Tyler's gaze flicked between us, exasperation leaking into his features. He dragged a hand down his face, growling. "Fine! But this time you do *exactly* as I say. No running off. Am I understood?"

"Yes, sir," I agreed readily as Ethan nodded. I was more than happy to take his lead. I had no idea what I was doing.

"They're everywhere. We'll have to go around this building and come around the back of the admin building to get to where they've set up the marquee for the event." He walked past us and away from the carnage we'd just caused, setting a rapid pace.

We circled around the building, sticking close to the walls, then darted across a clearing and into some trees. The woods at the periphery of campus provided decent cover as we looped around the massive admin building. The morning's rain had made the ground soft and muddy, and we made a mess of our clothing as we trudged through the undergrowth.

Tyler made us stop at the edge of the trees. The lawn where the event was to take place was clearly visible. It had stopped raining, but the heavy clouds were still casting a dull grayness over the whole scene.

Everyone had heard the explosion, but they didn't know what to make of it. People were milling about, talking to one another hastily, some of them walking away.

Finally I spotted the Reds near the entrance to the admin building, speaking with a man and a woman both dressed in suits. Beth was gesturing wildly behind her while Zara stood next to her, nodding.

"There!" I pointed. It looked as if they were having trouble convincing the staff to evacuate.

We were running out of time to get people to safety. Maybe we should go up there. Surely Tyler could convince them.

Just as I was about to suggest it, I heard movement in the brush behind us.

Tyler and Ethan had kept me behind them, peering between their shoulders to get a look at the lawn, so when we all turned, I ended up in front. Before us stood two people, bandanas over their noses and multiple weapons strapped to their bodies. They wore matching black clothing and had identical semiautomatic pistols in their hands.

We all froze.

A little machine in one of the gunmen's hands bleeped. He looked down at it in surprise, then lifted his gun to point at us. "We got one. Grab her."

They both moved forward, weapons raised.

The sound of gunfire from both sides was deafening. Tyler stepped up on my left and let off three quick shots, aiming at the gunman with the little machine.

The first two bullets thudded against his chest, knocking him back but not penetrating the Kevlar he was wearing. The last one went straight through his forehead. Blood gushed down his face as he crumpled to the ground, a spurt landing on Tyler's expensive shirt. The bright red was a stark contrast to the crisp white.

At the same time, Ethan came up on my other side, pushing me behind him with one strong arm and throwing his other arm forward. A blast of fire shot out of his hand, intense and angry, and hit the other gunman. The impact threw the man onto his back, enveloping him in fire immediately.

The man screamed—an animalistic, terrifying sound—and I found myself screaming too. The blood and the fire; the death and the pain—it was all happening too fast.

Tyler pulled me into him one-handed, his other hand still holding his gun at the ready, and blocked my view of the burning man. I clutched his shirt as if my life depended on it and screwed my eyes shut, my screams collapsing into long shuddering breaths.

After a moment, I forced myself to open my eyes. There were armed maniacs on the loose, and I needed to be aware of my surroundings.

I looked over to the two forms on the ground. Ethan was standing above the burned man, who was smoking and moaning on the ground. As I watched, the man stopped moving and lay still.

Panic rose in me again. "Is he . . ." My voice was shaky.

Ethan came over to stand with us, his eyes wide. "No. He just passed out from the pain. The other guy though . . ."

The other guy had a bullet in his brain. You didn't need to be a doctor to know he was dead.

Tyler had killed someone.

My hands were shaking, but his were steady, his hold on the gun firm.

That's when I realized the flames that had been licking up and down Ethan's arm had been replaced with streaks of crimson.

"Holy Thomas Edison!" I yelled.

Ethan's left bicep was red and glistening, macabre streams of blood trickling down his arm. A single drop from the tip of his middle finger fell to the forest floor.

I pushed out of Tyler's arms and rushed over to him. My hands hovered over Ethan's skin, unsure, panic beginning to set in. I couldn't figure out how badly he was hurt.

He pulled me into his embrace one-handed, as Tyler had. "Shh. It's OK. It only grazed my shoulder. I'm fine." He was the one that had been *shot*, and he was comforting me.

Before I had a chance to reply, a piercing woman's scream drew our attention back to the lawn. Tyler swung his gun in that direction as we all turned to look.

The field had erupted into chaos. Gunmen had swarmed the main area and begun shooting. This group, however, didn't look like the two assailants we'd just encountered. They appeared less organized, without the matching black clothing, their weapons a mishmash of handguns, shotguns, and automatic rifles.

The rain had started up again, and most people had gathered under the marquee to stay dry. They were easy targets. Bodies fell to the ground like ragdolls as terrified, guttural screams mingled with the menacing sound of bullets cutting through the air.

There was blood everywhere.

Just as Tyler had predicted, the Variants were not taking this lying down. While some people were running away in abject terror—many falling down lifeless in midstride—others were fighting back.

A man in a blue suit, one of the sleeves ripped, was standing in front of a group of huddled students. He had his hands up in front, feet wide apart. He must have had some kind of defensive ability, because there were several gunmen firing directly at them and the bullets were bouncing off, inches away from hitting him.

A girl about my age was standing in the thick of it all, holding hands with a boy, her Vital. She was using her ability to form the rain into icicles, their deathly sharp points embedding themselves in gunmen's chests. The pair took down three of the assailants before two attacked them from the back.

The two men who approached the Variant and her Vital looked identical to the ones who had attacked us in the woods, uniformly dressed and carrying identical weapons. The gunmen hit the boy and girl in the back of their heads, their bodies crumpling to the ground. Then they dragged the boy away, leaving the Variant girl lying lifeless in the rain.

Another young man was running through the crowd throwing bright bolts of lightning from his hands. I recognized Rick—the friend of Ethan who had introduced himself and his electric ability to me.

As Rick charged the bulk of the gunmen, Zara and Beth ran out from the cover of the admin building's entryway, trying to get away from a scuffle there. Their red hair was like a beacon, and I watched them run, terrified, into the crowd, straight into Rick's path.

I could see what was about to happen, but I was too far away to stop it.

With a panicked "NO!" I burst past Ethan and Tyler and ran straight for them.

Rick threw another bolt of angry electricity just as the Reds ran into his path. It hit Beth directly in the chest. She flew back several feet, her hand wrenched out of Zara's grasp, and flopped to the ground behind a row of chairs. The force of Beth getting blasted away knocked Zara to the ground too.

Neither one of them was getting up.

I pumped my legs faster, desperate to get to my friends, but I was no match for Ethan's athleticism. He caught up to me just as some of the gunmen noticed us, wrapping his big arm around me and twisting us sideways as bullets sailed past our heads. Tyler was right behind him and started returning fire.

We were out in the open and definitely outgunned.

An engine roared in my ears, and a motorcycle came to a screeching halt in front of us, blocking us from the gunmen. Alec climbed off the bike with grace and speed, turning his attention to our assailants, and Josh pulled up on his bike only a second later. They were soaked from riding in the rain, and they must have come straight from yoga, because they were both in shorts and tank tops.

I had a momentary spark of annoyance that they hadn't worn protective gear on their bikes, then nearly let loose a frantic giggle at the absurdity of that thought. Just as it had during the plane crash, my brain always seemed to throw useless information at me in moments when everything was falling apart. Was it some desperate bid for control? An attempt to feel better by focusing on the mundane—facts, statistics, the importance of wearing helmets?

People began moaning in pain. Everyone—human or Variant, crazed gunman or Bradford Hills student—was doubled over. Alec wasn't targeting specific people; he'd just unleashed the pain and let it incapacitate everyone. As soon as the bullets stopped flying, Josh flicked his hands up, and a shotgun flew over his head, landing somewhere behind us.

They were working as effectively and in tune with each other as Ethan and Tyler had in the woods. One by one, firearms sailed past as Josh pushed his ability to the edge.

I watched them for a few moments, transfixed by their abilities, and then remembered I could help. I pushed against Ethan's chest, trying to get to Josh, but he held me firmly.

"I need to juice him up!" I yelled, and Ethan let me go.

I ran to Josh and wrapped my arms around his middle, pressing my face into the cool wet skin at the back of his neck. He jumped in surprise, his muscles tensing, but relaxed as soon as he realized it was me. I pushed his tank top up and placed my palms flat on his stomach, letting the Light flow freely.

He rolled his shoulders, standing taller, more confident, more energized. I craned my neck to see around him as he lifted both arms, every remaining gun flying up into the air.

With a sharp motion, Josh brought his hands down, and the guns landed on the backs of the assailant's heads, all the Human Empowerment Network gunmen falling to the ground unconscious in perfect synchronicity. Then, with another gesture from Josh, the weaponry stacked itself into a menacing pile of metal behind us.

Alec took a shaky breath, and his shoulders sagged. The remaining people in the clearing stopped moaning and straightened, looking a little dazed.

Josh turned in my arms and crushed me to him. His breathing was erratic, the staccato rhythm only matching mine in its unevenness. He placed several firm kisses on my forehead and cheeks as he pulled away slowly. Then he held me by the shoulders at arm's length, his eyes raking over my body methodically, lingering on the cut on my cheek.

"I'm OK. I'm OK. I'm OK," I kept repeating in a quiet voice, my hands gripping his wrists until it sunk in. His green eyes finally looked into mine, and he breathed a sigh of relief.

"I'm OK." I said it once more, nodding for good measure. I needed to convince *myself* of the fact as much as I needed to convince him.

I was dirty from the mud in the woods, wet from having run around in the rain, and tense in every muscle. There was blood on me, but most of it wasn't mine. All the bullets had missed me, and thanks to the guys, none of the gunmen had gotten close enough to lay a hand on me.

"More are coming." Tyler stood a few steps away, looking in the opposite direction of where the first group had come from. He pushed a wet strand of hair off his forehead. The rain had settled into a steady patter, and we were all getting soaked.

"What?" Josh went to stand by him. "How do you know?"

"My ability. I'm able to see the truth of the situation, to an extent. At the moment, the most pertinent information is where the threat is, so that's what's most clear in my mind. They were holding this group back for something . . . I'm not sure. The extra Light Eve transferred is wearing off. But I know they're sending more in."

"Shit. How far out?"

"Two minutes. Maybe three. Alec."

Alec was still standing next to me in the same position, shoulders sagging, head bent.

"ETA on reinforcements?"

Without moving or even looking up, he answered, "At least nine minutes."

All three of them cursed profusely, and then Ethan piped in. "We need to get these people somewhere safe, and then we need to get Eve the hell out of Dodge." He was breathing hard, the white T-shirt stretched across his heaving chest nearly transparent from being so wet.

"Right." Tyler turned back to us, his face grim. A dark splatter of mud had joined the blood on his shirt. He directed the others to start maneuvering the crowd to safety, and he, Ethan, and Josh shouted at people to go hide, that there were more gunmen coming, that it wasn't over.

I kept my eyes on Alec. He was still staring at the ground.

I didn't understand it. Alec was the one who worked for the Melior Group in the field. Tyler outranked him and was a natural leader, so it made sense that he was taking charge of the situation, but Alec had the most combat experience. Shouldn't he be in his element here? Not standing there as if he had no clue what to do with himself?

He was breathing hard, his shoulders bunching with tension, each ripple of muscle making the visible tattoos under his tank top dance. His hands were clenching and unclenching at his sides, and his eyes were flicking around almost wildly, calculating, looking for the best course of action.

Around us, the others weren't having much success with steering people into hiding. Some had heeded the warning and taken off for the comparable safety of the buildings, but others, mostly Variants with active abilities, were insisting on staying and fighting. Rick was being very vocal about it, getting in Ethan's face and yelling about defending our people.

I wasn't allowing myself to wonder how seriously Beth and Zara were hurt. Many people had already died. Many more probably would.

And then realization dawned on me.

Alec wasn't trying to figure out the best course of action. He was trying to steel himself for it.

Ethan called my name, having abandoned his argument with Rick. He was saying we needed to go. I could see Tyler over Alec's shoulder, reloading his gun as he shouted something, and I could hear Josh somewhere behind me, still yelling at people to run.

But I focused on Alec. I knew just as well as he did what we had to do, and we were running out of time.

"Alec!" My voice was steadier than it should have been, considering the mess of emotions and fear writhing inside me. His eyes snapped up to mine, the blue more intense and yet brighter than I'd ever seen it, and I briefly wondered how eyes so light could hold so much darkness.

He held my gaze, but the overwhelming anger radiating off him nearly made me shrink away. He turned toward the sky and let the rain fall onto his face, teeth grinding, then took a deep breath and looked back at me with cold determination.

He gave one firm nod, and I launched myself at him.

I wrapped my arms around his neck and pressed my lips to his almost violently, our teeth knocking. He immediately pushed his tongue into my mouth, and his strong hands grabbed me under my ass, lifting me so I could wrap my legs around his waist. He grunted when the Light started to flow between us, and his fingers dug roughly into my thighs.

Even after all my practice transferring Light through my hands, this was still the quickest and most efficient way, and we were out of time. I could already hear the pop of gunfire in the background, the first line of more assailants coming upon us.

I pressed myself impossibly farther into him and let the Light flow completely free, focusing on the lines of his hard body pressed to mine, his hands gripping me all over. I moaned into his mouth, acutely aware how fucked up it was to be turned on at a time like this but consoling myself with the fact that the arousal would only make the Light flow faster and more intense.

A loud *bang* near us made my eyes fly open. I was glowing again; my arms, still wrapped around Alec's shoulders, were luminescent. He broke the kiss and looked at me with wide eyes, both of us breathing hard.

He began to shake lightly, and then, with me still wrapped around him, he dropped to his knees. His grip tightened around my flesh, then slackened, a little vein popping at his forehead.

Why wasn't he using his ability? Had the Light transfer not worked?

And then it hit me.

"Why are you holding it back?" I yelled into his face.

Anger fell over his features again, his head shaking a little with strain.

"Alec!" I was beginning to sound frantic.

He released me, sitting back on his heels and throwing his arms out wide, flicking droplets of rain off his fingers. I held on, planting my knees on the ground and using his shoulders to balance. He lifted his head to the sky and roared like a wild animal.

A massive burst of energy flooded out of him in all directions, like a sonic boom. His ability couldn't harm me, but I could feel the sheer power as it poured out of him.

I pressed my face into his neck. I wasn't going to let him do this on his own. I focused on the feel of the cool rain dripping down my neck and his body under mine, muscles rock hard with effort.

After only a few seconds, he went quiet and dropped his arms by his sides, his whole body sagging. I still held on. Chest to chest, heart to heart, we took shuddering breaths together.

Around us, everything had gone still.

When the body experiences too much pain, the brain shuts down as a self-preservation mechanism, resulting in unconsciousness. With my Light to power it, the blast of Alec's pain ability had been enough to knock everyone out cold. Only Tyler, Josh, and Ethan were still standing, watching us with varying degrees of shock on their faces.

As usual, Tyler was the first to take charge. "You guys can't be here when they arrive. They'll take one look at this and know about Eve and our Bond."

Alec moved to stand, and I untangled myself from him and stood up too. I wondered if he felt as drained as I did. He draped one heavy arm around my shoulders and held me to him but didn't meet my gaze.

The world dipped sideways and I lost my balance, but big warm hands steadied me. Ethan.

I vaguely registered them talking around me, discussing what to do, what to tell the authorities. Then somehow I was in the back of Tyler's car, my body cradled in Alec's arms and my legs resting across Ethan.

Then we were climbing the stairs of the mansion, a heavy silence weighing down our steps, making us all slow.

Then Alec was collapsing in the foyer. Ethan and Josh carried him into Tyler's study and deposited him on the couch, taking his soaking tank top off.

The pulling, urgent pain was in my chest again—just like the night Ethan had nearly died—and I took my soggy, blood-soaked, mud-splattered T-shirt off too. Josh and Ethan protested, saying I was too weak myself, but I shrugged them off and approached Alec on shaky legs. I had to try. The Light was demanding contact, and I didn't have the strength to resist it.

Josh supported me as I staggered over to the couch, the pain in my chest beginning to feel like tearing. Alec had given it all he had out there—he had unleashed the full, terrifying force of his ability, and it had taken a toll.

I draped myself over his body, the Light humming on my skin where we touched, my eyes already drooping closed. I could hear the guys bustling around the room, lighting a fire in the fireplace, bringing in extra space heaters. Someone draped a blanket over us, and then I was out.

TWENTY-SIX

I woke up a few hours later, but this time it was not slow and languid, as it had been when I'd awakened in Ethan's arms. I shot up on the couch, Alec groaning in protest next to me. Ethan was at Tyler's desk, his head resting on his forearms, and he jerked up in his seat at my sudden movement.

"Shit! The Reds!" Everything my overloaded brain had been incapable of processing earlier was flooding back, and I sprang to my feet. "I have to make sure they're OK."

Ethan rushed around the desk. He looked as awful as I felt—his clothing rumpled and dirty, his eyes bloodshot. It was lucky he moved so fast, because as soon as I stood, my knees buckled.

"Whoa," Ethan said as he caught me. "Take it easy. Just sit back down, baby."

He guided me back to the couch, where Alec was now sitting up. He looked like shit too. Dark circles under his eyes stood out against his otherwise pale face. He was probably out of the woods, but the Light inside me was still pushing me toward him; I reached over to squeeze his hand, sighing softly as the distinctive tingle of Light flow soothed us both.

"What happened?" My body may have been screaming at me to curl up next to Alec and embrace unconsciousness, but my brain was demanding answers. "I don't remember much after the . . . Are they OK?"

Ethan crouched in front of me, his warm hands on my knees. His left shoulder was bandaged, and the sight of the clean white gauze, stark against his tanned skin, reminded me of the blood dripping down his arm . . . the men pointing guns at us.

I broke contact with Alec to pull Ethan closer, pushing up the sleeve of his T-shirt so I could inspect the bandage. His hands on my knees flexed, and he swallowed hard, his gaze focused on the ground.

"Ethan?" I grabbed his face, forcing him to look at me. He had tears in his eyes.

"Zara's in the hospital. She's going to be OK," he whispered as one tear slid down his cheek.

My own eyes began to sting. Next to me Alec sat up straighter, shifting closer to me.

"And Beth?" I whispered back.

Ethan looked down, shaking his head sadly, and whispered into my lap, "I'm so sorry."

"No," I croaked, the tears spilling over.

"They said she died instantly. Before she even hit the ground. She took a direct hit at close range, and her fragile human body just couldn't . . ." He looked up at me, the amber in his eyes almost molten with emotion.

Beth was dead.

One of the only people I had ever referred to as a friend—sweet, thoughtful, kind Beth—was dead. The bandage on Ethan's shoulder was a sharp reminder that it could just as easily have been him. It could have been any one of us.

It felt like a stab in the guts. I doubled over, sobbing uncontrollably.

For a split second, I wasn't sure where I was. Was I sitting on the couch, crying over the death of my friend? Or was I in the hospital, crying over the death of my mother?

Ethan was running his hands through my hair, whispering calming things, but I couldn't hear him over my own grief. My body folded in on itself, trying to cover the hollow feeling in my stomach, just like in the hospital.

And just like that night, Alec wrapped his strong body around my weak one and held me together. He positioned himself behind me on the couch, one leg on either side of my sobbing, shaking form, and wrapped his arms around me firmly, his chest pressed to my back.

"You are not alone," he said. The same words he'd said to me that night in the hospital.

I had lost another person.

I had lost her after spending a year feeling as if I'd never find another soul to share my life with. I'd found Zara and Beth, Dot and Charlie, and my guys. These people had made me feel as though I had a place in the world.

Now one of them had been taken from me. It had hit me so hard I was thrown right back into that hopeless despair I'd felt in the hospital, staring down the barrel of a solitary existence.

And once again, my honey-voiced man was there.

He moved his head so his lips were right at my ear and whispered it again. "Evie, you are not alone."

My frantic crying calmed a little, the nightmare of my memories fading away. I took shuddering breaths as silent tears continued to stream down my cheeks, the falling drops mingling with the hair on Alec's forearms and sliding away.

He and Ethan spoke in hushed voices, and then Ethan left, shutting the door softly. Alec pitched his body to the side and gently laid us back down. He held me, just as he had in the hospital, and I drifted back to sleep.

When I woke up again some time later, it was much more slowly and gently. We had shifted positions in our sleep. Alec was on his back, stretched along the length of the couch, and I was tucked into his side, my head resting on his shoulder and my leg hitched over his thighs.

The heavy drapes in Tyler's office were drawn over the window, but a sliver of golden afternoon light cut across our waists. I could see tiny particles of dust floating in it.

Alec's chest was rising and lowering gently as he breathed, but I somehow knew he wasn't asleep either. The tattoos on his back curved over his shoulders and around his ribs, and now that my face was on his skin, I could see the scars that intermingled with the ink. The tattoos weren't placed carefully to cover the scars; they were just there. Unapologetic. Just like him.

Slowly I lifted my hand and dragged my fingers through the light spattering of hair on his chest, stopping at a ragged scar just under his shoulder.

"What happened here?" I whispered into his skin.

"I was stabbed," he whispered back, his voice quiet. Passive. The honey was gone.

My hand continued its exploration of the history of his pain, trailing a path over his shoulder and stopping just above his bicep. There was a smaller, circular scar there. "And here?"

"I was shot."

I drew my fingers down the length of his arm and ghosted them back over to his stomach. At his hip, disappearing below the waistband of his shorts, was a raised, uneven, pinkish scar. Some of it was covered by a tattoo. "And here?"

"Ethan. He was still getting the hang of it."

I let my finger trace the edge of the fabric before moving up. Under his ribs were three parallel jagged scars, raised and curving around his waist, disappearing where his side was pressed against mine. I ran my hand over each one. "And here?"

"Claws."

I paused. Did he mean it was an animal attack? But it seemed I'd have to wonder about that forever; Alec was done talking about it.

"I hate you," he whispered in the same detached tone he'd used to tell me about his scars.

I lifted my head to look at him, letting my confusion and hurt show.

"For what you made me do." His face was as detached and passive as his voice, his eyes half-closed. "I hate you for making me use my ability like that."

"Making you?" Anger rushed in to replace the hurt and confusion. It was easier to get angry than to deal with the pain of hearing my Bond member tell me he hates me. "I'm a hundred-and-thirty-pound science nerd. You're two hundred and fifty pounds of pure muscle. I couldn't *make* you do shit if I tried."

I lifted myself over him as I spoke, my hands on either side of his head. My hair fell in a messy heap over one shoulder. His eyes opened wider as he watched me, his anger rising to meet mine.

"You don't fucking understand anything, *Eve*." He sneered at me, spitting my name out as if it left a bad taste in his mouth. I was no longer Evie—my honey-voiced stranger was gone.

"No, I don't," I barked back at him. "I don't understand at all what your fucking problem is. We saved people's lives. I refuse to feel bad about that."

"Regardless of what it does to me, right? Regardless of the fact that it makes me into an even bigger *monster* than I already am? You've got three other guys foaming at the mouth to get into your pants and at your Light. What's one less?"

"What the fuck are you talking about?"

"Forget about it," he growled, his face twisted by anger and some other baffling emotion. He tried to raise himself up, but I had gotten really good at recognizing when he was about to run away, and I wouldn't let him.

I planted my hands on his shoulders and shoved him back down. My movement took him off guard, and he fell back, fixing me with a murderous expression as his hands flew to my hips as if to throw me off.

But he paused.

My body had shifted when I shoved him, and my leg had moved farther over his thighs, higher up. I could feel him getting hard under me. In complete contrast to his harsh words and angry looks, his erection was pressing into my thigh. Very high on my thigh. Just short of where I actually wanted it.

Feeling the undeniable evidence of his arousal had liquid heat pooling between my legs, and suddenly anger was no longer the only cause of my quickening pulse.

For a beat we stared daggers at each other, breathing hard, and then he bucked his hips slightly, rubbing his erection against my leg. The movement was subtle yet deliberate—it was a challenge, and I was not about to back down. Not one bit of me wanted to.

I didn't know who was more fucked up. We both had been turned on twice today—a day several people had lost their lives. But was he worse for thrusting into me, or was I worse for liking it and responding?

Purposely, I rolled my hips, grinding against him, and his mouth fell open in shock. He hadn't been expecting me to meet his challenge.

We leaned into each other, our lips crashing together as ferociously at they had hours before in the rain, our tongues fighting for dominance. His strong hands shoved my hips so that I was exactly where I wanted to be, and I moaned into his mouth. He met my moan with a guttural growl of his own.

We were frantic, our hands all over each other, grabbing, pulling, tugging, our hips finding a frenzied rhythm. He pulled away from my lips, yanking the left strap of my bra down and leaning forward to wrap his hot mouth over my nipple. His other hand remained on my ass, guiding me.

He groped my breast, holding it to his mouth, and sucked on my nipple with the perfect amount of pressure, eliciting another moan from me.

I wanted to taste him again.

I pulled away, causing us both to sit up, and mashed my mouth to his swollen lips. He continued to knead my breast, running his thumb over my nipple.

My skin felt as if it were on fire, and I opened one eye, momentarily paranoid that I'd gone nuclear again. Satisfied that my skin wasn't glowing, I reached one arm over his shoulder and raked my nails up his back. I was not gentle.

He grunted and bucked into me almost violently, sucking on my bottom lip, taking it between his teeth. He was not gentle either.

I wanted more. I wanted to chase whatever this frenzied feeling was—to forget about all the shit that had happened today.

I was only wearing leggings, and he was still in his thin workout shorts, so there wasn't a lot of fabric between us, but I wanted there to be less. None. I wanted to feel all of him.

I shoved him back down onto the couch and started kissing and biting his neck, trailing my hand over his incredible body and down to the waistband of his shorts. I had just lifted my hips and was about to slip my hand down between us when he slapped it away. I didn't have a chance to be confused though; in the next moment, he flipped us over, pushing one knee between my legs and pinning me to the couch with his body.

He started kissing me again as he did to me what I'd just tried to do to him. He dragged his hand over my breasts and down my front before pushing his hand into my pants.

He didn't tease me or try to build me up. He knew I was turned on and ready for it. He groaned when he felt how wet I was, and then he pushed two fingers straight inside and started moving them.

The suddenness of his fingers inside me, stretching me, made me inhale sharply, and he pulled away, kissing and licking down my throat. The way he touched me was nothing like the few high school boys I had been with in the past, who had been as unsure of what I would like as I had been.

Alec was a man who knew exactly what he was doing. He touched me deliberately, with confidence in every movement.

It felt fucking incredible.

I moaned again, throwing back my head and arching my back. My breath was getting more shallow and erratic, and I clawed at his shoulder as if I was trying to bring him closer. As if I was scared he would stop what he was doing to me and leave.

But he wasn't stopping. He set a steady, punishing rhythm, barely pulling his fingers out before driving them back in. The heel of his hand was grinding into my clit, and I couldn't stop my hips from rolling into his movements.

I bit down on his shoulder as my abdominal muscles tensed and other, internal muscles pulsed around Alec's fingers. An intense, almost savage orgasm spread from my core, sending waves of heat throughout my body and making me go still under his expert hands.

He kissed me roughly as I moaned my release into his mouth, stroking me a few more times as I came down off my high. Then he extracted his hand from my pants and rested his forehead on my shoulder, both of us panting.

It took me a few moments to calm down, to stop gasping as if I'd just been on a run. But when I did, I reached for his waistband again, eager to return the favor, to wrap my hand around his warm, hard . . .

But he slapped my arm away *again* and lifted himself onto his hands.

Our positions had reversed. Now he was the one balanced above me, looking down into my flushed face. I frowned, but that impassive look had fallen over his face again.

"Don't worry about it," he said in answer to my silent question. "I don't want *anything* from you."

He pushed himself up to stand next to the couch, his back to me, and stretched his arms over his head. The muscles in his back lengthened, his tattoos dancing with the movement, and I raked my eyes down his impressive form, lingering on his ass. My treacherous body wanted more.

What the fuck was wrong with me?

"What . . ." I breathed, still a little winded, and raised myself onto my elbows. Anger was bubbling up again, and his sudden disappearance from on top of me had left my flushed body cold.

He half turned toward me, adjusted his very prominent erection, and smirked, raising the eyebrow with the scar through it. Then he walked over to the door.

He smirked. He fucking *smirked* at me.

"You are such a fucking asshole!" I yelled after him as he disappeared through the door.

I reached over to the side table, picked up the first thing my hand landed on, and hurled it in his general direction. It shattered into a million pieces against the wall; whatever it was had been glass.

I growled, this time in frustration, as I flopped back onto the couch and threaded my fingers into my hair.

Footsteps echoed through the foyer—someone running, probably to investigate the yelling and the smashing. In some vain attempt to preserve my dignity, I scrambled for the blanket that had fallen to the ground.

Tyler came bursting through the door, sliding to a stop in his socks on the marble. He was in a baggy T-shirt and sweats, his brown hair even messier than usual.

His frantic eyes took in the glass littering the floor and me sitting on the couch, the blanket held up to cover my front, my hair disheveled, my lips swollen. It wouldn't have taken a genius to figure out what Alec and I had just been up to.

"Oh my god, Eve. Are you OK? What did he do?"

I averted my eyes and sat straighter on the couch, pulling my bra strap back into place and tucking the blanket securely under my arms.

"Nothing I didn't want him to," I murmured, the humiliation settling heavily over me. "I'm sorry about the . . . um, whatever that used to be. I'll replace it."

Tyler stepped gingerly over the glass and swept his messy brown hair off his forehead, coming to sit next to me on the couch. "It was just an ugly paperweight. Don't worry about it."

"OK. I'll clean up my mess." I made to get up, but Tyler placed a firm hand on my shoulder.

"Eve." He leveled a stern look at me.

"Don't," I whispered into my lap. "Please, Ty. I just can't . . . I can only handle so much, and I need to table this particular mess for now."

He sighed. "As long as you're OK."

"I'm OK. I promise. This can wait." I was so *not* OK, but I was really not ready to talk about it.

"Well, OK then." He gave me a weak smile. He knew I was lying, obviously, but something in my face must have told him not to press me. "If you want me to kick his ass, you just tell me. I'll get Josh to hold him down with his ability."

I chuckled, but it was weak. I couldn't find it in me to laugh, but I appreciated him trying to ease the tension. "What time is it? Is it too late to go see Zara in the hospital?"

"It's just after five. I'm sure we can make it before visiting hours end."

"OK. Can I use your bathroom? I really need a shower first."

"Of course." He stood and then paused. "There's something else . . ."

"What?" I stood too, my senses on alert. What now? Hadn't the past twenty-four hours been shitty enough?

He must have read the trepidation on my face, because he turned and walked out, speaking over his shoulder. "Never mind. Shower first. Ten minutes won't change anything."

"OK." I didn't have the will to argue.

He led the way upstairs and into the room across the hall from Josh's. I had never been in his room before. It was the mirror image of the one opposite—bed on the left, sitting area with fireplace on the right. It was decorated in a lighter, more neutral palette—the sheets were crisp white and made with military precision, the heavy drapes a cream color.

I followed him straight to the bathroom door, and he held it open for me.

"Help yourself to anything."

He made to leave, but I stopped him with a soft touch on his forearm.

"Thank you, Tyler." Before thinking about it too much, I leaned up, holding the blanket in place with one hand, and placed a chaste kiss on his cheek.

He cleared his throat and rubbed the back of his head. "It's just a bathroom." He chuckled but paused, his gray eyes returning my serious look.

We both knew I wasn't talking about the shower. He had shot a man to protect me—Tyler had literally killed for me. He had been my protector and defender through and through. I needed him to know I wasn't taking it for granted.

"What you did today . . ." I swallowed around the lump in my throat. "There are no words to express—"

"You're welcome," he whispered back, cutting off my rambling before it could even begin.

With a promise to hunt down some clothes for me, he backed away and left me to shower.

TWENTY-SEVEN

Fifteen minutes later I almost felt human again.

I used Tyler's shampoo and conditioner to get the knots and filth out of my hair. When I came out, wrapped in a towel, a ladies tank top and yoga pants were laid out on the bed, as well as a large, definitely not ladies hoodie.

Trying not to think too much about why a house full of men had women's clothes on hand, I dressed quickly and made my way downstairs, slipping the hoodie on as I went. A faint hint of expensive cologne and the scent of fresh air that lingered when clothing was dried outside in the sun wrapped around me. I paused halfway down and took a long inhale, bringing the fabric up to my nose and thinking of Josh.

I found them all sitting around the large dining table off the kitchen. Even Alec had reappeared—he was in fresh clothing and his hair was damp, apparently having showered himself. He was hunched over a laptop and didn't even spare me a glance.

"Hey." I smiled weakly at the other three boys, all of whom looked up when I entered, and I stared daggers at Alec's impassive face before sitting down between Tyler and Ethan. Ethan's hand went straight to my knee.

"How are you feeling?" Tyler asked, leaning back in his chair and giving me a warm smile.

"The shower helped. Thanks." His question was loaded. It could have been referring to what had happened between Alec and me in the study, all the violence we had witnessed and been a part of that day, or the fact that one of my friends was dead. But I chose to keep it simple and focus on the physical. I felt like shit, but physically, the shower had made me feel better.

Josh's foot nudged mine under the table, and I looked up into his intense stare. Those intelligent green eyes read exactly what I'd left unsaid; he knew I wasn't OK, but I was hoping he wouldn't push me to admit it. I stretched my legs farther and let them entwine with his as I gave him a pleading look.

A sad little smile played at his lips for a moment before he spoke. "Nice hoodie."

It was the perfect thing to say, and it even made me smile a little. I wrapped my arms around myself and inhaled exaggeratedly. "Thanks. It's a bit big, but I think I might keep it. I like how it smells." I said the last part softly, almost to myself, but everyone heard.

Alec finally lifted his head from his screen, glancing between Josh and me and frowning before going back to ignoring us.

I chose to ignore him too, focusing my attention on Josh's feet playing with mine under the table; Ethan's warm hand on my knee, rubbing gentle circles with his thumb; and Tyler's watchful gaze. At that moment, their unspoken support made me feel much better than talking about my confused feelings would have.

"All right," I said with a sigh, planting my elbows on the table. "Lay it on me."

Three sets of eyes averted their gaze.

"Shit. Guys, what is it?"

That little tingle of panic was welling up again. I sat up a little straighter, my senses on alert.

As usual, Tyler took the lead. "Charlie was taken."

"What? What do you mean *taken*?" But even as I asked, my mind rehashed the encounter in the woods—the weird beeping machine, the two black-clad, armed men stepping toward me menacingly.

Grab her.

Then I remembered the Variant girl forming icicles from the rain and the boy, her Vital, being dragged away by another two assailants.

Tyler explained even as my mind connected the dots. "It seems that causing chaos and baiting the Variants into a reaction wasn't the only aim of the attack. In all the confusion, a total of twenty-seven Vitals were abducted. Charlie was one of them. Unnervingly, they knew exactly which people had the Light and were very efficient in capturing them before the bulk of the violence even got to its peak."

He pointed to a familiar device, black and sleek with a small handle, sitting on the table in among some other stuff and papers.

"Whomever they were working with or for has developed a technology that is capable of identifying a Vital. It's how they were able to home in on them so fast."

"Shit." The breath rushed out of me, and I stared at the black device on the table. I knew this could potentially have some very serious ramifications for me and my guys, but all I could think about was Dot.

Charlie was her brother *and* her Vital. I had no siblings and had never been close enough to anyone growing up to know what that was like, but I did have a Bond of my own. In a way, that was a kind of family.

A sharp pain pierced my chest at the thought of one of my guys being taken from me. Even Alec. As much as he railed against it, as much as he'd been a total asshole to me only half an hour ago, he was still mine. He was part of my Bond. I was his Vital, and the Light inside me was not OK with the idea of him being taken away.

Then I remembered how the girl with the icicles and her Vital had been taken out, and I began to panic for Dot's well-being. I couldn't lose another friend today.

I pressed a hand to my chest, my breaths getting shallower, and looked frantically around the table from one somber expression to the next. "Dot . . ."

"She's OK," Tyler hurriedly said, reaching a hand out to me. I breathed a sigh of relief and took it gratefully, finding comfort in his touch. "She was knocked out, but she's fine. They're just keeping her in the hospital in case she has a concussion."

I squeezed Tyler's hand, then released it to run my hands through my hair. Taking a deep breath to calm myself, I leaned on the table again, trying to decide which question to ask first. "So, this was all about abducting Vitals?"

"No." Tyler shook his head sadly. "I was updated by the agents still on the scene about fifteen minutes ago.

We were in the thick of it, but assailants were attacking people all over campus. There are a hundred and eighteen confirmed fatalities and one hundred and ninety-two people hospitalized. But they're still counting."

"Holy shit," Ethan breathed. Across from me, Josh was shaking his head in disbelief, his eyes wide. Alec just continued to tap away at his computer, unaffected—he would have received the same updates.

"If this was just about abducting Vitals, they would have done it more quietly," Tyler continued. "It just doesn't make tactical sense to kill that many people when they were clearly well trained and highly organized. They used the carnage as a cover, but that wasn't the only reason for it."

"Then what? Who did this? Why?" Frustration was leaking into my voice. I couldn't fathom what could possibly motivate someone to do this.

"The massacre—all those people running around with guns, shooting anything that moved—that was the Human Empowerment Network. They weren't as well organized as the guys in black or as well armed, but they were united in their hate for Variants. They released a video about an hour ago taking responsibility for it. It's just their leader, someone they're calling Mr. X, in a mask spewing ignorant, hateful things at the camera, but the message is clear. The Human Empowerment Network is growing, and they're becoming militant. They're a much bigger threat than we realized."

"And the Vital abductions?"

"That was Variant Valor." Tyler ran his own hand through his hair. I took a closer look at him—he was in sweats and a T-shirt, his hair messier than usual, and big circles drooped under his eyes. He had been home long enough to shower but not long enough to sleep. While Alec and I were in each other's arms, letting the Light restore us, Tyler had been working his ass off to figure out what had happened, to keep us safe. He was spent.

"They haven't made any dramatic public statements about being involved," he went on. "That would defy the point of using the chaos to cover up the abductions. But we have intelligence that suggests it was Variant Valor." He shared a look with Alec, and I knew he wouldn't be saying much more on that front—clearly that information was classified.

"I can't go into details," he confirmed. "But the fact they were so well organized and armed—that alone points to Variant Valor. Plus I had an inkling of it while I still had excess Light." He pointed to his head. He couldn't share classified information, but we were his Bond, and he was willing to bend the rules to share what he'd learned through his ability.

Josh asked the most important question. "What do they want with the Vitals, Gabe?"

"We don't know." Tyler sighed. "We've been trying to figure that out since we noticed a pattern a year ago. There are a few theories, but we're not any closer to finding an answer. They've never been this brazen about it though. They've taken twenty-seven Vitals at once. Rumors have been flying around about the strange Vital disappearances around the world, but this won't go unnoticed. Whatever it is they're doing, they're gearing up for something big."

"Are you sure it's Variant Valor doing this?" I asked. Why would Variants abduct Vitals? Why would we do this to ourselves? It wasn't adding up.

Tyler and Alec shared another look before Ty answered, "That's classified."

So they *were* sure it was Variant Valor, but he technically wasn't allowed to tell us that, or how they knew.

"So, what?" Ethan was frowning at the table in front of him, his hand still firmly on my knee. "The human psychos and the Variant psychos are working together now?"

"No, we don't think so. Variant Valor probably just learned what the humans were planning and used it to their advantage, to cover up what they wanted to do. Look"—Tyler's voice became very firm—"I can't really tell you three much more. I've already said too much, but that's only because I want you to understand the gravity of the situation. The stakes have been raised, and people are really scared. This is only the beginning."

None of us were willing to push for more information now that Tyler had put his foot down, although, judging by Ethan and Josh's questions, they knew as little as I did. That made me feel somewhat better. I didn't want to be the only one out of the loop—especially in *my* Bond.

My mind was racing, struggling to make sense of it all while new questions constantly popped up. Both the Human Empowerment Network and Variant Valor had proven themselves to be very real threats. While the boys' initial insistence that we keep our Bond a secret had seemed overly dramatic and unnecessary at the time, after everything I had seen and experienced that day—and everything Tyler had told us—I completely understood it now.

I would take the secret of our Bond to the grave if it meant keeping us safe—if it meant protecting my Variants.

The table had gone quiet, everyone left to their own morbid thoughts. The soft sound of Alec tapping away on his laptop was the only sound in the room.

Josh broke the silence. "How did you explain all the unconscious people on campus?"

"I didn't." Tyler smirked. "I pulled rank and told them it was classified while putting on my authoritarian voice and ordering our operatives to do what needed to be done—helping the injured, gathering evidence, and so on."

"What about security cameras? Surely something would have recorded me transferring Light to you all." I clasped my hands in front of me, anxiety wrapping around my throat. It was only a matter of time . . .

"That's one thing that worked in our favor," Tyler answered. "They didn't just block the cell signal. All electronics were down—anything with a chip or a power cord was useless. I suspect they had a Variant with an ability to manipulate electronics."

"Won't all the people who passed out have some questions?" Ethan asked.

"Of course, but no one saw anything in the chaos, and then all they could focus on was the pain. The only people *I* need to answer to weren't present, and Lucian should be able to take care of them anyway."

"You told Uncle Lucian?" Ethan sounded shocked.

All of us snapped our heads up to look at Tyler, even Alec. It was a little disconcerting to know another person had learned our secret so soon after realizing why it was so important to keep it hidden.

Tyler nodded, fixing us each with a meaningful look but holding Alec's gaze the longest. "He already knew. He was giving us space, waiting for us to come to him when we were ready."

"Shit," Josh cursed softly.

"I trust him." Tyler shrugged.

They all murmured their agreement. They weren't worried about Lucian Zacarias betraying us; they were just surprised Tyler had told him.

It had been good to get some more information, but I'd spent the whole conversation keeping an eye on the time. I had to make sure I made it to the hospital before visiting hours were over.

I stood from my seat. "I need to see Zara and Dot. Can we continue this later?"

Ethan and Josh got up at the same time.

"Of course," Tyler said with a yawn. "I really need to get some sleep anyway. The boys will take you."

"While the men do the important things," Alec cut in, speaking for the first time since I'd entered the room.

"What is up your ass, man?" Ethan frowned. "You're even more surly than usual."

Josh just leaned in the doorway, watching everything as he usually did, not looking even slightly put off by his manhood being questioned.

Alec scoffed and tried to go back to ignoring us all, but if he was going to drop passive aggressive comments like that, I wasn't going to just let it go.

I leaned my palms on the table and spoke directly at him. "You may not think that other people are important, but some of us are actually capable of normal human connections. And *you* may not want anything from me"—I threw his words back at him—"but there are others who do."

He fixed me with an angry glare, but I didn't wait for him to respond, turning around and walking toward the door. The boys followed, as I knew they would.

Tyler called after us, "Kid, if anyone so much as looks at her funny, you fry them to a crisp and get the hell out of there."

"Goes without saying, Gabe," Ethan called back, overtaking me and leading the way into the garage.

Josh kept pace with me. "What was that about? And don't try to tell me it was nothing. You don't usually let him bait you like that."

I didn't say anything, hoping he would drop it, but he gently grabbed my hand so I couldn't run away. I mentally checked that my Light was under control, but it was out of habit more than anything. I'd expelled all I had to get Alec recharged—now was the safest time for them to touch me, and they weren't being shy about it.

"Something happened between you two in Tyler's study."

So much for him dropping it. Of course he'd figured out something more was up, but even Josh wasn't omniscient. He knew something big had happened, but he didn't know what.

"Josh, I don't want to talk about it. Please." It was bad enough that Tyler had seen the aftermath. I didn't need Josh and Ethan knowing how a member of my own Bond had hurt me in the most humiliating way.

I fixed him with a firm look, trying to pull my hand out of his, but he held on and pulled me back to his side. He watched me with concern in his eyes for a moment. Then he kissed me gently, sighing against my lips.

TWENTY-EIGHT

The drive to the hospital was quiet. They'd tried again to ask me what was going on with Alec as soon as we were on the road, but I shut it down, crossing my arms stubbornly and staring out the window.

It was hard to stay even a little mad at them though. Especially when they were touching me. They seemed to instinctively know there wasn't as much danger from my Light. Josh wrapped his hand around mine, prying it away from my chest, and Ethan leaned on the back of my seat, running his fingers through my hair.

As we reached the hospital though, they dropped it, and I was glad they did. I needed to focus on Zara and Dot. My personal shit wasn't going to get in the way of me being there for my friends.

We were a little surprised when the receptionist told us they were in the same room. I cringed, hoping they weren't making this whole situation worse on themselves by bickering, as they usually did.

Josh thanked her and took the lead down the hall. Now that we were in public, he was making sure to keep his hands off me. The events of the last twenty-four hours had been sobering—we had to be more careful. Ethan wrapped his arm around my waist, and I returned the side hug as we followed Josh into the elevators.

On the third floor, we walked together down the corridor, my guys flanking me like silent sentinels, but before we reached the door, I paused, wringing my hands.

Ethan draped an arm over my shoulder, but it was Josh who spoke from my other side.

"You got this, Eve."

He knew I was nervous. I had been keen to get to my friends to make sure they were OK, but now that I was actually here, I had no idea what I was supposed to do. I had no experience with having friends, let alone comforting them during a difficult time.

"Just be there," Ethan added.

I nodded and took a breath, squaring my shoulders. I could do this. If I could deal with Alec, I could deal with this.

With one final reminder to myself to put that asshole out of my mind, I raised my arm to knock on the door, but it swung open in front of me.

Dot and Charlie's mom stepped through it. Her face was streaked with tears, the mascara running down her cheeks, and her messy hair looked as if she'd run her hands through it a million times. Shoulders hunched, she looked up at me—or rather, *through* me—and blinked a few times.

"I'm getting coffee," she said in a detached voice.

"Mrs. Vanderford?" I placed a gentle hand on her shoulder.

She seemed to snap out of it, shaking her head lightly, some amount of clarity returning to her eyes.

"Oh, Eve." She drew me into a tight hug. "I'm glad you're here. They could both use a friend right now." Her voice broke on the last word, but she pulled away, making a visible effort to compose herself.

"I wouldn't be anywhere else. I just can't believe . . . Charlie . . ." My own voice was breaking as I struggled to find the words.

"How are you, Olivia?" Josh asked, saving me from having to find a way to finish.

"Is there anything we can do?" Ethan piped in.

"You're doing plenty by just being here," she replied in her shaky voice. "And we're holding up as well as can be expected. Lucian has already been in touch. He's furious, and he's promised to throw the full force of Melior Group at this. Knowing that something is already being done about it is helping. Henry is on the phone with him in the waiting room around the corner. I was just on my way to get us some coffee."

"Uncle Lucian won't rest until we find him, Aunt Olivia." Ethan stepped forward and wrapped his aunt up in one of his massive hugs.

"I know, sweetie." She sniffled. "I'll let you go see the girls. They shouldn't be alone."

She squeezed Josh's hand as she went past, her heels clicking on the gray floor.

I turned back to the door, taking a deep breath and wiping my eyes before pushing inside.

There were two beds in the sterile room, pushed up against the right wall, but I was surprised to find one of them empty. Zara and Dot were both in the bed closest to the window. Zara was lying under the covers, tubes sticking out of her arms, and Dot was sitting next to her, her knees pulled up.

They both looked in my direction, and I tried my best to hide my shocked expression. Not that I needed to.

As soon as she saw me, Dot flew off the bed and ran into my arms. We hugged tightly, just standing there, trying to find comfort in the embrace. Her delicate shoulders bobbed up and down softly as she cried. I'd been around her plenty of times without her massive heels on and knew just how short she was, but standing in the hospital room hugging her, she truly felt tiny in my arms—more fragile than I'd ever imagined my confident friend could be.

She pulled away slightly without letting go, and I saw she wasn't wearing any makeup either. Another first. Her bare face was splotchy and covered in tears.

"Charlie—" she croaked.

"I know," I cut in, saving her having to repeat it. "I'm so sorry, Dot. I can't even imagine."

Her face got a faraway look, and I guided her by the shoulders back to Zara's bed.

Zara watched us, silent tears soaking her pillow. With one last squeeze, I released Dot and slowly climbed onto the bed. I enfolded Zara in a much gentler hug, wary of hurting her, but she wrapped her arms around my neck tightly, and my own tears finally overflowed.

We held each other and cried for Beth—our beautiful friend who hadn't deserved this. An innocent, sweet girl who'd been dragged into a conflict that had nothing to do with her. She'd been there only because she was brave and wanted to warn people, and she'd ended up as collateral damage. Just another Dime that got in the way.

I pulled away and wiped my tears with the sleeve of Josh's hoodie.

"We're going to find out who did this," I said quietly, but the steel in my voice surprised even me.

Zara sighed and looked down. She didn't believe me, but she had no energy for a sarcastic reply.

Dot reclaimed her spot next to Zara, and I ended up sitting in the middle with my legs tucked under me, facing them. They were both staring into space, lost in thoughts of loved ones ripped away from them. I knew all too well how that felt.

"I'm a Vital," I blurted, and they both looked at me, a little confused.

I was trying to distract them, but I was also sick of secrets. If today had taught me anything, it was that life was precious and could be taken away at any moment. I'd lived my whole life lonely. Now I had two friends sitting in front of me, and I wanted them to know me. All of me.

"I know you guys already know that," I went on. Dot had figured it out ages ago, and Zara had put it together when I'd transferred Light to Tyler earlier that day. "But it feels good to say it. Do you want to know who's in my Bond?"

"Ethan," they both replied at the same time, but Zara added, "And Tyler Gabriel."

Dot looked at her in shock. "No, it's *Josh* as well as Ethan." Her eyes darted between Zara and me in confusion, the conviction in Zara's voice tripping her up.

"No," Zara replied. "It's *Tyler* and Ethan."

"You're both right," I piped in, stopping an argument before it started.

Zara gasped, lifting the hand not hooked up to an IV to cover her mouth in shock. "Ethan, Tyler, *and* Josh?"

I nodded, pressing my lips together and bugging my eyes out.

"Holy shit," Dot breathed. "Three Variants? That's so rare."

Sheepishly I raised my hand, holding up four fingers.

"*Four*?!" They spoke at the same time again, and I briefly wondered how they could be so hostile to each other. They were much more similar than they thought.

I nodded as they stared at me, mouths hanging slightly open. Having three Variants in a Bond was rare; four was almost unheard of.

"No, please, take your time in telling us who the fourth is. It's not like we're on the edge of our seats or anything." Zara managed to cock an eyebrow, and I smiled, glad to see some of her spunk back. I'd made the right decision in telling them, even if it made them forget for only a few minutes.

Dot gasped dramatically before I could speak. "In the square that day. You didn't get a headache."

She'd figured it out. I smiled at her and nodded. "Alec."

"As in Zacarias?" Zara asked for confirmation. "Kid's cousin. Brooding. Always wears black and scowls at people. Master of Pain. *That* Alec?"

"That's the one."

"Shut the fuck up. I don't believe you."

"I do," Dot cut in. "His power didn't affect her. I saw it with my own eyes. I can't believe I didn't put two and two together! Such an idiot! It's so obvious."

"Uh, no." Zara crossed her arms over her chest. "It's not. I've been living with this lying bitch for the last few months, and I had no clue she was even a Vital until today. It's like you've been living a double life."

"I'm so sorry for lying to you." I looked at her uneasily, feeling guilty. "It was not easy. And I felt like you could see straight through me every time I did. I was so awkward!"

She shrugged it off. "It's OK. I get why you're all keeping it on the down low. Especially considering . . ." She glanced over at Dot.

Dot began to cry again, her shoulders quivering, and I wrapped her hand in mine. Zara surprised me by grabbing her other hand.

Before I had a chance to say anything, though, Josh and Ethan walked in and announced that visiting hours were over. A stern-looking nurse was kicking people out, and they wanted to be gone before she set her sights on us.

Dot and Zara stared at them, my revelations heavy in their gazes. The guys shared a look.

Ethan crossed his muscled arms over his chest and frowned. "What?"

Instead of answering him, Zara looked at me. "You're going to have your hands full, girl. I don't know if I'm worried about your reputation or just jealous."

"Eew." Dot whacked her, but very gently. "You know I'm related to two of them, right?"

"What the hell are they talking about?" Ethan demanded, but instead of answering him, Dot climbed off the bed and gave him a hug. Ethan hugged his cousin gently, his big frame making her appear even smaller in his arms.

Josh made his way over to Zara's bed and spoke quietly to her. I heard them talking about her parents—they'd been in Canada at the time of the attack but had started heading to Bradford Hills as soon as they heard their daughter was in the hospital.

After a few moments, the boys swapped. Josh gave Dot a comforting hug while Ethan surprised me by propping himself on the edge of Zara's bed and leaning down to gently embrace her as well.

They'd had their differences in the past, but none of that petty shit mattered anymore. Not when Charlie was missing. Not when Beth was dead.

The stern nurse bustled in not long after and insisted we clear out, also ordering Dot back into her own bed. I gave the girls another tight hug each and, with a promise to come back the next day, left with my guys.

As soon as we were in the car, Josh turned to me. "You told them?"

"Told who what?" Ethan asked from the back seat.

"*Whom*," Josh corrected, keeping his eyes on me.

"Man, screw you and your grammatical shit," Ethan griped but with humor in his voice. "Tell me!"

I bit my bottom lip, worried I was in trouble for spilling our secret. It was done now, though, and I couldn't find it in me to feel bad. I'd shared something real about myself with my friends. Friends whom I cared enough about to feel their pain over what had happened to them today. Friends who cared enough about *me* to want to know this about me.

So I just nodded at him and turned away, strapping myself in.

"Eve told Zara and Dot about us. Our Bond," Josh filled Ethan in as he pulled out of the parking spot.

Ethan whistled from the back seat but didn't say anything.

"They already knew most of it anyway. Dot's known for ages, and Zara saw me with you and Ty today. I only filled in the gaps." I shrugged. "I trust them."

"It's OK. We were never going to be able to keep it secret forever." Josh reached over the center console to hold my hand as he drove.

"Yeah, I want everyone to know you're mine anyway." Ethan stuck his head in between our seats to give me a wink and a flash of his dimples. Of course, we all knew we needed to keep our Bond secret from "everyone" for as long as possible, but I still appreciated the sentiment.

"*Ours*," Josh corrected him for the second time in five minutes. "And everyone already thinks you're dating."

"Bro, it's not the same."

As they bickered lightheartedly over the semantics, I settled back into the seat and smiled to myself. I'd just come from seeing two people I could truly call my friends. I was a Vital with *four* guys in my Bond—four people I'd apparently known from birth.

It had been a bumpy couple of months, but I'd somehow found myself surrounded by people who cared about me, who knew me. I was beginning to learn what it felt like to have a family.

I belonged.

For the first time in my life, I was realizing that feeling as though you belong somewhere has nothing to do with geography. It didn't matter how many times my mother and I had moved, or that I'd never felt sentimental attachment to a family home. Belonging has nothing to do with that and everything to do with the people who make you *feel* as though you belong with them.

I had found my people.

Everything was still fucked up. Beth was dead. Charlie was missing. There was scary new tech that could out me as a Vital. There was a terrifying web of manipulation and ulterior motives, players I didn't have a scrap of knowledge about pulling strings behind stages I didn't even know existed.

And don't get me started on the most frustrating, worrisome, annoying asshole problem of all—Alec.

Yes, everything was a mess, but I had found where I *belonged*, and I refused to not be pleased about it.

EPILOGUE

The room was sparse but clean, the walls white, the two metal cots bolted to the floor. There was a toilet and a small sink in one corner.

Three times per day, two black-clad men pushed a trolley down the hallway and one of them slid a tray of bland food through a slot in the door.

Two times per day, two black-clad men accompanied another man or woman wearing a lab coat and carrying a clipboard. The lab coats peered into the room, pressed buttons on the panel next to the door, took notes, and moved away.

Five times per day Charlie tried to get answers from his regular visitors. As soon as he heard movement, he sprang off his thin mattress and rushed forward to the long, thin pane of glass set into the heavy door.

Charlie pleaded and asked questions, yelled and demanded answers. He had tried every way of speaking to them. He was always ignored.

He'd been in his white prison for three full days. He had no idea how long he'd been unconscious before that. A few days at least, judging by the amount of Light coursing through him. His arms and legs were almost constantly itchy, and it was spreading to his torso. Wandering around the bare room nude was beginning to seem like a good idea.

The mechanical clank of the door unlocking startled him, and he sat up. It wasn't time for food, and the last lab coat had come past only twenty-eight minutes and forty seconds ago.

For the first time since Charlie was dragged inside the cell half-conscious, the door opened. Charlie stood, unsure what to do. Should he dash forward, try to escape, or should he back away from the men with the large guns now entering the room?

At least the guns weren't pointed at him—they were slung over the shoulders of the two men half carrying, half dragging another man into the room. The new prisoner was wearing the same shapeless gray pants and top that Charlie had woken up in.

The two men dumped the unconscious form onto the bed and left the room without even acknowledging Charlie's presence. He rushed to the door and watched as the guards retreated down the empty hallway.

Moving back to the other bed, Charlie immediately started checking his new roommate. He knew just enough first aid to determine if the injuries were life threatening. After rolling the unconscious young man onto his back

Charlie checked his air passage and heartbeat. He was alive. With careful fingers, Charlie started checking for broken bones, moving the gray fabric out of the way to look for bruising. There weren't any obvious injuries, but there was no way to check for internal bleeding.

Even though the young man didn't look beaten or tortured, he hadn't regained consciousness, and his light brown hair was a mess, his skin clammy.

What the hell did they do to you? Charlie thought, running his hands through his own hair in frustration.

The sound of voices drew his attention back to the door. He stood facing it, putting himself between whatever was on the other side and the unconscious man on the bed.

" . . . shouldn't even be here!" a woman's voice carried clearly. "If I'm seen anywhere near this—"

"Why did you come then?" a deep man's voice interrupted her, sounding completely unfazed.

"Because you weren't taking my calls!" she yelled, frustration building in her voice by the second. "It's been over a week since that mess at Bradford Hills. I didn't agree to that many casualties. I *certainly* didn't agree to the Vital kidnappings."

A week? His family would be worried sick. Dot would be beside herself. At the thought of his sister, his Variant, Charlie's chest ached. It wasn't the consuming pain that came when she overused her ability and he needed to get to her. It was a longing—a need to be home.

He had no way of knowing if she was OK. All he remembered was trying to get to one of the residence hall buildings that was under construction, close to where they'd separated from Gabe, Ethan, and Eve. It would have been empty, a good place to hide. But halfway there, Dot crumpled to the ground next to him, her hand slipping out of his. Charlie had turned just in time to see the butt of a rifle coming at his face.

He knew now he'd spent the next few days unconscious and been moved to wherever this hellhole was. But he had no way of knowing what had happened to Dot. He was trying not to think about it.

He forced himself to focus on the voices in the corridor. He was getting more information from this one overheard conversation than he had from all the pleading with his impassive guards.

"Come now, Christine, you didn't think I would expend those kinds of resources without getting something out of it?" The man chuckled darkly. There was something familiar about his voice.

Charlie inched closer to the door, trying to catch a glimpse of the man's face, but it was the woman he recognized first. She came to a stop right in front of his cell, turning to face her companion.

"You're fucking deranged. What the hell even is this place?" Senator Christine Anderson screeched. She threw her arms up, looking around. The last time Charlie had seen her was the night of the gala as she'd stood on the stage and delivered her speech, waxing eloquent about her personal and professional mission to solidify peace and cooperation between Variants and humans, then announcing her intention to run for president.

"You want the presidency?" The man no longer sounded amused. "Well, nothing motivates voters like fear. Correct me if I'm wrong, but your poll numbers skyrocketed the day after the Bradford Hills invasion and have remained high. The fact that I used the opportunity to collect some assets for *my* interests is of no consequence. You will have the oval office, and I will have your cooperation as the leader of the free world when you do. Everything else is semantics. Now, calm down."

"*Assets.* You say it like you signed a contract for delivery of stock, not like you kidnapped nearly thirty Vitals in one day." Her voice had lowered, but she wasn't backing down. "Davis, you took Bradford Hills staff; children of prominent, influential Variants; a fucking chart-topping singer! People are going to take notice."

"They were already starting to. I need the Vitals. It's done now."

Davis. Just as the familiar voice and the name clicked into place in Charlie's mind, the man stepped forward, giving him a clear view of the dark hair, peppered with gray at the temples, and the broad shoulders draped in a three-thousand-dollar suit.

Davis Damari. Why was Uncle Lucian's business partner doing this?

Charlie had met the man on several occasions, usually at glitzy Variant events, a few times when Davis had been invited to dinner by Charlie's dad or Uncle Lucian. Surely Uncle Lucian didn't know anything about this?

Of course, Melior Group knew how to skirt the lines of legality—Charlie had no illusions about that, having done some slightly shady hacking work for them in the past. *But this . . .*

"What do you need the Vitals for? Stop evading my questions." There was more steel in Christine's voice now.

"Once I succeed, no one will even bat an eye at the methods. What's a couple of abductions and a handful of deaths when at the end of it, the world will be changed? I'm going to fix what science doesn't even understand yet. I'm going to show the world that Variants are meant to *rule* the world."

Charlie gasped and took an involuntary step back, the realization hitting him hard.

He was behind it all. Davis Damari was the one who had been orchestrating the kidnappings of Vitals for over a year. He was the one who'd been stirring up tensions between Variants and humans. He was the leader, maybe even the creator, of Variant Valor.

Charlie's movement caught the pair's attention, and they both turned to look. The senator averted her gaze immediately, recognition and then shame crossing her features.

Davis Damari didn't look at Charlie's face, to try to recognize the *person* in his clutches. He saw only an *asset*. His head cocked to the side slightly as his calculating eyes watched Charlie's twitchy movements. Charlie had been so focused on the conversation he hadn't even realized he was scratching vigorously. One hand was under the ugly gray top, the other trying to get at a spot on his hip.

Davis gestured to someone down the hall, and heavy booted footsteps approached. "This one's ready. Take him up and prep him."

As the sounds of the digital panel and the heavy lock sliding back filled the room once again, Davis turned away. "Come, Senator. We can talk in my office."

Davis Damari continued down the corridor, and Senator Christine Anderson followed him silently, her eyes still averted.

Two guards entered Charlie's room, and all thoughts about what he'd just heard fled his mind. Now, there was only fear.

VITAL FOUND

THE EVELYN MAYNARD TRILOGY
PART TWO

BY KAYDENCE SNOW

PROLOGUE

At the sound of three excited little voices coming up the drive, Joyce smiled, set down her book, and checked her watch. With the others here, Evie and Ethan wouldn't stay asleep much longer. They'd gone down for their nap a little later than usual, but one hour was still good.

Tyler was the first to let himself into the house, Alec hot on his heels.

"Hey, Auntie Joyce!" they yelled in unison, making a beeline for the fridge. At ten and eleven years old, they had more energy than they knew what to do with and needed unbelievable amounts of food to fuel it.

"There's cookies next to the stove," she called after them, coming around the couch.

Amanda came in a few moments later, a five-year-old Josh holding on to her hand.

"Can I have a cookie, Mom?" He looked up, tugging on her arm. It made the Thomas the Tank Engine backpack on her shoulder come loose.

Joyce caught it before it hit the top of little Joshy's head. She took the bulky handbag off her friend's other shoulder and set both down by the door.

"Yes. Go. Eat the cookies." Amanda heaved a massive sigh and then collapsed into a hug with Joyce, who patted her on the back.

"Long day?"

But before they could start their conversation, three-year-old Evie interrupted from the hallway, shuffling from one chubby foot to the other, her chocolate-brown hair a mess. "Mommy, I need to pee."

Joyce took her to the bathroom and put some shorts on her, then headed back to the living room.

Ethan was up too, rubbing his eye by the kitchen island, his favorite stuffed bunny hanging from his other hand; he always took a while to wake up properly. Joyce patted him on the head as she passed, grabbing a yogurt from the fridge for Evie.

"Enough." Amanda lifted the now half-empty plate of cookies high over her head as the two older boys groaned. "You have to eat something other than cookies or your parents will kill us!" She set it down on the island before pouring two mugs of coffee.

Joyce grabbed a cookie, but she paused with it halfway to her mouth and looked down. Ethan was hugging her leg, the bunny still clutched in his hand. He blinked his almost too-big eyes at the cookie, then looked at her and grinned. With those adorable dimples, how could she refuse? She sighed and handed it over.

He dropped the bunny and wrapped both hands around the sweet treat, devouring it.

"You spoil them," Amanda grumbled, perching on one of the stools and taking a long sip of coffee.

Joyce took a sip of her own, keeping an eye on the kids. "I know, but I love it."

After their snack, the children all piled out into the backyard to play. Joyce watched through the kitchen window as the boys broke into a run. Evie lagged behind, her little legs unable to keep up, but Alec shouted for the others to wait and turned around to take her hand in his.

Joyce smiled and pressed a hand to her chest. These kids were so precious, and she knew, she *just knew*, they would be friends for life. Just as all their parents were.

These people were her family—the family she had chosen—and they meant the world to her. She loved the chaos and laughter that came with having a bunch of kids around all the time. She loved how they all took turns watching them, picking them up from school and day care, feeding them, and having sleepovers. She loved Sundays, when they all got together, and it was the best kind of craziness.

And when she was with them, she could almost ignore the awful memories of that night . . .

Not a day went by that she didn't think about what she'd done. Guilt was a permanent part of her life now, choking her as she brushed her teeth in the morning, tightening around her lungs as she played with the kids, casting a dark shadow over joyful meals with close friends. Staying silent was killing her, but what other choice did she have?

All it took to strengthen her resolve was looking into Evelyn's dark blue eyes, so like her own. Joyce couldn't leave her little girl, couldn't stand the thought of her alone in the world. And maybe it was selfish, but she couldn't leave *him* either.

Motherhood had changed her—put things in perspective. Nothing was more important than Evie, and Joyce would protect her—here, beside the people who were her home.

After everything that had happened a few years back, she was finally finding true happiness in the simple pleasures of life.

ONE

I waded into the pool slowly, letting the sparkling water cool my skin and soothe my sore muscles. The midmorning summer sun was already scorching, and I ducked my head under, wading around for a few minutes before settling into a shady corner of the pool and leaning back.

The Zacarias mansion looked even more impressive from this angle. I'd been spending a lot of time there since the end of last school year—since the invasion and Charlie's abduction.

I couldn't quite believe it had been over two months.

It made sense the time had flown—we'd all kept busy. I'd taken a few extra classes to lighten my load for the coming year, and Ethan, Josh, and I had also been getting some additional training, as the guys had decided I needed to learn to defend myself.

With all the Vital abductions and the invasion of Bradford Hills Institute—an icon of the Variant community—I couldn't disagree. No one other than Zara, Dot, Charlie, and the guys' uncle Lucian knew I was a Vital and that Alec, Tyler, Josh, and Ethan were in my Bond. But with the appearance of new technology that could identify a Vital, I was definitely at risk.

Resting my elbows on the edge of the pool, I kicked my legs lazily through the water, wondering how long the large bruise on my left thigh would take to heal. I understood the need to learn self-defense—I just wished the process wasn't so brutal.

Tyler had arranged for an ex-Melior Group operative named Kane to come out several times per week and train us in the fully equipped gym in the basement. He was a Kane by name and a cane by nature, with a stocky build and light brown hair. I wasn't entirely sure how old he was or what color his eyes were, as I was too afraid to make eye contact long enough to find out.

Kane was told Josh and Ethan wanted to train in preparation for joining Melior Group in a few short years. That couldn't have been further from the truth; one of the reasons we'd kept our Bond a secret was that none of us wanted to become superspies, or whatever the hell Alec did. Melior Group's recruitment tactics for Variants with impressive abilities, and Vitals to enhance them, could be very persuasive. Kane didn't seem to care about that though, or the fact that he was also there to train me, stating, "All the recent tension between Variants and humans is making me nervous."

He didn't blink an eye when Dot joined us either.

She had spent a solid two weeks in bed, crying and hardly eating, after Charlie was taken. If being punished in the gym with us provided a distraction, none of us were going to say no.

The only other thing that had managed to take her mind off Charlie, if only for a few minutes, was finding out I was Evelyn Maynard.

Dot hadn't put two and two together until a few weeks after she'd gotten out of the hospital. Even though Dot's family had never met my mom, she'd heard the guys talk over the years about their missing childhood friend who was likely Alec's Vital. When she finally made the connection, she had a million questions. I didn't have many answers, but I did my best to keep her talking, keep her engaged, keep that vacant look out of her eyes for as long as I could.

Ever since then, she'd treated me like the sister neither one of us ever had.

Ethan, Josh, Dot, and I had just finished another murderous session with Kane, and I'd made a beeline for the pool while the others had gone to shower or do whatever they needed to recover.

At least the training made me feel as if I was doing *something*, as if I was strong—even though it always left my limbs feeling like jelly. The bruises from the sparring sessions always healed quickly—our Variant DNA allowed us to take harder hits and heal faster than a human—but it still hurt like a bitch

Thinking about the aches only made them worse though. Instead, I took a deep breath and dipped below the surface again.

I swam to the other side under the water, emerging at the deep end and gripping the edge. A big pair of black boots sat on the ground nearby. Just past them, in the farthest corner, was a body in the lounger, partially obscured by the shade of a tree.

The boots and the pile of black clothing were Alec's. He was facedown, his head turned away from me, his tattoos prominent on his naked back, which rose and fell rhythmically in his sleep.

I frowned. He was in the sun, and if he'd been too tired to go upstairs when he got back at some obscenely late hour, I was pretty sure he hadn't worried about putting on sunscreen.

We'd hardly spoken since our encounter in Tyler's study the night of the invasion. Dot had dubbed the incident "Studygate," and it annoyingly caught on. Both Alec and I were refusing to speak about it, but it had created even more tension between us, so the others were constantly trying to pry it out of us.

Regardless of my messed-up personal relationship with Alec, I saw how hard he was working to find Charlie. Family—including Tyler and Josh, even though they weren't related by blood—was incredibly important to him, and that I could understand, even grudgingly admire.

He was an ass to me most of the time, but he'd probably spent all night out on some dangerous mission. I didn't want him to get sunburned on top of it.

Deciding to blame it on the Light that tethered me to each member of my Bond, I lifted myself out of the pool and found the sunscreen near a basket of towels at the pool house, then made my way back to Alec. From this angle, standing over him, I could see the side of his face. His mouth was open slightly, his lips smooshed against the lounger.

I bit my bottom lip and fiddled with the lid of the sunscreen bottle. *Maybe I should just wake him up and tell him to go inside. Maybe I should just let him get burned. It would serve him right after the way he treated me.*

Trying not to think about it too hard, I squeezed some of the white gloop into my hand and spread it between my palms. As gently as I could, I rested one knee next to his hip for balance and leaned over his broad back. Starting at the tops of his shoulders, I spread the sunscreen in two big streaks down the length of his back with slow, gentle movements. When I made a pass back up and over his shoulders, he sighed.

I checked to make sure he was still asleep and smiled despite myself. Some part of me got satisfaction from the fact that he felt pleasure from something I was doing to him.

I'd moved on to his arms when he woke up.

He froze, the muscles in his back going rigid, his breathing halting completely for a beat.

He raised himself up onto his elbows, turning his head to fix me with a hard stare, his ice-blue eyes narrowed. I jolted away and back to my feet as soon as he moved.

"What are you doing?" His voice was low and gravelly from sleep.

"Umm . . ." I fidgeted with the strap of my bikini bottoms, suddenly feeling like a naughty kid caught with my hand in the cookie jar. "The sun is strong and . . . uh . . . sunscreen?"

He looked at me as if I were crazy, then lifted himself into a sitting position, giving me his back, and started rubbing his closely cropped hair with both hands.

"I didn't want you to burn in the sun, and I didn't want to wake you." I managed to complete a sentence. I was on the verge of saying "sorry" but managed to hold it back. His reaction made me feel guilty, but I hadn't done anything wrong. In fact, I was doing him a favor. Asshole.

He sat up straighter, ignoring my explanation, and stretched one arm over his head, holding his side with the other. The muscles in his defined back danced under skin riddled with scars and ink, drawing my eyes to the curve of his spine.

In a bold, clean font, the words "With pain comes strength" ran across the top of his back. Underneath that, some tattoos were jagged and warped by scars, and some scars were partially obscured by the black or gray ink. I ran my gaze over the box jellyfish and some kind of snake entwined in either a dance or a battle, a striking female face licking the sharp side of a knife, and a skyline that looked familiar with angry-looking lightning above it.

He stood up slowly, and I snapped my eyes up, not wanting to get caught staring. When he turned around, I gasped, my hand flying to my mouth.

Angry, mottled bruising covered his ribs on his left side. He'd obviously had a rough night, but I knew better than to ask what had happened.

He scooped his boots and clothes up, wincing in pain, and I winced with him. As he walked past me toward the house, he muttered, "Thanks" without looking at me, but I was so distracted by the evidence of how dangerous his job was that I didn't even register it until he was halfway to the house.

My chest was aching a little bit in a familiar way—the way it had the night of the invasion, when Alec had overused his ability to incapacitate all those people; the way it had the night when Ethan had overused his ability, and an inexplicable force had drawn me to him. I shuddered to think what that meant for whoever had been on the receiving end of Alec's ability last night.

He hadn't truly overused it though. The pain in my chest wasn't as urgent or overwhelming. He hadn't depleted himself to the point of putting his own life in danger.

That's why it had seemed like a good idea to rub him down while he was asleep instead of just waking him up. I hadn't even realized I was transferring Light to him while I rubbed sunscreen on his back—tiny, unnoticeable amounts, as though it knew it had to be careful not to gush out of me too fast.

I considered going after him—the pull was still there, faint as it was—but I knew he would flat out refuse, and it would probably end in a fight. A good sleep would get him back on track.

With a sigh, I flopped down onto the lounger, trying to focus on the feel of the warm sun on my skin and the sweet smell of summer in the air. Trying *not* to think about the feel of Alec's back under my hands and the way he'd sighed in satisfaction.

Ethan and Josh ran past my chair, one on either side, and cannonballed into the pool. I chuckled at their antics. Dot walked up a little more calmly, wearing a black one-piece with bold cutouts that looked perfect on her petite frame.

"You already been in?" She took the seat next to me, gesturing to my wet hair.

"Yeah. I had a quick dip to cool off."

A shadow fell over me, and I turned, shielding my eyes from the sun. Tyler was in gray pants and a teal shirt, the sleeves rolled up in his signature way. The sun was directly behind his head, making his messy brown hair look like a glowing halo.

"Just came to check if you needed to do a Light transfer." He sat across from me, swiping back the messy bit of hair that seemed to always flop over his forehead. His gray eyes looked bloodshot and tired.

"I'm all good. Thanks." I smiled. He was working as tirelessly as Alec, spending many hours at Melior Group headquarters or cooped up in his study—even disappearing with Alec from time to time.

"Good." He smiled back, leaning his elbows on his knees, drawing my attention to the corded muscle of his forearms. Why did he always have to roll his shirtsleeves up like that? It made me want to run my hand up from the expensive watch at his wrist to the fabric of the shirt, feeling the hair on his arm. "Let's do one later, just in case."

I nodded and made myself look at his eyes. "I'll come find you after lunch."

Even though I was getting better at controlling my Light flow, and Ethan and Josh were getting better at managing the extra Light and using it to develop their abilities safely, I was still mainly going to Tyler if I needed to expel excess Light.

"Great. I'll be in my study."

"Nope." I shook my head emphatically. I'd refused to step foot in that room since the night of the invasion.

Tyler and Dot both groaned. In the pool, the splashing and laughing stopped.

"Are you ready to tell us about Studygate yet?" Josh asked, treading water near the edge of the pool.

"Nope." I popped the *p* and crossed my arms over my chest.

Tyler had already shifted his attention to his phone, tapping away, his brows pulled together. He finished what he was typing and stood up. "I have to go debrief with Alec."

"Maybe let him sleep for a bit," I said quickly before he could disappear.

He turned back to me, one eyebrow arched in surprise. I was the last person to know what Alec needed and certainly not one to advocate for him, but the faint tightness in my chest was still there, a pull toward a certain room on the third floor. Tyler's eyes narrowed in on my hand lightly rubbing my breastbone.

"He's OK," I reassured him before he could ask. "I found him asleep out here. He was a bit banged up, had some bruising on his ribs." I winced as I said it. "I'm pretty sure he abused his ability a little too. I woke him and he went inside, but he's fine. Just let him sleep for a while." I left out the awkwardness with the sunscreen. No one needed to know about that.

"He'll recover faster if he lets you transfer the Light he clearly needs," Tyler huffed.

I didn't say anything. What was there to say? I was lucky I'd managed to transfer some before he woke up, but I wasn't about to share that with the group either.

"All right, I'll deal with him later." He turned to leave, then paused, running his eyes over me quickly. "Did you put sunscreen on? Don't get sunburned."

"Yes, Dad." I rolled my eyes, then scrunched my face up in disgust. I was pretty certain Tyler wasn't attracted to me like that, and I was still trying to sort through my feelings for him, but referring to him as "Dad," even jokingly, had left a bad taste in my mouth. I looked at him, and he was wearing the same expression.

He shook it off and walked away without another word.

I turned back around to find Dot holding back laughter.

"Oh, don't start with me." I groaned. Teasing me about my complicated relationship with the four Variant men in my Bond had become her new hobby.

She must have seen something serious in my eyes, because she took a deep breath and changed the subject. "Have you heard from Zara?"

"Yeah." I frowned as I squeezed some sunscreen into my palm and passed the bottle to her. "She's coming back tomorrow."

Zara had been spending the summer with her family in California. She'd been released from the hospital a few days after the invasion, just in time for Beth's funeral. Her parents had whisked her home straight after. We'd stayed in touch, sending each other messages while doggedly avoiding mentioning Beth or anything that had happened that day. It felt wrong to talk about it through a screen, but it meant our conversations felt superficial. Hollow. We hadn't spoken at all for the past week, and when I'd asked when she was due back, all I'd gotten in response was a date and a rough time.

It made my stomach clench—I was equally looking forward to and dreading seeing her again.

"She's cutting it close," Dot said. Classes were due to start the day after her return.

I shrugged. "I can't imagine she's too keen to come back to the res hall."

Dot just nodded, rubbing sunscreen into her shoulders.

Tomorrow would be Zara's first night sleeping in our shared suite since it all happened. Her first night back in the rooms she'd shared with Beth for three years. I'd known Beth for only a few short months before she was killed, and I felt the loss keenly. I couldn't imagine how people who had known her longer felt.

I'd been reluctant to stay there myself. It felt barren and sad without the Reds around. The guys refused to let me out of their sight anyway, so I spent most of my nights at the mansion in one of the many spare rooms. I still stayed at the res hall when I had an early class, but one of them would always insist on dropping me off, and someone would always be there in the morning to walk me to class. Between that and the Melior Group agents posted at all the gates for extra security, I was never far from a protective force.

Yet I never quite felt safe. I wasn't sure if I'd ever be able to walk the grounds of campus without reliving the horrors I'd witnessed there.

Josh stopped my dark thoughts from spiraling by using his ability to flick the corner of my towel into my face.

It brought my attention to his cheeky grin, his head disappearing under the water.

Just as I realized Ethan wasn't in the pool anymore, he grabbed me under the knees and behind my back and lifted me off my seat as though I weighed nothing.

I yelled and tried to wriggle out of his arms, but he just laughed, flashing me a wide grin that made his dimples appear, his amber eyes sparkling with mischief. One second we were standing at the edge of the pool, and the next we were flying through the air and hitting the water with a massive splash. He released his hold once we were in the water, but as my head broke the surface, I held on, twining my arms around his thick neck. I couldn't reach the bottom at this end of the pool, but he could.

"You are in so much trouble!" I laughed despite myself, pushing wet hair off my face.

"Oh yeah? What're you gonna to do about it?" Ethan was a hopeless flirt, turning every situation into an opportunity to make a double entendre, smirking with his full mouth and smoldering with his sexy eyes. Not that it worked on me. I was way too astute to let a little obvious flirting affect me.

"I'll . . . um . . ." I laughed again. Naturally my brain supplied the least helpful words possible. "I'll kiss you." Maybe I wasn't as immune to the flirting as I thought.

He started to walk us toward the shallow end, and I wrapped my legs loosely around his middle, trailing behind him in the cool water. He was tall, broad, and muscular, but his big hands were always gentle with me.

He didn't reply to my last statement. Instead he just watched me intently as he moved, keeping my gaze captive with his eyes.

He pressed his lips to mine as he continued to walk me backward, and I sighed, completely lost in his touch. I ran one hand through his wet black hair, but before the kiss could intensify, we came to an abrupt stop as my back hit something hard and warm and slick. Josh.

Josh was the shortest of the four, his physique lithe and athletic. But all the training with Kane was resulting in extra definition. His shoulders were looking a little broader, his crisp collared shirts straining a little more over his chest, and there was a six-pack becoming more noticeable every time he took his shirt off.

"That's not much of a punishment, Eve." Josh's voice was low, but it sounded semiserious. I pulled away from Ethan as Josh's hands found my waist. He tugged, and I leaned back into his chest, my legs still around Ethan's middle, not ready to let go but eager to have contact with Josh at the same time.

"Are you jealous, Joshy?" I teased, covering his hands with mine and turning toward him. His green eyes bored into mine, the lashes stuck together. His dirty-blond hair looked much darker when wet.

"Yes," he whispered, his breath washing over me. There was no hint of teasing in his voice.

My immediate instinct was to kiss him. The Light and I were in agreement when it came to wanting to even the score. I closed the small distance, pressing my lips to his. He sighed into the kiss, not hesitating to tease my lips with his tongue, but this kiss was cut short too.

A loud battle cry cut through the relative silence, followed by a huge splash as Dot launched herself into the pool, literally throwing water onto our heated moment. All three of us startled, and the boys released me. My feet found the bottom of the pool, and I stood between Ethan and Josh as Dot broke the surface.

"Did you three dickheads forget you had company?" Her voice was teasing. She wasn't actually upset, but I did feel bad that I'd forgotten she was there. "Save that ménage shit for when other people aren't around."

My eyes widened at her casual mention of threesomes. I stared at her, my lips pressed together, silently trying to communicate that she should stop speaking immediately. I mean, technically I had been in an embrace with both of them. So it was *technically* a threesome kind of situation. I just hadn't thought about it in any tangible way before, and we certainly hadn't talked about it.

I cleared my throat and chanced a look at Josh and Ethan. They were having their own silent conversation, their eyes locked on each other. Ethan was smirking, the dimple only just visible in his cheek, and Josh's eyes were narrowed, but there was a twitch pulling the corners of his lips up too. They turned to look at me as one, and I quickly averted my gaze, suddenly incredibly self-conscious.

I didn't want to examine too closely the thrill of excitement that jolted through me, settling somewhere low in my belly, at the charged energy between the three of us. I lifted my head to find Dot's smiling face. She was casually leaning on the edge of the pool, her elbows propped up behind her, looking satisfied.

I moved toward her as fast as I could in the water and splashed her viciously. She screamed and tried to get away, laughing and spluttering before changing tactics and trying to splash me back. The boys joined in, and the rest of the morning went by without any more awkward moments or teasing from Dot.

That moment in the pool was the first time I'd heard her laugh freely since Charlie had been taken. I knew by the way she retreated into herself for the next half hour—pretending to read a magazine on her lounger while not once turning a page—that she felt guilty about having fun when we had no idea what kind of awful situation Charlie was in or if he was even alive.

We gave her space, and not long after, she made an effort to join in the joking and fun. We all knew it was what her brother would want—for Dot to be happy.

TWO

That evening I sat on the edge of the kitchen island while Ethan cooked dinner. He moved around with ease, his posture relaxed, his smile coming easily as we chatted.

We talked about coursework, what he was cooking, how Dot was doing—and about our parents. Now that we knew we'd known each other since childhood, conversation turned to our parents a lot easier than it used to. We never reminisced for long or in much detail—it was too painful—but it felt good to talk about my mother in a context that didn't involve rehashing her death. It was nice to be able to ask them what she was like.

Ethan and Josh weren't much older than me, so they didn't remember much, but Tyler made an effort to describe in great detail whatever he could remember. Like how she used to bake cookies for us as after-school snacks, or how all of our families would get together on Sundays for these chaotic, joyful meals.

Alec was avoiding speaking to me at all, so I had no idea what he remembered of my mother or of me as a child.

We also never spoke about the day of the invasion outside the context of looking for Charlie. We had come so close to losing each other again . . .

"My power is so destructive." Ethan spoke low; we'd all become accustomed to lowering our voices when we talked about our Bond. He moved his chopping board closer so we could hear each other. "I just want to be able to do something positive with it, you know?"

"Ethan, it's not about the nature of the ability. It's how you use it."

He gave me a devious look, twisting my innocent statement into a double entendre. I rolled my eyes but couldn't help chuckling. Dirty jokes were now a daily occurrence.

"I know what you mean." He turned serious again, checking the pot on the stove before giving me his full attention. "But I still want to figure out how to put them *out.*"

Ethan was trying to develop a new level to his ability.

Tyler had discovered he could not only tell when someone was lying; with enough Light from me, he could also glean the basic truth behind their words. It was proving to be a handy yet slightly annoying development. He'd taken to constantly calling us out on our bullshit. Like when I asked if anyone wanted to watch *Cosmos* with me and they all said "yes," Tyler was quick to point out Ethan actually did not.

He respected our privacy when it came to serious things—he still hadn't asked about what had happened between Alec and I when his ability was enhanced with extra Light—but he was pushing us all to be more honest.

Josh, too, had noticed a new development. After he'd accidentally made Ethan float during one of our training sessions, we realized he could levitate not only inanimate objects but also people, even the members of his own Bond—as long as the intention to harm wasn't there. Recently he'd set his mind to making *himself* float. He was trying to learn to fly—and actually beginning to succeed. With extra Light from me and deep focus, he'd managed to get himself about ten inches off the ground.

Ethan's control had improved too, and the fire he wielded was becoming more powerful. But unlike Tyler and Josh, Ethan hadn't been able to discover a new aspect to his ability; he was just improving on what he already had.

A little frown formed above his bright eyes, and I sighed. He was beating himself up instead of acknowledging all he had achieved.

Putting fire out sounded deceptively simple. Ethan could make *his* fire disappear easily, but it was tinged with the Light that flowed through him to create it. He described it as pulling a limb back against his body. It was an extension of him.

What he couldn't do, and was trying his hardest to work out, was putting out regular fires. Fires started by someone else with non-supernatural means were beyond his reach.

"I know, hot stuff." I squeezed his shoulder, trying to distract him by starting up our nickname game. "You'll get there. Focus on the positives."

"I know, I know. Just imagine all the good I could do."

A slow grin spread across my face. It was fueled in part by how softhearted my big guy was—he just wanted to make the world a better place—but also by his not noticing my nickname. We'd become so used to calling each other increasingly ridiculous things that it was expected, and that, in turn, had given rise to a whole new game. We were now trying to slip them in so the other person wouldn't notice.

He smiled back but with some confusion. I plastered an innocent look on my face but couldn't wipe away the grin.

It didn't take him long to catch on. He pushed back from the bench and groaned in frustration even as he laughed. Playing every sport imaginable, Ethan certainly had a competitive streak. He loved these little games.

He checked the pot again, added the cilantro he'd been chopping, and quickly switched the burners off while I waited for him to concede defeat. With his latest culinary masterpiece no longer in danger, he placed one hand on either side of where I sat on the island, his big arms boxing me in, and fixed me with one of his dimpled smiles.

"You better hope Josh doesn't notice the cilantro in that stew—you know he hates it—and I don't know why you're smiling. You just lost a round," I teased, leaning back on my hands.

"Josh can suck it. And I may have lost"—he leaned forward, following me—"but you think I'm hot, so I figure I won as well."

I laughed softly, no longer trying to get away, maybe even tilting toward him a little. "Well, yeah, you do have a fire ability." My voice was almost a whisper.

"Whatever. You think I'm hot." His lips were inches from mine. "You want to hug me and kiss me and . . ."

I closed the miniscule distance between us and pressed my lips to his. We both sighed into the soft kiss.

Kissing Ethan felt as natural as it did exciting. With our continued training, my control of the Light and my guys' control of their abilities were getting better, which made it easier to be more intimate. Ethan and Josh were stealing more kisses, and so was I. It was only when things started to intensify that I'd lose control of my Light and we'd have to stop.

It was driving us all crazy. The three of us, that is. Tyler had maintained his platonic barrier.

He'd given me a hint of thawing out the night of the gala. The way he'd told me I looked beautiful as he dragged his fingers down the length of my exposed spine still gave me shivers to think about. It had felt like the beginning of something more between us.

But then he'd reestablished the boundaries. Despite his newfound fondness for calling out the cold hard truth at every corner, this was one thing he was keeping his mouth shut about. I knew if I asked him, he would tell me the truth, but I was afraid of the answer.

Alec had gone back to ignoring me as if we weren't even connected.

I may have been avoiding talking about intimacy with half my Variant Bond, but I was trying my best to make it past the make-out stage with the other half. So I did a mental check of my Light flow before deepening the kiss with Ethan.

Just as I scooted forward, opening my legs wider and pressing up against the hard planes of Ethan's body, the sound of the fridge opening interrupted the moment, and we pulled apart. The clang of bottles and jars in the fridge door rang through the kitchen as Alec slammed it closed.

We both turned to look at Ethan's obnoxious cousin. Alec was in sweatpants, shirtless and barefoot, breathing a little heavy, a light sheen of sweat covering his toned, tattooed body. He'd obviously just come up from the gym, and in our distracted state, we hadn't heard him.

He opened a bottle of sparkling water, the top making a distinctive hiss, and looked between us before taking a deep drink.

"Ah!" Keeping his eyes locked on us, he sighed exaggeratedly before wiping his mouth with the back of his hand, which, when it came away, revealed a crooked grin. He knew exactly what he was doing. He wouldn't even talk to me, let alone touch me in the way he had in Tyler's study, but he was determined none of the rest of my Bond would either.

Ethan dropped his arms and stepped away, sighing. He shot Alec a dirty look and got back to cooking.

Grinding my teeth, I jumped off the island and walked toward him. His eyes tracked me as he raised the bottle back to his lips, the eyebrow with the scar lifting slightly.

I stopped next to him and leaned in. "You are such a cockblocker." I spoke low, but my voice carried in the quiet kitchen.

His eyes widened, and he choked on his sip of mineral water, some of the liquid spurting past his lips and dripping down his tattooed chest.

It took physical effort to stop my eyes from following the droplets as they made their way down. I knew what it felt like to run my hands down that chest . . . But I refused to give him the satisfaction. I made myself look away and left the room.

Ethan's booming laugh echoed behind me, and I finally let a grin cross my face. Alec had tried to get to me, and he may have succeeded, but I'd gotten to him too.

~

Tyler and I had ended up skipping our Light transfer because he'd gotten tied up with work, and I woke up feeling a little itchy around the forearms.

The time between how often I needed Light transfers was getting longer the more I practiced mindfulness and control of the flow, but it still got away from me sometimes. The state Alec was in when I found him by the pool probably had something to do with it; the Light was pushing into me in an effort to get to him.

I went for a run with Ethan to try to work some of it off, careful not to touch him. When the Light was uncontrolled like that, the transfer could be sudden and violent, and that's when *he* would have to practice perfect control not to accidentally set something on fire.

After the run, which helped only slightly, I grabbed a quick breakfast and went searching for Tyler. I ran through the obvious areas of the house first—kitchen, living room, patio, even knocking on his bedroom door—before dragging my feet downstairs to his study.

The door was ajar, and I nudged it open while rapping on the frame. My feet stayed firmly planted on the outside of the room.

"Hey, got a minute?"

"Hey, Eve." He looked up from the pile of folders and newspapers on his desk before dropping his gaze again. "What's up?"

"We never got around to doing that transfer yesterday."

"Oh, yeah. The debrief with Alec went longer than I thought it would." At the mention of his name, we both looked over to the leather couch in the corner—the spot where he had lifted me to the highest peak of pleasure and then torn me down to the lowest point in the space of five minutes.

"I'll put the TV in the living room on." With one last glare at the couch, I left to wait for him.

He joined me after only a few minutes. "One of you is eventually going to have to tell us what happened on the night of the invasion." He sighed but sounded resigned. He knew I wouldn't tell him anything.

"Let's just focus, OK?"

He turned to face me, but I kept my eyes glued to the TV as he gently extracted the remote from my fingers and flipped to CNN. When he extended his hand, I grabbed it without hesitation, and immediately the Light poured out of me. Tyler grunted, and I worked at steadying the flow.

"Haven't felt it that strong in a while."

"Yeah, I think it might be because of Alec yesterday."

"Makes sense."

We turned our attention back to the news.

After the invasion, the media had reported on it almost around the clock for a full week. It had been the first large-scale, outwardly violent attack by an extremist human group—the Human Empowerment Network—against a Variant institution and Variant civilians in a very long time.

After the first week, the reports about the invasion became more sporadic, but almost every day contained a new report of a Variant business owner refusing to serve a human, or a gang of humans beating up a Variant with a passive ability. Variants were becoming less shy about calling humans *Dimes*—the derogatory term that had been so offensive a few months ago it was almost never heard in public. Humans were picketing Variant businesses and institutions all over the world. People were scared.

Today, we were staring at a story about how some senator was running for president. I sighed, exasperated, and tried to pull my hand away from Tyler's, but he held on tight. He was watching the screen intently, his eyes flying from side to side.

I got excited and wrapped my other hand around his, pushing more Light through our connection. If he was onto something, I wanted to make sure he had all the juice he needed.

Absently, I registered the sound of a commercial break, and Tyler gently pulled his hand away, moving backward until his legs hit the couch. He was staring into space, his brow furrowed.

Alec walked into the room in shorts and a sweat-soaked tank top, moving to the kitchen and rummaging in the fridge. After a few moments, he looked over, abandoned his snack on the bench, and came to stand in front of Tyler. "What did you see?"

In need of something to do, I grabbed the remote and turned the TV off. That seemed to snap Tyler out of his stare.

"Senator Anderson," he said, as if that explained anything.

When it looked as though he wasn't going to elaborate, Alec asked, "Christine Anderson? The Variant senator? What about her?"

Tyler had started to stare into space again, so I tried to keep the information flowing. "There was a news report about her running for president just now. Isn't she the one who gave the speech the night of the gala?"

Alec cleared his throat before answering, "Yes."

That was the night he'd first kissed me. The night he'd made me think I betrayed my Bond by kissing him back. I crossed my arms and refused to look at him.

Tyler shook himself out of his stupor. "Sorry. I was trying to make sense of it all. Anderson mentioned the invasion in her speech just then. She's running on a platform of unifying the humans and the Variants. I think . . . My ability doesn't work nearly as well when the subject is not physically right in front of me, but I think she knows more than she's letting on about the invasion, which means she may know . . ."

"Something about Charlie," Alec finished for him. "It's a lead."

"Yeah, but we're talking about government level . . ."

I didn't hear the rest of what Tyler was saying. They rushed out, talking over each other.

I was left standing in the middle of the room, my hands by my sides, stunned. "I'll just . . . stay here," I said to no one.

"Hey, petal pie!" Ethan beamed at me, emerging from the gym and looking as sweaty as Alec.

"Hey, snookums. Did you do *more* exercise after our exercise this morning?"

"Hells yeah!" He went straight to the kitchen, picking up where Alec had left off. "Takes serious commitment to look this good." He flashed me his dimples as he exaggeratedly flexed his arms.

"Modest as always." I perched on a stool across from him.

"How was your thing with Tyler?"

"Make me one of those sandwiches"—only Ethan could make a sandwich taste like fine dining—"and I'll tell you all about it."

"Way ahead of you." He slid a plate to me, and I told him what little I knew.

After our brief chat, he took two very large sandwiches into Tyler's study, and I went upstairs to grab my stuff. I would be staying in my res hall that evening. Zara was due back that afternoon.

Backpack slung over my shoulder, I made my way downstairs, but I knew better than to leave without telling anyone. The campus may have been teeming with Melior Group agents, but the three blocks between the Zacarias mansion and the front gates were completely unprotected. One of them would either drive or walk me there. Overprotective, maybe, but I didn't mind.

Thinking about why the extra precautions were needed made me feel sick, but I didn't want to end up like Charlie.

As predicted, Josh and Ethan were both waiting for me in the foyer.

"It's not too hot. Do you wanna walk it?" Josh asked. He was dressed in shorts and an AC/DC T-shirt. I looked pointedly at it, my eyebrows raised. He loved his band tees when relaxing at home but wouldn't be caught dead out in public without a collared shirt and pressed pants. He was preppy on the outside and wild rock on the inside.

He rolled his eyes. "It's not like anyone will see us. It's three blocks."

"Yeah, let's walk."

We all moved to leave just as the door to Tyler's study flew open. Alec poked his head out.

"You going?" he asked, looking right at me.

I stared back, trying to remember the last time he'd spoken directly to me. No one had been around to hear yesterday morning's "thanks" by the pool, and I wasn't entirely convinced it had happened.

"Eve's staying on campus tonight," Josh answered for me when I remained silent.

Alec came to stand right in front of me, digging his hand in his pocket. In the office behind him, Tyler had his phone to his ear, but he was watching us.

After a moment, Alec pulled a small item out of his pocket and let it hang on a chain between us.

We both opened our mouths to speak, but my words rushed out first. "You're giving me jewelry?"

Was I dreaming? Was this some kind of nightmare? Was he about to give me a necklace, and then when I tried to give one to him, he would throw it at me, declare he "doesn't want anything from me," and walk out?

"What?" His brows creased, and his lip turned up in a grimace. "It's a tracking device and distress beacon."

"What?" The item in question was still swinging in front of my face on a simple silver chain. It looked like a solid silver rod, a little thicker than a pencil and about half the length. The top third of it was matte black.

Alec rolled his eyes and sighed. "It allows us to know where you are at all times, and if you get in trouble, you can activate the distress signal." He delivered the speech as if he'd already explained it a thousand times.

"Wow. The stalking has gone to another level." I crossed my arms. "I'm not wearing that."

"Dammit! Tyler, talk to her." He let the little device flop to his side.

Tyler finished his call and came out to join us. "I thought you were going to give it to these two to give her." I turned on him. "You knew about this?"

Alec spoke at the same time. "I didn't have a chance to give it to them, and they were about to leave, so . . ."

"Yeah." Tyler sighed but had the decency to look a little sheepish. "We came up with the idea together."

I looked at them all one by one. "Idiots." I rolled my eyes.

"Eve." Tyler had his serious face on. "Vitals are disappearing every day. With those machines, it doesn't matter that we're keeping you a secret. If they track you down, they will take you. We want you to have the freedom to go on with your life, go to class, stay on campus—but we need to take precautions. Please—"

"It's either this or a subdermal implant," Alec cut across him, apparently done with civilized conversation. He stepped in front of me again, blocking my view of the others and holding the necklace up.

"No way in hell are you putting anything under my skin! That is so creepy."

He looked smug and shoved the necklace farther into my face.

Grumbling, I took it and slipped it over my head, giving him a "there, it's done" look—my eyes wide, my head cocked to the side. "Happy?"

He didn't answer, instead reaching out to grab the pendant in his hand. His knuckles brushed against my sternum where the long chain ended, and I gasped, surprised at the casual contact. He saw my reaction, his eyes boring into mine for the briefest of seconds.

"It's constantly transmitting your location," he explained. "But if you're in any kind of trouble, you just pull these two bits apart"—he yanked, and the bigger silver bit of the rod came away from the smaller matte black part—"and it will send an alert to us."

As if to illustrate his point, their phones went off, a high-pitched alarm bouncing off the marble. All four of them extracted their phones and turned the sound off quickly. Alec kept speaking: "If none of us responds with a password, an automatic message will be sent to Melior Group."

He joined the two parts together again.

"You try it." He dropped the heavy little bar, and it bounced on my chest. I picked it up, yanked the two bits apart, and braced myself for the alarm. It didn't disappoint, filling the foyer with its wail again.

I reconnected the two bits as the guys shut off the alarms.

"OK, got it." I sounded bored even to myself.

"Take this seriously, Evelyn," Alec growled at me. "This is not a toy. If that alarm goes off, I'm assuming your life is in danger, and we are coming in hot."

His intensity took me aback. "OK," I whispered, then cleared my throat. "OK, I get it. I'm not a child." A bit of frustration crept in at the end.

"Aren't you?" The question wasn't mocking. It was delivered with a completely straight face. An incomprehensible expression crossed his features, and then he disappeared into Tyler's study.

Tyler took his place in front of me, looking apologetic. "Sorry about Alec. He's just not used to . . ."

"Having normal conversations with actual people?" I finished for him.

"Something like that. Look, all we want to do is protect you, OK? This is the least invasive, least overbearing way we could think of."

I nodded. "I wish you'd included me in the conversation, but I get it." We had been isolated for the past few months, cocooned in the safety of the mansion's sprawling grounds. The escalating violence out in the world may have felt removed, but the threat was real. I just had to look into Dot's broken face to be reminded of it.

"Good." Tyler smiled warmly. "Now, it goes without saying that you can't take this off. You sleep with it, shower with it. It stays around your neck at all times, got it?"

"Yes, sir," I said a little playfully.

"And don't tell anyone about it either. It's inconspicuous enough that it should go unnoticed, but if anyone asks, tell them it was a gift from Ethan."

"Yes, sir."

He gave me an exasperated look, his eyes narrowing. Behind me, Ethan and Josh laughed quietly at some private joke. With one last lingering look at the unassuming pendant, Tyler waved goodbye and followed Alec.

Ethan, Josh, and I took off, walking most of the way back to campus in silence. I was lost in thought, trying to reconcile Alec's volatile treatment of me with his obvious desire to keep me safe. The boys mostly just watched me surreptitiously. As we passed the security checkpoint at the gate and moved away from the guards, I began to get exasperated with them.

"Stop it," I snapped.

Ethan stepped into my path and wrapped his big arms around my waist, leaning down to look at me. It was always Ethan in public. Josh couldn't touch me like this where someone might see. I glanced at him. He appeared casual, his hands in his pockets, his shoulders loose, but there was a tightness to his mouth. He was struggling with this more and more. I was too.

"We're just trying to keep you safe." Ethan's amber eyes were unusually serious.

"I know. Thank you." I hugged him, but I watched Josh as I did, putting as much warmth and meaning into my look as I put into Ethan's hug. He quirked his lips and nodded his head almost imperceptibly.

We said our goodbyes, and I headed to my res hall. As I approached the entrance, I kept my gaze fixed on the door, refusing to look at the building next to ours—the spot in the alcove where I'd last seen Charlie. My heart hammered in my chest every time I walked past there, remembering . . .

I ran up the stairs, the burn in my legs giving me a distraction, and made myself think about Zara. I'd sent her a few messages that morning—wishing her a safe flight, asking if she needed a lift from the airport, asking when she'd be back on campus—but she hadn't answered any of them.

THREE

The breeze drifting in through my window still carried the warmth of a summer morning. It was only a matter of time before it became too cold to have the window open at all, so I enjoyed the sweet smell of fresh air, the sound of early birds.

I sat on my bed in my PJ top, a heavy book on my lap: *Vital Myths in Medieval Texts*. The book wasn't as old as the parchment and vellum tomes it referenced—it was published in the late nineties—but it did have pictures of early texts depicting Variant life hundreds of years ago.

As I leaned back on my pillows, I stared at a depiction of a Vital found in a monk's tome from 1508. The Vital man stood in the middle of five women. Precious gold leaf had been painstakingly applied to the sections of the drawing that were supposed to be his skin, and a yellowish-white color had been drawn in all around him. Gold-leaf arrows pointed to each of the women, his Variants.

It was clearly representing what I'd experienced on the train platform, and again with Alec, yet the book was dismissing it as the overactive imagination and religious devotion of a person from a time before science. This was just how they saw Vitals at that time—sent from God and therefore glowing in the light of his divinity. It theorized that our modern terminology for the Light came from this idea.

Interesting, but completely useless. I sighed and let the heavy book flop onto my lap, abandoning it halfway through a sentence. I'd been almost obsessive in my research over the summer, trying to find any information I could about Vitals glowing—what it was, why it happened, if it was dangerous. But after two months, all I had were vague references in history books and a few conspiracy theories online about the government experimenting on Vitals with exceptional levels of Light. I had nothing.

At the sound of movement on the other side of my door, I set the book aside and swung my legs over the edge of the bed, then paused. Zara was up, but I wasn't entirely sure she wanted to see me.

When the guys dropped me off the day before, she still wasn't back. She hadn't arrived until after I'd eaten dinner, tidied up my room, and read half the latest issue of *Astronomy & Astrophysics* waiting for her. She'd let herself in quietly, pulling her suitcase inside as she backed through the door.

"Oh." She straightened when she saw me on the couch. "Didn't think you'd still be up."

"Of course I'm up." I went straight to her, giving her a tight hug. She stiffened for a moment, then returned

When we separated, I saw her eyes were as misty as mine, her jaw clenched. She didn't make eye contact, fidgeting with the handle of her suitcase and letting her silky red hair fall over her face.

"So"—I cleared my throat, trying to speak around the lump in my throat—"how was your flight?"

"Fine. Delayed." She rolled her eyes, then dragged the suitcase into her room, hefting it onto the bed and opening it to rummage inside. "I'm actually really tired. I think I'll just have a shower and go to bed. Can we catch up tomorrow?"

She gave me a tired smile as she held up her toiletries bag.

"Of course." I smiled back, and she shut herself in the bathroom. The sound of the shower starting reminded me I was still standing in the middle of the room, staring at the bathroom door.

I wished Beth were there.

I'd gone to bed, telling myself Zara needed space. Losing her best friend, having her own life put in danger— it was a lot to handle. Coming back to where it had all happened couldn't have been easy.

Which is why I was now hesitating, unsure if she wanted to walk to breakfast together.

I got dressed in jeans and a loose T-shirt, and as I was braiding my hair, she let herself into my room.

"Hey, ready for breakfast? I'm starving." She leaned on the edge of my desk.

I smiled, relief and longing fighting for strongest emotion. She and Beth used to both barge into my room like that. Beth would have been flipping through the clothes in my wardrobe by now, second-guessing her own outfit.

Zara was looking at the same spot.

"Yeah, let me just brush my teeth."

She gave me a weak smile before leading the way out of my bedroom.

Fifteen minutes later, Zara and I were walking toward the cafeteria. We enjoyed the lightness of our bags while we could; in a few weeks, we'd be buried in so many assignments that all the books we needed wouldn't fit inside them.

It was obvious things had changed, both with Zara and on campus. With the beginning of the semester, the bulk of the student body—those who had not hung around for summer classes—had arrived at Bradford Hills Institute, and at a quarter to nine on the first Monday, everyone was on their way somewhere. Several people had their faces in giant campus maps, looking a little overwhelmed, and I smiled to myself, remembering my own attachment to my map only a few months ago.

In a few weeks, the new students would be obsessing over the results of their Variant DNA tests, but for now, everyone's focus was on the heavily armed men making their presence known all over campus. Bradford Hills had always had its own campus security, posted at the gates and occasionally patrolling, like any other college in the country, but the new black-clad groups of hard-looking men were impossible to miss.

Melior Group had descended on Bradford Hills in the days following the invasion, and they hadn't left. The Variant community didn't take the safety of their best and brightest lightly. It had been officially announced that Melior Group would be handling increased security on campus for the foreseeable future. With Bradford Hills Institute offering free counseling to all staff and students, the two organizations were working closely to make sure their people were supported through this tough time.

I knew the frowning men and big guns were meant to make us all feel safe, but all it did was painfully remind me of why they were necessary.

Doing our best to ignore them, Zara and I took our time walking the curving paths of Bradford Hills, enjoying the morning sunshine peeking through the trees lining the laneways while we chatted about anything *other* than Beth. Now wasn't the time. I asked Zara about her summer, but she didn't give me much; she'd probably spent most of it grieving and closed off to the world.

"We should swap schedules," Zara suggested as we rounded the corner to the square containing the cafeteria building, "so we know when the other one is free."

"Yeah, sure." I smiled widely, happy she wanted to hang out with me. I'd been so worried about our friendship fizzling out, unable to withstand the pressure of losing Beth and two months of distance.

I was watching Zara's profile, so I saw the exact moment her eyes narrowed, her jaw clenched. My own body tensed in response, and I turned to see what she was looking at.

Sitting on a picnic bench facing us was Rick. The man who'd killed Beth was leaning his elbows on his knees and staring at the ground as people went about their morning around him.

"Why the fuck is he here?" Zara hissed between clenched teeth.

"I don't know. Come on." I pulled her by the elbow, trying to move toward the cafeteria. I didn't want to see him, didn't want to speak to him, didn't want to be reminded of his existence at all. But Zara was frozen to the spot, and Rick looked up and spotted us.

He sat up straight, eyes widening, and rubbed his hands down the length of his thighs a few times. When he rose and started walking in our direction, I gave up trying to drag Zara away and threaded my arm through hers. If we had to face him, I was glad neither of us was doing it alone.

The investigation into what had happened on the day of the invasion was still ongoing. With so many casualties and no surveillance footage, it would take a long time to unravel—to figure out who died by which gun, which Variants killed which humans in self-defense. Tyler was helping as much as he could with questioning the assailants they had captured. Alec was helping with the interrogations too. I tried not to think too hard about the kind of interrogating his particular skill set would be used for.

But Beth's death had been solved early. Zara's account of what happened, coupled with the electric burns on Beth's body, painted a clear picture. Plus, Rick had handed himself in almost immediately.

Had he walked up to the investigators looking as disheveled and tired as he did walking over the green grass now?

He came to a stop before us.

No one said anything.

Rick gazed intently at the ground, his shoulders tight, his breathing ragged. My eyes couldn't seem to settle on one thing; they flitted from Zara's profile to Rick's furrowed brow to the treetops swaying in the warm breeze to the people around us starting to slow down and take notice.

But Zara's eyes were glued to Rick. Her rigid body pressed up against mine as she watched him, not saying anything, her gaze almost daring him to.

"I want you to know that . . ." His voice broke. He swallowed, cleared his throat, and finally looked up. "That I am sorry. If I could go back and take her place, I would. I am so, so sorry."

He took a shaky inhale, his wide shoulders trembling as his eyes filled with tears.

Zara's voice didn't tremble. She lifted her chin and spoke with finality. "Fuck. You." She extracted herself from my hold and walked away.

"Zara . . ." I tried to call after her, go after her, but my knees were weak, and she was so fast.

"Eve . . ." My name sounded like a plea as Rick gave in to the tears completely.

I swatted at my own tears before turning away. I didn't have the strength to move, so I hugged my chest, breathing heavily, feeling cold and alone in the warm morning sun.

I missed her so much. I knew, logically, his intention hadn't been to kill her, but he was still the reason she was gone, and I couldn't look at him.

A hand touched my shoulder, but I didn't recoil from it; I knew the touch of one of my Variants. The loafers peeking out under neat trousers and the smell of expensive aftershave told me it was Josh.

I leaned into him, pressing my forehead to his shoulder, and his arms wrapped around me. We shouldn't have been hugging in public like this, but I needed him.

"Rick." Josh's voice reverberated through his chest. It was a comforting thing to focus on, and I tucked my face farther into him, circling my arms around his waist. "Maybe now's not the best time, yeah?"

Rick sniffled and coughed, trying to get himself together. He didn't say anything, but I heard footsteps retreating.

For a beat, Josh just held me, crushing me to his chest. Too soon, his grip on me loosened, and my knee-jerk reaction was to tighten my hold on his waist, telling him wordlessly I wasn't ready to let go.

"People are looking, baby," he whispered, sounding pained. "I want nothing more than to just hold you, carry you away from here, but . . ."

But I was supposed to be Ethan's girlfriend—not all of their Vital. That was a secret we still had to keep. I pulled away, nodded, and wiped my tears with the tissues he handed me.

Josh stuffed his hands into his pockets—something he was doing more and more when we were together in public—and we walked the rest of the way to the cafeteria in silence. He sat me down at a table in the corner, and while I rested my head on my hands and tried to get my emotions under control, he got me some breakfast.

I was halfway through the eggs when Ethan bounded up, loudly greeted us, and plonked himself in the chair next to mine, stealing a bite of my toast. When neither of us returned his greeting as enthusiastically, the bright look on his face fell.

"What happened?" He lowered his voice, draping a protective arm over the back of my chair.

As Josh explained, I leaned into Ethan's warm, strong body until I was practically in his lap. I took long breaths of his smoky smell and focused on the pressure of his hands holding me close.

Having some contact, even if we were still careful to avoid skin contact, helped clear the dark clouds Rick had brought with him.

The boys walked me to class and reluctantly left my side. Most of the early classes consisted of introductions and get-to-know-yous, the professors answering questions and going over the coursework. I was already ahead in most of it, so I tuned out to check in on Zara.

I sent her a message in our "roomies" group chat—the one Beth was in too. It made me feel closer to her, as if at any moment the little round icon with her smiling freckled face would zoom to the bottom, indicating she'd caught up on all the messages.

Zara said she was fine, that she only had a few classes that day, and since they were introductory ones, she was going to go catch up with a friend instead, get away from campus for a bit.

I hoped I wasn't one of those things she needed to get away from. I hoped our friendship wouldn't fall apart without Beth there to keep us together.

~

Summer was holding on, and the mornings were still hot, but I didn't have time to lie in bed and enjoy it. My first class started at nine.

I dressed in jean shorts and a loose tank top with a photo of Einstein sticking his tongue out on the front. I tried to be as quiet as possible, not wanting to disturb Zara; since our run-in with Rick a few days ago, she'd been especially withdrawn.

But when I tiptoed out of my room, she was already gone. Pushing the sadness aside, I rushed through my bathroom routine and pulled my hair up into a messy ponytail so it wouldn't stick to my neck. Then I grabbed an apple to tide me over until I could go to the cafeteria.

Slinging my light backpack over my shoulder, I opened the door and came face-to-face with Ethan, his fist raised and ready to knock.

"Hey, sugar." Ethan smiled with his whole being. Most people would pull their lips up at the corners, maybe show some teeth. When Ethan smiled, his face lit up, his dimples appeared, his amber eyes sparkled, his shoulders rolled back. It was like a breath of fresh air you couldn't help inhaling, making you smile back whether you wanted to or not.

"Hey, sunshine." I leaned in for a quick peck on the lips.

"Hey, snookums," Dot cooed in a high-pitched voice, popping her head around Ethan's frame.

"Hey, you weirdo." I laughed, giving her a hug. "What are you guys doing here? I have to get to class."

"Yeah. Biology. I have the same class." Dot leaned on the doorframe. She'd put her black hair in pigtails and was wearing what looked like a basketball jersey sewn up at the sides so my petite friend could wear it as a dress. Paired with the heeled Chuck Taylors (where did she even get those?), it looked perfect on her.

It was the first crazy, uniquely Dot outfit I'd seen her wear since Charlie was taken. There was still sadness in her heavily made-up eyes, but I was happy to see her doing something to make herself feel better—to feel more like herself.

"We went to the bookshop yesterday. Picked yours up too." Ethan held up a bulky-looking bag, then leaned around me to dump it just inside the door.

"Here's the biology textbook."

I shoved the heavy book Dot handed me into my bag while taking a bite of my apple. "Fanx," I said around the tart fruit in my mouth. "Les go."

Ethan slammed my door shut, then frowned at it.

"Is that the only lock that thing has?" he asked as we moved toward the elevator.

"Yeah . . ." It was a simple round door handle with a self-locking mechanism. It was basic, but if someone could make it past the armed, trained men downstairs, no door was going to keep them back.

"Hmm. Not very safe," he mumbled, pulling his phone out, probably to message my other overprotective boyfriend to complain about my door. I rolled my eyes at him.

Our walk to biology took us past the admin building, where Melior Group had set up a base of operations in the back rooms of the ground floor, much to the ire of the busy receptionists. One of the frowning, hard men clad in black was Alec. You could even say the asshole was the frowniest and hardest of them all, and he happened to come down the stairs just as we passed. Three identically dressed men followed close behind him.

I tried to pick up the pace, but Alec came straight for us, avoiding my gaze but waving Ethan down.

"Hey, Kid," he called out, "what do you mean her door is not safe?"

I turned to Ethan, shocked. I thought he was texting Josh about my "unsafe" door. I never would have guessed it was Alec on the other side of the message.

"Just has one standard entry handle, and the door isn't reinforced. Dunno." He shrugged. "Just seems flimsy. You're the security expert."

"My door is not flimsy." This was getting out of hand. "And anyway, with all the heavily armed men around campus . . ." I gestured to the men who had caught up with Alec and were listening in on our conversation, but Alec ignored me.

"Nah, good call, man. I'll make sure Gabe gets someone out today to deal with it."

I turned my shocked expression on Alec. I couldn't believe he was buying into Ethan's paranoia and even getting Tyler involved.

"Holy shit, it's Hawaii girl!" one of the men standing behind Alec called out, slapping one of his companions lightly on the chest.

Alec reacted immediately, speaking a little too fast as he turned to his Melior Group friends. "We should get to our post, guys."

But the one who'd spoken walked right past Alec to stand in front of me. He was of average height with straight black hair, cut very short—the standard among Melior Group employees. He reminded me a little of a teacher I'd had when my mother and I lived in Japan, only about ten years younger.

"You look much better than the last time I saw you." He smiled warmly, his intelligent eyes challenging me to remember.

I frowned. "Thanks? Have we met?"

"Well, you weren't really conscious, so technically we didn't really meet."

"OK. Well, that's creepy." I laughed nervously, taking an exaggerated step back. Neither Alec nor Ethan was going into protective Variant mode, so I was pretty sure this guy wasn't an actual threat, but not being able to figure him out was bugging me.

"Don't blame you for not remembering. It was dark and cold and wet. And you wouldn't have seen my face." He smiled again, raising his eyebrows expectantly.

"Uh, getting creepier by the . . ." Then realization dawned. I looked from the smiling man in front of me to Alec, who was frowning at us with his arms crossed, to the two other men behind them.

Images of water lapping at my face and the sensation of stabbing cold in my limbs came back to me as I finally understood: I was standing in front of Alec's team.

These were the men who had saved my life.

I inhaled sharply as my hands flew to my mouth.

"I think she remembers us." The man chuckled, turning to his teammates.

I rushed forward, regaining the distance I'd put between us only a moment ago, and threw my arms around one of my saviors, holding him tight around his middle.

He froze in surprise, but then his arms gently tightened around my shoulders.

"Thank you." I kept it simple but made sure to say it fast. The last time I'd tried to thank someone for saving my life, he'd made it outrageously difficult. "Thank you so much." I squeezed again to punctuate my statement.

"You're welcome. It's all part of the job, kitten." He was still holding on to me but letting me take charge and decide when the hug ended. I liked him already.

"Kitten?" Alec huffed, clearly bothered by my display yet unable to do anything about it. "You going to let another man hold your girl like that and call her 'kitten'?"

"He saved her life." Ethan's voice held a hint of teasing. "Our relationship is solid, bro. She can hug whoever she wants."

"Don't mean to be disrespectful." The man I was still wrapped around spoke to me, not my boyfriend. I released him and leaned back. "It's how I thought of you when I pulled you out of the water. You were soaked, shivering, and felt so light and fragile—like a drowned kitten."

"You're the one who pulled me out of the water?" I knew Alec had pulled me into the helicopter and stayed with me for the ride after.

He nodded, smiling again. I remembered the feel of his arms holding me firmly as my body lifted into the air, and another surge of thankfulness came over me. I placed a gentle, chaste kiss on his cheek.

Behind me Ethan let loose a full-bellied, mirthful laugh. I chanced a glance at Alec, and he was staring daggers at us. I hadn't intended to piss him off, but I put it down to a happy bonus.

I raised my eyebrows pointedly at him, hoping he would get the hint to get his shit together. Then I stepped around the man who had braved the freezing waters of the Pacific Ocean for me and quickly hugged the other two members of Alec's team, delivering my sincere thanks.

By the time I was done doling out hugs, Alec had managed to calm himself and was once again watching everything with a passive expression.

"I'm Kyo," the recipient of my kiss introduced himself, "and that's Marcus and Jamie."

"Eve. It's nice to meet you."

"So you're with Kid now. Gotta say, I'm surprised. And I'd love to know how you ended up in Bradford in the arms of Alec's cousin. When he went AWOL to stay with you in the hospital, we thought you might be his Vital. He was a little obsessive about it."

"Yeah, and that was a frightening thought for anyone who doesn't like excruciating pain," Jamie, the redhead who was nearly as tall as Alec, piped in, and they all chuckled. Alec just frowned more.

"You know we're just teasing, Ace," Marcus added, using a nickname I hadn't heard before. "You're terrifying even without a Vital." Marcus was bald with a dark complexion and the same height as Kyo. His full lips curved into a smile.

"Playtime is over. We're on duty. Time to get to our post." Alec's calm, even voice didn't give anything away, but it had a visible effect on his team. They all straightened a little, their shoulders pulled back, their expressions more serious.

"Yeah, and we really need to get to biology," Dot added. "And I'm Dot. Not that anyone cares."

"Oh, I care." Kyo flashed her a wide grin, dropping his serious soldier face for just a second.

"Mmhmm," Dot grumbled, turning to walk toward our lecture, but I caught the little smile before she fully turned away, and I caught the way Kyo's eyes lingered on her ass.

"Nice to meet you all. Bye," I called over my shoulder, jogging to catch up to her.

FOUR

The first week of classes had been hectic with everyone trying to settle into a new routine. I was way ahead on the reading, so by the time the weekend arrived, I wasn't stressed about schoolwork, but I was a little apprehensive about our next session with Kane.

Ethan picked me up from my res hall, and we walked to his house slowly, holding hands in companionable silence as the sun came and went behind fat clouds. The air had an edge of chill to it; fall was on its way.

At the gates to the property, one of the ground staff flagged us down, wanting to chat with Ethan specifically— because he treated them all like family rather than an army of servants paid very well to attend to his every need.

I gave Ethan's hand a squeeze and kept going up the tree-lined drive to the main house. Dot would be there, and I hadn't seen her in days. Other than that biology class on Wednesday, our schedules didn't overlap.

Lost in my worries for the little black-haired demon, I let myself in through the front door as usual but pulled up short, an embarrassing squeak escaping my lips.

Wandering out of Tyler's office, half-distracted by a stack of papers in his hand, was Lucian Zacarias. He was dressed casually in tan pants and a collared T-shirt and, for a second, looked as startled to see me barge into his house as I was to see him. He was never home.

A smile quickly replaced the surprise on his face, and for the first time I saw a hint of Ethan there. The resemblance to his other nephew, Alec, was evident in the strong jaw and intelligent, calculating eyes, but I could see only Ethan when he smiled.

"I'm so sorry, Mr. Zacarias. I should have knocked."

He chuckled, turning to face me fully and dropping the hand with the papers to his side. "Nonsense. My nephews have all told you to treat this as your own home. And please, Evelyn, call me Lucian. Or Loulou, if you prefer."

His eyes sparkled a little, clearly amused at some joke that had gone over my head.

"I'm sorry. What?"

"Loulou. It's what you used to call me when you were little."

"Oh . . ." I wasn't sure what to say to that. A strange kind of nostalgia for something I couldn't even remember swept over me, reminding me once again I wasn't a newcomer here. These people had known me since I was born.

As I mulled that over, Lucian watched me with kind eyes. Right then, he reminded me most of Tyler. I knew they weren't related, but it hadn't escaped my attention that he'd referred to them all as his nephews; they were obviously all close to Uncle Lucian.

"I think I'll stick with Lucian, if that's OK."

He smiled and nodded in approval, but before he could make another move, I blurted out another question. "Did you know my mother? I mean, I know you knew her . . . you all knew her, but . . . did you know her well? Do you remember her?"

"Yes. I knew her well." The sadness in his eyes was so similar to mine whenever I thought of her that it was simultaneously disconcerting and comforting.

A weight I hadn't realized I was holding lifted slightly. I wasn't the only one who remembered her. Keeping her memory alive was no longer my solitary burden to bear.

My mother had rarely spoken about her life before it was just the two of us, running all over the world under a cloak of anonymity, and here was a person who had known her well, who seemed open to talking about it. With a firm nod, I opened my mouth to ask Lucian more, but then Ethan burst through the door.

"Hey, Uncle Luce!" he boomed, grabbing me by the hand and dragging me toward the stairs.

"Hey, Kid. Try to get some studying done as well. Don't just slack off all day."

"Yeah, yeah!" he called back, already halfway up the stairs.

I looked back toward the first person I'd met who knew my mother before she was a mother, but the spot where he'd been standing was empty.

As Ethan and I barreled into Josh's room, I was distracted by the music coming from the high-quality speakers and the sight of my other boyfriend sprawled on the couch, so absorbed in a book he didn't even look up. He was in sweats and a Misfits T-shirt, listening to Muse and reading Orwell's *1984*.

I dropped Ethan's hand and leaned over the couch, pressing my face to the back of his book. Then I slowly peeked over the top of it. On cue, the corner of his lip twitched.

"Do you have any idea how distracting that is?" His green eyes danced with amusement as they finally looked into mine.

"Yes. That's why I'm doing it." I tried to keep a straight face but laughed.

With an over-the-top sigh, Josh dropped the book onto the coffee table just in time for Ethan to come up behind me and surprise us both. In one swift move, he swept my feet out from under me and flipped my legs over the back of the couch, making me land hard on top of Josh.

I screamed, but it ended in hysterical laughter.

"Oof!" Josh had the air knocked out of him, but he wrapped his arms around me. "Kid! A little warning!"

"Hey, is it because of your uncle that everyone calls you Kid?" I asked. My back was to Josh's front, and I made myself comfortable.

"Yeah, I guess so." The big guy shrugged, planting himself on the couch at our feet.

"He used to hate it when he was little." Josh chuckled, his breath tickling my neck.

"I'm the youngest, and after . . ." He still couldn't bring himself to say the words. "When we all started living with him, it would always be 'take the kid with you,' 'make sure the kid eats,' 'has the kid done his homework?' Tyler and Alec looked out for me and Josh, but Josh was always mature for his age, and it left me feeling like I wanted to be older all the time. Constantly being referred to as 'kid' definitely grated."

"But it stuck," Josh added.

"It stuck. I got used to it. I don't even notice it anymore. But I do notice that you don't call me that. You only ever say Ethan now, if it's not one of our nicknames." He smiled, flashing me his dimples.

He was giving me an out from a potentially heavy conversation, but I had a feeling he needed some reassurance. "After that night when I ran here like a crazy person because you'd overused your ability"—the smile left Ethan's face, and Josh held me a little tighter—"I just couldn't think of you as Kid anymore. It felt too casual. There is nothing casual about what you are to me, Ethan."

The smile slowly crept back, but it wasn't a playful one. He leaned forward, keeping himself suspended above us, and kissed me, unbothered by the fact that I was still in Josh's arms. The kiss was sweet and ended quickly, but it made me melt.

Ethan joked and laughed all the time, but he had a real vulnerable side that needed to be nurtured. Sometimes the big booming laugh and inappropriate jokes were just a cover for the scared little kid inside. And if he could be my protector, I could be his support.

Dot arrived just minutes before Kane, and we sweated and grunted through a heavy sparring session. After recovering, we spent the next few hours studying and practicing Light transfer. Dot floated in and out of Josh's room for a while, joining our study and conversations, but she ended up keeping mostly to herself in her usual room at the mansion. She was having a down day, her usual vibrant personality dulled by worry for her brother and Vital. I wanted to go be with her, but Josh stopped me, suggesting she needed some time to herself.

At lunch we wandered down to the kitchen, and Ethan made pizza—with handmade crust and Italian prosciutto and mozzarella. The incredible aroma brought Tyler, Alec, and Lucian out of the study. The men all sat around the big dining table stuffing their faces, and conversation turned to the search for Charlie and the other missing Vitals.

I finished my pizza but couldn't stop thinking about Dot, all alone in her room, so I put a few pieces on a plate and went back upstairs.

No movement or music was coming from her room, but the door was open. Thinking she might be taking a nap, I approached quietly, avoiding the creaky floorboard in the hall.

I stopped just outside her door, and my brows furrowed. Dot was kneeling in front of the bed, her butt resting on her heels and her hands on top of the mattress. For a moment I thought she might be praying, and I nearly backed away to give her privacy.

But something about the posture didn't fit that explanation, and a tiny movement in front of Dot's head caught my attention. Lying on her belly inches in front of Dot's face was Squiggles. The gray ferret seemed to be staring as intently at Dot as Dot was at her, both their heads resting on their folded hands/paws.

My usually feisty friend was trying to communicate with her ferret.

My heart sank. Dot was *really* struggling today. I hadn't, until that moment, realized how far-reaching the effects of losing her Vital were. She'd lost not only her brother but her access to the Light and, with it, the ability to communicate with animals that had been such a massive part of her since childhood.

Dot sighed deeply. Squiggles lifted her head and reached a tiny paw out, resting it gently on her human friend's cheek, her beady little eyes darting all over Dot's face.

"I know," Dot ground out between gritted teeth, her voice almost too quiet for me to hear. "I'm trying. I'm trying *so hard*." A soft sob escaped her and pushed me into action.

I walked into the room, setting the plate with the pizza on the bedside table and kneeling next to my friend.

She looked up at me with wet eyes. I pulled her into a tight hug, and she let her tears flow freely while I rocked us back and forth.

After a few minutes her crying calmed down, and she pulled away, leaning her side against the bed. "I'm losing Squiggles, Eve. Within a few weeks of him being gone, I started to lose the ability to connect to any animal within range remotely. But I've had Squiggles for years, and our bond is strong, so I could always reach her if I needed her. But in the last few days . . . I'm losing her too. I can only hear her clearly if we're touching."

"Oh, Dot . . ." I didn't know what to say. I'd never had an ability or a brother. I didn't know what it was like to lose either one, but I knew pain when I saw it.

"I've had this since I was, like, five, you know. With sibling Bonds, sometimes the abilities and the Light access manifest sooner, so it was just, like, a normal part of our childhood. Now all of a sudden I'm finding out how little I'm capable of without him, and it's like losing a limb."

My heart was breaking clean in half for her.

We both got lost in our own thoughts for a few minutes, staring into space. Hearing Dot talk about how much Charlie's Light made a difference to her abilities got me thinking about my own Bond and the nature of the Light in general. My mind randomly remembered some of the tutoring sessions I'd had with Tyler, specifically the very first one—before either of us knew he was mine.

I sat up straighter, an idea forming in my mind.

"Dot." I placed a gentle hand on her shoulder.

"Hmm?" She looked up, distracted.

"I want to try something."

"What?"

"The Bond is instinctual, right? And the Light flows easily between Bonded Vitals and Variants."

"Right . . ." She frowned at me. This was common knowledge.

"But it's possible for a Vital to transfer Light to any Variant—not just the ones in their Bond."

"Not as easy or natural but, yeah, entirely possible." The frown lifted as she caught on to what I was suggesting. I gave her a little smile.

"You would do that for me?" She sounded unsure, but a little hope had brightened her red-rimmed eyes.

I'd never transferred Light to anyone outside my Bond, but I couldn't think of a person more deserving or more in need than the one sitting in front of me. If I could do anything to ease the pain Dot had been living with for months, then of course I was going to try.

"I'm just sorry I didn't think of it earlier."

"Eve . . ." She looked so touched by the mere suggestion that it was already worth it.

"I don't know if I can do it," I added quickly, "but I'm willing to try. If you are."

"Fuck yes! Let's do this." Her enthusiasm was infectious.

"OK." I took a deep breath and sat up straighter, crossing my legs. Dot mirrored my pose and waited patiently.

I shook my hands out, not really sure why—it just seemed like a good preparatory action—and took another deep breath. I was getting a little nervous. What if I couldn't do it and she was disappointed? What if it hurt?

"OK, um . . ." I tentatively reached out in Dot's direction, then pulled my hand back. "Shit! I don't know how to do this."

Instead of looking crestfallen, Dot chuckled. "Just relax, Eve. Pretend I'm Josh or something."

I snorted. "I don't think you want me pretending you're Josh. Unless you want to make out with me, I'd better pretend you're Tyler."

We both laughed at that, which eased some of my nerves.

"Wait. Don't you want to make out with Tyler?" Dot looked a little puzzled. "I thought the Light pushed you to have the same level of intimacy with all your Variants. Isn't that a thing in non-sibling Bonds—if you're getting it on with one of them, you're getting it on with all of them?"

"According to all my research, yeah. But you try telling Tyler that—I'm not the one that doesn't want to make out. And other stuff." I couldn't believe I'd said that much out loud, but Dot didn't make me feel any more awkward about it. That's why I loved her.

"According to your research? What about the practical application, Eve? You have the perfect test subjects!"

"Yes, I know. And by all observable accounts, the Light is indeed pushing me to strengthen the Bond with all my Variants. Like I said—I'm pretty sure *he's* the one who's not interested."

"Interesting. I wonder why he's holding back."

"Maybe I'm just not his type."

"Pfft," she scoffed. "Please. You're his Vital—trust me, you're his type. There must be another reason. Got to admire his willpower though. Can't be easy. What about Alec, then? You said the Light was pushing you to all of them . . ."

"Stop distracting me. I'm trying to do something important here." I couldn't deny I was attracted to Alec, but he'd been such a colossal jerk to me I couldn't wrap my mind around my attraction. Plus, this conversation was sure to lead to Studygate, and I was definitely *not* talking about that.

Talk of Tyler, however, had reminded me once again of our first Light transfer and the way he'd held his hands out for me to take. It seemed to flow the easiest through my hands. Without letting Dot get another comment in, I held my hands out to her with more confidence, palms up.

She took a deep breath and placed her hands in mine.

I closed my eyes.

Using some of my mindfulness techniques, I located the barrier I'd carefully built up over time and lowered it a fraction, allowing the Light access. With the Light flow open, I drew a small amount into myself and then carefully restored the barrier. I didn't want to take in too much and have to run to Tyler if I couldn't expel it into Dot. It was like testing any new substance—you spot test in a discreet area first to see if it leaves a mark.

The pure power within me hummed faintly, and I tightened my grip on Dot's hands, putting all my focus on sending the Light to where we touched. With any one of my Variants, it didn't need to be directed. As soon as we had skin contact, it poured out of me and into them. I'd spent months learning how to *stop* the Light.

I'd never had to *push* it into someone. It was easy enough to get it to come to my hands, ready to release, but once it realized it wasn't one of my guys on the other side of the contact, it slammed the brakes on. It felt as if I were trying to push a toddler through the door to the dentist's office, and it had a death grip on the doorframe.

I focused on my breathing and reminded myself that I was in control here. Yes, the Light was pure, unadulterated power, but it was at my mercy. I got to choose when it flowed into me, and I got to choose when and how much of it flowed out. Most importantly, I got to choose *whom* it went to.

I was choosing Dot.

Slowly, reluctantly, the Light bent to my will.

Dot gasped, and her hold on my hands tightened, but she didn't say anything. She was controlling herself like a champ so I could focus. I smiled a little and put my full concentration back into what I was doing.

Thankfully, though, it didn't require much more hard work from me. The Light flowed just fine now that I'd established the connection. With my guys, it would gush out of me like a dam breaking anytime I let it; with Dot it was more like the flow of a shower in a cheap motel room with really bad water pressure—underwhelming but dribbling through steadily.

After a few minutes, we released each other's hands, and I opened my eyes. Dot was beaming. It was so good to see a genuine smile on her face that I couldn't have stopped returning it if I'd wanted to.

She launched herself at me, almost knocking me flat on my back, and squeezed with all the might her delicate arms could muster.

"Thank you, thank you, thank you!" she fired off, then shot up and ran to the window. Throwing it open with more than a little dramatic flair, she leaned out and shouted, "I'm back, baby!"

I laughed and lifted myself onto the bed next to Squiggles. The little ferret was bobbing up and down on her hind legs in excitement. Dot rushed back to the bed and leaned down.

"I'm back," she whispered before planting a kiss on Squiggles' head. The furry noodle did a weird excited turn on the spot, and Dot laughed. "I know, right?" she replied to whatever it was Squiggles had communicated to her.

Before I could jokingly ask if they were talking about me, Dot rushed back to the window and held her arms straight out. What followed was like a scene from a Disney movie.

All manner of woodland creatures—squirrels, mice, a racoon, and various brightly colored little birds—streamed in through the window. The birds perched on Dot's arms, and the furry friends crowded around her feet.

I sat on the bed, frozen, my mouth hanging open. Apparently Squiggles wasn't as impressed as me though, because she didn't rush forward to join the fun. When an actual *bald eagle* landed with a big flap of its impressive wings, Squiggles rushed up my arm and perched on my shoulder, giving me a very humanlike "are you going to do anything about this?" look.

"Let her enjoy it," I stage-whispered to the ferret. "I'll protect you from the . . . eagle."

When I looked back to the window, however, a snake was slithering its way in. I shot up and scrambled backward until my back hit the wall. One hand held on to Squiggles—who was trying to hide her face in my hair now that there were *two* potential predators at the window.

"Dot!" I said as firmly as I could, but my voice still wavered as I kept my eyes glued to the snake that was now halfway into the room.

She ignored me.

"Dorothy, cut it out!" I knew the use of her full name would annoy her enough to get her attention, and she looked at me over her shoulder, amusement written all over her face. "Squiggles is scared," I finished lamely, putting my attention back on the snake.

With a roll of her eyes, Dot turned back to the window and dropped her arms. Almost immediately the eagle flew off, the snake began to slither back out, and all the other creatures scurried off.

I took a breath, letting the tension in my shoulders release, and gave Squiggles a soothing stroke down her back.

"I don't know what the big deal is. We were just catching up." Dot waved casually in my direction as she wandered over to sit on the bed, enthusiastically biting into the cold pizza.

Squiggles untangled herself from my hair, scampered down my leg, and went to stand in front of Dot, making a sound that was something between the squeak of a mouse and the purr of a cat.

"You're being dramatic." Dot rolled her eyes as she answered whatever Squiggles had said.

Squiggles ran to the adjoining bathroom, let herself in through the crack in the door, and somehow managed to slam it.

I chuckled and, after checking that the snake really had slithered back out, pushed away from the safety of the wall. "How you feeling?"

Dot was stuffing pizza into her mouth so fast she was on her last slice already. "Arrazing!" she said around a giant mouthful, then paused, her eyes suddenly going sad. She swallowed slowly, staring very hard at the floor in front of her.

"Hey?" My brows furrowed. "What's going on?"

"I feel amazing," she repeated, but her tone suggested the complete opposite. "It feels so good to have my full ability again after all this time, but . . . Charlie."

She looked up at me, her eyes wide.

"Oh, Dot." I sat next to her and wrapped an arm around her shoulders. "Charlie wouldn't begrudge you this. You know he wouldn't. He might give you shit all the time, but really, all he wants is for you to be safe and happy. Wherever he is, he knows we're doing all we can to find him."

"I know. I just feel bad that for a moment there, I forgot about him. I felt so good and full of Light that it was all I could think about. I'm a shit sister."

"No, you're not!"

"Yes, I am!" She was on the verge of tears again.

Arguing with her wasn't going to get me anywhere. Dot was a proactive, energetic kind of person. She was a doer. So I would give her something to do. "You know what? No. I'm not going to let you wallow."

"But . . ."

"No!" I cut her off sharply. "We just had a win. I mastered a new part of my Vital powers, and you're fully juiced up for the first time in months. You might be feeling guilty, but I'm not going to let you dwell on it. Now, the boys are all gathered around the dining table downstairs discussing strategy again. So if you want to do something about Charlie, let's go down there and help."

By the time I finished my tirade, her tears had stopped, and she was sitting up a little straighter, so I threw in a joke to lighten the mood. "Help or get in the way and annoy them. Whatever."

She giggled softly, nodding, then stood up and took off, finishing the rest of her pizza as she walked.

FIVE

The guys were sitting where I'd left them, empty plates and napkins the only remaining evidence of the several pizzas. Lucian leaned back in his seat at the head of the table, arms lightly folded over his chest, his intelligent eyes observing the heated conversation Alec and Tyler were locked into.

They were on opposite sides of the table, both leaning on their forearms. They weren't yelling, but their shoulders were tense as they fired arguments at each other. As I walked past Tyler's chair, my fingers actually *twitched*—that's how strong the urge was to rub some of that tension out. But I held myself back. We didn't have that kind of relationship.

Why didn't we have that kind of relationship again? Why was it that one of my Bond members didn't want to touch me unless it was completely necessary? I shook my head, trying to sweep those thoughts away—now wasn't the time.

I plonked myself down next to Josh, and his hand immediately landed on my knee, giving it a gentle squeeze. He met my eyes with one of his knowing half smiles, and I wondered how obvious my thoughts were.

I returned his smile and, making sure my Light was locked down, placed my hand over his, reveling in the moment of intimacy.

"Alec, we've tried everything else." I'd so rarely heard frustration in Tyler's voice that he immediately had may attention.

"No, we haven't," Alec was quick to reply. "We're still waiting on intel to come in. Uncle Luce is pressing some of his other high-up contacts, and we're working on setting up an exchange of intel with some of the European governments. This shit takes time. We need to give it *more time*."

"It's been months." Now Tyler just sounded defeated. Again, I ached to soothe him in some way, but I threaded my fingers through Josh's instead.

"I can't believe you're even suggesting this, Gabe. Aren't you supposed to be the logical one?"

"We've explored all other avenues. And I appreciate that new info may come in anytime but . . ."

"But Charlie may not have time," Dot finished for him, making our presence known to everyone who'd been too absorbed in the argument to notice.

"Dot." Alec turned to his little cousin, the hard expression on his face softening considerably. "I know this is hard for you to listen to. Maybe you should—"

"We're not leaving," I interrupted. "We need to feel like we're helping too. Dot needs this."

Alec didn't look in my direction, but a muscle in his cheek twitched. I'd be lying if I said it didn't hurt that he'd been soft and caring toward Dot but the mere sound of my voice had him looking as if he wanted to hit something. There was only so much rejection a girl could handle, especially when it came from people who were literally made for me, supernaturally tethered to me.

"Do we even know where to find a Lighthunter?" Ethan's booming voice cut in, preventing an argument before it started. "I thought they were, like, a fairytale or something."

"Is this what it's come to?" Dot dropped her head into her hands. "Gabe, the most logical person I know, suggesting we use a *Lighthunter*. Fuck . . ." She started muttering to herself about Charlie being doomed and everyone losing their minds.

"There is some historical evidence suggesting they weren't just myth and legend," Josh explained. "I've been doing a little research since Gabe first floated the idea the other day, but there isn't much available from reliable sources and not much that's recent. The historical texts all point to them being real though."

"But even if they were, Josh," Alec argued, "you're talking in the past tense. There's nothing to suggest they're legit in this day and age."

Tyler crossed his arms. "That's not entirely true."

"Hold up!" I had to raise my voice to get everyone's attention. "What's a Lighthunter? I was raised as a Dime, remember?"

"Evelyn, please don't use that word," Lucian objected.

"Sorry," I whispered, appropriately chastised. Still, it made me smile a little. It had been so long since I'd had a parental figure in my life.

Lucian cocked his head at me, and his lips twitched too. Apparently he had some of Josh's talents for deciphering my feelings.

"The concept of the Lighthunter has been part of Variant culture and lore for thousands of years." Tyler stepped into his tutor role seamlessly, explaining everything in the same patient, calm voice he used during our study sessions. "In the last hundred years or so, it has fallen into the realm of myth."

"OK . . ." I nodded for him to keep going.

"According to legend, Lighthunters are Variants who have a special connection to the Light."

"Isn't that just what a Vital is?"

"Not like a Vital. Vitals have access to the Light and can channel it, passing it to Variants. Lighthunters don't do that. Their connection is less direct in some ways and more . . . informative in others."

I was fine with complex mathematical concepts and scientific theories. Those things were based in logic. This sounded more like fantasy.

At the confused look on my face, Tyler quickly continued. "Think of it like this: You, a Vital, can feel the Light as it flows through you. A Lighthunter can see it and sense it. They can take one look at a Variant and be able to tell who their Vital is and vice versa. Some of the texts suggest that with a deeper understanding of a particular Variant or Vital and their ability or Light access, respectively, they can locate members of the person's Bond."

As the implications began to sink in, I looked at Dot. She still had her head in her hands.

"For centuries Lighthunters were a revered part of Variant society," Josh jumped in. "They were instrumental in helping Variants and Vitals find each other. In a time when travel was limited to horse and cart, it was much more difficult for people to leave their village and 'network' in an effort to find their Bond. Having someone to point you in the right direction was incredibly useful, and Lighthunters were paid handsomely for their services."

"How exactly did they do that? Were some of them better at it than others? Was there a limit on the distance?" I fired off, my curiosity piqued. Tyler gave me an indulgent smile; I often did this in our sessions when something interested me.

"The historic texts aren't too clear on the specifics," Josh said, "and I've yet to find a text dedicated to the subject. So far it's been just obscure mentions here and there. Around the turn of the century, any mention of Lighthunters seems to just vanish. Until the forties. Some World War II books mention them being used to identify Variants in Germany. And we all know what the Nazis did to known Variants in the thirties and forties." Josh's beautiful green eyes turned sad, and I gave his hand a squeeze.

Now that I had a basic understanding of what we were talking about, I tried to bring the conversation back to the present. "So, how can this help us with finding Charlie?"

At the mention of her brother's name, Dot sat up straighter. She looked very skeptical but at least a little curious too.

"There are people who claim to be Lighthunters still," Josh went on. "They're hard to—"

"Yeah, but they're all nutcases! Carnies and fraudsters," Ethan interrupted. His deep voice sounded serious, rare for him, and I was reminded once again how much Charlie's disappearance was affecting everyone.

"Exactly!" Alec sounded as if he'd been bursting to interrupt the history lesson. "The scum who call themselves Lighthunters these days are no different from their human equivalent—psychics, clairvoyants, and mediums. They dress like hippies and prey on desperate young Variants, giving them some vague bullshit that's enough to give them hope while taking all their money. I don't even know why we're still talking about this!" He threw his hands up and leaned back in his seat.

Lucian gave him a weird look. "Calm down, Alec. We're only having a hypothetical discussion." He looked baffled by his nephew's behavior, although I was under the impression this was just Alec's default setting. I did my best to ignore him and focus on what Tyler was saying.

"We're talking about it because it's time to think outside the box, and I believe there's enough historical evidence to suggest Lighthunters were real. We don't know why they disappeared some hundred years ago, but I do think it's possible a few remain who are authentic. Also, I've already reached out to some contacts who can put me onto an individual who I believe could be the real thing." He delivered the last part in a slight rush, as if trying to get the words out before someone interrupted him, but his voice was still confident and sure.

There was a moment of silence.

Lucian's brows rose in surprise. Alec stood from his chair slowly, the muscles in his neck bunching, his jaw tight. Something in me was pulled to him in the same way I'd been pulled to soothe Tyler, and I squeezed Josh's hand again.

"You didn't. Please tell me you didn't." His intense blue-eyed stare was fixed on Tyler, who remained in his seat.

"I did. I think it's worth a try." I was impressed by Tyler's calm reply; I'd been on the other end of Alec's icy stare.

"You're a fool."

"Alec." Lucian winced as Dot sucked in a breath on the other side of the table, her hands flying to her head.

Alec looked between them, his eyes widening momentarily before he swore profusely and walked out of the room. Apparently he took the pain with him, because the only two people in the room affected by it visibly relaxed.

"Tyler, I think you'd better explain." Lucian had his serious, director-of-an-international-security-firm face on.

"Some years ago, through some contacts at The Hole"—he sighed and Lucian frowned, apparently not liking where this was going—"Alec and I made contact with a person claiming to be a Lighthunter. It was through underground channels, and it was not easy. This was not some hack at a carnival with a table you could just walk up to. That, combined with the fact that she couldn't help us—and said so instead of taking our money—makes me believe she may be the real deal."

Everyone at the table was quiet, their expressions thoughtful and a little sad. No one was looking at me except Tyler, who seemed expectant—as if he knew I would ask a question. Of course I had many, but one was at the forefront of my mind.

"Why were you two even looking for a Lighthunter?"

"He was trying to find you," Tyler said in a quiet voice.

I frowned and looked at the table. It didn't make sense. Why had Alec been looking for me? He hated having me around, hated the fact that I amplified his ability. So much hate . . .

"He never told me about this," Lucian said quietly.

"Probably because it was a bust. Like I said, she couldn't help us. She took one look at him and said no. He was convinced it was because of his ability—that she was keeping him away from his Vital so his 'curse' wouldn't be allowed to grow." He did air quotes around the word *curse*. "She explained it was because the Bond wasn't fully formed yet. She could indicate a general direction but couldn't pinpoint a specific location. The signal was just too weak. You know what he was like—he stormed out of there before we could even have a proper conversation, and that was the end of it."

"You really think she's the real deal?" Josh asked.

"I don't know. At the time I was only trying to be there for Alec. Had I known the Vital he was looking for was also *my* Vital, I would have insisted on staying." He gave me a warm smile before continuing. "That's why I've reached out to her again. I think it's worth looking into. Dot and Charlie's Bond has been building since birth. It's as strong as it can get. If she's legit, she might be able to lead us straight to him."

Dot was leaning forward and listening intently to everything. For the first time in months, her wide eyes had hope in them.

"Or she might lead us straight into a trap," Lucian added. The hope drained right out of Dot's face. "I appreciate the out-of-the-box thinking and the initiative, but this might not be worth the risk."

"Which is why I'm not doing it as an official part of Melior Group operations. At this stage it's just talking to some old shady friends. They may not even be able to find her. And if they do, what's the harm in just speaking with her?"

"All right, but this is strictly intel-only at this stage. The minute you need to use Melior Group resources to verify anything, you come straight to me. We'll need to be as by-the-book on this as possible."

"Yes, sir." Tyler's easy tone suggested what Lucian was saying went *without* saying.

Ethan stood to clean up the mess he'd made while cooking lunch. With a resigned sigh, Dot went to help him. Tyler planted his hands on the table as if to get up, but an idea was forming in my mind, and I had more questions.

"Ty?"

He paused at the sound of my new nickname for him. I was trying not to use it too much—it felt too intimate when he was trying so hard to keep me at arm's length—but it slipped through sometimes. "What's the litmus test?"

"I've been thinking about that too. We would need to verify she can indeed detect a Bond, and then we would need some way to test how accurate the locating portion of the ability is. We have no idea where Charlie is, so we'd need to know she can track him to potentially the other side of the world. Unfortunately, so much of the psychic-like stuff can be faked, and with today's technology, it's possible to find almost anyone if you know enough about them."

"But wouldn't you be able to tell if she was lying?" Surely Tyler's ability would provide all the information we needed, especially with extra Light from me.

He smiled sadly. "Unfortunately, no. I couldn't pick anything up from her, not even a hint. And when Alec lost his shit and stormed out, several other people in the room doubled over in pain, but she didn't even flinch. Lighthunters are immune to all other abilities. Josh's research suggests the same."

"A double-blind test would be ideal, then." I was thinking out loud.

"Yes." He smiled in that way he always did when I understood a complex issue. "Having her try to track someone she doesn't know and who doesn't know they're being tracked would be ideal, but it's impossible. There are too many variables we couldn't control. And Lucian's profile is too public. With enough research she could find some of the Vitals he knows in other parts of the world. That's the other problem. Vitals are so precious in our circles and Variants are so proud when they're located that you'd be hard pressed to find one who hasn't been interviewed by local media or bragged about on social media."

"Right." But we did have a Vital like that. *I* was a Vital like that. I was about 99.8 percent sure the idea I had brewing would not be received well by my overprotective Bond, so I quickly asked another question to prevent Tyler's ability from raising a red flag. "So how might this lead into a trap?"

Lucian answered this time. "The circle of people we can truly trust is dwindling. The tensions between the Human Empowerment Network and Variant Valor are increasing by the day, which means the tensions between humans and Variants are too. People do crazy things when they're scared. We have to consider the possibility that whoever is behind this might plant someone to pretend to be a Lighthunter and lead us into a trap to weaken Melior Group's combative forces."

It sounded pretty paranoid—planting people to pretend to be other people and setting elaborate traps. But then, he was the director of an international security agency, so what the hell did I know?

"I've got to get back to work." Tyler sighed, finally standing from the table and stretching his arms over his head.

"Let's do some training," Josh suggested. "Focus on something productive. I think I might have this flying thing down soon." He flashed me a playful smile and tugged on my hand as he got up.

As everyone dispersed, I excused myself to the bathroom, telling Josh and Ethan I would meet them upstairs.

On my way there, I came face-to-face with the last person I wanted to see. For someone who hated me so much, he certainly popped up an awful lot.

Alec was leaning on the elaborate end of the banister at the bottom of the stairs. He straightened as I approached, his ice-blue eyes looking right at me.

"What?" I demanded with a juvenile eye-roll.

He scowled. "I want to make sure you're not getting any stupid ideas with this Lighthunter shit. It's not going to happen."

"Don't call me stupid, you asshole."

"I wasn't calling you stupid," he ground out between clenched teeth, looking as if it took all his self-control not to yell the words in my face. Then he sighed, and his tense shoulders slumped. "I'm just trying to protect you," he said softly to my feet.

But I was over his attitude. "Are you? Well, that's hard to believe, because the only person who's really hurt me since I came to Bradford Hills is *you*."

His head snapped up. So much confusion crossed his face that for a split second I questioned if I'd hallucinated the shitty way he'd treated me and all the awful things he'd done and said.

"What are you . . . Is this about Dana? Just because you happen to own my fucking soul doesn't mean you get to dictate who I sleep with." His voice was hard, defensive.

"You think I'm jealous? Get over yourself." I crossed my arms and scoffed. I was jealous, but I wasn't ready to admit that to even myself, let alone him. "This isn't about what disgusting things you do with some slut."

"Then what the fuck is it about?" He raised his voice a little, his eyes bugging out as he leaned into me.

"You told me you hate me, you dumbass!" I replied before I could think, my voice rising to meet his.

"What . . ." Confusion clouded his face once again. The idea that I'd been feeling like shit about something so insignificant to him he didn't even remember it just turned the knife, but it was out now, so I might as well complete the humiliation.

"None of the shitty things you've done and said before and since that night even come close." The temptation to look down was strong, but I forced myself to keep eye contact. It may have been petty, but I wanted him to see the hurt in my eyes so he might feel some of it along with me. "You and I might not like that the Light has tethered us to each other, but it has, and I'm as powerless to do anything about it as you are. Do you have any idea how much it hurt to hear one of my Bond members tell me he *hates* me?"

Tears began to well in my eyes, and I only just managed to get the words out without my voice breaking. But I refused to give him the satisfaction of seeing the tears spill over.

"Fuck!" I yelled up to the ceiling and brushed past him, storming up the stairs.

"Fuck!" I heard him yell behind me and then the sound of a door slamming.

SIX

The sunlight filtering through the treetops jittered across the pages of the book in my lap, and I leaned my head back against the thick trunk of the oak tree. The leaves were changing, yellows and oranges dancing with the greens in the soft breeze. It would soon be too cold to sit outside, so Dot, Zara, and I were making the most of the warm October day.

We were supposed to be studying. One month in, we all had assignments and reading to work on, so we'd laid out a big picnic blanket in a quiet part of Bradford Hills' grounds. The spot was away from most of the academic buildings—it hadn't seen any violence on the day of the invasion; it was not soaked in the blood of the fallen.

We'd hoped the sunshine and fresh air would be motivating. And it was for about an hour, but I smashed through my chemistry homework and abandoned the textbook for another heavy old book from a dusty part of one of the campus's three libraries. My unwavering hunt for information about why I'd glowed had been reduced to a tome containing Eastern European folktales.

Next to me, Zara sat with her legs crossed, her elbows resting on her knees, her face in her phone. She'd been the first one to give up any semblance of study.

Dot was sprawled out on her belly facing us, still kind of reading her biology textbook, but her eyes were drawn more and more to Squiggles. The ferret was having the time of her life, chasing squirrels and darting in and out of piles of dead autumnal foliage.

I set my book aside and reached into Dot's tote for snacks, finding myself rewarded with the telltale crinkle of a chip bag. I opened it and set it in the middle, grabbing a handful for myself.

"Good idea," Dot mumbled before stuffing some into her mouth.

Zara barely spared us a glance before returning her attention to her screen.

"Who have you been talking to, Zee?" Apparently food had perked Dot up, and she was ready to break the comfortable silence.

"No one" was Zara's distracted reply.

Dot and I shared a look, a devious smile pulling at her delicate features. I was positive she was thinking the same thing: Zara was seeing someone.

I'd noticed her face in her phone more and more, her fingers flying over the screen. At first I thought she was just using technology to distract herself, but every time I asked her about it, she became cagey, hiding the phone away and changing the topic.

"No one?" Dot's voice was dangerously innocent. I narrowed my eyes at her in warning. Zara had been a bit more distant, but she'd also been quicker to anger than ever, snapping at little things and taking her frustration out on inanimate objects. It wasn't a good idea to push her.

Apparently Dot had a different opinion. She pushed herself up and nearly snatched the phone out of Zara's grip, but Zara pulled it back out of her reach.

"What the fuck?" she snapped, as predicted. "I said it was no one. Respect my fucking privacy."

A few people walking on a nearby track turned to look in our direction. Dot sat up, her eyes wide, her hands held out in front of her. "Sorry. Geez." She frowned at Zara and sat back on her heels, watching her warily.

"Let's all just take a deep breath." I channeled Beth, trying to defuse the situation as Zara breathed heavily through her anger and Dot remained silent.

I could understand why Dot had done it. After moving to Bradford Hills, Zara and Beth had both barged into my life in the most unassuming yet forceful way—invading my personal space, borrowing my clothes, reading my messages, entering my room without preamble. Dot had been just as quick to insert herself into my private business. It wasn't a stretch to assume that before their falling out, Dot and Zara had had the same easy closeness that allowed them to touch each other's stuff without asking.

But I could also understand Zara's reaction. None of us liked to be startled anymore.

My eyes drifted to a Melior Group guard walking past, clearly on patrol.

Zara closed her eyes and took a deep breath. "Sorry," she said softly. I knew it wasn't easy for her to say, and I was glad when Dot immediately accepted her apology.

I reached for the bag of chips, and the loud crinkle helped break the uncomfortable mood.

Zara left her phone sitting on the picnic blanket between us, and I caught a glimpse of the time as I leaned back.

"Shit." I swallowed my bite of chips as I hurried to gather my books. "I'm going to be late for my session with Ty."

"Have you noticed how she calls him Ty?" Dot whispered conspiratorially to Zara, a grin spreading over her face.

"Mmhmm." Zara nodded, eyebrows raised, a smile pulling at her own mouth. "No one calls him that. How sickeningly fucking adorable."

I rolled my eyes but didn't have time to come up with a witty retort. With a heavy pile of books in my arms, because I'd stupidly forgotten to bring a bag, I rushed off, only letting my smile through after I'd turned away. I was glad they weren't holding on to the earlier tension, even if it had been broken at my expense.

The admin building was a good ten minutes from our quiet picnic spot. I set a steady pace, hefting the books onto my hip.

I wasn't the only distracted one lately. Tyler had been as attentive as always during our tutoring sessions and training, but in the moments between, when our conversation would have turned naturally to more casual topics, he seemed more reserved. Our conversation didn't flow as easily. He didn't smile as warmly. He didn't even look at me with quite as much affection in his eyes.

I tried to tell myself he was withdrawn because of all the things everyone was dealing with—the invasion, the deaths, the search for Charlie—but the insecure girl-with-a-crush part of me couldn't help worrying that it had something to do with *me*.

"Need a hand with those?" The appearance of a black-clad man at my side startled me.

"Holy Copernicus!" My hand flew to my chest, and one of my books slipped and thudded to the ground. "Kyo, you scared the crap out of me!"

"Sorry, kitten." He chuckled, picking up the fallen book and taking a few more off my hands while I caught my breath. "It becomes second nature to move silently after a while. Didn't mean to scare you."

"Kitten? Really? That's happening? We're making that a thing?" I gave him a withering look.

"I like it." He shrugged, breaking into a grin.

I sighed. "OK, whatever. You did save my life, so I guess I'll let it slide."

"Yes, yes, I did! Where you off to?"

"I have a meeting with Tyler," I answered, resuming my walk.

"I'm headed that way too. You know, it's funny, with all this extra Melior Group presence, he's had to pull back on his Bradford Hills duties, but he still hasn't canceled any of his sessions with you."

"What happened that night? The night you saved me?" I deflected like a pro.

"Uh, what?" He looked a little taken aback, his eyes searching my face, but thankfully he didn't press the issue.

"I mean, I know the plane crashed. I was there. But I still don't really know what caused it or even why you guys were able to get there so fast."

"Right." He rubbed the back of his neck awkwardly, most likely calculating how much I already knew, how much I'd learned from my close proximity to the guys through my relationship with Ethan. But he had a precarious line to walk. He was bound by my least favorite word: *classified*.

"I've tried asking Alec about it, but for the longest time he refused to even accept my thanks, and he's just so frustrating to talk to." I frowned at the ground.

"Yeah, he can be hard to get close to. A lot of people are intimidated by him, so he's developed a shell."

Kyo was looking straight ahead, his brows furrowed. He'd nailed Alec and one of his many, many issues perfectly. He had to be pretty close to him—not an easy feat to achieve. I was equally happy Alec had support in his team members and frustrated he was capable of opening up to people outside his family—just not me.

"Yeah, I learned that the hard way." My baffling feelings about Alec weren't going to derail this conversation. We were nearly at the admin building's front entrance, and Kyo seemed to genuinely like me. I might actually have a chance of getting some info out of him. "My mother died in that crash."

His gaze flew to mine. "I'm so sorry. I had no idea."

"It's OK." I smiled reassuringly. "I just want to know what happened, you know? I still feel like I have no closure."

I was being more open about this with Kyo than I had been with most people. He was just super easy to talk to; it was probably a massive advantage in intelligence gathering situations.

"I can understand that. And I'd like to help as much as I can, but some things are . . ."

"Classified," I finished for him, with a tight smile. We'd reached the bottom of the steps leading up to the admin building. Several black-clad and suited-up people nodded to Kyo in greeting as they passed. "I hate that word," I mumbled, taking my books back. "Thanks for your help."

"I'll tell you what, kitten." His bright smile had me turning back to him, pausing with one foot on the steps. I was going to be late for Tyler, but he was probably still wrapped up in some important meeting that was going over time anyway.

"How about an exchange of intel?" Kyo leaned forward, lowering his voice conspiratorially.

I narrowed my eyes. What information could I possibly have that a Melior Group special agent couldn't get? "I'm listening."

"I'll tell you all I can without breaking the classification and losing my job."

"And in exchange?"

"You tell me some things about your friend Dot."

He smiled wide, not even a little embarrassed. I laughed; he might just be the kind of guy she needed.

"Deal." We shook hands, and then I hurried on my way.

Upstairs, I passed several people in the hallway outside Tyler's office. Melior Group people and Bradford Hills staff all ignored me as they filed out.

He stood at the door, speaking to Stacey from admissions, who always wore her hair in a neat bun and was always nearby, ready to give Tyler a helping hand. I swallowed the bitter taste of envy in my mouth but couldn't seem to look away from how their heads bent toward each other, how she nodded and smiled before touching him on the arm and strutting past me without even looking in my direction.

But Stacey was completely forgotten once I reached Tyler—chased out of my mind by the way his shirt stretched over the muscles in his forearm as he pushed the messy brown locks off his forehead.

"Hey." He gave me a tired smile.

Our session was shorter than usual, Tyler flying through the topics we needed to cover without pause, his shoulders slumped, his beautiful gray eyes almost never meeting mine.

We were interrupted by one of the admin staff coming in to ask Tyler a question. I packed up my books and excused myself, letting him get back to work. He barely spared me a wave goodbye as he rummaged through the pile of papers on his desk.

On the elevator ride down, I bit my lip and told myself yet again he was just busy, preoccupied, that his wavering attention wasn't personal.

It still hurt.

Outside, I patted myself on the back for not letting the tears overflow. Kyo spotted me at the same time I saw him and provided the perfect distraction, smiling widely from across the square and waving me over.

We found a picnic table near the cafeteria and sat down across from each other, both of us eager to get into our mutually beneficial exchange of information.

Kyo had a warm, relaxed manner that kept the conversation flowing naturally, despite my sometimes awkwardness and the way I asked a million questions without pausing. Unfortunately, he couldn't tell me much about the plane crash that I didn't already know. But he did help me get the pieces straight in my head, confirming what I'd managed to get out of Tyler and Alec.

Over the course of the past few months, I hadn't abandoned my quest for answers. The search for Charlie and the work to solve the mystery of who was behind it all was taking up most of everyone's time, but I'd still found a few opportunities to ask Tyler about the plane crash. Even Alec had answered some questions for me once, when he'd been in a good mood.

They told me the crash was not accidental; I'd suspected as much based on the crash investigators being so cagey about their findings. It was deliberately brought down by a targeted missile. They suspected it was an assassination attempt on the life of Senator Christine Anderson. She was supposed to have been on the flight but had ended up on a different one at the last second.

Kyo spoke about the crash not being accidental but didn't elaborate on the specifics, which told me Tyler had crossed the "classified" line by filling that detail in for me. They all remained tight-lipped about who they suspected was behind it though.

Knowing Ty had put my need for answers above his work made me feel better about his recent distance. I dug one nail into a groove in the timber tabletop, letting a smile cross my features. Maybe he really was just run down.

"So, the fact that the plane crash was deliberate is a good thing?" Kyo's laughter contained a hint of apprehension.

I lifted my head and laughed. "No! Sorry, I got lost on a tangent in my head. I do that sometimes."

"Care to share who was making you smile like that?"

I smiled again—I couldn't help it—and cleared my throat, looking away.

"Ah, so *not* Ethan, then." Kyo leaned forward on his elbows, grinning mischievously.

My face fell. *Shit!* I'd gotten so relaxed with this charming, friendly man I'd inadvertently clued him in to the fact that my boyfriend was not the only man in my life.

"I didn't say that." Remembering that deflection had worked so well earlier, I decided to try it again. "One of the other things I've been thinking about is why you guys were able to make it to the crash site so fast. It's like you knew it was going to happen . . ." I let the implications hang in the air between us.

Kyo watched me for a few moments, a challenge in his eyes, then chose to drop it and answer my unasked question. "That was pure coincidence. We were in Hawaii wrapping up another job. We were simply the closest team."

"What job?"

He grinned. "Classified," we both said at the same time, and I rolled my eyes.

Kyo chuckled. "It's my turn to ask questions."

I folded my arms on the table. "Shoot. But I have to warn you, I'm limited in what I can tell you due to the strict policies of girl code. Some things are *classified*."

He laughed, launching right in. "Is Dorothy single?"

"Yes, but don't ever call her that—she hates it. Call her Dot."

"Noted. Anything else I should avoid?"

"Leather. Foods containing palm oil. And anything tested on animals. Oh, and don't ever bring up dog breeders." I winced. Anything to do with animal welfare set her off.

Kyo fired off questions almost as fast as I had. I answered some and remained cagey about others.

As he was trying to squeeze info out of me about Dot's exes—and refusing to believe I didn't know anything, as she'd been single the whole time I'd known her—Jamie and Marcus walked up. They seated themselves at the table, and both greeted me warmly.

"Dude, you know this assignment isn't to embed yourself with the natives, right?" Marcus teased, pointing at the cafeteria nearby. "You embracing campus life? Gonna eat here?"

"Hey, the food here is actually not that bad." I defended my beloved source of sustenance.

"I say why not!" Jamie piped in, his red hair looking more orange in the midday sun. "This assignment is the easiest one we've had in ages."

"Shits all over the three months we spent in that hovel in Uzbekistan," Kyo agreed, and they all laughed at the inside joke. I smiled and tried not to be awkward.

"He means that literally," Marcus smiled at me, making me feel at ease once more. "We were in an actual hovel, gathering intel."

Kyo coughed and gave him a pointed look.

"I get the feeling that's classified." I raised my brows at him but let a teasing smile pull at my lips.

They all laughed, and Jamie pulled his phone out of one of the many pockets in his cargo pants, typing something into it quickly.

Despite joking about divulging restricted information, they were clearly very serious about their work. But I marveled at how easygoing and fun they all were. They shared things about their personal lives, their families, their hometowns. How in the hell did Alec fit with them? They were so warm and friendly, and he was so . . . not.

Kyo stretched his arms over his head and groaned, rubbing his belly. "I actually am pretty hungry. Wanna go into town?"

"Ace is on his way." Jamie whipped his phone out again to check it. I guess that's who he was texting. And that was my cue to bail.

Just as I moved to gather my books, Alec arrived at our table, an easy smile on his face. The sight of him looking relaxed was so shocking I abandoned my retreat and stared at him.

The smile fell as soon as he saw me.

"Wanna go into town for lunch?" Kyo asked as they all got up from their seats. "The Indian place looks good."

"Sure" was Alec's clipped answer as he avoided looking at me. Kyo frowned.

"You coming, Eve?" Marcus asked as I got up, holding my books close to my chest.

"I don't know . . ."

"Yeah, come with." Jamie smiled, his invitation genuine. "Don't worry, you'll be safe with us."

He was half joking, but clearly he thought my hesitation was because I felt unsafe off campus.

I smiled back but it felt forced. "Thanks, but it's not that. I . . . uh . . ." I couldn't help glancing in Alec's direction. I had no idea how to end the sentence; I couldn't think of a lie quick enough.

Alec's eyes met mine, and he made a visible effort to relax his posture. "You should come, Eve. I'm . . . I'd like you to come."

I stared at him, stunned. I would have assumed he was just putting it on for his team—trying to look casual so they wouldn't get suspicious—but his voice had that honey quality in it that told me he was being honest, genuine. *He actually wants me to come to lunch?* I couldn't quite believe it.

He'd been acting strange ever since I told him how much he'd hurt me. He no longer immediately left any room I entered and had been joining us for meals more often. Whenever I glanced in his direction, I would catch him staring at me as if he were trying to do algebra. It was creeping me out, but at least he wasn't looking at me as if I'd just kicked his puppy anymore.

The invitation to lunch—actively attempting to spend time with me—was another new development.

I blinked slowly, still gaping at him. The determined expression on his face was melting more and more into worry the longer I didn't reply. His eyes darted around, not focusing on anything, and he cleared his throat.

"Eve!" Zara waved to me from near the entrance to the cafeteria, snapping me out of my shock and providing the perfect excuse.

"Sorry! Gotta go! Enjoy your lunch!" The words rushed out, too loud and high-pitched, and I hurried away without waiting for a response.

Halfway across the grass, I couldn't resist looking over my shoulder. The four black-clad men were walking away in the opposite direction, heading for the main gate.

Alec was lagging behind as the others chatted, his hands in his pockets, his broad back rigid. He turned a split second after I did, and our eyes met. We both faltered in our steps. I had a strong urge to catch up to him, say I'd changed my mind. I wanted so badly for us to have that kind of easy relationship—one where every single interaction wasn't fraught with tension and hurt. But that wasn't our reality. I squeezed the books tighter to my chest, hoping to alleviate the heaviness I suddenly felt there.

Alec was the first to turn away. I was expecting him to be angry, frustrated, but more than anything, he looked . . . sad.

SEVEN

The distinctive rumble of Ethan's voice on the other side of my res hall door made me move to open it, but the seriousness of his tone pulled me up short.

"... sure about this. I don't like it."

I stared intently at the closed door, leaning forward to hear better.

"I don't like it either, man, but Alec needs us." Josh sounded just as somber. The mention of Alec immediately raised my suspicions. I glanced at the multitude of locks; they were all unlocked. I could get busted listening in at any second.

"I know. It's just ... if something happens, we'll all be at least an hour away ..." Ethan sounded torn.

"Trust me, I know how you're feeling. But she said she was staying in. I even sussed Dot out, and she went on about how we weren't invited to the girls' night in. Eve will be safe in her res hall all night. And Tyler has ordered a whole unit of Melior meatheads to monitor the building."

Ethan just grunted. He didn't sound convinced.

I knew I shouldn't be eavesdropping, but they were standing right outside the door and talking about me. I couldn't help myself. The talk of stalking me by Melior proxy wasn't all that surprising. Them being away from me, however ... I burned to know what it had to do with Alec.

I leaned a little closer, careful not to make any sounds.

"Maybe one of us should stay behind," Ethan offered. "Dana will be there."

"And what? Crash the girls' night? I don't think that would go down well." Josh sounded amused. "Plus, you know they don't let Dana in until after the match. And anyway, could you really stay back in Bradford Hills knowing what Alec is putting himself through?"

"No," Ethan growled. "Dammit. He's such an idiot. Why is he doing this?"

"I don't know, man. That's why I want to be there. That's why Tyler is using major Melior Group resources to keep Eve safe so he can be there too. Maybe he's not doing as well as—"

A warm body pressed up against my back, and since I was being sneaky as fuck, it startled the living daylights out of me.

"Whatcha doin'?" Zara whispered into my hair, and I jumped—literally jumped into the air—my heart flying into my throat as I gave a strangled shriek.

Zara threw her head back and laughed, thoroughly amused, just as the boys burst into the room.

"What's going on?" Ethan boomed as Zara's laughter quieted to giggles.

"Nothing!" I burst out before she could narc on me, giving them my best reassuring smile. "Nothing," I repeated, throwing Zara a warning look that I'm sure had a hint of panic in it. Thankfully she kept her mouth shut. "Let's get going."

I grabbed my bag and herded everyone out, even as Ethan started protesting, demanding to know what was going on. He really was on edge. Zara locked the door behind us and managed to distract him with chitchat. That bitch was sneaky, catching me off guard like that, but she was loyal too.

As we walked to class, I worked at calming my breathing. Of course, Josh noticed something was off. He cocked his head and raised a blond brow.

In answer, I rolled my eyes and nodded toward Zara just ahead of us, chatting with Ethan. His brows furrowed; he wasn't convinced my mood was just about Zara. I gave him a warm smile and twined my arm around his, leaning my head on his shoulder for a second before walking ahead into the lecture hall.

He was starting to rub off on me. His uncanny ability to notice things most people didn't, coupled with our always having to pretend there was nothing between us in public, had made us both excellent silent communicators.

He wasn't likely to let it go, but the busy day ahead wouldn't leave any chance to talk.

The little bit of information I'd overheard plagued me all day, my brain naturally filling in the gaps with the worst possible explanations. I was distracted in all my classes, wondering what Alec was up to, *with Dana*, that had the guys so worried. I couldn't just come out and ask them; that would mean admitting I'd eavesdropped.

So, naturally, I did the most mature thing possible—I obsessed over it until I'd whipped myself up into being pissed off at them for not telling me about it.

By the time our girls' night in rolled around, I was in a foul mood. I was flicking through channels and trying to take my mind off the situation while Zara studied in her room. When Dot knocked on the door, I stayed firmly planted on the couch.

She knocked again. "Open up, bitches! I have snacks!"

"I'll get it." Zara gave me a pointed look as she passed me, and I stuck my tongue out at her once her back was turned.

She undid the multiple locks, and Dot came into the room in a flurry of bags, pillows, and silky black hair, Squiggles darting madly in and out of the pile of stuff she deposited in the middle of the floor.

"Jesus, Dot. Are you moving in?" Zara started relocking the bolts.

"Whatever. I like to be prepared." Dot smiled sweetly, and I snorted.

They both turned to me, and I gave Dot an unenthusiastic "hey," pulling the blanket I'd draped over myself closer to my neck.

They exchanged confused looks. Dot gestured to me with her head, raising her eyebrow in silent question. Zara shrugged and crossed her arms over her chest.

I couldn't believe it. A couple of months ago these two weren't even speaking. Now they were having silent conversations?

"Don't look at each other about me! I'm right here, dammit!" I sat up straight, my hands in tight fists.

"What?" Dot laughed, but Zara had had enough.

"What's up your ass?" she demanded.

Her delivery left much to be desired, but she got straight to the point. That's why I loved her.

I groaned and flopped back against the couch, the fight draining out of me. It wasn't fair to take things out on them.

"What's going on, sweetness?" Dot sat beside me, and Zara lowered herself to the ground on the other side of the coffee table, rummaging through Dot's bags.

"I overheard Ethan and Josh talking earlier, and I shouldn't have eavesdropped, but I heard something, and I don't have the full story, and it's driving me mental."

"Aww. Did you have a fight with your harem? Is that why Alec's team are camped outside your building instead of one of your guys being here?"

"Don't call them that!" I whacked her lightly with the back of my hand, but I couldn't help laughing a little.

"Who's outside our building?" Zara walked over to the window as she devoured a bag of chips. After a few seconds, she whistled low. "Wow. They're not even being subtle about it. They just checked Pete's ID and frisked him." She chuckled. Pete was doing his honors in Variant studies and lived one floor above us; we'd exchanged polite chitchat in the elevator.

I finally peeled myself off the couch to stand next to her. In the waning evening light, I could clearly see Kyo and Marcus, fully armed, on the ground below us. I would've bet money Jamie was at the rear of the building.

"What did you do?" Zara asked around a mouthful of chips.

I sighed and sat back down. I told them everything I'd heard the guys say, hoping Dot and Zara could shed some light on what they were talking about.

"They won't let Dana in until after the match? That's what he said?" Dot asked.

"Yup."

She looked over at Zara, who was leaning against the window, frowning.

I looked between them. The fact that they weren't teasing me about eavesdropping on a conversation between my boyfriends and getting all worked up about it was making me nervous. This was exactly the kind of thing Dot liked to give me shit about.

"Guys, what am I missing here?"

They exchanged a wary look.

"The Hole?" Zara asked.

"Yeah, I'm thinkin' The Hole." Dot ran her hands through her hair.

"What's The Hole? Do I even want to know?"

"Probably not," Dot mumbled.

"It's a kind of underground club for Variants," Zara explained. "If Black Cherry is *the* exclusive place to be seen, The Hole is *the* shady, disgusting *literal* hole to be avoided."

I'd never been near it, but I knew Black Cherry by reputation; it was a VIP club in Manhattan, frequented by high-profile Variants, and often popped up in magazines like *Modern Variant*. This other place, The Hole, I'd never even heard of.

"OK . . . I don't get it. What's with the secrecy? It's just a shitty bar. Right?"

"Not exactly. The main form of entertainment is cage fighting—unregulated and completely illegal—and you have to be a Variant to get in. They have scanners at the door."

"Wait, does that mean that Alec . . ." I groaned. I didn't need to finish the question. *Of course* this was the kind of thing he would be involved with.

"Sounds like it," said Zara. "Yeah. I mean, I've only been once or twice, and I've never seen him there, but that doesn't mean . . ."

"Yeah. Alec will be fighting tonight for sure." Dot shook off her worried stare. "I've never been, but I know he used to go a lot. He and Tyler used to fight regularly."

"What?" Zara and I asked at the same time, incredulous. I could imagine Alec doing something stupid and destructive, but Tyler?

"Yeah. They went through some pretty hard times after their parents died. All the guys did. Alec and Tyler were angry young men with no outlet for their rage. This place was perfect for them. But then they started hanging out with a rough crowd, and Ethan and Josh got dragged into it. That's when they both joined Melior Group and sorted themselves out. Alec would still go back occasionally, but only to fight. He couldn't seem to walk away completely."

"Why?" I was slightly horrified, but I wanted to know more.

"Look I don't really know the full story, OK? Charlie would go with them sometimes, so I only know what he's told me and what I've gleaned from Ethan and Josh talking about it. And maybe a little from what Squiggles happened to see . . ."

"Dot . . ." She wasn't telling me something.

"Spit it out, tiny." Zara had my back.

"Fine." With a sigh and an eye-roll, she gave in. "The rules of the fight are simple. One on one. No gloves and no abilities. The first one to use an ability, tap out, pass out, or die loses."

"That's why they won't let Dana in," I mumbled, chewing on the corner of a nail.

"Yeah," Zara confirmed, "with Dana around, blocking everyone's abilities, it would be just a boring cage fight. You might as well go watch humans doing it. The whole point is to have enough control to keep your ability back while having enough skill to beat your opponent."

I chuckled darkly and shook my head. That was right up Alec's alley. I'd never met anyone with worse control issues than Alec. "Wait. So then why would Dana even be there?"

My two friends both shrugged.

I moved back to the window and crossed my arms, frowning down at the guards below without really seeing them. My mind was going wild with images of the only times I'd seen Alec and Dana interact—in the limo the night of the gala, her hands all over him; at his bedroom door when he was in nothing but a towel; at Ethan's party.

I ground my teeth, my breaths coming faster and shallower at the thought of her touching him after the way I'd touched him in Tyler's study that night.

What the fuck is wrong with me? He'd made it perfectly clear he didn't want me like that, or in any other way. Maybe his unattainability made me want him more? That probably had something to do with my never knowing my dad—what's more unattainable than nonexistent?—but I couldn't go down that train of thought. Not yet. That rabbit hole would take way too long to crawl out of, and I'd probably need the help of a mental health professional.

No, I needed to deal with the present situation, and I couldn't do that by seething silently in my room. There was no way I was going to sit around watching movies and braiding our hair while Alec did something so stupid. *Shit*, he was an asshole.

Clenching my hands into fists, I turned around. "We need to go there."

Dot and Zara wore matching looks of worry.

"How did I know you were going to say that?" Dot gave a small eye-roll, but her mouth quirked into a smile.

"Because she has a savior complex," Zara answered for me, crossing her own arms and looking as though she was about to try to talk me out of it.

"What? I do not have . . . whatever. Look, you guys don't have to come. Just tell me where this place is. I need to do something. He's not just hurting himself. It's not fair on the other guys, and it's . . . it's not fair on me."

I finished firmly with a little nod. The more I thought about it, the more I was convinced Alec was pulling a *really* dick move. Whatever messed-up shit he had going on inside his own head that made him want to get pummeled, or pummel someone else, was unfortunate. But he couldn't just go around doing stupid shit that hurt his family. Ethan and Josh were worried about him, and Tyler would certainly be stretching himself to take charge of the situation and make it easier on everyone.

"Relax." Zara's eye-roll was much more sarcastic than Dot's had been. "We'll take you to the dodgiest place in the tri-state area. What're friends for?"

"Really?" I was a little surprised it was that easy.

"Yeah." Dot shrugged. "He's your Variant. We know it would be impossible to sit here and do nothing when you know he might be getting hurt."

"But how do we get past the goon squad down there?" Zara pointed out the main problem.

"Yeah . . ." Dot dug through the pile of bags she'd brought, already figuring out an outfit. "Let's start by figuring out what we're dealing with first."

Squiggles ran over to the window and looked at me expectantly. I opened it for her, and she disappeared to do what she did best—reconnaissance.

"No." Zara's laughter dragged my attention back to my friends. "You can't wear a buttercup-yellow poodle skirt to The Hole."

Dot was holding the item up in front of her, frowning as if to ask why not.

We spent the next ten minutes getting dressed in dark, simple clothing at Zara's insistence. She was adamant we would be spotted within seconds if we went in outrageous outfits, if they let us in at all.

Riding down in the elevator, we were almost in matching outfits—all of us in black jeans and tops with dark jackets. Dot's jacket was some high-fashion mesh thing that probably cost a fortune, Zara's was her favorite leather jacket, and I'd just thrown on a dark gray hoodie. I really couldn't care less; I just *needed* to get to my guys before something bad happened.

Squiggles was waiting in front of the elevator when the doors opened. She and Dot stared at each other for a moment; then the little ferret ran off.

"Thanks, Squiggles!" Dot turned to us. "OK, so the good news is that it's just Alec's team out there. The bad news is that Squiggles overheard them talking about their orders, and they're specifically to guard the three of us—not the building."

"Shit." Zara groaned.

"What if I distract them somehow?" Dot suggested. "Maybe a flock of birds . . ."

Zara looked at her as if she were crazy. "I think an elite unit of trained fighters can deal with some birds, Dot."

"Yeah? Think they could deal with a bear?" Dot threw back defiantly.

"Yeah. They have guns."

Instead of listening to another bickering match, I marched past them to the front entrance, looking out the door's narrow window.

They followed me but didn't say any more.

"You said their orders were to 'guard' us, right?" I kept my eyes on Kyo as he slowly paced the stretch in front of the stairs, his arm resting casually on the butt of his automatic weapon.

"Yeah." Dot's voice was almost a whisper. "What are you thinking?"

"Not sure yet," I mumbled as I pushed the door open and stepped outside, my friends right on my heels. I was taking a bit of a gamble, but it was the most direct way of achieving what I needed. Get to the city; get to Alec. I just hoped there wasn't more to the orders than what Squiggles had overheard.

At the sound of the door opening, Kyo turned in my direction.

"Hey, girls. What's up?" He smiled casually, but his body language was no longer as relaxed.

"Hey, Kyo." I tried to keep the burning desperation out of my smile. "Whatcha doin'?"

"Working." His eyes narrowed. "What are you three doing?"

"Heading out." I held his gaze, my chin lifting a little in challenge.

"Are you?"

"Yep." I nodded firmly. As Marcus and Jamie emerged from the shadows, my friends stepped up next to me. They had no idea what I was planning, but they had my back. "What's it to you?"

Kyo's eyes narrowed, but his smile remained in place. He didn't say anything, so with a determined set to my shoulders, I walked down the stairs heading for the parking lot and Zara's car.

"I can't let you do that," he finally said on a sigh.

"Oh?" I kept walking, all five of them following behind. "Why's that?"

"Kitten, come on. I have orders."

"Do you?" I turned, making them all stop, our weird little group congregating in the light of an ornate street lamp. Marcus and Jamie hung back a little, keeping an eye on the darkness beyond. "And what are they exactly?"

"Can't say. Classified."

"I hate that fucking word. Look, I know it would be easier for you all if we just stayed in like good girls, but we all know your orders are to protect, not detain. Even Alec isn't stupid enough to order you to use physical force to keep me somewhere."

Kyo sighed and looked up, as if praying for patience.

"Either come with or fail your mission. It's up to you." Zara shrugged, unlocking the car and moving toward the driver's side.

"Come on. Could be fun." Dot smiled at him mischievously, and I could almost see his resolve breaking. Almost.

"No. I'm sorry, but this is the safest place for you. My orders are to keep you safe, but how I do that is up to me, and I will use force if I must." He wrapped his hand tighter around the butt of his gun. I didn't think it was meant to be threatening, just a subconscious reaction.

Zara whistled under her breath and propped her arms up on the roof of her car. Dot's eyes narrowed, and Kyo refused to look at her. He had an assault weapon and years of elite combat training, but I was pretty sure he was scared of my dangerously cute friend.

I decided to take a gamble. "Do you know where he is? Do you know where they all are? Why you're here guarding us?" I stepped into him, trying not to let the giant gun freak me out, and allowed the anger and frustration to finally enter my voice. "He's at The Hole right now, pummeling some poor asshole because he doesn't know how to deal with his own emotional shit. And Tyler, Josh, and Ethan are all there because they don't know how to stop him from doing it."

His brow creased in confusion, and he looked between the three of us, registering our serious faces, my desperate voice. "Why do you care?"

He wasn't stupid. My reaction to Alec being in danger was too strong for someone who was just his cousin's girlfriend. I hesitated only a second, weighing the risk of letting one more person in on the secret.

Dot tried to save me. "She's just worried about Ethan—"

"He's mine," I cut her off before I could change my mind. Alec didn't have many people in his life who truly cared about him, but I'd seen him with his team. They were more than just work colleagues. These guys genuinely cared about him. I hoped. "They're all mine. I'm their Vital."

I spoke low, but my voice was firm and sure.

Kyo took an involuntary step away, his wide eyes darting across the ground as he processed the implications. Then he looked at me again, a hopeful smile crossing his face.

"Fuck!" He huffed in frustration, and I knew I had him.

"Kyo? What's going on?" Marcus cut in. They couldn't hear what we were saying.

I ignored him, focusing on Kyo, pleading. "We need to go."

He nodded, finally realizing how serious the situation was for me. For Alec. For all of us.

"Change of plans, boys." He turned to his teammates, slinging his weapon off his shoulder. "We're heading into the city. Civilian clothes and concealed weapons only. We need to leave now, so we'll change in the car."

Everyone looked at Zara's purple Mini Cooper; it would fit maybe four people if we squished up. Zara just stared back, unflappable as ever.

Kyo rolled his eyes, walking over to a monstrous all-terrain vehicle with blacked-out windows and chrome wheels. "Obviously we're taking the company car."

EIGHT

About a half-hour drive past Manhattan, we pulled into a parking area in an industrial part of town. It looked like a massive lot for a giant factory, but the only building around was a brick structure that couldn't have been bigger than a four-bedroom house.

As we came up to a door recessed in the building, a very large man stepped out of the shadows, scowling. Kyo took the lead, and the bouncer's face relaxed measurably when he saw him.

"Kyo! Hey, man!" They did one of those manly handshake-hug things with lots of thumping on the back. "All the old crew is here. Should have known when I saw Ace slip in the back with his fight face on."

"Yeah, good to see you, man." Kyo launched into a catch-up session, keeping the focus off the rest of us.

I bit my tongue to keep from fidgeting impatiently.

"Anyway, better get in there." Kyo brought the chat to an end. "Don't want to miss anything."

"Cool, cool. It's gonna be an epic night." The bouncer gave him another slap on the shoulder and then turned to the rest of our group. "Bit young . . ." he remarked, eyeing me and Dot.

Kyo laughed.

"Since when have you guys bothered with legal drinking age?" Marcus asked. "Or legal anything?" He ended on a wicked little grin, slinging one of his arms around my shoulders. I leaned into him and smiled at the bouncer, doing my best to look relaxed.

"They're cool." Kyo drove the point home. Apparently that was all the convincing the "security" man needed to let three eighteen-year-old girls into possibly the seediest establishment in the city. He swung the metal door wide open for us.

The structure appeared to be completely empty, and I frowned, but everyone kept moving. Kyo made his way to a second door farther inside, opening it dramatically to reveal a stairway leading down and a pounding, heavy beat of music trailing up.

"Welcome to The Hole," he announced, resigned. "Remember what we talked about in the car. Stick to our sides and don't talk to anyone."

He took a deep breath and thumped down the narrow stairs, muttering about how crazy this was.

The Hole was quite literally a hole in the ground. The space spanned an area much larger than the brick structure above, and it was teeming with people. At least two scuffles broke out in the time it took me to reach the bottom of the stairs. My eyes struggled to adjust to the dim light; at first only the bar was clear, stretching along the left wall under the naked light bulbs hanging from the high exposed ceiling.

As "Can't Go to Hell" by Sin Shake Sin started playing, I stepped closer to a dark corner behind the stairs, tilting my head. There were two people back there, a woman and a man. I couldn't quite see what they were doing, but something about it didn't look right. The woman was leaning back into the man, her eyes closed and lips parted, while the man pressed one hand to her throat and one to the exposed skin under her crop top. If not for the look of bliss on her face, I would've thought he was hurting her.

Curious, I inched closer. Just as the woman's eyes opened, Kyo's firm grip on my elbow dragged me away.

"Stay the fuck away from the Lightwhores," he growled close to my ear. My eyes widened, and I looked back just in time to see the woman walking away as the man stuffed some cash into his pocket.

Not all Variants had Vitals, but the Light was craved by all, so some Vitals chose to sell their Light. The Bond was sacred for Variants; a Vital's Light was something precious and usually reserved only for his or her Bonded Variants. Selling Light as if it were a street drug was considered outrageous and dirty.

I let Kyo pull me along, taking in the rest of The Hole. The bar was on the highest and widest level—the one we'd emerged onto. The middle level had high tables and chairs. The only other well-lit area was on the lowest level, in the very center: a hexagonal chain-link cage raised on a platform. Bright floodlights illuminated disturbing stains on the cage's bare floor.

Zara leaned over my shoulder.

"Charming, isn't it?" she deadpanned. I just grunted in response. "The sides of the cage come off, so sometimes it's just a stage for live bands. But mostly people come here for the fights."

As if to illustrate her point, the next fight began. The music lowered, and the lights trained on the cage intensified as two people entered through a gap in the fence. A palpable buzz of excitement spread through the crowd. Several people shouted over everyone, openly taking bets on the outcome.

I moved over to the first-level railing to get a better look.

The two people in the cage were warming up. One was a bald man with a wiry physique, wearing a pair of shorts. The other was a woman with tied-back black hair, wearing shorts and a sports bra. They were both barefoot; neither one had any kind of protective gear.

My heart rate sped up. *Was it such a good idea to come here?* I wasn't so sure I wanted to watch a bare-knuckled fight, but I couldn't look away. I wrapped my sweaty palms around the steel barrier and braced myself.

"Keep an eye on the light above the ring, in the center there." Zara pointed at a flat, unassuming light—the kind of thing you might see in a garage—low wattage with a crappy plastic cover. "If it comes on, you know someone's used their ability. Although it's often plain enough to see anyway."

I nodded. I'd seen similar items before. Even though science didn't truly understand the Light or how it worked, we'd figured out how to detect its distinct energetic signature.

"What happens if someone in the crowd uses an ability?" I asked. "Won't that set it off?"

"Nah." She shrugged. "The sensors are placed around the top of the cage, and they point in. It's rudimentary but it works."

I didn't have a chance to ask any more questions; the fight was underway. A loud clanging bell was the only indicator it had begun—no presenter to get the crowd going, no introductions of the fighters.

The two people in the cage circled each other, and then the man lunged, throwing punches at the woman's head and torso. She shielded herself, then went from defensive to offensive in a heartbeat. She pummeled the man, giving as good as she'd got. Even from as far away as we were, the look on her face was visibly feral, blood already trickling from the corner of her mouth.

When she landed a particularly savage blow with her elbow to the side of his head, many people in the room gasped, me included, but more cheered, their bloodlust only intensifying the more violent the spectacle became. The woman pushed the man into a corner. He had his arms up, trying to find a way to push out.

The man's guttural growl of frustration could be heard even over the music; the woman wasn't easing up. Was I about to see a man die?

In the next instant, though, the woman sprang back, clutching her middle. She was facing the other side of the room, so I couldn't see her face, but I did see the light on top of the cage flick on.

The man remained slumped against the corner of the cage, but his hands were no longer hands—they were claws, something between bear and human. The woman turned toward the opening in the fence, where three bouncers were letting themselves in. She dropped her hands to reveal four jagged, parallel gashes oozing blood on her abdomen. Her hands and forearms glistened red, and she swayed as she exited the ring with the assistance of one of the bouncers, trailing blood behind her.

Her cuts were fresh, but I could guess what they would look like when healed. Alec had the same ones around his side. I could remember their texture from that night in Tyler's study. Right before he told me he hated me. Right before we . . .

"That was disgusting," Dot announced from my other side. I glanced behind us. Kyo, Marcus, and Jamie were standing close by, keeping a watch on us and the room.

"I told you not to watch." Kyo smirked at her.

"Yeah, I wish I hadn't. I need a drink." Dot's face held pure disgust. In contrast, Zara looked amused, even a little excited. Sadistic bitch.

"That asshole always ends up scratching someone. Like a petulant kitten. I've never seen him win. Don't know why he keeps fighting." She started toward the bar.

"Those didn't look like kitten claws," I grumbled, following her. If that was supposed to be the minor fight, I shuddered to think what kind of monster Alec would be pitted against. Or maybe Alec was the monster in this scenario . . .

Jamie stayed close to my side, while Kyo placed a gentle hand on Dot's lower back, guiding her forward. Marcus was glued to Zara. I guess they'd each assigned themselves one of us.

I needed a drink too. Alec wouldn't be happy to see me, and his shit would be easier to deal with if I had a little liquid courage.

"What do you want?" Kyo asked Dot, his hand still lingering on her back even though we'd reached the bar.

She arched a perfect brow. "You're allowed to drink while on duty?"

"Keep your voice down." Kyo leaned into her but made it look casual—as if he was flirting. Maybe that wasn't so far from the truth. "We're all just here to have some fun, have a few drinks."

He gave us all pointed looks. Clearly authority figures were not welcome here. Having a drink at the bar would help us blend in.

Dot looked worried for a split second, her eyes flying about the room, but she plastered a smile on her face. "Something refreshing to cleanse the foul taste that left in my mouth. Maybe a mojito?"

Zara and the guys all laughed. I wasn't in on the joke. I wasn't in on anything tonight. I crossed my arms, not feeling very jovial.

"*Mojito*. Oh, you crack me up." Zara wiped a tear from the corner of her eye. "They don't do cocktails, princess."

Dot gave her the middle finger. "Fine, then what do they do?"

"The core four and maybe vodka and OJ?"

"The core four?"

Zara counted off on her fingers. "Jim, Jack, Johnny, and Jose."

"Jose! I'll have tequila," I piped in loudly, and they all turned to me. "What? Might as well embrace the ambience."

Marcus ordered six shots of the amber liquid, and we slammed them back without salt or lemon.

Dot and Kyo started a private conversation, leaning into each other as if they were on a date, while I scanned the crowd for any of my guys.

Two women sauntered up to the bar next to us, chatting as they waited to order.

"Oh, by the way"—one of them raised her voice—"I heard that Gabe is here."

"Really?" The other one perked up.

"Yep. Apparently Ace is fighting tonight. Didn't the two of you have a thing a while back?"

I tuned in more closely to the conversation, making sure my gaze stayed trained on the crowd.

"Yeah, kind of. I only slept with him a few times, but god, it was hands down the best sex I ever had."

The two snickered, and I chanced a glance. They looked as if they fit right in. They were both brunettes, but one had some blonde highlights, and they both were wearing dark, tight clothing—cool, edgy, and a bit rough around the edges.

Zara noticed me looking and stepped closer, gripping my hand and asking me a silent question with her eyes. It was either "Are you OK?" or "Want me to punch her?" The options were equally likely.

I gave her a tight smile and squeezed her hand, turning away from the chicks at the bar as they resumed their conversation.

"Yeah, I remember. What was so good about it?"

I'd be lying if I said I didn't want to know the same thing. As much as hearing another woman talk about having sex with one of my Bonded Variants pissed me off, morbid curiosity had me glued to the spot.

"I think it was his ability honestly," the one with the highlights answered.

"What do you mean?"

Yes, what did she mean? It was painful for anyone to touch Alec. He had control over it most of the time, but if it was his ability this woman liked so much, what kind of kinky shit was he into?

"Well, he kept asking me questions." I frowned and nearly turned to look at them. "Do you like that? Does that feel good? That kind of thing. And while the dirty talk was hot, his ability meant he knew the answer every time and was able to . . . adjust accordingly. He knew exactly what I wanted, and he was more than happy to provide it. It was mind-blowing." They giggled, and it dawned on me.

They weren't talking about Alec. They were talking about *Tyler*.

My eyes widened. The extent of his ability always surprised me—how many and varied its applications were. This was just another one I hadn't yet considered. Another one I may never get to experience for myself . . .

The women were finally served, and their conversation came to an end. Dot appeared at my other side.

"Something to look forward to?" She winked, proving she'd heard the entire thing too and hadn't been as wrapped up in Kyo as I thought. They'd probably all heard.

"Not likely." I snorted, dropping Zara's hand and crossing my arms.

"Don't you like him like that?" Zara asked.

"Of course she does," Dot answered for me.

"I'm not the problem. I don't think it's what *he* wants." I spoke so low I wasn't sure if either of them heard, but Zara took a deep breath, and Dot's little hand landed on my shoulder. I shook it off as gently as I could. Now wasn't the time.

"Can we just focus on one infuriating, impossible Variant at a time?" I said much louder, getting the boys' attention too. "I've procrastinated enough. We need to find Alec. Maybe we should split up and—"

"Nope." Kyo's voice was firm. "No splitting up." I narrowed my eyes at him, but he kept talking before I could argue. "No need to. I know where they are."

"Well, why didn't you say something sooner?"

"Because I'm still not convinced this is good idea. And you're the one who demanded tequila, so . . ."

"What? That's not . . ." I took a deep breath, closing my eyes for a second. "Whatever. Kyo, where is he?"

He dropped the mischievous smirk. "He'll be in one of the back rooms—it's where the fighters wait until it's time."

He pointed to the opposite side of the space, where a corridor led off the main area. As I took off in that direction, a firm hand fell on my shoulder.

"I lead the way. Don't let the shots and music fool you. This is a dangerous place, kitten."

I nodded, and he took Dot's hand before heading down the stairs. Jamie appeared next to me, and Zara and Marcus followed behind. But as we made our way around the less-crowded middle level, the music lowered again, and the light on the cage brightened.

Our group stopped dead.

Alec was making his way to the cage. The other three were with him, but my focus was on the idiot in the front. He was wearing nothing but a navy-blue pair of shorts, every tattoo, scar, and ripped muscle on display, his face a hard, emotionless mask.

Jamie cursed. Kyo ran one hand over the top of his head in agitation.

"Shit." I made for the nearest stairs, but both Kyo and Jamie blocked my path, their hands closing over my upper arms.

"Get out of my way!" I was out of time. I needed to get down there immediately.

"Lower your voice," Jamie growled into my ear as I wriggled, trying fruitlessly to escape the grip of not one but two Melior Group agents.

"Eve," Zara said, "it's too late."

"What? Let me go. They haven't started yet. I can still stop him." Panic gripped my chest. Alec was already in the cage, another man stepping in behind him.

"No, you can't." Zara got in my face, blocking my view. "If you'd managed to convince him to pull out, then maybe this could have worked. But now that he's already down there, now that they've seen him . . ."

"Look around you." Kyo's grip on me loosened, his attention split between preventing me from doing something stupid and keeping an eye on Dot. She was hanging back, being way quieter than usual. "Listen to the crowd. If they don't get what they came for, all hell will break loose."

All around, people shouted over each other and pressed closer to the barriers.

"Thirty on the Master of Pain!" a guy with more piercings than I thought could fit on a single face yelled, and a bookie pushed through the crowd to take the bet. Similar exclamations echoed throughout the room. This round of bets was taking much longer than the first round. People were getting restless.

A fight broke out next to Dot. She grabbed a pitcher of beer and dumped it over the two Neanderthals throwing punches, and Kyo finally released me to yank her away from them.

I pushed past Zara and stood right up against the barrier, wrenching my other arm out of Jamie's grip to clutch the steel bar with both hands. They were right. These people were gagging for this fight; I wouldn't put it past them to kill me if I tried to stop it.

Alec had his back to us, his arms loose by his sides, his head slightly tilted to the side. He looked almost bored. In complete contrast, his opponent was a bundle of movement, bouncing up and down on his toes and punching the air. The other fighter was a mountain, bigger even than Ethan, but where Ethan's physique was toned and naturally large, this man was sinewy; he looked as if he had 0 percent body fat.

The bookies were nearly done taking bets, and my heart jumped into my throat. My eyes darted around the room, desperately looking for another solution, but no bright ideas presented themselves.

Then my eyes met calm gray ones.

Busted.

Tyler was gripping the chain-link as he leaned on it. When our eyes met, his widened for a beat, then narrowed, his lips pressing into a tight line. Ethan and Josh stood behind him, their postures screaming tension.

I refused to feel awkward for getting caught. Instead, a surge of defiance straightened my spine, lifted my chin. How dare they keep this from me? And then get upset when I kept something from them? I tightened my grip on the railing and allowed every bit of indignation I had to enter my gaze. Tyler didn't flinch, but he did break eye contact, turning to speak to the other two idiots.

I focused on the cage. Alec still looked bored; his opponent was still posturing, bouncing around the edges of the cage, gesturing and shouting to the crowd. They were lapping it up.

When I turned back to the spot where Tyler had been, it was empty. The next thing I knew, my hand was being removed from the barrier, and a male chest was completely blocking my view.

The reprimand in Tyler's beautiful gray eyes was even more intense up close, and it was tinged with something else—fear or maybe anger. I couldn't be sure. I was too distracted by what he was wearing to try to decipher his facial expression.

Tyler was in jeans and boots and a *leather jacket*. I'd seen him in a T-shirt maybe three times. Usually he was in perfectly tailored pants and collared shirts, his messy hair a constant contrast to his clean-cut look. The messy hair wasn't a bit out of place now.

"Get out of the way. I can't see," I ground out, twisting my wrist out of his grip. He released me, but big gentle hands landed on my shoulders, keeping me grounded to the spot. Ethan.

His eyes still trained on me, Tyler spoke loudly enough to be heard by the rest of our group. "Kyo, take Dot and Zara home."

His tone was pure authority, but it didn't escape my notice that he hadn't explicitly stated it was an order.

"Understood," Kyo replied, and Jamie and Marcus began shuffling Dot and Zara toward the exit. Even Zara didn't argue against Tyler's firm demand, his rigid posture, his deceptively calm eyes.

I was exactly where I wanted to be, but nothing was going right. And my anger and hurt at being lied to was not subsiding.

Just as I opened my mouth, Tyler spoke again. "I have to speak to a man about a Lighthunter," he declared in a quieter tone. He was still watching me with reproach, but he hadn't touched me again since I'd wrenched out of his grip. "You two stay with her. First sign of anything even remotely out of the ordinary, get her out." Without waiting for acknowledgment, he turned and disappeared into the crowd.

They were here to contact the Lighthunter? Had I misread this whole thing completely? I thought Alec was against it. Why would he offer to jump into a cage fight so Tyler could make his enquiries? It was far more likely this was Alec being his asshole self and Tyler was just using the opportunity to do something productive.

"You may not want to watch this." Josh took Tyler's spot in front of me, but he wasn't blocking my view as much. He was giving me a choice. The fight had begun.

I placed my hand on Josh's chest, intending to push him farther out of the way, but what I saw had me bunching the fabric of his Tool T-shirt in my fist.

Alec and the big show-off were throwing punches, and neither was holding back. Alec landed several blows to the other man's face, causing blood to spurt from his mouth, but that left Alec's torso unprotected, and his opponent took advantage of the opening. Large fists slammed into Alec's ribs and stomach.

The psychopathic crowd was loving it, yelling encouragement or taunts so loudly they drowned out the sound of flesh crushing flesh. It was the most violent thing I'd seen in my life, and I'd watched Tyler shoot a man dead right next to me.

Bile rose in my throat, and the back of my eyes began to sting. Every blow that connected with Alec's flesh had me cringing, yet I couldn't look away. If I looked away, something even worse might happen. Ethan's hands tightened on my shoulders, and I spared him a quick glance. He was watching the fight intently too, his body rigid.

A tiny bit of relief washed over me when I looked back to see Alec had the upper hand. Somehow they'd ended up on the ground, a tangle of limbs, but Alec was on top, and he was pummeling the other man mercilessly. It was in that moment I realized Alec was lethal even without his ability. His control was impeccable, his mercy for his opponent nonexistent.

Josh covered my fist with his hand and twisted slightly so he could see better. He was as tense as Ethan and me, even if he didn't show it as much. His face was a mostly calm mask, but his grip on my hand was flexing and relaxing in an unsteady rhythm.

A swell in the cheering had me whipping my head back to the cage. Alec was now the one getting the shit beat out of him. Somehow the beefcake had managed to get the fight back off the ground. He'd pinned Alec against the fencing and was raining down a stream of heavy blows.

Sweat mingled with the blood dripping from the man's nose and forehead. They were both getting tired. Yet neither one's concentration had slipped enough to allow their ability to take over.

"Why does he do this?" I gritted out between clenched teeth, not speaking to anyone in particular or expecting an answer.

Ethan's hands squeezed my shoulders again, and he stepped closer behind me, his heat pressing up at my back.

"To prove he's in control of his ability," Josh answered, his eyes never leaving the horror below. "That *he* controls *it* and not the other way around. To prove he's dangerous even without it. Those are the obvious reasons . . ."

"Sometimes I think he does it because he likes the pain." Ethan's voice was strained, and the lump in my throat became impossible to ignore. He was watching someone who was more than a brother to him get beaten. They both were.

I cursed Alec again for putting us all through this, even as I cringed at more blows landing to his ribs, his head.

"Not the pain." Josh picked up Ethan's comment. "I think he likes the punishment. With his ability, no one can touch him. But here, he can punish himself."

His words rang true. Too true. A deep kind of sadness settled into the gamut of emotions I was feeling.

As if he heard us talking about him, Alec turned into the metal fencing, trying to angle his front away from the onslaught of his opponent's fists, and his eyes met mine. My tears spilled over. I allowed every single awful thing I was feeling to pervade my gaze as I held his as steadily as I could through the blur of tears.

His eyes widened a fraction, and then his opponent was screaming. The massive, obscenely muscled man sprang away from Alec as the light above the cage flashed on. It didn't take a genius to figure out whose ability had triggered it.

Alec's opponent crumpled to the floor, his blood-curdling screams cutting through the music and the sounds of the cheering, gasping, writhing crowd. He curled into a squirming ball, his body contorting grotesquely. I'd seen Alec's ability in action—we'd taken down an entire campus full of people together—but that had been diffused over a wide area and so fast and intense that everyone passed out almost immediately.

This was something else; the full force of Alec's unassisted ability was making a grown man writhe and sob in pain.

As if surprised to hear the screaming, Alec whipped his head around to take in the man on the ground, then whipped back to me. The surprise in his expression was gone—he was pissed off. He sneered at me and pounded the fencing with his palms. I had the distinct feeling it was me he actually wanted to pound.

He turned around and took several deep breaths, visibly calming himself and getting his ability under control. The crowd started to boo, disappointed they'd been robbed of more bloodshed.

The man's screaming subsided into shuddering breaths. Only when it was clear Alec's ability was under control did the bouncers enter the cage. They went to the crying man, and Alec exited unassisted.

NINE

Alec disappeared down the corridor Kyo had pointed out.

"Let's go." Josh dislodged my hand from his T-shirt and pulled me in the same direction.

"What the fuck just happened?" Ethan's big hand stayed pressed to my lower back as we waded through the agitated crowd.

I let them take the lead, just glad it was finally over. "What do you mean?"

"Alec never loses like that," Josh explained as we entered the barely lit corridor. "Sure, he's lost from time to time, but never by using his ability."

"Shit . . ." He'd lost control because of me. He saw me and then his opponent started screaming.

I wasn't so sure I wanted to see him anymore. I'd done what I set out to do—I stopped the fight. Even if it was halfway through. Even if it had resulted in more pain for the poor man in the cage than he would have endured at Alec's bare hands.

But we'd reached the last door on the left, and it was too late to bail. Josh pushed the door open and dragged me inside.

He dropped my hand as soon as we stepped in.

"Alec, stop!" Dana yelled in frustration. "What the hell is wrong with you? Just sit down so I can clean your knuckles, you idiot!"

She was standing by a bench on the right wall, a small dark bottle in one hand and a wad of gauze in the other. Even in jeans and a hoodie she looked hot, her messy blonde hair falling around her shoulders. In the same outfit, I looked like a bum, while she looked like an advertisement for Calvin Klein. *So unfair.*

Alec was pacing the length of the room like a caged tiger, his shoulders bunched, his fists clenched by his sides—as if he were still in that cage, ready to throw a punch. He spotted us by the door and froze, his eyes trained on me. At the same moment, the door opened again, briefly letting the sound of the music and crowd filter in. Tyler walked halfway into the room, placed his hands on his hips, and sighed.

Alec's eyes on me didn't budge. I tried hard not to wither under his stare, but he'd had a lot of time to perfect it. It was a really good stare. I lowered my gaze and leaned into Ethan, who immediately wrapped an arm around my shoulders and held me close. Maybe if Dana hadn't been there, it would've been easier for me to speak up, or do anything other than shrink into my boyfriend.

Tyler took a look around the room. "OK, let's just—"

"Dana," Alec cut him off, his voice strained, "can you give us a minute, please?"

No one said anything for a few moments, and I finally looked up to see what was happening.

Alec was still staring at me. Dana was staring at Alec. Tyler's hands were still on his hips, his gun showing in the waistband of his jeans, and as he looked between the three of us, his serious gray eyes were wary.

"Did that steroid on legs damage your brain or something?" she snapped back, but I had a feeling she was similar to Zara in this respect—the sarcasm was a defense mechanism. "Your wounds need cleaning and dressing. You know your control slips after a fight. Is one of these spoiled brats supposed to whine through it? You need me."

At the less-than-kind evaluation of his family, Alec's gaze finally flew to hers. "Dana. Leave." His voice sounded barely restrained.

She looked between him and me, then dropped the bottle and the gauze on the bench and stalked toward the door.

She stopped right in front of me and stared at me for a beat, her breaths coming fast. "Who the fuck are you?" she half whispered, half growled.

Before anyone could spin another lie in our already complex web, she wrenched the door open and stormed out.

As soon as the door closed behind her, we all relaxed a little. Even in a situation as charged as this one, being alone, just me and my Bond, made everything feel a little easier to handle. Yes, our connection was rife with secrets and stresses, but it was there nonetheless.

Alec dragged himself to the bench. Tyler helped him sit up as Josh opened a few lockers on the opposite wall. Eventually he found a duffel and brought it over to them.

I remained in Ethan's arms, unsure what to do, but then a familiar ache in my chest made itself known. I rubbed at it. How much of his ability had he used? No wonder his opponent was left whimpering on the floor. Alec wasn't completely drained, but he was depleted. His physical wounds would heal faster if he had some Light.

I stepped away from Ethan's comforting warmth and tentatively made my way to Alec. Tyler was trying and failing to open a bottle of iodine with a childproof lid, muttering curses under his breath.

I placed a hand over Tyler's, and he looked up at me through the unruly tuft of hair over his eyes. I smiled and ran my other hand down his arm, giving his elbow a squeeze, asking him silently to move out of the way. He let me take the bottle, swiping at his hair as he stepped aside.

Alec's breathing was getting slower, the fight draining out of his slumped body. His legs were spread wide; his arms hung limply over his thighs. He was watching my every move with a blank expression. The scrutiny was making me a little uncomfortable, but I focused on the task at hand. Sure, I was still pissed at him for putting us all through this, but he was hurting and he was mine. I had to do something. I would tear strips off him later. And then I'd probably patch those wounds up too.

Yeah, our relationship was fucked up. Whatever.

I opened the iodine and, with a steadiness to my hands that surprised me, extracted some swabs from the first aid kit Dana had abandoned. Josh handed me a damp face towel; I hadn't even noticed him move to get it.

I paused, my eyes running over Alec, unsure where to start.

A gash above his eyebrow—the one with the scar in it—had created a trail of blood down the side of his face. His other eye was already puffing up, I didn't want to think about the state of his ribs, and he'd somehow managed to get a cut just above his right knee. But his knuckles were the worst by far, so that's where I started.

I gently cleaned away as much blood as I could, moving on to his other wounds once the knuckles were clean. I focused as hard as I could on my Light flow as I went, drip-feeding him tiny amounts as I touched him on his head, his hands, his legs, hoping he wouldn't notice.

"Can someone get some ice for his eye?" I said without turning, and the door immediately opened and closed. Probably Ethan; he was the closest.

As if my voice had roused him from his trance, Alec spoke. "What are you doing here?"

I paused for only a moment, trying to push aside the anger and frustration his question brought up. "What are *you* doing here?" I parroted, giving him a firm look as I dripped some iodine onto a cotton pad and dabbed at the wounds on his knuckles.

He hissed, and my patience with him ran out.

"Really 'Master of Pain'?" I said, dripping sarcasm. "You take that kind of beating and you can't handle a bit of iodine?"

He frowned, but as I swabbed the rest of his wounds, he didn't react, only wincing slightly for the worst ones.

I dressed his cuts and grazes as best I could. Just as I was finishing up with the one on his knee, Ethan came back with ice wrapped in a tea towel. Alec reached for it, but I snatched it from him.

He could easily do this part himself, but I needed another excuse to keep touching him. The ache in my chest had eased, but it was still there. The tiny amounts of Light I'd transferred were being used up as fast as I could give them, boosting his healing.

I pressed the ice to the swollen eye. With nothing left to do, I casually lowered my hand to his thigh, just above the dressing, and pushed just a little more Light to him, hoping the biting cold and the sting of his injury would distract him.

I was wrong.

"Eve . . ." He said my name on a sigh as he extracted the ice from my grasp, dropping it on the bench.

"You need to ice your eye." I reached for it, but his hand grabbed mine and held on.

"I know what you're doing." His eyes flicked down to my hand on his bare leg. I opened my mouth but hesitated, so he kept speaking. "Just do it properly." He placed my palm flat against his chest, over his heart, and looked away.

I didn't waste time questioning his sudden openness to having a Light transfer. I just closed my eyes and put all my focus on the energy flowing through me and into him.

With the now steady, strong flow, my palms tingled where they touched his skin. I carefully monitored the ache in my chest, using it as a guide for when to stop. Within minutes the ache was gone, and I pushed just a little extra to him for good measure before dropping my hands and stepping away.

He gave me a disparaging look that told me he knew exactly what I'd done. But he looked better. He was sitting up straighter, his face less pale. His Variant body would heal itself at the accelerated rate that it was capable of now that I'd given it all the Light it needed.

"Let's get out of here." Tyler handed Alec some clothing, and Josh packed the rest of his stuff into the duffel. "I'm going to kill Kyo for bringing you here."

"Disciplinary action for sure," Alec ground out as he pulled the sweatpants on.

"No one 'brought me here.'" I frowned. They were treating me like a child. "I *decided* to come here. Zara and Dot came with me because they knew I would go regardless. Kyo, very intelligently, made the same decision. You should be thanking them for having my back. Would you rather I showed up in this dump on my own?"

"That's beside the point." Alec's voice was muffled behind the T-shirt he was pulling over his head—black, of course. "You should never have known this was even happening."

Tyler crossed his arms, putting on his in-charge voice. "Eve, this might seem like a shady bar, but it's so much more. There are some seriously dangerous people here."

"What a load of shit." I kept my voice level, refusing to look immature by raising it.

"Eve, baby—"

"No!" I cut across Ethan. Even Josh was looking at me disapprovingly. "That's bullshit. You're all ganging up on me for coming here instead of focusing on the actual issue." I gestured to "the issue," who was now pulling on his shoes. "This whole thing is bullshit. You went on about how I'm part of your family. That our Bond is special and unbreakable. And then you *all* lie to me and come here without me. What the fuck?"

I was supposed to be their Vital—the thing that brought us all together as a Bond. Yet they'd lied to me and left me out. *They left me out.*

I'd spent my entire life feeling as if I belonged nowhere, had no family, was alone in the world, especially after my mother died. Then I'd found out I had four people whom I would always be connected to, no matter what. And they deliberately left me out? It cut me to my core.

Naturally Josh was the first to realize my anger was masking pain. He stepped over to me, remorse and worry in his beautiful green eyes, and reached out as if to hug me.

I took a step away. If I let him comfort me, I would break down crying, and I wasn't done ripping them all a new one yet.

Giving myself something to do seemed like a much better idea. I marched over to Tyler and took his left hand. My other hand went to his neck, and I pushed Light into him with a determination I hadn't felt since the night of the invasion. He looked surprised at the new way I was touching him, his hand coming to rest over mine on his neck.

Soon the surprise was replaced with suspicion as he felt the force of the Light flowing into him. His hand wrapped around my wrist, but before he could yank it away, I broke the contact myself and took a step back.

"Ask him," I demanded.

"Eve . . ." He sighed. "It's not that simple. My ability isn't destructive like the others, but it can be a real burden. You have no idea how many secrets I keep. Because they're not mine. I believe in truth above all else, but I also have to respect other people's privacy. Sometimes you need to let people tell you things in their own time."

"And sometimes they need a push. I'm his Vital. It's *my* business. Ask."

"I don't know . . ." He looked behind me, searching for assistance from the other three guys.

"You're the one who told me we should be more open with each other. That we need to trust each other.

That I should come to you if I ever want to know something. Well, I'm coming to you now. Alec's actions tonight have caused massive tension between all of us. I know me showing up as your Vital has changed a lot, but you need to accept it's changed things between *you* all as well. You're not just cousins and friends and brothers anymore. You're more. *Ask.*"

"I think you should ask." Ethan came to stand behind me. He didn't touch me, but I could feel his warmth at my back.

"Me too." Josh stayed where he was but added his support.

Alec cursed under his breath. "Fine. Whatever. Just ask me, man." He sighed, sounding resigned.

We all turned to face him. He was leaning back against the bench, his arms gripping it on either side of his hips. He stared intently at the ground, refusing to look at any of us.

Tyler sighed. "Alec, why did you come here tonight? Why did you fight?"

For a beat no one spoke or moved. Tyler's eyes lost focus as his ability gave him the answers that were left unspoken. Once his eyes focused on Alec again, they filled with despair.

Instead of filling us all in on the answer, he marched over to his oldest friend and gave him a hug. Alec returned it, and the two men held each other tight for a long time.

"Please, just talk to me." Tyler finally pulled away, his voice pleading.

"I can't. It's not just up to me." Alec looked straight at me, and Tyler sighed again.

"This is about Studygate?" Josh sounded surprised. "What the fuck happened, you guys?"

"Not entirely," Tyler answered.

"I came here for the same reason I always come here," Alec said, his voice hard. "I needed to prove to myself I have control. Of my ability, of . . . I don't know, my own life? Ever since she came back into it, it's like every ounce of control I'd built up over a lifetime just crumbles in her presence. Regardless of the fact that I'm not getting any extra Light from her. It's fucking terrifying. I needed to prove to myself I could still do it. That I'm not a danger to everyone around me . . ."

"Are you fucking kidding me?" Everyone turned to me. It was good to get an answer, but it wasn't complete. They'd hinted this had something to do with what had happened between us in the study, but I was artfully ignoring that. I knew, realistically, how selfish that was—to focus on Alec's shit while ignoring my own. But it was much easier to give in to the anger. Let it distract me.

"You came here for some manufactured sense of control? To prove some ridiculous point to yourself? Do you have any idea what you put us all through? These three are worried out of their minds for you!" I was too, but again, I wasn't ready to admit it. He had come here for a beating anyway, right? "Tyler used Melior Group resources so he could be here to watch you get your ass beaten. Ethan and Josh felt every blow as if it were landing on their flesh. Because they *care*. They love you, you complete fucking moron."

His face became redder as I continued my tirade, a thick vein appearing in the middle of his forehead, his fists clenching and unclenching, straining the bandages over his knuckles.

He stepped right into my space and opened and closed his mouth several times, as if about to say something. But instead he settled on just growling in frustration while making a choking motion with his hands. Then he turned around and stalked out.

Tyler shook his head wearily. "Let's just go."

We followed Alec up a steep set of stairs, through a back entrance off the dingy corridor, and past several rows of parked cars.

He stopped by a yellow Dodge Challenger. At least he was waiting for us.

"Give me the keys," he demanded. "I'll take the bike back. I can't be in the same car as her right now."

"You know what?" I moved forward, ready to get in his face again, but Tyler stepped into my path.

"Enough!" The finality in his voice made us both pause. "You're both acting like children, and I've had it. Alec, you're in no state to take the bike. Get in the fucking car. Eve can come with me."

Alec didn't wait another second, wrenching the passenger door open and folding his tall frame into the seat.

Josh closed the trunk, having swapped the duffel for a helmet, which he handed to me. A little surprised, I looked at Tyler. He already had his on, zipping his leather jacket up as he swung his leg over a motorcycle.

"Uh . . ." I'd never been on the back of a bike.

"You'll be safe with Gabe." Josh gave me a small smile, then took the helmet back and lowered it over my head. He secured it and gave me a little kiss on the nose before lowering the visor and getting into the driver's seat of the car.

Ethan helped me into a leather jacket. I was swimming in it, but it wasn't down to my knees, so it was probably Josh's and not Ethan's. He rolled the sleeves up, lifted the visor, gave me another kiss on the nose, and jumped in the back of the car. Josh pulled out of the spot immediately.

I pulled the visor back down. I didn't want Tyler to see the awkward look on my face. I may not have been on a bike before, but I knew we were about to be pressed up against each other for at least an hour. I had no idea how he felt about that. I wasn't entirely sure how I felt about it either.

I shuffled over and stopped just out of his reach. He finished putting on his gloves and looked up.

"It's OK. I got you." His voice was clear and confident even from behind the helmet. I couldn't see his eyes, but somehow I knew they were looking at me with warmth and encouragement. Despite the fact that I'd been a major pain in his ass.

I closed the distance and swung my leg over the bike, settling behind him as best I could without touching him. My toes brushed the ground on either side.

Tyler reached back, grabbed my right ankle, and positioned my foot on a little bar. I lifted the other foot into the same position. Then he started the engine, which came to life with a loud, angry roar.

Tentatively, I placed my hands on his waist. There was nothing else to hold on to. Not that I looked too hard.

He grabbed my wrists with his gloved hands and tugged until my arms wrapped around his chest and my front was flush with his back.

"Hold on tight." He had to speak up over the roar of the engine. "If something's wrong or you need me to pull over, tap my shoulder, OK?"

I gave him a thumbs-up; forming words was beyond me in that moment. With training and tutoring and all the Light transfers, I probably spent more time with Tyler than any of the others, but he wasn't the one I was closest to.

We'd hugged a few times, mostly in life-or-death situations, but touching him like this made me relive that first day at Bradford Hills, when I was trying not to get a crush on him and failing miserably. I tried not to pine for him, but with my arms feeling the taut muscles under his jacket, my chest and belly feeling his heat pressed into me . . .

We took off, and my heart hammered in my chest from fear as well as from the close proximity to Tyler, but after a while, I relaxed and started to enjoy the ride. We passed the Challenger on the freeway after only ten or fifteen minutes, but we whizzed by so fast I couldn't see inside.

I admired the twinkling lights of the city, then the darkness as we drove deeper into the country, the headlights illuminating trees and a short stretch of black road ahead. With every turn, every bend in the road, every little correction he had to make, Tyler's core muscles clenched and relaxed. Tight against him—my front to his back, my legs against his, my hips pressed into his ass—I was acutely aware of his every movement, of every inch of contact between us, and I reveled in it.

I may have been spending more time with Tyler than any of them, but I also craved him more. Ethan and Josh were giving in to their physical pull as much as they could without it becoming dangerous. With Tyler, I wasn't sure he even felt a pull.

I definitely felt it though.

The Light was pushing me to deepen the Bond with all of them. It was all I could think about at times. Every time I shared a heated kiss with Ethan or Josh, I remembered how Alec had made me feel that night on the couch, how his hands had touched me exactly how I'd wanted them to. Then I'd immediately start wondering what Tyler's hands would feel like on parts of my body I knew he'd never touch, what his lips would feel like pressed to mine.

I craved Tyler in a way I didn't crave the others—in the one way I couldn't have him.

The vibrations of the engine only added to my heightened state, driving me a bit crazy. All the drama of the night melted away. At least that was one good thing—the ride back, the fresh air, and the distraction of Tyler's body were enough to calm my rage toward Alec.

Too soon we were pulling through the gates of Bradford Hills Institute. Tyler checked us in with the guards at the gate, reminding them about their confidentiality responsibilities, and then we were at the back of my res hall, and he was shutting the engine off.

He straightened, leaning away from the handlebars, and my body reacted to his instinctively. I arched my back and rolled my hips forward, seeking more contact in the one place all my blood seemed to be flowing to—between my legs.

He paused, and because my arms were still wrapped around him, I felt him release a deep breath. He removed his gloves and placed his warm hands over mine. "Your hands are freezing."

Hearing him speak brought me out of my lust haze enough to feel embarrassed at how I'd basically ground myself on him. I'd practically sexually harassed him. He was handling it like a champ though, keeping his cool and not calling me out on it.

I pulled my hands out of his and got off the bike, immediately missing his warmth. My legs were shaky, and my numb fingers struggled to unclasp the helmet.

He stayed on the bike but reached out to pull me closer, then undid the helmet for me. I handed it to him and tried to gulp in the fresh cool air without making it obvious I was trying to calm myself.

"Thanks . . ." My voice was croaky, so I cleared my throat. "Thanks for the ride."

I turned to leave.

"Eve . . ." He sounded as if he was about to say something serious, something that might crush me, but I wasn't ready to hear it. His persistent and careful boundaries hurt enough. I couldn't stand to hear him *say* he didn't want me in that way, articulate it in no uncertain terms.

"Oh, right! You can't hold the helmet and ride the bike." I latched on to the first thing I saw. "Silly me."

I took the helmet back and forced myself to walk and not run up the stairs to my building. As I waited for the elevator, I heard the engine of the bike start up.

TEN

It was nearly midnight by the time I unlocked all the deadbolts on my door and stepped inside, but Zara and Dot were waiting for me. We dragged mattresses, blankets, and pillows into the living area, and I told them everything, completely giving in to all the emotions I'd been holding back and breaking down in tears several times. They listened, soothed, and plied me with junk food until we all fell asleep with the TV on.

When my alarm went off at eight the next morning, I nearly decided to skip my session with Tyler for more sleep. But regardless of how unbearable my pining for him was becoming, I couldn't pass up an opportunity to see him.

I managed to get ready without waking my still-sleeping friends and let myself out silently. I wished I had time to walk to the Starbucks across campus for coffee, but I was cutting it close and didn't want to be late.

The thick gray clouds threatening rain matched my somber mood perfectly. I was glad I'd thrown my oversized cardigan on over my jeans and T-shirt. It was the same warm one I'd worn on my first day at Bradford Hills—when I met Tyler and fell hopelessly in lust with him.

"Eve!" Ethan's loud voice pulled me up short, and I turned to see him and Josh jogging to catch up with me.

"Hey." I sounded flat and disinterested even to my own ears, but it had more to do with my sleep deprivation and not wanting to be late than the fact that I was still a bit pissed at them.

Neither one of them made a move to touch me in any way, and I wasn't in the mood for chitchat, so we just walked in silence.

Ethan ran his hands through his hair and sighed heavily. "I'm really sorry about last night, Eve. We shouldn't have lied to you."

Josh hastened to add, "I'm sorry too. Really sorry. We're still figuring this all out, and sometimes it's hard to know where the line between protecting you and excluding you is. We fucked up."

I sighed and stopped walking, turning to face them. "You're forgiven. Just don't exclude me anymore, OK?" The last part was delivered on a near whisper as I looked down at our shoes—my black flats, Ethan's sneakers, Josh's loafers.

Ethan rushed forward and wrapped me up in a hug that nearly lifted my feet off the ground. "Thank god! I barely got any sleep. I wanted to come over to your place so bad, but Josh made me leave you alone."

I hugged him back as I flashed Josh a grateful look. I needed to unload to my friends and have some time away from the guys to process—Josh knew that, as usual. He smiled and nodded.

We kept walking. I increased our pace, once again wary of being late.

"Where you off to this early anyway?" Josh asked. "We were coming to see if you wanted to get coffee while we groveled for your forgiveness."

I cocked my head at him, confused. "My session with Tyler." Had I gotten the days wrong?

They exchanged a worried glance before Ethan asked, "He didn't cancel?"

"No. Why would he?" I faltered. Had my behavior last night put him off more than I realized? Was he so repelled by me that he didn't even want to tutor me anymore?

"Today is his mom's birthday," Josh explained. "He usually takes the day off . . ."

"Oh." Tyler was grieving. That just made me want to go to him more. Maybe it was selfish, but I wanted to see him, see if there was anything I could do to help. After all, I knew exactly how he was feeling. We all did.

"Well, he hasn't told me not to come, so I might just check if he's up for it anyway." We'd already reached the front of the admin building.

"I think that's a good idea." Ethan nodded. "Maybe he could use the distraction."

Josh sighed. "I think you're right. Can't be worse than how he usually deals with it."

They both nudged me in the direction of the front doors, not giving me a chance to interrogate them about how Tyler usually dealt with this difficult day.

Riding in the elevator up to Tyler's office, I wasn't sure what to expect. After my mother died, I hated the look of pity in people's eyes. Their over-the-top reactions made me think about it all over again. I just wanted them to treat me normally so I could get through one hour without feeling like bursting into tears.

As I slowly approached his door, fidgeting with my cardigan sleeves, I took a deep breath and did my best to put a neutral expression on my face. I refused to look at Tyler with pity. I'd let him take the lead. If he wanted to tell me about his mother, I would listen. If he wanted to just have a normal session, I would ask a million questions and stick to the plan.

I rapped on the door and pushed it open. I never waited for him to invite me in anymore. But maybe I should have.

He was leaning back in his chair, and perched on the desk facing him was some woman. Dressed in a tight skirt and a soft blue sweater, her blonde hair in a neat, understated bun, she was leaning into him with her hand on his arm, speaking softly.

They both looked in my direction, and I saw it was Stacey from admissions. I resisted the urge to cross the room and rip her arm out of its socket. Tyler wasn't my boyfriend, I reminded myself; it was just the Bond making me react possessively, and I'd only a second ago decided I would do whatever he needed. The neutral look remained plastered to my face as I took my emotion out on the door handle, gripping it tight.

"Oh, Eve, right?" Stacey stood up. "Gabe is actually not feeling well today, so he's going to cancel all his appointments, sweetie. I'm sorry you came up here before I had a chance to let you know."

She placed a hand on his shoulder. It took all my self-control not to stare daggers at the exact spot where her hand rested.

Before I had a chance to answer, Tyler stood up, dislodging Stacey's hand. "Actually, I might keep this appointment." He lowered his voice, but I could still hear him perfectly well. "Might be good to have a distraction, you know? Focus on work for a bit."

"Of course." She had concern painted all over her face. Pity too. "You just let me know if you need anything. *Anything.*"

That last "anything" had an edge of suggestion to it. How transparent could a grown woman be?

"Right. Yes. Thank you." Tyler gave her a tight smile and turned his attention to me. "Come in, Eve. We have a lot to cover today."

Stacey finally went to the door and, with a last pitying smile, left the room.

Tyler and I stared at each other as her soft footsteps retreated down the carpet. When we heard the ding of the elevator, he slumped back against the side of his desk, his shoulders sagging. "I thought she would never leave."

I chuckled nervously, putting my bag down by the door before closing it. "I thought I was interrupting."

"Oh, you were," he said slowly, his eyes downcast. "And I'm so glad you did. The last thing I need today is . . ." He trailed off, staring into space.

It was so unlike him to have incomplete thoughts that my concern kicked up a notch. "I was so worried about Alec last night."

He kept staring, unfocused, at a spot low on the wall behind me. "He puts me through hell every time he fights. It's even worse for Kid and Josh. There's no stopping him, so I just try to manage the fallout as best I can—try to keep everyone . . . I don't even know. Safe? That's why I tried to keep you away last night. Not just because The Hole is dangerous. I wanted to protect you from seeing that, seeing how it affects us all. And then I see Dot, and I'm reminded of Charlie and what he must be going through, and I feel like we're not doing enough to find him. Like *I'm* not doing enough . . . and then my mom's birthday comes around, and I just feel like a twelve-year-old kid again, missing her, and I don't know how I can do it all anymore."

I twisted the edge of my cardigan between my hands. Tyler carried *so much* on his shoulders. How could I even begin to help him with the weight of that burden?

Should I ask about his mother? Should I make a start on our study session? I'd decided to let him take the lead, but he was just sitting there, looking broken.

I decided the best thing would be to ask what he wanted. It's what he would do. Be clear and direct.

I cleared my throat. "Tyler . . ."

As soon as his name was off my lips, spoken softer than I'd intended, he raised his head and looked at me.

The emotion in his gaze made me completely forget what I'd been trying to ask. His beautiful gray eyes, usually so bright with intelligence and curiosity, looked glassy and bloodshot, and his hair was even messier than usual, as if he'd been running his hands through it.

He held the intense stare for a few moments, then dropped his head again with a sigh. He needed something from me, but I wasn't sure what it was, and my attempt to ask him had failed miserably.

Without thinking about it too much, I raised my hand and ran it gently through his hair, pushing the mess off his forehead. He leaned into my touch, and I did it again, this time softly scraping my nails over his scalp. On my third pass, I rested my other arm gently on his shoulder, letting my fingers gently scratch the nape of his neck.

He raised his hands and tentatively placed them high on my hips, over my jeans. He wanted more of whatever it was I was giving him, and I was happy to oblige. I stepped farther into him, positioning myself between his legs but still not leaning into him fully. I didn't want him to get the wrong idea after the way I'd pressed myself into him on the bike the night before.

But as soon as I stepped into his space, he pulled me in the rest of the way and buried his head against my neck. And then his shoulders started to bob up and down, and his breathing became uneven. He was *crying*. After a split second of frozen shock, I wrapped my arms around him, one cradling his head and the other curving around his shoulders. He banded both arms around my middle and held me tightly.

He didn't sob or make any dramatic sounds. He just cried softly as I held him, my heart breaking.

A lump formed in my throat, and tears stung my own eyes. I was doing my best to be strong for him, but seeing him so upset was incredibly hard. The wetness in my eyes reminded me to keep my Light in check. It tended to go haywire when I got emotional, and I didn't want it to distract Tyler. He'd always been there for me to expel excess Light into when it overwhelmed me. This moment needed to be about what *I* could do for *him*.

I checked my mental barriers; my control had slipped, and excess Light was coursing through our contact. I took a deep breath and concentrated on keeping it in check while I gently moved my hand away from the skin on Tyler's neck.

His head snapped up. "Don't," he whispered softly, his hands once again landing on my hips.

"I'm so sorry. I've got it under control now. You don't have to do that for me today."

"No, that's not what I meant. Don't stop." He grabbed my hand and placed it on his cheek. "It feels good."

"Oh. OK." If he wanted whatever the Light made him feel, then I would give it to him.

I held his face on both sides and let my instincts take over, let his needs speak directly to the Light, let the Light flow. It trickled out of my hands as I wiped the tears off his cheeks with my thumbs, and his eyes widened slightly before drooping closed. A smile tugged at the corners of his lips, and he leaned forward with a small sigh until our foreheads were touching.

We stood like that for a long time, letting our supernatural connection tether us closer, healing unspoken wounds.

After a while Tyler started to speak. As if opening ourselves to our Vital Bond had opened some emotional block, he began telling me about his mother. He told me she was a single parent, and he never knew his father. She was a ballroom dancer and used to drag him to the classes she taught in the evenings.

As he told me how close she was to my mother, I got a lump in my throat. His pain directly mirrored mine. I felt every affectionate smile on his face, every chuckle at a silly memory, every wistful look as if they were my own.

We slowly moved to a more comfortable position on the floor, me leaning back against his desk, his head in my lap.

"And she loved ice cream. Used to make it from scratch. It was the creamiest, most delicious ice cream you would've ever tasted. And whenever it was her birthday or my birthday, there would be ice cream. It didn't matter that my birthday's in the middle of winter." He chuckled, his shoulders bumping against the side of my thigh. "She would make it anyway, and we would bundle up under a million blankets and eat it."

His ice cream story gave me an idea. "Keep talking, I'm listening," I murmured as I pulled my phone out of my pocket.

I absentmindedly ran my fingers through his hair again as I typed out a quick text to Josh.

Can you guys come to Tyler's office please? Bring ice cream.

I hit send and then hesitated, not sure I wanted to send the next bit. Reminding myself this was about Tyler, I typed it out quickly.

And bring the "Master of Pain."

Josh's reply came quickly.

Great idea! Done and done. :)

I smiled.

And get the good stuff. Ben and Jerry's or something. None of that cheap shit.

Yes, ma'am.

I put the phone away and focused on Tyler once more.

It couldn't have been more than ten minutes later that we heard footsteps in the hallway and the door handle turned.

Tyler sucked in a sharp breath and shot up from his horizontal position. He was propped up on his elbows, one knee bent and ready to push himself up farther, when he realized it was Josh walking through the door, with Ethan behind him and Alec bringing up the rear.

Josh paused but didn't allow any surprise to enter his expression. "Chill, man. It's just us."

Tyler relaxed, although he didn't return his head to my lap. Instead he shifted into a sitting position next to me, our backs against the desk. I immediately missed the warmth of his head on my legs and bent my knees up to ease the empty feeling.

The guys joined us on the floor, and Alec extracted three tubs of ice cream from a little plastic bag. It wasn't Ben and Jerry's, but it was amazing.

"It's from a small local producer," Ethan explained, getting that spark in his eye he had whenever he talked about food. "There's only one grocer in the area that stocks it. Luckily it was on Alec's way here."

He smiled at his cousin, a genuine smile that made his dimples appear. Surprisingly Alec smiled back. It was the most relaxed I'd seen him since Studygate, and it reminded me of honey-voiced Alec. A pang of longing slowly blossomed inside me and settled somewhere deep inside my chest.

What had caused such an improvement in his mood since last night? I studied his face as he'd been studying me lately, trying to puzzle it out, but all I could see was the physical damage from the fight. The cut over his eyebrow still had a dressing on it, but the eye was less puffy, and he wasn't moving as if he had a broken rib anymore.

Our talk of dead mothers was abandoned in favor of lighter topics. Josh played some music on his phone, and we chatted and joked, the guys teasing each other. Even Alec joined in, giving me a rare glimpse into their group dynamic. It was nice to see them like that, to see how people who weren't related by blood could still be a family. It was even nicer to be included in it—another stark contrast to the previous night.

I hoped things would keep moving in this direction. That we could have more of this and less of the tension between me and Tyler, less of the hostility between me and Alec, less of the barely restrained physical pull between me and Ethan and Josh. Less of the drama and angst of the night before.

We polished off the ice cream, passing the three tubs around our little circle as we talked. Then we picked ourselves up off the floor.

Stacey had canceled the rest of Tyler's commitments for the day, and Ethan, Josh, and I agreed we would ditch the rest of our classes. Even Alec made a few hushed phone calls before we piled into the elevator and headed off campus. The fat gray clouds hadn't dissipated, but it wasn't raining either, so we walked past the heavy security and headed into town on foot.

As we strolled the tree-lined streets of Bradford Hills, Tyler fell into step next to me, the other three having become engaged in a heated discussion around football, guaranteeing I'd tune out immediately. He grabbed my hand and gave it a firm squeeze before quickly releasing it.

"Thank you, Eve," he said softly into my ear.

I'd actually managed to make a difference. Even if it was only our supernatural connection that had done it, I walked with a lightness to my steps, knowing that something in me had helped to heal something in him.

"Don't mention it." I smiled, injecting every bit of my affection for him into my expression. I hoped he could see how happy I was to do something for him when he'd already done so much for me.

ELEVEN

Things settled down over the next week, and we all fell back into our routines. On the morning of my next session with Ty, I woke from a dreamless, deep sleep to the sound of my backup alarm.

I knew he wouldn't mind me being a little late, but I still swore under my breath as I threw back the covers and jumped out of bed.

The time for showering had long passed, so I just brushed my teeth, splashed some water on my face, and pulled my hair up into a messy bun. Rushing back into my room, I realized I had another problem. Between classes, the drama of the past week, training (of the Variant *and* the self-defense type), and taking care of basic human needs like food and bathing, I'd severely neglected doing my laundry.

I was pretty casual in what I wore, perfectly happy to get around in jeans, leggings, and loose cardigans, but even I wasn't so blasé about my appearance as to spend the day in public in a stained pair of sweatpants and one of Ethan's white T-shirts that I'd stolen. But that was all I could find that wasn't in my overflowing basket in the corner.

"Zara!" I yelled, reaching into the back of my closet and praying for a miracle.

"What?" she replied, sounding just as hurried.

"Can I borrow some clothes? Literally everything I own is dirty."

"Eew!" I heard her unlocking the several locks on our door. "Help yourself to anything in my room, you slob. I gotta run." The door slammed behind her just as I pulled an item of clothing I'd completely forgotten I owned out of my wardrobe—a white linen shirt. It buttoned up the front but was soft and flowy, not at all constrictive. Slipping it over my head, I ran into Zara's room. I only had five minutes to get out the door.

Zara and I were similar in size, but her hips were a little narrower than mine, so I ignored the jeans and grabbed the first skirt I found, figuring if I wore it a little higher on my waist, it should fit. I pulled the black plaid number on as I hopped awkwardly back to my own room. It fit pretty well but was a little shorter than I was used to. The only pair of socks I could find were a knee-high white sports pair. I shoved them down so they pooled around my ankles before quickly pulling on my Converse.

I didn't have time to check myself in the mirror, but surely I couldn't go wrong with black and white. Hopefully I wouldn't be too cold with my legs so exposed.

I grabbed my bag and my oversized cardigan, shoved an apple into my mouth, and rushed out the door, racing through campus.

I made it to the admin building in record time, dumping the chewed apple core in the trash as I approached the stairs. A large group of black-clad Melior Group agents were standing together off to the side, and I cursed mentally when I saw Alec with them, seemingly giving instructions. He had his back turned to me, one hand resting on his hip near his gun. Not that he needed a gun—I'd seen him incapacitate dozens of people with a single focused look. Hell, I'd helped him do it.

I slowed my pace and made my steps as light as possible, keeping an eye on his broad back. As if he had a sixth sense for people avoiding him, he turned just as I reached the bottom of the stairs and looked at me over his shoulder. The expression on my face must have been shifty, but his attention was drawn down, his eyes flicking over my body before he muttered something to the agents and walked over.

Before I had a chance to declare I was late and run off, he leveled me with an incomprehensible look, crossing his arms. "Is that what you're wearing for your session with Gabe?"

I blinked at him slowly, unsure I'd heard him correctly. A sarcastic comment, a grumble about my presence, an exclamation declaring I was the most irritating person in the world—any of those would have made sense. Alec caring about what I was wearing? It just didn't compute.

I went into worry mode. "Oh shit! Is there a stain or something?" I twisted awkwardly on the spot to try to look at the back of my outfit. "I woke up so late, and I didn't get a chance to check myself in the mirror, and then . . ."

My eyes narrowed in suspicion. He was smirking, mischief dancing in his bright blue eyes. His face had almost lost the constant underlying intensity and broodiness. Almost, but not quite. He was amused, but there was a cruel tilt to his smirk.

He was making fun of me. He broke his important work conversation, came over here, and was making me late just to make fun of me.

"You are such a fucking asshole," I muttered as I spun on my heel and stomped up the stairs.

"Have a great lesson, precious," he called after me with mirth in his deep voice.

I gave him the finger over my shoulder. As the glass doors slid closed behind me, I could have sworn I heard a chorus of manly voices laughing.

In the elevator up to Tyler's office, I huffed, annoyed, but then took a few deep breaths, trying not to let Alec get to me. My day had started off badly, and he'd made it worse, but I was trying to wipe the slate clean and go into my lesson with a fresh attitude.

As I entered Tyler's office, however, my day got weirder.

The door was ajar and I let myself in. "Hi."

He was sitting behind his desk, his face buried in a pile of paperwork as his pen scribbled furiously across the page.

"Hey." He glanced up, returning my greeting before dropping his head back down. "Let me just . . ."

The pen stilled, and he raised his eyes once more, slowly. His gaze flitted up and down my body very quickly, as if he were worried he'd go blind if he looked in my direction too long.

Eventually he cleared his throat and placed the pen down with unusual stiffness. His fingers raked through his hair, pushing that persistent messy bit off his face, as he glanced at me *again* before looking away.

"Have a seat." His voice sounded strained. "We should get started. We're behind."

As I took my notebook out of my bag and made my way over to his desk, my brow creased. Why was everyone acting so strange? "No, we're not. We're way ahead."

"Right. Yes. Ahead." He punctuated every word with a glance at me.

"Are you OK?" I was getting worried. Did this have something to do with the events on the night of Alec's fight? We'd never talked about the way I'd rubbed myself on him on the back of the bike. I was still mortified every time I thought about it and was living in fear of him bringing it up.

He took a deep breath, closing his eyes as he exhaled, then looked at me directly.

"Yes," he said with a reassuring smile. But it didn't reach his eyes, and I could still see tightness in his shoulders. "Let's begin."

I thought about pressing the issue, but he launched into the history of Variant suppression in Eastern Europe during the eighties, and I dropped it, focusing on our work.

The rest of the hour lacked the light atmosphere and casual back and forth of our usual conversations. He remained seated behind his desk, and considering that every other time so far he'd come around to sit with me, that was odd in itself.

By the end of the session, though, he was almost acting normally, telling me which journals were good if I wanted to do extra reading. "There's another one, but I can't remember . . . I think it was on one of the printouts . . ."

He started rummaging through the books and papers on his desk, but I knew what he was looking for.

"Oh, it's under this . . ." We reached for the same book at the same time, and our hands accidentally touched. I froze, my words dying in my throat. To my utter astonishment, he stopped moving too.

For a beat we just sat there, the tips of our fingers touching. Then his hand moved, brushing the backs of his fingers against mine. My lips parted, my breathing becoming shallow. I dared not look up for fear of breaking the spell.

With slow, cautious movements, I turned my hand to rest palm up on the desk. He responded by covering it with his, the tips of his fingers at my wrist. As he dragged his hand lightly over mine, our fingers caressing each other's palms, I slowly lifted my gaze.

His other hand was flat against the desk, fingers splayed, and his downcast eyes looked almost hooded. He was staring at my chest, which, I realized, was heaving with how hard I was breathing.

Sudden, loud laughter in the corridor snapped us almost violently out of the moment. I startled, flinching, and he pulled his hand back quickly. Our eyes met for the briefest of seconds; then he looked away and cleared his throat.

Both of us rushed through goodbyes as I scrambled to pack up, and I walked out of his office thoroughly confused and a little crestfallen. Despite the perplexing moment of intimacy, I saw him heave a sigh of relief as I closed the door behind me. I'd thought we'd taken a step forward last week, that he was finally letting his carefully built barriers down a little.

As I walked through the lobby on my way out, I saw Alec coming my way. With considerable effort I squared my shoulders, pressed my lips together, and avoided looking at him.

He laughed, drawing the attention of the women at reception, and then mumbled at me as he walked past,

"Went well, then?"

I kept walking, determined to ignore him, but as I stepped into the sunshine, I wondered if maybe Tyler had told Alec about our bike ride and Alec was using it to make my life miserable. They were both acting strange, and clearly I was missing something.

Ethan and Josh confirmed my suspicion when they came up to me at the bottom of the stairs. They slowed their walk, and both of their eyebrows shot up as they looked me up and down. Ethan grinned, while Josh puffed his cheeks and blew the air out slowly.

Either I'd been hallucinating the clothes on my body and had actually been nude all morning, or there was some tear in the space-time continuum and they were seeing something I wasn't. Either way, I'd had enough. My morning was ruined and I wanted answers.

I crossed my arms and jutted out one hip. "OK. What the hell is going on? Alec was a dick to me this morning, which isn't that weird, but he went out of his way to do it, and then Tyler was acting strange through our whole session. Now you two are giving me weird looks. Start talking."

They exchanged a glance.

"It probably has something to do with the fact that you're walking around dressed like Gabe's wet dream, honeybunch." Ethan sounded as if he was explaining things, but his statement only made me scrunch my face up in confusion.

Josh snorted. "Eloquently put, Kid."

"Thanks, bro!" Ethan slapped him on the shoulder and beamed at me. I just frowned and turned back to Josh.

"Tyler has a . . ." His eyes darted around uncomfortably as if looking for the right words. "A thing . . . for . . ."

"Eloquently put, Joshy!" Ethan mocked.

"He has a private schoolgirl fantasy," he whispered, pressing his lips together and shoving his hands into the pockets of his perfectly pressed pants.

"What?" The conversation had taken a turn I definitely hadn't expected.

"Like, sexually," Josh elaborated, looking a little worried.

I rolled my eyes at him. "Yes. Thank you, captain obvious. What the hell does that have to do with me?"

"Seriously?" Ethan couldn't seem to stop smiling. "You're basically wearing a school uniform."

"The knee-high socks." Josh pointed at my feet.

"The pleated skirt." Ethan lowered his voice, lightly caressing the fabric at the hem of the skirt in question.

"The white shirt." Considering we were in public, I was a little surprised when Josh stepped forward and gently tugged at the collar of my shirt.

"The sexy messy hair you have going on, and . . ." Ethan tucked a loose strand behind my ear. They were no longer smiling, the situation having apparently lost its humor. Stupidly, I was fixating on Ethan's use of the word *sexy*.

I got there in the end though. "I look like a disheveled private schoolgirl!" I said a little too loudly, and they both chuckled. "Shit!"

I wasn't sure how to feel. I didn't want Tyler to think I'd intentionally done this to provoke him. Or did I? Of course I was attracted to him, but I also respected him, and he'd very clearly set this particular boundary from day one.

Before I could continue to unpack the situation, I heard the man in question coming our way, his voice carrying through the building's front door. We were standing at the bottom of the stairs and off to the side, not immediately visible but close enough to make out his words.

". . . longest hour of my life." He groaned as he emerged from the building, Alec by his side. Ethan and Josh both turned at the sound of his voice, and Josh took a breath. Without even thinking about it, I shot my hand out and covered his mouth. Then I did the same to Ethan for good measure. I spent entirely too much time behind the eight ball in my own Bond. If they were going to talk about something pertinent in public, who were we to stop them? Ethan and Josh both gave me disapproving looks, but they stayed quiet.

"And you knew she was coming to see me dressed like *that*. You are such a fucking asshole." I smirked as Tyler echoed my words to Alec.

"What was I supposed to do, man?" Alec somehow managed to sound defensive and chastised at the same time. "Tell her to go home and change? Yeah, that would have gone over real well. Especially coming from *me*."

"You know I'm doing this for you, right?" Tyler was beginning to sound less amused. "I don't know how much—"

His mouth clamped shut. They'd seen us. We must have looked ridiculous, standing there, my hands over Ethan and Josh's mouths. Tyler's eyebrows shot up, his hand frozen in mid-gesture in front of him, while Alec threw his head back and laughed.

My eyes widened. I'd just been busted by my hot older tutor doing something naughty while inadvertently dressed like a private schoolgirl. The irony was not lost on me.

I dropped my hands, turned on my heel, and walked away as fast as I could.

I was mortified. About all of it—my unfortunate outfit, the new bit of knowledge about Tyler, the blatant eavesdropping on their conversation. *What was I thinking?* Of course he was going to spot us! And now Tyler surely thought my maturity matched my outfit—high school level. I couldn't fathom what Alec thought, but he was a mystery most of the time anyway.

The first words I'd heard Tyler say kept replaying over and over in my mind: *longest hour of my life.* Our session that morning had been awkward for me too, but I wouldn't say it was the "longest hour of my life." He hated it more than I realized. Not enduring my stupid outfit in his face for an hour. *Me.* It was our Bond he hated. Maybe even resented.

His power was passive; he'd never expected or wanted a Vital. It was a burden to him. That's why he'd put such clear boundaries in place. The few moments that made me think he might feel the same way as I did were simply Light-driven, instinctual reactions to our Bond. I'd probably completely ruined this fantasy for him.

I really wanted to go home and change, put on the stained sweatpants and questionable-smelling T-shirt, but we were already late for biology, and I didn't want to miss any classes. So I did my best to pull the skirt down as far as it would go and shove more of my hair into my bun in an attempt to look less . . . provocative.

The boys were following me, and I could hear them talking quietly behind me, probably *about* me. I forced myself to put one foot in front of the other and gripped the strap of my bag tighter. Ethan fell into step next to me. I didn't look at him, but I felt his fingertips gently drag down my arm from my elbow to my wrist—a warning he was about to take my hand.

I did a quick mental check and saw that, in my emotional state, I'd let more Light in than I wanted to. I took a deep breath and clamped down on the flow of Light, scrunching it up into a tight little ball deep inside me. Then I met Ethan halfway. His big, warm hand swallowed mine, giving me a little squeeze, and I instantly felt better. Josh was walking a pace or two behind us, allowing us to look like the couple the whole campus thought we were while still staying close enough to let me know he was there.

As we approached the science building, Ethan tugged me gently toward the side of the building as Josh overtook us. I wrenched my hand out of Ethan's grasp and planted my feet, facing both of them.

"No." I injected as much determination into my voice as I could. They were trying to pull that tag-team shit again—that thing where they crowd my personal space and fry my brain so I'll tell them what I'm thinking even when I'm not sure I want to. I refused. All I wanted to do was focus on science for a while. "We are going to class. I don't want to talk about it right now."

I gave them each a pointed look before turning around and walking to class. Thankfully they behaved, following me into the lecture hall and taking seats on either side of me. We made it just a few moments before class started, and Dot joined us, a few minutes late herself. We exchanged quick hellos before the lecture began.

I stared at the front of the room, oblivious to the information, my notebook remaining blank in front of me. After about ten minutes of this, Josh's hand landed on my leg. He gave me a little squeeze, his fingers digging into my skin below the hem of the skirt, and then he flipped his hand, his palm up in invitation. I placed my hand in his. It snapped me out of my distraction, and after a few minutes I took my hand back and started paying attention.

The rest of the day passed without incident. My classes went well, and no one commented on my outfit. I had lunch with Zara and Dot, but I stayed quiet for most of it, lost in my own thoughts.

When I got back to my res hall at the end of the day, I put on the stained sweats and dragged all my dirty laundry down to the laundry room in the basement. My third load was halfway through when Ethan and Josh came in.

I looked up from the assignment I'd been working on and groaned.

Ethan chuckled. "Well, hello to you too, cutie." He dropped a kiss to the top of my head. I stayed seated, not making it easy for him.

"Hey, pumpkin," I finally replied. I wasn't actually mad at them. "Hey, Josh."

Josh tapped me under my chin, and I raised my gaze to his face. The pure affection in his green eyes made me relax a little. He kissed me softly on the cheek before going to lean against a dryer across from me. Ethan sat on top of the one next to him, and I briefly worried for the structural integrity of the machine; his hulking frame looked as if it could crush it.

They weren't crowding me, as I'd worried they would earlier in the day, cajoling confessions out of me with their searching eyes and probing hands.

"Look, Eve," Josh started, "we don't want to force you into talking about anything. We just want to clear shit up. In case you may have gotten the wrong idea."

"OK." I folded my hands on the table, resting them on the pile of forgotten textbooks and notepads. "Clear away."

"When we told you about Gabe's . . ."

"Proclivities," I finished for him, raising an eyebrow.

"Yes. Thank you. When we told you about that, we didn't consider that it might make him out to seem more . . ."

"Like a perv," Ethan supplied helpfully.

Josh threw him an annoyed glance. "Like he's crossed some boundaries when he actually hasn't."

"What the hell are you talking about?" I was really struggling to keep up with conversations today.

"We just don't want you to think he's actually crossed that line with a high school student before, or even with someone who's underage. He used to watch a lot of anime, and it's just a harmless fantasy he's shared with us because . . . well, we're guys and we talk about that shit. Anyway, Ethan and I gave you an incomplete picture of the situation, and we figured it was up to us to make sure it was cleared up. Because, you know he would never, *ever* . . ." Josh was beginning to ramble, and it was adorable. His perfectly put-together preppy outfit was in total contrast to the slightly frantic look in his eyes.

"Stop." I looked between the two of them—serious, if a little sheepish—and laughed. "It didn't even cross my mind. I think I know Tyler fairly well by now, and I can't imagine him abusing his position of power to do something so . . ."

"Pervy?" Ethan once again supplied helpfully.

"Pervy," I confirmed, giving him an affectionate smile and hoping we could drop the conversation and forget this whole day had happened.

Naturally, Josh was not going to let me off the hook so easily. "Then what's had you so preoccupied all day? What's going on?"

. . . *longest hour of my life.* Tyler's words ran through my mind again, and I slumped in my seat.

I didn't know how to talk about this with them. They both had feelings for me—feelings that were returned and getting stronger by the day. I loved Ethan's infectious smile, his boundless energy, his gentle touch despite being bigger in stature than anyone I'd ever met. I loved Josh's unpretentious intelligence, his calm nature, his ever-vigilant eyes.

How was I supposed to tell them it wasn't enough? I had two amazing guys, and I spent the day pining for a third. I sounded selfish and petulant even to myself. I was attracted to Tyler, I wanted him badly, and he didn't want me back. But I couldn't say that out loud.

"I'm just embarrassed, that's all." It wasn't a lie. I *was* embarrassed. I just wasn't specifying *what* I was embarrassed about.

"Understandable." Josh nodded. "But you shouldn't be. It's not a big deal."

"Agreed!" I spat out a little too enthusiastically, and they both chuckled. "So can we just stop talking about it and move on? Please."

"Sure," Josh agreed readily.

Ethan opened his arms wide in invitation. I didn't hesitate to leave my seat and step into them, my thighs flush with the dryer he was still sitting on as I relaxed into his chest. After a few moments Josh stepped up behind me to rub soothing circles into my shoulders. With my hands still resting on Ethan's knees, I leaned back into Josh, and his arms encircled my front. I sighed contentedly.

It felt so good to be surrounded by them, Josh pressed to my back, Ethan inching forward to press into my front, his hands snaking into my hair, Josh's breathing becoming shallower, Ethan's eyes looking at my lips as he swallowed . . .

As Ethan leaned in for a kiss, movement in the corner of my eye made me stiffen. We all turned to see various bits of my dirty clothing floating around the room.

"Shit." Josh stepped away and visibly composed himself, returning all the floating items to their spots.

Ethan groaned in frustration, and flames flicked into existence all up and down his muscular arms. Luckily his hands were still in my impervious-to-his-ability hair and not touching something flammable.

I stepped out of his reach and wrapped my arms around myself, bringing my Light back under control as Ethan extinguished his flames. My emotional day had resulted in lack of control, and I was frustrated that they were the ones who had to deal with it. I was also *sexually* frustrated; once again we had to stop things before they'd really started.

Even so, it wasn't the best time or place for all that anyway. While the basement laundry room wasn't exactly public, anyone could walk in at any moment. Plus, I had to finish my laundry. That was of paramount importance.

Josh shifted the bulge in his pants as he turned away, and Ethan jumped down off the dryer.

We all took a few deep breaths at opposite ends of the room, then Ethan folded all my newly clean clothes while Josh helped me with my assignment. I didn't really need the help, but it was good to have a discussion partner and get another perspective on the problem.

After helping me carry all my washing back upstairs, they left with chaste kisses on my cheeks.

TWELVE

The next day, I found a way to use the whole embarrassing situation to my advantage.

Walking out of my last class, I slung my bag over my shoulder and made a beeline for my res hall. I was supposed to be heading to the boys' house for more training, but I needed to speak to Dot privately, and there hadn't been a chance for us to do that in weeks. Zara had messaged me telling me she'd be back late but hadn't specified when.

I texted Dot to come over ASAP without actually telling her what I wanted to discuss. Hopefully the message was firm enough despite the vagueness. I also texted the guys, telling them I needed some alone time and was skipping the afternoon's sessions. I hoped they would leave it at that, but of course that was naive.

"Eve!" Ethan's distinctive voice pulled me up short just around the corner from my building. I mouthed *fuck* before schooling my features into a neutral expression and turning around. He jogged a little to catch up to me, dressed in his standard jeans and white T-shirt. I tugged my jacket tighter around my body to ward off the chilly wind and wondered for the hundredth time how he wasn't cold.

"Hey, snuggleface." I gave him a big smile, which he returned, showing off his dimples.

"Hey, cuddlebum." He rested his hands on my hips and leaned in. "What's going on? You never miss an opportunity to play around with our abilities. I mean, to train." He chuckled lightly. My fascination with Variant abilities had not even remotely waned since I'd learned I was a Vital. If anything, it had intensified.

"I know. I just . . ." I tucked my face into his chest, giving myself some time to think of something. The previous day's events provided the perfect excuse. "I'm just not ready to see Tyler yet," I mumbled.

He sighed and gave me a squeeze, pulling back so I had to look him in the eyes. "I thought we cleared all that up yesterday. You have nothing to worry about."

"I know, I know. But it's easier said than done. I'm still embarrassed, and I just need a day. OK?"

He looked skeptical. "I get it, but I haven't seen you all day."

"I'll come over tomorrow, I promise. Dot's on her way over, so I'd better get going."

"Oh, cool. We can just hang with you. I'll text Josh." His boyish face looked ridiculously eager.

"No!" I blurted out too quickly, then panicked. Thinking quick, I pushed up onto my toes and pressed my lips to his, sparing a moment to make sure my Light was in control. He responded immediately, as he always did, tenderly kissing me back.

Eventually we pulled apart with reluctance. My plan may have backfired; my brain was as fuzzy after that kiss as I was hoping to make his.

"Are you trying to distract me with your womanly wiles?" He wiggled his eyebrows suggestively.

I laughed. "Would you be opposed to that?"

"No . . ."

With a conscious effort, I stepped out of his arms, giving myself some space to breathe and think. "I just need some girl time with Dot, OK? I'm not trying to avoid you, big guy. I swear."

Over his shoulder I spotted Josh coming our way, impeccably dressed as always; his checked shirt looked as if he'd only just put it on, not as if he'd been sitting in classes all day, and not a blond hair of his slicked-back style was out of place. I knew I had to get going before he joined us. I couldn't hide anything from Josh.

"I don't want to keep Dot waiting, OK? I gotta run. Can you update Josh?"

Ethan nodded, and I gave him another peck on the lips, waving to Josh as I rushed toward my building. His brow creased as I turned to leave, but I didn't give him a chance to stop me.

Dot was waiting outside my room. Her face in her phone, she was leaning next to the door dressed in jeans and a plain sweater, her hair pulled up, her face clear of makeup. My heart broke to see her like that.

She'd been less and less herself. Her moods had been a little better since I'd figured out how to transfer Light to her, but the transfers always made her feel guilty, and she only let me do it whenever she started losing the ability to call out to animals remotely.

Watching her turn into a shell of the vibrant, enthusiastic woman I'd first met—it only solidified my determination to do what I was about to do.

My footsteps echoing down the hall caught her attention.

"Finally." She rolled her eyes. "What's with the vague text?"

"Nothing. I just wanted some girl time." She watched me suspiciously as I unlocked the million locks.

"Is Zara joining us?" She dumped her bag on the couch and rifled through the stash of snacks we had in the little makeshift kitchen.

"Um, no. She has a thing," I said over my shoulder as I checked the window. Then I checked the bedrooms too, just to be sure. It wasn't that I didn't trust Zara, but the fewer people knew about my plan, the more likely I was to succeed, especially considering Tyler's ability. I wouldn't even be telling Dot if I could avoid it, but I needed her help.

As I shut the door of what used to be Beth's room, Dot gave me a funny look while stuffing chips into her mouth. I could tell she was about to ask me what the hell I was doing. I shook my head at her and bugged my eyes out, which made her look even more confused.

"So"—I cleared my throat—"something kind of embarrassing happened yesterday."

At this she perked up. That girl lived for gossip. I slipped my necklace off and placed it gently on the couch. I wouldn't put it past Alec to have placed a listening device in there along with the tracker and distress beacon. Sure, I was being paranoid, but I had no idea who on campus had which ability—which student or Melior Group guard might have super hearing and could grind this thing to a halt before it even started.

"OK . . ." Dot stopped eating and fully focused on me.

"Yeah, so I was on my way to my session with Tyler and . . ." I double-checked that the locks on the door were secure. "Actually, while we talk, can you help me with . . . um . . . my hair? In the bathroom?"

I led the way into the tiny bathroom and closed the door behind us. Immediately I turned the shower on and stood as close to it as I could without getting soaked, gesturing to Dot to come stand next to me.

She hesitated for a moment, looking as if she was questioning my sanity, then finally joined me.

"I have a plan," I rushed out. I knew we couldn't have much time if someone was listening.

"Eve, what the fuck . . ." Her voice was much louder than mine, bouncing off the bathroom tiles.

I slammed my hand over her mouth, putting my finger to my lips. Her eyes bugged out but she stayed silent.

"Just listen, OK?" She nodded and I removed my hand. "I couldn't stop thinking about the Lighthunter and how there's no way to authenticate that she can do what she says, but there *is* a way. *I'm* the way. She doesn't know me. She's never met me. No one even knows my real name, and how would they find out? Plus, if there's one thing my mother taught me to do well, it's disappear."

I paused, waiting for her reaction, but Dot just stared at me for a few moments, dumbfounded. "What exactly are you saying?"

"I'm going to run. And the guys can't know about it." I cringed even as I said it. I knew exactly how hard this would be to pull off, and I knew how pissed they would be when I did it. But it would all be worth it. For Charlie.

"Eve, no. I can't ask you to do that." She shook her head, but I didn't miss the spark of hope in her eyes. "It's too dangerous."

"You're not asking." I took her by the elbows, leaning my face close to hers. "I'm offering. No, I'm not just offering. I'm telling you I'm doing this. For Charlie. I've felt so useless and helpless the past few months, and finally here's an opportunity to actually do something about it. I'm not going to miss it."

"I get it, but why can't we ask for help? I would be livid if Charlie pulled something like this. Your Bond is fucking scary, and they're not gonna like it. Why can't some of them go with you while the others stay behind to test the Lighthunter?"

"They have rare abilities, they're Lucian Zacarias's nephews, they're too high profile. It would be way too easy to track their passports, find them using facial recognition. I can't have them with me, and they'd never let me go alone."

"What about Alec? I'm sure he has secret identities, considering what he does."

"Probably. But again, that would mean using Melior Group resources, which would leave a paper trail. No one knows me, Dot. If they knew I was Evelyn Maynard and heard some of the stories about us as kids, they might have connected the dots and guessed I was Alec's Vital. But no one even knows I *am* a Vital. There is nothing to connect me to them in any way."

"What if something goes wrong? What if they catch you? There has to be another way." She had three questions for every answer I gave, but she was looking at me as though she hoped beyond hope I would keep answering them.

"It's a risk I'm willing to take." I didn't want to think too hard about the ominous "they"—about the possibility of ending up in the same position we were trying so hard to get Charlie out of. "Having a good plan and thinking through the contingencies will help us minimize it."

"But Tyler might not even be able to get in touch with this so-called Lighthunter."

"But if he does, I want to be prepared. The second we hear that he's made contact, I want to be ready to go."

"I still think we should tell them. They can help—"

"Dot," I cut her off, "you and I both know they will never let me do this. They won't even let me out of their sight from the mansion to the campus. And the only way to be sure is if I go alone."

She watched me for a moment, chewing on her bottom lip. "What does that mean? What would you need to be ready to go?"

I smiled, finally allowing a little excitement to take over. She hadn't said it outright, but Dot was in.

"I'll need ID, and I can't trust some hack to do it for me. I'll need some equipment so I can make a passport and maybe a driver's license. And I'll need a disguise—just something to get me out of Bradford Hills without being recognized."

"A passport? Where would you go?"

"I can't tell you. All it would take would be for Tyler to ask, and . . ."

"He'd know," she finished for me. "Right."

"I'll make you a list, you let me know if you can get the stuff, and we can take it from there. We'd better get out of the bathroom now. If someone actually is listening in, they'll think we're getting it on in here."

I chuckled, and Dot let out a big laugh. "That explains the paranoid behavior."

I turned the shower off and followed her into the living room. We spent the next few hours working on our biology homework and expertly avoiding any mention of what we'd discussed in the bathroom. She clearly had a bunch of burning questions—I could practically read them in her eyes—but she controlled herself like a pro. Dot loved gossip, but this was about saving her brother's life. There was no way she would jeopardize that.

On her way out, she gave me a big hug, holding me longer than usual, and whispered into my ear, "Thank you. I don't deserve you."

We pulled apart and shared a meaningful look before she walked away, her head held a little higher, her steps a little lighter.

Dot was halfway down the corridor when the elevator dinged and Zara stepped out. She appeared to be deep in thought, staring at the ground, so she didn't see Dot until the smaller girl was wrapping her up in a hug.

I laughed, both delighted to see Dot happy and amused by the surprised look on Zara's face.

"I'm heading off, but I'm glad I bumped into you, Zee." Dot gave her a kiss on the cheek and rushed to catch the elevator before the doors closed.

"See ya!" Zara yelled after her and rolled her eyes, tucking a silky strand of red hair behind her ear. A reluctant smile pulled at her lips.

"How was your night?" I asked as she let herself in, removing her leather jacket and sitting down on the couch to get her boots off.

"Yeah, OK." She struggled with the left one. They were the pull-on kind—no zips.

I stepped forward to yank on the heel. "Who'd you catch up with?"

We both strained until the boot slid off, and I stumbled to catch my balance.

"No one you know." Zara held her other leg out, and we repeated the process until she was boot-free.

"What'd you do? Where'd you go?" I started to tidy up the main living area. Neither one of us had really had time to clean. The place was a mess.

Zara narrowed her eyes. "What's with the interrogation?"

I paused halfway through wiping down the little dining table by the door. I was deflecting, trying to keep focus on Zara in order to avoid talking about what Dot and I had discussed, and it was getting obvious. I hadn't even realized I was doing it. I felt like shit not telling Zara, excluding her from something so important.

"Sorry." I hoped my smile didn't look too guilty. "Just making conversation. I didn't mean to pry."

I finished wiping down the table, then braced myself as I moved on to the little bar fridge. Something had gone off in there several days ago, and I was about to find out what it was.

"That's OK. Oh . . . ugh!" Zara and I both gagged at the putrid smell. I had to lean back and cover my nose with my elbow as I extracted every single item, not willing to get close enough to identify the culprit.

Zara put some music on. My cleaning frenzy must have infected her—either that or she felt guilty I was the only one doing it—and she put on some gloves and started scrubbing the bathroom.

We spent the next hour cleaning, chatting about easy, pointless things. By the time I went to bed, I was sure she didn't suspect anything, but the spot just under my ribs was no less twisted at the thought of deceiving her.

THIRTEEN

Dot's black hair was gliding through the straightener when "Side to Side" by Ariana Grande began to play through the speaker in the corner.

It was Dot's nineteenth birthday, and we were in the spare room of Lucian's apartment on the Upper East Side. I hadn't been back there since the night of the gala, when I was too drunk and then too hung over to really appreciate it.

The beautiful apartment was modern and sleek in every way the mansion in Bradford Hills was old-world and classic. Every room had stunning views of Manhattan. While we put on makeup and did our hair, Dot and I watched the city lights start to twinkle as the sun went down.

I paused, holding the straightener over Dot's head as I grooved along to the beat. "I like this song."

I'd been listening to a lot of rock, discovering bands I'd never heard of thanks to Josh and his obsession. With all the new playlists he'd been making for me, I hardly ever heard the radio, let alone a new pop song, anymore.

"Me too! It's so dirty." Dot grinned at me in the mirror.

"Dirty?" I frowned as I pulled her shoulders back against the chair, trying to finish doing her hair.

"It's pretty much about being fucked so hard you can't walk straight." She chuckled. "What did you think it was about?"

I laughed, throwing my head back. "I don't know. I've never really paid attention to the lyrics. I just like the beat."

"I hope tonight ends with me walking side to side," she declared. "It's been way too long since I had *good* sex."

"You and me both. Except it's more like *never* for me. All the sex I've had has been mediocre at best." I shook my head as I finished smoothing out the last section of her perfectly straight hair, then set the hot straightener down on the vanity, somehow finding a clear space in among all the makeup, hair products, jewelry, and for some reason, a bra.

"Well it's lucky you have four seriously hot guys in your Bond who won't be able to resist hitting that pretty soon." Dot jumped out of her seat, smacked me on the ass, and rushed over to the little speaker.

I snorted. "Whatever. I think it could be pretty good with Josh and Ethan, anyway." I didn't want to get into the whole "half my Bond finds me repugnant" thing.

"At the same time?" She wiggled her perfect brows suggestively and restarted the song.

"That would certainly leave me walking side to side," I answered, intentionally vague, as she cranked the volume up.

She bounced over to me as the lyrics began, doing the silliest, least sexy dance I'd ever seen. "Dance with me!"

I rolled my eyes at her, but her excited energy was infectious, especially when seeing a genuine smile on her face felt so great. For the next three minutes, we bounced around the room with the kind of energy I got when I had an overflow of Light.

Once the song ended, more upbeat "going out" music blasted through the speaker. We left it on loud as we finished getting ready.

When Dot had declared she wanted to have a night on the town for her birthday, we were all a little surprised. But she'd explained we'd all been working like crazy and worried out of our minds for Charlie, and it was time to put a pause on it all.

"I just want one night to pretend like everything is normal, go out, have too much to drink, and just . . . forget for a little while."

No one could begrudge her that, and within two days, she and Ethan had organized it and invited more people than I'd ever met.

Dot was in all white, a dress that combined patent leather and velvet and somehow managed to look high fashion and edgy, especially when paired with her white thigh-high boots.

In contrast, I was in all black. Dot had talked me into a pair of very tight black pants—which, admittedly, did make my ass look pretty good—and a shimmery top that left way too little to the imagination. My distress beacon necklace was tucked snugly into my cleavage, out of sight except for the silver chain. Because it was her birthday and she kept gushing about how hot I looked, I let her complete the look by straightening my hair and putting it in a very high ponytail.

Before we headed to the front door, I put my coat on. I was a bit self-conscious about the outfit and wasn't ready for everyone to see it in the bright hall lights; hopefully I'd be more comfortable in the dim lighting of a club. Dot complained that with her birthday being in December, it was always too cold to go anywhere without a coat, which ruined her outfit—even though the coat she had on was faux polar bear fur that matched what she was wearing perfectly.

As Dot and I, along with my four Variants, squeezed into the elevator, she sighed. "I wish Zara was coming."

"Me too." I gave her a sad smile.

Zara was reluctant about any event involving a large group of Variants together in one place, but she'd reluctantly agreed to come celebrate Dot's birthday. Then, the day before, she'd come down with a stomach bug. Dot and I were both suspicious; the timing was just a little too convenient. But hearing her vomiting in the bathroom as I packed my overnight bag had convinced me she wasn't faking it.

"You think she'll be OK?" Dot asked. "Maybe we should've just canceled it."

"Stop looking for excuses to cancel this!" Ethan gave her a nudge with his shoulder—or rather the side of his arm, because his shoulder was level with the top of her head. "It was your idea, and Zara will be fine."

"It's just a stomach bug, and she said a friend was coming over to check on her," I reassured her.

"Who?" Dot frowned. "Everyone we know is coming tonight."

I shrugged. Once again, Zara had been vague about who she was spending her time with, and I wasn't going to pry. I was keeping things from her too. "I think it might be the mystery man or woman she's been seeing."

"Do I need to run a background check on this person?" Tyler held the door open, frowning, and we all filed out.

I gave him a warning look. "Can we rein in the stalking for one night?"

He laughed and held his hands up in surrender, but Alec brushed past and said simply, "No."

I chose not to engage. It was Dot's birthday.

We decided to walk to the club. It was a clear night, and while the crisp air hinted at snow, it was likely to stay clear. The six of us bundled more tightly into our coats as we started the four-block walk.

Ethan and Josh took the lead, joking and laughing, their broad backs covered in thick wool. Dot and I walked arm in arm behind them, much more quietly. I had a feeling she needed some time alone with her thoughts, and I was more than happy to simply walk with her. Alec and Tyler stayed behind us, speaking softly and, I'm sure, keeping an eye on everything.

When we were about halfway there, something occurred to me. "Wait a minute. How are we going to get into a club? Isn't the legal drinking age here twenty-one? I could have made a fake ID if you guys had given me notice."

In response, everyone laughed. Ethan turned around without missing a step, walking backward as he spoke. "Uncle Lucian owns the club." He flashed me his dimples, then turned back around and kept walking.

Of course he did. Why wouldn't he own an exclusive club in New York?

"That's a useful skill to have," Alec piped up.

I flashed him a confused look over my shoulder before I realized I'd casually announced I could falsify identification documents. "Oh, that. Yeah. My mother taught me when I turned twelve, I think, or eleven. Around then. She wanted me to know how to do it in case she . . ." *died*. But I really didn't want to go there. The mood of the night was heavy enough, with Charlie's absence constantly hanging over us. "Umm . . . In case I needed to."

I felt a squeeze on my arm. My eyes met Dot's, and we shared a meaningful look. We were both missing people we loved, but tonight was about having a little fun. About allowing ourselves to feel good for one night.

As we rounded the corner into a side street, I got my first glimpse of an exclusive New York nightclub. A line of people at least fifty deep, cordoned off behind a long stretch of velvet rope, led to the front doors. We walked past them, none of my companions even missing a step, and stopped in front of the entrance. The sleek doors were painted black, like the rest of the building, and were at least ten feet tall, with chunky round handles in their centers. Above them, red neon spelled out the words *Black Cherry*.

In front of the doors stood two large men, the bouncers, dressed in matching suits. "You'll have to go to the back of the line." One of them leaned forward and pointed, his tone not aggressive, simply matter-of-fact.

The two girls at the front of that very line, their hair pulled back tight, their makeup slightly overdone, smugly looked us up and down. I gave them a sickly sweet smile and turned my attention back to my friends.

Tyler, phone in hand as he texted, held up his other hand to the bouncer in a "wait just a sec" gesture, not even looking at the man.

He finished his quick text, returned his phone to his pocket, and just stood there casually as the other guys chatted. The bouncer looked to his companion, neither of them sure what to do. Before either could say anything, however, the doors behind them opened, and a tall thin man in a gray suit emerged. The music's booming bass released into the night for a brief moment before the doors closed again.

The man smiled wide as he hopped down the stairs, and the two bouncers went back to ignoring us.

"Tyler!" He moved in for a firm handshake, then repeated the same greeting with the other three guys.

"He's the manager," Dot stage-whispered to me. "We could have just told the bouncers we were on the list, but that would have meant going through an ID check. This way, we go straight in."

I nodded and chuckled to myself. I guess there really is no need for such pesky things as proof-of-age when your family is loaded and owns the club.

He greeted Dot with a kiss on each cheek and a jovial "happy birthday." He greeted me last but just as warmly.

As he led us past the bouncers and straight through the big doors, I caught the looks of the two girls at the front, their faces much less smug now. I couldn't help myself; I gave them another wide smile before heading inside.

The inside of the club was draped in black, the walls covered in expensive-looking intricate wallpaper, the bars the same slick black finish as the doors, the seating a rich velvet. It was spread over a few interconnecting levels, with several bars and a large central dance floor.

The manager said a few quiet words to Tyler and then disappeared up a side staircase. Dot took the lead, taking me by the hand and walking to a VIP area in a back corner, which had its own bar with bench seating running the length of the wall and small tables scattered throughout. A large sign above the seating read, "Happy Birthday, Dot" in curving script.

At least twenty people were already there, a few of whom I recognized from the Institute. Dot made her way around, saying hi to everyone. The guys led me to a corner near the bar, all taking their coats off and handing them to the pretty blonde bartender. I started to unbutton my coat, but just as I reached the top, Josh stepped behind me.

"Let me help you with that." The music wasn't quite so loud in the VIP area, but he still had to lean in close to be heard, and it sent a little shiver down my spine. He grabbed my coat by the collar and dragged it down my arms. With the heat in the club, I was glad to be rid of it, my hesitation at the outfit momentarily forgotten.

I turned slightly, thanking Josh with a smile. He swallowed hard, returned my smile, then promptly handed my coat off to the bar girls. When I turned back to the front, Tyler and Alec were both staring at me, their gazes taking in the tight pants, the cleavage, the sliver of skin between the hem of my shimmery top and the waistband of the pants. They exchanged a charged look and, as one, turned to the bar. Alec barked something at the poor bar girl, and she immediately poured two shots of some clear liquid. As soon as they were full, the two men threw them back, smacking the little glasses back down.

Tyler lifted his hand, calling the bartender back, but my view of them was suddenly blocked by a very wide chest in a white button-down, open at the top. I looked up into Ethan's face and returned his naughty smile.

"You look smokin'." He planted his warm hands on my waist and pulled me in.

"Thanks, puddin', you look pretty hot yourself." I lifted my hands to his shoulders and gave him my best flirty look.

Making sure my Light flow was in check, I lifted onto my toes and softly pressed my lips to Ethan's. He smiled gently against my mouth and pulled me closer. The kiss didn't last long, but it was enough to give me butterflies. Endorphins released; mission accomplished. I was a little wary about the night, but feeling Ethan's strong body pressed to mine, I allowed myself to let go and embrace the party.

"Let's get you a drink." Ethan kissed me once more on the mouth before leading me to the bar.

Tyler and Alec were still in the same spot, now facing us, their elbows leaning on the bar behind them and their gazes trained on where Ethan's hand met my exposed lower back.

Dot appeared out of nowhere. "What're we having?" she asked, a hint of the lightness that had disappeared along with Charlie back in her voice.

"Whatever the birthday girl desires!" I answered, injecting some pep into my own voice. Anything to keep that easy look in her eyes.

"Cocktails it is then!"

I watched, horrified at the amount of alcohol being poured into the small martini glass, but Dot clapped her hands excitedly. If me drinking copious amounts of alcohol would make her feel better, then I was prepared to be carried home.

Surprisingly, it didn't taste like turpentine, as I'd expected. You could definitely taste the alcohol, but it was fruity and not too sweet. I raised my eyebrows in surprise and gave her a thumbs-up as I took another sip.

"Careful." I hadn't noticed Alec move to stand next to me. "It might taste like peach tea, but there is a lot of alcohol in that."

I rolled my eyes. "Yes. Thank you. I did watch her make it."

He frowned, disapproving, and I felt that familiar Alec-fueled irritation sneaking in to ruin my good vibes. "Look, can we just agree to stay on opposite sides of the room? Then maybe we can both have a good night. Yes? Great!"

I didn't wait for a response before turning back to Dot and Ethan, who had a drink of his own now.

More people began to arrive, slowly filling the VIP area, and Dot was pulled away to accept birthday wishes and gifts. I sipped my cocktail and chatted to a few people I knew from my classes, but either Ethan or Josh was always nearby, if not right next to me. We were all doing our best to have a good night for Dot, but their less-than-subtle hovering was sending a clear message: they were still on alert for any potential threats. It didn't escape my notice that Josh was only drinking soda, and the others were nursing their drinks slowly.

By the time Dot managed to find her way back to us, I was on my third delicious cocktail. As much as I hated to admit it though, Alec was right. They were potent, and I was beginning to feel a little happy.

"I'm so over talking to these posers and pretending I like them while they pretend they care about how I'm doing. You know, with 'the whole Charlie thing.'" Dot made air quotes around 'the whole Charlie thing,' putting on a fake voice as she rolled her eyes. She was being sardonic, but I could see the angry downturn to her lips.

"Let's get you walking side to side!" I burst out at the top of my lungs, gaining a few weird looks and a laugh from Dot and Ethan. "Let's dance and see if we can find someone to . . . !"

A wide, knowing smile reappeared on Dot's face, and I slammed the rest of my cocktail back, smacked the empty glass on the nearest table, grabbed Dot by the wrist, and marched out toward the mass of writhing bodies.

Ethan stuck to our side like glue, his intimidating size keeping sleazy guys far away. At first he crossed his arms over his chest and just stood there, glaring at things as we danced, channeling his cousin a little too well. But after Dot and I poked him repeatedly until he cracked a smile, he gave in and started to dance. Surprisingly, he was pretty good at it. A few of Dot's other friends joined us too.

Every few minutes my eyes were drawn to the VIP area. Every single time, Josh, Tyler, or Alec was looking in our direction. Sometimes more than one of them would be casually leaning on the railing, sipping a drink. They were taking turns, swapping out every so often so it wouldn't be so obvious. At one point all three of them stood there, looking impossibly gorgeous in their collared shirts and their unique eyes and their perfect faces. I waved at them, and they all waved back at the same time in the exact same way, reminding me once again how close they were despite not being related by blood.

Tyler and Alec seemed to be hanging back more. I wasn't sure if it was a conscious effort on their part or simply because people gave Alec a wide berth wherever he went and Tyler refused to leave him alone. Probably a combination of both. They were deep in conversation every time I spotted them—not the light, laughing kind you usually have in a club, but the heads bent and eyebrows furrowed serious kind.

Someone delivered another round of drinks to the dance floor, and I managed to down most of mine without spilling too much as the music changed to a more sultry rhythm, the beat deeper and slower.

A flash of white to my right caught my attention: Dot was dancing with Kyo. I smiled and nudged Ethan, pointing them out.

Several Melior Group operatives were present—some on security detail for specific Vitals, others for added security—but Alec's team were all off duty. Marcus and Jamie were nearby talking to a curvy blonde, but they were both watching Dot and Kyo as intently as I was.

The two of them were completely engrossed in each other, moving to the beat, their bodies inching closer and closer until they wrapped their arms around each other and started kissing! Ethan and I whooped, and Marcus and Jamie hollered from the other side. Kyo grinned against Dot's lips, and Dot just flipped me off, not taking her focus off Kyo for a second.

I got back to dancing but couldn't wipe the smile off my face.

Ethan stepped up behind me, placing one hand flat against my stomach and pressing his body against my back. We started to move together, our bodies swaying. I was tipsy but still had the presence of mind to make sure my Light was locked down tight. I covered his hand with mine and reached my other hand up behind his neck, bringing his head closer.

His free hand brushed my jaw gently, nudging it to the side, away from his face, and then he placed a feather-soft kiss on my neck. I dropped my hand and let it hang loose at my side as I bent my knees lower, arched my back a little more.

With my head turned, I realized we had an audience. All three of my other guys were at the barrier staring at us, their expressions indecipherable.

Ethan dragged his lips up the side of my neck, and I gasped, my lips parting as I kept my eyes trained on the others. Alec's hands on the barrier tightened, the muscles in his forearms popping, and a stormy expression crossed his features. He turned abruptly and stalked off. Tyler whispered something to Josh, took one more look at us, and went after him. Josh leaned his elbows on the barrier, settling in, and flashed me a secret smile.

A guy with bright blue hair and a full tattoo sleeve came up to him, and they started to talk. I looked away so we wouldn't get caught making eyes at each other while I dirty-danced with my "boyfriend."

We let the music hypnotize us, ignoring everything else. Ethan's hands trailed up my sides, his fingers tracing the curve under my breasts. Blessedly the music was loud enough to cover my groan. The several cocktails swimming through my bloodstream, the sultry beats of the music reverberating through my body, and Ethan's confident, smooth moves were just about unravelling any sense of propriety I had.

I turned to face him and pressed my body flush with his, wrapping my arms around his neck. He pushed one knee between my legs and pressed his lips to mine. We kissed and we danced, not an inch of space between us, and I couldn't help imagining what this would be like without any clothing in the way.

Deciding it was probably not a good idea to have sex in the middle of the dance floor, I reluctantly leaned away to give myself some breathing room. We shared a heated look and then put a bit more distance between us.

I looked around, hoping for a distraction. When I glanced toward the VIP area, the guy with the blue hair was still there.

Josh was keeping an eye on us while also maintaining a conversation with the stranger, but there was something off about their body language. I cocked my head, distracted. Behind me, Ethan froze, and I turned to look at him, the question in my eyes. He cringed slightly.

"Who is that?" I asked, raising my voice over the music.

"Uh . . . Just an old . . . um . . ."

An uneasy feeling settled into the pit of my stomach. I turned back to Josh, and he looked as awkward as Ethan sounded. To the casual observer he would have seemed fine—just having a chat. But I could see the tension in his shoulders, the way his usually careful, attentive eyes darted around the room. The guy with the blue hair was leaning into Josh as he spoke, gently touching his arm from time to time. He seemed interested . . .

My eyes widened, and I stepped out of Ethan's arms. He shoved one hand into his pocket, the other rubbing the back of his head as he eyed me warily. I crossed my arms and gave him a stern look.

He sighed, defeated, and leaned down to speak into my ear. "That's Ben. Josh's ex."

What? My mind wasn't sure what to do with that information. Was Josh gay? Was our Bond forcing him into a relationship he otherwise wouldn't have even considered? I didn't want that. I didn't want him to push down a vital part of who he was because of the stupid Light. Because of *me*.

I looked back at my beautiful, kind, observant Joshy, and my heart sank. Was I about to lose another one of my Bonded Variants before I even had him? Was I reading them *all* completely wrong?

FOURTEEN

"Is he gay?" My voice was high and uneven.

Ethan chuckled and gave me an odd look. "Ben? Yeah, he's gay."

"I meant Josh and you know it."

"No. He's bi. Eve, you know how hot we are for you. He's mad about you."

Now that he mentioned it, I knew our attraction was mutual. I'd felt it on many occasions. Tyler and Alec fried my brain, I was so unsure of where they stood when it came to a romantic relationship, but Ethan and Josh had never given me a reason to wonder. They'd been into me, and all in, from day one. It was only alcohol-fueled insecurity making me question it. And yet . . .

I nodded and gave Ethan a reassuring smile before looking back at Josh. Ben was leaning right into him, saying something into his ear, his tattooed hand on Josh's shoulder. On *my* secret boyfriend's shoulder!

My eyes narrowed, and Josh saw me looking. He shook his head a little, warning me off. But it was too late; I needed to get to him.

"Shit!" Ethan yelled, taking off after me, but his big frame couldn't navigate the crowd as easily, so I managed to get to the VIP area before he had a chance to divert my attention.

As much as I wanted to, walking up and removing Ben's tattoo sleeve with a cheese grater would probably draw too much attention, so instead I headed to the bar, ordering another cocktail for myself and a soda for Josh. Ethan caught up to me just as the bargirl served me the drinks.

"God, you're fast," he said, sounding a little impressed. I gave him a devious smile as I grabbed the drinks and ducked past him, narrowly skirting past Tyler and Alec, who were walking in the opposite direction. Both of them shot me confused glances.

When I reached the railing where Josh was still speaking with Ben, I pasted a friendly smile on my face, then shoved the arm holding the soda between the two men. "Hey, Josh! I got you another drink. Who's this?"

They both stared at me as if I were a crazy person, and then Josh took the drink. "Uh, thanks, Eve. This is Ben. He's . . ."

Ethan came barreling through the crowd again. "Would you stop doing that?" he admonished me. Then he turned to Ben, his signature wide smile on his face and his hand out to shake. "Hey, man, how you been?"

"Good, good. You?" He shook Ethan's hand while giving all of us a confused look, finally settling on me.

"And who's this?"

I inched closer to Josh, my arm pressing against his.

"This is Eve." Ethan pulled me away from Josh and wrapped his arms around me. "My *girlfriend*." He put a bit of emphasis on the word, trying to remind me that the rest of the world thought we were exclusive. I couldn't seem to find it in me to care, the Light-driven instinct pushing me to remove any perceived threat to my Bond. In this case, the perceived threat was a tall guy with blue hair, lots of tattoos, and sharp cheekbones.

"Nice to meet you, Eve." Ben smiled politely. "How long have you guys been together?"

Alec and Tyler chose that moment to join us.

"Oh, hey, the whole gang's here!" Ben smiled wide and greeted them both in turn, although he didn't shake Alec's hand.

They engaged him in conversation, diverting his attention from me and, thankfully, from Josh. After five minutes of this torture, Dot showed up. Ignoring Ben, she declared she needed me to come with her, extracted me from Ethan's iron grip, and pulled me toward the dark corridor leading to the bathrooms. I threw Josh a pointed look over my shoulder.

We rounded the corner and she released me. "So, I'm guessing you know that's Josh's ex?"

"Yep." I crossed my arms and tapped my foot, fighting the urge to run back there.

"You OK?"

"I don't know. What are we doing here?"

"I figured you guys needed to talk before the situation imploded."

"Yeah, probably. But that would require us to be in the same place."

"No shit. Don't get bitchy with me. He'll follow."

I flashed her an apologetic look. It was her birthday, and here she was dealing with *my* drama. She smiled back before looking over my shoulder and walking back out to the club.

Josh took her place in front of me, but I couldn't look at him, opting to focus on his very expensive shoes instead. They were deep red suede, and he'd combined them with black pants and a midnight-blue shirt, the dark hues accentuating his light features.

"Eve?" Josh sounded as unsure as I felt. He sighed and moved a little closer. "Please say something. Is it . . . Do you have a problem with the fact that I'm . . ."

"No!" My head whipped up, and my hands went to his shoulders. His green eyes were mesmerizing, dark in the dim lighting of the club. I'd never seen so much insecurity in them. "That's not it, Josh."

He nodded, still looking unsure, and covered my wrists with his hands, dragging them down to his chest.

"I mean, when Ethan first told me Ben was your ex, I thought you might be gay, and I was horrified the Bond was *making* you have feelings for me, but that's it. I don't care what label society puts on you. As long as this"—I gestured between us awkwardly, his hand still closed around my wrist—"is genuine and you don't have to be someone you're not in order to be Bonded to me."

"That's not what's happening here. I was attracted to you from the start, before I even realized what you were. Remember? In my room that night, the first time we kissed. How could I have known? That was pure chemistry."

I smiled and gravitated farther toward him. "I know. Ethan covered that too."

Josh rolled his eyes. "Ethan's been covering a lot of things I'd like to cover tonight." His eyes trailed unashamedly down my body, and I smiled, feeling better already. "So, if Ethan explained these things, what's going on? What was with the weirdness back there?"

I cringed.

"Eve." His voice had that slight scolding tone to it; he wasn't going to let this go. He released one of my wrists and ghosted his fingers down my jaw, tilting my chin up.

"Fine." I caved. "I was jealous." I put on the most stoic look I could muster, trying to hide my embarrassment "I know that part of it was Light-driven, this force that gets all agitated whenever it feels threatened. But I would be lying if I said it was all Light. I don't like seeing another person all over you."

He smiled, not mocking or indulgent, just open and loving. "I can understand that. I broke up with Ben last year. It wasn't working. Tonight he was hitting on me. He hopes we might be able to get back together, but I'm not even remotely interested. OK?"

I nodded and swallowed around the lump in my throat. The possessive jealousy, the worry, the happiness at hearing how he felt about me were all a little overwhelming. The four cocktails probably weren't helping either. I took a shaky breath, struggling to pull myself back together so we could go back to the party.

As if he knew what I was feeling, he flicked his eyes over my shoulder, in the direction of the music and flashing lights, then pulled me into himself, wrapping his arms around my waist and pressing a searing, determined kiss to my lips. He'd told me how he felt; now he was showing me, and it was exactly what I needed. The feelings Ethan had stirred on the dance floor slammed back into me with a vengeance, and I moaned into his mouth as his tongue found mine.

A booming laugh made my eyes fly open.

"So this is why you were so disinterested before, J. You're into girls now?" Ben walked into the corridor, some vaguely familiar blonde girl by his side. "Your best friend's girl, apparently." His eyebrows rose in surprise as Josh and I took a small step away from each other.

This was bad for our cover story. Really bad. But I had no idea what to say or do. Something in me demanded I stick close to Josh though, and since my brain had checked out, I went with my instincts. I wrapped an arm around his waist, pressing my side to his.

"This isn't what it looks like." Josh's voice was calm, even a little bored, his arm draping casually over my shoulders. It was a complete contrast to the tension in his muscles, which pressed up against me like stone.

"Really?" The blonde girl's smile was ecstatic as she tossed her perfectly styled hair. "Because it looks like *Eve* here is cheating on Kid. With you."

I recognized her. The reason I'd had trouble placing her at first was because I'd never seen her smile. The only time I'd seen her she was crying, sitting between Zara and Beth on the couch in my res hall.

"Anna?" Fantastic. Another ex to deal with. Wasn't one enough for the night?

"Oh, good. You remember me." She sneered, her face taking on a slightly manic quality. "You took my spot at Bradford, my friends, and my boyfriend, bitch. I want you to know it's *me* who took him away from *you* this time. Kind of poetic, don't you think?"

I frowned; she was clearly unhinged.

"Ooookay then." Ben rocked back on his heels, looking between the three of us. "Nice to see you, Anna. Nice to meet you, Eve. Josh, call me if you get over your boobs stage. I'm out. Bye." He turned and casually walked out of the corridor.

"Oh, this is gold!" Anna laughed heartily, waving goodbye as she sauntered away.

Josh cursed under his breath and ripped his phone out of his pocket, shooting off a quick text to Ethan. "Let's go. Time for damage control."

I followed him back out into the writhing, loud, craziness of the club, where we pushed past drunk people to get to Tyler at the bar. Josh leaned over and spoke quickly, pointing at me. Tyler's face fell and he nodded, his mouth forming a tight line.

Without looking at me, Josh took off again, leaving me with Tyler.

"This is all my fault." I groaned and leaned back against the bar, defeated.

"No, it's not. Something like this was bound to happen eventually. Much as I'd like to, it's impossible to control everything." He gave me a lopsided smile, and amused by his own dig at himself, I returned it.

"We can't control everything, but I should have at least been able to control myself."

Tyler shrugged. "The Light is a powerful force. It influences our emotions more than we realize, pushing us to act in ways that are truer to what we're actually feeling rather than ways that are . . . socially acceptable."

I was pretty certain he was referring to the fact that many Vitals ended up in romantic relationships with two or three people at once—their Variant Bond members. But why was Tyler bringing up polyamory in the Variant population now? Was he trying to distract me? The topic had been on our list of Variant studies subjects to cover for some time, but we always seemed to skip it.

Before I could dwell on it further, I was distracted by Alec. He was at the opposite end of the bar, ordering.

"You have got to be fucking kidding me," I ground out, my nails digging into my palms.

Tyler stood up straight, on the alert. "What?"

"Oh, nothing," I answered in my best sarcastic voice. "Just yet another ex for me to have an overwhelming and confusing reaction to."

My eyes glued to Dana as she stepped up behind Alec. She was in a black dress that revealed just the right amount of skin, somehow sophisticated and scandalous at the same time, and her dead-straight blonde hair accentuated the strong lines of her cheekbones. Alec hadn't noticed her yet. She leisurely looked him up and down in a predatory way, her eyes lingering on his ass. Then she wrapped her annoyingly sexy body around his from behind, whispering something in his ear.

His shoulders tensed when her hands first made contact, but he threw his head back and laughed at whatever she said.

Tyler cursed, his hand closing around my forearm, as if I might take off at any second to gouge someone's eyes out. I couldn't blame him.

Alec's eyes found mine, staring at me down the length of the bar. The crooked, mischievous smile slowly dropped from his face.

I turned away. I couldn't look anymore. My relationship with Alec was the most confusing of all. He had been there for me during some of the toughest moments of my life, in a way that was hard to put into words. Yet he'd been so antagonistic—avoidant and downright hurtful at the same time. I was drawn to him, yet he made me want to throw things. *At him.*

I didn't *want* to be attracted to someone openly hostile toward me.

Regardless, watching Dana's hands crawl all over him made my gut clench. Flashes of what I'd seen in the limo on the night of the gala kept popping into my mind, unbidden and disturbingly detailed. I knew what her bare ass looked like, and I really didn't want to. The thought that he could end up in that situation with her again tonight . . .

I faced Tyler, zeroing in on one particular button of his shirt as I tried to calm my breathing. One of my hands was resting on the bar, my fingers clenching and unclenching in time to my grinding teeth. Tyler's grip had loosened, and he was now rubbing my arm soothingly.

"Try to breathe, Eve." He lowered his voice. "Your Light is flowing like crazy."

"Shit!" I slammed my fist down onto the bar, drawing a few looks. I was fighting the urge to march over to Alec and cause another scene, to drag Dana off him by the hair. My control had completely slipped.

"Just breathe, Eve," Tyler soothed, taking a relaxed sip of his drink.

Once no one was looking in our direction anymore, he nudged me and led the way to a back corner of the VIP area. It was next to another smaller bar that was closed for the evening, and the lack of lighting provided some semblance of privacy.

I leaned on the abandoned bar as Tyler once again reminded me to breathe. Trying to get my Light flow back under control was, at least, a good distraction from what was happening at the main bar. I focused on my breathing, on the loud music, on the thumping base reverberating through my feet, and within a few minutes I had it contained again.

"Good." Tyler smiled encouragingly, and I smiled back.

Now that one potential catastrophe had been averted, the other one refused to be ignored. I tried, I really did, but I couldn't help myself. I turned to look.

They were gone.

My heart sank, a hint of panic sending adrenaline through my system. While I was having my Light overflow crisis, they'd left to . . . Ugh! I couldn't think about it. I turned to Tyler, hoping he could do something to distract me so I wouldn't go looking for him, but just then, Alec approached us through the crowd.

Relief flooded through me. He was here. He wasn't with her. But I didn't know how to express the clusterfuck of emotions that had slammed through me in the space of half an hour, so I switched to my default Alec setting— sarcastic and baiting.

"That was quick. I didn't take you for a one-minute man." I propped one hand on my hip and smirked at him in what I hoped was as cruel and detached a way as he so often smirked at me. "Or did you decide not to have slutty car sex tonight?"

His eyes briefly widened. "You're one to talk, precious. I'm not the one who's made out with two separate people in one night, in a very public place."

He crossed his arms over his chest and cocked an eyebrow, the scar becoming more prominent. He was in all black, as usual—black jeans and a black shirt that pulled tightly over the taut muscles in his arms.

"It's not the same and you know it," I spat.

"Guys." Tyler tried to get between us. "Don't start. We've got enough fires to put out for one—"

"Oh, don't I know it!" Alec cut across him. "I just turned down a sure thing for . . ." He waved his arms up and down in my general direction. "I don't even know what!"

Tyler sighed, rubbing the bridge of his nose. "I guess we're doing this, then," he muttered.

"Wait. Did you reject Dana?"

"Yes, OK?" He stepped closer, but I stood my ground, squaring my shoulders and looking up to meet his stormy eyes. I'd never seen the blue in them look so dark. "Yes. You want to know what happened? She came on to me, in no uncertain terms. I mean, we could have been . . . like, right now. But no. I said no to the only woman I've ever met who makes me feel normal. Because of *you*."

He ground the last bit out between gritted teeth, punctuating his statement with a stab at my chest. He left the finger there, leaning in as he continued. "I looked down the bar and saw you, with that broken yet somehow furious look on your face, and all I wanted to do was come over and wipe it off. Is that what you want to hear, Evelyn? That I watch you so closely I feel like I can read your mind? You want to know how I haven't gotten laid since Studygate because I can't *fucking* stop thinking about it? You want to know that if it wasn't for the fact that you gush Light out of every pore every time one of us touches you, I would be slamming you up against a wall and bruising your lips with mine? There, now you know!"

He finally dropped his hand and took a small step back. I hadn't shrunk away from him during his tirade. I'd frozen, my eyes wide with shock, but I'd kept my gaze steady on his and my feet planted.

The tone in his voice and the tension coursing through his body were palpable. He was furious. But in a fucked-up, intense, uniquely Alec way, he'd told me he wanted me.

I blame what I did next on the haze of desire that coursed through my veins at hearing his words. They were violent and slightly disturbing—he'd spoken about slamming and bruising—but they made me think of the way we'd all but battled each other on the couch in Tyler's study that night. Something had to be fucking wrong with me, but I wanted more of that. It made me feel alive.

I blinked, breaking the stare we were in, and my lips parted to release a shuddering breath. "If that's all you're worried about, I have a solution," I rushed out, barely considering what I was saying.

Ethan had run his hands all over me on the dance floor, and Josh's kiss had been exactly what I'd needed in that moment, but they'd both left me needing more. The Light was straining to strengthen my connection to each of them by any means necessary, and my body was providing the means, reacting to each touch, each look, each hint at deeper intimacy with a longing so fierce I had no idea how much of it was my own desire and how much could be attributed to our supernatural Bond.

Now, here was Alec, telling me in his own messed-up way that he desired me too. That it was only the Light transference that was holding him back. For the first time since we'd met, we seemed to want the same thing, and for once I had a solution.

I glanced at Tyler, then reached out to grasp his hand in mine. "Accidental transfer is not an issue for at least a few hours after I've expelled excess Light to Tyler. It would be perfectly safe for us to . . ." I trailed off, partly because in my rush to explain how we could get it on, I hadn't properly considered how to phrase it, and partly because Alec's eyebrows shot up in surprise.

"You can't just . . ." Tyler stared at our joined hands, his brows creased. "I'm not . . . how can you . . ." He looked up at me, his mouth forming a tight line, his eyes turning hard. He wrenched his hand out of mine, making me tip to the side and grab on to the bar for balance.

"You know what? Screw you both." He gave each of us a stern look and then stormed away, shoving Alec with his shoulder as he passed.

I turned to Alec, completely confused. "What the hell just happened?"

He looked as deflated as I felt, his shoulders drooping as he watched Tyler disappear into the crowd. But unlike me, he didn't look confused.

"Fuck." The curse was not an outburst of emotion. It sounded resigned and defeated. Instead of answering my question, he went back to the bar and ordered a drink, giving me his back.

I'd been dismissed and rejected, and I still had no idea why. I needed to get out of this club and away from all these people and all this noise. My best bet was probably to try to find Ethan or Josh, so I headed toward the main club area. Just as I reached the velvet rope, Alec appeared, halting me with one hand around my wrist.

I tried to twist out of his grip, but he rooted me to the spot with an intense look.

"Where are you going?" he demanded as his grip loosened.

"Anywhere but here."

"Ethan and Josh took off a while ago, trying to fix the clusterfuck you three created tonight. They're meeting us at the apartment. And Tyler is going to need some time to get over the fact that his Vital just made him feel used. So we're stuck with each other, precious. I'm the only protector you have left tonight, and I'm your only way home."

"Used?" That was the only thing he'd said I could fixate on. Just the suggestion I'd made Tyler feel bad was giving me an awful tightness in my chest.

"Don't worry. It wasn't just you. I fucked up just as badly. I should never have asked him to keep his distance for my . . . Never mind. The point is, every man has his limit. You trying to use him so it would be safe for us to fuck was his limit."

He shoved my coat—which he must have collected at the bar—at me before taking the lead toward the exit. I followed, absentmindedly putting my coat on as my mind processed what he'd said.

As we emerged into the cold night, the full realization of what I'd done hit me.

"Fuck!" I pulled up short on the sidewalk, shoving my hands into my hair and ruining the perfectly sleek style.

Alec turned to look at me, his expression annoyed.

"Oh, I am such an *asshole*!" I whined. Alec wasn't my first choice of confidant, but he was the only one there.

"Don't worry about it. I'm an even bigger one. Let's go before we freeze." He nudged me forward with a firm hand on my lower back.

I crossed my arms, partly to ward off the cold and partly to stop myself from crying.

Tyler had been there for me from the beginning. Before he even knew I was his Vital, he'd been willing to help me with excess Light flow. He'd taught me about the Variant world, guided me through an incredibly confusing part of my life, and been a solid, constant presence I could always rely on. And I'd taken him for granted.

I didn't even think about how he would feel when I reached for him to expel Light so I could fulfil a physical urge. Of course he felt used.

Despite my best efforts, as we stepped into the warm, brightly lit lobby, my tears spilled over. I turned my head away from Alec and tried to surreptitiously wipe the wetness from my cheeks, but I couldn't stop my shoulders from shaking a little.

As the doors of the elevator closed, shutting us away from the prying eyes of the doorman, Alec surprised me by wrapping one big arm around my shoulders. He pulled me into himself and sighed heavily. The unexpected gesture of comfort made me cry even harder, and I leaned into him.

"It's going to be OK, Evie. He'll get over it. This is mostly my fault anyway."

I had no idea what he meant by that, but before I had a chance to ask, the elevator doors were opening and he was stepping away from me.

As he unlocked the front door of their apartment, another thought struck me.

"Fuck!" I yelled into the quiet hallway.

"God, you have a mouth on you tonight." Alec looked back with a mixture of amusement and worry. "What now?"

"Dot!" If it wasn't bad enough that I'd made Tyler feel like crap, I'd completely forgotten about Dot. "We just left her there. We have to go back! I am a terrible person."

I made to march back toward the elevator, but Alec grabbed a fistful of the back of my coat.

"Dot came home half an hour ago with Kyo. They left around the time you were propositioning me at the bar." He nudged me into the apartment as he spoke, punctuating the last sentence by closing and locking the door. "She's in her room, but I wouldn't go checking on her. I don't know what you might walk in on."

With that, he stalked off down the dark hallway and disappeared into his room.

I trudged to another of the rooms, my irritation with Alec returning. He'd been nice in the elevator—sweet even—and then he had to go and ruin it by making baiting comments about me propositioning him.

I was pissed off at him, but I went to bed more pissed off at myself than anyone else.

FIFTEEN

The next morning I was equally looking forward to and dreading seeing Tyler.

They'd come in about an hour after us, and I'd lain there in my giant bed and expensive sheets, straining to hear what they were saying in the hall. All I could make out was the low bass of Ethan's voice, the whispered responses from Tyler.

Then the door handle rattled. I'd locked it, and after a heavy pause, two sets of footsteps moved away. I couldn't stand to have Ethan and Josh hold me, comfort me, make me feel better when I knew Tyler was down the hall on his own, feeling like shit. Because I'd *made* him feel like shit. I rolled away from the door and stared at the beautiful city view, my silent tears soaking the pillowcase.

I'd hardly slept all night.

The large windows were letting in the morning sun as I slowly walked into the living space, wringing my hands. Everyone was already up.

Ethan and Josh were in the kitchen making breakfast. Dot was curled up in an armchair by the windows, a mug of coffee in her hands, looking out over the city. Tyler had his head in his phone, eating a bowl of cereal at the dining table. Alec was nowhere to be seen. The only noise came from the kitchen and a news program playing softly on the TV.

Ethan spotted me first.

"Morning, babe," he said in a much more muted tone than what I was used to. He came over, dropped a kiss on my head, grabbed a frying pan from a drawer near me, and got back to what he was doing.

I kept my eyes trained on the dining table. Tyler froze, his spoon halfway to his mouth, his thumb midscroll. For a beat he just stared at nothing, and then he lowered the spoon and the phone and took a few deep breaths, still refusing to look at me.

Indecision rooted me to the spot, my heart hammering in my chest. I had no idea how to fix this, how to make him understand I hadn't meant to hurt him.

Josh must have been watching me as intently as I'd been watching Tyler, because he stepped up behind me and placed a firm hand on my shoulder. "Don't overthink it," he whispered before kissing me softly on the cheek and giving me a gentle push toward the dining table.

I took a deep breath and cleared my throat. "Ty . . ."

He shot out of the chair. "I have to go," he declared in a flat voice, stuffing his phone into his pocket and walking toward the front door.

I panicked. I couldn't let him run out again. I jumped into his path, hands held wide as if I were wrangling velociraptors, and yelled, "Stop!"

Amazingly, it worked. He huffed and put his hands on his hips but still wouldn't meet my eyes. "Move, Evelyn," he demanded in a quiet, cold voice.

"No," I replied in a much shakier one. "We need to talk. Can we go into the other room, please?"

"I have nothing to say," he told the lamp behind me, every muscle in his body tense. Despite his original statement, however, he had quite a bit to say. "I shouldn't have waited this long to tell you I want you in the exact same way the others do. That's on me. But even if I didn't, even if *you* don't feel attracted to *me* like that . . . I'm not going to be your supernatural contraceptive. I am not OK with that."

My jaw dropped. I knew I'd hurt and insulted him, but I hadn't expected him to tell me he was attracted to me. As fast as joy raced through me, it was snuffed out by anxiety. Just because he was attracted didn't mean he wanted to act on it—not after I'd wounded him as much as I had. I *needed* him to forgive me, for things to be OK between us again; my skin crawled with the knowledge I'd hurt one of my Bond members.

"Fine, then just listen." I dropped my arms to my sides tentatively. He still seemed ready to bolt at any moment.

He rolled his eyes. As controlled as he usually was, Tyler could be a little juvenile when he was hurt. But I really had no right to judge his reaction. "I don't want to hear—"

"I'm sorry!" I cut over him loudly.

He crossed his arms, his brow pulling down stubbornly. He still wasn't looking at me. His body language said he didn't believe me, but considering his ability, he had to know I was telling the truth. I guess emotional pain can be a powerful distraction.

"Ty, just use your ability. *Please*. Tell me if I'm lying."

His eyes started to dart left to right, his mind calculating.

I kept speaking, hoping I'd appealed to his rational side. "I'm sorry about the way I treated you last night, Tyler. Am I telling the truth?"

With a huff, he nodded, a quiet "yes" falling from his lips.

It was working! "I'm sorry I hurt you. Am I telling the truth?"

"Yes." A tiny bit louder.

"Knowing I made you feel used or unappreciated has made me feel completely gutted. Am I telling the truth?"

"Yes." But his eyes were still locked on a spot on the ground behind me.

"Tyler, I appreciate so much all you do for me. The lessons, the Light transfers, your protecting me, *everything*. I would be lost without you. Am I telling the truth?"

"Yes." A slightly defeated tone this time, and he dropped his arms to his sides. I was getting through to him, but it wasn't enough.

I didn't want to go back to the way things were.

Tyler had built his defenses up so high I had a better chance of cracking Alec again. But he needed to know I wanted intimacy with him as much as I did with the others. I needed to bring this issue we'd been skirting around for months into the forefront. I tried not to think about everyone around us listening as I steeled myself for my next move.

"I care about you. Am I telling the truth?"

"Yes."

"I enjoy your company. Am I telling the truth?"

"Yes."

"I think you're an amazing, intelligent, caring man. Am I telling the truth?"

"Yes."

"I'm . . ." I faltered, incredibly nervous, but I had to get it all out. "I'm attracted to you. Am I telling the truth?"

Finally his head whipped up, and he looked at me, his gray eyes intense. "Yes."

"I like you, Tyler, and not because of all the things that have forced us together. I like you for *you*. Am I telling the truth?"

"Yes." A tiny twitch of his lips pulled them into a near smile.

"I want *you*. Am I—"

"Yes," he cut across me before I could finish my question, taking two long strides forward. With determination, he cupped my face in his hands and pressed his lips to mine.

Finally, *finally*, Tyler kissed me! I'd wanted this since the day we realized we were connected, and now, at last, it was happening. He was knocking down that barrier between us. I didn't even care that three other people were in the room watching us make out; I was so fucking happy to finally touch him how I really wanted to, to have him touch me.

I clasped my arms around his middle, leaving not even an inch of space between us. He deepened the kiss, leaving one hand cradling my cheek and pressing the other to the curve of my spine, making me arch my back. His tongue darted out, and I didn't even hesitate, opening my mouth and embracing every level of deeper connection to him. He was an amazing kisser, his lips soft but firm on my mouth, his tongue finding a steady rhythm against mine.

For minutes, or maybe hours, Tyler kissed me as though he was in the desert and I was a waterfall. It was intoxicating. My Light flowed freely in and out of me; I didn't have to worry about containing it with Tyler.

I was giving in to my desire in a way I couldn't with the others, and it was consuming my mind and my body, making me completely forget where we were. I lifted my right leg slightly, wanting to wrap my body completely around his. The hand that had been holding my face flew down to grip the back of my thigh firmly. I moaned into his mouth and started thinking about where the nearest flat surface was. I wanted more; I needed to feel him on top of me. Maybe the floor would be fine. Marble tiles were totally comfortable.

But thinking about the floor made me remember where we were. Tyler must have realized the same thing, because we reluctantly broke apart.

I found myself staring directly into Tyler's eyes, the gray almost swirling. I'd seen the amber in Ethan's and the green in Josh's just as alive plenty of times, but during the many instances Tyler had willingly taken my excess Light, I'd never been close enough to see it in him so clearly.

I was mesmerized, and he looked away first, his eyes darting around the room. He removed his hand from my thigh and took a measured step back, and I followed his lead. The chair by the window was empty. Dot had slipped out to give me some privacy with my Bond.

Ethan and Josh were standing shoulder to shoulder, staring at us with varying degrees of shock and excitement playing over their expressions. I started to feel a little awkward. I wasn't ashamed of my attraction to Tyler, but I was worried about how this decidedly more physical development between us would make them feel.

By equal measure, I was also a little . . . excited. To know they'd been watching us sent a jolt of confusing arousal through me. I decided to examine it later, but before I could say anything, a fire erupted in the kitchen.

It wasn't Ethan losing control of his ability; the bacon grease in the forgotten frying pan had ignited. Before I even had a chance to react, Josh made a small hand gesture, turning the knob controlling the burner to the off position. Ethan, glancing back almost absently, made a lazy swipe of his arm, and the fire went out.

A big smile crossed my face. Tyler stepped up behind me, wrapping his arms loosely around my front. I looked up to see him beaming at Ethan. Both of us had realized something the other two hadn't caught on to yet. Their focus was on Tyler's arms, so casually draped around me.

"Kid," Tyler said, his voice excited. "Do you realize what you just did?"

Josh realized it before Ethan. He gasped and turned to face him, his finger pointing to Ethan and then to the stove. "Dude! You put the fire out."

Ethan's confused eyes flicked between us and Josh. Slowly, the crease between his eyebrows smoothed out, and his face broke into a big smile. "I put the fire out . . . I put the fire *out!*" he repeated, much louder, and laughed excitedly before jumping and punching the air.

Ethan's excitement was infectious, and I found myself laughing with him, folding forward a little at the hips. But that resulted in my ass bumping back against Tyler, and the evidence of his arousal pressed into me for the briefest of moments before he took a step back, clearing his throat.

"This is great, Kid." Tyler moved next to me. "We should practice—"

"Oh, I don't think so!" Josh cut across him. "You don't get to deflect from talking about that little show you two just put on."

"Can't we deflect for just a little longer?" I shot him a pleading look. I didn't want to overanalyze it.

"No," Josh and Ethan answered together, standing side by side again, presenting a united front. My shoulders slumped and I huffed.

"They're right, Eve," Tyler said, the ever-present voice of reason. "If Anna has anything to do about it, everyone will be gossiping about what she saw. We need to get on the same page, and we need to get ahead of it."

He walked over to the dining table, sat down in the chair he'd abandoned earlier, and looked at us all expectantly. The three of us joined him, me dragging my feet, trying to delay this as long as I could.

I really wanted to bask in the fuzzy feeling that had settled around my shoulders now that I'd deepened my Bond with Tyler. Kissing him had been like a daydream come true. I didn't want to ruin that warmth in my belly by talking about complicated things.

But my mind could never resist the opportunity to gain more knowledge, so I sat next to Tyler.

Ethan placed a plate full of waffles with berries and ice cream in front of me, and Tyler scooted his chair closer to mine, resting his arm on the back of it. He swiped my hair to the side and placed his gentle fingers on the nape of my neck. I smiled into my waffles, biting my bottom lip.

A simple touch was giving me butterflies. I shoved a huge bite of waffles into my mouth to cover up my embarrassing reaction. When Josh set a latte—made on a very expensive espresso machine they had in the kitchen—next to my plate, I finally looked up.

They were all watching me. Josh and Ethan were sipping on their own coffees across from us, and Tyler was just smiling, his eyes trained on my mouth.

I swallowed my food, and in the interest of not getting sidetracked by wondering what he was thinking while he looked at my mouth like that, I started the conversation I'd so wanted to avoid.

"What made you change your mind?" I asked, drawing Tyler's focus away from my mouth to my eyes.

He frowned. "What do you mean?"

"I told you how I felt about you because I couldn't stand the thought of you thinking I didn't care. I knew you didn't want me like that, but I needed you to understand that you matter to me more than you know. But what made you change *your* mind?"

"You thought I didn't want you like that . . ." A sad look crossed his face.

"Have you given her any reason not to, Gabe?" Josh's words were gentle, but they cut right to the crux of the matter.

"No, I suppose I haven't." Tyler sighed and half faced me in his chair, the hand at my neck beginning to stroke me softly. "Eve, I've always wanted you like that."

I frowned and took another bite of the amazing waffles. I didn't know how to respond; his behavior had told me otherwise for months.

"From the first day you walked into my office, I was attracted to you. But you were a student, and even with Bradford's lax attitude in regard to some staff dating students, it felt like I would be crossing a line of propriety to even consider it. Then we learned you were Bonded to Ethan and Josh, and I knew I needed to put your safety and theirs above all else."

His fingers kept up the gentle massage at my neck, and I kept eating my waffles, my eyes on my plate. I couldn't make myself look at him.

"When I realized we were Bonded too, I could have cried from happiness, but I knew immediately how much more danger we were in—how powerful you really are. I resolved to keep our connection restrained so you could have time to learn to control your Light, so these two could learn to control their dangerous abilities."

He gestured to Ethan and Josh. Ethan was leaning on his elbows, listening as intently as I was, and Josh was reclined in his chair, casually sipping his coffee, as if he'd heard this all before.

"The night of the gala"—at his mention of that night, my eyes whipped over to Tyler—"my resolve broke. You'd gotten closer to Ethan and Josh, and even me, in every other way, but that day, the physical connection stepped up a notch, and then you came down those stairs in that dress, and I just wanted to rip it off you."

I swallowed, the sweet taste of my breakfast still on my tongue, but I'd already forgotten how good it was. At his words, all I could think about was tasting his mouth again.

"I made the decision that night to pursue you romantically as enthusiastically as the others, and I'd deal with the consequences of the increased levels of Light. But then Alec . . ."

I cringed, looked away. The memory of what had happened between us that night still made me sick to my stomach. "And then I ran away, and then Bradford Hills was invaded, and everything turned to shit," I deadpanned.

He chuckled, nudging my chin with his free hand until I was looking at him again. "Yeah, things got more complicated. And once the truth about Alec was revealed . . ." He sighed. "He asked me to keep my distance. He begged me to keep things platonic between us until he could deal with some of his shit. That night after you ran away, you slept in the arms of Ethan and Josh while Alec pleaded with me for time. Maybe it was the wrong thing to do, but I agreed."

I stared at him, eyebrows raised in growing disbelief. "Maybe? *Maybe* that was the wrong thing?"

Un-*fucking*-believable. Hours after promising to be honest with me, he had vowed to keep a massive secret. With Alec of all people.

"Oh shit," Josh whispered, sounding genuinely worried.

"Dude, even I know that was a bad move." Ethan shook his head. I looked between him and Josh, my eyes narrowed. It was a small relief to see they both looked just as shocked as I was.

"Tyler, you promised me no more secrets, and then you went and made another one." Just as quickly as the anger had risen, it dissipated, leaving me feeling deflated and hurt.

"Eve, I'm sorry." He took my hands in his and looked into my eyes, his gaze brimming with sincerity. "It wasn't my secret to tell. You don't know all that Alec's been through. You weren't around all those years to see how much he struggled with his ability, with losing you, with losing our parents. I was afraid I would lose *him*."

I pulled away from Tyler and stood, teeth clenched. My hands tightened into fists at my sides. "So you couldn't stand to lose him, but you could stand to never have me?" I ground out, tears blurring my vision.

"No!" Tyler stood too, his face determined. "Every second I stayed away from you, every moment I kept myself back, was torture, and I never intended to keep this distance forever. But I didn't do it just for him."

"Then *why*?" I hugged myself with one arm, wiping the tears away with quick, frustrated movements. I didn't want to be crying, weak.

To his credit, Tyler kept explaining, *pleading*. Alec would have stormed out in a huff ages ago.

"It was the right thing to do for all of us."

I wasn't the only one who huffed at that. Ethan and Josh added their protests to mine, and we all started speaking over each other.

The sound of the front door slamming broke the cacophony, and we all turned to look at Alec. He came to a stop halfway between the door and the dining table, taking the scene in.

"So you told her?" he asked in a calm, clear voice, removing his coat and dropping it over the back of the couch. There was no anger or resentment; he said it as if he'd expected as much.

"Yes. I kissed her too. I can't do this anymore, man." As he spoke, Tyler moved to stand next to me, wrapping an arm over my shoulders.

And I forgave him. I still didn't fully understand why he'd done it, but he'd apologized immediately, hadn't run away from a difficult situation, and now had my back, standing by his decision to be honest and to be with me. His actions spoke louder than his words, and I couldn't stay mad at him.

To my utter astonishment, Alec didn't rage and yell, storm out and push us all away. He nodded and took a deep breath. "I should never have asked you to do it in the first place."

He looked down and placed his hands on his hips, looking all kinds of awkward and apologetic.

But he hadn't actually said he was sorry.

"So that's it? You're not even going to apologize?" I crossed my arms and leaned into Tyler.

"I was getting there." His ice-blue eyes snapped up, his ire rising to meet mine, as it always did.

A loud, deep groan brought all our attention over to Ethan, who was looking up at the ceiling. "Can we not get into another screaming match, please? I feel like we have bigger fish to fry."

I was a little taken aback that Ethan, the goofball, was the one talking sense. The others must have agreed, because we all sat down again, Alec joining us at the head of the table.

"So how did things go with Anna?" Tyler asked, his hand returning to the nape of my neck.

But before the guys could fill us in, Alec interrupted. "Wait, I just . . ." He looked between me and Tyler uncertainly, his knee bouncing under the table. "I need to apologize to both of you. I am sorry . . ."

"We both made a bad call. Let's just move on." Tyler reached out, and they gave each other a quick hand squeeze while I stared in astonishment. That was it? *Men.*

I could only give Alec a little nod. I couldn't find it in me to speak the words. I wasn't sure if I meant them yet.

"Eve." Alec directed the next part just at me. "I know this doesn't excuse it, but I want to at least explain it. It's not easy for me to talk about this, but I do want you to understand."

When I didn't say anything, he took it as a sign to keep speaking. "Please just know it wasn't personal. I wasn't being malicious or deliberately trying to keep your Bondmates from you to hurt you. I just . . . you don't know how . . . I *hate* my ability," he finally spit out.

I leaned forward. Alec was showing vulnerability, being honest and real for once. I didn't want to blink and miss it.

"What do you mean?" It was the best I could manage to encourage him.

"They call me the 'Master of Pain' like it's something I lord over people—like I enjoy it. But I hate hurting people, and there is nothing I can do to switch it off. Having you . . . being with you, in your Bond, it makes my ability stronger. Eve, your Light is so fucking bright it's blinding."

I stared at him, at the intensity in his eyes. The way he looked at me, with so many conflicting emotions in his face, reminded me of the night in Tyler's study.

Even if it makes me an even bigger monster than I already am? His words rang through my mind, and they finally made sense.

Being with me, letting my Bond deepen with all four of them, would have meant amplifying Alec's ability—the thing about himself he despised the most. He was so stoic most of the time, so solid in his frame and posture, hard in his voice and actions. But underneath all that, he was suffering—had been for a long time.

I stared at him, not sure what to say, how to express that I understood but it still didn't excuse the lying.

"You could have just told me." My voice was low, sad. "Both of you."

"I should have." He nodded. "I didn't know how."

"And it wasn't my story to tell," Tyler piped in. "I'm sorry I deceived you, Eve. I am. But I've watched Alec struggle with this since we were kids. I've watched it bring him to the brink of destruction. It was too heavy for me to just blurt out to you. He needed to do it when he was ready."

"He was never going to be ready." Had they planned to just hold off sex with me for life for the sake of Alec's messed-up attitude? I got the sense the three of them had been letting him get away with a lot over

319

the years. I wasn't about to fall into the same pattern.

"No, I wasn't," Alec agreed, "but it's out now, and I'm glad, because at least now I'm not hurting you both anymore. Regardless of my ability, I'm constantly hurting people." The last part was spoken more to himself as he sat back, dragging his hands down his face.

"If I'm being completely honest, that's not the only reason I held off getting physical with you, Eve." I turned back to Tyler, frowning. "I wasn't ready either."

"What?" Ethan said. He and Josh had been very quiet, letting Tyler and Alec put everything on the table, but they both looked confused at this.

I threw my hands up. "Do guys talk about anything?"

Tyler chuckled, catching my hand and pressing a kiss to my palm. "I never even thought I'd have a Vital. The . . . sharing thing is much more accepted in Variant society, regardless of whether you're in a Bond or not. But I kind of always figured I'd find that one person, and that would be it. I never expected I'd have to share you—and that's OK," he rushed to add. "It really is. I just needed some time to get used to the idea."

At the mention of "sharing," everyone went silent. I glanced around the table to see they were all looking at me, as if waiting for my lead. Josh had a smirk on his face. Fucker.

Yes, there were worries and insecurities about how we would make this work—how we would balance all the emotional scars, needs, and strong personalities without being at each other's throats all the time. But there were other thoughts too—dirtier, more difficult to verbalize thoughts.

I averted my gaze and squirmed in my chair.

"Are you guys done making out?" Dot chose the absolute perfect moment to interrupt. I loved her a little more for it, even as I wondered if she'd been eavesdropping; her timing was a little *too* good. "Because we really should talk about the 'Eve getting caught kissing Josh' debacle." She stopped next to Alec's chair and gave us all a withering look. "I love gossip, but you guys are doing a shitty job of keeping all this"—she gestured around the table with one hand—"a secret."

"Yes, we need to talk about that. Any news?" Tyler slipped back into his leader role seamlessly.

"Oh yeah!" Dot held her phone up as evidence. "All the news. You're trending, and it's not even ten a.m."

"Trending?" Alec asked, even as Josh groaned and Ethan started softly banging his head on the table.

"Hashtag ScandalAtTheClub, hashtag VariantSlut."

"Oh, Lord Kelvin." I dropped my head into my hands.

"What happened with Anna?" Tyler's voice still sounded even; I held on to that to keep myself from descending into full-blown panic. "Did you catch up to her?"

"We couldn't find her," Josh answered. "She left pretty fast, and we decided calling her would only add fuel to the fire, so we left it. Obviously that was a mistake."

"No," Tyler assured him, "it wasn't. Urging her to keep it a secret would only have given her more to gossip about. This way we can have some control over what we say about it."

"What do we do?" I turned my pleading eyes to my friend—the gossip expert.

Her lips widened into a crafty smile, and she tossed her messy black hair. It was still unbrushed from whatever she'd been doing with Kyo the previous night, adding to the slightly unhinged vibe she had going.

"We confuse the fuck out of them," she declared, as if it were obvious.

SIXTEEN

As I zipped up my boots and gathered my stuff for the first day of classes since Dot's birthday, I tried my best to remain calm. I'd woken up before my alarm, and worst-case scenarios had been running through my head all morning.

What if Dot's plan didn't work? What if no one believed us?

I hated being the center of attention. I'd spent my whole life learning how to disappear, and I much preferred the company of dead scientists. But what really had me taking deep breaths to calm my nerves was the thought of my Vital status coming out and putting us all in danger.

I could've really used some of Zara's no-bullshit straight talking—she would have told me to calm the fuck down with an eye-roll—but she'd left for an early class.

She'd asked me what happened as soon as I'd come home after Dot's birthday. Her stomach bug seemed to have completely passed, and she'd held her phone up to show me the gossip all of the vulture Variants of Bradford Hills were eating up.

I told her the whole awful story, including the bits no one else knew about—how I'd been terrible to Tyler and come on to Alec. I told her about the kiss with Tyler too, barely concealing the grin on my face.

She agreed Dot's plan was probably the best course of action but did try to present another option.

"Have you thought about just coming clean?" She asked as we sat on the couch, sipping hot chocolate—it made us both think of Beth, in a good way. "I mean, maybe it's not worth the effort anymore. And you might be more protected if it comes out you're a Vital. They'd probably give you a Melior Group personal bodyguard."

She'd rolled her eyes, and we'd both chuckled, but she wasn't far from the truth. Most Vitals were under some kind of protection, especially at Bradford Hills. The Institute was probably the safest place for a Variant or Vital to be. But after talking about it for a bit, I'd dismissed the idea. The longer we kept this on the down low, the better. Especially considering how tenuous my connection still was to all my Bond members. We weren't steady enough to present a united front yet.

I put on my thick coat and took one final deep breath before opening the door. Josh was standing on the other side, his fist poised to knock.

He was in a peacoat, his dirty-blond hair parted on one side and styled meticulously, a Burberry scarf around his neck. He gave me a brilliant smile, flashing his perfectly straight teeth, and held up his other hand. "Hey. As your boyfriend, I figured it was my duty to bring you coffee."

"You bring me coffee all the time." I chuckled, taking the cup and inspecting it. "And the boyfriend thing is not new."

I was focused on the double helixes covering my new reusable cup. When I looked back up at him, he was smiling from ear to ear.

"What?" I smiled back, uncertain.

"I just like hearing you call me your boyfriend." He shrugged, taking a sip from his own reusable cup. His had the Rolling Stones mouth on a black background.

I pulled the door closed behind me and gave him a kiss. The taste of coffee on both our lips mingled with the warm, clean smell that always clung to Josh, and I sighed. "You know you're much more than that," I whispered against his lips, eliciting another smile.

Outside, I was glad for my coat and boots. The snow hadn't arrived yet, but the chill in the air announced it was just around the corner. As we walked toward the science buildings, some of the nervousness returned.

"What's going through that head of yours?" Josh leaned in as people started looking in our direction, not being at all subtle about the fact they were talking about us. It reminded me of the day my blood test results came out and every Variant on campus wanted a piece of me. All the attention made my skin crawl.

Unfortunately, Dot's plan hinged on us gaining that attention.

"I'm not entirely sure how to go about this," I admitted. "I don't like having everyone watch my every move."

"How about we just start with this?" He intertwined his fingers with mine, giving me another brilliant smile.

I squeezed his hand, double-checking that my Light flow was under control. If that slipped, the whole plan would crumble.

"It feels so good not to have to stop myself from doing that anymore." He kept his voice low, his words just for me. To anyone looking, we were simply whispering sweet nothings to each other, our hands locked and our sides pressed together, our steps synchronized as we walked.

"Guess this means Ethan's single again," a girl said to her friend, throwing me a smug look.

"It was only a matter of time," her friend responded, and they moved off, not waiting for a response. Not that I was going to dignify them with one. But my hand did tighten around Josh's, my baser instincts driving me to defend what was mine.

"Deep breath," Josh whispered. "We know the truth."

I nodded and did as he said, letting the cool air in my lungs push the mean comments out of my mind.

"I'll see you at lunch." He leaned in and kissed me. It was a chaste kiss in comparison to some of the others we'd shared, but it was still intimate, and it was in front of all the people walking past us into the building.

We separated, but before he had a chance to walk away, Dot marched up to us in black thigh-high boots and her polar bear coat, with a confidence I hadn't seen in her for a long time. She stopped right in front of me, a devious smile on her face.

"Hello, lover," she said at a volume that wasn't trying to be heard or hidden. Then she draped her arms over my shoulders and pressed her lips to mine in an over-the-top kiss.

I chuckled against her lips, and the kiss ended as abruptly as it had begun. She pulled me into a hug, and I returned it, but I wasn't expecting her to rub her whole body up against mine in a deliberately sexual move. If people hadn't been paying attention earlier, they certainly were now.

"What are you doing?" I whispered into her ear. "I don't recall this part of the plan."

"The plan was to confuse them," she whispered back, finally pulling away, "act so erratically that no one has any idea who you're dating or screwing or what the hell is happening."

"She's a little too good at this." Josh sighed, lowering his own voice. "But when you factor in the fact that you've been giving her your Light, I might actually be getting jealous."

He narrowed his eyes at us, but a smile was playing on his lips. He dropped one last kiss on my forehead and headed off, hunching his shoulders against the cold.

Dot looped her arm through mine, and we headed inside to our classes. People who'd been stealing looks before were outright staring now. A few even had cameras out.

I did my best to ignore it and focus on my classes, but I was on my own until lunch, and all the eyes on me made me feel vulnerable. At lunchtime, I speed-walked to the cafeteria.

Zara and I reached the entrance at the same time.

"How's it going so far?" she asked, not bothering with petty things like greetings and pleasantries.

"It's been half a day, and it already feels like torture," I deadpanned, removing my coat as she did the same. We picked a table and sat.

"Well, it's already working, if that makes you feel any better. Some of the rumors I've heard are ridiculous." She smirked, leaning forward so we could keep our voices down.

"Excellent." I rolled my eyes. It was what we intended, but I hated that there was an element we couldn't control.

Dot and Josh joined us soon after, and we were about halfway through our meals when Ethan made his entrance. No doubt it was by Dot's design that he arrived late, his big frame ensuring all eyes were on him as he came through the doors.

He paused, removing his bomber jacket as he scanned the crowd. He found our table and smirked, the dimple appearing for only a moment, but he moved off toward the food instead of joining us.

The chatter in the room lessened, everyone watching Ethan's every move as he piled his tray high with food, then marched straight over to us, his big shoulders pulled back, his eyes dancing. I could tell he was fighting laughter; he found the gossip as amusing as I found it frustrating and awkward.

He lowered his tray, deposited his bag and jacket in a chair, and faced Josh. Josh remained in his seat, one arm resting on the back of my chair, the picture of relaxed.

There was a moment's pause.

The two of them looked at each other.

The room held its breath.

"Hey, bro!" Ethan finally released his brilliant smile.

"What's up?" Josh reached his hand out, and they did some weird horizontal high five before fist-bumping.

I figured if we were going to do this, we may as well do it right. I stood up and wrapped my arms around Ethan's neck. He had to bend to meet me halfway, but we shared a brief kiss hello.

The room descended into confused murmurs. Some people went back to their food and conversations now that the drama they'd been expecting hadn't happened. Others started whispering.

I reveled in Ethan's warmth, the strength of his gentle arms around me, and used it to ground myself.

He stole my seat and pulled me into his lap, and we spent the rest of the hour talking about anything other than the plan we were, so far, flawlessly putting into action.

Two weeks later, Dot's plan was working like a charm. The attention had died down after some furious speculation about who I was actually dating. When no dramatic fights or breakups happened, everyone got bored and moved on to other things. I was no longer trending.

No one had even speculated that I might be a Vital; Dot throwing her attention into the ring had put a stop to that. Everyone knew Charlie was her Vital, and no one wanted to be reminded of the fact he was missing.

Even Zara had joined in the fun, walking through campus with me with our arms around each other. She probably only did it because she enjoyed glaring death at anyone who dared to look at us, but I was grateful anyway.

But there was one unexpected side effect of having the whole campus think I was dating multiple people.

The bitchy comments from girls when they realized Ethan wasn't actually back on the market and people calling me a slut were not a surprise. But the extra advances I received, just the sheer volume of attention, were a bit unsettling. I'd been asked out and propositioned more in two weeks than I had in my whole life before. Both guys and girls were coming up to me, some of them subtler in their flirting than others.

I would have thought that with most Vitals having multiple partners, the Variants of Bradford Hills wouldn't be quite so affected by the idea of someone dating more than one person. But I was wrong. So wrong.

As I headed to my next session with Tyler, yet another guy zeroed in on me, stepping into my path and waving. "Hey, girlie!"

I scowled at him. We were both bundled up in warm clothing, but I could see his face clearly. The last conversation I'd had with Franklyn was at Ethan's party, when he'd come on to me in the grossest way possible on the dance floor.

He kept pace with me as I sped past him. "No bodyguards today?"

The guys had been sticking closer to me than usual with all the extra attention; it hadn't gone unnoticed.

I didn't spare him a glance. The admin building was in view. "No, but I have snipers watching my move at every moment."

Franklyn faltered for a beat, his eyes scanning the bare treetops as if he actually expected to see a gun pointed at him. "Haha! Good one."

We reached the square housing the admin building. There were more people there, and I felt a little safer.

"So, I'm not really into guys, but I'd be up for a three-way with you and the short one with black hair. Her brother's dead, right?"

His words were so insensitive, so rude and presumptuous, that I actually did stop. I stared at him, slack-jawed, wondering how he didn't know Dot's name when they'd been in the same classes for years, how he could talk so casually about Charlie's disappearance, how he thought it was OK to say shit like that to a woman.

He took my pause as a sign to move in, and before my stunned mind could process what was happening, he was lowering his face as if to kiss me.

The invasion of my personal space snapped me out of my shock. A jolt of fear tinged with anger shot through my limbs, and I stepped back, shoving him with my hands flat against his chest. Adrenaline was coursing through me, my fight, flight, or freeze instincts settling on *fight*. My nostrils flared, and I bared my teeth as I prepared to shove him again, to tell him exactly where he could shove his callous comments.

But before I had a chance, his face scrunched up in pain, and he flinched away from me.

"Every time I see you near her, I'll zap you," a deep, angry voice said from behind me. "I won't even pause to find out if you're behaving yourself, understand?"

Franklyn looked as if he was considering fighting back, but then he just turned away and stalked off, rubbing a spot on his chest.

I turned around to see Rick scowling at Franklyn's retreating form. Electricity was still dancing between his fingers, but he snuffed it out as his gaze focused on me.

"Thanks." I didn't really know what else to say. Every time I saw him, the image of his electric ability slamming into Beth assaulted my mind.

He looked like shit. I hadn't spoken to him since he'd come up to me and Zara on the first day of classes, but I still saw him occasionally around campus. He kept to himself these days, seeming to focus more on his studies instead of goofing around with all the loud, athletic guys who hung around Ethan. He looked older too, more tired.

I knew Ethan still hung out with him occasionally, trying to be a good friend. He'd asked me if I was OK with it, and I'd told him he should follow his conscience; I just didn't want to hear about it or see it. I respected that he had a big heart and couldn't help seeing the good in everyone.

We were all still reeling from Beth's death, but as I stood in the square in front of Rick, feeling the cold wind whip my hair around, I realized it couldn't be easy to live with the knowledge you'd killed another person either.

"Anytime," he responded, then hesitated. He looked over my shoulder, then spoke again, his words coming a little quicker, his voice low. "I don't know exactly what you guys are playing at, but be careful, OK?"

"What?" I narrowed my eyes, leaned in a little closer. The hairs on the back of my neck were standing up, and it wasn't because of the cold.

"Just be careful. Watch your back. Don't be precious about your . . . friends being overprotective. You may have confused all these *children* with the show you've put on, but there are other people paying closer attention." He flicked his eyes over my shoulder again and backed away. "I have to go," he rushed out, turning to leave.

"Wait!" I grabbed his arm, and he flinched, hissing as if I'd hurt him, but he pulled a neutral mask over his features quickly. "I don't believe you meant to . . . I believe it was an accident." I'd meant to question him further, demand what he was being so cryptic about, but this had been in the back of my mind too long. Zara may have drawn strength from her anger, but I couldn't hold on to mine. Beth wouldn't have wanted me to.

He nodded once, the barest of smiles pulling at the corners of his mouth. Then he turned and rushed off.

The thud of boots on concrete made me turn back toward the admin building. Kyo and Marcus were jogging up to me.

"You OK?" Kyo demanded as Marcus kept his focus on Rick's retreating back, his hand on the gun at his waist.

"I'm fine." They both looked skeptical. "I'm fine, I swear. Stand down."

The pair relaxed visibly and chuckled at me.

"Only Alec can order us to stand down, kitten." Marcus crossed his arms over his chest.

"Technically, so can Tyler. And I don't know how Alec would feel about either of you calling me 'kitten.'" I raised my eyebrows at them. Alec was still keeping his distance from me, but he was pretty intense about my safety.

Marcus looked genuinely worried, even checking that Alec wasn't standing behind him, but Kyo just laughed. I waved at them as I rushed off for my session with Tyler.

For the first time in weeks, I found Tyler alone in his office. No Melior Group operatives asking for direction, no Bradford Hills staff wanting updates, no Stacey being "helpful."

I dropped my bag by the door and removed my coat while he finished up a phone call.

"Perfect. Thanks, man. I really appreciate this." He sounded more casual than he usually did on official calls. He was standing by the window, one hand in his pocket, the sleeves of his slate-gray shirt rolled up, as always. "I'll wait for your call. Bye."

He hung up, dropped the phone on his desk, and turned to face me with a brilliant smile. I hadn't seen him smile like that since the day after Dot's birthday, when we finally kissed.

He'd been so busy and stressed, jumping straight back into work. But he was much more affectionate. The look he was giving me held all the warmth and caring it used to when our relationship was closer to friendship, but now it also held a little heat. He wasn't shy about letting his eyes trail down my body, checking out what was visible of my curves under the layers of warm winter clothing.

He also didn't hesitate to meet me halfway when I walked toward him.

I wrapped my arms around his neck, but he surprised me by gripping tightly around my middle and lifting me into a spin on the spot. I let out a startled whoop, and we both paused, our eyes flying to the door to double-check it was closed.

Then his lips were on mine, and I didn't care about anything anymore. His hands roamed up and down my back as we kissed, and I lost myself in the feel of him. I didn't care who might have heard me; I forgot about Rick and his cryptic warnings, Franklyn and his disturbing comments.

There was only Tyler.

I let my hands explore his back, feeling the tight muscles I'd noticed within minutes of first meeting him. I traced downward all the way to his ass. He had such a tight ass, and I'd recently learned I quite enjoyed groping it. Not that he minded. He mirrored my movements, dropping both hands to my ass and giving me a firm squeeze as he ground his very prominent erection into my front.

With a grunt he pulled away, resting his hands on my hips and raising a warning brow.

"Hey, you started it." I was unapologetic, punctuating my statement with another grope of his butt.

He was starting things whenever he could—we both were, as if we were making up for lost time. He constantly stole kisses in his office, pulling me into private corners of the mansion to get a brief hot moment alone. I reveled in being able to touch him, in being able to drop every guard and reservation with him.

"What's got you so excited? Not that I'm complaining." I finally released my hold on his ass, lifting my arms back to his shoulders. His messy brown hair had fallen over his forehead again, and I pushed it back, running my fingers through the soft locks. I was doing that every chance I got.

"I just heard from my guy at The Hole. He's made contact with the Lighthunter." He grinned, releasing me to return to his desk.

My heart jumped into my throat; I made myself swallow around the lump and respond in an even voice.

"Oh? That's great. When can you meet?" I had to be very careful about what I said. I'd just transferred a massive amount of Light to him; his ability would be hypersensitive.

"Hopefully next week. He's going to get back to me. I really have a good feeling about this." He turned back to me with some papers in his hands and sat in one of the chairs, gesturing to the other.

I took a seat, pulling my books out of my bag. "Well, I know I wouldn't bet against one of your feelings."

"Just have to wait and see what happens. Let's focus on what we need to get through for today."

Relieved he'd changed the subject, I forced my mind to focus on the textbooks and the academic discussion. I waited until I was out of the building before texting Dot. We needed to get things in motion.

SEVENTEEN

The plan was simple. The biggest chance of it getting derailed was before I even made it out of Bradford Hills: I had to make it past the Melior Group guards posted at Dot's house.

I'd been doing more sleepovers at her place over the past few weeks instead of hanging out at the Zacarias mansion. We explained it as wanting more "girls only" time and invited Zara as much as we could, even though we hadn't told her what we were planning.

That night it was dumb luck that Zara had something else to do. Dot and I did the same things we always did—we ordered a pizza and watched a movie while Dot did my nails. But we were so quiet, knowing what was to come, that her mom asked us several times if everything was OK.

Eventually we headed upstairs and went through our usual bedtime routine. Then we shut ourselves in Dot's room and waited for the house to fall silent. Her mom's footsteps came past Dot's room a little after eleven.

"Are you sure about this?" Dot whispered. She'd been asking me some variation of that question ever since I'd clued her in on my plan, even as she procured everything I needed to make a fake passport and helped me pack my go bag.

"Yes." There wasn't an ounce of doubt in my voice. "For Charlie." That always shut her up.

Quietly, we got ready. Dot inserted bright pink and purple hair extensions into my hair as I applied heavy black makeup and fake nose and eyebrow piercings. It couldn't have been more different from my casual look.

I put on some of Dot's ripped-up, crazy clothes, slipped on my sneakers, and grabbed my duffel. It was small enough to not draw too much attention but big enough for the essentials.

"OK." Dot looked around the room, swallowing hard and taking another nervous breath.

I slipped the tracker necklace off. Holding it in the palm of my hand, I felt a pang of guilt. They would be so worried. And mad. Alec was going to lose his shit. And Ethan . . . I'd promised Ethan I would never leave him again, and here I was doing exactly that. I was a shit girlfriend.

I reminded myself I was doing this for Charlie. And Dot. My guys would understand once it was all over.

I pulled the note I'd written from my pocket and handed it, along with the tracker necklace, to Dot, and she hid them in a desk drawer.

I'd agonized over the note for a good hour, staring at the blank page with no idea what I could possibly write to make this easier for them. When I finally realized nothing I could say would alleviate their worry and anger, I decided to keep it simple.

I'm sorry.

Come find me.

I miss you already.

"Say it back to me," I whispered under the light of the one lamp we'd left on.

"I give the note and the necklace to Gabe. He's the only one who can't stop me or slow me down with his ability. I don't wait for him to read it or ask questions. I just tell him to use the Lighthunter, and I hightail it out of there. I camp in the woods for a night, and I keep this on me." She held up a disposable cell phone. I was the only one with the number.

I nodded. We'd gone over the plan a million times, but it made us both feel better to repeat it. With everything ready, there was only one thing left to do. Dot and I stepped closer and held hands. I closed my eyes and let the Light flow out of me while making sure none was allowed in to replace it. I'd been practicing this too—expelling all my Light to see how long I could go without it leaking back in and becoming unbearable.

It was difficult to test, as the guys constantly wanted to train and Tyler asked for boosts almost daily as he tried to puzzle out who was behind the kidnappings.

I'd managed to somehow get a stretch of nearly three days without transferring; that seemed to be close to my limit. By the end of the third day, I was feeling the itchiness at my wrists and ankles, the increased levels of energy, the pull toward my guys to release it.

"Twenty-four hours." I nodded, dropping Dot's hands.

"Twenty-four hours," she whispered back. "I'll come back after one day, and if the Lighthunter is bogus, you tell me where you are, and we come get you."

We stared at each other, then we hugged, holding tight.

"Thank you so much for doing this," she whispered, her voice shaky.

"Hey." I pulled back, my own throat getting tight. "None of that. We need to stay focused. And you can stop thanking me."

Because you're my family. I left that unsaid. I wasn't ready to verbalize it, but that's how I thought of them. It felt good to be so close to people, to feel so safe with them, that I could give them the same label my mother had—*family*. But on some level, it also felt like a betrayal of her.

But I couldn't afford to get into that now, to get emotional. My full focus needed to be on getting past the Melior Group guards posted outside and keeping my Light in check.

I put on a dark coat with a hood, and we quietly made our way downstairs and into the garage. The plan was to hide me in the trunk of Dot's hatchback and have her drive out, telling the guard she was popping out for snacks. The guards were there for general security, but anyone Tyler posted on duty near me was briefed to make me a top priority. If the guard thought I was still in the house, he wouldn't try to accompany Dot. I hoped.

In the garage, we left the light off and walked straight to the car. As Dot opened the driver's side and I reached for the trunk, the side door leading outside opened, and a light flicked on, illuminating the space in a harsh fluorescent light.

Dot's mom, Olivia, stood at the door, one hand clutching the handle, the other holding a half-smoked cigarette between elegant fingers.

"Mom?" Dot sounded outraged more than surprised. "When did you start smoking?"

"I . . . well, I quit a long time ago. But lately, with all the stress, I just . . ." The guilty look on her face melted away as she zeroed in on the bag slung over my shoulder, my new look. She straightened and crossed her arms, keeping the lit tip of the cigarette away from her fluffy white robe. "What are you two up to?"

"Uh . . ." Dot's eyes flew between me and her mom's. If their relationship was anything like mine had been with my mother, Dot wouldn't be able to lie to her. There was no point anyway. Even if we managed to convince her we were just going for snacks, she would insist on the guard coming with us.

"It's for Charlie!" I blurted out. Trying to convince her of some half-baked, last-minute lie would never work. Olivia was too smart and already suspicious. The only chance we had was to appeal to her own worry. Her own grief. Her own need to do whatever possible to find her son. "This could help us find Charlie. But we don't have a lot of time. Please . . ."

I wasn't sure how to finish. Her eyes narrowed, looking between me and Dot but eventually settling on me. "Explain."

"There's no time." The plane ticket was booked, and I had a narrow window to take a convoluted enough path so I disappeared before going to the airport. "I need to get to the train station without the nice men in black knowing. Then, hopefully, in a day or two, we'll know where Charlie is."

It was the best I could do, giving her as much info as I could without jeopardizing the plan.

"Evelyn." She sighed, flicking her cigarette. "I can't let you head out without a guard. It's too dangerous, sweetie."

She wasn't convinced. I was touched that she cared enough about me to want to keep me safe. It was so motherly . . . But once again I couldn't let myself think about mothers and family. I had a mission.

"I miss him, Mom." Dot's voice was low, but it broke on the last word.

She was standing by her car, her fingers clasped around her keys. Every bit of worry, grief, frustration, fear, and longing that Dot had felt since her brother and Vital had been taken was written all over her face. It was in her upturned eyebrows, her hunched shoulders, her glassy eyes. Every painful emotion she'd dealt with in private, or even tried to push down, came out.

"I can't do this anymore." Fat tears started rolling down her face, her breathing becoming labored. "I need him. I need to know . . . Charlie deserves this. We have to try."

Olivia's own expression was full of pain as she watched her daughter break down for her son. "Shit," she cursed under her breath. Then she took one last long drag of her cigarette and threw it to the ground, putting it out with her fluffy white slippers.

"Dorothy, go back inside." Her tone brooked no arguments. "Evelyn, get into the back seat of my Escalade. The windows are tinted."

Dot made a sound that was something between a sob and a surprised laugh, watching with wide eyes as her mother disappeared inside and came back a few seconds later with the car keys and her purse.

"Get in," she ordered, jumping into the driver's side and starting the engine, "before I change my mind." Dot and I exchanged one more meaningful glance, and I climbed into the back seat.

Olivia pulled out of the garage as soon as I closed the door. I covered myself with a blanket and crouched in the footwell for good measure.

At the gate, there was a quick exchange. Olivia said she was out of cigarettes and moved off without incident. The guard didn't even look in the back seat, hardly even giving her an answer past a polite "yes, ma'am." It was so easy. I hoped I hadn't just cost a man his job, but I couldn't afford to worry about that either.

"Where am I going?" Olivia asked uncertainly.

"The train station," I replied, making sure *my* voice sounded nothing but confident. "But park around the corner, on Baker Street." There weren't any cameras there to record which car I'd arrived in, and my altered appearance should be enough to keep me anonymous from the cameras in the station. Dot and I had cased the joint on one of our coffee dates.

She nodded and kept driving. It took only ten minutes to get there, and Olivia spent most of the time nervously adjusting her grip on the steering wheel and muttering to herself. "Must be out of my mind . . . so stupid . . . I should turn this car around . . . supposed to be the adult . . ."

But the car continued to move at a steady, sure pace toward the station, so I kept quiet.

When we came to a stop, her muttering stopped too. She remained facing forward, her breathing labored. "Maybe this isn't such a good—"

"It's for Charlie," I cut her off. "Mrs. Vanderford, Olivia, I need to do this for him. For Dot. For *me*. For all of us."

She finally turned to look at me, her eyes watering. She searched my face for a long time and then, as her tears spilled, gave me a tiny nod and turned back to the front.

I didn't wait for her to change her mind; Dot would make sure she didn't crack. I got out of the car and walked away without looking back, keeping my pace steady, my head turned down under the hood.

My train pulled in just as I made it onto the platform, and I chose a seat near the back. Other than one other guy in a safety vest—probably a shift worker—I was the only one to board. The train moved off, and the shift worker almost immediately fell asleep, his head propped up against the window.

I leaned back in my seat but kept my hood up and my face down. I spent the hour-long ride into the city fortifying my control of my Light and mentally going over the next steps, keeping a careful eye on the handful of people who boarded the train as we got closer to my destination.

But I couldn't help my mind wandering a little, remembering the last time I'd taken this trip. The two experiences couldn't have been more different.

When I'd tried to run away all those months ago, I'd been overly emotional, paranoid, and irrational, constantly looking over my shoulder and completely ignoring the amounts of Light pouring into me. I hadn't even had a go bag ready. I hadn't created a new identity in months!

This time, I was nothing if not prepared. I'd created a passport and other IDs, with the name Gracie-Lou Freebush on the perfect forgeries. I'd altered my appearance. The cash I'd been slowly withdrawing from my account and storing in the pages of my physics textbook was now tucked into my purse. I'd remembered every lesson my mother had taught me.

And I'd thought of every possible outcome. Some of them were more daunting than others, like the scenario in which black-clad men jumped out of the shadows with one of those black devices, identified me as a Vital, and made me disappear for real. But I'd never get through this if I allowed fear to enter my mind. I had to be brave.

I could do this.

I got off the train a few stops before Grand Central. It was easy to get lost in the jostling New York crowd and make my way outside, where I hailed a cab.

I spent the next hour taking several cabs and walking around between them in various directions. I changed my coat twice and put my hair up and down, altering my appearance when I could.

The last cab deposited me at World Trade Center station with just enough time to get onto the train heading to JFK.

Another uneventful train ride later, I was at the airport, making my way past more armed guards to get in line for passport control. My work was impeccable, and the man checking my ID hardly even looked at me.

Waiting in the departure lounge, another pang of doubt stabbed my gut. The guys would be pissed—and worried. And what if I was caught, abducted, killed? Maybe we should have included them in the plan. But they would never have agreed to it!

No, it was better this way. I shut my worries down and, after a tense hour, boarded the plane with the other tourists, businessmen, and families with screaming children. Before I had a chance to doubt myself again, we were taking off as the sun began to rise over New York.

~

New York to Melbourne is one of the longest routes in the world. I had to do two layovers, and one of my connecting flights was delayed, but thirty-five hours of travel time later, I arrived—tired, disheveled, and smelly. All I wanted was to collapse into a bed and sleep until my guys found me, but I couldn't let my guard down just yet.

I still had to get somewhere safe—somewhere without police and CCTV. But for that, I needed help.

After brushing my teeth and changing my top in the airport bathroom, I stuffed my jacket into the duffel bag—both to change my appearance again and because it was a hot day. I made it past customs and passport control without incident and took another paid-in-cash taxi to my old stomping ground of Fitzroy.

It was midmorning as I slowly rounded the corner. The café was two doors down, a post office and a milk bar separating us. I wanted to take it all in before making my move.

Greville's Café was our regular hangout when I lived in Melbourne. It took up two shop fronts in the middle of a small strip of stores located in a mostly residential area, a few blocks from my old school and within walking distance of both where I'd lived and Harvey's house. People drove out of their way for the best fair-trade, organic coffee in the city, as well as the homemade jam doughnuts.

At least a dozen alfresco tables were situated out front, boxed in by low planters with succulents. Several oversized umbrellas provided necessary shade—a respite from the harsh Australian sun.

Harvey was sure to come here at least once, although I worried he'd already been today and wasn't planning to come back. I had no idea what his schedule was. He'd finished high school the year before and would have started his graphic design course by now. It was all he could talk about when we were together.

I really didn't want to go to his house and risk his sister or parents answering the door. I couldn't hang out inside all day either—too many people I knew frequented the place. But loitering on the corner of a residential street all day would be way too suspicious.

I chewed my bottom lip, fidgeting with the strap of my duffel. The strong sun beat down on my back, making me sweat, and when my stomach growled, I decided to take the risk and go in.

The morning rush had ended, and I didn't recognize any of the few seated patrons. I ordered a cheese toastie, a friand, and a latte. The food came out before the coffee, but when the barista placed the little glass full of happiness down in front of me, I abandoned the sandwich and immediately took a slow sip. I moaned loudly, my eyes closed, as the exquisite, smooth, creamy flavor hit my tongue.

When I opened my eyes, the hipster barista was looking at me with raised eyebrows, fighting a smile.

I cleared my throat. "I really needed that—rough morning. It's really good."

"No worries." He chuckled, moving back to the coffee machine to make more liquid pleasure.

I stayed at my table for nearly two hours, ordering another coffee and taking my time with the food while pretending to read a magazine. But as the lunch rush started, I got worried about looking suspicious; I'd already drawn the barista's attention.

I paid with cash and got up to leave. Halfway across the room, the little bell above the door tinkled as two girls my age walked in, chatting. My heart flew into my throat. They'd gone to my school when I lived here and had hung out with us sometimes at Harvey's house. I cast my eyes down and hunched my shoulders, hoping my heavy makeup and crazy hair were enough of a disguise.

One of them glanced in my direction as we passed each other, but by some miracle, she didn't seem to recognize me.

I walked to the park across the street, on the opposite corner, and hid behind the slide, my heart hammering against my ribcage until they came out and strolled away. I stayed in the park to keep watching the café, praying to the universe Harvey would show up.

It was two thirty, the café buzzing with moms grabbing an afternoon caffeine hit before school pickup, when I spotted him. He was with two other guys I didn't know. *Uni friends?* I smiled to myself.

I wondered from time to time what might have become of Harvey and me had I not screwed up and started us on a course that changed my entire life. But I'd realized, ultimately, there was no avoiding that course. I was made for those four incredible, loving, frustrating men. I was their Vital, and we were always going to find each other, one way or another.

What I'd had with Harvey was superficial by comparison. I was sad about how it had ended—he would have been confused and scared when I just disappeared like that—but I harbored no unresolved feelings for my old boyfriend, just a strange kind of nostalgia and a hope that he was happy. Seeing him laughing and joking with friends made me feel better about it all.

I crossed the street again and stood around the corner, watching. When they came out of the café, takeaway cups in hand, I started to worry they would leave together and I'd have to go to his house. But his two friends took off in the opposite direction, and Harvey headed toward me.

I pulled back and leaned against the rough brick, my palms a little sweaty and not just from the oppressive heat. What if he was really mad and refused to speak to me? What if Variant Valor had somehow got to him, and *he* kidnapped me? What if he didn't remember me?

My paranoid thoughts were interrupted by their subject walking around the corner. He was in a Deadpool T-shirt, his backpack slung over one shoulder. He looked taller.

He was tapping away at his phone and didn't even notice me standing there.

"Harvey," I called out.

He pulled up, turning distractedly, his attention still half on his phone. He lifted his eyes to mine, a mildly curious expression on his face, before dropping them down to his screen again. Then he froze, his fingers tightening around his takeaway cup, his eyes flying back to mine.

Shock and disbelief were heavy in his raised eyebrows, his parted lips. "Holy shit." The words came out on a breath.

Suddenly unsure what to do, I gave him an awkward smile and a pathetic little wave.

"Holy shit, Eve!" That time he practically yelled the words, throwing his almost full coffee to the ground as he lunged forward.

"No need to waste perfectly good coffee . . . *oof*." He knocked the breath out of me as he enveloped me in his arms, giving Josh a run for his money when it came to lung-crushing hugs. He was definitely taller. We used to be about the same height, but now he had almost a head on me. His voice sounded deeper too. The boy who had been so many firsts for me had turned into a man.

I returned his hug, feeling comfort and nostalgia in his arms but not a scrap of the angst-ridden pining I used to feel. I'd found something much deeper with my Bond than Harvey and I could ever have had.

"Can't breathe," I managed to get out with the last bit of air in my lungs.

He released me only to grasp my shoulders and stare into my eyes. "My god. It's really you!" His volume was still high.

"Shh!" I glanced around.

His eyebrows pulled together in suspicion. "Eve . . ." He dropped his arms by his sides but kept staring at me as though he couldn't quite believe what he was seeing.

"I know this is a lot—me showing up like this."

"I . . . there are just so many questions. I don't even know which one to ask first."

"Do you hate me?" It wasn't exactly the question I'd planned to ask, but it had been playing on my mind since the night my mother forced us to pack up and leave. Of course he would have worried, but how long had that lasted? How long before he'd turned to anger, looked for someone to blame? If he still held a grudge, my chances of getting his help were significantly lower. Harvey could be almost as stubborn as Alec. Almost.

"Hate you? No." He chuckled, shoving his phone into his pocket. "Eve, I knew you would never leave like that for no reason. I could never hate you . . ." He looked a little awkward, and it struck me in that moment that we'd never actually broken up. It would be the logical conclusion after not seeing each other for over a year and a half, but technically . . .

I breathed a sigh of relief, choosing to focus on my current situation. The afternoon was slipping away and taking the light with it. I needed to get on the road soon.

"Harvey, I'm sorry for so many things, and I wish I had all the time in the world to explain them to you, but . . ."

"But you're in trouble." Tension returned to his posture.

"Kind of, I guess." I wasn't technically, but I could be. "I need your help."

"What do you need?" I knew he burned for answers, but he put that aside and was willing to do what I needed. He reminded me of Ethan in that moment; my big guy was the most selfless, caring person I knew.

I pushed the longing down, making sure to shut my Light flow down with it. "I need to borrow your car, and I need the keys to the Carboor house, just for a few days, and then everything will be OK." I didn't sound convinced, but I really hoped what I was saying was true.

"Who are you running from, Eve?" He stepped closer, lowering his voice. "Is it the same people as before? Is that why you left? Maybe I can help. Maybe we could call my uncle Steve. He knows some guys in the federal police . . ."

"No!" My voice rose. "Harvey, no police." I fixed him with a firm look, poised to just run away from him again if I had to.

"OK, OK. No police. Just please tell me what's going on?"

"I can't." I sighed. "There just isn't time. I need to get going before it gets too dark to navigate the dirt roads. Please, Harvey!"

I injected as much desperation into my look as I could. He watched me for a beat, then sighed and rolled his eyes, and I knew I had him.

"Come on then." He headed toward his green Range Rover. "Don't suppose there's time to get another coffee."

"I wish." I looked longingly back toward the source of the best coffee I'd ever tasted.

EIGHTEEN

Harvey drove in silence, and it almost started to feel awkward, but his house was really close, and we were pulling up in no time. I took in the big eucalyptus tree in the front yard, the red mailbox, the curving path to the front door. It looked exactly the same as when I used to come over after school, and another pang of longing shot through me for something that almost was but never really could have been.

Harvey wasn't getting out of the car. "It's getting late, Eve. It could be dark by the time you get out there. Maybe you should just stay the night. Mum and Dad won't mind, and Mia will be ecstatic to see you—"

"Harvey," I cut him off, "you can't tell them I'm here." The fewer people knew I was in the country, the safer. Plus, while Harvey had talked about his family's holiday property often, I'd never been and would be relying on GPS to get me there. I needed to get going.

It had been over forty hours since I'd left. Dot would have told my guys about it by now. If the Lighthunter was legit, they were probably already on a plane on their way here. I needed to be somewhere isolated, and I needed to stay put until they found me. It was safer for me—away from creepy little Vital-identifying machines—and it was safer for the general public; I wasn't sure how well I could control the amount of Light that would come gushing out when we reunited.

"Will you explain things after . . . whatever this is? When you bring my car back. You *will* bring my car back, right?" He flashed me a smile, but it didn't reach his eyes.

"I'll do my best to explain it all." I owed him that much.

Harvey nodded, got out of the car, and walked up the curved path. I shifted over to the driver's side and fastened the belt, ready to head off.

He came back after ten minutes, just as I was beginning to panic he'd blabbed to Mia. But he emerged on his own, carrying a bag and a cooler. He dropped both in the back before coming around to the window, playing with a set of keys.

"I packed some extra supplies for you."

"Thank you, Harvey. For all of it."

"Just be safe." He handed the keys to me.

Not knowing what else to say, I nodded and started the engine. He stepped away from the car as I moved off. I could see him for a while in the rearview mirror, watching me drive away.

Once I was past the rush-hour traffic of the city and on country roads, the rolling hills in shades of muted green and brown soothed my nerves. No cars followed me out of the city, and Harvey's GPS guided me toward my destination.

The sun had set by the time I had to navigate the dirt roads on the approach to Harvey's vacation home, so I put the high beams on and took it slow, looking out for wombats and kangaroos. I finally arrived around nine, unloaded the car, took a quick shower, and collapsed into the first bed I found, not willing to walk even the few extra steps to the master.

It had been over forty-eight hours since I'd slept in an actual bed, and I was beyond tired. I fell asleep as soon as my head hit the pillow.

When I woke up to the sound of kookaburras outside the window, my arms and legs were itchy. I'd done my best to keep the Light at bay, but there wasn't much I could do while I slept.

I groaned, getting out of bed. After another long shower, I removed my brightly colored extensions and got dressed in shorts and a tank top; even though it was only ten, it was already sweltering hot. Scratching at my arms, I rifled through the supplies Harvey had packed. The extra bag had spare blankets, flashlights, a first aid kit—the kind of things I'd need if the car broke down. The cooler had food.

Thank the Milky Way. Food was the one thing I hadn't thought about. If my ex-boyfriend hadn't raided what looked like half his fridge, I would've had to drive into town, and I couldn't risk being seen or having the guys find me there.

Ten minutes later, I was sitting on the porch with a plate of scrambled eggs and bacon, a mug of instant coffee (it would have to do) next to me. I took my time eating, watching the birds fly from tree to tree and breathing in the warm air. The beautiful view helped me focus as I tried for the millionth time that morning to bring my Light flow under control.

But the itchiness had already spread to my shoulders and hips, and it wouldn't be long before it reached my torso. I had no doubt that within twenty-four hours, I would be glowing like a Christmas tree.

Sighing, I took another sip of coffee, turned on the phone only Dot had the number to, and dialed. It had barely started ringing before she answered.

"Are you OK?!" my crazy friend shouted down the line, startling a flock of birds that had settled into the branches of a nearby tree. I cringed, pulling the phone away from my ear. Then I chuckled.

"Yes, Dot. I'm fine. Everything went to plan. Are you OK?"

"Oh, thank fuck." She sighed. "Yes, just . . . just wait, Mom . . ." I could hear Olivia in the background. "I'm talking to her . . . She's fine . . . You can't talk to her because *I'm* talking to her . . . Mom!"

I laughed, listening patiently to scuffling sounds on the other end of the phone, followed by a door slamming.

"That woman has been driving me mad. I had to take her camping with me so she wouldn't blab. You owe me for that one."

"I am eternally in your debt."

"You put your life at risk to help me find my brother—we can call it even."

"Haha! Deal!"

"So how you holding up?"

"I'm fine. No issues getting here, but my Light levels are starting to get uncomfortable. What happened after I left?"

"Well, I didn't sleep all night. Partly because I was worried sick about you and partly because Mom was worried sick about you. She regretted her decision, like, immediately. She walked through the door and started freaking out, and the only way I could keep her from running off to Uncle Lucian was to answer her million questions. Thank god Dad is away or this whole plan would've imploded the second he saw her."

"So rough night, then?"

"Yeah, you could say that. The next day I somehow managed to convince her to come camping with me. So we drove to campus, and I made her stay in the car while I waited for Gabe. He showed up with Alec."

I cringed. "Shit."

"Yeah. Shit. So I pretty much threw the scrunched up piece of paper at him and sprinted to the car, and Mom and I sped out of there. But, man, was he pissed."

"Who?"

"Who do you think? Gabe just stood there frowning at the note, but Alec . . . the words coming out of his mouth made even me blush. I could hear him loud and clear despite the fact that we were already driving away."

"So are they on the way? Did it work?" I needed to know if it had all been for nothing. I'd never received the call from Dot—the one we'd planned on if the Lighthunter was bogus and I had to tell them where I was—but I needed to hear it.

"Well, after another sleepless night in the woods, once again courtesy of my mother—I mean, I had a bear guarding us from all the dangerous animals, but apparently that made her uncomfortable. I swear . . ."

"Dot!" I laughed, the itchiness creeping up my collarbones momentarily forgotten.

"Anyway, I called them in the morning, and they were already in the air. I·spoke to Josh. Gabe was busy ordering people around, and the other two were pissed and refused to speak to me."

"Ethan was pissed?" I knew he'd be hurt and worried, but I'd never seen my big guy lose his temper.

"Yeah. Punched a hole in the wall, apparently."

"Shit."

"Yeah, you're in *so* much trouble."

I groaned. "How did they know where to go, Dot?"

"The Lighthunter." She sounded excited. "Josh said they drove to The Hole immediately and demanded to know where to find her from Gabe's contact. The guy needed a little persuading, but he spilled eventually." I didn't want to know what kind of "persuading" they'd done, but I could guess. "Then they went straight to wherever that was, and within an hour they were in the air. So how's your ex?"

I spluttered, dribbling coffee all over myself as I laughed and coughed at the same time. "What?!"

"Well, Josh said they were heading to Australia. I figured you hit the Aussie up for some help. Is he still hot?"

"Yes. I mean, no! I mean, yes, I did ask Harvey for some help, and when it comes to his level of hotness, I don't know. I don't look at him like that anymore. I have three new boyfriends, remember?"

"Four boyfriends," she replied without missing a beat, and I rolled my eyes. "Alec has issues, but he's into you. Trust me. And bitch, please! You cannot tell me that you reunited with a guy you've seen naked and didn't appraise whether he got hotter or notter."

"Notter?" I chuckled.

"I'm coining a new term. Just roll with it."

"You know what? This conversation has turned pointless. I need to go burn some of this Light off."

"Fine. Be like that. Just don't get eaten by a kangaroo out there."

"Aren't you supposed to be an animal expert? You know kangaroos don't eat humans, right?"

"Oh, hey, my mom is calling me. Gotta go!"

"Whatever." I was barely containing my laughter.

Before I could actually hang up though, Dot spoke again, her tone much more serious. "Thank you for doing this, Eve. I love you."

"I love you too, Dot."

"Good luck with your boyfriends."

"All three of them? Thanks!"

"Fou—" I hung up before she could get the word out.

I propped my feet on the railing and sipped my coffee, smiling to myself. Now that I knew my guys were on their way, I felt much more relaxed, despite the itchiness.

It had worked. The Lighthunter was real, and we might actually have a chance at finding Charlie.

After a punishing, hour-long run, I jumped into the shower to wash away the dust of the dirt trail. As I headed into the bedroom, wrapped in a towel, my hair piled on top of my head in a messy bun, I heard the distinct sound of a car engine.

That can't possibly be them yet. Fear spiked, making my stomach clench, my spine straighten.

I peeked out the window at the dark truck approaching, leaving clouds of dry dust in its wake. It was too late to make a run for it. I had no way of getting away, and they were already pulling up next to Harvey's Range Rover.

I pulled the towel tighter around myself and swallowed around the ball of fear that had lodged in my throat, making it hard to breathe, talk, or scream.

And then all four car doors opened at once, and I breathed a sigh of relief.

The mental walls I'd so diligently constructed were instantly dust, pulverized by the mere sight of my Variants within touching distance. The itching was all over my body, but now it wasn't just itching. My skin felt as if it were humming, practically vibrating with the amount of Light straining at my seams.

To my dismay, a soft glow illuminated my skin, making me look like a nightlight. It was the first time since the invasion my Light overflow had gotten this bad. The glow faded and then intensified again, appearing and disappearing as though it weren't sure if it wanted to be there yet. But I couldn't waste any more time.

I rushed onto the porch as they all piled out of the car. I was down the few stairs and halfway to them before I realized Tyler and Alec both had their guns out.

My steps faltered. "It's OK. We're safe here . . ."

They ignored me. Everyone was moving forward, but none of them were looking directly at me except Ethan. He was the only one heading straight for me, and he was the only one unarmed.

"Stop!" Tyler's commanding voice halted them all. "No one fucking touch her until I do. I can practically smell the amount of Light coursing through her body. Alec, Josh. Perimeter. Kid, watch her."

I huffed and rolled my eyes. "This really isn't nec . . ."

But the three of them had already moved off. Only Ethan stayed, his gaze never having wavered from mine.

A fifth person had also exited the car, but I barely registered what they even looked like. My focus was on my big guy.

His shoulders were hunched, his huge chest heaving, his fists clenching and unclenching. He looked as if he was a split second away from ignoring Tyler's command and launching himself at me. I knew because I felt the same way. The Light inside me was throwing its full weight against the inside of my skin, reaching with outstretched hands to get to one of my Variants.

But it was his face that kept me glued to the spot. His eyes were blazing, and considering his ability, that was scary in itself. He somehow looked both furious and scared at the same time.

I really just wanted to hold him, but I tried speaking to him instead, my voice soft. "Hey, marshmallow."

Apparently now was not a good time for our nickname game. His lips pressed together, and he looked away, staring at the gravel by his feet.

My heart cracked in two, and I couldn't wait any longer to go to him, to try to wipe that devastating look off his face. But before I could take a step, Alec's serious voice sounded behind me. "Clear."

"Clear" came Josh's reply, followed by his footsteps pounding down the stairs.

"Clear." Tyler finished off the routine, but it was *his* voice, the voice of my logical leader, that sounded uneven, insecure. I turned to face him, completely shocked for the second time in fifteen minutes. He was striding toward me, tucking his gun into the back of his pants.

Alec and Josh were halfway between me and the house, Alec's hand on Josh's shoulder, as if to hold him back. But Tyler was demanding my full attention. He took me in his arms, one hand banding around the middle of my back, the other splayed flat against the bare skin above the towel. My hands instinctively flew to his neck.

We both grunted at the force of the Light that gushed out of me and slammed into him as soon as we made contact. And then he kissed me—one searing kiss, filled with all the intensity of the moment. Too soon he pulled away, but he didn't let go. If anything, his grip on me tightened, his fingers pressing into my skin.

"Don't hold back." He panted into my mouth, his lips nearly on mine again. "Let me have it all. I want it all."

I had a feeling he wasn't just talking about the Light, but I didn't have a chance to think about it; my body was already reacting to his words. Lifting onto my toes, I pressed my lips to his and pushed my tongue into his mouth.

He responded, kissing me with a passion I hadn't felt in his kisses before but had sensed all along, underneath his careful control.

He broke the kiss again but only to pick me up and hold me against his chest as he turned and walked purposefully toward the house. I wanted to lift my legs and wrap them around his waist, but I remembered just in time I was in nothing but a towel, and my ass was already an inch away from being exposed to the Australian countryside, as well as our other companions. So I left my legs hanging, bending them at the knees to avoid kicking Tyler in the shins as he went up the steps.

I lifted my head just as Tyler carried me into the house.

Josh's eyes were glued to the spot where Tyler and I were touching, and the envy in his narrowed eyes was warring with another emotion, one that had his lips almost twitching into a smile.

Alec was watching my face, his hand still on Josh's shoulder, and his expression could not be mistaken for anything other than longing. The intensity in his ice-blue eyes as they met mine surprised me and confused me so much that I had to look away.

I only caught a glimpse of Ethan before Tyler carried me deeper into the house. He was still standing in the same spot, still not looking at me.

I ached for them. Each of them. I wanted to comfort Ethan, reassure him I was OK. I wanted to make Josh's smile break through, prove I wanted him as much as any of them. I even wanted to wipe that look of longing off Alec's face, show him he could have what he longed for if only he would drop his stubbornness, reach out, and take it.

I wanted to be touching them all. But I was touching Tyler, and that was nothing to complain about.

He carried me into the bedroom. His hands were everywhere—fast, frenzied—as if he didn't know where he wanted to touch me first. He was more out of control than I'd ever seen him, his breathing ragged, his blue shirt crumpled.

I pushed his messy hair back, threading my fingers through his soft locks as he came in for another kiss. I got completely swept up in the taste of him, the smell of his cologne mingling with a hint of sweat, the feel of his perfect body against mine, his greedy hands grabbing my arms, my back, my waist, my ass.

We ended up on the bed, Tyler half on top of me. One of his legs pushed between mine, and I could feel his arousal pressing into my side. I moaned into his mouth. After all those months of being sure he didn't want me in the way that I wanted him, feeling the evidence of his desire was the ultimate turn-on.

I hiked my leg over his hip and drew him even closer, wedging my hands between us to access his shirt buttons. I had half of them undone before he broke the kiss, his breathing uneven. His gray eyes were bright, almost silver, and swirling.

"Why"—his voice was low and strained—"are you wearing a towel?"

He was holding himself above me with one arm, but his other hand was gripping my hip, his fingers flexing and relaxing on my bare flesh. The towel had come completely untucked, and the whole right side of my body was exposed.

"I wanted to be naked when you all got here." I meant it to come out more lighthearted than my breathy voice and swollen lips made it sound. Tyler's eyes narrowed, and he groaned, dropping his forehead to mine.

"Kidding." I chuckled. "I was in the shower and . . ." I didn't bother to finish, focusing instead on what my hands were doing. I undid the top button on his black pants and dragged the zipper down, sliding my hand inside his underwear.

The silky-smooth skin was warm in my hand as I wrapped my fingers around him and started to stroke. His eyes closed, and his hips started to move in rhythm with my hand.

He trailed his fingers up my side, over my shoulder, and down my front. He paused at my breast long enough to give it one firm squeeze that made my back arch off the bed just a little. Then he moved lower.

I dropped my leg off his hip to give him better access. His fingers reached the spot where I wanted them most, spreading the moisture with slow, deliberate movements that made me falter in my strokes, and then, as he started to push his finger in . . .

"Gabe!" the hard, almost growl-like quality in Alec's voice was punctuated by loud thumps on the bedroom door.

"Fuck," Tyler whispered against my lips. He pushed his finger in the rest of the way in one swift move, swallowing my exclamation of surprise with one last searing kiss. Then he pulled away, extracted my hand from his underwear, and left me panting and naked on the bed.

He fixed his pants and ran a hand through his hair as he opened the door a crack, murmuring something too quietly for me to hear.

Alec's voice wasn't quiet at all. "You have two minutes."

Tyler shut the door and turned, his hands going to the buttons on his shirt, but he paused when he noticed I hadn't moved.

"Much as I love this view," he growled, pausing to bite his lip and rake his eyes all over my nakedness, "you need to get dressed. The others are getting impatient."

I took a deep breath, relishing the way his eyes followed my chest's rise and fall. Then I got up and pulled on some shorts and another clean tank top.

He moved to open the door. "It's probably better that we stopped."

"What?" I halted, his words bringing back every insecurity I'd ever had about his feelings for me. Did he regret taking our relationship to this new physical level? Was I a disappointment? "I thought we were past this shit." I somehow managed to get the words out on a firm, annoyed tone, my arms crossing over my chest.

"Oh, Eve, no . . ." He abandoned the half-open door and faced me fully. "I'm not saying I wanted to stop."

"OK . . ." What was he saying, then?

I had a feeling this was related to what we'd briefly talked about the morning after Dot's birthday: Alec's conflicted feelings, Tyler's getting used to sharing me, both of them needing time. Maybe I just needed to be more patient? But I kept my mouth shut, waiting to hear what he had to say.

"It's just . . . the physical stuff is a little complicated. You know how intense and steady the Light transfer is when you're touching us, especially in that way."

"Yeah." I propped my hands on my hips. "Stop being obtuse. It's not your style. Spit it out, Ty."

He smiled and wrapped his arms loosely around my waist. I returned the embrace, resting my hands on his shoulders and doing my damnedest not to let his proximity distract me.

"When you give to one of us—when you share your affection and your Light—the others are naturally drawn to you. When the"—he paused, searching for the right words—"pleasure is received by you, it's a little easier to resist the urge. But when it's *given*, it's almost impossible. It's like my ability has a mind of its own, instincts of its own, and it demands I claim you—get my share of the Light and the attention that comes with."

My mind went to the night of the invasion, when Alec had refused to let me touch him in the way he'd touched me, refused to let me give him the kind of pleasure he'd given me. He wasn't just denying me the closeness I craved; he was making sure the others wouldn't have extra temptation to cross the same line. I wasn't sure if he was being thoughtful or selfish. Once again my feelings toward Alec were ambiguous.

"So you're all refusing to let me pleasure you because you know the others will be tempted too?" I arched a brow, skeptical.

Tyler chuckled but nodded. "That, yes, but also . . . Eve, I'm trying to be mindful of you. Of what you are and aren't ready for. It's—"

"That's my decision to make. Not yours." Who did he think he was to decide when I was ready to have sex?

"I'm not trying to control you!" Tyler wasn't quick to anger, but he wasn't one to back down when he believed in something. "I'm just trying to give you the space to make that decision yourself—to not have it made for you by the pull of the Light. Eve, there's four of us. Once you cross that line with one, the other three won't be able to resist much longer. You won't be able to either. Are you sure you're ready for that?"

My immediate gut reaction was "Yes! Sweet baby Einstein, yes!" But I didn't speak. My instincts were screaming at me to jump him, tear his clothes off, and deal with the consequences later. But my pesky logical brain was throwing up all kinds of doubts. Like how it could be dangerous if my Light control slipped. Or how I wasn't entirely sure Alec wanted it. Or how I wasn't sure I wanted it with *him* after the way he'd treated me. I wanted the physical—the way he made me feel was undeniable—but did I want all the emotional baggage that came with the physical pleasure?

"We're just trying to give you time." Tyler smiled reassuringly before giving me a kiss on the forehead. "At least some of us are," he mumbled under his breath, and it made me smile.

It also made me realize I had yet to have a proper reunion with the rest of my Bond.

I followed Tyler out of the bedroom only to find Alec stalking across the living room toward us.

"Well, at least you're dressed this time," he grumbled, crossing his arms. "I can't get Kid to move or speak or anything. He's starting to freak me out. Fix it, precious."

I ignored his pompous attitude, already brushing past him on the way to my big guy.

NINETEEN

Ethan was still in the same spot in front of the car, his shoulders tense, his gaze fixed on the ground.

I marched right up to him, my heart aching, but he wouldn't meet my eyes. I'd expected him to be upset with me—he'd been the most hurt when I'd attempted to run away the first time—but I hadn't expected this.

"Ethan? Talk to me," I pleaded, petrified I'd pushed him too far—that yet another one of my Bond connections was about to fracture—but I knew he needed more than words.

I burrowed up against him, pressing my face into his chest and tucking my arms under his to wrap them around his waist. The back of his shirt was damp with sweat, and I could feel the tension in every rigid muscle. But it was the million-miles-per-hour hammering of his strong heart under my cheek that took my breath away.

He was scared.

My eyes started to sting, an unbearable ache growing in my chest that had nothing to do with the Light.

"I'm sorry," I murmured into his white T-shirt.

I pulled away only long enough to lift onto my toes and move my arms upward. He still wasn't looking at me, but his body was responding to mine, his head dipping so I could reach his neck.

I took it as a positive sign and forged on, doing what felt natural. I lifted one leg, winding it around his hip, and then held on tight to his shoulders as I lifted the other too, wrapping myself around him completely.

His hands remained by his sides, so I ended up clinging to him like a monkey. I didn't care how ridiculous I looked or that my arms were already starting to ache from the effort. I'd hang there all day if that's what it took to wipe that heart-wrenching look off his face.

"I'm sorry," I murmured again into his neck and pressed a soft kiss to the same spot. His breathing shallowed, his big chest jostling me with every inhale.

My thighs were already in a jellylike state from what Tyler had done between them. My legs started to tremble, and I slipped just a fraction, nearly losing my grip. I caught myself, but Ethan moved in the same instant.

The sensation of me slipping away from him once again, even a tiny bit, was enough to break whatever spell he was under. He took a sharp breath as his arms finally flew around me. One went to my ass, holding me up, and the other banded around my back.

His head dipped, and he took a long inhale before mirroring my action and lightly kissing my neck. His lips lingered as I spoke again.

"I'm so sorry I put you through this again, baby. I wasn't running away from *you*. I was only trying to help save Charlie. I would never run away from you again, ever."

He sighed, his breath against my neck sending goosebumps over my entire body despite the stifling heat—and despite the fact that every inch of me was flush against someone who was known to spontaneously combust from time to time.

He pressed his lips once more to the same spot, darting his tongue out just a little before trailing his lips up the side of my neck, across my jaw, and over to my mouth. He kissed me, pouring all his frustration and fear into it. I kissed him back with all I had, pushing my tongue into his mouth, crushing my breasts against him, grabbing a handful of his hair.

He needed me to show him I wanted him as much as he wanted me, but I did it because it felt right.

Someone cleared their throat.

"I hate to break this up"—Josh's quiet, steady voice made us pull away from each other—"but we have company."

Ethan's eyes finally met mine, and I was more than relieved to see a smile pulling at his mouth. I pressed one more quick kiss to his full lips, and he lowered me to the ground.

I kept my hands on his shoulders. "Are we OK?"

"Not by a long shot." His usually booming voice was pitched low and ragged. "But I'm glad you're safe."

Before I could say anything else, he grabbed me firmly by the hips and turned me to face Josh.

Josh's green eyes were practically shining in the bright Australian sun, and his gaze was making up for the way Ethan's had avoided me.

He didn't come to me as Tyler had. I didn't go to him as I'd known Ethan needed me to. No, with Josh, I was always on an equal footing. We leaned into each other at the same time, and he pulled me into one of his bone-crushing hugs.

I dropped my forehead to his shoulder. Ethan let me go, even encouraged me to go to Josh; he knew that's what we both needed. But he stayed close because that's what *he* needed. I could still feel his heat behind me, one of his hands on my hip.

Josh pulled back, threaded one hand into the hair at the base of my head, and kissed me. I returned the kiss with all the intensity he was throwing into it.

He grunted and stepped forward farther. My back connected with Ethan's chest as the evidence of Josh's arousal pressed into my front. Solid as always, Ethan didn't lose his footing; he only lifted his other hand to grab my hip, his fingers seeking out the exposed skin above my shorts.

Knowing Josh was hard and ready to go made me want to drag him into the house to finish what Tyler had started—maybe grab Tyler on the way too. My desire, my need for them, was dizzying. I didn't even think before I arched my back, rubbing my ass against Ethan. The hardness I felt there as he met my grinding motion with one of his own proved he was just as ready.

I was trying to decide whose shirt to remove first when Josh broke the kiss. I gave him a questioning look, both of us breathing hard, and he licked his lips and glanced over my shoulder, having one of his silent conversations with Ethan. Ethan took a deep breath and squeezed my hips one last time. Then his searing heat at my back disappeared.

It helped sober me up. Tyler was right; I was having trouble controlling my sexual impulses, and I couldn't entirely be sure if it was my own desire—the estrogen, dopamine, and oxytocin my brain was releasing—or the Light that was driving it.

I also remembered the extra person. My eyes widened, and I backed away from Josh while still keeping my hands on his shoulders, not quite ready to let go. I was a little surprised to see Tyler standing close on my left, his hands on his hips, his body blocking us from the striking woman behind him.

He gave me a smile and a little nod, and I turned back to Josh.

He had that knowing look in his eyes. Of course Josh would have been aware Tyler had come over to give us some semblance of privacy while the three of us pawed at each other like animals with no impulse control.

I kept my eyes locked on Josh's, reveling in the connection we shared, but his smile slowly dropped from his lips, his eyebrows knitting together as he searched my face. "When are you going to stop running?"

His words hit me with the weight of an eighteen-wheeler. The question cut to the core of who I was as a person.

I'd spent my life running, spurred on by my mother, her eyes always looking over her shoulder. But I'd run from her too, hiding things about myself I knew she would disapprove of—like Harvey. I'd grown so much since meeting my guys, but I was still running from some things. Like the fucked-up situation with Alec and what that meant for the rest of us.

Josh watched me intently as half-formed thoughts and conclusions ran through my mind. But after a moment he simply kissed me on the forehead and stepped out of our embrace. Now was not the time for that conversation.

He turned to face Tyler and cleared his throat. "Eve, this is Nina. Nina, this is our Vital, Eve."

Tyler stepped out of the way so I could face the woman, the Lighthunter, properly. She was tall and had an athletic build—the toned muscles in her arms and midsection making her every movement seem effortless—and her complexion was a rich umber. The black hair on her head was buzzed very short, but her graceful movements and the delicate lines of her face and hands made it impossible to mistake her for a man. She was wearing a red crop top and tan pants with rips all over them.

She looked right at me with almost black eyes and smiled wide. "So this is your Light? Hello." She spoke with a heavy French accent. "Nice to meet you."

"Nice to meet you too." I stepped away from my guys, extending my hand in greeting. If I could blush, I would have. She'd seen every kiss, heard every moan, as I reunited with my Bond. "Sorry about . . . uh . . ."

"Not to worry." She shook my hand. "I am well acquainted with the dynamics of Bonds."

"Right. Because you're a Lighthunter?"

She nodded with a small smile.

"Nina has more than proven she's the real deal," Tyler said, placing a hand at my lower back and making me sigh with pleasure. Even though I no longer felt as if the Light were about to burst out of my skin, tearing me apart in the process, something still felt off; there was still an *almost* pulling sensation in my chest.

"You scared your Bond half to death. I don't know what they would have done to me had I refused to locate you." Her words were ominous, but she looked very amused. Then her smile faltered as something behind me drew her eyes. "Why do you not reunite with all your Bondmates?"

"What?" I'd never heard the term *Bondmates*, but it was obvious she was talking about my Variants. Specifically the one Variant I had yet to properly deal with.

"Your Light clearly flows through him, but it is dim. The connection is strained." Her gaze wandered to the spot on my chest right where I could feel that dull ache. I raised my hand to rub at it, not particularly wanting to discuss with a total stranger the clusterfuck that was my relationship with Alec.

She stepped forward and gently pulled my hand away, immediately replacing it with hers. My eyes widened, and my mouth opened to say something, but all that came out was a small gasp of surprise.

"So much tension . . ."

For some reason, I felt compelled to explain it to her. "Yeah, Alec and I, we—"

"Not just that one thread," she interrupted. "All your threads are tense. Your Bond is unsteady."

"What? No . . ." I knew where I stood with the others. I knew where I wanted our relationships to go.

"Yes." She chuckled and dropped her hand. "You are all connected. You are *as* one. But you are *not* one. If there is tension with one Mate, there is tension with the whole Bond."

"Oh . . ." The complicated situation between Alec and I was making things more difficult with the others too. They felt they had to take sides at times, and hadn't I just had a conversation with Tyler about why they were holding off on physical intimacy?

"Why does he not come to her?" Nina asked Tyler.

"He doesn't feel it would be received well. And he doesn't think he deserves it. It's complicated . . ."

"Oh, for Galileo's sake." I rolled my eyes and marched over to where Alec sat on the steps. If we could just hug it out and mute this annoying ache in my chest, maybe we could all get on with the important stuff—finding Charlie.

I stopped in front of him, determined, tiny puffs of dust settling around my feet. He had his head in his hands, his fingers digging into his scalp, his elbows resting on his knees. It reminded me a lot of the first time I'd seen him. He'd been sitting exactly like that in the corner of my hospital room after he'd saved my life.

Suddenly, I found myself wanting more than a means-to-an-end hug. I wanted him to look at me with those ice-blue eyes and speak to me with the honey in his voice.

I wanted the man who'd been kind and made me believe I wasn't alone in the world. Not the one who had been cruel to me, ignored me, and pushed me away. I was finding it increasingly difficult to reconcile the two.

"Alec," I said uncertainly.

He looked up, his eyes searching mine, his expression somehow simultaneously vulnerable and angry. "I know that I . . . I'm sorry . . . I just . . . fuck!"

He leaned back and looked up, rubbing his thigh with one hand. His other was tightening and relaxing rhythmically around something in his fist.

Usually he bailed well before this level of emotion was allowed to surface.

He reached out as if to touch me but pulled his hand back. I shuffled my feet, unsure.

Then I huffed—at him, at me, at this whole situation. My gaze zeroed in on his clenched fist and the delicate sliver string peeking out from between his fingers.

I reached out and covered his fist with my hand, and his nervous movements stilled. Using both hands, I uncurled his fingers to reveal my necklace—the tracking device. I took it and slipped it over my head.

His striking eyes followed my movements. I gripped the little silver rod pendant with one hand and placed the other back in his still upturned one. His calloused fingers closed around mine immediately.

I gave him a nod, hoping it conveyed what I couldn't seem to find words for.

Part of me wanted to apologize for running away, for putting him through that again. The words had come easily with Ethan, but with Alec they just didn't sit right. I couldn't make myself say sorry to him when he hadn't said sorry to me for so many things.

He gave me a little nod in return, the tension in his shoulders relaxing slightly. Folding both his big hands around mine, he opened his mouth to say something, then closed it again, his eyes flying from side to side.

I waited patiently, my heart beating a little faster. This was the most sincerity I'd seen in his face for a long time, the most vulnerability.

He looked back into my eyes.

"Evie." His voice was like honey, and I nearly melted. "I am so sorry . . ."

Whatever he was about to apologize for, it was interrupted by Tyler rushing up to us, his gun by his side. "We have company."

Alec stood and pulled his own weapon immediately, his face going hard again, all the rigidity returning to his posture. They moved together and nudged me behind them, shielding me from the oncoming threat.

I craned my neck and spotted an unfamiliar car coming up the driveway. This must have been the most action that driveway had seen in months.

A tiny jolt of fear spiked in my chest. I stepped closer to the two broad backs in front of me, resting a hand on each. I needed something to hold on to.

Tyler reached around to hold me closer to his hip. Alec leaned back into my touch but kept both hands firmly on his weapon. Ethan and Josh moved cautiously to stand off to the side and in front of us. Nina simply got back into the car; it was most likely bulletproof if it had come from Melior Group.

The silver Holden Commodore slid to a stop in the gravel, the driver having slammed the brakes a little too hard.

When Harvey got out and raked his confused glance over the scene, I breathed an audible sigh of relief. The sound drew his attention, and he spotted my face between Alec and Tyler's shoulders. Then his eyes took in the weapons in their hands.

"Hey!" He marched toward us. "Get away from her!" His voice carried, the squawk of nearby galahs punctuating it further.

He had no idea these guys were my Bond; he knew only that I was on the run from someone dangerous, and here were a bunch of armed men literally holding on to me.

My guys had no way of knowing Harvey wasn't a threat either. This could turn ugly real fast.

"Wait, wait," I rushed out, tapping both Alec and Tyler on the shoulder. "It's OK, he's—"

"Stay back." Tyler's command was calm but firm.

"I said get the fuck away from her!" Harvey was undeterred by the fact that both Tyler and Alec were raising their weapons, but it was Josh who reacted first.

He moved both hands in a shoving motion, and Harvey was thrown off his feet, sliding on his back almost all the way back to his car.

My eyes widened; Josh looked furious. I'd never seen him like that. He was always the calm one.

My attention shifted to Ethan and the angry ball of blue fire in his hand.

Harvey slowly got to his feet.

Tyler and Alec's guns were both pointed at him.

To say their show of force to protect me from a *human boy* was overkill would be a massive understatement. But I was fast learning their protective instincts knew no bounds. Just like my own toward them.

I wrenched myself out of Tyler's grip and planted myself between my ex-boyfriend, who had managed to regain his feet, and my four Bondmates, as the Lighthunter had called them.

Tyler and Alec immediately dropped their guns but kept their eyes on Harvey.

"Stop!" I held my hands up to either side, as if I were separating misbehaving children. "He is not going to hurt me. This is his house. He helped me. He kept me *safe*."

Logic worked with Tyler; his posture relaxed visibly, and he even tucked his gun away. Alec kept scowling at everything, but that was nothing new. I turned to check that Ethan had extinguished that angry flame, and breathed a sigh of relief when no fire was in sight. My big guy was doing a good impression of his older cousin, scowling with his arms crossed.

That's when Harvey made another mistake. He came up behind me and placed a hand on my shoulder, speaking in a low, suspicious voice. "Eve, what the hell is—"

His words were cut off by Josh using his ability again, only this time it wasn't directed at Harvey. I found myself flying through the air backward, the wind knocked out of me. The sensation was like when you miss a step walking down stairs, and your stomach ends up in your throat while your whole life flashes before your eyes.

But unlike Harvey, I didn't land on my ass. In a split second my back hit something, and strong arms encircled my waist protectively. Josh had used his ability to pull me to himself. I was equally annoyed at his overreaction and proud that his telekinetic control was improving.

"Josh, it's OK. He's not a threat. This is—"

"Harvey," he finished for me, his green eyes meeting mine over my shoulder. "Yeah, I know."

I narrowed my eyes.

"His first reaction when he got here was to protect you. He ran *at* two loaded guns to get to you. I knew he wasn't a threat. I figured he must be the ex."

I gaped at him. "Joshua," I scolded, extracting myself from his arms and turning to face him with my hands on my hips. "Not cool!"

He had the decency to look sheepish, rubbing the back of his neck and looking down at his feet. His dirty-blond hair was a mess, and he was in one of his band T-shirts and shorts. His neat chinos-and-shirt combo was nowhere to be seen.

"Sorry," Josh mumbled to the ground.

"This is your ex?" Ethan came to stand by me, another ball of fire appearing in his hand, his signature cocky grin pulling at his lips. "This should be fun."

"Ethan!" I was just about at my limit of testosterone for the day.

The fire was yellow, meaning it was harmless and would fizzle to nothing if he threw it, but Harvey didn't know that. To his credit he stood his ground—a human facing the crazy Variants down despite the growing fear in his eyes. This was why I'd fallen for Harvey; he really stood up for what he believed in. He was brave.

"If the one who pulled you away with his ability, which is totally cheating, by the way"—Harvey was scowling, his fists clenched by his sides—"is your boyfriend, then who's this fuckwit?"

"What the fuck did you just call me?" The fire in Ethan's hand started to turn blue.

"Enough!" I yelled. "Unless you want to whip 'em out and measure 'em, it's time to behave like adults."

All three of them looked as if they actually considered it for a moment, sizing each other up, but finally Ethan extinguished the fire, Josh stuffed his hands into his pockets, and Harvey rolled his neck while taking a deep breath.

"That's better." I looked over my shoulder, wondering why Tyler hadn't stepped in sooner. He and Alec were standing shoulder to shoulder, both wearing matching amused expressions. He was too proud to act as juvenile as Ethan and Josh had, but he was enjoying the way they were staking their claim.

I shook my head.

"Guys, this is Harvey." I chose not to put a label on him. He was definitely no longer my boyfriend, but he was much more than just a friend. "Harvey, this is Josh."

"Her boyfriend," Josh added as he waved, but at least his tone was friendlier.

"And this is Ethan."

"Her boyfriend." Ethan dropped one big arm over my shoulders, his grin widening at the confusion on Harvey's face.

Tyler walked over to us and took my hand. He extended his other to Harvey. "I'm Tyler, her boyfriend." I rolled my eyes, but laughter was starting to bubble up in my chest from the ridiculousness of it all. "Sorry about the rocky start."

"Um . . . OK." Harvey shook Tyler's hand, then looked at me with raised eyebrows. "How many boyfriends do you have?"

We all turned to Alec, who was now leaning on the railing, his arms crossed and his cool blue eyes narrowed.

"Uh, it's complicated," I answered. "And that's Alec. You should probably just . . . stay away from him."

"Yeah, you definitely want to steer clear of Alec," Tyler reinforced my warning.

But we'd spoken of the devil, so he appeared. Alec walked right up to Harvey, a smile tugging at his lips. There was nothing friendly about it. He extended his hand. "Hi, I'm Alec."

Harvey's manners won, and he returned the greeting, reaching his hand out.

As soon as their hands clasped, Harvey yelped in pain and yanked his back to his chest, rubbing at the palm.

The creepy smile was still on Alec's face. "That's just a little taste of my ability."

I rounded on him. "Alec, what the fuck?"

His fake smile fell away. "So this is why you flew halfway across the world? To see your ex?"

"Man, you know she came here to help find Charlie." Tyler sounded as frustrated as I was angry. "Calm down."

"I'm not a fucking moron," I seethed. "I'm not going to put my life in danger to have a chat with an old friend. I came here for Charlie. I went to Harvey for help. He was gracious enough to provide it."

"How convenient. Isn't four enough? You looking to add another to your collection?"

I flinched but didn't hesitate in my response. "I don't have four. I have three."

He watched me for a long moment, neither one of us willing to back down, look away.

"You have four," he said with such certainty I almost wavered and reached out for him. Almost.

"You've got a funny way of showing it."

"What?" It was his turn to look confused.

"Dana," I ground out between clenched teeth. I'd tried to pretend I wasn't jealous. I'd tried to tell myself Alec and I weren't together, so he was free to do whatever he wanted. But I was his Vital. He was in my Bond. He was *mine.*

"Dana?" Bit by bit, the confusion in his furrowed brow turned to anger. "Dana?! I haven't fucking touched Dana in . . . since the fucking gala. I told you that the morning after Dot's birthday. I fucking want *you.*"

"Oh, I'm sorry, am I supposed to read your mind? How the fuck am I supposed to know . . ."

"Stop fighting!" Ethan's voice was so loud and sudden I actually startled. "Just stop. I'm so sick of this. I can't take it anymore. Please . . ."

His voice lost its booming quality, his shoulders sagging. He looked so tired. Had he slept? Had any of them? They all looked disheveled and haggard, hair messy, expensive shirts rumpled.

"I have never seen so much tension in a Bond." Nina had exited the car and was standing next to Harvey, who looked somewhere between confused and uncomfortable. "She has more than enough Light to sustain all four abilities."

"Light? Abilities?" Harvey's eyes widened. "Eve, what is going on?"

Harvey deserved answers. Though he wasn't a part of my life anymore, at one point he'd been my whole world. His kindness had meant everything at a time when I'd felt so isolated. Then I'd just disappeared. And now I'd just shown up out of nowhere, bringing all my drama and baggage into his life. I was surprised he wasn't being more forceful about getting the truth.

"A lot has changed since we saw each other last, Harvey." I smiled sadly, nostalgic for how simple my life had been back then, when all I had to worry about was keeping my boyfriend a secret from my mother—and occasionally about what we were running from. Simpler times . . .

"Yeah, I'm starting to get that." He smiled back.

"Put the kettle on?" I nodded toward the house. "I'll tell you all about it over a cuppa."

He nodded and walked into the house, running his hands through his brown hair and releasing a deep breath.

"Eve," Tyler said tentatively, "we don't really have time to—"

"Yes, we do," I interrupted with a smile. I wasn't going to run off on Harvey again. There were very few people I'd ever gotten close enough with to care about. I needed to stop hurting them. Might as well start here, in the scorching heat of a dusty Australian sun.

TWENTY

My cup of tea with Harvey turned into lunch. The seven of us crowded around the little round table, and the guys let me do most of the talking. Nina observed every interaction, every little touch between us, as if she were trying to put together a jigsaw.

Harvey wasn't stupid; the talk of Light and all the guys' abilities led him to the conclusion I was a Vital. But he had a million questions. I answered them all, despite the other men's disapproving looks and even attempts to stop me. I trusted Harvey, and other than the Melior Group stuff I wasn't supposed to know, I wanted him to have the truth.

I did, however, make the gravity of the situation clear. "You understand you can't repeat any of this to anyone, right? You can't tell Mia or your parents you even saw me. People's lives are at stake. *My* life could be at stake."

Harvey frowned but nodded. "This have something to do with the Vital abductions I've been seeing all over the news?"

Tyler's voice was patient but firm. "Yes. It's very complicated, and we can't tell you much more—for your own safety as much as anyone else's."

The guys, realizing they couldn't stop me from telling him as much as I could, ended up just imploring Harvey to stay quiet. Tyler used logic and his naturally authoritative demeanor; Josh had seen how much he genuinely cared for me, so he appealed to those feelings; Ethan poured his big heart out, telling him how much I meant to them, how much it would hurt to lose me. He made me get all emotional, but he still wasn't meeting my eyes most of the time. Alec just glared, his threat evident in his posture and facial expression.

After lunch, we drove for hours, past the city and to a private airstrip. At least that explained how they'd gotten to me so fast. Leaving as soon as you want and refueling in the air certainly saves time.

I gave Harvey a brief hug on the tarmac, hyperaware of the four sets of eyes watching us intently.

"Keep in touch this time?" he joked, but his smile didn't quite reach his eyes.

"I'll text you when we land. Thank you so much, Harvey."

He nodded, and I turned away, walking to my guys and onto the plane.

In a much shorter time than it had taken me to cover the same distance, we were back home.

Everyone filed through the entryway and into the massive foyer of the Zacarias mansion. Extravagant Christmas decorations had appeared in the few days I'd been away. Next to the curving staircase stood a massive tree, resplendent in red and gold decoration, and poinsettias had replaced the usual vase of fresh flowers on the side table. Even the banister was decked out in garlands.

Nina smiled as she stepped inside, lowering her bag onto the pile of coats and luggage by the door. "You must be Dorothy."

Dot looked more nervous than I'd ever seen her. She was standing between her parents, Lucian hanging back by the stairs. "You can call me Dot." She cleared her throat uncertainly.

"Hi, I'm Olivia." Dot's mom waved. "And I have to be honest here, I don't really understand how this works, and I'm not entirely convinced it's a good idea."

"I understand your concerns, madame. My name is Nina, and I would be happy to explain to you as much as I can how my connection to the Light works, but I have a feeling everyone in the room would prefer if I tried to track your son first?"

"Yes, please!" Dot's eyes were wet, and my own throat tightened. We'd been waiting for this so long; the anticipation, the hope that we could be so close to finding Charlie, was palpable.

Josh circled his arms around my front. Ethan had been very quiet the whole way back, and while he wasn't rejecting me when I hugged him or leaned on him, he wasn't initiating any affection. He was still pissed at me.

"Come." Nina gestured to Dot. "Let me get a proper feel for you."

Nina took Dot's hands in hers and closed her eyes. After only a moment, she opened them again and sighed, giving a sad, tight smile. "I'm sorry—"

"No!" Dot wrenched her hands back as her mom started to cry. Dot's dad, Henry, folded his wife into his arms, his own eyes tired and misty.

"No, you misunderstand," Nina rushed out, her French accent becoming more pronounced. "I am not saying he has, how you say, passed away. Only that I cannot track him as—"

"I knew it!" Alec burst out. "This was a waste of fucking time. She's a fraud. Now she'll ask for money."

Everyone started speaking over each other, and Nina looked more than a little frustrated.

"Let her speak!" I yelled, and miraculously, everyone quieted down. Alec huffed and crossed his arms over his chest. The frown on Lucian's face was just as skeptical, but at least he was controlling himself.

"I cannot track him *now*," Nina continued, "but I will be able to once the foreign Light is out of Dot's system."

"What do you mean?" Dot asked, wiping tears away.

"I mean that you have too much of someone else's Light coursing through you." She looked pointedly in my direction. "The connection is not strained toward your Vital because your ability is sustained. Once Eve's Light is cleared, I will be able to track your brother."

"Shit." Guilt gripped my lungs, making it hard to breathe. It was my fault we couldn't get to Charlie right away. I'd only been trying to help Dot, make her feel better, but I'd ruined everything.

"You could not have known." Nina smiled at me, then frowned. "You have been very generous with your friend. There is more of your Light in Dot than in some of your Variants."

Her dark eyes traveled to Alec. She had very expressive eyes.

"OK, how does this work?" Henry stepped forward, demanding answers, daring to hope.

"I will be more than happy to answer any questions you have, but I do need a shower. We may have flown in a private jet, but twenty-two hours on a plane is still twenty-two hours on a plane."

"Of course!" Tyler stepped in. "I'll show you to the guest room."

He took off up the stairs, carrying Nina's bag. The other guys dispersed too, in search of showers and fresh clothes.

Dot came up and enveloped me in a big hug. "I'm so glad you're OK," she whispered into my neck, "but you smell like shit." She pulled back, making a face.

"I'm sorry about the Light." I looked down, not finding any humor in the situation. "If I'd known . . . and now we have to wait longer."

"Stop." Olivia pulled me into another hug. "You have nothing to apologize for, Evelyn. I'm glad you're OK. Thank you for doing this. You have no idea how much I appreciate it."

She was starting to cry again. She gave me another squeeze and moved off after Lucian and Henry, muttering about making tea.

Olivia may have let me off the hook, but I was still nervous about what Dot had to say.

"Don't even worry about it." She waved me off, moving to sit on the stairs. I breathed a sigh of relief and sat next to her.

"So, you took the private jet, huh?" She nudged me with her shoulder. "I've never been in it. What's it like?"

"It was actually really cool." I couldn't help grinning. Extravagant things didn't usually faze me, but the jet was amazing. "I loved not having to deal with customs or passport control or waiting for ages to board, and it has a bed!"

"A bed, eh?" She gave me a knowing look, but I rolled my eyes.

"As if. We had company. Plus, Alec won't touch me, Tyler had to work most of the time, and Ethan's still pissed at me. I took a nap with Josh though."

"Yeah, Ethan was pretty upset."

"I know. I feel really bad. I'm constantly hurting someone or letting someone down. I've just never had this many people in my life, you know? I'm still learning how to not only think about myself."

"Speaking of pissed . . ." Dot cringed, and I groaned.

"What now?"

"Zara. I talked to her, explained the situation. I think she gets it, but she feels like we lied to her."

"We kinda did." I sighed.

"I know, but this was about Charlie, and I'd do it again a hundred times over if it meant getting him back. I just think you should talk to her."

"I will. I'll go home . . . soon." I yawned, leaning my head on Dot's shoulder.

My phone vibrated. It was Harvey, replying to the text I'd sent him when we landed. It felt good to have him back in my life, to have some connection to my past. I smiled as Dot read over my shoulder.

"So, how'd the guys do with meeting the ex?"

I groaned. "About as well as could be expected."

"Oh, so he's dead? Then who's texting you?"

I laughed. "OK, slightly better than expected. They gave him a hard time, and it started a fight with Alec. But I made them all be nice."

Dot chuckled, jostling me on her shoulder.

I lifted my head to glare at her. "It's not funny. He could've been hurt. You should've seen them all when they realized his last name is Blackburn."

"Wait! You gave yourself his last name? Oh, this is gold!"

"I created this identity before we got together, OK? I had a crush. How was I supposed to know I'd be stuck with it indefinitely?"

"Maybe not indefinitely. You could start using your real name once it's safe. Have you figured out why your mom ran in the first place?"

"No. It's on my long list of mysteries to solve." I sighed and stared at the beautiful, glowing tree.

"OK, Veronica Mars." Dot chuckled and followed my gaze, leaning her head on my shoulder.

I'd been meaning to raise it with Lucian, but it was proving more difficult than I'd anticipated, partly because he worked more than even Tyler and partly because I had no idea how to broach the subject. I'd spoken to the guys about it at length, but they knew about as much as I did—jack shit.

Part of me was afraid to find the answer, but what terrified me even more was a lack of any insight at all.

Would I live the rest of my life not knowing why my mother had taken me away from our home?

~

Josh, Ethan, and Dot had already headed off to shower, but I needed another minute for my breathing to recover. It had been a leg-heavy session in the gym, and I was skeptical the noodles currently attached to my hips could make it up the next two flights of stairs. It didn't matter that it was three days before Christmas; Kane refused to give us a break.

"Your enemies will not take a break to bake gingerbread cookies while plotting your downfall" was his reasoning, delivered with a scowl. He had a point.

I pushed the sweaty strands of hair off my forehead and hobbled toward the front of the house. At the bottom of the curving main staircase, I paused, resting one hand on the banister.

"Come on, Eve," I whispered to myself. "You can do this. It's just stairs. You climb them all the time."

But my legs refused, so I lowered my forehead to rest on the back of my hand and took a little standing nap.

Voices from Tyler's office drew my attention, and I turned my head, resting my cheek on my hand instead of my forehead.

The door was ajar, and Tyler's voice came through clearly.

" . . . don't understand. It's been confirmed and verified as well as we could have hoped for. What are we waiting for?"

"It's not that simple. I may be the director, but I still have a board I have to answer to, Gabe." Lucian sounded just as frustrated. "And it would seem we don't have the full support of the board."

There was a pause, and I found myself straightening up, leaning toward the door in order to hear better. Then I realized what I was doing and shook my head.

If it was important, Tyler would tell me. They knew what they were doing when it came to Melior Group operations.

"So this has become political, then." Tyler sounded resigned, if a little angry.

I abandoned the stairs and headed back toward the kitchen.

"It always was," Lucian replied. "We need to tread carefully, be smart about . . ."

The voices faded as I continued to the back of the house.

I looked at the pool longingly. It would have been great to jump in and cool off, let the water support my aching muscles for a while. But it was covered up for the winter and way too cold anyway.

It wasn't too cold for a steam though. There were multiple studies expounding the benefits of a steam room post-workout for recovery, heart health, respiratory health, and skin, just to name a few.

I grabbed one of Ethan's hoodies off the back of the couch before rushing across the yard to the pool house. The smell of snow was in the air, and the cold was biting. As a freezing gust of wind cut through Ethan's big hoodie as if it were a scrap of lace, I envied Zara.

She was spending the holidays with her family in California. She'd sent me a photo of herself at the beach just that morning, and I'd sent one back of the heavy gray clouds that had been hanging over Bradford Hills for the past three days.

She'd left a few days after my return from Australia. I'd done my best to explain to her why we'd kept it from her, but understandably she still felt left out. I'd spent as much time with her as possible before she left, but there was still a distance, a coldness in her eyes when she said goodbye.

Hopefully the warm Californian weather would thaw her out.

Inside the pool house, I headed straight to the large bathroom at the back, taking my shoes off at the door and moaning when the heated tiles made contact with my frozen toes.

"Hello?" a heavily accented female voice called out, and I looked up. The steam room was already occupied, the heavy moisture behind the glass making it difficult to see inside.

"Oh, hey, Nina. It's Eve. Sorry, I'll come back."

I turned to leave, but she called out again. "No need, darling. There is plenty of room."

"Oh, OK." I hesitated. I'd been planning to steam naked, but I eyed the pile of thin Turkish towels on the bench next to the sink. I guess that would work too.

I undressed and wrapped the pale purple cloth around myself before stepping into the steam room and closing the glass door.

The hot, humid air enveloped my body, relaxing me almost immediately. I took a deep breath and rolled my shoulders, releasing the tense posture I'd held since the frigid air first hit me outside.

Nina sat in the middle of the bench, leaning against the wall, completely relaxed and completely naked. Her lithe body, her long legs, and all the private bits were just . . . there. The humidity glistened against her smooth skin.

Once again I hesitated. She cracked one eye open. "Are you going to sit? The steam can make you dizzy."

"Oh, yeah." I averted my eyes and quickly sat to her left, leaning back against the warm tiles. I tightened the towel around my chest, then paused. I was being ridiculous.

She was an adult, I was an adult. There was nothing sexual or inappropriate about sitting in a steam room together.

Making a conscious decision not to be ashamed of my natural human state, I let the towel fall at my sides, reveling in the warm moisture caressing every inch of my skin, the heat soothing my aching muscles.

"How are you finding your stay here?" I asked. I hadn't had too many opportunities to speak with the

Lighthunter one-on-one. After everyone had showered and slept off the massive trip, Nina had sat down with Dot and her parents, with Tyler and Lucian present, and answered all their questions.

I wasn't there for that conversation—I was busy having my own big conversation with Zara—but Dot had filled me in later.

It would take a few weeks at least for my Light to drain out of Dot enough for her ability to strain toward her Bonded Vital, Charlie. They would continue to check in regularly, but in the meantime we had to wait. Alec had insisted that Nina stay at the Zacarias mansion, with thinly veiled threats to inflict pain if she put any more of his family in danger. As if it were her fault I ran away. Lucian smoothed it over with an invitation to *host* her for the duration of the wait and a promise to pay her generously for leading them to Charlie.

She'd refused any kind of payment until she could prove herself to even the staunchest of skeptics—namely Alec and Dot's dad, Henry—but had accepted the offer of a place to stay, as she didn't know many people in the area.

She mostly kept to herself but did join us for meals and the occasional discussion. No one could resist Ethan's food or Josh's subtle ways of pulling you into a fascinating chat.

"It is very comfortable. The Zacarias family has a lovely home," she answered.

"I'm sorry if Alec has been difficult. He's just . . . I don't even know. He treats me with the same level of hostility, if it makes you feel any better."

She chuckled. "Alec does not bother me." She waved a lazy hand in the humid air. "He is only motivated by his strong protective instincts toward you. It is plain to see."

"Not to me," I mumbled.

"You know, I can see the ties in a Bond almost as physical things at times."

"Really?" I turned to her. She and the things she could do fascinated me, and there wasn't a single book on the topic I could read. "How does that work?"

She shrugged. "It does not matter how. I just can. Just like I can't tell you how I track a Variant or Vital through the others in their Bond. Just like you can't describe the color green or any other color."

"What do you mean? Green is the color of leaves, grass, the combination of blue and yellow—"

"Yes," she cut me off, "you can point to things that are green, but you cannot describe the color itself. We both know what a Variant is, what a Vital is, the DNA behind it. There are theories behind what exactly the Light is, but no one can really explain it. I can't really explain how I do what I do. I just do it. It is like breathing."

I thought about what she was saying. The stuff about colors was blowing my mind a little. How *do* you describe green without pointing to something green? My default was always to understand things, to learn them, unpack them. But some things just . . . are.

"What does it look like? The Bonds?" I decided to focus on what information she *could* give me—her own experience of it.

"When the Bond members are in close proximity, sometimes it's like a wisp of smoke from one to the other, moving and shifting like it has a mind of its own. Usually, though, it is just a feeling. A sense of something that is difficult to articulate. I just know that two people are connected."

"Kind of like Tyler just knows when someone is lying?"

"Yes, very similar."

We fell silent for a few moments. The heat had completely relaxed my muscles, and I was taking long, deep breaths.

"I have never seen so much tension in a Bond as I have in yours, Eve." Her tone had become more serious, and I stayed silent, waiting for her to elaborate. "With Tyler, Josh, and Ethan there is a lot of positive energy, even if it is restrained, not fully actualized. But with Alec, so much uncertainty, so much resistance. Yet it is the most established of all."

I frowned, running my hands down my slick thighs. "What do you mean? How is that possible?"

"The connection to Alec was made many years ago. Before the Light had begun to course through you even. The Bond was made but not actualized."

The glass door opened, letting some of the steam out and a gust of fresh air in. Dot waltzed in completely nude and plonked herself down on Nina's other side.

"Yeah, even an idiot could see that the Bond is strained because of Alec." She inserted herself into our conversation seamlessly, leaning back and taking a deep breath. "No offense. I've just known him for a long time."

"None taken." Nina's voice held a bit of humor. "But it is not only because of Alec."

"Do tell." Dot angled her body toward us, giving Nina her full attention.

"Yes, Alec is . . . ambiguous. He is already irrevocably connected to you, but he is fighting it."

"He hates his ability, and I only amplify it. Therefore, he hates *me*." I couldn't keep the bitterness from my voice.

"Dramatic much?" Dot added helpfully as Nina chuckled.

"He definitely does not hate you. But that does explain the tension. The others are holding back too for this reason? To help him have distance?"

"Yeah, pretty much," I grumbled.

"But you do not wish to wait any longer." That was not posed as a question.

"Yeah, my girl has a major case of blue ovaries." I was beginning to think Dot had only joined us to make my life difficult.

"I do not understand this phrase 'blue ovaries.'" Nina looked between us, confused.

"What my friend is so helpfully trying to say is that, yes, I would very much like to . . . take the next step." I'd pretty much just admitted I wanted to fuck four guys. "The attraction is getting difficult to hold back. My feelings toward Alec are complicated—he hurt me a lot recently—but I'm even attracted to him . . . physically."

"Naturally. He is in your Bond. There is nothing to be ashamed of, Eve. But the longer you drag this out, the more tension there will be, the more intensely the Light will pull you together. If you let nature take its course, follow your instincts, trust your body, the Light will settle. Alec is afraid of his ability, you are all cautious about the damage Ethan and Josh could do, but you fail to realize that once it is settled—once the tethers of the Bond are sealed—the Light will not be quite so intense. It will be easier for you to control, easier for them to manage. The amount that transfers will not be excessive, because the Light will not be straining you to deepen the Bond."

"So you're saying once I sleep with them, the Light will be *less* intense, not more?"

"Exactly. Lean into it, and everything will fall into place. Dot can tell you. Her Bond is established and settled.

You only receive the exact amount of Light you need at any moment, unless your Vital consciously pushes more at you, correct?"

"Yeah, but he's my brother. I didn't have to sleep with him to seal the Bond." She shuddered. "Plus, it wasn't something we had to build—it was always there. It was a normal part of our sibling relationship growing up."

"I think I know what you're saying." I sighed. We were all so concerned about keeping our distance—keeping the Light at bay so we could learn to control it, so Alec could get his shit together emotionally—that we weren't allowing the Bond to deepen and settle naturally. "I don't know how to even raise this topic with them," I grumbled.

"Why must everything be discussed?" Nina stood as she spoke. "You are perfectly capable of making your intentions clear with your actions and your body."

She winked at me and exited the steam room. A minute later we heard the shower start up.

I sighed. "Why does this have to be so fucking hard?"

Dot snorted. "That's kind of necessary for the sex stuff."

I rolled my eyes. She was almost as good as Ethan at making everything into a dirty joke. "I'm serious, Dot. Things are impossible with Alec, but it's not just him. We keep hurting each other. I can understand why they're holding off on the physical stuff for now, but I can't understand why they keep hiding things from me—not including me in the decisions. I'm supposed to be their Vital. We're supposed to be this tighter-than-family unit, but it doesn't feel like it."

"Maybe it's *because* you're their Vital that they do it? All I've seen from them is that they're trying to protect you."

"They can't protect me while keeping me in the loop? That's bullshit." I crossed my arms, then dropped them down to the bench immediately. It was too hot to have any part of my body touching another.

"We didn't keep them in the loop about Australia either," she pointed out.

"I know." I looked down. "I knew they'd be pissed—Ethan's still keeping his distance, even while he watches me like I might evaporate if he blinks. I just didn't realize how hurt they'd be. I was on my own for so long. I guess I'm still learning how much my actions impact them too. I just . . . How do we stop doing this to each other?"

"Look, those boys have been tight for a long time. I mean, I'm their cousin, and we moved back here not long after their parents died, but even Charlie and I aren't a part of their little inner circle. They've spent so much time together, sometimes they communicate without speaking. You may be their Vital, but having you be a part of that is going to change that dynamic. And you're still learning what it means to have a family. Those kind of changes take time."

"So what do I do? I can't wait for them to slowly realize I'm part of their little group now, and I don't want to feel like an invader in my own Bond."

"Just be patient." She shrugged. "Try to make your feelings on the matter clear, but try not to get too frustrated when they fail from time to time."

I leaned back, watching the white steam obscuring the top of the steam room as I thought about that. It was actually really good, mature advice. And then she had to go and add to it.

"Or if you want, I can get Squiggles to spy on them." She smiled wide.

"No!" I stood up slowly and wrapped the thin towel around myself. "No more spying." Before I closed the door, I added, "But thanks for the advice."

She just smiled and closed her eyes, settling in for a bit longer.

As I showered and dressed, I thought about all I'd discussed with Nina and Dot. Relationships were complicated enough with just two people trying to navigate life together. I had to deal with *four* guys who all had their own issues and insecurities, a supernatural force that tied us all together, and dangerous, powerful people who were after Vitals like me for an unknown, probably horrific reason.

It was probably easier to deal with the sex stuff first.

TWENTY-ONE

As Zara and I strolled in the direction of the town center, I fingered the cool metal pendant hanging around my neck. Zara was right—we needed to get out for a bit—but one of the guys was most likely monitoring the tracker at that very moment. I kept expecting my phone to blow up with calls and messages demanding to know why I'd left the safety of campus.

It was early January, a few days before classes were due to resume, and both of us were in boots and coats, mine big and black, Zara's fitted and almost the same color as her bright red hair.

"I'm not sure about this, Zara. Ethan is still pissed at me. I'm just going to text them so they know I'm off campus."

"Nooo," she whined. "Come on, Eve. You know one of them will come down here, and it's supposed to be just you and me. And do you know the things I had to do to get Derek to agree to this?" She grinned, hinting that she actually rather enjoyed those things.

Derek was the Melior Group guard currently manning the east gate at Bradford Hills Institute. On our way out the gate, Zara had planted a kiss on Derek's lips. "I really appreciate this, babe."

He'd winked at her as he let us pass. "You have one hour max. I don't want to lose my job."

I'd gaped at her. The mystery of who she'd been seeing in secret had been solved, but as we continued into town, she'd persisted in acting totally unaffected by it all, even under my onslaught of questions

Normally students had to sign in and out at the gates. All Vitals had a personal security detail, but I wasn't a Vital as far as anyone knew, so all the agents were under instructions to report my absence to Tyler. This was really only a safety precaution in case someone forced me to leave under duress; I never left campus without one of my guys or someone under Tyler's orders.

At least, not until today.

"I don't know." I chewed on my bottom lip, feeling as if I was doing something behind my guys' backs. "What if something bad happens?"

Zara rolled her eyes. "We are literally in the most heavily guarded place on the East Coast right now. Even if shit goes down, there are Melior Group badasses everywhere."

As if to illustrate her point, two black-clad, armed women passed us, heading in the opposite direction. Bradford Hills was crawling with them.

We fell into a companionable silence, walking side by side. As we rounded a corner onto Main Street, Zara turned to me.

"OK. We need a better distraction. Want to get some ice cream?"

"I don't know. It's freezing." I pulled my scarf a little tighter around my neck, tucking the pendant into the front of my shirt. If I couldn't see it, maybe I would stop worrying.

"Who cares? Do you want ice cream or not?"

I smiled, glad she seemed to be getting over the fact that Dot and I had lied to her. "Let's do it."

With a satisfied nod, she pulled me along. "There's a little gelato place at the other end of Main."

"Thanks for talking me into this." I kept my eyes on the street ahead as we passed boutique shops, little cafés, cozy restaurants, and lovely old buildings, with giant oaks lining the street the whole way, their branches bare. "I hardly know the town, and I've been living here almost a year. It's really nice. And I wouldn't mind trying some of these restaurants."

Zara remained silent. I looked over to see a deep frown on her face, her eyes fixed on the sidewalk.

"Red? You OK?"

"Huh?" Her head snapped up. "Sorry. I was in my own world."

I smiled warmly. "That's OK. I was just saying thanks for talking me into this. It's nice. I wish Beth was here."

"Me too," she whispered sadly as we slowed to a stop in front of the gelato shop. It was a little separated from the rest of the Main Street buildings, its front door on a diagonal, almost hidden from the main road.

"Oh no. I think it's closed." The shop's Closed sign hung unmistakably on the door. I glanced around for another café, but there were no other establishments at this end of Main, the street curving up a hill and disappearing into the trees.

"Is it?" Zara stiffened next to me, the arm looped through mine going rigid. "You sure?"

She dragged me right up to the door.

"Pretty sure." I chuckled. "I know you want ice cream, but the sign is pretty clear."

"Yeah . . ." She looked behind me, scanning the street with nervous eyes.

I frowned. She was acting strange.

"Let's just walk back up the street. We can get coffee and cake instead." I tried to tug her away, but her grip on my arm was like steel. "Zara, what the hell—"

An unassuming gray van suddenly pulled into the driveway leading to the back of the building, cutting my words short. It stopped right next to us, blocking the footpath and the view of the rest of Main Street.

I hardly had time to register the prickles on the back of my neck before the door slid open and two masked men stepped out.

They moved fast. Two sets of rough hands closed, vicelike, around my upper arms. As they wrenched me away from my friend, she released her hold. I didn't even have time to try to run, yell at Zara to run, do *anything*.

They dragged me backward toward the van, and one of them shoved a face mask over my nose and mouth—the kind you would see in a hospital operating room. Something sweet smelling with a sharp alcoholic tinge filled my lungs, probably some form of ether.

All the training I'd done had been for nothing. The endless hours of torture in the gym with Kane, the runs with Ethan, the sparring—I still had no idea what I was doing.

As the ether did its job, stealing my consciousness away at an alarming rate, my mind registered only two things.

The first was the chemical formula of ether: $C_4H_{10}O$. Completely useless in this situation.

The second was the cold, hard look in Zara's eyes as she willingly climbed into the van after us.

The last thing I heard before blacking out was the thud of the van door slamming shut as the betrayal slammed through my heart.

~

My eyes slowly opened, the sense that something wasn't right pushing through the haze in my brain.

I groaned and rolled onto my back, screwing my eyes shut again. The ground was cold—concrete—and I could hear rain, a rhythmic metallic sound in the background. If it weren't for the fact that I was freezing and on the hard ground, the noise would have been soothing. I lifted my right hand to rub my temple, and my left came with it.

They were bound at the wrists with a zip tie.

A jolt of adrenaline shot through me, fear finally catching up to the murkiness in my head, but I tried to shove it down. I had to remain calm. I had to assess the situation.

I was in what looked like a basement. The concrete floor matched dank, dirty concrete walls, and timber beams ran across the low ceiling. It was dark, but thin windows situated high on one wall were still letting in some faint light, so it couldn't have been more than a few hours since I was taken. Zara and I had headed out around midafternoon.

Zara!

The detached look in her eyes as she closed the van door flashed through my memory.

Confusion, worry, betrayal, and fear churned inside me, all battling for dominance. But I couldn't give in to the overwhelming feelings. I needed to stay focused.

Moving my legs, I realized my ankles were bound too. I tried to push myself up, but halfway there my stomach did a flip, and I collapsed onto my elbows, vomiting—a side effect of the large dose of ether they must have given me to knock me out so fast. I puked until there was nothing left, fighting my body to stop dry retching.

Once my breathing calmed a little, I managed to scoot into a sitting position, away from my own vomit, and look around for something, *anything*, to tell me where I was or what was happening.

There didn't seem to be anyone around, but the basement looked large, the area farthest away from the windows cast in shadow. Stacks of crates sat at intervals along the length of one wall, and multiple shelves held neatly arranged gardening implements and tools. A wall was at my back, and stacks of crates towered over me on either side. Metal bars stretched between the two stacks and, I realized as my eyes adjusted, all the way around, completely enclosing me.

A cage.

Panic began to set in. I lifted my bound hands to swipe away the tears pricking at my eyes while my brain grasped for control by providing relevant statistics. Kidnapping statistics for US adults are elusive, as the *crime* of kidnapping is not recorded separately to all missing persons cases. When it comes to minors, 86 percent of perpetrators in non-family kidnappings are male, while the victims are predominantly female. Nearly half of all victims are sexually assaulted.

I was fairly certain my particular situation had more to do with my being a Vital than with someone wanting to rape me, but the idea only added to the terror clawing at me from the inside out.

My wrists were beginning to hurt from the tight restraints, but they were also itchy. I cursed under my breath; I'd completely dropped my control of the Light flow, distracted by dread and nausea.

I leaned my head against the cold metal bars and closed my eyes, consciously taking deep, slow breaths. Without any of the guys here to transfer to, the Light could get overwhelming very quickly.

My eyes flew open. *The guys!* I had a way out! It was on a chain around my neck. My bound hands flew to my chest, where the feeling of the little metal bar had become so familiar I forgot it was there most of the time.

I couldn't find it.

How could they have known to take it off me? I hadn't told Zara about the little distress beacon.

Forcing myself to take another calming breath, I pulled my scarf away, running my fingers over my throat more carefully. The chain was there! The pendant had just gotten twisted so it hung down my back.

I tugged on the chain, pulling the little metal bar to the front, and didn't waste any time, yanking the two pieces apart with shaking fingers.

I knew four alarms on four cell phones had instantly gone off, but for me it was a little anticlimactic. I was still bound and caged, sitting on the cold concrete with no idea where I was or how long I'd been there.

My shoulders slumped. I stuffed the silver bit into the pocket of my jacket, then did my best to pull the jacket closer around myself. The adrenaline was beginning to wear off, and the cold seeping into my bones was taking its place. All I could do now was wait and hope they got to me before . . . I didn't let myself entertain the myriad horrible possibilities, focusing instead on bringing my Light flow under control.

But my mind wouldn't stop trying to puzzle things out. The men who had grabbed me were trained, efficient, and identically dressed in black, with masks that brought back gruesome memories of the invasion. Judging by what I knew about Melior Group's suspicions, and about how the Vitals had been taken, I was pretty certain I was firmly in the clutches of Variant Valor.

And Zara had told them my secret.

My gut twisted. I pushed the thought out of my mind and counted my breaths instead.

After at least an hour, I managed to get into a meditative state and bring my Light flow under control. But it slipped away again violently the moment a painful tugging sensation stabbed through my chest. I gasped, my hands flying to the spot to try to rub the ache away.

One of the guys was in trouble. I hadn't felt the pull this bad since that first night when Ethan had blown up a car and I'd run to him in the middle of the night.

Panic squeezed my lungs as the Light poured into me, desperate to be released into whoever had me feeling as if I might die if I didn't get to him *now*. Would I have to sit here, feeling the pain in my chest get worse and worse as one of them lay dying? A sob of hopeless frustration choked me, my body folding in on itself; the pain and the pull were becoming unbearable.

Just as I was about to curl into a fetal position, a loud metallic clang shattered the basement's quiet.

A light flipped on, illuminating the area in front of my cage as boots thudded down the stairs.

I sat up straighter, on alert, but the tears continued to slide down my cheeks, the pain in my chest refusing to be ignored.

As the group came into view, I released a strangled sound—something between a sob and a wail.

Two men were hauling a limp Josh across the concrete. They each had a firm grip on one of his arms, his feet dragging across the ground, his head hanging. His chinos were covered in dirt from the calf down, and his white shirt was torn at the right shoulder and crumpled.

Blood was everywhere. A thick, gluggy drop of it fell from someplace on his face I couldn't see and, as his feet dragged through it, left a macabre streak on the dirty concrete floor.

Behind them walked Zara and another woman, whose pantsuit and neat hairdo seemed out of place in the dank basement. The woman was looking down at her phone as she walked, her heels clicking.

The two men dragged Josh over to my cage, one of them reaching for the lock. I awkwardly shuffled over to the bars, everything in me screaming to get to Josh.

"I wouldn't put him in there. She's his Vital." Zara's detached voice made them pause, and they both looked over to the older lady. There was something vaguely familiar about her, but all my attention was on Josh.

She looked up, sparing me a disinterested glance. "Put him in another cage. We can't have a fully charged telekinetic disrupting the schedule." Her voice was quiet, her words articulate, and I once again got a pang of familiarity before she turned and focused again on her phone.

My kidnappers dragged Josh away from me, and the ache in my chest got impossibly worse, making me sob. They opened the door to another cage, on the other side of the crates to my left and at a right angle, and dumped him inside, his body crumpling lifelessly to the concrete.

They locked the door and walked back the way they'd come, the fancy lady leading the way.

"Right, now I'd like a full report. How the hell did he find us? Are you idiots sure you weren't followed?"

"Yes, ma'am," one of them answered. "We followed protocol to the letter and . . ." His voice trailed off as their footsteps got fainter.

I switched my attention to Zara. She was just standing there, looking at Josh's prone form. I couldn't make myself look at him again. Not yet. I needed to talk sense into Zara. There was no point in pleading with the black-clad men or their boss, but Zara was my friend. Or so I thought.

"Zara." My voice was strained and gravelly. More tears fell down my face.

She just kept staring at Josh, her expression disturbingly flat.

"Zara!" I managed to yell, and she turned her blank eyes to me slowly. A sick, hollow feeling settled in my stomach. She was *not* OK, and I'd been so wrapped up in my own shit, in supporting Dot through losing Charlie, that I hadn't paid attention to what was going on with my other friend. I'd always seen Zara as such a strong person; it never occurred to me that she could be the one struggling the most.

"What are you doing, Red?" My voice broke again, but I hoped the use of my nickname for her would spark some emotion. "Why?"

All she did was blink slowly, her arms slack. I began to worry she was having some kind of mental break.

Another sickening stab of tugging pain made me double over, struggling to breathe. When I looked back up, she'd moved closer to my cage. Her expression was still indifferent, but she'd tilted her head to the side and seemed to be focusing on me better.

"Zara?"

Before I could formulate another way to get through to her, she spoke. "We're doing important work. We are. We need Vitals to fix it. And you're a Vital. I told them. I helped them get a Vital. A powerful one. We need more powerful ones. The others keep failing. Dying. It will all be worth it in the end. She'll understand once it's over. Once we fix it."

She looked away as she spoke, gazing at some imagined sight in the middle distance. Her right hand began to twitch next to her leg, little flicks of the wrist that didn't look deliberate.

"Fix what? What are you trying to fix, Zara?"

Her hand stilled. "The genes. The Light can switch them on. I think Josh is going to die."

She wasn't making any sense, and the rapid change of topic had me crying harder. I'd lost another friend. She was standing right in front of me, but Zara was gone. And if the excruciating pain in my chest was anything to go by, I was about to lose one of my Variants too.

"I think you're right. Josh is dying." I fought hard not to break down completely, my breaths becoming more and more erratic, my tears soaking the scarf at my neck. "Help me save him, Zara. Just let me touch him. He doesn't have to die. Please, we can—"

"No," she cut me off. "He doesn't matter. Only you matter."

She turned on her heel and left. I crumpled to the ground, watching my last hope of saving Josh walk away, indifferent.

With my face on the cold hard ground, my tears staining the gray concrete black, I finally looked through the two sets of bars at a dying Josh. He was on his front, his head angled toward me. The half of his face that wasn't squished into the ground was red with blood.

He didn't even look as if he was breathing, but the awful pain in my chest told me he was still alive. As long as the pain was there, there was something for the Light to be drawn to. I was dreading the pain disappearing.

I pushed my hands between the bars, reaching in his direction; it was pointless—our cages were feet away from each other—but I couldn't help trying. The tight zip ties around my wrists dug in, angrily chafing my skin, but that wasn't what demanded my attention as I moved my arms in front of me.

I was glowing. There was so much Light pushing inside of me in anticipation of releasing into Josh that I had gone nuclear again.

TWENTY-TWO

At the sight of my glowing skin, I cracked. The pain, the worry, the despair, and the hopelessness churned together into something closer to frustrated anger. I growled, screwing my eyes shut and bunching my hands into fists, my nails digging into my palms hard enough to leave marks. Then I opened my fingers, stretching them wide.

My eyes flew open at the warm, tingly sensation that spread through my hands, as if I were holding them under a giant faucet, the running water firm but pleasant. But it wasn't water flowing over my hands. It was Light. And it wasn't flowing over me. It was flowing *out* of me.

I watched, mesmerized, as the Light shot across the distance between the two cages and slammed into Josh.

I didn't dare move a muscle or think a thought. I had no idea how the Light could transfer without contact, but I wasn't about to question it. Not when it was saving Josh's life. I knew I'd done it that day on the train platform—my Light had leaked out to Ethan and Josh even though I hadn't been touching them—but I hadn't done it since, and we still had no idea how it worked.

The glow on my skin slowly faded, the pain in my chest abating until it no longer felt as if I were being torn in two. Eventually the Light pouring out of me stopped.

Josh's eyes flew open, and he took a deep, shuddering breath. Trying to push himself up, he coughed, spluttering blood everywhere, then groaned and rolled over onto his back.

"Josh!" I did my best not to shout. I didn't want the guards to come back.

He looked over at the sound of my voice, his eyes widening as they landed on mine. He tried to get up again but winced, clutching his side.

I winced too. "Don't move. Just take it easy, OK?"

"Are you OK?" His voice sounded strained. I'd been drugged, kidnapped, and betrayed, and I'd nearly had to witness him die. I was definitely *not* OK.

He watched me in that way only he could, then nodded. Our gazes stayed locked across the space of the dirty concrete floor, both of our heads on the ground, both of us reaching for the other through the metal bars.

"We need to get out of here," he ground out after a few minutes, pushing himself to a sitting position.

I sat up too, my restraints cutting painfully into my skin. "How?" I was really hoping if he had a plan, it was better than the one that had gotten him all bloody and caged. "And where are the others?"

"I was the closest when the alarm went off. Hopefully they're not too far behind." He looked around the basement, paying special attention to his cage. Pulling himself to his knees, he studied the cage door intently. I heard the metallic *click* of the lock turning, and the door swung outward.

The tug in my chest increased a little. My glowing Light transfer had managed to get him off death's doorstep, but he was nowhere near fully healed and shouldn't have been using his ability at all. I kept my mouth shut though. He was doing it to save our lives, and there was nothing I could say to convince him not to.

He rushed over to my cage. As soon as he was within reach, my bound hands went to his, and I immediately started pushing Light into him.

He paused and sharply inhaled as his eyes closed for a moment, but he didn't indulge in the sensation for long. He unlocked my cage the same way he'd done his. In an instant, he'd pulled me to my feet and wrapped me in one of his crushing hugs, my bound hands squished awkwardly between us.

The hug didn't last long either. Someone could come in at any moment.

"I need something to cut you free," he whispered into my hair before moving off. I only nodded. I didn't want him away from me, but short of hopping around with my feet bound and probably face-planting onto the concrete floor, there wasn't much I could do to follow him. So I just stood there in the open door of my cage, my heart hammering in my chest, listening intently for the sound of boots on rickety stairs.

Josh returned quickly, a pair of giant bolt cutters in his hands. "It was all I could find." He shrugged before bending down and cutting the zip tie around my ankles. He made quick work of my wrists too, and I rubbed them, wincing at the raw skin.

Josh grabbed me with one hand and held on to the bolt cutters with the other, taking the lead toward the far end of the basement—the area cast in shadow. We couldn't risk going through the same door the kidnappers had taken. There had to be another way out.

Unfortunately, we hadn't made it more than a few steps before the dreaded metallic sound of the door opening rang through the cold space.

". . . why we have to knock her out again. She's tied up already," one of the kidnappers whined.

"Man, shut the fuck up and pass me the tank." His gruffer-voiced companion didn't sound as if he was in a good mood.

They were on the stairs, about to come around the corner—too close for us to make a run for it, and we had nowhere to hide. I started to panic; we didn't have time to jump back into the cages and pretend we were still tied up and knocked out.

Josh reached the obvious conclusion before I did. We had to fight.

He pushed me behind him, raised the bolt cutters over his head, and waited. I prayed that neither one of them had their guns drawn as I stuck my hands under Josh's shirt and pushed as much Light into him as possible.

But as the two men came into view, three quick, loud bangs—the sound of muted gunfire—came from somewhere above us, followed by shouting voices. The two men turned their heads, their hands going to their weapons.

Josh didn't hesitate, bringing the heavy metal tool down over the first man's head. His target crumpled to the ground, the tank I recognized from my kidnapping clanging to the ground next to him. But it was the other man who howled in pain, doubling over and clutching his head.

Had I not seen countless other people doubled over in pain just like that, I would have wondered if my mind was playing tricks on me. But I knew exactly what was causing it.

"Alec," I breathed, a tentative kind of relief flooding through me. We were still in danger, we had no idea how many people we had to fight through to get out of this situation alive, but at least the reinforcements had arrived.

Josh dropped the bolt cutters, and with a flick of his wrist, a heavy wooden crate tumbled off a nearby shelf onto the second man's head. He joined his companion on the ground, unconscious.

I crouched next to the pile of passed-out kidnappers and extracted the first man's gun from its place on his hip. Josh picked up the other weapon and reached over for mine, but instead of taking the gun away from me, he flicked the safety off and fixed me with a steady look.

"Hold it with both hands, point, squeeze the trigger, and be ready for the recoil."

I gave him a shaky nod, swallowing around the lump in my throat. He nodded sharply and turned back around, positioning himself at the corner and pointing his gun up the stairs. I stayed behind him, the heavy gun trembling in my raised hands, my brain helpfully reminding me I had no idea what I was doing.

A *bang*, like a door slamming against a wall, came from the top of the stairs. I jumped, nearly firing the gun I had no business handling. The loud noise was followed by the sound of several feet on timber.

Josh lowered his gun and slumped against the wall, but I couldn't make myself do the same. Logically I knew by his reaction that whoever was coming toward us wasn't a threat, but the horror of the situation was catching up to me, and something at the edges of my being was starting to crumble. The gun provided an illusion of safety I wasn't ready to part from.

Tyler came into view first, his gun raised as he moved forward purposefully. He was wearing a thick black vest, which was probably bulletproof, and the pale yellow shirt underneath jarred with the gritty situation we were in. The color was too cheery; his signature rolled-up sleeves, too casual. He cast his eyes over me and Josh but kept moving past us, still on alert.

Alec followed, wearing the same vest, but his combat boots, black pants, and long-sleeved top fit right in. Despite his pain ability, he too was armed, his stance almost identical to Tyler's. With his ice-blue eyes, he scanned me, then Josh, just as Tyler had, but he didn't move off immediately. He lowered his gun, extending his left hand toward me, palm out.

"Eve." His voice was level, his face blank. My eyes were darting between his face and the gun I was pointing directly at his chest. Or almost directly—my hands were shaking so badly I couldn't even aim properly.

A split second later, Ethan came around the corner. He wasn't armed, but one raised hand held a deadly ball of blue fire. His eyes went straight to me, and all the emotions he must have been holding back cracked through and poured into his expression. All the fear and worry and anger were right there in his amber eyes.

"Evie." Alec drew my attention back to him.

Fat tears began rolling down my filthy cheeks. I took my finger off the trigger, my shoulders slumping as I finally let my arms go slack.

Alec grabbed the gun by the barrel, removing it from my tenuous grip in one swift movement.

"Watch them," he said to Ethan over his shoulder, passing him the gun. Then he raised his own weapon and went after Tyler.

Ethan secured the gun in the back of his pants before stepping forward and enfolding my terrified shaking body in his big warm one. He tucked me into his side, standing between me and Josh and keeping a vigilant eye on our surroundings. I clutched at his bulletproof vest but couldn't find anywhere to grip the rigid material, so I settled for nestling my arms between us and turning my face into his shoulder.

I could feel Ethan trembling, tiny little shivers coursing through his body as he gripped me as if I might disappear into thin air at any moment. As confident as he'd looked coming around the corner, he was clearly just as freaked out as I was.

After only a few moments, Tyler's firm voice yelled, "Clear." A beat later Alec answered him with a "Clear" of his own, from the opposite end of the basement.

I lifted my head. Tyler was stalking back toward us, holstering his weapon at his hip. His gray eyes, usually so calm, were staring right at me, filled with fear. As he got within a few feet, I instinctively reached for him, and he took hold of my outstretched wrist and tugged me out of Ethan's grasp. I winced from the friction on the spot where the zip ties had cut in, but he didn't see it. He'd already pulled me into a hug.

He wrapped his arms around my shoulders, one hand at the back of my head, holding me firm to his chest. I focused on the feeling of being held by one of my Variants, on the way his fingers were flexing against my scalp.

Ethan turned to Josh and gave him a hug too before pulling away and letting Alec take his place. Alec grabbed the back of Josh's neck and pressed their foreheads together, his back and shoulders rigid. As he straightened, he said something I couldn't hear. Josh nodded weakly, raising his hand up to squeeze Alec's shoulder before they both took a step back.

"We've got company," Alec ground out, his eyes on the little windows near the ceiling.

"What about our guys?" Tyler released me to reload his gun.

Alec turned back around. "On the way. Probably another five."

"This basement is a death trap, we can't let them corner us down here." Tyler didn't wait for a response, taking the lead up the rickety stairs.

"Wait." My voice was shaky. So were my knees. "What are we doing? What do I do?"

But Ethan was already helping Josh up the stairs, and Alec was firmly nudging my back with one hand. I started climbing, my heart simultaneously climbing into my throat. At least the extra adrenaline was helping energy return to my limbs.

"Just stick close to me." Alec spoke low. "I'll keep you safe, Evie."

I had no other choice but to let them take the lead. Alec overtook me at the top of the stairs, placing his body between mine and the rest of the house.

Then things started happening fast.

Shouting and banging—the sound of glass breaking.

Alec pulled me through the door and darted down a hallway, stopping near a bathroom. When Tyler appeared next to me and grabbed my hand, I barely managed to stop myself from calling out. Josh and Ethan crowded next to us in the bathroom doorway.

"I need a little more Light, baby," Tyler whispered close to my ear, his eyes glued on the hallway, his gun raised.

Immediately, I pushed as much Light into him as I could. He dropped my hand within seconds and took off again, gesturing to Alec. I didn't understand what the hand movements meant, but Alec must have, because we followed Tyler in the opposite direction to where we'd been heading. Ethan supported a limping Josh, and we moved as a unit though the house.

Eventually I forced myself to look up from the back of Alec's bulletproof vest. We were at a front door, waning afternoon light streaming in through the side panel.

"Bulk of force coming in through the back. This is our best chance, but they're not stupid—they have a few out front as well," Tyler filled us in.

Before anyone could respond, deafening gunfire made me jump again, and this time I couldn't hold in the panicked scream that came tearing out of my throat.

It was Tyler who'd started firing. Armed men were coming down the hallway toward us. They took cover in the rooms off the hallway but soon returned fire.

Alec spun around, firing over my shoulder with one hand and pushing me behind him with the other.

To my right, a large cabinet tumbled to the floor with a tremendous *crash*, blocking the path of more assailants who were coming at us from an elaborately decorated sitting room. It wouldn't stop them, but it would slow them down.

Unfortunately, the use of his ability would slow Josh down too. The sudden pain in my chest made me cry out, the Light desperate to get to him. He wavered, but Ethan caught him, at the same time throwing an angry blue ball of fire that engulfed the cabinet in flames.

Bright light streamed into the foyer from the now open front door, and Alec pulled me through, once again keeping me behind him.

But as soon as we were outside, the gunshots started up again. Three more assailants came toward us, big black vans blocking the street behind them.

We had danger behind us and danger in front of us, and Josh was fading fast.

I didn't hesitate. I made everything else fall away—time itself seemed to stand still—as I put all my focus on Alec. My fingers tightened around his hand, and I pushed Light to him almost violently, raising my other hand to the back of his neck—the only other bit of exposed skin I could see.

I grit my teeth and growled. I was weak too. Bringing Josh back from the brink had drained me, and I couldn't get that level of power again so soon, but I pulled Light into me as hard as I could, and I shoved it all into Alec.

Within seconds, everyone was on the ground, moaning in pain, gripping their heads and stomachs. It wasn't instantaneous, as when we'd done it that first time at Bradford Hills, but eventually they all lost consciousness.

At first, my own wheezing breath was the only sound I registered. Then traffic, a loud car alarm nearby. As the wail of sirens announced we were about to have more company, my other senses joined the party too. I let go of Alec and stepped back.

We were at the top of the stairs leading into a large, elegant home.

At that moment, something clicked into place—the reason why the woman from the basement had looked so familiar. She was Senator Christine Anderson—the same woman who had delivered the rousing speech the night of the gala and was all over the TV lately. How deeply connected was she to Variant Valor? And how the fuck did Zara know her?

This had to be the senator's house. Similar homes lined both sides of the street, and tall concrete-and-glass buildings cut into the skyline a little farther away. Were we in Manhattan? Surely they couldn't have been so brazen as to keep people locked in the basement of a home in the city? And come to think of it, where was the senator?

Where was Zara? Had they been involved in the gunfight inside? Had my friend shot at me? Tried to kill me?

My eyes scanned the quiet street, the bodies on the ground. When they landed on Josh, I remembered the pain in my chest.

Rubbing at the ache, I took the few steps to reach him, my hands going straight to the sides of his neck. I let the Light do its thing as best I could. I was running on empty; anything coming into me was going straight back out to him.

"Time to go," Tyler announced, reloading his gun. "Ethan, are you hurt? Help Josh to the car?"

"Yeah, I got him." Ethan's voice was shaky.

"Alec, go." Tyler turned to Alec, who was still facing the unconscious assailants. "I'll try to clean this mess up."

"What?" I croaked, whipping my head around to look at him. "You're not coming with—holy shit!"

Tyler's chest was drenched with blood. Crimson covered the entire right shoulder and right side of his shirt, the original color of the fabric not even discernible.

I was torn. Josh needed me—he was leaning heavily against Ethan, his eyes closed as he enjoyed the sensation of the Light transfer. But I ached to go to Tyler too, check where the blood was coming from, how badly he was hurt.

He must have read the torment in my face, because he came to me, pulling the collar of his shirt down. "A bullet grazed my neck. I barely felt it. I'm OK." He kissed me on the forehead, one hand in my hair, before looking me level in the eyes. "Evelyn, I'm OK. It's already stopped bleeding. Josh needs you. You need to get him home. Alec!"

But Alec was already moving. He wrapped one of my hands around Josh's, took the other, and hurried down the stairs. As we headed up the street, I looked over my shoulder to see Tyler standing by the door, watching us.

"Wait!" I tugged on Alec's hand, but he kept a firm grip, a steady pace. "Alec, we can't leave him there alone. What if they wake up? What if more come?"

He stopped, then turned me by the shoulders to fully face where we'd come from.

"Melior Group has arrived," he said evenly. "See Kyo?" He pointed to a group of three heavily armed men moving toward Tyler. More followed behind them. "Tyler is fine." He turned me back toward himself, his hands on my shoulders. "We have to go, precious. Josh needs you more than any of us right now."

I nodded. Tyler was OK—I'd seen it with my own eyes—and the panic was beginning to settle. My head didn't feel so light; my ears weren't ringing quite so much. I'd made it out. Now I had to make sure Josh did too.

TWENTY-THREE

Alec resumed his lead, and I tried to focus on his wide back, his shoulders tense under the black fabric. Some people had come out of their homes to see what all the noise was about; a crowd had gathered on the street, and phones were out. I tried to take in their faces, anything to distract me from how loose Josh's grip was on my hand, how much my chest still ached even though I was transferring as much Light as our contact would allow.

As we rounded a corner, coming to a stop next to Tyler's black Escalade, it began to snow.

I had to let Josh's hand go for the few seconds it took the guys to get him into the car, and those few seconds just about tore my chest open. He lost consciousness as I doubled over in pain, the ache and urgency unbearable.

As soon as Ethan had lifted Josh's legs inside, I shoved past him and found contact at the exposed part of Josh's neck where his shirt was torn. He was slumped in the middle of the back seat, his head lolling to one side, his blood-streaked hair falling over his eyes.

The boys tried to get me to move so they could strap Josh in, but I ignored them. "Just go!"

I didn't even know where I wanted them to take us; I just needed to be on the move.

The door behind me slammed shut, and a moment later Alec was behind the wheel with Ethan in the seat next to him. He started the car and pulled away with a jolt. They'd both taken the time to strip down to T-shirts, and Ethan was cranking the heat up.

Josh needed me and my Light more than anything, but keeping him warm would help. He could use every advantage we could give him.

Sitting on my knees, I had one hand on his neck and the other clutching his limp hand on the seat. It wasn't enough. The Light was practically humming with how quickly it was flowing between us, but it was still straining against my skin. Josh needed more.

Making sure to keep contact with the backs of my hands as I went, I undid what was left of his shirt and pushed it off his shoulders. Then I pressed my forehead to his as I shrugged off my jacket and sweater, pulling my top over my head in one swift move.

After lifting myself over his lap, I removed my bra for good measure. I vaguely registered protests from the front seat about seatbelts and nudity before pressing my front flush with Josh's.

Slowly, as the car warmed up, my breathing evened out, and Josh's became stronger. We all settled into silence. Thoughts fell away, and I was lulled by the motion of the vehicle. I can't be sure how long we drove, but it must have been at least an hour or two, because my hips were aching from staying in that position for so long.

The sudden absence of the engine's rumble made me open my eyes and lift my head from Josh's shoulder. He roused at the same time, placing his hands flat against my back.

Our eyes met, all we'd been through passing between us unspoken, but the stare wasn't uncomfortable. I could look into those green eyes all day and never get weirded out or bored.

"Let's get you both inside." Ethan was the first to get out of the car, Alec following close behind.

As their doors slammed shut, Josh pressed his forehead to mine and whispered a heartfelt thanks, his hands moving to my hips and giving them a gentle squeeze.

The light pressure made me shift, my hips rolling forward, and he froze. I suddenly became very aware of how naked I was from the waist up. As if to emphasize the point, my breath hitched, and my breasts pushed farther against his chest.

I felt him grow hard under me. And then the car door opened. Alec draped a jacket over my shoulders and stepped back.

"Are you sure we shouldn't take him to a hospital?" Ethan sounded hesitant. I finally lifted my head. We were in the Zacarias mansion's underground garage.

"There's nothing better for him right now than her," Alec answered decidedly. "We'll get him checked out in the morning."

I pushed my hands into the sleeves of the jacket. The view Josh got of my breasts as I pulled back to do so was unavoidable, as was the jolt of desire that shot down my spine at the hungry look in his eyes.

I scrambled out of the car, holding the jacket closed with one hand and trying to balance on my almost numb legs with the other. Alec steadied me while Ethan helped Josh out of the car, and we all headed inside.

Much as I dreaded climbing the two flights of stairs to Josh's bedroom, that's where I suggested we go. He had regained consciousness, but he was still severely depleted, and I itched to get that skin contact back. The pull was still there; the healing was not done.

"I really need a shower first," Josh said.

Despite all our protests, he insisted he felt disgusting. There was a smear of something on his cheek that was such an odd color it couldn't be identified, and his grimy hair looked more brown than blond.

"OK," I conceded, "but then straight to bed. You still need more Light." I chewed on my bottom lip, uncertain. But now that he mentioned it, I really needed a shower too.

"I know." He smiled weakly, and then Ethan practically carried him up the stairs.

I watched them go and took a deep breath, preparing myself for what felt like a climb up Mount Everest. I lifted one foot but couldn't seem to find the energy to follow through, so I ended up twisting awkwardly and lowering myself onto the step.

I leaned my head on the banister. *I may have to ask Ethan to carry me up too.*

Then I noticed Alec standing in the foyer. He looked almost as worn out as Josh, but the ache in my chest was still pulling me up to the third floor, not to the impossible man standing in front of me, so he hadn't overused his ability. He was just emotionally and physically spent.

"You OK?" The words were out of my mouth before I could really think about them. It just seemed like the right thing to say.

His shoulders sagged, and he dragged his feet as he came and sat down next to me, resting his elbows on his knees.

"I'm fine, Evie." His voice was low and tired, but it had honey in it, and it was making my heart ache. "Not that it matters right now. But you're safe, so I'm fine. It's Josh who needs you."

"I know . . ." I was replying to what he'd said about Josh, but it felt loaded all the same. "I bet you're burning to say I told you so." I wasn't sure why I was giving him an opportunity to be an ass. I guess it just felt like our default, a bit of familiarity after so much turmoil and fear. To his credit, he didn't rise to my bait.

"I take no pleasure from any part of this situation, believe me." He looked at me with those icy eyes of his and raised his eyebrows, nothing but sincerity in his voice. "I know I don't deserve it"—he averted his gaze before continuing—"I know I've made a lot of mistakes, but can I please just hold you? Just for a moment?"

He looked so vulnerable, his eyes darting about the room, his hands clenching and unclenching. I leaned into him and rested my head on his shoulder. He released a massive breath and, in one swift move, picked me up and settled me on his lap, crushing me to his chest and burying his face in my filthy hair.

My arms were squished between us, but I managed to extract one to curl around his neck. I hadn't realized how much I'd been craving his embrace. The distance between us had begun to feel insurmountable, but I needed him. I needed him as much as I needed the others. We were incomplete without Alec. I just hoped he realized how much he needed me too.

"I keep losing you," he mumbled into my neck, his voice shaky. "I can't keep losing you, Evie. It's killing me."

"So do something about it." I had so little energy. I knew he was trying to tell me he needed me, that he regretted how things had turned out between us, but I couldn't muster much of a response. It was just too much. My brain was mush.

"I will," he whispered. Then he lifted his head and touched his hand to my cheek, nudging softly until I was looking up at him. "I will," he said with steel in his voice. "I'm going to fix this."

I stared back, at the sincerity in his face, the intensity. I knew how fucking stubborn he was; when he decided something, there was no changing his mind.

But I also knew how much he'd hurt me.

"I need a shower." I wasn't ready to accept his declaration. I wasn't in the right place, mentally or physically, to entertain the idea of trusting Alec with my heart.

He pressed his lips together, and I braced for another screaming match. But he surprised me yet again.

He stood, holding me close to his chest, and started to climb the stairs.

"I can walk." Even my words came out sounding weak.

"I know" was his quiet reply.

I didn't have the energy to struggle, so I let him carry me up the two flights of stairs, through his bedroom, and into his en suite. He set me down on the counter and turned on the hot water in the shower, then disappeared into his room. He returned a few seconds later with a bundle of clothing.

"Do you need help?" He wasn't coming on to me or looking at me with hunger in his eyes, even though the jacket was unbuttoned and my breasts were on display. He didn't look uncomfortable either. He was simply asking what I needed.

"No, I'm OK." I got off the counter. The hot water was filling the bathroom with steam, and the pure white water particles were reminding me how dirty I was. A clump of something disgusting was matted into my hair, and my mouth still tasted like vomit.

Alec nodded and left me alone, closing the door softly.

Slowly but efficiently, I managed to get myself scrubbed, my hair clean, and my teeth brushed. I was painfully aware that it was Alec's bathroom, his shower, his toothbrush I was using, and it was hard to relax under the hot spray sluicing over my aching shoulders. On top of that, the ache in my chest, pulling me to Josh, was impossible to ignore.

I dried off and put on the boxer shorts and soft black T-shirt Alec had left out for me. They smelled like him, and I had no idea how I felt about that.

The room beyond the bathroom was dark. Alec was already in bed. The brightness from the bathroom behind me cast one harsh column of light across his gray sheets. He was under the covers, his face in darkness. I couldn't see what he was looking at, couldn't guess at what he was thinking or feeling. I never could.

I switched the bathroom light off and remained in the threshold. I should go, run to Ethan or Josh—to someone emotionally safer. But then I realized I was doing what Alec always did: standing in a doorway and getting ready to run.

So I chose not to.

I did what I really wanted to do. I sought out what I craved—the comfort he'd provided that night in the hospital what felt like a lifetime ago.

I walked over and sat on the bed, my back to him. He was silent and unmoving behind me. But he wasn't throwing me out, and he wasn't leaving.

I lay down on my side, my back still to him, and screwed my eyes shut, pulling my knees up, hoping beyond hope . . .

After an excruciatingly long second, the sheets rustled, the mattress shifted. My mind convinced me he was getting up, leaving. According to psychological theory, assuming the conditions are the same, the best predictor of future behavior is past behavior.

But he didn't leave. He scooted closer and curved his body around mine. His strong arm wrapped around my front, and he held me tight, his face in my damp hair.

I didn't know what had gotten into him, but I was in no state to question it. Because my honey-voiced stranger was holding me together, and it felt so fucking good.

But that's what he was—a stranger. This side of Alec was much less familiar than the hard, cruel asshole he'd been showing me since I came to Bradford Hills. On some level I knew that wasn't really him. I couldn't describe the reasons why—it likely had more than a little to do with the supernatural tether of Light between us—but I felt as if this was the real him. *This* was how it was meant to be between us.

With his arm holding me tight, just as it had on the two worst nights of my life—when I'd lost my mother and my friend—I mourned for the relationship we could have had, *should* have had.

Pile that on top of everything else I'd been through in the past twenty-four hours, and the emotional breakdown was inevitable.

Tears stung my eyes. Heat spread up my chest, and my breathing became shallower and louder in the dark room. As the tears soaked Alec's pillow, he shifted, lifting himself up a little on his elbow. His strong presence enveloped me like a blanket of steel—comforting, protective, and suffocating all at once.

"It's OK, Evie," he crooned into my ear. "You're OK. I've got you. *We've* got you. You'll never be alone again."

In a moment of indulgence, I let all the emotion come. His declaration had probably been more in relation to my physical safety, but it had hit on one of my biggest fears—being alone in the world. And here was the man who'd pushed me away more than anyone in my life, telling me I wouldn't be. I sobbed into the pillow as Alec stroked my hair and held me, whispering things I could no longer hear.

After a while, the tears subsided, and I nudged him so he would back away a little. He responded immediately, and I rolled onto my back, wiping the tears and snot away with a wad of tissues he handed me.

"I have to go to Josh," I said in a raspy, strained whisper, rubbing my chest. "He needs me. I need him."

I needed all of them. I needed Alec to keep doing exactly what he was doing—it was soothing my soul in a way that was too scary to examine—but Josh needed me more. No, he wasn't going to die, but the ache in my chest wasn't abating. I couldn't keep ignoring it for my own selfish reasons.

Alec nodded and gave me a reassuring smile as I sat up, swinging my legs over the edge of the bed. I braced myself, fighting the fatigue in my muscles in preparation for standing, but Josh beat me to it.

He appeared in the doorway, the light from the hall casting his face in shadow but making his dirty-blond hair look like a halo. He walked over, and I pressed my hand to his bare stomach, finding skin contact as soon as possible. The ache in my chest disappeared immediately, and we both sighed in relief.

I wrapped my arms around his waist, pressing my cheek to his belly, letting the Light flow freely.

After a moment, he pulled back, and I tilted my head to look at him. He gave me a weak smile, rubbing my cheek with his thumb. Dark bags sagged under his eyes, and a cut on his chin looked as if it would probably bruise. His shoulders were slumped, but nothing but warmth emanated from his eyes.

He looked over my shoulder, but the gaze didn't linger, didn't go into a silent conversation with Alec. He just took in the scene, then got into the bed, shuffling me into the middle of the mattress.

We faced each other, my head resting on his arm, our limbs instinctually entwining. Josh's eyes closed. His mouth parted slightly, and he fell asleep almost instantly.

I was ready for oblivion too. Exhaustion was pulling my eyes closed, making me feel as if I were sinking into Alec's soft sheets and Josh's fresh, warm smell. But the sound of movement from the door caught my attention. I lifted my head—it felt like an anvil—and saw Ethan dropping a bundle of bedding on Alec's couch.

Alec sighed. "What is this?" he whispered. "A fucking slumber party?"

Ethan walked over to Alec's side of the bed, making me crane my neck to see him. He was shirtless too, his glorious, muscular body on full display. Why did they all have to sleep in nothing but underwear? It was incredibly distracting—not that I was in any state to do anything about it.

"We all need to be close tonight, bro," Ethan whispered back. He leaned over his cousin to kiss me on the lips, then on the forehead. "It's part of being in a Bond. Sometimes we *all* need her. You're just going to have to get used to it."

I tucked my head back into Josh's chest. I didn't want to see Alec's face, his reaction to Ethan's words. I didn't have the energy to deal with it.

The soft rustle of bedding as Ethan set himself up on the couch lulled me toward sleep. But as I started to drift off, Alec shifted, his movements slow and careful so as not to disturb all the sleeping people who'd dared invade his fortress of solitude.

He grabbed the blanket that had pooled around our knees and pulled it up, covering us all. But his hand lingered on my shoulder, his fingers tentatively caressing it over the fabric of the T-shirt. I stayed still.

His fingers trailed up until they found the exposed skin on my neck, but he didn't pull away. There was no Light left over for him; all I had was going to Josh. My skin tingled where Alec touched it but not because of the Light.

He removed his hand and replaced it with a kiss so soft I questioned whether it was really still him in the bed with us, but there was no denying the honey voice, the one I always craved.

"I promise," he declared, finishing some private train of thought on the barest of whispers. Then he settled himself behind me, resting his hand on my hip.

With Josh in front and Alec behind, I finally felt safe, warm, and unconsciousness took me. I would have to wonder about Alec's promise when I woke up.

TWENTY-FOUR

I woke up flat on my back, my head turned toward Alec, my left hand resting on Josh's chest. Slivers of morning light peeked past Alec's heavy drapes, but most of the room was still cast in hazy darkness.

The weight of all that had happened was nudging at me, trying to wake me fully, make me think about it and dissect it and figure it all out. But I pushed it aside, covered it with a warm blanket, and made it go back to sleep. I wanted just a little longer to look at Alec's peaceful, sleeping face in the muted light, feel the steady rise and fall of Josh's chest, feel them there with me.

I sighed softly, letting my eyes rake over the little scar in Alec's eyebrow, the very slight kink in his nose, the stubble on his strong jaw. My fingers itched to reach out and touch the rough prickles, but I didn't want to risk waking him.

Josh was already awake though. He turned onto his side, making my hand drop to his hip. When he pressed his palm against my belly, I turned to face him.

His eyes were half-open, and he was watching me as I'd been watching Alec. I covered his hand with mine and inched it up.

I was making sure to keep the difficult, heavy thoughts away, but I couldn't help remembering the previous times I'd woken up from spending the night in the arms of one of my Variants, restoring their Light—the possessive way Ethan had held me that first night, the way Alec and I had crashed into each other in the study.

My skin was sensitive to every touch, my body painfully aware of the two nearly naked men on either side of me, and all the heat was pooling between my legs. My breathing got faster, my lips parted. It drew Josh's attention to my breasts under the black cotton of Alec's T-shirt.

I nudged his hand again, just a fraction, in the direction I wanted it to go. He trailed it up my ribs and cupped my breast through the fabric, gently but with confidence. The slow, deliberate movements he used to knead the soft flesh were driving me mental, but I let him take the lead for a while. He *had* nearly died after all.

His lips parted, his breath grew heavy. His hooded green eyes watched me with *need*. When I felt his rock-hard length press against my hip, my breath hitched.

Josh rocked his hips against me, and knowing he wanted me as much as I wanted him turned me on even more. I squirmed, rubbing my thighs together.

Our subtle movements must have woken Alec.

He shifted, and I froze, but Josh hadn't noticed, his hips still rocking against me in a steady rhythm, his mouth now at my neck, pressing soft, moist kisses to my burning flesh.

My heart was on the edge of a cliff, ready to fall as soon as Alec realized what was happening and put a stop to it.

But instead, I felt Alec's hand nudge the T-shirt aside, wandering up my torso until my other breast was in his hand. Instead of plummeting, my heart soared, and I moaned—a soft breathy sound as much surprise as it was arousal.

Josh paused what he was doing to look. He took in the fact that Alec had joined in, as well as the desperate, needy look on my face, and smiled a sleepy but excited smile right before he kissed me, *hard*, his hand on my breast becoming less gentle, his tongue immediately invading my mouth. But the kiss didn't last long. He pulled back and nudged me so I faced away from him.

Suddenly I was face-to-face with Alec, Josh's hardness now pressing into the curve of my ass. Alec's stare was laced with lust but a hint of uncertainty too. His hand had come away from my aching flesh as I shifted, and he wasn't making another move. So I did.

I leaned forward and kissed him as forcefully as Josh had kissed me. He responded immediately, fighting my mouth for dominance, growling a little as his strong hand went to my ribs. He was rock hard too, his arousal making itself known against my front.

Squished between them like that, not a breath of space between our writhing bodies, hands roaming everywhere—it was intoxicating. Almost too much. Too much skin, too much heat, too much sensation.

Yet it wasn't enough.

As if he'd read my mind, Josh pushed forward, giving me more. His hand thrust its way between me and Alec to the throbbing flesh between my legs. Alec moved away just enough to give him access, and Josh started rubbing me over my borrowed boxers. The friction was exquisite, and I followed his lead.

I reached down and started rubbing Alec's length the way Josh was rubbing me.

Alec growled again, a low sound that reverberated through his chest, through mine, and elicited a moan from Josh behind me. Alec pressed his forehead to mine, watching how I touched him. Encouraged by his enthusiasm, I moved my hand higher, to the waistband of his underwear. I didn't let myself pause, didn't let the memory of what had happened the last time my hand had been in this position stop me. I reached inside, pushing the fabric down, and wrapped my hand around his warm, engorged flesh.

He didn't swat my hand away. He just closed his eyes and reveled in the sensation. And I smiled in triumph.

I started slow, pumping him up and down in deliberate strokes, slowly increasing the pressure, the speed. He began to move with me, his hips bucking slightly in time with my movements.

Josh moved his hand to the waistband of my boxers before pushing his long fingers under the fabric.

"So wet . . ." came Josh's strained whisper at my ear. He licked a path from the curve of my neck to my ear and started nibbling. His words sent a shiver down my spine, and I moaned softly, making Alec open his eyes.

I closed the miniscule distance between us and licked his lips. He crushed his mouth to mine, pushing his tongue inside my mouth.

But just as fast as he'd kissed me, he pulled away. His hips stilled.

The atmosphere between us changed.

Something heavy settled in the pit of my stomach. Alec closed his eyes and took a deep breath. My hand slowed, stopped. I didn't want to suffer the pain of having him remove it again, so I did it myself.

Josh stopped what he was doing too, pulling his hand out of my underwear and resting it on my hip.

Alec rolled onto his back and rubbed his closely cropped hair with both hands, sighing loudly before dragging his hands over his face. He pulled his underwear back up and turned to face me again.

"I want this so bad." His eyes may have been icy in color, but they were *burning* with intensity.

I frowned, confused, disbelieving.

"I do," he declared with more steel in his voice. Steel but also honey. He wasn't returning to his cruel, detached self, but he was still pulling away. "I'm just not ready. I always thought you were mine. Just mine. And now I have to share you—and that's OK, it is—I just need some time."

I was still breathing hard, but I pressed my lips together and looked down. I couldn't think. The throbbing between my legs was relentless, my body not yet aware of the rejection. I knew what he was saying, the words made sense, but I just couldn't process them. All I understood was that I wanted him. I wanted him and Josh and Ethan and Tyler. I wanted them closer, more, *completely*. But he was rejecting me again.

He was ruining it *again*.

"Alec . . ." Josh's whisper sounded exasperated.

"I'm sorry. I'll fix everything. I promise," Alec said softly, answering Josh's unfinished question and all my unspoken ones. Then he pressed a kiss to my head and left, his bare feet silent on the plush carpet.

The soft click of the door closing felt almost worse than if he'd slammed it.

I sat up, staring at the closed door in bewilderment. My mind was struggling to process it all. My body was still wired, still *craved*.

Josh sat up too, resting his chin on my shoulder, his hand running up and down my arm soothingly. Ethan got up from the couch and came to sit in the spot Alec had just abandoned. I'd forgotten he was even in the room. He frowned at the closed door, but when he turned his amber eyes to me, they softened.

"How about I go down and make us some pancakes?" he whispered, cupping my cheek, rubbing his thumb over it softly.

He was always so gentle with me. But I didn't want gentle. I wasn't done. My mind was reeling, but my body was still on fire, my skin tingling, every nerve ending on edge.

"No," I whispered back. For some reason, we were all keeping our voices, our moans and sighs, low. The curtains were still drawn, the room deceptively dark despite the light threatening to burst from behind the heavy drapes.

"No?" Ethan frowned, cocking his head.

"No." I licked my lips, and his eyes dropped to my mouth for a split second. He was in nothing but underwear, the bulge under the thin fabric impossible to hide. Even if he hadn't been a participant, he'd been affected by what we'd started in the bed. He'd heard the rustling of the sheets, our whispers, our soft moans. He was setting his desire aside because he thought that's what I wanted. They both were.

But that wasn't what I wanted. I wanted *more* intimacy with them, not less. If Alec didn't want to be a part of that yet, that was his problem.

"Fuck him," I breathed an inch away from Ethan's mouth. Then I wrapped a hand around his neck and crashed my lips to his. His response was instant, the hand at my cheek threading back into my hair as his tongue met mine.

Josh's hand pushed up under my T-shirt to find my breasts again. My nipples were hard and sensitive, and every touch, every caress, felt impossibly heightened, as though beyond what a human brain was normally capable of processing.

I broke my frenzied kiss with Ethan to rip the T-shirt off over my head.

We all fell back to the pillows in a tangle of limbs and bedding and heavy breathing. Two hands—one with long artistic fingers, one with strong athletic ones—dragged the last scrap of clothing off my body. Alec's boxers disappeared into the void beyond the edge of the mattress.

Nothing existed but the bed; nothing was going to interrupt, stop, or ruin what I'd started up again. While Ethan assaulted my mouth with his, his tongue pushing in and out steadily, Josh moved his hand between my legs once again.

This time there was no fabric hindering his movements. He teased me, spreading the wetness around, circling my clit.

"So fucking wet," he whispered again, his hot mouth at my cheek, inches away from mine, from Ethan's.

Ethan broke the kiss and looked at Josh.

"Is she?" he whispered, his eyes dancing, the amber vibrant even in the dim light of the bedroom.

"Oh yeah. Feel it." Josh punctuated his statement by pushing one finger just inside me and then pulling it out again. We both groaned.

Ethan bit his lip, his eyes flicking between my flushed face and Josh's, all our mouths so close that if I were to lean up just a little, I could probably taste them both.

I tilted my face, and Josh's lips met mine, his tongue darting out. Ethan pressed his forehead to the side of mine, watching us kiss. He didn't join in, but he didn't pull away either, his lips inches from ours. He trailed a big, warm hand down the length of my naked body, and his fingers joined Josh's between my legs.

"Fuck," he groaned, his breath washing over our wet lips. Ethan's face was glorious, his eyes half-closed, his mouth hanging open as he panted, running his fingers up and down my folds.

"I want to taste it . . ." he whispered so quietly I wasn't sure he meant to say it out loud. But his face was so close to mine I heard every word, and it filled me with curiosity and desire so strong I finally broke the kiss with Josh.

Whatever Ethan saw in my face made him smile, his lips slowly turning up into a devious smirk. When he licked his lips, in what I'm sure was a deliberate move to make me imagine what his tongue would feel like on *my* lips, I couldn't help smiling back and nodding.

It was all the encouragement he needed. He shimmied down the bed, kissing and licking my body as he went, taking his time with my breast, nipping at the sensitive spot on my ribs. All the while, Josh kept kissing my neck, his hips rocking against me from behind.

As Ethan's face came level with my hips, Josh moved his hand out of the way. He grabbed my ass firmly and bit down on my neck, making me gasp. Then he moved his fingers back between my legs, only from behind, giving Ethan full access to the front.

Ethan grabbed the inside of my thigh and held my leg out of the way, giving himself enough room to press his mouth to my molten core.

As Ethan's lips started kissing, then sucking my most sensitive flesh, Josh pushed two fingers inside. I was completely lost in the sensations of what the two of them were doing to me. The licking and sucking and pushing and stretching . . . It was almost too much. My mind completely shut off, and I became nothing more than what they were making me feel.

They worked in perfect synchronicity, Josh's fingers and Ethan's mouth finding a steady rhythm that had my ecstasy climbing with increasing intensity.

My body started to tremble, soft little shivers spreading from my core down my limbs. When Josh leaned over and took one of my nipples in his mouth, I reached the peak of pleasure and came plummeting down all at once.

I cried out, a guttural, almost surprised sound that broke the relative quiet that had enveloped the room. The intensity of the orgasm made my back arch off the mattress, lifting me onto my elbows.

Once the stars obscuring my vision cleared, things beyond the edge of the bed faded back into reality.

Tyler was standing in a pile of bedding near the fireplace, wearing tight black briefs and a crumpled shirt, half the buttons undone. He was holding his gun loosely by his side and staring at me as I panted through the aftershocks of my orgasm, his mouth slightly open, as if he didn't quite believe what he was seeing.

Josh laughed—a surprised yet unabashed chuckle, as if he couldn't quite hold it in. That made Ethan lift his face from between my legs. He glanced first at us, then over his shoulder.

His big shoulders started to shake too, and I deliberately, slowly closed my legs. I hadn't known Tyler was in the room. With his mussed hair and glassy eyes, he looked half-asleep. I must have woken him with the unrestrained sound that Ethan and Josh had elicited.

"You all right, Gabe?" Josh asked, the laugh still in his voice as he gently kissed my shoulder, keeping his eyes on Tyler.

"Uh, yeah, I'm . . ." Tyler finally looked away, casting his eyes about the room, to the bedding at his feet, as if he was only just realizing where he was. His mind was catching up, but his voice still had that gritty, sleepy quality to it. "I heard a shout, and I . . . uh . . ."

He lifted the weapon in his hand and frowned at it. Obviously, when my orgasmic outburst had startled him from sleep, his training had kicked in, his senses looking for the threat.

"That was just us," Ethan teased. His head was turned away from me, but I was sure his dimples were showing. "Giving our girl the wakeup call she deserves."

He punctuated his answer by biting the top of my thigh and making me yelp.

Their laid-back attitude put *me* at ease. I'd had a moment of hesitation when I realized someone had been present for such an intimate experience. But it wasn't just someone; it was Tyler. He was part of my Bond, and I was no longer unsure where I wanted our relationship to go.

I laughed too, throwing my head back and letting my sweaty, perfectly satiated body flop back into the soft bedding.

"I'll just . . . ah . . . I need a shower," Tyler mumbled, walking out of the room without waiting for a response. I peeked over Josh's body just in time to see Tyler adjust himself before reaching for the door handle. I laughed again. To know he was as affected as we were—that he wanted it too—filled me with joy. Much as he fought for control of the situation with his mind, there was no hiding what his body wanted.

"Fifty bucks says he's rubbing one out in the shower." Ethan crawled up to settle himself on my other side, still chuckling.

"No way am I taking that bet!" Josh fired back, but he was grinning too. "He's *definitely* rubbing one out in the shower. Plus, how would we settle it? Someone would have to go in there to check."

"I volunteer as tribute!" I yelled, and we all descended into laughter once again. I wasn't even self-conscious about how various parts of my body might be jiggling in unsightly ways. I was too busy wiping tears from the corners of my eyes.

Our giggles subsided, and we all just lay there, catching our breath and staring at the ceiling. Ethan's hand rested easily on my bare thigh while Josh traced lazy patterns up and down my upper arm.

I didn't want to get out of bed, didn't want to break this sickeningly happy, naked bubble we were in by opening the curtains—letting the light illuminate all the shit we still had to deal with.

But my stomach had other ideas. It growled loudly, breaking the moment.

"OK." Ethan slapped me on the thigh and sat up. "Pancake time."

Josh pressed a quick kiss to my cheek and jumped out of bed too.

My eyebrows creased, and I shot up. "Wait."

They were already standing, but they paused and looked at me.

"What about . . ." I gestured to the still obvious bulges in both their underwear. I was beyond satisfied—they'd been generous in the way they'd worshipped my body—but neither of them had finished. "I want to, you know, return the favor."

I let my expression fill with lust, raking my eyes over their amazing bodies, taking in the tattoo on Ethan's strong shoulder and the lithe muscles of Josh's abdomen, dragging my eye lower . . . I wanted to make them feel as good as they'd made me feel. It was making me excited all over again.

They exchanged a loaded look before focusing back on me. Ethan growled and rubbed his short black hair with both hands.

Josh exhaled sharply. "You look so fucking hot, lying there in the tangled sheets, naked and inviting." I arched my back, pressing my breasts forward at his words, illustrating his point for him. "There is nothing we want more than to just crawl back to you and let you . . ." He growled too and rubbed his erection with the palm of his hand, as if it was painful not to touch it any longer. "But if we cross that line, if we receive from you in the same way you've received from us . . . I think it's better that we sort out the situation with Alec first. You need to be sure you're ready for this with all of us."

He was talking about what I'd discussed with Tyler, what I'd done my best to research. The Light demanded equality in my connection to my Bondmates. The deeper the connection—the stronger the next level of intimacy—the harder it was to resist evening the score with the others.

Alec wasn't ready; he'd expressed that clearly. I *was* ready; I wanted them all. But I was apprehensive about taking that step with Alec while so much was unresolved between us emotionally.

Once again, they'd thought of the consequences of our physical relationship, managed to push their own lust aside to put my emotional well-being first. What the fuck I had ever done to deserve them was beyond me.

I pulled the sheet up to cover my naked body and nodded, giving them both a genuine smile to show I understood.

They smiled back, then headed for the door.

"I guess we're all rubbing one out in the shower this morning," Ethan mumbled, but we both heard him clearly. I laughed, happy the moment was ending on a light note.

Once they were out of the room, I started looking for my discarded clothing, focusing on the promise of pancakes as I headed for the shower myself.

TWENTY-FIVE

As I headed downstairs, dressed once again in borrowed men's clothing, the heaviness of the past twenty-four hours started to settle in. With every step, the weight on my shoulders increased, wiping the smile off my face.

Step. Alec ran away from you. Again.

Step. You were kidnapped . . .

Step. . . . knocked out . . .

Step. . . . nearly killed.

Step. Zara betrayed you—had possibly been plotting to do it since Beth's death.

As I allowed myself to think about what Zara had done for the first time since coming face-to-face with her in that basement, I had to pause. One hand flew to the railing; the other went to my abdomen as I bent over. I felt sick—both as if I might vomit and as if my stomach were hollow.

After a few deep breaths, I straightened and continued to the kitchen. I was trying to convince myself the hollow feeling had more to do with the fact that I hadn't eaten in nearly a day. Maybe food would help.

Alec and Tyler sat side by side at the dining table, laptops in front of them, both absorbed in what they were doing. They had the exact same posture—shoulders slightly hunched, hands moving furiously over keyboards—and they wore matching creases between furrowed brows. Tyler paused what he was doing and reached for a steaming mug of disgusting black coffee. Alec reached for his own only a beat behind him.

They were so similar in their mannerisms I wondered for a second if they weren't related by blood after all.

I padded into the large open-plan room, the thick socks I'd taken from one of Alec's drawers making my movements soundless.

"Morning, Eve." Tyler greeted me without lifting his eyes from his screen.

"Morning, Evie." Alec did the same thing.

I guess I hadn't been as stealthy as I thought. I cleared my throat before mumbling my own "morning" and shuffling into the kitchen.

At the fridge, I frowned. Alec had called me Evie, and he hadn't sounded pissed off or hostile *at all*. In fact, his voice had that honey quality I craved like an idiot. It was so contradictory to his behavior earlier that it was confusing the shit out of me.

Again, I put all my focus on food instead, pulling a bunch of stuff from the fridge for scrambled eggs. I'd cracked a dozen eggs into a big bowl when Ethan came into the kitchen.

"Morning!" He grinned widely.

The two at the table grunted in acknowledgment. Ethan planted a kiss on my cheek, replaced the fork in my hand with a fancy whisk, and started chopping vegetables, chattering about the omelet we were apparently making.

Josh joined us not long after, giving me a kiss and making coffee. Since I'd started staying over, a shiny new espresso machine had appeared in the butler's pantry. I was never without a good latte anymore.

No one spoke about the heavy shit for the next half hour. We expertly ignored the shaky camera-phone footage of ourselves playing on the muted TV as we ate the omelet and sipped our coffees.

As I finished my latte and dropped my dishes into the sink, Tyler cleared his throat, closing his laptop.

"Eve, in light of the events of last night, I'd like you to consider moving permanently into our place." His voice was even as always, his hands clasped on top of his laptop. But the slight tightness around his eyes gave him away. He was worried about my response.

Ethan's head snapped up, looking from Tyler to me as a huge grin spread over his face.

Josh nodded. "I was going to suggest the same thing."

I leaned back against the sink, gripping the edge of the bench on either side of me. I was trying so hard to ignore all the things threatening to tear us apart; I hadn't expected that to be the first thing he raised. I hadn't even thought about it.

"None of you have even asked me out properly, yet you're asking me to move in?" I joked, trying to buy myself time.

Instead of taking up my teasing tone as he usually did, Ethan fixed me with one of his rare serious looks.

"I think we both know I was never pretending, baby. I'm yours through and through," he declared without a hint of doubt, his big shoulders rolling back.

I couldn't help looking over to Josh as an unfamiliar emotion threatened to choke me, the smile falling from my face.

Josh smiled at me with his knowing look, answering my unasked question, "Me too. Goes without saying."

I looked back to Tyler, and he beckoned me to come away from the sink and rejoin them. When I did, he wrapped his warm fingers around mine. "If words of commitment are what you need, then, yes, I'm in too. Mind, body, and soul. I just want you to be safe, and since Zara . . . I don't like the idea of you staying in the res hall alone."

I didn't like the idea of being alone either. I never wanted to feel alone again.

"You know about Zara?" I asked.

"We saw her at Christine Anderson's house when we arrived." Alec broke my flimsy bubble of pretending he wasn't in the room. "She wasn't tied up or locked in a basement, so we figured she had something to do with your abduction. According to reports from my team, she and the senator are the only ones who got away—with the help of Zara's parents. We're trying to track them down."

"Shit." I pulled my hand out of Tyler's and wiped it across my eyes. Talking about Zara was making it all come back. Betrayal was the worst kind of . . .

"And just so it's clear"—the hard edge in Alec's voice had me lifting my head to look at him—"I want you here just as much as the others. Don't let me stop you from moving in here. I said I would fix things, and I meant it."

"Oh, was that you fixing things this morning?" The snipe was reflexive, born out of the need to protect myself emotionally from Alec's behavior.

"What happened this morning?" Tyler frowned, looking between us. He didn't like not knowing things.

"Dude," Ethan said, "you slept through a lot."

"Evie . . ." Alec's voice was soft, his eyes pleading. Something clenched deep in my gut, but I wasn't ready to let him off the hook.

"You basically pulled the same shit you did that night in Tyler's study. You know how much that hurt me." I crossed my arms and stared him down, challenging him to disagree.

With a deep sigh, Tyler dropped his head into his hands, running his fingers into his messy hair and leaving them there. "We can't keep doing this." He spoke to the table. "It's getting dangerous. Everyone else knows now anyway."

The rest of us shared confused looks. He was talking to himself, but he wasn't making a lot of sense.

"Gabe?" Josh leaned forward, but before he could formulate a question, Tyler jumped up out of his seat, coming around the table to stand in front of me.

"Enough is enough," he declared in a louder, confident voice. I stood up a little straighter. His shoulders were back, his face determined as he grabbed my face in his hands and kissed me firmly.

I made a muffled sound of surprise, and then my eyes closed of their own volition, my hands lifting to rest on his hips.

He pulled away just a fraction, his lips not even an inch away from mine.

"Let it flow, baby," he whispered, his warm breath washing over my face.

Then his lips were back on mine with a renewed intensity. One hand threaded into the still damp hair on the back of my head while the other circled around my back, pressing our bodies firmly against each other.

I wrapped my arms around him and completely dropped my mental barriers, letting the Light flow freely. It always came most easily when one of them was kissing me—when all my logic went out the window, chased away by the heady feeling at the base of my spine.

Tyler pushed his tongue into my mouth, and I moaned softly, his hard chest pressing against my breasts. With a new wave of desire, a fresh wave of Light came pouring out, and he moaned in response.

"Uh, guys?" Ethan's voice only just managed to penetrate the fog of lust Tyler had so expertly got us lost in. With a few more soft kisses to my swollen lips, Tyler pulled away but still held me close.

"My ability is not dangerous." He spoke at a volume the others could hear, but his gray eyes focused on mine. "But it can be hard to live with sometimes. I know so many things I'd rather not know. Sometimes I'll ask an innocent question, and my ability fills in the answer in ways I don't expect. It can be a burden carrying others' secrets."

I frowned, not sure where he was going with this, but didn't interrupt. I ran my thumb across his cheek in what I hoped was a soothing gesture and waited for him to continue.

"So when I know that someone has a secret, something they don't want to talk about, I try my best to respect that. I don't ask them about it because I know they don't want me to know."

"Oh, shit." As usual, Josh was the first to figure out what was going on.

"I've respected your privacy." Tyler looked at me pointedly. "I've tried to be there for you in the hope that you would come to trust me enough to tell me yourself, but you're more stubborn than I anticipated."

His mouth quirked up just a fraction, but my eyes widened as I realized what he was doing.

"Shit! Tyler, no!" I injected as much steel into my voice as I could, my shoulders tensing as I pushed him away. He let me put a little distance between us, but his hands came to rest lightly on my hips.

"Eve, we've come so far, the five of us. We're getting closer and working as a team more every day. But this thing between you and Alec, it's hanging over us like a cloud. Shit's getting really serious, and we just can't afford to have any more surprises. Not ones we can prevent. No more secrets."

"This is none of your business, Tyler." Outrage surged through me, my breathing erratic for all the wrong reasons now. But I couldn't seem to make my hands leave his shoulders. I was scared of this thing coming out— this thing festering between Alec and me. I was scared of what they would think of me, how they would react. But even as my anger rose, I knew it wasn't Tyler's fault for pushing it. I *needed* a push.

"It is though." His eyes were sad, as if part of him wished that weren't true. "I'm yours. Don't you get it? This isn't some human relationship with human rules. I'm a Variant and you're my Vital. Your relationship with each of us doesn't exist in a vacuum, separate from the others. We're your Bond—we're *all* yours, and we're *all* in this together. When something affects you, it affects us all."

He was right. The connection we had was far beyond anything that could be described adequately with words. Each one of them was a part of me, and I hadn't known how incomplete I was until I found them.

Tyler had stopped speaking. He'd forced out of me the means by which he could get the information himself, but he was still giving me a chance to tell it first. He'd nudged me to the ledge, but the final leap was mine to take. I just didn't think I had the words. I wasn't sure I could get them all past the emotions lodged in my throat.

I looked up at his patient gray eyes, took a deep breath, and nodded once, giving him permission to finish what he'd started.

"Alec," he said immediately, not giving me a chance to change my mind, "the night of the invasion, when you and Eve—"

"No!" The sound of a chair scraping on the floor was accompanied by Alec's firm voice. "Tyler, I refuse to speak about this."

Neither one of us was looking at Alec. Tyler was focused on me, and I was returning his gaze, even though every fiber of my being wanted to avoid his eyes.

"When you and Eve were in my study, alone"—Alec started cursing, but Tyler just raised his voice and kept speaking—"what happened between you two?"

"Fuck!" Alec stormed around the table, coming to stand right next to us. I could see him out of the corner of my eye but kept my focus on Tyler.

I watched his face closely, making a conscious effort not to cringe at what I knew must be running through his head. His eyes darted back and forth, and his mouth dropped open slightly. I replayed the main highlights of Studygate in my head as I watched him: Alec holding me and telling me I wasn't alone, the matter-of-fact way he'd said he hated me, the frenzied make-out session on the couch, my incredible orgasm, Alec rejecting me, my outburst and the smashed glass all over the floor.

With a sharp intake of breath, Tyler's focus slammed back into the present moment. I dreaded to see what look would cross his face now. Would he be disgusted with me, disappointed in me, pity me, or some other unfathomable combination of awful things?

But none of that came. Instead, he released me, only to push me behind him and give his full attention to Alec.

"What the fuck is wrong with you?" he seethed, and I braced for Alec's response, sure he would explode and start shouting and throwing things. But he remained silent.

I leaned around Tyler to peek at him. Alec was breathing hard, his head hanging low and his shoulders slumped. Ethan and Josh were both staring at us with wide eyes, out of their seats and looking as if they were poised to move at any moment.

"So many things," Alec finally replied, his voice quiet and a little shaky. "I fucked up, OK? I didn't even realize how badly I fucked up at the time, but I know now. I'm an asshole."

I snorted and rolled my eyes. I'd called him that as I threw the glass paperweight in the general direction of his head. I'd been calling him that in my head and out loud for months.

"What were you thinking, man?" Tyler's shoulders were tense, one arm still holding me back protectively. He was keeping me away from Alec. He was protecting me *from Alec*. His ability had shown him not only the facts of what had happened but the truth about how I felt—about how Alec made me feel most of the time—vulnerable.

"I wasn't." Alec finally looked up, pleading. "You've never been depleted like that. You don't know what it's like to feel like you're fading into nothingness, and then you feel the most incredible thing—it's what sunshine would taste like, what warm summer nights smell like, what it feels like to be wrapped up in a warm blanket, naked. And it's the only thing keeping you tethered to this world. And then you start to get some conscious thought back, and you realize all those things are *her*. It's fucking impossible to resist."

I didn't know what it felt like to be on the other side of Light transfer. I knew what it was like for me, but I'd never asked what it felt like for them.

"That's not an excuse." Tyler echoed my thoughts.

"Can someone please clue us in on what the fuck the three of you are talking about?" Ethan's booming voice could never be ignored, but I knew him well enough to hear the note of insecurity in it. He didn't like feeling left out. His big arms were crossed over his chest where he stood, frowning at us.

Josh had sat back down, but he was watching us intently too. "Yeah, even I'm having trouble keeping up."

Tyler rubbed his temple. "I don't even have words . . ."

"Now you know why I refused to talk about it." I stepped around Tyler and fixed him with a firm look.

Alec sighed and turned to face the table. He still hadn't looked at me, and it was beginning to piss me off. "Look, I'm not proud of it, OK? But that night—"

"No. I'll tell it." It was time to put my big-girl panties on anyway. I was sick of people speaking for me, and I was getting sick of Alec's voice. It sounded like honey—gentle and genuine—which told me he was being honest, but I wasn't ready to forgive him. Not that he'd even asked for forgiveness.

Calling up every scrap of maturity I could muster, I took a deep breath and spoke in as even a voice as I could manage. "You both know what happens when you idiots overuse your abilities and I have to juice you up." I looked between Josh and Ethan, fighting the urge to look down out of embarrassment, to hunch my shoulders, to fidget. "You know how drawn we are to each other. The Light pushes me . . . and the urge to just . . . get closer is . . . So

I'm sure it's not a surprise that things got physical between Alec and me. But things went further than they'd gone with any of you at that point, and I'm not even entirely sure how, because I tried to . . . and then . . . Fuck, I'm mumbling!"

No one was saying anything, giving me the time I clearly needed. I took a breath and crossed my arms. It made me feel a little stronger.

"OK, basically Alec got me off, and then—"

"You two had sex?" Ethan's voice was higher pitched than I'd ever heard it. Josh's eyebrows shot up. I could almost see the gears turning in his head.

"There is more than one way to get a woman off, little cousin." Alec chose possibly the worst thing he could say at that moment, and he said it with that cocky grin, the one that turned one corner of his mouth up.

Fucking asshole. I stared at him, my mouth agape, my brain trying to process that *he'd actually said that* while also trying not to think about all the other ways he could get me off. I was decidedly pissed off at him, wanted nothing more than to be away from him, yet I was getting turned on at that mere suggestion of feeling his hands, and other things, on me again. I hated it. But that's what the Light did. That's what it meant to be in a Bond. You were drawn to each other no matter what.

"You did not just crack a joke." Tyler groaned.

"Dude, what is wrong with you?" Josh bugged his eyes out at him.

"I thought we already established that many things are wrong with me. I was trying to lighten the mood." Alec groaned. "It came out before I could think about it. I can't fucking think straight when she's around."

"Enough!" I banged my fist on the table. Like the mature adult I was trying so hard to be, I ignored that he'd just blamed his stupid comment on my presence and got back to the task at hand. "I am speaking. No more interruptions."

I fixed each of them with a serious look, and they all looked appropriately chastised. Even Alec.

"As I was saying, he got me off—and I'm not going to elaborate on the details. Then when I tried to return the favor, he pretty much told me I was worthless and ran out of the room." Josh and Ethan were staring at me with horrified expressions on their faces. "He rejected me twice that night, but none of that hurt as bad as when he told me he *fucking hated me.*" I ground the last part out between clenched teeth and felt the sting of tears. Blinking furiously, I finally allowed myself to turn away from them and toward the picture windows, staring at the heavy clouds hanging over the massive yard.

Silence filled the room for a beat.

Then sudden movement drew my eyes back around just in time to see Ethan's fist flying at Alec's head.

TWENTY-SIX

We all knew Alec was lethal and could've stopped Ethan's punch from landing, but he just stood there and took it. The muscles in Ethan's arms and back bunched as he delivered the blow. Alec's head snapped to the side, and he stumbled a little, catching himself on the edge of the island.

My hands flew to my mouth in shock. Tyler and Josh sprang into action, getting between the two cousins. Tyler pressed both palms flat against Alec's chest, and Josh used his ability, floating Ethan a couple of inches off the ground to drag him back.

"I'm not gonna hit him back." Alec held his arms out at his sides, and Tyler lowered his hands. "I'm not gonna hit any of you back. If that's what you need to feel better, I'll let you all have a free hit."

"Would you stop being a fucking martyr?" Josh rolled his eyes, releasing Ethan once it became clear the big guy wasn't struggling either.

"I didn't punch you to make myself feel better." Ethan frowned, his voice hard. "I did it because what you did was low, and there need to be consequences for treating our Vital like shit."

He pointed at me as if to illustrate his point. I lowered my hands from my mouth to my chest. I didn't like the violence, but I could appreciate the sentiment. They were standing up for me—defending my honor. It was positively chivalrous, and I was beyond relieved they weren't upset with me, that they weren't judging me.

"May I speak?" Alec asked in a quiet, serious voice, finally looking directly at me.

I sighed and made a "whatever" gesture, then turned back to face the windows, having trouble holding his intense gaze. His footsteps approached, but then he just stood there, not saying anything.

Frustration built inside me, creasing my brow and making my heart rate speed up. I whipped around, ready to demand what the hell he wanted to say.

"I'm sorry!" he blurted out before I'd even opened my mouth.

I don't know what I'd been expecting, but it certainly wasn't that. He knew how much he'd hurt me. He'd had plenty of opportunities to apologize. I'd all but given up on it.

"You're sorry?" My tone suggested it wasn't good enough. Because it wasn't.

"Yes. I'm sorry. I know I should have said it sooner, but I just didn't know how. I tried so many times, but something would interrupt, or I would realize what I was about to say just wasn't . . . enough. I didn't know how to make sure you understood that I meant it. That I fully recognize how much I fucked up."

His shoulders hunched forward, and his eyes darted between mine, pleading, refusing to release me.

I crossed my arms and let him fill the silence.

"I'm sorry I rejected you. I'm sorry I made you feel worthless." He looked disgusted at the mention of that word. "I'm sorry I blamed you for something that was all on me. I'm sorry I suggested that the fact we saved all those people was somehow a bad thing. *I'm sorry I said I hated you*."

His voice broke a little at the end, and the lump returned to my own throat. I was already on edge, and here was the strongest, hardest man I'd ever encountered getting emotional. It had nothing to do with the fact that he was finally saying what I'd needed to hear from him since that night. Nothing to do with the fact that I was maybe starting to believe him. At least that's what I was trying to convince myself of.

"That's what I'm most sorry about, Evie." At the sound of my childhood nickname, the tears spilled over, and I had to take a shuddering breath. "Because it's not true. It couldn't be further from the truth. It's *me* that I hate."

Tears tracked down my face, but I was also confused. Why was he saying he hated himself?

"My ability makes people literally recoil from me. It causes so much pain. And I've been living with that since I was twelve. It's who I am, and I know I can't change it, but I *hate* it. Your mere presence makes the one thing I hate about myself amplified exponentially. I blamed you for that when I should know better than anyone that you can't control that. It just is what it is. I took my own fucked-up feelings about myself and projected them onto you."

He took a step closer, his hands in front of him, palms turned up. We were both breathing a little hard, both trying to hold back the tears. He was doing better than I was. His eyes were red and misty, but my tears were already soaking the collar of my hoodie.

"I'm so, *so* sorry."

I was finding it really hard not to believe him. The layers of defensive anger I'd built up were slowly crumbling, torn down by the sincerity in his face and words.

And then he delivered the final blow.

"Because the truth is"—he took a deep breath—"I don't hate you at all, Evelyn. I fucking love you."

I definitely was not expecting *that*. My arms dropped to my sides as my jaw unhinged. The tears were still trickling down my cheeks, but I didn't even know why anymore. I was frozen to the spot, no idea how to react.

I chanced a quick glance in the direction of the table. Tyler was wearing a look very similar to mine—shocked. Ethan looked surprised too, but he was also smiling a little, the dimples only just appearing. Josh had a smug grin on his face, suggesting he wasn't surprised at all. Naturally . . .

Alec didn't bother to check the others' reactions. His focus was all on me.

"I've loved you since the day you were born and we went to the hospital to meet you and my mom insisted I hold you. I love you with that same protective, nurturing feeling I had toward you when we were kids. I love you in that uniquely fucked-up, impossible-to-describe way that all Variants love their Vitals—because I can't help that one. I love you for making Ethan feel like he has a family again. I love you for drawing Josh out of his books and making him rejoin the real world. I love you for making Tyler realize he doesn't have to be the strong one all the time.

"I tried to fight it—*railed* against it. But then I saw how fucking smart you are, and I watched you repeatedly get this close"—he held his thumb and forefinger very close together between our faces—"to finding me several times before I could stop it. I watched you show up and fall into this world like you belong here—because you do.

I watched you as you embraced the news that you're not only a Variant but a *Vital*. And I watched you constantly push every damn button I have. I realized you're *strong*. Much stronger than I ever gave you credit for. And I loved every fucking minute of it, even while I was constantly getting frustrated and pissed off. I loved it because I was finally around you all the time. And I love you."

"Stop saying that." Something warm and fuzzy—but also incredibly confusing—was igniting in my chest.

"I can't." He chuckled darkly and looked up to the ceiling. "It's out now. There's no putting it back in."

"I don't want you to put it back in," I replied as Ethan chuckled. His mind was always in the gutter, but I ignored him. "I just don't understand. I'm . . . what does this mean? What do you *want*?"

That was the main issue—what the hell did he want from me? Did he expect us to just start acting like a couple? Going on dates? Cuddling on the couch?

"I want you to forgive me. And I know it won't be this easy—that's why I haven't tried to make it right yet, because I didn't know what I could possibly do or say to atone—but at least it's all out there now. It's a start."

He stopped speaking and just stared at me, the tattoos running up and down his arms projecting the tough guy exterior that completely contrasted with the vulnerable look on his face.

"It's a start," I conceded in a low voice. Because it was. He had at least admitted he was an asshole and apologized for it.

He breathed a massive sigh of relief and nodded. "OK. I'm just going to . . . go. For a little while."

I frowned at him. He was leaving?

"I'm not running away," he rushed out, holding up his hands as if approaching a wild animal. As though *I* was the one who might bolt at any moment. "I'm just going for a walk, and I'm coming right back. *Not* running away. Just giving you some space. OK?"

He wasn't actually leaving. Not this time. I nodded, and he turned around, finally releasing me from his intense stare, and walked toward the front of the house.

I released a massive breath I hadn't realized I'd been holding. Then I turned to Tyler. If he was determined to break every barrier between us, if he felt entitled to know what was between me and Alec, then I felt no qualms about asking him to use his ability to give me some clarity.

"Was he telling the truth?" I braced myself for a fight—for him tell me he had to toe a line between being truthful and betraying others' privacy. But he didn't. He smiled and leaned on the table, staring after Alec, his posture relaxed.

"Alec can be hard to read sometimes." He kept his eyes trained on the middle distance. "He's so conflicted about himself, his place in the world, his feelings about it all, that often, even when I detect truth in what he's saying, it's laced with doubt. But, Eve"—finally he turned his eyes to me—"I have never heard him sound so sure of anything in my life. I've never sensed more truth coming off him than I did just then."

I let his words sink in for a moment. "Still doesn't excuse the way he treated me."

"No, it doesn't." The way Tyler pressed his lips together, a frown pulling at his eyebrows, told me he'd be having another chat with Alec. "But he *is* sorry and he *does* love you. That much you can be sure of."

I nodded and sighed. I didn't know what to say. In true Alec fashion, he'd dropped a massive bombshell and then promptly made his exit, leaving the rest of us to deal with the fallout. Only this time, I needed the space too.

Ethan used the stretching silence to bring the conversation full circle. "So, will you move in with your four boyfriends?"

He flashed me his dimples, obviously attempting to lift the mood, even though I could tell he was anxiously awaiting my answer.

"Yes." I smiled. "I'll move in with my four stalkers. I mean my four Bonded Variants. Tomato, tomato." I waved a hand, but he whooped and lifted me clean off the ground, mashing his lips to mine and making me remember what we'd been up to earlier in Alec's bed.

As soon as Ethan set me down, Josh enfolded me in one of his bone-crushing hugs. "Thank god," he whispered into my hair. "I was already planning a roster so one of us could stay with you on campus every night. This is much more convenient."

"Oh, well, I'm happy to make your stalking habit easier on you." I chuckled as he released me.

"Come on." Tyler pulled me over to the couch and tucked me into his side. "We need a break from the heavy stuff."

He flicked through channels, making the news disappear until he found some shitty sitcom, and we all settled in.

Alec came back and sat in the empty spot next to me, taking my feet and putting them in his lap. Tyler's hold on me tightened, and he placed a reassuring kiss on the top of my head. I decided to leave my feet in Alec's lap. I wasn't sure how I felt about his declarations, but he could have my feet for a little while. I was willing to give him that much.

Halfway into the third episode, Dot bounded into the room.

"What the fuck is this?" She put her hands on her hips, furious. "You assholes promised to tell me when she woke up, and I show up here to find you . . ." She gestured wildly to our various reclined states on the comfy couches. Ethan was snoring lightly, not in the least disturbed by her dramatic entrance.

"Sorry, Dot." Tyler looked guilty. "We had some things to discuss. She's fine, see?" He held up one of my wrists as proof.

"No, I don't see." She sniffed, turning her nose up. "I need a closer look."

I peeled myself off the couch with a groan and went over to her. "I'm fine, Dot. I promise."

She sprang forward and wrapped her arms around me. I held her for a long time, only pulling away when she did.

"I was so worried it had happened again," she whispered, not looking at me.

"It nearly did." I wasn't going to lie to her. "But my guys got me out."

She nodded, taking a few deep breaths.

Tyler and Alec went back to their computers, declaring break time over, and Dot joined me on the couch. We spent most of the day lazing around, watching movies and eating. Nina joined us not long after Dot, saying she was happy to see me well but not asking any questions.

By late afternoon we had cleaned the fridge out of leftovers, which gave Ethan an excuse to start making dinner from scratch. Tyler and Alec moved to stools at the island bench and opened some beers, chatting with him as he chopped things. I ended up in Josh's lap, reveling in messing up his perfectly styled hair with my fingers.

When Lucian walked into the room, his suit crumpled and his tie hanging loose, shoulders hunched from the weight of his day, the mood in the room changed.

He stepped up to lean heavily on the island, palms flat on the cool stone, as Dot muted the TV.

"What the fuck were you thinking?" His quiet voice carried in the now silent room.

I'd never heard Lucian swear. I stood, moving to the opposite end of the island, my full focus on Lucian and whatever fresh hell he was about to rain down on us. Alec and Tyler's postures were rigid in their seats, almost as if they were at attention.

"Lucian," Tyler started, "we—"

"What the fuck were you idiots thinking?!" the older man cut across him, raising his voice. "That shit is all over the news, the senator hasn't been seen since this morning, and now they're starting to speculate that there's some conspiracy in Melior Group to take her out. Not to mention the fact that you've exposed yourselves. Exposed Evelyn."

He finally raised his head, looking mostly at the two older Variants in his employ but also casting his furious gaze to Ethan and Josh, who had joined me at the other end.

"We couldn't just sit around and do nothing. All we knew was that Evie was in danger. We acted to protect her." Alec kept his voice even.

"By bursting in there and causing a national incident, getting on the fucking news?" He gestured to the muted TV, slapping his hand down on the bench. "You should have told me and waited until we could get a stealth team down there to sort this out *quietly*."

"With all due respect," Tyler replied, "we reported it to you immediately, but we couldn't wait. Every second we wasted could've been a second she didn't have. Not to mention Josh happened to be in the city and got to her first. He has barely any training, and it was a stupid move, but he couldn't have stopped himself any more than we could have. They were both in danger. We couldn't wait."

"You should have," Lucian ground out between gritted teeth.

"As if *you* could have." Frustration leaked into Alec's voice. "If it had been Joyce, if it had been *your* Vital, you really think you could've waited?"

Lucian's eyes went wide. He turned to me as I gasped, my hands tightening on the edge of the bench.

"Your . . ." I couldn't get more than a single word out. The room felt as if it had tilted on its axis, and my grip on the bench was the only thing holding me upright. My mother was a Vital? My mother was *Lucian's Vital*?

"Holy shit." Josh laid a comforting hand on my shoulder, but my eyes were fixed on Lucian. "You didn't know Lucian was Joyce's Variant?"

"What?" I couldn't seem to get my voice above a stunned whisper. "I didn't even know my mother *was* a Vital."

I tore my gaze away from Lucian's to look at the guys. They all had varying degrees of shock and confusion on their faces. They thought I knew, but Lucian knew I didn't. Another realization crawled into my mind, and I looked back at him, holding on to the bench tighter. My knees were weak.

"Are you my father?" My voice sounded steady, but there was a tempest raging inside me, and I hoped I could hear his reply over the noise in my head.

"No!" He held a hand out, pleading. "Your mother and I met when you were already six months old. There's no way . . . I would never have kept that from you."

I released a tense breath, relief flooding through me. If Lucian were my father and had been keeping it from me this whole time, I don't think I could have coped. And the implications of him being Ethan and Alec's uncle . . . that would have made us cousins. The things we'd done were certainly *not* familial.

I scrunched up my nose in disgust, and when I looked up, both Ethan and Alec were wearing matching expressions, no doubt thinking about the things they'd done to my body.

Next to me Josh chuckled, and I rolled my eyes at him. Of course he was amused by it. Shit stirrer.

"How is it possible that my mother was a Vital and I had no idea?"

Lucian had been staring into space, but at my question he looked up, eyebrows raised. "Hmm? Oh, yes, she was . . ." He sighed deeply, running his hands through his salt-and-pepper hair in a move that reminded me of Tyler. "I think it's time you and I had a long talk, Evelyn. There are things I haven't said because I didn't want to hurt you, and there are things I simply didn't know if you knew or not. But in light of recent events . . . it's all coming out now, and it won't be long before your father puts two and two together, if he hasn't already."

"My father?" My back straightened, my hands closing into fists. If there was any topic my mother had avoided more than why we were on the run, it was the issue of my paternity. My heart kicked up a beat. Even as the vulnerable, young side of me that pined for a dad got excited, the grown-up, logical one reminded me there was a reason Lucian hadn't told me yet.

"Yes. I think once I explain who he is, and what I suspect him of, you will understand why your mother and I both kept it a secret. Maybe we should sit—"

"Oh!" Nina's surprised exclamation cut Lucian off, and we all turned to her.

She was sitting up on the couch, the loose gray hoodie covering her bald head askew as she stared at Dot on the chair opposite her. Nina's wide dark eyes had a faraway look to them, and a tense silence settled over the room.

Dot sat up straighter in her armchair, dropping her feet to the ground.

"Dot." Nina tilted her head to the side, a tiny twitch of her lips hinting at a smile. "Come."

Dot practically fell over the coffee table in her rush to sit next to her, launching herself into the spot next to Nina and grabbing her outstretched hand.

We all held our breath, watching them intently. After only a fraction of a second, Nina smiled. "I feel him. I have a location," she declared, and Dot burst into tears.

The room exploded in a flurry of activity. Ethan called up Dot's mom, letting her know the news. Lucian, Tyler, and Alec converged on Nina, firing a million questions and already starting to strategize. I wasn't sure what Josh was doing—probably something no one else had thought to do.

I went to Dot and just held her close in the second highly emotional hug we'd shared that day.

"He's alive," she whispered into my shoulder, and I smiled.

TWENTY-SEVEN

The formal sitting room off the foyer had not changed one bit since Josh had given me an amazing dress and I'd kissed him silly. It was still immaculately clean, the two velvet couches positioned perfectly on either side of the coffee table, the drapes hanging precisely, a fire roaring in the fireplace. Even the Christmas decorations had disappeared as fast as they'd arrived, leaving the room looking untouched.

I sat on one of the soft couches, reading the latest edition of *New Scientist* and trying to take my mind off the fact that my father was alive and the man who knew his identity was in the house somewhere.

While the room remained unchanged, so much else hadn't. The day I'd first stepped into it with Josh, giddy about the gift and the kiss, I'd had no idea Alec was part of my Bond, no one knew I was a Vital, Beth and Zara were my closest friends, Charlie was safe and well and getting ready for the same gala we were.

Now . . .

We knew where he was, but we still couldn't get him. The news that Nina could now track him had pushed everyone into action the previous night, but my assumption that we would be commandeering the jet within hours was grossly misguided.

There were preparations to be made, approvals to be gained, strategy to finalize. Dot's parents were almost manic in their attempts to get things moving, but Lucian insisted we do things properly.

"We could get him killed if we march in there unprepared," he'd explained. "We don't know what we're walking into, what we're up against. We don't know how big it is, how many Vitals they're holding, who's behind it. The more information we have, the better our chances of success."

Tyler and Alec agreed; it was important to do recon first. They copped some sarcastic remarks from Lucian, considering how they'd handled saving me from the senator, but they were all determined to do this right.

Which left the rest of us sitting on our asses with nothing to do—and left me dying to ask Lucian who my father was. The man didn't have a spare second to eat, let alone talk to me about shit that happened before I was even old enough to remember. Hopefully things would calm down enough for us to have a proper conversation soon; I wasn't sure how much longer I could wait.

I'd spent the previous night in my usual room, in a giant, ridiculously comfortable bed, but I'd spent it alone. As much as I loved being around my guys, I needed the space. I needed to not worry about who was sleeping where, who might be feeling left out, and if I was being a good enough Vital.

I'd grown up pretty much alone, and I was still getting used to being around so many people all the time.

I was *still* alone by midmorning. Everyone was busy preparing to rescue Charlie, and Josh and Ethan had headed to Bradford Hills Institute to pack up my stuff. I'd considered going with them but decided in the end to let them do it for me. I wasn't ready to walk into those rooms and look at the empty beds—reminders of the two friends I'd lost as fast as I'd made them.

"Eve?" Lucian's call came from somewhere in the house. I stretched, taking my time getting off the couch.

"*Eve?*" His voice was closer this time, mingling with the sound of his loafers on the foyer's marble floor. This time it held a panicked edge.

I rushed to the door, catching him on his way to the kitchen. "Lucian?" He spun around, eyes wide. "What's wrong?"

"Evelyn." He rushed over and placed both hands on my shoulders. "I'm sorry I don't have time to explain everything properly, but I need you to listen and do exactly as I say."

"OK . . ." I fiddled with the hem of my white sweater.

Alec came bounding down the stairs, phone in hand. He ended a call as he reached the bottom. Tyler was hot on his heels, buttoning up a fresh blue shirt.

"She's on the way. She should beat him here," Alec said.

"Good." Some of the anxiety drained out of Lucian's face, but he kept his eyes trained on me. "This is what I was afraid of when visuals of you transferring Light to Alec were plastered all over national television. Now everyone knows what you are, and some people know *who* you are too. One of those people is on his way here now."

"What? Who?" My voice was high. "Why are you guys so freaked out? You're freaking me out!"

"Uncle, you're scaring her." Alec placed a hand on Lucian's shoulder, and the older man released me.

"Sorry, it's just we have no time . . ." Lucian looked more rattled than I'd ever seen the distinguished man look. I wondered how much he'd slept in the past few days.

"Eve, Lucian's business associate Davis Damari is coming here," Tyler said evenly as Lucian visibly pulled himself together, tucking his shirt into his slacks and smoothing his hair.

"OK . . ." I frowned. Davis had popped up in my reading a few times—in the news and online when I was doing research about Variants—but I didn't remember anything alarming.

"He's made up some flimsy excuse to invite himself over," Lucian explained, a little more collected, "but he's really only coming to see you for himself."

"What? Why?" Why would some super-rich hotshot business guy want anything to do with me?

"Because he knows you're *Evelyn Maynard*. He knows what you're capable of."

"How?" Alarms started going off in my mind. Why did everyone seem to know more about me than I did?

"I wish I'd made time to have this conversation with you sooner. Now it's too late." He sighed. "The most important things for you to know are that he's dangerous and he's trying to find out what we're up to. He also has a mind-reading ability—"

"Which is the only reason why we invited . . ." Alec cut in, then trailed off.

"Who?" I was asking all the *W* questions, trying in vain to piece together the puzzle with whatever snippets of information I could drag out of them. I was so sick of being out of the loop.

The doorbell rang. All three of them looked to the door.

"It's not him," Tyler announced, moving to open it.

Dana was the last person I expected to come through the door. She looked almost as irritated as me. As soon as we saw each other, we both crossed our arms.

She was in black pants and combat boots—standard issue gear for Melior Group operatives—but once she took her thick coat off, the white top underneath looked as if it were painted on, showing off her voluptuous breasts and toned arms.

Tyler took her coat and hung it up. "Thanks for coming, Dana."

"Just following orders," she replied.

Lucian inclined his chin. "We still appreciate it."

"What exactly do you want me to do?" She was having trouble keeping her eyes off Alec. He was standing eerily still, his hands in his pockets, and avoiding everyone's eyes.

"Davis is on his way, so just the standard," Lucian answered. "He's here for"—his eyes flicked to me—"other reasons, but we can't have him picking up that we suspect he's behind the Vital disappearances. It would unravel months of hard work."

"Got it." Dana pulled her phone from her pocket, looking bored. From the way Lucian spoke to her, it sounded as if she did this all the time.

But my brain was still processing the bombshell Lucian had dropped. Davis was behind the Vital disappearances?

"Your mouth is hanging open," Tyler whispered into my ear as his gentle hands rubbed my shoulders. I snapped my mouth shut.

"Maybe we should just hide her?" Alec spoke for the first time since Dana had arrived. "Have Tyler take her out for a few hours and say she's not here."

"He'll just find an excuse to stay until they get back," Lucian answered. "He won't leave until he's seen her with his own eyes. It's better if we get it over with quickly, and then I'll steer the conversation toward business. The sooner we can get him out of here, the better."

"I don't want him anywhere near—"

Whatever Alec had been about to say was cut off by the crunch of tires on gravel.

A rush of panic and adrenaline made me fidget again, my eyes darting about the room. I needed to move—to do something—but Tyler's grip on my shoulders tightened, and he leaned in, his heat at my back soothing.

"Calm down, Eve," he whispered. "You need to be calm and polite, and we'll get you out of here in a few minutes. You can do this."

I breathed deep, focusing on the mindfulness techniques Tyler had taught me months ago. He released my shoulders and stood next to me.

Lucian moved to the door, opening it wide and blocking my view. Pleasantries were exchanged, comments about how cold it was, and then three men entered the Zacarias mansion.

Two of them were clearly security detail—dressed almost identically, with weapons strapped to their hips and beady eyes taking everything in. The third was Davis Damari. I recognized his broad shoulders and dark hair, peppered with gray, from the few images I'd seen online, but he was a little taller than I expected.

Their coats were taken by a maid who appeared out of thin air and disappeared just as quickly while the men continued to chat. Davis greeted Alec with a polite head nod in place of a handshake and then shook Dana's hand.

"What a pleasure to see you again, Dana." He smiled warmly but showed just a hint too much teeth for it to not look menacing.

"Nice to see you again too, sir." She smiled politely, her face pleasant but her posture at attention.

"I can't remember the last time we had a meeting without Dana present, Lucian." Davis turned to him. "I must say, it's a pleasure to have a break from the constant chattering in people's heads. Although if I didn't know any better, I'd think you were keeping her around to keep something from me, old friend."

Those teeth again. To his credit, Lucian just chuckled, not looking even slightly nervous about Davis's pointed teasing. As soon as we'd heard the car pull up, Lucian had drawn himself to his full height, and any hint of the panic he'd shown moments before had been wiped off his handsome face. He was giving nothing away.

"You know my ability blocks yours anyway. Dana has been working closely with me lately on a special project."

The guys had mentioned their uncle's ability when I first met him at the gala. While Dana was a blocker—neutralizing the ability of any Variant in her vicinity—Lucian was a shield. He was impervious to others' abilities but could only protect himself, and it worked best against more passive abilities, like Tyler's truth telling or Davis's mind reading. I wondered what he'd been capable of when he had my mom, his Vital, around.

"Oh?" Davis's eyebrows rose. "Sounds intriguing. I don't suppose you can tell your old friend what you're working on?"

"It's classified." Lucian smiled, an amused glint in his eyes, and stuffed his hands into his pockets casually. He looked so relaxed that even I almost started to believe these were just two old friends teasing each other. But Davis wasn't quite as good at covering his true feelings; his eyes narrowed just a fraction.

"Excuse my rudeness." Davis turned toward me and Tyler. "I have yet to greet your right-hand man." He sauntered over and shook Tyler's hand before fixing his intense gaze on me. "And you must be Evelyn Maynard." He smiled wide, looking at me in the same way I'd seen women look at shoes they loved but couldn't afford—with longing and greed.

I patted myself on the back for not flinching at his use of my full name, the name I'd spent my whole life hiding. Hearing it used so casually by someone who was making my skin crawl felt like a siren going off.

Danger! Evacuate! Take cover!

I breathed through it, taking inspiration from Alec's unflappable uncle, and smiled back. "Yes, pleasure to meet you, sir."

I kept my hands loosely clasped. I didn't think I could suppress a shudder if I had to touch him.

"You have no idea how it warms my heart"—he pressed his hand over the organ in question, his eyebrows turning up in a decent imitation of sincerity—"to see you safe and well."

"Yes." I cleared my throat. "It's been a crazy couple of days."

"Couple of days?" He chuckled. "My dear, I was referring to the past dozen *years*. I am sorry to hear your mother is no longer with us. You look so much like her."

I kept my mouth shut, unnerved. How the hell did he know so much? Once again, I wished the guys had told me more, that I'd had time to interrogate them. I looked away from his intense stare but didn't know what to say.

"I don't mean to upset you. I see now that you don't know who I am. It's not all that surprising that your mother kept it from you, I suppose. She did, after all, keep you from *me*."

I looked back into his face, frowning. He seemed to be insinuating *he* was the reason my mother and I had been on the run all those years. Was he threatening me?

Except that didn't sit right. His words weren't *menacing*, they were *griping*. They were the kind of thing a person would say if they were bickering about custody.

My breath hitched.

The ground fell out from under me.

I had my mother's hair, her eye color, her build, but in front of me stood a man with the same *shape* eyes as me, the same full lips, a more masculine, bigger version of my nose.

All sound disappeared as the implications fell into place. I retreated completely into my own mind, momentarily cut off from my senses, incapable of movement, as I processed the bombshell that had gone off inside me.

I tuned back in in time to see Lucian leading Davis to Tyler's study, turning the conversation to business. Tyler said something about getting them coffee and looked at me with concern.

I looked back at him, letting my eyes go wide, letting the realization crash over my features. He pressed his lips together and shook his head before heading off toward the kitchen.

Alec came to stand in front of me, worry and a question in his eyes.

I had questions of my own. Now that my senses had returned, all I had were questions.

What the fuck? I mouthed.

He pressed a finger to his lips and took my hand in his, leading me up the stairs and past a scowling Dana. She was leaning on the wall next to the door to Tyler's study, arms crossed, eyes fixed on Alec's hand gripping mine.

We made it up only one flight of stairs before I couldn't keep quiet any longer.

"He's . . ." I pulled on Alec's hand. I needed to stop, sit, think. "He's my . . . that man is . . ."

I needed to hear someone say it, but I couldn't form the words myself. The word *father* was too unfamiliar to my lips; they didn't know how to shape the letters.

Alec gave up on dragging me up another flight, instead nudging me a little farther down the hall. "He is your biological father, yes." He kept his voice low, looking both angry and wary at the same time.

"Did you know?" I yanked my hand out of his, my rising anger giving me added strength. Was this another thing they'd kept from me? Would the secrets never end?

"No." His answer was firm and definitive. "Lucian did, but it's not something he shared with us until half an hour ago, when he heard Davis was on his way. We've suspected he may be behind the Vital kidnappings for some time—there's a special task force in Melior Group dedicated to investigating the theory—but we haven't been able to find anything concrete. He's very good at keeping his dealings private. A little *too* good for it to not be suspicious. But that had absolutely nothing to do with you, as far as we knew. Now . . ."

His voice had dropped so low I had to strain to hear him, hanging on every word. I believed him that he hadn't known, but I had so many more questions. I needed answers, and almost as much, I needed *comfort*.

I leaned forward and pressed my forehead to his chest, breathing in the clean male scent of him. He closed the remaining distance, wrapping one strong arm around my back and cupping the back of my head with the other.

"He'll be gone soon," he whispered into my hair, pressing a kiss to the spot, "and then we'll have a nice long chat with my uncle. You will have your answers. I promise."

When Alec set his mind to something—like stopping me from finding him for a year, or resisting the pull of the Bond, or keeping my identity a secret from his family—there was no stopping him. He was like the most solid tree in the forest. It was nice to have that force of will on *my* side for a change.

After a while, we separated, and I slid down the wall to sit on the ground. Alec stayed with me, but when we heard movement downstairs, he went to make sure Davis was leaving.

For a few minutes, the sound of several male voices drifted up to me. I caught my name a few times but didn't have the energy to try to listen in. I couldn't even be bothered to move, try to hide, when I heard footsteps coming up the stairs.

A pair of boots, too small to be a man's, came to a stop next to me. I sighed and leaned my head against the wall, drawing my knees up.

Out of the corner of my eye, I watched Dana turn around, but instead of heading back downstairs, she sat on the top step. We were a few feet apart, facing opposite directions but sitting in line with each other.

"He was never mine, was he?" There was no anger in her voice—just a resigned kind of sadness.

"If it makes you feel any better, he fought it really hard. For a long time," I told the ornate hall table in front of me.

"It doesn't," Dana answered.

"I'm sorry." I was just as surprised as anyone to hear myself directing those words at her. But I really did feel bad about how it had all played out. She'd got caught up in our mess, and it wasn't fair to her. Alec had hurt us both.

"Don't be. You didn't do anything. I see that now. I just wish he'd told me."

But I had done something. I'd let him kiss me; I'd kissed him back when I'd thought he was with her. I wasn't sure she knew that, and I didn't want to rub salt in the wound. "He kept things from me too."

"Fucker."

I turned my head in her direction. She met my gaze and rolled her eyes, a tentative smile pulling at her lips.

I smiled back and shook my head.

At least there was one fewer person I had to watch my back with.

TWENTY-EIGHT

Ethan and Josh got back just as Dana was leaving, so I let Alec and Tyler catch them up. I needed some time alone. I spent most of the day shut up in my now-permanent room, staring at the ceiling or out the window.

After a subdued dinner where Lucian didn't join us and the guys kept looking at me warily, I decided I couldn't put it off any longer. The guys all got up to go with me, but I wanted to speak with Lucian alone. Much as I appreciated having Alec's determination on my side, he tended to escalate situations.

The older man was on the balcony off his study on the first floor. A single desk lamp cast the room in an eerie yet cozy glow, throwing shadows over the vast bookshelves. I walked through the classically decorated room to the balcony doors.

Lucian stood at the railing, looking out over the yard. I grabbed a blanket off the leather couch and draped it over my shoulders before stepping out to join him.

It was a perfectly still night, so there was no biting wind. Just the snow falling softly, coating everything in white and silence.

A silence it was time to break.

I stood next to him, both of us looking out over the white powder, and waited. He knew all my questions; there was no need to voice them.

He sighed deeply, his breath misting in the cool air, and held a glass out for me. I took it reflexively; he had a matching one in his other hand, and both held a generous amount of scotch. Something exorbitantly expensive, I was sure.

I brought it to my lips but couldn't discern any fancy undertones in the flavor. It just tasted like alcohol. It burned my throat on the way down and made my lungs burn, but it did make me feel warmer.

"Your mother glowed too," Lucian finally said, "when the Light flow got really intense. I only saw it a handful of times, but it was exactly like what you did."

"They told you about that?" I looked at him out of the corner of my eye.

"I saw it in the footage from the train station."

"I thought Alec took care of that."

"He had Charlie delete it all, but I *am* the director of the top security firm in the world. Give me a little credit."

"Fair point." But if he'd found it, who else had?

"Have you figured out yet that when you glow, it allows you to draw Light from Variants?"

"No. Only that I can transfer *to* them remotely. Although I don't know what it is or how it works. My research is yielding no results." I frowned at the amber liquid and took another sip. Could I really draw Light *out* of others? I couldn't remember doing that, but the few times I'd glowed had been under extremely stressful circumstances. I'd been acting on instinct.

"I only experienced it for myself once and saw her do it a few more times, but she told me about it—what little she knew herself. Evelyn, you need to be very careful with it. When you glow like that, when you tap into such intense power, it allows you to *give* a Variant an ability. Someone who doesn't have one, you can give it to them."

"Whoa . . ." I whispered, my mind racing.

"But it kills the Variant you're drawing Light from."

I whipped my head around to look at him. He didn't meet my gaze, continuing to stare out into the silently falling snow.

"The only way to give a Variant an ability is to draw it from another, but you take every scrap of Light they've ever possessed, and it kills them. Have you ever wondered how Davis got his ability?"

"No," I whispered, dread trickling down my spine.

"You may have seen mentions in the media about his ability manifesting in his early thirties—much later than is common." Lucian took a sip of his own whiskey. "Well, it didn't *manifest*. Your mother *gave* it to him."

The implications of that settled in the silence between us.

The snow continued to fall. Soundless. Steady. I knew the answer was right there in front of me. In the icy flakes, in the amber liquid, in Lucian's unsteady voice.

But I just couldn't wrap my mind around the idea that my mother had killed someone.

"What do you mean?" I sniffled, not entirely sure if it was from the cold or the emotion beginning to choke me. I lifted the glass to my lips once more; my hand was shaking.

"She didn't mean to do it. She knew as little as you did about how it works, why she glowed. But Davis is very manipulative, and she thought she was in love. So she drained another Variant dry, not knowing it would kill him. In the weeks after, she realized she was pregnant, and Davis, drunk on his new power to read people's minds, dumped her."

"How do you know all this? You said you didn't meet my mother until after I was born."

"I didn't. I lived in London for most of my youth, working for my father there. When an opportunity with Melior Group came up in New York, I moved back here, returning to my childhood home"—he gestured to the sprawling yard and the beautiful mansion—"and my sisters. Olivia was living in London with her family too. They came back not long after you and Joyce disappeared.

"I met your mother when I moved back, and realized she was my Vital. You were only a baby, but your father—"

"Don't call him that." My voice had the bite that was missing from the cold. I hadn't thought before I spoke, but the reaction felt right. "I don't have a father."

"Fair enough." Lucian nodded. "He was already out of the picture. He got what he wanted from your mother, and he was off, using his new ability to build his empire. It was only when he decided he wanted more from her that he came back."

"What did he want?"

"He wanted her to do it again. To kill for him again. To take another Variant's ability and help him figure out how she did it. He became radicalized, obsessed, had crazy ideas about how he could make more Variants. He wanted to change humans—give them abilities. It's not scientifically possible. Humans simply don't have the DNA, but he was . . . persistent."

"What did he do?" I was afraid of the answer, but I needed to know. I couldn't shy away from asking all the relevant questions, even if the answers pained me.

"Your mother felt awful about what she'd done. She thought a lot about turning herself in to the police, but she didn't have any family, and that would have left you alone in the world. She just couldn't do it. When Davis came back a few years later, he threatened her with exactly that. He said he would turn her in, make it sound like she was the one who'd orchestrated the whole thing. It would be his word against hers—a prominent businessman with friends in high places versus a single mom, trying to figure things out. She was scared. She knew what he was capable of, and once again she chose to put you first. So she ran."

And there it was—the answer to the question I'd been asking for as long as I could remember. I finally knew what my mother had been running from: my father.

I took a deep breath, trying to calm my racing heart. "Why didn't you come with us?"

If he was really her Variant, how did he ever let her leave? If she was his Vital, how could she stand to be away from him? The mere thought of separating from my guys sent a jolt of pain through my chest.

"It was the single hardest thing I've ever had to do, but it was the best way to keep you both safe. I was already well-known in Variant circles, in the business world. My face was recognizable. I had a large family. I couldn't just disappear. I would have been a liability. But by staying behind, I was able to help. I helped her stay hidden, stay one step ahead of him. I used every Melior Group resource at my disposal. Who do you think taught her how to make fake documents?"

I looked over at him and smiled. She'd taught me, but I'd never really thought about who taught her. "Yeah, she passed that skill on. Thanks, I guess."

"You're welcome." He smiled into his glass before taking another sip. "And I've seen your fakes. They're exceptional—better than some of the forgeries my professional guys can do."

"Thanks." My chest swelled a little. He didn't strike me as a man who gave praise frivolously.

"Evelyn, Davis's dogged pursuit of your mother and her ability is why we suspect he might be behind the Vital kidnappings. I never heard him mention it once since Joyce ran, despite the fact I kept him close, made deals with him, pretended to be friends with him—but I believe he never gave up on his mission to give others abilities. I think he just refined it. The fact that you're like your mom—not only a Vital but one with all the extra power—is why she had to keep you from him. She couldn't risk him using you like he did her. Hurting you."

"So she knew. You guys knew I was a Vital even that young?" Abilities and Light access usually didn't manifest until the teens.

"Alec was twelve when his ability started to manifest. You were only four but already showing signs of access to the Light. You weren't transferring to him or anything like that, but it was clear you had a special connection. You felt particularly safe and comforted with him, and he was crazy protective of you. Playing with a toddler for hours on end doesn't exactly top the list of desirable activities for most preteen boys. We all suspected. When you actually glowed one night during a temper tantrum, it was confirmed. Not long after that, Davis showed up again, making his threats."

"And she ran," I whispered, my breath misting in the cold.

"And she ran," Lucian repeated, his voice low, sad.

We were both silent for a while, staring at the snow still falling steadily. If it kept up this pace, we wouldn't be able to get a car down the driveway in the morning. I tried to digest all I'd learned, but it sat heavy in my stomach, making me feel a little lightheaded. Or maybe that was the whiskey.

I put my empty glass down on a table behind me and pulled the throw blanket tighter around myself. "Why did you keep me in the dark? You must have known who I was when you saw me at the gala. Why didn't you tell me?"

"Alec—"

"Fucking Alec," I cut him off.

"He's trying."

"I know."

We both sighed in the exact same way, mutually frustrated and grudgingly understanding.

"When your mother didn't check in at our designated time, I knew something was wrong. Unless, of course, it was a last-second decision, she usually kept me informed about where you were heading next—sometimes I would help her set it up. Then she would check in once she got there."

He looked at me expectantly, his eyes burning with the need to know why we'd abruptly left Melbourne.

"She found out I had a boyfriend," I explained. "We were on a plane within hours."

"Ah." He nodded. "I assumed you were both . . ." He swallowed audibly. This was clearly difficult for him to talk about, and I felt a pang of guilt for putting him through it. But I shoved it aside. I'd been lied to so much my whole life. I deserved some answers.

He refilled his glass and took a big sip. "I knew your mother was gone. There was no way she would have gone that long without getting in touch. When I saw you at the gala, you can't imagine how happy I was, Evelyn. To know you'd survived whatever it was that happened to her. To know we hadn't failed after all . . . but I was so mad at Alec for keeping it from me. For a long time."

"Still doesn't explain why you didn't tell *me*."

"What was I supposed to do? Walk up to you in a room full of gossiping Variants and say, 'Hey, I know you don't know me, but your mom was my Vital, and I was in love with her, and I know who and what you are—by the way, why are you dating Ethan and not Alec?'"

I rolled my eyes. "You could have come to me after."

"Alec begged me not to. He wasn't ready to face it all, and if I'm being completely honest, neither was I. You didn't know any of it, but you were where you belonged. You were safe and happy, and that's all that your mother and I ever wanted, so I decided to let you enjoy it for a little while. Plus, I had to do all I could to keep Davis from finding out you were alive. That's what I focused on."

I should have been angry—what was it about Zacarias men that made them so determined to keep secrets from me?—but I just couldn't seem to find the energy. He may not have handled it how I would have liked, but maybe he'd handled it how *my mother* would have wanted, and I couldn't fault him for that. Besides, considering all he'd told me, all that had happened recently, we couldn't afford to be at odds.

This was my new family. It was time to move forward.

I opened my mouth to say just that, but he beat me to it.

"I'm sorry, Evelyn." It came out on a whisper, his voice quivering slightly. "I only ever wanted to protect you and your mother."

"I know," I answered quickly. "But no more secrets and lies and *classifieds* and keeping things from me for my own good. I'm not a child anymore. I have a right to make my own informed decisions about my life."

"It's hard for me to think of you as anything other than that little four-year-old who was the light of our . . . of your mother's life, but I agree. No more secrets."

His little slip didn't go unnoticed. I was taken aback by just how much he seemed to care for me—I hadn't even known who he was until a few months ago—but knowing what he was to my mother changed everything. I was a Vital too; I knew what it meant to have Variants.

I couldn't trust myself to speak without crying. Instead, I took a tiny step closer to him and slowly lowered my head to his shoulder. After a beat, he wrapped a tentative arm around me and took another sip of whiskey.

~

The first day back after Christmas break was about as awful as I expected.

Walking to my last class, a Variant studies lecture, I was one-hundred-percent over it. I'd done my best to ignore the whispers and stares all day—to focus on the feel of Josh's hand in mine, the heaviness of Ethan's arm over my shoulder—but it was hard.

Dot's mood wasn't much better; any Light I'd transferred to her was gone, and she'd lost all ability to talk to animals without touching them. Zara's absence was excruciating when I had to attend classes we'd shared and sit by myself—nothing but her betrayal in the seat next to mine and people's gossip settling over me like a heavy cloak of deceit and pain.

I took my bulky coat off inside the building and headed for the lecture hall, juggling it with my book bag.

"Is it true?" A blonde girl who used to date Ethan blocked my path. I remembered her from when we first started dating; she'd never been shy to let me overhear her talk about how there was nothing special about me.

"Hi, my name is Evelyn. How nice of you to finally introduce yourself." Maybe because I was so acutely aware of Zara's absence, my reaction was pure sarcasm. Although it did feel good to finally use my real name. It was freeing, despite the fact that I was introducing myself to a total bitch.

"Come on, are you really a Vital?" She crossed her arms over her chest. She had some friends with her, but a few other people also stopped to listen. Everyone wanted to know; she was just the first one to actually ask.

"I'm sure you've seen the news." I refused to lower my voice. Let them listen. "Clearly I am."

"And you have *three* Bonded Variants?" She asked skeptically. "That's really rare."

"Yeah, I know." I matched her bitchy tone, laying a little more snark on top. It was all out in the open. I had nothing left to lose by being honest. A Melior Group agent was never far away, and they were all on orders to keep an eye on me. "And I don't have three."

She looked satisfied, turning to her friends. "I told you. No one—"

"I have four," I cut her off.

They all turned to face me.

"Bullshit." One of her friends scowled, but her eyes held a heavy dose of uncertainty.

"Believe whatever you want." I sighed, shifting my bag off my shoulder; it was getting heavy.

"Four Bonded Variants is unheard of," the blonde declared, as if I didn't already know. As if everyone in the hallway didn't already know. "You expect us to believe you have four and that the 'Master of Pain' himself is one of them? Please! You're probably just using this to explain away the fact that you're fucking half the school."

"Not half the school. Just four guys—*my* guys." I leaned forward for that last part. I was done being called a slut. I wasn't technically sleeping with them yet, but she didn't know that.

"I don't believe you. No one goes near Alec . . ." Her eyes widened at something over my shoulder. The crowd shifted, shuffling away while still trying to stay within earshot.

Then I felt Alec's solid presence at my back. I could just imagine the scowl he was wearing. If there was anyone who hated attention more than I did, it was him.

"Is there a problem here?" he asked in his cold, unyielding voice as Kyo, Marcus, and Jamie stepped into my field of vision, looking every part the tough Melior Group team they were.

No one answered. I leaned back a tiny fraction and let my back make contact with his chest. He placed one possessive hand on my hip, and I tilted my head up until I was looking at him upside down.

He was wearing the exact scowl I'd pictured—the one that pulled at the scar in his right eyebrow—and I could see up his nose. I don't know why, but that made me chuckle.

He looked down at me, amusement playing at his lips. Instead of explaining myself, I decided to ignore the whole thing.

"Hey, Alec," I whispered, giving him a genuine smile.

"Hey, Evie," he whispered back and smirked at me. "You good?"

"I am now."

He leaned down and planted one quick kiss to my head.

Everyone left me alone in my last lecture, some people even actively avoiding me. Apparently their fear of Alec now extended to me, and I was OK with that, especially if it provided a small reprieve from all the attention.

TWENTY-NINE

At the end of the day I got a ride home—I was still getting used to calling it that—from Kyo and Dot. They were now officially an item. Since they'd first kissed on the dance floor on Dot's birthday, every moment that Kyo wasn't on duty they spent together. They weren't the kind of couple who were sickening in their PDA, but Dot had no filter and told me all about it. In great detail. Including their sex life. And about the time Marcus joined them for a threesome. I always told her she was oversharing, but secretly I paid close attention . . . for future reference.

Judging by the way she'd whispered to Jamie before jumping in the car, her hand on his bicep as she leaned in close, I wouldn't be surprised if she ended up in bed with all three of them by the end of the week.

Alec had taken Josh and Ethan into the city to meet with Melior Group management. That was the only reason it wasn't one of them escorting me safely back to where I belonged. Instead, Marcus and Jamie followed us through the streets of Bradford Hills in an unmarked vehicle.

We'd managed to hold off this dreaded meeting for the past few weeks due to all the intense stuff that had happened, but the board had stepped in, and now even Lucian couldn't stop it from happening.

They'd managed to keep me out of it somehow—Lucian, Alec, and Tyler had probably all pulled some serious strings. I suspected Ethan and Josh had also offered themselves up much more easily than they otherwise would have to keep me away a little longer. But even so, one of the things we'd dreaded—one of the reasons we'd kept our Bond secret—had come to fruition. Both Josh and Ethan had formidable abilities, and now that it was known they had a Vital, Melior Group was recruiting them.

That was the first purpose of the meeting. The relationship between Variants and humans had only gotten more strained. There were constant protests outside Variant organizations and businesses. Groups of humans were ganging up on Variants with more benign abilities. Politicians were making outrageous comments in the press, capitalizing on the fear to gain more voters. And throwing fuel on the fire, Senator Christine Anderson was still missing.

The Variants were saying humans had taken her out because of all the work she was doing to bring Variant interests to the forefront in Washington. The humans were saying she'd been plotting to make them second-class citizens, so good riddance. Things were getting increasingly violent. Melior Group wanted all the help they could get.

The second reason for the meeting was even more serious. When any Variant finds a Vital, they have to register the Bond with the government. If the abilities are as dangerous as Alec's, Ethan's, and Josh's, this is taken particularly seriously. We hadn't technically broken any laws—because we *had* reported it to Melior Group (i.e. Lucian), which is tasked with handling the registrations and managing the risk to the general public—but we'd skirted the line by not keeping the humans in the loop.

Now that it had come out in such a public, spectacular way, they were pissed. We'd made them look bad.

Alec, Josh, and Ethan would be gone most of the evening; they might even stay the night in the city apartment if the meetings went long. Tyler was the only one home, working in his study.

That's where I found myself after changing into comfortable leggings and a soft black sweater—pacing the marble floor in front of the study's half-open door. I could hear Tyler inside speaking on the phone, but I wasn't paying attention.

I was thinking about the day I'd had. How freeing it was to say my real name, to not have to hide anymore, to have Alec at my back.

My talk with Lucian flashed through my mind too. How much more I felt like a part of his family with fewer secrets between us all.

Then I remembered what Nina had told me that day in the sauna. How much stronger we would be as a unit if we let the Bond strengthen naturally—if I followed my instincts instead of my mind and let the Light guide me.

I considered how much easier it was to control the Light—that I didn't really even *need* to control it—when we were relaxed and together and connected in the way I wanted us to be. As I'd been with Josh and Ethan in Alec's bed . . .

Decision made, I marched into Tyler's office and closed the door.

He looked up, the phone still to his ear. He was beautiful. He'd been at Bradford Hills most of the day and was still in his slacks and a patterned teal shirt, the sleeves rolled up, of course. His brown hair was messy as always, but his shoulders weren't as slumped as I'd come to expect these past few months; his face wasn't as drawn.

Locating Charlie and knowing he was still alive had lifted all our spirits.

"OK, just get it to me by morning so I can review. I have to go." He listened for a bit and then hung up.

I sat down on the edge of his desk. "You didn't have to hang up on my account."

"I'd been trying to end that call for five minutes." He chuckled, leaning back in his chair. "How was your first day back?"

"I don't want to talk about that." I waved my hand dismissively.

"OK." He stood, stretching his arms over his head and rolling his neck. My eyes couldn't help wandering down to where his shirt was straining to pull out of the waistband of his pants. "I need a break. Want to watch some TV?"

He made to move past me, but I placed one hand firmly against his hard chest.

"No." I shook my head, my voice betraying my nerves. I wanted this, I was sure of it, but I'd been rejected so many times . . .

"Then what do you want to do?" Tyler's voice lowered, and he stepped closer, resting one hand lightly on my knee.

In answer, my hand wandered over his defined shoulder to the back of his neck, and I leaned up, pressing my lips to his. He kissed me back, trailing both hands up the outside of my legs and resting them on my hips. I pulled him closer, opening my legs so he could step between them, and deepened the kiss. His tongue met mine.

After losing myself in his embrace for a while, I knew it was time. I pulled back, my hands still wrapped around his neck, my fingers playing with the crisp collar of his shirt.

"Ask me what I want to do," I demanded on a whisper, holding his gaze.

He indulged me, his swollen lips twitching in amusement. "What do you want to do, Eve?"

As his ability told him my intentions, I drove my point home by slowly and deliberately dragging one hand down his chest, over his abs, and all the way to between his legs. I stroked him, feeling the hardness through the fabric, as realization entered his face.

His breathing sped up and his hands flexed on my hips. "Are you sure?"

"I'm positive." I leaned forward and placed soft, sensual kisses on his neck, keeping a steady pace with my hand.

He groaned, stepping out of my reach. "This will mean taking it to the next level with all of us. You understand that, right? The Light is a powerful force. We're not animals, we can resist it, but it won't be easy. And you won't *want* to either. Are you positive you're ready for that with Alec?"

"Yes." I wasn't, not entirely. Judging by his disapproving look, his ability had told him as much, so I rushed to explain. "Look, I know Alec and I still have a lot to sort out, but I'm done pretending he's not in my Bond. I'm done allowing distance and insecurity to create more tension. Mentally, I may have some doubts, but in every other way, I'm ready. I want this, Tyler. I want you."

I kept my gaze locked on his, even though I felt incredibly vulnerable. His ability had told him I wasn't sure what to expect from my relationship with Alec, but it would also have told him how sure I was about everything else. I was choosing to follow my instincts—put my faith in the Light. I just hoped Tyler would see that.

I finally dropped my eyes, the potential of another rejection weakening my resolve, but that's what seemed to break him out of his own thoughts

He grabbed my hands and pulled me to my feet, then toward the door.

"You're not even going to talk to me about it?" I tried to tug my hand out of his grasp, frustrated, but he held on.

"I'm not saying no." He smirked over his shoulder as he reached the door. "This door doesn't have a lock."

He yanked the door open and quickened his pace toward the stairs.

I snapped out of my shock as we started to climb up, the frustration and fear of rejection wiped away by Tyler's cheeky grin and the lust in his eyes. Giddy anticipation replaced it, giving me a burst of energy, and I overtook him on the stairs.

Now I was the one pulling him behind me, and we ended up running and laughing all the way to his room.

As soon as his bedroom door was locked, the energy changed again. It turned more serious as we came together, his lips devouring mine as he held me close. It turned more intense as he walked me backward toward his bed.

When the backs of my knees hit the mattress, I broke the kiss, and before I could reach the hem of my sweater, Tyler was yanking it over my head.

I wanted his hands all over me. I wanted his mouth on my skin. Once again, he gave me exactly what I wanted, licking and kissing my neck as he unclasped my bra.

My breathing was heavy, my heart hammering with anticipation. The thought alone that I wouldn't have to stop, wouldn't have to hold myself back, was sending jolts of pleasure straight to my core.

I threw my bra aside and made quick work of Tyler's buttons, shoving the shirt off his shoulders. As he pulled it off, I pressed my lips to his chest. He was warm and smelled like the body wash I'd taken to using since the night of the invasion—when he'd let me use his shower. It smelled so much better mingling with his natural scent.

I kissed my way up the flat planes of his chest to his neck, running my hands up the muscled arms that had caught my attention that very first day.

His breathing was loud in my ear as he pressed himself closer and closer, his hands gripping my hips, my waist, my ass; kneading my breasts; never lingering in one spot for too long. As if he didn't know what he wanted to touch first.

But I knew exactly what I wanted. I ghosted my fingers over his shoulders and trailed them down his back as my mouth found his. Once my hands reached the waistband of his pants, I pushed my tongue into his mouth and, without wondering when I should stop, undid the clasp.

I didn't waste time, shoving both the underwear and the pants down. I touched him in the way I'd wanted to for so long, wrapping my hand around his erection and basking in the way he moaned into my mouth, the way his hips thrust forward, encouraging me.

Just as I was increasing my pace, intoxicated by his every reaction to what I was doing to him, his hand clasped around my wrist, and he pulled away.

"If you keep doing that, this will be over before it starts."

"I thought it had already started," I teased.

"I want to come inside you, not in your hand." He looked me dead in the eye as he said it, reminding me that was exactly where I wanted him. *Inside me.*

Suddenly I couldn't think about anything else.

The Light was *purring* as it flitted over my skin and into him in a slow, steady trickle, unrestrained. My body was flushed and ready.

My mouth, however, was apparently determined to ruin the mood.

"You mean you want to come inside a condom inside me, right? Safety first." My breathy voice betrayed how aroused I was, even if my words weren't exactly seductive.

Tyler's lips pulled up in a brilliant, amused grin. "Yes, that's exactly what I meant."

"Sorry . . ." That wasn't the sexiest thing to say with his dick in my hand.

"Don't be. I would never be so reckless."

I circled my arms around his middle, leaning my forehead on his shoulder.

His hand threaded into my hair and nudged my gaze back to his. He looked at me with so much affection and understanding it took my breath away. Or maybe it was his mouth that took my breath away. The kiss he pressed to my lips was intense yet gentle, but he kept his tongue back. He was being sweet and patient, putting me at ease.

But I didn't want gentle; I was ready for *more.*

I smiled against the kiss and then sucked his bottom lip into my mouth, biting it. He gave me a devious grin that reminded me of bad-boy Tyler—the one I'd briefly glimpsed at The Hole, who wore leather jackets and had women gossiping about how good he was in bed.

He stepped out of the pants and underwear that had pooled around his ankles and picked me up roughly. His hands gripped my ass, and I wrapped my legs around his waist, my hands flying to his neck so I wouldn't fall.

He dropped open-mouthed kisses on my collarbone as he moved, then he dropped me onto his bed. I bounced a little on the mattress, giggling, as giddy and excited as I was turned on and ready.

Tyler stood in front of me, gloriously naked, for only a beat before crawling over me, his knees on either side of my thighs. He placed another searing kiss to my lips, but before I could pull him closer, he was moving down my body.

He kissed a trail down the center of my torso, deliberately bypassing my breasts as his hands dragged a path down my sides.

Once his face and his hands reached the waistband of my leggings, he leaned back and pulled them off along with my underwear. He threw the clothing over his shoulder dramatically as his eyes raked over my completely naked body, from my toes all the way to my face. When our eyes met, he leaned forward, and I lifted up onto my elbows. We couldn't resist coming together anymore. We didn't want to.

He crawled back onto the bed and pressed the length of his body over mine as I pulled him down. We kissed deeply, breathing heavily through our noses, our hands roaming, our bodies starting to move to the rhythm of our mouths. I opened my legs wider and felt his hardness. We both groaned, and Tyler broke the kiss, pressing his forehead to mine as his hips continued to grind against me.

"I want you inside me," I whispered against his lips. I'd never been more sure of anything in my life; his ability would have made that clear to him.

"Fuck." He groaned before getting up and going to his bedside table.

As he ripped open the foil packet and put the condom on, I took in his glorious body.

He was a little bit taller than Josh but just as lean; hard muscle hid beneath his pressed shirts and tailored pants. I let my eyes linger on his tight ass before my attention was drawn to a large tattoo across his upper back. Scrawled in a bold but intricate font were the words "Knowledge Is Power." The simple sentiment was so him, and the fact that he had ink under his clean-cut appearance reminded me of his slightly shady, dangerous past.

Condom in place, he came back to the foot of the bed. I moved backward against the pillows as he crawled over the top of me, his eyes full of need, almost feral.

He was letting his instincts take over. And judging by the narrow-eyed look he was giving me, his instincts were to claim me.

He pushed my legs apart and settled between them, holding himself up on one arm. His lips crushed fiercely to mine—repayment for the way I'd bitten him earlier—and his hand roamed, grabbing and feeling and teasing my skin on its jagged path to the spot between my legs.

Once there, he broke the kiss, his eyes closed, his mouth panting.

His fingers trailed up and down, spreading the wetness and rubbing the most sensitive spots with the perfect pressure. He alternated pushing his fingers inside and rubbing my clit, tormenting me in the most delicious way, giving me a taste of exactly what I wanted, then changing it up.

Just as I was starting to get frustrated with his antics, he shifted and slowly, deliberately pressed his length into me. Inch by glorious inch, Tyler filled me until he was all the way in, and we both groaned at the sensation.

Finally, *finally*, I was breaking down one of the last barriers between me and my Bonded Variants, and everything about it felt so fucking right—his smell, the way his hands caressed my body, his weight on top of me, the feel of him inside me.

For a few moments we just stared at each other, the connection deepening in a way clearly fueled by the Light but also in ways that had nothing to do with our supernatural Bond. Yes, I was his Vital and he was my Variant. But I was also a woman and he was a man, and we'd wanted each other in this most intimate, carnal way for a long time.

A messy brown lock fell over his forehead, and I didn't hesitate to brush it away, threading my fingers into his hair, moving my hand to the back of his head and attacking his lips with mine again. He started to move, and I met every thrust with my own hips.

Tyler seemed to know exactly what I wanted. Just as I imagined his fingers twining into my own hair, there was his hand, pulling gently at the strands. Before I'd even fully formed the thought that I wanted my breasts crushed against his hard chest, he was letting a little more of his weight onto me. As I let the sensations take over my mind, chasing the highest form of pleasure, Tyler adjusted his movements and angled his hips in exactly the perfect way.

His thrusts became harder but shallower, barely even pulling out as he ground himself against me.

I pressed my head back into the pillow, not even caring about the sounds coming out of my mouth as I rode the waves of pleasure.

The orgasm lasted longer than I was used to. As I clawed desperately at Tyler's back, the heady, molten sensation built and built. My stomach muscles clenched as I lifted my legs and wrapped them around his hips, making it possible for him to drive deeper into me, drive me higher. I moaned loudly and my vision went blurry as wave after wave washed over me. My thighs started to tremble, and I put my feet back down onto the mattress.

Before I had a chance to catch my breath, Tyler changed it up again, pushing in and out with more force— longer, faster strokes that drew out my own pleasure—then groaned his release into my neck.

He rolled onto his back beside me, and our hands found each other between our naked, panting bodies.

As my breathing evened, I turned my head to him. "You cheated."

He looked at me and smirked. "Are you complaining?"

"No. I couldn't be more satisfied."

THIRTY

Alec arrived back from his meeting at Melior Group headquarters while Tyler was still inside me—for the second time. He pounded on the door, demanding to be let in. We thought he was just feeling the Light's pull and ignored him until we finished. But it turned out he'd been trying to call us for over an hour.

The Melior Group board had finally approved the large-scale attack they'd been planning for weeks, and we needed to move out immediately. The jet was being fueled.

He pointedly ignored the fact that Tyler opened his door in nothing but underwear, as well as me on the bed, nothing but a crisp white sheet covering my still-flushed body. It was only when Tyler disappeared into the bathroom that Alec looked at me.

So many emotions crossed his face I struggled to unpack them, but the way his hands clenched and unclenched by his sides told me at least some of his urgency actually had been driven by his need to get to me.

"Fuck," he breathed, finally letting the lust hood his eyes. Despite my just having had sex with Tyler twice, my body reacted to the desire in his gaze, and I squirmed on the bed. But he turned on his heel and rushed down the hall.

The next few hours were a flurry of activity, everyone packing, preparing, bustling to the airport. Olivia cried on and off, Dot worried about whether to bring Squiggles, and Tyler and Lucian were constantly on the phone, making last-minute arrangements and giving orders.

We hadn't had time for the guys to update me on their meeting. I hadn't had time to tell them about Tyler and me either, but they knew.

I'd showered and dressed and was packing when they got home, but Josh took one look at me, kissed me passionately, and grinned from ear to ear, anticipation and happiness dancing in his eyes.

"Well, OK then," he said before releasing me. Ethan kissed me just as passionately, lifting my feet off the ground, but the look in his face was a little more confused.

Josh dragged him away so they could get packed, and I saw him whisper something, their heads bent together. Then Ethan's back straightened, and he looked back at me with wide eyes. If Josh hadn't pulled him along, I had a feeling he would have marched back to me, locked the door, and forgotten about the mission entirely.

Since then, they'd both been throwing me knowing looks full of promise that made my heart beat a little faster and my mind wander to lascivious thoughts.

Before I had a chance to process though, we were in the air. Then, hours later, we were landing in Bangkok and making our way to the compound.

Only then did Tyler explain to Josh, Ethan, and me that we weren't technically allowed to come. I was only permitted to be there because I was an active operative's Vital. If something happened to Alec in the field, I needed to be close by to transfer Light to him.

It was stinking hot and humid in Thailand. We were in the wilderness somewhere, well off the beaten tourist track, but Melior Group had managed to find a compound with modern amenities and multiple dwellings to use as a base of operations. Charlie and another eighty or so suspected captive Vitals were in a low building a few miles to the south.

For the past week, teams of Melior Group operatives had been moving into the area—some into this compound, some into resorts and other places nearby—and we now had a small army, as well as all the information we could gather about the target location through observation and bribing locals.

All this I'd overheard in the strategy meeting Josh, Ethan, and I had just been thrown out of.

I hadn't been able to help myself; I'd asked a question to clarify something, and everyone in the room had turned to look at me as if I were insane.

"Let me make this perfectly clear . . ." Tyler lectured us in his stern man-in-charge voice as he promptly escorted us out. "You three are here as civilians, just like Nina, Olivia, Henry, and Dot. You will not be assisting in the strategy, and you will not be going in with the highly trained Melior Group agents. Am I understood?"

We all grumbled a response, and he nodded before turning back to the main house.

"We might as well get some sleep." I sighed and started walking toward the cottage at the back of the property. Hopefully we'd only be there a night or two.

"I'm going to see if I can get back in there." Josh gave me a light kiss on the forehead and followed after Tyler. His need to know everything burned as bright as mine. I smiled after him.

"I need to cool off. I'm gonna jump in the pool first," Ethan said. Personally, I was enjoying the break from the freezing New York winter, but the heat had Ethan struggling to breathe most of the time, and he always planted himself under the AC in every room.

As I walked through the manicured grounds, my flip-flops slapping on the pavers, I pulled my loose tank top away from my sweaty skin and briefly considered joining him. But I desperately needed to lie down. It was early evening, the sun only just dissipating into twilight, but none of us had slept much in the past twenty-four hours.

Anyone here *not* as a civilian spent most of the day planning and going over maps and reports, making sure they were as prepared as possible. They would be going in at four in the morning—while it was still dark and silent.

Hopefully they'd get some rest before.

The cottage was the designated civilian area. It had four bedrooms and a small open kitchen and living space. Dot's parents had one room, Dot and Nina were sharing the one with single beds, and the guys and I had yet to arrange ourselves between the other two rooms.

I showered and crawled into the bed of the closest free room, wearing nothing but underwear and a tank top. Everyone besides me and the guys had already gone to bed, although I'm sure no one was sleeping. We all wanted to be in that meeting, but Tyler was right; we were too emotionally involved, and we needed to let the professionals do their work. It was Charlie's best chance.

As I lay on my back, enjoying the breeze coming in through the window, I tried to will my body to relax, my mind to stop obsessing over what was to come. But it was pointless. My mind was wired, and my body was humming with need.

As if on cue, the door opened, and the perfect distraction entered.

Ethan was shirtless, his broad muscular chest bathed in moonlight. He dropped his towel and shirt to the floor and took two steps toward the bed before stopping.

"You need to tell me if you want me to sleep in another room." His low voice was strained. His jet-black hair was still wet from the pool, and a droplet landed on his shoulder, glistening in the blue light. "Because I can't lie next to you all night and not . . . do things."

"What do you mean?" I put on my best innocent voice. "What things?"

I dragged my fingertips up the front of my thigh, up my belly, between my breasts and propped my head on my hand so I could see him better.

He groaned, dragging his hands down his handsome face, but when he took them away, he was smiling, the dimples showing. "You're teasing me?"

"Nope." That time the innocence was gone. "I fully intend to follow through."

He closed the distance, and I lifted myself onto my knees to meet him. We crashed into each other with such intensity we nearly lost our balance. Kissing and giggling, we ripped the last few scraps of clothing from each other's bodies.

He ran his big hands all over me, and I did the same to him. As he pushed his tongue into my mouth, I grabbed a handful of his ass. It was cool from where the wet fabric of his swim trunks had clung to him, and the skin warmed under my touch.

With Tyler it had been intense, and more serious, and everything I'd needed it to be. With Ethan it was playful, our movements less restrained. I felt giddy. I was aroused but also just plain happy to be in his arms and touching him how I wanted to.

I spared a moment to make sure my Light control was locked down, but I'd transferred to Tyler just an hour ago to give him an extra edge in the planning, and now that I was giving in to my Light-driven instincts, it was nowhere near as pushy as it usually was. I was doing what it wanted me to do.

Satisfied I wouldn't be complicit in starting a bushfire in the Thai wilderness, I finally let my hands drag around to Ethan's belly, eager to properly explore the hardness pressing into my front.

I broke our kiss to see what I was doing as my hand wrapped around the base of his erection. I paused, letting myself fully take in the size of him before dragging my hand up . . . and up and up.

Ethan was a big guy and *every* part of him was in proportion. I took a deep breath, a tiny bit of worry breaking through my lust. He was bigger than Tyler, bigger than any guy I'd ever slept with. But he was my Variant—meant for me in every way. It would be fine. *Right?*

He must have noticed my hesitation, because he chuckled and pressed his forehead to mine. "You'll be fine, baby. We just need to make sure you're real relaxed."

"Mmhmm." I couldn't seem to manage words, let alone entire sentences.

Effortlessly, Ethan picked me up and dropped me onto my back. But instead of lowering himself on top of me, he sank to his knees and put his mouth right between my legs.

I gasped, not having expected him to go straight for the sweet spot, but he was a man on a mission, and my lucky stars, was he good at that! His tongue, his lips, the occasional scrape of his teeth . . . And then he put two fingers inside me, and I was a goner. The orgasm washed over me quickly and intensely, but I somehow managed to stay silent, remembering there were other people on the other side of the walls.

Ethan kissed his way up my body as I caught my breath, but once again, instead of lowering himself on top of me, he pulled me up by the hands and picked me up. I wrapped my legs around his thick waist, and he sat down on the bed with me in his lap, producing a condom seemingly out of nowhere.

He must have had it with him, but I couldn't care less where it had come from. I was as relaxed and wet as I was going to get. He slid the condom down and held his erection at the base.

"You're in control," he whispered, his deep voice sending a shiver down my spine. A light sheen of sweat covered my skin, and I could feel dampness at the nape of Ethan's neck as I held on to it for balance.

I lifted myself onto my knees and looked him in the eye as I slowly took him in. His eyes fluttered at the sensation, his full lips parting as his breathing deepened. My hips met his, and we both groaned, my eyes finally falling closed.

The feeling of fullness was almost overwhelming, and I gave myself a moment to adjust. Ethan waited patiently; the only sign he was aching to move inside me were his hands on my waist, his fingers pressing almost painfully into my flesh.

When I started to move, slowly, deliberately, he released me and leaned back on his hands. The only part of him that moved were his hips, thrusting up to meet mine as we found a steady rhythm. His abdominal muscles clenched and relaxed with every roll of his hips, and I could feel his thick thighs under me.

My hands on his shoulders, I focused on the feeling building deep inside me once again—almost as deep as Ethan's impressive length could reach.

I rolled my head back, and the wavy ends of my hair tickled my lower back.

We were panting, little moans and groans escaping here and there, but we were doing our best to stay mostly silent.

"That's it, ride my cock." Ethan's words came out on a low growl as his hand found my breast and he massaged it, running his thumb over the nipple.

Those words and that hand pushed me over the edge again. I leaned forward, biting his shoulder so I wouldn't call out. He kept pumping his hips under me, losing the rhythm a bit as his movements became more frenzied.

The hand on my breast moved down to grab my ass, squeezing and guiding me on top of him, and then he stiffened too, his groan of release a little too loud. He leaned forward and brought his other arm around my middle, burying his face in my neck.

Then he leaned back, letting me fall on top of him. Despite the oppressive humidity, I pressed my sweaty cheek to his chest and listened to the pounding of his heart.

I was exactly where I wanted to be, and I dozed off with Ethan running his hands through my hair.

Some time later, as I lay half-asleep in Ethan's arms, I heard the door open and close softly. Someone shuffled about the room, and then the bed dipped behind me.

I caught a hint of expensive aftershave as Josh's long, soft fingers caressed my shoulder. He trailed a line down my arm and over my hip, his touch so soft it almost tickled.

And that's all it took to get me going again.

I'd known it was going to be hard to resist them after I crossed this line with Tyler; I just hadn't expected giving in to be so *easy*. It was effortless the way my body responded to his touch, the way I rolled over so I was facing him, the way our lips came together in the softest of kisses.

Tyler and Ethan had both checked with me, making sure I was ready for what we were about to do, but this was Josh. He didn't need to ask; he knew I wanted this, and he was ready to give it to me.

I hadn't bothered to get dressed after Ethan and I had sex, and Josh was completely naked too. He kissed me slowly—his lips pressing into mine in the most torturous way, preventing our tongues from deepening it just yet—and I let my hands explore his body as he was exploring mine, with soft, slow movements.

As I tugged on his hip, shuffling closer, he finally ran his tongue over mine, pressing his body flush against me. He pulled my knee until my leg was hitched over his hip, then he ran his hand down the outside of my thigh until he had a firm but soft grip on my ass.

I felt his erection between us as we both started to rock gently against each other, our bodies no longer able or willing to keep still.

Josh moved his hand just a little farther over and felt how wet I was. He moaned softly into my mouth. It was getting hard to breathe, but neither one of us was willing to break the kiss, which was becoming frantic as the rest of our bodies reacted.

Without taking his lips from mine, he rolled us over so he was on top of me, and I could feel him—hard, smooth, and right where I wanted him. He rocked his hips, rubbing his length up and down, spreading the moisture between my legs with every movement. The friction was driving me wild, making me almost forget there were other people in the house, that Ethan had been lightly snoring right next to me when Josh got into the bed.

I finally pulled away, nudging his shoulders lightly, and he lifted himself higher to look at me. His perfect face was as flushed as my whole body felt, his usually immaculate hair a mess, his vibrant green eyes hooded.

I *needed* him inside me.

"Condom," I whispered, hating that I was breaking the spell of silence but not willing to risk unsafe sex.

I bit my swollen bottom lip, showing him I didn't want to wait any longer.

He smiled, flashing me his perfectly straight teeth, and moved to do as I'd instructed, but a condom appeared instantly between us. It was already out of its packet, pinched lightly between Ethan's fingers.

We both turned to look at him, doubt bubbling up in my chest. Maybe Ethan didn't want to watch Josh fuck me in the exact bed where we'd just done the same thing. Maybe Josh didn't want an audience. It felt right to me—I had nothing to hide from either of them—but I hadn't stopped to consider how *they* wanted this to play out.

Wordlessly, Josh took the condom and sat up to put it on.

Ethan caressed my cheek with the back of his knuckles. His eyes were hooded with lust, but they also held a hint of uncertainty. "I can leave if . . ."

I looked at Josh as he lowered himself back down and caressed my hair.

"Doesn't bother me." To prove his point, he started to press into me slowly, pulling back out and watching my face.

I looked back at Ethan. "Stay."

I returned his lazy smile, and then my focus was back on Josh.

He pushed all the way into me in one slow, smooth movement. He didn't stop, didn't wait for me to adjust. He was done taking his time.

Josh was sure and quietly confident in all he did, and this was no different. He started moving in and out of me at a pace that completely contrasted with the sensual and languorous way this had started. Hard and intense. He watched me the whole time, his eyes drinking in my expression, the way my lips parted on a moan, the way my eyes struggled to stay open.

His hips hit a particular spot every time he slammed into me, and it was driving me to an orgasm; it was going to wash over me any second.

"I can't . . ." I panted, but he was relentless. "Can't keep quiet."

In answer, Josh turned my head gently toward Ethan. As the orgasm crashed through my body like waves against a cliff, Ethan pressed his mouth to mine, swallowing all the noise I couldn't contain. He pulled away just in time for me to watch Josh finally lose control.

His eyes closed, the most beautiful look of serenity wiping the intensity from his features as he held himself inside me, riding out his own release.

He collapsed next to me as Ethan pressed a soft kiss to my cheek.

Once Josh's breathing evened out, he raised one hand in a fist above me. "Thanks for the assist, bro."

Ethan didn't even skip a beat, and they fist-bumped over my naked, sweaty body. "Anytime, man."

"You're both idiots." I rolled my eyes but wasn't entirely able to contain my giggles.

This felt so right. I couldn't believe I'd waited so long to do it.

THIRTY-ONE

I never did fully fall asleep that night. The apprehension about what was due to happen in a few short hours was palpable. I stayed in bed between Josh and Ethan, dozing and letting my mind wander.

Ethan's light snores filled the quiet, mingling with the sound of insects from the open window, but even he didn't stay asleep all night. Josh didn't even try. Every time I looked over at him, his eyes were wide open, even though he was lying perfectly still.

As I was contemplating checking the time, the door opened, and Tyler stepped inside. He paused, taking in our naked bodies sprawled on the bed, not a scrap of clothing or sheets in sight.

"Sweet fucking Christ," he breathed, running his hand through his hair.

"No Christ here," Josh answered as Ethan rolled over, rubbing his eyes, "but there was plenty of fucking."

I sat up. "Is it time?"

Tyler took a deep breath and nodded. "It's time. I thought you'd want to know. Plus, I think Alec could use some juice."

I was already half-dressed by the time he finished speaking. I pulled on some shorts and a tank top, not bothering with underwear. I wouldn't know where to look for it anyway.

Tyler led me through the manicured grounds back to the main house; the bright lights still on made me squint.

There was a flurry of activity, some black-clad men strapping on gear, others testing the communication devices that sat snug in their ears. Alec was strapping a belt with more knives than I could count to his right thigh. His team was nearby, also arming up.

I walked straight up to him, weaving through the busy people.

"Hey." I had to raise my voice to be heard over the hubbub. He straightened and turned to face me, his ice-blue eyes taking in my haphazard appearance—the shorts inside out, my hair an absolute mess.

His expression was unreadable; he was already getting into his "dangerous secret organization badass" frame of mind and wasn't giving much away.

"Ty said you might need . . . um . . ." I didn't know why I was so reluctant to voice that I was there to transfer Light to him. He was my Variant. Everyone in the room already knew that.

"Yeah." He nodded, giving me a little smirk before darting his eyes about the room and frowning. Maybe he was feeling as unsure as I was. This wasn't exactly our usual dynamic.

"Just . . ." He lowered his voice and rubbed the back of his neck, scowled at the ground, then straightened to his full height. He looked pissed off, but I didn't feel as if it was directed at me. "It'll be good to have a bit of an edge but not too much. I haven't had a chance to train with extra Light, and it could be a distraction."

I nodded. He'd spent years training to be a killing machine without what I could provide. Giving him too much could actually be counterproductive.

I held my hand out, offering the Light to him in the least intrusive way I knew. But he surprised me by wrapping his calloused hand around my wrist and tugging me forward.

I found myself chest to chest with him, and instead of focusing on the task at hand, my mind helpfully supplied vivid images of what I'd been doing just hours before.

He must have seen the lust in my face, because he smirked again, narrowing his eyes. "Just a little, Eve."

Then he took a breath before pressing his lips to mine.

I wrapped my arms around his neck, his buzzed hair prickling my fingers, and Alec kissed me in a way that was sweeter than I'd thought him capable of.

I knew this was an important moment for him, for us. He was trusting me to do my job as his Vital. I needed to keep that trust by not getting distracted by the ache between my legs.

And so, even as I delighted in his lips on mine, I focused on the tingly, humming sensation of the Light flowing into him. I replenished what he was missing and gave him a little extra—just enough to make his ability reach a little farther, make the pain a little more intense, let him use it a little longer. Then I cut it off. It was easier than I'd ever thought possible.

He took that as a sign to break the kiss, pulling away while still keeping me in his arms.

I licked my lips, wanting to taste him again, drag him back to the dark room in the cottage and complete the connection to my Bond. "Be careful."

I fixed him with a look that I hoped conveyed my sincerity and stepped out of his arms. He nodded once, and I watched him pull his hard, unfeeling mask back into place. He started barking orders as Kyo handed him a very large gun, and I turned away, going to stand just outside the back door.

I couldn't watch them leave.

Dot was sitting on a log, her elbows on her knees. I leaned on the wall next to her, and we listened to the sounds of heavily armed men and women heading out to bring her brother home.

I reached a hand out, and she took it, squeezing it firmly.

~

I was pacing the kitchen, arms crossed, listening intently to what Tyler, Lucian, and the other Melior Group operatives were doing a few feet away.

A swell of panic within me kept fighting to break through. It would bubble up to my chest, and I would squash it down with a deep breath. It would gurgle up to my throat, and I would only just hold it back by focusing on moving my feet, step by agonizing step, on the pale green tiles.

It couldn't have been more than an hour since the organized force of Melior Group fighters had taken off for the compound. They'd converged on the low structure, taken out the few guards posted at gates, and breached the building.

And then all communications had gone down.

Anyone associated with or employed by Melior Group was keeping their cool.

Lucian leaned on the dining table, still strewn with maps and tablets from the strategy meeting, his intelligent eyes watching everything, monitoring for any missteps.

Tyler flitted from one place to another, typing furiously at a computer one minute, then issuing commands to groups of people the next.

Ethan was sitting on the kitchen bench, his head in his hands. Josh leaned next to him, watching the whole room, but even he couldn't keep the worry off his handsome face.

Dot had run back to the cottage as soon we'd lost contact with our teams, updating her parents. I couldn't imagine how difficult this must be for them.

"Fuck," Ethan growled and looked up, hugging his big arms around his middle. He looked more like a scared kid lost in the mall than he did like the six-foot-four, 250-pound man he was.

Tyler glanced in our direction, murmured something to the computer tech he was standing next to, and came over. He placed a comforting hand on Ethan's shoulder and tucked me into his side.

"It's OK, Kid." He gave Ethan's shoulder a squeeze, then addressed us all. "Guys, we knew this might happen. The comms all went down that day at Bradford Hills. We're pretty sure it was due to a Variant with an ability related to tech. We expected to come up against it again. We're prepared for this. OK?"

"Lucian?" Olivia's panicked voice came from the back door. She'd arrived just in time to hear Tyler's little speech. Dot stood next to her, holding her hand, and Henry was behind her, his eyes bloodshot and drawn.

Lucian got up and went to stand by his family

"He's right, Olivia." He pulled her into a hug. "We've got this under control."

We spent the next hour on a knife's edge. Olivia would burst into tears sporadically, Dot or Henry rubbing soothing circles on her back.

I continued to pace.

Tyler and Lucian continued to work.

The clock continued to tick with no news, not even a report of movement from the scouts watching the area.

"It's time," Lucian finally declared, his voice firm, and the Melior Group staff sprang into action.

"Time for what?" I asked. Tyler had started strapping weapons to his body near the kitchen, and I went to him. "Time for what, Ty?"

"We're going in," he answered, and Josh stepped forward to help him strap on his Kevlar.

"Going in?" The past hour of waiting had been so tense my mind couldn't seem to process the fact that things were happening.

"Yeah." Tyler checked his gun and holstered it. "This is part of the contingency. We gave the A team time to do their job. They haven't been in contact and haven't returned. It's time for backup. That's us."

I looked around the room. By "us" he meant every Melior Group employee left. They may have been computer geniuses and tactical masterminds, but they were all just as highly trained as anyone else permitted to attend this mission. They were all gearing up.

Within five minutes, another twenty people were ready to move out. Other teams from other locations were calling in their readiness over the speakers.

"All right, there won't be anyone left here with you guys, but you're perfectly safe, OK?" Tyler addressed the three of us, then tipped his head in the direction of Dot's family. "Olivia and Henry both worked for Melior Group at some stage. They've had training. They'll know what to do in an emergency." At last he turned to Josh, the only one of us as seemingly calm as the professionals in the room. "If all else fails, stick to the plan. Get her out."

Josh nodded, and I squashed my annoyance at the fact that there was some last resort plan I was unaware of. Instead I focused on Tyler.

I stepped into his space, and he embraced me without hesitation. Pressing my lips to his, I let the Light flow freely, even giving it a little push. I wanted him to have every advantage he could out there, and unlike Alec, he didn't need to worry about controlling his ability in the field.

We pulled apart, and he placed a kiss on my forehead. "I'll be right back." He smiled, but the anxiety threatening to choke me wasn't pacified.

Most of the others were already out the door, but Lucian stood to the side, waiting for Tyler. Without thinking about it too much, I walked up to him.

"Would it help if you had a little boost too?" I asked. His ability was defensive, and I'd perfected transferring Light to non-Bonded Variants. If this was the only way I could help, I'd drain myself dry so my family could be safe.

"It can't hurt." He smiled tentatively.

I reached out my hand, and he took it gently in his. Closing my eyes in concentration, I pushed a decent amount into him, and he gave me a little squeeze when he'd had enough.

"Thank you, Evelyn." His eyes were a little brighter, his posture a little straighter, and I wondered if he'd had any Light transferred to him at all since my mother had taken me and run off into the night.

Acting on instinct, I gave him a quick hug before scurrying back to Ethan's side.

Then they were gone, and we went back to waiting.

Nina joined us not long after they left, and Dot updated her on the situation in minute detail. I think it made her feel better to have something to do, something to say. Nina listened to it all with patience and understanding.

As the first hints of light started to announce the dawn, I rubbed at my chest, feeling a pang of alarm. Had it been too long? Should we be doing something? Calling someone?

The weight on my chest grew heavier, and I started to wonder if I was experiencing the beginnings of a panic attack. I leaned on the bench with one hand as the pressure increased—except it wasn't exactly pressure. It wasn't caused by the crushing anxiety of waiting to see if they were all OK.

It was *pain*. It was that pain that was becoming more and more familiar to me every time one of my Variants put himself in danger and used too much of his ability. And it was getting worse.

"No!" I cried out as I bent over double. The urge to run, to get to him *now*, felt as intense, though not quite as all-consuming, as it had the night I'd run to save Ethan.

"Eve?" That was the first hint of panic I'd heard in Josh's voice. His hands were all over me, checking for injuries. Ethan was on my other side, doing the same.

"Oh no." Nina shot up from the couch. "She feels the pull. Something is wrong with one of her Variants."

There were only seven people in the room, but it erupted into chaos, most of it centered around me. Some of them were talking over each other, trying to decide what to do; some of them were asking me questions.

I focused on my breathing and on Ethan and Josh's soothing touch. The pain, the pull, was still in my chest, but it had stopped getting worse. Whatever my Variant had been doing, he'd stopped doing it. He was drained, weak, but he wasn't dying. *Yet.*

"I have to go there," I whispered. No one heard me over the cacophony of voices. I straightened, squared my shoulders, and looked around. Slowly, one by one, they returned my stare and grew quiet. "I have to go there. I have to help."

"Evelyn, I can't possibly let you do that." Henry was putting on his parent voice, but he wasn't my parent, and I wasn't a child.

"With all due respect, I'm not asking for your permission. Two of my Variants are in there. One of them could be close to death. I'm going." To my surprise, neither Ethan nor Josh was arguing with me.

"What other choice do we have?" Ethan growled, crossing his arms.

Josh sighed. "Tyler is going to kill me, but I can't live with myself if we do nothing and . . ." His unfinished sentence settled heavily over the room.

Olivia stopped crying and stood from the couch, wiping her tears away angrily. "I'm with Eve. I'm sick of sitting around, losing more of my family as every hour passes."

"Olivia!" Henry turned to her, horrified, but the rest of us were already springing into action.

"Henry, Charlie is in there. My brother is in there. Alec, Tyler . . ." She started ticking names off on her fingers.

"Kyo," Dot added, her face desperate. I wondered if she'd realized yet how hopelessly in love with him she was.

I went to Dot and pulled her into a hug.

"I'm thinking it might be a good idea . . ." I started at the same time she said, "I think you should juice me . . ."

We both nodded, no more words necessary, and I took her hands in mine, doing the most efficient and quick Light transfer I'd ever done. When we pulled apart, she ran for the door.

"I'll do recon as I change," she yelled over her shoulder.

Ethan and Josh had already dressed in the leftover gear, decked out from head to toe in black, looking every part the Melior Group agents they weren't.

The next few things happened so fast they were mostly a blur. I must have got dressed in tactical clothing too, because I was in all black when I pressed my lips to Josh's, slamming Light into him as if our lives depended on it. Ethan adjusted my Kevlar before I turned to him and did the same.

When we made for the door, I stopped short and gaped at the sight of Nina with an automatic rifle hanging off her shoulder, her delicate frame draped in weapons.

She smirked as she took the lead toward the jungle. "What? I know a few things I have not told you about."

Even though Henry tried to talk us out of it the whole way there, eventually he gave up and started giving us all advice and instructions on how to stay alive. "This is madness," he ground out between clenched teeth as we crouched in the underbrush about an hour later, near an unassuming green door.

Dot had used her ability to perfection. An orange-bellied leafbird had informed her no one had gone in or out since the backup team. But a mouse that had scurried inside the building said there were "a lot of men in black unconscious inside."

Unconscious gave me hope. Unconscious wasn't dead.

We crept forward. At a flick of Josh's wrist, the door swung open, and we moved inside.

Immediately, everything became fuzzy, muted somehow. I was having trouble holding on to my gun, which felt foreign in my hands anyway. I lost track of the others. My vision kept fading in and out. I couldn't remember where we were.

"You're early, daughter dear."

A voice drew my eyes up. *When did I sit down?*

"I didn't even have to kill him to get you here." A face with eyes similar to mine, only much darker and more cruel, hovered over me.

As Davis Damari grinned, the world around me dissolved into blackness.

THIRTY-TWO

I came to slowly, my limbs heavy.

". . . takes time. Everyone is different," a female voice I didn't recognize said.

"I need her to wake up. This won't work unless she sparks up." Davis sounded more than a little impatient.

The ache in my chest had returned along with my consciousness, and that made everything else come crashing back. Reflexively, I tried to lift my hand to rub at the pain and discovered I was tied down.

My eyes flew open.

I was in a padded chair, not unlike a dentist's chair, half-reclined, my wrists bound to the armrests. A large circular piece of opaque glass housed in a thick black frame hung above, pointing directly at my chest. I couldn't even begin to guess its purpose. Monitors stuck to my torso and head fed into thin wires leading somewhere behind me.

"Ah, you're up." Davis moved to my side, his hands in his pockets, his posture the picture of casual calm—as if he were about to ask what I wanted for breakfast. I ignored him, my eyes flying about the room.

It was cavernous, white walls and no windows. Benches and workstations were scattered throughout, as well as beds on wheels. The beds were all empty, but I shuddered to think what they were used for.

"I told you, you just needed to wait." The woman speaking had short black hair and sharp glasses perched on her nose. She was holding hands with a man who looked vaguely familiar.

"Yes, yes." Davis moved over to one of the benches. "And the others are still subdued? Wouldn't want any interruptions."

"Yes." The woman rolled her eyes. "Just get on with it."

"Gina." The man holding her hand spoke over his shoulder, directing his words to someone else. "Do you need more Light?"

A short, stocky woman with curly brown hair stepped out from behind him. "Nah, I'm good." Her gaze was fixed on me, as if she were watching fish in a tank. "I'm only shielding us from the passive abilities. I could do this all day."

The man nodded and closed his eyes again. He was clearly a Vital; the two women, I assumed, were his Variants.

Davis murmured to a few other people gathered around the bench, some of them jotting things down on tablets, others fiddling with screens and knobs. Then he sauntered back over to me.

I knew it was pointless, but I pulled on my restraints all the same, testing them. Every instinct I had was screaming at me to get the hell away from this man—not to mention the horrific pain in my chest urging me to do whatever I could to get to my Variants. It now felt as if more than one of them was drained.

I looked around, trying to spot them, but both my brain and body were sluggish from whatever they'd used to knock me out.

"What did you do to me?" I growled.

"Me?" Davis pressed a hand to his chest, amusement playing in his eyes. "Nothing . . . yet. It was my colleague Sarah who incapacitated you and all the others. A very handy ability to have when armed men come storming onto your property, don't you think? And Gina here made sure young Tyler Gabriel knew nothing about it."

The impressive nature of both abilities sent a chill down my spine. To be able to knock people out but choose to leave others in the vicinity conscious was a scary thing to be up against. The fact that the other woman—Gina—was seemingly able to shield whomever she chose explained why Tyler hadn't seen this coming, why they went in not expecting any of this. He would hate that he hadn't been able to warn his teams.

Once again, I frantically scanned the room for my guys, but all I could see were sterile walls, fluorescent lights, clean steel surfaces. The pull in my chest was tugging me to the left, but I couldn't see around the Vital and his two Variants.

"Move out of the way so she can see her Variants, would you?" Davis waved, and they shuffled to the side.

Behind them, all four of my guys were slumped, unconscious and unarmed, on the ground. Guarding them was another couple, one I recognized from when Ethan had pointed them out at the gala. The man was tall; the woman had Zara's silky red hair. Con and Francine Adams—Zara's parents.

A few feet over, leaning on the wall, was Zara herself. She had her arms crossed over her chest, her head tipped back, and she was watching me with a blank look in her eyes.

Seeing her again would have upset me on any day. Seeing her now, as I was strapped to a chair and out of my mind with worry that one of my Variants was about to die, just about pushed me over the edge.

I ground my teeth as a half growl, half wail ripped from my chest, and hot tears started trailing paths into my hair.

Crouched down next to her, his elbows on his knees and his arms extended in front of him, head hung low, was Rick. For every bit of apathy in Zara's posture, his held defeat.

It shocked me to see them next to each other. He was responsible for Beth's death. Zara *held him responsible* for our friend's death and had refused to even hear his apology. Yet there they were, side by side, watching me fall apart under the hands of a man who I may have called father had my life turned out differently.

Rick looked up, his red-rimmed hazel eyes meeting mine. His jaw trembled as if he was trying to hold back tears. I looked away, and my eyes landed on the Vital whose name I didn't know—the one with the two powerful Variants currently thwarting our rescue mission. He looked familiar because he was an older version of Rick. He had the same honey-blond hair and hazel eyes. I wondered if Sarah or Gina was Rick's mother.

"Bring me one of them." Davis gestured in the general direction of my Variants. Two of his thugs hauled Tyler up and dragged him across the smooth, clean floor as I tried to control the sobs, uselessly struggling against my restraints again.

They propped him up in a chair identical to mine, directly opposite me, not bothering to fasten the straps.

Davis yanked a tablet out of the hands of one of the people—I was reluctant to call them scientists—near the bench and pressed some buttons. The odd glass circle above Tyler's chair lit up with a dull blue light, the machinery in the room making a soft humming, whirring noise.

Immediately, the ache in my chest began to throb. It felt as if someone had sliced me open, reached a hand into my sternum, and was tugging me by the ribcage toward Tyler. My back arched off the chair, and I screamed.

They were draining him.

Whatever the fuck Davis Damari and his lackeys had been doing in this hellhole, one thing was certain: they'd figured out how to harness the Light, and not just from Vitals. They'd figured out how to drain it from anyone with the Variant gene.

They were killing him.

Gritting my teeth against the pain, I sat up as straight as I could and focused on Tyler's prone form. My skin had begun to glow, reacting to his need, and even though I didn't want to expose my secret to these people, I couldn't just sit there and watch them kill Tyler.

I embraced the energy, the power, coursing through me and directed it all at him. With a rush like a waterfall washing over my skin, the Light released and went where it was needed most.

Immediately, the ache in my chest subsided, and I was able to breathe again.

Davis turned his horrific machine off and, before I could turn my attention to my other Variants, came right up to me, grinning maniacally.

"Perfect!" he yelled. "Even brighter than your mother. Dare I say I'm proud, daughter?"

"You're fucking sick, is what you are." My voice was hoarse, my body strained from being under so much stress, despite the fact that it was humming with Light.

He just chuckled as if I'd made a joke and started untying my restraints. He yanked me out of the seat as his thugs dragged Tyler back to the others, dumping him unceremoniously on the ground.

Rick had moved away from Zara and was standing next to his parents. Sarah still had that look of concentration on her face, his father still transferring Light to her, but Rick was pleading with them.

"Come on, Mom, please!" He raked his hands through his hair, not even trying to hide his tears or wipe them way. "We don't have to do this. Let's just go. You're hurting people. I *killed* someone!"

"She was just a Dime, son." His father frowned at him. "Stop worrying yourself over it."

I suppressed the urge to gouge the man's eyes out for referring to my dead friend in such a dismissive, derogatory way, and my eyes flew to Zara. For the first time since before I was abducted, I saw a glimmer, a tiny hint of the old Zara. Her eyes narrowed, and her lips almost pulled into a scowl. But then she met my gaze, and whatever she'd been thinking disappeared from her features as she watched, unblinking, while Davis shoved me toward my Variants.

I didn't question why he was letting me go to them. I just ran.

A blur of movement was all that preceded Zara's father appearing next to me, and I remembered belatedly that he and his wife both had super speed. He jerked me to a stop, his grip on my upper arm painful. I clawed at his hand and thrashed against him, but he pulled me tight against his chest.

"Probably not a good idea to let her recharge the one with the pain ability," he spat out, the sarcasm rolling off him so similar to what I was used to from Zara.

But Davis wasn't paying him any attention. He held his hand out to Zara. "Come, my dear." She went to him without hesitation. "Now that Evelyn has so graciously helped me configure the machine, we can see about gifting you with an ability."

The smile on Zara's lips was a little too wide, her eyes glassy. I may have seen a hint of my friend for a second there, but the promise of an ability—of being everything she never could be before—had driven her to insanity.

"Which ability would you like?" Davis cooed, helping her onto the chair I'd just been torn apart in. Her mother stepped up behind it, running her hands lovingly through Zara's silky hair, as if she were comforting her on a routine visit to the doctor.

All these people were completely unhinged.

"A powerful one" was her answer, her eyes zeroing in on the unconscious bodies just out of my reach. "That one." She lifted her arm and pointed—right at Ethan.

Davis snapped his fingers at his lackeys, and they moved to obey.

"No, no, no!" I thrashed against my captor again. "Leave him alone! Put him down. I will *fucking destroy you*!" My hoarse voice sounded feral; my legs kicked so violently they were leaving the ground.

No one even remotely reacted to my outburst.

The guards struggled under Ethan's weight, and a third stepped forward to help. They hefted Ethan into the chair Tyler had occupied and stepped away, panting with the effort.

"Are you sure this won't hurt her?" Zara's mother asked.

"Her?" Davis answered as he punched buttons on the tablet again. "No, completely harmless to *her*. Him? Well, this is the new part of the experiment. One we haven't been able to test without a particular kind of Vital to configure the machine." He glanced in my direction, and I deflated.

Whatever it was he'd been doing here, I'd just provided him with the final piece of the puzzle. I'd done my glowing thing, drawing Light and sending it remotely to Tyler. I'd walked in here and offered myself to him on a platter. I may have had an IQ of 153, but I was a fucking idiot.

Lucian had told me how Davis had gained his ability. Now he was about to attempt the same thing with Ethan and Zara.

"It may kill him." Davis shrugged as he confirmed my fears, sounding positively chipper. "Let's find out, shall we?"

He pressed one last button, and the machines started to whir to life, the circular glass above both illuminating.

Something inside me cracked.

There was no time to dissect the implications of what was before me. To puzzle out the quantum mechanics behind this new technology. To analyze the unique abilities of the Variants in the room. To *think* of a solution.

I needed to *do* something.

Wrapped in a bigger man's iron grip, with my Variants knocked out cold, there was no way I could do it with my body. So I put my faith in the most powerful aspect of myself.

I planted my feet on the ground, took a deep breath, and unleashed.

I allowed the Light to take over.

I drew on every bit of Light I could access—every tendril I could find. I pulled the Light that was naturally and plentifully always available, but I also drew it from every other source in the room. I counted twelve—twelve other people with Variant DNA and therefore some amount of Light. I pulled it from all of them.

I glowed brighter than I ever had before, the warm white light bouncing off the white walls and shiny surfaces.

And I pushed it all into them. Every bit of Light I siphoned I sent to the four men who each held a piece of me.

At the same time that Davis's macabre machine came to life and I started transferring Light to my Variants, Rick lost his shit.

His pleading with his parents had failed, and in a moment of pure desperation, he used his ability. Other than the day he'd protected me from Franklyn, this was the first time I'd seen Rick use his ability since the day it had killed Beth. Only this time it wasn't an accident, and it wasn't random. The electricity came to his hands effortlessly, and he let out a pained yell as he aimed it right at his mother, hitting her square in the chest. Her eyes flew open and then went dull as she crumpled, falling into her Vital's arms.

With most people in the room shielding their eyes from my lightshow, I was the only one who saw Rick take down his own mother, then run to Ethan. With strength I didn't know he possessed, Rick hauled his friend out of the seat, shoving him out of the way and taking the brunt of whatever the machine was doing.

As the intensity of my glow began to fade, Rick collapsed onto the chair, facedown.

People started to get nervous, fidgety, but Davis remained fully focused on finishing his experiment. His shouted orders were now all about keeping everyone away from the range of his machines so the process could be finished.

I stopped pulling Light and transferring it to my guys; they were replenished and overflowing. Now I just had to wait for them to come to.

Con's grip on me loosened. He was the closest Variant to me, and I'd pulled the most Light out of him. He was weakened, so I seized my opportunity.

I braced, remembering some of the ruthless drills Kane had put us through, and leaned forward as far as I could before slamming my head back into his face. It hurt like a bitch, but his grip loosened further. Just as I was about to kick him in the shin though, he was wrenched away.

I turned just in time to see Alec swing his fist, knocking the older man out cold.

I'd never been happier to see his scowling, cruel face. Behind him, Tyler and Josh were getting to their feet, shaking the rest of the daze from their heads.

Alec shoved me almost harshly in their direction, and I heard a low growl as he launched himself at the guards between us and Davis.

Before any of them could take a shot, Josh disarmed them, their weapons twisting into unusable chunks of metal over their heads.

"Could've used one of those, man," Tyler grumbled as he pushed me behind him. Josh closed in on my other side until they were boxing me in.

"There you go," Josh answered, and a handgun came flying toward Tyler. He caught it effortlessly and fired, taking out an assailant who was about to hit Alec from the back.

I bent to see around Tyler, and the first thing I caught sight of was Ethan, still sprawled on the ground near that awful machine. Why wasn't he waking up like the others? He was too close to all the dangerous people, all the flying fists and whatever that machine was doing.

I ducked past Tyler and Josh and ran, sliding on the ground to come to a rest next to Ethan.

"Dammit!" Tyler swore, hot on my heels. Josh was swearing too but not following, so I had a feeling he was dealing with something else.

I ran my hands over Ethan's bulky form, placing my palm flat to his neck, but he didn't need more Light, and he was breathing. He was just taking a little longer to wake up. A tiny bit of relief leaked through the panic as he moaned and started to shift beneath my hands.

The machine next to us had finished what it was doing, and the cold light emitting from the round bit of glass faded until it was dull once more.

"Did it work?" A frantic female voice asked, and I looked up to see Francine brushing hair from Zara's forehead, her fearful eyes darting about the room. The guards were managing to keep Alec at bay—only just. There were so many more of them, and for some reason he was refusing to use his ability, mowing them down with his fists.

Gunfire and shouting could be heard from behind the white walls and closed doors. The rest of the Melior Group forces must have come to when Alec did, but who knows what they had to fight through to get to us.

"Time to go!" Davis shouted. He gathered up some items from the bench, and his other scientists did the same, lifting out of their hidden positions behind benches.

Zara sat up in her chair, seemingly oblivious to the chaos. She held shaking hands out in front of her, her head bent, as she took shuddering breaths. She was turning her hands this way and that, seeing or feeling something the rest of us weren't privy to.

Davis yanked her out of the chair by the wrist and dragged her to a discreet door in the back of the room, her mother and some of his other staff hot on his heels.

As more men in black burst into the room, Davis and his group disappeared through the door, slamming it shut behind them.

THIRTY-THREE

For a split second my heart sank, convinced the people streaming into the room were Davis's guards. But then Jamie's red hair caught my attention, and I started recognizing the Melior Group operatives who'd been at the compound. Lucian appeared at my side and started helping Ethan sit up as Kyo and the guys fell in beside Alec.

We gained control of the room within seconds, but it was seconds too late to stop Davis.

Lucian looked as if he'd aged ten years as he checked his nephew for injuries, finally pulling him into a hug as Ethan shook the lethargy from his head. As soon as Ethan's eyes found mine, he pulled away from his uncle and scooped me up, one hand holding me close and the other running over me, looking for any harm.

"You OK?" He asked my hair.

"Are you?" I threw back at him.

Neither of us answered the loaded question. We just pulled apart and got to our feet.

Tyler was barking orders to detain the thugs Alec hadn't killed, and a group of agents were trying to force open the door Davis had disappeared through.

With everyone else occupied, Lucian turned to me. "What is this place? What happened?"

My heart was ripped out of my chest. I was betrayed. We nearly died. I didn't know where to start, so I stuck to the facts. "Some kind of fucked-up lab." Lucian didn't even flinch at my swearing. "You were right. He's been trying to figure out how to switch on the dormant Variant gene in Variants without abilities—epigenetics taken to the criminally insane level. He did it. He nearly killed . . ." I swallowed around the lump in my throat, my gaze going to Ethan's back. He was turned away from us, staring at the machines. "I glowed and . . . I couldn't help it, but . . . I gave him . . . I . . . I . . ."

I was losing my shit, but Lucian put one comforting hand on my shoulder and held my gaze, his expression calm. Instead of asking more questions, he gave me some positives to hold on to. "We found the Vitals. We've been getting them free slowly. They should nearly be all out. When the others started waking up, we moved to clear the rest of the building and—"

"The others?" Tyler came to stand next to me, and I leaned into him. "I thought everyone was knocked out."

"When we breached, almost everyone fell. But I had a little help." Lucian gave me a wink. "The extra Light I had from Eve allowed me to shield myself and the three closest operatives to me. We faked being unconscious, and when everything was quiet, we started taking the guards out and moving through the building slowly. After a while we found Nina too, fully conscious and fighting off *two* of Davis's men. If there was any doubt that Lighthunters are impervious to other abilities, she more than dispelled it. She's in the lower levels, helping to free the Vitals."

While we talked, Ethan moved to Rick's side. He checked the spot on his friend's wrist and his neck for a pulse, and then his big shoulders slumped.

The moment Rick had gone limp in that chair, some part of me knew he wouldn't be getting up again. But seeing it in Ethan's defeated posture, his misting eyes and quivering lip as he turned to look at us, was almost too much to bear.

It could have been him lying dead in that chair. It nearly was.

Tears blurred my vision as I wrapped my arms around my torso and tried to stay strong. I couldn't fall apart.

But Ethan reacted differently. Something changed in him. It took maybe a second—his gaze flying around the room, taking in the implications of it all—but then his eyes narrowed; his lips curled in anger.

Without warning, Ethan started conjuring angry blue fireballs and throwing them at the machine, the computers, the walls. He was destroying the room.

I knew his ability couldn't hurt me, but I backed away, frightened by the intensity of his anger.

A massive *boom* sounded from the door Davis had escaped through, and Tyler turned to shield me from the blast. Apparently the door was somehow reinforced, and Melior Group was using explosives to try to remove it.

"Kid, you're destroying evidence!" Lucian yelled, stepping into Ethan's space, despite the fact that Ethan's ability definitely *could* harm him.

Between him and Alec, they managed to calm Ethan down. At the same time, Josh finished off what the detonators around the door had started. He used his ability to twist the door in on itself, and it finally came open.

"All right, let's move!" Alec yelled, his team already forming up at his side.

I grabbed his forearm with both hands. "No!"

That one word came out so forcefully and loudly that several people turned to look before getting back to what they were doing.

Alec turned to me, and I braced for him to sound angry, annoyed that I was getting in his way, but the look on his face was regretful. "I have to go, baby. It's my job."

I tightened my grip on his arm. "Alec Zacarias, don't you leave my sight right now. Don't any of you leave me."

I turned to look at them all, proud of how steady my voice sounded despite the tears that had once again started falling.

By this stage, two other teams had already gone through the busted door after Davis.

"Get these civilians out of here." Lucian rolled his shoulders back. "That's an order."

He gave Alec one firm look before following the last few agents through the busted door. I could have kissed him, but he moved fast for an older guy.

"All right, team, let's move." Alec gently pried my hands from his forearm and took my hand in his. Kyo and Marcus took the lead, and we all headed through the opposite doorway, Jamie bringing up the rear.

As we made our way through the building, which was much larger underground than it looked from the outside, evidence of the fighting was clear: bullet holes in the wall, macabre splatters of blood, doors hanging off their hinges. But Melior Group was efficient, and all the actual people were gone. We came across only one Melior Group operative helping a teammate with an injured leg. Marcus stepped up to assist them, and before long we were emerging into a wide warehouse-like space.

It was much dirtier and rougher than the pristine white lab and maze of corridors we'd just come through. A few all-terrain vehicles were lined up on one wall; massive shelving stacked with different sized boxes took up the other.

And in the corner closest to us were cages.

I shivered, remembering the last time I'd seen black bars like that, in the basement of a house in Manhattan. There were so many of them, more than I could count as we kept walking, heading for the ramp on the other side of the open space. The morning light streamed in through the wide opening at the ramp's top, beckoning us to freedom.

But before we'd even made it a few steps, a massive *boom* reverberated through the structure, shaking the walls, the very ground we stood on. We all bent our knees, throwing our hands out for balance.

We were still one floor below ground level, and it looked as if the structure above was about to come crashing down. Cracks were appearing in the ceiling.

Another *boom* sounded from farther away. People were screaming, yelling. Jittery shadows cut across the sunlight ahead as people ran about frantically.

"We need to get the fuck out of here." Tyler took the lead, but as he stepped forward, a giant chunk of concrete landed in front of him.

Josh pushed past him and threw his hands into the air, every muscle in his body taut, as if he were physically holding the bricks and mortar up with his hands rather than his ability.

I dropped Alec's hand and pressed my palm flat against Josh's bicep—the biggest bit of exposed skin I could find. The only problem was I wasn't sure I had anything left to give. Yes, the Light constantly coursed through me, but I'd used so much recently, and in such an intense way. I was spent, tired, weak.

My skin took on that ethereal glow once again, but there just wasn't that much Light available for me to pull from. I reached mentally for my Variants, for what energy they had.

Ethan's big warm hand found my free one, and the connection made it so much easier to draw Light from him. Next, Tyler's firm grip closed on my forearm. I took from them and gave to Josh—just in time. The ceiling was completely collapsing. We were the only thing holding it up.

At Alec's command, the other operatives with us started to make their way across the wide expanse, keeping to the edges.

"Can you keep that up and move?" Alec asked, panic tinging his words.

Before Josh could answer, another dozen people streamed through the door from where we'd just come. Some of them were Melior Group agents; others were in nothing but gray pajama-looking outfits, the looks in their eyes pure terror and confusion. Many of them were dirty and sooty, their clothing torn. They stayed close to the wall, unwilling to brave the massive piece of concrete now hovering above our heads.

As Alec spoke to his subordinates—asking how many people were still coming, if everyone was out, what the situation was—the slab of concrete burst into flames.

Some of the fire burned blue, and for a moment I wondered why. That only happens when high levels of oxygen are present or when copper, chloride, or butane are added to the flame. But the blue flames were random and flickering in and out, so neither of those explanations fit. The only other blue flame I knew of was Ethan's . . .

But the time for curiosity was over. A mere second after the concrete caught fire, another explosion, farther away, went off.

"Run!" Alec roared, waving at the group of people by the door. "Go! Now!"

They obeyed, shuffled forward by Kyo and the other operatives, some of them helping the injured as they ran for their lives. The five of us were the only ones left on this side of the room.

"We need to secure it!" I yelled.

Ethan was freaking out but keeping his hand firmly around mine. "Why the fuck is everything on fire?"

"Josh, use the shelving!" Tyler gestured to the steel constructions at the edges of the room.

"I'm barely holding it up, Gabe!" Josh's voice was strained with effort.

"Maybe we should retreat, let it fall," Tyler thought out loud.

"No." Alec appeared in front of me, pressing his palm to my cheek. "We'll be trapped. Take it all if you have to."

The last part was directed at only me, his ice-blue eyes determined.

I pulled—took the extra connection and drew on Alec's Light, slamming it all into Josh.

Josh took his first deep breath. He held the concrete in place with one hand and swung the other out, dragging the tall shelving over, letting the boxes and crates stacked there fall to the ground. He positioned the shelves under the collapsing ceiling and lowered it a bit. It was still on fire, the flames licking fast and angry, spreading to some of the cardboard and timber crates.

The concrete slab must have weighed several tons, not counting the above-ground building on top of it. The shelves, solid as they were, wouldn't last long. They simply weren't made for it. Not to mention that the intense fire was weakening the metal and making the concrete crumble further. There was no amount of math I could do to figure this out; I wasn't an engineer. We just had to hope for the best.

"Now!" Tyler yelled, and we ran.

All five of us sprinted across the warehouse floor as flaming chunks of concrete fell around us. Once we made it to the relative safety of the bottom of the ramp, I chanced a look back, and my heart froze, *seized* in my chest.

Halfway to us was Henry, an unconscious Charlie in his arms, dressed in the same gray pajamas I'd seen on the other prisoners. Keeping pace with them was a Melior Group operative carrying one of his comrades in a fireman's hold. Olivia was limping, lagging behind, but they all hauled ass. Menacing balls of fire fell all around them, making them zigzag.

Without even thinking, I turned, ready to launch myself back into the thick of it. But before I could take a step, strong arms closed around my middle and pulled, knocking the wind out of me.

"God dammit!" Alec yelled. He threw me over his shoulder and carried me the rest of the way up the ramp. I struggled against him, but the way he held me allowed me to watch the others make it to safety, my guys helping them up the ramp as Josh used his ability to swat away the flaming obstacles.

As we emerged into the sunshine and the chaos above ground, Alec set me down.

"Where's Dot?" I immediately demanded, craning my neck to see around him. I had to make sure everyone was OK.

Alec grabbed me by the shoulders and turned me toward several parked black vehicles. Dot was enveloped in Kyo's arms, her head on his shoulder, but she was standing, conscious, unhurt.

As soon as the rest of her family emerged, she broke out of Kyo's arms and ran to them, but I didn't get to witness her finally reunite with her brother and Vital. Alec turned me back to face him. With both hands on my shoulders, he leaned down so his intense eyes were level with mine.

"Is Charlie OK?" I tried to ask, but he spoke over me, his expression somewhere between frustration and fury.

"Have you no regard for your own safety whatsoever?"

"Huh?" I lifted my hands, resting them on his elbows.

"You don't have to be the one to do it all. You don't have to save everyone, Evie. There are other people here just as invested in helping and certainly more qualified and trained. It's not all on you." With one thumb, he wiped a tear I hadn't even realized was streaming down my cheek. "You have us. You're not alone anymore, precious. You're *not alone*."

A sob broke out of my chest, and I leaned into him. He held me tight, as if to enforce his statement, as I absorbed the truth of what he'd said.

For all his fucked-up issues, his antisocial tendencies, the giant chip on his shoulder, his emotional stuntedness, Alec always seemed to know when I needed to hear those words the most.

I relaxed against him, finally letting go, and when he passed me to Ethan, I didn't struggle. I let my big guy scoop me up into his arms and buried my head in his neck. I didn't check on what Alec and Tyler were doing. I didn't demand to know what needed to happen next. I just let Ethan hold me—let Josh run his hand through my hair, removing the hair tie and dislodging some of the knots with his fingers.

People were still rushing about—some working to put out the fire, others tending to the wounded—but Davis's remaining men were all restrained, and the sense of danger had abated.

Sitting in a shady spot with her knees drawn up, her shirt torn and her face dusty, was Nina. She chugged an entire bottle of water in one go and took several heaving breaths. Our eyes met, and I gave her a tired smile, hoping it conveyed my gratitude. She winked at me.

The sound of helicopters drew my gaze up.

"Medevac," Josh murmured just as medics began to move some of the worst injured toward a clearing in the distance. One of the people being rushed to the choppers was clearly Charlie; Dot and his parents were running beside his stretcher. I wanted to rush after them, comfort my friend, find out what was happening, but I reminded myself Charlie was in good hands. Kyo jogged to catch up with them and took Dot's hand right before they disappeared behind some trees. I let myself relax a little more to the steady beat of Ethan's heart.

But soon Josh's fingers in my hair faltered, then stopped completely. He cursed low under his breath. Ethan's whole body stiffened, his arms around me tightening.

I hadn't even realized I'd closed my eyes, but I made myself open them, ready for whatever new catastrophe was befalling us now.

Medics were rushing about frantically near the vehicles. Tyler was pointing at things, yelling at people. Alec just stood there, his hands on his hips, his head hung low, his shoulders heaving.

All their attention was centered around a man on a stretcher.

"Who do you think . . ." Josh's question died when a gap in the crowd revealed a glimpse of distinguished features, dark hair peppered with gray.

The man on the stretcher, the man I'd watched be carried out next to Henry and Charlie, was Lucian Zacarias.

The three of us rushed forward at the same time, fear choking the air out of my lungs.

THIRTY-FOUR

The blood on Alec's knuckles had crusted over. There were so many people with serious, life-threatening injuries that a couple of busted hands just weren't important.

I focused on the deep red, the bruising already beginning to show, the streaks of dried blood mingling with dirt and dust all over his arms. Anything to distract myself from the screaming.

Charlie's latest blood-curdling scream came to a whimpering stop, and we all took a small breath of relief.

Alec was sitting in a plastic chair across from me, his head in his hands, his shoulders stiff. Ethan mirrored his older cousin's posture in the seat next to him. I could see the resemblance clearly in the dark shade of Ethan's longer hair and Alec's buzz cut, in the set of their tense shoulders, in the way both of their feet were planted wide, the toes slightly turned out.

Josh sat next to me. I had a feeling if he wasn't scared to crush the bones, he would have been gripping my hand as hard as I was gripping his.

Davis had managed to get away with Zara, her mom, Rick's dad, and a small group of the mad scientists.

In the ensuing battle, forty-eight people had died, and several hundred were wounded. There were bullet wounds, broken bones, blunt force trauma, and a myriad other injuries. But the worst were the burns.

They were still trying to figure out what exactly had caused the fire. It had spread fast to many parts of the building, and several people had serious burns. Charlie was one of them.

The medics had managed to stabilize Lucian at the scene, but his injuries were horrific. He'd been shot multiple times in the chest and left arm as he joined the teams trying to stop Davis from getting away. Then, as the last few people were evacuating the building, a wall had collapsed, knocking him unconscious and pulverizing his hips.

He was still in surgery, doctors battling to save his life, while Charlie screamed through his first change of dressings.

"This is my fault," Ethan growled, rocking back and forth, pulling on his hair.

"No, it isn't." I didn't even hesitate to refute him. He'd started blaming himself once we'd realized how badly some of the victims had been burned. By the time we'd arrived at the hospital in Singapore where the worst cases had been airlifted, nothing could convince him his ability hadn't caused the fires.

His anguish had Alec sitting up straighter. "We don't know what happened yet. But, Kid"—he put a firm hand on Ethan's big shoulder—"no one would blame you even if your ability did start it. We were all there because of that fucker in the first place. Aim your anger at him, not at yourself."

The sound of approaching footsteps preceded Tyler's arrival. He came to a stop near the waiting area and propped his hands on his hips.

"Hey." He sighed. We were all tired, dirty, and aching. Tyler's hair was all kinds of crazy, but he was dressed in black, just like the rest of us, so the filth wasn't as visible. "How's Charlie doing?"

We all winced. The doctors had rushed him to surgery as soon as we'd arrived, doing their best to repair the damage to the right side of his body. He'd been resting until a few moments ago.

"They're changing his dressings now. What's going on out there?" Josh asked.

"Chaos, but we're doing our best to contain it. The press has already gotten wind of things. We told everyone to keep it quiet, but a lot of Vitals were being held, and they're reuniting with their families. It's impossible to keep that many people quiet. Also, we found the senator."

"Christine Anderson?" My eyes snapped to his, my back straightening. That woman had been at least partially responsible for my kidnapping, for Josh nearly dying, and she was definitely involved in all this. But she hadn't been seen or heard from since that day.

"Yeah. In one of the cells. And she's not shy about talking. She's a little delusional about her political prospects after all this, but it seems she was working with Davis early on—until he decided she was a liability and locked her up."

"But she's talking?" It was the first time in hours I'd seen a hint of a smile on Josh's face. The hope in his eyes gave *me* hope.

"She won't shut up." Tyler smiled. "She confirmed Variant Valor orchestrated the invasion at Bradford Hills Institute, manipulating the Human Empowerment Network to cause a distraction so they could kidnap Vitals. How they've been transporting them and where to. She's also saying some interesting things about how Variant Valor began—how deeply Damari is involved. There's a long way to go to corroborate her stories but—"

Another gut-wrenching scream, barely recognizable as human, came from Charlie's room. Tyler reached for the gun at his hip, but we all just flinched.

I squeezed Josh's hand again, gritting my teeth. Alec dropped his head back into his hands, and Ethan growled—a sound between pain and frustration.

Josh held his other hand out to Tyler, gesturing for him to lower the gun. "It's the pain from changing the dressings."

"Fuck," Tyler breathed, threading a hand through his hair. "Can't they give him some painkillers or something?"

"They've given him as much as they can," I explained. "This is one of the most painful things a person can experience. The dressings are often put on wet and pulled off dry to tear away dead tissue. There's only so much morphine can do."

My brain was in that weird state where it started firing related yet unhelpful facts and statistics in moments of high stress. Apparently, I was now comfortable enough with my Bond to spew this information out loud instead of just going over it in my mind, despite them all watching me with horrified expressions. "Burns are categorized by thickness. Charlie's burns are bad but *not* full thickness, which means the nerve endings weren't destroyed completely, which means he can still feel it all. Yeah. It fucking hurts."

Alec growled, throwing his hands in front of him as if he could physically throw off the discomfort he was in, and leaned heavily back in his chair. He started rubbing his thighs, then sat up again. His eyebrows were threaded together, the scar in the right one puckering.

Out of all of us, Alec had the most experience with pain, yet he seemed to be struggling the most with listening to Charlie go through it. But he wasn't leaving.

"Has anyone called in a healer?" Tyler asked in the next break between screams.

"Uncle Henry did," Ethan said to his shoes. "But they're coming from Egypt, and it's going to be a while. They can't just not change Charlie's dressings."

Healing abilities were extremely rare—rarer even than the four unique abilities my guys had. There were only a couple of dozen healers in the world, and half of them could only handle minor injuries. The more powerful ones—the ones with Vitals—were in high demand.

"I'm sure this is the best thing for him, then." Tyler frowned.

"I think we all just feel helpless." Josh nailed it. All four of my guys were proactive, and I hated having a problem I couldn't solve. Sitting in a waiting room, listening to someone scream in pain only feet away—it was beyond frustrating.

But maybe there *was* something we could try.

Chewing my bottom lip, I extracted my hand from Josh's iron grip and stood, taking the three steps necessary to move in front of Alec.

He saw what I was planning written all over my features. His face fell, worry and disappointment replacing the frustration. "I can't," he whispered, narrowing his eyes at me.

"So you have thought about it?"

"Of course I've thought about it," he huffed, throwing his arms up and letting them flow back down to his knees. "But now is not the time to test it."

"Why not? What's the worst that could happen?"

He stood, his hands in fists, but I didn't step back, so we ended up chest to chest. "Are you fucking serious? I could make it worse."

"You won't." I had to look up to meet his icy stare, but I held it, refusing to back down.

"You don't know that."

"Yes, I do, Alec." I placed my hands on his chest. "I've never met anyone with more control in all aspects of his life than you. You have more control of your ability than anyone I know. I don't for a second doubt that you'll be able to hold back that part of it. It's second nature to you. The worst that could happen is nothing."

He was breathing hard, his eyes searching mine.

"You can do this, man." Josh's voice was steady.

"What makes you think it's even possible?" Alec kept his gaze trained on me.

"Logic." I moved my hands to his shoulders. "With my Light, Tyler can tell not only that someone is lying but what they're lying about. With my Light, Josh can not only levitate a few books in his room but hold up an entire floor of a building, make himself fly. With my Light, Ethan can not only set fires but put them out. Alec, he can *put out* fires he didn't start. There's no reason you couldn't take away pain you didn't inflict."

"I've been waiting for a good time to raise this, Alec." Tyler sighed. "But she's right. The research supports it, study after study showing that with access to a Vital, the ability can be used far beyond what—"

Charlie screamed again, cutting Tyler off. Ethan stood and placed a big hand over mine on Alec's shoulder.

"Alec, please try." His voice was hoarse, tears threatening to spill over. I wanted to take him into my arms and comfort him, but in that moment, Alec needed me more.

"You can do this." I injected as much confidence and intensity into the statement as I could.

Alec wrapped his arms around my waist, drawing me to him so tightly my feet almost lifted off the ground. I circled my arms around his neck and held on. I would hold on for as long as he needed, prove to him I was there— that I was in this with him.

He'd told me hours before I wasn't alone, that I didn't need to do everything myself. Now it was my turn to show him the same thing.

"I'm so fucking scared, Evie," he whispered into my dirty hair, too low for the others to hear.

"I know, but I'll be there with you. You're not alone." He released me, and I pulled back to look at him. "You can do this, Alec. I know you can."

He took a deep breath, rubbed his hands over his cropped hair, and nodded.

I didn't wait for him to change his mind. I grabbed his hand and pulled him in the direction of the screams.

Inside the room, three nurses hovered over Charlie, moving quickly but efficiently, piles of bloody bandages in a heap next to the bed.

Olivia sat next to Charlie's head, holding his unburned hand, tears streaking her cheeks even as she murmured soothing things into her son's ear. In the opposite corner, Henry cradled Dot with one arm, her face turned into his chest.

"Stop!" I may have yelled a little too loudly, but I didn't want to waste another second.

"You not permitted to be here," one of the nurses said sternly in heavily accented English, pointing harshly to the door.

"We're family." Alec stepped in front of me, his voice hard and even despite the level of emotion it had trembled with only moments before. Charlie needed him to be strong. "And we can help."

He stepped forward and explained his ability to the nurses.

"I don't know about this." Olivia stood, her brows creased, one hand still on Charlie's forehead. "What if you just hurt him more?"

"We should let him try, Mom!" Dot piped up, her hoarse voice breaking on every second word.

Everyone started talking over each other, arguing for or against the plan, while the nurses continued to try to get us to leave.

I kept my eyes trained on Charlie. He was breathing hard, his teeth gritted, his eyes drooping, but he was meeting my gaze. After a few moments, he nodded and squeezed his mother's hand, cutting off whatever it was she'd been saying.

She looked down at him, and the whole room quieted.

"I want to try," Charlie breathed, his voice weak and strained.

Olivia closed her eyes, pushing more tears down her cheeks, and took a deep breath. Then she nodded, kissed Charlie tenderly on the forehead, and went to stand with the rest of her family.

Alec and I took her place. He rubbed his palms on his pants, blowing out a breath—the first signs of nervousness he'd shown since we'd walked into the room.

Charlie lifted his hand in invitation, and Alec took it. I threaded my fingers through Alec's other hand and waited for him to take the lead.

"Just give me a little to start with," Alec murmured, and I obeyed, letting the warm, tingly feeling in our hands take over. I released just a little Light, then shut it down and waited.

Alec closed his eyes, a look of intense concentration on his face. He bent over Charlie, gripping his hand just a little tighter.

"More," he whispered, and I gave him more—the same amount as before. As I was about to stop the flow, he spoke again. "Keep going. I'll tell you when to stop."

I let a steady, controlled stream of Light course through my hand and into his, briefly marveling at how effortless it was. The closer I got to my Bond—not just physically but on all levels—the easier it was to not only control the Light but understand it. Knowing exactly how much I needed to transfer and when and who needed it most was becoming second nature.

"OK." Alec squeezed my hand but didn't let go. I cut the flow.

For a few moments, everyone held their breath, the whirs and beeps of the machines in the room the only things penetrating the silence.

Then, Charlie sighed. Olivia sprang forward, looking poised to tackle the Master of Pain himself to the ground, but she stopped in her tracks when she saw the look of serenity on Charlie's face.

Pride swelled in my chest, as if I'd just done the impossible and not Alec. I grinned, rejoicing in the little twitch of his lips that indicated he was pleased too.

"How does that feel, Charlie?" Alec spoke low, caressing his cousin's hand with his thumb. Charlie loosened his grip, but Alec was holding firm.

"Like . . . nothing."

Finally, the smile broke out on Alec's face.

"Not like a pleasant sensation or anything, just . . . nothing." Wonder filled Charlie's voice, and his eyes closed; his body visibly relaxed. "The pain is just gone."

"You think you can keep it going?" one of the nurses recovered enough from her shock to ask.

Alec and I both nodded, and they sprang back to work.

We didn't speak, but we worked perfectly together—me pushing more Light at him as soon as I registered he needed it, him focusing fully on keeping the pain at bay.

The process wasn't flawless. A few times Alec's hold on the pain slipped, or I didn't push more Light in time, and Charlie would wince or cry out. But we quickly adjusted, and the nurses worked fast. They soon finished changing the dressings, and as they cleaned up, Alec finally released Charlie's hand. He was asleep.

Olivia pulled Alec down into a hug.

His face froze in an expression of shock. As much as people avoided him because of his ability, Alec had pushed people away too. It may have come as a surprise to him that his aunt was hugging him, but it was not a surprise to me. His family loved him.

Dot wrapped her delicate arms around his waist straight after, holding on to him for a long time, then turned and hugged me too. Over her shoulder, I watched Henry pull Alec in for a third hug, relief palpable in his red-rimmed eyes.

As we stepped back into the hallway, the others looked up expectantly.

"Well?" Ethan asked, his hands on his hips.

Instead of answering, Alec swept me up in his arms and kissed me. His arms banded tight around my back, he lifted me off the ground, and I twined my legs around his waist.

Kissing Alec was always intense, usually a surprise, and never failed to satisfy. This was no different, yet it had a new energy to it. He kissed me deeply, his tongue massaging mine in steady movements, his arms pressing me against his chest. I enthusiastically returned the embrace, still riding the high of what we'd been able to do for Charlie.

The kiss was everything it always was with him—all-consuming, making the rest of the world fall away—but it held none of the reluctance or restraint I'd felt from him in the past.

I felt giddy. Horny but giddy.

My surge of lust had me forgetting where we were, and I rolled my hips against the steadily growing bulge in Alec's pants. He had the presence of mind to break the kiss.

He pressed his forehead to mine and smiled in a way I'd only seen a handful of times—wide and genuine, his beautiful blue eyes sparkling with happiness. "Thank you." His warm breath washed over my face.

"What for? You did all the work." I chuckled as he set me back down.

He held my gaze, his eyes boring into mine with so much emotion, so much *hope*.

I had a feeling he wasn't thanking me for helping him take Charlie's pain away; he was thanking me for making him see it was possible. For showing him he was more than a monster, that he could use his ability for positive things.

"You're welcome." I smiled, hoping the look in my eyes conveyed my understanding.

"So it went well, then?" Josh chuckled.

"Knew you could do it." Tyler looked smug as Alec and I finally separated.

Ethan clapped a hand on Alec's shoulder and beamed, making his dimples appear.

But before we could explain to them exactly what happened, a doctor in scrubs came rushing down the hallway, one of the nurses from Charlie's room right behind him.

"Oh, shit." I pressed myself closer to Alec.

"Are you the man with the pain ability?" he demanded.

Alec nodded. "I am."

Without hesitation, the man held his hand out for Alec to shake, and after a pause, Alec took it.

My face nearly split open, I was smiling so wide. Someone casually touching Alec was an insignificant, everyday thing, but I knew how much it meant to him.

"Can you do it again? I have more burn victims than this facility is equipped to handle, and it would go much faster if patients weren't in pain." The doctor's face was wild with desperation and hope.

Alec looked at me, raising his brows.

"I'm up for it if you are." I shrugged. I was spent—absolutely exhausted, dirty, and sore in places I didn't want to think about, but I'd managed to have a nap on the plane, and I'd been sitting in the waiting room for hours letting the Light replenish. If there was anything we could do to help some of these people, I was on board.

"Lead the way, doctor." Alec's chest puffed out just a fraction as he threaded his fingers through mine and followed the doctor down the hall.

Tyler followed after us, heading for the exit. "I'll go try to deal with the press."

"I'll check in with Aunt Olivia." Ethan was already halfway through the door to Charlie's room.

"I'll get us all some food and coffee." Josh gathered his jacket from the plastic chair.

"Espresso!" I yelled over my shoulder. "Latte if you can get it."

He flashed me a grin and shook his head.

We all did better when we felt as though we had something to do—some way to contribute.

We had no idea if Lucian would make it through the night, Davis had escaped, Zara very likely had a dangerous new ability, and once again people had been maimed and killed. As soon as details made it to the public, I had no doubt tensions between Variants and humans would turn nuclear. We had one hell of a clusterfuck to deal with.

But in that moment, rushing down the hospital hallway hand in hand with Alec, at least I could take comfort in the fact that we would deal with it *together*. I finally felt as if I was part of my own Bond, and I knew they'd have my back no matter what.

EPILOGUE

"G'day, love. You right?" The trucker was about as cliché as you could imagine, standing between his rig and the back wall of the rest stop—potbelly, wifebeater, dirty red cap half covering his weathered, frowning face.

But what choice did Zara have? "Yeah, just tired."

"Strewth! American." He smiled, showing crooked teeth, but it seemed genuine. "Backpacker?"

Why did Australians insist on shortening everything? What was wrong with full sentences? She resisted the urge to roll her eyes and made herself stand up taller. "Yeah. Trying to get to Melbourne. Can I get a lift?"

"It's your lucky day!" The trucker pulled his shorts up, puffing his chest out. "Heading right through the city on me way to Geelong. Just gotta take a piss. Head off in fifteen."

He didn't wait for a response, walking around the block of toilets and leaving Zara alone in front of the semi-trailers. She let herself slump forward again, giving in to the shake in her arms.

She was somewhere just past Sydney. The couple in the minivan had dropped her off at the truck stop; they were heading into the center, and Zara needed to keep moving south.

It was a long way to Melbourne. Hopefully the trucker wouldn't want to do it in one long drive. Even though he didn't make the best first impression, she still didn't want to kill him. And she wasn't sure she could stay in control for that long.

She could feel the electricity now. It was always there, under her skin. Writhing, straining, demanding to be released. As if it knew it didn't belong there—that it wasn't Zara's to command.

Davis had a fucking contingency plan for everything, and it was almost laughable how easy it had been for them to slip away in Thailand. They'd been hiding out on a remote property in northern Australia, in another underground lab, as his scientists continued their work. But as Davis's plans moved forward, he had less and less interest in Zara and helping her bring her new ability under control. He'd all but given up trying to figure out why it was so unsettled—despite the fact she'd accidentally killed one of his men.

Even her own mother was paying her less and less attention. Zara was pretty sure she was fucking Davis, judging by the disgusting looks she threw his way any time they were in the same room. Apparently her father hadn't meant all that much to her, and neither did her daughter anymore.

"Right, let's get a move on." The trucker reappeared, climbing into the driver's side and not offering Zara any help with her backpack.

She'd packed only the essentials when she'd made a run for it. Not that she was entirely sure anyone gave a shit she was missing. But Davis was possessive of his creations, and he might come after her, which was why she was avoiding trains and airports. That and she was running out of money; the odd plastic Australian bills were dwindling.

She threw her bag up and hefted herself into the passenger seat as the giant engine of the truck rumbled to life.

Zara couldn't see any other way out of the fucked-up situation. She needed to get to the one person who'd made it all possible—the one person whose very existence had given Davis what he'd needed to make Zara into an even bigger *freak* than she was before.

She needed to get to Evelyn Maynard.

There was only one way she could think to do that without getting caught by the police, the Melior Group, or worst of all, Davis Damari.

She only hoped Eve's ex Harvey wouldn't be too difficult to find.

VIVID AVOWED

THE EVELYN MAYNARD TRILOGY
PART THREE

BY KAYDENCE SNOW

PROLOGUE

Sneaking around Bradford Hills Institute at night with Davis always sent a thrill of rebellious exhilaration through Joyce. Doing *anything* with Davis had an edge of adrenaline to it.

He was the model student during the day—even friendly with some of the lecturers—but at night, he was a bad boy. And he spent most of his nights with Joyce. That made her feel special, as if she were the only one who knew who he really was, the only one who saw his dangerous side.

"Where are we going?" George was keeping pace with them, walking slightly behind as the trio navigated a dark curved path by nothing but moonlight.

Davis hushed him. "Keep your voice down. We're going to the construction site."

"Oh." George's steps faltered. "Aren't students banned from there?"

Joyce detangled herself from Davis to loop her arm through George's. "Yeah, but that's what makes it fun." She grinned and pulled him along. "It's not like we're gonna do anything bad—just have a few drinks and check it out. It's totally safe, I promise."

Construction on what would be the new admin building had begun several weeks ago. During daylight hours, the area was teeming with contractors, buzzing with the noise of power tools and manual labor. At night, it was pretty much abandoned. Joyce and Davis had snuck in there a few times already, having sex up against the rough concrete of the structural walls and smoking pot, feeling on top of the world.

When Davis had suggested they invite George, Joyce had been surprised. She had Variant Studies with the smart, shy seventeen-year-old and had chatted with him a handful of times—they'd even done a group project together once—but she couldn't recall Davis ever speaking to him. George didn't really speak to anyone. His mind-reading ability made it difficult for him to be around people, and most students steered clear, worried he might expose their deepest secrets.

It was really sweet of Davis to notice the kid needed some friends. Joyce had agreed readily and invited him herself.

Davis placed the six-pack of beer he was carrying on the ground and held the chain-link gate wide enough for them to squeeze through.

They climbed to the third floor on staircases without railings and sat with their legs hanging off the edge of the building. The faint lights of the town twinkled past the treetops as they drank their beers and chatted about classes, gossiped about their classmates.

George kept pretty quiet at first, but the beer and easy conversation soon loosened him up.

"Hey, Georgie." Davis had started using the silly nickname as soon as they'd picked George up at his res hall, and he hadn't dropped it since. "You know, Joyce here is a bit special—like you."

"Really?" George's eyes flicked between the couple as Davis slung an arm around his girlfriend's shoulders. "You have an ability? I thought you were a Vital."

"Yeah, I am." Joyce nodded but eyed Davis. He had that look in his eyes—the one he always got just before he pulled something really daring. Usually it was fun, but sometimes . . .

Davis was the only one she'd told about her Vital status, about the way she sometimes glowed, but he wasn't in her Bond; there had been no spark between them when they touched. His ability hadn't even manifested yet—a sore subject for him.

"Wait, how did you know I'm a Vital?" Joyce asked.

George tapped the side of his head. "Heard you think it once or twice."

"Right." Joyce laughed. "I almost forgot."

"She's not just any Vital." Davis leaned forward, tipping them almost dangerously over the ledge. "She's a *special* kind of Vital. She can do things other Vitals can't."

"Davis." Joyce leaned them back to a safe distance. What was he doing? He knew how stressed she was about the glowing, how much she worried there was something wrong with her. Wasn't he the one who'd convinced her not to say anything to the social worker or the nurse? They might treat her like a freak, even take her away from him if they thought she was dangerous.

She couldn't risk that. She loved her life and her friends too much. She loved Davis too much to even think about being away from him.

"It's OK, sweets." Davis kissed her on the cheek. "Georgie won't tell anyone. I just want to help him."

"Help me?" George asked at the same time as Joyce said, "How?"

"You see, Joyce can draw Light from any source, including other Variants. And when she does, she can temporarily transfer the Variant's ability to another Variant."

George's eyes narrowed, as if he couldn't quite figure out what Davis was saying . . . or thinking.

"Davis." Joyce shrugged his arm off her shoulders and fixed him with a firm look. "What are you getting at?"

They'd used her glowing Light a handful of times. She'd once drawn from a shape-shifter and transferred to Davis so he could make himself look older and buy them beer. Harmless fun, but it took a lot out of her. Any time she used the glowing Light she felt drained and weak, and it took days to feel like herself again. But Davis loved having an ability for a little while, so she did it whenever he asked.

"He wants you to take it all," George answered for Davis.

Joyce wasn't entirely sure whether George's ability had clued him in to what Davis wanted or if he was just smarter than her and had figured it out quicker—most people were smarter than her—but it suddenly made perfect sense.

"You want to take his ability permanently?" Joyce stared at Davis with wide eyes. "We don't even know if that's possible. We don't know what it'll do to George. I may not even be able to do it. I'm not that strong."

"Yes, you are." Davis said it with such conviction, such certainty, the doubt almost completely evaporated. He fixed her with that look she loved, the one that made his eyes shine, that made her feel as if they were the only two people in the room—in the *world*.

He cupped the side of her face, his hand warm, and she instinctively leaned into the touch. "I know you can do this, Joycie. I love you."

"I love you too . . . but . . ."

"Please try." George's plea reminded her they weren't actually alone in the dimly lit construction zone.

"George, I don't know what it might do to you."

"I don't care. Even if it doesn't work. Even if it only works for a little while. Do you have any idea what it's like to have voices constantly in your head? To not be able to sleep until everyone else in the building is asleep? To not be able to make friends because . . . because you're a *freak*? Just try. *Please*."

His eyes pleaded with her as much as his words. He was desperate.

Joyce chewed on her lower lip. Davis wanted this. George wanted this. Who was she to say no?

"OK." She nodded.

Davis clapped his hands once, the sound bouncing off the concrete. "Excellent!"

Joyce took George's hand and concentrated hard. She'd never tried to pull *all* of it before—she had to focus.

It took time, but eventually the Light became the only thing she saw in her mind's eye, the only thing she felt. She pulled harder than ever before.

She was so focused on her task, so determined to give them what they wanted, she didn't notice when George tried to pull his hand out of her grip, when he whispered weakly for her to stop. She didn't see Davis place his hand over George's mouth, holding him in place.

When she'd pulled all the Light out of George, she gasped and her eyes flew open. Her body and mind couldn't handle the pressure, the overwhelming weight of that much pure power.

She passed out.

Davis caught her before her head hit the concrete and lowered her gently down. Then, when he was sure George had no pulse, he kicked the young boy's body off the edge, hoping it would look like an accident.

"Fuck." With a growl, he grabbed two fistfuls of Joyce's coat and shook her. "Wake up."

This *had* to work. He hadn't put in months of effort hanging out with this desperate, pathetic chick for it to all be a waste.

"You better not be dead." He huffed and unzipped her coat, reaching for her neck to check for a pulse.

As soon as his skin connected with hers, he felt it. There was so much Light coursing through her she didn't even need to be awake to transfer it to him. It was *gushing* out of her.

A manic smile spread over his face as the sheer power coursed into his veins.

He considered throwing her off the edge along with George—he couldn't risk her freaking out and telling someone about what had happened—but he dismissed the idea. He had to make sure it was permanent first. And if it was . . .

He resolved to keep his new ability a secret as long as possible; he'd reveal it only at the most opportune time. He was already in his early twenties—no one expected him to manifest an ability at all.

As Davis lifted Joyce into his arms and climbed down the stairs, he allowed himself to think about what this could mean for him. He would be the most powerful man in America, maybe even the *world*.

Oh, the mind reading would certainly help, but it wasn't as if the ability was unique. No, the real prize was lying unconscious in his arms.

If he was right and Joyce really could take an ability and give it to someone else, he'd have to make sure he kept her close for a long, long time. He was a bit young to be a father, but if that's what it took to lock her into his life permanently, he'd start poking holes in condoms as soon as he got her back to his place.

ONE

One of Josh's carefully curated playlists drifted softly from the high-tech system in the corner of my room. Although it had taken him all of five minutes to throw it together, he knew exactly which songs to choose, and they were all perfect "getting ready" songs.

It had been way too long since one of Ethan's epic parties, and apparently the masses were getting impatient. Plus, my big teddy bear loved to throw a big party.

Dot unclipped the last little chunk of hair at the top of my head and separated it into sections. I was seated between her legs on the floor, my back leaning on the mattress as she meticulously straightened my hair. I hadn't cut it more than a trim since my mother's death. When straightened, it nearly reached my ass.

"Should I put it in a ponytail or something? It's getting really long." My nervousness about this party was manifesting as self-consciousness.

"What're you nuts?" Dot bent around me to look into my face, her brow creased. "I just straightened it to perfection. Girls would kill for this kind of hair."

"OK, OK." I held my hands up but chuckled. It was nice to see her spunk back. Her vibrant, loud, over-the-top personality had faded each day her brother and Vital had been missing.

Charlie had been rescued over a month ago, along with dozens of other Vitals. He sat on the bed behind us, leaning on the headboard, flicking through my latest edition of *New Scientist*. He must've found something to hold his attention, because we hadn't heard a comment or a page flip in a while.

Bradford Hills Institute had given him the rest of the year off; he was to resume his studies for his master's the following year, but for now, he was spending most of his spare time with us. He'd obviously missed Dot. I couldn't imagine what he'd been through, locked up in a little cell for so long, never knowing when he might be dragged off to the lab of horrors.

It made me sick to my stomach.

"Apparently neural stem cells from Variant donors are seventy-six percent more effective than those from human donors in treating patients with chronic spinal cord injuries. The transplanted stem cells develop into new neurons that replace severed or lost nerve connections and almost completely restore motor and sensory function," Charlie piped up from behind us, solving the mystery of what had him so engrossed.

"Oh, really? I guess it makes sense when you consider the accelerated healing and better resistance to injury and disease in people with Variant DNA," I answered, itching to read that article myself.

Dot nudged my head to face forward again. "No nerd talk! Stop moving. I've only got one section to go."

I kept still as she dragged the last section of my chocolate-brown hair painfully slowly through the straightener. I had a feeling she was doing it just to bug me.

"There. Done," she declared, finishing it off with some anti-frizz shit that smelled sickly sweet and made me sneeze. She went straight to my closet and flicked through the hangers. "You sure I can't convince you to wear a dress?"

Hanging next to my mother's poppy-print dress were rows of clothes I'd purchased on a recent trip to the city with Dot. Charlie and Ethan had come too, as well as a full Melior Group security detail. We were able to pretend the agents weren't there for most of it, and I'd learned how enjoyable spending money could be when you didn't have to worry about packing all your purchases into one easy-to-carry bag.

For tonight, I'd opted for skinny jeans and a blood-red sweater with a V-neck. My suede ankle boots—one of *three* newly purchased pairs of shoes—went perfectly with it. The outfit was nowhere near as dressy as Dot's was going to be, but I thought I looked nice, and I was warm and comfortable. A chill still hung in the March air, but so far the rain had remained trapped in the fat gray clouds above.

"Nah," I finally answered. "I like what I'm wearing, and it's too cold for a dress."

"Fine." She rolled her eyes. "But you know you'll get drunk and start dancing and you'll be way too hot in that later, right?"

"Well, then it's lucky the party is only downstairs, just a short walk away from my closet with all these clothes in it."

In place of an answer, Dot just stared at me with raised brows and pursed lips. Then, slowly, she held her hand out. Squiggles came running out of the hallway, scampered up her side, and dropped a tube of mascara in her palm.

Dot thanked her gray ferret while keeping her eyes on me, then turned to face her. "I know. She's being sassy. I don't like it."

Charlie snorted and flopped the magazine down on the bed, leaning back against my multicolored, geometric-patterned sheets. I flashed him a conspiratorial smile and went over to the side table. It held a cluster of framed pictures: the one of my mother that had survived the crash, one of her with the guys' moms, one of the five of us as kids, and one of Dot, Charlie, and I mugging for the camera. Nestled among the frames was an old, ornately carved jewelry box. It was way too heavy and bulky to have been anything I would've owned before, but Josh had given it to me as a Christmas gift and then promised to fill it over the next unspecified period of time.

I knew he meant forever—Variant Bonds were unbreakable—but none of us were ready to say that word out loud yet.

Alec had told me he loved me, but I hadn't said it back, and none of the others had broached the subject. I suspected they were giving me space and letting me take the lead—as they had with the sex—but an insecure part of me also wondered if maybe they weren't ready for that level of emotional commitment yet either. I mean, really, we'd only known each other for a year. We may have played together as kids, but I didn't remember that.

The box only had a few items in it—a bracelet Dot had given me that same Christmas, a gold pair of earrings (I was wearing them when the plane crashed, and they were the only piece of jewelry I had from my mom), a silver caffeine molecule necklace I'd bought for myself, a few bits of costume jewelry. I lifted out the simple rod pendant that was also a panic beacon and tucked it under the fabric of my sweater. I wasn't wearing it for protection. It was the first thing they'd given me. It may have been delivered in the worst way possible by Alec, but it was from all of them, and I'd come to love the heavy weight of it around my neck.

"What're you wearing tonight, Dot?" I asked to distract her from further bitching about my outfit. Charlie was in jeans and a shirt-sweater combo, his black hair falling over his forehead.

"Something new." She grinned before she got back to applying her makeup. The look she was going for tonight was heavy and dramatic—exactly her signature style before Charlie went missing. I looked forward to seeing what she came up with, even if I wasn't entirely looking forward to the actual party.

I still hardly knew anyone that well, and with Davis Damari—my psychotic biological father whom my mother had kept us on the run from my entire life, aka the man responsible for kidnapping and torturing Charlie and dozens of other Vitals, aka one of the richest men on the planet, aka the biggest asshole to have ever lived—still underground, it felt wrong somehow to celebrate.

But Ethan insisted we had plenty of reasons, and Dot agreed wholeheartedly. My birthday was only a few days away; I'd refused to allow them to make this party all about that—not after the track record I had with birthdays— but they'd waved me off and said it was a multi-celebration. My birthday would be toasted, but so would Charlie's safe return, our win in solving the mystery of the missing Vitals, and Uncle Lucian's recent recovery and release from the hospital.

I wandered over to the window as the song changed to something a little more upbeat. The room I'd moved into in the Zacarias mansion was a little smaller than the others on this wing, but it faced the backyard and caught the afternoon sun beautifully.

Ethan was standing halfway between the house and the pool, completely in his element, dictating the final preparations. He gestured to someone I couldn't see around the corner. In the next moment, the string lights came on, and he clapped his big hands together.

People had already started to arrive—some of Ethan's sports friends and a few other people he and Josh were close with but I didn't know that well. Getting into deep conversations was hard when you were hiding a big secret about yourself. Thankfully we didn't have to worry about that anymore. My identity and my Vital status were public knowledge now.

A few more people streamed out of the house, and Ethan welcomed them enthusiastically, wrapping them all in big hugs, high-fiving, and carrying on.

I couldn't see them from my window, but I knew at least three Melior Group teams were stationed around the perimeter. Every Vital in attendance had their own personal security detail, a very visible team was at the front gates checking vehicles, and another was at the front door, checking each person before they entered the house.

At the first party I'd attended here, security had been nonexistent.

The air was getting brisk as dusk settled in—not that it bothered Ethan. My fire fiend was dressed in his signature jeans and a white T-shirt stretched over his defined, broad chest.

Everyone else, however, would be feeling the cold. Of course, Ethan and Dot had thought of that too.

After saying something to the group that had just arrived, Ethan summoned a ball of blue fire and threw it almost lazily over the still water of the pool. It hit its target—a brazier on the other side—and a bright warm flame rose instantly. He lit two more braziers, then paused and turned to face his audience, a cocky grin on his face. He held his arms out at his sides and lifted them dramatically. The other dozen braziers lining the perimeter of the area, as well as the big firepit opposite the bar, all flared to life.

I couldn't help smirking. His friends were loving the show, shouting and clapping Ethan on the back. He was reminding me of the confident, full-of-life jock I'd first been warned against by the Reds. But that memory was making me think of Beth—poor Beth—and Zara . . .

I couldn't go there. Instead, I focused on the small, pulling ache that had appeared in my chest. It had been a while since I'd transferred any Light to Ethan, and he'd just used up every extra bit he had with his little magic trick. He wasn't depleted to a dangerous level—not by a long shot. I wouldn't have even registered this mild of a pull a few months ago, but our Bond was deepening by the day, and I could sense their needs more and more effortlessly.

I pressed my palm flat against the windowpane and called up the Light, making my skin glow that ethereal white, and remotely transferred just enough to replace what Ethan had used up.

His chest puffed out on a deep breath, and he paused midsentence and looked straight up at my window. Even from this far up, I could see the dimples from his smile—or maybe I just knew them so well I could picture them without having to see them.

I smiled back, shutting off the flow and snuffing out the weird glow with it.

"That is so fucking creepy," Dot murmured, staring at me from her spot on the floor, one hand still holding the mascara wand in midair. "But so fucking cool." She smiled wide, then half turned to Charlie. "Why can't you glow and transfer Light to me remotely? Underachiever. You know how handy that would be?"

He just flipped her off with a sweet smile on his face.

"It's not exactly all sunshine and rainbows," I grumbled. We still didn't fully understand *what* it was. Not to mention the fact that dozens, if not hundreds, of Vitals had been kidnapped, experimented on, and tortured by Davis Damari in his demented search for another like my mom. Like *me*.

"Hey." Charlie's gentle voice drew my attention back to him as he scooted to the edge of the bed. "None of that. I can see you overthinking it again. Blaming yourself."

We'd had several conversations about this—I wasn't hiding how I felt from my friends. They knew all about my guilt, my remorse, my worry.

"None of that was your fault. None of it. *He* did that. You saved me, Eve. You saved us all. If it wasn't for you and your impromptu trip to Australia, I don't know how long they would've taken to try the Lighthunter. I don't know if it might've been too late . . ."

He trailed off, reliving horrors I couldn't even imagine. I sat down next to him. Dot sat on his other side but remained silent.

"I'm really glad you're OK, Charlie," I whispered, resting my head on his shoulder and wrapping my arm around his waist. When I felt Dot's delicate arm over mine, I knew she was mirroring my pose.

Beneath the soft fabric under my cheek was scarring. The day after Alec and I had helped the nurses and doctors manage the pain of the burn victims, the healers had finally arrived. They'd repaired the worst of the damage, made sure the muscle was strong, the bone unaffected, the skin stitched back over it all. But even they weren't miracle workers.

Almost the entire left side of his body had been covered in burns, some more severe than others. Most of it had returned to smooth skin after the healing, but Charlie still had scars on his hip, his elbow, and over his shoulder and neck. Most of it could be covered by clothing, but he didn't seem to care too much.

He gave us both a squeeze and then extracted himself. "All right, enough of that. This is supposed to be a celebration, no?"

"Yes!" Dot hopped up. "No more moping. Only fun and merriment from now on."

She turned back to the mirror, but I saw her wipe some of the moisture under her eyes before she went back to doing her makeup.

"I'm going to head down and get a drink." Charlie stuffed his hands into his pockets and wandered out of the room with an easy smile.

"Do you think he's OK?" Dot kept her eyes trained on her own face in the mirror but pitched her voice low.

I went to stand behind her, placing a comforting hand on her shoulder. "I think he will be. With time."

It always took time. I could attest to that. But this family I was suddenly a part of was made of tough stuff.

"I can't wait to meet Eduardo." I smiled at her, hoping to lighten the mood.

"Me too. Wish he could've been here in time for the party."

While locked in a cell, Charlie had met the love of his life, his cellmate Eduardo—the only other Vital with a sibling for a Variant that I knew of. The two of them had slowly gotten to know each other, tended each other's wounds, kept each other sane, and eventually, fell in love.

Eduardo and his brother lived in Colombia, and he was due to arrive for a visit in a few days. I'd never seen Charlie—who was sometimes even quieter than Josh—so excited.

We were excited to meet him too. In all the chaos of the rescue, Ed was taken to a different hospital and went home with his family, so none of us even knew how important he was to Charlie until he demanded a laptop so he could track Ed down.

"We'll just throw him another one." I rolled my eyes.

"Brilliant idea!"

I wasn't entirely sure if Dot was joking. I groaned, not eager to repeat this madness again so soon, and she laughed maniacally. Next to the mirror, Squiggles bobbed her upper body up and down and ran around in a few excited circles. I think it was her way of laughing.

"You two are creeping me out. I'm going downstairs." I gave them one last frown and turned for the door.

As I passed Josh's room, I poked my head in. He had music playing—some band I didn't even recognize.

I crossed the room to the bathroom. The light was on inside, and the door was ajar. I nudged it the rest of the way open and smiled.

Josh was standing at the sink, doing his hair. His preppy look was impeccable as always—navy chinos and a cream cashmere sweater, a checked shirt collar peeking out from underneath. I leaned in the doorway and checked out his ass as he put the finishing touches on his now perfectly styled dirty-blond hair.

Just one hour ago he'd been reading a book in sweats with a tear at the knee and a Warrant T-shirt. His favorites were the Metallica, David Bowie, and Linkin Park ones, but other than those, I hadn't seen him wear the same shirt twice.

"Can I ask you a question?" I asked. His beautiful green eyes met my dull blue ones in the mirror.

"Of course." He smiled. We were all making more of an effort to be honest with one another.

"You're obviously more comfortable in jeans and band tees. Why do you dress like an Abercrombie and Fitch model every time you're in public?"

He rinsed the hair product off his hands. "You think I look like a model?"

"Well, yes, but that wasn't my point." I smiled smugly.

He laughed, his eyebrows rising in surprise, then dried his hands off on a towel and pressed a sweet kiss to the tip of my nose. "Don't you want to go down to the party?"

Not really. "I want to know more about you. I thought we all promised to be more honest, answer each other's questions." I looked at him expectantly.

He grabbed my hand and gently pulled me into his room. "Come on, I'll show you."

He led me to the impressive bookcases on the opposite side of the room and stopped in front of the complicated sound system. The shelving reached almost to the top of the twelve-foot ceilings, and neither one of us could reach the top without a stepladder. He pointed up, and I craned my neck. The entire top shelf was lined with identical brown leather-bound spines without titles.

"Those are my dad's journals. He used to write in one every day." Josh's arms circled around me, his chest pressing into my back. "When our parents died, I was so lost. The only people I would even talk to were the guys. Then I hit puberty, and I was just angry *all the time.* Some of that anger was directed at my parents. I nearly threw all these out. I packed them up and dragged them all the way down that ridiculous driveway"—we both chuckled— "to dump them on the curb. I figured if they weren't going to be around, I didn't want to get to know them any better. But Alec saw and dragged them right back, and then a few years later, he gave them back to me. It was right around the time he and Gabe were getting heavy into the fighting scene. Kid and I started tagging along, getting mixed up with shady people. That's when they got their shit together and Alec pulled these out of his closet. I was so happy he'd saved them I cried like a little baby."

I didn't speak, riveted.

"I started reading them and couldn't stop. It's what started my obsession with books. I inherited all the vinyl from my dad, but all the books were my mom's. It's funny that reading my dad's journals is what got me to start reading at all. Anyway, my dad was dirt poor growing up. He lived in a trailer with his aunt and went hungry more than a few times a month. But he studied hard, stayed out of trouble, and got himself a scholarship to Bradford Hills Institute. That's where he met my mom. But everyone judged him for his worn, old clothes. No one took him seriously. People constantly dropped jokes about how he was punching above his weight with my mom, wondering what the hell she was doing with him."

I frowned, my heart aching for Josh's dad. I knew what it was like to be on the receiving end of derisive comments about who you were dating—I'd been subjected to months of it from Ethan's exes.

"My dad wasn't a vain man, but he firmly believed in making a good impression—that if you presented well, people were less likely to judge you on what you looked like and more likely to listen to what you had to say. He got pretty successful in the music business, made his own money, and dressed in a three-piece suit every day of his life. He was only relaxed and casual with his family."

"Like you," I whispered, and he smiled.

"Yeah. I didn't grow up poor like my dad—they left me a lot of money—but I learned a lot reading his journals, and this place . . . much as I love Bradford Hills and my family, Variants can be judgmental, bitchy, and gossipy. I refuse to give them any reason to say I'm less than, that I don't belong here because my dad was trailer trash. I make an effort with my appearance not because I care too much what people think but because it was important to my dad, and because it makes me feel closer to him."

For a beat, we fell into silence, Josh's revelations sitting heavy between us. I didn't know what to say. On one hand, it seemed like a massive burden—feeling as if you had to look a certain way so your place in society would never be questioned. But on the other, it didn't feel as if Josh was pandering to the stuck-up Variant elites. He was just trying to do his dad proud.

"Plus, have you felt how fucking soft this cashmere sweater is?" Josh grinned, obviously trying to lighten the mood. "It's like butter."

I smiled. "I think your dad would be proud of you."

A wave of emotion crossed his features, and he cleared his throat, looking down. I wrapped my arms around his neck tightly, and he crushed me to him in one of his signature hugs.

When the giant speakers came to life downstairs, the heavy bass of some hip-hop song interrupted the moment. Josh kissed me firmly on the lips, only just teasing me with his tongue before pulling away.

"Let's get down there before Ethan comes looking for us." He took my hand and led me down the stairs. I was worried for a second I'd upset him by unwittingly bringing up his parents, but if anything, he looked a little lighter—as though a burden had been lifted, now shared with me.

But to me, it didn't feel like a burden. I knew more about Josh and his history, and I couldn't wait to hear even more—to learn more about each of them. It felt like a gift. I smiled and squeezed Josh's hand as we descended into the growing chaos of the party.

I was looking forward to seeing Ty. He'd been at work all day but had promised to be at the party. Even Alec had grunted noncommittally when we asked if he'd come. It wasn't a yes, but it wasn't a no either.

I wasn't sure if he'd be there, but I wasn't sure of a lot when it came to Alec. He'd relaxed considerably since all the secrets between us had been laid on the table; he wasn't flinching away from my touch now that we knew his ability could take pain away as well as inflict it. But his unreturned declaration of love sat awkwardly between us. Over the past couple months, he'd become quiet—not necessarily angry or defensive like before, but certainly more thoughtful. Add that to the fact that any time I tried, he found a way to avoid sex with me, and I knew something more was festering in that complicated, broody mind of his.

I was hoping the party would give us all an opportunity to relax a little, but I was also hoping it would allow me to get to the bottom of the Master of Pain's latest issue with me.

TWO

The setting sun cast the vast, open spaces of the Zacarias mansion into shadow. As Josh and I reached the bottom of the stairs, someone flicked the lights on, and the ostentatious chandelier in the foyer tinkled to life.

A maid opened the heavy front door, letting another few partygoers in. I didn't know them, but they waved to Josh as they passed, following the music to the back of the house.

We trailed after them, our hands swinging between us.

"You kids have fun tonight. You've all more than earned it."

We turned to see Uncle Lucian emerge from the corridor leading to the west wing. A black-clad Melior Group agent walked ahead of him, carrying a small piece of luggage toward the garage.

"Thanks, Uncle Luce." Josh leaned down slightly to give Lucian a hand slap–fist bump combo.

Lucian had survived the rescue mission, but not unscathed. He was in a wheelchair, and despite the healer's best efforts, it didn't look as if he would ever walk again. The damage to his hip and spine was just too severe.

"Are you sure you don't want one of . . . the guys to go with you?" I was about to say one of us, but I wasn't entirely comfortable including myself. The guys were incredibly close to their uncle, and I still wasn't sure how I fit into that dynamic.

"I'll be fine." He smiled. Despite being confined to a wheelchair, Lucian Zacarias was all poise and dignity—his clothes impeccably fitted, his salt-and-pepper hair trimmed, his face clean-shaven. "I have a whole Melior Group team for security, and two nurses to tend to my every need."

He was staying in his city apartment for the night. He said it was because he had early appointments with specialists and doctors, but I was pretty sure he was just leaving so we would have his gigantic house to ourselves.

"And me." Olivia, Lucian's sister and Dot and Charlie's mom, came out of the nearest room. She stopped behind her brother and rested her hands on the back of his chair. "What am I? Chopped liver?"

Lucian rolled his eyes, but humor crinkled at the edges. "Yes, Olivia, you're a damn saint. I don't know what my team of well-paid, highly skilled people and I would do without you."

I stifled a laugh.

Olivia whacked him on the back of the head. "Ungrateful little shit. Do you have any idea what you put us all through while you took the world's longest nap?"

"Nap? I was in a coma! And isn't it politically incorrect to hit people in wheelchairs?"

"Whatever. Come on, wheelie, Henry's meeting us for dinner. I don't want to be late." She pushed his chair forward, giving us a stern motherly look as she passed. "Don't get into too much trouble."

Lucian yelled over his shoulder, "Get into as much trouble as you can. In fact, try to trash the place! We have all these contractors around. I wouldn't mind an excuse to keep them longer and get the kitchen remodeled!"

They bickered all the way to the parking garage door, where two burly Melior Group agents picked Lucian's chair up and carried him down the stairs. The contractors Lucian had mentioned were working on making the mansion more accessible, but most areas still didn't have ramps installed.

"Come on, let's get a drink." Josh tugged me in the direction of the kitchen.

~

A few hours later, I was sitting on the kitchen bench facing the dance floor, my third cocktail in hand. The bright orange drink perfectly matched Dot's outfit.

She was in tangerine from head to toe. She should've looked like a traffic cone or a Teletubby, but she didn't. The high-waisted pants and crop top fit her small frame so perfectly I had a feeling they were tailored. Paired with bold black jewelry and dangerous black platform heels, they made her look like a supermodel.

She was tearing it up on the dance floor while I chatted with Charlie and a couple of his friends about their theses. We'd gotten into a lively discussion about Variant abilities and how they seemed to evolve with other advancements—like the ability to control electronics.

I spotted Alec moving slowly along the edge of the room but kept my focus on the conversation, animatedly waving my drink in the air to emphasize my point. A tiny bit spilled, and when I looked for a spot to set the drink down, I glimpsed blonde hair near the dining table. Leaning up against the wall was Dana.

She was dressed in all black, no hint of the revealing top she'd looked like sex in the last time, and she was alone, her arms crossed, her gaze focused on something in the crowd of dancers. I glanced in the same direction but couldn't figure out what she was looking at.

"Eve?" Charlie brought my attention back to the conversation.

"Sorry!" I blurted out. "I just have to go do something."

I knocked back the rest of my drink and discarded the empty glass on the counter. It didn't take me long to spot Tyler.

In jeans and a casual shirt—with rolled-up sleeves, of course—he stood at the other end of the island, speaking to a colleague from Bradford Hills Institute's Admissions Department. Where the last party had been mostly college kids, this one had a mix of ages and, according to Dot, fewer attendees. It still looked like a concert crowd to me, but either way, it was definitely mellower.

As I approached, Tyler took a sip of his scotch, and his eyes found mine. He smiled and pulled me into his side. After he introduced me to his colleagues, I excused us and pulled him a few steps away.

"I have a question," I said close to his ear. His intelligent gray eyes looked at me lovingly, but I didn't actually want to voice my question.

I pressed my lips to his cheek, letting the kiss linger for a moment as I transferred a little extra Light. I could've just glowed and done it remotely, but while the Variant crowd was used to Vitals with multiple Variants, and therefore multiple partners, they were still wary of the glowing. No one really knew what to make of that yet. Least of all me.

When I pulled away, Tyler had a knowing look in his eyes and an amused smile playing at his lips. "What's your question, Eve?"

His ability would've immediately filled in the gaps: I wanted to know why Dana was there. I wanted to know who invited her and why she'd come when she looked so miserable.

Tyler looked over my shoulder, but I made sure not to turn. The last thing I needed was for her to think we were talking about her. Even though we were.

"She's on duty." He pulled me closer. "She's security detail for one of the Vitals here. He hasn't spoken to her in months, other than at work."

He watched my face for a reaction. I nodded and smiled, hoping my expression looked relaxed and didn't give away the confusing mess of feelings writhing inside me.

I knew Alec wasn't interested in her anymore. He'd told me so himself. He loved me. He'd told me that too. But he hadn't said it since, and he was once again keeping his distance. My insecurities were getting to me. I hadn't said it back to him—I wasn't sure I felt it yet—but I still didn't like the idea of him being with another woman. Especially her.

The very fact that I was overthinking this shit pissed me off, and I rolled my eyes at myself. I was just letting past hurts and worries get to me. She hadn't said it in so many words, but even Dana had made it clear she was no longer after Alec.

"Thanks, Ty." I pressed another kiss to his cheek and, before he could stop me, pushed through the crowd.

"Hey." I smiled a little too brightly when I reached her.

She frowned, then went back to scanning the crowd. "Hi."

"Um, do you want a drink?" I gestured to the bar outside.

She didn't look at me. "I'm on duty. I can't drink."

"I mean, like, juice or soda or something . . ."

After a few moments of awkward silence, I sighed and turned to go, but at that moment, she spoke. "I could go for a lemonade."

"Coming right up!" I sped away from her, on a mission. Once I'd grabbed her a lemonade at the bar, I wriggled back through the crowd, handed it to her wordlessly, and smiled.

She took a sip. "We don't have to be friends. I don't need your pity."

I crossed my arms. "Trust me, there is no pity. And no, we don't have to be friends. But we don't *not* either."

"What?" She finally looked at me, confused.

"Look, all I'm saying is, what's in the past is over, and we have enough *actual* enemies—people trying to kidnap and maim and kill us—that there's no point being hostile over petty shit."

She sighed. "OK. Fair point."

Even though trying to make peace felt all kinds of awkward, Dana hadn't done anything wrong. She'd fallen for Alec—they'd found solace in each other when the rest of society had shunned them. She hadn't known I was his Vital. I had a feeling Dana, just like Alec, didn't really have any friends. If nothing else, I could understand her on that front. I'd gone my whole life feeling lonely until I came to Bradford Hills.

I'd extended an olive branch, but that was enough for one night. "Anyway, have a good night." I smiled, more genuinely this time, and turned to leave.

"Thanks for the drink," she called after me. I could've sworn it sounded sincere.

I made my way back toward the bar. In my awkwardness with Dana, I'd forgotten to get myself another drink, and after that, I needed one. Ahead of me, people started laughing nervously and jostling each other out of the way. Next thing I knew, I was face-to-face with the Master of Pain himself.

He looked just as calm and unyielding as he always did, at least to the casual observer, but I could see the panic in his slightly wide eyes, his clenched teeth. I flashed him a smile and kept going. Judging by how easy it suddenly was to walk through the crowd, he followed close behind.

He sidled up next to me when I reached the bar. Once I'd placed my order, he spoke. "I didn't invite her. She's here on duty. Just so we're clear, I meant what I said—I only want you."

He kept his voice pitched low, so I answered the same way: "I know."

He frowned, confused. He'd expected drama. I tried not to let the amusement show on my face.

I'd seen him a few times throughout the night, sometimes speaking to someone, sometimes with one of my guys, but always off to the side and always watching me. Which made me wonder . . .

"Are you on duty?" I asked.

"Working? Not tonight. But I'm always on duty when it comes to your safety." He leaned in a little as he said it, making the statement that much more dramatic.

I rolled my eyes. The buzz of the alcohol was making me bolder. "Why do you have to be so fucking intense all the time?" I flashed him a cheeky smile. The bartender slid two Long Island iced teas across to me, and I thanked him.

Alec was frowning so hard the scar in his right eyebrow was puckering. "I'm not—"

"You're pretty fucking intense, bro." Ethan did not keep his voice down as he slapped a big hand on Alec's shoulder, gaining a few nervous laughs from the people nearby.

"Hey, my little pony." He flashed me a dimpled grin. The nicknames were getting ridiculous.

"Hey, care bear." I smiled back and took a long drink.

Alec snatched the other cocktail. It was intended for Dot, but he threw the straw on the ground and gulped the drink in one go, not even flinching at the amount of alcohol. "I am not—" he began again, but Ethan's and my burst of laughter interrupted him. The look in his eyes was just so . . . *intense*!

"Come dance with me!" Ethan demanded and, without waiting for an answer, threw me over his shoulder and headed for the dance floor. I shrieked but managed not to spill too much of my drink. I waved at Alec, who was staring after us, his hands in fists.

I finished my drink as Ethan and I found Dot in the middle of the dance floor. Someone coming past took the empty glass, and I wrapped my hands around Ethan's neck. His hands went to my hips. Every inch of my front was pressed up against the hard muscles of Ethan's body.

After a few songs, I felt the heat of another body at my back, but Ethan smiled mischievously and the touch felt familiar, so I didn't panic. Another pair of hands landed on my waist, just above Ethan's, and when I turned my head to look, my eyes found intelligent gray ones.

I was a little surprised to see Tyler and not Josh, but I wasn't complaining. He caught my lips with his, teasing my mouth with his tongue as he pressed closer. The three of us moved seamlessly in time with the music, and I lost myself in their touch.

To see Tyler, who was always so careful and controlled, with a little bit of glassiness in his eyes—to feel him gripping my waist with his hands, kissing me so passionately in a room full of people—was driving me nuts! I loved to see him let loose a little. It was so rare, but when it happened, I just about went weak at the knees.

As the music changed to a slightly slower, more sultry beat, he broke the kiss and, always the leader, set the pace. It wasn't long before the three of us were pretty much just grinding on each other, and I was loving every second of it.

I glanced around the room. Alec stood near the hallway leading to the front of the house, his stare fixed on me. I didn't care how much he denied it—he was intense in everything he did. But as much as I teased him, I wouldn't change that. Alec didn't do anything by halves, and something about that was intoxicating, even as I got more and more frustrated by his assholeish behavior.

I kept my gaze fixed on his as Ethan and Tyler swayed with me, their hands running up and down my sides, gripping me, stroking me. Having Alec watching added another layer of desire to my already heated state.

The music changed to a loud and fast crowd favorite that had everyone jumping up and down to the beat. It broke our lust haze, and we pulled apart to join in.

My skin was still flushed, and the ache low in my belly wasn't going away. I looked back to where Alec had been standing. He was walking toward the front door, one hand rubbing his closely cropped hair. He must have reached his quota of peopling for the day, if not the week.

"I'm gonna check on Alec," I yelled close to Tyler's ear, and he gave me a look that somehow managed to be both skeptical and knowing.

I rolled my eyes and took off through the crowd.

Alec was being as up-front as the others when it came to our unspoken commitment to brutal honesty, but he was still avoiding deepening our physical connection. He'd relaxed about the extra Light since we'd discovered he could use it to take pain away and not just inflict it, but he was still hesitant, still insisting we needed to train and practice and be controlled about the levels. I couldn't get it into his head that controlling how much I transferred to them was effortless now, that knowing exactly how much they needed was second nature.

Of course, I hadn't crossed that physical barrier with Alec yet as I had with the others, so the Light was pushing me to him, drawing me to connect. On the rare occasion I did slip, it was always with him, and he always used it as ammo to argue we still needed to be careful.

But there was more to it. My mind kept filling in the "why" with the worst-case scenario: He didn't want me like that. He'd given in to the Light and accepted the Bond, but it wasn't what he truly wanted.

I could've asked him, of course, but I was being a coward. Once again, we found ourselves at a standstill, things between us strained.

As I descended the stairs past the front door, I had just enough liquid courage to push the issue, and I knew exactly how I wanted to push it.

The gravel crunched under my boots as I rushed to catch up to him, the light and noise of the party fading behind us. He must've heard me chasing him, but he didn't slow down—unyielding as ever. The tattoos I knew were all over his body peeked out from under the sleeves of his black T-shirt. The fabric stretched over his broad shoulders, tension making the corded muscle even more prominent.

I caught up and slid my hand into his, tugging lightly. He huffed but stopped immediately. "I'm not leaving, Evelyn. I just needed some air."

"I know." I tugged again, and he let me lead him between two of the massive trees lining the driveway. The party was in full swing, no one was around, and we were about halfway between the security at the gate and the security at the front door. We were alone, but I craved more privacy, more darkness. I always did with him.

I could've started a conversation, asked if he'd had enough of the party, made small talk. But I didn't feel like talking. There was more than one way to sort shit out between us.

I faced him, playing with the hem of my red sweater. Without thinking about it too hard, I whipped the soft fabric over my head and dropped it to the ground. The air was cool, but my skin felt as if it were on fire.

His eyes narrowed but stayed glued to mine, refusing to look down at my matching red lace bra. I pushed the pang of rejection aside, placed my hands on his hips, and tilted my face up, practically begging him to kiss me.

He was so still, every muscle in his body strained as if poised for an attack. I couldn't reach his lips if he didn't lower his head, so I pulled the neck of his T-shirt down and kissed his chest. He smelled like smoke from the bonfire and some other fresh, manly smell—probably his aftershave. I darted my tongue out for a tiny lick.

As if my tongue had flipped a switch, he grunted and sprang into motion. He grabbed under my ass with both hands and lifted me. I wrapped my legs around him, and my back slammed into the rough surface of the tree just as Alec's lips slammed into mine.

I groaned and rolled my hips. He was rock hard already. This was that all-consuming intensity I loved so much. I knew it wasn't healthy to avoid talking about our issues, but fuck if my body couldn't care less. When Alec kissed me like that, nothing else existed.

But as suddenly as it started, Alec broke the kiss and stepped away, dropping me to my feet. He leaned one hand on the tree next to my head and dragged the other down his face. We were both breathing hard.

"What are you . . . *why*, Alec?" I hated how desperate, how hurt, I sounded.

"You don't want this," he ground out, his eyes downcast.

"What?" I was not expecting that to be his answer. "You don't get to decide what I do and don't want, you fucking jerk."

His eyes flicked up, now full of defiance, his anger rising to meet mine. "You are so fucking impossible sometimes."

I took a deep breath. I hadn't come after him for this to become another screaming match. "Please explain what you mean, because I'm getting really confused, Alec. I can't keep doing this."

He sighed. "It's just the Light. You've done it with the other three, and the only reason you want me is because of the fucking Bond. It's pushing you to make it even."

I blinked and stared at him. He was keeping his distance because he thought I didn't want to be with him?

I threw my head back and laughed because I didn't know what else to do. The laugh ended on a groan, and I opened my eyes to look at him.

His teeth were grinding, his eyes narrowed, but there was hurt behind the anger.

"I'm not laughing at you," I rushed out. "I'm laughing because I've been having this exact same doubt—worrying that you didn't actually want to be with me. That you resented the Bond. Sometimes it's eerie how similar we are." I ended on a whisper.

"I want you." He ran his thumb over my cheek, and I leaned into the touch. "Don't ever doubt that. But I don't want to do this if it's not for the right reasons. I want you to want me too, and not just because the Light makes you."

"I *do* want you, you idiot," I whispered back, but he just gave me a skeptical look.

I rolled my eyes and swatted his hand away. "*You* can resist the pull of the Bond, have enough self-control to not fuck my brains out while the others are doing exactly that, but you don't believe *I* can decide for myself whether or not I want to be with you? So, what—you're not controlled by the Light but everyone else is? Give me a break."

He opened and closed his mouth a few times, then just sighed, defeated.

"Fine," I declared. "Then I'll prove it to you."

I sank to my knees, keeping my gaze locked on his, and slowly but confidently reached for his pants.

"What are you doing?" he asked, exasperated, as I started undoing the buttons on his jeans.

"Showing you I can control myself." I pushed down his pants, but before I could reach for the underwear, he wrapped his hands around my wrists.

"Get up, Evelyn, you don't know what you're doing."

I gritted my teeth. His assumption was patronizing and just plain mean, but I refused to allow my anger to rise. I had something to prove. I may not have been as experienced as him, but I'd been with enough guys to know how to give a blowjob.

I stayed exactly where I was and stared him down. He'd stopped what I was doing, but he wasn't leaving. That meant he didn't actually want to. I was *so* close to breaking him.

"Alec, remove your shirt, put your hands on the fucking tree, and shut up." I didn't let any frustration leak into my voice. He ground his teeth, his icy eyes glaring at me, his nostrils flared. Then he huffed, released my wrists, and did as he was told.

His shirt joined mine on the ground, and I spared a moment to appreciate his amazing body—the tattoos, the scars, the V at his hips leading right where I needed to focus. As he lifted his head to the dark sky on another sigh, I grinned.

He wasn't leaving, and he was actually listening to me. He was *trusting* me.

By the time his gaze returned to mine, I'd schooled my features into a neutral expression. I placed my hands on his hips, rubbing his hip bones with my thumbs to let him get used to my touch. Before I went any further, I checked in with my Light. The strain of it wasn't unbearable, but it was definitely nudging me to Alec, wanting to bring him into the fold of our Bond. I locked it down tight. I closed the flow in and out of me and bolted that shit.

Then I moved my fingers to the waistband of his briefs and pulled them down, freeing his erection.

As I slowly stroked him up and down, I could feel that pressure building at the base of my spine again, the desire to take more, to demand more from him. But I did my best to lock that down too and focused on the silky-smooth feeling of him in my hand.

I looked up at him. He was looking down, but he wasn't watching my hand; he was watching me, his eyes boring into mine, the emotion swirling there incomprehensible. I kept eye contact as I leaned forward and took him into my mouth.

His eyes narrowed, hooded; his lips parted on a sigh.

I loved every fucking second of it. I loved watching Alec give in, let go of some of that fear and self-loathing and just feel *good*.

It was *my* hands, *my* mouth making him feel good, making him let go.

I took him deeper into my mouth, swirling my tongue around the tip as I pulled away. One hand stayed at the base of his cock, the other at his hip as I set a steady rhythm.

He groaned, his breathing coming in pants. After a while his hips started making little involuntary jerks, and I knew he was close. But I refused to let him have any control.

I released him from my mouth and squeezed his hip to get his attention. He looked down at me, a hint of surprise and a little fear in his gaze.

"Don't move," I whispered, an inch away from his throbbing hardness. My eyes were challenging. "I am in control here. Understand?"

He nodded and bit his bottom lip.

I nearly groaned. I knew what it felt like to have those teeth biting *my* lip.

Once again, I took him into my mouth. He sighed, the sound pure ecstasy. I heard light scraping as he tried to grip the bark.

As Alec dug his nails into the tree, I dug mine into his hip, reminding him I was in charge. His breathing had become completely erratic, moans and groans escaping his mouth more and more often, eliciting my own sounds of pleasure.

My lips were starting to go a little numb from the constant friction, but it wasn't long before he released a guttural sound and came in my mouth. I swallowed it, gagging slightly as I wasn't prepared, then stroked him gently and sat back on my heels.

I rested my head against the tree and sighed. Above me, Alec was shaking lightly through the aftershock of his orgasm.

I stood slowly and pressed a kiss to his chest, letting his trembling arms box me in. When my lips touched his skin, he dropped his arms and wrapped me in a hug.

"Maybe you should sit before you fall down," I whispered into his neck, smiling.

"No." He nuzzled into my hair. "I have a favor to return."

He dragged his rough hands down my sides, then cupped my ass over my jeans.

I leaned away and put that serious look back on my face. "No. I don't want that from you today."

His brow furrowed in clear confusion and hurt. I realized I'd echoed the cruel words he'd left me with in Tyler's study, just after he'd driven me to the brink of ecstasy and not allowed me to return the favor.

"I want *everything* from you, Alec." I injected as much conviction into my voice as I could, saying the exact opposite of what he'd told me back then. "I want you in every way, and I don't know why you think I don't. But this is about me proving to you I have control. *I* have control over my Light and my desire. I'm *aching* for your touch. You have no idea how hard it is to say no, to remove your amazing hands from my body." As I spoke, I grabbed his wrists and took his hands off my ass. "But I'm going to walk away now to prove to you I can. I have just as much self-control as you, Bond be damned."

For a few seconds, I took in the stunned yet hopeful expression on his face, then I kissed him on the lips once, grabbed my sweater, and pulled it back on as I walked away. I made my point and left him there, his dick hanging out, shocked but satisfied and, hopefully, convinced.

The thumping bass from the house reminded me there was a party still in full swing, and I headed in search of my guys. I'd lit a spark with Alec that I hadn't allowed to ignite fully, but the music was pulsing and so was my desire. Someone was getting lucky tonight . . . maybe a few someones.

THREE

I was trying to finish my cereal before Ethan got back from his run. He loved feeding me, and it was always waffles this and poached eggs that. I loved it most of the time, but it was next to impossible to match the enthusiasm he had from the second he woke up. I needed coffee before I could even speak coherently. Sometimes, I just wanted to sit at the bench, eat my Wheaties, and drink my delicious latte.

I'd put the TV on for background noise but soon remembered why we were all avoiding it—except for Tyler, of course. The four TVs in his office were always on, and he scrolled through news sites on his phone as much as he sent messages and emails. I wondered if it was this aspect of his nature—the desire for knowledge—that had determined his Variant ability or if it was his ability that made him crave knowledge more and more. It was a chicken-and-egg problem. According to evolutionary biology, eggs in general have been around for roughly 340 million years, whereas chickens evolved some fifty-eight thousand years ago. Science had solved that problem, but I didn't know how to solve it in Tyler's case.

The news for the past month had been all about the events at the lab in Thailand. They were getting some of it wrong and just plain making up the rest, but the Melior Group board had put a gag on any of their staff discussing the events, and they'd encouraged survivors and their families to stay quiet too. They wanted to avoid spreading panic about the kind of experiments that had happened down there, as well as prevent tensions between humans and Variants from escalating.

I shoved another spoonful of cereal into my mouth and frowned at the TV. I hadn't registered the channel when I turned it on, but the remote was so far away, in the living room, I didn't have the energy to get up and change it.

It was on a conservative human news network. They had a rotating stream of politicians and social commentators making wild assumptions and whipping up fear.

"... and why won't the mighty Melior Group comment on what exactly they found?" demanded a heavily made-up middle-aged woman in a blue pantsuit. The rest of the panel nodded in agreement. "Surely they've finished their investigation by now, but they won't even tell us *that* much. How can we be sure it wasn't actually *them* running these experiments—trying to make themselves stronger or inventing new abilities. I mean, this could be a real threat to national security, Tom." Her face was nearly purple as she finished her tirade.

"What a moron," I mumbled into my cup, taking another sip of my latte.

"Who's a moron?" Tyler came into the kitchen dressed in a white shirt with a tie, his hair the neatest I'd ever seen it.

I pointed at the TV with my spoon. "Some nutbag."

He frowned, went over to the living area, and changed the channel to a breakfast show. "Don't watch that crap, baby. We know the truth. That's all that matters."

I huffed but couldn't help smiling. He'd called me "baby." I'd been having regular sex with him for weeks now, but I still had a massive crush. Any time he flirted or used a pet name, I got butterflies in my stomach.

"Why are you all dressed up?" I asked.

He was standing at the fridge, eating strawberry yogurt from the tub. "I have a meeting." He looked at his watch. "And I'll be late if I don't get going."

He shoved three more giant spoonfuls into his mouth, gathered his messenger bag, kissed me on the lips (butterflies!), and ran off.

I'd just stood up to put my bowl in the dishwasher when Ethan and Josh came into the kitchen. They were both freshly showered after their workout, Ethan's hair slightly damp but Josh's perfectly styled and parted on the side.

"Hey, pumpkin tits!" Ethan grinned at me as Josh wrapped his arms around me from the back, nuzzling his nose into my hair. "Want some breakfast?"

I absentmindedly rested my hands over Josh's. "No thanks. I ate."

I didn't throw a ridiculous nickname back at him—the TV had distracted me again. The cooking segment had given way to a news report. "Protests against Variant-run institutions and businesses have turned violent as tensions between human picketers and frustrated Variant business owners begin to boil over. In Los Angeles, a large group of protesters outside a Variant abilities training studio started breaking windows, and a fight broke out when the business owner—a Variant with a water ability—attempted to disperse the crowd by dousing them with water. Similar incidents have occurred in other cities the world over, with some of the worst violence seen in Moscow, where a riot erupted. The widespread violence resulted in several deaths and many injuries with . . ."

I hardly registered Ethan's protestations about me having fed myself. I waved him off, my full focus on the TV.

Variant Valor were getting louder and more brazen in their discriminatory rhetoric, and more and more Variants were no longer ashamed to say they subscribed to the organization's extremist views. Some had even set up local branches and held meetings. We'd been invited to more than one in Bradford Hills. Tyler and the administration at the Institute were doing all they could to shut it down, but there wasn't much they could do about people meeting off campus.

The Human Empowerment Network had taken on a life of its own. Melior Group investigations had all but confirmed that the HEN had been started by Variant Valor and Davis Damari himself to create more fear and unrest, making it easier to push the boundaries of what was acceptable in terms of controversial legislation and risky experiments and business ventures. Davis had no qualms about breaking the law when it came to his demented science experiments. He had enough power and influence to build an underground facility in Thailand without anyone knowing or questioning it.

"It's going to turn into World War III at this rate." I groaned and rubbed my forehead as images of the riots in Russia flicked across the screen.

Josh used his ability to press the power button on the remote. "Hey, look at me." He turned me in his arms, and I looked into his kind green eyes. "The news always makes it seem worse than it is. They're fearmongers. That's exactly what Davis wants—more fear—but it doesn't change the facts. There's a whole private security firm, hundreds of highly trained operatives, working against him. All you have to worry about today is focusing on your lectures and your chemistry lab. OK?" He raised his eyebrows.

I nodded and went to get ready for school, but the heavy feeling of dread still sat in the pit of my stomach. I focused instead on the weight of the books I stuffed into my bag and the hint of Josh's cologne as I slipped on his Bradford Hills Institute hoodie.

When I'd grabbed everything I needed, I went back downstairs, sitting on the bottom step to put my boots on. They were a cute black pair of ankle boots that went great with my skinny jeans.

"Has Tyler left already?" Lucian came out of the west wing corridor dressed in a suit and tie, a briefcase on his knees. "I thought we were heading in together."

He looked around and I followed his gaze. Plaster dust covered the marble floor of the foyer, and various piles of building material and tools littered one side of the wide space. Lucian had to navigate slowly around some timber to join me at the staircase, and I frowned at the offending wood. I would have to have a chat with the contractors about being mindful of their client.

"He said something about having an important meeting and ran out about half an hour ago." I shrugged.

"Oh. Must've come up last minute." Lucian shrugged too, not at all put out by the fact that his adopted nephew and righthand man had left him behind.

Boots thudded down the stairs. I turned to see Alec jogging down, dressed in his Melior Group blacks but not armed. His ink was snaking out of the sleeves of the tight long-sleeved T-shirt and crawling up his neck. I wanted to tear the fabric away to see them fully, move my hands down his defined, scarred chest and undo his belt . . .

"You're going in with me and my team, Uncle Luce." Alec's deep voice drew me out of my lascivious thoughts, and I was glad I couldn't blush. "Gabe had to rush in."

"Ready when you are." Lucian smiled and started to wheel himself over to the garage door. "Have a good day, Evie."

"You too!" I yelled after him.

Alec held a hand out, and I took it, letting him pull me up to standing. His jaw tightened as he watched Lucian navigate the new ramp down into the garage.

His focus was on his uncle, but his hand was still wrapped around mine. We'd come so far from the days when he couldn't even stand to be in the same room as me, but every step forward with Alec felt like a step up an impossibly steep incline, and the path was along a cliff with no railings. Shit could turn catastrophic at any moment.

But the blowjob I'd given him at the party had made my point. We hadn't talked about it, but I knew Alec needed to process things in his own silent way. Sometimes that took him a long time. Meanwhile, every time I laid eyes on him, I wanted to jump him and tear his clothes off. Part of that was the Light pushing me to even the connection to my Bondmates, but part of it was *me*.

I just hoped I'd proven I could control that aspect of our connection. He was more affectionate, slowly thawing out. He was getting there. But would he get there before my ovaries exploded?

I gave his hand a squeeze. "He'll be fine. He's a strong man. He raised your stubborn ass, didn't he?"

Alec looked down at me and blinked in surprise, but his beautiful lips pulled up into a smirk. Rather than acknowledge my assumption about what he was thinking, he pressed those smirking lips against mine, pushing his tongue into my mouth.

I couldn't even remember what I was teasing him about.

"Upstairs . . ." I whispered against his lips. I couldn't even fully form the thought; I just wanted to get him into a locked room. He groaned and ran his teeth over the curve in my neck before placing a gentle kiss in the same spot.

"Duty calls," he growled. He gave my ass one last squeeze and stepped away.

"And we'll be late to class if we don't get going." Josh sounded amused as Ethan grabbed my bag off the bottom step, flashing me a wink and a dimple. When did they even come into the room?

Alec kissed my forehead and disappeared into the garage. I took several deep breaths and made myself think about the chemistry lab I had that afternoon.

Two silent agents drove us to campus in a blacked-out, bulletproof vehicle, another car following close behind. The bald man in the passenger seat was my security detail for the day. Since I often had Alec or Tyler with me, I didn't have a regular guard, so when they were both busy, it was always someone different.

I stared out the window at the trees swaying in the light wind and soft sunlight. All the snow had melted weeks ago, and despite the lingering chill, it would've been a nice day to walk. But our days of walking to campus were over. Being exposed outside of a safe zone—like the Institute, the mansion, or Charlie and Dot's place—had been deemed too much of a security risk.

Thinking about chemistry, the weather, and the constant threat on my life helped to distract me from Alec's lips and body, and by the time we were pulling through the security checkpoint at the gates, the throbbing between my legs had almost completely stopped.

My bald companion stayed glued to my side the entire morning, opting to sit next to me in the lecture instead of standing in the back of the room with the other agents. Despite his closeness, he refused to engage in conversation, replying with short monotone answers while his eyes constantly scanned our surroundings. I eventually just started to ignore him.

He stayed one step behind me as I walked between classes, got myself a coffee, and picked up a book from the library. He was still half a step behind me as I headed to a café in a quieter part of campus to meet Dot and Charlie for lunch.

It was the same café where Dot had interrogated me about Alec while Charlie watched with careful interest. It seemed fitting it would be the place I would meet yet another new friend. Charlie's boyfriend, Eduardo, had landed late the previous night.

The three of them were already seated at one of the outside tables, coffees steaming in front of them, outdoor heaters keeping the chill at bay. I picked up my pace, my shadow sticking to my side.

"Hey!" I waved as I reached them, slightly winded. "I'm so sorry I'm late. My last class was on the other side of campus."

"Totally fine, girl." Dot jumped up to give me a hug, and I held her tightly for a moment. The horrific shit I was seeing in the news every day made me want to hold all my loved ones a little tighter. "We ordered you a latte."

"I love you!" I was hungry, but I needed coffee just as badly.

"Hey, Beau! Haven't seen you in a while, man. How've you been?" Charlie shared an enthusiastic handshake with my shadow, and the man's seemingly permanent scowl actually relaxed.

"Good to see you up and about, Charlie. I had to take some medical leave after rescuing your ass in Thailand. Had a couple broken ribs and shit."

Charlie laughed. "Well, thanks, man, and good to see you back on the job too. Wanna join us for lunch?"

Beau flicked his gaze to me before straightening his posture. "Thanks, but I'm on duty. Better get back to it." With a nod, he stepped back and positioned himself near the corner of the building, where he could see the whole square and keep me in easy reach.

"Eve!" Charlie didn't miss a beat. He was more animated and talkative than I'd seen him . . . probably ever. "Meet Eduardo."

He reached his arm out. A guy with short curly hair and a tan complexion stepped into Charlie's embrace and smiled at me shyly, his dark eyes meeting mine for only a fraction of a second.

"Hello." His voice was smooth and masculine but soft, almost hard to hear.

"Hi. I'm Evelyn. It's so nice to meet you!" I stuck my hand out and plastered a wide, genuine smile to my face.

He stepped away from Charlie and squared his shoulders, but instead of shaking my hand, he wrapped his arms around my waist and pulled me in for a hug.

"Oh!" He seemed so shy and quiet. The sudden display of familiarity took me aback.

I returned the hug, but he pulled back quickly.

"Thank you, Evelyn." He had a slight Spanish accent. "You saved our lives. More and more Vitals were not coming back from the lab. I don't know how much time we had left before he went too far and . . . I don't know how to repay you."

Now it was me who was unable to keep eye contact. I'd received multiple emails and DMs on social media from grateful Vitals and their families. Many people had approached me at Bradford Hills with the same depth of gratitude Eduardo was showing now. It always surprised me.

"You're welcome." I smiled, keeping it simple.

"For someone who hounded Alec for months trying to deliver your own 'thanks for saving my life' speech, you sure don't know how to take it," Dot teased, breaking the moment.

"Hey! At least I accepted the thanks." I wagged a finger at her, and we all settled into our seats and ordered.

Once our food arrived, I turned to Charlie's new boyfriend, eager to get to know him. "So, Eduardo—"

"Please," he cut me off, "call me Ed."

"Ed." I smiled. "Your brother is your Variant?"

"Yes." He swallowed his bite of pasta before continuing. "He has a strength ability. It was hard for him to have me leave again, but he couldn't get time off work, and I had to see Charlie."

"I wish you could stay longer." Charlie pouted.

"I'm staying for a whole month!" Ed laughed but rubbed Charlie's knee.

We chatted easily for the next half hour, the sun pleasantly warm on my back. As the waitress cleared our table, a familiar noodle of fluff caught my attention. Squiggles came running out of the trees. She scampered up Dot's leg but then immediately shot across the table straight at Eduardo.

"Hey, girl!" I reached out to give her a little pat—we were becoming friends, despite only being able to communicate through Dot. She usually went straight to me after checking in with her.

Dot groaned, throwing her head back. "She can't even talk to you! How was she supposed to let you know?" She bugged her eyes out at Squiggles, and the ferret gave her a death stare, lifting her little paws onto Ed's chest.

"What's going on?" I chuckled.

"She's upset we didn't tell her we were having lunch. *Really* she's upset she lost sight of Ed for an hour. It's not my fault you don't like the food I buy you and insist on hunting your own." Dot rolled her eyes.

"Squiggles has taken a liking to Ed," Charlie explained as Ed started to scratch her little head.

"It's because I give the best head scratches," Ed cooed at the ferret.

"He does." Charlie nodded seriously, as if we were discussing Ed's qualifications for a high-paying job. "He gives the best head scratches."

Ed just smiled and lifted his other hand to the back of Charlie's head, giving him the same treatment. Both Charlie and Squiggles closed their eyes and melted into his touch.

Dot bugged her eyes at me and shook her head. *Can you believe this shit?*

I laughed silently, my shoulders shaking. *Who cares? I'm happy they're happy.*

I really was. It warmed my heart more than I could describe. Charlie still struggled with what happened to him, but he was seeing a therapist specializing in trauma, and he was safe and happy. That would always make me smile.

My phone vibrated on the table, and I picked it up and opened the email without thinking.

Dear Miss Maynard,

You don't know me, and I hope you don't mind me messaging you out of the blue. But I saw the footage of you where you glowed, and it was so similar to my own experience that I just had to reach out and . . .

The smile fell from my face, and I exited the email without finishing it, dropping my phone on the table a little harder than intended.

"What's the matter?" Dot's voice was heavy with concern. A split second later, Squiggles leaped into my lap, her little face looking up at me.

I stroked her back, feeling the soft fur under my fingers. "Nothing really. I'm fine. Just keep getting these emails."

"What emails?" Charlie leaned forward. "Is someone bothering you?"

I waved him off. "It's nothing like that. I just keep getting messages from people claiming . . . They're from other Vitals saying they can glow like me."

"Have you been replying?" Charlie reached down for the messenger bag he usually had with him—the one with his computer. He was already going into super-hacker mode, ready to look into it, but he didn't have his computer with him. With a frown, he returned his hand to the table.

"No, I've just been ignoring them. After everything that's happened, how can I trust any of them are genuine? I mean, statistically I know it's improbable that I'm the only one with this . . . quirk. But any one of them could be Davis trying to lure me in. It's too risky and too convenient. Why have none of them come forward before? How is there absolutely no mention of this glowing bullshit anywhere? Like, *none* whatsoever?" I was starting to ramble, frustration leaking into my words as I gestured wildly.

Charlie caught one of my hands and held it on the table between us. I took a deep breath and returned the other to Squiggles's fur.

"You're right to be suspicious, Eve." Charlie gave me a hard look. "But I'm sure some part of you is curious?"

"Of course! But with Davis breathing down our necks, Variants and humans tearing each other to pieces, my GPA needing to be kept up, and Alec's stubborn ass refusing to have sex with me . . ."

I clamped my mouth shut. I couldn't believe I'd just blurted that out. Dot knew most of it anyway, and I didn't mind talking to Charlie about it, but the last thing I wanted to do was make Ed uncomfortable. When I looked in his direction though, his expression was nothing but concerned, if a little amused.

"We can deal with the Master of Pain's sexual hang-ups another day." Dot waved her hand.

"And we can deal with the emails whenever you want." Charlie patted my arm. "I can look into them, do some digging, see if they're at least legit people. But you're entitled to a private life, Eve. You don't have to answer them if you don't want to."

I nodded and let Dot change the topic. I could see Charlie's point; I was under no obligation to reply to any of these people. But the main reason I was avoiding the emails wasn't privacy—it was fear. The idea that this was another way for Davis to suck me into his clutches again—that it could put my Variants, my friends, my family in danger—terrified me.

But my mind was naturally curious. Surely some of them were legitimate, honest calls for help? If these people were telling the truth, they were likely just as scared and confused about their glowing as I was. Maybe getting together could help us solve the riddle of what the glowing was. Was that worth putting us all in potential danger again?

On the other hand, could I live with making decisions out of fear, especially at the expense of truth and knowledge? Did I want to live like that?

FOUR

The morning of my nineteenth birthday, I wasn't entirely sure how to feel. I'd found the answers to questions I'd been living with for years. I had my Bond, and we were getting stronger every day. For the first time in my life, I was introducing myself as Evelyn Maynard. I was even starting to feel as if I was part of a family.

Yet the first thing I thought about was the fact that it had been two years since I lost my mom.

I missed her so much.

I wanted to remember all the good things about her, not the gut-wrenching way her hand had been yanked out of mine as she fell to her death. That was the visual my brain kept replaying in vivid detail.

Regardless of all the positives in my life, bad things always happened around my birthday. Why should that change now?

Shit could go horribly wrong in so many different ways. Maybe this was the day Davis ordered another attack by Variant Valor. Maybe Zara would come for me with Rick's lightning ability. Maybe some other horrific thing would happen—something my mind couldn't even fathom. I was tempted to stay in bed with the curtains drawn.

But I also had people to spend my birthday *with* now. I knew my guys would have something planned, despite my telling them how I felt about birthdays. They would all be downstairs, waiting for me. Tyler and Alec would've taken the day off work. Ethan would be planning an elaborate feast. Josh had probably put an insane amount of thought into a present. I couldn't pass that up.

Ignoring the whispering what-ifs in the back of my head, I got out of bed. I brushed my teeth, stuffed my feet into my astronaut boot slippers, and headed downstairs.

As soon as I reached the bottom, Lucian came out of the corridor leading to the west wing.

"Good morning, Evie." He rolled to a stop in front of me and smiled. "Happy birthday."

I smiled back, but it didn't reach my eyes. "Thank you."

Before I could continue to the kitchen, he spoke again. "I know this day is incredibly difficult for you." He took my hand. I was expecting it to be awkward, but it was comforting. "I was hoping you would let me take you out for breakfast."

"Oh." My eyebrows rose in surprise. "Like, all of us or . . . ?" I could hear the espresso machine working in the kitchen, several male voices chatting.

"Uh, that's not what I had in mind, no. But if that's what you'd prefer . . ." He dropped my hand, gripped the wheels of his chair, and cleared his throat. "When the boys came to live with me, we kind of started a new tradition. On their birthdays I take them out, and we spend some one-on-one time together. Sometimes it's just a meal or a coffee. Other times it's a movie or an entire day. The idea is to have some quality time that's just theirs. You're a part of this family, and I'd very much like to include you in this tradition. Of course you should spend the day with your Bond, but I'd love to at least take you for coffee."

I swallowed around the lump in my throat. "I'd really like that."

I gave him my first genuine smile of the morning. I had a feeling Lucian would've been a great father. Then I realized that's exactly what he was. He was a father to the four orphaned men in the next room.

He was being a father to me.

It was the best birthday present I'd ever received.

"I'll just go get dressed." I turned for the stairs just as Ethan burst out of the kitchen.

"You're up!" He headed straight for me as he yelled over his shoulder, "Guys! She's up!"

Ethan lifted me off the ground with a firm grip around my waist and planted a dramatic kiss on my lips. "Happy birthday, sugarplum." He flashed me his dimples.

"Thanks, honey bear."

He set me back on my feet. Tyler wrapped his arms around me from behind and gave me the sweetest kiss on the cheek, whispering "Happy birthday" in my ear. I melted into his embrace, closing my eyes.

But the next thing I knew, the distinct sensation of Josh's ability tugged along my skin, and I was pulled out of Tyler's arms and straight into Josh's.

A burst of joyful laughter bubbled out of me. Josh's hugs were always a little too firm—as if he thought I'd disappear if he didn't hold on tightly enough—but I loved them.

After a barely there kiss, he whispered "Happy birthday" against my lips and slowly, reluctantly released me.

I looked over his shoulder. Alec stood slightly apart from the group, his hands in his pockets, his bright eyes watching. His strong features were relaxed—not frowning or scowling—as he waited patiently.

He'd spent a long time waiting for me.

He extended his hand, and I stepped forward and took it. As he pulled me to him, a little pang of excited nervousness shot down my spine. Would he kiss me tenderly and whisper in that honey voice? Would he bruise my lips with his intensity? I never knew.

It turned out to be a combination of the two. His sexy smirk appeared, and my honey-voiced stranger told me, "Happy birthday, Evie." He pulled me against his chest and threaded his hand into the back of my hair. Then Alec Zacarias, Master of Pain himself, kissed me silly. I sighed, my arms brushing against the prickles of his closely cropped hair.

Someone cleared their throat. I froze and extracted myself from Alec's grip, taking a moment to catch my breath before turning back to the rest of my Bond and Uncle Lucian.

Ethan clapped his hands, the booming sound bouncing off the walls. "OK. Pancakes for breakfast?"

"Actually," I said, and they all pulled up short, "I have plans."

"Plans?" Tyler arched a brow, but Josh's eyes flew to the kind man in the wheelchair, and his lips turned up in a smile.

"Yeah. I promise I'll spend the day with you guys, but Uncle Lucian is taking me out for breakfast. Just the two of us."

I couldn't stop the grin. I hadn't intended to call him Uncle Lucian, but now that it was out there, it felt right. If things had turned out differently, I may have grown up calling him Dad, maybe never even knowing he wasn't my birth father. But that title didn't sit right. Calling him what the guys did felt natural.

I ducked my head to hide my goofy grin and made my way back upstairs before anyone could say anything.

Twenty minutes later, my hair was brushed, and I was dressed in jeans and a long, thick cardigan, an oversized scarf wrapped around my neck to ward off the cold. Lucian's driver chauffeured us—in a brand-new, wheelchair-friendly vehicle—to the little café that made the best coffee in town. The waiter seated us at a corner table and handed us some menus.

Two agents sat at a nearby table, but the rest of the security detail remained outside.

After perusing for only a few seconds, Lucian dropped the menu back on the table. "Pancakes," he breathed sadly. I frowned. "Maybe we should've stayed at home, had Ethan make you pancakes. I'm sorry . . . I forgot . . . She kept it going, right? She mentioned it several times, that she still made pancakes for you every year and . . ."

"Yes, she kept it going." I reached out and covered his hand with mine. "You know, come to think of it, I've never missed a year. Even last year, when I was in foster care with this older couple—Marty and Baz—Marty made me pancakes." I smiled fondly, reminding myself to send them an email when I got home. "They weren't Mom's pancakes, and all it did was make me think harder about the fact that she's gone, but I appreciated the gesture."

Lucian opened his mouth to say something just as our waiter walked up to the table.

"Ready to order, folks?"

"I'll have the pancakes and a latte." I didn't hesitate as I handed over my menu.

"I'll have the same." Lucian nodded. "But make mine an English breakfast tea, milk on the side."

The waiter took our menus and moved off.

I made a disgusted face. "English breakfast tea?"

Lucian laughed. "What? I lived in London for years. I picked up some habits. It's pretty good when the tea is high quality."

"I never took you for a tea snob," I teased.

"Look who's talking, miss 'fair-trade, organic espresso or nothing.'"

"At least you don't make your tea in the microwave," I conceded as we both cringed. America was the only country I'd lived in where the concept of a kettle was foreign.

"I have to admit, it's good having those espresso machines at the house and the apartment for when I want a decent coffee. Don't know why I didn't put them in sooner."

"Maybe because you can wave a distinguished hand and someone rushes out to get you one whenever you want."

He rubbed his chin in an exaggerated way. "You might be onto something. Maybe it's the novelty of doing it myself—experiencing how average people do it."

We both laughed. I was happy to see he had a sense of humor about his obscene amount of money. Just like Ethan, he didn't let his privilege go to his head.

We spent the next half hour eating the fluffy, sweet pancakes and sipping our tea and coffee while we chatted, avoiding the heavier topics of my mother and all the tensions in the world. When our plates and cups were empty, a comfortable silence settled between us. I stared out the window at the people strolling past on Bradford Hills' main street.

"Evie, before we head off"—Lucian's expression became solemn—"I wanted to speak to you about something. And if you don't want to discuss this today, just say so. It's totally fine. But I wanted to talk to you about setting up a memorial plaque for Joyce."

"Oh." I didn't know what to say. The idea hadn't even occurred to me. I'd spent the past two years trying to just survive without my mom.

Suddenly I felt as if I was letting her down. She deserved to have something permanent to mark her life. She deserved to be remembered and honored. Tears stung my eyes, and I took a labored swallow around the lump in my throat.

Lucian sighed. "I'm sorry I brought it up. I know this must be an incredibly difficult day for you, and I just wanted to do something to focus on the person she was instead of dwell on the way she died. We can discuss it another time."

I looked at the ceiling, trying to dry up my tears before they fell. "No. It's just a really emotional day for me. To be honest, I'm feeling bad I didn't think of it."

He smiled. "You've had a lot to deal with, and honestly—"

Whatever he was about to say was cut off by a loud whooshing that drowned out all other noise. A wind so strong it overturned tables and chairs exploded through the café, making it difficult to breathe.

I threw my hands up instinctually to protect my head, but through a gap in my forearms, I saw one of the Melior Group agents get taken out—by *water*.

All the liquid in the area—the teas and coffees, the dishwater in the sink, the water in the small fish tank on a side table—congregated into one ugly, gray, writhing ball of water, which affixed itself to the head and upper body of one of our protectors.

The man pulled his gun but quickly realized it was useless. What good were bullets against a seemingly sentient ball of liquid? He thrashed, bumping into people and furniture still being tossed about by the wind. After a few minutes of frantic scratching and clawing, he fell to his knees, then onto his front, his body convulsing as he drowned.

Once he stopped moving, the water lost its shape and pooled around him. His empty eyes stared upward, wide and unblinking.

The unrelenting wind whipped my hair around my face, making it almost impossible to hear or move. I jumped as someone's hand closed around my wrist, but when I turned, it was only Lucian. His chair had been pushed up against the wall. He pulled on my arm, gesturing for me to get behind him as his eyes flicked to something over my shoulder.

I dropped to my knees, and the chair I'd been sitting on flew into the cyclone. Struggling to keep my balance, I crawled over to lean against Lucian's legs and try to get my bearings.

Most of the people in the café, as well as the furniture, had been pushed to the walls. Some cowered in fear; others appeared to be unconscious or dead. I had no idea where the agents outside were or if they were even alive.

The drowned agent's partner lay half-behind the counter, a snapped-off chair leg sticking out of his chest.

Blood dripped from his mouth and the wound, puddling beneath the gun next to his outstretched hand. The wind slowly dragged the weapon across the tiles, marking a crimson streak along the ground as it skittered past a pair of small purple boots. I followed the legs up until I was looking at a young woman. She was the only one in the room standing, not at all affected by the wind. The blonde hair in her messy ponytail didn't even stir.

She was short, maybe a half foot taller than Dot, and dressed in jeans and a black long-sleeved T-shirt. A dirty apron hugged her hips. She looked like one of the kitchen staff—an unassuming twenty-something, maybe even a Bradford Hills student—except for the crazed look in her narrowed eyes and the way her teeth gritted as she arced her hands in wide sweeps.

She was coming straight for me and bringing *fire* with her.

The wind didn't abate, but now she was drawing fire from the grill in the back, pulling it forward, letting it swirl with the wind and ignite everything it touched. Her intense gaze never left me as she approached with small, slow steps.

If the chaos and destruction so far hadn't already scared me stiff, the intention in her look and posture certainly would have. My heart hammered in my chest. Every muscle in my body tensed as my mind went crazy with options, but they flew through my head too fast for me to grab on to an idea and run with it.

I couldn't move, couldn't call for help, couldn't do anything to attack her or defend myself.

Defend. *Block*!

Maybe I couldn't do it, but Lucian could.

I reached a hand up, and his warm grip closed around my wrist. As soon as I had skin contact, I pushed as much Light into him as I could.

Transferring to a Variant outside my Bond always took more time and effort, but I forced the Light to bend to my will quickly. It poured into Lucian almost as fast as it did to my Variants.

Before the woman was halfway to us, Lucian raised his other hand over my shoulder. Finally, I could breathe properly.

I heaved a few gasping breaths, my limbs trembling as the intense pressure of the cyclone released. My hand stayed tightly wrapped around Lucian's wrist to maintain the flow of Light.

He'd thrown up a shield. The wind and fire lashed against it angrily, revealing its invisible domelike shape.

Smoke choked the air. The wind had whipped the flames into a furious blaze. People were coughing and spluttering, trying to move away from the woman and the fire.

Lucian's shield kept growing. I didn't know how far it could expand, but it was the only thing we had at the moment, so I kept pumping him full of Light until we could figure out another way out of this. Several people got encased in his protective ability and scrambled closer to us. Some started trying to open the door, but it wasn't budging.

We only had half the people protected, and some of the others were starting to get burned. Their screams mingled with the deafening roar of the wind.

The woman's voice rang out, loud and clear over it all. "Give her to me!"

If there had been any doubt she was after me, it was just smashed to pieces. People were dead because of me; they were getting hurt, injured, burned. How many more would die? Lucian couldn't seem to make his shield expand farther, couldn't reach the people on the other side of the room.

Fear, desperation, and hopelessness constricted my throat like a noose. I looked around desperately for something, anything . . .

My wide eyes locked on the gun that had slid past her. It was just out of my reach, but I didn't hesitate. I dropped Lucian's hand, hoping he could sustain the barrier for even a few moments, and lunged for it.

It was sticky with the dead man's blood, but I lifted onto my knees and held it with both hands, just as Ty had shown me. I pointed it right at her chest—the easiest target for inexperienced shooters to hit—and pulled the trigger.

The recoil threw me off balance, and I dropped one hand to the ground to steady myself, unable to follow through with another shot. By the time I recovered, the chaos had stopped.

The woman stood in the middle of the café, a stunned look on her face as she clutched a spot just under her right breast. Blood oozed between her fingers.

Moans of pain filled the café. Some people scrambled up and moved toward the door, which was barred with pretty much all the furniture in the building. Others remained frozen, watching the woman warily.

Shouts and barked commands could be heard from outside. They would have access to us in a matter of moments.

I kept my gun on her.

"He's never going to stop coming for you." Her steady, if a little high-pitched, voice was directed to the ground. "Do you understand?" She looked up at me, her eyes wild. "He's *never* going to stop."

I adjusted my grip on the weapon, ignoring the shuffling behind me as people shifted furniture away from the door. I kept my laser focus on her.

"It's better if you just . . ." Her free hand curled into a fist. Blood dripped from her wound onto the floor, and she swayed a little, widening her stance. "It's better for all of us if you just . . . *die.*"

Behind her, fire from the grill rose several feet into the air, then swirled toward me like a striking snake.

The gun was snatched from my grip. Lucian pointed and fired. Unlike me, he knew how to handle a gun. He fired off three shots in quick succession—two to her chest and one to the head.

The fire fizzled out inches from my face as the woman crumpled to the ground, dead.

Despite his messy clothes and tangled hair from the gale-force winds, Lucian's face was calm, determined. He lowered the weapon and looked at me.

Melior Group agents streamed into the space from the newly cleared front door and the back of the building, guns raised, shouting orders.

"Are you hurt?" Lucian's sole focus was still me.

I slumped against the side of his chair. "I don't think so. But I don't think I can walk just yet." My voice was hoarse, and I dropped my head, taking deep breaths.

Lucian's hand went to the tangled mess at the back of my head—I didn't look forward to brushing through that later—but he didn't ask any more questions.

The next few hours both dragged on painfully slowly and were a blur of activity. The guys showed up around the same time as the ambulances. Tyler's black Escalade screeched to a halt at the curb, the doors opening before it had even fully stopped. They flocked to me like birds—big, muscled, tense, angry birds. But their hands were gentle, their kisses soft.

Eventually the EMTs made them back away so they could check me for injuries. Alec lingered the longest, his hands on either side of my head, his forehead pressed to mine. He was in full gear now. I had no idea when he'd had time to put on the vest and strap all the weapons on.

"Alec, I'm OK. Just let them check me so we can go home."

He kissed my forehead and leaned away. "You're going to the hospital for a thorough check-up, but I have to stay here for a while. I . . ." He hesitated, but I could see the *love* in his eyes, could practically feel the words trying to tumble off his lips. "I'll be there as soon as I can."

He turned and walked away, his shoulders stiff. Kyo fell into step beside him, with Marcus and Jamie following close behind.

As the EMTs started checking me for injuries, I turned to Tyler. "I didn't know he was working today."

"He was on call. He'll have to stay until things are finalized here." Tyler cast his eyes over the scene, his brow creasing. The place was crawling with Melior Group operatives, as well as local police. "It's good for us to have someone we trust on the ground anyway."

I wasn't sure what he meant by that. Couldn't we trust anyone employed by Melior Group? Weren't they all under Lucian's orders and at Tyler's beck and call? I kept my mouth shut; this wasn't the best time to raise the issue.

Lucian lost patience with the EMTs before I did, insisting he was fine and wheeling himself over to one of the senior police officers.

Josh sighed. "I'll go talk him into going home."

Law enforcement interviewed everyone while the street was still shut down. Businesses had been evacuated while we were still fighting for our lives inside. No one was permitted to return yet, but a crowd was gathering at both ends of the street, held back by police tape and armed men.

When a news van rolled up, I groaned. Soon after that we left. We managed to convince Lucian to come with us, but he refused to go to the hospital. Despite the guys' arguments, I insisted that if Lucian wasn't going, neither was I. I just wanted a shower, something to eat, and the safety of home.

Grudgingly, and with a cavalcade worthy of a president, Tyler drove us back to the mansion.

"Food or shower first?" Ethan held my hand all the way home, up the stairs from the garage, and through the foyer. I really wanted a shower, but the mention of food had my stomach growling. It was well past lunchtime, and near-death situations really took it out of a girl.

I tried not to dwell on the fact that I'd been in enough near-death situations to know that.

Ethan was all too happy to feed us, whipping up some mac and cheese. We all slumped around the dining table. Lucian wheeled into his spot at the head, and Josh pulled me into his lap, crushing me to his chest.

Tyler was on the phone, demanding updates and answering questions while Lucian threw in his two cents over his shoulder.

As Ethan dropped bowls in front of us, Tyler hung up. "It's confirmed. Our guys raided the woman's apartment in Bradford Hills East and found all kinds of Variant Valor paraphernalia, including propaganda material. On her computer they also found some direct communication between her and some of Davis's higher-ups. They're discreetly telling some of their more zealous followers they need you."

He looked right at me, tired, resigned. Considering what she'd said, it wasn't much of a surprise.

I picked up my fork and started eating. The mac and cheese was delicious, as Ethan's food always was—

THE COMPLETE EVELYN MAYNARD TRILOGY

creamy and rich with little bits of bacon through it. Perfect comfort food.

"Why did she try to kill me?" I asked my empty plate, interrupting whatever it was they were talking about. I'd tuned out, but now my food was gone; I couldn't stop my brain from demanding answers.

I looked into Tyler's calm gray eyes. "At the end, after I shot her and she lost control of her ability, she said something about it being better for everyone if I just died, and then she came straight for me. If Davis needs me, why would she try to kill me?"

Had we read the situation wrong?

Tyler shared a loaded look with Lucian but didn't try to evade the question. He was getting much better about the whole "keeping secrets to protect me" bullshit. "We also found some evidence that Variant Valor was threatening her family. I suspect she realized she was going to fail to capture you, that she was probably going to die, so she decided to kill you"—his eyes darkened and his hands curled into fists, making the roped muscles in his forearms twist—"in order to prevent others from going through what she was going through."

"He's getting desperate." Lucian took a sip of his whiskey.

"He's always been desperate. He's just no longer hiding it as well as he used to," Josh observed.

Davis had been obsessed with my mother's glowing Light for years. That fixation had driven his every decision. And now here I was—capable of even more—and I was just out of reach. There was no doubt in my mind he would do whatever he deemed necessary to get to me. My shoulders slumped. How many people had to die?

I cleared my throat and pushed the despair deep down into a dark, soundless part of myself where I could avoid dealing with it a little longer, right between Zara's betrayal and Alec's undying love.

"What was her ability exactly?" I gave my mind something else to think about. "I've never seen it before."

"It was a rare one," Tyler answered. "She had the ability to control the elements. Not like Kid—she couldn't conjure fire like he can, but she could control existing fire, water, air."

I thought back to how the liquids formed a ball to drown the agent, how the fire only came from the grill in the back.

"It's a bit of an evolutionary throwback." Tyler had answered my question, but he was giving me what I needed—a distraction. "We've found that the types of abilities that manifest in Variants are sometimes affected by environmental factors. A lot of defensive abilities happen during periods of war and unrest, for example. And it's only in the last thirty to forty years that we've started seeing things like being able to control electronics. That woman's ability would've been incredibly useful a couple hundred years ago. Not that it wasn't useful in this day and age, but back then, it could've been the difference between life and death."

"Yeah, I read a paper on this a while back in the *Journal of Variant Studies*. They looked specifically at never before reported abilities throughout history and were able to pinpoint a specific environmental factor that served as a trigger for each one. Doesn't explain things like telekinesis"—I gestured to Josh—"or Alec's pain ability though, so environment is clearly not the only factor."

"Definitely not," Josh agreed. "Some abilities have been around since before recorded history and show no signs of disappearing. Genetics play a factor, but they're still doing research on that."

Tyler, Josh, and I kept talking about Variant abilities and science for a while longer, but when I yawned three times in one sentence, Ethan pushed his chair back.

"Let's get you showered, baby." He pulled me out of Josh's lap, but before I could take two steps, he picked me up and held me to his chest.

"I can walk just fine, big guy." I wrapped my arms around his thick neck and ran my fingers through his black hair. It was getting long, starting to fall over his forehead the way Tyler's did. "I wasn't hurt."

"I know." He kissed me on the cheek and started to climb the stairs. "I just wanna hold you."

Those words in that deep, gruff voice just about melted me. If he wasn't careful, I would trickle right out of his big arms. I buried my head in Ethan's chest and rested in the comfort of his strong hold, all the way to my en suite.

FIVE

Ethan left me alone to shower, and I spent a long time under the hot spray. I scrubbed every inch of my body and painstakingly detangled my hair, using nearly half a bottle of conditioner. Then I just stood there, letting the water soothe my muscles until I no longer felt like a tension wire.

When I started to get wrinkly fingers, I dried off and put on one of my soft cotton sleep shirts. I picked the towel back up off the end of my bed and tried to squeeze more moisture out of my hair.

The thud of boots on carpet was my only warning before the bedroom door burst open and a furious Alec stormed into the room.

The sudden loud noise startled me, and I dropped the towel. "Fucking knock, Alec!"

He just strode inside, still in his full uniform. "Why the fuck aren't you at the hospital?" His voice was hard and unyielding, his hands in fists by his sides.

"Because there's nothing wrong with me, asshole."

"Get your shit. I'm taking you to the hospital."

"No." I took a few steps away from him, stopping near the open window. The evening breeze had a chill on it. "The EMTs checked me out and I'm fine."

Alec growled. He turned away and ran his hands over his buzzed hair before swinging his furious, wide eyes back to me. "I can't believe those motherfuckers didn't take you to the hospital. I'm gonna kill them."

He stalked forward until we were chest to chest. "Evelyn, I'm not going to say it again. Get your shit and let's go."

I crossed my arms and tilted my chin up. "No."

He pressed his lips together, breathing hard through his nose. Frustration and barely restrained anger laced every exhale. He was practically throwing a temper tantrum, and I refused to pander to his ridiculous demands.

"Alec, would you calm the fuck down? The EMTs said I was fine. I just wanted a hot meal and a hotter shower. What is going on with you?"

He moved so fast it was almost a blur, his hands going to my waist and gripping tight, as if he were about to lift me and just carry me to the hospital kicking and screaming. His hands moved up my ribcage, then back down to my hips as the rage in his face melted away, replaced by . . . fear?

"I just . . ." He closed his eyes and took a deep breath. "I'm fucking terrified of losing you, OK? I need to make sure you're not hurt."

"I'm fine." I covered his hands with mine and pressed my forehead to his. "I'm right here, arguing with you." I smirked and moved one of his hands up to my neck. "I'm standing and breathing. I don't have a concussion or even a scratch on me. A few bruises, but that's it. I'm *safe,* Alec." I squeezed his hands, making him feel my flesh in his fingers. "I'm safe."

For a few moments we just breathed, him holding me, me feeling more and more grounded by his strong hands. Rain started to pitter-patter outside, giving the cool breeze a distinctive fresh smell.

As the rain picked up, Alec pulled me into his arms, making me lift onto my toes.

The rain started hitting my ankles, but I ignored it, waiting until Alec was ready to let go. I was the one who'd nearly been killed, but it was *me* who needed to reassure *him* that everything was OK. Alec was strong in so many ways—formidable even—but he would always have a weakness for those he loved. And he'd told me in no uncertain terms that he loved me.

When he finally loosened his grip, I kissed him but didn't linger long. The rain was going to ruin the carpet, and the cold wind was giving me goosebumps. I turned and pulled the window shut, enjoying the soothing, steady rhythm of the rain hitting the glass.

"Are you sure I can't convince you to go get checked out?"

The stubborn jerk just wasn't dropping it. I rolled my eyes. "If I'm not feeling well in the morning, you can take me. I promise. Now can we drop it?"

He frowned, not liking my compromise, not liking any compromise ever. His eyes raked over my body but not in that lascivious way I loved; he was still looking for injuries.

I was done arguing. Better to give him something else to focus on.

I stepped into his personal space once more, wrapped my arms around his neck, and pulled him into a kiss. Not the gentle reassuring kiss I'd given him moments ago, but that all-consuming, desperate kind we'd perfected—only I wasn't entirely sure who was desperate in this scenario. Was it him? Desperate to make sure I was safe, to feel me in his arms. Or was it me? Desperate to feel alive after coming so close to death.

Reflexively, his hands gripped my hips, almost bruising, then grabbed my ass. He rolled his own hips, rubbing his erection against my front.

Then all at once, his hands and his mouth were gone.

I stumbled as he stepped back, but I leaned into the fall, kept going, refused to let him speak or leave or stop. With a sudden, aggressive move that made his eyes widen, I shoved him in the chest. His back collided with the mirror on the wall next to my bathroom, cracking the glass. He grunted in surprise, but I was already crushing my breasts against his front, clutching two fistfuls of his shirt, and hitching a leg over his hip. He grabbed my thigh with one calloused hand, his other arm banding around my back and pulling me impossibly closer, and then he was kissing me again.

We writhed against each other—teeth scraping, hands roaming—ignoring the destruction, the cracks.

I pulled back slightly and reached for his zipper. His movements stilled and his hands dropped away from my body.

Defeated, I dropped my leg and stepped back, keeping my gaze on his boots. My bare feet looked so small next to them.

He cleared his throat. "The broken glass. I just—"

"Don't," I cut him off and crossed my arms.

He sighed and pushed past me, walking to the door. As his hand reached for the knob, I turned to my dresser and began digging through my underwear drawer. I couldn't stand to watch him walk away again.

After an extended moment of stillness, he huffed, and I heard him moving around behind me.

I paused, my hands running through my damp hair. Alec had never been in my room. He hung out with us in Josh's room more than he used to, and I'd crawled into bed with him a few times—mostly after he got back from some days-long mission and the Light was straining me toward him. Once he'd crawled into bed behind me when I was sleeping with Tyler.

I turned to find him sitting on my bed. He didn't look at me—just started to unlace his boots.

"Are you here to sleep or . . . ?" I wasn't entirely sure how I wanted to end that sentence, but what I'd said at the party still held true. It didn't matter that I'd been attacked, that he was freaked out about it. I wasn't going to allow him into my bed if he wasn't ready to be with me fully.

Just thinking about it had my pulse quickening, and I was suddenly very aware of the fact that I wasn't wearing any underwear. I'd been heading to the dresser to get some when he barged in.

He stared me down for a beat. "Or," he declared, a challenge in his eyes. He was still testing me. Still unsure.

I crossed my arms. "I meant what I said, Alec. You can't stay here if you're unwilling to let go of your martyr crap and be with me. I want to fuck."

It may've been a crude way to put it, but he seemed to respond to me best when I was fired up. I just hoped it didn't backfire. His eyes narrowed, but his lips twitched into an almost smile—something between pleased and amused.

In answer, he pulled his black T-shirt over his head and threw it to the ground, putting his glorious, tattooed, scarred body on display. I raked my eyes over the muscle and the ink, the raised pink scars, and the smooth skin. My lips parted slightly.

I walked over to him and dropped my hands to his shoulders—these shoulders had carried so much. So much pain, so many worries, so much responsibility.

"Are you sure you—"

"Shut the fuck up, Alec," I rushed out before leaning forward and crushing my mouth to his. He responded with a low growl, his hands going to my hips and tugging me closer. I lifted one knee to the mattress and left one foot planted on the floor between his feet. He had to tilt his head up to kiss me, and I liked having the upper hand. I was the one guiding the kiss, controlling the angle.

As we kissed—our tongues battling, our teeth scraping—he dragged his hands down my sides until his palms found skin at my legs. Then he trailed them back up, lifting the cotton hem of my shirt. When he reached my hips, where his fingers should have found my underwear, he broke the kiss and stared at me.

His stunning eyes were hooded with lust, but there was also a hint of surprise, as well as some other, more perplexing emotion.

He didn't let himself get lost in it though. He moved his hands to cup my bare ass and squeezed, kneading the cheeks. His breath washed over my chest, tickling the spot just above the neckline. His mouth was so close to my breasts—I couldn't stop remembering how good his tongue had felt when it circled my nipples.

I yanked my top off and threw it somewhere behind me. I was completely naked, hovering above the Master of Pain as his hot breath washed over my breasts and his hungry eyes took me in. I had a feeling he was hovering too—hovering on the edge of giving in to our relationship, our Bond. If he needed more pushing, I would push, but I knew I nearly had him.

I moved backward to remove his pants, but he stopped me. Apparently he was done letting me take charge.

He held me to him with one strong hand still on my ass. The other moved to the back of my knee, nudging until I was right where he wanted me—both knees planted on the mattress, straddling him. I was spread open, and a shiver crawled up my spine as the cool air hit the heat and wetness between my legs. But he didn't let me lower onto his lap. The hand on my ass kept me upright as he leaned forward to wrap his mouth around my right nipple, just as I'd hoped he would only moments ago. As his teeth bit down lightly, I moaned. He moved to the other breast, giving it the same treatment. My nails dug into his shoulders, one hand going to the back of his head to hold him close. I didn't want him to stop.

But he did, releasing my left breast after one last bite that bordered on painful—if anyone knew how to walk the line between pleasure and pain, it was Alec. His hot tongue licked a trail between my breasts and up to my collarbone; his hands ghosted along the inside of my thighs.

He ran two fingers over my already slick folds before making a circle down, then back up my thighs. His fingers ran over me again, this time with more pressure—feeling how wet I was for him before he'd even touched me there. He groaned and pressed his face into the bend of my neck, kissing, licking, and biting between pants. His chest pressed flush against my front, and all I could do was try to remain upright as he slipped his fingers inside.

He didn't give me a chance to adjust—didn't check if I was ready or if this was how I wanted it. He just held me to him and pumped his fingers in and out, deep and fast, his mouth sending gasping breaths over my neck.

I groaned and pressed my breasts against him, loving the pressure, the extra friction. The orgasm came fast and wild—as everything always did with Alec. It exploded out from his fingers, and I involuntarily rocked my hips.

My knees were weak as he finally let me lower to his lap. I rested my forehead on his shoulder and took a moment to catch my breath. One of his hands rested at my hip while the other stroked my back tenderly. But judging by the straining bulge in his pants, there was nothing too tender about his thoughts.

I sat up and kissed him softly, taking a deep, satisfied breath.

But I wasn't done with him.

To break the kiss, I sucked his bottom lip into my mouth and bit down hard. He grunted in surprise, and his hand slapped my ass. The crack of his palm connecting with my flesh reverberated through the dark room.

I leaned back, surprised—half at the fact that he'd done it and half at the fact that I was kind of enjoying the warmth as the sting faded.

I didn't let either of us overthink it though, quickly moving my hands to his fly.

His fingers wrapped around my wrist, and for a split second, my mind flashed back to that night in Tyler's study when he'd rejected me, made me feel worthless. Uncertainty clawed at me, but I forced those thoughts away and met his gaze.

"Don't," I whispered and narrowed my eyes. My body still craved his. "Don't try to bail again."

He released my wrist and cupped my cheek, but his harsh words contrasted with his gentle touch. "Would you fucking relax? I'm just trying to get the condom out of my pocket before you tear my pants off."

"Oh . . ." I bit my lip and waited for him to pull the foil packet out—then did exactly as he'd said. I ripped his pants and underwear off in one go and settled back over him. We were both completely naked now. Another surge of excitement coursed through me; we were even, and he wasn't leaving.

"The guys told me you're a contraceptive Nazi so . . ." His tone was teasing as he slid the condom down his perfect, erect cock.

"Well, *excuse me* for not wanting to catch some disease from one of you man-whores." I shoved his shoulders, and he flopped down on the mattress with a crooked smirk.

"Ex-man-whores. None of us have been able to so much as fucking look at a woman since we touched you."

Now probably wasn't the best time to bring up Dana, so I went with a simple yet classic retort. "Fuck you, Alec."

He rolled his eyes. "Would you stop talking about it and fucking do it already?" He held his erection by the base and moved it up and down, teasing me, spreading the wetness.

I reached down and covered his fingers with mine, stilling his movements, then started to lower myself onto him.

We both sighed in pleasure. When I was halfway down, enjoying every slow inch of this moment—the moment I'd been dreaming about for so long—he removed both our hands from between us and thrust his hips up mercilessly.

"Ah!" I cried out in surprise and pleasure, but outrage quickly followed. "Fucker!" I frowned at him. *What a dick.*

He just smiled his cruel smile, and despite myself, I smiled back. I couldn't worry about that anymore—Alec was inside me, and it felt fucking amazing.

I started moving up and down in a slow rhythm, trying to draw this experience out as long as possible. I wanted to feel every inch of him as he moved inside me. I wanted to revel in his hands roaming my body. I wanted to commit every lascivious image to memory.

He lay back and let me have my way with him.

For about two minutes.

Then he sat up. With one hand gripping my ass and the other threaded in my hair, he flipped us over as if I weighed nothing. His hand in my hair tugged roughly, almost too painfully, yet it sent a jolt of desire straight to my core. My pussy tightened around him as I gasped. He pressed me into the mattress, still inside me, and kissed me. His hips remained perfectly still as his tongue explored my mouth, the kiss building and building in intensity until we were both breathing hard through our noses. I kept trying to move my hips, roll them, do something to get that friction happening again, but he kept me pinned as his mouth devoured mine.

When he decided he'd had enough, he broke the kiss, lifted himself onto his hands, and started pounding into me—long strokes, nearly all the way out before driving back in. Where I wanted to prolong and savor every moment, apparently Alec had decided we'd waited long enough. He wasn't holding back anymore.

I loved that he was giving in to it, but why did it always have to be a battle of wills with him? Why did it always give me a little thrill to challenge him? To *be* challenged by him? What the fuck was wrong with me?

But I didn't have time to unpack that. Alec's hips were chasing all thought from my mind as he drove in and out of me mercilessly.

He watched me with piercing blue eyes as he fucked me, taking in my flushed face and swollen lips, watching my breasts bounce in response to his movements, watching his cock disappear into me repeatedly. He couldn't get enough.

I could feel another orgasm coming. The tingling heat spread from deep inside, and my core muscles clenched in preparation. I started making incoherent sounds between panting breaths, clawing at his shoulders, trying in vain to bring him closer.

He hissed as I accidentally drew blood with my nails, smearing the crimson over his shoulder. But he didn't stop pounding into me, and I was too far gone to care.

When I closed my eyes and rolled my head back, he growled, "No," and I snapped my eyes open again. "Look at me. I want to watch you come."

"Oh, fuck." His words were the final push that sent me toppling over the edge. I watched Alec watch me come apart under him, the orgasm crashing through me in waves.

He didn't stop or even slow down, didn't give me a moment to recover. He just kept up his merciless pace. I was hypersensitive to his every movement, every nerve ending on fire. His eyes raked up and down my body, and it wasn't long before he found his own release.

With his gaze fixed on mine and his lips parted on an O, he groaned. The soft but guttural sound rumbled from his chest, and I had to admit, I understood why he'd insisted on watching me come. Watching him do the same—seeing him unravel on top of me in pure ecstasy—was mesmerizing.

He dropped to his elbows, and I locked my ankles behind his back, keeping him buried inside me as he caught his breath.

His hands threaded into my hair, much more gently this time. Nuzzling his nose against mine, he kissed me, then drew back just a fraction. I smiled, letting my happiness and satisfaction show—hoping he could see there wasn't even a hint of regret.

He smiled back, a rare genuine smile that almost made his eyes sparkle. Happiness shone in his gaze too, and . . . *love*. He had that same look on his face as when he'd first declared his love to me.

To stop him from voicing it again, I tilted my head up and kissed him. I wasn't ready to hear him say those words again. I wasn't ready to say them back. Alec and I were moving forward in our own stunted, fucked-up way, but I couldn't go that far yet.

He kissed me back, then pulled out and headed into the bathroom to clean up.

Fuck! I mouthed to the ceiling, running my hands through my hair. I went into the bathroom after he'd finished and rushed through my nighttime routine, petrified he'd be gone when I was done. But when I came back out, he was under the covers, staring at the window with one hand under his head.

I flicked off the bathroom light, casting the room into almost complete darkness. The curtains weren't drawn, but rain still pattered outside, and there was no moonlight.

I crawled into the bed next to him, pleased to find he was still as naked as I was. He wrapped himself around me from behind, and I fell asleep in his arms.

The next morning I woke to the sound of birds chirping obnoxiously and bright sunlight streaming through my window. One of my arms was slung over Alec's waist, and when I cracked my eyes open, I found myself staring at his tattooed back. But someone was pressed to *my* back too, sandwiching me between two muscled male bodies.

I rolled over as carefully as I could, but Josh was already wide awake. He smiled when I faced him fully. He was shirtless too, and I wondered how the hell I got so lucky—most mornings I woke up next to at least one Adonis of a man, usually two. If any of our beds were bigger, I'd probably be waking up with even more from time to time.

I smiled back, biting my bottom lip.

"How was it?" he whispered, gripping my hip over the covers.

I didn't know how to answer that—it was way more complicated than my brain could manage before coffee—so I just grinned in response.

He raised his eyebrows, a cheeky smile pulling at his lips. "Shall we wake Alec and ask him?" It was an empty threat, but my eyes widened in warning anyway.

He laughed silently, his smooth shoulders shaking, and leaned forward to kiss me. I kept my mouth shut to his probing tongue though, paranoid about morning breath.

He propped himself up on his elbow just as Alec yawned and rolled over.

"Morning!" Josh grinned at Alec and jumped up. He used my bathroom, put his shirt back on, told us Ethan was making pancakes downstairs, and left.

I chuckled but looked at Alec, a little worried about his reaction.

"I'm not used to sharing." His voice was gritty from sleep, but it didn't sound angry or hard—it sounded like raw honey. "But I'll *get* used to it."

He smiled and pulled me into the crook of his elbow.

"You OK?" I asked. I didn't know what else to say. I wasn't about to offer to be with only him. Not one part of me wanted to—they were all mine equally, and they would all have to share equally.

"I'm fine, precious, I promise. It helps that it's them. That we're already close. That they already know all my dark secrets."

"Do I know all your dark secrets?" I ran my hands over his torso, tracing his scars. They fascinated me. They were like a roadmap of his pain, his history. I wanted to know the story behind each one.

"Not all. But I'm sure I don't know all yours either."

I shrugged. "My biggest secrets were my real name and the fact that I'm your Vital."

We were both silent for a while, him trailing his fingertips up and down my back, me paying special attention to the scar that usually disappeared into the waistband of his pants. I could see now it went over his hip and all the way to the top of his thigh.

"Maybe you could tell me about some of your scars."

"I'll tell you anything you want to know, but not today, OK? I want to just focus on the nice things today—fucking pancakes, and that sickening sunshine and rainbows and unicorns and shit."

"OK." I chuckled and decided to take the focus off him. "You know, I only have one significant scar, and I don't even know how I got it."

I pushed the blanket down, revealing both our naked bodies, and lifted my knee over his belly so I could point to the long scar on the side of my right knee.

"I think it happened when I was little, before my mom took off. She refused to talk about anything in the past. She never mentioned any of you my whole childhood—not even Lucian. That's probably why I don't really remember much."

"I know when you got that."

I propped myself onto my elbow. "What? How'd it happen?"

"I was around twelve, I think. You were three, maybe? I was hanging with some friends after school. I don't even remember what we were doing, but I decided I needed to go home. I had this urge to just . . . go. Then for some reason, I found myself walking to your mom's place. So I get there, and you're crying. Like, at the top of your lungs, hysterical crying, and there's blood trailing down your leg. Your mom couldn't get you into the car, and it wasn't serious enough to call an ambulance, so she'd called a doctor to come out, but this guy couldn't even get close enough to clean the cut. Anyway, I walk in, and you reach your fat little arms out to me, and I take you, and they're finally able to treat it. I don't even remember how you got the cut in the first place. I think that was the day they realized you might be my Vital. Not that anyone said anything to me . . ." His voice took on a note of bitterness.

"I'm so sorry, Alec." I rested my chin on his chest, keeping my eyes on his face. "If I hadn't been a kid, I never would've let anyone take me from you."

"I know." He ran his thumb over the scar on my leg. "It's just that for the longest time, I thought that was the reason she took you. That my ability was so horrid and disgusting the adults decided it would be better if I never had my Vital. That your mom decided I wasn't good enough for her little girl. I know now why they couldn't tell me more at the time, but yeah, my mind filled it in with the worst explanation possible."

I sighed, my heart breaking for him, for me, for all the shit we'd been through because of things beyond our control.

"Anyway"—he planted a kiss on my forehead and sat up, swinging his legs over the edge—"we said we weren't going to talk about heavy shit. Let's go get some fucking pancakes from one of your other boyfriends, the one who happens to be my cousin." He shook his head, but when he turned around, a teasing smile tugged at his lips.

I laughed, letting the conversation drop. We got dressed and headed downstairs, following the smell of freshly ground coffee.

SIX

Tyler drove us into the city early in the morning, our security detail close behind. The butterflies in my belly wouldn't leave me alone; they'd been flapping all night. We'd spent so much time keeping our Bond a secret it was hard to let the paranoia go.

I'd agonized over what to wear the night before. I even called Dot to get her opinion—she said it didn't matter, that I could show up in my underwear. All they were interested in was my status as a Vital. Eventually she took pity on me and told me to look presentable but not too dressy. No jeans but probably not a collared shirt either.

I settled on pale blue woolen tights, a simple long-sleeved dress that fell to my knees, and my favorite cardigan for warmth. Tyler wore one of his endless supply of perfectly fitting shirts and light gray pants. He looked sophisticated and smart.

I fidgeted with the hem of my dress and huffed, regretting not wearing pants.

"You OK?" Tyler placed a gentle hand on my knee, keeping his other firmly on the steering wheel.

"I don't know. I'm obsessing over my outfit. I think it's my brain's helpful way of distracting me from freaking out about this." I played with his fingers instead of the hem.

He squeezed my hand, halting my nervous movements. "It's going to be OK. It's standard protocol to go in and register. They'll sit you down—"

"But you were so adamant it was dangerous. You wanted to keep it a secret."

"When we first realized what you were, yes, that was the biggest threat. Some of the things I've seen in reports, the places Alec's been, the things we've both done in this job . . . The work we do is important, but it's not pretty."

"Not helping."

He turned a bend in the road, and the early spring sunshine streamed in through my window, making me even more hot and uncomfortable.

"Let me finish." He chuckled. "At the time, I was really worried about Ethan and Josh getting recruited. If they decided to join on their own, then so be it, but I wanted them to finish college first, to have a *choice*. Once Melior Group knows a powerful Variant has found a Vital, they put a lot of pressure on. They offer a lot of money, promise travel around the world, put on the guilt trip about using their rare ability for good. It's not how Lucian and I would run things, but the recruitment side of it isn't up to us. I wanted to save them from that, and I wanted to protect you from the kidnappings. Now . . ."

"That's the least of our worries."

He sighed. "Yeah. Now we have a face and a name to put on the threat, and if Ethan and Josh join up with Melior Group, I don't even care anymore. I just want us all to be safe, and we won't be until Davis is rotting in a hole somewhere."

His grip on the steering wheel tightened, his knuckles going white.

"What about the humans?" I asked. Part of this meeting would involve an interview with a representative from the government. All Variants had to be registered—it was the humans' way of feeling in control. They thought if they could list and catalogue all the Variants, everyone would be safe.

"That's just a standard, boring part of the process." Tyler waved his hand dismissively.

I'd asked most of these questions already over the past few days, but he patiently answered them anyway. He knew I felt better if I had all the facts. I'd even badgered Alec to tell me the layout of the building so I would know what areas to avoid. He looked at me as if I was losing it, told me I would never be left unattended, and shut me up with his mouth and hands.

They all seemed to be using sex as a distraction—I'd had more sex in the last few days than I'd had in the few *years* since I'd started having sex. Or maybe that had more to do with Alec *finally* completely being in. The Bond was even, the connection as deep with each one as it was with the others.

Tyler battled the Manhattan traffic, then the next thing I knew, we pulled into an underground garage. Two armed guards checked Tyler's ID—even though they greeted each other by name—and signed me in, and we parked in a spot with a little "Reserved for T. Gabriel" sign above it.

My heart hammered in my throat. I swallowed around the pressure and rubbed my hands on my thighs, but Tyler wasn't about to let me sit there and freak out. He got out of the car, slung his bag over his shoulder, and went to the elevator. I followed him, trying my best not to show my nervousness.

In the elevator, he tapped away at his phone with one hand and threaded his fingers through mine with the other. We got off on a really high floor, stepping out to a stunning view of Manhattan through a floor-to-ceiling window.

"Whoa." My trepidation was momentarily forgotten as I took it in, spotting the Empire State Building and the Chrysler Building and straining to glimpse the Statue of Liberty in the distance.

"Come on." Tyler tugged me along. "I've got the same view from my office."

"Of course you have an office here." I rolled my eyes as I followed him past the shiny reception area, through another keycard-protected door, and into a vast open-plan office area.

"Hey, kitten."

I turned to see Kyo smiling and coming toward me.

"Hey!" I grinned and gave him a hug.

"Here for your induction?"

"I guess."

"We couldn't put it off any longer," Ty jumped in.

"You'll be fine, Eve. There's nothing to be nervous about." Kyo smiled in his easy, relaxed way.

"Oh, shit, we're really scraping the bottom of the barrel if they're letting you join." Marcus sidled up to us, grinning.

I flipped him off. "You'd be lucky to have me."

"Yeah, we would." Jamie slapped Marcus on the back of the head and also gave me a hug. "Just promise you'll let us be part of your team when you steal our Master of Pain."

"Huh?" I frowned and looked at Tyler.

"When, *if*, a Vital decides to join Melior Group, they're automatically placed in a team with their Variants. It's the easiest arrangement—Bonds naturally work well together. If you join, Alec will automatically be assigned to your team, and I'll probably have less desk time and more field time too."

"Oh." I didn't want to break up Alec's team. I didn't even want to join Melior Group! I wasn't a spy. I was a scientist. "None of you have anything to worry about. The scary, dangerous, brooding thing isn't really up my alley. I'm finishing college and figuring out why the fuck I glow."

Everyone chuckled, but Kyo also surreptitiously looked around the office before leaning in. "Just be careful about what you say. Pretty much everyone here is trained in intelligence gathering. There's always someone listening."

My eyes widened and I gripped Tyler's bicep. All the banter had done a good job of distracting me, but now the nerves came slamming back.

Tyler sighed. "Thanks. That's real helpful, Kyo."

I shot Kyo a dirty look as Tyler led me away to a boardroom, which looked surprisingly mundane. Surrounded by glass windows, it had all the elements you'd expect—comfortable chairs, a projection screen, a conference phone.

Tyler barely had time to deposit his bag on the long table and rub a few soothing passes up and down my arms before other people started arriving. A woman in an ill-fitting suit was one of the first. She introduced herself as Susan from the Variant-Human Relations Department and shook Tyler's hand and mine before taking a seat. The next few were Melior Group employees and greeted Tyler as if they knew him.

"Shall we begin?" At Susan's invitation, we'd just moved to take our seats when the door opened again.

"Victor." Tyler greeted the man in the sharp blue suit, and the others in the room sat up a little straighter.

"Hello, Tyler. I thought I might sit in for this one. Please carry on like I'm not here." He sat at the far end of the table and motioned for us to continue.

Tyler cleared his throat. "Evelyn, this is Victor Flint. He's our recruitment manager and a member of the board."

"Nice to meet you, sir." I was too far away to extend my hand, so I just waved. He returned it with a tight smile. The anxiety twisting my gut doubled down, but I made sure to keep a neutral expression on my face and my hands steady as I laid them gently on the glass tabletop.

"I hope you don't mind if I go first," Susan said. "I have another meeting to get to."

No one objected, so she pulled a small stack of papers from her bag and slid them over to me. She explained the forms were standard and just a way to verify my identity and register me as a Vital in the database. Each one had Evelyn Maynard written on it, and most of my other details were already filled in. I signed in all the marked spots. She handed me a brochure about my responsibilities as a person with abilities in the wider community, said goodbye to everyone else in the room, and left.

"OK, Evelyn," said a short woman who'd been speaking with Tyler but hadn't bothered to introduce herself to me. "I'm Gemma, and it's my job to make sure you understand what it means that you're a Variant and that you're receiving the appropriate training."

I nodded. She handed me pamphlets, then spoke about Variant DNA and how Variant Bonds worked. It was barely scratching the *surface* of stuff I already knew. Between Tyler's tutoring and my own obsessive study, she really couldn't have told me anything new. But protocols had to be followed. She ticked boxes on a tablet screen as she went through each topic.

"Have a glance at this list, and if you agree that I've explained all the items on it, please tick agree." I ticked it without even looking at the list properly. I was getting bored. My focus kept wandering to my periphery where Victor sat, observing me as keenly as I wanted to observe him.

"Now, you're attending Bradford Hills Institute, which means it should be easy to make sure you get the necessary education and training from now on. Tyler here can make sure you're moved into the necessary classes."

"Actually," Tyler interjected, "that won't be necessary. I've been tutoring Evelyn in the relevant Variant studies topics since we first learned of her status as a Vital, and she's already enrolled in several Variant studies units. She's a keen student and her knowledge is not lacking."

"Oh, OK. Perfect. That takes care of that then. I'm done." Gemma smiled at me and pressed some more buttons on the tablet.

Victor shifted in his seat. "Thank you, Gemma." He leaned back and folded his hands casually in his lap, his head tilted to the side. Everyone paused and gave him their full attention.

"Evelyn, there is one last item I'd like to discuss with you." His gaze was relaxed but intent on me.

I cleared my throat, not sure what to say, but Tyler spoke before I could. "What's this about? I wasn't informed of another item for discussion."

Victor waved his hand dismissively. "Oh, you're free to leave, Mr. Gabriel, if you have something else to attend to. It's a last-minute item that I didn't have a chance to add to the agenda. I only need a few more minutes of Evelyn's time."

No one got up. If anything, they settled into their seats, paying rapt attention to whatever this was.

There was no way in hell Tyler was leaving my side. His shoulders tensed just a fraction, but he managed to keep a neutral look on his face as he leaned his forearms on the table. "I have time."

Victor nodded before turning his full attention to me. "I'm a busy man, so I won't beat around the bush. Evelyn, I'd like to make you an offer. The standard offer that Gemma outlined stands, of course—we're always happy to offer positions to extraordinary Variants and Vitals. You would be an asset. But I'd like to extend an additional, rather unique offer to you also. We all know you're more than an exceptional Vital. Despite your Variants' refusal to discuss the matter, which I completely understand"—he held a hand out to Tyler, giving him a conciliatory look—"I think we've all seen the footage of the unfortunate incident at the senator's residence in Manhattan. The glowing."

I narrowed my eyes and wrapped my arms around my chest before I could stop myself. I had no idea what the glowing meant, and I didn't like being confronted with it.

"What is this about?" Tyler asked.

Victor kept his keen gaze on me. "I'm offering you the opportunity to figure out what it is. How it works, what it can do, what the limitations and dangers are." My eyebrows rose as he continued. "I would like to offer you access to some of our top researchers and scientists, a safe environment in which to test your particular . . . situation."

"Why was I not consulted on this? Or even informed of it?" A hint of frustration leaked into Tyler's clipped tone. No one else at the table spoke, but they watched the two men verbally sparring with ravenous eyes.

"I didn't have approval to make the offer until earlier this morning. There was nothing to inform you of. And to be quite frank, I wanted to bring this directly to Evelyn. I know you've shut down offers of a similar nature from Bradford Hills Institute."

Bradford Hills Institute had made offers like this?

My immediate reaction was to get pissed off at Tyler. How dare he make such a decision for me? Did the others know too? But I made a conscious effort to keep the irritation from showing on my face. After the initial knee-jerk reaction, I realized exactly why Tyler hadn't entertained the idea. We knew I could use my glowing to kill a Variant—draw the Light right out of them—but the rest of the world didn't. I had enough of a target on my back without exposing me, us, to more suspicion from powerful people.

Tyler looked at me out of the corner of his eye, but this time, I spoke first. "The reasons why we turned down the offer from Bradford Hills Institute are between my Bond and me." I placed my hand lightly on Tyler's forearm, surprised at how calm my voice sounded. "But since you took time out of your day to make this offer to me personally, I'm happy to consider it."

I smiled politely, pushing as much Light to Tyler as I could before removing my hand. Hopefully the extra boost would help him figure out what Victor's angle was, but I also hoped he'd use it to see what I was about to do. We needed help figuring this glowing shit out; Victor Flint had the resources—I just needed to make sure we got as much out of this as possible.

Clasping my hands together, I leaned on my elbows. Tyler moved in the same instant, settling back in his chair and placing a comforting hand low on my back.

He was sending everyone at the table, including me, a clear message—I was taking the lead now.

Victor didn't miss a thing. His calculating gaze flicked between us, and he tilted his head, an amused smile briefly passing over his features.

"Excellent." He leaned forward too, mirroring my position. "A team of researchers would be at your disposal. Ideally, we would have you come in two to three times per week for a few hours. They'll run tests to see if we can identify any anomalies in your blood, your DNA, and your physiology, then they'll observe and measure you in the glowing state both alone and with one or several of your Bonded Variants present so they can observe the transfer. We will leave no stone unturned until we know all modern science can discover about your situation."

I didn't like how he kept referring to it as a "situation," as if it had happened by accident and wasn't permanent. This was part of who I was. Yes, it could be dangerous, but it was pretty fucking extraordinary too. Even so, I was glad to see how hard he was trying to sell me on his offer. "Thank you for not beating around the bush. I'll offer you the same courtesy. I'd like to know what's in this for you?"

"Whatever do you mean?" He smiled, his tone slightly teasing. He knew I'd figured him out; he just wanted to hear me say it.

"Firstly, as you said, you're a busy man—you wouldn't waste your time on something if it wasn't important to you. Second, Bradford Hills Institute is an educational facility. Their primary focus is education, knowledge. Melior

Group is a *business*. Your bottom line will always be *the bottom line*. Clearly you believe you can learn something from studying me that will allow you to make money. My best guess would be a new method for delivering Light to your active agents remotely. That would be invaluable in the field."

His smile only widened. "Very clever. I would genuinely like to help you, Miss Maynard." I was no longer Evelyn. That was good—he was treating me with more respect. "But of course, you are correct. This is a business, and my team's secondary purpose would be to develop technology with what we learn from studying you."

Tyler remained reclined. "Victor, you're trying to use my Vital as a prototype for new tech that could make you billions. Can you not see why I would have an issue with this?"

"Of course I understand your reluctance, but—"

"I'd like to be paid," I cut him off. I was done with pleasantries and I was getting hungry. "This is business, and you stand to make a large amount of money. I want an hourly rate and a cut of the profits from whatever prototype comes from these experiments. I want my Variants to be compensated for their time too."

For a beat, Victor watched me with a calculating look. "Fair enough. We can arrange an hourly rate for yourself, Mr. Paul, and Mr. Mason. As Mr. Gabriel and Mr. Zacarias are already employed by us, this will simply be part of their working day. And you can have two percent of the profits for the first five years on the market. In exchange, you make yourself available two times per week for a minimum of three hours."

"Ten percent for the *lifetime* of the product, and Tyler and Alec get extra pay—this is well outside either of their roles." Neither one of them needed the money, they were all rolling in it, but I needed to ask for things so Victor would feel as if he won when I finally agreed. "Three hours, two times per *month*. We all have lives, Mr. Flint. And you leave Josh and Ethan alone. Your recruiters don't go after them. Ever. If they choose to join Melior Group at some point, then so be it, but they will not be pressured into it. No offense." I threw a quick glance at Gemma, barely registering the look of surprised respect on her face. "And I'd like clearance for the three of us. I'd like Tyler and Alec to be able to tell me about their day at work without holding back any details. Those last two points are not negotiable." I leaned away to drive my point home, crossing my legs.

"Five percent for the lifetime of the product, no extra pay for Tyler and Alec, three hours one time per week, and we'll not actively recruit Ethan and Josh for the next five years. I'll have to see what I can do about the clearance—it's not only up to me." He remained leaning on the table, his hands in front of him.

Tyler had told me as much about the clearance level—that it may be difficult to get, even with him and Lucian pushing for it. It couldn't hurt to have another person arguing for us.

"You leave Josh and Ethan alone for good—as I said, that's not negotiable—and we have a deal."

He pressed his lips together and sighed, then stood and reached a hand over the table. "You have yourself a deal, Miss Maynard."

I stood up and shook his hand firmly.

"I'll have our legal team draw up the paperwork."

"I'll have mine look it over before I sign."

"I would expect nothing less." He laughed as he left the room. Everyone filed out after him, and Tyler led me to his office down the hall.

As soon as the door closed, I collapsed against it and took a massive, shaky breath.

"Holy shit." I laughed and ran my hands through my hair, trying to calm my breathing, stop my heart from hammering in my chest. I had no idea a conversation could result in so much adrenaline.

Tyler tugged my hand from my hair and pulled me into his arms. He kissed me passionately, the hard planes of his chest flush against my body, and then just as suddenly pulled away. His hot breath washed over my face in panting breaths as he leaned his forehead against mine. "That was the hottest fucking thing I've ever seen."

I chuckled and kissed him again, high on the rush of the negotiation and the feeling of Tyler's arousal pressing into my belly.

I stepped out of his arms.

"I'm not happy that you kept the Bradford Hills offer from me." I wagged a finger at him.

"It's not that I was keeping it from you." He adjusted his pants, moving his prominent hard-on. "I just knew we wouldn't be able to take them up on it. I was saving us all some time by cutting the conversation off before it began. And we've had quite a bit on our plate. It just never made it to the top of the list of priorities to discuss. I'm sorry."

"Apology accepted, but please don't turn things down on my behalf again. I agree with your assessment of the situation, but I need to be included in these conversations. We need to make these decisions together, even if it takes up some of your precious time."

"OK. I get it."

"Good. Now take me to lunch so we can discuss this situation I just got us into without speaking to you first."

He laughed and stuffed some papers into his messenger bag before leading the way out of his office. "Alec is going to be so pissed at you."

I chewed my lip as we reached the elevators. He was right. Alec didn't want me anywhere near Melior Group. Now I was about to be there every week, potentially exposing some serious vulnerabilities. "Yeah, he is, but I have boobs to distract him with. And the angry sex is phenomenal."

Tyler groaned. "Now I'm thinking about how to make you angry."

SEVEN

Halfway through my first lecture of the day—Synthetic Organic Chemistry—I had three pages of notes and several new books on my TBR list. My phone vibrating in my backpack was an unwelcome distraction. With a huff, I pulled it out to silence it and saw it was an incoming video call from Harvey. I frowned and waited for it to ring out.

Once it stopped, I tapped out a quick message.

Did you butt dial me? LOL!

I'd kept in contact with him since my impromptu trip down under. We chatted online from time to time, and I'd even reconnected with Mia, Harvey's sister. It was the first time I'd reconnected with anyone from my past. My mother had always forbidden it. Being able to chat with him was really nice—he was my friend first, and that friendship was still there. But we didn't do video chats. I'd mentioned I had an early class when I spoke to him the night before, so the call was a little unusual.

Wasn't a butt dial.

I sat up a little straighter at his reply, confused. The three little dots told me he was typing.

I need to speak with you urgently. Can you call me please?

I chewed on my bottom lip. I didn't really want to get up in a silent lecture theater. I'd had enough of the Variants of Bradford Hills staring at me to last a lifetime.

My lecture finishes in about half an hour. I'll give you a call right after.

His reply was instant.

This really can't wait. Please hurry.

That got my alarm bells ringing. Keeping as quiet as possible, I packed up my books and shuffled to the end of my row. The professor didn't even miss a beat, continuing to educate everyone else on azobisisobutyronitrile and radical initiator mechanisms. I rushed to the doors, my mind full of questions, my gut telling me I may not like the answers.

Alec stood in the hallway, talking to a Melior Group woman I'd never seen before. The black-clad operatives were all over the place. Most of the ones assigned directly to Vitals were in the lecture theater.

Alec was officially assigned to me for the day but preferred to wait outside during my classes; it was less distracting for me and allowed him to get a little work done, making calls and barking orders at Kyo, Marcus, and Jamie. When he saw me come out, his posture straightened, and he excused himself immediately.

"Evie? What is it?" He loomed over me, but before I could answer, my phone started buzzing again. We shared a look and I rushed outside. Alec stayed glued to my side.

I sat down on a bench in the courtyard, under the shade of a maple tree, and answered. Alec remained standing in front of me, his arms crossed.

"Harvey? What's wrong?"

"Hey, Eve." It was way past midnight in Melbourne. His voice sounded hoarse, and heavy bags sagged under his eyes. "I really need to talk to you."

"OK . . ." I waited, but he seemed to be struggling to get the words out.

"Just . . . uh . . . don't freak out or anything."

My spine straightened, and I threw a wary look in Alec's direction.

Another more feminine, more sarcastic voice came through the phone. "For fuck's sake. Just let me talk to her, human boy."

My heart flew into my throat, and I sprang to my feet, gripping my phone tightly. I knew that voice.

"Harvey!" I yelled, my voice shaking. Alec was making a call, keeping his eyes on my screen but staying off camera. "Harvey, listen to me."

At the same time, Harvey replied to Zara, "You asked me to talk to her. What the fuck . . ."

The video feed went shaky, as if they were fighting for the phone. Then a blinding flash of electricity cut across it, and the call cut out.

"Shit!" Hot, panicked tears stung my eyes. Did I just watch another friend die? Did Zara take another person from me, just as I got him back? "No! No no no." I prodded my phone with shaky fingers.

"What do I do?" I turned my panicked gaze to Alec.

He tucked his phone into his pocket before placing both hands on my shoulders. "We're going to call him back. She had him call for a reason, so they'll take the call. I've already arranged for it to be traced. Take a deep breath."

I nodded and tried, but it just made me hyperventilate more.

Before I could calm myself enough to call him back, Harvey's name popped up on my screen again.

Another jolt of cold panic shot up my spine, and I gritted my teeth, making myself answer it. Alec stepped out of the camera's way once more as Harvey's face appeared, Zara's right next to it.

"Harvey!" The panic in my voice was palpable. "Get away from her. She's dangerous, do you hear me? She is *not* my friend. I don't know what she's told you, but—"

"Deep breath, Eve," Harvey interrupted me, his eyes wide, his hand held out in front of him. "I'm OK."

Zara rolled her eyes. "Would you chill the fuck out? What do you think I'm going to do?"

She leaned back heavily in Harvey's computer chair, scowling. As if I was the one being unreasonable.

"Chill the fuck out?" I gritted my teeth, aware of the danger in angering an unhinged person, but my rage was rising fast. "You have Rick's power. The same power that killed Beth. Remember Beth? *Your friend?* And now you're holding *my* friend hostage, so *excuse me* for getting worried."

"Yes, I fucking remember Beth!" she nearly yelled, and Harvey shushed her with a hand on her arm, checking over his shoulder. Why was he trying to hide the fact that a dangerous lunatic was in the house?

Zara took a very deep breath, visibly calming herself. "Eve, I need your help."

I blinked slowly at my screen, waiting for the punch line to the sick joke she was clearly making before killing Harvey in front of my eyes.

She stayed silent, and when her eyes started darting about the room, it sunk in. "Holy shit, you're serious."

"Yes, I'm fucking serious. I made a mistake. I fucked up *real* bad, OK? And now my life's in danger, and things are so much worse than you know."

"I don't care!" I screamed. The lecture I was supposed to be in must've finished. Students were streaming out of the building, a few throwing me curious looks.

"Eve, please, just hear us out." Harvey's voice was calm, and I tried my best to take my cue from him. I couldn't risk her hanging up again.

As if he read my mind, Alec's warm, calloused hand wrapped loosely around my forearm. I glanced over the top of my screen to see him holding up a thumb as he mouthed, *Got her.* I focused back on my phone as Alec pressed his earpiece and listened in.

"Harvey, I'm so sorry you got dragged into this," I said, "but it's going to be OK." I chewed on my bottom lip, wary of revealing too much. Melior Group operatives were on their way, and I didn't want to give her a chance to run.

"You suck at this." Zara rolled her eyes. "I don't know how the fuck you lied about your identity your entire childhood. You can tell whichever Melior Group lackey is standing next to you to come out. I know they've tracked me to Harvey's house. I called to tell you where I am. I need help."

I couldn't help glancing up at Alec again. He wore his signature scowl as he reached a hand out for the phone. I passed it to him and, with shaky legs, lowered myself back to the bench.

"Oh, hey, Ace." Zara's tone was saccharine, and I wondered why she was being so antagonistic if she really wanted our help. This could all be a trap, but Alec knew what he was doing. I had to trust he would take care of it.

When he spoke, his voice was hard but professional. "Zara, if you're serious about handing yourself in, don't struggle. They're under orders to detain you. Do not resist. Do you understand?"

I didn't hear a response before Alec kept speaking. "If you use your ability and any of the men and women coming your way are harmed, you will spend the rest of your life rotting in a windowless cell." Most people wouldn't have picked up on the emotion in his voice, but I detected the hint of anger in the slight growl in his throat, the way his free hand curled into a fist.

"Harvey," he continued, "just stay out of the way, man. And show them your hands so they know you're not a threat."

Without warning, he hung up. I took the phone numbly as he sat down next to me.

"You hung up?" I stared at the phone, then at him as prickles of panic started to poke at me again. "Wait . . . what . . . *why?*"

Alec put an arm around me and spoke in a low, soothing tone. "Our team was thirty seconds out. She can't get away now, and Harvey will be better off if he's not distracted. It's handled. Wanna go grab some lunch?"

"Do I want to . . . *what?*"

I guess he was used to dealing with life-and-death situations, putting it out of his mind once he'd done what he could, trusting the people on the ground. But I wasn't. My mind and heart were still in that dark room in Australia.

"Evie." He nudged my chin until I was facing him, then gently held the side of my neck. "There's nothing more we can do. The team will report as soon as it's done. You need to clear your mind. Focus on me. Look at my eyes, precious."

My mind beat against his words, my thoughts going faster than I could articulate them. But I made myself look into Alec's piercing eyes. His stare had always been arresting, but now when he looked at me, love permeated his gaze, not hostility. My shoulders relaxed slightly as my breathing slowed to match his.

He smiled, then leaned down and placed a gentle kiss on my lips. Pulling away just a fraction, he spoke in almost a whisper. "Feel the cold breeze on your skin."

I listened, feeling the breeze.

"Listen to the voices, the leaves, the cars in the distance."

I listened, remembering where we were. The people, the sounds, the sun streaming through the leaves—everything slowly came back into focus. Alec's honey voice and strong hands calmed me down despite myself.

He leaned away, a faint smile on his face, just as Charlie walked up to join us.

"Good work." Alec fist-bumped him, and Charlie gave a smug smile.

"What was that all about? Or should we not discuss it in public?" Charlie looked around. The courtyard was clearing again as students and staff moved off for their next classes and commitments.

"I think we're safe," Alec answered.

I sat up a little straighter. "Wait, that was you? Tracking the call?"

"Yeah." Charlie shrugged before casually sitting down on my other side. "So why was I tracking a call from your ex-boyfriend to your ex-boyfriend's house?" He raised his eyebrows, his amused gaze moving to Alec. "Interesting use of Melior Group resources."

Alec leaned around me and smacked his cousin on the shoulder. "Smartass. Zara surfaced."

Charlie whistled low. They were both men of few words, and while it was annoying sometimes, it had its benefits when you were discussing sensitive information in public.

"I thought your stalking ways had reignited. But, just for the record, she saved my life, so my allegiance is to her now." Charlie gave me a warm smile.

I smiled back and looked down. "I didn't really do anything. Just helped find you."

"Always so modest," Charlie teased.

"Wait, what do you mean about stalking?" Something clicked in my mind as I remembered what Alec had told me about the year I spent in Idaho. I pushed the residual hurt down as Alec ran his hand over his buzzed hair.

"How you gonna throw me into it like that, man?"

"I told you. I'm on her side now. Besides, what difference does it make? She already knows most of it."

"Yeah, well, maybe it's better not to rehash old—"

"It was you?" I cut Alec off, staring at Charlie. "That year I lived in Nampa? You were the one blocking me from finding Alec."

It made sense now that I knew how Alec's mind worked. He wouldn't have wanted it to be easily traced by Melior Group, nor would he have wanted to justify the use of resources, but he would've needed someone he trusted to do it. Charlie was the obvious choice.

"Yep. Kept you well away from this asshole but kept him informed of your every damn move. Made a good amount of money that year. He *really* wanted to keep you a secret, and he was willing to pay well."

I smacked him on the shoulder too. "Charlie!"

"But!" He leaned out of my reach. "In my defense, I put a stop to it."

"What?" Alec and I both said.

"Why do you think you were offered a scholarship here?"

"I'm gonna fucking kill you," Alec growled, but I was pretty sure he wasn't serious. "I want my money back."

I just gaped, a smile tugging on my lips as Charlie argued, "Technically, you paid me to block her from finding you and to report on her movements and 'anything suspicious.'" He used air quotes. "You never expressly said I couldn't do anything to help her out a little."

"Wait." I finally found my voice. "So I didn't actually earn my scholarship? You just . . . hacked me into the system?"

"Oh, Eve, no!" Charlie waved his hand. "All I did was bring you and your brilliant science mind to the attention of the admissions board, nudge them to get in contact with your school. The rest was all you, babe!"

I let out a relieved sigh. Of course I belonged here. The idea that I didn't get into Bradford Hills Institute on merit should've never crossed my mind. If there was one thing about myself I was sure of, it was my intelligence. I was excelling in all my classes, even despite the constant disruptions and catastrophic, traumatizing events.

I pulled Charlie into a tight hug. My gratitude was threatening to burst out of me—pop open my seams and pour out like the stuffing in a teddy bear. "Thank you, Charlie. You changed my life."

"Well, you saved mine, so we'll call it even."

I chuckled and pulled away, taking a deep breath to ease the persistent pressure of tears behind my eyes. Charlie's eyes looked a bit misty too.

"Are you two *crying*?" Alec sounded perplexed, and we both burst into quiet laughter.

I cleared my throat. "I really appreciate it, Charlie, but why?"

"I didn't know you were Evelyn Maynard, or Alec's Vital, but I knew you were damn important to him. For him to spend that kind of money and insist I keep it confidential under threat of excruciating pain, not to mention that he went out there every chance he got to keep an eye on you himself . . . I knew you were something special. Secrets never last long, and the sooner they come out the less damage they do."

"I was handling it," Alec grumbled.

"No, you were sticking your head in the sand while developing an obsession. I know I meddled, but I did what I thought was best for everyone. I did it because I love you." Alec just grunted, but Charlie kept speaking. "When I saw you two meet for the first time in the square that day, I knew who and what you were."

"Holy shit." Charlie knew I was a Vital before I did. He knew my true identity and kept it to himself. "You knew the whole time? But Dot said she told you."

He chuckled. "She did when she figured it out, but I already knew."

"Oh man, don't tell her she was actually the last one to figure it out. She'll *hate* that."

Charlie cringed. "Yeah, good point."

"Why didn't you say anything?"

"I was a virtual stranger. I may have known a lot about you, but you'd only just met me. What would you've done if I'd walked up to you and announced I knew your real name and oh, by the way, you're a Vital and this asshole is your Variant?"

"Yeah, fair point, I would've disappeared."

"No, you would've *tried*. I was never letting you out of my sight again," Alec declared, and because I'm just a little fucked up, I felt warm and fuzzy at his stalkerish declaration.

"Plus"—Charlie shrugged—"much as I wanted to give Alec a push, there was a good reason he was keeping it all a secret. I may have meddled a little, but once you were in the same place, it was up to you."

Alec and I both scoffed. If it wasn't for Charlie "pushing things," who knows where we would've ended up?

Before we could continue the conversation, both their phones went off. They glanced at the screens and got up.

"What's going on?" I slung my backpack over my shoulder.

"We're being summoned." Alec took my hand and pulled me in the direction of the admin building. "The team in Australia has checked in with an update."

The anxiety Alec and Charlie had so expertly distracted me from flooded back, and I picked up the pace, leading the way to Tyler's office.

EIGHT

It was unseasonably warm for April, warm enough to be outside in shorts and a tank top while Ethan grilled hamburgers for lunch. Ed, Josh, Tyler, and Charlie played some fast-paced card game on the patio table that had them shouting and laughing while half the cards ended up on the ground.

Dot and I sat by the pool. She flipped through the latest edition of *Modern Variant* while I perused Josh's copy of *God is Dead* by Nietzsche—a welcome break from the complex scientific theories I usually read. It'd been a long, taxing week.

Alec and his team were at work. Zara had landed at a secure private airstrip the day before, and they'd been tasked with getting her safely to Melior Group HQ. Another two teams had assisted, along with Dana. With Dana there, Zara would be as harmless as any other twenty-year-old college student, but they weren't taking any chances.

Alec had checked in a few hours earlier; everything had gone off without a hitch. Zara was secure in a specially built cell, protecting her from abilities outside of it and protecting everyone else from her. Alec wanted to be present for her questioning that afternoon.

I wasn't sure if I was more worried about him or her.

Josh's, Ethan's, and my clearance hadn't come though yet, so he couldn't give us too many details. I suspected Victor was dragging the process out—just to show me he was in charge. I'd mentioned it to Lucian over breakfast, and after raising his brows in surprise, he'd grumbled, "Leave it to me," then disappeared once more behind his newspaper.

I had a feeling the clearance would be sorted out quickly.

But ultimately it didn't matter. Alec would tell me whatever I wanted to know, right after he crawled into my bed in the middle of the night and we had sex. Again. Since our first time together, hardly a day had gone by that I didn't have him inside me.

Even though the intimacy levels with the others remained the same, I still wanted him. I wanted them all. I was insatiable, as if we were making up for lost time—playing catch-up on all the sex we could've been having if it wasn't for the secrets and the pain and the holding back.

"Do you think Zara did it on purpose?" Dot's voice was sad, her eyes downcast but not focused on the magazine.

"What do you mean? It's not like she tripped and accidentally nudged me into a van with people who wanted to kidnap me."

"No, I know." She turned her almost too big eyes on me, and the scowl on my face melted away. "It's just . . . I don't even know what I'm saying. Forget it."

She waved her hand and turned back to the magazine, but she wasn't even remotely reading it. It was upside down.

"Dot. What's going on? Talk to me."

"I know she didn't do anything to me directly." She stared at her lap. "She didn't shove me into a van or stand by while I was experimented on. But after Beth died, I felt like I was getting her back as a friend, you know? Like the three of us were getting really close. It felt almost like old times. It just hurts to know it was all a lie. And I also feel like I should've known. Out of everyone, *I* should've picked up that something wasn't right with her. I guess when I say I wonder if she did it on purpose, I'm hoping maybe it wasn't her. Like maybe Davis had some kind of mind-control Variant or machine that made her do all those things."

I sighed. Zara's actions had affected so many people, in ways I didn't even fully comprehend. The fact that Dot was hurting made me so fucking mad . . . but I breathed through it. I needed to be there for her.

"I wish I could tell you that was the case—that Zara's as much a victim as we are—but we both know there are no recorded cases of Variants with mind-control abilities. And when I spoke to her on the phone, she said, 'I fucked up.' She owned it. I'm sorry, Dot, but she did this, and now she has to pay for it."

"I know. I'm not suggesting she should get away with it. I just . . . I don't know!" She threw her arms up and let them flop back down to her lap. "This whole situation is so fucked up. What happened to Charlie is fucked up. What happened to you is fucked up. What Zara did is fucked up. Her whole childhood was fucked up. I mean, it wasn't a surprise to anyone that her parents were involved with Variant Valor from the start. They're about as elitist and bigoted as you can get. And they were so hard on her. *So* mean. I remember this one time I was at Zara's place—we must've been, like, thirteen—and her mother came right out and said, 'You don't even have an inkling of an ability; you're a disappointment and a waste of space.' It was awful. I can't imagine the kind of shit they said when no one else was around. I just wonder if she would've done all those terrible things if she'd had a better family life."

"Maybe. Maybe not. Zara couldn't choose her parents, and neither could I. But at some point, we have to stop making excuses." Maybe it was a harsh way to look at things, but I just couldn't accept any argument that absolved Zara of the responsibility she had for her own actions. I was simply too angry.

We settled back into silence. I didn't want to argue with Dot or take my anger out on her. None of this was her fault.

She reached a hand between the loungers, and I took it without hesitation, squeezing her fingers. We held hands until the rage in my chest subsided, until she stopped staring into her lap as if the weight of sadness made her head impossible to lift, until the warmth of the sun and the sound of laughter behind us reminded us we had things to be happy about.

The silence once again turned comfortable, and we got back to reading.

After barely ten minutes, Dot let her magazine flop onto her chest and gazed at the glistening pool. "That water looks so inviting."

I dropped my book to the ground beside me. "It really does. I'm just trying to figure out if it's warm enough."

"Food's up!" Ethan yelled, sending a flock of birds flying out of some nearby oaks.

My stomach grumbled.

"Let's test the water after we eat." Dot led the way to the outdoor dining area.

We spent a relaxed few hours eating, drinking, joking around, and decidedly *not* talking about Zara, Variant Valor, the Human Empowerment Network, or Davis.

We did brave the pool in the end, Ed leading the charge as he pulled his shirt off. "I've been dying to get into that pool since I got here, but it's been too damn cold!"

His defined, tanned chest was narrower and more delicate than Charlie's, sprinkled with black chest hair that matched the curls on his head, but the two of them had one distinct thing in common. It wasn't until Ed ran for the pool that I saw his scars. Charlie's burn scars covered his right side, but Ed's were mostly on his back, starting at his shoulder blades and disappearing into the waistband of his shorts.

"I passed out from the smoke, and he shielded me from the fire with his body until they came to get us out. I'm so lucky to have him." Charlie stood next to me as the others stripped down and jumped in after Ed.

I took Charlie's hand. He gave me a squeeze back, and we shared a sad smile. There were so many things I could've said, questions I could've asked. But the best way—the only way—to get Charlie to talk was to just *listen*. I waited patiently, happy to abandon the rest of the afternoon and sit with him as long as he needed.

Instead, his smile widened, and he pulled me toward the pool. He wasn't ready to talk more about it, and that was completely fine. He knew I was there whenever he needed me. We all were.

I followed Dot's lead and stripped down to my simple black bra and underwear, not wanting to waste any time hunting for a bathing suit. I was the last one in . . . and apparently a rotten egg . . . because apparently we were all in elementary school again.

We splashed around and joked and then started getting out one by one.

The sun peeked in and out between fluffy white clouds. The heat that had made it just warm enough to be in the water was fading fast, chased away by a cold breeze.

As everyone else ran for the house, shivering, I huddled under the water. If I stayed there, the cold wind couldn't freeze me to death.

Apart from me, Ethan was the last to pull himself out of the pool, the fire tattoo dancing as his muscles bulged under his weight. Naturally, he didn't seem to feel the cold.

"You coming?" He half turned to check.

I shook my head and crouched farther, dipping my neck and chin into the water.

He laughed, flashing me a dimpled grin, and launched himself back in.

I screamed and jumped up, trying to avoid getting my head drenched from the tsunami he'd caused with his cannonball.

He swam to my side underwater before emerging, his jet-black hair plastered to his head. "What do you feel like for dinner?"

That boy always had food on his mind. I smiled and waded around, trying to ward off the chill. "What do you feel like making?" I rarely got a craving for a particular food. Whatever he chose to make was always delicious.

He flashed me another brilliant smile, leaning his elbows on the edge of the pool. "I found one of my mom's

Mediterranean cookbooks, and I've been wanting to try some more stuff. I really want to do the moussaka, but I've never made it before and I'm not sure I have time to experiment, so I was thinking I could do this pasta dish. Now, I know what you're going to say—pasta's not really original, and there's more to Mediterranean food than just Italian, but . . ."

I chuckled as he kept talking. I wasn't going to say that at all, but he was on a roll, and there was no stopping him from geeking out. I slowly treaded water, watching him.

Light reflecting off the water made his amber eyes sparkle, and his hair was dripping, the droplets meandering down his broad chest. His big shoulders were pushed forward, and the fire tattoo contrasted starkly with the blue water and light tiles. He'd started to tan over the last few weeks; his naturally olive skin soaked up even the meager spring sun and had taken on a golden glow.

He was beautiful.

A fuzzy, overpowering feeling bubbled up in my chest, and I froze, transfixed, almost overwhelmed by its intensity. I wanted to hold Ethan close and never let him go. I wanted to kiss him silly until he was laughing and the dimples became permanent. I wanted to see that carefree, happy look on his beautiful face every day for the rest of my life.

As I realized what this feeling was, what I'd been feeling for a long time but hadn't allowed myself to examine, I shot through the water and wrapped my arms around his neck.

". . . the balsamic vinegar can be—" When I plastered myself against his front, he cut himself off, dropping his arms to hold me loosely around the waist.

"Ethan?" I struggled to hold back my smile, a tinge of nervousness mingling with the excitement.

"Yeah, bubble butt?" he half teased, searching my face.

"I love you." I let the grin break out in full force.

He blinked as all the teasing and lightheartedness left his features, replaced by that rare intense gaze. Then his arms tightened around me, and he pulled me against his chest as the most brilliant smile I'd ever seen crossed his face.

"I love you." He said it back without hesitation. "I think I've loved you since I first laid eyes on you."

I chuckled. "So that was an expression of love, was it? Throwing a ball of fire at my face and scaring me half to death?"

He grinned. "You weren't scared. You hardly even flinched. That's what made me want to know you."

He cut off my witty reply with a soft, gentle kiss. I tightened my arms around his neck and wrapped my legs around his waist, drawing him impossibly closer. We made slow circles in the water, moving deeper into the pool as his tongue waded into my mouth and he waded further and further into my very soul.

We broke apart, panting, and I opened my eyes to see beautiful flames covering the entirety of the pool's surface. They licked four feet into the air, banishing the cold wind.

I looked around us in wonder, smiling, warm and fuzzy on the inside *and* outside. It was almost exactly like the day we'd first tested our Bond connection, except this time, the flames weren't raging as high, didn't have that jerky, uncontrolled, volatile energy. Ethan was in perfect control; the fire was only high enough to hide us from view, an even height all over. He was doing this on purpose.

"What—"

My question was cut off when he leaned forward and started kissing and sucking my neck, then moved his hot mouth up to my ear.

"I want you," he whispered, and I groaned at his words, my thighs tightening around him reflexively.

I kissed him again, pushing my tongue into his mouth. With one hand, I undid his swim trunks while he nudged the fabric of my panties out of the way. Our movements weren't jerky or desperate—we knew we had the rest of our lives to spend together—but we weren't taking it painfully slow either. Neither one of us wanted to wait much longer to start that life.

Within minutes of declaring our love, Ethan was inside me, filling me up in every way. We both sighed into the feeling—warm, safe, and so fucking good. It was the first time I'd had him inside me without a condom, feeling every inch of silk-covered steel as he slid in.

We made love in the pool, staring into each other's eyes as his bright flames lit up the water around us. I'd never felt closer, more connected, to him.

We came at the same time, our foreheads together, our soft moans mingling as we watched each other unravel in the sweetest kind of surrender, our souls bare.

I rested my head on his shoulder, and he just held me as the flames flickered out completely. It was now dusk. A gust of wind reminded me we had no business being in a pool at night in April unless we wanted to freeze, but I didn't care. I was safe and warm in my fire fiend's arms.

When we finally got out of the pool, Ethan froze, his back tense as he turned to me, wide-eyed. "Shit! Condom."

I chuckled and took his hand in mine. "It's OK. I got the implant over a week ago, remember? We're safe."

He took an exaggerated sigh of relief. Tyler had used his ability to make sure we were all clean before I had the procedure.

Another chilly gust of wind made my teeth chatter, and Ethan wrapped a big towel around my shoulders. We headed back to the house hand in hand.

"Maybe I'll do the moussaka after all," he mused. "I think I have enough time. I'll have to get more eggplant though."

"Sounds perfect." I smiled up at him.

NINE

I forced myself to sit up straighter in the lecture theater seat. The coffee Josh had brought me after lunch just wasn't cutting it.

It had been nearly two weeks since Zara's capture—or surrender, depending on how you looked at it—and I was trying to maintain a routine, refusing to let her disrupt my life any further. But the Variant history lecture, a compulsory unit for all students with Variant DNA, was not holding my interest. Shaking my head to clear away the fuzziness, I noticed I wasn't the only one having trouble concentrating.

It started with a few whispers, pockets of people shifting in their seats, bending their heads together. Then it spread farther. People were getting louder and looking at their phones.

The professor shushed them, a stern look on her face, but whatever was happening had them ignoring her. People were starting to get downright rowdy.

A pang of worry shot down my spine, and I looked to the back of the room, searching for my security detail. The agent was standing near the door, his finger pressed to his ear as he spoke softly into his unseen mic. He was the only black-clad figure there—apparently I was the only Vital in the lecture today.

Without even meaning to, I reminded myself of the exits. The closest was the one next to my security detail. Two emergency exits were on either wall at the bottom of the room, and I was pretty sure the office behind the professor's lectern had another door leading to a corridor on the other side of the building.

The professor gave up trying to wrangle the crowd and demanded to know what was happening. One of the students in the front row got up and showed her his phone. The professor frowned.

"Surely this is a hoax," said a boy a few rows down.

"How is this possible?" a girl sitting near me asked no one in particular.

"I have to call my mom." A young boy, no more than sixteen, haphazardly gathered his things and rushed out of the room. Others followed, the theater erupting into disorder, the lecture forgotten.

I packed my books and stood just as the crowd parted. Alec came down the few stairs to stand at the end of my row. He was in uniform, a gun strapped to his hip, his tattoos almost completely covered by the long sleeves.

I swung my bag over my shoulder and took his hand. "What's happening?"

"Not here," he growled over his shoulder as he pulled me along.

When we exited the lecture theater, my other bodyguard fell in behind us. Alec marched us across campus, glaring at anyone who got too close. Several other people were rushing in various directions too, while some just stood around talking animatedly or looking at their phones.

I was dying to know what the hell was happening, but clearly it was serious, so I kept my mouth shut.

We jogged up the stairs to the admin building and marched straight past the reception desk, Alec's boots thudding on the polished concrete floor as I struggled to keep up. The receptionists barely spared us a glance. At the elevators, Alec ordered the other Melior Group agent to stay there, and we headed up to Tyler's office.

Once inside, Alec finally dropped my hand.

". . . you understand? Stand down." Tyler was on the phone, every muscle in his body stiff. "We can't risk turning this into an international incident. We'll just have to deal with it as best we can *quietly*." He was silent for a few moments. "Good. Report as soon as you have something." Then, without saying goodbye, he hung up.

"Guys, I'm starting to freak out here." I found myself shifting closer to Alec, pressing myself into his side.

Alec wrapped one arm around my shoulders as Tyler sighed and leaned on his desk. He picked up the remote, pointed it at the TVs on the wall behind me, and turned up the volume.

Staring back at me from the screen, a charismatic smile pinned to his face, was Davis Damari—my so-called father and the reason for everything that had ever gone wrong in my life. I stiffened, the blood rushing to my ears making it hard to hear. Alec squeezed my shoulder.

Davis was giving some kind of speech in front of a crowd. Cameras and microphones were everywhere.

"This is, we believe, one of the greatest scientific breakthroughs in modern history. Not only can we now isolate Variant abilities, we have developed technology that enables us to give Variants *without* abilities the gift of an ability."

The news program cut to a reporter summarizing the situation. Apparently Davis had given an impressive speech only an hour ago. My eyes flicked around the other three screens. Each one was covering the news; each one had his ugly face plastered all over it.

Tyler stepped around his desk and planted himself at my other side. But even Alec's and Tyler's comforting arms around my shoulders and waist couldn't stop me from feeling as if the world was crumbling around me.

"What the fuck is happening?" I muttered to myself. No one answered.

After the incident in Thailand, Davis, his core group of scientists, and some of his more fanatical Variant Valor supporters had completely disappeared. Melior Group had worked tirelessly to find him, but Davis was rich and well connected. He had friends in high places everywhere to keep him safe.

I'd had several arguments with Tyler over why it *wasn't* all over the news that Davis Damari was behind Variant Valor, the attack on Bradford Hills Institute, the Vital kidnappings. The whole world should know what a piece of scum he was. But Tyler and Alec kept explaining it wasn't that simple.

Much of what happened in Thailand was classified and therefore couldn't be discussed. Plus, apparently Melior Group's board had decided it would be bad for business if it got out that dozens of their best elite operatives had been knocked out in one fell swoop by a single Variant with an impressive ability. They were trying to save face.

Senator Christine Anderson was talking, but she refused to front the media or go on record with human law enforcement for fear of her life.

Zara was cooperating too. She'd told Melior Group about another of Davis's secret labs in Australia, but by the time Melior Group had got a team there, the place was empty, completely cleared of people or any trace of useful information.

While we knew the truth, the rest of the world was left to wonder what the hell had happened in Thailand, and Davis's name was not once mentioned in relation to the incident. This had resulted in more suspicion, fear, and worry in the general public. They were filling in their gaps in knowledge with the worst-case scenarios.

And now the psychopath behind it all stood, untouched, in a three-thousand-dollar suit, announcing a "scientific breakthrough" as if it was just another business day and he had nothing to do with the chaos erupting all over the world.

Davis Damari was winning. It made my blood boil.

He didn't go into detail about how exactly he gave abilities to Variants who hadn't manifested any, but people were losing their minds, reporters clambering over each other to ask questions.

One of the main sound bites they kept repeating was that the technology was nearly ready, but there was one last kink to figure out. They were close, really close, but something stood in their way. At this point, Davis announced he was out of time and walked away from the frenzy of questions.

"It's me," I breathed, stepping out of their embrace. "I'm what's preventing him from figuring it out."

The attack at the café, the woman's declaration that he would never stop coming for me—it made sense now. When he'd captured me in Thailand, he hadn't had enough time to test his process, perfect it, poke, prod and torture me until he understood my glowing Light better. He still needed me to figure out how to not kill people during the procedure, because even *he* couldn't sell *that*.

The door swung open, and Ethan and Josh burst into the office, finally tearing my attention from the four screens.

"Why haven't they arrested him?" Ethan's booming voice bounced off the walls. "Why the fuck was he able to just walk into a car and be driven away?"

Josh remained silent, a deep frown on his face. He crossed his arms and leaned back against the door.

"Keep your voice down." Tyler's commanding tone had an immediate effect on Ethan. He didn't back down completely, his big shoulders still tense, but he did unclench his fists and take a deep breath.

"Sorry." He sighed. "I just don't understand."

"It's OK, Kid." Alec slapped a hand on his cousin's shoulder as Tyler muted the screens.

"He's in fucking Dubai. We have operatives in the area, but we couldn't get them there before the cameras showed up. We couldn't take him into custody with the whole world watching—not when no one knows all the shit he's done. And now this . . ." Tyler groaned, running his hand through his messy hair and looking out the window. "He planned this perfectly. He disappeared off the face of the earth, forced us to spread ourselves thin looking for him, then reappeared in a location where we couldn't get to him in time. Now with this announcement, the press will be on him like a bad smell, not to mention all his supporters and lackeys. He's basically made himself untouchable."

He was looking out at the campus grounds below, and I knew what he was seeing—people rushing about, some excited, some worried, *everyone* talking about it.

"So what do we do?" I asked. I needed a plan. I always felt better with a plan.

Alec lowered his tall frame into one of the tub chairs.

No one answered.

"Guys!" I nearly yelled, a bit of panic leaking into my voice. "What do we do?"

Tyler squared his shoulders. "We keep an eye on him, and we work on our own strategy."

"Which is what exactly?" Josh spoke for the first time.

"We have to be smarter than him, stay one step ahead. If Eve is right, and I think she is, that he needs her to complete his machine, then we learn everything we can about the glowing Light. Maybe we'll be able to use that against him somehow. We've already agreed to work with Melior Group's research team—may as well use that to our advantage. But let's keep as much to ourselves as we can, OK?"

Ethan frowned and shared a look with me and Josh. "Are you saying we can't trust Melior Group? What's going on?"

"Nothing I can put my finger on yet." He exchanged a loaded look with Alec. "All I'm saying is, we should keep our cards close to our chests. People are scared, and scared people do stupid things. In the meantime, now that he's surfaced, we have eyes on Davis. He's hiding behind powerful men with even more questionable morals than his, but at least we can track him now. As soon as we can take him down discreetly, we will. All we can do now is stay vigilant and gather as much information as we can."

"And above all"—Alec rose to his feet, turning to face me—"we protect Evelyn."

TEN

After ten minutes of focused mindfulness, I opened my eyes.

Controlling my Light flow had become second nature, almost instinctual. Our Bond was settling; it was formed, strong, *equal*. No one held back and created an imbalance in the connection, and the Light no longer gushed dangerously out of me in order to solidify our Bond. Transferring Light was just part of my physiology now—almost as effortless as breathing.

But the *glowing* Light required more intention. I'd only glowed in a handful of situations—most of them highly stressful and potentially deadly.

Continuing to take deep breaths, I uncrossed my legs and dropped them to the ground in front of the couch. Ethan and Josh sat in matching armchairs across from me, a heavy stone coffee table between us. The rest of the room was decorated like a modern living space—polished concrete floors, leather furniture, open bookshelves styled meticulously, hints of metallics and marble in the decor—but the heavy white drapes had nothing but thick brick walls behind them, and the giant mirror to my left concealed a team of Melior Group researchers, watching my every move.

This session was meant to be as "natural" as possible, hence the living room setup. They wanted me to do my thing without external influence so they could observe—from behind the safety of the glass, of course. Dana was in the next room on standby in case anything went wrong.

My first session had consisted of a battery of medical tests and basic observations of my Light levels when I let it flow into me unobstructed, when I mentally shut it off, when I transferred to someone in my Bond, then someone outside of it. Those were baseline tests.

This session would be the first time they observed the glowing, and since we couldn't be sure it wasn't dangerous, I had to have my Variants there to transfer to. I didn't want to find out what would happen if I took in that much Light and had no outlet for it.

I sat up a little straighter and focused purely on the Light, letting my instincts take over to an extent. I not only dropped my mental barriers—unlocked the doors, so to speak—but threw them open and shouted, "I'm here."

The Light was all around us, in the air, in every Variant, and in very tiny amounts, in every living thing.

I pulled, imagining the warm white glow on my skin. As if imagining it had made it manifest, I started to glow. It slowly got brighter and stronger.

Ethan and Josh wore matching brilliant grins. Both of them sat forward, their elbows on their knees, their faces full of pride, wonder, *love*.

Before the glow became blinding and made it impossible for anyone to observe anything, I reached my hands out. Neither of my Variants took my hand. They just waited, patiently.

I sent the Light to them; it felt like warm water running over my skin.

After a quick transfer, the glow faded, and I stopped the flow of Light.

We sat in silence for a few moments. The head researcher, Karen, usually used the intercom system to give us instructions, her calm voice filling the room through the built-in speakers.

But after I finished my glowing transfer . . . nothing.

I shared a confused look with Ethan and Josh before turning to the double-sided mirror. My own reflection stared back at me.

Just as I was about to get up, Karen's voice came through the speakers.

"That was incredible!" She sounded more animated, more excited than I'd ever heard her. So did the cacophony of chatter in the background. "Just amazing!" She cleared her throat, shushing some of the other excited nerds before speaking again in a slightly calmer tone. "Now we need to observe the abilities in action—to illustrate that Light has indeed been transferred."

Needing no further instruction, Ethan and Josh got to their feet. Ethan curled his fingers, and a bright blue ball of menacing fire appeared, while Josh lifted the solid stone coffee table up to the ceiling with a flick of the wrist.

They had us repeat the process a few times, measuring the levels of Light and my vital signs, sometimes taking the guys into other testing areas where they could use their abilities to their full potential by basically blowing shit up.

While practicing was good, none of this was new to us. We were almost bored, going through the motions for the sake of the scientific process, to make sure everything was recorded accurately.

It wasn't until toward the end of the session that we learned anything interesting. We were discussing what I'd observed about how the process of drawing Light to me worked, and I explained that I seemed to be able to draw it directly from specific individuals. In the next round of tests, Karen asked me to draw directly from Ethan and transfer to Josh.

Ethan stood at my back, his hand resting lightly on my hip. His other hand gripped mine, and I threaded my fingers through his.

Josh stood several feet away, his hands in the pockets of his chinos, his perfect lips turned up in a slight smile.

I was getting tired, but I inhaled deeply and focused on my connection to the fire fiend behind me. I took my time, making sure to block all other sources of Light while drawing on Ethan's alone.

As with all things, when it came to my Bondmates, it came easier than anything. I didn't even have to pull—I just opened my arms and his Light charged into my embrace.

As soon as my skin began to glow, I lifted my free arm and sent the Light to Josh. I nearly gasped as the sheer power of Ethan's force flowed through me. For a few seconds, we were all connected. It felt incredible on a soul-deep level—so good I absentmindedly arched my back, a familiar ache in my lower belly building unexpectedly.

Ethan's hand on my hip gripped tighter, and I shut the flow down, the glow fading.

Josh didn't look so casual anymore. His hands were out of his pockets, his smile replaced by a much darker, more heated look.

Karen's voice came through the speakers, throwing cold water on the moment. "Mr. Mason, if you would . . ."

She sounded a little amused, but Josh squared his shoulders and, as he'd done countless times already, lifted the coffee table into the air. The heavy piece of furniture burst into bright blue flames, singeing the ceiling and startling us all.

Josh's panicked eyes flew to us. He was effortlessly keeping the flaming table off the ground and away from other flammable things, but he clearly had no idea what to do about the angry blue flames.

Ethan wrapped one big arm around my waist and reached the other over my shoulder. It took him longer than usual, but he put the fire out, and Josh lowered the charred, smoking mess back to the ground.

"What the fu—"

The door burst open, interrupting Josh's confused utterance, and the entire research team swarmed into the room.

Some threw a barrage of rapid-fire questions at us, furiously writing everything down, while others inspected the coffee table. I was so fascinated myself I didn't even mind the session was going past time. A flurry of theories buzzed through my mind, but I carefully avoided sharing too much of my own thoughts. If there was one thing I'd learned from both my upbringing and my time in Bradford Hills, it was when people knew things about you, they could use them against you.

After a solid half hour of this, and declarations that we had to repeat it in future sessions, they finally allowed us to leave. Everyone trickled out of the room, chatting excitedly. As Josh, Ethan, and I passed the door to the observation room, a man in a navy-blue suit broke off his conversation with Karen and came toward us.

"Miss Maynard." Victor Flint flashed me a grin, all teeth, and shook my hand.

"Mr. Flint." I smiled politely, and he turned to my Variants.

"You must be Mr. Paul." He shook Ethan's hand, then Josh's. "And Mr. Mason. Pleasure to meet you both, and I am deeply sorry you won't be joining Melior Group in any capacity other than as test subjects. But a deal is a deal."

He flashed me that grin again.

"You were watching," Josh stated, stuffing his hands in his pockets. Ethan wrapped a protective arm around my shoulders. Either they didn't trust him or they were picking up on my unease.

"I caught the tail end of the session, yes. I must say, I was very pleased by what I saw. We're learning so much already. I have every confidence we'll be able to give you some clarity about your condition, Miss Maynard."

"I certainly hope so." I resisted the urge to cross my arms—I didn't want to appear rude or standoffish—and settled for clasping my hands.

"Oh, I *know* so." He laughed deep in his chest. "And the process is shedding light on things I didn't even expect, like the events in Thailand. You've just solved a problem that's been plaguing the investigators for months."

"Oh?" I raised my brows but didn't say any more. Sometimes the best way to get people to talk was to just be quiet. But Victor didn't seem at all reluctant to share information.

"Yes, the fire in the parking garage. We determined early on that Davis remotely detonated several explosions as he made his escape." I remembered the booms, the ground shaking. "But those were primarily on the other side of the facility, where the labs and files were. He was destroying evidence, or trying to—we still managed to recover a good deal. Anyway, those explosions resulted in fires, which spread quickly to other areas, including the holding cells where they were keeping most of the Vitals. But they did not spread as far as the garage, where I believe you were . . ." He looked pointedly at Josh and held his hands above his head, miming the way Josh had kept the ceiling from collapsing on us.

Josh nodded and Victor kept speaking. "There really was no discernable reason for that part of the structure to have caught fire. We couldn't work it out. Until today. It seems Mr. Paul's fire ability transferred to Mr. Mason through you, Miss Maynard, just like what happened here today."

I blinked. Of course, it made sense for one of the head honchos of Melior Group to be across the major points in the investigation, but I didn't think he was looking into such minute details.

His assessment seemed accurate. I'd suspected the same thing when I saw Ethan's ability manifest at Josh's command, but I'd been waiting until we were somewhere private to raise it with them.

Josh appeared unfazed, his posture still relaxed, his curious eyes studying the middle-aged man in front of us. Ethan, on the other hand, was suddenly breathing more rapidly, his arm tightening around my shoulders.

"But I see this isn't entirely shocking news to you." Victor kept the smile plastered on his face, but his eyes narrowed. Before any of us could respond, he pulled something out of his pocket.

"In other news, your clearance has been approved and finalized. These passes will give you access to all parts of the building that your clearance level is permitted to enter. Not that you'll need to access other areas, but it will make coming and going to these sessions easier. Pleasure meeting you, gentlemen. Goodbye."

He handed the plastic passes to us, turned on his heel, and disappeared down a corridor.

Ethan backed away from me until his broad back hit a wall. He slid to the floor, threading his hands through his hair.

Josh and I exchanged a worried look and crouched down next to him.

"Baby?" I scratched the back of his neck, my other hand going to his knee. Josh placed a comforting hand on his shoulder.

"It wasn't me," Ethan whispered into his lap. "It wasn't me, you guys. I didn't burn them."

He took a massive, shuddering breath and looked up to the ceiling, relief palpable in every fiber of his being. Ethan had been convinced it was his fault the fires had started. That it was his fault all those people had been burned, even killed. Tyler had explained the investigators' findings, but Ethan couldn't be dissuaded, couldn't forget the distinctive blue tinge of the fire we'd all seen.

Hearing Victor spell it out and seeing for himself how the glowing Light transfer worked had finally made it all click. He wasn't to blame.

He gave me a brilliant smile, dimples on full display, and pulled us both in for a hug. We sat on the floor laughing, shedding a few happy tears, and then Josh got to his feet.

He held his hand out to me. "Come on. I need to get back to my thesis, and you're going to be late for lunch with Dot."

"Shit!" She was probably furious. I was surprised she hadn't sent Squiggles to find me—or a bear.

While I was in the bowels of Melior Group doing my best impression of a lab rat, she'd spent the morning shopping with Kyo, Marcus, and an entourage of security guards. The plan was to have lunch together at one of

Dot's favorite cafés in the city. She'd been trying to take me there for ages.

When we finally made it to the lobby of the building, Dot grumbled about my lateness but still gave me a hug. Marcus had some work to get back to in Bradford Hills, so he was getting a lift back with Josh, along with all of Dot's purchases.

Dot kissed Marcus goodbye openly, her short frame plastered to his tall one, then took Kyo's hand and led the way toward the exit.

"I don't know about this." Josh frowned as he held me close. "Maybe we should all head home and Ethan can make you lunch?"

I wrapped my arms around his neck, fiddling with the stiff collar of his shirt. "We have a full Melior Group detail, we have Kyo, and we have my big fire fiend. We'll be fine."

After what had happened at breakfast with Lucian, they were all understandably cautious. I was shaken too. The fact that he could get to us in Bradford Hills—probably the most guarded place on the East Coast—was disconcerting, to say the least. But I refused to live my life in fear. That's what drove the division, the unrest.

"Text me as soon as you're heading home," Josh demanded, holding me almost too tightly.

"I promise." I breathed in his expensive aftershave, resting my cheek on his shoulder.

"Maynard!" Dot yelled, her voice echoing in the cavernous marble-lined lobby. She and Kyo were waiting for us beside the revolving glass doors. "Move it! I'm hungry!"

Josh planted a little kiss on my nose and turned away, taking some of the countless bags off Marcus and heading for the parking garage.

The security detail wanted to take armored cars to our destination, but it was only three blocks away, and Dot and I insisted on walking. It was a beautiful spring day, though a bit chilly in the shade of the tall buildings, and we wanted to enjoy the sunshine and the blossoming trees.

It might've been better to take the cars though—the walk turned out to be less than relaxing.

Seeing high-profile Vitals with a couple of security guards had never been uncommon, but lately, it seemed as though anyone with Variant DNA who could afford it was hiring either Melior Group or another security company to follow them around.

Walking down the street, we saw several people being followed closely by frowning armed guards, but nothing compared to the entourage we had. No fewer than eight Melior Group operatives surrounded us, all of them taking their job very seriously and making the lives of anyone walking in the opposite direction a nightmare.

Dot either was oblivious to it or just didn't care, walking confidently with Kyo just ahead of us. They were downright adorable, hand in hand, leaning into each other, giggling like schoolkids.

I smiled, overjoyed that my friends had found happiness in each other. Ethan squeezed my hand and gave me a knowing look.

"People are staring," I whispered out of the corner of my mouth.

He chuckled and slung an arm over my shoulders. "People always stare at you. You're beautiful. You just never notice."

I huffed and slapped him on the stomach, but I couldn't stop a wide smile from crossing my face.

We came to a stop next to an older Beaux Arts–style building. The café had cute striped awnings, planter boxes hanging off the low windows, and a door angled into the corner.

"I can't wait for you to try the crumpets!" Dot grabbed my hand and bounced on the spot. "They make them from scratch, and they're so good."

"What's a crumpets?" Kyo frowned, but Ethan's face had lit up.

We weren't allowed to go inside yet though. Several of our guards held their hands out in a halting motion while two headed for the front door to ensure it was safe.

As they reached the door, it swung open, and a furious middle-aged man in a sunflower apron marched out. The guards all reached for their guns, on high alert. Ethan pushed me behind his wide frame as Kyo did the same to Dot.

I couldn't see what threat this man with narrow shoulders and more salt than pepper in his hair could pose. But then, the short young woman who'd tried to kill me hadn't exactly looked like a crazed murderer either. Considering what happened with Zara, I was the worst judge of who could and couldn't be trusted.

"Oh no you don't!" He wagged a finger in our direction, not even slightly intimidated by all the heavily armed men and women giving him warning looks.

One of our guards, his voice calm, tried to keep him back with an extended arm. "Sir, you need to step—"

"This is *my* café, and I'll do whatever the hell I want. You haven't taken that right from me yet, so I'm exercising it. And *you're* not welcome here."

"Excuse me?" Kyo bristled.

"I may be just a Dime, but I still have rights. This is my establishment, my *home*, and I refuse to allow guns inside. I refuse to allow people like you . . ." he sputtered, obviously frustrated. "Variant abilities may as well be weapons. I want my patrons to feel safe. *I* want to feel safe. Leave! You are not welcome here."

For a moment, no one said anything. The man crossed his arms and planted his feet wide, guarding the door with nothing more than a furious glare and sheer determination.

Ethan sighed, his big chest puffing out, and gave me a sad, worried look over his shoulder.

I reached out and took Dot's hand. Her eyes met mine.

"Let's just go," I whispered, and she nodded. It wasn't worth it. We didn't want to make anyone feel more unsafe than they already did. I knew what that felt like, and I refused to add to it.

Kyo was the most frustrated. "It's not right. This is discrimination. He can't just . . ."

Dot took his arm and pulled him along, doing her best to soothe him as our entourage closed in tighter.

We ended up in a diner a few streets over, the four of us seated in a booth. Our protectors spread out, some sitting close by, some posted at the exits.

It was a somber lunch. The food was mediocre; even Ethan didn't finish his BLT. They didn't have an espresso machine, so I went without coffee. I really needed it too, judging by the building headache behind my eyes.

After a long, heavy silence, Dot pushed her plate away. "Everyone is acting weird and doing strange things, and it's scaring me."

Kyo rubbed her back. "Everyone is scared. That's why they're acting weird. I've got your back."

"I know you do, but that's not really what I mean. I'm scared for my immediate safety, yes. It's hard not to be, considering . . ." She looked at me, her perfect brows pulling together.

"Considering the constant attempts on people's lives?" I deadpanned.

"Yeah. But when I say I'm scared, I mean in a bigger sense. I'm scared about what the world is turning into.

I'm scared about what all this fear will lead to. I don't want to spend the rest of my life being followed around by an entire team of agents while I get kicked out of my favorite restaurants and shops."

"We got turned away from a lingerie boutique earlier today as well," Kyo explained. "The owner there wasn't quite as dramatic as the guy at the café, but she made herself clear. Variants aren't welcome."

I sighed. "I hate this. And I can see both sides. I mean, I was raised human, never believed there was anything special about me whatsoever. You do kind of feel like Variants get privileges, advantages that we don't. It's worse in some parts of the world, but I can see how it breeds resentment. You fuel that resentment with fear—suggest that now, not only do human kids have less access to the opportunities Variant kids have, but their lives are in danger too? I wouldn't want my family anywhere around us either."

"But we're not like that!" Dot sounded equally pleading and outraged. "Most Variants are normal, happy people trying to live our lives, just like humans. I'm not interested in blocking anyone from having a better life. I'm certainly not interested in killing little human babies."

"No, and most Variants would agree with you. But then you see more and more of them joining Variant Valor, and not shy about talking about it. You see people using the word *Dime* with abandon. It would be pretty hard not to feel attacked."

"Yeah, I get that." Dot flopped back against the back of the booth.

"Variant Valor aren't the only ones getting louder," Ethan grumbled. "I'm seeing more and more mentions of the Human Empowerment Network too."

"Yeah." Kyo drew Dot to his side. "Both the boutique and that café had big posters in the windows—'Human Safe Space' in big bold letters with HEN's branding all over it. They're taking the safety-in-numbers approach, and they're not being subtle about it."

"It's just creating more division," Ethan agreed.

"The most frustrating thing"—I clenched my hands into fists—"is that none of these people, Variant or human, realize they're pawns and playing right into that asshole's hand. Davis is behind all of this. It's no coincidence that this divisive rhetoric got more intense after he did his press conference. This is what he wants. He *wants* the Variants scared of the humans so they'll spend all their money on his sick invention. He *wants* the humans scared so the division continues to breed."

"I wish we could just hunt him down and lock him in a dark hole where he can't touch or hurt anyone," Ethan muttered. He was such a sweetheart. Davis may have been my biological father, but I wanted him dead, not locked up.

"Do that, and he becomes a martyr. Even harder to fight against a legacy than a man," Kyo argued. "Toppling Dictatorships 101—discredit and besmirch the charismatic leader. *Then* take him out."

I wondered just how many governments Kyo and Alec's team had been involved in tearing down, but I had a feeling even my new clearance level wouldn't be high enough to gain me access to that information.

"I. Hate. Him." My voice was clear and level as my eyes narrowed on the table, not seeing our half-empty plates or the condiment bottles. Only his ugly face.

My friends watched me warily.

ELEVEN

The late afternoon sun bathed the yard in a golden glow. I put in one earring and watched from my window as Ethan got out of the pool, his lean muscles effortlessly lifting his heavy frame out of the water.

The mid-May weather still wasn't warm enough for most of us. Other than that one blissfully hot day a few weeks back, it had been too cold for swimming. But Ethan never felt the cold. As he dried his hair off with a towel, all that muscle glistened in the sun, making me want to go down there and lick the water droplets off his smooth chest.

I shook myself out of it and put my other earing in, then turned and paused.

Josh was at my door, leaning on the frame and watching me as I'd been watching Ethan.

"You are so beautiful," he stated, his boyish face full of sincerity.

"Thanks. This dress is stunning." He was in sweats and a Queen T-shirt, and I was in eveningwear, my feet tucked into bright red heels. The strapless dress tapered in at the waist and stopped at about midcalf. Black tulle surrounded my legs, but a red lace top layer popped against the black. Dot had painstakingly braided my hair into a pattern almost as intricate as the bold design of the lace.

The dress had appeared on my bed a few hours earlier when I emerged from the shower, just as I'd started to panic about what to wear.

When Tyler had first told me about the event, I'd groaned. But he never asked me for anything, and after he explained why he needed the extra Light boost, I agreed quickly.

The formal evening had been organized under a cloak of secrecy; it brought together security, law enforcement, and intelligence bigwigs from all over the world. The situation with Variant Valor and the Human Empowerment Network was continuing to escalate, and some leaders wanted to increase their efforts to work together, hoping more cooperation would help. They were holding a massive meeting, hosted by Melior Group, but it wouldn't take place until the next day. This evening was a welcome cocktail event with a formal dress code. Because we couldn't possibly solve the world's problems in smart casual.

I smiled as I walked toward Josh. "I'll never get over your uncanny ability to choose a dress that's perfect in every way, right down to the fit."

"Actually, Ethan helped this time. We went together."

"When did you two have time to go shopping?" Between our sessions at Melior Group, the continued training with Kane, studying for exams, and preparing for summer classes, we were all busy.

"We invited you to go with us, remember?" Josh raised his brows. When I gave him a blank look, he rolled his eyes and smiled. "But of course, you had your head in a science book, so I should've realized you barely heard a word I said."

I chuckled, wrapping my arms around his neck. "It really is beautiful. Thank you. You guys spoil me."

"Actually we're holding back. You don't know what spoiled looks like. And I wasn't talking about the dress. *You* are beautiful."

He squeezed my sides for emphasis and pulled me fully against his front. My breath hitched. I stared into Josh's knowing green eyes, my smile falling away. It really hit me once more how much he thought about me, how in tune he was not just with the size of my body when buying me couture but with my thoughts, feelings, wants, and needs. I could've put it down to the Bond, but that wasn't it. The level of attentiveness was uniquely Josh.

"Josh." My voice was low. I bit down on my bottom lip, suddenly a little nervous. The words were at the tip of my tongue, but a tightness squeezed the base of my throat, making it difficult to get them out.

Of course, he knew what I was thinking.

He smiled. His whole face lit up, and his eyes practically sparkled, just as Ethan's had in the pool when I told him.

"I love you too, Eve." He beat me to it.

"You stole my moment." I slapped him lightly on the shoulder, my own matching grin already breaking out on my face.

"I love you, Josh." I said it anyway.

"I know, but it's really nice to hear it." He pressed his lips to mine in a passionate kiss that definitely ruined my lipstick.

We heard footsteps coming up the stairs but didn't break apart. When I felt a hard, warm chest at my back, I knew it was Ethan and I was at risk of ruining more than just my lipstick.

I broke the kiss, but Ethan's lips were at my neck, his breath tickling my skin. "Don't stop," he whispered, breaking up his words with the occasional soft kiss. "I like seeing you all dolled up like this, kissing Josh when he doesn't look even remotely in your league in his ratty clothes."

As Josh started kissing the other side of my neck, all I could do was hum in acknowledgment, although it came out more like a moan.

"What's wrong with what I'm wearing?" Josh whispered before licking a particularly sensitive spot.

"Nothing," Ethan answered, "but it's such a contrast to what *she's* wearing that I can't stop thinking about . . . ruining that dress."

I moaned again. I was just about to ask them to show me exactly how they planned to ruin it when I was suddenly yanked away. Strong, calloused hands pulled me out from between Ethan and Josh so swiftly the two of them nearly bumped into each other. Ethan caught himself on the doorway, and Josh leaned a hand against Ethan's bare abs.

I looked between them, then up and around to Alec, cocking one eyebrow to show my disapproval.

"We're going to be late if you start that now. You two need to make yourselves scarce." He kept my back against his chest, his hands on my bare shoulders.

Josh sighed and hung his head, and Ethan immediately lifted his free hand to the back of Josh's neck. It was a reflex, a comforting gesture, but standing so close, with their hands on each other and Ethan shirtless, they almost looked like . . . lovers.

Their eyes locked for the briefest of moments before they pulled away. As Josh walked past, there was no mistaking the little smirk on his face. Ethan looked more confused, but curiosity definitely gleamed in his eyes too as he headed for his room.

"Why are you always cockblocking me?" I sighed, leaning back against Alec.

"Because we really are going to be late." He ran his hands down my arms slowly and pushed his hips forward, pressing his erection into my ass. "And because I want to ruin that dress myself later."

When he kissed one side of my neck, then the other, I shivered, my lips parting on a heavy exhale.

"Now hurry up." He pulled away, smacked me on the ass, and thumped down the stairs.

Fucking tease. I rolled my eyes before fixing my lipstick and grabbing my clutch off the bed.

~

Tyler's left hand rested on my leg, playing absentmindedly with the tulle, while his other scrolled through messages on his phone. Alec had a firm, unmoving hand on my other leg as he looked out the car window at the dusky sky.

Apparently taking a limo for just the three of us was overkill, but we couldn't possibly drive ourselves, so we were on our way to Manhattan in an Aston Martin town car driven by the same driver who had taken us to the gala. His name was Joe.

Important people were flying in from all over the world—we couldn't *not* throw a fancy event for them, although this would be much more low-key than the gala. Only about 150 guests were expected.

"So how come they're all coming here?" I asked. "Why aren't we flying off to Geneva or something?"

"It's New York," they both answered at the same time, as if it were obvious. Joe's shoulders shook with silent laughter.

"Americans . . ." I sighed. "You know there are cities just as vibrant and just as important as New York. And probably more convenient to get to for most of these people."

"I'd like to remind you that you're also American." Alec turned to face me. "And there's nowhere in the world like New York."

Tyler gave me a more serious answer. "Melior Group is hosting the event. Our HQ is here. It made sense. Plus, it gives us the chance to make sure it's well protected, allows us some control over who's invited, and puts us in a leadership position before any of the conversations have even started."

He stuffed his phone into his jacket pocket and smiled in a way that reminded me of our study sessions, when he was waiting for me to understand something complex, already believing without a doubt I'd get it.

I nodded. The choice of New York wasn't just arrogance—making everyone come to them; it was strategic. I should've known.

Joe pulled the car into an alley and then . . . stopped. I frowned, craning my neck to look out the windshield. It was just a dark and dingy alley, complete with trash cans and back entrances.

But the guys both got out of the car. Tyler held his hand out to me, and I let him help me out, still confused.

"Stay close, Joe," Tyler said to our driver as Alec went to a nearby recess in the wall. It was so dark I couldn't tell if a door or a vampire was in the shadows. "It'll be at least two hours before we can leave, but we may want to leave early."

I had no idea why Tyler would want to leave early when we were here to gauge the other leaders, but I'm sure it was part of his master plan.

"Yes, sir." Joe nodded and drove off toward the other side of the alleyway.

"Uh, where exactly are we?" I finally asked.

"Dammit." Tyler huffed and reached into his pocket, pulling out a hundred-dollar bill. He handed it to a smug, smirking Alec, who promptly pocketed it.

I just got more confused and crossed my arms over my chest.

"I bet that you would hold yourself back from asking any questions until we were in the building." Tyler sighed.

"*I* bet that you'd crack before we made it inside. I won!" Alec looked a little too pleased with himself.

I rolled my eyes at them both. Betting money on me. *The nerve.*

As another set of headlights illuminated the dirty alley, Tyler guided me toward the dark recess in the wall, his hand at the small of my back. Alec pulled a heavy steel door open, and we all walked into a brightly lit corridor.

A team of agents stood on the other side, in suits but fully armed. They nodded to Alec and Tyler and waved us past.

Alec took the lead, stopping at a set of elevators and pressing a button. The fabric of his perfectly tailored suit stretched over his muscular shoulders. He was in all black, as usual, but the simple suit and shirt—no tie—fit him perfectly. I was pretty sure it was the same one he'd worn to the gala.

Tyler, on the other hand, was in a beautiful gunmetal gray three-piece suit, the crisp white of his shirt providing a contrast to the dark, smooth fabric. A pale blue tie and pocket square finished off the polished look. The colors went together seamlessly and made his gray eyes pop. Even his messy hair was in a somewhat neat style, held in place by product. I couldn't stop looking at him.

"Well?" I asked again as we waited. I couldn't help myself. I hated not knowing things.

They both chuckled before Tyler took pity on me. "This isn't like the gala. The point isn't to be seen and make a spectacle. This is a private, secure event. It's being held in an event space at the top of an office building with no ties to Melior Group. There are three separate access points through which guests will arrive. Each has a team posted. Plainclothes officers on the street are keeping an eye on it as well."

I nodded as we entered the service elevator.

As we rode up in silence, the butterflies returned. Did I really have any business being here? I was a nineteen-year-old science nerd—what the hell did I have to talk about with leaders of militias and heads of state? I blew out a big breath and straightened the front of my dress.

Alec wrapped an arm around my shoulders, and Tyler took my hand and squeezed.

"You'll be fine, and you look beautiful." Tyler smiled.

"Just let Gabe do the talking," Alec added, "and give him some Light when he signals you. Smile and be polite and don't drink your weight in Dom Perignon like last time."

I glared at him. "That would be my volume, not my weight, as champagne is a liquid. And that's rich coming from you, considering you were the cause of my drinking that night."

Alec groaned and removed his comforting arm. But before we could really get into it, the elevator doors opened, and the distant sound of chatter and clinking glasses reached us.

"We've gone over this. You've got this. And Alec will never be far. He's your personal security detail tonight."

We followed the sounds of people down the plain corridor, then crossed an open foyer area into a stunning, sleek, modern event space that felt as if it were floating above the city.

Along one entire wall, floor-to-ceiling windows jutted out at an angle, making it feel as if you could just walk right off the edge. The furniture was all sharp angles and shiny surfaces. Candles in geometric holders sat on the bar and on the edge of the stage, where a blonde bombshell sang a slow, sultry tune in front of a small band.

I was pretty sure I was the only one in the room with a *teen* on the end of my age. It made me feel even more awkward and self-conscious.

Tyler placed my hand in the crook of his elbow, like a real gentleman, and led me into the room through the dead center of the double doors. He was making an entrance. I wanted to make sure I looked the part, so I plastered a smile on my face and hoped like hell no one saw the slight twitch in my lip. Alec fell back, blending into the crowd while still staying close.

Tyler walked up to a man in an expensive suit and turban. He introduced me as his Vital and then spent a few moments in conversation—mostly just pleasantries. I stood there and nodded and hummed a few times before it was time to move away.

He repeated that process with a handful of other people—all men, most of them middle-aged or older, and each with a beautiful woman on his arm.

"Can we get a drink?" I blurted out before we could get into another conversation with another boring person.

"Sure." Tyler smiled and started to lead the way toward the bar, but halfway there we were intercepted.

Victor Flint stepped into our path.

"Miss Maynard." He nodded and I managed a smile. "Tyler. How's everything going?"

"All to plan so far, Victor. You'll know if there are any issues."

"Good." He flashed us that toothy grin, and I did my best to keep a pleasant, neutral look on my face. I wasn't sure if it was his no-nonsense, borderline rude way of speaking or the fact that I felt he always had an ulterior motive, but I wanted to get away from him. I had to play my part though—be the good little Vital.

"Alec." Victor shifted his gaze to somewhere behind us. "You don't usually attend these events, do you?"

Alec's voice was flat, his face emotionless. "I'm on duty, sir. Protection detail."

Victor's eyes met mine just as Karen joined our group.

"Evelyn." She beamed, and I gave her a greeting and a smile much more genuine than the one I'd given Victor.

"I didn't know you were going to be here, Karen." I was beyond happy to see a familiar face.

"Oh, it was last minute. Lucian wasn't able to attend, and the other board members asked me to step in. I don't usually deal with this side of the organization." She smoothed the front of her blue velvet gown, looking almost as uncertain as I felt.

Lucian was usually the one to attend these events, and more public ones like the gala, but despite returning to work, the pain from his injuries was sometimes too much. Tonight he was home in bed, sedated into a painless sleep while one of his nurses kept an eye on him.

Victor interrupted our conversation. "Let me get you a drink, Karen. We should let Mr. Gabriel focus on his task." He took her by the elbow and was already turning away when he addressed Tyler. "Report to me in the morning, before the meetings, so we can debrief." He walked away, barely giving Karen an opportunity to wave goodbye.

"Dick," I muttered under my breath. I couldn't help it—the man had no manners.

Tyler shushed me, even as he chuckled, and led me the rest of the way to the bar.

"There are ears everywhere." Alec leaned in and tapped the earpiece that allowed him to communicate with the other agents. "Both electronic and of the Variant kind. Several people here have enhanced hearing."

As if I could know which ones they were by looking at them, my eyes scanned the room. Enhanced hearing was one of the common abilities, often overlooked and easy to hide once the Variant learned to turn it on and off. But it was probably one of the most underrated too, especially in the spy game. I made a mental note to watch my words and accepted the champagne flute Tyler offered me.

I took a sip and was not at all surprised to find it tasted incredible. I looked behind the bar; instead of Dom Perignon, as Alec had insinuated, they were serving Cristal. Just as expensive, and it would be just as much of a shame if it ended up being vomited out in a back alleyway.

My nerves calmed significantly once I realized how little attention most people were paying me, and the next hour crawled by. Tyler and I floated about the room, engaging in brief and seemingly insignificant conversations as I sipped on my champagne and he nursed a scotch. Waiters carried around finger food, and the band kept playing pleasant background music.

We schmoozed with dignitaries, military leaders, and directors of intelligence organizations and other private security firms. None of them were recognizable or particularly famous, but the people in this room, if they chose to work together, could change the world . . . or control it.

Occasionally, I was even included in the conversation.

It seemed like boring chitchat on the surface, and for the most part it was, but Tyler was getting more from it than anyone could possibly know. I kept transferring Light to him in controlled doses as he needed it.

It felt good to know I was doing my part, despite it being a bit boring. Seeing as how I couldn't just glow in the middle of a crowded room, I had to stay right at his side, and because he was wearing a suit, I had to be crafty in how I transferred.

It was a brush of our fingers there, a straightening of his perfectly straight collar here, a push when his hand came into contact with the bare skin at my back. I was quite literally glued to him.

And Alec was glued to me. He wasn't always in sight, but I could feel him nearby, feel his eyes on me. I would look over my shoulder, and there he was, giving me a slight nod, his blue eyes piercing into mine.

As I finished my second glass of champagne and dropped it on a nearby high table, another couple approached us.

The Japanese couple both looked to be in their late forties. The man wore a perfectly tailored blue suit, and the woman was in a stunning traditional kimono, her black hair in an elaborate updo.

They bowed, and the man spoke in perfect, if slightly accented, English. "Good evening. I am Itsuki Takata. This is my wife and Vital, Yui."

Tyler and I returned the respectful bow.

"Pleased to meet you, Mr. Takata. I'm Tyler Gabriel, and this is my Vital, Evelyn Maynard."

A spark of recognition entered Mr. Takata's expression, but he quickly hid it behind a warm, polite smile.

I thought back to the months my mother and I had spent in Japan and greeted them in their own language. They both looked pleasantly surprised. Mrs. Takata immediately started talking to me, explaining that she didn't speak much English and had been unable to chat with almost anyone. I apologized for how rusty my Japanese was, but we managed to carry a short conversation while Tyler asked Mr. Takata some seemingly innocuous questions.

As they moved off, I seized the opportunity to take a little break.

"I have to go to the bathroom," I whispered to Tyler.

"No problem." He smiled and grabbed my hand. We stood together for just a moment, and I gave him a good dose of Light, making sure he would have enough until I returned.

As I headed across the foyer, Alec silently fell in at my side.

"You know, you can't go into the ladies room with me," I teased, not even looking at him.

He scoffed. "I take my job very seriously."

At that I did turn to look at him, my eyebrows raised. Was he being serious? We couldn't just clear out the ladies room so I could pee. But then he smirked, the glint in his eyes telling me he was teasing, and I slapped him lightly on the stomach. He wasn't in a bulletproof vest, but it still felt as if I were hitting steel.

He positioned himself right outside the door. Just as I entered, he lifted his sleeve to his lips, murmuring something I couldn't hear without taking his eyes off me.

Only two other women were in there, and I didn't have to wait for a stall, so I finished in no time, fixed up my makeup, and headed back out.

I walked straight past Alec—I couldn't resist provoking him a little. As we were about to enter the main room again, his warm hand wrapped gently but firmly around my elbow and pulled me to the side.

"What are you doing?" I asked. My instincts weren't telling me yet that Tyler needed more Light, but I still wanted to be there for him.

"Just following orders from my superior" was Alec's cryptic answer, but his lips twitched, and his voice had turned to honey—the professional, neutral tone gone. It sent shivers of anticipation down my spine, and I let him lead me into a side room that shared a wall with the main function area.

An oval table in the center of the room looked as if it could seat about a dozen people, but at the moment there was only one. Tyler was leaning on the table, his legs crossed at the ankles, his suit jacket hanging over the back of a chair. He looked so fucking sexy in the vest as he rolled his sleeves up and looked at me sideways, as if he were preparing to get his hands dirty.

My breath quickened and I swallowed. "Your superior, eh?" I had no idea why they'd dragged me into this abandoned, dark room—the city lights behind Tyler were the only illumination, casting his face in shadow—but I could take a guess.

"Yes." I could feel Alec's heat at my back. "Tyler is my superior . . . technically. I was following his orders to bring you here."

"Good work, Alec." Tyler's voice was pitched low, and it was doing things to me . . . also somewhere low.

Alec wasn't touching me, and I leaned into him, hoping to get a reaction. But Tyler issued another order.

"Bring her to me."

Alec wrapped an arm around my middle and slowly walked me forward until we were inches away from Tyler.

"You've been exceptional tonight, Evelyn," he whispered, leaning in. My lips parted. "I know this has been a little boring for you, so I thought we might reward you with a little break."

He didn't wait for my response before crushing his lips to mine, pushing his tongue right into my mouth. I moaned and lifted my hands to his neck, returning the kiss eagerly. Alec remained mostly still, but his chest rose and lowered a little faster against my back, his breath tickling my neck.

Just as suddenly as he'd initiated the kiss, Tyler broke it. He stood up to his full height and removed my arms from around his neck.

"Turn her," he demanded, and Alec obeyed. With firm hands on my hips, he pushed until I was facing him.

"I think Alec's getting a little hot," Tyler whispered against the nape of my neck before placing a firm kiss there. "I think you should remove his jacket."

"Yes, sir," I breathed. Tyler froze, his lips on my skin. I felt him smile, and pleasure welled up inside me.

I slowly pushed Alec's jacket off his shoulders, and he let it fall to the floor behind him. As I ran my hands over the hard planes of his chest, then his shoulders and muscular arms, he watched my every move as if he had all night, his lips parted, his breath quickening even more.

I rested my hands on his hips and tilted my face up to kiss him, but before I could crash my mouth to his, Tyler's hands covered mine. He caressed my fingers until his hands were wrapped around my wrists, and then he tugged my arms to his sides, pulling me flush with his chest and away from Alec.

"Not yet." His voice was deceptively calm—I could feel his arousal pressing into my ass. I leaned my head back on his shoulder, sparing a fleeting thought for my appearance and hoping they didn't ruin my hair and makeup too much. "Alec, remove her underwear. Take your time."

Alec and I both moaned lightly. I was like putty in his hands, loving this side of him, and Alec wasn't arguing either. Maybe he could learn to share after all—maybe he just needed someone to order him to do it. But I would have to puzzle that one out later.

Alec inched forward.

The way Tyler had my arms pulled back made my chest jut out, my breasts rising and falling with every labored breath. I was ready and wanting. When Alec got his hands on my underwear, it would be soaked through.

Alec bent down just slightly, then placed both hands flat over my thighs. He dragged his palms up, bringing the layers of tulle with him. His fingers crawled over the dress bit by bit until the hem was in his hands.

With his fist full of tulle, he pressed the fabric against my belly while his other hand found my hip under the dress. Gently, very slowly, he traced my hip, then once again dragged his palm up my thigh. It took all the willpower I had not to squirm, move to the side, try to get his hand where I wanted it most. When he reached the top of my underwear, he dipped one finger under the fabric and ran it from one hip to the other, his nail scaping lightly just above my pubic bone.

He watched me the whole time, his icy blue eyes boring into mine, his lips parted. He watched as my breath hitched, as my eyes drooped, as my chest heaved and pushed my breasts out.

He snapped the top of my panties against my skin as he removed his fingertip, but he didn't pull away. With the backs of his fingers, he trailed a path over my pubic bone and down to my most sensitive area. As his knuckles grazed my clit through the fabric, I nearly gave in, ready to beg them to end this torture. But the look of pure lust on Alec's face and the impossibly hard erection against my ass kept me quiet. They were enjoying this as much as I was—it was just as exquisitely torturous for them as it was for me.

Alec's fingers found the lower hem of my panties, and he slipped two fingers underneath, hooking the front of my underwear through the leg holes. He held it as if he was about to rip it away from my body. I wished he would. The visual made me moan, and Tyler's hot breath at my neck started to come harder, his hips rolling against me in tiny, slow movements.

Alec just kept doing what he was doing, the picture of control except for his heavy breathing. His knuckles grazed my pubic hair as he dragged his fingers lower—lower, lower, between my legs. When he reached the warm, moist apex of my thighs, with his fingers caught between the wetness of my flesh and the wetness of the fabric, he showed his first sign of weakness. He swallowed hard, his Adam's apple bobbing, and a barely audible "fuck" passed his lips. But he didn't stop. He rubbed his fingers up and down my folds, spreading the wetness.

Nothing escaped Tyler's notice though. "Alec. Report," he demanded, his voice still pitched low but suddenly strained.

Alec cleared his throat. "It seems our girl's more responsive than we anticipated. She's soaked through her underwear."

"Mmm." Tyler hummed his approval and pressed a sensuous kiss to my neck. "Excellent. I want to see the evidence myself. Remove them. No more teasing."

"Yes, sir," Alec answered with a smirk just as I moaned a "yes" of my own.

Tightening his grip on the crotch of the panties, Alec pulled down, but before the fabric was past my hips, he froze. His shoulders tensed, and the hand holding the dress up clenched tight. His gaze fixed loosely on my chin, but I had a feeling he wasn't really paying attention to me anymore.

Even as my skin still burned with lust, a cold chill ran down my spine.

"Alec?" Tyler's voice lost that smoky, sultry quality, and his grip on my arms loosened.

In answer, Alec pulled my underwear back into place and dropped the front of my dress. He straightened to his full height. "Building is breached. We need to go."

TWELVE

"Shit." I was anything but calm as Tyler released me and they both put their jackets back on. "Shit, shit, shit."

Not this again. Not more guns and fighting and people trying to hurt us.

I backed away from the door and stumbled against the boardroom table.

Both of them pulled their guns out, and Alec pressed his left hand to his ear. "K, I need an exit." He was quiet for a few moments, listening to whatever Kyo was saying on the other end.

Tyler's face appeared in front of me, and only then did I realize how blurry my vision was. I blinked, and fat tears fell down my cheeks.

"Eve." Tyler held his gun firmly in one hand, but his other cupped my cheek, wiping the tears away with his thumb. "I need you to be strong. We'll get you through this. We'll get you out. But you need to keep your shit together, baby."

I can't do this. Not again. I can't.

"Yes, you can." Alec crowded me in on the other side, his hand squeezing my waist. Apparently the filter between my brain and my mouth had disappeared. "Evie, you're the strongest person I know. It's time to pull those soaked panties up and get the fuck out of here."

He flashed me his cocky, lopsided smirk that immediately made me want to call him an asshole—but it helped. It was dragging me out of my head, pulling me out of my panic, making my back straighten.

"Is this really the best time to make inappropriate jokes?" My voice still shook, but I was getting there. Feeling their touch grounded me. I placed my palms flat against the sides of their necks and pushed Light into them—giving them as much as I could in a short burst.

"There's my girl." Tyler smiled. Alec just nodded and moved to the door.

I took a deep breath, squared my shoulders, and walked to the door by Tyler's side. Music still drifted out of the main event area, along with the sounds of polite conversation and clinking glassware.

"Why aren't we hearing chaos?" I asked, my voice low.

"Wait for it," Tyler replied. A mere two seconds later, the music cut off, and the timbre of the voices changed, growing more intense, more panicked.

"Wait, why aren't you ordering everyone around?" My question was directed at Tyler, but he didn't have a chance to answer.

"Time to go." Alec pulled the door open and stepped through. I followed, staying as close as I could without impeding his range of movement. I could feel Tyler doing the same behind me.

In the foyer, beautifully dressed people were filing out of the function room and, to their credit, calmly if hurriedly making their way toward the exits. Melior Group agents ushered some people down in the service elevator, while others were sent up the few flights of stairs to the roof.

Alec led the way toward the same service elevators but headed past them. "Kyo said there's a large balcony off the eighty-ninth floor—three floors below the roof, where the choppers are being sent. He said it looks abandoned and doesn't appear to be a target. He's sending Jamie up with gear. Is this the best option, Gabe?"

Tyler thought about it for only a few seconds. "Yes. For now. But things are changing fast—it's like they had a plan, but they're changing it as they go. They're either really disorganized or really fucking good."

"We'd better haul ass then." Alec picked up his pace, and I had to jog to keep up.

We climbed up a dingy back staircase. A faulty fluorescent light kept flickering, making my nerves even worse. After the first flight, I made them stop so I could take my heels off, after which we were able to climb faster without making as much noise.

"Who. Is. Doing this?" I asked between panting breaths, not daring to slow down. Tyler was breathing only a little harder than usual—as if he were going for a light jog, not sprinting up stairs with his life in danger. Alec wasn't even breaking a sweat.

"I'm not entirely sure." Tyler's voice echoed off the concrete walls. "It's not my focus right now. We just need to get you out of here."

I was about to argue, demand he give me answers, when the sound of gunfire startled me so badly I flung myself against the wall. Alec didn't even flinch. Tyler grabbed me firmly by the elbow and pulled me forward.

"Move," he ground out, keeping his voice low. I obeyed.

The gunfire sounded way too close. It came in bursts, separated by silence and occasional shouting. Whoever it was had made it to the higher floors of the building, but it wouldn't be an easy win for them. There was a small army of Melior Group agents to get through.

At a door marked with a plain red "89," Alec stopped. I leaned on the railing, trying to catch my breath quietly.

He cracked the door open, peeked through, then swung it wide and stepped into the service corridor of the eighty-ninth floor. We followed close behind, Tyler closing the door soundlessly.

The gunfire and shouting sounded farther away now—as if someone had left an action movie playing on the TV in the next room—but I knew it could catch up with us at any moment. Both my guys crept forward cautiously, guns raised.

Alec led the way down the corridor and back into the nice part of the building. The plush carpet soothed my bare feet after all those rough concrete stairs.

We made it into another bigger boardroom without meeting anyone on the way. The room was just as dark and quiet as the one we'd been in several floors below.

"J. Report," Alec said, his hand pressed to his ear. "Copy that." He moved to the windows and opened the glass door. A cold breeze lifted the light curtains as he stepped out onto the balcony. With a firm hand at my back, Tyler pushed me out after him.

Plants and seating dotted the edges of the enormous balcony, which was twice the size of the boardroom.

Manhattan spread out spectacularly far below us, but the wind this high up was biting.

I wrapped my arms around myself. Tyler faced the door, his gun lowered but ready, as Alec pushed a bench up against the glass railing and leaned over. My heart jumped into my throat—he was bent double over the edge, looking as if a light breeze would send him hurtling down eighty-nine floors to the concrete below. But he didn't fall—he holstered his weapon and reached down. The next thing I knew, Jamie was climbing over the railing, dressed in all black with heavy gear strapped to his back.

I rushed forward to help him take the gear off.

"Hey, kitten," he panted out and smiled, as if we'd just bumped into each other in the mall. "Ready to blow this party off?"

"Yes." I nodded emphatically, my eyes wide. I just didn't have it in me to crack jokes.

Within moments, the two of them had secured thick, heavy ropes to the bolted railing, and Alec strapped a harness on. He removed his suit jacket and draped it over my shoulders. "Put this on. The wind is even worse at the side of the building."

"OK." I nodded.

I went to put my arms through the sleeves and realized I still had a death grip on my heels—one beautiful red shoe in each hand. I dropped them and finished putting Alec's jacket on, rolling the sleeves up several times so I could have use of my hands. The jacket reached the middle of my thighs, and it smelled like him.

"Wait." It suddenly dawned on me what they were about to make me do. "No. Fuck. Alec, I can't rappel down the side of a building! I . . . I'm . . . I do *science*."

Eighty-nine floors, at an average of twelve feet per floor—that was 1,068 feet! We were more than a thousand fucking feet off the ground!

It was Tyler who answered, his harness already in place. "You won't be. Alec will carry you down."

"What? How?"

"Does she ever stop asking questions?" Jamie piped in, sounding way too amused. I was starting to think there was something seriously wrong with all the guys in Alec's team—it was probably why they all got along so well. They were all nuts.

"No," Alec and Tyler answered at the same time.

Before I had a chance to defend my curious mind, Tyler was shoving a harness in my face. He made me put it on while I continued to protest the next phase of their crazy exit strategy. They all just ignored me.

The harness was like something you'd expect to wear when bungee jumping—tight around my thighs, making my beautiful dress bunch up, and with straps over my shoulders.

"She's ready," Tyler announced.

"No, I'm not!" I protested, but Alec spoke over me.

"Ready."

"Ready," Jamie parroted.

They all moved in unison, like a well-oiled machine.

While I continued my stream of protests, Alec attached my harness to his, then attached his to the rope. I kept arguing that I couldn't do this, had no idea what I was doing, was scared, all while following their quick instructions. Before long I was holding on to Alec in a piggyback position.

When he swung his leg over the railing, I squeezed my mouth and eyes shut, my heart jumping into my throat. The wind whipped the soft tulle of my skirt around my legs, which were clenched tightly around Alec's middle.

He didn't give me any warning or ask if I was ready. He just pushed off the wall, and we went plummeting. My eyes flew open, and my stomach joined my heart in my throat as I released a high-pitched, breathy scream. Sleek glass sailed up as we went down. The sound of the rope feeding through the device attached to Alec's harness was almost drowned out by the wind.

We jolted to a stop, and Alec propped his booted feet against the building. I took a breath.

"Evie." He spoke just loud enough to be heard over the rush of the wind. "We're trying to get out undetected here. This is a *stealth* mission. I need you to keep your mouth shut."

I was about to snap back at him—even if we were flying down the side of a building in a life-and-death situation, I was not about to let him get away with telling me to keep my mouth shut—but without waiting for a response, he pushed off again.

Again fear wrapped its cold claws around my throat. But I stayed silent. I focused on my dress whipping almost painfully around my naked legs, on the harness digging into my skin, on a little mole on Alec's neck I'd never noticed. I made a mental note to give that a proper look when we weren't running for our lives. Fear of skin cancer never leaves you after you've lived in Australia.

After several excruciating seconds, movement to my left and above us caught my eye.

Jamie and Tyler came sailing down the side of the building, overtaking us in seconds. Alec cursed and picked up speed. At first I thought he was just being competitive, but then I saw Jamie pull out his gun.

Jamie and Tyler took several shots in quick succession at the glass just below them. They holstered their guns, swung out wide, and threw themselves at the glass. It shattered around them as they disappeared into the building.

With one more gut-wrenching drop, Alec lowered us to the same spot, and Jamie and Ty pulled us in.

"What's going on?" I demanded as soon as we were out of the screaming wind.

"They made us," Tyler explained as he detached my harness from Alec's. "They were keeping all the people upstairs hostage, but as soon as someone spotted us coming down the side of the building, they pulled everyone to come after us. We think they're after you. Some of our people made it upstairs, and the hostages are saying they're looking for a girl."

My heart sank. Of course they were looking for me. More people were getting hurt because of *me*.

"We have to move," Alec growled, loosening his harness. I just stood there, trying not to let the despair take over.

"They're trying to get to us, but our guys are heading them off where they can. It's pandemonium out there, and we need to use this opportunity to get out another way."

"There's no clear exit," Jamie announced, as if that wasn't a big deal. "The most lightly guarded one is the east stairwell. They have four on the ground. We can take 'em."

The others didn't answer as they finished taking off their rappel gear. When Tyler started to remove my harness, I jumped, but there was no time for him to try to calm me, comfort me. The others were already walking out the door, guns cocked and at the ready.

Ty pushed me forward, remaining at my back. We rushed down the hallway. My bare feet helped me stay quiet, but my dress still made an obscene amount of noise, the layers of fabric rustling with every step.

We passed the front desk of whatever business had their offices on this floor and exited through the massive glass doors. There were elevators on our left, another set of giant glass doors on the opposite side, and a corridor with an emergency exit sign above it on our right.

Just as the doors swung closed behind me, several masked men emerged from the corridor, guns raised.

For a split second, everyone froze.

Then one of the men spoke. "Just hand her over, and no one has to die."

I took an involuntary step back. It didn't take a genius to figure out these were Variant Valor dickheads—Davis's thugs.

Alec laughed, a low, menacing sound. "If you want her, you'll have to kill us first."

As if to prove Alec's point, Tyler inched forward, blocking me from their view.

I opened my mouth—to stubbornly declare I'd die too before I was taken—but I never got the chance.

A gun went off. I had no idea whose, but it must've been one of the ones pointed at us, because the door behind me shattered. I hunched my shoulders and covered my head with my hands. Glass shards showered over me, getting stuck in my hair and slicing into my exposed back.

Tyler fired, his precise aim taking out one of the thugs before all the glass had even fallen to the tiled floor.

Everyone started shooting, the sound deafening. The glass behind the assailants exploded too, littering the floor with more glittery particles.

More assailants poured out of the corridor and the office on the opposite side of the building, but at the same time, Melior Group agents stepped off the elevators and appeared behind us too. Even people in formal wear, the important dignitaries from the party, were there—diamonds and tuxedos mixing with the bullets and blood.

After the initial surge of gunfire, both sides took cover—in doorways, in offices, behind desks and chairs.

Alec was at the front of our group. Once the reinforcements arrived, he gestured to Jamie and Ty. They closed in, and Alec roughly pushed me back the way we'd come.

My mind felt slow, as if I were wading through syrup. I didn't even turn around when Alec started nudging me; I just walked backward, flinching at the shattered glass under my bare feet.

After a moment, Alec simply swept me up with one arm and carried me the remaining few steps. He set me down behind the reception counter, and Tyler tugged me down into a crouch beside him.

Alec remained standing. When I looked up, he was looking down, a somewhat confused expression on his face. Time seemed to slow as he pressed a hand to his chest, then pulled it away and stared at it.

He grabbed the edge of the desk with the same hand, but it slid right off, leaving a trail of red on the white surface.

My eyes widened.

My heart stopped.

My throat constricted, cutting off my air.

Alec dropped to his knees as his gun slipped from his grip. The confused expression melted away, replaced by something else, something harder.

Ty, Jamie, and a few other people who'd taken cover behind the reception desk were focused fully on fighting off the assailants. Gunshots and shouts echoed all around me.

None of them had noticed yet. None of them had seen the blood. *So much blood.* It oozed between the fingers of the hand Alec pressed to his chest.

"NO!" My guttural scream immediately drew everyone's attention. My hands became a blur as they flew to his neck, then his shoulders, then the bloody, slick hand at his chest.

Together, Tyler and I lowered Alec to the ground.

As another person came to help, my mind supplied a list of all the vital organs in the area he was shot—lungs, small intestines, heart . . . *So many ways to die.*

"There's no exit wound," someone declared from his other side. The lethal piece of metal was still lodged in his body somewhere. Killing him.

Why wasn't he wearing a vest? Was Tyler wearing a vest?

I whipped my head around frantically, but Tyler was right next to me—fine. He looked as panicked as me, his eyes wide, his hair all over the place, but he was upright. He was moving. He wasn't bleeding.

I wasn't losing them both.

But I might lose Alec.

Our guys were administering first aid with speed and precision. Alec was still conscious, but his eyes kept rolling back in his head. His breaths came in short pants, as if he couldn't quite make the air reach his lungs.

Every time he managed to get his eyes to focus, he looked right at me.

"Ev . . . Evie . . . I . . ."

I grabbed his hand, struggling to keep my grip against the slippery blood.

"I love . . . y . . . you."

He said, "I love you," but he meant "goodbye." I heard *goodbye.* And I was not going to accept that.

As Alec's eyes closed and his limp hand slid from my grasp, a heavy steel barrier shuttered over my emotions. All that was left was white hot rage and a determination fiercer than I'd ever felt before.

No one noticed me rise slowly to my feet; they were too focused on saving Alec's life. By the time I was standing, my skin had already begun to glow.

I embraced the Light. I let it flood me, consume me, until it filled every fiber of my being. My glow became so bright that some of the people fighting stopped to shield their eyes.

Several guns pointed right at me, and I barely registered Tyler's panicked yell as the triggers were pulled. I didn't even flinch. I already knew a shielding ability was coming up behind me. The representative from Japan, Mr. Takata, appeared at my side, his hands held out in front of him. The bullets harmlessly bounced away.

I continued to push Light to Alec remotely, as much as he needed. It would by no means save him or heal his wounds, but at least it would assist the healing.

As long as Alec held on, I had something to fight for. And I was *so ready* for a fight.

THIRTEEN

I pushed some Light to Mr. Takata, and as I stepped out from around the reception desk, he stayed beside me, keeping me shielded. Tyler stuck by my other side; he kept his gun raised but didn't fire. I was keeping him juiced up too, and his ability would've told him what I was doing. Soon there would be no need for bullets.

My instincts were taking over. I surrendered to the Light and watched in awe as all the Variants in the room became obvious to me, almost as if I were playing a video game and all the guys on my team were marked.

I held my hands out at my sides and closed my eyes; I could *feel* them. I could feel the ones who were using their abilities most; the ones without Vitals who were getting depleted; Mr. Takata with his shield; a woman with an ability to freeze a person on the spot, trying to get close enough to touch people without getting shot; a man with a fire ability like Ethan's, but instead of throwing fireballs, he had to intensely focus to make an object or person erupt in flames.

I could feel Davis's men too. They had a shield, a man with a water ability thwarting our fire guy, a few others with common speed and strength abilities. I felt the Light inside them, and I *pulled* until they fell to the ground unconscious.

The Light flowed through me with the force of a waterfall—making my skin buzz until it almost went numb—and went straight into the Variants who needed it.

With the Variants on the other side incapacitated and our guys overflowing with Light, we overpowered them in seconds.

Most of the Melior Group operatives moved off immediately to clear the building and neutralize the rest of the assailants. The others started tying up our captives—the ones who still lived.

As my glow faded, I dropped my arms to my sides and opened my eyes. The first thing I saw was Tyler's worried expression.

My chest heaved, and my teeth gritted from exertion. I wanted so badly to fall into his arms, let him hold me and take charge of the situation as he always did. But I wasn't done.

I pointed to a slight woman in a stunning black gown who was helping to tie someone up. She had the freezing ability, able to suspend a person in motion—essentially put them on ice.

Tyler rushed over to her, spoke hurriedly, and ushered her to my side in seconds. She looked nervous, her wide brown eyes darting from mine to his, but she took my hand when I held it out. I was fading, and I needed the contact to transfer to her.

I could see Tyler's lips moving as he spoke to her, hear his voice, but his words weren't registering. I turned and led the way back to the reception desk. Halfway around it, I stumbled, but a firm, warm hand steadied me. Mr. Takata was still by my side. As soon as it was clear I wasn't going to face-plant, he released me, tipping his head forward in a little bow.

By the time I turned back, Tyler and the woman were already kneeling beside Alec, nudging Jamie out of the way.

I lowered myself to my knees on his other side. Taking his hand in mine again—it was sticky now, not slippery—I kept pushing Light at him, but there was no point anymore. No amount of Light could help him now. And I had nothing left to give.

I had nothing left.

My eyes drooped, and my head felt heavy. Even as my mind fought to the last second for consciousness, my muscles ultimately gave in. My vision faded, and I fell in a heap next to Alec, our limp hands stuck together with his drying blood.

~

I came to just as the paramedics were taking Alec away and discussing having me taken to the hospital in another ambulance. I refused, demanding to stay with Alec. They were stubborn, but so was I, and in the end we tailed Alec's ambulance to the hospital.

Lucian was already there. Josh and Ethan rushed forward as soon as we stepped inside, hugging me tight despite the gore clinging to me. They fired off questions, demanded I see a doctor, spoke over each other while frantically running their hands over me.

During the surgery to remove Alec's bullet, I was checked over by a doctor—not even a concussion, thank you very much—and despite my protests, everyone insisted I should go home, clean up, have something to eat. Alec was stable, but they were keeping him sedated so his body could have some time to heal.

"I won't leave this room, and Olivia is on her way," Lucian reassured me.

Tyler had to go back to the scene and do some damage control, make sure his guys were doing what needed to be done. He ran his hands through his hair, his worried gaze darting to Alec, then me. He pulled me into a hug and held me for a long time. I gripped his filthy suit jacket, my eyes closed.

"Please, Eve. Please go home. I need to know at least one of you is safe and warm." He spoke into the top of my head, his chest reverberating under my cheek.

Grudgingly, I realized he was right. I couldn't do anything more for Alec—he had all the Light he needed and then some. The hospital, under medical supervision, was the best place for him. But I *could* do something to ease Tyler's worry.

I nodded against his chest.

We peeled apart—the front of my dress had stuck to his suit jacket. That's how much drying blood I was coated in.

I looked down at myself and really took it in for the first time. My arms were smeared with blood. It covered my chest, my shoulders, even my hair. My beautiful dress was ruined, but not in the fun way Ethan and Alec had both hinted at. It felt as if the dress itself were blood, soaking into my skin.

"OK." I lifted my eyes. "I, uh . . . I need to get out of this blood . . . the dress . . ."

Tyler leaned forward and placed a gentle kiss on my forehead. "Kid, Josh, take our girl home. I'll send two teams to meet you in the underground parking garage in the north wing. Uncle Luce . . ." He ran his hand through his hair again as he eyed Alec lying helpless in the hospital bed.

"I'm here." Lucian's tone was calm and firm. "I won't leave his side, and I'll call if there are any changes. Go. All of you, get out of here."

The finality of his words pushed us into action. Knowing he was staying made me feel better. It may've been one of the most fucked-up situations I'd been in, but I couldn't help thinking it was nice having a family.

Tyler marched down the hallway first. Ethan, Josh, and I went a little slower, making our way to the parking garage.

We were driven back to the apartment in an armored vehicle with another following close behind. Both were filled with agents armed to the teeth.

All ten of the agents escorted us up from the underground parking garage, through the lobby—where we got some shocked looks from the doorman—and all the way to the penthouse. They made us stand outside the front door while four of them swept the space. I leaned on Ethan and held Josh's hand while we waited.

When they were finally satisfied, they allowed us to enter. Josh locked the doors, and we all breathed a sigh of relief. No doubt the agents were positioning themselves around the building to ensure our safety. I wouldn't have been surprised if they were waking up all the other residents and sweeping the entire building top to bottom.

The guys took their shoes off as I stood there, not quite sure what to do. I needed someone else to make the decisions, maybe even move my limbs for me. Plus, I didn't have shoes. My feet were barefoot and bloody.

And my dress felt as if it were squeezing the air out of my lungs.

"Get it off," I whispered to the ground. Tears began to track down my cheeks for the millionth time that night. "Get it off me!" My raised voice sounded more than a little manic as I pulled at the collar of the dress, trying to tear it away from my skin.

Both Ethan and Josh were beside me in an instant. One of them pulled my hands away from the dress while the other undid the zip at the back. They pushed the filthy fabric down over my hips and let it flop to the floor.

My breathing calmed but only slightly as my blurry eyes met Josh's worried ones. Ethan's big, comforting hands rested on my shoulders, lightly caressing, but his clean fingers pulled at my tacky skin. I started rubbing my arms, trying to get the crimson off, but it was nearly completely dry, and I couldn't unzip it like the dress.

"I need to get it all off," I pleaded.

Josh looked over my shoulder, sharing a worried look with Ethan, and then they moved at the same time.

Ethan hurried down the hallway as Josh picked me up. I wrapped my legs around his waist and my arms around his neck as he carried me into the bathroom. Ethan had already started the shower, and steam was billowing from it.

Josh set me down and, once he was sure Ethan had a hand on my shoulder, started undressing. Ethan kneeled before me and gently took my underwear off, letting me use him for balance as I stepped out of it.

I stood before him naked, bare, and bathed in blood. He took my face in his big hands and leaned in, placing a tender kiss on my chapped lips and wiping my tears with his thumbs.

"We got you, baby," he whispered against my lips. His breath was minty, his clothing and hair clean. Not draped in death like mine.

Josh finished undressing and adjusted the water temperature. The shower had limited space, and there was no way we would all fit in there.

Ethan released me and Josh took my hand, pulling gently forward.

"I'll make us something to eat and a warm cup of tea while you get cleaned up." Ethan picked up the discarded clothing and closed the door behind him.

Josh coaxed me into the shower with gentle but sure hands. He pulled me in close, then walked me backward until the almost too hot spray hit my shoulders. I gasped, the water waking me out of my stupor a little. I was pretty sure I was experiencing shock, my reflexes slow, my breathing shallow.

"Is the water too hot?" Josh immediately reached for the tap, but I shook my head.

"No, just . . ." I didn't know how to finish the sentence.

Josh settled his hands on my hips, holding me down to earth so I wouldn't float away into a full-blown panic attack. I tried to focus on his slow, even breathing, the way his chest rose and fell, the very fine bit of blond chest hair between his pecs. Droplets of water sprayed off me to land on his chest, shoulders, and belly, gathering together until they started to trail wet paths down his body.

Within a minute of standing under the hot spray, the droplets started to take on a pink tinge. I furrowed my brow, worried I was starting to hallucinate. Then I remembered—the dried blood was finally melting off me.

I lifted my hands to his chest, covering all the red droplets, and looked down. Mesmerizing swirls of red circled the drain, fed by crimson tracks of water traveling down my legs.

Josh reached behind me for a loofah and a bottle of something that smelled like Tyler. He worked some of the bottle's contents into a lather in his hand, and then with slow, careful movements, he washed me.

He cleaned my neck and shoulders, then reached around to do my back, my ass. My breasts and belly followed. He added more bodywash to do my arms.

I kept my eyes on the drain. The blood mixed with the suds, fluffy pink swirls disappearing into the pipes. For some reason, that made it a bit easier to watch.

Josh moved my hands up from his chest to his shoulders, then slowly kneeled down. He cleaned my legs one by one, lifting one foot, then the other. I'd completely forgotten about the cuts on my feet, which stung as the sudsy water washed over them. Thankfully, Alec had carried me over most of the glass.

When Josh stood up again, I let my hands drop back to his chest. I liked feeling his breaths, the faint thud of his heartbeat. I leaned my forehead on my hands. The water running into the drain was now perfectly clear.

Once again, Josh moved, and then shampoo was in my hair. He lathered it slowly, massaging my scalp and spreading it all the way to the ends.

"Lift your head so I can rinse the shampoo." He didn't raise his voice, but the way it bounced off the tiles made it sound louder than it was.

I tipped my head back into the spray. Josh rinsed the shampoo and wiped it away from my eyes.

I lowered my head to look at him and took my first deep breath. My shoulders were relaxing; I was no longer covered in blood. I couldn't be sure if I was still crying or not as my whole face was wet, but my nose wasn't blocked, so that was a good sign.

Josh's vibrant green eyes fixed on me, and as always, I felt as if he could see right into my soul. The water had turned his dirty-blond hair dark, and he licked the moisture off his full lips.

He reached behind me again. Conditioner this time. As he spread it through my hair with care, I trailed my hands over his shoulders to play with the damp hair at his neck. Then I leaned forward and kissed him gently beneath his ear.

It was meant as a thank you—to show I appreciated how attentive he'd been—but as my lips tasted his skin, my body began to crave more.

Maybe it was fucked up that I wanted sex after the horrific shit I'd just been through, but it was never just sex with them. It was healing and comfort and connections and coming home all at once.

After he'd finished working the conditioner into the ends of my hair, he brought his hands back to my hips and swallowed audibly. "Eve?"

He was waiting to figure out what I needed, but his body was already reacting to mine. He was getting hard.

Maybe now wasn't the time. I looked up at his clever, watchful eyes and thought about getting out of the shower, drying off . . . but then I'd have to deal with the rest of it. I'd be out of this steam-and-tiles cocoon, and I'd have to think about the blood circling the drain, Alec unconscious in the hospital, all the people who'd died. *Because of me.*

My eyes stung, and a relentless, unbearable tightness squeezed my chest.

I wasn't ready.

"Just . . . I need . . ." I struggled to articulate my jumbled thoughts between increasingly erratic breaths. "I don't want to think about the blood . . . I can't . . . make me forget . . . please, just . . . make me forget, Josh."

He pulled me against him and kissed me hard, pushing his tongue into my mouth. I threw my hands around his neck and held on, focusing fully on his perfect lips, on my stiffening nipples, on his wet body plastered against mine, on his hard cock against my belly.

He broke the kiss, his mouth trailing a path over my jaw, then my neck, as his hands kneaded my ass. He sucked up the water with licks and kisses against my skin, but they were much gentler than that first kiss had been.

I tugged on the hair at the back of his neck. "More," I whispered hoarsely.

He looked searchingly into my face. Whatever silent question he was asking, he must've found his answer, because in the next instant, he spun me around so I was facing the wall and pressed into my back, the shower's spray still hitting our shoulders and sides.

He pulled me back against him, one hand on my hip, one on my shoulder.

"Feel my body against yours, Eve." He moved against me, our slick skin making it easy, then ground his erection into my ass. My lips parted. *Yes*, this was exactly what I needed.

"Listen to my voice." It was low and all kinds of sexy. He spoke close to my ear, then bent his head and gently bit my shoulder.

"Feel my hands." He squeezed my hip and shoulder. Then he moved one hand to my breast and the other between my legs.

I gasped, my breaths coming faster and shallower.

I placed my palms flat against the slick tiles, my elbows half-bent as I leaned forward. My ass ground into

Josh's rock-hard erection, and he groaned. The sound bounced off the tiles and sent another wave of desire straight between my legs, where his hand started moving against my aching flesh.

Josh's long, artistic fingers were nimble, and it wasn't long before the sound of my heaving breaths filled the bathroom. I closed my eyes.

But that was a mistake.

As soon as I didn't have anything to look at, images assaulted my brain: Alec falling to his knees, the blood pooling around him, the blood swirling around the drain.

I forced my eyes open just as Josh pushed two fingers in. It felt incredible, but I wanted more. I leaned forward until my forehead rested against the tiles, my hands on either side of my head.

"More," I demanded with my words and my body, arching back into him.

He removed his fingers and replaced them with his cock. He wasn't slow or careful. He drove into me in one precise thrust. I was ready for him—his hands had made sure my pussy was as dripping wet as the rest of my body—but the sudden sensation of having him completely inside me, the wonderful fullness, surprised me in the best way.

"Yes," I grunted.

All the bloody images were driven from my mind as Josh started to move. As I knew he would, he figured out exactly what I wanted. What I *needed*. He pounded into me, deep powerful strokes that had my whole body moving, my breasts bouncing.

He squeezed my hip hard with one hand, pulling me back onto him as he drove forward. His other hand went back to where we were joined. This time his fingers weren't so gentle and exploratory. He went straight for the most sensitive spot and started rubbing firmly in time with his thrusts.

I kept my eyes open. I watched his hand moving between my legs, my boobs bouncing, his calves and thighs flexing with every movement. I focused on watching us fuck, listening to our grunts and moans echoing in the hot bathroom, feeling Josh slide in and out of me.

The pressure built low in my belly, and I chased it, let it take over. Pleasure traveled up my spine and spread to my chest, my head. Almost animalistic noises burst past my lips as I completely gave in to the orgasm. Stars burst across my vision, the intense waves of pleasure making me stiffen and press my cheek against the wall.

Both Josh's hands gripped my hips as he continued to push in and out of me, but his movements had lost intensity. Now he was taking it slow, making me feel every inch of him as he slid in and out, careful and gentle as I came down from my orgasm.

As I started to catch my breath, I realized my eyes had closed. Images of blood and violence once again seeped into my mind. Alec falling . . . blood pooling . . . blood circling the drain.

I ground my teeth and grunted in frustration, pushing against the tiles until I was upright again.

"More," I demanded. I wanted him to drive every bad thing from my mind until I couldn't think straight. I wanted him to make me forget.

Josh stilled behind me. "Eve . . ." He sounded unsure, worried.

"I don't need your pity."

"I'm not pitying you. I'm trying to take care of you." His voice was calm and patient as he nudged me around to face him.

I immediately felt bad for snapping at him. "I know. I'm sorry. I just . . . please make me forget."

Without waiting for an answer, I reached between us and started stroking him. He was impossibly hard and covered in the evidence of my orgasm, mingled with the spray of the water.

He let me touch him as he searched my face again. Then he gave me what I wanted.

He pushed me back against the tiles and kissed me forcefully, teeth scraping, tongue battling for dominance. One of his hands slapped the wall next to my head, and the other lifted my leg. He hooked my knee over his elbow and pressed his palm flat against the wall near my hip, keeping my leg angled out. I guided him back inside me, and he pressed his forehead against mine, his breath washing over my wet face.

Then he started to move, driving into me as he had before, his intense eyes watching my face. After a few moments, I felt the nudge of his ability. I lifted my other leg and wrapped it around his hip as he held me up with his mind. The new position allowed me to spread my legs wider, tilt my hips forward. Josh's strokes reached deeper and deeper, and I held on to his shoulders and let my head rest against the tiles.

I watched him as intently as he watched me. He was beautiful—his full lips parted, his soft hair falling over his forehead in a wet mess, his green eyes hooded yet still watching, seeing, *knowing*.

His movements became more erratic as he chased his own release. I could tell he was close. I was too. He was hitting just the right spot with every slap of his hips, and that heady feeling was building again.

"Come with me," he growled out as he drove into me one last time and ground his hips against mine.

Just as he'd obeyed all my demands, I now obeyed his. We both crashed into orgasm the same way our bodies had been crashing into each other—with intensity and urgency.

We cried out but kept our eyes open, our gazes locked.

As our breathing slowed, Josh pulled out and lowered me to my feet. My knees shook, but he kept me steady. He moved me back under the spray and rinsed out the conditioner I'd completely forgotten about. I held his gaze, reading his unspoken message even as he read every expression on my face.

He'd given me what I asked for, but now he was taking care of me.

As the last of the conditioner left my hair and the water washed our sweat away, I leaned forward and kissed him gently.

He sighed against my lips, and his shoulders relaxed under my hands. I hadn't realized how tense they were until I felt the muscles soften.

I pulled back and looked him in the eye, running my nails over his scalp. "Thank you, Josh. I love you."

"I love you too." He gave me a small smile, and I knew we would be OK. I was where I needed to be.

I shut off the water as Josh stepped out of the shower and reached for the towels.

I dressed in a pair of Josh's sweatpants and Alec's T-shirt. It smelled faintly like him, and even though it made my heart ache, it also made me feel closer to him.

We came out to the kitchen just as Ethan dropped the last plate of steaming food onto the counter.

"Creamy pasta with some of last night's leftover roast pumpkin and crispy bacon bits," Ethan explained as he pulled out a stool for me. "Nothing fancy, but it's comfort food."

"Ethan, everything you make is fancy and delicious." I gave him a smile, but it didn't feel like it reached my eyes.

Josh took the chair next to me, and as soon as I started eating, I realized how hungry I was. We both stuffed our faces. Ethan ate half of his, then jumped up and disappeared down the hall. He came back moments later with a hairbrush and positioned himself behind me.

"You don't have to . . ." I trailed off as his warm, comforting hand landed on my shoulder, rubbing lightly.

Silently, I got back to eating as Ethan brushed my damp hair. He was so careful, so gentle, I never felt a painful tug at my roots, never had my head jerked back.

Once we were done, they led me to the bedroom in the back.

My body was ready to give in. All my basic needs were taken care of—food, hygiene, sex. Now it was time to rest. But a faint blue glow was peeking through the curtains, and I made myself stop at the threshold. "It's morning. We should go back to the hospital."

Josh reached out to me. "Eve, you need to rest."

Ethan, on the opposite side of the bed, did the same. "Uncle Luce said he'd call as soon as there was any news."

I looked between them. I couldn't crawl into a warm comfortable bed when Alec was lying in a hospital with a bullet wound—that he'd taken to protect me. "He needs me."

"Yes, he does." Josh didn't argue. "But you're no good to him dead on your feet. You can't pour from an empty cup."

As if to illustrate his point, I swayed and caught myself on the doorway. In two long strides, Ethan reached me and swept me effortlessly into his arms.

"Sleep for a few hours, and then we'll go straight back," Ethan said close to my ear. "The doctors said they were keeping him under for most of today anyway." He didn't give me a chance to argue before he lowered me to the bed and pulled off my pants.

I didn't have any more energy to object. The pillow was really soft, and my limbs felt heavy. My guys climbed in on either side of me, cocooning me with warm, hard bodies and gentle, tender caresses.

FOURTEEN

Alec had a private room at the hospital, but even Lucian's money couldn't buy more space, and it was crowded with all of us in there.

I sat in a chair, holding his hand in both of mine and trying to stay calm. It really wouldn't help if I started crying again. I'd been doing it on and off all morning—when Lucian called to tell us they were going to wake Alec up, as we hurriedly dressed, when we made a quick pit stop for pastries and coffee. I was so over it; I felt as if I had no control over my own tear ducts.

Lucian looked like I felt. He was in the corner by the door, disheveled, his head drooping. He looked as if he might pass out at any moment but was refusing to leave until Alec woke up. *If* he woke up . . .

The doctors had kept Alec in an induced coma overnight. They'd already given him the medication that would wake him up, and we'd spent the past twenty minutes holding our collective breath.

He *had* to be OK. I needed him to wake up and scowl at something, or I was going to lose my mind.

Tyler was asleep by the window, in the only other chair. His head rested against the back, and his legs were splayed out in front of him. It didn't look comfortable at all, but he'd been up all night. Soft snoring sounds drifted from his slightly open mouth.

Ethan and Josh leaned on the wall behind me, too on edge to sit down.

No one spoke. We just breathed and waited.

Dot, Charlie, Olivia, and Henry were in the waiting room just outside. So were Kyo, Marcus, and Jamie, still in their Melior Group uniforms. Dana was there too, along with a handful of other agents I hadn't met. For someone who pushed people away so expertly, Alec sure had a solid group of people who genuinely cared for him. Loved him, even.

There was that word again—*love*.

I could see it in his eyes every time we had sex, every time we shared a moment of tenderness, a deepening of our fraught bond. I'd said it to Ethan and Josh easily. I was so sure of my feelings for them. They were my world, my home. They all were.

I was waiting for the right time to tell Tyler, but when it came to Alec . . .

Did I love him?

I raised my head to look at him. My eyes landed on his strong, stubbled jaw first, then his nose with the slight kink in it. His eyebrows were relaxed as he slept. His beautiful ice-blue eyes—the eyes that had haunted me for a year, watched me with derision, studied me with abandon, then stared directly into my soul with love—were closed. And I was terrified they would never open again, never watch me tell him I loved him. Because I did.

I loved Alec. It was time to let go of the last scrap of a barrier between us. I was barely holding it up as it was, exhausted by the vain attempt to protect myself from further emotional pain.

He loved me. He was committed. Everything he'd done since he'd said those words had only put them into action.

I propped my elbows on the edge of the bed and pressed his limp hand to my forehead, willing him to wake up, to come back to me.

The big hand in my grip twitched. I whipped my head up. Alec lay still, his face blank, his breathing even. I focused on his hand, inches away from my face.

This time, I saw his fingers move, his hand just barely closing around mine. I gasped and sat forward in the chair, my heart hammering in my chest.

The movement caught everyone's attention. Ethan and Josh were by my side in a heartbeat. Lucian wheeled himself forward, his questioning eyes hopeful.

Kyo appeared in the doorway the same moment I said, "His hand twitched," as if it was the greatest thing to have ever happened.

"I'll get someone." Kyo rushed away without waiting for a response, but his loud voice finally woke Tyler. He sprang to his feet and pulled his gun out, his eyes searching for the threat before they were even fully open.

"Chill, bro." Ethan tried to keep his booming voice low. "There's no one to shoot. We think he might be waking up."

Tyler took another second to survey the room, then put the gun away. Yawning, he leaned one hand on the foot of the bed and rubbed the sleep from his eyes with the other.

Kyo came back with a nurse and doctor in tow, but fitting everyone inside the room was impossible. The medical professionals needed to be there, I refused to leave Alec's side, and the guys refused to leave mine, so Kyo and Lucian were promptly kicked out. The nurse started fiddling with the machines attached to Alec, intermittently jotting things down on a clipboard, while the doctor checked his vital signs.

She turned to me and looked over the rim of her bright orange glasses. "You said he twitched?"

I nodded. "His hand. Twice."

"OK. According to his vitals, he's not showing any signs of coming out of it just yet. Which is fine, it'll happen any moment now. The twitching is perfectly normal. Sometimes—"

Whatever she was about to say was cut off by a grimace of pain. Her mouth opened on a silent scream, and she doubled over, clutching her head. Behind her, the nurse did the same—moaning as she collapsed against the wall and started to slide to the ground.

The smile that pulled at my lips as I took in the all-too-familiar pain was almost manic. A surprised, delighted laugh burst out of me as my wide eyes darted between the people writhing in pain and Alec's face.

Tyler and Josh rushed to the women and tried to keep them upright.

"I'll get Uncle Luce. Maybe he can shield them." Ethan rushed toward the door, but halfway there, the pained groans stopped.

Alec squeezed my hand.

Everyone paused. Tyler and Josh helped the panting, shaking women into chairs while I kept my full focus on my Master of Pain. His fingers were still wrapped loosely around mine, and his brows furrowed, making that scar pucker.

"How is he scowling while passed out?" Josh shook his head. He came to stand next to me and Tyler, and Ethan took up the other side of the bed.

"Not out, dickhead," Alec croaked, slowly opening his eyes. It looked as if it took quite a bit of effort.

We all breathed a massive sigh of relief. Ethan's eyes were definitely misty as he took his cousin's other hand. Tyler leaned on the bed, his head drooping.

I just kept staring into Alec's beautiful, drawn face as he worked to open his eyes fully. As soon as he managed it, he looked directly at me.

A barely there smirk pulled at his lips. "Did I just hear you laughing at someone's pain?"

I shook my head, trying to hold back more tears. I couldn't speak around the lump in my throat.

He squeezed my hand again, and his smirk grew. "My little fucking sadist."

I laughed, throwing my head back as the lump in my throat began to ease. My hand stayed tightly wrapped around his as I leaned in close. "Thank fuck you're OK."

I kissed him, softly brushing my lips against his and nuzzling his nose.

Pulling back, I stared into those ice-blue eyes, the ones I'd worried about never seeing again. And again, all I saw there was devotion and love. He looked at me as if I was the only person in the room.

I stroked the side of his head, his cheek. The words were on the tip of my tongue—I felt it, and I'd resolved to tell him—but my stupid brain decided to throw up a roadblock.

I didn't want him to think I was only saying it because he'd nearly died—that it was some knee-jerk reaction to fear. I wanted him to know it was genuine and heartfelt.

So instead I held his gaze. Every other time he'd looked at me like that—with love practically bursting out of his pores—I'd turned away, unable to handle the intensity, the pressure. This time, I returned the look. I thought about how much I loved this impossible, frustrating, broken man, and I let it all show on my face.

His smile widened, and he opened his mouth to say something, but the doctor interjected.

"Excuse me. Make room, please. I *do* need to examine him." She nudged her way past Ethan's bulk and made him and Tyler step back. The nurse joined her and got back to recording things on her clipboard. I had to hand it to them, they were handling the whole "struck down by excruciating pain" thing like champs.

I held on to Alec's hand as the doctor poked and prodded him, asked him a bunch of questions, checked the bullet wound before the nurse changed the dressing.

At the end of it all, she said she was very pleased with how he was doing. The bullet had managed to avoid major organs, so the worst damage was the blood loss and the injury to his muscles. He needed rest and another blood transfusion, but he would be fine. "I'd like to keep an eye on you a little longer, so you're staying for another night, but if all goes well, I should be able to discharge you tomorrow."

She gave him an encouraging smile.

Alec frowned. I could tell he was about to argue, demand to be released immediately, but before I had a chance to chastise him, Tyler beat me to it.

"Wipe that look off your face." Tyler wagged a finger at Alec. "You were fucking shot. You're staying here until the medical professionals say you can leave."

"What he said." I had to add my agreement. Ethan stepped up next to Tyler and crossed his arms, adding his support firmly but silently. Josh chuckled, endlessly amused by our dynamics, as usual.

Alec may've been stubborn, but he knew when he was outnumbered. Plus, no one argued with Tyler when he put his authoritative voice on.

"Fine," Alec grumbled. "I could use another nap anyway." He ended on a yawn.

The nurse cleaned up and left the room, but the doctor paused in the doorway. "Honestly, you're lucky I'm letting you go tomorrow." She stuffed her hands in her pockets and looked at Alec reproachfully. "You had *open surgery*. If you were human, you'd be here for at least a week, and you'd be on bed rest for another month after that. We normally keep Variants in the hospital for three to four days, but since you have a Vital, your body has all the extra Light it needs to accelerate healing. So behave for another day, and thank your lucky stars you have *her*." She pointed at me, flashed him another challenging look, and left the room.

He turned back to me and didn't even hesitate. "Thank you."

I looked down and cleared my throat. "I just happen to be a Vital. Your Vital. I didn't do anything."

"Just accept the thanks, Evie." His voice held a hint of teasing, and I rolled my eyes. We really didn't have a good track record with thank yous.

Tyler interjected before I could answer with another smartass comment. "What do you mean you didn't do anything?"

He stepped over to my side of the bed and turned me by the shoulders to face him, frustration evident on his face.

"You literally saved his life. Several others. You transferred Light to every single Variant on our side, and then when we crushed those bastards in a matter of seconds, you immediately made sure the woman with the freezing ability went to Alec. You bought him valuable time. You're fucking incredible, and I'm proud to be in your Bond."

He leaned forward and kissed me, hard. Alec caressed the back of my hand with his thumb as Tyler sighed against my lips.

"All right, what the fuck happened last night?" Ethan looked between the three of us, his hands on his hips.

Josh lowered himself into Tyler's vacated chair. "Yeah, we still don't have the full story. We got a call in the middle of the night and rushed to the hospital. All Kyo told us was that there was an attack on the event? How did anyone even know about it?"

Someone knocked on the door. Dot stood just outside, Charlie behind her with his hands on her shoulders. Olivia and Henry craned their necks to see in.

"They said you were awake . . ." Dot sounded uncertain.

"I'm still getting reports from operatives in the field and the police. Let's talk about it later," Tyler answered Josh, then stepped out of my embrace.

Alec waved to Dot. "Hey, pipsqueak. What's up?"

Dot took that as an invitation and walked into the room, Charlie hot on her heels. "Don't 'pipsqueak' me. And would you all stop nearly dying and shit? You're making me age faster. I'm going to have to start getting Botox!"

"Glad you're OK, man." Charlie stuffed his hands in his pockets—it couldn't have been easy for him to be in a hospital again—but the look he gave his cousin was genuine and warm.

"Are you comfortable, sweetie?" Olivia went into mom mode, fluffing Alec's pillow and pulling the thin blanket up to cover his shoulders. Of course, that made his bare feet poke out. She huffed. "This is ridiculous! There must be more than one measly blanket in this whole hospital. I can't believe . . ." She muttered and fussed, found a spare blanket, and made sure Alec was tucked in as tight as a cinnamon roll. He grumbled and rolled his eyes, but I think he secretly liked the motherly affection.

When Henry came back, wheeling Lucian in front of him, the guys and I left the room. There just wasn't space for everyone, and I knew his work friends would want to see him.

In the hallway, I leaned my forehead on Ethan's chest. He rocked us lightly back and forth as I listened to his steady breathing, his strong heartbeat. After a few minutes, I turned and rested my cheek on him instead.

Farther down the hall, Dana was chatting with another black-clad woman and man as they waited their turn to see Alec. She glanced over, and our eyes met.

Her questioning look held a hint of concern. *Are you OK?*

I gave her a tight smile and shrugged. *Not really. Could be worse.*

She inclined her head, gesturing to Alec's room with another question in her eyes. *And him?*

This time, my smile was more genuine. I nodded and breathed a deep sigh. *He's going to pull through.*

She smiled back, then said something to her companions. As she passed us on the way to Alec's room, she squeezed my shoulder briefly but didn't say anything.

I lifted my head off Ethan's chest and blinked. Did I just have a silent conversation with *Dana*? Did she let her humanity show by giving me a gesture of comfort? This had to be some kind of dream.

Josh's amused chuckle brought me out of my stare, and I craned my neck to look at him.

"I can hardly believe it myself." He shrugged, but his grin was full of mischief.

I rolled my eyes at him as Ethan looked between us. "Can't believe what?"

My big guy hated being out of the loop, but before I could explain, we were interrupted once more.

"Excuse me." A polite accented voice drew our attention to the older Japanese man standing a respectful distance away. It was the same man I'd met the night before, the one with the shield ability who'd refused to leave my side.

I stepped out of Ethan's embrace, but he stayed close. Josh took my other hand, and Tyler boxed me in from behind. Their protective instincts were in overdrive.

"My deepest apologies for interrupting." The distinguished man bowed low. "I am happy to hear your Bondmate is well and will recover."

"Thank you." Tyler spoke for all of us, but his voice was cautious. "And thank you for your assistance last night, Mr. Takata. Has anyone from Melior Group spoken with you?"

"Oh, yes. I have given my statement to the authorities, and your people have debriefed me. I am hoping to speak with you about the . . . Light." He seemed uncertain about the last word.

"Yes?" Tyler prompted him as I frowned.

"My apologies. I am very tired, and my English suffers for it. Uh . . . *kagayaku*." He said the word in Japanese, and by some miracle, my addled brain remembered its meaning.

"Glow?" I supplied, and his face lit up.

"*Hai.*" He inclined his head. All three of my Bondmates stiffened. I didn't see anything threatening about him, and my Light-driven instincts had put him squarely on our side of the fight last night, so his intentions were pure, or at least they had been then. Still, their hesitancy put me on edge. Now that I thought about it, he had used the term *Bondmates*—not *Bonded Variants* or *Bond members* as most Variants did. Was that just a cultural thing—a quirk of translation? I'd only ever heard one other person use the term—Nina, the Lighthunter. And why did he want to speak to us about my glowing?

"I am honored to meet one such as yourself. I have known only one other with a glow such as yours, and she was extraordinary also."

He smiled as my eyes widened in shock. Did he know what it was? Why I glowed? Was I finally about to get some answers?

Within minutes, Tyler had commandeered a small meeting room at the other end of the corridor and stationed two guards in front of the closed door.

We settled around the small table. Tyler looked downright exhausted as he collapsed into a chair and leaned forward on his elbows. I took his hand and pushed a little Light to him, hoping it would be both a pleasant sensation and a boost to his ability for the conversation we were about to have.

"Thank you for understanding our need to be cautious." I smiled at the man across from me. The guys were still throwing him worried, suspicious glances. If Alec had been here, he probably wouldn't have even let this conversation happen.

I understood their suspicion, but I was more excited than anything. Trying to find any information on this had been one dead end after another.

"Of course." He nodded.

"Please tell me about . . . uh . . ." The Vital? The other glowing chick? What was the correct terminology?

He smiled and leaned forward, wrapping his hands around his plastic cup of water. "When you glowed last night, the way you drew the Light into yourself and were able to transfer it remotely not only to your Bond but to others, to me"—he pressed a hand to his chest—"I had never felt anything like it. But I saw the glow, and I couldn't quite believe what I was witnessing. You truly are extraordinary, Miss Maynard."

"Thanks," I mumbled and fiddled with the rolled-up sleeve of Tyler's shirt. Tyler threaded his fingers through mine, stilling my hand.

The man continued. "When I was a boy, I would spend summers with my grandmother. She was a Vital, and she had three Variants. She would tell me stories of the ones that glowed—their power and potential. On a few occasions, I even witnessed her skin glow as she transferred Light to one of her Bondmates. But as I grew into an adult, I relegated her stories to the stuff of myth and folktales, put the glow I'd seen down to a child's overactive imagination. The few times I raised it with my parents, they dismissed the topic. For forty years, I put it out of my mind. And then last night, I saw you, *felt* you, and it all came back to me. I knew it was real."

"Is your grandmother still alive?" I was hanging on every word, leaning forward over the table. I didn't mean for the question to sound so harsh—I was simply ravenous for more information. "I'm sorry. I don't mean to be insensitive."

He bowed his head but waved my concern away. "It is quite all right. Yes, my grandmother is still alive. She is one hundred and three years old, but she still tends an herb garden and has tea with her friends every day. Or so she tells me in her letters. She lives in the same village, high in the Hida Mountains, but I have not been to see her in many years."

"I'm sorry"—Tyler leaned forward, suddenly all business—"why are you telling us this? Excuse my bluntness, but what do you want?"

Tyler's ability would've alerted him if any of Mr. Takata's story so far had been a lie—the fact that he hadn't raised any alarms yet gave me confidence—but in most situations, Tyler had to ask questions for his ability to give him the answers. I wasn't sure how much Tyler's ability filled in before the man answered, but he kept a straight face and allowed him to speak.

"Mr. Gabriel, I understand your concern, but I am aware of your ability, and I would like to remind you of mine. I have kept my shield down, allowing you to see the truth in my words. I have no agenda other than to offer my support and my services to you." He looked directly at me. "You are proof that the stories my grandmother told are true, and if that is the case, you must be protected. I am at your service."

Again, he bowed.

A little taken aback, I leaned back in my chair, unsure how to respond. I turned to Tyler for guidance. Ethan and Josh were looking at him expectantly too. He gave us all a glance and relaxed his posture. "He's telling the truth. He has a shielding ability, perfectly capable of blocking me, but he's keeping it lowered."

I cleared my throat. "Thank you, sir, but I'm not sure that I really . . . need anything right now?" I sounded unsure and awkward, even to my own ears. I'd never had someone declare their "service" to me. Was I supposed to assign him a task?

Tyler saved me. "Do you know any others who glow, like Evelyn and your grandmother?"

"No. I'm sorry."

"Does your grandmother?"

"I don't know. It's possible."

"Our top priority is to keep Evelyn safe. I'm sure, considering your line of work, you appreciate how valuable information can be in a situation such as this." They shared a look of mutual understanding. "If you'd like to help, then help us learn more about what this is. Could you speak with your grandmother?"

"Of course. It may take some time. There aren't phones in her village, let alone Internet. I will have to travel there and then back down the mountain before I can get in contact, but I will leave at once."

Apparently he wasn't one to waste time, and neither was Ty. They both rose from their seats. I scrambled to follow suit, as did Ethan and Josh.

"I'll organize a secure line and wait to hear from you," Tyler said.

"Perfect."

Tyler and Mr. Takata bowed to each other. Mr. Takata repeated the gesture with Josh and Ethan, then turned to me.

He took a card out of his pocket and held it out with both hands. "Evelyn, this is my private, secure line. I am always reachable on this number. Please don't hesitate to use it."

"Thank you." I took the card with both my hands, as I'd learned to do when I was a child in Japan, and bowed.

He left and closed the door behind him.

"Got any more cult followers waiting to declare their undying devotion, or can we get the fuck out of here?"

Tyler wrapped an arm around my shoulders, his tone teasing but tired. "I need sleep."

"Let's get you home." I hugged him around the middle as Josh opened the door for us.

We checked in on Alec, but he was asleep again. Lucian had been ordered home by Olivia, and the only reason I felt comfortable with all of us leaving was because she and Dot promised to stay until we came back. That and the Melior Group guards crawling all over the building.

We left the same way we arrived—inconspicuously and heavily guarded—and headed back to the apartment.

Tyler fell asleep in the car, then again in the elevator, leaning his head back against the mirror. Once we made it inside, he shuffled to the first bedroom, flopped face-first into the bed, and immediately started snoring.

I felt so bad for him. He hadn't slept in over thirty-six hours. He was always cleaning up the messes, taking care of us.

Well, now he had *me* to take care of *him*.

I pulled his shoes off and unbuckled his holster, then managed to roll him over to remove his pants. I grabbed an extra blanket from the next room to cover him and drew the curtains. Lying down beside him, I ran my hand through his messy brown hair.

I was itching to call Mr. Takata on the number he gave me. In the short time since he'd left, my mind had made a shopping list of questions. But I knew it was better to let him go to his grandmother and get more information first. I so badly wanted to go there myself—meet someone else like me.

But for right now, I was exactly where I needed to be.

FIFTEEN

We spent another night at the Manhattan apartment, then most of the next day at the hospital with Alec. He slept through most of it. The doctors assured us he was in the clear, but I just wanted to be close to him, hold his hand, even lie down in the bed next to him. I wanted to be there for him just as he'd been there for me when my mother died and I thought I was alone in the world. How wrong I'd been.

Much to Alec's ire, the doctor decided to keep him for an extra night. The next morning Tyler headed into work, and Ethan, Josh, and I drove home to Bradford Hills with an entourage of armored vehicles. Alec would be released that afternoon, and we wanted to get home ahead of him to make sure we had everything set up for his recovery.

But we were so spent we ended up piled on the couch, curtains drawn, and spent the morning watching movies and eating takeout.

Around lunchtime, Josh started flicking through live TV channels to see what was on. I was trying to decide if I needed to pee badly enough to move—I was ridiculously comfortable.

Ethan was reclined in the corner of the big, soft couch, his body slightly turned inward, a cushion half over his lap. Josh had his head on the cushion, the rest of his body spread out. I was squished between my blond bombshell boyfriend and the back of the couch. My head rested in the crook of Josh's shoulder, and one of my legs was hitched over his hips.

Ethan was running his hand through my hair absentmindedly. I was so relaxed I couldn't even be bothered to cover my mouth as I yawned. It was a big one, stretching my jaw wide.

Ethan's hand in my hair stopped. As my yawn ended, I unexpectedly closed my teeth and lips around his finger.

My hand flew to his as the two of them cracked up laughing, making me laugh around Ethan's digit too. But I couldn't let him off that easy. Still struggling to contain my giggles, I tightened my grip on his hand and held his finger hostage with my teeth.

I wrapped my lips around Ethan's finger and sucked.

Both their laughter died in their throats, and I felt their full attention on me, on my mouth.

Excruciatingly slowly, I dragged Ethan's finger out, lightly scraping it with my teeth, then swirling my tongue around the tip. He groaned and Josh gripped my thigh, pulling my leg higher over his growing erection.

I sucked Ethan's finger back into my mouth while rolling my hips against Josh.

I had no idea how the energy between us changed so fast, but I was drunk on it. I loved hearing Ethan groan when I was barely touching him. I loved feeling Josh's arousal pressing into my thigh. Witnessing the effect I had on them made me feel powerful. Loved, safe, and powerful.

I drew Ethan's finger all the way out of my mouth and, with Josh's help, drew myself up, straddling him.

That heavy, needy feeling was building deep inside me, and I rubbed myself up against Josh, seeking the friction that would both ease and intensify it. With Josh's hands on my waist, I leaned up. Ethan met me halfway and kissed me passionately, his tongue invading my mouth.

Josh trailed his hands up my sides, pushing my sweater up, and Ethan broke our kiss to yank it completely off and throw it to the ground. He leaned back in and started kissing and sucking on my neck. I moaned and turned my head to the side, giving him more access as Josh grabbed my ass, his hips rolling under me to meet my movements.

But with my head turned, I caught a glimpse of the TV and froze.

It was turned down, but the rolling script at the bottom said "Live," and Davis Damari's ugly face filled the screen as he walked up to a podium overflowing with microphones. There were those eyes, the same shape as mine; my full lips; a more masculine version of my nose.

"Stop," I murmured, a cold chill dousing my desire. But they were caught up in the moment. Josh's hips were still pitching under me, Ethan's mouth still nibbling on my neck.

"Stop." I put more force behind the word that time, pushing on both their chests.

That time they heard me.

"What's wrong?" Josh sat up.

Ethan spoke at the same time. "You OK?"

I kept my eyes on the TV as their hands and eyes searched my body for injuries, but they caught on pretty quickly. Ethan grabbed the remote and turned the volume up.

". . . mixed news for you all today." Davis flashed his perfect teeth at the cameras, displaying that charismatic smile that made me want to vomit. "Our team of scientists and engineers have been working tirelessly to bring you our latest technology, which I announced recently. As you all know, this will allow us to transfer an ability from a Variant and give it to any person with Variant DNA who happens to not have manifested one naturally. We have worked out the legal and financial side of the process, ensuring that the donating Variant is compensated adequately for their generous decision to part with their Light-given ability. All that's left now is to make sure our technology, our machines, are perfectly optimized and safe for all parties involved. Safety is our number one priority."

Ethan scoffed. "Please. Safety, my ass."

Josh shushed him and turned the volume up even more. Davis launched into all the wonderful things his company was doing to ensure the safety of its customers—all the amazing things this would do for Variants around the world. The spiel was delivered with ease and practice, the touch of a marketing professional clear in the phrasing. He discussed how Variants who disliked their abilities would be able to rid themselves of an unwanted burden. How Variants with common abilities but no clear use for them would be able to make a substantial amount of money by giving them up.

As if his proposed system wasn't rife with opportunities for exploitation. As if it wouldn't turn into another way for the rich to get what they wanted at the expense of the poor and desperate. As if it wouldn't encourage Variant trafficking.

The reporters were eating his words up, asking enthusiastic questions and flashing their cameras. How did they not see that this could turn nasty overnight? That it was just like what the Lightwhores did—Vitals selling off their precious and sacred Light for a couple bucks? Except this was *permanent*.

His blatant lies made me feel sick. I wrapped my arms around myself, and Ethan handed me my sweater. As Davis kept twisting everything with his clever, poisonous words, I pulled the sweater over my head, and Josh held me close to his chest.

"Unfortunately we've had to push back our timeline." The look of disappointment on Davis's face was so exaggerated I almost laughed. "We were hoping to make the procedure available to the public next month; however, we've hit . . . a snag." He sighed. A flurry of questions flew at him from the reporters, who all spoke over one another. He gestured for them to calm down. "I can't go into too many details regarding the process—there is the matter of intellectual property to consider." He flashed that greasy grin. "But the technology is developed from studying Vitals and the process of transferring Light. There is one particular individual who is very unique in this aspect, and her Light is what allowed us to get this far with these incredible advancements."

I leaned toward the TV even as I gritted my teeth and gripped Josh's T-shirt, my knuckles turning white.

A reporter cut in. "Are you referring to the girl who glows?"

Davis sighed, another exaggerated, fake look of regret crossing his face. "I'm sure most people have seen the footage of the young lady who glowed as she transferred Light. Yes, her talents are more than just a visually impressive display. Yes, she was instrumental in assisting us with developing the technology. And yes, we still need her assistance."

"He makes it sound like you were working together," Josh ground out, "not like he fucking kidnapped you and nearly killed us all."

My fists, still wrapped around the poor fabric of his T-shirt, started to shake in anger.

Davis just kept spewing his lies. "I'm very saddened to say she is no longer working with us, especially considering . . . but I won't go into sharing private family matters at this time."

But by saying that, that's *exactly* what he'd done. My mouth dropped open. What the fuck was he up to?

Intrigued murmurs rose from the reporters, but they settled down quickly, eager to hear more from Davis.

"It's all about to become public knowledge now, so I won't deny that the Vital in question is my daughter. The only thing I'll add is that my deepest wish is to see her again. Despite the delays with our project, regardless of the wider implications, I only wish to speak with her again." At this, he turned and stared straight into the camera. "Evelyn, you've left me no choice but to implore you, to plead with you in such a public way—please, darling. Come home so we can make up for all those years apart. So we can get back to our important work and change people's lives. So we can make sure you're safe *together*." I wanted to throw something at the TV, at his ugly face. It felt as if he were staring right at me, the fake sincerity infecting the crowd, reporters, and viewers like a disease.

"Is she dangerous?" Someone shouted.

Davis shook his head immediately, but I caught a glimpse of a satisfied smile. He'd been hoping someone would ask this, maybe even planted someone in the crowd. "My daughter would never knowingly harm anyone." He pressed a hand to his chest, his eyes imploring, then paused, sighed, and leveled everyone with a serious look. "Her Light is incredible, and the glowing is merely a visual representation of how formidably powerful she is. It is this particular brand of Vital Light that allowed us to figure out how to draw the ability from a Variant. But the process can be . . . deadly."

The reporters erupted in a hectic hubbub of questions, shouting and elbowing one another to coax more information from Davis. But he just waved them off and turned away, wiping a fake tear from the corner of his eye.

That son of a *bitch*!

"Fuck!" Ethan and Josh cursed at the same time.

This was bad—really bad.

Josh handed me off to Ethan, stood up, and reached for his phone. Ethan's big arms boxed me in as my heart slowly plummeted, hammering in fear all the way down.

The world's journalists had already figured out my identity. My photo and real name appeared on the screen now that the press conference had ended and Davis had walked out.

"Did he see it?" Josh barked down the phone. He paced as he talked. "The press conference. You didn't see it? . . . Good. Make sure he doesn't turn the TV on in his room . . . I know . . . Fucking bribe the nurse to knock him out if you have to . . . I know . . . I *know* . . . Yes. OK, thanks, Kyo."

He was making sure Alec didn't fly into a rage and rip his stitches open. Because that's exactly what he'd do if he saw this shit—tear the hospital down to get to me. Josh hung up, and his phone immediately started ringing again.

"Hey." He rubbed his forehead as he paced. "Yep . . . She's safe. In Ethan's lap as we speak . . . No way in hell. We're never leaving this fucking house again . . . Good. Agreed . . . I know, Gabe . . . I will . . . OK, bye."

As Josh hung up, Lucian wheeled himself into the room. He flicked on the kitchen light. With the heavy curtains drawn, we'd been sitting in the dark, the glow of the TV the only illumination.

Lucian came to a stop next to the couch. "You saw it?"

"Every damn word," Ethan growled, his grip on me tightening. Josh lowered himself onto the coffee table, his expression grim. "How did we not know about this?"

"We were told he was calling a press conference," Lucian said, "but that was only an hour ago. No one, not even the reporters, were given any inside info. We had no way of knowing he would—"

"Paint a target on my back?" I stared at the corner of the coffee table, next to Josh's knee.

Lucian sighed, but none of them contradicted me.

That's exactly what he'd done. He'd named me, outed me, and twisted it to make it sound as if I were the bad guy—the petulant teenager preventing scientific advancements with petty temper tantrums. Meanwhile, he'd all but announced I could kill people with a simple touch and left it to people's imaginations to fill in the horrific details.

Now every person with Variant DNA who'd failed to manifest an ability would see me as the bitch standing in their way. The one person stopping them from getting what they'd wanted their whole lives. The selfish asshole preventing a scientific advancement that would benefit the entire Variant community.

Every human would fear me too. His description of what I could do with the Light was accurate, but the language he'd used made me sound downright dangerous. To the humans, I was now another threat in a world where they already felt scared for their lives, scared for their children's future, scared for their very right to freedom.

I could see it from both sides. Could already see the kinds of things Variant Valor and the Human Empowerment Network would say about this, about *me*. Hell, I could probably write their propaganda for them.

Whatever way you looked at it, I was a fucking monster.

SIXTEEN

The doorbell rang as I was coming down the stairs. Alec stepped out of Tyler's study to answer it, favoring his right side. Whoever was at the door made his shoulders stiffen, his hand tighten around the doorknob.

He really should've been in bed, not rushing to answer doors. He'd only just been discharged from the hospital a few days ago. I hastened to his side, my heart beating a little faster with unease.

Logically, I knew the guards at the gate wouldn't let anyone who was unknown or uninvited step foot on the property. But every time I walked outside, part of me still half expected cameras and microphones shoved in my face, just as they had been the day after Davis made his passive-aggressive announcement. We'd been on our way to class when reporters had swarmed our vehicle, shouting questions and flashing cameras. Our security detail beat them back before they could get very close, but it was still confrontational.

So were the stares I was getting from students and even a few staff. I did my best to grit my teeth and avoided speaking to anyone for fear I'd tell them exactly what I thought of my so-called father.

Thankfully, that had been my last day of classes before summer. I had a few assignments to finish and one lab exam, and then I'd get a short break before summer classes started. I could stay home and ignore the chaos until it hopefully went away. It was wishful thinking, but it was better than the encroaching panic that gripped my chest whenever I thought about the alternative—that this would probably get worse before it got better.

It didn't help knowing he was still out there—that he could make another grab for me or continue to twist things to the press, and there was nothing we could do about it.

After Davis's press conference, a stealth team had been sent to apprehend him in the dead of night. They'd had eyes on him since his speech, he was in a new location, they had the numbers. But once again, the attempt was unsuccessful; by the time they arrived, the new hideout was abandoned. Tyler said it was almost as if they knew we were coming. He shared a worried look with Alec while Lucian hung his head in his hands, grumbling unintelligible things for a long time.

Feeling confident about anything was hard when the smartest, most competent, most dangerous men I knew were sharing looks tinged with fear. Every passing vehicle, every unfamiliar face, every ring of the doorbell made me cringe.

When I made it to the door, I heaved a sigh of relief.

". . . not even here to see you, Alec." Dana stood on the ornate doormat with her arms crossed, glaring at Alec and looking as hot as she always did. "Although I'm mildly pleased you didn't, you know, die and shit."

"Then why are you here?" Alec's low voice grated, a hint of annoyance coming though, just as Dana's eyes met mine.

I smiled at her as Alec took my hand. "Hey."

She smiled back but answered Alec instead of me. "I'm here to see Eve, actually."

"What? Why?" His hand tightened around mine. Having his ex show up at his front door and demand to see his Vital must've been awkward, but in his usual manner, he was handling it like crap.

"Alec." I tugged on his hand and shot him a reproachful look. "You're being rude."

"Yeah, *Alec*." Dana smirked at him as I ushered her in. "Eve and I are, like, totally BFFs now. She's my bae!" She slung an arm over my shoulders and delivered her speech in an exaggerated SoCal accent.

Alec stood in front of us, frowning.

I couldn't help the laughter that bubbled up, and my shoulders started to shake with my efforts to keep it contained.

Dana let out one long guffaw and dropped her arm. If someone had told me on the night of the gala that Dana and I would be laughing *together* at Alec's expense, I would've suggested they get their head checked, but here we were . . .

When Dana spoke again, her tone was more serious. "I'd prefer to have this conversation in private."

"No," Alec answered without hesitation.

Ethan chose that moment to come bounding out of the kitchen wearing nothing but shorts, his impressive muscles glistening with sweat. He'd clearly just come up from the gym. He faltered as he registered the scene, the easy smile falling from his face. His bulk and height made him look even more awkward as he ran a hand through his sweaty hair, then turned on his heel and went back the way he'd come without a word.

I stifled another laugh. "It's OK, Alec. I'll be fine."

"If you're talking about me, I get to listen," he said, his petulant side coming out. He crossed his arms, then winced and immediately dropped them.

"Why are you even out of bed?" I asked reproachfully, but he ignored me.

"Not everything is about you, oh mighty Master of Pain." Dana's voice practically dripped sarcasm.

"What's it about then?"

"Alec. Go." Dana and I spoke at the same time, in the same exasperated tone.

Alec's eyes widened as he looked between us. Finally, with a groan, he dragged his hands over his buzzed hair and down his face, then rushed out of the room as fast as his injuries would allow, muttering, "This is too fucking weird."

"Lie down on the couch, please!" I yelled after him as he disappeared in the direction of the living room. "Before you tear your stitches!"

I bugged my eyes out at Dana and shook my head.

She chuckled. "This one time we were on a mission in Morocco, and he got typhoid. We were just on recon, but instead of taking two fucking days to rest, he kept pushing it and ended up being evacuated and hospitalized for a *week*."

I groaned but laughed darkly as I led Dana toward the formal sitting room. None of that surprised me whatsoever.

"Your problem now," Dana finished as we sat down on the plush velvet couch under the window.

"Yeah . . ." I trailed off, not really sure how to address that. Even though Dana and I were now on good terms, it was still a bit odd to be sitting next to a woman—a very sexy, beautiful woman—who'd had sex with my Variant.

I cleared my throat. "Can I get you anything? Tea? Coffee? We have this ridiculous state-of-the-art espresso machine I've recently learned how to use."

"No thanks. I don't have a ton of time, so I'll get to the point."

"Oh, OK." I angled my body slightly to face her.

She leaned forward, propping her arms on her knees and taking a deep breath. "I'm here to speak to you about going to see Zara."

She looked at me, her expression wary but determined.

My eyes widened even as my brow furrowed. I leaned back against the plush pillows, at a loss for words. "What?"

"There are only two people employed by Melior Group with an ability like mine—blocking other abilities. Zara's held in a cell that blocks Light and scrambles the use of abilities, but any time she's taken out, one of the two of us has to do it. She's too unpredictable, has very little control of her ability. She's dangerous."

"I know she's dangerous," I growled. She'd handed me over to a man who would have happily seen me die to achieve his goals; her actions resulted in countless deaths and put all my Bonded Variants in danger.

"I'm just trying to explain," Dana rushed out, keeping her voice calm. "I spend a lot of time with her, see her almost daily. And every damn day, she asks about you, *begs* to see you, Eve. She pleads with me to get you to come. You have clearance now, so you can just walk in any time you want."

"Why would I?" I couldn't believe she was asking me to do this. My heart pounded in my head; my fists clenched. "Why the fuck would I give that traitorous bitch another second of my time, another scrap of my energy?"

"I get it." Dana held her hands out in front of her. "Trust me, I understand. Which is why I'm not trying to talk you into it. I'm just passing on information."

"I don't care!" My voice got high. "I don't want to hear it."

"Eve, I'm sorry. I really didn't come here to upset you. I just feel like you deserve to know. You of all people deserve to have all the information in this situation."

She kept looking at me with that calm expression, those expertly made-up, understanding eyes. Stupid, beautiful bitch was being all kinds of patient and mature, which was more than I could say for myself.

If I was being completely honest, I'd avoided thinking about Zara—about how she'd betrayed me, about the cold look in her eye as she'd slammed that van door. It was no wonder having it brought up made me explode; it was the only time I ever expressed anything about it.

Sitting on that plush couch with Dana, the mild spring breeze that came through the window tickling the back of my neck, I realized I hadn't processed the situation with Zara. At all. I'd shoved it into a black metal box and slammed the lid shut with a clang.

I stared at the emerald velvet cushion between us, running my hands over the soft fabric and taking a few breaths.

Finally, I lifted my gaze to meet hers. "What does she want, Dana? I can't handle any more of her manipulation. I seriously don't think I can take another . . ." I trailed off, not entirely sure what I was getting at. Another betrayal? Another drama? Another bombshell I didn't see coming?

Dana wrapped her hand around mine. Her fingers were warm and strong, but she didn't linger. She just gave me a squeeze and released my hand. "I get it. That's why I'm not here to plead her case. I'm not trying to get you to forgive her or whatever. I'm just keeping you informed. What you choose to do with the information is completely your call."

Dana was going out of her way to not keep anything from me. She had no obligation to tell me anything, no stake in my happiness, but there she was, doing the right thing and giving me the truth. It couldn't have been easy to raise such a difficult topic with her ex's Vital and girlfriend. She was beautiful *and* gutsy.

I nodded, and she continued.

"She just keeps asking about you. How you are, what you're doing, how you're coping. I never give her any info—it's against policy to give detainees information about the outside world, and I would never share anything without your consent anyway. Still, she never stops trying. More than anything though, she keeps begging me to bring you to see her. She keeps saying she needs to see you. Not wants—*needs*. She's a little manic about it. I mean, she wasn't exactly mentally stable to begin with, but I think the isolation and the removal of autonomy is only pushing her further into madness."

"Am I supposed to feel sorry for her?" I remained calm, but I was defensive too.

"You're not supposed to feel anything. Just sharing the facts," Dana reminded me yet again.

"I know. I'm sorry." I sighed. "This is just really hard for me. What do you think this is? Is she giving you guys intel? Or is she being difficult until she gets her way?"

"Nothing like that. In fact, she's cooperating fully. She's answered all our questions, even giving us extra information without us having to ask. She genuinely seems to hate Davis and even her own mother, although I don't think there was ever any love lost there. As to what I think this is about—honestly, I have no idea. All I know is that she's desperate to see you." Dana shrugged.

"OK. Thank you for coming here to tell me."

"It's all good. Call me if you have any questions. Gabe has my number, even if Alec has deleted it. I have to get going or I'll be late for work." She got to her feet.

"I will. Thanks, Dana." We shared a genuinely friendly smile.

After seeing her off at the front door, I wandered back into the sitting room and flopped onto the couch with a huff. I didn't appreciate being forced to deal with my feelings around the Zara situation, but it was probably best I did anyway. It was on me that I hadn't talked to anyone about it yet—let alone a mental health professional.

My mind rifled through the implications and possibilities. A big part of me wanted to go see her just to satisfy my curiosity; I never could resist a puzzle. But maybe that was her plan all along—to get me curious and manipulate me into seeing her. Then again, what if I was just being paranoid? Still, Zara had more than proven she could be devious.

As my mind raced, so did my heart—sadness, anger, and frustration all vying for first place.

With a groan, I sat up straight. For the next half hour I tried to meditate—on the couch, the wingback chair, the floor—but my thoughts constantly wandered. I managed to slow my breathing and heart rate somewhat, but after a while, I gave up.

I needed advice—someone to talk it over with. I could've gone to Dot, Charlie, any of my guys. Even Uncle Luce would have been more than happy to give me his sympathetic ear.

But I needed to feel in control of how much I discussed this, how much time and energy I chose to give it. All of them would push me to talk more, would bring it up the next day, would look at me with cautious worry in their eyes.

So I called Harvey.

At the second ring, I realized it was around four in the morning in Australia, but just as I was about to hang up, he answered.

"Hey, Eve." He didn't sound tired or groggy at all.

"Oh, hey, Harvey. I didn't wake you? Sorry."

He chuckled. "No. I couldn't sleep. Been up drawing for a few hours now. What's up? How are you?"

He sounded relaxed, and I could hear music playing softly in the background. I could picture him sitting at his desk with the drawing pad, a lamp illuminating his work while the rest of the room was cast in darkness.

"What're you drawing? Is it for your course? How's that going?"

He told me about his studies and the friends he'd made but didn't tell me what he was working on. He'd always been very secretive about unfinished projects. We talked about my science subjects too, about our families and the crazy stuff happening all over the world. He indulged me for a while, then pushed. "What's going on, Eve?"

"Maybe I just really wanted to catch up. We did promise to stay in touch."

"Eve. What's going on?" His voice was still warm, but it held a hint of firmness this time.

I sighed. I did call him to ask for help with the Zara situation, so why was I avoiding it? "Fine. I need your advice."

"About?"

"Zara."

"What happened?"

"Nothing? I don't know. She's been locked in a cell since they dragged her back here. It's just . . ."

"Dude! Spit it out."

I rolled my eyes—at myself. Why was this so hard? "She reached out to me, kind of. Through Alec's ex Dana."

"Alec . . . he's the tall, scary one? With the pain thing?"

"Yeah, that asshole."

"He has an ex? Like, some chick was ballsy enough to touch him long enough to sleep with him?"

"Harvey! I don't need reminders of that, thanks!"

"Hey, you're the one who brought it up. Clearly as a distraction tactic from talking about what you actually want to talk about. What did Zara want?"

"Why do you have to be right about everything?"

"It's what I do—I draw and I speak the truth. Zara?"

"She wants to see me. Dana has a blocking ability, and because Zara's electric ability is so unstable, Dana is on guard duty with her a lot. She just came over to tell me that Zara won't shut up about me and keeps begging to see me. I don't know what to do."

"Do you want to see her?"

"No. I hate her." I paused, a little taken aback by how intense those words sounded coming out of my mouth. I'd never said I hated Zara, but maybe that was the feeling I'd been stuffing down. Or maybe suppressing all my thoughts and feelings about this had made them fester and turn into hate. Did I really want to be capable of hating another person? Harvey just sat silently on the line, waiting patiently for me to continue.

"I . . . I don't know, Harvey. I don't want anything to do with her, but it all feels so unresolved."

"You say you don't want to see her, but you're calling me for advice on what to do. Dig deeper, Eve. Use that logical mind of yours. Give me the reasons *not* to go and then the reasons why you *should*."

"I don't want to see her. The thought of speaking to her makes my stomach turn. She betrayed me. She keeps asking for me, and I don't want to give her the satisfaction of getting what she wants."

"And the other side?"

"I need to know *why*." I sighed. That was what it came down to—I wanted to understand why she betrayed me. To an extent, I could guess at some of the reasons, like her zealot parents, her need to belong, her desperation to stop feeling like a failure for not having an ability. But I still couldn't understand why she'd done that to me. It felt so personal. "I want to look her in the eye and ask if our friendship ever meant anything to her."

"OK, here's my advice. Forget about this 'giving her what she wants' bullshit. It's petty reasoning, and you're better than that. Think about what *you* want and need. Really think about it, Eve. If you need to protect yourself emotionally from dealing with her again, then don't go. If you think you'll learn something or get some kind of closure from seeing her, then go. Just do what's right for you."

"Yes, but what is right for me? Tell me what to do, Harveyyy." I dragged his name out on a whine. His advice was solid, but I still kind of wanted someone to tell me what to do. Or did I? I knew that if I went to Alec, he'd tell me to stay the fuck away from her, and I really didn't like being ordered around.

"OK. Go talk to your four boyfriends about this. I'm happy to give you some advice, but this is big, and they need to know. Also, I still can't believe you have four fucking boyfriends!"

I laughed. "You get used to it."

"I bet. I could get used to it in a heartbeat."

"Having four boyfriends?"

"What?! No! Clearly I meant girlfriends."

"I don't know if you could handle four women, Harvey."

"You mean they couldn't handle me."

We both laughed.

When I hung up, I felt lighter. Zara had been a strong presence in my life, one of the only friends I'd ever made. She meant a lot to me, but she wasn't my only friend. I had other people I could rely on—other people who had my back and wanted me in their lives. I had their support through this.

I dragged myself off the couch and went in search of my four boyfriends to tell them what was going on in my life. Look at that—I was learning not to keep secrets from my loved ones. All kinds of personal growth was happening today.

SEVENTEEN

My gin and tonic was nearly empty, but I waited for Tyler to take his turn before deciding whether to finish the last of it.

"Come on, man! Say your thing!" Kyo chuckled, taking a swig of his beer. His other hand gently caressed Dot's ankle. She was in Marcus's lap on the couch, and Kyo was sitting on the ground next to them.

We were all in Josh's room—me, my Bond, Alec's team, Dot, and Charlie—keeping Alec company as he recovered. He kept saying he'd be more than happy to just shut himself in his room and . . . scowl at his wound until it went away or something, but I think he secretly liked us all taking care of him.

It had been only a week since his release from the hospital, but he was healing fast. He'd be going back to work the next day—office work only for a while, much to his ire. He was still on pain medication and not allowed to drink, but the rest of us were celebrating for him.

We were also secretly distracting Charlie from the fact that Ed's visit had ended. He'd been moping around for the last two weeks, ever since his boyfriend had gone home.

Josh had put on some music, and "Want You Bad" by The Offspring was playing. He mouthed the words, his back to the bookshelves. Barefoot, in sweats and a Blondie T-shirt, he looked the epitome of relaxed.

"OK, got one." Tyler leaned forward, casting his eyes over the group. Dot and Marcus were on his right, Alec on his left. One of Alec's arms rested on the couch; the other held a soda casually between his knees.

"Never have I ever . . ." Tyler started, then paused until he had everyone's full attention. Ethan shifted at my back, breaking off his conversation with Jamie about football or something. I don't know—I tuned out any time sports came up. We were both sitting next to the fireplace, me between his legs.

The fire crackled, making the room slightly too hot, despite the cool early summer breeze coming through the open French doors.

Once everyone was paying attention, Tyler finished: " . . . had sex with a man." He leaned back on the couch, his knowing eyes watching us all carefully.

I downed the rest of the gin and tonic. I'd slept with several men, four of them in this very room. That thought made me giggle. Or maybe it was the four gin and tonics in my system making me giggle. I really wasn't much of a giggler. *Giggler*—was that a word?

Ethan gripped my hip, holding me still against him, but his beer remained untouched by his side.

Dot, Charlie, Josh, Kyo, and Marcus each took a healthy swig of their drink, and then we all gave our full attention to Tyler. Playing "Never Have I Ever" with a truth-telling Variant in the room was way more fun than the regular version.

Tyler's eyes scanned the group, dramatically taking his time even though his ability would've pinpointed the lies immediately.

"Jamie." He barely held back his laughter, his eyes dancing as they zeroed in on the tall redheaded man on my left. "Something you want to share with the group?"

Jamie's head snapped up, his eyes wide in what looked like genuine surprise. "Me?" His pale cheeks started to turn the same color as his hair.

Laughter bubbled up in my chest, and my cheeks ached from the strain of keeping the smile off my face. Dot had given up and was covering her mouth with one hand, her shoulders shaking uncontrollably.

Jamie's brow furrowed. Then, as he looked out into the middle distance, a look of recognition came over his face. "Oh . . . yeah, I guess that counts." He shrugged and took a long drink of his beer.

"You had a penis inside you! It doesn't matter if there was a woman in the bed. I'd say that fucking counts, bro!" Tyler managed to shout before completely doubling over in laughter. Everyone else let loose too, and the room filled with deafening sounds of mirth.

As the noise started to recede, Jamie managed to shout over everyone, "Gabe, you can see that much detail?" He looked a little horrified.

Tyler chuckled. "Not exactly. It's not like there's a porno playing out in my head or anything. I just kind of . . . know the information." He shrugged.

"For a second there"—Josh held his middle, gasping and letting the odd laugh out between words—"I thought he was looking at you, Kid. I thought you were holding out on us." He descended into laughter again. I was right there with him, throwing my head back and letting Ethan steady me.

Ethan lifted me so I was sitting on his lap instead of between his legs. "I've never left a woman unsatisfied." His deep voice rumbled through me, making me shiver. "So you can suck on my big hairy balls."

I had no idea how his answer related to the suggestion he'd slept with a man, and neither did anyone else, because we all erupted into another laughing fit.

When I managed to calm down enough to breathe, I wiped the tears from the corners of my eyes. "To be fair, his balls are pretty fucking big."

Tyler choked on his bourbon and coke, spraying the coffee table with it.

I managed to keep my laughter in check long enough to point at Ethan. "And you be careful what you wish for"—my pointing finger traveled to Josh—"because he just might."

Tyler made the mistake of trying to take another sip just then, because he choked on that one too. Next to him, Alec leaned his head on the back of the couch and ran his hand down his face in exasperation, but when it came away, I saw the amused smirk pulling at his lips.

"Fresh drinks before the next round!" Dot announced, getting up.

"I'll help." Charlie shuffled forward too. "Everyone having the same again?"

"No!" Josh sat bolt upright, halting them and everyone else's conversation. "Sit down. I got this."

He crawled past the coffee table and over to me, his vibrant green eyes intent on mine.

"Uh, Josh," Alec teased, "the door is in the opposite direction."

Josh just flipped him off and leaned into me, kneeling over Ethan's outstretched legs. His perfect, full lips connected with mine, and I caught on to what he was doing. I kissed him back, caressing his tongue with mine in slow, luxurious movements as I gave the Light free rein to flow into him. A groan reverberated through my chest, but it wasn't me—it was Ethan. His hands gripped my hips as I felt him grow hard under me. Josh had more than enough Light to lift an entire liquor store, but he kept kissing me, pressing against me as Ethan reclined further.

We were nearly horizontal when Kyo's voice finally broke the spell. "Unless you want this to turn into a gang bang, you may want to cut that shit out." He chuckled, but there was no denying the hint of lust in his voice.

Josh finally pulled away, flashing me a brilliant smile and a wink. Then he moved back to his spot against the bookshelf, adjusted the bulge in his pants, and closed his eyes. A look of pure concentration fell over his beautiful face.

Not even a minute later, the door to his bedroom opened, and a cooler full of drinks floated into the room. He deposited it near the door, and several beers and other mixed drinks flew straight into the hands of almost everyone seated around the little coffee table. We all clapped, genuinely impressed.

Josh bowed, grinning from ear to ear, his eyes a little glassy. Then he changed the music—"Bring Me the Horizon" came blasting out of the speakers.

"My turn!" I yelled, sitting up straighter on top of Ethan. His hands on my hips tightened, using me to hide his still prominent erection.

"Never have I ever had group sex!" I blurted the statement without letting myself think about it too much. The alcohol had made me brave, and I was deeply curious what my guys' answers would be.

Poor Tyler nearly choked on yet another sip of his drink, but this time, he managed to cough it back between laughs.

Before anyone could answer, Dot held her hands out. "Hold up! I need clarification. What are we classifying as 'group sex'? Like, anything more than just two people doing it?"

Charlie groaned, clearly uncomfortable hearing his sister talk about sex. "Gross."

I laughed at the disgusted look on his face.

"Threesomes?" Marcus pulled her back against his chest. "Three is technically a group."

"No." Tyler laid down the rules. "A threesome is a threesome. Group sex is four or more people."

He gave a definitive nod, and no one argued. After a beat, we all started looking around to see who would drink. My gin and tonic stayed firmly by my side. Charlie's drink remained untouched, as did Ethan's and Alec's.

Dot, Kyo, Marcus, and Jamie all drank while sharing knowing glances—it didn't take a genius to figure out they'd all had sex at the same time.

I wasn't sure if I was more surprised by Ethan's or Tyler's response. Ethan leaned forward and whispered against my neck, "I'm a one-woman kind of man, and you're all the woman I need."

I melted at his words, but my eyes flew to Tyler. He necked his beer, finishing the bottle in one go. When he was done, he took a deep breath, dropped the bottle down on the table, and grinned wide. That, coupled with his answer to the previous question, had me wondering just how many women he'd slept with. With his ability and his skilled hands, how many women had he given the greatest pleasure they'd ever known? How many bitches did I need to be jealous of? Was Stacey from admissions one of them? Is that why she was skirting the line of propriety every time they were in the same room?

Suddenly I regretted asking that question. I didn't want to think about their whorish pasts. Chatter and joking filled the air around us again, and I dipped my head and took a long sip of my drink, letting the cold, tart liquid cool my racing heart.

Once again, Ethan's hot mouth brushed against my neck, and he placed a soft kiss just below my ear. "You're all the woman *he* needs too, baby."

I chewed my bottom lip, surprised Ethan had picked up on my insecurities. My big guy wasn't always the best with subtlety—usually it was Josh who watched me like a hawk and figured out what I was thinking.

I glanced in Josh's direction and was rewarded with the kind, knowing look I'd expected, laced with more than a little heat. I couldn't make myself look at Tyler, so my eyes naturally moved to my honey-voiced stranger next.

He was slumped in the corner of the couch, his knees wide, his head resting against the back. He looked down his nose at me, wearing that little smirk I both loved and hated—the one that made things tingle low in my belly, sometimes from frustrated anger and sometimes from pure, scorching lust. He was looking at me as if I were the only person in the room.

Slowly, he lifted his hand from the arm of the couch and crooked his finger, beckoning me over. I bristled at being summoned like that even as my body began to respond. Ethan released his hold, pushed me up, even nudged me in Alec's direction. After a few wobbly steps, I stood in front of him.

He wrapped his strong hands around my waist and pulled me between his legs. I had an urge to lift one knee, then the other, and straddle him, but before I could, he lifted me up, wincing slightly at the pain from his wound, and deposited me in Tyler's lap.

Tyler circled his arms around me, drew me into his chest, and with a gentle hand at my cheek, made me look into his serious gray eyes. "Do I need to kick everyone out of this room so I can show you how much I want you and no one else?" he murmured against my lips.

What was I thinking? This was my Bonded Variant. I was his Vital! Nothing could ever compete with that; nothing could break that connection. Alec and I had tried to resist it. It was impossible.

My paranoid insecurity melted away, and I shook my head. "No, let's keep playing."

I smiled and he nodded, his ability confirming the truth of my feelings. He placed a searing kiss on my lips but didn't open his mouth to me when I darted my tongue out. It left me wanting as he raised his voice and asked whose turn it was.

As the night progressed and the game continued, most of us got more and more drunk. At one point, Dot and Charlie ganged up on me, apparently determined to see me get wasted, as they fired off statements like "Never have I ever falsified identification documents," "Never have I ever lied about my identity," and "Never have I ever tried to run away from my Bond because I thought they were out to get me."

I threw them dirty looks over the rim of my glass while fighting giddy laughter.

At some point, well past midnight, we all started to disperse. Dot and Charlie's plan had worked—I was well and truly drunk off my ass. I only vaguely registered Alec guiding me up the hall toward his room, the sharp pain in my hip as I barreled into a side table, Alec's grunt as he picked me up and carried me the rest of the way.

As he wrangled me out of my clothes, I blabbered on in half-finished sentences. " . . . evil Dot and Charlie ganging up on me . . . I love them. They're so nice. They're like my family now . . . They *are* my family . . . Everyone is my family." I giggled, stumbling backward, but Alec caught me and lowered me to the bed. He kept me sitting upright so he could pull one of his soft T-shirts over my head.

I inhaled. "You smell good. This is a really soft T-shirt. Why are all your things so soft? What was I . . . oh yeah! The whole world is my family. You know, we need more love in all the . . . um . . . in the . . . the world needs more love. I love Dot and Charlie and everyone else. I have *so much* love."

I grabbed on to the front of his shirt and pulled him down to eye level. My vision was swimming, but he looked as if he was smirking at me, amused. I steadied my swaying as best I could, blinked a few times, then said in an intense whisper, "I have so much love in my heart, Alec, for all of you."

His smile fell, but he kept staring at me with those intense eyes of his, dark blue in the low light of the bedside lamp. "So do I," he whispered, pressing his forehead to mine.

I smiled and nuzzled his nose. The last coherent sliver of my brain—the only little bit not swimming in alcohol—managed to stop me from saying, "I love you." I didn't want to say it to him drunk. It felt cheap and fake, and I didn't want to give him any reason to doubt me.

My eyes widened and I leaned away, my hands flying to my stomach as my mouth filled with saliva.

"Oh shit," I managed to get out before my stomach heaved. Alec sprang into action, shuffling me to his en suite.

The last thing I remember before I blacked out is Alec holding my hair as I vomited gin and tonic into his toilet.

~

I woke with a groan to the sound of a door banging open.

"Gym?" Ethan's booming voice was like a sledgehammer to my already throbbing head.

Heavy curtains slid across the rail to reveal bright sunlight, which sent even more pain stabbing through my skull. The sledgehammer had the back of my head covered, while the stabbing focused on my closed eyes. I buried my head in a pillow, and my forehead bumped into another forehead. We both groaned.

Vaguely I registered I was in Alec's bed, but his voice came from somewhere behind me, where the stabby light was coming from.

"Yep! I'm feeling much better today. The bullet wound's nearly healed completely."

"Sweet, bro!" Skin slapped against skin; I was pretty sure they'd high-fived. Thankfully, the sound of their obnoxiously loud, manly voices soon moved off down the hall. But the assholes had left the curtains open, and a dull thudding was coming from another part of the house. I couldn't be entirely sure if the thudding was hammers and ongoing construction in the west wing or if it was just my head.

Alec hadn't touched alcohol the night before, so it was no surprise he was up, bright eyed and bushy tailed, but I was about 87 percent sure Ethan had downed at least two six-packs of beer. He'd been giggling like a schoolgirl at one point . . . I just couldn't remember what the joke was.

He'd definitely drunk more than me, and yet he was up and ready to do a workout. *Jerk.* Far more annoying, though, was the bright light still stabbing me in the fucking eyes.

I groaned and cracked one eye open. Josh was in the bed with me, his forehead against mine and his mouth slightly open. I nudged him. His eyes flew open, but then he cringed and tried to roll over.

With a grunt of protest, I halted his movements and gestured vaguely in the direction of the windows. Thankfully, his hangover didn't hinder his ability to know exactly what I was thinking. With a lazy flick of his wrist, the curtains drew closed, casting the room into blissful darkness once more. Then, without me even having to grunt at him again, he did the same to the door.

He rolled over, and I snuggled into his back, playing the big spoon.

~

I'd spent enough time in Alec's and Tyler's rooms to know the afternoon sun streamed in through the windows on this side of the house. It was *early* afternoon, but I'd still slept half the day away. And I was in the bed alone. Why did they all recover faster than me? Didn't we all have Variant DNA? Why did I still have to suffer the dull headache at the back of my head, the sick, empty feeling in my stomach?

I sighed and crawled out of bed, then used Alec's bathroom to shower and brush my teeth. I really needed to buy another four toothbrushes. Because I stayed with them—one or more of them—several times per week, I ended up using their toothbrushes way more than was hygienic. According to the World Health Organization, the mouth is home to more than seven hundred species of bacteria, and each person has their own unique mix of bacteria that don't take kindly to other bacteria being introduced.

I put thoughts of gum disease out of my mind. The shower and tooth brushing had me feeling almost normal, but there was one more need to attend to. My stomach grumbled as if to punctuate my thoughts.

On the ground floor, I had to step around sheets of drywall and several wheelbarrows full of debris. I frowned, cursing myself for not stealing a pair of Alec's socks. What the hell were they doing up there? This renovation was taking forever.

As I walked into the kitchen, the smell of coffee drove all thoughts of swinging hammers and messy demolition from my mind. I inhaled deeply and followed my nose, walking around the corner with my eyes half-closed.

Like a vision of hotness, all my desires incarnate, Tyler stood at the island holding a fresh latte out to me. I took it with both hands, hugging it to my chest and then taking a sip. I moaned and nearly closed my eyes, but I couldn't tear them away from the perfect man in front of me.

It was Sunday—usually the only day I saw Ty in sweats, relaxing—but clearly, he had to do some work. He was in gray slacks, and the rolled-up sleeves of his crisp white shirt cut into his defined forearms. Despite his neat clothing, his messy brown hair stuck up all over the place, that pesky wayward bit hanging over his forehead, and his gray eyes watched me with so much affection, so much . . .

"Mmmm, I love you." Was I talking to the perfect coffee or the perfect man? My brain was still struggling to keep up. He just kept watching me, his face the picture of patience even though he clearly had somewhere to be.

I took another sip, but it wasn't the amazing coffee spreading warmth through my chest. I set the cup down and leaned my hip on the bench, mirroring his posture.

He tilted his head and smiled. "How are you feeling after—"

"Shh." I cut him off with a hand over his perfect mouth. His eyes widened, then crinkled in amusement. He kept one hand flat on the bench next to his hip, but the other went to my waist.

I removed my hand from his mouth and trailed my fingers over his freshly shaved jaw, coming to rest at his neck, just under the crisp collar of his shirt.

"Ask me what I'm thinking about, Ty." I held his gaze, steady and sure as I let my Light flow into him unobstructed.

I love you.

I love you.

I love you.

I repeated the words over and over in my head, waiting for him to ask the question.

"What are you thinking about, Eve?" His voice was low but playful, his eyes still amused.

I watched, mesmerized and awed, as his ability filled him in. I was thinking the words so hard, with so much intention, it must have sounded like someone shouting in his head.

The playfulness left his expression, replaced by something . . . more, deeper. He smiled and licked his lips as he pulled me against his chest.

"Wait!" I stopped him before he could speak. "I want to say it." A thrilling, light giddiness bubbled up in my chest and burst out of my lips. "I love you, Tyler Gabriel."

He grinned, his whole face lighting up. "I love you, Evelyn Maynard."

I returned his grin and leaned up to kiss him. We held each other close, our kisses messy and erratic, punctuated by laughter and broken by toothy smiles.

By the time we pulled out of each other's arms, my latte was going cold.

He made me a fresh one, pouring coffee into his travel mug as he went. Ethan and Josh came into the kitchen, laden with grocery bags, as Tyler slid my second latte over to me.

"Did you two go grocery shopping?" I frowned as they each gave me a kiss on the cheek and deposited the bags on the island. "Don't you have, like . . . people for that?"

"Yes." Josh chuckled. "But we wanted to get out of the house for a bit, and Kid started getting ideas for dinner and . . ." He gestured to the food.

"But how about some breakfast first?" Ethan flashed me his dimples, twirling a pan in his big hand before setting it on the stove to heat.

"I have to head into the city for a meeting. I may need to stay the night, depending on how late it goes." Tyler gave me a kiss on the top of my head and turned to leave. "Love you."

"Love you." It was amazing how easy it was to fall into those words, how effortlessly they came tumbling out considering we'd only said them for the first time a few moments ago.

As Tyler left, Alec came around the other side of the island in sweats and a hoodie.

My heart sank even as it started to hammer in my chest.

Ethan cracked an egg into the pan, the oil sizzling.

Alec pulled his hood up over his head, avoiding eye contact.

He'd heard. He must have. He was too close *not* to have heard me tell Tyler I loved him as if I'd been saying it my whole life, as if it were just part of our daily repertoire.

I watched him, chewing on my lip, horrified and feeling like shit.

He collected a bottle of mineral water from the fridge and walked out, not saying anything or looking at anyone.

I couldn't see the look on his face, but his unhappiness was clear from the tension in his shoulders, his hurried steps, the way his fingers gripped the bottle. I couldn't imagine what was going through his head, what he was feeling.

Was he kicking himself for the way he'd treated me? Or was he mad at me for torturing him like this?

I was mad at me.

I folded my hands on the cool stone and dropped my head onto my forearms. Why couldn't I just say it? I felt it. I knew he felt it. He'd said it to me. So why couldn't I say it to him? Why wasn't I rushing out after him to tell him this instant?

Alec and I had come very far, but I was still worried he'd hurt me. No one had ever been quite as good at tearing my heart out of my chest and stomping on it to make himself feel better. If I went after him now and tried to tell him I loved him, would he throw it back in my face, reject me yet again? That was how Alec reacted when hurt; he pushed people away, hurt them more than they were hurting him. I just couldn't bear the cold look in his eyes, couldn't stand the thought of hearing his hard, detached voice.

Soothing hands rubbed my shoulders as tears pricked my eyes.

"Just tell him, baby," Josh whispered next to my ear.

My silent tears spilled over. If only it were that simple.

EIGHTEEN

I took the bottle of water from Karen gratefully, downing half of it in one go. When I'd first arrived for my session, I regretted wearing a summer dress and sandals. It was a hot day, but the AC inside the building was pumping. It hadn't taken me long to wish for a cardigan.

But once the session got underway, I was hot and sweaty in no time. They hadn't requested any of the guys for this one. Tyler was in his office some thirty floors up, and Alec was somewhere in the building too, so they were on standby if we needed them, but the research team wanted to test my ability to transfer Light to Variants *outside* my Bond.

"You OK?" Karen took a seat on the couch next to me. We were finished for the day, and it had become a bit of a routine for the two of us to sit down and debrief after each session. We mostly used the area they'd set up as a living room—the couches were comfortable.

I stretched. "I'll be fine. It's just a lot more effort outside the Bond."

"It's to be expected. But if at any point you feel like it's too much, you just say so, sweetie." Karen had gone from barking cold, impersonal commands into the speakers to having semi-casual chats with me and calling me sweetie. I must have grown on her.

The session had been grueling. I could transfer Light to other Variants without a problem. Yes, it required more concentration, but I'd done it enough that it wasn't that difficult. But none of that was new; all Vitals could do that. What they wanted was for me to use my glowing Light to transfer to Variants outside my Bond *remotely*.

I'd done it at the Melior Group event about a month earlier, so it *was* possible, but I'd been acting on pure adrenaline and survival instinct, not to mention the feral need to protect my Variants. I tried not to think too hard about that night. Doing so made vivid, disturbing images invade my mind—the blood, Alec falling to the floor . . .

I couldn't stand the thought of losing any of them.

Naturally, Melior Group had footage of the whole thing, so Karen and the team had studied it. I'd tried to watch it myself, but as soon as the armed men appeared on the screen, I panicked. The thought of seeing Alec get shot from a whole new angle made bile rise in my throat, and I raced out of the room.

Karen didn't make me watch the rest of the video, but she did push me to try to replicate the transfer.

I was grateful for the push. My own mind was curious about this development, but I was scared to try it again. Left to my own devices, I might have avoided the issue indefinitely.

By the end, I'd managed to draw the Light, get the glow up, and remotely transfer some to a researcher with super hearing on the other side of the room. He smiled wide and pushed his glasses up his nose when my Light hit him. Then, to prove the transfer was successful, he started answering people on the other side of the reinforced concrete wall.

It had taken the entire session to get to that point, and now I was exhausted, drained, and starving. Karen kept our chat brief and shooed me out, sending me in the direction of the cafeteria on the fifth floor.

The elevator stopped on the ground floor, and I found myself face-to-face with Dana. Her blonde hair was up in a neat ponytail, her curvy physique covered, but not hidden, by the signature black uniform.

"Hey," she mumbled around a mouthful as she stepped in. She had a giant burrito clasped in both hands.

"Hey," I told her burrito and licked my lips. It smelled amazing. The elevator doors closed again, and we started moving up.

"Research sesh?" she asked, taking another giant bite.

My mouth filled with saliva, and I had to swallow before answering. "Yup."

"How was it?"

"OK. Long and draining. I'm fucking starving."

Finally she realized I was giving her burrito looks that would make even Ethan blush, and she paused with it halfway to her mouth.

"You're on your way to the cafeteria, right?" She took another bite, protectively angling her body away from me.

"Mmhmm." We were already passing the third floor. Food was minutes away. But all I wanted was that damn burrito.

Dana sighed and rolled her eyes, then wordlessly handed over the burrito.

I snatched it out of her grasp and took a giant bite. It tasted just as good as it looked and smelled—tender beef, crunchy lettuce and corn, and she'd doused it in guacamole and salsa. I moaned right as the elevator doors opened on the busy fifth floor.

Several people paused and turned toward my decidedly sexual noises. I couldn't care less. I took another delicious bite as we stepped off the elevator.

Marcus and Jamie stood a few feet away, shoulder to shoulder, barely containing their grins. Marcus's black hair and dark skin couldn't have contrasted more with Jamie's red hair and pale complexion, but their posture and the slant to their smiles were so similar it was clear they spent a lot of time together.

"You doing chicks now, Dana?" Marcus teased.

"I might be." She shrugged. "What's it to you?"

They laughed, and Jamie answered, "Nothing at all, but her Bond members might have something to say about it."

I rushed to swallow my bite. "Knock it off, or I'm telling Dot you were making rude jokes." They just grinned wider. They knew she wouldn't care—Dot loved a dirty joke. "And anyway, I'm all about the burrito."

I took an exaggeratedly slow bite, moaning and rolling my eyes into the back of my head.

All three of them laughed, and Dana slung an arm over my shoulders. "Keep the fucking burrito. That was gold!"

They got food from the cafeteria, and the four of us sat together as we ate, chatting. Judging by some of the questions Jamie and Marcus asked Dana, they didn't seem to know her that well, which was odd considering she and Alec had seen each other for some time. But Alec and Dana could both be standoffish.

Dana didn't seem to mind the questions and even joked around with us. I hoped this would be the beginning of some new friendships for her; I had a feeling she was lonely, not that she'd ever admit it.

"OK. Back to the strategy meeting. Kyo will have our asses if we're late." Marcus got to his feet.

Jamie groaned. "Why do we have to go to that again?"

"Because Ace can't, and we're stepping in for him."

"What's Alec doing?" Dana asked, picking up everyone's rubbish and dropping it in a nearby trashcan.

Marcus and Jamie looked at me, wary.

"It's OK." I waved them off and held up my shiny badge. "I have clearance now."

"It's not that." Marcus rubbed the back of his neck.

"Come on. We really can't be late." Jamie tugged him along, and they rushed off.

"That was weird." I frowned after them.

Dana shrugged. "Men."

"You heading up? I think I'll have to wait for Tyler to finish some stuff before we can go home."

We stopped at the elevators, and she pushed the down button. "Nah. Heading down."

She gave me a tight smile. Other than the labs, the only thing below ground level were the holding cells. Dana was on Zara duty.

I'd spoken to the guys at length after my chat with Harvey. None of them particularly wanted me around Zara for fear of my physical and emotional safety, but they were fine with whatever I decided.

So far, though, I was still avoiding it.

I sighed, thinking back to just that morning, when Karen had pushed me to deal with another painful thing I could've easily kept avoiding. I was on the other side of that now and better for it. I knew more about my glowing Light, had better control of it. I'd worked hard, and it felt good. By the end I was glad she'd pushed me.

The situation with Zara wasn't remotely the same, but I could feel it festering deep in that dark hole I'd locked her up in, twisting my insides any time it stirred.

The elevator doors opened, and Dana stepped in. She raised her hand to wave goodbye, but before she could say the words, I stepped in after her. Her eyes widened in surprise for a second, but she recovered quickly and pressed the button.

I took a deep breath and pushed it out loudly. Did I really want to do this?

"Wait. Is this a good time? Are you, like, taking her to . . ." *be interrogated? Have a toilet break?* I didn't really know how these things worked, and I was looking for an out.

Dana shook her head. "Now is fine."

"Shit." I took another deep breath. Why was I so nervous about this?

Dana placed a hand on my shoulder and squeezed. Surprisingly, it helped. Knowing she was there, and not on either my side or Zara's, made my fidgeting stop, and I took a few calmer breaths.

After that, we didn't speak. The elevator doors opened, and Dana led the way to an anteroom with several corridors leading off it. I had no clue what differentiated them or what they contained. The only signs above the doors showed series of letters and numbers completely meaningless to me.

Dana went to a door on the right, swiped her access card, and pushed it open. I followed her down a long, brightly lit corridor with heavy steel doors on either side. About halfway up, she stopped in front of one of the doors and turned to me.

"The cells in this corridor are reinforced steel on all sides." She pointed to the roof and ceiling. "Plus, they have an extra layer of a special material that's impenetrable by any Variant ability. It's like a thin, clear plastic. No one can hear anything while these doors are closed, but we monitor these detainees at all times."

She tapped a tablet-sized screen next to the door, and a view of the room beyond appeared. It was exactly as you'd expect a prison cell to be—small bed, desk and chair in one corner, toilet and sink in another—but more modern and clean, everything in shades of gray and white. Zara was on the bed, reading.

I looked away from the screen as Dana continued. "There are seven detainees in this section, and only two of them are considered nonthreatening enough to have regular time outside their cells."

Clearly Zara was one of them. I wondered who the other person was and what they were in for. And what about the other five? What made them so unstable that even having Dana around to neutralize their abilities wasn't enough to deem them nonthreatening? I also wondered what that ability-blocking material was, how they'd developed it, why it wasn't available widely. I was grateful to Dana for giving me all this information; it provided a much-needed distraction from my nervousness and gave me a sense of control.

"When I open the door"—she gestured to the handle—"there'll be another one behind it made out of the clear material I mentioned. You have clearance to be here and speak with her, but you don't have the training or permission from management to be in the same room as her. You'll have to speak through the membrane."

"Good." I nodded. I still wasn't entirely sure how I would react.

"Ready?" She held her pass poised over the scanner, waiting for my OK.

I nodded. Dana swiped the pass and pulled the door open.

The sound drew Zara's attention, and she dropped the book and sat up, swinging her legs over the side of the bed.

She opened her mouth to say something, probably sarcastic, but she saw me and froze.

For a beat we just stared each other down. She was in blue pants and a gray T-shirt. Her hair was brushed, but it needed a trim and looked messy at the ends. She had no makeup on—no signature dark eyeliner and bold lipstick.

She looked healthy but . . . bare. Stripped of anything that could exhibit individuality. She probably hated that. Good . . .

After a moment the shock in her eyes was replaced by something much more complex. Sadness, maybe? A hint of longing and . . . something else? Something messy.

She cleared her throat and slowly stood up. "I'd given up hope that you were going to come."

"Well, I'm here now." I crossed my arms. "So get on with it. Say what you have to say so I can get on with my life and forget you ever existed."

"I deserved that." She nodded, moving to the front of the door.

"You think?"

We were close enough to shake hands, the translucent film of ability-resistant material the only thing separating us. The only sign it was there at all was the slight iridescent quality it had and the fact that Zara's voice sounded just a little muffled.

"How have you been, Eve? How are your guys? Dot and Charlie? I heard they got him out." She looked as if she genuinely cared—as if she genuinely wanted to know how I was.

But I knew how well she could fake it. I'd seen it firsthand—right up until she slammed that van door shut.

"As if you give a shit," I spat.

"I deserved that too, I suppose." She sighed. "But I do. Everything was . . ." She made a circular gesture with her head. ". . . twisted. I fucked up. Big time. Like, *epically*. But I do really care, Eve. I'm so sor—"

"Save it!" I rolled my eyes. "You don't honestly expect me to believe that you spent months plotting against me, pretending to care, yet now, all of a sudden it's real? How fucking stupid do you think I am?"

"I wasn't pretending to care, even then. I love you, Eve, and I was incredibly conflicted about what I was doing, unsure about it until the last minute, but . . ."

I just arched a brow, silently showing her my skepticism.

"I've thought about this for so long—what I would say to you, how I would explain and beg for your forgiveness—but it's all coming out wrong."

"Maybe it's coming out wrong because *you're* wrong. There's got to be something seriously fucked up about you that you could do that to someone you called a *friend*. That you could go and join the very people responsible for Beth's death. Have you ever truly cared about anyone in your life?"

I was being cruel, but I needed to say all the things I'd been refusing to acknowledge for months. I didn't think I'd ever see her again; I had to let it all out.

At the mention of Beth's name, anger flared in her eyes and her fists balled up. For the first time, I saw a glimpse of the Zara I knew—the one I'd called my friend.

My heart clenched.

The biggest thing I'd been avoiding was how much I fucking missed her. It hurt *so much*.

I expected her to throw a cutting remark in my face, but the anger crumpled just as fast as it had come. She hung her head as tears streamed down her face.

Next to me, Dana shuffled and crossed her arms loosely. She wasn't particularly comfortable with emotions, and Zara and I were flinging them around with abandon.

Zara sniffed and swiped at her tears. "You're right." Her voice was strained, but she raised her red-rimmed eyes to mine. "Beth would've hated what I did. What I became. She probably would've stopped being my friend a long time ago."

"No, she wouldn't have." I sighed. "Beth was selfless and kind. She would've stuck by you. She would've stuck by us both and made us make up. Maybe none of this would've even happened if she was still around."

"I miss her so much." Zara sobbed.

"Me too," I croaked. I hated myself for it—I didn't want to show her any weakness.

"She always pushed me to be a better person, you know? Even when we were kids. She would've forgiven Rick right away, probably made really good friends with him too."

I chuckled through my tears. She was right. Making the man who'd killed her a friend was exactly the kind of thing she would've done. I didn't get to know him very well before he died, but I had a feeling Rick would've embraced the friendship—would've embraced any opportunity for redemption.

I guess, in a way, he did redeem himself. He'd tried to warn me to be careful, and in the end, he stood up to his parents and sacrificed himself to save his friend. To save Ethan.

Did Zara deserve the opportunity to redeem herself too?

Beth would've wanted me to be kind, to not hold on to resentment, but I just couldn't get past my hurt and anger. Thinking about Rick and that awful night in Thailand brought it all rushing back, as uncontrollable as a hurricane.

"I know Beth would've wanted me to forgive you, but I can't, Zara. You were one of the closest friends I'd ever had. I loved and trusted you, and you betrayed me. You broke . . ." *my trust? Our friendship? My heart?* ". . . so many things."

I ran my hands through my hair and took a step back. I didn't even know what I was saying anymore.

"Wait!" She stepped as close to the doorway as the clear membrane would allow, her eyes puffy and panicked. "Please don't go."

"What else is there to say, Red?"

"Please, I haven't explained about . . . I want to tell you about my parents and the way I was raised and . . . and how angry I was after Beth, and then Davis . . . He's so good at twisting things. And I know—I *know*—none of it excuses what I did, but I wanted to at least *explain* some of it so you would understand."

"I get it." I spread my arms, then let them drop to my sides. "OK? I know about your childhood and your asshole parents. You told me all about it when we were roomies. I know what a manipulative prick Davis is—I know better than anyone what he's capable of. I know how you must've felt after Beth . . . but you know what I can't get over? Why you didn't come to me. Why you didn't confide in me, let me be there for you. I just . . ." I groaned. The tears were welling up again, and I'd had enough. "I can't do this anymore. Let's go."

Dana nodded, nothing but sympathy in her eyes, although I wasn't sure if it was for me or Zara. Probably a bit of both.

"No!" Zara's voice took on an edge of desperation. "Please! Please, Eve, I know I have no right to ask anything of you, but please, take it. Take it away!"

I paused, mainly out of confusion. What the hell was she talking about? "What?"

"I know you can. Your mom could do it, and you glow, so you can do it too. That's why he wanted you—so he could figure out how you take the abilities away. *Please*, take Rick's ability away again. I don't want it anymore. It's not right. It feels *wrong* in every way."

"You want me to . . ." I was stunned. The last thing I'd expected was for her to ask me that. "Zara, it could kill you. I've never actually done it, and you know what?" There was that anger again, bubbling up like a geyser. "Where do you get off asking me for anything?"

"I know I don't deserve anything from you, but I don't want it. I don't want to be this . . . this . . . *person*. It doesn't belong to me, and I want to give it back."

"You can't give it back. Rick is dead, remember? And you can't ask me to risk taking your life. I may think you're the scum of the earth, but I don't want to be a killer."

I wasn't entirely sure it would kill her. The electricity wasn't Zara's—it was Rick's. I would technically just be removing something that didn't belong in the first place. But I couldn't be sure. Once it was transplanted, perhaps it fused to her Light, to her very essence.

I had no problem defending myself, but I couldn't stand there and deliberately and calculatingly do something that could end a person's life, no matter how mad I was at that particular person.

"You made your bed, Zara." I nodded at the narrow cot in the corner. "It consists of a thin mattress and a scratchy blanket. Now lie in it."

"I don't care if it kills me." Again, her words floored me. She was no longer yelling and pleading; she was calm now, resigned. "I've got nothing left. I'd be better off dead."

She looked broken. Her shoulders were hunched, and silent tears streamed unhindered down her face and neck.

She shuffled slowly back to the cot.

I turned away before she reached it, and Dana softly closed the door.

I walked to the end of the hall, my steps rushed. I needed to give my body something to do—some other reason for my labored breathing.

Dana caught up to me as I reached the door to the anteroom. She placed a gentle hand on my shoulder. "I'm sorry, Eve. I never would've asked you to come if I knew it would be so . . ."

"Fucked up?" I supplied.

"Yeah." She sighed. "She's been so cooperative and pretty much OK. Honest about the shit she's done but accepting responsibility, you know? Never even hinted at suicidal thoughts . . ."

"Is there anything in that room she can use to . . ."

"No. It's strict policy. They're not allowed much."

"Good. Is she allowed other visitors? Like, maybe a psychiatrist? Maybe I should . . ." I looked back down the hallway. It was so long. Impossibly long.

"No." Dana shook her head. "You didn't even have to come see her. This is not your responsibility. She's in Melior Group custody. I'll make sure she gets some help."

I nodded, taking a few deep breaths, and then Dana surprised the hell out of me by pulling me into a hug. "You've got enough on your plate, Eve. I got this."

I held her tightly, not saying anything—partly because if I started talking about this clusterfuck again, I would start crying, but partly because I was a little speechless.

A year ago, even a few months ago, if someone had told me Dana would one day hug me, be there for me, share her burrito with me, I would've figured one or both of us was certifiably insane.

But there we were. Hugging. In a secret underground prison.

"Thank you, Dana," I whispered as we pulled apart.

"Don't mention it." She smiled, swiping her pass to open the door. "Seriously. If you tell anyone I hugged you, I'll kill you."

I laughed—a loud, full-bellied laugh. It was exactly what I needed to lift the heavy weight sitting on my chest, threatening to suffocate me.

Dana was fast becoming one of my favorite people. Who would've thought?

NINETEEN

Dana pulled the door shut just as the one on the opposite side of the anteroom beeped and opened. Alec stepped out, a deep frown pulling at his brows, his shoulders tense.

When he spotted us, he took a deep breath and blew it out of his nose. "What the fuck?"

"What?" Dana crossed her arms and bristled. "Evelyn asked to see her."

"She's not supposed to have visitors, and *she*"—he pointed at me but didn't look—"is supposed to be upstairs with Gabe."

"Zara can speak with anyone with level four clearance and above." Dana lifted her chin. Considering how stubborn they both were, I wouldn't be entirely surprised if this ended in violence. I took a tentative step back.

Alec threw me an incredulous look before dropping his arms. He rubbed his closely cropped hair and dragged his palms down his face. "Let's go."

He didn't look at either of us, but I knew his words were for me. Without waiting for a response, he walked down the corridor.

I looked at Dana and cringed. "Are you in trouble?"

"Nah." She shrugged. "I followed the rules. He can't do shit to me. You, on the other hand . . . "

I rolled my eyes. "Don't worry. I can take it."

She cocked her head to the side. "You're not at all what I first thought you were, Evelyn Maynard."

"Yeah, I'm a real mystery, wrapped in an enigma, dipped in a glow stick." I waved my hand as I walked away from her, trying not to lose sight of Alec as he rounded the corner.

Behind me Dana laughed, and a door beeped as it unlocked.

I jogged to catch up, but Alec was leaning on the wall around the corner, waiting for me. He didn't spare me a glance before swiping his security pass and opening a door next to the elevator. I followed him into the stairwell and groaned. Kane would be proud of all this extra exercise I was getting in.

Alec took the winding stairs two at a time. I had to jog to keep his tense back within view. His hands were in fists, but his butt looked amazing in the tight black uniform—it stretched over his defined glutes with every unnecessarily large step he took.

I was getting puffed and pissed, and I was done chasing him.

"Alec!" I yelled, but he kept walking.

"Alec, stop!" He reached a landing and froze. I was a little glad to see his shoulders were heaving too. Not as bad as mine, but still.

I climbed the last few stairs to reach him and stood at his elbow, looking at his strong profile. "What the fuck is your problem?"

"Really?" He turned to fix me with a scowl. It reminded me of how he used to treat me at the very start—with disdain. I flinched away, but a lot had happened since then, and I was no longer backing down.

"Yes, really. So I went to see Zara! So—"

"I don't give a shit about that!" His deep voice bounced off the concrete walls. "That's your decision to make, and you were safe with Dana."

"Then what the fuck is your problem?" I threw my hands up and let them flop down at my sides.

"Don't pretend you didn't see—like you don't know what I was doing in that room." His nostrils flared, his posture and expression radiating anger, but I could see something else in his icy eyes too.

"You're pissed because I saw you doing your job?"

"I'm pissed because you saw what I'm capable of." We were chest to chest now, breathing hard and glaring.

"I know what you're capable of. I'm not a fucking idiot. You have a pain ability. You work for a secretive security company that keeps people detained in the basement of their fancy building in Manhattan."

"Evelyn, I just tortured a man," he ground out, as if I still wasn't getting the point.

I sighed in frustration. "Yes, Alec, I'm aware. Do I like it? No, of course not. Torture has been proven to be an ineffective interrogation strategy. According to several studies, 'rapport-based' interrogation techniques, such as finding common ground and demonstrating kindness and respect, are generally the most effective. But I mostly don't like it because I know you hate doing it. But just like you acknowledge that seeing Zara was *my* choice, I acknowledge that you doing this is *your* choice and part of your job. I don't know what the fuck you're so upset about."

"I've read the fucking torture studies, Evelyn, and it's rare that we use 'enhanced interrogation techniques,' but when it's necessary, guess who they ask to do it? Now stop pretending that you're not repulsed by this. That you don't find me abhorrent for doing it. Everyone else does."

"I'm not everyone else, asshole!" I yelled, right into his face. I couldn't help it. But I did manage to lower my volume, if not the level of intensity, for the next part. "I'm Evie. I'm your Vital. I'm completely and irrevocably tethered to you in every conceivable way. I . . .."

The words were at the tip of my tongue, but I couldn't say them. Not like this. Not through gritted teeth and growling tension.

He was feeling like shit about himself again, as if he didn't deserve my understanding and affection. He'd spent his whole life building that wall. My mind got stuck on those three little words I couldn't say, and what else *could* I say? Would he even hear me anyway?

So I decided to *show* him.

I closed the distance, wrapping my arms around his neck and attacking his lips with mine. He grunted and circled his arms around my middle, pushing his tongue into my mouth. He didn't drive me away with his body as he had with his words. Instead he drew me closer, pouring all his rage and frustration and desperate need into that one frantic kiss. I took it all and gave it right back, our hands pawing at each other, his threading into my hair, mine pulling on his shirt.

The sound of a door slamming echoed through the stairwell, and we broke the kiss but still clutched each other. I held his icy stare as the sound of voices and several footsteps reached us from below. It sounded as if we were right in their path.

I groaned in disappointment. No one could get me going as fast as Alec. More and more often when we got into each other's faces, neither of us willing to let our stubbornness go and concede, it would end in frenzied, passionate sex. I couldn't seem to get enough. It was as if I'd psychologically primed myself to associate our bickering and arguing with sex, like some fucked-up version of Pavlov's dog. Pavlov's cock?

It couldn't have been healthy, but that didn't change the fact that I was so ready to go that my abdominal and vaginal muscles were clenching and relaxing in anticipation. How the hell was I supposed to face people in this state?

Apparently Alec didn't want to wait either.

"Fuck it," he growled and grabbed me by the wrist, climbing the few stairs up to the next level. He swiped his access card and pulled me through the door. Most of the fluorescent lights inside were off. The only light came from the "Exit" sign and the flickering indicators on rows and rows of computers stacked on top of each other in glass cabinets.

As soon as the door clicked shut behind us, Alec picked me up and slammed me against the wall next to the door, crashing his lips to mine once again. I looped one arm around his shoulders and put the other at the back of his head, mushing his face closer to mine. Our teeth knocked. I wrapped my legs around his waist and rolled my hips. He rolled his back, and we found a rhythm, grinding against each other as our tongues fought for dominance.

A few torturous minutes later, his hips stilled, and he pulled his mouth from mine.

I made an incoherent sound of protest and shoved against his shoulder. "Alec, what the f—"

"Shh." His hand clapped over my mouth, and he fixed me with a hard look.

Did he just shush me? I frowned, about to claw my way out of his grip, but then he gestured to the door with his head, and I heard voices. It must've been the same people we'd heard earlier. They were making their way past the door, their voices and footsteps muffled.

I understood now why he'd stopped, but I still thought it was unnecessary to hold a hand over my mouth. So I bit him.

He flinched but only slightly, and instead of giving me a disapproving scowl as I'd expected, he smirked at me. The naughty look, coupled with the lust in his hooded eyes, shot another pang of desire straight to my core. As if he felt the rush, Alec started moving his hips again, his arousal rubbing against me through our clothes.

As the voices moved away, my eyes rolled into the back of my head, and I let my jaw go slack under Alec's hand. I panted, feeling an orgasm building. The excitement of doing this somewhere we really shouldn't only heightened every sensation. With my mouth open, it was easy to dart my tongue out and lick his palm. It tasted just a little salty but smelled like soap—clean.

Alec dragged his fingers across my mouth, pulling my lips to the side, then stuck the tip of his finger into my mouth and let it catch on my bottom teeth. I wrapped my lips around it and sucked it in farther, opening my eyes to watch him. He groaned and leaned forward to bite my neck, then immediately licked and kissed the spot to take away the sting.

He removed his finger and replaced it with his tongue. His big hand held my jaw, keeping my head pinned against the wall.

I loved it when he tried to take charge. It made me want to give in to every demand his body made of mine . . . for about a second. Then it made me want to fight him. In the best way possible.

I pushed hard against his shoulders, and he released me, letting me back down to my feet. My lips were throbbing—both of them—so I didn't waste any time getting more of what I wanted.

I had his belt undone in seconds, freeing his hard length and stroking it.

"I want you inside me," I panted.

He groaned and reached under my dress to pull my panties down. I stepped out of my flats and underwear in one go.

A desk chair in the corner caught my attention. It was an old one, on wheels and without armrests. I twisted out of Alec's arms and took the few steps necessary to grab it and spin it around. "Sit."

His eyes narrowed. "You're in my domain now. You don't get to bark orders."

But he pushed his pants down over his hips and sat in the chair anyway. I smirked as I swung one leg over his lap and hovered above him. With my legs wide, I was completely exposed, and another thrill raced up my spine.

Alec dragged a hand up from my knee, over my thigh, and right to the wetness between my legs. He pushed two fingers inside, and I gasped at the sudden intrusion, nearly losing my balance. I held on to his shoulders as he moved his fingers inside me, making me grind my hips against his hand.

But I didn't want to come on his hand. I wanted to come with his cock buried deep inside me. I shoved his hand away and reached for his rock-hard cock, holding it at the base. I teased myself with the tip, moving it up and down my folds, before sinking down onto him.

He let out a growl that ended in a moan, leaning forward to lick my lips. His big hands held me tight against him, his legs spreading wide under me.

I didn't give either of us a chance to adjust, to get used to the heady sensation of complete connectedness—of feeling, seeing, hearing, breathing nothing but the other person. I started moving on top of him, rolling my hips as I used my legs to push up and down.

I was on top. I was supposed to set the pace, but Alec fought me. His strong hands had a firm grip on my hips, and we once again battled for control. Eventually the battle settled into a dance—a hard, intense dance that had his cock sliding in and out of me, hitting a spot deep inside.

It wasn't long before the orgasm bubbled up again. It had been building since the frenzied kiss on the stairs. I'd been close when he'd had me against the wall, grinding into me. I'd been close when he'd buried his fingers inside me and played me like a stringed instrument. And I was fucking close as I bounced and ground on top of him.

He shoved one of his hands up my dress, pulling my bra out of the way to knead my breast.

The combined sensations, coupled with the knowledge that someone could walk in at any moment, had me crying out as I finally gave in to the climax. It washed over me, making my vision blur as every muscle in my body tensed. I rocked against him and bit his neck, hard, and he responded with a grunt that sounded like a mixture of pain and pleasure. I relaxed some of the pressure of my teeth and licked the skin between them.

Alec's hips were still rocking under me, his movements erratic and desperate. I used his shoulders to balance and, with shaky legs, met his movements with mine, bringing him to release.

He did that sexy as fuck growling moan again as his head dropped back and his chest heaved.

After a few moments, he pulled me against him and buried his head in my neck. I nuzzled his jaw and smiled. This was exactly what we needed. We started out shouting at each other and getting riled up, frustrated, hurt. And we ended up in each other's arms, planting soft kisses all over each other's faces, caressing and holding and showing our devotion.

After one last lingering kiss to my lips, Alec craned his neck, then used his legs to push the wheelie chair over to a side table with a box of tissues. It was only once I had a wad of tissues in my hand that he let me up. We cleaned up as best we could and started fixing our clothes.

"Is there a bathroom on this level? I don't want to get a UTI." I looked around—all I saw were rows and rows of servers.

Alec chuckled as he zipped up his pants. "Don't know. But the level above does."

"Don't laugh, you dick. UTIs hurt like a . . ." I caught sight of a camera near the ceiling, high up in a corner.

"Alec!" I hurriedly pulled my underwear up the rest of the way and fixed my dress.

"What?" His attention was on his phone.

"There's a fucking camera?" I gestured to the item, my tone half question, half chastisement.

He glanced at it and then smirked at me. "We're in the most secure area of the most secure building in Manhattan—except maybe the cells below. Of course there are cameras, precious."

"Fuck. Alec!" How was he so relaxed about this? Yes, the *risk* of getting caught had given me a thrill, but I didn't actually want strangers to watch me having sex. The other guys, maybe . . .

Alec wrapped an arm around my shoulders. "Relax. I'm on it."

He put the phone to his ear, and I covered my face with my hands, leaning into him. I was close enough to hear the ringing on the other end and Charlie's voice as he answered. "What's up, dickhead?"

"Hey, jerk-off." Alec's teasing tone turned serious in the very next word. "I need you to make some security footage disappear."

"Shoot."

"HQ. Main server room on subbasement level 1. The past twenty minutes should do it."

Charlie sighed. "Seriously? Do you have any idea the kind of security I have to get through?"

"You saying you can't do it?"

"No!" Charlie sounded outraged. "Of course I can do it. I'm just saying it won't be easy and you owe me one."

"Good. Also, I need you to do it without looking at the footage."

There was a pause on the other end. "Alec, what's going on?"

At his worried tone, I piped in. "Hey, Charlie."

"Eve?"

"Yeah. Don't stress, OK? He's just trying to prevent some poor Melior Group minion from getting an eyeful of my bare ass."

There was another pause, and then Charlie started laughing, big infectious guffaws that had Alec and I both chuckling despite ourselves.

When he finally calmed down, he spoke between giggles. "You two horny fuckers are lucky I'm in the building.

This would be way harder if I was trying to do it remotely, and the fact that . . . hmmm."

Alec stiffened, his arm around me tightening. "Charlie?"

"Meet me in Gabe's office." The line went dead.

"Shit." Alec pocketed the phone and led the way to the elevator.

As we stepped inside, I took his hand and gave him a worried look. "Alec? What's going on?"

"Nothing good. Gabe's office is soundproofed and the only place we can speak freely." He gave me a pointed look, and I pressed my lips together.

As we walked through the halls and past offices and desks, it suddenly felt as if every person was watching us, every wall had someone on the other side listening in.

We reached Tyler's door at the same time Charlie did. He was dressed simply in black jeans and a gray sweater, a laptop tucked under his arm, his expression blank.

We let ourselves in without knocking. Tyler lifted curious eyes at the intrusion, took in our serious expressions, and stood up from his chair.

Alec locked the door as Charlie dropped the laptop on Tyler's desk and propped his hands on his hips.

Tyler didn't speak. Didn't ask unnecessary questions. He just let Charlie talk.

"Something's not right. When I went in to get rid of the server room footage, I noticed something off."

"In what way?" Tyler pressed. He didn't question the fact that Charlie was erasing security footage, which made me wonder how often he did this for them. How many secrets did they have?

"I'm not the only one that's been in the system, which isn't surprising in itself, but I'm the only one that goes in and out undetected. The others I can track. I can see what they've done, changed, erased. With enough digging, I can find out who it was. But I think I just found evidence of someone else—someone as discreet as me."

"What?" Tyler's eyes widened as he leaned on the desk. "Do we have a breach? Should I be initiating protocols?"

"It's not that simple."

"What do you mean?"

"I need to do a little more digging, but so far, from what I can see, they're not taking anything. They're not copying data, trying to access the encrypted files. They're doing the same thing I was doing—deleting security footage, maybe security pass logs as well."

Behind me, Alec cursed under his breath.

"It doesn't make sense. It's like they're trying to cover their tracks, but they haven't actually done anything."

"It makes perfect fucking sense," Alec growled. He and Tyler exchanged a hard look.

Tyler hung his head and sighed. "This is worse than an external attack, a hacking attempt. This sounds like an inside job."

"Fuck." Charlie sank into a chair and dropped his head into his hands. "I wouldn't have even seen it if these two hadn't decided to have a quickie in the server room and needed me to cover it up."

Tyler shot us an amused look before getting back to business. "All right. Charlie, I need you to keep digging— get me as much information as you can. You have complete access to my office. From now on, we work under the assumption that this building is no longer secure. Keep this between us. Stick to the secure channels—text only. And we discuss this in secure rooms. That's this office, my office at Bradford Hills Institute, and my study at the manor. Alec, update Uncle Luce when you get back. I'm going to fill in Ethan and Josh, but Charlie, I think we should keep Dot out of it."

"Agreed." Charlie's focus was already on his screen, his fingers flying across the keyboard.

"I think you can trust Dot, guys. She wouldn't blab about something like this." I crossed my arms. Keeping things from people was kind of a sore spot for me.

"It's not that we don't trust her." Tyler smiled at me warmly. "It's that it's safer if she's kept out of it. For her."

Grudgingly, I nodded. I'd happened to be right next to Alec when this all happened, but would they have told me had I not been? I had the clearance now. Tyler would certainly have discussed it with me had I pressed for information, but they would've probably preferred to keep me out of it, just like Dot. Because it was "safer."

Well, I was there, and I did hear. I couldn't undo that. All I could do was focus on the issue at hand and try to be useful if I could be. All I could do was prove they didn't need to keep hiding things to protect me.

TWENTY

I'd been to Dot and Charlie's house dozens of times. I'd had sleepovers with Dot, been around for dinner, hung out with Olivia and Henry. Yet as we drove in Tyler's Escalade toward their house, a bit of nervousness still twisted my gut.

Josh took my hand. "What's going on?"

I glanced toward the front—Ty and Alec were engaged in a soft conversation as Tyler drove through the leafy streets of Bradford Hills.

"I don't know." I shrugged. "I'm just a little nervous. It feels really . . . formal or something?"

"It's just dinner." Josh squeezed my hand. "There just happens to be more of us tonight."

We were on our way to Sunday dinner. Lucian and Ethan were being driven in the car behind us, a Melior Group vehicle with armed guards led the way, and one brought up the rear. Jamie and Marcus had to work, but Kyo was going to be there too, representing Dot's harem for the night. She'd been referring to each of the men as her "boyfriend," and none of them were seeing other people. It wasn't uncommon for Variants to be in polyamorous relationships, but whenever I asked her how it was going with them, she insisted they "weren't putting a label on it." I called bullshit every time. They worshipped the ground she walked on, and now Kyo was coming to family dinner—shit was getting serious.

When we pulled up, the big metal gates opened to admit the cavalcade of cars, and we drove to the main house.

As the driver of the car behind us lowered Lucian in his wheelchair, we all headed toward the front door. Another pang of nervous uncertainty shot through me—should we knock?

Ethan bounded up the stairs, beating us all there, and let himself straight in. He left the door wide open as he disappeared toward the kitchen, yelling about basting the turkey or something. I chuckled, some of the tension easing. He'd really wanted to do the cooking but had to work on an assignment, and Olivia had ended up having the dinner catered.

We spilled into the large kitchen and dining area, everyone saying hello and hugging. Henry uncorked several bottles of wine, and Alec handed me a glass.

"Thanks." I smiled and brought it to my lips. I'd never really had wine and wasn't sure if I liked it, but as the burgundy liquid hit my tongue, I moaned a little in surprise and appreciation.

Alec smirked at me. "I'm starting to think you have expensive taste."

"Why?" I took another sip.

"That's a Chateau Margaux Merlot." When I gave him a blank look, he elaborated. "It's, on average, one hundred and fifty dollars per bottle, depending on vintage."

"Holy shit." My eyes widened at the unassuming liquid in my glass, and Alec took a slow sip of his own.

After a moment I shrugged and kept drinking. I hadn't grown up with drivers and houses with bedrooms in the double digits, but they *had*, and there was nothing wrong with enjoying the finer things in life. Galileo knows, we'd all had enough shit to deal with—we deserved it.

"We used to do this every Sunday when we were kids." Alec had one hand in his pocket, the other holding his wine glass as he looked out over the room of laughing, talking people—our family.

I frowned. "I thought Olivia and Henry didn't move here until after my mom and I left?"

"They didn't." Alec wrapped an arm around my middle in an uncharacteristically sweet gesture, and I melted into his side.

It was Lucian who answered me. He pulled his wheelchair up beside us and gave me a warm smile. "Your mom was close with my sisters and Josh's and Tyler's mothers. They were all like a big family by the time I moved back here from the UK. The Sunday dinners were a regular occurrence. It was actually at a Sunday dinner that we first met—that we first realized we were connected."

I sat down on the arm of the couch so I could see him better, and Alec's arm moved from my waist to my shoulders.

Lucian kept speaking. "The dinners were a bit more somber after you and your mother left, and then the accident in Japan . . ."

"We stopped doing the dinners after our parents died," Alec finished for him. "It used to be, like, twenty people, massive amounts of food, and all kinds of ruckus. Then all of a sudden, it was just us. It wasn't the same."

"Olivia and Henry moved back a few months after that. The plan was for Alec and Ethan to move in with them, but by that stage all the boys were staying with me, and they didn't want to be separated." Lucian gave Alec the kind of nostalgic look a father might give his son. "But we did pick the Sunday dinners back up. It was more sporadic than it had been before, but even when Alec and Tyler were hanging around The Hole, getting their asses beat, they showed up for the dinners. They sulked and hardly spoke to anyone, but they still showed up."

"Maybe we can make it a more regular thing now," Alec mused.

Olivia and Ethan were in the kitchen, helping the catering team finish off the food preparation. Josh was deep in conversation with Charlie, and Henry and Dot and Tyler were looking at family pictures on the wall.

It was so . . . domestic—and a little foreign to me. Or maybe it was the entire concept of family that was foreign. Maybe that's why I'd been so nervous in the car. I still wasn't entirely sure how to be part of a family.

"Sorry I'm late!" Kyo rushed into the room, and Dot practically bounced over to him, giving him a kiss hello that was just on the border of too intimate for a family gathering. He greeted everyone just as the food was ready, and we sat down at the big dining table.

As we ate the amazing food and drank more bottles of the delicious, expensive wine, I relaxed. We may have been a large group, but I knew and was comfortable with each and every person at this table. The conversation flowed as easily as the wine.

By the time we were ready for dessert, we were all wiping tears from our faces as Kyo told a story of how a mobster's spoiled daughter fell head over heels in lust with Alec when they were infiltrating the operation. She hadn't even been deterred by the fact that he kept "accidentally" zapping her with pain any time she tried to touch him or go in for a kiss.

"Do you have any idea how hard it was to keep a straight face?" Kyo said between bursts of laughter as Dot leaned her head on his shoulder and completely lost it. "You got this constipated look every time she walked into a room."

Alec scowled through the whole thing, but I could see his shoulders start to shake and his lips twitch from keeping the laughter in.

After everyone's giggles subsided, the conversations became a bit more subdued. Ethan leaned forward, draping an arm over the back of my chair and speaking to Tyler on my other side. "Do you think there'll be time to go to the fish markets in Tokyo? I really want to try some fresh tuna sushi."

Mr. Takata had been in touch. He'd visited with his grandmother, but the older woman had simply smiled and asked to see me. He was extremely apologetic, but he was stuck between his duty to respect his elders and his newly declared fealty to me.

Now we were trying to find time to plan a trip, but between classes, demanding work schedules, and security concerns, it wasn't easy.

Tyler shrugged, spinning his empty wine glass on the spot with his dexterous fingers. "Don't know. We'll have to play it by ear."

"Have you not been to Japan?" I asked, my cheeks still a little flushed from the laughter and the wine. "The food is incredible!"

My big guy surprised me by answering silently, with a sad nod of his head. He started playing with the corner of a cloth napkin, his eyes not meeting mine.

I frowned and turned to Tyler, but he was watching his wine glass with a look very similar to Ethan's. Confused, I searched for answers across the table. Alec's hands were clasped in front of him, his brows furrowed and his eyes fixed on the table. Next to him, Josh was the only one meeting my gaze, understanding in his eyes, as always, but also sadness.

The whole room had fallen silent, but Josh put me out of my misery. He cleared his throat. "Our parents were killed in Japan. In Tokyo."

My heart sank. "I am so sorry for bringing it up."

"You didn't, baby." Ethan's hand went to the back of my neck. "I did."

"A lot of people died that day." Henry spoke up from the head of the table. He held Olivia's hand as she discreetly wiped away a tear. "It was tragic."

"Yeah, it was all over the news, even here," Lucian added. "Joyce had just arrived there and then went radio silent. Those were the worst twenty-four hours of my life, thinking I'd lost half my family *and* both of you too."

I gasped, my eyes going wide. "Holy shit! I remember this. I was only eight years old, and we were in Tokyo for, like, a day, and then this awful *thing* happened, and next thing I know we're on a train out of there. Were you guys all there? Were we mere streets from each other?"

Alec remained silent, his eyes still glued to the table in front of him, but Tyler answered. "We'd crossed the street—the four of us. We were ahead of them and just made the crossing signal, but they had to stop. If they'd called out, made us wait with them . . . or if they'd rushed to catch up with us . . ."

Josh picked up where Ty left off. "We were thrown to the ground and knocked unconscious, but they all . . ." He cleared his throat again. "I don't remember it. I was told all of it when I woke up in the hospital, but they were all killed pretty much instantly."

The room once again descended into tense silence. No one made eye contact with anyone else. Dot and Charlie looked from their parents to Lucian to my guys with just as much curiosity as compassion in their eyes. I had a feeling no one had spoken much about this before, and they probably didn't know all the details.

Before I could make an awkward attempt at changing the subject, Alec spoke. "It was like all the sound was sucked out of the air, and there was a split second of perfect stillness—everyone paused, knowing something wasn't right but not knowing what. Then I felt this . . . surge. Like something crawling over my skin but also *through* me— something intense and powerful. And then the world just . . . exploded. There was fire and shit floating around in the air—like cars and concrete bolsters. Everyone just dropped. Fell to the ground and never got up again. I was thrown down with the others, but I didn't get knocked out. My cheek was pressed into the concrete." He lifted a hand to his face absentmindedly, ghosting his fingers over his skin. "And I lay there, and I watched the life drain out of my mother's eyes."

Tears pricked at my eyes as my heart broke clean in half for him. For all of them. Images of the last time I'd seen my own mother attacked my mind—her hand slipping out of mine, her terrified yet surprised face. That image would haunt me for the rest of my life. Knowing my guys were dealing with that same pain—that they knew exactly what that felt like—just twisted the knife.

Yet in some perverted way, it also felt good. The fact that all four of them had experienced the same depth of pain and loss I had made me feel even closer to them. It was yet another thing threading us closer together, strengthening our relationship and Bond.

Our Bond . . .

I gasped, my hands flying to my mouth as the tears spilled over, trailing messy, wet paths down my cheeks and over my fingers.

Alec finally broke his stare-off with the table to look at me, Ethan dropped his arm to my shoulders, and Tyler gripped my knee, leaning forward to look into my face.

"Let's stop talking about it for a while." For once Josh hadn't picked up on what was really happening; he assumed the topic of conversation had upset me. He wasn't entirely wrong, but I was also coming to a realization that made bile rise in the back of my throat.

I shook my head. A sob escaped from between my fingers before I finally forced the words out. "You were all there. And I was there. And your abilities can't harm each other because of me. And *I* was there. And . . . and I can transfer Light remotely. But I'm not . . . I don't remember glowing, but maybe I did. What . . ." I couldn't hold back another sob, dropping my head into my hands. "What if I did this? What if I killed . . ."

I couldn't get the word out, couldn't fully voice that I may have been responsible for the deaths of their parents, not to mention all those other people. I couldn't shake the feeling that my proximity to them had resulted in a massive transfer of Light that they couldn't control. What if their abilities going haywire had caused all the destruction . . . and the death?

"Eve. No." Tyler squeezed my knee. "Think this through. Our abilities can't harm each other now—now that we have you and the Bond has formed. Before that we were definitely able to hurt each other with our abilities. Trust me."

"You didn't do this." Josh's hands landed on my shoulders. I hadn't even heard him get up. "It's not likely you were able to glow at such a young age. You said yourself you'd never experienced it before."

"Yes, but it has happened. Even Lucian"—I gestured in his general direction—"told me I'd glowed once or twice as a kid."

Lucian piped in, reminding me we were still in a room full of people—people whose family I may very well have killed. "Evelyn, that was nothing like what you can do now. It was a flicker of a glow at best, enough for us to know what you were but not enough to do anything with it."

"Yeah, but—" My chair was suddenly yanked backward. The guys' hands disappeared from my knee, shoulder, and neck as I was spun around to face Alec's furious gaze. He lowered himself to his knees, putting his face level with mine and planting his hands on either side of the chair's seat.

I stared at him, expecting him to go back to hating me but really just wanting him to take me into his arms. He did neither.

"Evie, I don't know what the fuck happened that day, but I'm sure as fuck not going to blame an eight-year-old kid. It may've taken me a while to get there, but I'm so glad to have you in my life, baby. Please don't do this to yourself."

"How can you live with even the *possibility* that it may've been my fault, Alec? How can I live with that? How long before you start looking at me with that derisive, mean look again. I can't take that again."

"Evie, please . . ." His thumbs rubbed my hips as his eyes flew about the room, looking for help.

"I really didn't want to bring this up yet"—Lucian's resigned yet determined tone drew everyone's attention—"but we may potentially have some new information on that day."

I had to turn in my chair to see him properly. He was leaning back in his wheelchair, a worried expression on his face.

"Luce?" Olivia looked confused, but there was no denying the hint of fear in her wide eyes. "What is this about?"

"We don't have the full picture yet, and I'm technically not meant to reveal this, as it's classified." He eyed Dot and her parents—the only people in the room without clearance. "But I can't let this go on any further. We've all suffered enough at that man's hands."

Alec's arms stiffened around me, and I leaned into him, angling my body so I could see Lucian better.

"Evelyn, that was in no way your fault. It was a complete coincidence that you and Joyce were there. In Sweden, where you were staying previously, you were discovered by one of Davis's men, and your mom had to get you out immediately. She didn't get in touch until the next day to tell me where you were, and I didn't receive the message in time to tell her that the others were in Japan on holiday, that she needed to leave immediately. By the time I saw her message and replied, she was already offline."

"Lucian, what do you know?" To my surprise, Ethan growled the demand, but my big guy was prone to anger when really pushed. I held his hand in both of mine as Lucian got to the point.

"We never knew what happened. The local police got there before we could get any of our people out. They cooperated with us, but we couldn't find anything definitive. It was only after Thailand that we found some evidence on a hard drive . . . Davis has offices all over the world—that's not a secret—and he had a building in Tokyo. Apparently he had a lab in the basement levels. Not much on the drive we recovered was salvageable, but there is enough to suggest he was running experiments even then. We have no way to prove it, but the logical conclusion is that whatever he was doing down there went horribly wrong and resulted in the chaos and death above ground."

"Why haven't you said anything?" Despite his hard tone, Tyler sounded hurt.

"The techs only just delivered their report two days ago," Lucian explained. "They're still trying to get more information from the drive, and we're nowhere near done going through all that we found in Thailand. He did a good job destroying most of it with the explosions, but we were able to recover a decent amount of evidence. Anyway, I was never planning to keep it from any of you. I'm done keeping secrets from my family." He gave me a meaningful look. Memories of the night we'd stood on his balcony drinking scotch flickered through my mind. "I just wanted to give the techs another day or two to see if they could find anything more. I didn't want to bring it up during this evening, but I can't sit here and watch Evie blame herself for something that was not her fault."

"Thank you." I wiped the tears from my cheeks.

Rather than unleash a barrage of questions, the guys had all gone silent and introspective. If they were anything like me when it came to talking about their parents' deaths, I couldn't blame them.

After a few tense moments, a chair scraped loudly and Dot stood up.

"How about some dessert?" She smiled, but it didn't reach her eyes. The others all murmured their agreement, and Alec and Josh returned to their seats.

"I'll help you." Charlie followed Dot into the kitchen.

Henry grabbed the open bottle of wine from the buffet, refilling glasses until it was all gone, then opening another bottle. Dot and Charlie delivered individual servings of tiramisu to everyone, and conversation got back to normal. It wasn't as lively as earlier, but the heavy emotions had lifted.

I sat back and sipped on my third glass of expensive red, my tiramisu half-eaten. Lucian's last few words kept repeating in my mind.

I can't sit here and watch Evie blame herself for something that was not her fault.

No matter how I looked at it, that statement didn't sit right, didn't ring true. I wasn't completely blameless. I couldn't escape the fact that at least some of this was my fault.

I hadn't set out to hurt anyone, hadn't asked to be born this way, with this much Light and connected to such powerful Variants. I would never intentionally hurt anyone.

But at the end of the day, Davis was doing all this precisely because of what I was. He lied, manipulated, and tortured people in his dogged mission to figure out how my Light worked—so he could exploit it for money and power. He'd driven my mother and me from our home and family, from our Vital Bonds. He'd practically started a war between Variants and humans in an attempt to gain more power.

As I sat at the table with my new family, I looked at each one of them. We'd all lost people because of him.

I had two choices.

I could down another bottle of wine, wallow in my self-flagellating misery, and fall deeper into depression.

Or I could fight. I could do whatever I could to show that, despite the fact that my glowing Light could be dangerous, it could be *good* too. Even though I couldn't fully understand it yet, I firmly believed my glowing was a tool. It would only be a negative destructive force if I chose to use it that way.

I couldn't fight Davis with guns and abilities and secrets—Alec, Tyler, and Lucian had that covered. But I could do what I did best: figure out the puzzle. I had to get to the bottom of why I glowed, and I couldn't do it on my own.

It was time to reach out to some of the people who claimed to be able to glow as I did. It was time to put my mind to figuring this shit out.

"We *need* to go to Japan," I announced.

Tyler stopped midsentence to turn to me. His cheeks were a little rosy; the wine was probably getting to him. "Sorry?"

I cleared my throat and raised my voice. "We need to go to Japan. I need to speak to Mr. Takata's grandmother myself. And, Charlie, I need help determining which of those messages I've been receiving are legit and safe to reply to."

"Done." Charlie nodded, not hesitating or questioning me at all. Most likely he'd secretly already started looking into it.

When I looked across the table, Josh had a little smirk pulling at the corner of his lips, his knowing eyes full of pride.

TWENTY-ONE

As usual I lost track of time at the library. It was nearly dusk when I emerged, but when I checked my phone, I was relieved to see I hadn't missed any calls—*Tyler must still be in his office working late.*

My security detail for the day was a young guy with brown hair and a baby face. He'd reluctantly told me his name early in the day and then resisted any further attempts at conversation, insisting on remaining one step behind me wherever I went. That's exactly what he continued to do as I turned my steps toward the admin building.

I hefted my heavy bag higher on my shoulder. The agent didn't offer to help carry anything, and checking out that last book had probably been a mistake. With a statistics assignment due just before we took off for Japan next week, I wouldn't have time to read about the emergence of technology-related Variant abilities anyway. My yawn turned into a groan and my steps slowed. Despite the sun setting, the temperature remained high and sticky. At least with summer in full swing, there weren't as many people on campus. I'd almost had the library to myself.

The lights lining the leafy walking path came on. Dusk was beginning to cast a quiet gray light over everything, throwing twisted shadows from the tall trees.

As I made my way past the cafeteria—which was lit up brightly, bustling with students having their dinner—a couple came out, swinging their own bags over their shoulders. I flashed them a polite smile, but they were caught up in their conversation and didn't see me.

The most direct way to the admin building was down another tree-lined path that cut through the grounds and weaved behind some of the residence halls. Readjusting my bag yet again, I threw the agent a withering look. He just stared at me, his face completely blank.

A few feet along the path, I noticed the couple from the cafeteria heading in the same direction. I could hear their chatter, the occasional light laugh. I looked over my shoulder, making sure they had enough room to pass us if they wanted to.

I made eye contact with the girl and gave her another smile. She was wearing a cute scarf with French Bulldogs all over it and a flowy dress. This time, there was no question she saw my smile, but she still didn't return it. She just watched me with a slight frown as the guy continued to speak to her, his voice low. I faced forward and wrapped both hands around the strap of my bag.

What's her problem? She was probably one of Ethan's exes. They'd significantly backed off when it became known I was his Vital, but some of them were still salty.

I tried to put it out of my mind and think about the pasta waiting for me at home, but when their chatter turned to whispers and then complete silence, a cold chill shot down my spine. I attributed it to the sudden gust of wind, which made the branches above dance grotesquely, but still found my steps speeding up. My emotionless shadow matched my pace.

Any fatigue I'd been feeling was chased away by adrenaline. I looked at my agent again, letting my worry and uncertainty show. He kept his stern gaze fixed ahead and didn't even meet my eye. I eyed his gun and told myself this was why he was here—to protect me if anyone tried anything—but the unsettling feeling wouldn't go away.

All my senses were on alert, my ears listening for any little sound, but I dared not turn around again. As my steps almost doubled in speed, I could clearly hear theirs keeping pace behind me.

We rounded a bend, and the brightly lit square and a corner of the admin building came into view past the trees.

"What makes you think you get to decide who can have Variant abilities and who can't?" a deep male voice growled from behind me.

My heart flew into my throat as the female voice added her own hateful words. "You arrogant bitch!"

Instead of telling them to back off or putting himself between us, my supposed protector *chuckled*.

I didn't think, didn't turn around to argue, didn't even falter in my steps. I just dropped my bag and books and took off running.

My sparring may not have been advancing as well as Kane wanted, and my upper body strength still left much to be desired, but I could *run*. I'd been doing it for years, and it was one thing I had confidence in. I took off so fast and so suddenly that I halved the distance to the end of the path in no time.

But just as fast as I'd taken off, I ground to a halt. Something wrapped around my ankle, and I flew forward. My palms and cheek slammed against gravel.

I didn't focus on the pain shooting through my wrists and head or the fact that all the air had been pushed out of my lungs. I immediately started pushing myself up.

But once again I found myself flying—this time up instead of down. Whatever had wrapped itself around my ankle snaked up my leg and banded around my middle, lifting me clear off the ground until my feet hung below me uselessly.

I thrashed and wriggled as a scream tore through my throat. Desperate, I reached for my distress beacon necklace, but as my hand closed around it, another two branches snatched my wrists and yanked my arms behind me.

I was being restrained by the very grounds of Bradford Hills Institute—tree branches, vines, and shrubs moved like tentacles on a sea monster to hold me hostage.

Tyler's name came out on a screech. He was the closest, in his office in the building I could see *right there*, but I had no idea if he'd be able to hear me.

"Would you shut her up?" the agent growled, his youthful features twisted with hate.

The girl took her scarf off and handed it to the other guy, who rushed up to me. He had to reach up, but his rough hands tied the scarf around my head, the light fabric shoved into my mouth.

The chick wasn't saying much. The muscles in her forearms strained as she held her hands out in front of her, teeth gritted, panting. Clearly, she had some kind of plant-control ability similar to Dot's animal control—the flora to Dot's fauna—but it didn't seem as though either of the guys was her Vital. She looked as if she was using all she had to hold me up. Impressive, to be sure, but I didn't know how long she could maintain it without a Light boost.

The Light!

I gasped. I wasn't completely powerless, despite being bound and gagged.

I dared not close my eyes for fear of missing what their next move might be, but I concentrated as hard as I could, tapping into my own Light deep inside me.

I was going to drain that bitch of every last drop until she released me.

"Shit!" The guy who'd gagged me threaded his hands into his hair, panic evident in his wide eyes. "What the fuck do we do with her now?"

The agent answered. "We get her to Damari so he can fix us."

"How? Do we knock her out? How do we even get her past the guards at the gate? How do we even contact Damari? I don't know him personally, do you? And what about . . ."

"Shut the fuck up!" said the agent. "I'll take care of the guys at the gate, and we can worry about the rest after. Just help me find something to tie her up with. Elena can't hold her forever."

I bit down on the scarf and narrowed my eyes. Just as I began to glow, footsteps came thudding toward us.

I kept my focus on the Variant in front of me, letting my instincts take over and latching on to her distinct energetic signature. Then I *pulled*.

She gasped, her eyes going wide, and wrapped her hands around her middle, as if the action could hold the Light in. But it was at my mercy; she was powerless to stop me now.

The branch around my middle loosened, making it easier to breathe, and the vines circling my wrists were no longer cutting off circulation.

I'd never pulled Light like this before—from a single, direct source that wasn't one of my Bonded Variants. Sure, I'd pulled it from other Variants in Davis's lab and in the gun fight as Alec lay dying at my feet, but those times I'd simply pulled from all directions, letting the Light drain anyone it recognized as a threat.

This was different—it was personal. I wasn't trying to boost my guys' powers, to give us the upper hand in a life-or-death situation. I was using my glowing ability as a *weapon*, homing in on the one person who posed the biggest threat to me and coaxing the Light right out of her.

It was almost too easy.

She fell to her knees and sat back on her heels, folding in on herself. Her arms stayed wrapped around her middle.

As several Melior Group guards ran toward us, she completely lost her grip on her ability. The branches and vines detangled and retreated slowly.

The guards had their guns drawn, yelling at everyone to get down on the ground, but they didn't seem sure of whom to point the weapons at.

On the one hand, it looked as if I was being attacked, but on the other, I was glowing like fucking plutonium as the plant life lowered me to my feet. Meanwhile, the agent who'd turned on me was yelling that I needed to be restrained, confusing the crap out of his colleagues.

The girl—Elena—wavered and toppled to the ground.

"No!" I shouted, dread crawling up my spine to grip my throat. I shut my glow down immediately and stopped pulling Light from her.

I'd wanted to defend myself—I couldn't just hang there and let them kidnap me. It was never my intention to kill her.

I rushed forward, but a black-clad woman stepped into my path, pointing a gun at my chest. "Do not move!"

I froze and put my hands up, but I shifted from foot to foot, my darting eyes trying to take it all in, trying to see if I'd just killed someone.

One agent had a gun trained on me, and the other was checking to see if Elena was OK. When she coughed and moaned, I breathed a shaky breath of relief as my tears spilled over.

Other people started pouring onto the narrow path from both ends, drawn by the shouts and commotion. The two agents were struggling to maintain control of the situation.

"She's the dangerous one!" Elena's friend gestured to me, his other hand in a fist by his side. "We should be tying her the fuck up. Handing her over to Davis Damari. Don't you assholes want abilities?"

"I'm human, dumbass!" another guy shouted.

People started yelling over one another, ignoring the firm demands of the armed guards to remain calm and step back. Some of the Variants seemed to know the couple, and most of them wanted my head—or my Light, as it were.

As more and more people piled into the tight space between the trees, it started to feel like the beginnings of a mob. *Someone should really run and get the torches and pitchforks.*

I took tentative steps back, the leaves and twigs crunching under my feet, as the angry, arguing crowd closed in. More guards arrived, but short of firing weapons, there wasn't much they could do to stop what was fast turning into a riot.

A Variant with super speed blurred through the crowd, and I suddenly found myself restrained once again, my wrists in a tight grip and my shoulders pulled back.

People in the crowd cheered, started pushing forward.

The guard pointing a gun at me faltered, looking between me and my captor with uncertainty. "Everyone calm the fuck down and step back!"

But the yells and angry words of the crowd drowned out her voice. Scuffles began to break out.

"Let me go or I'll drain you," I growled, doing my best to look at the asshole holding me. I caught a glimpse of stubble, a sneering mouth. "I'll drain you like I drained her."

He hesitated, the hands around my wrists loosening just a fraction, but then he yanked me back roughly.

Whatever he was about to say was interrupted by a deafening roar behind us. The crowd immediately quieted down, looking around warily and shuffling backward.

The roar came again, louder, closer. But I couldn't turn to see what was making the terrifying sound. My latest captor finally released me, turning to face the new threat.

The sound of snapping twigs and branches mingled with yet another growl as two towering, dark shapes moved through the shadowed trees.

At the same time the grizzly bears came into the light, Dot and Charlie stepped forward between them, their hands clasped. One of the bears reared up on its hind legs, making us all crane our necks, as the other let out another deafening growl, showing its lethal teeth and jaws.

More fearful shuffling and a few terrified shouts came from behind me, but for the first time, I wasn't scared. These were Dot's animals; there was no way they would hurt me. I looked into my short friend's fierce eyes and gave her a tiny, shaky nod of thanks. She smiled, dropping her death glare, but it was Charlie who spoke.

"Anyone who does not wish to get mauled by a bear tonight should kindly back the fuck away." His voice was calm and even, his free hand in the pocket of his black pants.

Tyler's voice, on the other hand, was full of barely restrained anger. "Why is there a gun pointed at my Vital?"

I turned to see him standing only feet away, his full focus on the agent whose weapon was still trained on me. His jaw was clenched, his hands in tight fists.

I had an intense urge to run to him, feel his comforting arms around me, bury my face in his neck and ignore this whole fucked-up situation. But I stayed back, knowing he needed to take charge and not wanting to distract him.

"I . . . I'm just . . . she was . . ." The agent's wide eyes flicked from me to him uncertainly.

"Agent, lower your weapon. That is a direct order," Tyler barked.

Immediately, she dropped the gun and stood at attention, her lips in a tight line. As Tyler turned his murderous gaze away from her, her eyes narrowed.

There was division in the ranks; Melior Group was falling apart. That sent a shiver down my spine more than anything else—more than the grizzly bears, the people crying for my blood, the guns pointed at my face. When institutions and organizations of that scale and influence began to show cracks, we were all fucked. We were about three weeks away from the Hunger Games. I just wasn't sure if it would be the humans or the Variants killing the other for entertainment.

"I want these four detained." He pointed to my attackers. "Bradford Hills Institute will not tolerate this kind of behavior. We take the safety of *all* our students extremely seriously."

Operatives pushed through the crowd to obey him. He wasn't armed or in a badass black uniform, but Tyler was the most formidable, commanding presence there. I ached to touch him yet again—that authoritative power made me feel safe.

My treacherous bodyguard had remained quiet after failing to immediately convince his colleagues to detain me. He'd shifted farther back into the crowd, but there was no hiding from Tyler. His men brought the man forward as he struggled to get out of their grip.

Tyler looked at him as if he were a sticky piece of shit on the bottom of his shoe. "I'm going to ruin you." His voice was low, menacing, and full of intent. "The rest of you, head back to your residence halls and expect a visit from a Melior Group agent in the next twenty-four hours. Those of you not living on campus, head to the cafeteria for temporary accommodation. The campus is officially on lockdown. No one is to go in or out."

Some people started to move away, warily eyeing Dot's bears, but others grumbled about not being allowed to leave.

"Move!" Tyler bellowed, his patience wearing thin, and the rest of them flinched and scattered.

Once the only people in sight were us and another four agents, Tyler turned to Dot and Charlie. "You can send them home, Dot." He gestured to the bears. "Thank you. Both of you."

"Anything for Eve." Charlie wrapped me up in a hug as Dot shooed the bears away. One of them nuzzled her tiny frame with its giant muzzle as a goodbye.

She shoved her brother out of the way to squeeze her arms around me. "Would you stop trying to get yourself kidnapped?"

We both chuckled, but a cold, heavy weight settled at the bottom of my ribs. It could have been so much worse.

"Kyo and Marcus are at the east gate." Tyler stepped closer. "They'll get you home, but you better hurry before the announcement is blasted through all the speakers."

Dot and Charlie hurried away, and Tyler finally held a hand out to me, his warm gray eyes full of an emotion I couldn't nail down.

I rushed to him, fully intending to wrap myself around him and never let go, but he took my hand firmly in his and set a fast pace toward the admin building, the four agents closing in around us.

TWENTY-TWO

I gripped Tyler's hand and struggled to keep up, but we reached the brightly lit lobby in no time.

Stacey was behind the reception counter, looking harried as Bradford Hills staff and Melior Group staff rushed around. She saw us but kept speaking to the man beside her.

Tyler bypassed the elevators and ushered me into a small meeting room. He slammed the door shut with his foot and finally pulled me into his arms.

As the announcement that the campus was on lockdown reverberated through every speaker on site, Tyler held me close. I buried my face in his neck, curling my arms around his waist and holding tightly to the fabric of his shirt. An arm around my back almost crushed me, and another pressed against the back of my head.

His heartbeat was erratic, a staccato rhythm hammering under my cheek, and his labored breaths fanned over my hair.

We didn't speak. We just held each other. He was my anchor—something to keep me tethered to this world, to keep away the panic once again clawing at my throat.

I focused on his firm grip, his warm breath, the texture of his cotton shirt in my fists. But I didn't close my eyes. If I closed my eyes, I would start to relive it, along with all the other things that resided in that festering, fucked-up, traumatized part of my brain.

The branches restraining me, making it hard to breathe.

The blood pooling around Alec's still body.

The steel bars of a cage in a basement.

Beth getting knocked off her feet.

My mother's stunned face as her hand slipped out of mine.

I had to keep my eyes open, keep my focus on the here and now. Or I'd completely fall apart.

After a few minutes, or maybe it was days, Tyler's heart rate began to slow down, his breathing became more measured. My own inhalations and exhalations matched up to his instinctually.

"Nowhere is safe, is it?" My voice was flat—just stating a fact, even if I posed it as a question.

He loosened his grip and leaned back. His eyes searched mine as his mouth opened, then snapped shut again. Finally he sighed and pressed a kiss to my forehead.

Tyler couldn't lie to me—not anymore—and there was nothing else to say.

The sound of the door opening made us pull apart, and then I was crushed to another broad, strong chest. Alec lifted me clear off the ground, both arms around my middle and his face buried in my neck.

I returned the embrace. It felt good to have him holding me up—both physically and metaphorically. His strength made me feel stronger.

The sound of a female voice made me lift my head. Stacey had followed Alec into the room and was speaking with Tyler in hushed tones, their heads bent together. A Bradford Hills Institute staffer and another Melior Group operative joined us too. The black-clad woman closed the door behind her.

Suddenly, I didn't want to be held off the ground like a child anymore. I wanted to stand on my own two adult feet.

I gave Alec a squeeze and pulled back. Instead of setting me down, he lifted his face and mashed his lips to mine. The kiss was desperate—full of the fear and frustration I was feeling myself. Alec didn't give a shit that we had an audience. He needed to feel me, safe and warm in his arms, needed to reassure himself that I was OK.

I held the back of his head, feeling the demanding strokes of his tongue and the prickles of his buzzed hair under my palm.

Tyler cleared his throat loudly, and we pulled apart. Alec's ice-blue eyes stared me down, searching, but I looked away.

"Faculty and students have all been informed of the lockdown. The protocols are being put into place," the Bradford Hills staffer informed the room as Alec slowly lowered me to the ground.

"All the gates are secured," the woman in black reported, "and we have extra men in place along the perimeter. Every twenty feet, as ordered."

"Can we go home?" I kept my voice low, but we were in a small room and everyone heard me. "I wanna go home."

I wanted to take my Bond and just lock us in a room. What I'd do with all four of them in there, I wasn't entirely sure, but my Light instincts had never done me wrong before. I just wanted them close.

I turned to face Tyler, my eyes pleading.

His expression softened. "Soon, baby."

Stacey gave him an odd look, a slight furrowing of the brows that she quickly wiped off her face. I only saw it because she was standing right next to him, because I was hyperaware of her elbow brushing against his arm as she tapped the tablet in her hands. As usual, she looked sophisticated in a pencil skirt and sweater, though her usually sleek bun had a few bits of hair sticking out of it. That seemed to be the only sign she was stressed.

I moved toward Ty again, but Alec pulled me back, holding me against his chest. I covered his hands at my hips with my own and let him ground me. I needed to be touching at least one of them, and there was a distinct possibility I'd growl at Stacey like one of Dot's bears once I got my hands on Ty.

"We knew there was a risk of some kind of violent or disruptive event," Stacey said to the room, "but considering the circumstances, I think we need to discuss Miss Blackburn—"

"Maynard," Alec and I cut her off at the same time, but I explained, "It's Evelyn Maynard. Can we get that changed, please?" Everyone knew my secrets now anyway. My so-called father had laid me bare for the world to see. Weren't parents supposed to protect their children? Shield them? What a joke.

"Yes, very well." A bit of frustration cut into her perfect demeanor. Stacey didn't appreciate being interrupted.

"As I was saying, I think we need to consider having Miss Maynard take a break from classes."

I looked at her sharply and frowned. "You're kicking me out? But I have a scholarship . . ." Of course this had nothing to do with my academic performance. It just seemed as if it needed to be said: I had a right to be there. I'd worked hard and earned my spot.

"Oh, no, sweetheart." Stacey reached a hand out to me, her expression sympathetic if a little fake. "No one is kicking you out. Your scholarship is secure. What I'm talking about is taking a break. Just until things calm down."

"Until things calm down." I crossed my arms and looked at my feet.

"The safety of the staff and students has to be our primary concern, Eve," Tyler explained, his expression resigned, sad. "After the way you were attacked tonight, I simply don't believe Bradford Hills Institute is a safe place for you anymore. And as much as it frustrates me to say it, removing you from the situation would make the other students safer too."

"Right." I'd crossed my arms in defiance, but now I was hugging myself more than anything. They were right— I was dangerous. I could drain any Variant to death if they pissed me off enough, and the fact that Davis had basically put a bounty on my head meant that anywhere I went, I was at risk of starting a riot.

An indignant part of me wanted to argue. This may never get resolved. It wasn't fair. How was it *my* fault that idiots were getting dragged into Davis's bullshit? Why should I suffer because Melior Group couldn't do their damn jobs? All I ever wanted was to study science and find a place to settle down.

But another, bigger, more sinister part of me understood how naive my indignation was.

"Maybe I should just leave. Permanently." It would be less of a headache for Tyler, Stacey, and the Bradford Hills Institute board if I just quietly went away. There would be less drama, and they wouldn't be forced to take sides in a war that no one would ultimately win.

If I was being honest with myself, none of this would be happening if it wasn't for me. Davis wouldn't be trying to make his own Frankenstein monsters if my mother's Light hadn't shown him it was possible. He wouldn't have started two extremist organizations in his pursuit for answers. He wouldn't have kidnapped all those Vitals. Rick would still be alive. Beth would still be alive. People wouldn't be starting riots in the streets if Davis wasn't so determined to get *me*.

I could just hand myself over to him, but then he would have exactly what he wanted, and I shuddered to think what the world would look like if a man like him had that much power.

Really, this would all go away if I didn't exist.

"Maybe I should just . . ."

I trailed off, not quite able to say the word. The fact that this thought had even crossed my mind scared the absolute shit out of me. My whole world tilted on its axis as cold dread trickled down my spine.

Tyler propped his hands on his hips. "You should just what, Eve?"

He asked and his ability filled him in. His eyes widened in shock, horror, *fear*.

I looked away, willing myself not to cry even as my eyes started to sting from impending tears.

"Evelyn, no one is suggesting you leave permanently." Stacey was oblivious to what had just gone through my mind, but Tyler cut in.

"Don't," he growled, stalking forward to stand directly in front of me. His hands cupped my cheeks and lifted my face until I was looking directly into his intense gray eyes. "Don't you dare think like that, Evelyn."

Panicked, I glanced around as much as his grip would allow, worried he would expose to the whole room the single darkest thought I'd ever had.

But he just said what I needed to hear. "You are mine and I love you. You are the most important thing to me. I won't stand for it. Do you understand?"

I nodded weakly, and Tyler closed the distance, placing a searing kiss on my lips. I wrapped my arms around him, and he didn't stop at what would've been proper in a room full of people. He darted his tongue out and I met it with mine.

Alec had no idea what we were talking about, and he wasn't asking—although I was sure there would be questions later—but he could clearly tell something was wrong. Instead of giving us space, he closed in and pressed his front against my back. Tyler continued to assault my mouth, driving any depressing thoughts right out of my mind for those blissful few moments. I was exactly where I wanted and needed to be—with them.

Tyler broke the kiss and touched his forehead to mine. "I love you," he whispered against my lips. "Please don't leave me."

I took a shuddering breath. He'd gotten to the crux of the matter. If any one of them was taken from me, left me, I would be a mess. A broken twisted mess. How could I possibly do that to them?

When Tyler finally stepped away, giving me some room to breathe, the first person I made eye contact with was Stacey. The other two were averting their gazes, but her full, stunned attention was on me—on us.

I think that was the first time Stacey had seen Tyler and me together—*really* together—the first time she'd glimpsed what it meant to be in a Bond. On some level, I felt a little bad for her; she clearly had a crush on Ty, and I knew what that was like. I was still crushing on him too. But as a human, she could never fully appreciate the level of devotion and connection we shared. We were tethered in every way imaginable and in one way even science couldn't explain—by the Light.

She'd finally seen for herself that she truly had no chance with him. He was mine, always was, and always would be.

With a little cough, she looked down at her tablet. To her credit, she didn't give much away, didn't throw me any jealous looks or childish sneers. She simply fixed one of the many stray hairs that had fallen out of her bun, smoothed down her skirt, and got back to business. I had to admire her strength and professionalism.

Before she could speak again, Tyler did. "Can we finish this conversation tomorrow, Stacey? You have the lockdown under control, and Melior Group are all in place with additional agents called in for backup—all bases are covered. I'll speak with Evelyn about her classes at home, and we can finalize the details tomorrow."

"Of course." She smiled politely. "You should get her home. I have a free hour at eleven tomorrow morning?" She tapped at her tablet, and Ty took out his phone.

"That works. Lock it in."

They set the meeting, Tyler made sure everyone was clear on their orders, and we headed into the underground parking garage.

It wasn't until we were safely inside the house that any of us spoke again.

"Hey! That was a late study session." Ethan flashed me his dimples, meandering out of the living room in sweats. He gave me a quick peck on the lips, then paused, his smile faltering.

Josh appeared in the doorway, also in sweats and a band T-shirt. "What happened?"

He rushed over and gave me a kiss too, holding on to my hand.

Alec was the first to speak, but he didn't answer their questions; he just posed another one.

"What the fuck was that in there?" He looked between Tyler and me, his mouth set in a firm line but his eyes full of fear.

"We have a lot to discuss, but I think we should do it on the plane." Tyler ran his hands through his messy hair—a sure sign of stress.

"Plane?" I asked. Josh, Ethan, and I all turned confused looks on him. "What plane? Didn't you just set a meeting with Stacey?"

"We couldn't risk anyone getting suspicious," Alec answered for him.

"You all know there's a mole in Melior Group." Tyler sighed. "Well, considering tonight's events, things are worse than we thought."

"How?" Josh kept his questions simple and to the point.

"We had agents disobeying direct orders. Some are outright siding with Davis. There's a faction within the organization that believes we should align with him—that his goals for Variants are in line with Melior Group's. It's a load of shit, but it goes as high as management. We can't trust Melior Group anymore. We have to go dark," Tyler explained.

"Dark? What does that mean?" I thought I was being somewhat dramatic when I said nowhere was safe anymore, but it looked as if I was more right than I thought.

"We're gonna run." Alec took my other hand and gave me a sad smile.

"We were planning a trip to Japan anyway." Tyler shrugged. "We just have to move it up from next week to, well, right now. And we'll have to take a roundabout way to get there."

"Get packing, you three," Alec barked.

Instead of obeying, Ethan crossed his arms over his big chest. "Is someone going to tell us what the fuck happened?"

Alec's eyes narrowed, but I stepped between them. "I'll fill them in while they pack. My go-bag is ready anyway."

"Of course it is." Alec chuckled darkly as I led the way up the stairs. It felt good to have a task, something to keep my mind off the dark thoughts threatening to creep back in at any moment.

I gave the guys the abridged version of the evening's events, sticking to the facts and leaving out my insidious thoughts. After several bone-crushing hugs and my repeated assurances that I was fine—something I wasn't entirely convinced of myself—they reluctantly left my side to go pack.

I rushed through a quick shower, washing off the heat of the day and the mess of the evening. Meticulously and precisely, I tied my damp hair back, dressed in simple dark clothing, and grabbed my go-bag from the bottom of my wardrobe. I didn't give myself time to slow down and think. Our best chance to get away undetected would be under the cover of darkness, and we had to hurry.

I rushed downstairs, worried I was holding everyone up because of my shower, but I still beat Ethan and Josh. They came jogging down the stairs just as I reached the bottom.

Once we'd all converged in the foyer, I unzipped the front pocket of my backpack and handed each of them a new passport with a new identity.

"Oh, right." Ethan took his wallet out of his pocket, stared at it as if he didn't know what it was for a second, then dropped it onto the side table.

"Jonathon MacLaine?" Alec scoffed, but his eyes danced with amusement.

I gave him a smile and shrugged. I'd toyed with the idea of giving them all action hero–adjacent names but decided against it. This was serious, and I took it seriously. Unfortunately, Alec's *Die Hard* identity was already created by the time I came to that conclusion.

"These are really good, Eve. Thank you." Josh tucked his new passport into his pocket just as Lucian came rolling out of his wing.

"OK, you're all set." He came to a stop before us. "The more stops you make, the better, but you're leaving at night and when no one expects it, so that'll help. Evelyn, do you have those new passports you've been working on?"

"Yes, Uncle Luce."

Everyone held up their new documents, but Lucian was already barreling on. "Just keep your heads down, and don't draw attention to yourselves."

"We know." I went to stand in front of him.

"Crowds are good if you need to lose a tail and—"

"Uncle Lucian," I cut him off, taking his hand in mine. "We know."

I'd spent my entire childhood doing this. Alec and Tyler were highly trained. Ethan and Josh weren't idiots.

He took my hand in both of his and sighed. "Please just . . . be careful. I can't lose any more family."

He gave us all a pointed look, and I leaned down to hug him. He held me close before finally letting go.

Tyler cleared his throat. "I've informed Mr. Takata, through a secure channel, that we're on our way. The only decision left to make is how we actually get off the property."

"Well, then you're lucky I'm here." Olivia strode out of the back of the house, purse over her shoulder, wearing a tracksuit and a determined expression.

"Olivia came to make sure I eat a decent meal for dinner." Lucian rolled his eyes, but I could tell he was happy to have his sister around more. "We're lucky the garage was open when she showed up. No one will see you all getting into her SUV, and no one will question her leaving now."

Once again, Olivia ended up playing my getaway driver. She was much calmer about it this time—no nervousness or second thoughts, no muttering to herself or questioning her decision. She just kept her eyes on the road, and we all crouched in the back.

When the car finally stopped, she paused, pretending to rifle through her purse. "Take care of my boys, Evie."

Then she got out of the car and walked away.

They didn't need taking care of. They were the ones with incredible, dangerous abilities. She was just telling me in her own way to be strong—that she believed in me.

We waited for ten minutes, then slunk out of the car into a sprawling department store parking lot. There weren't many people around but plenty of cars.

By the time I'd gotten my bearings, Alec had already disappeared without a sound, and Ethan and Josh were making their way over to the next row of cars.

Tyler tugged on my arm, two helmets held in his other hand. He led me to a motorbike parked in a dark corner and swung his leg over. If there was any doubt in my mind that we were about to steal a motorcycle, it was wiped away once he started to hotwire it.

I settled in behind him as the engine came to life.

He grabbed my arms and wrapped them tightly around his waist as he turned to flash me a grin. "This time I don't have to pretend I don't want your hands all over me."

Despite the tense situation, I laughed. "This time I don't have to feel bad about groping you."

I reached between his legs and gave him a gentle yet confident squeeze. He chuckled and pulled his helmet on, forcing me to abandon my grip on the growing hardness to do the same, and we were off.

We drove to Boston, switching vehicles several times, sometimes splitting up into different groups. Josh booked tickets on a flight to Japan as we drove, and we arrived at the airport with plenty of time to clear customs and passport control without a hitch. My fakes were damn good.

TWENTY-THREE

When we got to the gate, most of the passengers still hadn't been called for boarding. Business class was being given priority, so we got in line behind half a dozen other business-class people and waited.

Ethan had his face in a cooking magazine, his bicep bulging. I smiled at him indulgently and leaned into Josh, but when I rested my head against his shoulder, it felt tense. I looked up at him. The expression on his face was one of careful concentration, his full attention on something over his shoulder.

I followed his gaze to the reception desk. In front of the counter stood a woman with short black hair, dressed impeccably in slacks and a white business shirt. She was saying something to the young woman behind the counter, gesturing with her hands. She looked upset, and even though I couldn't make out what she was saying, I had a feeling it wouldn't be long before everyone could.

"Shit." I gripped Josh's arm a little tighter, glancing around the busy terminal, clocking the exits.

Without tearing his gaze away from the unfolding scene—as predicted, the woman was beginning to raise her voice—Josh inclined his head and called out quietly, "Gabe?"

"I see it." Tyler sounded as if he was close behind me, which made me feel a bit safer.

"What?" Ethan whipped his head up, the magazine still clutched in both hands.

The woman's voice finally raised to an audible volume, answering Ethan's question.

". . . not be that difficult!" She huffed, slapping her hand on the counter and propping the other on her hip.

Around us, conversations hushed as others started to take notice, making the flight assistant's response easy to hear.

"Ma'am, as I already explained, the economy section of the flight is full. I simply can't move you. You're welcome to book another flight, but we are under no obligation to accommodate your request."

"This is ridiculous." Again she huffed, her voice more high-pitched. "You have a duty of care to your passengers. I have a *right* to feel safe. How can you expect me to sit next to a . . . *person*"—she spat the word—"like that?"

"We do not ask people if they are human or Variant when they buy their tickets, and we certainly don't segregate our flights as such. That would be against the law. Now, you can either lower your voice and board the flight or you can purchase another ticket, but if you continue to behave in an aggressive manner—"

"Don't you threaten me!" The woman wagged her finger in the young girl's face.

"Motherfucker," Alec growled. He was standing on my other side, watching the scene unfold with a scowl.

An older woman joined the young girl behind the counter. The boarding was getting delayed, and people were becoming fidgety.

"I demand to be moved to a seat that's not next to a *Dime*, or I want a full refund!"

Several people gasped at the derogatory term, but a few exchanged sympathetic looks. One person even nodded.

Fear jolted down my spine.

The fact that seemingly normal businesswomen felt it was acceptable to say that word and demand to be kept away from humans in such a public way was downright terrifying. People were losing their fucking minds.

"If you don't lower your voice, you will not be permitted to board this flight." The older worker's tone was firm, her mouth set in a hard line.

Before the woman could go on another rant, a man stepped up to the counter. He was middle-aged, his hair more salt than pepper, and dressed casually in jeans and sneakers. A backpack was slung over his shoulder.

"Excuse me." He leaned forward, extending a hand to get their attention but keeping a safe distance. "I'm happy to take a later flight, if that's possible. I really don't want any trouble."

Tyler grumbled something under his breath as he stepped around us and went to the other end of the counter.

"*Don't touch me.*" The woman flinched away from the man dramatically, disgust all over her face. He took a step back, his hands out in front of him, and sighed in frustration.

The ground staff started talking again, explaining that the circumstances wouldn't allow them to move either person to another seat or flight—it was outside the airline's guidelines. The younger woman looked as if she was calling security on a walkie-talkie as the other staff began boarding the business-class passengers.

Meanwhile, Tyler stood tall and confident at the other end of the counter, speaking calmly to the man at the computer. Within minutes, he was handing the attendant a wad of cash. When he had his change, Tyler took two steps to reach the commotion.

"Excuse me." His loud, authoritative voice demanded everyone's attention. "I'd like to assist. I don't believe anyone should be subjected to sitting next to such an abhorrent person for any period of time, let alone a long-haul international flight. I've taken the liberty of purchasing a business-class ticket."

He spoke to no one in particular, addressing the group with one hand in his pocket. He was casual but commanding. Calm but intense.

The woman crossed her arms and threw a smug look at the human man and the ground staff. "I'm glad some people understand what—"

She was cut off by the younger flight assistant stepping up to the counter and addressing the casually dressed man. "Here is your new boarding pass, sir. Your section is now boarding. We apologize for the inconvenience." She smiled professionally as he slowly took the boarding pass, a stunned look on his face.

He looked at Tyler and smiled tentatively. "Th . . . thank you."

"My pleasure." Ty smiled, and they walked back to us together, getting in line just as it moved forward.

The woman snapped out of her shock and *lost her shit* just as four security personnel rushed to the scene. They dragged her away kicking and screaming as several people clapped and cheered.

I beamed at my man, so proud. As he rejoined us, I took his hand and gave him a kiss on the cheek. "You're a good man, Tyler Gabriel," I whispered in his ear.

"I'm just sick of watching this shit get worse and worse." He frowned as his fingers tightened around mine. "We need to start standing up for one another. If ignorant people are going to get more brazen in their bigotry and hatred, we need to get more bold in the way we stand up for what's right."

~

Thankfully, the flight was completely uneventful, even free from turbulence. It wasn't as luxurious as the flight we took in Melior Group's private jet on the way back from Australia, but it was still better than most of the flights I'd been on. Being able to stretch out and lie down was pure heaven.

We landed in Tokyo in the middle of the night. I wanted to call Mr. Takata and head to his grandmother's village immediately, but the guys insisted on petty things like showers and sleep.

In order to avoid drawing any more attention to ourselves, we decided not to book a suite, opting instead to go with three regular rooms in a hotel. They were pretty small—we were in Japan after all.

After several rounds of aggressive rock-paper-scissors, Ethan won the privilege of sharing a room with me. He threw me over his shoulder and carried me into it along with all our luggage, making me laugh too loudly for a hotel hallway late at night.

His feet hung off the end of the mattress, but he snuggled into my side and fell asleep quickly. Unfortunately, finding my own sleep was more difficult. My mind raced: Were we careful enough getting here? What would tomorrow hold? I slept in fits and starts, and when the gray morning light peeked in through the curtains, I got out of bed.

After a shower, I called room service and ordered enough food for all of us in a whisper, trying to let Ethan sleep as long as possible. Then I called the others and told them to meet us in our room. Tyler grunted, and I heard him call Josh's name as he hung up. Alec had already been up for an hour and been to the gym.

The food arrived just before the rest of my guys did, and for the first time, I was the one delivering breakfast in bed to Ethan. I may not have made it myself, but I ordered the fuck out of it like a pro. It totally counted.

He somehow managed to sleep through the room service being delivered and the others filing into the cramped space. Alec took the desk chair, Josh made himself comfortable on the ground, and Tyler leaned on the headboard next to Ethan, each of them holding a plate of eggs and pastries.

With a warm, delicious-smelling chocolate croissant in hand, I climbed on top of Ethan, straddling his hips. I waved the croissant under his nose as I kissed the stubble on his jaw.

He took a deep breath and groaned lightly. Lazily, his hands went to my hips, and he shifted me just a little lower—until I was settled over his morning wood.

I chuckled, and his mouth and eyes opened at the same time. He took a quick bite of the pastry before leaning up and planting a kiss on my lips.

"Delicious." His voice was croaky and deep—all kinds of sexy.

"Me or the croissant?" I teased.

"Hmm. Not sure. I think I need another taste." He took another bite of the croissant, but instead of kissing me, he pulled at the hem of my shorts, giving me that cheeky grin that made his dimples appear—

and usually made my clothes *dis*appear.

"We have company," I informed him.

He looked around the room and shrugged. "They can watch. Or join in."

His hands traveled up my sides, cupping my breasts.

"If you don't eat these eggs, I'm going to," Alec announced.

I climbed off Ethan. He groaned in protest, but Alec's mention of eggs reminded me I was hungry too. One basic need at a time.

We polished off all the food and ordered more.

Ethan went to shower while we waited, and I planted myself on Alec's lap, studying the tourist map and pointing things out past the window.

"The Imperial Palace is that way, and just past that is Tokyo Tower." I consulted the map again. "And just a few blocks that way is Shibuya Crossing." I knew they hadn't been back since the accident, but I wanted them to know I was there for them. "We can go there if you guys want to. We can make time."

"No." Alec didn't hesitate. His voice wasn't hard or angry, just sure. "You guys can go if you want to, but I won't. I want to remember them for how they lived. Not how they died."

I stared at his profile as he looked out the window. My Master of Pain could be really poetic when he wanted to be.

"I have no interest in seeing it again," Tyler agreed.

"Me neither," Josh murmured before taking another sip of coffee.

"Yeah, fuck that!" Ethan yelled from the bathroom, proving how thin the walls were in this tiny room.

I hugged Alec and gave him a kiss on the cheek.

"Evie, are you OK?" he murmured against my cheek.

Tyler had filled them in on my dark thoughts after I was attacked. They'd all chastised, pleaded, and questioned me every chance they got while we traveled. I'd been brushing them off, trying to tell them I was fine, but they just weren't dropping it. I sighed and looked away. Tyler and Josh were both staring at me; Ethan was leaning in the doorway to the bathroom, a towel wrapped around his hips.

"Not really," I finally answered, deciding to be honest. "But I'm going to be, and I'm already feeling better than I was last night. Can we just focus on why we're here? One crisis at a time." Being around them, seeing the concern in their eyes, really had made me feel better.

Reluctantly, Alec nodded and gave me another gentle kiss.

More food arrived, and we talked about lighter topics until I received a text message from Mr. Takata; he was waiting for us in the lobby.

We packed up and headed down, dressed in comfortable clothing light enough for a walk in the Japanese wilderness in the middle of summer. I wasn't entirely sure where his grandmother lived, but he'd mentioned it was remote.

In the lobby, Mr. Takata greeted us with the same level of respect and reverence as when we first met, bowing low.

I returned the gesture.

"How was your flight?" he asked as Alec went to reception to check us out.

"There was some drama at the gate—a loud-mouthed, entitled Variant—but the flight itself was fine, and we've had most of the night to rest. I'm excited to get going. I can't wait to meet your grandmother."

He smiled. "She is very eager to meet you also."

"Careful what we discuss in public." Tyler leaned in, giving us meaningful looks.

"Naturally." Mr. Takata inclined his head. "And just so you're aware, my security team will be accompanying us most of the way."

Tyler frowned, clearly not too happy about men with guns being in our general vicinity, but Mr. Takata waved him off. "It is a small team of three men whom I trust implicitly. They have been with me for over twenty years, and one of them is a cousin. I have not told them of your situation, but they have been briefed to defend your life as they would mine, Evelyn—with their own lives."

"Thank you. I really appreciate that."

"Yes." Tyler finally nodded decisively, satisfied with whatever extra information his ability had provided. "Thank you."

Mr. Takata led us out front to a black van with tinted windows. We all piled into the back, with two of Mr. Takata's men in the front. The third man was to follow behind discreetly.

We drove west for hours until the city disappeared, replaced by low buildings and residential streets, then verdant green hills and traditional dwellings. The road continued to narrow, going from a six-lane freeway to, eventually, rough gravel and dirt.

We stopped once for a toilet break and once for lunch at a small ramen restaurant on the side of the road. The owner spoke no English, but the ramen was amazing. Ethan had two bowls.

Around three in the afternoon, just as the road was becoming unbearably bumpy and slow, the van came to a stop.

"From here, we walk." Mr. Takata got out of the van and strapped on his backpack. We followed suit. Two of his men took off into the trees, following a narrow path, while the third waited patiently to bring up the rear.

Mr. Takata took the lead. Tyler shot everyone a stern look I wasn't sure how to interpret, but they arranged themselves so I was surrounded as we hiked. Tyler walked with Mr. Takata, Ethan kept pace with me, and Alec and Josh stayed close behind us.

No one spoke, all of them on high alert, and Mr. Takata abandoned his attempts at small talk quickly. I understood why they were cautious—we were in the middle of nowhere, in an unfamiliar place. This would be the perfect opportunity for an ambush or a double-cross. But I trusted Mr. Takata, and Tyler's ability would certainly warn us of any danger.

I was really excited to meet another Vital like me—one that had more Variants than was supposed to be possible and glowed like a nightlight. Nothing was going to ruin my mood. I took in the tall trees, listened to the birds singing, breathed the fresh air. Despite the heat, it was invigorating, especially after sitting in a van most of the day.

The uphill path was wide and clear—wide enough for a small horse and cart but way too narrow and uneven for a car. Maybe an ATV could've worked?

I'd never had even a passing interest in ATVs, but an hour into the trek, that was all I could think about through my panting and sweating. Training with Kane was no joke, but this kind of prolonged, long-distance style of exercise—*up a hill*—was way more than I was used to.

Ethan was fine, even with both our packs slung over his broad shoulders, and Alec hadn't even broken a sweat. Tyler and Josh were starting to breathe heavily, and Mr. Takata was struggling about as much as I was.

Still, none of us seemed willing to stop for a break. A heavy tension had settled over our group, probably due to how suspicious my guys were, how leery they were being. I couldn't blame Mr. Takata for wanting to get to our destination as soon as possible, and I couldn't blame them for wanting to determine whether we were really safe here or not.

My legs burned, but the promise of what awaited me on the other side pushed me forward.

After nearly two hours of walking, the trees thinned. Mr. Takata's pace slowed considerably, and we all had long drinks of water.

Voices and the sounds of life started to reach my ears, and I couldn't stop the smile from breaking over my face.

In my excitement, I tried to rush forward, but Ethan caught me by the hand and held me firmly in place, in the middle of their protective circle.

"Welcome to Urahidaka," Mr. Takata announced. We emerged onto the outskirts of the most picturesque place I'd ever seen.

The houses were mostly wooden, built close together near the center of the village and more sparsely at the edges. Smoke rose from several chimneys, which jutted up from thatched and tiled roofs. Goats and geese wandered as freely as the villagers along cobblestone streets. The village was set into the side of a hill overlooking a valley. A few fat white clouds floated by lazily, but the afternoon sun cast a golden glow over the whole scene.

The air was crisp and fresh, tinged with that light hint of smoke and animal smell that was so unmistakably "countryside." The faint, steady sound of running water indicated a nearby stream we couldn't see.

It was like a postcard!

"It's so beautiful," I breathed. Standing there, looking at the calm valley, the Japanese maples swaying in the light breeze, I could almost pretend all the horrible things happening in the rest of the world weren't real. How could they be when this valley and this village sat here so peacefully?

A middle-aged woman rushed up to us. Her hair was tied back neatly, and she wore a plain yukata.

"*Konnichiwa. Youkoso,*" she greeted us and bowed to each person individually.

"*Konnichiwa.*" My Japanese was rusty, but I still remembered the basics. I bowed a little lower than she did as a sign of respect.

"This is Youko, my cousin. Our grandmother lives with her and her family. She will take us to her home now," Mr. Takata explained in English.

She gestured politely down the cobbled path toward the squat buildings, and we followed. We passed through the village's main square, which was centered around what looked like a few teahouses and one small grocery store. A large cherry blossom tree grew in the very middle.

After passing down several winding lanes, we stopped at a house. It was similar to all the others in the area—slightly raised and mostly constructed of wood with a tiled roof. A front garden displayed an array of brightly colored, artfully arranged plants.

After we all took our shoes off, Youko led us inside. Most of our group had to duck their heads in order to pass through the doorway.

The home was as traditional inside as it was outside—tatami mats, low tables, and cushions to sit on. As we rounded the corner into the main living space, I froze, my eyes going wide.

If any doubt lingered in my mind about Mr. Takata's story or motives, one look at the elderly woman in front of me instantly dispelled it.

Her face was creased, her white, almost translucent hair tied into a knot. She hunched slightly over the gnarled hands she'd folded neatly in her lap.

She looked like any number of dignified, old Japanese women, but what made her remarkable—what had me gasping—was her glow.

It wasn't nuclear. It wasn't the warm white that emanated from my skin when I was under extreme pressure or, lately, when I called it up intentionally. No, this was a very subtle, almost hazy luminescence that seemed to hover around her.

I didn't have to check with everyone else in the room—I was pretty certain I was the only one who could see it. I felt drawn to her, inexplicably connected in a way that was bigger than both of us, bigger than *all* of us. In a way we weren't capable of understanding yet, no matter how hard we studied or how rigorous our scientific process was.

This was *pure Light*.

I knew she could do what I could do, because I felt it in every fiber of my being.

I moved forward. Her eyes fixed on me as mine did her, completely ignoring everyone else in the room. They all had the presence of mind to remain silent.

I dropped to my knees in front of her and bowed low. "*Konnichiwa. Watashi wa* Evelyn *desu.*" Fumblingly, I expressed my gratitude for her time and for welcoming us into her home.

A light touch brushed the back of my head, and I rose into a sitting position, resting my butt on my heels.

Her hand dropped to my shoulder—a very familiar, even *familial* gesture. She had tears in her eyes as she looked at me for a long moment.

I must've had the same hazy luminescence she did. How long had it been since she'd seen another glowing Vital? I'd never come across another my whole life, and I'd traveled the world. She'd lived most of her life in this remote village. Had she *ever* seen one?

"My name is Tomoko Takata. It is a pleasure and an honor to meet another *azayakana* again. You bring an old lady much joy."

She spoke in Japanese, but I understood most of it, only tripping up on a few words.

"*Azayakana?*" I turned to Mr. Takata, frowning. "I'm sorry. My Japanese is mediocre at best."

He smiled and stepped forward. "The best translation into English is 'Vivid.' It is the word that is used to describe Vitals who glow, such as you."

"Vivid." I smiled to myself. It was kind of appropriate.

I turned back to Mrs. Takata. I had so many questions, and for the first time, I was in front of someone who could actually answer them.

TWENTY-FOUR

Before I could start barraging the old lady with questions, her granddaughter insisted she show us to the bathrooms to freshen up.

"It is nearly dinner time. By the time you finish in the bathroom, I will have dinner on the table."

Dutifully, we all followed her to the small bathroom in the back of the house and took turns. It was basic, but it had running water—an impressive feat considering how remote the village was.

I changed out of my sweaty clothes, splashed some water on myself, and tied my hair back into a braid.

The living space was abuzz with chatter when I came back. Several low tables were laden with food. There was room for everyone, including Youko's husband and daughter and Mr. Takata's three bodyguards.

Mrs. Takata was at the head of the table. She waved me over and patted a cushion next to her, so I settled myself down between her and Tyler. The rest of the guys spread themselves out among our gracious hosts.

The delicious spread contained a plethora of traditional Japanese dishes, such as noodle soup with vegetables, steamed trout, marinated duck, and of course, plenty of steamed rice. As the plates emptied, several carafes of sake appeared. I clinked glasses with Mr. Takata and took a drink, doing my best not to wince at the strong alcohol.

I managed to fumble through some chitchat with his family and grandmother in Japanese, but my knowledge of the language was far too lacking to have the kind of conversation I wanted to have with her.

"Would you mind translating for me?" I asked Mr. Takata.

He nodded and waited for me to speak.

I chewed on my lip, suddenly unsure where to start. I had so many questions; they were all trying to elbow to the forefront of my mind, creating a bottleneck.

Something had been bugging me since I first laid eyes on her, so I decided to start there. "Can you please ask her why I could tell she was Vivid—why I could see luminescence around her, but I couldn't see it on my mother? She was like us too."

Dutifully, Mr. Takata translated the discussion I'd been waiting to have since that day on the empty train platform.

"Your mother has not been around since you met your Bond?"

Technically, we'd "met" as kids, but I was pretty sure that wasn't what she meant. "My mother died before I knew what I was."

She nodded and patted my hand. "You did not see your mother's glow because you had not yet formed your Bond. The Bond makes us stronger in all things, especially our connection to the Light."

"Does she know what it is? The glow? What am I?"

"You are a Vital. There is no question about that. You have the Light and you have a Bond. Your Light shines brighter than others'. It is Vivid. You are Vivid."

"Are there others like us? Has she met others? Why does no one know about this?"

"I knew two others—many years ago—a woman from a village nearby and a man from very far away. They told me of others but not very many. Both of them died in World War II. There have been no other Vivids in younger generations that I know of. In my time, it was something that was not understood, but it was respected. It was said that the glow was sent to us by God, his way of shining his light on our village and sending us strength. It was said that the birth of a Vivid heralded both a great blessing and a grave warning. Death and danger were sure to come, but God had sent us a Vivid to protect us. And indeed, my Bond and I had to do many things to protect our families, our village, our country. But when there is peace, there is no need for the Vivids. We have had a great many years of peace."

I nodded, my mind whirling with the practical applications of what she was saying. What was the most probable scientific explanation?

I turned to Tyler. "Evolution? Could it be as basic as the idea that nature is compensating for the loss of life by providing a line of defense?"

"It makes sense." He nodded, leaning his elbows on the table. "This could be a Variant DNA quirk. When certain levels of cortisol are in the pregnant mother's system, indicating high levels of stress, it could result in the baby being born Vivid. But that doesn't account for all the stresses of life. Why aren't women in domestic violence situations giving birth to Vivids?"

"Maybe there needs to be more at play? I mean, we don't really fully understand the Light. Maybe it has a better sense of what's happening in the world than we do? But I'm not sure if that adds up either. While most of the Western world has had relative peace for decades, how do you explain the fact that there haven't been any reports of Vivids popping up in the Middle East, for example?"

"Maybe there have been," Josh jumped in. "But the number of Variants relative to humans is much lower in that part of the world, thanks to the discriminatory laws during the sixties and seventies. A lot of Variants flee that area. And if it's dangerous to even have a common ability like super speed, I doubt anyone would be shouting from the rooftops that they can *glow*."

"True." I nodded and turned back to Mrs. Takata. "Do you know why the world is so oblivious to our existence? Why there aren't even any mentions in history books?"

"The Lighthunters." She smiled and took a sip of her sake.

Lighthunters? The time we'd spent with Nina a few months prior had certainly confirmed they were real, but any time I'd tried to question her more deeply about her nature, she'd managed to artfully change the topic.

She'd told me all I wanted to know about Variant Bonds, my own Bond and the connections within it, how to follow my instincts when it came to the Light, even about her own Lighthunter abilities. She was a well of knowledge, but sitting there, I realized just how well she'd avoided my questions about other Lighthunters and why the world thought they were a myth.

"I'm sorry. I don't understand." I frowned. "What do the Lighthunters have to do with it?"

"They are called Lighthunters because they are most well-known for finding the threads, connecting the Bonds. But they are also our protectors. Or they were. They shielded us from those who thought Vivids were dangerous, who thought it wasn't natural to have that much Light. They did a very good job hiding us, and we were so rare already. Then there were fewer and fewer Vivids being born. I hadn't heard of a single other like me until my grandson came with news of an extraordinary American girl." She smiled at him, then at me, the deep laugh lines around her eyes and mouth crinkling. By this stage, the whole table had fallen silent, their full attention on the matriarch and her wisdom.

"It is not surprising to me that between how rare we are and the Lighthunters' work, the world simply . . . forgot."

"I remembered." Mr. Takata spoke in Japanese, but the words were simple enough that I understood them. "I remembered your stories, grandmother."

She patted him on the hand, pride in her eyes.

"Please excuse me if this is rude, but where are your Variants?" I asked before I could stop myself. I had a feeling I knew the answer, since none of them were by her side.

"Passed. All four of them. Two were killed a very long time ago, one died in an accident, and one about fifteen years ago from old age."

I looked down the table at my Bondmates—my strong, beautiful, fiercely protective men. I couldn't imagine losing any of them. The mere thought sent pain shooting through my chest, and I involuntarily rubbed the spot. When I turned back to face the old woman, she was watching the hand at my breastbone.

"Yes, it is painful. Your connection is strong. You would not be Vivid without it." She stared into my eyes as though she could see right into my soul. I remained silent.

"You were made to make them strong." She gestured down the table with a swoop of her hand. "But they make you strong too. They cannot do what they do without your Light, but you cannot do what you do without them. That is why Vivids have more Variants in their Bonds than regular Vitals do. With practice, you may have learned to draw and transfer Light without a Bond, but it would have required an extreme amount of focus, would have been very taxing on your body. I have not glowed since my Variants died. I am old and weak and no longer have their strength to make it possible. Your Bond is the same. You can take not only from them but from all sources of Light around you because they give so freely. It is the ultimate symbiotic relationship."

"I make them strong, but they make me strong too." I parroted her words, and she nodded. I'd never thought of it like that, but it made sense.

In a regular Bond, the Vital channeled the Light and transferred it to their Variants; the Vital made the Variants strong. But in a Vivid Bond—in our Bond—they also made me strong. I could take from one and transfer to another. I could draw Light into me simply by willing it to come, and I could push it out to them without moving a muscle. The longer I'd been with them, the stronger our connection had grown, the easier it had become.

Yes, training helped, but my Light undeniably became more a part of me the more I used it. Every time my Bond and I got closer physically, mentally, emotionally, spiritually, I got stronger.

I brought us all together, tied us irrevocably to each other. I made them stronger than they ever could've been alone.

But they provided the foundation on which our collective strength was built. Each one of them was a solid, unwavering pillar in his own way.

Ethan always craved family, and when we found each other, he was immediately all in. I represented what he'd lost and all that he could have in the future. I was family, and he was devoted heart and soul.

Josh observed everything quietly from behind his clean-cut look and his books. It was his way of feeling in control in a chaotic world that had taken his parents away. But I saw the real him. From the start, I saw who he truly was, and I loved him for it. We showed each other that letting go of control could be freeing.

No one exercised greater control than Tyler. He'd resisted the pull from the first moment, before he even knew what it was. He'd continued resisting after he knew everything, even the things I didn't, even when it required him to sacrifice his own wants and needs. Because that was what was best for me, best for all of us. We'd needed time, and Tyler had made sure we'd had it.

Alec had been there from the start. And I don't mean that day in the hospital after the crash; I mean the *very start*, when we were all kids and had no idea of the hurdles we'd have to jump in order to be together. He was the one who'd made this possible. Because he never gave up on me, even when he knew it would make him more the monster he believed himself to be. Even when he resented it, he kept looking for me. He yearned for me and what I represented.

And he yearns still.

He was engaged in a conversation with Mr. Takata's cousin, but as though he felt my gaze on him, he looked up and met my eyes.

He'd been an asshole—a jerk of epic proportions. We'd both made mistakes, and he'd hurt me more than I thought possible. But he'd also changed. He'd worked his ass off to let me in, to embrace our Bond. He'd told me he loved me, and he'd been showing it every day since. Even as I continued to push him away. Even as I told the others I loved them.

Even as *I* continued to hurt *him*.

"You all must be exhausted." Mr. Takata's cousin started clearing the table. "Let me show you where you will sleep."

Youko and her family were staying with her husband's family, giving up their entire home so my Bond, Mr. Takata, and his security guys could have somewhere to sleep. We were set up in the biggest room in the back, on futon mattresses. A paper screen provided the only privacy.

All five of us were to sleep in the same room together. We'd never done that before—not intentionally. I'd shared a bed with more than one of them on numerous occasions, and there had been those few times, usually after someone tried to kill one of us, that we'd all ended up in the same room. Some of them usually wound up squished on a couch or making do with a pillow on the floor.

But this was the first time we were essentially all sleeping in the same bed.

We were strangely quiet as we got ready for sleep, taking turns in the bathroom, undressing, getting under the covers. Maybe it was because we were so tired, or because the walls were literally paper thin and we could hear Mr. Takata snoring lightly in the main living area.

I wasn't sure where the silence was coming from, but it didn't feel uncomfortable, and I couldn't stop smiling.

Naturally, I ended up in the middle, with Tyler on one side and Josh on the other. Ethan was behind Josh;

Alec on the other side of Tyler. The others fell asleep quickly, but I lay on my back, feeling safe and *right* between them but unable to sleep despite how tired I was.

Yes, the new information was running through my mind, making a million new questions pop up. But mostly, I couldn't stop thinking about Alec.

He was just on the other side of Tyler, but he felt so far away. That was my fault.

I felt it, so why couldn't I say it? It had come so easily with the others, so why was it so damn hard with him to wrap my mouth around those words?

Careful not to wake the others, I lifted myself onto my elbows. I just wanted a glimpse of his face, the strong jaw, the scar through the eyebrow, the tiny kink in his nose.

But when I looked over, his stunning ice-blue eyes were staring right back at me. Alec was on his back, one arm propped behind his head, the blanket pushed down around his hips. He was just as wide awake as me.

At the same time, we smiled, an exchange that wordlessly said both "Why aren't you sleeping?" and "You can't sleep either?"

I sighed lightly and inclined my head toward the door, raising my brows.

He nodded and, with lithe, completely soundless movements, managed to get up without jostling the three sleeping men jammed into bed with us. I knew he was highly trained in how to be super stealthy and shit, but that was seriously impressive. I'd have to get him to teach me how to do that.

I crawled over Tyler much less gracefully while Alec silently laughed at me. I flipped him off as I grabbed a light cardigan off the top of my bag and he pulled on a pair of pants.

I led the way through the house, past the sleeping men in the main room, and out the front door. Alec closed it softly.

He was in nothing but a black pair of pants; I was in a tank, shorts, and my loose cardigan. Thankfully, the cobblestones were still warm on my toes from the hot summer sun, and it was a mild night.

We threaded our fingers together and slowly wandered down the curving lane. There were no streetlights, and half the houses probably didn't even have electricity, but the light of the moon was more than enough to light our way. At the end of the lane, warm stones gave way to soft grass as we reached the edge of a wide grassy knoll, the beginning of the steep hill into the valley.

Darkness stretched below us in the valley, but above, billions of stars shone down from a magnificent, cloudless sky, taking my breath away.

For all my travel, I'd never been in a place with so little light pollution. I knew how vast the universe was—how many stars, planets, and other celestial bodies were visible in our night sky—but I'd never seen it so clearly.

The curve of the Milky Way started behind the blue-black outline of the mountains across the valley, then curved above us to disappear somewhere to our backs and to the left. I craned my neck to follow it, my mouth hanging open in awe. Alec wrapped his arms around me from behind, and I rested my head on his chest, just staring up.

I picked out several constellations and planets: Ursa Major, Pegasus, and the brightly glowing, slightly reddish spot that was Mars, some 33.9 million miles away.

If the lifetime of the universe were put into the span of a day, humans would have only existed for the past four seconds. Thinking about that made all the drama and conflict around us feel somehow lighter. When all this was over and no one even remembered our names, the universe would still be shining bright; the Earth would still be here. Life would go on.

The longer I stared, the closer the night sky seemed. Eventually it almost felt as if I were among the stars, as if I could reach out and touch them and they would feel like smooth velvet under my fingers.

Without realizing, I reached a hand out toward the sky. Alec chuckled, his warm chest jostling my back, and I lowered my arm, smiling to myself.

Neither of us had spoken a word. This place was almost magic in its peace.

It was time for me to break the silence.

There was one pressing thing that still mattered, even though we were barely a speck in the dust that was the universe.

I turned in his arms, putting my back to the most amazing view I'd ever seen.

He'd kept a long-sleeved shirt on at all times since we'd arrived in the more remote areas, where tattoos didn't have positive connotations. But now his ink and scars were on full display—his art and pain worn like armor. I ran my hands over his chest and shoulders, feeling the strong muscle under the soft skin.

The blue in his eyes was almost silvery—reflecting the stars. He smiled at me, no sign of the frowning, brooding, tense asshole I'd first met. This was the real Alec. This was *my* Alec, my honey-voiced stranger who was a stranger no more.

This was the man I loved.

"I love you, Alec." I looked right into those mesmerizing eyes as I told him.

He blinked, his eyes widening just a little, and then so many emotions passed over his face that I couldn't have named them if I tried. There was surprise, for sure, happiness in the tentative curve of his lips, even relief in the way he sighed.

I hated that one. I hated that I'd waited this long to tell him, that I'd given him reason to doubt.

But I didn't dwell on it, because the most dominant emotion of all, the one that shone most clearly from his eyes, was *love*.

"I love you, Evie." There was that honey voice I lived to hear. And then he was kissing me.

Alec drew me up against his chest, making me lift onto my toes as I wrapped my arms around his neck and held on. I was never letting go again.

He kissed me deeply—as if we had all the time in the universe. As if the billions of stars shining down on us would just have to wait until we were done expressing our love.

~

The next morning, I slept in. Alec and I had thrown caution to the wind—or the light summer breeze, as it were—and made love under the stars.

Love! Because he loved me and I loved him and I'd told him. Finally!

We'd crawled back into bed in the wee hours of the morning and told each other again before falling asleep.

I woke up with a smile on my face, alone on the futons with bright sunlight streaming in.

Ethan was in the kitchen with Mr. Takata's cousin, getting a lesson in traditional Japanese cookery. He looked even more giant in the small space but managed not to knock anything over. As he delivered a traditional breakfast of rice, miso soup, and grilled fish, Alec and Josh wandered into the main room.

"Morning!" Josh gave me a kiss on the top of my head and kept heading for the door. "We're going for a run."

I mumbled around a mouthful of food, gesturing for them to wait. I wanted to go for a run too.

Tyler plopped down next to me. "Just eat, baby. I'll go with you later."

I grumbled but kept eating.

Alec kissed the same spot Josh had. "We won't be long. Love you."

"Love you too!" I called after him, smiling like an idiot over my food as he walked out.

Tyler kissed me on the cheek softly and gave me a wide smile, but he didn't comment.

I spent most of the day with Mr. Takata and his grandmother, asking all the questions I could think to ask. Her answers were rooted in myth and tradition. She couldn't give me scientific explanations for how my glowing Light worked and why I had it, but she told me all the stories her mother and grandmother had told her.

She impressed upon me the significance of this "gift." Through both her stories and her straightforward explanations, she told me what I was capable of—the immense amounts of Light I could channel; the remote transfers; the ability to draw from one Variant and give to another, temporarily giving them the other's ability.

She also explained the responsibility that came with having this gift. She spoke candidly about her own experiences of draining the Light from a Variant, taking their ability and killing them in the process.

"There is a reason we have this ability," she explained. "It would not be possible for us to do this if there was no purpose for it, but it must not be taken lightly. You have great power, Evelyn, but you must wield it wisely."

Practically speaking, she didn't give me any new information about what I could do. I'd experienced this all for myself, short of actually killing someone by draining them dry. But she confirmed many of my theories, and talking with someone who truly understood what I was going through was beyond satisfying.

She also told me the glow was a visual representation of my power, a beacon to draw people to my side.

I'd already seen evidence of that: the way Mr. Takata had devoted himself to me without even knowing me, the way strangers had come to my defense on countless occasions—when I was attacked at Bradford Hills, when I glowed the night of the formal evening in Manhattan, even when Rick had risked his life to warn me of the danger I was in from Davis's plans. And that wasn't even counting all the emails and private messages I'd received from Variants and Vitals all over the world.

Yes, the likelihood of a lot of those being fake was high, but I could feel in my gut that plenty of them were genuine too. That's why I'd asked Charlie to wade through them to check which ones might be legit.

People were scared and were looking for a spark of light in the darkness. Maybe it was time they had something to turn to besides the twisted views of Variant Valor and the Human Empowerment Network.

After lunch we wandered into the town square and sat outside a charming traditional teahouse, sipping on sencha as we continued our chats. It wasn't long, though, before we were interrupted by a buzz of excitement— kids rushing through the square, women chattering.

I frowned. "What's going on?"

Mr. Takata sat up straighter, craning his neck to look around. "It seems there is another visitor approaching the village on the path."

Alec and Tyler strode into the square, both of them clearly on alert.

TWENTY-FIVE

"There's someone approaching." Alec told us what we already knew while Tyler simply extended his hand to me.

I took it and pushed Light to him reflexively. He turned toward the path to the village, not visible past the low buildings and winding lanes. His eyes lost focus, but instead of sharing what his ability was telling him, he just frowned and cocked his head to the side.

"Ty?" I tugged on his hand. "Who is it?"

He shrugged. "The most I can sense is that they're not a threat."

I scratched my head. Even with all that extra Light, Ty couldn't tell who it was?

Before I had a chance to think about it too much, the person in question walked around the corner, solving the mystery of why Tyler's ability seemed to be malfunctioning.

Nina was in linen shorts and a loose white shirt, stark against her dark skin. Her hair was once again cropped close to her scalp, and she carried only a large backpack, which no doubt contained several weapons and countless secrets.

"Nina?" Alec and I said at the same time. What was the statistical probability of us meeting up in such a remote place? Maybe she knew we were here? But if she'd found us, did that mean others could too?

When she was about halfway across the square, she spotted me.

"Evelyn?" She smiled and rushed over.

"Fancy meeting you here." I laughed as we hugged. I'd missed her, and I held on for a long moment.

She greeted Tyler and Alec just as warmly and, to our surprise, seemed to know Mr. Takata's grandmother very well. Her French accent was as thick as I remembered, but she spoke to the old woman in Japanese.

Nina pulled up a chair and joined us. "How have you all been? I have seen some things on the news, but I am taking most of it with a large dose of salt."

"How have *we* been? Nina, how have *you* been? Seems you left a few things out the last time we met." I folded my arms, jokingly scolding her but unable to wipe the smile off my face.

"And I see someone has filled you in on it?" She threw Mrs. Takata a look, to which the old lady just chuckled, no remorse on her face whatsoever. "There wasn't exactly complete trust between us when we first met." She eyed Alec, and he looked down, rubbing the back of his neck. He'd been a jerk to her.

"Sorry," he mumbled and stole a sip of my tea. Mr. Takata motioned for the proprietor and ordered more tea for everyone.

"It is quite all right. You were being cautious. I understand. But I was also limited in what I was permitted to tell you at the time. There are some Lighthunters who have been pushing for us to remove ourselves from Variant society fully." She sighed.

"What? Why?" Tyler questioned.

"It is complicated, but it seems that it is proving impossible regardless. That is why I have come here. You were going to be my next stop. You've saved me a flight to America. Thank you!"

"Nina, what's going on?" I leaned forward.

"We are . . . I suppose you could say, investigating? The Lighthunters are visiting Vitals we know, the most powerful ones—even the few Vivids we are aware of. We are trying to get some understanding around what is happening with the Light."

"What's happening with the Light?" I asked. That sounded ominous.

"It is difficult to explain." She sighed. "Remember how a Lighthunter's connection to the Light is different? How we do not have the abilities or the access that Variants and Vitals have, but we do have a different—in some ways, a deeper—understanding?"

I nodded.

"Sometimes, I see the Bond connections. Like tendrils, tethering individuals together. Your Bond is much more settled, by the way." She smiled. "No more tension. Whatever you've been doing, keep doing it."

I looked between Alec and Tyler. Our commitment to be more honest and open had no doubt played a big part in that, but ultimately, I was convinced it was our love that had made us stronger.

"Please go on," Mr. Takata prompted. He looked just as worried as Alec and Tyler.

"Right. Yes. Lighthunters have a sense of Bonds, connections. We can tell what state a Bond might be in. We can point people in the direction of their potential Variants or Vitals. We can track Bonded Variants and Vitals, like I did to help you find Charlie. How is he doing?"

"Really well. He was hurt badly in the rescue. A lot of people were, but we managed to get a healer to the hospital. He has some scarring from the burns. Lucian will probably have to be in a wheelchair for the rest of his life though."

"Oh no. I am so sorry."

"We're just happy he made it out alive."

"Nina, please." Alec's knee bounced impatiently. "We'll catch you up on everyone later. What's happening with the Light?"

"Right! Sorry. Part of why we're able to see individual connections is because we have a deeper link to the Light. It is like a constant presence—both in me and all around me. A tapestry or a mist hanging over everything. Most of the time it is just a part of how I experience the world, another sense, like sight or smell. But when I need to use it, I become more aware of it. Like when you're looking for an item in a messy room, you use your sense of sight with more intention. When I am looking for a particular Variant, I am more acutely aware of my connection to the Light.

"On the other hand, sometimes it makes itself known to me. Like when a loud noise startles you, you are suddenly more aware of your sense of hearing. When something is significant, it's hard to ignore—sitting here with you, for instance. Your access to the Light is immense, Evelyn, your threads to your Variants solid and strong. It is not something I can avoid noticing." She sighed and threaded her fingers in front of her.

"The same is true when there is something not so positive in the Light. I can tell when there are . . . I believe you call them *Lightwhores* completing a transaction—selling their Light like it's a cheap thing. The Light feels heavy, tainted, in these moments.

"Over the past few months, the Light has been feeling more and more . . . off. It is not a particular incident or location we can pinpoint. It is more like a general sense of it being tainted somehow, strained, tense. It has us all on edge. We have never experienced a sense of wrongness of this magnitude. We are worried—worried enough to set aside our internal politics and try to figure it out. That is why we are visiting some of the more powerful Vitals we know. We are hoping by being near you, studying the way the Light is behaving, we may get a clue as to what is happening."

I shared a worried glance with Alec and Tyler. "Nina, it's probably Davis—what he's doing with his machines."

It was bad enough he was causing political and social unrest all over the world. I hadn't considered that his fucked-up experiments could have an impact on the very thing fueling Variant abilities, the very thing that made us what we were. He was rotting everything he touched.

"Yes." She nodded solemnly. "That is what I and most of my fellow Lighthunters believe also, but we thought it prudent to rule out any other potential issues. Plus, visiting with the Vitals allows us to explain the precarious situation, to urge them not to support this lunatic in any way. Maybe even to fight."

Alec perked up. "Fight? How?"

"We do not have all the answers, but we do feel strongly that he cannot be permitted to continue unresisted."

"Agreed." Tyler took a sip of his tea and crossed his legs. "But if fighting is even an option, and you have the kind of resources you seem to be hinting at, why haven't you done anything yet?"

"It is complicated." Nina sighed. "There is a reason we have managed to remain secret. We rarely get involved in any way that's not discreet. I am hoping that will change very soon."

Mr. Takata sat up even straighter, his expression serious. "Knowing what I know due to my work, and knowing what I know due to my connection to two Vivids, I can't in good conscience sit by and do nothing. Regardless of what the Lighthunters decide to do, I am prepared to take whatever action is necessary to put a stop to this. I am at your service, Evelyn."

"Thank you." I smiled, still a little uncomfortable at the intensity of his devotion.

His grandmother patted his hand and smiled, the lines in her face deepening. He'd spoken in English, but she'd gleaned the gist of it.

"I don't know what the answers are." Alec took a sip of his own tea, scowling at the little cup as if he wished it were something stronger. "I'm not even sure what the right questions to ask are. But one thing I know for certain is we have to keep Evie safe."

No one disagreed with him. Nina started to chat with Mr. Takata and his formidable mother in Japanese while Alec continued to scowl into his tea.

Tyler was leaning back against the wall of the teahouse, frowning, his unfocused gaze pointed at his feet.

I was just about to ask him where he'd gone when his shoulders tensed. The change in posture was barely discernible—something I wouldn't have even noticed if I hadn't been staring at him. His eyes remained unfocused but started to dart around, as if he were looking for something the rest of us couldn't see.

I moved without thinking, my Light reacting to his body's need for it. My hand covered his, and after only a few moments, he whipped his head up.

He flipped his hand so he could hold mine in a firm grip. "We need to leave. They found us."

"What? How?" I demanded at the same time Alec shot to his feet with a growled, "Fuck." He looked ready to throw me over his shoulder and just run down into the valley.

"We have about an hour until they reach us. They've been watching you since we met in New York." Tyler nodded at Mr. Takata, and the older man frowned in confusion.

"It's not possible. I've taken every precaution."

"Your countermeasures were excellent, but some footage from the hotel lobby slipped through. It took them a while to put it together, but now we have a team of six, disguised as tourists, coming up the main path." He pointed across the square.

"Are there any other ways in or out of the village?" Alec asked as everyone else got to their feet.

"No," Tyler and Mr. Takata answered at the same time. The latter elaborated, "Climbing the peak of the mountains is too treacherous, and the descent into the valley can only be managed if you're a goat."

Alec cursed again, but Mrs. Takata cut in with a gentle touch to her grandson's arm. She spoke in rapid Japanese, impossible for me to follow, but he translated for us.

"There is a young man in the village with an invisibility gift. He does not have a Vital, but if you are willing to share your Light, Evelyn, he can hide you all."

"But what about you? What about the village? These men are dangerous." I took Mrs. Takata's hand. Her skin was paper thin, her hand fragile, but her grip was strong. I'd only just met her, yet I'd already learned so much. Now I was about to leave just as I'd brought danger to her doorstep.

A heavy, twisted feeling settled in the pit of my stomach. Destruction followed me everywhere I went.

"If they are claiming to be tourists, there should be no issues." Mr. Takata waved his hand. "If they ask questions, well, I am simply here visiting my grandmother. And if they get violent, we are more than capable of defending ourselves."

He was such a calm, pleasant man I sometimes forgot Mr. Takata was in the same line of work as Alec and Tyler. I nodded reluctantly.

"We have a way off the mountain, but then what?" Alec asked. "We can't trust any of our Melior Group contacts on the ground here. Not anymore. What's our next move?"

"You come with me." Nina crossed her arms, nothing but determination on her face. "I can get you out and somewhere safe, and it may be just what we need to convince the rest of the Lighthunters to take action."

Alec looked to Tyler. We had no other ideas, and it sounded good to me, but Alec was letting him make the final call.

Tyler propped his hands on his hips and sighed. "I can't tell if what you're proposing is safe—your immunity to my ability is irritating, to say the least—but I think it's the best chance we have. The Lighthunters have managed to evade discovery by the entire world for hundreds of years. Can't think of a better group of people to keep us hidden, keep Eve safe."

He shrugged, and it was decided.

Nina nodded and turned to Mrs. Takata, expressing her disappointment that their visit had to be cut so short. In my broken Japanese, I expressed the same sentiment, giving the old lady a low bow. She pulled me into a hug and patted my cheeks.

"We will meet again." She nodded with a tranquil smile.

Ethan and Josh wandered into the square, chatting and joking as they strolled. As they approached us, Josh noticed something was off first, his easy smile falling.

"Pack your shit," Alec barked before they even had a chance to greet anyone. "We've been made. We have twenty minutes to get out of here."

"Nina?" Josh ignored him and came forward to say hi.

"Oh man." Ethan groaned. "I was just about to get something to eat." His shoulders slumped as he turned to follow a marching Alec back to the house.

I took his hand. "Yeah, but you're always about to get something to eat."

"True." He grinned at me.

Within fifteen minutes we were packed and at the start of the path. We said our goodbyes, and the villagers all went about their daily lives as if we'd never been there.

The young man with the invisibility—he didn't look older than seventeen—was so excited to put his ability to use he was practically bouncing on the spot. He needed contact to keep us hidden, but as I reached for his hand, Nina grabbed my wrist and stepped between us. Without any thought for personal space, she placed her hand on the man's chest and cocked her head. After a few moments, she smiled.

"When you can, head east," she told him. "Your Vital is in Africa, somewhere south of Ethiopia."

"Thank you!" The young man beamed, bowing repeatedly and grinning.

Nina stepped away, and I took the man's hand, pushing Light to him in a steady stream. The others made a chain behind us, and we stood at the side of the path and waited.

It was almost too easy. The six men came walking up the path, barely breathing hard after the long, difficult climb. They were casually dressed, like tourists, but their expressions were hard, their eyes searching, and they barely talked.

They passed us without so much as a glance. Once they were well on their way to the center of the village, we moved down the path.

At the bottom of the mountain, we said our goodbyes to the youth who'd probably just saved our lives. He grinned, clearly happy to have been useful, as well as overjoyed at the knowledge Nina had shared about his Vital.

A beat-up old van pulled up next to us, and we piled in. The driver said a few short words to Nina but generally ignored us until he deposited us at a small airstrip.

We rushed from the van into a small plane, the engines already firing up as the door was pulled shut. The pilot was as quiet as the driver, not asking any questions and not sharing anything either.

As we settled into our seats, I finally took a few full breaths.

Ethan took my hand in his big one and promptly fell asleep. I smiled at him affectionately even as I cursed him out of envy. He really could sleep anywhere.

Just as fast as we'd arrived, we were leaving Japan, this time, hopefully, completely undetected.

I leaned my head on my fire fiend's big shoulder and closed my eyes, hoping to get some sleep too.

TWENTY-SIX

Nina unbuckled her seatbelt and stood in the aisle, hands on her hips and an excited look on her face. "Time to go."

She started pulling bags down from the overhead lockers.

"Time to go?" I shared a worried glance with Ethan. "Uh, in case you haven't noticed, we're in the *fucking air*."

"We're somewhere over the Mediterranean, right?" Tyler questioned, picking up one of the bags and starting to strap it to his body.

Holy fucking Heisenberg! They were going to make me jump out of this plane.

"Extraction?" Alec asked.

"Naturally." Nina had her parachute in place and was adjusting a pair of goggles. "I have a boat coming to get us."

Alec nodded, a smile pulling at his lips as he started to strap his parachute on. "Nice."

"*Nice?*" I screeched. Ethan and I stood, holding on to the backs of our seats. He looked wary but not panicked like me. Josh remained in his seat, unfazed, still reading his book. "Not nice! No one said anything about jumping out of a plane! I'm not jumping out of a *fucking plane*!"

Alec grabbed my wrist and pulled me into the aisle. He planted both hands on my shoulders, piercing me with his blue-eyed stare. "Bailing out now while the pilot keeps going and lands somewhere far away means we evade anyone who might be tracking our flight on radar. We have all the equipment. This is the best move."

I fisted my hands in his shirt, as if I could stop him from hurling me out of a plane. "Jumping out of a fucking plane is the best move? I don't fucking think so!" My voice sounded frantic as my heart hammered in my chest.

"You get so sweary when you're stressed." Alec chuckled. "It's cute."

Tyler handed Ethan a harness. "You and Alec are closest in height—you can tandem jump with him."

"Cool!" Ethan started putting the harness on. He looked more excited than scared now, as if this were an adrenaline experience and not a life-or-death situation.

We were twenty thousand feet in the air. Tyler said we were over the Mediterranean. We'd be landing in water. I quickly calculated terminal velocity—we would be falling somewhere between 120 and 150 miles per hour. Water is incompressible fluid, so hitting it at terminal velocity would be like hitting concrete. The likelihood of surviving a fall like that was . . . practically nonexistent.

My body screamed at me to sit back down and strap on my seatbelt. My mouth just started screaming. "No no no no no! Don't make me do this! I'm not fucking doing this! We're all going to die! Oh my god!"

"Did she just say *god?*" Ethan chuckled, leaning over Alec's shoulder to look at me.

"Fuck, she's really freaking out." Tyler leaned over Alec's other shoulder, frowning.

"Evie." Alec shook my shoulders lightly, his voice firm. "Calm down."

"Calm down?" I finally released his shirt and pulled myself up to my full height. "Calm down?! Never in the history of calming down has being told to calm down resulted in a person. *Calming. Down. Alec!*" I screamed into his face, letting all my fear and frustration loose.

Instead of getting pissed off or yelling back, he smirked as if I was amusing him. Then, before I could start yelling again, he leaned forward and kissed me. With one hand on the back of my neck and the other at the base of my spine, he pinned me against him and devoured my mouth with his. Involuntarily, I wrapped my arms around him and closed my eyes. It was one of those searing, all-consuming Alec kisses I loved so much.

Logically I knew this was a distraction—he was using physiology to override psychology. The tactic annoyed me slightly, but damn, if it wasn't working.

After a few dizzying moments, he pulled back. "You're safe. We've got you. Tyler and I have done this hundreds of times. Josh has a skydiving license. We know what we're doing."

Reluctantly, I nodded.

"Better?" he pressed.

"Better." I nodded again, breathing him in. He made me feel strong, but I'd made it a point to avoid planes since . . . and now I was about to jump out of one, into water no less. Talk about triggering trauma. "I'm still scared, Alec."

"I know. This isn't like that night." He knew where my freak-out was coming from. "We're not crashing. You're safe. You have to trust us, precious. We'd never let anything happen to you."

I closed my eyes and took a deep breath. If there was one thing I could be sure of, that was it. They put my safety above all else. I had to trust this was the best move.

"Two minutes!" Nina yelled from her spot near the door, one hand on the handle.

"Alec, Kid, get in position," Tyler ordered. Alec dropped one last kiss to my forehead and went to stand next to Nina.

Ethan let him pass before pulling me into a hug. "Love you, baby. You're gonna be fine." He kissed me on the cheek and followed Alec. They attached their harnesses together, and Alec started giving Ethan instructions.

"Eve, you're with me. Josh, gear up." Tyler handed me a harness, not dissimilar to the one they'd forced me into just before we rappelled down a building in Manhattan.

"Actually"—Josh closed his book and stood, the picture of calm—"I think Eve should go with me."

I looked between them. Did Josh have more skydiving experience? Alec said he had a license, whatever that meant.

"One minute!" Nina called.

"Good thinking!" Tyler slapped him on the back. "I still want you strapped together though."

Josh nodded, already putting his harness on. It didn't seem to be attached to a large backpack containing a parachute though . . .

"See you down there." Tyler gave me a brief kiss on the lips and moved toward the door, taking his position in line to jump out of a *fucking plane*.

I couldn't believe we were doing this.

"Nina's about to open the door." Josh pulled me to him. "It's going to be windy and loud." As I tied my hair back, he explained the best way to skydive, what to expect, how to hold my arms and legs out.

He flashed me his perfect teeth in a grin just as Nina turned the lever and the door went flying.

Frigid wind whipped all around us with a deafening roar.

I gripped the back of the seat. Nina waved and flashed me a smile as if she were popping out to grab us some coffee, then she stepped out and disappeared. My stomach dropped.

Alec and Ethan shuffled forward, Ethan's back strapped to Alec's front. They leaned forward in the door, and Ethan whooped as they went plummeting.

Tyler checked his straps one last time and stepped out without hesitation.

Josh nudged me to face the aisle, and I felt him attach my harness to his. "It's our turn," he yelled over the noise. "Now, juice me up, babe!"

I turned my wide eyes over my shoulder, and he caught my lips in a kiss. I pushed Light to him as if my life depended on it, focusing on the feeling of his perfect lips on mine, the tingling, warm sensation of the Light transferring.

As he kissed me, Josh walked us forward, down the aisle and toward the open door.

He broke the kiss and smiled. "Ready?"

I faced forward. We were already at the door, Josh's hands gripping the sides of the opening, bright sunshine and a few fluffy clouds visible beyond.

I dared not look down.

"No." I shook my head. Every instinct I had, every scrap of self-preservation in me, screamed to *step the fuck back*!

But Josh shoved forward, and we were officially jumping out of a plane.

My heart lodged in my throat and stopped beating.

I tried to scream, but the intense rush of air whipping at my face took my breath away.

We don't have a parachute!

My mind reminded me of this little fact now that we were already free-falling.

Somehow, some part of my brain was with it enough to follow Josh's instruction. I held my arms out loosely at my sides, my knees bent slightly, and tucked my chin against my chest, creating a little pocket of air so I could breathe before I passed out.

My eyes watered, and my face felt numb from the frigid air.

Josh's arms banded around my middle, and he reminded me why jumping without a parachute wasn't a fatal mistake.

Our plummet toward certain death slowed. After a few moments, I felt the unmistakable nudge of Josh's ability.

He was using his telekinesis to fly.

In a moment of panic, I slammed more Light into him. I had to make sure he had enough! I knew how draining it was for him to do the flying thing, how hard he'd had to train to get it, how much Light and concentration he needed to do it for any length of time.

He grunted, and his arms tightened around me. Then he chuckled. "Ease up, Eve. I've got plenty. I won't drop us."

He didn't have to shout at all for me to hear him. Actually, all the overwhelming noise had ended. I stopped the Light flow, leaving the connection open in case he needed more, and looked around.

We'd come to a complete stop and were floating among fluffy white clouds.

My shoulders relaxed just a fraction, and I took a deep breath of the fresh air. I hugged Josh's arms around myself, feeling the muscles and tendons in his forearms as I craned my neck to look at him.

He smiled, relaxed, confident in his ability and my Light needed to fuel it. I smiled back, some of the fear finally dissipating. I couldn't even feel the harness tugging me or cutting into my legs; Josh held me in his arms and with his ability with no extra help needed.

I looked down just in time to see one, then two, then three parachutes unfurl and slow the others' descent.

The bright sun sparkled off the water below, and coastline and islands gleamed green and gold in the distance. It was beautiful.

Josh started floating us down toward the water. Unlike the pace we'd been rocking only moments before, his speed now was closer to a rollercoaster than a missile. Much more enjoyable.

"This is like the coolest ride at the fair!" I told him through a smile.

He laughed, but instead of replying, he sent us sailing through the air in a perfectly smooth loop.

I couldn't contain my laughter. I'd gone from abject terror to giddy glee within a matter of minutes. I decided not to consider the implications for my mental state too closely. That was just what being in a Bond meant. They could make me feel incredible no matter how bad things seemed.

As we continued our easy glide toward the glittering turquoise water, I relaxed into Josh's embrace. He was so good at this, as if he'd been born with wings and had been flying his whole life.

As if to illustrate my point, he planted a soft, lazy kiss to the curve of my neck, not even paying full attention to keeping us both airborne. I smiled and wriggled against him, which made me think about how closely he was holding me. His front was against my back, not a breath of space between us, our feet tangling playfully.

"Hey, Josh?" I half turned my head so he could hear me.

"Hmm?" he hummed, his lips still at my neck.

"How long do you think you could keep us both in the air? Theoretically? And how hard would you need to concentrate for the duration of . . ."

He smiled against my neck, making me bite my bottom lip. I had no doubt he knew exactly what I was insinuating, but he decided to tease me anyway.

"For the duration of what? What exactly do you have on that fucking dirty mind of yours?"

I shivered against him. I loved it when he cursed. It gave me a glimpse of his freaky side—a side only *I* got to see . . . and sometimes the others.

"I think you know exactly what I have in mind." I arched my back, pressing my ass into his groin. I wasn't at all surprised to feel his erection.

He chuckled but put a tiny amount of space between us. "I think that can be arranged, but not right now, unless you want an audience?"

I looked back down. We were barely twenty feet away from the surface. The others had all landed and disconnected their parachutes, the colorful fabric floating in the water. A speedboat pulled up next to Nina, and a person reached down to help her over the side.

Ten feet. We were close enough to hear their voices but not make out what they were saying.

Ethan went next, Nina and the other man pulling him up while Alec and Tyler helped from the water.

Five feet.

It was Tyler's turn. He was light and agile, only needing a hand over the edge from Ethan. Alec lifted himself into the boat before anyone could offer him help.

"Shit!" We were about to hit the water. I'd been too distracted watching them all climb to safety to notice. "Josh! I don't want to go in the water, Josh. Josh!"

Our toes only just touched the surface, then he spun us around and farther up, away from the boat.

"It's OK. It's OK, Eve. I've got you." He tightened his grip around my middle, and I realized I was digging my fingers into his forearms. I released my grip immediately and rubbed over the nail marks I'd left in his skin.

"Sorry. Shit, I hurt you."

"No, you didn't. You OK? What's going on?"

"I . . ." I wasn't sure how to articulate it. I couldn't remember hitting the water when the plane crashed, but apparently my body could. Approaching it from the sky made me panic in a way that was hard to explain. "I just *really* don't wanna go in the water."

"We don't have to." He was already steering us back toward the boat, coming in slower and slower. "Tuck your legs up."

I wrapped my arms loosely around my knees. Josh approached the boat with such control I barely even felt us land. His feet touched down on the wooden boards, and the sensation of his ability disappeared.

Alec was at our side instantly, holding me in his arms as Tyler disconnected my harness from Josh's, then set me on my feet. He watched me with a question in his eyes while his hands roamed, looking for injury. Tyler and Ethan eyed me warily too, clearly on edge.

"I'd love to meet you all properly, but it's probably best if we don't linger here too long." The man at the front of the boat drew our attention, speaking in a thick Greek accent.

Working as a team, we pulled the soaking, thin fabric of the parachutes out of the water and dumped them in a corner. Everyone took a seat. Ethan pulled me down between him and Alec, and the speedboat took off.

It was a pretty smooth ride. The hot summer sun beat down from above, and the salty air whipped past our faces as the Greek man pushed the boat faster and faster. There weren't any massive waves or bumpy bits; we just glided along the waters of the Mediterranean . . . for hours.

The noise made it hard to talk, so we spent most of the ride in silence, watching the water and the occasional bit of land in the distance. By the time the roar of the engine started to calm down, I was starving, a little seasick, and completely over the novelty of being in a speedboat.

We pulled up to a small dock jutting out of the side of a cliff face. There was no beach or easy approach to speak of, but three other boats identical to ours were docked there. We got out of the boat and took some time to stretch and look around as the man tied the boat to the dock.

"I'm Stavros." He smiled at us—crooked teeth and deep laugh lines on a tanned face. "Pleased to meet you all."

Nina introduced us one by one. "Stavros is a Lighthunter, like me."

"It's a pleasure to meet you." I smiled, but I couldn't stop my eyes from wandering up the cliff. I had to lean back to see the top. "Um, where are we, exactly?"

"If I told you, I'd have to kill you," Stavros deadpanned, his voice low and gravelly. My eyes widened. Alec stiffened and stepped between the man and me. He couldn't use his ability—none of them could on the Lighthunters—but Alec was deadly for more than one reason.

Nina slapped Stavros on the shoulder and rolled her eyes. "Not funny, old man."

His serious mask dropped, and they both laughed. "It was a little funny."

The scowl on Alec's face suggested he disagreed.

"Come on." Stavros picked up his backpack and waved for us to follow him.

Alec grudgingly brought up the rear. At the end of the dock, stairs zigzagged all the way to the top of the cliff. Most of them were carved directly into the rock, but every once in a while, timber ones filled in gaps.

"We are in the Greek islands." Stavros puffed his chest out. "This island is called Naxonnos, and as far as the authorities are concerned, it is barren and unlivable with no wildlife or plant life of note. It is remote, about three hundred kilometers past the nearest island frequented by tourists or locals. It is also Lighthunter HQ."

He delivered the last line as we crested the top of the cliff. This island definitely wasn't barren or abandoned. Before us was an entire city! Or what I imagined a city would look like without really tall skyscrapers.

Paved streets and low buildings stretched out in front of us. People were milling about; ATVs and golf carts zipped past. I could even see a helicopter on a landing pad to our right. I couldn't believe an operation like this had managed to go undetected by all the world's authorities and operations, including Melior Group.

Ethan echoed my thoughts. "Man, Lucian's gonna be pissed he didn't know about this."

Nina leaned forward, sticking her head between ours to stage-whisper, "Wait until you see what's underground." She winked and grinned at us. "Let's get you settled and fed."

She pushed past us and led the way down the main street. Stavros waved goodbye and wandered off.

A few people threw us curious glances, but for the most part, people just went about their business. I was a little surprised to see so many children running around among the adults.

"Nina, what's with all the kids? I thought this was, like, a secret lair or something."

She burst out laughing, then cocked her head and hummed. "Yes, I suppose it kind of is. A lot of our work happens from here and a few other sites like it across the world, but it is also a settlement of sorts. Lighthunters call this place home. It is a sanctuary as much as it is a lair."

The hot summer sun was beating down on us, and I was grateful when she gestured us toward a shaded table outside a café. She ordered food and drinks for everyone in Greek as we settled in.

"How many languages do you speak?" Josh asked as Ethan fanned himself with the menu. Alec and Tyler sat back, looking relaxed, but I knew they were watching everything closely.

"Twelve," Nina answered as if it were no big deal.

My eyes bugged out. "Fluently?"

"Yes. French is my native tongue, and my accent is stubborn, but I speak, read, and write the other eleven languages fluently."

Before we could ask more, the food was delivered. We all dug in, Ethan the most enthusiastically.

After half his meal was gone, Tyler leaned forward. "You said there was something underground?"

"Yes, about twice as much as you see above ground. Most of the dwellings and everyday life is above ground—cafés, shops, the school, the library, and so on. Below is a large bunker, offices, a server room, surveillance, our secret texts and teachings. Our work is below ground, safe."

Tyler abandoned his food, his full focus on Nina. "What's with all the secrecy? How is this even possible?"

It was killing him that there was something he didn't know—that an entire organization managed to exist without his knowledge.

"At the start, it was about protecting ourselves." She waved her hand dismissively, speaking around mouthfuls of food. "We're talking about hundreds of years ago, when it was believed the Light was a gift from God and Lighthunters were kind of like prophets. We had a connection that no other mortal being did. We understood it, saw it like no one else could. Eventually, some assholes figured out they could make money from this. Between the snake oil salesmen—the ones pretending to be Lighthunters and charging a fortune to send hopeful young Variants on veritable goose chases—and the more sinister practice of capturing, torturing, imprisoning, and exploiting Lighthunters . . . yeah, we decided to go to ground.

"At the time, we were led by a charismatic man named Father Lightwood. He believed we were truly God's prophets, sent here to guide the masses to better live according to how God wanted us to live. He convinced us the best way to do that was silently—that our work was too sacred to risk having it perverted. We withdrew from society, disappeared from the villages and emerging cities, took all our texts and any other texts we could with us.

"Over the years, we continued to erase any trace of ourselves from history. We worked in secret, orchestrating the meetings of Variants and Vitals by setting up scholarships, overseas exchange programs, and job offers to bring them into proximity with one another. We only stepped in where we felt we needed to—like the incident in Thailand."

"I'm amazed you've managed to keep this a secret for so long." Tyler shook his head.

"What happens when a Lighthunter is born? Do you take them from their family?" I questioned.

Nina smiled. "That is not necessary. We are not like Variants and humans. A Variant can be born to entirely human parents and vice versa. A Lighthunter can only be born to Lighthunter parents—our gift is hereditary. Not every child is born with the sight, but no child *outside* a Lighthunter family is ever born with it. There are one hundred recorded bloodlines of Lighthunter families. Sixty-six remain to this day. It is frowned upon and very rare for us to marry outside the community."

I nodded. "I guess not living among the rest of the world would help with keeping the secret." All the kids running around made much more sense now. This wasn't just a hippie commune on steroids or a headquarters for a secret society; this was an entire civilization, living in secret.

Nina smiled sadly. "You have to understand, for us, this secret and the work we do is sacred. We have evolved with the rest of the world—hell, some of the technology widely available now we developed first and then leaked—but our traditions are strong and lasting. The fact that we are even having discussions about getting more involved is momentous. People are scared, but it is time for change. We have the resources to help, and we *should*."

"Why are you telling us all this now?" Josh asked one of the things I'd been wondering too. "You were so secretive when we brought you in to find Eve, then Charlie. Why lay it all out now? Why even bring us here?"

"I trust you." She shrugged. "I think our goals are aligned, and I think it is time. We know more about the outside world than your Melior Group does, but we are still isolated from it. I am hoping that by bringing you here, the reality of what is happening beyond those cliffs will become more concrete for those who rarely leave."

She was helping us, keeping us safe from Davis's greedy clutches, but she was also trying to effect change—in her own community and in the wider world. I admired her for that.

"Nina!" The exclamation was half reproach, half disbelief.

We all turned to look down the street. A small group of people were marching in our direction, varying degrees of anger and confusion on their faces.

Nina groaned. "If they don't excommunicate me first," she mumbled before standing to face the group.

The man who'd shouted, the one in the lead, was tall, his full head of white-gray hair a contrast to his dark olive complexion.

"What were you thinking?" he demanded as he reached us. "You brought non-enlightened here? Have you gone completely mad?"

"I understand this goes against our traditions, but I felt I had no choice." Nina spoke in a low voice, her head bowed, her hands crossed in front of her. "Elders"—she raised her head, looking at them all before turning slightly to us—"this is Evelyn Maynard, a Vivid with great power. She is in danger, and she may just be what we need to help us come to a decision. These are her Bondmates."

A dozen sets of eyes focused on me. I resisted the urge to hunch my shoulders and sink into the chair, opting instead to wave and smile awkwardly.

TWENTY-SEVEN

The first few days with the Lighthunters were like a holiday. They freezed us out of most of their discussions while they decided what to do with us, and we were placed in a cottage on the quiet side of the island. There were no beaches, but the hill was slightly less steep—not like the sheer drop we'd had to climb up on the way in. It was still impossible to walk down, although the goats didn't seem to have any issues.

Our cottage was nestled in among about a dozen others. They were temporary accommodation for Lighthunters who didn't live on the island. As most of them were currently out visiting Vitals and Vivids, all the other cottages were empty.

Ours had a kitchenette, a dining table with four chairs, and a living area with a couch. At the back was a small bathroom and a decent-sized bedroom with two queen beds. Once we'd pushed the beds together and Josh had dragged an extra chair over from the cottage next door, we were actually quite comfortable. A little patio with chairs overlooked the cliff and the stunning view beyond, and farther down, there was even a pool and a traditional Turkish hammam.

We spent the days exploring the island; the perimeter could be walked in under two hours, and we were banned from some areas, so it didn't take long. Josh found a library in one of the main buildings, so he ended up doing a lot of reading. Alec and Ethan exercised frequently, and I joined them for daily runs.

Tyler struggled the most. He was so used to being in control, calling the shots, and knowing everything. Now, suddenly, he was supposed to just stay out of it. There were no newspaper deliveries on the island and no TV in our cottage. We'd all left our phones behind, and he immediately started having major tech withdrawals.

The sun hadn't even set on the first day by the time Tyler talked someone into giving him a laptop with a secure connection. He was able to keep an eye on the news; speak with Lucian, Kyo, and Charlie for short periods of time; and with Charlie's help, even keep an eye on restricted intelligence channels. He didn't share the info unless someone asked, but he was looking more and more worried each day. It wasn't a surprise to any of us that things were going downhill.

We spent the evenings eating slow dinners on the patio and sipping Mediterranean wine. We played truth or dare, laughed, and had conversations that started with statements like "Remember that time we snuck out to follow Alec and Gabe to The Hole?" (Josh) and "OK, real talk, I actually hate mushrooms, and I wish you'd stop putting them in the stir fry" (Tyler) and "I'll kill you all if you ever tell anyone, but . . ." (Alec).

I learned more about Alec and Ty's bad-boy stage, their time hanging with the rough crowd from The Hole.

"Alec did it for many reasons, not least of all for the sense of control it gave him," Tyler mused, swirling his pinot grigio. The corded muscle in his forearms danced with every movement. "But for me it was more about the challenge. My ability is passive. I never had to control it or rein it in. I just had to learn to keep my mouth shut when I accidentally learned something private. But other than that, I was free to use it all day and at any time. Fighting at The Hole made me learn how to control it, how to turn it off. I loved the mental challenge of figuring out how to do that more than learning how to fight, although that was fun too."

"Eventually." Alec smirked. "You got your ass handed to you the first few times."

"Not the first time." Tyler laughed. "The first time I didn't even last two minutes before that fucking light went off telling everyone I'd used my ability. It was second nature. It took me ages to learn how to turn it off. *Then* I started getting my ass handed to me."

Later that night we got onto the topic of food, and Ethan told us he really didn't want to play pro sports. He had the talent and natural affinity for it, could probably have his pick of football, baseball, and ice hockey teams if he chose to really focus and train. "But honestly, all I want to do is cook." He shrugged his big shoulders and looked around at the guys sheepishly.

"Bro, if you wanna cook"—Alec leaned forward, resting his elbows on his knees—"then fucking cook. Who cares?"

Josh jumped in. "Life's too short, man, filled with bad shit, pain, and loss. Follow your fucking dream."

"You can totally do it. I know." Tyler tapped the side of his head, half joking about his ability in an attempt to lighten the mood. It worked, and we all laughed.

I took Ethan's big hand in mine and squeezed. I had no doubts at all he could do whatever he set his mind to. All of them could. And with each other's support, we would be unstoppable. If we managed to survive the clusterfuck our lives had turned into. If the *world* managed to survive.

It seemed none of us really wanted to talk about that though—it was too heavy and bitter a subject for the sweet, warm night. It was too hard to talk about the future when we were precariously balanced on the tip of a sharp knife, unsure if we were about to slide down the smooth side, unharmed, or go plummeting down the sharp edge, leaving streaks of red behind.

Despite the way Tyler frowned at the laptop every day, his shoulders sagging under the weight of his worry, we managed to ignore the world for a few days and just enjoy one another. If my mother had taught me anything, it was to find joy in these moments—to seize the times of laughter and positivity, hold them tight, and let yourself embrace them. Because you never know when the next threat will come.

So I enjoyed the fresh food, the wonderful wine, the honest conversation with my Bond. I reveled in the warm sun on my shoulders during the day, in their embrace at night as I made love to one or sometimes more than one of them.

For a few blissful days, I let the rest of the world fade into the background as I lost myself in their stories, their smiles, their affectionate yet possessive touches. I knew I was sticking my head in the sand, but I couldn't bring myself to care. For the first time since I'd met them, there were no secrets—not from everyone else and not from one another—and no immediate threats to our lives.

So fuck it! I was treating it like a Greek holiday and enjoying every minute.

The morning of the fourth day, we all had a slight hangover from the wine, and we lounged around the cottage and the patio. After days of summer heat, the sky was finally a little overcast, the air blessedly breezy.

By the early evening, it was cool enough for me to go in search of a cardigan. The sun peeked out from behind the clouds for the first time that day, just in time to disappear into the azure water in a stunning sunset.

"I'm gonna go give that steam room a try," Josh announced, dropping the third novel he'd finished in as many days and stretching his arms over his head.

"Great idea." I abandoned my search for warmer clothing and took Josh's hand instead.

"Talked me into it!" Ethan flashed his dimples and followed us out.

Tyler grunted, still buried in his laptop at the table. Alec was napping in the bedroom.

The three of us took a slow, lazy walk in the post-sunset glow, following a cobbled path to a building near the back of the cottages. A couple of outdoor showers stood in the building's little courtyard, just outside a spacious changing room and bathroom. Past that, a glass door led to the steam room.

Josh fiddled with the controls on the wall, and it started to fill with steam.

"Shit." I grimaced. "We don't have bathing suits."

"Who cares? There's no one around." Ethan shrugged, whipping his T-shirt over his head and pushing his shorts and underwear down in one go. Every large, defined muscle was on display; his fire tattoo curved tantalizingly over his shoulder, making me want to lean forward and lick the flames.

"This is a Turkish hammam," Josh mused as he too stripped down to nothing. "Traditionally, they were used in the nude, the men and women having separate facilities or times of the day to visit."

Now there were *two* glorious specimens of male beauty before me—all that corded muscle, masculine spatterings of hair, smooth skin, and abs . . . so many abs.

Josh startled me out of my trance by stepping around me to grab three thin Turkish towels from a shelf. "They did, however, use towels from time to time." He handed one to Ethan and one to me, then secured one around his own hips before giving me a light kiss on the cheek.

He opened the glass door and walked into the steam that billowed out, his ass looking incredible even in a light pink towel. Ethan flashed me another mischievous grin and followed Josh, not bothering to wrap the towel around himself. I could've sworn he put a little extra swagger into his gait, and I stared at his bare ass unashamedly. It was *my* ass after all.

They were right. We hadn't seen anyone else in the cottages. It was unlikely anyone else would be coming to use the steam room any time soon.

I still wrapped the towel around myself after undressing, just in case.

I walked into the steam room and took a deep breath, letting the warm, moist air envelop me and drain some of the tension from my shoulders.

The room was an octagon; each side, apart from the glass-doored entrance, had tiled bench seating. Two of them, on opposite sides of the room, had a little sink on the bench with a beautiful mosaic pattern over it.

The entire room was tiled in dark gray and teal marble, including the pitched ceiling, which met in a point in the middle of the room, like a tent. Everything was very symmetrical and oozed opulence.

Ethan and Josh sat on the bench opposite the door, leaning back against the wall, their towels haphazardly resting over their laps.

In the center of the room was an octagonal, low platform, about the height of a coffee table. I wasn't sure what its purpose was, so I stepped around it and sat between Josh and one of the little sinks.

Steam had already filled the room and warmed the tiles. Even the light fabric of the towel felt heavy and sticky on my skin. Just as I reached to undo it, the door opened, and I paused just shy of exposing my boobs to the newcomer.

"This was a great idea, Josh." Tyler's voice echoed around the room. Alec closed the glass door behind them. They both had matching towels around their hips, which—except for one corner covering their crotches—they removed as they sat down. Tyler settled in on the other side of the little sink, and Alec sat on the opposite side of the room.

Once I was sure no one else was following them, I let my towel drop at my sides and leaned my head back against the tiles, closing my eyes. For a few moments we just sat in silence, breathing the steamy air and letting the heat warm us from the inside out.

I cracked one eye open and laughed. All four of them were staring at me, lips parted, gazes hungry. As if they didn't see my boobs on the daily. As if I hadn't had a threesome with Alec and Josh the night before. As if Ethan hadn't woken me that morning with his fingers sliding inside me. As if Tyler hadn't joined me in the cramped little shower afterward.

It was as if they couldn't get enough. I couldn't get enough of them either.

"I'm getting lightheaded." Ethan kept his deep voice low, but it echoed anyway.

"That's because you're freakishly tall." Tyler chuckled. "Your head is higher and therefore hotter."

"No." Josh's eyes hadn't left my body. "It's because Eve is sitting there completely fucking naked like the goddess she is."

I smiled but didn't reply, instead closing my eyes again. I wasn't embarrassed or self-conscious—I had nothing to hide from them anymore—but I wasn't exactly used to receiving constant compliments either.

"Maybe you should step outside," Alec suggested.

"Nah . . ." Ethan didn't elaborate.

"Then here, cool down a bit." Josh leaned over me to turn on the little tap, his arm brushing against my breasts in what was clearly a deliberate move.

I rolled my head to the side, curious. The sink didn't have a drain, and Josh turned the tap off once it was full. Then he picked up a little metal bowl sitting next to it, scooped up some water, and flung it at Ethan.

Ethan didn't even flinch, but his shoulders shook in silent laughter. "Refreshing."

The sound of splashing in the opposite sink pulled my gaze to Alec. He shut the water off and dipped his hands into it instead of using the bowl, sloshing some onto his forehead.

He dragged his hands down his face and pinned me with his icy stare, leaning forward and resting his elbows on his knees. The movement made the towel slide down, exposing dark hair and just a glimpse of silky-smooth skin lower still.

I turned to the side and copied him, scooping some cool water into my hands and splashing my face with it. Refreshing droplets trickled down my neck, dripped off my chin, ran down my chest. Alec's gaze followed their progress, his eyes drinking in every detail of my body. I could practically feel the caress of his eyes even from the opposite side of the room.

"What's the stage thing for?" I gestured to the tiled octagon in the middle of the room, looking for something to distract me from Alec's lascivious stare.

"Traditionally, bathing was a ritual as much as it was a part of daily routine," Josh explained. "People would take their time in a hammam. Usually an attendant or masseuse would provide an olive oil scrub and use a Kese mitt to exfoliate. That platform in the middle—the *göbektaşı*—is where most of the bathing, scrubbing, and massaging takes place."

"Why do you know so much about this?" Tyler chuckled, scooping some water with the bowl and splashing himself with it. Now it was me watching droplets cascade down his chest, following their path down his abs and past the tantalizing V at his hips, and seeing them get absorbed into the towel that would come away completely at the lightest tug. My fingers twitched, but I kept them on the bench by my side.

"It's history." Josh shrugged. "I find it interesting, and the library had a book about the cultural and historical significance of bathing houses, so . . ."

Tyler smiled, a glint entering his gray eyes. "Why don't you give us a demonstration then?"

He nodded at the platform, then swiped his hair off his forehead. Even wet from the water he'd been throwing on himself, it still managed to get in his face.

The grin Josh flashed him was downright wicked. "Great idea."

But it was Ethan who stood first, not even trying to grab at the towel. "If we're spending more time in here, I need a drink of water, and I need to turn the steam down or I'll pass out."

"Good thinking." Josh nodded as he stood too, coming to stand directly in front of me. Apparently we were all abandoning our towels now, because suddenly I had a half-erect dick in my face. Not that I was complaining. I licked the moisture off my lips and looked up at him.

The sound of the door closing behind Ethan mingled with the echo of Josh's voice.

"Come on, let me worship your body." He held his hand out, and I took it without hesitation, letting him guide me to the platform in the middle.

I sat on the edge, and Josh sat down next to me, nudging my shoulders until I turned my back to him. He started massaging my neck. His nimble fingers worked at the muscles in firm but gentle movements, slowly moving to my shoulders and my upper back.

My skin was damp with steam and sweat, and Josh's hands glided over me with ease, as if he'd used massage oil. I closed my eyes and rolled my head from side to side, giving his fingers room to move and stretching into the pressure.

The sound of the door opening again made me lift my eyes. Ethan waltzed back in, handed us each a bottle of water, and sat down in front of me. We drank deeply.

I knew it was dangerous to remain in a steam room or sauna for too long—you could get lightheaded or even pass out. But the water was helping us rehydrate, and Ethan must've turned the steam down very low. It was still hot and steamy, but it wasn't oppressive and difficult to breathe.

Besides, there was nothing that could tear me away from Josh's hands at the moment. If I passed out, so be it.

"Lie down on your front," he instructed, and I climbed farther onto the platform, my head near Alec's spot on the bench, my feet hanging off the end. The smooth, slick marble surface was almost too hot but pleasant against my skin.

Splashes echoed around me, and then Josh's hand was at my ankle, massaging gently before gliding up my leg. His touch was followed closely by the exquisite shock of cool water, trickling along my ankle and up to the top of my thigh. With my eyes closed, I felt every droplet as it caressed my skin.

He repeated the motions on my other leg—the gentle touch followed by the cool trickle of water up my calf, the back of my knee, my thigh.

Metal clanged against the stone bench, echoing in the dimly lit space. Then two sets of hands appeared at my feet. Judging by the size difference, Ethan had joined Josh in massaging my legs.

They started at my feet, moved up my ankles, calves, the backs of my thighs. They worked in perfect synchronicity, as they always did. It was both perfect—ideal pressure, exact amount of time spent on each muscle— and nowhere near enough.

As they paid special attention to the spot just under my ass, their fingers passing lower and lower between my thighs, the tap came on again. I kept my eyes closed as it turned off, and then a trickle of water started at my neck and traveled painfully slowly down the center of my spine. The droplets tickled a little along my ribs, but I was so lost in all the other sensations that it wasn't unpleasant.

Whoever it was repeated the action, using a little more water this time, covering my shoulders and then continuing past the base of my spine and between my butt cheeks.

Cool, velvety water trickled down between my thighs, adding even more moisture to my already wet folds, teasing my most sensitive parts in the most delicious way. I gasped, the sound startling in the heavy silence.

The air had already been thick with steam; now it became even heavier with taut, breathless anticipation.

TWENTY-EIGHT

As soon as the gasp left my lips, the hands at my thighs moved up and over my ass. They glided up my back, then separated over my shoulders. Ethan and Josh took my wrists and stretched my arms out to either side. Then the two of them started a slow, sensual massage, giving my arms the same treatment as my legs. The water appeared again, trickling over my wrists, up my arms, and to my shoulders.

The third set of hands picked up where they'd left off at my thighs, zeroing in on my ass. Immediately I knew it was Tyler. His hands were strong, firm, but smooth. Alec had rough, calloused hands, despite how tenderly they touched me.

Tyler kneaded my butt with slow, deliberate movements. His outspread hands ran all the way up and over, then caressed down my sides and hips, dipping into the crease before circling back up.

Every time he passed the underside of my ass, his fingers came within a hair's breadth of where I craved their touch the most. The teasing was maddening, and since this was Tyler, I was positive he knew exactly what he was doing.

After hours of this torture—OK, it was probably just a few minutes—his thumbs finally passed over my aching lips, pausing to massage the area for just a moment before moving away again.

I groaned, mostly in protest. I wanted *more*.

But they remained silent. Josh and Ethan's caresses had nearly reached my shoulders, and Tyler started massaging my back in long, slow strokes.

They worked together until every inch of my back was given the same treatment. Finally, Tyler's lips pressed between my shoulder blades, and he gently trailed kisses all the way down my spine. Once his mouth reached the sensitive area of my lower back, he kissed, nipped, and licked my skin as he moved his fingers up the inside of my thigh, up to my core, and slid two fingers inside in one smooth, slick movement.

I arched my back and moaned.

As Tyler moved his fingers, sliding them in and out painfully slowly, more water was poured down the length of my spine. Tyler removed his fingers and licked all the way back up my body, his tongue gliding over each little bump of vertebrae. He kept his body low over mine, his heavy breaths loud in my ear, his hot chest trapping me against the hot tiles.

"Turn over," he commanded, his voice thick with lust. And then he was gone. All their touch was gone.

I was at their mercy, ready to do whatever they asked, and I moved to obey immediately. I lifted onto my elbows but paused.

Alec was still in the same spot, his shoulders propped against the wall, his head leaning back.

Sharing me didn't come naturally to him, and he'd worked to get used to the idea. I'd had sex with more than one of them before, even with Alec involved, but we'd never done *this* before. I'd never had them all in the same room during sex, let alone have them all at the same time.

And that's exactly what I wanted. I hadn't been thinking about it—or much of anything really, I was so lost in the sensations—but now I realized that was *exactly* how I wanted it to play out. I wanted them all, at the same time, equally. As in all other things.

Alec met my gaze unflinchingly. He wasn't paying a lick of attention to the other guys or what they were doing. His full focus was on me, the lust in my eyes, the anticipation in my face, the way my boobs pressed into the tiles every time I took a breath. He was here for me and nothing else, and he wasn't leaving.

In fact, I was pretty sure he was enjoying himself. His lips parted as his hooded eyes took me in. The towel was still in the same spot, just barely covering his crotch, but now the tip of his erect cock was visible over the top of the fabric.

But I still needed to make sure. I focused on his eyes and mouthed, *OK?*

He smirked in that delicious, intense way that could equally mean he was about to hurt me or kiss me. I'd take either at this point. I'd take everything Alec had to give and politely ask for more.

He gave me one nod and pulled the towel away. I couldn't have stopped my gaze from wandering down if I'd wanted to. He wrapped his hand around his shaft and took one long, slow stroke that made me want to crawl over there and help him out.

But the others were getting impatient. Working together, they gently nudged and eased me onto my back.

Now that I was facing up, my back pressing into the warm tiles, I couldn't bring myself to close my eyes. Not with three such amazingly hot men leaning over me. So much glistening skin and corded muscle, the broad shoulders, the tight abs, the erect, proud cocks. They were all hard. For me.

It was intoxicating.

But their eyes, despite looking at me as if they each wanted to take a bite, were full of love. I felt safe, adored, *worshipped*.

The metal bowls were refilled once more, and Ethan and Josh poured refreshing water over my neck, my sensitive, hard nipples, and down my belly. As they reached the apex of my thighs, Tyler pushed my knees apart and let the water sluice down. The sensation was a little weird, almost as if I were about to pee, but it was pleasant. The bowls were set aside, and then their hands were back—*all* their hands, kneading my body all over.

Ethan and Josh concentrated on my top half, massaging my arms, shoulders, and chest; teasing me by avoiding my breasts; and moving down to caress my stomach. Meanwhile, Tyler settled himself between my legs and worked on my thighs, his fingers pushing harder and firmer, his movements sliding closer and closer to where I wanted him most. His ability would've been telling him exactly where I wanted those hands. Any of those hands, all of them.

Usually when we made love, he blew my mind, picking up on every little thing I wanted and doing it before I could even voice the desire. But this time, he was deliberately denying me, teasing me. They all were, and I was starting to unashamedly writhe under their touch, looking for more friction, more . . . *anything* to satisfy this ache.

As Ethan and Josh finally stepped it up, their hands caressing my breasts, Tyler followed through and swiped his thumbs over my folds, rubbing in an up-and-down motion but still avoiding the most sensitive spot. The frustration was becoming unbearable.

"Please." The word came out on a desperate whisper.

"Enough." Alec spoke for the first time, his voice low but commanding. "Make her come."

Tyler paused and looked up, one eyebrow arched, his lips quirked into an amused little smile. I couldn't see Alec's face behind me, but I could picture the challenge in his gaze.

Tyler was the leader. It came naturally to him, and the others followed his lead because they trusted him. But every once in a while, Josh would step in to point out another option, and Alec would go completely off-script.

I had a feeling we were going to have a lot of fun exploring this power dynamic between them. Little did they know, I was the one truly in charge. If I demanded something with enough seriousness, they would all willingly give it to me. That's why I loved letting Tyler take the lead, take control of my pleasure—I trusted him without question and knew he would do as I asked if it came down to it.

So I kept my mouth shut, waiting to see who would win this tug of war . . . this time.

"Why don't you come and do it yourself?" Tyler resumed his movements, making me moan, but kept his gaze locked on Alec.

"I'd prefer to watch for now. I want to see the look on her face when she shatters."

Tyler chuckled. "All right."

He slid his hands down my legs, shuffling back as he went. Before I could wonder where he was going, he lowered his head between my legs, wrapped his hands around my thighs, and stopped teasing. He didn't nip and lick and ease me into it. He stuck his tongue out and licked me firmly and decidedly.

I moaned in both relief and desperation. Tyler alternated between licking and sucking my clit and working the other areas with perfect pressure. His hands held my hips down, at his mercy.

Josh wrapped his hand around the front of my neck and, before I could think about whether it made me more turned on or less, dragged his hand down my chest and took a firm hold of my left breast. His perfect mouth closed over my nipple and made me cry out again.

Ethan laced his fingers through my right hand and kissed and licked his way to my other breast. His mouth was gentle, his tongue moving in wide, languorous swoops; Josh was a little rougher, raking his teeth over my sensitive flesh.

I was moaning with every breath, the sounds echoing off the tiles. My entire body was a ball of sensation, pleasure, *sex*. The amount of build-up I'd had to endure meant I was close to climax within just a few moments of having their mouths on me. Every swipe of a tongue on my aching flesh sent me closer and closer to the edge.

I gripped Ethan's fingers and threaded my free hand into my hair, rolling my head back. As soon as my eyes connected with Alec's, he moved toward me. He dropped to his knees, his cock inches from my face. I wanted it in my mouth, but I didn't think I'd be able to give him a proper blow job—I was moaning and writhing too much, too lost in my own pleasure.

But Alec surprised me anyway. He sat back on his heels and pulled my hand out of my hair with rough fingers. His other hand held my jaw as he kissed me.

The stubble on his chin brushed against my nose as he kissed me upside down, his tongue claiming my mouth.

I had all their mouths on me, all their tongues working to give me the greatest pleasure I could ever imagine. Just as Alec pulled away and licked my lips, I came.

He watched me, just as he said he wanted to. His eyes took in every detail of my face and body as I came undone beneath them, wave after wave of pleasure washing through me; I moaned into Alec's face, and he panted above me.

Tyler slowed down as I rode it out. Ethan and Josh did the same, giving me little kisses.

They all backed up and stood around me, watching with heavy eyes and heaving chests as I slowly melted into a puddle on the platform. I liked having their eyes on me, their undivided attention. It made me feel powerful. Strong.

As my breathing calmed, I struggled up onto my elbows. Alec rushed forward to support me, so I gave up trying to sit up and leaned on him instead.

"Water." I reached my hand out, and Ethan placed a bottle of water in it immediately. I drank half the bottle and handed it back.

Alec was rock hard—he was pressing into my back, his hands starting to roam my body—and I could see how hard the others were too. Seeing and feeling the evidence of their desire had my body responding again already. Alec's touch was becoming more demanding, his hips rocking lightly behind me. Ethan sat on the edge of the platform and leaned in to kiss me, gentle at first but more insistent with every second.

Tyler sat down on the bench and drank his water as his eyes drank in what we were doing on the platform.

He'd started this, probably orchestrated the whole thing, and now he was sitting back to watch it play out. He looked so fucking cocky, with that knowing smile on his face, my favorite little bit of hair falling over his forehead.

I pulled away from Ethan's kiss, and he started kissing my jaw, moving down to my neck as his hand gripped my hip.

Josh walked around the platform until he stood before me, then gave me a brilliant, lust-filled smile. I just loved how freely they moved while completely nude, not even a little shy about the raging erections standing to glorious attention.

Untangling myself from the hands and mouths that already had me ready to go again, I lifted onto my knees and pulled Josh in for a kiss. He groaned into my mouth, grabbing my ass firmly and rubbing himself all over me. The steam made everything slick and slippery.

I pulled out of his embrace, turning to the other two.

"On your back." I didn't specify which one of them I wanted to lie down. I just pointed to the platform. Ethan obeyed immediately, flashing me a dimpled grin. He spread out on one side of the platform, one leg stretched out, the other hanging off the edge with his foot planted on the ground, his thigh muscle bulging. Who was I kidding? All of Ethan's muscles were bulging. All the damn time. He stared at me with adoration, patiently waiting for me to do whatever I wished to his body.

Alec, on the other hand, looked as if he was contemplating scooping me up and running out of there to find somewhere dark he could fuck me hard and fast against a wall, all to himself. I was all for that, but not today.

He was breathing hard, his eyes narrowed, his shoulders tight. He didn't like me telling him what to do. It was always a battle of wills with us. I kept my gaze steady, resolute, and eventually, his eyes still glued to mine, he lowered himself to his hands and knees and spread himself out on his back for me. Because while he didn't like me telling him what to do, he also fucking loved it when I told him what to do. It was fucked up and confusing, but I understood it perfectly. Because it was exactly how I felt about *him* telling *me* what to do.

I wanted Alec first. He'd been first in so many ways—my first Variant; the first one I saw after being kept away for years; the first one to bring me to orgasm, despite the less than ideal circumstances. I wanted him to be the first one inside me now.

I straddled his legs and gripped his cock, giving it a few slow strokes. His breathing got shallower at my touch, but he kept his hands by his sides.

I leaned down and kissed the jagged scars curving around his side. Crawling up his body, I let my breasts drag over his cock, his belly, his chest. He still didn't touch me.

Ethan watched my every move, lying patiently next to us, and all I had to do was lift my eyes to see Tyler staring at us too. Josh leaned down on one elbow on Alec's other side, his eyes appreciatively raking over both my body and Alec's.

Gripping the base of his cock again, I put all my focus on Alec. He was looking only at me.

As I sank down onto him, inch by excruciating inch, we both moaned. Those intense eyes, still fixed on me, threatened to close, roll into the back of his head. Getting that implant was the best decision I'd ever made. Feeling them inside me, skin on smooth skin—there was no better feeling in the world.

His hips bucked up to meet mine, and I splayed my hands on his stomach for balance. Finally, he lifted his hands off the tiles, but instead of touching me, he reached over his head and gripped the edge of the platform. His abdominal muscles stretched under my fingers, and I gave them a less than gentle scratch. I dragged my hands up his chest, then raked my nails back down as I moved my hips. The tile was slippery under my knees, and I couldn't get a good grip, but it just meant I ended up riding him deep, his hips rolling to meet mine in a delicious grind.

He grunted and finally gave in to the need to close his eyes, rolling his head back. His neck muscles pulled taut as his hands gripped the edge even tighter.

I gave up trying to lift my hips up and down and reveled in the feeling of him deep inside me. He was holding himself back from touching me, letting me take control.

Tyler's moan drew my attention. He was stroking himself slowly. I could tell by the tension in his shoulders and the unhinged, hungry look in his eyes that he wanted to finish himself off. But he was holding back, holding out for me, once again showing me how much discipline he had.

Looking at Tyler broke my Alec tunnel vision. Ethan and Josh were still in the same positions on either side of us, Josh's eyes roaming our bodies, Ethan's gaze stuck to my bouncing tits.

I wanted to kiss them, touch them, hold them.

I curled my hand around the back of Josh's neck, and he leaned up to meet me halfway in a searing kiss. With one hand, he kept himself propped up while he dragged the other over the curve of my ass and up my back. My damp hair was sticking to my neck, and he pulled it away with gentle fingers before gently dropping his mouth to my moist skin.

I turned my head to Ethan, and he was halfway up before I even had a chance to reach out to him. He mirrored Josh's pose, leaning his weight on one hand, and let me pull him to me. I kissed him hard, our teeth bumping, our breath mingling as we panted and licked and sucked.

I pulled away for some air, and he immediately bent down to take my breast into his mouth.

With one hand around each of them and Alec under me—surrendered to my touch, letting me use him however I saw fit—I *felt* like a fucking goddess.

My second orgasm tore through me like a dam bursting, a rush of sensation making me forget everything but this single moment in time. I cried out but kept my eyes open and locked on Tyler's lust-filled ones, holding him with my gaze just as surely as I held the others with my body.

Ethan and Josh supported me as I started to relax against them, strong hands at my back. But Alec had other ideas.

Finally, he touched me, tearing me out of their grasp and pulling me down on top of him. One hand gripped my hip possessively; the other grabbed a fistful of my hair as his hips pumped mercilessly. I met his fast, erratic movements as best I could and wrapped my arms around his shoulders, kissing his face, his chin, his neck.

He came with a guttural roar, gripping me even tighter and then collapsing under me. I rested my forehead against his, then gave him a soft kiss, pouring all my love into it, letting my lips linger even though I was breathing hard through my nose. When I pulled away, he smiled and kissed me on the tip of my nose.

As I lifted my hips, his cock slid out of me, and his cum dripped down the inside of my thigh. One of the Turkish towels, sopping wet and ready, slapped down on the tiles next to me. I looked up, and Ty gave me a wink.

I wiped up the mess between my legs and got off Alec.

I didn't want a break, didn't need my body telling me I'd had enough, that I should pause. I was on a mission to have them all.

Ethan helped me crawl into his lap and straddle him, then he kissed me tenderly.

I appreciated his soft touch, his patience and willingness to take it easy, but I didn't need it. I deepened the kiss, rubbing my breasts against his chest, massaging his tongue with mine.

Alec scooted to the edge of the platform and took a few breaths before getting up. I heard the tap behind me running and then water splashing, but I was already consumed with Ethan's touch, his big, gentle hands caressing my body as I started to rock against him. I slid up and down his impressive length, spreading my moisture all over him without actually taking him inside me.

My body was so wired, every nerve ending at attention; it was as if I was constantly on the verge of another orgasm. Judging by Ethan's erratic breathing, the soft moans escaping his lips, he was pretty close too. Not wanting to wait another minute, I pulled back.

Ethan still had one foot planted on the ground next to the platform, and my leg was draped over his thick thigh. With a hand on my ass, he helped me rise up and impale myself on him. I slid down his length and paused, letting myself adjust. Ethan was the biggest in every way, and despite the fact that we'd been having sex for months, it still took me a moment to adjust to his size—to adjust to the stretching, the almost too full feeling. But as soon as I relaxed, it felt amazing.

I rolled my hips and wrapped my arms around his neck. He kept one hand planted on the tiles for balance as the other pushed the sticky hair out of my face. With his big, gentle hand, he caressed my brow, his thumb swiping across my cheek, the tips of his fingers caressing my jaw. All the while, his amber eyes watched me with awe.

My heart felt as if it were bursting as I stared back at him, my sweet, loving, gentle man.

He threaded his hand into the hair at the back of my head and pressed his forehead against mine. We only needed to rock slightly for his big cock to caress every inch of the sensitive nerves inside me.

My hands glided over his shoulders and chest, caressing him as gently as he caressed me, and I kissed him.

Keeping my mouth trapped against his, Ethan leaned back slowly until he was flat on his back and I was riding him. My breasts rubbed against him with every thrust as his hands dragged down my back to hold my ass firmly.

As another orgasm built—heat spreading up my chest and down to my fingers and toes, like molten lava—I kept kissing him. I came, shuddering on top of him and moaning into his mouth as I panted and licked and sucked.

His grip on my ass tightened, and he came with me, his release only a few seconds behind mine. He grunted and moaned but was just as unwilling to break our kiss, his tongue caressing mine, his lips just as greedy.

Panting, I finally pulled away and collapsed on top of him. My cheek pressed against his slick chest as he lazily ran his fingers through my hair.

I'd had three orgasms so far—the most I'd ever had in a single session—and as much as I wanted to have them all, I wasn't sure my body was capable of it.

But Josh wasn't going to let me be a quitter. As if he could sense my doubt, he appeared at my back, his mouth at my ear.

"You like feeling his big cock inside you? Filling you up?" His whisper was hoarse, but his words still bounced off the tiles, making my pussy clench around Ethan's cock.

"Yes," I hissed. Josh gripped my hips and lifted me until I was on my knees hovering over Ethan. Immediately I missed the feeling of him inside me, and just like that, I was ready to keep going, all doubts about my body's limits driven out by Josh's dirty words. I was so lost in my lust I barely registered Ethan cleaning up his hot seed with gentle hands and the wet towel.

"You want me inside you?"

"Yes." I was panting again, or still. I wasn't sure I'd ever stopped. Ethan was trying to catch his breath too, his eyes raking my body.

"You want us both inside you?" Josh nipped my ear, and I shivered. He reached between my legs from behind and stroked me, his fingers gliding easily over the slick flesh. I was so sensitive I nearly came again. Ethan grinned and started playing with my breasts.

"Fuck. Yes." I moaned.

"Who?" Josh dragged his fingers back farther, between my ass cheeks. "Tell me who you want inside you."

"You." I arched my back, desperate for more now.

"I'll take your ass." He pushed the tip of one finger just inside. "I'll be the first one to stick my cock here. But who do you want inside your pussy at the same time?"

"Any of you. All of you." I was incoherent, drunk on sex. I had no idea what I was even saying. I did want them all, and logically, I knew it was physically impossible, but Josh was making me crazy with his dirty talk.

We'd discussed anal sex. I couldn't stop fantasizing about having two of them at the same time, so I'd sat Josh and Tyler down and told them what I wanted. A brand-new butt plug had appeared in my drawer the next day, and we'd started experimenting, working up to it.

"Next time, you can have whoever you want. But right now you'll have me." Josh put a second finger into my ass, his breath still hot on my neck. At the same time, he finally pushed his cock into me—slowly, so I could feel every inch of him sliding in as he pulled his fingers out of my other hole at the same time. It was such an intense sensation, a unique kind of friction.

My arms started to shake as I struggled to stay upright, and I let myself collapse on top of Ethan's chest. Ethan stroked my shoulders with his gentle hands while Josh kept my hips angled up with a firm grip.

After starting things slowly, taking a few deliberate, languorous strokes, he set a fast pace, his hips slamming against me as though he couldn't seem to keep himself from chasing his release.

His breathing became erratic, but in between moans he managed to make another demand. "Come with me. Fuck. I'm so close."

"Don't know if I can," I panted. It was almost too sensitive, too much. Maybe my body topped out at three.

"Yes, you can." He sounded so sure. His chest pressed against my back as his arms slapped down on either side of Ethan's shoulders. "Ethan, give us a hand here."

His hips never stopped pounding into me as Ethan dragged his hand down my side, then pushed it between us.

"With pleasure." I could hear the grin in his voice as he found my clit and rubbed in rhythm with Josh's fast pace.

"Fuck!" Josh sounded as frustrated as he did satisfied; he couldn't hold it back any longer. He slammed into me one last time and spilled inside me.

The way his hips ground into me through his release pushed him deeper, hitting the sweet spot. Combined with Ethan's unrelenting fingers on my clit, it was enough to send me over the edge yet again.

"Yes!" I cried out. Josh's tendency to verbalize everything made me more vocal too. I shuddered through my release, pressed between two hot, chiseled chests.

Josh pulled out and collapsed onto his back next to us.

"Just in time." He smiled at me. His wet hair looked almost as dark as Tyler's brown locks, and I ran my hand through it.

Josh kissed me tenderly on the lips, the forehead, and the tip of my nose, then leaned back and closed his eyes as his breathing evened out.

Over the steady rise and fall of his chest, my eyes locked with serious gray ones. Tyler was still in his spot on the bench, slowly stroking himself with one hand. I couldn't believe he'd been touching himself this whole time and managed not to come. The man was the epitome of control.

As he rose to his feet and came around the platform, I had the distinct feeling I was about to see that control shatter.

I rolled off Ethan, onto my back, and propped myself up on my elbows. The movement made Josh's semen come dripping out of me. Ethan was there in a flash, towel at the ready.

Ethan and Josh pushed themselves up off the platform and went to the sinks to freshen up. Behind me, Alec was lying down on the narrow bench, one foot planted on the ground for balance and an arm slung over his eyes.

My attention snapped back to Tyler when he firmly grabbed my ankles. His touch was searing, demanding, and jolts of excitement and desire shot up my legs.

The muscles in his arms and shoulders contracted as he dragged me toward himself, and I dropped to my back, my messy wet hair trailing behind me. When my ass was at the edge of the platform, he let me go, and I lowered my feet to the ground and sat up.

He straightened to his full height and gripped my shoulders as if to push me back down, but my hand was already wrapped around the base of his cock, and I took it into my mouth.

The hot tiles felt good against my pussy, and I rocked my hips back and forth as I sucked Tyler's cock.

"Fuck." His voice was unsteady, strained. He dug his fingers into my shoulders as I took him as deep into my mouth as I could. I swirled my tongue around the head, tasting the salty precum, but before I could repeat the motion, he threaded his hands into my hair and pulled my head back.

I looked up at him and waited. His dick twitched inches away from my mouth, and I licked my lips. Tyler shuddered, the look in his eyes wild as his gaze darted over my face, my body, the proximity of his cock to my lips. His hands in my hair tightened as he breathed through his mouth.

"I . . ." He trailed off without giving me even a hint of what he wanted to say. I'd never seen Tyler so flustered, so out of control. He may have orchestrated this whole thing, but watching it play out was making him unravel.

"Her mouth feels incredible." Josh appeared at his side, caressing my cheek with the back of his hand. "But you want to come inside her."

Finally, Tyler snapped out of it and released my hair. Ethan leaned in, his mouth suddenly devouring mine, and gently pushed me back until I was lying down again.

Ethan and Josh backed away as Tyler dropped to his knees. The low platform put me at the perfect level for him. He pushed my knees wide apart and then entered me in one smooth thrust, burying himself balls deep. I was so wet, slick all over from the steam and multiple orgasms, he slid in with ease, igniting all those nerve endings once again.

I was nearly spent, my body pushed to its limit. But I still wanted him, still craved him, still started to roll my hips against him, begging him with my body to move against me.

His eyes were closed, his hands gripping my thighs with more and more pressure as he struggled to take deep, even breaths. He was trying not to come, not yet, but knowing he was *that close*, I just wanted to push him.

I reached for his hands, intending to pull him on top of me, but something halted my movements.

Alec appeared over me and grabbed my hands with his rough ones. He kneeled on the other side of the platform and pulled my arms over my head, giving me a devious smirk.

With Alec firmly holding my wrists and Tyler gripping my thighs, I was at their mercy once again. I allowed them to take control, too spent to fight them even if I wanted to.

Tyler finally opened his eyes, took me in, and gave Alec a little nod of thanks.

Only when he was positive he was once again in control—of the situation, of his own pleasure and mine—did he finally start to move.

He fucked me deep and hard, barely pulling out before sliding back in. Every time his hips connected with mine, bursts of electric sensation shot from my core through my body, an orgasm building *again*.

Tyler repeatedly dragged his hands over my hips, up my body, over my breasts and back down. His palms slid over my skin like silk.

When his damp hair fell over his eyes, I ached to brush it away, feel the soft locks between my fingers. I tugged against Alec's grip, but he only tightened it, pulling my arms tighter above my head, making my torso stretch like a lazy cat.

Tyler picked up the pace, and on his next pass, squeezed my breasts in his hands, making my back arch. He pinched my nipples lightly just as he ground into me and leaned forward, putting firm pressure on my clit.

I threw my head back and cried out as I came, my vision going blurry, my body writhing under his.

With another few deep thrusts, Tyler groaned, his gravelly voice echoing around our chamber of sex and depravity. He came deep inside me, his fingers digging into the flesh of my hips.

As my vision cleared, ice-blue eyes and a sultry smile came into focus—Alec leaning over me.

"I fucking love watching you come." He released my wrists and moved away to make room for Tyler. Still buried inside me, Tyler lowered himself until his chest was flush with mine. I wrapped one arm around his shoulders and finally ran my fingers through his hair, pushing it off his forehead as he leaned in to kiss me.

We kissed for a long time, lazy and slow, our tongues caressing. Then he finally pulled out and struggled to his feet.

I couldn't even fathom trying to sit up. My eyes were already drooping closed. I could totally sleep here for the night—it was warm enough.

Luckily, I had four Variants to take care of me. Water was once again sluiced over my body, a wet cloth and gentle hands cleaning me all over. Then I was wrapped up in dry towels and lifted into strong arms.

Someone cracked a joke about making sure the steam room was thoroughly cleaned and disinfected before someone else used it, but I was already relaxing against a strong chest.

I was asleep before we made it back to our cottage.

TWENTY-NINE

A warm breeze caressed my naked body as the soothing sound of crashing waves drifted in through the open window. It was still nighttime, the only light coming from the partially obscured moon.

So what had woken me?

I snuggled closer into Ethan's side and closed my eyes.

Murmuring voices made me open them again. I recognized the deep honey quality of Alec's voice and the firm, calm response coming from Tyler, but I couldn't make out the words.

As safe and comfortable as I was boxed in by Ethan and Josh, my curiosity wouldn't allow me to go back to sleep.

With careful movements, I shimmied to the edge of the bed and managed to slip out of the room, grabbing the abandoned sheet off the ground as I passed.

I was sore, every movement reminding me of what we'd done in the steam room only hours prior. But the aches in my arms, legs, and abdominal muscles were nothing to be alarmed about—if anything, they made me smile.

I wrapped the sheet around myself and padded through the little cottage, following their voices toward the front door.

"I just feel so impotent." Tyler's frustrated voice rose, and Alec shushed him. I paused halfway to the door and clutched the sheet to my chest.

"I know, man. I just want to go out there and . . . punch something," Alec growled, "but it's starting to feel insurmountable. What are we supposed to do?"

"I don't know. That's the problem. I have all the relevant information. I have so much of her Light coursing through me I hardly even need to focus to draw out the truth. It just comes to me. But I don't know what the next move is. Every possible scenario puts her in danger."

Alec sighed.

My days of eavesdropping on conversations and coming to erroneous conclusions were over, and I didn't feel the need to hide from them. So I walked to the door and out onto the patio.

Neither of them so much as raised an eyebrow. They'd probably heard me coming. They sat side by side, their chairs facing the edge of the cliff. The moon, half-hidden behind a cloud, reflected off the inky water in the distance. It was eerily beautiful.

I sank into Tyler's lap, and he wrapped his arms around my middle and kissed the back of my neck. Reaching out, I threaded my fingers with Alec's, and he kissed the back of my hand before dropping it into his lap.

"I'm sorry." I wasn't entirely sure what I was sorry about. So many warring feelings writhed inside me it was difficult to decipher them.

"You have nothing to apologize for," Tyler said firmly,

"None of this is your fault," Alec agreed.

"I hate how messed up everything has gotten." Neither of them replied. What was there to say?

We sat like that for a while, just holding each other and staring out at the moon, listening to the water crash rhythmically against the cliffs.

Eventually, we went back to bed, but I couldn't get to sleep.

I kept staring into space, thinking about all the things I'd avoided thinking about for days, if not weeks. Then I'd stare at their beautiful faces and feel my chest tighten at the mere thought of losing one of them.

As soon as the first rays of sun streamed into the room, I got up—careful not to wake them—got dressed, and went for a run. I pushed my body despite the soreness, letting the burn in my lungs distract me, letting the crisp morning air clear my head. I went around the island twice, waving to some of the Lighthunters we'd met.

By the time I got back, the sun was casting bright rays over the kitchen, where Ethan was cooking eggs. The others sat around the dining table, sipping coffee.

"Hey," I panted, pouring myself a big glass of water and chugging it at the sink.

A chorus of "mornings" accompanied tired, lazy smiles. Ethan kissed my sweaty cheek.

After a hot shower gave me an extra dose of determination, I came back to the dining area and pulled Tyler's borrowed laptop toward myself. He looked up from his coffee with raised brows.

I sighed. "I need to know what's happening out there. I can't pretend anymore."

They all paused and watched me warily.

"Breakfast first." Ethan dropped a plate of eggs and bacon in front of me. His smile didn't reach his eyes.

"Breakfast during," I stated, picking up the fork and opening the laptop at the same time.

Tyler draped an arm over the back of my chair and leaned in, bringing up news articles, intelligence reports, and updates from people we trusted.

"I'm not gonna lie." He sounded resigned. "It's not good."

For the next hour, he updated me on what was happening past the azure waters at the bottom of the cliffs.

The protests and violence had escalated. Some countries had been forced to declare a state of emergency; in other places, curfews and security checkpoints were coming into effect. Variant Valor had branches everywhere. They were well funded by the generally better-off Variants, and their propaganda was all over billboards and the media. The Human Empowerment Network was taking a more grassroots approach—graffiti, human-only areas, Molotov cocktails, and radicalization through social media.

Davis's face and voice were all over the reports—both news and top-secret intelligence.

So was mine.

He was holding press conferences to tell the world I was the key to everything, making it sound as if the technology he was creating would solve everyone's problems.

According to Lucian and Kyo, Melior Group was struggling to keep up with him. They were stretched thin.

Part of the forces were tasked with assisting human law enforcement, trying to make the streets safe, but some of the elite teams were still hunting Davis, trying to take him down discreetly.

Lucian happened to connect while we were going over the reports. He explained, "Part of the problem is that he keeps moving and he's well protected by his own lackeys, some of them with dangerous abilities. Then there's the issue of discretion. We need to take him quietly, if possible. We can't just tackle him to the ground in front of a dozen cameras. But by far the biggest problem is the mole we have. Whenever we get a solid lead and set up an operation, he disappears. We suspected it before, but now it's undeniable that someone high up, maybe even someone on the board, is leaking information to Davis." He sounded tired and far away on the other end of the line, and I felt bad we'd abandoned him. Tyler was his righthand man, and he was here with both hands tied behind his back. "There is serious division in the management here, and it's starting to trickle down the ranks. The number of people I can trust is woefully small. Charlie is doing all he can to weed out who the problem is, but they're covering their tracks very well. I don't know how much longer it'll be before I lose complete control over any aspect of operations."

He had to get off the phone then, and Josh made more coffee as we kept going over everything.

Bradford Hills Institute was on partial lockdown. Scared parents were pulling their kids out of school, and even some faculty had stopped showing up. Classes continued amid tight security, but the situation was tense and tenuous. Schools all over the country were in a similar situation.

An encrypted message from Charlie described the mood: "People are terrified. It's like they're all hunkering down and preparing for Armageddon. The US isn't in a state of emergency, nor do we have any curfews in place, but there are outbreaks of violence from time to time. The streets are deserted, half the businesses closed. It's eerie."

"Who can we trust?" I looked between them all. I needed to know where we stood when push came to shove.

Alec leaned forward on the table. "Uncle Lucian. Aunt Olivia and Uncle Henry. Dot and Charlie. Ed and his brother, maybe. Kyo, Marcus, and Jamie, definitely. A handful of other agents you haven't met. I know they're loyal. Other than that . . ."

It was a short list.

"Dana." I nodded firmly. "She may be jaded and frustrated with the way she's been treated her whole life, but deep down she's a good person. She's shown me that more than once. Plus, she likes me. We're practically best friends now. Also Mr. Takata and his men. He's more than proven himself. What about the Lighthunters?" I questioned just as one of them walked through our front door.

Nina had clearly heard the tail end of our conversation, but she didn't seem offended by it.

"Yes." She nodded, perching on the arm of the couch. "You can trust the Lighthunters."

"Are you positive? They were pretty pissed you brought us here." Josh made a good point.

Nina nodded. "They were, but mostly at me for not informing them. We take the security and secrecy of this facility very seriously. Honestly, we are all horrified at what Davis is doing, the way he is perverting the Light for his own sick reasons, the division it is causing all over the world. We can feel it more than anyone. It is painful. We want to help, but we have stayed silent and secret for so long. Honestly, we just don't know where to start."

Nina ran her hands over her cropped hair and stood, starting to pace. "A lot of the meetings recently have been about what our next step needs to be. The more reports that come in from our people on the ground, the more helpless we feel." She huffed.

I folded my arms and leaned forward. If a super-secret, mega-rich society of badasses was at a loss, what hope did the rest of us have?

Nina kept ranting. I had a feeling she needed to get it all off her chest. "There are some advocating for gathering up as many Vitals as we can, especially the Vivids, and bringing them to our secure locations. They want to bunker down and ride it out from the sidelines, just as we have for centuries. But that is ridiculous! We can't continue to ignore the tension in the Light, not to mention all the humans! Who is supposed to protect the humans? Granted, some of them need protecting from *themselves*—I mean, who runs at a Variant with a paralyzing ability armed with nothing more than a baseball bat and their convictions?" She bugged her eyes out incredulously as she referred to footage of one of the riots in Russia that had gone viral.

"Others are arguing we should get involved—come out to the world and tell them of our existence, fight to bring back peace. But people are scared of that too. There is a reason we went underground. I am just not so sure those reasons hold up any longer."

"Something that unifies people could go a long way. A revelation like this—that Lighthunters are real—could bring real hope to Variants," Josh mused.

"Yeah, but what about the humans?" Tyler argued. "They could see this as just another advantage the Variants have."

"Not if you present it in a good light," Ethan argued. "I mean, shit's bad, but there are places managing to stay peaceful—look at Iceland, Canada, New Zealand. They're all managing to keep their shit together. Their governments are pushing messages of unity, and people are following through on the ground, working together and refusing to get whipped up into . . ."

We were all staring at him, struggling to keep the slight shock off our faces. Ethan wasn't usually this vocal in these discussions. He listened and made sure he knew the important parts, but he left the questioning and arguing to Tyler, Josh, and me.

"What?" He frowned. "I read the news. I just prefer to read about the good bits." He folded his arms and looked down into his lap.

"No." Nina stopped pacing. "That is brilliant!"

"It is?" Ethan looked at her, surprised, a smile pulling at his lips.

"It is! And it is so simple. Marketing makes the world go round, does it not? Isn't that what Davis is doing—just really clever, aggressive marketing? If we are careful about the message we send . . ." She muttered to herself in French. "This could make all the difference. If someone can take Davis out, and then we go public with a message of peace and equality . . . We would need to put action behind our words, maybe pick both a human and a Variant organization to support. . . Yes, that might just work. I have to go!"

She ran out of the cottage, probably on her way to convince her leaders that all they needed was a good marketing plan. I hoped they still planned to provide support with their impressive resources—not the least of which were weapons and people highly trained to use them.

Yes, changing public perception and getting people to work together once more would go a long way. But sometimes, it was necessary to fight.

"None of it will make a difference as long as Davis is out there," I declared.

Tyler gripped my knee. "They're trying, baby."

They.

The people we'd left behind were doing all they could to bring down the pathetic excuse for a man I had the displeasure of calling my biological father. While we took a holiday in the Greek islands.

I stood, sending my chair scraping back.

"We need to help. We need to stop hiding and take out the root of the problem or . . ." *die trying.* I couldn't bring myself to say it. The thought of a world without the four of them in it was more than I could bear, but this was so much bigger than us, so much bigger than me.

Yet, somehow, I was the key. I was the only one who could get to Davis. Because I was the only one he wanted.

"What we need to do is keep you safe." Alec leveled a hard stare at me.

I knew that look, the tension in his shoulders. He was gearing up for a fight, but I didn't want to waste any more time fighting him.

I gave him a sad smile. "I know. That's why we ran. That's why we've been staying hidden. I get it. Trust me, I do. My mom made every argument you could possibly think of in support of the whole 'running for safety' thing. But the thing is, much as I love her and believe wholeheartedly she was just trying to protect me, *she was wrong*. And we're wrong by continuing to hide now. The longer we run from this, the worse it'll get."

"What exactly are you suggesting?" Josh raised his voice—so unlike him.

They all started speaking over one another, arguing with points I hadn't even made. They were scared. I let them get it all out, patiently standing at the table and keeping my mouth shut.

When they finally quietened down, they all stared at me with sad, resigned looks.

"You're determined to do this." Tyler had already figured out the gist of my plan.

I nodded. "I am."

"Eve, think about this." Josh looked defeated.

"Please . . ." Ethan's eyes just about broke my heart. I didn't think even he knew what he was pleading for.

"I can't lose you again, Evie." I'd never seen Alec cry, but he was close in that moment, his jaw trembling. "This isn't on you. It's not fair."

I so badly wanted to give in, to let them talk me into staying in hiding and maintaining the illusion of safety. But I had to be strong.

"Life's not fair." I shrugged. "The five of us know that better than anyone. And no, this shouldn't be on me—I don't want this responsibility. But that doesn't change the fact that I'm the best chance we have of drawing him out. He wants me. He's not even hiding it anymore. He's practically obsessed."

"What are we supposed to do?" Josh was really struggling with this. "Just knock on the door to one of his secret facilities? He'll see us coming a mile away. We'll be outnumbered and unprepared. What's the point?"

"No. We make him come to us," Tyler explained, and I knew I had him. We were moving from whether to do this or not to the practicalities of it. "We level the playing field and draw him out."

"How?" Ethan growled.

"I stop running." I moved to my bag in the corner of the room and dug around in one of the pockets for my stash of passports. It took only a moment of flicking through them to find the one I was looking for.

I slapped my Evelyn Maynard passport down on the table—the only legitimate passport I'd ever had, the one

I'd applied for as soon as my true identity became known.

"How do we know this will draw him out? How do we know it'll work? How can you just put yourself in danger like this?" Alec continued to argue. I understood why. I didn't want them anywhere near danger either, but it was time for us to do what we'd been working so hard to do since we met. It was time to be brave and honest and work together as a Bond.

"I don't know the answers to any of those questions." I looked around at them, squaring my shoulders. "But I know without a shadow of a doubt that I can't keep sitting here, hiding and doing nothing, while the world burns. And I know you can't either. I know in my soul that this is the right thing to do, and I know I have the strength to do it. Because I'm not alone anymore."

~

We took a day to prepare.

Whatever Nina's impassioned speech had been to her leaders, it worked. The Lighthunters were going public. They hoped to burst onto the world stage with a message of hope and unity to distract from Davis's hateful crap.

They were also putting the full weight of their support behind any organization focused on peacekeeping around the world.

Tyler and Alec reached out to the few people we trusted and filled them in on the plan. Every call met with resistance and arguments, but once we'd made a decision together as a Bond, we were united. My guys may not have liked what we were about to do, but they supported me one-hundred-percent.

We packed our meager possessions and went over the plan repeatedly. Alec's team and a handful of other agents would be with us, prepared to go rogue and defy orders if necessary. A few other players in the Variant world were behind us too, including a good number of Mr. Takata's trusted contacts.

When I spoke to Dana, however, she was so quiet on the line, her answers so short and reserved, by the end of it I was questioning my faith in her.

"Look, I know it's a lot to ask—this is really fucking dangerous—so I completely understand if you can't be there to back us up, but please, at least don't tell anyone about it. Give us a fighting chance."

"Yeah . . . I gotta go." She ended the call without even waiting for a response.

"Shit." I dropped the phone and dropped my head into my hands. "Shit fuck fucking tits."

Ethan chuckled as he leaned over the back of the couch to massage my shoulders. "Nothing you can do about it now, baby. You had faith in her humanity—you trusted her. I, for one, am glad you haven't lost the ability to trust altogether after all the shit you've been through."

His words were comforting, as were his strong hands on my shoulders, but I still worried I'd made a colossal mistake.

Once we'd spoken to everyone we could trust, we fell into silence, sitting about the room lost in our own thoughts.

Tyler's computer pinged, and he shook himself out of his contemplation to look at it. "It's Charlie again," he announced, then smiled as he kept reading. "He's asking if the phone is free to set up a secure line? Dot's demanding to speak to you, Eve."

He typed as he spoke, and a few moments later, the phone next to me on the couch rang.

I took a deep breath and answered. "Hey, girl."

"Don't 'hey, girl' me! If you fucking die pulling this shit, I'm gonna be so mad at you. *So mad!* I mean, I know when we did that whole 'go rogue to Australia,' that was a stupid move, but this is some next-level shit. Didn't you all run off so you could be *safe*? And now you're gonna walk right into the lion's fucking mouth! Girrrrl, you *better* not fucking die!" She ranted on about how her friends kept dropping like flies, then went on a tangent about how I'm not even a friend, I'm family. That last bit made me choke up, but I let her get it all out of her system.

When the sounds coming down the phone were more heavy breathing than shouted threats, I asked, "You done?"

"No!" She huffed, then after a pause: "Yes . . . I'm scared, Eve. I don't want to lose any of you."

"I'm scared too. But this is the right thing to do."

"Eve?"

"Yeah?"

"I'm really fucking proud of you."

I had to swallow around a lump in my throat, and even then, my answer still sounded choked. "Thanks, Dot. Love you."

"Love you."

I cleared my throat and wiped the tears off my cheeks. "What's been going on with you? I've only been gone a week, but it feels like a year."

"I know what you mean. So much has changed. I've stopped going to class. Mom and Dad are too freaked out, and the guys are on their side." I could practically hear her rolling her eyes. "I'm still doing a few classes by correspondence, but I'm starting to get cabin fever. I haven't left the house in, like, three days. But I have had a ton of extra Internet time. At least that's still up and running—we haven't gone full *Walking Dead* yet."

I chuckled. Only Dot would be excited about still being able to check social media during a time of crisis. "Been doing some online shopping to fill the time?"

"As if! I'd have nowhere to wear my new clothes. No, I'm using my uncanny digital communication skills to do some good. There's a resistance happening, and it's taking off. Eve, our generation, most of the young people I speak to, want nothing to do with this conflict, and we're sick of being ignored. I started to see these groups pop up all over the world, independent of one another—people using social media to organize peaceful protests and sit-ins, that kind of thing. So I thought, why not connect them? Make a global network of resistance?"

"Holy shit, Dot, that's amazing."

"Yeah, Charlie helped me set some stuff up, secure webpages and shit, and even connected me with some of his hacker buddies. Anyway, we're all working together to spread more messages of unity. There's gonna be a worldwide peaceful protest next week. Oh! And we're getting T-shirts printed!"

I had to laugh at that. Of course she was getting T-shirts printed. I'd been gone a week and my best friend had managed to set up a global resistance movement. "I'm gonna make sure you speak to some of the Lighthunters. What they have planned is really in line with what you're doing too. After . . ."

I had no idea how to finish that sentence.

Nina walked into the cottage, backpack slung over her shoulder. "Ready? The boats are waiting."

The guys started to gather up our last few things while my heart jumped into my throat. I gripped the couch cushion. "I have to go."

"Shit! OK, um . . ."

"I'll see you tomorrow, Dot." Considering how fucking terrified I was, I was surprised at how even my voice sounded. I didn't want to say goodbye to her. I didn't want to say goodbye to anyone.

"Yeah . . ." She was crying again. "Yep. I'll see you then."

I hung up and stood. Immediately, Josh took my hand, giving it a comforting squeeze. Ethan waited by the door. Alec and Tyler were just outside, watching.

I squared my shoulders and walked toward what I knew would be a defining moment of my life—if it didn't kill me.

And my Bondmates would be with me every step of the way.

Three speedboats carried us and a delegation of Lighthunters to the mainland. No one spoke much, and in Athens, we split up. The Lighthunters headed off on various assignments to prepare for what they were about to reveal to the world, and the five of us headed straight for the airport.

I gave the airport worker a weak smile as he checked my passport. In all my years of using fake documentation, I'd never been as nervous as I was to hand over my actual, legitimate passport. The man scanned it, stamped it, and handed it over.

It was done. Evelyn Maynard was officially checked in to the international airport in Athens. I could just imagine some warning system in one of Davis's buildings going off, alerting them I'd surfaced.

I made room for Ethan, then Alec, behind me. Josh and Ty waited just past the little booths. As I moved to join them, I gripped the strap of my backpack, my knuckles going white, and looked up for the security camera. I spotted it in the corner, near the ceiling.

Davis would get access to it.

With every bit of determination and anger I possessed permeating my gaze, I stared it down as if it were the devil himself perched in the corner and not an inanimate object. Just for good measure, I mouthed, *Come and get me.*

Then I turned and marched to our boarding gate.

THIRTY

We had fifteen hours—the time it took to travel from Athens to Washington DC—to mentally prepare for what was to come. I'd expected to find it impossible to sit still, expected to fight against the adrenaline, but as we reached cruising altitude, a kind of calm fell over me.

Alec and Tyler slept most of the way, conserving energy while they could. Ethan dozed too, but he found it difficult to get comfortable in the tight seats, which were definitely not designed for someone his size. Josh and I didn't sleep a wink, both of us lost in our thoughts.

We needed to give our people on the ground time to prepare, but I still wished the flight wasn't so long. We'd debated taking a shorter one, just going somewhere in Europe or even waiting for him in Athens, but in the end, we'd decided to go home.

According to intelligence reports, Davis was somewhere on the West Coast, and I wanted to make sure he came for me himself. Mostly, I wanted to send him a message—I was done running. He was not going to keep me from my home any longer, stop me from being where I belonged. While we weren't flying into New York, it was close enough. Besides, DC was a smaller airport and would be easier to evacuate.

We landed in late afternoon, the hot sun casting golden light over the vast planes of the airport, but when we parked on the tarmac and didn't move for a long time, it became clear something was wrong. Passengers were getting restless by the time the pilot finally made an announcement. "Folks, we have an emergency situation, and I've been instructed by ground control not to approach the airport terminal. We're going to deploy the emergency slides and disembark. I've been assured we're safe here, but we do need to evacuate the aircraft in a calm and timely manner. Please pay close attention to what your flight attendants are saying. Thank you for your cooperation."

The level of chatter rose among the passengers as they started to get a bit panicked, but he flight attendants were professional and efficient, deploying the slides and ushering people down.

Once on the ground, all the passengers were herded onto waiting buses. Men clad in black and holding automatic weapons stood by, watching everything carefully. As we approached the bus, one of the armed men stepped forward and gestured for the five of us to follow him to the side. I could feel the eyes of the other curious passengers burning a hole in the back of my head.

The buses drove off, leaving us with the four armed men on the deserted tarmac. As soon as the other passengers were out of sight, the men relaxed their tense stances and greeted Alec and Tyler.

"Everything's in place. Airport buildings should be cleared within the next ten minutes," the man who'd stopped us in line reported.

"I don't know if this is brilliance or pure fucking madness," another said to Tyler, but his eyes kept darting to me. I must've looked like a mess after the long-haul flight, my hair crazy, my clothes wrinkled, my skin drenched in sweat from the summer sun. It must've been ninety degrees out there.

"We're not paying you to wonder about the merits of missions," Tyler said with a teasing grin.

"Man, you ain't paying any of us for *shit*. I don't even know if we'll have jobs after this, if we even make it out alive. Anyone from Melior Group that's here today is going rogue, acting against direct orders from the board and siding with Lucian Zacarias and you fuckers."

People were putting their jobs, their lives, on the line to help us. Some of the resigned calm that had fallen over me on the plane was chased away by uncertainty.

In place of a reply, Alec clasped the man's hand, and they patted each other on the back. He repeated the gesture with the other three, and I had a feeling they'd known each other a long time.

We parted ways, and a short golf buggy ride later, we walked into the terminal building.

I sighed, glad to be in air conditioning after the oppressive heat. Or maybe it was the situation itself that was oppressive.

Walking through an abandoned airport was kind of surreal, like something from a post-apocalyptic movie. Stores were still lit up and wide open while plates with half-eaten meals and still steaming mugs of coffee littered the tables of restaurants.

We settled in near a wall of windows overlooking the tarmac. Ty and Alec sat calmly on either side of me at one end of a heavy wooden table. Ethan leaned against the window, his feet crossed at the ankles. Josh paced slowly, looking down the wide corridor every once in a while. Really, we had no idea where any potential threat could come from. It could crash through the ceiling for all we knew.

None of us spoke.

Should I be more nervous? I was waiting to face head-on the threat my mother had been running from my entire childhood. But I was eerily calm, as calm as the abandoned airport. I'd made peace with whatever happened next. If I was to die, I was taking him down with me.

The sharp sound of glass shattering in the distance was the first sign we were no longer alone.

We all rose to our feet, and the guys positioned themselves in front of me. Tyler and Alec pulled their guns, and Ethan conjured an angry blue fireball. I'd already transferred all the extra Light I could to them. We were as prepared as we could be, so I just planted my feet wide and waited, craning my neck to see through the gap between Alec and Tyler's broad shoulders.

Davis's men barely made a sound as they approached. The breaking glass had likely been a distraction to get us all looking down the wide corridor, because when they appeared, they converged on us from all directions.

A shadow caught my eye, dancing jerkily on the concrete floor to my left, and I turned just in time to see several masked men rappel down the tall windows and shoot the glass. It all happened so fast, their movements so precise and practiced that I barely had time to blink before one of them landed mere feet from me.

The guys tightened their position around me, boxing me in, as the masked men approached. Despite the assailants' dramatic entrance, they weren't shooting or moving to attack. They just surrounded us, guns pointed.

One of them stepped forward and spoke, his voice muffled through the mask. "Hand over the girl, and we'll kill you quickly."

For a moment, no one spoke. My heart battered against my chest, and my breathing sounded obnoxiously loud.

I couldn't see Tyler's face, but I could see the way his cotton shirt pulled taut over his tense muscles; I could imagine the way his gray eyes narrowed on the piece of shit threatening to kill them. When he spoke, his voice was firm and loud. "No."

As soon as the word left his lips, Tyler and Alec both fired in rapid succession, taking out two men each with clean headshots before anyone else could react. Ethan threw the fireball, the blue flames engulfing his victim faster than any fire I'd ever seen; he threw more as fast as he could conjure them.

Josh simply backed up, his back connecting with my right arm, and watched everything with a look of intense concentration.

Davis's men started firing.

Every bullet came within a foot of us and then dropped to the ground. The tinkling sound of ammo piling up at our feet mingled with the deafening gunfire.

"Take out the blond one!" someone shouted.

So far, only bullets had been flying at us, but when more assailants started running up, it became apparent Davis had sent in his Variants too.

Unnaturally fierce wind started to lift anything in the area that wasn't tied down. At the same time, several machines—transport buggies, vacuum cleaners, anything electronic and on wheels—started careening straight for Josh.

Alec isolated the Variant with the wind ability and the one with the tech ability and took them both out, their screams of pain audible even over the rest of the cacophony.

As Alec defended Josh, Ethan paused throwing fireballs. Instead, he lifted his arms over his head and sent wave after wave of bright golden fire in every direction: the signal for our own backup to come charging in. From every back room, storage area, and hidden location, our people burst out to join the fight.

The Lighthunters—being impervious to Variant abilities, highly trained in combat, and as yet unknown to the rest of the world—were the biggest secret weapon. With deadly proficiency, they incapacitated the confused Variants, who couldn't figure out why their abilities had suddenly stopped working.

My heart skipped a beat when I caught sight of Dot and Charlie, walking slowly hand in hand at the edge of the fighting. I ducked as all manner of winged creatures came flying through the now wide-open space where the glass used to be. Several wings clipped my head and shoulders as pigeons, woodpeckers, kites, hawks, and eagles swooped down on our enemies.

Even Olivia and Henry were there, not that I should've been surprised—they'd both worked for Melior Group at one time. They stuck close to Dot and Charlie, shooting anyone who came close with lethal accuracy.

Lucian had stayed behind, even though doing so had probably pissed him off. But we needed him on the outside. He was managing communications and organizing all he could between the different groups that had come together.

Ed and his brother were there too. Ed was keeping one hand on his brother's shoulder, transferring Light to him, as the bigger man used his strength ability to barrel through assailants, knock people unconscious with a single punch, and throw tables as if they weighed no more than a sheet of paper.

Kyo, Marcus, and Jamie were leading the Melior Group agents who had gone rogue to join this fight. They were in their element, working perfectly as a team, almost every gunshot meeting its target.

Mr. Takata's people were at the same level—highly efficient, deadly, precise. Mr. Takata himself was in a room in the basement, near where they sorted the luggage, with his wife and Vital. His sole focus was on keeping everyone shielded from another potential threat like Sarah, the Variant whose ability could cause unconsciousness on a large scale. We couldn't risk something like that happening again. Mr. Takata couldn't isolate this many specific people to shield—there were simply too many of us to keep track of—but he could, with the help of his Vital, throw a large shield over the whole area to defend against any such remote attacks.

My eyes darted about the room. I wasn't a fighter; I still struggled in the sparring sessions, and I hated guns, so I'd only learned the basics at Tyler's insistence. But I was a *survivor*, and I wasn't completely helpless.

I let my glowing Light surge through me and tipped my head back. Replicating what I'd done on the night Alec nearly died, I drew Light from those meaning to do us harm and pushed it to those fighting on our side. But I couldn't keep that up too long. Davis still hadn't shown himself, and I had to conserve my energy.

As prepared and well armed as we were, we still weren't fighting children. We were up against trained killers and people with formidable, dangerous abilities.

A man with a water ability was throwing massive sprays at Dot's birds, making it difficult for them to fly and attack. Another person with a speed ability was blurring about the room so fast it was impossible to distinguish their appearance, but every once in a while one of our people dropped, blood gushing from a slit throat, after the person whizzed past.

Both cool water and warm blood splashed me, making me wince as if I'd been slapped. I wiped the mess off my cheek but refused to look at my palm as I rubbed it against a dry spot on my shorts.

A middle-aged woman took slow, careful steps through the chaos, her hands clasped in front of her. Every time someone went for her, she cocked her head to the side, and her attacker dropped to their knees, whimpering in terror. I wasn't entirely sure what her ability was, but I didn't want to find out.

Both sides were taking heavy losses.

We couldn't keep going like this.

"Alec!" I yelled, even though he was standing only a few feet away.

"I know!" he growled as he reloaded his weapon.

"We got you covered." Tyler stepped to the side, and Ethan and Josh shifted to cover the gap Alec created as he turned to face me.

One second my head was spinning from all the chaos, all the violence around me. The next my head was spinning because Alec was kissing me. His mouth devoured mine, intense and urgent. One of his hands gripped my hip while the other still held on to his gun. For few blissful seconds, there was nothing but Alec.

I let the Light gush through our connection. He really didn't need to kiss me to get it. I could've given him all he needed with a simple touch. I could've done it without touching him at all. No, Alec was kissing me so intensely because he needed it—needed the comfort before doing the one thing he hated most: using his ability.

But we didn't have time for this. After only a few moments, I pulled away and gave him a firm nod.

He squared his shoulders and turned, blocking me from most of the action. With a deep breath, he lowered his head and clenched his fists, every muscle in his body tensing as he unleashed the full force of his pain.

We'd been practicing as much as we could, but it was more difficult to do that safely with Alec; someone always had to volunteer to be exposed to excruciating pain in order for us to test his limits. But he'd managed to work out how to isolate specific individuals when sending out a massive blast of his power. Still, his technique was far from perfect, especially in such a hectic environment.

I felt the sheer force of Alec's ability as it blasted out of him. Some people screamed, clutching their heads or stomachs before falling to the ground. Most just crumpled immediately, unconscious, their brains incapable of processing that much pain.

All the noise of people killing one another ceased. Bullets stopped sailing through the air. Things stopped crashing and smashing. People stopped barreling into each other. All was silent as I breathed heavily, my chest rising and falling in an unsteady rhythm.

As soon as bodies hit the floor, Tyler reloaded both his guns. "Regroup! Assume there are more coming! Let's get the wounded to a safe distance and restrain the enemy operatives!"

I lifted my head, letting my surroundings soak in. Smoke billowed from the corridor to our left, which was choked with debris. Most of the furniture—tables and chairs, lounges belonging to various airport cafés—was strewn about or pulverized. But the worst of it were the bodies. A lot of them were just passed out, taken down by Alec's ability, but many more were surely dead. A heavy metallic smell mingled with the smoke—blood.

Blood was everywhere. It wasn't as obvious on the black clothing of the Melior Group operatives or Davis's men, but it was stark against skin. It dripped off the counter near where we stood, giving Jackson Pollock a run for his money with how far and wide it had splattered.

Bile rose to my throat and saliva filled my mouth; I struggled to take a deep breath. Everywhere I looked there was blood. With every breath, I could smell it. My eyes started to water as I clenched my jaw, willing myself not to lose it. Not yet.

"Jamie!" Dot's shrill scream echoed in the now silent, cavernous space.

Just a few yards in front of me, Dot sprinted over bodies and dropped to her knees in a slide, Kyo and Charlie hot on her heels. Her frantic hands ran all over the body of a man dressed in black. Jamie's bright red hair stood out among the dusty gray debris.

Marcus rushed over from the opposite direction, holstering his gun. I rushed forward too but stopped just short of them. What could I possibly do?

"Was it Alec?" Dot sounded frantic as Kyo hurriedly checked Jamie. "Please tell me it was just Alec. He'll wake up. He'll be fine. He just needs to sleep it off."

I hadn't even realized Ethan and Josh had followed me or taken my hands in theirs, but I squeezed them tightly, dreading what Kyo would say next. I could see the devastated look on his face.

Kyo closed his eyes and swallowed slowly before straightening up.

"No." Dot shook her head, her expression something between angry and broken. "No, no, no, no . . ." She kept repeating the little two-letter word as if it would bring him back, as if the rapidly widening puddle of blood around him would magically retreat, as if his chest would start rising and falling once more.

As Dot fell apart, cradled between Kyo and Marcus, another layer of steel shuttered down over my heart.

I couldn't afford to fall apart.

Not yet.

I needed something to focus on, so I took deep, measured breaths and counted off the people Alec had managed to keep safe from his ability.

Dot and Charlie. *Don't look.*

Olivia and Henry. Bloody and dirty but still standing. *Don't linger.*

Kyo and Marcus. *Don't think about Jamie.*

Ed and his brother. Helping to carry all the unconscious enemies to a secure room in the back. *Don't focus on the smell. Just breathe.*

Several of the rogue Melior Group agents. Is that Kane? Our ruthless trainer didn't look injured at all as he methodically reloaded his weapons, standing tall in a sea of bodies. *Don't think about it.*

And all the impervious Lighthunters, of course.

"Eve?" Josh turned to me, reaching up as if to cup my cheek. I dropped their hands and stepped back, out of his reach.

"I'm fine," I rushed out. If I let them touch me, comfort me, draw me into their arms and hold me, I would fall apart.

Not yet. Don't think about it.

"We need to get all our wounded to a safe place." It was a pointless statement. We were already doing that. The more bodies we moved, the more the concrete floor was revealed. It used to be gray; now it was bathed in crimson.

Thankfully, Josh knew I needed to stay strong. He nodded and moved off, helping to carry the injured and unconscious with his ability. Ethan stayed by my side. I wasn't sure if having one of them always beside me was a good or bad thing. They gave me strength, made me feel as if I could handle this, but at the same time, I was a giant glowing target, and anyone close to me could die at any moment. I couldn't stand the thought of any of my beautiful, loving, kind men . . . *Don't think about it.*

Not yet.

I looked around and spotted a camera near the table we'd sat at when we first arrived. The heavy timber table was the only piece of furniture still standing. I marched over, tilting my head to stare directly into the camera.

"Come and get me yourself, you fucking coward!" I yelled, imagining his face. I knew he'd be watching. I would be if I were him.

Keeping my eyes on the camera, I bent down, picked up a chair, and took a seat at the table, finally looking away to stare straight ahead.

With every steadying breath I took, I reminded myself why we were here, what I had come here to achieve. That strange calm slowly settled over me as the room was cleared of bodies. One by one, my Variants came back to my side.

Ethan leaned on the end of the table opposite me, his big arms crossed. Alec stood tall near him, his feet planted, his gun drawn. Josh was at my right shoulder, his hand resting on the back of my chair, with Ty at my left.

Dot and Charlie, Ed and his brother, Kyo and Marcus, and Nina and the Lighthunters were scattered about the room, catching their breath but on the alert.

Dot's tear-streaked face was set in a hard, steely mask. Her men were one down, but they stood at her back, supporting her just as mine were.

Our eyes met across the room. All my deeply buried pain and worry, all my determination and barely contained rage, I saw reflected in her eyes. We didn't get up and go to each other for a hug.

Not yet.

We didn't say anything or even nod. We simply held each other's gaze for a few long seconds—a moment of pure solidarity.

I understood the look on her face perfectly. And I intended to do something about it.

I wasn't leaving here until Davis Damari showed his face. Until I did all I possibly could to remove his toxic influence from the world.

As the sun set behind me, taking the last bits of natural light with it, I looked away from Dot and narrowed my eyes on the vast open space before me. Half the lights had been busted in the battle, casting the area in an uneven, eerie light, but it was still enough for me to see my so-called father as he approached.

The sound of several footsteps preceded his arrival. He wasn't alone.

THIRTY-ONE

As Davis came around the corner, his expensive shirt and pristine tailored pants a stark contrast to the destruction and gore around him, I knew one thing without a shadow of a doubt.

One of us would not be leaving alive.

"Such heavy thoughts, daughter," he called out, pretending to frown before his face split into a disturbing grin.

I stayed silent. I had nothing to say to this monster. This was another distraction technique, another attempt to get a rise out of one of us. Just like the way he'd made us all wait. It was just another stupid power play.

"Oh, got me all figured out now, do you?" His mind-reading ability was something we guarded against carefully. Lucian had been successfully avoiding it for years, but it didn't matter anymore. I didn't care what he knew. The games, the planning and plotting, the chasing and running—it was all over now. We had no secret twists to throw at him. We'd deliberately gone into this without a concrete plan. We were betting on our Bond connection and our ability to work well together under pressure, hoping beyond hope it would be enough.

"So sorry to keep you waiting. My last meeting ran late." He walked forward confidently, unperturbed by the death stares and the several guns pointed at him. He was arrogant, but he wasn't stupid, and I never expected him to waltz into this alone and unprotected. He had his own entourage.

Several heavily armed people walked ahead and behind him, guns raised. Zara's mom was keeping close to his left side, hardly able to keep her eyes off his profile, and the short, stocky woman from Thailand, Gina, was with them too. I recognized her immediately—I didn't think I'd forget anything from that day as long as I lived.

Rick's mother, who'd had the ability to render people unconscious, was dead—killed by her own son—and his father had been captured and was still imprisoned by Melior Group. Gina, the other Variant from that day, had a shielding ability. She may not have been able to shield as far or as well without her Vital, but I had no doubt she was keeping Davis covered.

A few other people I didn't recognize trailed behind Davis as well.

We were at an impasse. Both sides had guns pointed; both sides were protected by formidable Variants. I didn't think he gave a shit about his people, but I didn't want any more of mine to die. Everyone was on alert, tense, silent.

He stopped just feet away from Alec and Ethan. I could imagine the looks they were giving him, but I kept my face neutral, my breathing calm and even.

"You wanted me here." He spread his arms wide. "I'm here. What now?"

The smile didn't falter, the little gleam in his eye suggesting he had something up his sleeve. That was his advantage—we had no idea what he had planned, while he could read all our minds.

But we had something he didn't have too—we had *me*.

"Don't even fucking think about it," he growled, his amused mask slipping for the first time. "I see even a hint of illumination on your perfect skin, and my men will fire. Your telekinetic may be able to stop bullets, but can he stop them all at once?"

Without needing to hear the order, his goons pointed their weapons at my Variants—more than a dozen guns, trained directly at the people I loved most in the world. I thought Josh could stop them, but I wasn't entirely sure. Those were automatic weapons. I had no doubt he would keep me protected, but could he keep the others safe too? For how long?

Davis gave a satisfied nod and smoothed the front of his shirt. "Good. Now, let's negotiate."

"Negotiate?" Tyler spoke for us all. "You have nothing we want, and there isn't a person in this room willing to bend to your will."

"Everyone wants *something*, and I promise you, I can make it happen. Money? Fame? Power? Everyone has a price."

"And what is it you expect in return?" I knew the answer, but I wanted to hear him say it. For once in my entire existence, I wanted to look at this despicable man and hear him speak the truth.

He cocked his head to the side, watching me for a few moments. Then, for some reason, he decided to give me what I wanted.

"I want you, Evelyn." He folded his hands. "I think we all know why. I've gone as far as I can with my research and engineering team, and they can't figure out how to keep the donor Variant alive. I need to study you to fix it." He held his hand up, stopping any questions before they could be asked. "Because I want to rule the world. I want to walk into any room on the face of the planet and be the most powerful man there. Everyone wants power, *everyone*. Anyone that says they don't is either resigned to the fact they'll never have it or lying to themselves. I'm just willing to do whatever is necessary to get it."

"Why me?" It was the one thing I couldn't work out. "There are other Vivids. You could use any one of them to achieve the same thing." There had been so many people sending me messages; surely some of them had tried to go public with their own ability to glow, despite the unrest and the fear. Davis was surely aware of each and every one.

The look that twisted his features then was so grotesque and full of rage that I wondered how far gone his mind was.

"Because you dare to defy me!" Spittle flew from his mouth as he roared, his hands clenched into fists. Some of the people around him shifted uncomfortably. Zara's mom took a tiny step away.

"Pay attention, Evelyn." His breathing quickened as he visibly tried to calm himself. "You're supposed to be a smart girl. You get that from me, you know. I just told you what my ultimate goal was. I intend to be the most powerful man alive, but what's the point if I don't have you? I can't very well say I am if you continue to defy me. You get *that* from your mother." He wagged his finger at me, eyebrows raised, as if he were telling me off for kicking a ball inside the house.

"Don't you see? It all started with her. Joyce made me what I am—made it possible for me to do what I do. She gave me the greatest gift, my ability. Then the bitch ran off on me!"

"Because you threatened her. Threatened me!" For the first time, I let him get to me, my own anger rising. He smirked, just a tiny twist of his mouth. Josh's hand landed on my shoulder, giving it a squeeze that was both comforting and restraining.

"I simply explained to her what needed to happen next. She could've been by my side, my queen, as I built my empire. You could've been my princess. But that bitch chose to run. So this is how it has to be. She started it, and you're going to end it. Kind of poetic, don't you think?"

"You delayed finishing your masterpiece of machinery for poetry?" I scoffed.

He didn't like being mocked; his hands curled into fists. "You are the fruit of my loins. How could I move forward without your submission? I mean to have *supreme* power over *all* things, Evelyn! Including you! It has to be *you*!"

When he was done with his little tantrum, we all fell into silence for a few moments. Davis's entourage shuffled farther away from him; even his armed guards threw cautious looks over their shoulders. With them all spread out a bit more, I noticed another familiar face.

"Karen?" My eyes widened, and I slapped my palms on the table and pushed myself up. The woman who was in charge of my training and testing at Melior Group, the one who was as excited as me about the science side of Variants, the one who'd been kind to me—she was right there, standing at Davis's side. Was she there against her will? Had he kidnapped her in an attempt to get to me? Maybe he was blackmailing her?

Karen smiled at me, her lips a thin line, but it was Davis who answered my unspoken questions. "I assure you, Karen is here of her own free will. We've been working together for a long time. You see, we have the same goals when it comes to empowering the Variant community. She's been quite the useful resource."

He smiled at her, and she beamed, wide-eyed, as if she were a puppy and he was dangling a piece of chicken in front of her.

I couldn't believe it. I'd been half-convinced Victor Flint was the mole in Melior Group, but Karen had the highest level of clearance too. She could just as easily have gained access to all the information that was leaked.

I'd been fooled again. Was I so desperate for friendship, human connection of any kind, that I blindly trusted anyone who showed me any kindness?

"What do you want, Damari? How exactly do you think this is going to end?" Tyler still had his gun pointed, as did Alec and everyone else in the room. You could cut the tension with a hacksaw. But why was Tyler pushing him? To break the stalemate?

Davis spread his arms wide. "You summoned me here. What is it *you* want?"

"I want you to die," I declared without even thinking.

Davis chuckled. "So dramatic. But since we're on the topic, here's how this is going to go. You summoned me here, dear daughter, and here I am to collect you. You will come with me, you will cooperate, and you will help me complete my machine. In exchange, I'll let your Variants live."

"I'm not going anywhere with you."

"Well, then everyone dies."

"In case you haven't noticed, we have just as many guns pointed at you as you have at us. What makes you think you'd be able to walk out unscathed?"

"I think I can help with that." Dana sauntered in from around the corner. She was in jeans and a skin-tight tank top, all her curves accentuated, her silky blonde hair tamed in a braid.

Walking in step with her, their hands clasped, was Zara.

I took an involuntary step back. It felt as if someone had stabbed me just under the ribs and twisted the knife. I could understand Dana not wanting to be involved in this fight, wanting to steer clear of trouble, but to go out of her way to thwart us? To work with Davis? To break Zara out and bring her here to betray me *again*? It was just so cruel.

Davis gave her a wide smile and waited patiently until they were standing next to him.

"Fucking bitch," Alec growled, tightening his grip on his gun. I knew he wanted to shoot her in the face, but he was smart enough to resist the impulse. If he started firing, *everyone* would start firing.

"Why?" I hated how hurt I sounded.

"Aww, poor naive little Eve," Dana cooed, a cruel tilt to her mouth. "Haven't you learned by now not to trust everyone who says they're your friend? I thought you were supposed to be smart."

Zara snorted and picked at her nails.

"I'm gonna kill you both!" Dot launched forward, but she'd barely taken a step before Charlie wrapped his arms around her middle and picked her clean off the floor, her feet kicking. Kyo and Marcus stepped in, placing themselves between her and Davis.

Everyone tensed, but thankfully, no one fired. With Dana neutralizing everyone's abilities, we were all equally vulnerable. Josh wouldn't be stopping *any* bullets, let alone all of them.

"Thank you for bringing her back to us, Dana." Davis lifted his hand and caressed Zara's cheek with the backs of his fingers.

"Yes, I'm so glad you're OK, darling," Zara's mom rushed out. Apparently now that Davis had welcomed her daughter back into the fold, it was OK for her to do the same. Twisted bitch.

For the first time since they walked in, I saw a crack in Zara's sarcastic mask. She covered it quickly, but her free hand started to twitch—little, jerky movements, just like when I was in a cage begging her to help me save Josh's life. When had she slipped back into her delusions? Had she ever truly turned against Davis, or was it all an elaborate lie?

Zara ignored her mom, practically speaking over her. "I'm sorry I ran away. I was . . . confused."

"Water under the bridge." Davis's focus was still on her. "You were my first creation. You're more of a daughter to me than Evelyn ever was."

I rolled my eyes. Was that supposed to make me feel jealous?

"You're about to make up for it, aren't you?" The smile Davis gave her then was nothing short of deranged, and the one she gave him back was just as unhinged. "But first things first. Dana."

"Right." Dana dropped Zara's hand. "I'll wait in the car or something," she deadpanned, then walked off at a leisurely pace.

The exact moment Dana was far enough away to no longer be blocking anyone's ability, electricity started to flitter along Zara's skin, every twitch of her hand eliciting a little spark. Everyone took a collective breath. Her ability was volatile, and she'd had little to no training with it. Josh's telekinesis wouldn't do shit to stop Zara's electricity.

If she could focus enough to direct it at any of us, we were fucked.

Davis had the upper hand. Again. Because despite my impressive IQ, I'd done something colossally stupid. *Again*.

"I meant what I said, Eve." The crazy look disappeared from Zara's eyes, replaced with sincerity and determination. The twitching stopped, and electricity that had flickered over her a moment ago now rushed with purpose to her still hand. "I fucked up. But I learn from my mistakes."

"No!" Davis roared, raising his arm as if to punch her. He'd read what she was about to do, but he was too late to stop it.

Zara turned to face him fully and, before he could land his punch, lunged forward, pressing her electrified hand against his chest.

He roared in pain, every muscle in his body tense as the electricity coursed through him.

His goons hesitated, confused by the fact that none of the people they were pointing guns at had done anything. Half of them turned to check what Davis was screaming about, losing sight of their targets.

It was enough for us to act. Tyler and Alec fired off several shots in rapid succession, as did Kyo and Marcus.

Zara's mom lunged, clamping her arms around her daughter's waist and tackling her to the ground. Once the electricity released Davis, he swayed, his eyes droopy, but managed to stay upright.

In the same instant, my legs moved, my instincts carrying me forward. I stepped onto the chair, then onto the table, took two running strides, and launched myself into the air, aiming straight for Davis.

As I sailed through the air, my skin started to glow, filling me with Light and confidence and illuminating the dark space. Almost immediately, the sensation of Josh's ability tugged on my body, and my heart sank. Of course they wouldn't want me anywhere near that maniac! But instead of yanking me back into his strong embrace, it gave me an extra push.

I would've landed short, but with Josh's help, I barreled directly into Davis. We fell hard, my left elbow crunching against the concrete and making me cry out in pain. But I didn't stop, didn't pause to cradle my aching limb. I found exposed skin on his right forearm, wrapped my hands around it, and pulled.

I'd never pulled Light so forcefully before. All my focus was on the pure, unadulterated power surging into me, the Light-fueled instincts telling me to *just hold on*.

"No! Stop! How is this possible?" A frantic voice drew my attention. Gina stood a few feet away, staring at me intently. Karen and a few other Variants huddled around her, seeking the protection of her shielding ability.

"She's not using an ability." Dot took measured steps forward, Charlie and Kyo close behind her with guns pointed. Dot's eyes were narrowed, looking for someone to hurt. "You can't block her."

Before Gina could answer, Dot sprang forward and landed a punch right to her nose. As blood started to pour down Gina's front, the birds returned, lifting messy wisps of Dot's black hair as they sailed past her, straight for Gina. The woman screamed but was completely engulfed.

With Gina eliminated, the other Variants were left vulnerable, but of course, Davis always had another plan.

More people poured into the area, guns raised, abilities ready. I couldn't focus on them enough to know if they were ours or theirs. The last bits of Davis's stolen Light streamed easily into me. It felt like a relief, as if the Light had been waiting for someone to beckon it away from its usurper.

When the last tendrils left Davis's body, I gasped and let go of his arm. The power surging through me was terrifying—it was difficult to stand under its weight. I looked around for help, but my throat felt tight, and I couldn't seem to unclench my teeth. My skin was glowing so brightly some people were shielding their eyes.

But it wasn't just me creating so much light. Ethan stood with his broad back to me, his arms raised, commanding a *wall of fire*. Rising twenty feet into the air and burning a furious blue, it encased the three of us, protecting us from whatever chaos was happening out there.

There was a massive tear in the back of Ethan's T-shirt, and the exposed corded muscle strained with the effort of keeping the wall up. He was burning through Light quickly, but I couldn't transfer to him. Not yet, not alone. Instinctively I knew that if I transferred to any of them, they would end up with Davis's mind-reading ability.

I followed the blue flames up, taking in the sheer scale of what he was capable of. Above us, Josh was flying, hovering close by while making throwing movements with his hands. Crashing and banging followed the gestures.

Failing to get to my feet, I finally looked down at my father.

I had no idea if draining his stolen ability would kill him, and I'd done it without a moment's hesitation. It was time to find out if I'd just committed patricide.

He was prone on his back, his eyes closed, his head to one side. I couldn't tell if he was breathing or not. I leaned forward, reaching out to check for a pulse.

Before my hand connected with his neck, he took a giant breath, his eyes flying open as he shot up into a sitting position. He breathed hard for a few seconds, his eyes darting about and then, finally, landing on me.

"No," he breathed, pressing his hand to his chest. "What did you do?" he roared into my face. "Give it back! Give it back to me *now*, you stupid bitch!"

He lunged for me, and I didn't have the strength to fight him. My back hit the floor hard, knocking the air out of me, and we slid back dangerously close to Ethan's fire wall.

Davis started slapping and hitting me, his movements jerky and messy as he shouted incoherent things into my face. I barely had enough strength to lift my arms and protect my head from some of his blows, but I refused to let my hold on the Light slip. To come this far and then end up accidentally transferring his ability back to him would be tragic.

He smelled like sweat and desperation, the foul odor mixing with the metallic tang of blood in the air.

Searing pain exploded in my side, my shoulder, my neck, my temple. My vision blurred. I was vaguely conscious of several voices calling my name.

I searched for a way out—something, anything to make the blows stop.

But I had no chance. I could hardly move as he kept taking all his madness, all his fear and anger and inadequacy, out on me. He'd been doing that my whole life in one way or another.

He reared back onto his knees, one on either side of my torso, and backhanded me. My cheek burned and my ears started to ring.

With my head turned, I could see Ethan frantically looking between me and something in front of him, his arms still raised to hold up the fire wall as protection from whatever was the bigger threat on the other side. Josh hovered just over Ethan's left shoulder, bullets coming within inches of his face before falling to the ground. So many bullets.

I couldn't hear it over the ringing in my ears, but I could see Ethan yelling, his eyes wide.

Was he calling for help? Telling me to hold on? I supposed it didn't matter anymore.

Davis's hands circled my neck and squeezed.

I doubled my own chokehold on the ability I refused to let him have again. Even if he killed me, I'd die knowing I took from him what was never his to begin with. I'd die knowing I'd crippled him.

I refused to look at Davis. I didn't want my last image of this world to be his ugly, hateful face as he choked the life out of me.

Instead, I kept my gaze on the beautiful rage of the blue flames.

THIRTY-TWO

As though I'd summoned him, Alec burst through the fire.

He ran at full speed, taking the scene in and reacting with precision. He raised his gun and pulled the trigger, but it was empty. Without missing a step, he threw it aside, dropped a shoulder, and tackled Davis off me.

They crashed into some furniture beyond the fire wall, and Davis's screams filled the air.

I took spluttering, excruciating breaths, my lungs burning as they filled once again with air.

Tyler burst through the flames a second later, gun raised, the look on his face feral. Blood was running down one side of his face, and his right shirtsleeve had completely ripped off. He lowered the gun and rushed straight to me just as Josh landed at his side.

I managed to lift myself onto my elbow and hold my other arm out. "Stop," I croaked, the word sending a hundred razor blades down my throat. They both paused inches from me and crouched down. Their eyes raked over my body, but they kept their hands back as I coughed and spluttered through the pain. "Need to touch you all at once."

Tyler nodded, but an abrupt escalation in noise distracted all of us. We couldn't really see past the blue fire wall, but it sounded as if more people had joined the fight.

"What's going on out there?" Tyler checked how many bullets he had left, then slammed the magazine back into the gun.

"A bunch of humans just showed up," Josh answered. "I saw them coming and flew down to get to Eve."

"Humans? As in, civilians?" Tyler looked aghast as Josh nodded. We had some humans with us, but they were trained and knew how to handle themselves. A bunch of civilians would get slaughtered.

I'm not sure if Ethan had the same thought or if he'd just had enough of not being able to get to me, but he roared and threw his hands out. The blue wall of fire separated into a thousand fireballs and shot out in every direction.

The fire was so intense that Ethan's targets didn't even have a chance to scream before they dropped to the ground in a smoking, charred mess. He'd executed the maneuver perfectly; only Davis's men had been hit. Everyone else in the room stopped to catch their breath.

The only sound now came from Davis, his screams of pain echoing in the vast space.

Ethan turned to me but swayed. His big body toppled to the ground. He reached for me, eyes drooping, then passed out.

Pain instantly tore into my chest. They were all running low. Now that I was paying attention, I could tell they'd all just about reached their limits, but that last stunt had pushed Ethan over the edge. He needed Light. *Now.*

"Eth . . . Ethan . . ." The massive burden of the Light inside me weighted me down so much I could hardly speak. It was begging, *demanding* to be released. I reached out to him, but I couldn't risk touching him, not without touching them all.

We needed Alec.

But Alec was still pummeling my father, lost in his rage.

Josh rushed to Ethan's side, checking for injuries. I looked up at Tyler, gritting my teeth with the effort of controlling all the Light, and hoped the pleading look in my eyes was enough to convey what I needed.

Tyler looked in Alec's direction, shouting his name.

Alec was kneeling over Davis, landing punch after punch to his face, ribs, anywhere his fists could connect. Fountains of blood sprayed in gruesome bursts every time Alec's fists connected. I couldn't be sure how much was my father's and how much belonged to the Master of Pain.

By some miracle, Davis was still conscious, screaming between blows. That's how Alec must've been keeping him awake—just enough pain inflicted by his ability to keep his adrenaline pumping and his mind still connected to his body.

Or maybe he was screaming from the pain of the burns. Being pushed through Ethan's fire wall had left half of Davis's face a gruesome, charred mess, with a black hole where his eye used to be. The right side of his body was almost as bad. The smoking flesh seemed to be fused with the fabric of his clothing.

Alec was determined to make him suffer, fully embracing all he hated about himself to hurt the man who had ruined our lives. His expression was feral, his teeth bared, his eyes wild. Blood dripped down his face, and his muscles bunched with every movement.

I knew he'd hate himself for getting lost in the pain later, but I couldn't worry about that yet.

Alec wanted Davis to suffer, but I just wanted this to end.

"Ty!" I managed to yell. Tears of frustration streamed down my face, mingling with the blood and dust in my hair. He was refusing to leave my side, but he saw the desperate look in my face, knew Ethan didn't have much time.

"Josh!" he yelled as he rose to his feet, raising his gun.

Josh whipped his head around, figured out what was needed in under a second, and lifted his arm. Using his ability, he yanked Davis out from under Alec and lifted him into the air.

Davis stopped screaming. His one good eye rolled into the back of his head before it focused on me. Somehow, he managed to smile, the good side of his face pulling up in a twisted, horrific way. "You're all—"

Tyler pulled the trigger, shooting him through his good eye and finally ending his life. Josh released his hold, and Davis fell to the ground next to a slightly confused, panting Alec.

With the screams and the sound of punches gone, my weak voice carried. "Alec."

He finally looked at me, the violent haze clearing from his eyes.

"Need you," I panted. He was rushing to me before the words were even out of my mouth.

Josh's ability lifted me so gently that not a joint was bent, not an injury jostled. He lowered me next to Ethan just as Alec and Tyler dropped to their knees on my other side.

I reached for Ethan, knowing they'd follow my lead. As I grabbed Ethan's cold hand—his hands were never cold—Josh wrapped a hand around my ankle, Alec took my other hand, and Tyler cupped my cheek.

I hoped to the vastness of the universe, to whatever divine power was behind the Light and all that was made possible because of it, that this would work.

I let my hold on the Light go.

My skin lit up, glowing brightly for a few intense seconds before fading once again. My Bondmates grunted and steadied themselves as the force of the Light slammed into them.

I sighed in relief—finally, I could breathe.

Ethan groaned, stirred, then sat up, looking disoriented. It should've taken him at least a day or two to recover from being depleted of Light to the point of unconsciousness. He looked down at our joined hands, and his eyes widened.

"Eve." My name on his lips was a combination of question, plea, and sigh of relief.

I sat up, and Ethan pulled me into his arms. "You scared me, big guy."

"You scared me too, baby."

Ethan would've held on to me for days if he could have, but within moments, I was pulled out of his embrace and into another set of strong arms. Then another and another. We held on, making sure we were all there, all still breathing.

We weren't unscathed by any means. Ethan had nearly died overusing his ability, Josh was limping, the gash on Tyler's head was still oozing blood, and Alec was so covered in gore I wasn't sure what his injuries were. My own body ached all over. Muscles I didn't even know I had were burning, my elbow still throbbed, and I could feel the bruises and scrapes from Davis's bashing.

But we were all still there. We were alive and he was dead.

Once I was sure of the most crucial things to my existence—the functionality of my own vital organs and the survival of the loves of my life—other things started to come into focus.

The airport was trashed. Debris and damage covered everything. Holes in the walls, charred furniture, lights hanging half off the ceiling, bodies everywhere.

I'd never seen so many dead people.

Most of the survivors were either sitting on the ground or leaning on things, catching their breath and evaluating their own injuries. They were all watching us. I looked around at their faces as I rose to my feet. I didn't recognize most of them, but no one was looking at me with hostility or hatred or fear. Mostly it was curiosity and awe, even a few uncertain smiles.

Dot stood nearby, leaning on Kyo.

As soon as our eyes connected, we moved toward each other, wading through the debris and gore to finally wrap each other in a big hug.

"I'm so glad you're OK," she whispered into my neck as I said at the same time, "I'm so sorry about Jamie."

We took shaky, uneven breaths, fighting tears. As we pulled apart, we looked into each other's faces. I wondered if she saw as much strength and determination in my eyes as I saw in hers.

She would survive this. I had no doubt.

When she stepped back, her knees gave out. I lunged for her, but Marcus caught her, sweeping her up into his arms and planting a gentle kiss on her cheek.

"Let's get you some water." Kyo led the way to the heavy timber table that was somehow still standing. He found a few chairs, righted them, and the three of them settled in.

A sob drew my attention back to where Kyo and Marcus had been standing a moment earlier.

Charlie held Ed in a tight hug, his eyes red from crying as his boyfriend fell apart in his arms. Josh took my hand, and I followed his gaze to one of countless bodies near the couple's feet. Ed's brother lay on the ground, a knife sticking out of his chest, his eyes wide but unseeing.

Once again, I fought tears, my lip trembling. I didn't even get to meet him.

I felt frozen. Simultaneously I wanted to turn my face into Ethan's broad chest and forget it all, and I wanted to rush around and look into every single dead face to know exactly who we'd lost.

More and more sniffles and sobs started to fill the air as people took stock of the aftermath.

Olivia and Henry, Mr. Takata, and a handful of other people who'd been hidden away came out of a back corridor. Olivia and Henry went straight to their children as others started to help tend to the wounded.

A spark of electricity drew my eyes to a spot nearby, near where I'd tackled Davis to the ground.

Zara was on her back, her left leg twisted at an unnatural angle, her face scrunched up in pain as sparks flitted over her skin. I stumbled over to her, the guys sticking close by, and dropped to my knees.

"Eve." Her eyes widened, then scrunched up in pain as another flash of electricity skittered over her body. "Are you . . . is he . . . did we win?"

I nodded, swallowing around the ever-present lump in my throat. "He's dead."

She smiled, showing teeth covered in blood. She moaned in pain, and the electricity came more suddenly this time, a violent bolt shooting out of her chest and connecting with the high ceiling above.

"I can't . . . hold . . . you have to . . . Eve, you have to . . ." She was struggling to control Rick's ability. With all the pain she was in and how weak she was, I was surprised she hadn't fried us all already.

"Someone find Dana!" Tyler roared, and several agents dropped what they were doing to rush in various directions. But they didn't get far before Dana came running up.

"I'm here." She sprinted directly for us, a big group of paramedics rushing up behind her. The electricity stopped sparking as Dana approached, and Zara sighed in relief.

Dana skidded to a stop and took Zara's hand. "I told you not to die, you bitch."

Zara laughed, then coughed, the sound wet and dangerous sounding. "Fuck you."

A paramedic appeared next to her, and we backed up so they could work. I wasn't sure if Zara would make it. The blood she was coughing up indicated internal bleeding, and that was pretty fucking serious. But with paramedics here, she had a fighting chance. That was more than I could say for her mom, whose body lay lifeless several feet away.

Had Zara killed her own mother, just as Rick had? Or was she felled by another's hand? Was it Zara's own mother who'd inflicted such damage on her body? It was beyond disturbing to think about, but then, my own father had been beating me only minutes earlier. Had it only been minutes?

"Where the fuck did all these humans come from?" Tyler scratched his head and winced when he accidentally scraped the gash in his forehead. The paramedics were moving through the wounded quickly, prioritizing the worst cases.

"Oh, that was me." Dana waved a hand dismissively, her worried gaze fixed on Zara. "I've been working with some HEN groups in the area. I took a chance and told them what was happening, and most of them decided they wanted to help."

"Why didn't you say something when I called you?" I asked. I'd been so worried after our talk.

"Couldn't. I was about to go into a meeting with Variant Valor—too many of Davis's people around."

The sneaky bitch had been playing both sides, biding her time to make the best move.

"I'm really fucking glad you're not a treacherous bitch," I told her.

As the paramedics lifted Zara's body up on the stretcher, Dana finally looked at me and smiled. "Had you going."

"Yes, you did." I pulled her into a hug.

"And I'm glad you're not, like, dead and shit. I guess." She shrugged, but it didn't escape my notice how tightly she was returning my hug.

"This will never not be weird." Alec sounded disturbed, and we pulled apart. I couldn't believe I was able to smile so soon, but if we were to have any chance of getting through this, we had to hold on to these moments of positivity.

Dana rushed off with Zara and the paramedics as they evacuated the worst of the injured. The few people on Davis's side who'd managed to survive were being led away in handcuffs. Karen was one of them. She was cuffed to a stretcher, her head wrapped in bandages, blood seeping through the crisp, white fabric already.

"Eve." Tyler pulled on my good elbow, his voice laced with urgency.

I turned to look behind us.

Near what used to be the windows and was now a big gaping hole in the wall, a group of people were gathered around something.

I didn't want to know, wasn't sure I could handle losing another person, but I made myself ask. "Who?"

"Nina." Tyler was already pulling me along. I wasn't sure I could've made my feet move otherwise.

I had no idea what time it was, but it was night, and the giant hole just looked like a black pit of darkness and despair. Nina was lying close to the edge of it, the other Lighthunters surrounding her.

"Why didn't the paramedics take her?" I said angrily as we got close enough to see her broken body. They were supposed to be taking the worst of the injured.

Tyler's ability answered the question better than anyone could've. "Her injuries are too extensive. She's got minutes if she's lucky."

The anger evaporated, replaced by a heavy longing feeling it was hard to put my finger on. Nina was a friend, but she was so much more. She'd been there when we needed her most. She was the reason we'd been able to save Charlie. She was the one who'd explained my nature to me better than anyone. She was wise and kind and selfless. The world would be worse off without her. *I* would be worse off without her.

I went to kneel next to her, but she rose into the air, as though floating on a cloud. Her body was lifted upright, her feet hovering above the floor.

Frowning, I turned to Josh, but he looked just as confused.

The other Lighthunters made a semicircle around us, facing the black night.

"Evelyn." Nina's voice sounded weak but calm. Her features were smooth, not at all creased with pain, her eyes tired but relaxed.

"Nina." Tears trailed down my cheeks, but I managed not to sob. I reached up to touch her, but I hesitated, scared I would hurt her. She caught my hand in hers and held it.

I squeezed her fingers, as though if I held on tightly enough, she'd stay.

"Please . . ." I knew it was silly, that it was way beyond anyone's control, but I couldn't stop my plea. "Don't leave me."

So many people had left me, abandoned me, betrayed me.

She smiled. She was dying, her clothes filthy, her umber skin covered in gray dust that only made the blood appear brighter. Her other arm hung limply by her side, the shoulder angled down in a sickening way, but she managed a smile.

"But you are not alone." Her French accent seemed thicker as she glanced behind me to my Bondmates. "You will never be alone again. Just remember to lean into the Light. Let it guide you. Trust your instincts."

She started to glow in much the same way I did when I used my Vivid Light. Her hand felt tingly in mine, and when I looked down, it started to disintegrate before my eyes.

I gasped in shock and looked back into her face just in time to see her close her eyes and smile. She looked at peace as she faded. It was as if she was absorbed by the glowing Light and as if the Light came from within her all at once.

Slowly, softly, she disappeared. Eventually I stood with my hand held out in front of me, staring into the darkness.

As the last few sparks dimmed, the Lighthunters sighed in unison. They held hands for another moment, then all at once, let go.

I couldn't quite believe what I'd seen. It was some kind of molecular disintegration, the very fiber of her being coming apart on a microscopic level and transforming into pure Light.

I filed it away to wonder about later.

"Does that happen every time?" Josh asked. "I mean, do all of you . . ."

"Yes," one of the Lighthunters answered, a stocky man with dull brown eyes. "The Light takes us at the end. Death is never painful or unpleasant for us. We die knowing we continue to serve that which we dedicated our lives to."

The Light absorbed them back into itself, and they lived on in anyone with Variant DNA.

I took a deep breath and leaned back, knowing Alec was there to wrap his arms around me. He always had my back.

The Lighthunters started to clear out, and the five of us gravitated toward the big timber table where Dot sat in Marcus's lap, her feet in Kyo's. Ed and Charlie were with them. Ed had stopped sobbing, but silent tears still streamed down his cheeks as he stared into the middle distance. Charlie was rubbing soothing circles into his back.

Ed had lost his brother and his Variant. My chest felt too tight to breathe at the mere thought of losing one of my Bondmates. I couldn't imagine the pain he felt.

As Josh righted some more mismatched chairs with his ability, I paused at what used to be a bar. Half of it was disintegrated, still smoldering from Ethan's fire, and glass covered every surface. My attention snagged on a few bottles that had miraculously survived the violence. Just as we had.

I stepped past the debris to reach them. Two were some kind of liqueur that looked like it contained more sugar than alcohol. I grabbed the third, a bottle of tequila.

Alec searched the cupboards and found a tray of glasses.

Everyone settled into chairs and stared into nothing, trying to process in their own way. I stood at the table and looked around at all the people I *hadn't* lost. I looked at each one of them in turn and thanked the Light they were still here, still breathing, still living and loving . . . and grieving.

As I opened the bottle, I turned my thoughts to those I'd lost. I poured a bit into each glass and then lifted one.

"To Nina." I slammed it back and immediately reached for the bottle again.

Everyone else watched me, either with blank expressions or as if I were crazy. Then Ethan reached forward and grabbed a glass.

"To Nina." He downed it. Slowly, one by one, they all reached for glasses and toasted the Lighthunter.

I refilled them and raised mine again.

"To Jamie."

We drank. Dot had to take a few deep breaths before she could down the strong alcohol.

We toasted Ed's brother next, then name after name as we remembered the fallen.

As I poured the last drops of the bottle into the last glass, Tyler stood and raised his.

"To everyone we've lost. Their deaths will not be in vain. We will fight to make this world a better place."

As one, we drank.

As I dropped the glass back to the table, I swayed a little. I wasn't sure if it was from exhaustion, the alcohol, or a combination of the two, but just like always, my Bond was there to catch me.

Ethan pulled me into his lap, and I relaxed into his embrace.

Everyone fell into silence. All the injured had been tended to or taken away to hospitals. Those who hadn't needed medical attention had left. Where had they gone? What do people do after an epic battle? Just . . . go home? Have a shower and go to bed?

I could use a shower, and my body already seemed to be shutting down, ready for oblivion. But I wasn't sure if I'd be able to sleep—if I'd be able to close my eyes without seeing crimson.

Ethan's booming voice broke the silence. "Can't believe he called you 'the fruit of his loins.' Who the fuck talks like that?"

For a beat, everyone remained silent. And then we all burst into laughter. We laughed for a solid minute, bent over the table, wiping tears of both mirth and grief from the corners of our eyes.

It was exactly what we needed to break some of the thick tension. As our laughter receded, we slowly got up and started making our way home.

THIRTY-THREE

I stood at the foot of my bed in my underwear, my hair falling down my back in waves, my makeup done, staring at what I'd decided to wear.

It was only a dress, but this felt important, momentous even.

The black fabric and bright poppy prints contrasted starkly with the creamy white linen sheets.

I ran my hand reverently over my mother's dress, the only piece of her I had left. I'd saved it like the precious artifact it was, hardly even touching it where it hung in my closet for over two years.

It was time to honor her memory by wearing it. It was time to remember all the times I'd seen her in it, smiling and happy. It was time to remember all the good and, instead of feeling sad about what we'd lost, feel happy about all we had to look forward to.

It was what she fought for—my future.

I slipped the dress over my head and did up the zip on the side. It was a little loose around the middle, but the top fit perfectly, and the understated A-line shape reached just below the knee. I remembered us being the same height, but I was sure it used to reach midcalf on her.

I smiled and took a deep breath, squaring my shoulders.

At the last moment, I decided to grab a cardigan. I picked a red one, the color almost a perfect match for some of the poppies on the dress. I slipped my feet into black flats and came out of my massive walk-in wardrobe, pausing in the doorway.

I would never get enough of the view from our bedroom. And I would never forget the day they showed it to me.

Ethan had practically been jumping up and down from excitement. Josh had hung back, a smug, knowing look on his face. Tyler had led the way up the stairs, and Alec had held my hand and walked by my side, his posture more relaxed than I'd ever seen it.

They guided me into the newly renovated section of the third floor and paused in front of an ornate set of double doors.

"Ready? Ready?" Ethan's grin was wide, his dimples prominent.

I chuckled. "Ready."

Josh flicked a wrist and the doors flung open.

I gasped, my eyes darting about the room. I'd had no idea what was taking the contractors so long, but it had never crossed my mind that they were converting the space into a giant-ass bedroom for me. For *us*.

I couldn't decide if I wanted to jump on the massive bed first or run past the light, gauzy curtains and take in the view from the balcony.

"The bed is big enough to fit us all." Ethan rushed over to it, then buzzed around the room, showing me all the different features. "My feet don't even hang off the end! But this is *your* room, really. The bed is just for when we all want to be together, you know. There are four bedrooms just off the hallway, two on either side, so we're close, but you still have your privacy. I know how you like your alone time. Oh, and there's a walk-in closet! Look! Josh and I have been buying some things and filling it up already. I hope you like them. And on the other side—I mean, there are bathrooms off the hall too, but this is the main one." He grabbed my hand and dragged me over to another set of double doors.

"We already have a steam room in the pool house." I laughed. The en suite was insane! Massive shower with two showerheads, two sinks—it was the size of the bedroom I'd been using, and half of it was taken up by a steam room. It wasn't as big as the one on the secret Greek island, but it would fit us all comfortably, and the tiles were almost identical. There was even a little sink with a modern mosaic pattern behind it.

"Yeah, but this one's more private." Alec's breath fanned over my neck, making me want to test it out immediately.

"And it has the best view of any room in the house." Ethan was already leading us back out.

A pair of cushy armchairs and a little side table sat in front of the windows. Ethan rushed around the furniture, flapping at the curtain to reveal the stunning view.

"Do you like it?" Finally he stilled and clasped his hands in front of him. I realized he was nervous.

Ignoring the view, I wrapped my hands around his neck and drew his face down to mine. "I love it, big guy!" I gave him a brilliant smile and a soft kiss. "Thank you."

Pulling out of Ethan's arms, I went to each of them in turn, giving them kisses and thanks and appreciation. Then I rushed out of the room, the giddy excitement infecting me.

"Where are you going?" Josh called after me, but I could hear his footsteps following.

"I have to get something!" I knew exactly what I wanted to add to this room first.

I rushed into my old bedroom and over to my dresser, Josh and Ethan only a step behind me. I grabbed the jewelry box they'd given me and handed it to Josh as I gathered up the framed photos—my friends and family cradled in my arms. Needing something to do, Ethan threw my closet open and scooped up a bunch of hangers, then led the way back to my new, magnificent room.

Ethan set to putting the clothes away as Josh and I arranged the photos on the side table near the door. I'd added a photo of Lucian with my mom, my three-year-old self cuddled between them.

"I want more photos on this. We need to take more photos together."

"You got it, precious." Alec, surprisingly, was the first to agree.

"Where do you want this?" Josh held up the jewelry box.

Before I could answer, a piece of paper I'd forgotten I was keeping under the box dislodged itself and fluttered to the floor. I reached for it, but Tyler got there first.

I chewed on my lip as he opened it, his slight frown of curiosity slowly giving way to amusement as he realized what it was.

He smiled at me. "You kept this?"

"What is it?" Josh leaned over, and Alec stepped around to get a better look. Ethan came back out of the walk-in to peer over all their heads.

I was once again grateful I couldn't blush. I had no secrets from them—I loved them more than I loved my own life—but I was still a little embarrassed.

"It's a note I wrote to Eve when she first got to Bradford Hills," Tyler answered as Ethan gently took the piece of paper and they all looked at me.

I rolled my eyes and huffed; it was silly to be embarrassed. I mean, I'd been having sex with the man. We lived together. So what if I'd kept a silly note about school supplies?

"I had a crush on you from the first second I saw you, OK? You were a hot older guy, and you did something really thoughtful for me." I shrugged.

They all looked as if they were trying really hard to hold back laughter, even Ty. He wrapped his arms around my waist and kissed me through our chuckles while the others descended into full-on guffaws.

"It was wildly inappropriate at the time." Tyler pulled away just far enough to look into my eyes. "But I was attracted to you too. I couldn't stop thinking about leaning forward and just closing the distance between us. And then you showed up in my damn office wearing that fucking schoolgirl outfit."

"Oh man, that skirt." Alec groaned.

"You know I spent that whole session with a raging boner?"

"That's why you didn't move from behind your desk." I slapped him on the chest.

We spent the afternoon reminiscing about the way I met them all, teasing each other and laughing as we wandered between my old room and my new one. I was fully moved in before dinner.

The view from the balcony that day had been a bit different. Summer had been ending; the leaves on the oaks lining the drive had only just started to turn.

Now, we'd come through another harsh winter. Summer was just starting. Trees budded with new growth as the morning sun streamed over the manicured grounds. The balcony was smack-dab in the middle of the mansion, and the view overlooked the massive driveway, the top of the iron gates just visible over the trees. Beyond, some of the taller buildings of the Institute peeked over the lush trees littering all of Bradford Hills.

I grabbed my bag off the bed and made my way downstairs.

They were waiting for me in the foyer, reminding me of the day of the gala when I'd come down these same stairs, feeling sexy and confused at Alec's lascivious stares.

This time, there was nothing but love in their eyes as they looked up at me one by one.

I'd asked that people not wear black—I didn't want it to feel like a funeral. Ethan was in jeans, a white short-sleeved shirt stretching over his broad chest. Josh was in chinos and a green polo shirt that made his eyes pop. Tyler wore gray slacks and a crisp blue shirt, the sleeves rolled up. Alec had been wearing more color lately—lifting the blackness from his heart had opened him up to all the vibrancy of life in other areas. His jeans were black, but his shirt was an electric blue.

"You look beautiful." Tyler took my hand as I reached the bottom. I could hear it in his voice—he was speaking for all of them.

Lucian joined us, stopping his wheelchair near the ramp to the garage.

"Ready?" He looked as distinguished and dapper as ever in slacks and a light sweater.

"Ready." I nodded, and he looked at me properly for the first time. His eyes widened a fraction as they flicked up and down my body, his gaze more disbelieving than anything.

I knew it was the dress giving him pause. He would've seen her wearing it before we left—I'd seen pictures of her in it from before I was born. But I was surprised at how much emotion he seemed to be feeling. His chest rose and fell a little faster, and his eyes were even getting misty.

"Uncle Luce?" I took a step closer to him, worried.

"That dress . . ." His voice was choked, and he cleared this throat before taking my hand in his. "She was wearing that dress when we met. I had no idea she still had it—that you still had it."

"It was one of the only things that survived the crash. She wore it a lot, always on happy days."

"For a second you looked exactly like her. You have the same eyes, the same hair—she had it long like yours when we met."

"I can change if this is too much—"

"No." He shook his head and smiled. "It looks beautiful on you. It's a nice reminder of her. It just took me by surprise, that's all."

"We should get going," Tyler gently reminded us.

We piled into two cars and headed off to a memorial that Lucian and I had organized for my mother.

This was not another funeral. This was a way to acknowledge the past and focus on the future.

In the weeks after the confrontation with Davis, we went to *so many* funerals, sometimes more than one in a day. There were a few days where all we did was eat, sleep, and go to funerals. I almost felt numb to it by the end, but then I'd hear the loved ones start to cry, and it would all come flooding back, my own emotion, my own tears bubbling up.

I cried at every single one.

I bawled uncontrollably at Jamie's, Dot's grief amplifying my own.

The reprieve was brief. We took some time to say goodbye to the fallen, but there was a lot of work to do. We'd taken Davis out—we'd removed the cancer—but we had to make sure his poison didn't keep spreading. Our cuts and bruises were fading, the broken bones healing, but the world still had a long way to go.

All of Davis's properties and holdings were seized and searched, all his secrets revealed. His horrific experiments were stopped, his machines destroyed. Any research that could be useful was handed over to ethical, educational institutions.

The world learned how he'd stolen his ability, how he'd lied, cheated, and manipulated to get ahead. Everyone knew he was responsible for the Vital kidnappings, for countless deaths in incidents like the one that killed the guys' parents. Everyone knew it was on his orders—in an attempt to assassinate Senator Christine Anderson—that an entire plane of civilians was shot out of the sky.

He killed my mother, but I took *him* down.

With Davis dead, his reputation in tatters, and no one willing to defend his memory or his legacy, Variant Valor started to lose steam.

The world was more stunned to learn of the Lighthunters' legitimacy. Their "coming out" went as well as we could've dreamed. They had insurmountable evidence to prove they were the "real deal," not to mention decades' worth of evidence to prove Davis was shady, manipulative, and a downright murderous psychopath.

At every turn, they preached peace between humans and Variants, vowing they were on the side of order and peace. It's what the Light demanded, and that included the human population.

After initial mistrust, the Human Empowerment Network began to calm down too.

The work Dot and Charlie were doing with other grassroots organizations across the world was helping. There were peaceful protests, Human-Variant community meetings, reconciliation speeches, forums, all kinds of small and large events in local communities all over the world that fostered cooperation and togetherness. Their main aim was to dispel fear through education.

As we drove through Bradford Hills—Lucian, Alec, and Ethan in an accessible SUV, Tyler, Josh, and I in Josh's Challenger—we had the windows down, enjoying the warm breeze. No armored cars tailed us. There were no security checkpoints to pass at the gates, no black-clad agents crawling over every inch of town or following every Vital.

The violence had stopped. Some residual unrest lingered in Bangkok, Moscow, Mexico, and a few other spots, but for the most part, the world was getting back to normal. People were getting back to their lives. Businesses were opening, schools were back in session, Bradford Hills Institute was back at full capacity. Some changes in staff had been called for, and a handful of students had been expelled after it was discovered they'd worked closely with Davis and committed serious crimes, but the reputation of the Institute was intact. Most people were just happy to get back to learning.

Me most of all.

I'd decided I wanted to major in genetics with a focus on Variant studies. I'd spent so much time not knowing what I was, then struggling to understand what it meant. I wanted to contribute to the wider understanding of what the Light was and how it functioned.

With the Lighthunters rejoining society and all the other Vivids coming forward, several new areas of study would exist by the time I finished my degree.

Lighthunters were working closely with Bradford Hills Institute and other prestige organizations all over the world to help identify which claims of Vivids were legitimate. There were, so far, forty-eight confirmed Vivids. Forty-eight of us in the whole world. About two dozen were coming to Bradford Hills next week to get to know one another and do some experiments.

Lucian, Victor, and Tyler had retaken control of Melior Group within days of Davis's death, but I still refused to continue our research sessions there. No one dared to make me stick to the contract.

Karen had died in the hospital a few days after the battle with Davis, and most of her research team had been disbanded while they investigated who knew of her treachery. Tyler's ability helped enormously, especially now that Davis's shield was dead and no longer protecting his people from being discovered. But it was a large organization, and things took time. Melior Group was doing a massive restructuring, and they let a lot of people go. Some were arrested and prosecuted, their transgressions going further than just disobeying orders.

Even so, I needed to not be surrounded by black-clad agents. I'd had enough of that. Further research and testing was happening in the well-equipped labs at Bradford Hills Institute with professors I knew and liked. They would be in charge of welcoming the Vivids and working with us all.

They were the ones I allowed to observe and gather as much information as possible the last time I glowed.

Zara was released from the hospital maybe a month after the altercation. Her injuries were extensive, and she'd have scars to rival Alec's, but she survived. Considering all that was revealed about Davis and how deeply his manipulations went, coupled with the fact that she'd cooperated and provided information early on, no charges were pressed against her. She was free to leave the hospital.

I appreciated beyond measure how selflessly she'd acted to help us bring Davis down, but I wasn't ready to forgive the way she'd betrayed me. I just had too much emotional baggage to wade through, and I wasn't sure we could ever get back to how we were at the beginning. But to make it safe for others around her, to give Dana a break from having to stick by her side twenty-four seven, and as a gesture of gratitude, I took her ability.

We did it under the watchful eyes of Bradford's professors, my guys all standing by to take the excess Light as soon as it was done.

We sat facing each other on the ground in the small research lab, legs crossed, and I took her hand. She smiled at me with a multitude of emotions in her face, but the one that seemed strongest was relief.

I pulled the Light out of her much more slowly than I had with Davis, careful not to take too much and kill her. She passed out anyway, collapsing onto her side as I dragged the last tendrils out of her. It weighed me down, the sheer force of that much Light making me grit my teeth as I glowed brightly.

But my guys were right there, ready to step in and take it all from me safely.

That was one thing I was sure of without a shadow of a doubt—they would always be there for me. They would always stand at my back, ready to support, defend, and love me in every way I needed, just as I would for them. We would lay down our lives for one another. After all the shit we'd been through, I knew there was nothing life could throw at us that we couldn't survive.

My Bond was complete and unbreakable. In them, I had the family, the connection, I'd craved my entire life.

We turned the corner, driving slowly through the manicured grounds of the memorial park. The rest of my family had already arrived and were waiting for us on the grassy area near the parking lot.

Olivia and Henry were standing in the shade of a tree, talking with their children.

Charlie and Ed were getting married in a few months, giving us all another positive thing to focus on. Ed had moved to Bradford Hills permanently and fit so perfectly with our family we sometimes forgot he hadn't been around from the start. He sometimes had to remind us to catch him up on inside jokes and conversations he hadn't been around for.

Dot, Kyo, and Marcus were looking for their own place in Bradford Hills—somewhere close to campus so Dot could finish her veterinary course. It still wasn't possible to marry more than one person, but the way Dot ranted about it, I had a feeling she would make it her own personal mission to change that law.

They were all dressed in bright spring colors—as if we were about to have a picnic and not a memorial.

Dot rushed over to me, her black hair shining in the sun, and gave me a hug.

"How you doing, girl?" She scrutinized me, but I smiled and pulled away.

"I'm good. Focusing on the positive memories. You?" Like me, she'd struggled with all the funerals we had to attend, each one reopening the wound of her own grief and making it hard for the skin to stitch over.

"I'm pretty good." She sounded a little surprised. "This one feels different."

"Yeah, it does."

I threaded my arm through hers, and we wandered over to the others while the guys helped Lucian out of the car.

"Hey, kitten." Kyo stepped forward and gave me a hug. Not to be outdone, Marcus lifted me clean off the ground when he hugged me.

"How you doin'?" he asked as he set me back down.

"Wishing people would stop asking me that." I raised my brows at him, and he flashed me a brilliant smile.

"It's because we care." Charlie nudged me, and I gave him and Ed hugs too.

"I know." I smiled at the way they linked hands as soon as their hugs were delivered. Their happiness was contagious, made even sweeter by the bitterness of all the recent loss.

"Evelyn." Olivia held me at arm's length, her gentle hands on my shoulders. "You look beautiful, darling." She pulled me into a hug and stroked my hair in a gesture that was so motherly I almost felt as if my mom were holding me.

"I love you, Auntie O," I whispered into her neck.

"I love you too." She pulled away and smoothed my hair before wiping her eyes discreetly.

Henry surprised me by going in for a hug too. He was a quiet man who traveled a lot for work, and out of everyone, I knew him the least.

The hug was brief but warm and not at all awkward. And if the hug was surprising, his words just about floored me.

"Your mother would be incredibly proud of you, Evelyn. I know I am." He nodded and turned to lead the way up a small hill, leaving me standing there feeling as if my chest were about to burst. I had to take a second to breathe through the emotion.

Lucian appeared next to me. "Let's do this." He gave me a smile, and Olivia pushed his chair up the hill— even though that damn chair was the best money could buy and was fully electric. I think she just liked feeling useful.

We climbed the hill as a group. We could've taken the winding gravel path to where my mother's memorial plaque was installed in a low wall surrounded by trees and flowers, but we took the most direct route, even if it wasn't necessarily the easiest.

As we crested the hill, I had to pause again.

Lucian let his chair race down the hill, a joyful laugh escaping him as he overtook Henry, and Olivia chased after him, half chastising and half laughing. The others jogged down behind them, but my Bondmates stood at the top of the hill with me in a line, looking down at the scene below.

I couldn't quite believe how many people had shown up.

A handful of chairs faced the plaque, and a simple lectern had been set up for speeches. The sea of people there to show their respects, to share memories of my mother, was overwhelming.

"She was loved." Tyler echoed my thoughts.

"More than you know." Alec nodded.

"So are you," Josh added quietly.

While many people were there because they wanted to remember my mother, many others had never met her—like the Lighthunters and some of the students from the Institute. They were there for me, to show their respect and support for me.

"How could she not be? Look at her." Ethan lightened the mood, and we all chuckled.

I adjusted my bag on my shoulder and headed down the hill to join my family and friends. Ethan, Josh, Tyler, and Alec were with me every step of the way.

EPILOGUE

I heard Alec thudding through the foyer and snapped my head up to check the time.

"Shit." I cursed under my breath. "Alec!"

"Yeah?"

"You may wanna skip the workout. We should probably head to the hospital soon." I leaned over my desk, rushing to finish the section of the research report I was working on.

Alec appeared in the doorway. "What do you mean? Now? It's happening now?" His eyes were wide, his shoulders tense. He looked like a really sexy, tattooed deer in headlights.

Before I could answer, Uncle Luce wheeled himself out of his office. Mine was next to his on the ground floor. I'd had it set up just before I started my PhD. As I researched how Vivid Light could be used to treat terminal diseases, it was handy to have a space to work from at home.

"Yeah, you may want to get going," Lucian said. "I'll meet you all down there later."

"Shit!" Alec ran his hands over his buzzed hair. "Should I change? Never mind. No time. Let's go." He waved his hands maniacally, trying to shoo me out of my chair.

I groaned and got up, reluctantly giving up on getting any more work done. "Alec, calm down. These things take time—sometimes days. We're not in any kind of rush."

"You don't know that," he argued. "Sometimes they happen fast. Really fucking fast. Like in the back of the car on the way to the hospital fast."

I chuckled as I took my time walking down the hallway; Alec buzzed around me like a toddler on a sugar high.

Josh came down the stairs just as Alec and I reached the foyer. He had my bag and shoes in his hands.

"Heard Alec losing his shit." He gave my Master of Pain a teasing grin. "Figured it was time to go."

Alec flipped him off as he grabbed his wallet and keys and I slipped my feet into flats.

Josh drove, the leather pads on his elbows stretching every time he changed gears. When he'd started teaching Variant studies at Bradford Hills Institute, he'd taken to wearing tweed. He was pairing the traditional, preppy Ivy League uniform with his band T-shirts and jeans, combining his two signature styles into one delicious one. When he wasn't at the front of a lecture theater, he was leading a program that provided Variant studies teaching in public, predominantly human, schools. All the girls had crushes on Professor Mason—human and Variant.

As we walked up to the maternity wing in the hospital, Tyler and Ethan got up from their seats in the waiting area.

Ethan wrapped me up in a big, warm hug and gave me a soft kiss that I just about melted into. He was in a white T-shirt but still had his chef pants on. He was the head chef at a painfully trendy restaurant in Manhattan and chasing his first Michelin star. In the next year or two, he planned to open up his own restaurant.

"We don't have time for this." Alec tried to wedge an arm between us, and we pulled apart, chuckling.

Tyler pulled me away from both of them with a hand around my waist. "Would you calm down? You'd think it was Eve about to have a baby and not Dot, the way you're carrying on."

He gave me a kiss too, taking his sweet time—no doubt to irritate Alec. Tyler was the youngest headmaster Bradford Hills Institute had ever seen. One of the first things he'd done was create a new position—a human liaison who worked on building ties with human communities and broadening the Institute's admissions guidelines. Tyler had just come from a meeting in the city. His tie was loose, his crisp shirt rolled up at the sleeves.

I smiled against his lips and pulled away, putting Alec out of his misery.

"OK, which room are they in?" I asked.

"This way." Tyler took my hand and pulled me down the corridor.

Outside the door to Dot's birthing suite, Olivia sat casually flipping through the latest edition of *Variant Weekly* while Henry slowly paced the corridor, a very serious frown on his face.

We shared hugs as Alec scowled at us all impatiently.

Everyone else stayed outside as Alec and I went in.

"Your pain management plan has arrived." I grinned.

Dot looked up from her phone. "Thank fuck. The contractions are getting really close, and I'm more dilated than all the pupils of every rave attendee *ever*. I think it might be time soon."

"I told you so." Alec huffed, and I rolled my eyes.

"We're here now. It's all good." I rubbed his arm in a half-apologetic gesture. We'd all been giving him shit.

"Hey, kitten." Marcus gave me a kiss on the cheek, then gave Alec one of those thumping man-hugs.

I gave Kyo the same greeting, but he just stood in front of us looking kind of dazed.

"I'm going to be a father," he stated in a monotone, then blinked once. Alec and I shared a look.

Lucian was still the managing director of Melior Group, but he was looking to retire soon, and he was grooming Kyo to replace him. Having that kind of responsibility didn't seem to faze him, but the prospect of becoming a parent was proving a little intimidating.

"Yeah, man." Alec slapped a hand on his shoulder. "That's how this works."

"So am I," Marcus piped in from his spot next to Dot. "We'll figure it out."

Dot was having twins. After two years of trying to conceive naturally without success, they'd decided to try IVF. Dot immediately decided she wanted a baby from each one of her loves and insisted she be inseminated with both embryos. "Plus," she declared at family dinner one night, "it'll be good to get all my breeding out of the way at once." Miraculously, it worked.

"Shit." She cringed and leaned forward.

"Ace, you're up." Marcus took Dot's hand and waved us over with the other.

Alec rushed to his cousin's side and took her free hand. I held on to his arm and transferred the perfect amount of Light so he could take her pain away.

We'd perfected this process.

From time to time, after a really bad natural disaster or in a situation where it was difficult to get people to proper medical care, Alec and I volunteered our time to help manage pain—if it was safe, of course. Their protectiveness never really waned.

Alec had toyed with the idea of somehow making it his full-time work, but that would've required me to go with him everywhere he was needed, and I had my own scientific goals to kick. He'd also realized pretty quickly that he actually didn't want to spend that much time surrounded by people in pain. Even if he wasn't the one inflicting it, it still triggered bad memories. Yet he didn't want to stay with Melior Group either.

After Alec spent a few months moping around the house and bemoaning how useless he was and how he could just be "the house husband," Tyler slapped a pile of college brochures down in front of him and told him to get his shit together.

He was in his second year working as a specialized counselor at Bradford Hills Institute. He worked exclusively with kids with rare, dangerous, or isolating abilities. No one understood them like he did. He was kind of perfect for it.

Despite Dot's colorful evaluation of what stage of labor she was in, she actually wasn't ready to push for another few hours. We stayed with her the whole time, managing her pain through the contractions and then through the delivery.

Both babies were the picture of health, twenty little fingers and twenty little toes, wailing to announce their arrival into the world.

Alec and I stepped out to update the rest of the family while the nurses did their thing. Charlie and Ed had arrived too, and they all swarmed us for information.

"A boy and a girl." I grinned. "Both healthy. Dot did amazingly."

We all knew they were having one of each—Dot had left no aspect of this pregnancy a mystery—but it still felt as if I was announcing a surprise.

Henry started crying, which got Olivia going too. Charlie pulled a sniffling Ed into his side. Ethan got misty eyed, and Alec was somewhere between dazed and ecstatic after witnessing his first birth.

It was my first birth too, but I'd researched the fuck out of it. As soon as Dot announced she was pregnant, that became my side project. We even got together one night and watched a bunch of birthing videos together, a giant bowl of popcorn balanced on her giant belly.

Kyo and Marcus came out, kicking off another round of hugs, shouts of congratulations, and more tears.

We took turns going in to visit with Dot and holding little Jamie and Nina. I made sure I was sitting down when one of the fragile little bundles was handed to me, desperate for a cuddle but terrified I might hurt her.

Ethan was confident holding Jamie, the baby not even close to the length of his giant forearm. He cooed to him and even started singing a lullaby.

Josh wasn't remotely fazed by it either, holding both of them with assurance, although I suspected he was using his ability to make sure both precious babies were safe at all times.

Alec was still a little dazed when Kyo deposited a baby into his arms. His eyes were a bit wide, his shoulders more tense than I'd seen them in years. He looked down into little Nina's face and relaxed a bit, a smirk pulling at the corner of his lips, but he passed the baby off to Tyler quickly and heaved a sigh of relief.

Ty was uncertain and looked around the room for help.

"Just make sure you support her head." Marcus showed him. "And hold her like this. There you go."

Eventually he eased into it, rocking the baby. After a few moments, he cocked his head to the side and stared off into space as the rest of us chatted quietly around him. Then he smiled to himself, and his knowing gray eyes met mine.

I didn't know what truth had been revealed to him or if it was even related to having kids—I just liked looking into his eyes. He still gave me butterflies.

"Do you think you guys will have any?" Dot asked from her reclined position on the bed. I smiled at her and shrugged.

Maybe one day, but for now we had each other, and that was enough. We were happy.

BONUS SCENES

LAYOVER

Author's note: This is a deleted scene that takes place after the end of Vital Found but before the events of Vivid Avowed.

The Melior Group private jet was not available, so we flew first class, but the guys all complained about having to do a layover. We had three hours to waste. After having a delicious meal in an exclusive lounge and freshening up, Tyler and Alec pulled out their laptops. Ethan, Josh, and I decided to go for a walk.

We wandered around the airport, checking out the stores. Considering how well he dressed, it shouldn't have surprised me that Josh enjoyed shopping. It wasn't long before he had several bags swinging in his hands. Ethan and I mostly just followed him, window shopping and messing around, but when we went past a lingerie store, they both pulled up and shared a look over my head.

"I don't think they sell men's underwear here, guys," I said innocently, knowing full well what they were thinking.

"Let's just look around." Josh had that mischievous glint in his eye. I sighed but followed him in. I couldn't resist him when he had that cheeky look, and we did have time to kill.

"Great idea!" Ethan boomed, grabbing my hand and dragging me the rest of the way in.

The store was all dark displays and velvet chairs—tasteful and opulent. Josh slung his shopping bags over his shoulder and wandered around as if he browsed crotchless panties all the time. Ethan glued himself to my back, his hands on my hips, as we moved about the store slowly, pointing at every single item and saying, "That's the one. No, that's the one."

For the most part, I wasn't even looking at the hangers, just enjoying spending some time with my guys, but a silky black number caught my attention, and I reached for it. It was a one-piece, like a bathing suit—except you would never wear something like this at the beach—and constructed of a series of black bands covering the breasts and crotch and crisscrossing over the body. It was also nearly a thousand dollars! I gasped and went to put it back, but Josh appeared next to me and took it out of my hand.

"This was a bad idea." Ethan's voice was strained as he backed away from me and surreptitiously adjusted the bulge in his pants.

I ignored him, focusing on Josh.

"You should try it on." He shrugged, holding it out to me along with several others. "These too."

"Josh, they're really expensive," I whispered, eyeing the smartly dressed shop assistant behind the counter. She was keeping her distance but also keeping an eye on us as she served another customer.

"Yeah, but who cares? We can afford it." I went to protest again, but he cut me off in a lowered voice. "I want to see you in them. Trust me, this is more of a present for me—and the others—than it is for you."

That cheeky, smoldering look was back. I couldn't deny him when he looked at me like that.

I took the hangers without looking at the sizes, confident he'd probably chosen better than I would have, and headed to the back of the store. The assistant finished with the other customer and smiled at me as I approached.

"Would you like to try those on?" she asked, a polite smile pasted to her face.

"No—" I tried to say we'd just buy them, but Ethan cut me off.

"Yes. She's trying them on." He nudged me toward the changing room, and the smile on the assistant's face became more genuine.

"Are you OK with sizes?" she called after us.

"Yes, thank you!" I called back.

Josh stayed in the store, looking at a display near the counter, but Ethan shoved his way right into the changing room and pulled the heavy velvet drape closed.

I cocked one eyebrow and pointed to the padded low stool in the corner. "You can sit and you can watch. No touching." I kept my voice low. I didn't want to have sex in a changing room in the airport, and the look written all over his face said that was exactly what he was planning.

"I'm OK with watching." He raked his eyes up and down my body—not that there was much to look at yet. I was in leggings and an oversized, soft cardigan.

I took my clothes off and piled them in his lap until I was completely naked except for my underwear, and the look on his face became much more serious. His broad chest rose and lowered with heavier breaths, his amber eyes hooded.

I pulled on the first set, a pretty tame, simple deep blue panties and bra with white lace detail.

Skimpy bits of lace and leather flew about the room as I tried each piece on, and Ethan's grip on my cardigan got tighter and tighter.

Each piece was a little more risqué than the last, until I finally stood before him in the expensive black number I'd balked at before Josh insisted I try things on. Soft leather-feel strips of fabric barely covered my breasts, while thinner strips crisscrossed over my belly and disappeared between my legs, the whole thing held together with fine silver rings. It was luxurious and sexy but definitely hinted at bondage.

Ethan took in all the spots where the strips of fabric were cutting into my skin and swallowed, his Adam's apple bobbing. He was struggling, but he was being a good boy and staying put.

"So, you like it?" I trailed my hand down my cleavage, fiddling with the straps over my ribs before looking up at him through my lashes. He dumped all my clothes on the ground and took a step toward me, his bulk making the tight space feel even smaller. I backed up against the mirror, the glass cool against my bare back.

He planted a hand on either side of my head and leaned in, still behaving and not touching me.

"I don't like it." He leaned all the way in to whisper in my ear, his breath tickling my neck. "I fucking love it."

His warm, sweet smell surrounded me—his ripped, muscled body inches from mine—and I kicked myself for teasing him. I was suddenly seriously considering having sex in a changing room in an airport.

I reached for the buttons on his jeans, but he took a step back, out of my reach, and flashed me a grin. I wanted to lick those dimples right off his face.

"Tease," I grumbled, taking a few deep breaths before peeling the scandalous lingerie off my body.

"Takes one to know one," Ethan growled, but his eyes were still dancing with mischief.

He took several deep breaths himself while I put my clothes back on. As we exited the dressing room, he adjusted his pants, hissing.

Josh was leaning on the counter and chatting with the shop assistant. He was perfectly put together, as always, not a dirty-blond hair out of place, and the assistant was looking at him through her eyelashes.

I pushed down the jealousy and stepped up to the counter. "I like these two the best."

Josh flashed me his perfect smile. "We'll take all of them."

My eyes bugged out. "Josh—"

"We'll take all of them." Ethan leaned around me, pushing the pile of fabric toward the assistant.

She went silent, her eyes flicking from me to Ethan to Josh and back to me, her mouth slightly parted as she connected the dots. Ethan had gone into the dressing room with me; now here was Josh, paying for the racy items, snaking an arm around my middle and pulling me to his side.

I leaned into him, deciding to have a little fun with her. Polyamorous relationships were common in the Variant communities, but it was still somewhat taboo with the humans. Some of them had embraced it and were taking the Variants' lead; others were wary and judgmental. It also varied from country to country, religion and culture having an impact too. Most people were fascinated by it. I wasn't sure how this shop assistant felt about it, but she obviously wasn't exposed to open displays of it that often, judging by her surprise.

Watching her out of the corner of my eye, I leaned forward and pressed a decidedly not friendly kiss to Josh's neck. "Thanks, baby," I whispered and bit my lower lip, giving him a flirty look.

His lip twitched. He knew exactly what I was doing, and he was amused.

"Can't wait to see you in them." He gave my ass a squeeze, then looked over my shoulder. "Can we?"

Ethan's warmth pressed into my back. "I just saw every single one, and I already want to see 'em all again."

I wasn't sure if Ethan was playing along or just still trying to process what he'd watched in the changing room.

The shop assistant's face was priceless. She stared at us, mouth slightly parted, eyes wide, a scrap of lacy fabric held in midair. As one we all turned to look at her. She visibly snapped out of it, hurriedly getting on with scanning the items as a deep blush spread across her cheeks. She was no longer making eye contact with any of us.

"There you all are." Tyler's timing couldn't have been better. I smiled wide and felt Josh's shoulders shaking in silent laughter, his jaw clenching to keep himself from smiling.

"Hey, baby." I turned, extracting myself from between Ethan and Josh and taking the two steps to get to Tyler. I wrapped my arms around his neck and gave him a kiss on the lips. He was a little surprised but kissed me back, holding me to him.

I broke the kiss and looked back. The assistant was back to staring and frozen in mid-scan.

"You two got this?" I asked. "We'll meet you back in the lounge."

They both waved me off and turned back to the counter.

"Thank you for your help." I smiled sweetly at the shop assistant, and once again, she snapped out of her daze.

"Oh, you're welcome." She smiled back. Then she looked at all three of my guys one by one. "You're a lucky woman."

She blanched, making me think she hadn't meant to say it, and I felt mean for toying with her. "Thank you." I made sure my voice was genuine. "I know I am."

As Tyler and I reached the entrance to the store, Alec stalked in, looking just as intense and menacing as he always did—shoulders tense, eyes narrowed, dressed all in black.

"We're going to miss the flight." He frowned at us all.

I stepped forward, wrapped my arm around his middle, and led him out the door. "Let's go then."

I smiled up at him. He frowned suspiciously at me but wrapped his arm around my shoulders and let me lead him away.

Behind me, the other three burst into laughter.

SIXTY-TWO PUSH-UPS

Author's Note: This takes place at the beginning of Vital Found. *It was originally going to be the beginning of Chapter 1, but I decided to change that up as this didn't have the impactful, tense beginning I wanted. Still a fun scene though!*

"Again!" the man in the tracksuit at the front of the room shouted, and we all obeyed.

My muscles were aching. Sweat gathered at my hairline, in my cleavage, running down my back. Next to me, Dot was panting so hard she was beginning to sound wheezy. I knew not to suggest she take it easy though—I had done that only once during a training session, and I would never do it again.

Dutifully, we repeated the sequence we had been taught earlier in the session, punching, kicking, and ducking in almost perfect unison.

We were in the basement of the Zacarias mansion, in their very well-equipped gym. Ethan and Josh had mentioned doing workouts down here in the past—but I had only visited this part of the property a few short days after the Bradford Hills Institute invasion. Once everyone had gotten some sleep, and Alec and Tyler were done with the lengthy debriefings with Melior Group and the federal law enforcement, I found myself being ordered into this dungeon.

They marched me down here and put me through an hour of torture to assess my level of fitness, reflexes, strength, and self-defense skills. I had been doing a lot of running since my mother died to expel what I now knew was excess Light I'd had no outlet for at the time, so my cardio fitness was good, but my reflexes and strength left a lot to be desired. My self-defense skills were nonexistent. I preferred to spend my time in a science lab doing experiments rather than in a gym lifting weights. *Sue me!*

Then they wanted me to show them what I would do if someone attacked me. Without a second of warning, Josh stepped up behind me and wrapped his arms around me in an aggressive way. I squealed in surprise and cracked up laughing, going completely limp in his arms. He released me, and all four of them sighed in unison, Tyler running his hand through his messy brown hair.

Alec had declared, "She's going to get killed, and then we'll try to save her, and we'll all get killed too." He didn't even look at me as he spoke or as he walked right past me and out of the gym. Things were still tense between us.

Their solution was to bring in a Melior Group trainer to whip me into shape.

Of course, no one knew I was a Vital yet—or that Alec, Tyler, Josh, and Ethan were in my Bond—and they wouldn't waste their precious resources on some random potential Variant, which was all I was as far as anyone outside our circle was concerned. So the story was that in light of recent violent events and increasing tensions between the Variants and the humans, Ethan and Josh needed to begin training for when they were old enough to join Melior Group as recruits. Melior Group had been trying to get them on board with this for years, so they were more than happy to oblige.

Josh's telekinesis and Ethan's fire ability were rare and coveted and would be a massive asset to Melior Group. They would be foaming at their collective mouth if they knew Josh and Ethan had found their Vital, *me*, and their abilities were stronger than anyone could imagine. That was a big part of why we were keeping our Bond on the down-low. None of us were particularly interested in becoming guns for hire. That and the fact that known Vitals were disappearing without a trace all over the world.

It worked out well anyway. Ethan and Josh really did need to get serious about their training. Once Dot found out, she insisted on joining us. No one wanted to say no to her. We were all still reeling from Charlie's abduction, but she was his Variant *and* his sister. It was hitting her really hard. If joining us for brutal training sessions helped take her mind off it, who were we to say no?

Kane, the Melior Group trainer, showed up at the house five times per week to run us all through punishing drills, complicated sequences, and sparring sessions where the boys and us girls would pair up and try to slam the other to the floor. I was taller than Dot, and when we did weights training, it was clear I was stronger too, but she was fast and channeled all her rage and frustration into whatever she was doing. We were pretty evenly matched.

Kane would stand in front of the mirrors that lined one entire wall of the room and watch us with a frown on his face, barking at me to watch how Dot had quickly ducked away from my attack, or grumbling at Dot that her punches would never hurt if she didn't put on some muscle.

We had been training regularly for two months, and I didn't think I'd ever seen the man smile. He was a Kane by name and a cane by nature, constantly whipping us with his words and punishing our bodies with his training sessions. He had light brown hair and was a little shorter than Josh. I had no idea what color his eyes were—I was too afraid to make eye contact long enough to find out.

As the summer passed, I spent my time training in the basement gym with Kane and the others, going for longer and longer runs with Ethan to keep my fitness up, and attending summer classes with Dot at Bradford Hills Institute to lighten my load for the coming semester. I also spent a lot of time practicing my control of the Light flow, both alone and with the guys so they could practice controlling their abilities when they had extra juice.

Not with Alec though. Alec didn't join in any of our summer activities. He was constantly in tactical meetings at Melior Group headquarters in New York and disappearing for days at a time on missions no one was willing to give me any details on. I didn't doubt he wanted to do all he could to find his cousin, but I had a feeling he was using it all as a very good excuse to completely ignore me and the fact that I was his Vital. Speaking of . . .

Kane had us end the session on push-ups. He did this "fun" thing where he would demand we complete some arbitrary number of push-ups—"the correct way," he would bark, "none of this girly bullshit doing push-ups on your knees"—say fifty-three, and we would have to do them as one, all four of us counting them out as we went. If one of us faltered or collapsed, we would all have to start again. It was torture.

We got through the sixty-two push-ups he had ordered and all collapsed onto the ground, panting and groaning.

Kane grunted, looked at us with a disgusted expression on his face, and collected his bag on his way out without saying goodbye.

As usual, Ethan was the first one to recover, sitting up next to me and giving me a view of his wide, sweaty back. The boys trained shirtless, and it was always distracting at the start of the session when they both lifted their shirts over their heads, but the intensity of the training made it impossible to focus on anything else once we got started.

I dragged my eyes from Ethan's sweaty neck, the black hair sticking to his glistening skin, and down the length of his spine, watching the muscles move rhythmically as he worked to calm his breathing. Ethan had always been big—taller than the others even though he was the youngest, and broad in the shoulders, his size intimidating to most people—but all the training was giving his form extra definition. Josh, on the other side of Ethan, was still lying on the ground and panting like I was.

I looked over at him, and he smirked at me. He had seen me checking Ethan out. I grinned back and ran my eyes over him too. Because I could.

They were both in my Bond, and now that Kane had left, there was no one around we had to keep this secret from. I had a feeling Josh was doing extra weight training. He was the shortest of the guys and had the most lithe and athletic physique, but lately his shoulders were looking a little broader, his crisp collared shirts straining a little more over his chest. My eyes lingered on the six-pack that had recently made itself known too. Kane liked to make us do sit-ups as much as he liked to make us do push-ups, and it was paying off.

Ethan flipped over to his hands and knees. "I'm going to take a shower," he told no one in particular, breaking my shameless examination of Josh's abs with his hulking form, which was now leaning over me. My eyes widened, and I lifted my hands in front of me, stopping just short of actually touching his chest.

"No! Sweaty!" I scrunched my face up and turned it away from him. He laughed, the big infectious laugh he was known for, before leaning forward. His sweaty chest made contact with my palms, and he planted a wet kiss on the side of my forehead before pulling away. Josh got up too, and they left together, disappearing up the stairs.

Dot and I remained on the ground, taking our time and letting our limbs regain energy before attempting to move.

"Wanna jump in the pool?" She lolled her head to the side so she could look at me, messy bits of her black hair stuck to her forehead. I nodded, and we both made exaggerated groaning sounds as we peeled ourselves off the rubber floor.

"Ugh! I'm getting too old for this shit," she grumbled as she pushed herself into a standing position.

"I'm going to need a hip replacement if I'm not careful." I lifted my leg up and down, wincing at the slight pain in the side of my thigh. It was just soreness from all the side kicks, and it would be healed by the morning. People with Variant DNA recovered much faster from illness and injury. It was why we could have such hard training sessions almost daily. We didn't need much time to recover.

"Oh, my poor back," Dot complained, rubbing it.

"My shoulder is killing me. You slammed me down hard that last time."

She laughed, the cruel bitch. "Ah, my knee is in agony!"

"My elbow is falling off!"

"My cataracts! I can't see!"

We burst out laughing, heading for the stairs.

My chest constricted with a bittersweet kind of hope for my friend. That was the first time I'd heard her laugh since Charlie was taken.

"I'm going to take a shower first," Dot said at the top of the stairs, her laughter dying, her brows furrowing. I could practically see the guilt wrapping around her like a cape.

I sighed and headed straight outside. I had left my swimsuit in the pool house bathroom the other day, and the blue water of the pool was glistening so temptingly.

SNOWFLAKE

Author's Note: This scene was written early on in the process of writing Vital Found (I write out of order), and I couldn't include it due to continuity. It just didn't fit the timeline, and Alec was not in the headspace of the below scene for most of the book—he was much darker and broodier. But I love this little moment of connection between them!

When we emerged from the building, the world was white. I froze, and Alec took a few steps ahead of me before realizing I wasn't following him and doubling back.

"What?" he asked, frowning down at me and shoving his hands into his pockets.

"Snow," I breathed out, wonder in my voice, my hand pointing to the white bits of fluff floating ethereally down from the heavens.

I knew snow was just tiny ice crystals that fell through cold, dry air. But as I stood there, I couldn't help feeling as if it were magical, as mysterious and unexplained as the Light.

"Yeah." Alec's eyes looked from me to the rapidly whitening world before us, then back to me. "It must have started snowing while we were inside. We should probably get going before it gets worse." He made to leave but stopped, huffing when he saw that I was still rooted to the spot, a goofy look on my face.

In all our travels across the globe, my mother and I had managed to never be around during winter in any place where it snowed. I didn't know if it was just chance or if it had more to do with how much we both loved summer. Probably a bit of both. The end result was that I'd never seen snow. I hadn't seen it falling. I hadn't seen everything transformed into a winter wonderland. I hadn't heard the muted, peaceful silence it brought with it. I was mesmerized. Alec was getting worried.

"Shit. Are you broken?" he asked, half joking. Then when I didn't answer him, he placed a hand on my shoulder and asked in a more serious voice, "Eve, you OK?"

"I've never seen snow." I finally turned to look at him, my voice still hushed and awed. "It's so beautiful."

His eyes widened a little, and the corners of his lips twitched. We turned as one, both of us now watching the fat snowflakes tumbling to the ground. His hand trailed a slow path down my arm until our hands met. Instead of pulling away at the skin contact, he wrapped his fingers around mine. Immediately, I made sure my Light control was impenetrable. I didn't want to give him a reason to pull away. I wanted to show him that he could trust me with this, that I could keep a lid on it.

But it was fine; I already had it under control. Once I made sure all my mental blocks were in place, I returned my attention to the snow and the feel of Alec's hand wrapped around mine. It was the first time we had ever held hands, and it was strangely more intimate than the things we had done on the couch in Tyler's study. We were sharing a moment, and he was trusting me enough to risk getting juiced up by holding my hand.

It wasn't windy; the snow was falling softly to the ground, undisturbed, so the chill in the air didn't have a bite to it. It just felt as if we were cocooned in a tub of vanilla ice cream. But other than the icy kiss of the cold air on my cheeks and nose, I didn't feel cold. In complete contrast to the weather, the sensation that sparked up in the center of my chest was warm and fuzzy. It spread, leaving a soft and safe sensation as it filled my chest, melting me from the inside in the most wonderful way.

I sighed, and a wide smile crossed my face. I looked up at Alec. The strong lines of his jaw, covered in a five o'clock shadow, were softened by a smile that matched mine. His eyes were a brighter blue than I had ever seen them, the white all around us bringing out the lightest hues in them.

I squeezed his fingers reflexively, and he looked down at me, both of us grinning at each other when our eyes met.

"Come on." He surprised me by springing into action, yanking me along behind him as he rushed over to where I was pretty sure a grassy area lay under all the snow, his big boots leaving deep prints in the perfect powder. I held on to his hand with both of mine, feeling the snow begin to fall on my face, an uncontrolled laugh falling from my lips.

Just as suddenly as he had started to move, he came to a stop. Turning to face me, he flashed me another smile before extracting his hand from mine and leaning backward until he fell flat on his back in the snow. I laughed again, wondering at the whole situation and reveling in it even as I hoped it wasn't all a dream or hallucination.

He spread his arms and legs wide, like a starfish, and then began to move them in arcs, creating streaks in the snow.

"Come on!" His voice had honey in it, and my breath hitched a little at hearing it. I loved it when his voice sounded like honey. "I can't make a snow angel on my own. It's against the law here in America!"

I didn't need any more encouragement. I moved to the side of him and flopped down into the snow, copying his movements. When a bit of snow made its way under the collar of my jacket, I squealed, and Alec laughed loudly next to me.

His face appeared above mine, his eyes sparkling as he offered me his hands. I reached out and let him pull me up, and we stood back to look at our work. Our hands made their way to each other once again, our fingers intertwining this time.

"I know you don't remember, but we used to do this as kids." He was looking at our angels as he spoke, mine significantly smaller than his and a little more wobbly. "Your angel would be half the size of mine. It's not half the size anymore."

A silence fell over us, and I had a feeling he was thinking about how different our relationship had turned out from how he had probably expected it to. I wondered what our Bond would have looked like if we had grown up together. If my mother had never gone on the run, taking me away from him, would we have ended up with a Bond more like what Charlie and Dot had—close but completely platonic? Would we have grown to see each other more as siblings than anything else? Would I have ended up having the other three in my Bond at all?

It was painful to think about not having them tethered to me as strongly as they were, and it was pointless to think about what-ifs, so I put it out of my mind and focused on the present. On the man I was sharing this new experience with.

We must have come out of our reveries at the same time, because our eyes met, and we once again smiled at each other. The Light inside me relished how calm and easy our connection felt. The tension and hostility that had kept our link taut and dissonant was gone in that moment, and we both felt it.

We turned toward each other, our hands still clasped at our sides. His eyes flicked down to our entwined fingers, a hint of curiosity entering his expression, and then they flicked down to my lips before he looked into my eyes fully.

I knew he was about to kiss me. I could feel it in the soft silence all around us, in the way his fingers flexed around mine, in the way he stepped closer to me with intention in his eyes. It didn't matter what our Bond would have looked like if we had grown up together. This was what it was now, and he had decided to try giving in to it. I wasn't about to give him a reason to pull back again.

He had noticed I'd kept a tight hold on my Light while we held hands, not allowing any of it to transfer to him whatsoever, and apparently he was ready to test my control.

I took a breath, mentally checking in on my control once more as his eyelids lowered lazily and he watched my face. He knew what I was doing, and he was giving me space to make sure it was done right. I gave him a tiny nod, letting him know I was ready, and one corner of his mouth twitched up in that crooked smirk I loved and hated in equal measure. But there was no cruelty in it this time as he leaned down.

I lifted my face up to his, meeting him halfway. His lips found mine and kissed me softly, testing out what it felt like. My face was no longer cold, having warmed up from all the frolicking in the snow, and I could feel little snowflakes falling gently onto my skin and melting on my warm cheeks. I sighed against Alec's lips, and he wrapped his free arm around my shoulders, pulling me farther into the embrace.

Much as I wanted to, I didn't deepen the kiss, and neither did he. With another soft peck, we pulled away to look at each other.

"Your control is improving." He spoke softly, but the smile on his face betrayed his calm words. He was excited.

He leaned forward again, his enthusiasm getting the better of him. Seeing the desire in his expression sent a jolt of excitement down my back that settled at the base of my spine, making me acutely aware that this was very different from the innocent, childlike excitement I'd felt at experiencing snow for the first time. This was definitely not innocent. It was dangerous.

Terrified that my control would slip and allow Light to transfer to Alec, setting our relationship back an immeasurable amount, I yanked my hand out of his and practically jumped out of his grasp.

I held one hand out in a stop motion as I took a few calming breaths. Alec looked surprised at first, but he recovered quickly, shoving his hands into his pockets and watching me with an easy expression, giving me the space I needed.

"My control is improving," I finally said, letting my hand drop to my side. "But let's not push it, OK?"

He nodded. "OK." I was relieved to see that the easy expression didn't leave his face as he flashed me another crooked smile.

We walked back to the car, not holding hands but side by side and in companionable instead of tense silence. It was a definite improvement.

When we settled into the car and started driving, he spoke quietly. "Your control is improving in more ways than one." He was referring to the fact that I had managed to think through my own desire and make the smart decision. It wasn't easy. "Thank you for . . . just, thank you."

He was being hard on himself for not being the one to stop it before it potentially became dangerous, but there were two of us in this mess, and I couldn't expect him to be the responsible one all the time. That wasn't what an adult relationship was about. And that's what I wanted—an adult, open, honest relationship where we could rely on each other equally. While I also relied on three other men. And they relied on me. And I did other things with them too.

In place of a "you're welcome," I reached my hand out and covered his. He flipped it, and we held hands as he drove.

ALONE

Author's Note: This is a deleted scene from somewhere around the first half of Vivid Avowed.

As soon as the forkful of cheesy pasta hit my mouth, I thought of my mother. The image of her smiling face burned so clear in my mind and appeared so suddenly that it made me gasp a little. I closed my eyes and chewed slowly, savoring the simple yet perfectly balanced flavors of the meal. Images of my mother bustling around several of the different kitchens we had called ours flashed through my mind.

I could see her grating the cheese, pulling the heavy dish out of the oven, smiling at me from across the table as we devoured our meal for two. I could hear her laugh as clearly as if she were standing next to me.

I opened my eyes and focused on the bowl in front of me, scooping another big bite of something I hadn't tasted in over a year into my mouth. The boys' chitchat and the sound of the TV had faded, and I couldn't see anything past the rim of the bowl I held in my hands. I was in the living room with my Bond, but I was also with my mother. Somehow, Ethan had made my favorite meal that my mom used to make. The creamy sauce, the chicken and mushrooms, the aromatic herbs and way too much cheese.

The first bite had been like turning on a bright light in a pitch-black room to reveal all the things you knew were there but couldn't see. The second bite was much more bitter. As the warm cheesy pasta made its way down my throat, I remembered why I hadn't tasted my favorite meal in so long. The person who used to make it was gone. My mother was dead, and I missed her *so much*.

Unbidden tears welled in my eyes, and my throat became tight, making it impossible to eat another bite. I took a shuddering breath as a tear escaped my eyes and plopped unceremoniously into my bowl.

"Eve?" Josh was the first to notice the effect our dinner was having on me. "What's wrong?"

"Are you hurt?" Tyler piped in, placing a gentle hand on my shoulder.

Ignoring them both, I looked up and focused on Ethan, the look in my eyes so intense that he sat up a little straighter, surprise crossing his features.

"Where did you get this recipe?" I managed to ask around the thick lump in my throat.

"Uh . . . what?" He looked really confused.

"The recipe, Kid. Think." Alec saved me from having to ask again. I spared him a quick glance. He was standing in front of the armchair, radiating tension, but his voice had sounded like honey.

"Oh, um . . . it's an old one. It's not from any of the cookbooks. It's from one of the notebooks Mom left me." He looked down; sadness at being reminded of his own dead mother replaced the confusion on his face.

"I'd almost forgotten." Alec's voice was sad. "It's been so long . . . This is Joyce's recipe."

"Oh my god." Ethan sounded horrified, his eyes wide, and he looked as if he was about to launch himself out of his seat opposite me. "Baby, I am so sorry. I swear I didn't know."

As Tyler's hand reached for my shoulder again, I stood from my seat, wiping the moisture off my cheeks with the sleeve of my sweater. If he touched me in his comforting way, if Ethan hugged me with his warm arms, if Josh looked at me with that knowing look in his eyes, I just *knew* I would lose it. So I stood up, out of his reach, and with as much composure as I could muster tried to excuse myself.

"It's OK, Ethan." I focused on him, careful to avoid Josh's gaze. "Really. It's delicious, like all your food. I think I'm full though. Might go upstairs for a bit and, um . . ." I didn't know how to finish the sentence, and my voice sounded dangerously shaky, so I just turned and walked out of the living room, focusing on putting one foot in front of the other until I had climbed two flights of stairs and shut myself in my room.

As soon as the door closed and I was alone, the tears spilled over once again. I didn't sob dramatically or throw myself down on the bed. The emotion I felt was powerful but quiet. Lonely. The tears flowed freely, and I slowly lowered myself onto the soft sheets, grabbing a pillow to grip tightly.

Tasting my mother's food so unexpectedly had taken me completely off guard. The memories it brought back were simple yet incredibly vivid. I missed her every day, but that was more about the general sense of her. The flavor of the pasta bake had made me miss very specific aspects of who she was as a person, very specific things about our close relationship.

It made me remember seemingly inconsequential things I hadn't thought about in a long time. And that was part of the problem. Yes, I missed her every day, but I hadn't thought about the little things in a while. The way her hair was almost exactly the same shade as mine. The way she tried to make every day a little bit of an adventure so I wouldn't focus on the fact that we were running from something. How she hummed while doing the dishes, even when she was in a bad mood.

I had been so preoccupied with starting my new life in Bradford Hills, discovering I was a Vital, getting to know my Bond, making friends, and dealing with the aftermath of the massacre that I had forgotten to be broken about the fact that my mother had died. I was moving on, and it felt as though I was betraying her.

I hugged the pillow a little tighter as a fresh wave of emotion washed over me. Tears soaked the sheets under my head, and my shoulders shook.

It couldn't have been more than ten minutes before I heard the door behind me open, the hallway light spilling in before several sets of soft footsteps followed behind it. The door closed as softly as it had been opened, and the light disappeared once more.

I tried to stop crying, not wanting them to see me like this, but once the floodgates had been opened, there was no closing them. The tears continued to flow, but I did manage to stop my shoulders from heaving so uncontrollably. With a shuddering breath, I half turned to look at them over my shoulder.

I was surprised to find four dark shapes standing in the dark with me. It wouldn't have surprised me if Ethan and Josh had come after me on their own, even Tyler's calm approach would have made sense, but to have all four of them there . . .

The shock made me sit up slowly, my eyes adjusting to the dark and starting to see them a little more clearly. My tears seemed to slow down too. Maybe it was the distraction of having something new to think about—the puzzle of why all four of them had come after an overreacting crying girl. Or maybe it was just their proximity. I was still curious, in a scientific way, about why it felt so good to be near them physically, but I was past denying or questioning that there was something supernatural and instinctual about it.

"Um . . . what . . ." My brain may have been curious about their strange behavior, but apparently it wasn't entirely capable of forming full sentences. I was just so confused at seeing them all standing there in the dark that I wasn't entirely sure what I even wanted to ask.

"Eve." Josh stepped forward first, the light from the window illuminating his face. The cool moonlight made his blond hair appear silver, but his green eyes looked almost black. "Look, I know you're not used to having anyone around to comfort you since your mom died."

At the mention of my mother, I took a shuddering breath. I sat up fully and hugged my knees to my chest but tried to focus on what Josh was saying.

"I know you've learned to just deal with shit on your own, but you don't have to do that anymore. You can't, baby."

It was the first time he had used any kind of pet name with me, and it somehow made the ache in my chest better and worse at the same time. He came to the bed and sat right in front of me.

"You have us now. When you're hurting, we're hurting. And you can't hide it from us either. I can always tell when something is not right."

He reached a hand out and gently nudged my chin, making me look at him, not even bothered by the fact that my face was wet with tears that now coated his fingers. "I will never stop looking out for you, Evelyn. I will always have your back. You know you can't hide these things from me."

To punctuate what he was saying, he wrapped me up in his arms. I was still in a little ball, my knees held to my chest, but he just pulled me to himself and held me while I held myself. It was exactly what he was trying to tell me with his words—I could hold myself together, but he would always notice I was doing it and would hold me too. Josh always knew what I was thinking, and he was so bloody smart he could usually guess what I was overthinking. Somehow he always managed to put it all together.

"Yeah, sweet thing." Ethan's usually booming voice was quieter and softer than I had ever heard it, so smooth it almost reminded me of his cousin's when the honey was in it. "You know you can't hide anything from Josh. He watches you like a hawk."

The bed dipped behind me as Ethan's heavy frame gently landed on it. Josh released me, holding on to my hand as Ethan's big arms wrapped around me from behind. They were slowly untangling my body from the tight ball I had rolled it into.

"Josh will always know when you're worried about something or sad about something or upset about something. And I will always be there to cheer you up, to make you smile, to help you look on the bright side."

He placed a gentle kiss to the back of my head and gave me a squeeze.

"And when you can't look on the bright side, I will sit with you in the dark." Alec's voice drew my attention to the door, where he was still standing with Tyler. They were both leaning on the wall, out of the reach of the light from the window. Both their faces were cast in darkness.

Josh and Ethan had slowly been dragging me out of myself with the comforting words and gentle touches, but it was Alec's declaration that made it all start to sink in.

Josh always knew what was happening with me, and Ethan's smile was infectious, but sometimes the heavy things needed to be acknowledged before you were ready to be cheered up. Alec was telling me he would be there with me while I dealt with the heaviness.

I stared into the darkness, focusing on the outline of his face. I could almost feel him staring at me in that intense way he had. He pushed off the wall and started moving toward me. In perfect synchronicity, Josh pressed a kiss to my cheek and scooted away, Ethan moving only a fraction of a second after Josh did. They leaned on the headboard as Alec came to a stop in front of me.

I could finally see his face in the light of the moon. It carried all his scars, physical and emotional, and the expression was unfathomable. But this wasn't about figuring out what he was thinking and feeling. This wasn't about what they wanted or needed—it was about what *I* needed.

"I will always be there to help you carry the heavy shit until you're ready to put it down. You hear me? I have battled enough of my own demons to know that sometimes you need to just cuddle up with them for a little while instead."

Ethan and Josh had made room for him, and as he spoke, he climbed onto the bed and positioned himself behind me, extending his legs to either side of mine and draping his tall frame over mine. He held me as he had several times now. When I was at my lowest, Alec always seemed to be there to hold me, his honey voice washing over me and soothing the ache in my chest.

I took a deep breath, letting myself melt farther into him as I covered his hands with mine.

Tyler stepped out of the dark too, coming to the side of the bed and squatting down so his face was level with mine.

"And when you're ready to talk about it, I'll be there. Whether you want to try to figure it all out or you just want to vent, I will drop everything I'm doing, and we will sit and talk as long as you want."

He reached a hand out and wiped the tears from my left cheek, his fingers lingering on my face, caressing it with a lover's touch. I wiped my other cheek with the back of my hand, realizing that at some point I had stopped crying.

"You are not alone, Evie." Alec spoke softly, but we were all sitting so close we could hear him as clearly as if he had shouted it.

He had said that same thing to me several times in the past, and it had made me feel comforted every time. But in that moment, in that dark room, surrounded by my Bond, the words had a new layer of meaning. For the first time, the words started to really sink in, the evidence behind the sentiment surrounding me with their thoughtfulness, strength, and support.

For the first time since my mother died, I really started to believe I wasn't alone in the world. They were *making* me believe it.

Josh always knew when I needed their support, even if he didn't always know exactly why.

Ethan always made me cheer up, his dimples and positive attitude impossible to ignore.

Alec had proven time and time again that he would have my back in the darkest hours.

Tyler was always there to help me figure it all out, knowing exactly what to say to help me work through a problem or see a situation from a different point of view.

Separately, the four of them were unique, interesting, and attractive in their own ways. Together, they balanced each other's personalities, their virtues and vices. They were exactly what I needed at any given moment. They were perfect.

No amount of research or reading would help me understand this thing inside me—the Light that tethered me to them—more than that exact moment. Because I could feel in my soul what it meant, and there were no words for it. They were perfect *for me*, and I was *theirs*.

THE GALA

Author's note: This is Alec's POV of Chapter 19 in Variant Lost—the first time he kisses Eve at the gala and the events that follow.

They were being discreet enough that no one else would notice the Light transfer, but I noticed. I noticed every fucking thing about Evelyn Maynard—or *Eve Blackburn*, as she was going by. Her Light was so damn strong, and I'd spent so long resisting its pull, I could practically smell it in the air now.

The senator started her speech, and I inched closer to my family and *her*, keeping behind the pillar near the bar.

Everyone's eyes were on the stage, and mine were on *her*. When Gabe reached up and ghosted his hand down her bare back in a move that was definitely not platonic, I wanted to march over there and rip his arm right out of its socket. He whispered something in her ear, and her breath hitched. What the fuck was he playing at? They were supposed to be cooling it, keeping their distance to protect her secret. Unknowingly, they were also protecting *my* secret—the biggest one I'd ever kept.

Her life was at stake, and they all lost their tiny little minds at the sight of one provocative dress. Although I was pretty sure they weren't thinking with the heads on their shoulders. And I had to admit she looked incredible in that damn dress.

When she'd walked down those stairs, I'd realized for the first time that she was a woman and not the little girl I'd pictured in my mind all these years. Evie was all grown up, and my dick was making sure I knew all about it. I'd been at half-mast most of the evening.

Problem was, I still had to stay the fuck away from her—for her own good and mine. But Josh had to get her a damn backless dress, Kid had to have his hands all over her, Gabe had to choose this moment to let his perfect control slip. Bunch of douchebags . . .

The glass in my hand was in danger of getting pulverized in my grip, so I turned away and left the room, dropping it on a nearby table. As I headed for the bathroom, applause went off behind me—the speech had ended.

I spotted Dana out of the corner of my eye, standing near the entrance and talking on her phone. I didn't glance in her direction. Between dodging her and my uncle, I was almost better off spending the entire evening hiding in the men's room. But someone had to keep an eye on the children, so I took a quick leak and headed back out.

Evie stood at the opposite end of the corridor, the look on her face pure determination. I had to hand it to her—she was almost as stubborn as me. Whatever those assholes were playing at had the Bond straining me toward her. Coupled with how fucking angelic she looked all dolled up, I almost didn't want to tell her to fuck off this time.

Almost . . .

She was a little buzzed from the two and a half glasses of champagne she'd had. She slurred the tiniest bit as she pleaded with me to hear her out.

I needed to stay as far away from her as possible, couldn't stand the sight of her most days, but I still found myself holding the damn door to the cloakroom open for her.

Better to get this shit over with.

As she passed, I caught a whiff of her perfume, mingling with whatever Dot had sprayed her hair with, and resisted the urge to take a deeper breath. That desperate part of me wanted to give in to every Evie-related urge, but I had to be stronger. It was safer for all of us. It was safer for *me*. She was so strong I was half-convinced even *breathing* too closely to her would amplify my fucking ability.

I was hoping she'd just rush through the thanks so this torture could be over, but now that she had something to focus on, her words were perfectly clear and measured. "I don't think you understand how much it meant to me what you did. And I'm not just talking about pulling me out of the water and getting me medical attention. I don't know what happened to you to make you think that you don't deserve thanks, but you do."

I tightened my arms across my chest and looked away, frowning. This was exactly why I didn't want to have this conversation with her. She made me think about all the worst things in my life. Why didn't I deserve thanks? Because my ability was so abhorrent I didn't even deserve a Vital. Isn't that why Joyce took her away from me in the first place?

Not to mention how long it then took me to find her again, and then the only reason I did was by pure fucking chance. I didn't do jack shit and should've done more.

Maybe if we'd had a chance to grow into our Bond together, I'd have better control of my pain ability with her extra Light. Maybe I wouldn't be such a fucking pariah if I'd had a Vital from the start. Maybe people would've seen that the Light saw my ability worthy of a Vital.

There was real determination in her voice as she thanked me and my team for saving her life, her hands tightening into fists at her sides. But it wasn't until she started talking about *after* the crash that I looked at her again.

With an adorable little crease between her eyes, she laid her soul bare to me and told me exactly how low she'd been in that hospital bed when I told her Joyce was gone.

I had to admire that—it wasn't easy to speak a truth so heavy to a virtual stranger.

That was the last time I'd held her in my arms—in the damn hospital as she fell apart. After she'd sobbed herself to sleep, only after I was certain she was passed out, had I allowed myself to remember Joyce. That woman was pure light and love. I hated her for taking Evie from me, but I still couldn't help loving her and the love and kindness she'd shown me as a kid. She was part of our family. Which was why it hurt so much more that she didn't think I was worthy of her little girl.

Tears had welled in my eyes as I'd buried my head in the back of Evie's neck. I'd let myself cry like a little bitch for about thirty seconds. Then I let her go. I had to. It was the only way to keep her safe. From whoever was kidnapping Vitals . . . and from me.

I just had no idea she remembered our interactions in the hospital that well, let alone that it meant so much to her. She'd been so out of it.

The obsessive way in which she'd tried to find me for a whole year made a little more sense now.

"I had no idea . . ." I let my words trail off before I went and spilled the whole sordid truth to her. "If it meant that much to you, I accept your thanks. You're more welcome than you know."

She leaned back against the door, closed her eyes, and sighed, a tiny satisfied smile pulling at her perfect, full lips.

She didn't know it yet, had probably put it down to her stubbornness to find me, but she craved me just as badly as I craved her. I got a kind of sick satisfaction from knowing that I affected her just as strongly as she affected me. I loved it, even as I fought against it. The Light was a force of nature, drawing Bonds together, but I was determined to build a hurricane-proof shelter around myself and ride out this storm.

I refused to put my family in danger because of her. I refused to have people look at me with even more fear and disdain than they already did. *Because of her.*

I hated her . . . but just like the other three douchebags, I was weak and I couldn't resist her.

Not tonight.

Not after what she'd told me.

Not when she looked like *that* in that stupid dress.

I took the few small steps necessary to stand directly in front of her in the dark, cramped space. With her eyes closed, that look of relief mixing with satisfaction on her ethereal face, I could almost believe she wasn't the source of every single fucking thing that had gone wrong in my life. How could she be with a face like that?

She opened her eyes. There was no fear in them, not like most people had when I got this close.

I glanced down at her lips without meaning to. They parted, and she tilted her face up.

I almost couldn't believe she wanted this after how hard I'd tried to push her away, how badly I'd treated her. Maybe she was just as fucked up as me . . .

"Put your hands behind your back," I demanded, keeping my voice low so I wouldn't give away how fast my heart was hammering in my chest. "Don't touch."

She obeyed immediately, and another piece of my crumbling control chipped away. She'd been told I was dangerous. She'd seen my ability in action—she should have been scared of me. But standing there, with her hands tucked behind her back, she looked excited more than anything.

I lifted my arms and propped them on the wall on either side of her head. The less we touched the better—I couldn't risk her feeling the Light transfer or realizing it wasn't hurting her when we touched. I just hoped she'd assume I had control of my ability enough to not make the kiss hurt.

I pressed forward. Her breath hitched, but she kept her hands behind her back.

Even as I leaned in, I knew this was a bad idea. A horrible, terrible, *fucking disastrous* idea.

I kissed her anyway, and all thought went out of my mind.

Her lips were incredibly soft, and she tasted faintly like expensive champagne. The sweet perfume I'd resisted inhaling as she walked past me hit the back of my nose, and I breathed her in.

She moaned into my mouth, and it was the most erotic sound I'd ever heard.

I was intoxicated, completely lost in her.

And the Light. *Oh God*, the Light. It was just the tiniest bit of a transfer, a tingle at my lips—the only place where we were touching. I'd be surprised if she even noticed it. It was downright heavenly.

I wanted more.

I wanted all of it.

I wanted to strip us both down to nothing and tangle myself up in her until her Light was gushing into me through every inch of skin I could reach.

Why did it feel so right?

I wasn't an idiot—I knew it was the Light that made kissing her feel like home, but I couldn't do this. It would make everything worse. It would make *me* worse. And I couldn't endure that. Even for her.

Just as my body screamed at me to lick at the seam of her lips, to mold my body to hers, to rub my insanely hard dick against her soft curves, I somehow found the strength to stop.

I pulled back. Her lips were glistening and parted, begging me to bite, but her eyes widened. The lust was replaced by horror in her gaze.

As if I'd slapped her and not kissed her, she spun around, yanked the door open, and ran away from me. *Again.*

She was always running away from me. Figured—eventually, everyone left me. The only people I could always count on were Gabe, Josh, and Kid, and I probably just fucked that up too.

"Fucking cunt shit . . . dammit," I growled and dragged my hands down my face. Then with a hiss, I adjusted my boner.

This shit was ridiculous. I may have been avoided like a leper by most people, but pain was the other side of the coin to pleasure, and there were always women who wanted to push their own boundaries. I'd had some depraved, crazy-ass sex in my time. But nothing had ever left me as horny as that single innocent kiss from a teenage girl. She didn't even slip me any tongue, for fuck's sake, and I was standing there, willing my dick to just . . . *go down.*

Thinking about her tongue did not help . . .

My nails dug into my palms, and I gritted my teeth. *Stupid.* How could I have been so stupid to allow myself to be in the same room as her, alone? How did I always manage to fuck everything up?

I stormed out of the cloakroom and headed straight to the bar to order a double shot of whiskey. I downed it in one go and slammed the glass down on the bar a little too hard.

Two men watched me. I had vague recollections of being introduced to them by Uncle Luce—business types. They looked perturbed, warily eyeing the empty glass while surreptitiously trying to inch away from me. People who'd met me, or even knew of me, didn't really like it when I drank. It made them nervous that my ability was at risk of hurting them. That I didn't have it under control.

Fools. I had the best control out of every damn Variant in this room.

My family and my team were the only people who seemed to know that.

I wished Kyo, Marcus, and Jamie were here. We were all on leave for a few weeks after another failed mission to track down a missing Vital. They were visiting with their families while I dealt with my own personal hell.

I wouldn't tell them what was going on, but they'd be able to distract me at least. They'd be able to take me away from my brothers—who were also now my Bondmates, not that they knew it—away from *her*, and just let me be . . . me. Fuck around and crack jokes and get drunk somewhere where no one knew me enough to throw me worried glances.

But they weren't here, and I wasn't about to call them to drop everything and come here to braid my hair and make me feel better.

I just . . . really fucking wanted to hit something. I hadn't been back to The Hole in months, but I found myself thinking about it more and more since Evie had shown up and ruined everything.

The lights in the ridiculously opulent ballroom were dimmed, and the music was turned up. I'd known where Evie was the entire evening, keeping her at the edge of my consciousness whether I wanted to or not. I kept her in view still, even though she couldn't see me in the dark corner next to the door. Creeping . . . like a motherfucking creep.

I was doing my best to ignore her, not look in her direction, but when she snatched up her third glass of champagne in the short time since running from me, I narrowed my eyes and stared directly at her. Even though it hurt to look—like staring into the sun. It was both mesmerizing and dangerous at the same time.

Did kissing me repulse her so much that she had to get wasted to wash it from her memory? She was cleansing me from her being with alcohol. She was getting wasted, dancing with Dot while the others hovered nearby. At least I knew she was safe with them around.

Just as I decided to do the same and turned for the bar, my uncle appeared at the grand entrance to the ballroom. He gave me a narrow-eyed look and turned on his heel.

I contemplated ignoring him and ordering the drink anyway, but I sighed and followed.

He'd given his official goodbyes and taken his public leave for the evening already. He was being as sneaky and creepy as me.

I followed him out into the street. The night wasn't warm, but it wasn't freezing either. The sound of a siren wailed in the distance somewhere. A few people were milling about on the sidewalk, chatting, smoking, waiting for their cars to pull up, but thankfully the protesters and the paparazzi had cleared out.

Lucian walked away from the front doors and the prying ears, going almost all the way to the corner before stopping and leaning back against the building.

I took up a position next to him and folded my arms.

"How long?" Lucian's voice was low, calm, but I saw the tic in his jaw. He was pissed.

"The mission near Hawaii—about a year ago," I answered.

"Jesus fucking Christ," he breathed. "That must've been the night that Joyce . . ."

He trailed off, and I turned to look at his profile, frowning. My uncle was never speechless.

"Joyce didn't make it, Uncle Luce. I would've told you had we pulled her from the water too." I couldn't have kept it from him that I'd found his Vital—I wasn't that cruel.

"I know." He was staring into the dark street, not really seeing anything.

I frowned again. "What do you mean you . . ."

Now it was me who was speechless, my mouth falling open in shock as things started to click into place in my head.

"You son of a bitch," I growled, tightening my hands into fists again. The man was like a father to me. He'd raised us all, taken care of us when we lost our parents. I fucking looked up to him. *And he'd been lying to me this whole time*. He knew they were alive. He knew they were out there somewhere while I tore myself apart wondering *why*.

He grunted and screwed his eyes up, leaning forward and gripping his head with his hands. "Alec," he managed to get out through gritted teeth. Even with his shield ability, my pain was affecting him, although not as badly as it was affecting the people milling about near the entrance. They were all doubled over. Someone had fallen to the ground; a woman screamed.

I growled and made myself take deep breaths through my rage. It didn't take me long to rein in my ability, but I should've never lost control of it in the first place.

Lucian straightened up and took a few deep breaths of his own. The other people all calmed down too but looked around in confusion. An agent I'd worked with a few times threw me a questioning look. I gave him a terse nod, letting him know I was good, and he rushed over to the people to smooth things over.

"Sorry," I mumbled.

Lucian faced me and picked up our conversation as though nothing had happened. "Alec, nothing is as simple as it seems. Doing what we do for a living, we both know that."

"Screw you."

"She was my Vital." There was understanding and a bit of pity in his eyes—I hated that pity—but there was a determined set to his lips too. "I was doing what I thought was best for her. I think you can understand that now." He gave me a meaningful look. "There's a lot you don't know."

"Then fucking enlighten me." If it was anyone else, anyone other than the man I loved and respected most in the world, I would've already punched him in the nose and walked away. I still might . . .

A couple walked past us on the sidewalk, swinging their clasped hands, leaning into each other to whisper. He waited until they were out of earshot to answer.

"Not here. Come to my office in the morning, and I'll tell you everything. But you have to tell me your side too. How the fuck have you kept this secret for so long?" He shook his head and ran a hand through his salt-and-pepper hair, incredulous. "And what is she doing with Kid? And don't think I didn't notice how Josh was looking at her either."

I sighed. Those idiots were going to get us caught. "Gabe too."

"What?" His eyes widened.

"They're hers. We all are."

His face paled, and a hint of fear entered his eyes. "She has four?"

I nodded, gritting my teeth. I wished she only had three. I wished she only had one . . .

"I can't believe I didn't know any of this." As the director of a security firm, he really didn't like not knowing things. He had that in common with Gabe.

"You've been preoccupied lately." My uncle, just like all of us, had been busy with trying to get to the bottom of the Vital disappearances, but now that I thought about it, it was more than that. For the past year or so, he'd been quieter, more withdrawn and sullen, away on longer trips. Since Joyce had died . . .

"Tomorrow. Early. I have to fly to London for a meeting."

"You'll answer all my questions?" I fixed him with a firm look. He returned it.

"If you answer all mine."

I nodded.

He gripped my shoulder and gave it a squeeze. I looked away. After a moment, he sighed and left, getting into his town car and disappearing, unseen by anyone else.

For the millionth time that night, I wanted to punch something. I wanted to punch *myself*. I was hurting the people I loved and not just with my ability. I hadn't lost control like that since I was a teen, definitely not around my family.

Then *she* came along, and people were suddenly doubling over in pain all over the place again.

If I was being honest with myself, that was the worst part of this whole situation. Her mere presence made me feel as though I had no control. No control of my ability, no control of her, no control of what happened to my family, no control of who I wanted to be with for the rest of my miserable life. It was downright terrifying.

I dug my nails into my palms again and leaned my head back against the brick. Thinking about her was making me lose my shit—again. Just when I'd gotten myself under control.

I took deep, cleansing breaths and focused on the crisp night air going into my lungs and the warm air rushing out through my nose.

The dark, tumultuous, writhing thing inside me calmed bit by bit, my ability bowing before my will.

I knew Dana was nearby as soon as I felt that darkness ebb away. It was always there, always percolating under the surface, waiting for me to unleash it so it could hurt, maim, destroy. It was always a part of me, with me. Except when she was around.

When I was with Dana, that dark, dangerous part of me was muzzled, sedated and restrained. It was as if it were buried under a mile of dirt and unable to move or do anything.

It was bliss . . .

I heard her heels clicking on the concrete, but I kept my eyes closed, feeling the tension drain out of my shoulders. The next breath I took was one of relief, not another desperate attempt to keep my shit together.

She stopped right before me, and I opened my eyes to look at her.

She was wearing black, my favorite color, the color of my cold dead heart. The dress was simple—spaghetti straps, a slit up one leg, a plunging neckline—but it clung in all the right places.

I wondered what Eve would look like in it . . .

She smirked and raised one blonde eyebrow. "Why are you still hanging around?"

"The perks of being related to the director. You?" I rolled my eyes. It was a load of shit. Yes, I had to make an appearance, but I could've left hours ago, and no one would've batted an eye.

"The perks of still being on duty." She moved the front of her dress aside and up, just enough to show me the gun holster attached to her thigh. The move was clearly deliberate, making me drop my gaze to where she wanted it. The holster was digging into her thigh, and I pictured my fingers digging into the same spot on the other leg.

I licked my bottom lip and looked into her face. She was staring right at me, keeping her features neutral, but I could see her pulse thudding in the vein in her neck.

My dick twitched. I was doing all I could to pretend I hadn't been at least at half-mast this whole night, that it was reacting to the woman standing before me and not the one who'd run away from me.

Every instinct I had was screaming at me to leave, get away from Dana, and go find Evie. The Light was driving me to be with *her*, close to *her*, at least watching her if I couldn't touch.

But fuck the Light.

I needed a break from it all. I wanted to forget the mess my family was in, forget how much Uncle Luce and I hurt each other, forget how out of control Evie made me feel, forget how much of a plague my own ability was to myself and all those around me.

No one could make that last one possible other than the woman standing in front of me.

"That's our limo." I nodded to the long black car parked on the street behind her. "No one's going to need it for a while. Can you take your break?"

A flash of surprise broke out on Dana's face, but it was quickly replaced by lust. I'd been keeping my distance from her lately, so I could understand why she was surprised to have me coming on to her. It wasn't that I was doing it on purpose; I just found myself preoccupied with other things. Work things and family and stuff—nothing to do with Evie. Nope. Not me.

I knew I was being an ass to Dana, but I couldn't seem to stop, and she wasn't one to lie down and take it; we were getting in more fights, butting heads. The best thing, the honorable thing, to do would've been to just break it off with her, even if I had no intention of getting together with Evie. But as everyone liked to remind me every day—I was not a nice guy. I was dangerous and I hurt people.

The fact was, I was addicted to what Dana made me feel—or rather *didn't* make me feel. She took my ability away and, some days, that was the only way I felt as if I could breathe. So I was being selfish, defying the Light, disrespecting both women in my life because trying to detangle the clusterfuck my life had turned into was just too damn hard.

Dana raised her wrist to her mouth and spoke into the hidden microphone I knew was installed in her bangle. "This is Vulture—calling in my twenty-minute break."

She stared at me, her eyes raking up and down my body. I pushed off the wall and gripped her hips, dragging my teeth up the side of her neck. She gasped, then cleared her throat and spoke into the bangle again. "Copy that."

Then she turned in my arms and opened the car door.

As I climbed in after her, I was determined to close that car door on all the bullshit I wanted to avoid. I just wanted twenty goddamned minutes to breathe. But as Dana climbed into my lap and started popping the buttons on my shirt, I knew it was a losing battle. All I could think about was *her*.

THE MORNING AFTER

*Author's note: This is Josh's POV of the second half of Chapter 20 in Variant Lost—*the conversation that happens in Tyler's study, the day after the gala.*

"Alec kissed me." Eve's words washed over me like icy water. A sick feeling that had nothing to do with the hangover I was sporting settled in the pit of my stomach

As Eve struggled to finish a sentence, looking all kinds of broken and beat down, Gabe and Kid asked questions. Gabe was furious; the way his lip was curling up and his knuckles were turning white reminded me of what he used to be like before he joined Melior Group and got his shit together. I hadn't seen that side of him in years.

Kid looked about as broken as Eve.

I was speechless. I knew there was something going on when I saw her glaring at him in the limo, but she shook her head and I dropped it. I figured it was nothing more than her having tried to thank him again or Alec having said or done something idiotic—he was really good at that lately.

I would never in a million years have guessed it was because my brother had gone for my girl, my *Vital.* I could practically feel my heart cracking down the middle—Alec pulling on one side and Eve holding on to the other, both their hands bloody.

As Eve tried to take more of the blame, tears marring her perfect face, every fiber of my being knew it wasn't her fault. I just couldn't figure out why Alec would do this.

Was it that he felt left out? He had been keeping his distance from all of us, not just Eve, since we realized she was ours. I missed him. I missed doing yoga together, spending time together, just hanging out. Alec had never really had anywhere he fit in. His whole adult life people avoided him, and he wore that shit like armor. He embraced his "Master of Pain" status and used it to push people away before they could recoil from him. But with us, he was just himself. We were his family—a family forged through time, loss, and pain.

If there was one thing I was sure of, it was that the four of us would always have one another.

Now that was being threatened, and I didn't know which way was up. Did he kiss her because he wanted to be in the Bond—because he couldn't stand to be left out in the cold by us? By the only people in the world who accepted him no matter what?

Or was it because he resented her presence in our lives? Did he do it to cause a rift between us? To drive a wedge into our Bond and push Eve away? Surely he wasn't that fucking selfish?

Eve was feeling like the scum of the earth, and he was just standing there, staring at the back of her head as if she was the one who had fucked up! Man, Alec could really be a dick sometimes. I had never had it aimed at me, but I knew how much he frustrated other people. Now I was experiencing it for myself.

Gabe was hurt, Kid was crushed, and I. Was. Livid.

I hardly even thought about it. I just reached with my ability for the copy of *War and Peace* I knew was on the shelf behind me, and I flung it at his stupid head as hard as I could.

He didn't even twitch as it bounced away from him harmlessly.

"What the fu—" I stood up straight, my eyes wide. Deep down I knew the implications of that book flopping to the floor like that, but my mind couldn't quite grasp it yet. I couldn't quite *believe* it.

When Kid leaped forward and threw a fireball at Alec and it did the same thing my book had, there was no doubt in any of our minds.

"You can't hurt me." Alec's words just drove the point home.

"Holy shit." Gabe and I spoke at the same time. He was in our Bond.

Motherfucker!

Naturally, my girl put it all together just as quickly as I had. I watched her back as her shoulders began to heave with heavier breaths, her hands tightened into fists. I wanted to step forward, lay soothing hands on those delicate shoulders, ease her pain. But I knew she wouldn't want to be touched, wasn't ready to have her rage pacified—she needed to let it out.

"Wait, does that mean she's *that* . . . I can't believe I didn't see it before . . ." Gabe was reeling. In the second that thick book bounced off Alec's thick head, I realized she was Evelyn Maynard—Alec's suspected Vital and our missing childhood friend. Gabe was only just connecting the extra dots. I didn't remember much from before she and her mom disappeared, but ever since, I'd watched Alec struggle with losing her, then losing our parents, just as much as he struggled with his ability. Those things were connected in more ways than one.

"Yeah. Look—" Alec started to explain, but Eve was finally ready to let it all out, and man, was she pissed!

She let him have it, not holding back at all, and then she left, slamming the door behind her and making us all flinch.

I wanted so badly to chase after her, wrap her in my arms and wipe the tears away. Her eyes were a stormy kind of blue when she cried, and I wanted to look into them and tell her it would all be OK. It's what I'd been doing since that kiss in my room. I'd been chasing after her like a lost puppy while Kid got to be her "pretend" boyfriend.

It was so clearly *not* pretend for him. She was still trying to make sense of it all, but it was clearly not pretend for her either. Even someone who didn't pay as much attention as I did could see that—that was why they were so convincing as a couple. I saw the way they looked at each other. It was exactly the way I looked at *her.*

But I held myself back. She had been clear about wanting to be alone, and I respected that. I knew that feeling all too well.

I knew the others would be wanting to go after her just as badly. The urge to protect her, hold her close, was almost impossible to resist. She was our Vital—nothing mattered more than her happiness and well-being.

Kid took an involuntary step toward the door. But he made himself stop, his shoulders tense, and refocused his energy on his older cousin.

We all started speaking over one another, none of us hearing what the others were saying. Alec just stood there, scowling at the expensive rug in Gabe's office, not meeting any of our eyes. *Coward.*

I was most upset about how his actions had clearly made Eve feel, but my admonishments were getting lost in the cacophony of voices, so I cut myself off and went to stand right in front of him.

Gabe growled and turned away, leaning heavily on his desk and taking deep breaths—reminding me of the old Gabe once again. Kid crossed his massive arms over his chest and waited for my lead. We were a good team like that—the brains and the muscle.

I wanted to check out—shut myself in my room, blast Rise Against out of the speakers, and read Richard Dawkins (or someone equally angry with the world). But I couldn't do that anymore.

Eve needed me. So did Alec. Kid needed us all. Come to think of it, even Gabe needed me in the moment. He was usually the one to take charge, make us focus on the most pertinent things, but he was really struggling, so I stepped up.

"Alec, man, why?" I kept my voice as level as possible and watched him like a hawk, his expression, his posture, the way his shoulders slumped. His eyes looked glassy and red, but I couldn't be sure if it was emotion or if he was just tired. I didn't think he'd slept at all the previous night. I didn't like not being sure one way or the other. I didn't like that he'd managed to keep any of this from me at all.

Before I could study him further, he sighed and dragged both hands down his face.

I watched him shuffle over to the couch and collapse his tall frame onto it, resting his elbows on his knees.

My question was loaded. But that's exactly why I'd asked it and why I didn't elaborate. I wanted to see how he'd take it. What was the most important thing to him? What was driving him?

"She makes it worse" was his low, resigned answer. I had suspected as much. We had watched him become more bitter and cold to the rest of the world as he grew into a man and his ability grew with him. The more they feared and avoided him, the more he used that fear to build up his armor—to shut everyone out. Except us. He had never shut us out, never lied to us. Which was why his lies were leaving us all reeling now.

"You knew who she was in the hospital that you apparently visited her in?" Gabe asked, still leaning on his desk and facing away from us, but his voice was calmer, lower.

"I knew the second I pulled her out of Kyo's arms and into that chopper. Every fiber of my being wanted to wrap itself around her and *protect*. It took everything in me not to growl at my own fucking team to stay away from her," Alec explained.

"Do they know?" Gabe had to consider more than just the personal angle—this could affect both their jobs.

"No. I reined in my reaction and kept them out of it."

"Fuck." Gabe finally turned to face us, looking absolutely exhausted, but his eyes had widened with realization. I frowned. I didn't like not knowing things. "Joyce . . ."

There were no survivors in that crash other than Eve and the copilot.

Eve's mom was dead.

"Yeah." Alec looked as though he might cry again, but he coughed and looked away.

"Does Lucian know?" I asked. The implications of this situation just kept getting wider and heavier. The tangled web that had started to weave when we were only kids was getting more and more knotted. I wasn't sure how we would go about detangling it. I didn't like having a problem I couldn't solve. That was something Eve and I had in common.

I loved how a little crease would appear between her eyebrows whenever she encountered a complex theorem or mathematical equation she couldn't immediately wrap her brilliant mind around. As if she was outraged that any scrap of knowledge in the known universe dared to elude her understanding. But now wasn't the time to think about all the little things I loved about her. I needed to focus on Alec.

The asshole on the couch sighed. "If he didn't before, he does now. She's the spitting image of Joyce, and he saw her last night at the gala."

"Jesus Christ, Alec." Gabe was starting to get frustrated again. Alec seemed to be the only one capable of getting that reaction out of him. "You didn't think to warn him?"

"I didn't know how!" Alec's frustration rose to meet Gabe's. "I had no idea how to raise it without giving it all up, and I couldn't bring myself to tell anyone before I told all of you. And it didn't feel right talking to *you* about it without coming clean with *her*. So yeah, I got myself into a giant fucking mess and had no idea how to get out, and now it's all exploded in my fucking face."

I rolled my eyes. If he was expecting sympathy, he wasn't going to get it.

"How could you keep her from us for this long?" Kid spoke for the first time, not even trying to hide the hurt in his voice.

"Kid, I had no idea she was your Vital. I thought she was just mine. And just as much as I couldn't handle what that meant for *me*, I also needed to protect *her*. Keeping her away, hidden, meant keeping her safe."

"You may not have known she was all our Vital, but you knew she was as good as family. You knew what she meant to Lucian." Kid propped his hands on his hips and scowled.

"I'm sorry." Alec didn't hesitate to say it. He never hesitated to show his vulnerabilities to us. But he had lied about so much for so long that even though I could see the sincerity in his eyes, the pleading in his posture, I still questioned it. Alec kept speaking: "I'm sorry I kept her from you. I'm sorry I lied. I'm sorry for this whole fucking mess. But I don't know how to fix it."

Kid and I looked to Gabe. Gabe stared at Alec for a beat before sighing and looking up to the ceiling.

"He's telling the truth." Gabe confirmed what I'd already seen in Alec but wasn't letting myself believe. We fell into silence. There were so many questions, so much to unpack, that none of us knew quite where to start. Least of all Alec.

Kid was the one to break the silence, his voice low, resigned. "I'm glad you're in our Bond."

Alec's head whipped up to look at him, his expression shocked but hopeful, as Kid kept speaking. "You fucked up, bro, and I'm still mad at you. But I was starting to feel like I was losing you, and . . ." He trailed off, not quite able to finish the sentence.

"You're never gonna lose any of us, Kid." Alec sprang to his feet and wrapped his little cousin up in a big hug. They held each other tight, neither of them speaking.

Gabe and I watched them, and I realized Kid was right—I was glad Alec was part of our Bond too. It was a fucked-up situation, and I was beyond pissed off at how he'd handled it, but I, too, had noticed how much Alec had pulled away from us ever since Eve crashed into our lives and made us all feel alive again. I'd missed my brother, and I'd been starting to worry that in finding the light of our life—our Vital—we would lose him. I was terrified this was just another thing that would isolate him further from the world.

I, too, was a little happy that wouldn't happen now.

I looked over their still hugging shoulders and met Gabe's eyes. We had a silent conversation.

Can you believe this shit? He rolled his eyes.

Not really. I bugged mine out and shook my head.

What do I do with this? He gestured in the general direction of Alec, huffing.

I let the tiny bit of hope I was feeling quirk my lips up in a barely there smile and shrugged. *Don't know, but I'm glad we have him back.*

Gabe pinched the bridge of his nose and watched as Alec and Kid finally separated, then answered out loud, addressing both my silent hope and Kid's last words. "Me too."

"Me three," I agreed but quickly added to Alec, "But you gotta fix this shit, man. And tell us everything. Like, *every* fucking thing. And no more lies."

Alec nodded and blew out a big breath. "I think someone should check on Evie."

It wasn't lost on me that he was referring to her by her childhood nickname—something I'd only heard when the people who were old enough to remember her spoke about the past—but I knew he was the worst possible person to go after her.

"Just stay there and practice your groveling face." I held a hand out in a stop motion, already moving toward the door. "I'll go talk to her first."

Much as she needed answers, craved them in every aspect of her life, I knew Alec was the last person Eve wanted to see. I had studied her like the creep I was for the past few months—it was all I had when Kid was all over her in public—and I knew she needed time to process, to set it all straight in that brilliant mind of hers.

Kid was great at cheering her up, distracting her, making her feel good, but she wasn't ready for that yet either. Gabe may have been able to give her what she needed just as well as I could in that moment, but they didn't have that kind of closeness yet, and I knew she wouldn't be as comfortable talking about the heavy emotional shit with him. *Yet.*

No, she needed to make sense of it all, to have someone understand it from her point of view, to have someone focus completely on her—her thoughts, her feelings, her reactions. I made my way up the stairs to be what she needed.

THE LONGEST HOUR

Author's note: This is Tyler's POV of Chapter 11 in Vital Found—*the day when Eve accidentally comes to their study session dressed like a schoolgirl.*

The phone rang, and I immediately knew who it was. It didn't matter that it was the desk phone without caller ID— my ability told me all I wanted to know as soon as I wondered.

Victor Flint was on the Melior Group board and a pain in my ass.

"Hi, Victor," I answered.

"Hello, Tyler." His deep voice sounded chipper on the other end, as it always did. I could picture his ever-present, wide salesman smile. "Just checking in on how the meeting went yesterday."

"As well as could be expected. The details will be in my report." I provided a weekly report to Melior Group, updating them on any issues, concerns, or developments on the Bradford Hills Institute side. I provided the same, if more carefully worded, report to Bradford about Melior Group. But Victor always wanted to know everything immediately, and yesterday's meeting had people on edge.

"So you don't need me or Lucian to step in? Maybe having a board member address it would help?"

I held in my sigh but let my eyes roll. "It's not necessary. I managed to placate everyone. If it arises again, I won't hesitate to ask for assistance."

Bringing a Melior Group bigwig to a Bradford Hills Institute meeting would just escalate the situation. With the increased security, some of the staff were feeling as if Melior Group was encroaching too much already. The security checks at the gates were tedious and time consuming—they couldn't understand why they had to be subjected to them when every single person employed by the Institute had to have a vigorous background check. They were complaining it was disruptive, distracting for the students, and inconvenient.

I'd sat at the table with Stacey on one side and the dean on the other and listened. I let them get all their frustrations and complaints out while my ability told me exactly what the biggest issue was for each person. Then I reminded them why the added security was necessary—the invasion from only a few months ago, the Vital kidnappings—and did my best to subtly solve each of their problems without making it too obvious my ability had told me exactly what they wanted to hear. People didn't like it when they realized I was using my ability to gain the upper hand. They thought it was cheating. I thought it was just good negotiating.

It wasn't as impressive as Ethan's fire, as practical as Josh's telekinesis, or as formidable as Alec's pain, but my ability was damn useful.

Not that it didn't take some getting used to when Eve strolled into my life, flipped it upside down, and made my ability about a million times more intense.

I would never forget that day, in this very office, when we realized we were connected. If I'd given in to my instincts in that moment, if I'd pulled her close and kissed her as I so badly wanted to, I wondered how everything would've played out. But that wasn't something my ability could provide an answer to, so there was no point dwelling.

With that much extra Light in me, those first few weeks made me feel like a teenager all over again—trying to manage an overwhelming ability while covering up the fact that I was horny all the fucking time.

When I first got my ability, it took a while to get a handle on it. I had to learn not to always call people out on their lies, to keep things to myself, to not ask questions I didn't want to know the answers to. Then Eve came along, and the amount of information my mind was bombarded with made me want to drink myself into a stupor in a cabin in the woods just so it would stop.

Eventually I got used to it. Putting to use the mindfulness techniques Uncle Luce had taught me, focusing on work, and making sure Eve was OK got me through it. Now the constant stream of information was more like a dull buzzing in the background—a wealth of knowledge I could call on at any moment if I chose to.

I spoke with Victor for another few minutes, dodging his questions about Ethan and Josh and if I thought they planned to join our ranks, then managed to hang up.

I knew he had a meeting to go to, so it wasn't hard to finish the call. I also knew Stacey had spent half of yesterday's meeting getting distracted by wondering what my hands would feel like on her bare breasts. I knew that the dean was happy with how the meeting went, that there were currently 208 people in the admin building, that Ethan was singing at the top of his lungs along to an Offspring song in the passenger seat of Josh's Challenger as they pulled up at the security checkpoint at the east gate. I also knew that Eve was running a little late. I had time to finish the report I was just telling Victor about.

I shut the mental door on my ability. If truly dangerous or life-threatening information came up, there would be no blocking that from my mind even if I wanted to.

Fifteen minutes later, the number of people in the building went up by one. I was only aware of it because I knew it was Eve. I rushed to finish jotting down some notes before she came in.

I heard her enter the room, my pen flying across the page.

"Hey." I glanced up and dropped my eyes back to my page. "Let me just . . ." It took my mind a moment to catch up to what it had seen, and I had to take another look to make sure I wasn't imagining it.

That skirt, those socks, her plump lips and uncertain eyes. She was simultaneously the picture of innocence and every depraved fantasy I'd ever allowed to play out in my mind.

My heart threw itself against my ribcage, feeling as if it might burst through at any moment. Blood rushed from my head, leaving me a bit light-headed, and went straight to my cock. Within seconds I was so fucking hard it was almost painful.

She said something, then I said something. The *wrong* something, obviously—she looked confused. I tried to get my shit together, but every anime I'd ever seen—from innocent classics like *Sailor Moon* through to the nastiest *hentai*—was running through my mind.

None of it compared to her.

She wasn't even trying. My ability made that glaringly obvious as soon as I realized she'd walked into my office dressed like a private schoolgirl. She wasn't trying to goad me. It wasn't deliberate; it was an accident.

The socks were pooled around her ankles, at the bottom of her toned legs. The shirt was crisp white but looked comfortable, soft like her creamy skin. The skirt . . . *fuck me*, the skirt! And her eyes—her beautiful, expressive, intelligent eyes that I could drown in—were confused.

Get your shit together, Tyler. She needs you.

I made myself take a breath and focus. She had enough uncertainty in her life, enough confusion and worry. I refused to add to it. Not when I'd been working so damn hard to be the one true and constant thing, the one place where she felt confident and supported.

I stayed behind the desk and forced my mind to focus on the study session. Despite the fact that there was nothing remotely sexual about what we were doing, that I was making a conscious effort to cast lascivious thoughts from my mind, my dick stayed hard for the entire hour. It twitched from time to time, straining against my slacks like a toddler trying to get to its favorite toy. It made it impossible for me to move from my desk-prison and sit at her side as I always did. I wanted her to know I was on her side. Always.

I knew that must've confused her, but it was necessary.

Despite the fact that I managed to keep my voice even and my head on the books, going over her lessons and even managing to carry a conversation that made sense, that dark part of my mind that *craved* kept throwing up images.

Eve chewing on the end of a pencil, her sexy, plump lips curving into a smile.

Me running my hands up her calves, then thighs, until I reach the hem of that skirt.

Her taking a seat on my desk, right in front of me, spreading her knees as she leans back.

My hands undoing the buttons on that shirt, one by one, until her perfect, perky tits are spilling out.

My knees hitting the carpet as I lift the skirt and bury my face in what's hidden under it.

Somehow, we got through the hour. And then . . .

I reached for a book.

She reached for the same book.

Like a cliché moment in a rom-com, our fingers touched.

My dick twitched again.

Her warm, soft touch under my fingers was impossible to resist.

She turned her hand, offering me her palm.

I knew if I asked, if I showed even a hint of wanting her as badly as I did, she'd give me much more. She'd give me everything.

She wasn't ready.

I wasn't ready.

Alec *definitely* wasn't ready.

So I let myself revel in this brief moment. I dragged my fingers, feather light, over her hand, the connection between us fucking electric.

She was breathing hard, her full focus on our hands, her chest heaving.

She wanted me. That wasn't arrogance talking. That was just the fact of the situation, confirmed by my ability. She'd wanted me as badly as I'd wanted her from the first moment we touched all those months ago.

I knew she fantasized about what it would feel like to kiss me, hold me, touch me. I knew she thought about it when making out with Ethan or Josh. I knew she pictured my hand in place of hers as she touched herself in the dark at night, releasing some of the tension that was building between us all.

I was a millisecond away from wrapping my hand around her wrist and pulling her over the desk into my lap. My resolve was on a knife's edge.

Someone laughed out in the hall, popping the tension like a balloon.

I cleared my throat and drew back.

She scrambled to her feet, gathered her things, and left just as my phone rang.

I answered it, made an excuse to whoever was on the other line, and hung up, but she was already gone. I was both glad the torture was over and already missing her.

But that's exactly why it was good I hadn't acted on my more primitive instincts. She needed to feel safe with me. I needed to give her time to process. *I* needed time to process.

I was glad my brothers had found their Vital. She was exactly what they needed—what *we* needed. But every time I saw Josh wrap his arms around her and nuzzle her neck, every time my ability told me Ethan had dragged her into a corner and was running his hands all over her body, I found myself pushing down this choking feeling. I wanted her all to myself. That was never going to happen, so I needed to get over it. Before I took her into my bed, because I'd never let her out of it otherwise.

I leaned back in my chair and closed my eyes, taking deep, measured breaths. I put some mindfulness into practice until my thoughts and urges were under control once again.

The raging hard-on went down enough that I was able to stand up and adjust myself so I wouldn't be poking people in the thighs as I went past them. I abandoned the report on my desk and tucked my phone into my pocket before heading for the door.

Alec was on his way up, coming to see if I wanted to grab lunch.

The elevator doors opened, and I stepped in with him as he jabbed the button for the ground floor.

"How was your session?" He sounded nonchalant, calm. If my ability hadn't already told me he knew, the fact that he'd asked would've been suspicious in itself. He preferred to avoid talking about Eve as much as possible, trying to deal with his insanely complicated feelings toward her and our situation in the worst possible way—alone.

"You are such a cunt." I punched him on the arm, but it was half-hearted, and the release of physical energy was already making me smile.

He flinched back, laughing even as he took a defensive stance.

In the past, he always had the upper hand when we wrestled and sparred. But now that we were both in Eve's Bond, his ability didn't affect me, and we were pretty evenly matched.

"Don't take your sexual frustration out on me." His bright eyes still danced in amusement. It was nice to see him laughing, relaxed.

"Considering the fact that my sexual frustration is your fault, I'd be well within my rights to take it out on you." I shoved him in the shoulder one more time as the elevator opened and we stepped out.

"Are you coming on to me?" He bumped my shoulder with his as we crossed the lobby and I avoided meeting Stacey's eyes. She was hoping I'd look up so she could have a reason to wave me over and invite herself to lunch. I kept my eyes trained on the front doors as I answered Alec.

"You wish."

What he was feeling about seeing Eve dressed like my fantasy, then watching her go up to my office, was way more complex than simple amusement. But there was no point pushing the issue with him, especially not in public. He would just shut down and walk away. I'd rather enjoy a nice lunch with him and broach the subject later. Maybe after everyone had gone to bed and we could talk uninterrupted.

And as much as I'd insinuated that I was keeping my distance from Eve solely because he'd asked me to, that wasn't the entire reason. I was still working through my own shit with this situation while trying to keep everyone safe and happy.

It was time to start pushing past all that. It was time for me to get over myself, and it was time to push Alec to do the same. This wasn't just about him anymore.

Now wasn't the time to begin that monumental conversation, but I could plant the seeds at least.

"I was ready to knock out any fucker that even looked in her direction." Alec kept his voice low as we stepped outside, rolling his shoulders to release some of the tension from even thinking about another man touching her. I knew the feeling. "I've spent the last hour talking myself out of following her around campus all day. I was glad she was on her way to see you—you've got more self-control than anyone I know."

I wasn't sure if that was entirely true. People feared Alec, but he had his ability under perfect control—no easy feat. "That may be so, but fuck was it tested. That was easily the longest hour of my life. And you knew she was coming to see me dressed like that? You are such a fucking asshole."

The least he could've done was warn me. But then what was I going to do? She was already on her way up.

"What was I supposed to do, man? Tell her to go home and change? Yeah, that would've gone over real well. Especially coming from me." Alec's voice went up a little as he ran his hands over his short hair. He felt bad for leaving me to deal with that alone, but he really had spent the last hour fighting the urge to do physical violence to anyone who looked at Eve. Even if her outfit wasn't overtly sexual to the common observer.

Fuck, he had it bad. He was so in love with her it was taking everything I had not to shout in his face to just tell her. I was shoving that urge into the back and locking it down tight—right next to the urge to ask about what happened with Studygate, as Dot had dubbed it. It was killing me that I didn't know, but I was trying to respect their privacy. Whatever semblance of privacy any of us had. We were in a Bond, and eventually we were going to have to accept that there was no hiding shit from one another anymore.

But not yet. We weren't ready. Alec wasn't ready to tell Eve he loved her. Shit, he wasn't even ready to admit it to *himself*. And Eve wasn't ready to hear it.

"You know I'm doing this for you, right?" Some of my weariness seeped into my voice. I had so many things to worry about. Sometimes it got exhausting. It was time to plant that seed for a later conversation. "I don't know how much—"

I froze, my eyebrows shooting up.

There stood the subject of our conversation, of my every waking thought, looking just as fucking hot as she had in my office not fifteen minutes earlier. She was covering Kid's and Josh's mouths, clearly eavesdropping.

Naughty girl . . .

My dick twitched *again*.

Alec did the worst possible thing and laughed.

Eve's eyes widened in horror. She dropped her hands, turned, and rushed away, wrapping her arms around her middle and dropping her head.

I focused on the two dumbasses in front of me as they turned to face me with guilty looks. I asked the question under my breath, and my ability filled in the gaps of the conversation they'd been having parallel to the one we'd been having.

I closed the distance and leaned in so I wouldn't be overheard. "Why the fuck would you tell her that?" I growled.

Ethan hunched his big shoulders, looking like an overgrown toddler, while Josh stuffed a hand into the pocket of his chinos.

"Trying to lighten the mood?" Josh's answer came out as a question. "She was confused."

"Yeah, we just got carried away." Ethan glanced up and cleared his throat.

I pinched the bridge of my nose and took a breath before speaking again. "The three of you keep trying to get into one another's pants, while this one"—I gestured over my shoulder at Alec—"is ignoring the whole situation like if he just keeps his eyes closed, it'll go away. *Meanwhile*, we're keeping so many damn secrets from so many people that even *I'm* struggling to keep track of them all. She needs to have someone she feels safe to talk to—someone who doesn't have any expectations of her. I am that person. Fix. This."

I gave them one last "don't fuck with me" look, and they sprang into action.

"You're right, Gabe. We fucked up." Josh nodded as he turned, pulling Kid along behind him. "We'll talk to her."

They rushed off after our girl, and I forced myself to take another breath.

"Wanna fill me in?" Alec stepped up next to me.

"Not particularly."

He frowned, taken aback. There wasn't much we kept from each other. But he didn't have a leg to stand on, considering he'd kept her from us for a whole fucking year. "I need you to get your shit together, man. Before this situation explodes in all our faces."

I didn't wait for a response before walking away. So much for waiting for a better time to bring it up.

I expected him to lose his shit and walk off, have a pity party, and blame us for ruining his day, but he surprised me when he kept pace with me. He stayed silent, but he stayed by my side while I walked toward lunch and thought things through. Maybe there was hope for him yet.

THE PACKING

Author's note: This is Ethan's POV of Chapter 27 in Vital Found—the day after Eve is kidnapped and agrees to move in with them.

Twirling Eve's keys in my hand, I pressed the button for her floor. Next to me, Josh leaned on the wall of the elevator and yawned, crossing his arms over his chest, although it looked more like he was hugging himself.

"You OK, man?" I did my best to keep my voice casual, but I was worried that maybe he was in pain. He'd dressed in black pants and a perfectly pressed shirt but left his hair messy. It wasn't like him. It had only been a day since he overused his ability to a dangerous level. He could've *died*.

I could hardly think about it without losing my shit. I couldn't lose him. I couldn't lose any of them.

"Yeah, I'm fine," he answered around another yawn. "Just fucking tired. Hardly got any sleep last night. I tried, but I just wanted to . . ." He sighed.

"Hold her. Yeah, same." I was wrecked too, but I knew how to hide it. The first thing people saw when they met me was the size; the second was the confident, happy attitude. I knew how to hide the heavy stuff behind a wide smile and a joke. Because who wanted to talk about that shit?

But just like Josh, I hadn't gotten much sleep. Between tossing and turning, practically aching to hold her in my arms, and worrying about the dickhead next to me, I didn't know why I bothered to stay in bed.

I understood why she wanted space. Logically, I got it. It'd been a crazy couple of days. She was kidnapped and taken from us—I still balled my hands into fists every time I thought about that, the urge to punch something practically making my muscles twitch—was betrayed by Zara, and nearly lost Josh, then Alec pulled his disappearing act again just as they were getting it on. God, he was *such* an asshole. I loved my cuz, but he really needed to get his shit together. He was lucky I'd only decked him once after they told us about Studygate.

We were all damaged, fucked up from what happened to our parents, but he was taking it out on her, and that was not cool.

Then he turned around and told her he loved her. I was still figuring that out. Because honestly, it made me realize I did too. I'd never said that to a girl, and now that I realized I felt it, I was bursting to tell her. But one thing Gabe was right about—why was he always right? So damn annoying—was that we needed to give her time and space to navigate this Bond on her terms.

Which was why we all suffered through a sleepless night, hours after almost losing her, because she wanted to sleep alone in her new bed. I was consoling myself with the fact that her new bed was in my house. I would get to see her every day. Hold her, touch her, cook her breakfast.

A small smile tugged at my lips as the elevator doors opened. I stopped twirling the keys and took the lead down the corridor.

As I unlocked the final deadbolt, my phone vibrated in my pocket for the hundredth time that morning. The damn thing was constantly going off—the football guys talking about practice, friends inviting me out, even girls still trying to hook up despite the fact I'd been making it clear I was with Eve for months now. Usually I ignored most of it, but today I was checking it every time it went off.

As Josh pulled the flat boxes and a spare suitcase inside, I pulled my phone out—just a notification from a group chat. I sighed.

"What's going on?" Josh dropped the boxes and went to the little fridge in the makeshift kitchen area, pulling out two bottles of water and tossing one to me.

"Haven't heard from Rick. He's not replying." Rick and I'd been friends since elementary school. His family was as old and rich and steeped in the Variant community as mine. I could never get as close to him as I was to Josh—Rick still had both his parents and would never really understand what it was like to lose them—but he was as close to me as any friend could get. But after the shit that went down on the day of the invasion, it was getting harder to be his friend.

He killed Beth, someone Eve loved dearly, but he was devastated about it. Thankfully, my girl would never ask me to stop being his friend, and he never asked me to plead his case to her. It made being there for both of them that much easier. He was so withdrawn and quiet since it happened, stopped doing all the sports we used to do together, stopped hanging out with all our friends. I was pretty sure I was the only one he still hung out with, and even then it was mostly because I initiated it.

He'd really opened up to me about how much guilt he felt over Beth's death, how it changed his perspective on shit. On several occasions he'd been on the verge of tears, but there was something else. Something weighed heavily on him, and I couldn't figure out what it was. Every time I tried to ask him about it, he clammed up. I was pretty sure it had to do with his parents. He'd never gotten along with his dad, but lately he was talking about them as if he wished he didn't even *have* any parents.

As a guy who'd lost his, that was hard for me to listen to.

"You worried about Rick for Rick's sake?" Josh questioned. "Or because you think he might be involved in this shit?"

I ran my hands through my hair. "I don't know, man."

There was a heavy feeling in the pit of my stomach. Rick's parents were old school, like Zara's. I wouldn't be surprised if they were secretly involved with Variant Valor, but the thought that my friend had a hand in kidnapping my Vital . . . It made my insides feel all kinds of twisted.

Josh squeezed my shoulder. "We can try to see him tomorrow if he doesn't answer, but I think you should tell Gabe."

I nodded. If nothing else, Gabe might be able to use Melior Group to get some more information on Rick's parents.

"Now," Josh continued, "let's get this stuff packed up so we can get home to our girl. And maybe take a nap."

He yawned again as he reached for the boxes, and I smiled. Our girl. Home. Our girl living with us in our home. Making it feel more like a home already. Silver linings, man!

We did a quick scan of the communal living area and the other two rooms. A Melior Group investigation team had already been through, removing most of Zara's stuff for evidence. They would've gone through Eve's stuff too, but I was sure Gabe would've instructed them to leave it as they found it. A cleaning crew would be through to remove the food and the last few items after us.

Josh emptied all the drawers in the bathroom into a small box, I gathered the few nerdy magazines from the living room, and we moved into her bedroom.

Josh propped the suitcase open on the bed and started dumping the clothes hanging in the closet into it. I moved to the dresser, opened the top drawer, and came face-to-face with a lacy black bra.

I'd seen hundreds of fucking bras—with tits in them—but *her* bra made me pause, made my heart rate speed up. Slowly, I picked up the delicate thing with the thumb and forefinger of my right hand and turned to face Josh.

"Dude." I bugged my eyes out at him as he turned to face me.

He saw the item held gingerly in my fingers, then the look on my face, and cracked up laughing. Then he groaned and looked up to the ceiling.

"God, she's got great tits. Perfect handful." He held his hands out in front of himself as if he were squeezing a phantom pair of tits.

"Not quite a handful for me." I held up my free hand, definitely bigger than his. "But still perfect."

We shared a knowing grin, and I tossed the bra into the suitcase, turning back to the greatest drawer to ever exist in the history of bedroom furniture.

I badly wanted to pack this particular drawer up one item at a time—really inspect each bra and pair of panties. Even the socks. She had the cutest little toes . . . but that would take forever, and I wanted to get home already.

I scooped up as much as I could in one go and dropped it all into the suitcase. Turning back around to get the last few bits, I saw I'd dropped a piece and bent down to pick it up. It was tiny, barely a scrap of delicate lace that looked as if it would match the bra. I held it out between my hands, inspecting it properly, and groaned. It definitely matched the bra. The pair of lace panties wasn't like a proper type that covered everything, but it wasn't a thong either. It was the kind that sat sort of on the top of the ass, the bottom of the cheeks hanging out. I had no idea what any of these things were called, and all I could do was imagine her ass in them.

I bunched them up and pressed them against my nose before I could stop myself. They just smelled like clean laundry, and I dropped them into the suitcase.

"OK, you're starting to creep me the fuck out." Josh was looking at me with raised brows and barely containing his laughter.

"Dude, I'm starting to creep *myself* out!" I laughed, then groaned again. "I haven't gotten laid since I met her. Do you have any idea how much I jerk off? Every damn day! Usually twice! It's getting to a point where I'm worried that when we actually *do* have sex, I won't last longer than thirty seconds."

"I know, I know. I'm rubbing one out at least daily too. I'd bet my inheritance that those other two dickheads are as well, despite how hard they're working to resist it."

"I get it—I know why we're giving her time and space and shit. I want her to be sure when she decides to take that step too. But *fuck*, man! I just want to . . . like, all the time!"

Josh threw a pillow at my face. "Stop talking about it! Just talking about it is making me hard. Here, I'll finish off the dresser. You do the desk."

I caught the pillow before it hit my face. Josh adjusted the bulge in his pants as he moved past me.

The pillow smelled like her—Tyler's fucking shampoo that she'd taken to using and that warm feminine smell that was so uniquely her. I lifted the pillow. I just wanted to press my cheek to it, just for a second, breathe her in.

The pillow disappeared before I could mush my face into it, pulled out of my grip by Josh. He threw it back onto the bed and pointed at the desk in the corner. "Get back to packing, you creep."

I flipped him off and started packing the heavy science books into another box. It took only a few minutes to dump all the books and school supplies into a box, and all the clothes from the closet and dresser fit into the suitcase with room to spare. We left the sheets—her bed at home was much bigger, and she'd have no use for them. I started zipping up the suitcase.

"Oh! Bedside." Josh threw me the book sitting on top of the little table, and I added it to the suitcase as he opened the one small drawer.

He paused, leaving the drawer open, and straightened, staring at it with his hands on his hips. Frowning, I went over to see what it was and found myself rooted to the spot next to him. Our girl was full of surprises.

Sitting in the middle of the drawer, on a piece of white fabric, was a vibrator. It was small to medium size, slightly curved, and a pale blue color; it looked like soft, smooth silicone. The only other things in the drawer were a packet of tissues, a bottle of lube, a bottle of toy cleaner, and a charging cord.

We both stood there as though we'd never seen a damn sex toy before.

Josh's voice was low when he finally spoke. "I simultaneously want to use it on her and throw it the fuck away so she'll use me every time she has a need for it."

"Yeah . . ." He'd perfectly summed up my own feelings on the situation. I turned away and dragged my hands down my face. "Now I'm picturing her using it."

"Fuck. Now *I'm* picturing her using it." After a beat, Josh took the items out of the drawer. The fabric turned out to be a cotton pillowcase, and he put everything into it before adding it to the suitcase and zipping it up quickly.

I had to get my mind out of the gutter. We couldn't go walking through the building with tents in our pants.

It was just so hard (pun intended) when everything made me think about her. Especially now that I'd tasted her. It was only twenty-four hours earlier that Josh and I made her writhe and moan and shake with pleasure in Alec's bed. But I already wanted more. I wanted to feel her tight body on top of mine, run my hands over her smooth skin, taste her lips. Both of them. Even if one of the others was in the bed with us, like Josh had been.

I always figured I'd end up in a threesome at some stage—Anna had even brought a friend over once, but she chickened out before things got too far. I just never thought it would be with another guy.

I wasn't sure how I would've felt about it if it were some random dude. But Josh, Gabe, Alec, and I were closer than brothers. Especially me and Josh. We pretty much told each other everything, shared everything. It was only fitting we would end up sharing a Vital.

I didn't mind feeling his hands on her as I caressed her, seeing how she reacted to his touch. If anything, it was a turn-on for me because it was a turn-on for *her*. I didn't even mind feeling his fingers right next to my face as he pushed them in and out of her pussy while I went down on her. Because it drove her wild.

Shit! I was supposed to stop thinking about that, and here I was fantasizing about what other positions we could get her into—especially once she decided to take things to the next level.

I adjusted myself again and seriously considered just rubbing one out in the bathroom before we left.

"Just take a few deep breaths, and let's get going." Josh nudged me with his shoulder, carrying the two boxes out and leaving the suitcase to me.

I picked it up and followed after him, scanning the space for anything we may have missed, then frowned.

"We sure this is all of it?" I asked as we reached the elevator. I left the door unlocked—there was nothing in there to keep safe anymore.

"Yeah." He shrugged.

I looked at the two boxes he held with ease—the contents of her desk, her toiletries, a few pairs of shoes—then at the half-empty, light-as-fuck suitcase in my hand.

"This is all her stuff? Don't girls like to shop and shit?"

"She spent most of her life on the move, man. She's used to having the bare essentials and being able to pack up quick."

I sighed. She'd perfected the disappearing act. Just like when she ran away to Australia a few weeks earlier. I was so fucking mad at her for that. *So mad!* But I couldn't exactly take it out on her. I took it out on the drywall in Tyler's office when he called us there and told us what stunt she'd pulled. Then I took it out on Dot, yelling down the phone at her on the way to the airport for helping Eve do it. But she started crying and telling me how much she was worried about Charlie, and I instantly felt bad.

At the end of the day, that was what it came down to—it made me feel bad. I hated that she felt as though she couldn't tell us her plans. But I could understand why she didn't—there was no way any of us would've let her out of our sight!

It still hurt. In the few seconds between Tyler telling us she'd run away and him telling us *why*, my heart broke. I immediately assumed she didn't want me, didn't want us or the Bond or all the crazy-ass shit that came with it.

I was sure she'd run because I wasn't enough. That all the bad outweighed the good.

I was mad at her for making me feel like that, and I pushed her away because I didn't want to rage at her, and I didn't know how else to explain it.

Then she actually *was* taken from us—nearly ended up in the hands of the very fuckers we were trying to hide her from. And my heart broke again. I wasn't sure how much more it could take. But it did make me realize I needed to let the hurt go. I couldn't keep being mad at her, pushing her away when she might be taken from me for real.

And then we nearly lost Josh . . .

If any one of them was taken from me, I'd raze this city, the entire fucking East Coast, to the ground. There would be no controlling my fire and my fury.

It's why I refused to believe Charlie was dead. I had to have hope. My family was everything to me. *Everything.*

We dropped the stuff in the trunk of Josh's Challenger and just stood there for a beat, staring at it. All our girl's stuff fit into two small boxes and a half-empty suitcase.

"I don't like this." My voice was low and rumbly even to my own ears.

"Neither do I."

"I'm gonna buy her so much stuff she won't know what to do with it all."

"Yes. Good. I'll help."

We looked at each other and nodded before he slammed the trunk closed.

We made a pit stop in Bradford Hills so I could get some ingredients for dinner, and since we were already there, we went to Eve's favorite café and got a latte for her and bagels for everyone for lunch.

As Josh pulled the car up to the house, Dana came jogging down the front stairs. She didn't wave or acknowledge us in any way, simply getting into the car and driving away.

Josh and I shared a wary look and rushed to get inside.

As we came through the front door, Alec came down the stairs, a hard look on his face, tension in his shoulders. As if he wanted to punch someone. I knew the feeling.

"What did you do?" I got in his face.

Just like the day before, he didn't fight back. Instead, the intense, pissed-off look left his face, and he raised his hands in front of himself in surrender.

He opened his mouth to answer, but just then Tyler came out of his study. "Kid! Back off. He didn't do anything."

I gave him another stern look and took a step away.

"What's going on?" Josh asked.

"We had a visit from Davis Damari." Alec's voice was hard, the pissed-off look back on his face.

I frowned. "Uncle Lucian's business partner? So what?"

"At least that explains why Dana was here." Josh gestured to the door. "Is that why everyone's tense? Did she say something to Eve?"

"No." Tyler pinched the bridge of his nose. "Apparently Davis is Evelyn's father. She just found out. So did we. It's been a weird morning."

"Holy shit," Josh whispered, his eyes wide. "Aren't we thinking he might be behind the Vital kidnappings?"

"Yeah." Alec still looked as if he wanted to punch someone. At least now I knew who.

Damari came to the house to meet with Uncle Luce from time to time. He gave me the creeps on a *good* day. That sleaze was her father? I had so many questions. But all that would have to wait.

"Is she OK?" I needed to give my girl a big bear hug. I moved toward the stairs, but Alec stopped me with a hand against my chest.

"No, Kid, she's not." He moved the hand up to my shoulder, making the gesture more comforting than confrontational. "Her whole world was just turned upside down. She's upset and confused, and she wants to be left alone."

I sighed. We were back to the whole boundaries-and-space shit. I just wanted to hold her, tell her everything would be OK.

"Come on, let's get the stuff from the car." Josh pulled on my arm, and I followed him for something to distract me from running up the stairs and beating her door down.

Then we all sat around the kitchen island and ate the bagels while Gabe and Alec caught us up on everything we'd missed. It seemed that Uncle Lucian was keeping some pretty big secrets of his own. I guess it ran in the family.

Eve missed lunch and stayed locked in her room all afternoon. We took turns sneaking up there, tiptoeing to the door and straining to hear anything. It was silent every time I went up—no music or crying or anything. She was either sleeping or reading or just . . . I didn't even know! But she'd asked for privacy, and I was doing my best to provide it.

I started dinner early, in need of something to do, and just as Alec was setting the table, she joined us.

I hadn't seen my uncle since that morning, and it was probably for the best—I was worried I'd say something I didn't mean—but he didn't join us for dinner either.

It was just the five of us, Eve sitting at the head of the table and the four of us on either side of her, ready to cater to her every need like a bunch of lovesick puppies. I imagined myself as the rottweiler in this scenario—big and strong and ferociously protective.

But she hardly looked at us, didn't eat much, and said even less.

Her hair was messy and unbrushed, as though she'd been running her hands through it. I still thought it looked sexy.

She wasn't crying or upset, but she did look tired, drawn, kind of flat. Her beautiful deep blue eyes were downcast. I wasn't sure if she was deep in thought or just checked out and trying not to think about anything.

I was too scared to say anything or ask a question that would draw attention to the elephant in the room if she didn't want to talk about it. I think the others were all thinking the same, because it was a very quiet dinner as we all shared worried looks over mouthfuls of pasta.

After we finished eating and Eve's plate had sat on the table half-empty and untouched for ten minutes, she stood up.

"I'm going to talk to Lucian."

We all got to our feet at the same time, ready to go with her, show a united front.

"Yes, you deserve answers." Alec said what we were all thinking.

She raised her eyes and finally looked at us each in turn—*properly* looked at us—as she managed a barely there smile.

"I really appreciate your support. All of you. But I think I need to do this alone. I'm sorry." She frowned and looked down again.

"You have nothing to be sorry for, baby." Josh spoke up first. "You handle this in whatever way is best for you. We're all right here if you need us, OK?"

She gave him a nod and a warm smile, her eyes misty, her shoulders hunched. She looked so fucking fragile, and I couldn't take it anymore.

As she turned to leave, I reached out and gently took her hand. She looked up at me, making her eyes look even bigger. She was so fucking cute.

I knew she was fragile in that moment, and I treated her as such, my every touch and every movement careful and slow.

I knew my size and strength. I knew the kind of destruction I was capable of, even without my ability. But I also knew I could be as gentle and delicate as she deserved to be treated.

Slowly, I drew her to me, giving her plenty of time to back away if she really didn't want a hug. But she met me halfway and melted into my chest, her arms wrapping around my waist. I held her to me, stroking her messy hair and just feeling her in my arms.

Her shoulders relaxed just a tiny bit, and she pushed her face into my chest and breathed me in. I kissed the top of her head, and she kissed my chest through the fabric of my T-shirt.

My chest swelled with pride that I was able to provide even a tiny scrap of comfort to her, that she *let* me.

All the shit Josh and I'd joked about in her res hall earlier was insignificant. I would wait my whole life for her. She was worth it.

PEACHES AND CREAM

Author's note: This is a deleted scene that takes place somewhere around Chapter 20 in Vital Found—*after Eve's little trip to Australia.*

I regretted not putting socks on as I padded in bare feet across the cold marble of the foyer. The nights were getting chilly, and goosebumps crawled up my legs. Crossing my arms over my chest, I also wished I'd grabbed a sweater. The loose, oversized T-shirt with the wide neck that I wore to bed was fine when I was tucked into the luxurious bedding of the Zacarias mansion's spare room, but it did nothing to ward off the chill downstairs.

As I entered the open-plan area at the back of the house, almost tasting the leftovers I knew would be in the fridge, the marble under my feet gave way to polished timber. I turned toward the kitchen and saw the fridge doors wide open, casting light over the pristine stone countertops, but I couldn't see who it was rummaging in there. I came around the island just as Ethan straightened and turned toward me, a bowl held in one hand and a plastic container in the other. He was barefoot too, but at least I had clothing on. He was in nothing but his boxers.

"Hey," I whispered as he kicked the door closed, throwing us into darkness. "Looks like our stomachs had the same idea."

"Hey," he whispered back. There was something about the cocooning silence of 2 a.m. that neither of us was willing to disturb by speaking at a normal volume or turning on the lights. I heard the contents of his hands being deposited onto the counter as I waited for my eyes to adjust to the dark. Moonlight was streaming in from the wall of windows at the back of the room, the pool visible beyond. The water looked black in the night.

Once Ethan's features became clearer and I could make out the outlines of items in the room, I shuffled over to the island and tried to haul myself up next to Ethan's containers. "What you got there?" I asked, still whispering as I willed my half-asleep limbs to work well enough to get me up onto the counter and away from the cold seeping into my bare feet.

"Fruit and some leftover cream from the pie we had at dinner." He spoke low too as he gripped me firmly by the waist and helped me situate myself on the counter. "Want some?" His hands were warm. His whole body radiated heat, as usual, regardless of the fact that he was practically naked and it was a cold night.

"Sure," I all but breathed out. Instead of making a move toward the food, I just sat there, my hands gripping the edge of the counter, and watched Ethan. He lifted the plastic wrap off the bowl of cream, then removed the lid from the container and extracted a wedge of something—apple? Orange? He dipped it into the cream and popped the whole thing into his mouth.

After sighing, satisfied, around the treat in his mouth, he reached into the container again, dipped another wedge into the cream, and held it out to me. I opened my mouth and wrapped my lips around what I realized was peach. I bit it in half, the juice dripping down my chin and over Ethan's fingers. We both laughed quietly as I wiped it away.

A dollop of cream fell onto my knee. I mumbled around the sweet peach and cream, gesturing at the blob on my knee with sticky fingers as I twisted to one side, then the other, looking for a tea towel. Ethan just grinned at me before popping the other half of the peach into his mouth. He surprised me by leaning down and licking the cream off my knee, his hands planted on either side of me on the counter.

The move was playful, but it sent a jolt of something heavy and thick through my body, making me feel breathless and completely eliminating any cold still clinging to my skin.

He looked up at me, sensing a change in the air between us, or just a change in my breathing—it was suddenly deeper. He straightened up slowly, watching me, the playfulness on his face replaced by something more serious and urgent.

I gripped the edge of the counter tightly, trying to get a hold of myself. Ethan kept staring at me, waiting for my lead. I swallowed loudly and took a deep breath. I could make a casual comment about how hungry I was, and I knew he would back off, go to the fridge, make me something more substantial than peaches and cream. Or I could choose to embrace the magic of the silence and darkness of 2 a.m. and lean into this moment. Lean into Ethan.

He was waiting for me to decide how this would pan out. And I realized that was what he'd been doing for months. Him and Josh and Tyler, and even Alec to an extent. They were holding back and giving me space. Waiting for me to decide when, where, and how I wanted to get more intimate with them.

I watched Ethan watch me as the moonlight filtered in through the windows, nothing but patience in his demeanor, and my decision was easy. I leaned into this moment, my mind curious to see where it would go, my body eager for that deeper connection. My Light was doing all kinds of happy dancing inside me, straining for stronger ties to the Variant abilities it existed for.

I quickly made sure it was reined in, my mental barriers strong so I wouldn't accidentally leak Light to him with what I was about to do. Keeping my eyes on his, I slowly reached out and fumbled around until I found the edge of the bowl. I grabbed it and dragged it closer to me, scooping some cream out with one finger. Ethan's eyes narrowed. He could see what I was doing out of the corner of his eye, but he was just as unwilling to break the gaze we'd locked ourselves into.

I brought my hand up slowly between us and smudged the cream in the curve between my neck and shoulder, where my wide-necked sleep shirt had slipped down.

"Oops," I breathed out, not a hint of remorse or even playfulness in my voice, then popped my finger into my mouth and licked the rest of the sweet cream off.

Ethan managed to maintain eye contact with me, but the muscles in his arms became rigid, his fingers gripping the countertop on either side of my thighs very tightly. When I pulled my finger out of my mouth, his gaze finally dropped, and he watched, transfixed, as I lowered my hand and licked my lips.

He mirrored me, licking his own lips as his gaze traveled to my neck.

He leaned forward painfully slowly, and I held perfectly still, my breaths becoming labored just from his close proximity and the knowledge of what he was about to do. I dared not move for fear it would somehow disrupt this moment and break the 2 a.m. spell.

I could feel his breath on my shoulder, his lips inches from my skin. What was he waiting for? Just as doubt began to creep in, he moved closer, his tongue driving all thought from my mind.

He licked the cream off in one smooth motion. I heard him swallow, and then his mouth was back on my neck. He kissed the same spot, his warm lips sending a little shiver down my back. I felt him smile against me, and then he was moving back to put his face level with mine again.

Without warning, he leaned in and kissed me, his lips pressing to mine firmly. He took his time, his kiss as slow and measured as all his movements so far. I was impressed by his control, but I wasn't sure how much abuse the counter could take. He was still gripping it tightly, the muscles in his strong arms rippling as he flexed and relaxed his fingers.

He broke the kiss and leaned back to lock me into another stare. The patient, neutral expression was back, but the tension in his body betrayed him. Maybe the darkness made me feel more bold, or maybe the fact that he'd made it so clear I was in charge of where this went lulled me into a false sense of security, but some mischievous part of me wanted to test that unwavering control.

Working hard to keep the smirk off my face, I slowly reached my hand toward the bowl. He must've seen something in my eyes though, because when his narrowed again, I could just make out a hint of amusement mirrored in the languid amber.

Once again, he kept his eyes trained on my face as I dipped my finger into the cream. With my other hand, I reached for the neck of my shirt, pulled it low in the front, and smeared the cream on the top of my left breast, dangerously close to my nipple.

As I went to stick my finger in my mouth like I had the first time, Ethan's hand shot out and grabbed me by the wrist. It was the most sudden movement he'd made thus far, and it sent a shot of adrenaline through me, mixing with the other thing—the heady, heavy feeling that had settled low in my body.

He held my arm between us with a firm grip, my finger pointing up, and then he wrapped his own lips around it. He kept his gaze on me as he swirled his tongue around my finger and slowly extracted it, lowering it to my lap and returning his hand to the edge of the counter.

All sense of mischief had been pushed out of me with the way Ethan wrapped his mouth around my finger. My lips were parted slightly, every inch of my being paying attention to only him. He leaned his head down, and my eyes followed his movements. As he had at my neck, he paused, his face inches away from my breast. I was breathing hard, my chest moving up and down, and I resisted the urge to push it forward just a little more, to force the connection I suddenly realized I'd been craving long before tonight.

He didn't torture me too long. He closed the distance and licked the cream off my breast in yet another slow, controlled movement. A little moan escaped me, and at the sound of it filling the silence of the dark kitchen, he leaned his forehead against my collarbone, his fingers flexing around the edge of the counter once again as he took a shuddering breath. His breath fluttered down into the front of my shirt, and I could feel it feathering over my belly. It made me squirm, opening my knees a little wider.

Ethan responded to me as immediately as I'd responded to him. He lifted his head and stepped closer, between my legs. This time, his kiss was more urgent. He pushed his tongue into my mouth, and I wrapped my hands around his neck, scooting forward, desperate now to get closer. To feel him pressed up against me.

But his hands remained planted on the counter on either side of me; he hadn't lost as much control as I thought. He broke the kiss again and leaned away, a small smile playing at his lips, hinting at the dimple I knew would appear if he smiled fully.

I watched, transfixed, as the calm, patient expression came back into his features while I all but panted, only just managing to stop myself from wrapping my legs around him and forcing his body to mine.

He was still letting me take the lead, still waiting to see how far I would take this, but it had also turned into a bit of a game. I was now determined to break him.

I let my arms drop from around his neck and, with a now shaky hand, reached for the bowl again. I dipped a finger in, working to calm my breathing and ignore the ache building between my legs. I hadn't thought about my next move, and I paused, cream-covered finger in the air as I stared at Ethan's infuriatingly calm expression.

I needed to get him to release his grip on the countertop, to put his hands on me, to break this tightly restrained standoff we were in.

I reached my free hand between us and was satisfied at the way his eyes widened slightly.

I bit my lower lip as I slowly lifted the hem of my shirt, exposing my thighs. I smeared the cream on top of my right thigh, *high* on my thigh. With the same slow, deliberate movement, I raised my finger and held it up in front of his mouth. He wrapped his lips around it almost immediately, then let me draw my hand away, but he didn't move otherwise. He was ignoring the dollop on my thigh. His expression remained calm, but his eyes swirled with intensity.

The urge to say something, move toward him, do something to get him to make *his* next move was almost unbearable, but I knew I had to be as patient as he was. He'd let me take the lead; I'd made my move, and now he had to make his.

To keep from launching myself at him, I leaned back onto my hands and widened my knees just a little farther. It had the desired effect. His gaze was drawn by the movement, his eyes falling to my lap.

"Fuck," he cursed, so low I almost didn't hear him, and then his body followed his gaze, bending down over my lap. His hands finally left the counter and landed on top of my knees. He didn't hesitate or take a breath as he had the last two times. My breathing became labored once again as his tongue snaked out and traced a line from the outside of my thigh to the top, collecting the cream as he went.

He looked up at me and placed a kiss to the same spot, his hands flexing around my knees as he lifted himself into a standing position. My eyes traveled down his body as he straightened, taking in the broad shoulders, the wide chest, the flame tattoo that covered one shoulder and continued down his torso. They trailed lower to the only item of clothing he was wearing—his boxers. But before I could really focus on what I was looking at, he squeezed my knees again and stepped between them, the edge of the countertop obstructing my view.

I looked up at him. His lips were parted too.

His throat bobbed as he swallowed, looking now as if he was struggling for control as much as I was. His hands flexed and relaxed on my knees in an unsteady rhythm.

I leaned forward, pushing up from my reclined position, and he met me halfway, mashing his lips to mine. The kiss was more urgent, both of us moaning a little into each other's mouths. Ethan's hands trailed up my thighs, resting just below the hem of the shirt. He was leaning into the moment just as I was, but he was managing to have some restraint.

But I wanted *more*.

I wanted his hands all over me.

I wanted the few scraps of clothing between us to be gone.

With a little grunt of frustration, I sucked his bottom lip in between my teeth and pushed my hips forward. We were already very close, so the movement brought me into contact with the evidence of his arousal.

Instinctively, he bucked his hips, meeting my sudden movement tit for tat. A liquid warmth spread through my body at the friction, and I reveled in the sensation of Ethan's tongue pushing into my mouth once again as he ground his length into me.

But the sweet friction lasted only a few moments before he pulled away. He moved his hips back just out of reach, panting hard.

"Wha . . ." I was panting too. "Why?"

He chuckled low, leaning his forehead against mine.

"I just need a minute." His hot breath fanned over my face.

"What for?"

"I just . . . I can't . . . I mean, I won't want to . . . fuck!" He chuckled again, leaning back farther to look at me. "I can't even think straight."

"You won't want to what?" With potential rejection as close to the edge of this situation as my ass was to the edge of the counter, my mind grabbed on to those words, and I needed to know their meaning.

"Stop." He lowered his voice to a whisper again.

"What's going on? I thought you wanted this."

"I do. I've never wanted anything more in my life." It was a dramatic statement, but it was delivered without much humor. I just frowned, waiting for him to explain. He'd leaned away enough to be able to speak to me, but his hands still had a firm grip on my thighs, and his hips were still only inches from mine.

"Look." He took a deep breath. "Do you remember how you went to your lesson with Gabe dressed . . ." He trailed off. He was talking about that unfortunate day I accidentally walked around campus dressed as a private schoolgirl. It made for a particularly awkward lesson.

"Yeah." I ducked my head. I was embarrassed and confused about why he was bringing that up. It was kind of ruining the vibe.

"Well . . . uh, that's his particular . . . fantasy, and . . . um . . . well . . ." He was stumbling over his words, so unlike the boisterous, confident guy I knew, and he was moving farther away from me. Frustration began to set in.

"Spit it out, Ethan. Why are we talking about Tyler's wet dream?"

"Because I needed a segue to tell you that this is *my* wet dream," he rushed out, looking at me with an intense expression.

"What is?" I wasn't getting it, but at least the conversation was getting back onto a track more in line with what I wanted to be doing.

"You know how much I like to cook."

I nodded.

"And how much I like to eat." He smiled a little, the tension leaving his features.

I nodded again. Getting more and more confused.

"Well, my fantasy involves a kitchen and . . . eating, and we're dangerously close to acting it out."

"Do you have some sort of food fetish?" I asked, partly joking and partly serious.

"No." He chuckled. "My fantasy involves a kitchen and a *midnight snack.*" He looked at me meaningfully and dragged his hands up the few centimeters of thigh still covered by fabric, his fingers slipping underneath and coming very close to the edge of my underwear. His hands moved with purpose, his eyes trying to convey a message I'd yet to grasp.

I'd been distracted by the confusion and worry and strange conversation, but what Ethan's hands were doing brought me right back to the worked-up state I was in moments before. My breath quickened once again, my heart pitter-pattering in my chest. The desire was a distraction, and I didn't grasp the meaning of his words right away. When I did, I gasped, my eyes going wide.

Before I had a chance to formulate a response, he kept speaking. "I don't want you to do anything you're not into—not everyone likes it. But yeah, it's a big fantasy of mine, and if we keep going, I'm not going to want to stop." His voice had gotten husky at the end, barely discernible.

The implications of what he wanted to do slammed into me as my body remembered how his tongue had swirled around my finger to get the cream off, how his hot mouth had felt on my knee, neck, breast, thigh . . . The fact that he was so up-front about it being his fantasy only made me want to do it more. The Light inside me was jumping for joy at the prospect of doing something to make one of my Bond members happy, but I would be lying if I said it was all Light. *I* wanted to make Ethan happy.

"Ummm . . ." Ethan's uncertain voice brought me back out of my stare, my brain going through all the information. I cut him off before he could finish what he was about to say, wiping the worried look off his face.

"Do it," I rushed out on a shaky whisper and smiled. Anticipation was now adding to the desire, intrigue and adrenaline running through my veins, and it made for a heady cocktail.

Ethan smiled back, all dimples. Not needing to be told twice, he leaned in and kissed me. It was like no kiss we'd ever shared. This kiss had an urgency and purpose behind it I'd never experienced from him before. His mouth devoured mine. His body pressed up against mine as his hands gripped my thighs and pulled me closer before moving to run up and down my back. His hands were everywhere, but he was denying me the friction I wanted most, keeping his hips just out of reach.

He started kissing down my neck, my heavy breaths filling the silent kitchen. His mouth trailed a path down my neck and over my collarbone, heading lower. With one big hand on my back and one at my ribs, just under my breast, he firmly but gently lowered me onto my back, leaning over me as he went. The stone countertop was cool under me, but I barely registered it as Ethan wrapped a hand around one of my breasts, his mouth covering the other over the fabric.

He teased me through the fabric before pulling the front of the shirt down, the wide neck exposing both of my breasts. His hot mouth immediately went back to the same spot, tasting my nipple, his tongue swirling as it had around my finger. With a light suction that made me arch my back a little, his mouth left my flesh. He released the neck of the shirt, and it snapped back up, just covering my nipples.

He dragged his hands down my sides, my ribs rising and lowering under his palms as I panted. He reached under the fabric and hooked his fingers around the edge of my underwear. I angled my hips up, and he pulled the fabric away, sliding it down my legs until it disappeared.

I glanced down. He was on his knees, and all I could see was the top of his chest, his broad shoulders, and his head. He was looking at me, but not at my face. His eyes were hooded and his lips parted, so he seemed to like what he was seeing, but it still made me feel incredibly exposed. I quickly looked away, letting my head fall back to the hard stone and looking up at the dark ceiling.

Instinctively I tried to close my knees, but he stopped me. One hand landed on the inside of my thigh, not pushing it wider but not letting me give in to the insecurity either. His other hand reached up and found mine, and his warm fingers closed around mine and reminded me I was safe with him. He'd been up-front about what he wanted to do, had made sure I was comfortable with it, and I knew he would stop if I asked him to, regardless of the fact that he said he wouldn't want to.

I reminded myself I was safe with Ethan, and my body reminded me I wanted this—it was beginning to tremble with anticipation. I gave his hand a little squeeze in return, letting him know I was OK, and released it. To drive my point home, I moved my knees apart just an inch, inviting him to continue.

He sighed, and then his hands were trailing up the inside of my thighs. He started to rub me with his thumbs with a light pressure, very careful to avoid the most sensitive areas. All the buildup was beginning to drive me nuts. But before I had a chance to complain, his hands gripped my thighs firmly, pushing them apart wider, and then his mouth was on me.

The sensation was like nothing I'd felt before. It was warm and wet and soft and wonderfully surprising. I moaned into the darkness, breaking the silence we'd maintained with whispers and careful movements since I walked into the kitchen. My hands slapped down onto the counter on either side of me as incoherent sounds escaped my lips.

I felt a little naughty doing what we were doing in the kitchen. Anyone could walk in at any moment. But I didn't feel bad about the fact that we were doing it. That part felt *so* right. I wanted more of Ethan. I wanted to be closer to all of them. And as Ethan's tongue did incredible things to my body, it was impossible to pretend that the closeness I craved was driven solely by my Light.

My moans were becoming louder, but I didn't care. All I could think about was the feeling of his hot mouth on me, his hands gripping my thighs, my back arching as my hips started to thrust of their own volition, meeting Ethan's rhythmic movements with my own.

"Yes," I hissed out between moans when he hit a particularly sensitive spot. My frazzled mind couldn't seem to find any other words to tell him to keep doing *exactly* that. Thankfully, he was paying attention. He was so in tune with my body. He kept doing that same thing with his tongue, maintaining the same pressure and speed, just how I liked it.

It was exactly what I needed to get over the edge, my orgasm washing over me in waves as Ethan's mouth maintained its steady rhythm on my swollen flesh.

My left hand brushed against fabric—a tea towel on the counter. I grabbed it and shoved it into my mouth, biting down and using it to muffle the guttural sounds I was making. My other hand reached down and grabbed a fistful of Ethan's hair, keeping his mouth in place, making sure his tongue kept doing that thing. Exactly. Like. *That.*

The swells of pleasure subsided, and I collapsed, releasing Ethan's hair and drawing the tea towel away from my face as I caught my breath. After a few moments, I lifted my head and looked down. Ethan was still on his knees, his hands rubbing up and down my legs in soothing movements. He was grinning from ear to ear, the dimples on full display.

CHERRY PIE

Author's Note: This takes place not long after the events of Vivid Avowed.

I'd done all the research I could, watched a bunch of videos, and practiced in front of the mirror, feeling silly. But this was one part of my plan that required more than just research—it required skills I didn't have.

It was the morning of Josh's birthday, and I needed to make this happen *now*.

I stared at the ingredients on the countertop, laid out neatly in the order they appeared in the recipe, and chewed on my bottom lip. I'd never baked a single thing in my life. I was genuinely worried I might set the Zacarias mansion on fire but consoled myself with the fact that Ethan was nearby to put it out.

Maybe I should just buy the pie? I was about ready to give up and go to the store when the fire fiend himself walked into the kitchen, sweaty from his workout—which had ended much sooner than expected.

I gasped, my eyes going wide, and scrambled to shove the evidence into the cutlery drawer.

Ethan froze, his eyes narrowing on the drawer.

His gaze flew up to mine, his expression aghast.

One of his big hands went to his hip, and the other pressed flat against his chest. "Evelyn!" His voice came out sounding higher than I'd ever heard it. "Please tell me you did *not* bring store-bought pastry into my kitchen!"

"Uh . . ." I had no idea what to say, and I was running out of time. Josh would be home in a matter of hours!

Ethan marched around to my side of the counter, and I turned and pressed my back against the drawer, trying to keep him from it.

"Go away!" I yelled, but it came out sounding whiny. "This is my thing. It has nothing to do with you."

He grabbed me around the waist and moved me out of the way effortlessly, the muscles in his big arms flexing. I tried to fight him, but it was half-hearted—he was twice my size.

He pulled the drawer open all the way, the knives and forks clattering inside.

"I knew it!" he declared, holding up the packet of pastry triumphantly. "What were you thinking? What are you trying to do, baby?" He was genuinely upset to see the counterfeit pastry in his precious kitchen, but his lips quirked into a smile by the end, the dimples showing.

I sighed, and my shoulders slumped. "I was trying to bake a pie for Josh's birthday," I told the smooth stone surface of the counter, my voice low.

Ethan chuckled. "What? Why? I'm making him a croquembouche. The profiteroles are already done."

I chewed on my bottom lip, suddenly unsure of my plan, then leaned forward and whispered to Ethan what I had in mind.

He leaned away and raked his eyes up and down my body, no doubt imagining it, his eyes amused yet heated. His gaze made me think about the last time he'd looked at me like that in this very kitchen, the dirty yet delicious things his mouth did to me on this very countertop. It nearly made me abandon the baking altogether for another activity. But this was for Josh.

Ethan moved to the trash and dropped the pastry into it dramatically.

"Lucky son of a bitch," he declared as he started pulling ingredients out of the pantry. "I'll help you make your dirty pie."

I grinned and watched the corded muscle under his white T-shirt move as he reached for something on the top shelf. This was a double win—I'd have a delicious pie, and I'd get to spend some time in the kitchen with Ethan.

A couple of hours later, I was covered in flour because we got into a flour fight that ended in a make-out session, but there was a perfect cherry pie cooling on the counter, so I wasn't complaining.

Josh was out with Lucian—it was a birthday tradition of theirs since they were kids. He would take the birthday boy out and spend some one-on-one time with him. I thought it was sweet that they'd kept it going into adulthood. I suspected I only had a bit of time left before they got back, so I jumped in the shower to wash off the flour and get ready. As I shampooed my hair, I did my best to distract myself from the self-doubt creeping in. I'd never done anything like this before. I did some complex mathematical equations in my head to take my mind off it, and I made myself concentrate on the jolt of excitement that sparked in my chest whenever I imagined Josh's face as I gave him my surprise.

After drying my hair and leaving it tousled and loose around my shoulders, I raided Josh's wardrobe for my outfit. I'd seen the perfect band tank top in there a few weeks back, and it sparked this whole idea.

Fifteen minutes later, I sat on the edge of Josh's low coffee table, leaning on my knees, my chin in my hands, the pie next to me. Josh was running late, but Ethan had promised to find out where he was after he delivered the pie.

At the sound of voices and footsteps outside Josh's door, I sat bolt upright, another surge of nervousness and insecurity making my heart leap into my throat. I ignored it and picked up the pie, getting into position.

". . . need to pop back into town for—" Josh sounded annoyed, but Ethan cut him off.

"Dude! Just trust me! Go to your room." Ethan's voice was firm, but there was a hint of amusement.

After a beat of silence, Josh answered, "You're acting really fucking strange, man."

"Yeah, yeah. Whatever. You can thank me later." Ethan opened the door as he spoke and shuffled Josh inside, then closed the door behind them and leaned back on it, a massive grin on his face.

Josh sighed and shook his head as he turned toward me. When he spotted me, he froze on the spot, his eyes going wide. He was in beige chinos and a pale blue Oxford. The cashmere sweater tied around his shoulders, the loafers on his feet, and his perfectly styled dirty-blond hair finished off the preppiest outfit I'd seen him in to date. He looked as delicious as the pie I was holding flat on my palm, like an over-the-top waitress.

"What's going on?" Josh asked, even as his perfect lips quirked into a tentative smile and his eyes took me in from head to toe.

"Just a little birthday treat." I put on my best teasing, innocent voice, hoping I didn't sound like a dickhead. Judging by how both their eyes narrowed in lust, it would seem I succeeded. Bolstered by their reactions, I propped my free hand on my hip and jutted it out, arching my back and pushing my boobs out too.

That drew Josh's eyes to the Warrant tank I was wearing, and he swallowed, the smile falling from his face. I'd paired the tank with a pair of outrageously short cut-off jean shorts, and I was barefoot, standing in the middle of Josh's coffee table. The only other scrap of clothing I had on was a thong. I never wore the tiny torture devices, but it was perfect for this, and it peeked out of the top of the shorts.

"What kind of treat are we talking about?" Josh finally moved toward me and stopped directly in front of me.

"I made you a cherry pie." I scooped a bit of the cream off the top and licked it off my finger. "Have a seat, and I might let you taste it."

"Might?" Josh raised his eyebrows, finally taking his gaze away from my lips. "I thought it was *my* birthday pie?" He reached his hands up as if to put them on my waist, but Ethan moved forward and planted one of his big hands on Josh's shoulder.

"Nuh-uh." Ethan shook his head. "No touching the lady, sir. I'm going to have to ask you to take a seat."

He crossed his muscled arms over his chest and kept a straight face, perfectly playing the part of the bouncer. I felt giggles bubbling up in my chest, but I kept it locked down, kept the mirth off my face. I'd planned to do this all alone—a special treat just for Josh—but I was really glad Ethan was there. He'd helped me make the pie, and he was helping me keep the pretense up. I would probably have let Josh touch me otherwise—I really couldn't resist any of them.

But I did want this to be about Josh, so I gave him the option. "Josh, this is a special treat for you, so it's up to you whether Ethan stays or goes for the next part."

Josh sat down on the couch, right in front of me, and looked from me to Ethan and back again. His face lit up with a wicked grin before he answered. "He can stay, but if I can't touch, he can't touch."

Josh pointed to the armchair in the corner, and Ethan flashed us his dimples before quickly planting himself in the chair.

My audience had doubled, and it sent a rush of excitement up my spine, making me bite my lip in anticipation. It was time to get this show started.

With both of them watching my every move, I stepped down off the end of the coffee table and placed the pie on the shelf next to Josh's sound system. Then I pressed play and turned to face my audience.

I propped one bare foot on the edge of the table as the first upbeat notes of "Cherry Pie" by Warrant came blasting out of the speakers. Josh's smile widened, but there was no surprise in his eyes at my song choice.

Starting things off with a bang, I did a couple of wild head rolls, flinging my hair back and rolling my body as I ran my hand up my leg, from my ankle to the seam of the tiny shorts. Then I stepped back onto the table—my stage—and faced away from Josh. I could only see Ethan out of the corner of my eye as I planted my feet wide and moved to the music, dropping my hips low, practically sticking my ass into Josh's face.

For the first half of the song I used every dirty move I'd seen in the videos I'd watched online and practiced in the mirror. I lifted my hair off my neck while arching my spine. I swayed my hips from side to side. I looked at him through my lashes as I trailed a hand down my body. I got on my knees and gyrated like a fucking pro!

Moving my body as if I were actually having sex, coupled with the tightness of the shorts, had me panting from desire and not just from how physically demanding stripping actually was.

My nipples hardened, reminding me I was supposed to be taking my clothes off. I stood back up and played with the hem of the tank top, pulling it down to expose my cleavage while leaning forward and pressing my boobs together. Josh watched every move, his hungry eyes taking it all in.

Out of the corner of my eye, I saw Ethan shift in his chair, but I kept my focus on the birthday boy.

I whipped the tank top off, using it to flip my hair again, exposing my bare breasts, and threw the fabric at Josh. He caught it midair and threw it to the side, already forgotten.

I stepped down off the table and planted myself directly in front of Josh, then ran my hands up my boobs, letting them bounce a little as my hands moved away and up into my hair. His lips were parted; the cheeky, wide grin he'd been sporting was gone. His eyes were hooded. His hands gripped the tank I'd thrown at him on one side and a cushion on the other. I loved every second of it. I was drunk on his reaction to my body.

I leaned forward, bringing my breasts mere inches from his face, and did a body roll as I leaned away again. He leaned forward like a snake following the music, then sat back once he realized he'd moved.

The song changed to "Pour Some Sugar on Me" by Def Leppard—I hadn't been sure how long this would take, so I'd made a whole playlist of classic rock stripper music—and I took that as my cue to remove the scrap of denim passing as shorts.

First, I turned around and leaned forward, arching my back and moving my hips to the music, giving Josh a glimpse of the red, lacy thong. I could've sworn I heard him groan, and I grinned. I was loving his reactions to me, and I couldn't help glancing over to Ethan.

Ethan was gripping the arm of the chair with one big hand, his knuckles white, but his other hand was in his lap right over his prominent erection, his thumb rubbing circles.

His eyes were narrowed, tracking my every move.

Both of them were enthralled by my body, and it was fucking intoxicating, sending a shiver down my bare spine and making me wonder if it was a good idea to wear the thong—it was pretty much soaked with my arousal already.

I turned back to face Josh and undid the buttons on the shorts one by one, then slowly slid them over my hips until they fell to the ground. I stepped out of them, planting my feet wide, and trailed my hands up my nearly naked body. Josh followed my hands' progress, over my hips, up my belly, lingering at my breasts, and up into my hair again.

Our eyes met, and I let every bit of arousal I was feeling enter my gaze, showing him exactly how this was making me feel. He shifted in his spot and took a deep, shuddering breath. His erection was straining through his chinos—I could practically see it throbbing.

Moving with the music, I turned around again. I backed up until I was standing between Josh's knees, and he automatically spread them wider, giving me room. I dropped it low and let my ass brush his lap as my eyes went to Ethan.

He was now rubbing himself through his jeans, his eyes drinking in my body without shame. Our gazes locked as my right hand moved over my belly and down between my thighs. I bit my lip, and Ethan leaned his head back as his gaze finally dropped, zeroing in on the hand between my legs. I stroked myself, matching his movements with each roll of my hips.

Josh was being a good boy and keeping his hands to himself, but he surprised me when he snapped the strap of my thong, making the spot sting just a little. A startled laugh escaped me, and I straightened, turning to face him once again.

I put one hand on my hip and wagged a finger at him with the other. There was absolutely no remorse in his cheeky smile.

It was his birthday, and I couldn't stay mad at him.

Planting one knee on either side of his hips, I straddled him but didn't lower myself into his lap. I kept gyrating on top of him, my movements sensual, my nipples brushing the fabric of his shirt. It wasn't long before his hands were on my hips, his thumbs caressing the string of the thong.

Holding on to the back of the couch with one hand, I lifted the other behind my head, tilted my head back, and closed my eyes. Then I lowered myself fully and started grinding myself on him. He was rock hard, and I completely lost the rhythm of the music, my desire taking over and making me give in as I enjoyed the friction.

Josh groaned, and his hands moved to grip my ass firmly, helping to guide my movements. I opened my eyes and met his green ones, blazing with desire. We leaned toward each other at the same time. The kiss wasn't gentle or sweet. It was passionate and desperate, our lips parting immediately, our tongues finding a steady rhythm.

He was still fully clothed, and I was practically naked. Something about that felt dirty, lascivious—as if he had the upper hand somehow, or I was so wanton that I couldn't keep my clothes on. It was turning me on even more, but I was beyond ready to feel him inside me, so I started unbuttoning his shirt.

Just as I got to the last button, the music was turned down, and I heard rustling behind me. I broke the kiss with Josh and helped him get the shirt off, then glanced over my shoulder. Ethan had moved to sit on the coffee table directly behind me. He was shirtless, every big, bulging muscle and the fire tattoo on full display, and his jeans were unbuttoned.

He was moving in for a closer look, but he still wasn't reaching out to touch me—he was respecting the instructions that he could only watch.

The birthday boy smacked my ass, and I yelped in surprise, turning back to face him. He had that grin on his face as his hand rubbed the spot that was stinging—the spot that was sending jolts of desire straight to my core.

Josh trailed a path up my exposed back and into my hair, then mashed my lips back to his. We were all tongues and panting and hands all over each other again. But I could feel Ethan's eyes on me from behind, and that was only spurring me on.

I kept kissing Josh as I scooted back just a little so I could reach the buttons on his pants. I undid them as fast as I could, then I did break the kiss when I moved farther back to remove them.

Josh watched my every move as I slid onto my knees in front of him. I pulled both his pants and underwear down at the same time. He lifted his hips to make it easier on me.

As I pulled the fabric down Josh's legs, I leaned farther down, arching my back more, shifting backward. And then my ass was in Ethan's lap, but I didn't feel denim on my bare butt cheeks as I expected—I felt warm, silky skin.

I groaned and closed my eyes as another wave of arousal washed over me, brought on by the surprise of finding out Ethan had opened his pants and whipped his impressive cock out. It was pressing up perfectly into the crease of my ass.

I pulled Josh's pants off all the way while I ground myself against Ethan.

"Fuck, she's soaked through the thong." Ethan's voice was a growl. He was letting me rub myself up on him, but he was still being a good boy, keeping his hands to himself. I had a feeling his control was slipping though.

I leaned away from him, immediately missing the friction and the warmth, and looked up at Josh.

He crooked his finger at me, and I started to crawl back up his naked body. He already had a condom on, and I smiled, happy to see he was as eager to be inside me as I was to feel him there.

As I rested one knee next to his hip, he shook his head. "Stand up." His voice was firm and low, sexy.

I did as instructed and stood before him. He sat forward, his face level with my belly button, and hooked a finger under the strap at each hip. He didn't tease; he just pulled my last scrap of clothing down and abandoned it on the floor.

With one hand firmly on my hip, he moved the other to between my legs and put two fingers straight in. I moaned loudly and threw my head back. I was so fucking turned on I felt as if I would come from just a few minutes of Josh's long, gentle fingers moving with slow strokes inside me. But just as quickly, he removed his hand and nudged me to turn.

I faced Ethan and let Josh take the lead.

Ethan had one hand wrapped around his big cock, the other leaning back on the table behind him. He was stroking himself slowly, his lips parted, his amber eyes sparkling and taking in every inch of my body.

Josh guided me backward, my legs on either side of his, and helped me lower myself down slowly. He held his rock-hard cock at the base, and I slid down, reveling in the feeling of fullness, the satisfaction of finally having him inside me. He entered me smoothly with one long stroke—I was wet and ready for him.

When my ass met his hips and he was fully inside me, I released my weight fully on top of him, leaning my back against his chest, and moaned in relief as much as in pleasure.

For a few moments we both just sat there, Josh's hands on my hips, my hands over his, both of us breathing deep and just feeling the connection.

With a roll of his hips, Josh elicited another moan from deep in my throat. We started to writhe against each other, his length barely pulling in and out of me, the feeling of fullness almost too much. I sat up a little straighter, changing the angle, wanting to feel him even deeper.

He gripped my hip firmly with one hand, guiding my movements, as his other moved to between my legs. His fingers found my clit and started rubbing it up and down, in time to the movement of our hips.

I wanted to close my eyes, lose myself in the sensation, but I couldn't tear my gaze away from Ethan. His chest was heaving, and his eyes were everywhere—taking in how Josh's fingers were digging into my hip, how my tits were bouncing, how my hair was falling over my face in a mess, how Josh's hand between my legs picked up its pace. He couldn't seem to focus on just one thing, greedy to take it all in as he pumped himself faster.

I could see Ethan's abdominal muscles beginning to tense as my own climax began to send that tingly feeling out all over my body.

"Come with me," I ordered, my words strained between panting breaths.

His eyes connected with mine, and we both exploded together. I moaned, grinding myself into Josh, letting his cock and his fingers drive me to orgasm as the tingly feeling turned more intense and spread to my fingers and toes. I managed to keep my eyes open and watched, fascinated and turned on, as hot cum came spurting from the tip of Ethan's cock, making a mess on his belly. He couldn't keep his eyes open. They closed, a look of pure ecstasy smoothing out his features, a low groan escaping his full, parted lips.

I flopped back against Josh, and he went still under me, letting me recover. But his hands trailed feather-soft touches up and down my body, my arms, my breasts. It felt amazing.

So did the hardness inside me.

I rolled my hips just a little, giving him a silent signal that I was ready to keep going, and he chuckled, his chest vibrating at my back.

"Ready for more?" he whispered in my ear before licking the spot just under it, making me shiver.

I nodded and reached a hand down to play with his balls as I turned my head to kiss him. Our tongues moved in synchronicity with our bodies—slow, languorous movements.

I felt the couch dip next to me, and I opened my eyes to find Ethan's face mere inches from ours. Josh and I stopped kissing as he spoke. "I know I'm not supposed to touch, but can I have just one kiss?"

His black hair was falling over his forehead, and his cheeks were still flushed from his orgasm. I bit my bottom lip; he looked adorable and sexy, but Josh spoke before I could agree.

"Nope." With a firm grip on my chin, he turned my head so I was facing the other side of the room. "*My* birthday. If you want to kiss something, you can kiss her other lips. Our girl's ready for round two."

I wasn't sure when the balance of power shifted from me having their rapt attention and commanding the room with my slutty clothes and lascivious dance moves to Josh ordering everyone around . . . but I liked it. It sent another shiver down my spine.

Josh removed my hand from his balls and placed both my arms gently on the couch on either side of us. As Ethan kneeled between my legs and lowered his mouth, he licked his lips, looking up at me and giving me a grin that made his dimples appear. Then his mouth was on me, and all I could do was moan.

Fuck, he was so good at that. The way his tongue moved, the pressure of his lips, the suction, his big hands gripping my thighs . . . he was a pro and he knew it. He didn't seem even remotely bothered by the fact that Josh's balls were, like, *right there*, that his tongue must have been hitting the underside of his friend's cock where it was buried inside me. He just unabashedly went to town on my pussy.

Josh kept moving his hips, ensuring I was getting bombarded by sensation both on the inside and the outside. His hands went to my breasts, squeezing and kneading, his fingers pulling on my nipples as his own breathing became ragged. Soft moans escaped his lips right next to my ear, his warm breath tickling my neck.

He moved one hand down and rested it on Ethan's head, threading his fingers through Ethan's hair. Ethan's hand moved up to cup the breast Josh had abandoned.

Our hands were everywhere, perfection entwined, and seeing them so comfortable with touching each other in the most intimate of ways was making my mind go crazy with possibilities.

The second orgasm was more intense than the first. I gripped the cushions on either side of me as it crashed over me, making it feel as though every muscle in my body was clenching and pulsing, especially the ones between my legs.

I rode it out and collapsed back onto Josh. Ethan took a few last, long strokes with his tongue before sitting back and grinning, satisfied with himself. I smiled back at him as I worked to catch my breath, but Josh wasn't going to let me have a break.

I felt the distinctive nudge of his ability on my skin as he used it to help lift me up.

I gasped as he pulled out of me, but in the next instant, I was on my back on the couch, and he was pushing in again. My right leg was hanging off the edge, my toes just touching the ground, and Josh positioned my left so it was propped up on the back of the couch. The position allowed for an interesting angle, letting him drive into me deeper.

He held himself up with his hands on either side of my head as he moved, not waiting even a second for me to come down off my orgasm, to catch my breath.

But it felt incredible, drawing the pleasure out, so I wasn't complaining. His intelligent green eyes were hooded as he watched me, his perfect plump lips parted as he moaned and grunted.

His thrusts were fast but shallow, his cock barely pulling out halfway before he was slamming it back in. I met him thrust for thrust, rolling my hips up, as I ran my hands down his cut chest, his abdominal muscles straining and popping out with his efforts.

He tilted his head back and cried out as he came deep inside me. I held on to his hips, pressing him impossibly deeper into me, and ground myself against him.

Josh lowered himself onto his elbows, nuzzling my neck.

"Best birthday present ever," he whispered between panting breaths.

I chuckled and held him close, planting a wet kiss on his shoulder. "Happy birthday."

He gave me a brilliant smile and kissed me. Our sweet, soft kisses were interrupted by Ethan.

"Done?" he asked with a smile on his face, and I became aware of the sound of running water. He was still completely naked, his dick half-erect.

Josh kissed me on the forehead as he pulled out and sat up. "Yep."

"Is that on its way down or back up?" I pointed in the general direction of Ethan's junk.

He looked up at the ceiling, as if considering it, before answering. "Bit from column A, bit from column B."

Josh and I both chuckled, but I also groaned. "I need a break," I said, covering my swollen, satisfied pussy with both hands.

"I know." Ethan leaned down and lifted me into his arms effortlessly. "That's why I ran a bath."

"Great idea," Josh agreed, overtaking us and reaching the bathroom first.

It was lucky Josh's en suite had a very large corner tub that fit three people comfortably.

APPLE

Author's note: This takes place a few years after the end of Vivid Avowed.

If I missed my first lecture of the day, it wouldn't really be that big of a deal. It was nearing the end of the year; I was nearing the end of my degree. I was ahead in the coursework and ready for the final exams. It would be worth it to see the look on Tyler's face when I walked into his office wearing the same outfit I wore that day.

Summer was fast approaching, but I still wore a long cardigan so my outfit wouldn't be too obvious. I'd been toying with this idea for years, since Ethan and Josh first told me about Ty's *particular* interests. Since Tyler finally embraced our Bond and I realized I could have him in every way I desired.

But then people kept trying to kill us and betray us, and we went running around the world, and school and work got in the way. Or maybe I was just nervous, subconsciously putting it off. Because deep down I was worried that the real thing could never live up to the fantasy in his head.

But I was running out of time. In only a matter of weeks, I would be done with undergraduate study and moving on to my doctorate, and Tyler would be cleaning out his office for a bigger one. He was about to become the youngest dean Bradford Hills Institute had ever had. I was running out of time to make this happen while we were still in these particular . . . roles in our lives. It was now or never.

I'd saved the blouse—the one with the loose sleeves and soft fabric—but I'd lost Zara's skirt and had to buy a new one. This one was blue with gray in the tartan. The long white socks were pooled around my ankles, my feet in Chucks, as I adjusted my bag on my shoulder and headed for the admin building.

There were butterflies in my stomach. Tyler always gave me butterflies, but this morning it was worse. I was excited and nervous and a little distracted. I didn't see Alec coming down the stairs.

He blocked my path, startling me, and I pulled up just short of barreling into him.

"What are you up to?" He crossed his arms over his chest, the fabric of his suit stretching over his biceps. I had to crane my neck to meet his ice-blue eyes—narrowed in suspicion but with a hint of amusement.

"What do you mean? Nothing." I took a step back. His days of wearing Melior Group black were over, and I kicked myself for forgetting he had his interview that morning. Between providing pain relief at the local hospital and helping out as necessary in emergency situations, he'd applied to be a guidance counselor at Bradford Hills. He wanted to work with kids who had dangerous, frightening abilities. He didn't want anyone to feel as isolated and angry as he once did.

"I came to see how your interview went." I nodded decisively, happy for the convenient excuse.

"Fine." He drew the word out, stepping into my personal space and gripping my hips. "You know it was a formality more than anything." He leaned forward to whisper into my ear. "Now stop lying. What're you up to?"

I swallowed as my breathing kicked up a notch. I didn't know why I was being so secretive about it. It wasn't as if Alec didn't know about Ty's fantasy. It wasn't as if he hadn't seen us having sex a hundred times—or joined in, for that matter. We didn't have any more secrets.

I was being self-conscious about it, but I made myself square my shoulders and lean back so I could look at him.

He looked good enough to eat in a suit perfectly tailored for his tall frame. A crisp white shirt and a gray tie completed the clean-cut look. His tattoos only just peeked out of the top of the collar. I resisted the urge to lean forward and lick them.

But I did lean forward and reach for his tie. "I'm not up to anything bad, baby. It's something good. For Ty." I bit my lip and batted my eyelashes at him. As predicted, his gaze narrowed in on my mouth. "Actually, you can help. Can I borrow your tie?"

Before he could answer, I'd already loosened it, popped his collar, and lifted the tie over his head.

Finally, his focus left my lips, and he took in my outfit as I slipped the tie over my own head.

"You dirty girl." He grinned, then lifted my hair out from under the tie.

I laughed and fiddled with my collar, some of the nervousness coming back. "Do you think he'll like it?"

"He'll fucking love it. Can I come too? Pun intended."

I slapped him on the chest lightly. "No. This is for Ty. Now, should I do up the shirt or leave the tie loose?"

"Leave it loose." He didn't hesitate, his eyes taking in the hint of cleavage on display before moving back up to my face. "When's my turn?"

I cocked my head at him. He was teasing, but there was a hint of seriousness there.

"Ethan had his midnight snack in the kitchen, Josh got his dirty dance, and now Gabe is about to have his naughty schoolgirl. When's my turn?" Alec asked.

I lifted onto my toes and wrapped my arms around his neck before giving him a firm, long kiss.

"When you least expect it," I whispered against his lips. I wanted to make all their fantasies come true. I would make sure Alec got his—as soon as I figured out what it was.

He groaned. "Can't wait."

He took a tiny step away, putting some much-needed distance between us, and grabbed the two sides of my cardigan. After pulling it closed to hide most of the tie, he flashed me his crooked smirk. "I'll see you at home."

I took a deep breath and crossed my arms over my chest, keeping the cardigan closed. "See you at home."

I felt his eyes on me as I turned and marched up the stairs, through the lobby, and up to Ty's office.

At the end of the hall, I looked around to make sure the coast was clear. Then I pulled up the socks, grabbed an apple out of my bag, and took the cardigan off.

His door was ajar, and I knocked on it lightly before walking inside.

"Yes?" He didn't look up from the papers on his desk.

I dropped my bag and cardigan on the ground and closed the door, leaning back against it, my hands folded behind me.

"Excuse the disruption, Mr. Gabriel, but I needed . . . to see you."

At the sound of my voice, he finally looked up, swiping that adorable tuft of hair off his forehead. His eyes met mine, confused, then flicked down the length of my body and back up to meet my gaze again, widening. His brows rose as he sat up straighter in his chair.

I held my breath and gave him a tentative smile. Did I look ridiculous? Would he laugh? I would die of mortification and never have sex with him again if he laughed. Well . . . maybe not *never* . . .

Finally, his eyes narrowed, lust taking over his expression, and he cleared his throat. "Miss Maynard. Aren't you supposed to be in class?"

Excitement sparked in my chest, and I only just managed to contain the grin threatening to break out.

"My Variant Studies lecture doesn't start for another twenty minutes, sir."

"Very well." He leaned back in his chair, gripping the armrests. The action made the corded muscle in his forearms strain against his blue shirt, the sleeves rolled up, as usual. "What is it that you need?"

He put only the slightest inflection on the word *need*, his manner and tone of voice perfectly professional otherwise.

"I'd like to give you something. As a token of my appreciation."

"Oh?"

With a shy smile, I moved my hands out from behind me and held the apple up next to my face. It was a shiny Granny Smith, without a single mark. I'd spent an obscene amount of time picking it out.

"My, that looks . . . *plump*." He smiled, narrowing his eyes and suddenly looking a little less professional and a little more predatory.

With the shiny green apple held at my side, I walked over to his desk. His eyes tracked me intently. As I came to a stop next to him, he leaned back in his chair and swiveled so he was facing me.

I leaned on the desk with one hand and dropped the apple in front of him. His eyes dipped to stare down my top. Alec's borrowed tie brushed his knee. After taking his time staring at my tits, his eyes lifted to mine once more. Keeping me locked in his gaze, he reached out, grabbed the apple, and took a big bite.

His lips glistened with the juice of the fruit as he took his time chewing it. It sounded crunchy. I wanted to lean forward just that little bit more and lick the tart sweetness off his lips. Instead, I licked my own and stood up straight.

Tyler swallowed, his throat bobbing, then licked his lips clean.

"Juicy." His voice came out low, but still more even than I felt. "Want a taste?"

He held the fruit up to my face, and I took a bite, chewing slowly. I left the sticky juice on my lips, just as he had, but unlike me, he didn't resist the urge to taste it.

He grabbed the tie and pulled me down until my face was inches from his, then licked my lips. I opened my mouth, ready for the kiss and everything else that was about to come.

But before my lips met his, Tyler pushed his chair back and got to his feet, making me stumble and right myself.

He strolled to the door, then turned to face me, putting his hands in his pockets. It did nothing to hide the bulge in his pants. I didn't hide the fact I'd noticed, letting myself smirk.

His eyebrows rose slightly. "Are you amused, Miss Maynard?"

"Yes." I let my smile widen.

"Hmm." He looked displeased, but I knew this was all a part of the game. "Well, I'm willing to bet you're not the only one with cause for amusement. Shall we find out? Take your panties off. Bring them to me."

My heartbeat kicked up a notch, my whole body ready to take this to the next level. It was going way better than I could've imagined.

I walked to the front of his desk and stopped, facing him. I reached up under my skirt at the sides, the front still covering me; hooked my thumbs into the waistband of my underwear; and pushed them down until they were loose enough to fall to my ankles. After stepping out of them, I leaned down slowly to pick them up, giving Ty another good look down my shirt.

He was playing his role infuriatingly well, the hardness in his pants the only clue that he was affected at all. But then I shouldn't have been surprised at Tyler's control.

He held his hand out, and I walked to him and dropped my panties into it. I expected him to inspect them, tease me about how wet they were already as payback for smiling at his erection. But he just scrunched them up and shoved them into his pocket.

"I have a meeting in fifteen minutes, and you should get to class. Let's continue this . . . *discussion* this afternoon. I have a slot available at three." His voice was infuriatingly level.

"What?" But I was ready now. I was *so* ready.

Tyler licked his lips and leaned in close. My breath hitched. He fiddled with the hem of my skirt, then dragged the backs of his fingers up the front of my thigh.

His voice was low and seductive when he spoke again. "Just so we're clear, Evelyn—you are not to go home and change, and you are not to put on any form of underwear. I want you to go about your day thinking about this very moment. Every time the fresh air caresses your bare pussy"—he reached between my legs and touched me, ever so lightly, before dragging his fingers back down the other thigh—"I want you to think of me and all the things I'm going to do to you this afternoon."

I had to swallow before I could form words. "Like what?"

"You'll have to wait and see." He removed his hand from under my skirt and leaned back. "And one more thing. You are not to come for the rest of the day. Whether it's with one of the other guys or by your own hand. Your next orgasm is mine."

He was torturing me. I'd gone there to do something nice for him, to have some fun, and he was going to torture me all day. I kind of liked it . . .

I bit my bottom lip and smiled.

Tyler pulled the door open and stood to the side. "I'll see you this afternoon, Miss Maynard."

I scrambled to pull the cardigan back on before someone came past his office and saw exactly what we were doing. "I'll see you then, Mr. Gabriel," I said, swinging my bag over my shoulder.

Thankfully, the elevator was empty on the way down, and I was able to take a few cleansing breaths before taking the tie off and shoving it into my bag. With the socks pushed back down around my ankles, I didn't look so much like a bad porno character.

I forced myself to put one foot in front of the other and just focus on getting to the lecture theater. I could do this. I'd just focus on my classes and study, and I wouldn't think about Tyler or the dirty, sexy, hot things he was going to do to me that afternoon.

But I'd never walked around without underwear, let alone in a short skirt, and it was impossible not to be aware of just how *exposed* I was under it. And that stupid light breeze. Halfway across the courtyard, it kicked up a bit, and I felt the gentle wind right between my legs. Immediately my mind went to Tyler and his intense gaze and the way he'd almost touched me.

"Hey, Eve!" A girl from my study group smiled and waved at me, heading in the opposite direction. I smiled and waved back. She had no idea what I was thinking or feeling, and for some reason that made it even hotter.

The entire day was fucking torture.

Every time I sat down, walked outside, had to bend over even a little, I thought of Tyler and his heated stare, his hand under my skirt. I had to go to the bathroom several times to make sure I didn't leave wet patches on any seats I happened to occupy.

But none of it was as bad as what I was forced to endure during that very first lecture.

I'd just managed to settle myself into the seat, the hem of the skirt just covering all the important bits under me, when Josh sat down next to me. Not a moment later, Ethan swung himself over the back of the chair on my other side.

I looked between the two of them. "What are you doing?" Josh didn't even go to lectures anymore, and Ethan wasn't in this class.

"Gabe told us about your little visit this morning." Ethan flashed me that dimpled grin, his eyes full of amusement.

"If you're here to make fun of me—" I gritted out, but Josh swung an arm over the back of my chair, cutting me off.

"Not at all, baby," he whispered into my ear. "We're here to make sure you don't break the rules."

Shit.

The lecturer walked in then, and the room fell into silence, preventing me from saying anything snarky.

"Fine. Whatever," I whispered. "Just let me focus."

Ethan chuckled, and Josh leaned in so close I could feel his breath on my ear. It made me shiver. "You didn't put on panties, did you?"

I shook my head and gritted my teeth. The lecture had begun. Several dozen people were learning, and here I was sitting at the back of the room with no underwear on, being tortured by my boyfriends—at my other boyfriend's request.

"We'd better make sure," Josh whispered. I whipped my head around to gawk at him. What did he expect me to do? Lift my skirt in the middle of the lecture theater? But he turned to face the front, ignoring me, a way-too-amused smirk on his face.

Ethan's warm hand landed on my knee, and I jumped, turning to face him. He was facing the lecturer too, his smirk making a dimple pop out.

"Pay attention, Eve," he whispered, and I forced myself to turn to the front.

Ethan's hand began its slow trek up my leg. I squeezed my thighs together, but he wasn't deterred. He just kept dragging his fingers until they were up under my skirt and touching my pubic bone.

Heat spread through my chest and up my neck, and I knew I'd be blushing if I could, but the heat wasn't pure embarrassment. It was desire too. To my utter surprise and a bit of horror, I widened my knees.

I could see them both grin from the corners of my eyes. Never one to ignore an invitation, Ethan dragged his fingers lower until they were nestled between my legs. He dragged them through my wetness, and then it was my turn to be smug. Ethan clenched his jaw and took a deep breath before removing his hand.

Involuntarily, I made a little sound of disappointment.

Josh leaned in really close again. "You're not allowed to come."

His hot breath, saying hot things to me in the middle of a lecture . . .

But . . . wait. It actually felt as if he was *doing* things to me. It felt as if someone was caressing my breasts, tweaking the nipples. With a gasp, I realized it was Josh using his ability on me. He'd pretty much mastered his telekinesis. He could move colossal objects with my Light, but he could also do things that were incredibly precise— like moving clothing and parts of my body to make it feel as if he were actually touching me, caressing me, running his palms over my breasts and down my torso, rubbing me between my legs.

I gripped the armrests and tried my hardest to keep my eyes open and not moan as the pressure built and built and . . . then it all disappeared.

I panted through my nose and threw a glare in Josh's direction.

Around us, people started talking and gathering their things. The lecture was over.

"You're not supposed to come, but Gabe didn't say we couldn't tease you." Ethan grinned before getting to his feet. I had to take a few moments before I could gather my things and move toward the exit.

"I'm not talking to any of you." I rushed ahead of them, my nose in the air, my core throbbing with need. I was mostly joking, and they both laughed loudly as they trailed behind me.

They hovered for the rest of the day—popping up in my classes and the library when they wouldn't usually be there—but they were smart enough not to pull that shit again. I could only take so much before I got pissed off for real. Having them follow me around campus "inconspicuously" kind of reminded me of when I'd first met them. It made me feel nostalgic. But I was still mad at them for teasing me, so I didn't tell them that.

They finally disappeared when I made my way back to the admin building in the afternoon. I was practically buzzing with anticipation as I pulled up my socks and looped Alec's tie over my neck once more in the elevator.

At Tyler's office, I took a breath and knocked lightly before letting myself in.

He was at his desk, his head in some paperwork. He glanced up, then returned to his work. "Miss Maynard."

"Mr. Gabriel." I dropped my bag and cardigan by the door.

"Lock the door, please," he said, still not looking at me.

I did as he asked. He continued to ignore me, even when I crossed the room and leaned over the desk in front of him, my tie brushing the edge of the paper he was writing on.

"I believe we had an appointment, sir," I said, adding a little edge of annoyance to my tone. *Give me attention, dammit!*

Tyler's pen froze on his paper, and he placed it down deliberately before raising his eyes to mine, pausing to look down my shirt. "We do. I'm a busy man. Sometimes I need to finish what I'm doing before I move on to the next thing."

"And what are you doing now?" I bit my bottom lip, then let it pop out from between my teeth.

He smirked briefly and leaned back in his chair. "Come here."

I walked around to his side, and he took my hand, guiding me to sit on the desk right in front of him.

Keeping intense eye contact with me, he reached down to grab my right ankle and lifted my foot to rest on his chair. Then he did the same to my left foot and scooted his chair closer. I had no choice but to spread my knees.

Tyler's hands went to my bare knees and caressed down my sock-covered calves, then back up, over my knees and up my thighs. His lips parted as his fingers went under my skirt, but just before he reached the apex of my thighs, his hands were gone again. He moved back to my knees, then dragged his hands back up, over the skirt and all the way to my boobs. He squeezed and kneaded them confidently, his eyes devouring my body and what his hands were doing.

I gripped the edge of the desk and just panted under his touch, letting him do whatever he wanted to me. He undid the buttons on the shirt one at a time, pulling it out of the skirt's waistband at the front but leaving it in place otherwise. I'd considered not wearing a bra, but as Tyler unclasped the lacy white one in the front, I was glad I'd decided to wear it. He groaned when my tits popped out enticingly.

His hands went back to my breasts and pushed them together, squishing the tie in the cleavage, before he leaned forward to lick each one. I sighed and gripped the desk harder. He laved each nipple, licked and sucked and scraped his teeth.

Releasing my breasts, he left a trail of hot kisses down my front and, before I could react, lifted my skirt to put his face right between my legs.

I jumped and cried out at the sudden contact—the touch I'd been craving all day. I moved one hand farther behind my back for better balance and widened my knees even more. I couldn't resist touching him, so I ran my fingers through his hair and gripped it, my hand holding the soft strands and the tartan of the skirt as Tyler's head moved under my touch.

He didn't tease or take it slowly—he got right down to business, no doubt using his ability to read exactly what I wanted. The pressure was perfect, the pace was perfect, his tongue and his hands on my hips and his mouth, *oh god*!

It barely took a few minutes before I was crashing, moaning on Tyler's desk with my tits out and his head between my legs as my orgasm washed over me. It was beyond erotic, and I knew I should be keeping my voice down, but I just couldn't. I *couldn't*. After being teased and tormented all day, the pleasure was too intense.

Tyler sat up and wiped my orgasm from his mouth before grinning at me, then cleared his throat and put on a serious face. "I hope that's taught you a lesson."

"That if I interrupt your work, you'll go down on me and give me orgasms?" I panted. "Lesson learned."

His eyes narrowed. "So mouthy, Miss Maynard."

"I thought you liked it when I expressed my opinions, Mr. Gabriel."

"I do. But good, *stimulating* conversation involves back and forth. Give and take." He leaned back in his chair and undid his belt—just his belt—and rested his forearms on the armrests.

He looked so fucking sexy, draped in his executive chair, his eyes drinking me in, his open belt both an invitation and a command.

I pushed his chair back with my feet and slid to my knees.

761

"Don't let it be said that I don't take instruction well," I said as I undid his pants and pulled them down just enough to set his erection free. He wasn't wearing underwear either, and I wondered if he'd been free-balling it all day just like me. It made me smile.

Since we seemed to be tit for tat in everything, I wrapped my mouth around him and got to pleasuring him with as much enthusiasm and vigor as he'd shown me just moments before.

He jerked his hips slightly and cursed under his breath as I sucked him deep. His reaction was beyond satisfying. Anytime I managed to surprise Tyler, it brought me a deep sense of accomplishment.

With one hand, he gathered my hair and held it, his fist moving in rhythm with my head. His other hand gripped the edge of the desk tightly, the corded muscle in his forearm taut. I used my mouth and my hands and went to town, determined to make him come as fast as I had. I knew that would likely be the end of this encounter, but I couldn't help myself. I wanted to see Tyler fall apart.

He groaned and threw his head back against the chair, and I pumped him harder, sucked him deeper.

Then, all at once, he tugged my hair harder and pushed the chair back, bringing, frankly, my best blowjob ever to an abrupt end.

"Did I say something wrong, sir?" I sat back on my heels and smirked.

Tyler took several deep breaths, then looked down at me and groaned again.

"No. You're fucking perfect." He leaned forward and tucked my hair behind my ear. His touch light, he caressed my cheek gently—in complete contrast to the almost feral desire in his eyes. He brushed my jaw, then rubbed his thumb over my bottom lip, dragging it down. I stuck my tongue out and licked it.

Tyler got to his feet and pulled me up with him. His pants dropped to his ankles, and his steel-hard erection pressed against my belly as he pulled me in for a kiss. It was an intense, consuming kind of kiss. We moaned and groped each other, and my desire grew and grew until I thought I might explode if he wasn't inside me within the next *second*.

Just as I was about to pull away and demand exactly that, he broke the kiss and whirled me around, making my head spin for more than one reason.

There was no more talking, no more teasing. There was just raw need.

Tyler pushed me up against his desk, and I threw my hands out to lean on it, folders and newspapers crinkling under my fingers. He pressed his body to my back and palmed my breasts. I arched my back and ground my ass against him, then leaned forward and propped myself on my elbows.

He flipped my skirt up, exposing me, and kneaded my ass. I pushed it back into his touch, practically begging.

But he dragged his hand down the back of my left leg to grip my knee. With a firm touch, he guided my leg up until my thigh was propped up along the edge of the desk.

I didn't think I could feel any more exposed, but I did. I was spread open for him, vulnerable, and I fucking *loved* it.

Finally, *finally*, Ty rubbed his hardness against me, coating it in my arousal, and then he slid inside. Inch by slow inch, he pushed into me until his hips were flush with my ass.

He took his time at first—even though we were both panting and desperate for more—sliding in and out with slow, deep strokes. His hands gripped my hips, caressed my ass and my back, and I leaned down farther until my cheek was on the desk.

That's when he picked up his pace. With one hand on my upper back and the other on my elevated thigh, Tyler rammed into me faster and harder. The desk started to rock with our intensity, a pencil falling off the edge. Our moans and grunts filled his office and mingled with the wet sound of our fucking.

It was so raw, so naughty to be doing this in his office, in the middle of the afternoon.

My second orgasm was even more intense than the first. My toes curled, my fingers wrapping around whatever paper was under them and scrunching it up as pleasure coursed through every fiber of my being. The Light flowed between us, pulsing in rhythm with my climax.

Tyler came at the exact same moment, his hips grinding mine into the desk, his fingers digging into my flesh as he groaned low in his throat.

After several moments, both of us panting and coming down from the high, he pulled out of me with a hiss. I pushed myself up on shaky arms and legs, but Ty didn't let me fall. He pulled me into his lap and sat us down in his chair. We wrapped our arms around each other and just took a moment to bask in the afterglow.

"Teaching is so rewarding, Miss Maynard. Thanks for stopping by," he said, his voice husky, his eyes lazy.

I grinned and leaned my head on his shoulder. "So is learning, Mr. Gabriel. Thanks for making time for me."

HONEY

*Author's note: This takes place several years after the end of Vivid Avowed.

I checked my reflection in the bathroom mirror and adjusted my hair. I was in a floor-length, gauzy slip thing that couldn't even pass for sleepwear, let alone an actual dress. It was a deep teal color and had lace details and the thinnest straps and was completely sheer. I liked how it made my boobs look—perky and shapely. My hair was out, styled in silky waves around my shoulders, but I hadn't put any makeup on. Alec preferred me without makeup, and tonight was all about him.

Josh walked into the bathroom and moved something into place next to the massive tub with a flick of his wrist, his ability second nature now. He came to stand behind me, his hands on my hips.

"You look . . ." Instead of finishing the sentence, he hummed a satisfied sound against my neck and dragged his lips up to my ear, giving it a little nibble.

"Thanks." I smiled at him in the mirror. He was dressed casually, his dirty-blond hair falling over his forehead as he nuzzled my neck. "You smell amazing."

Josh always smelled amazing—like sunshine and something fresh and expensive. He ran his hands up my sides, bunching the delicate fabric, and grabbed my breasts gently.

"Do we really have to go?" he whined, grinding his erection into my ass. I pushed back against him instinctually and nearly gave in. I loved the nights when we all came together, all four of them pleasuring me for what felt like hours.

I made myself step out of his embrace. "No. Tonight is about Alec."

Josh sighed and followed me out of the bathroom, grumbling about provocative outfits.

I shot him a look over my shoulder. "You bought this for me. Specifically to wear tonight."

"Yeah, yeah. Alec's gonna love it." He waved his hand and rolled his eyes.

I paused to give him a kiss, making sure it was a quick one and backing away before he could take it further. I only had so much self-control. "He will. Thank you, Joshy. I love you."

He gave me a perfect, brilliant smile. "Love you too."

Josh had helped me set up our room and the bathroom, and even made a few suggestions to make the evening perfect. His attention to detail was amazing.

We headed downstairs and into the kitchen, where Ethan was making dinner for two. The gigantic dining table was set with two settings and an obscene number of candles.

Ethan looked up from the salad he was tossing and dropped the tongs, his mouth falling open and his eyes bugging out. "Fuck me," he breathed, raking his eyes over my body.

"Not tonight, sweetness," I teased and cocked one hip. My leg peeked out through the suggestively high slit in the dress.

"This is so unfair." His eyes were glued to the most private part of my body as he licked his lips. Anytime Ethan and I found ourselves alone in the kitchen, and Lucian was not home, he'd abandon whatever he was doing, lift me onto the counter, and eat me out as if I were his favorite meal. Sometimes he did it when the others were around too; he just couldn't help himself. He loved it so much, and I wasn't one to say no to orgasms. He was looking at me like that now—as though he wanted to devour me.

I pointed a warning finger at him. "No."

He stuck his bottom lip out and wrapped his big arms around my waist. "Please."

"Don't pout." I smiled against his lips.

"Flash her your dimples—she can't resist the dimples," Josh teased from behind me, his chest suddenly pressing to my back.

Ethan's mouth slowly curved into a grin, flashing those damn dimples, while Josh's hand teased its way into the slit in the dress. I could feel my resolve breaking. Maybe we could fit in a quick three-way before—

The sound of voices in the foyer made me come to my senses, and I slid out from between them. I pulled on my sparkly silver heels and rushed out of the kitchen, glaring at them over my shoulder. They both adjusted their junk and made themselves busy.

My heels clicked on the marble floor, and Alec and Tyler paused in the middle of the foyer, right next to the round table with the giant floral arrangement.

They both worked at Bradford Hills Institute now. Tyler had been the dean for nearly two years, and Alec had been in his guidance counseling role for nearly the same amount of time. When their schedules lined up, they went to work together and came home at the same time. Tyler had made sure their schedules lined up today, then delayed them just a little bit so we'd have time to set everything up.

"Evelyn!" Alec hissed. He rushed forward, whipping his sweater off and holding it out to me as he looked down the hall. "Uncle Luce could come out here any moment."

I chuckled and took the sweater from him, then dropped it on the table. "Lucian is catching up with some friends tonight. He's staying in the city."

"Oh." Alec relaxed, his eyes finally appreciating what was before him. "Oh."

"And Josh, Ethan, and I are heading out for the evening." Tyler leaned in and kissed me on the cheek. "Hey, baby. You look fucking amazing."

"Thank you." I smiled. It didn't escape my notice that he kept both hands balled in his pockets as he headed for the kitchen. Part of me wanted to follow him and really test his control, see if I could make him crack without even taking the slinky dress off. But tonight was Alec's night.

"Welcome home, darling." I wrapped my arms around Alec's neck and gave him a soft, slow kiss.

His eyes were hooded when I pulled back, his hands gripping my hips. "What is this about?" His voice was melted honey, and it made me feel warm on the inside.

"I just love you." I shrugged. "You deserve to be spoiled, so I'm spoiling you."

I took his hand and led him to the dining table, gesturing for him to sit. He reclined into the chair, his black slacks stretching against his defined thighs. Now that he worked an office job, Alec dressed in shirts and slacks more. But he still worked out like crazy, and his body was amazing.

"Hey, bro!" Ethan greeted his cousin, placing two steaming plates on the table.

"Hey, guys." Alec waved, looking a little dazed.

Josh popped the cork on a bottle of wine and poured two glasses.

Tyler pulled my chair out for me, and I lowered myself onto it, crossing my legs. He pulled my hair over one shoulder with a gentle touch, then caressed my neck, my collar bones, and just teased my cleavage. I kept my eyes on Alec.

"Enjoy your evening," Ty said and leaned down to give me a kiss. Josh kissed the back of my hand, and Ethan kissed my cheek, copping a naughty feel of my boob. He glanced down the length of the table, and several dozen candles flamed to life at once. I was positive he'd just lit all the ones upstairs too so I wouldn't have to later. Tyler flicked the light off on their way out, and then Alec and I were alone.

I pushed my chair in and picked up my cutlery. "How was your day?"

Alec chuckled and leaned his elbows on the table. "Do you really expect me to just eat dinner with you sitting there looking like pure sin?"

"I don't know what you're talking about." I popped a bit of chicken into my mouth and moaned. It was succulent and full of flavor. Ethan had outdone himself. "But if you don't eat your dinner, you don't get dessert."

Alec stared at me, his icy eyes intense, and picked up his wine. After a sip, and another moment of smoldering, he started eating too. I breathed a silent sigh of relief. There was only so much I could do to resist him, and I wanted him in that moment. I wanted him bad. But I'd planned out a whole evening, and I wanted to draw out the anticipation. It was always better with a good dose of anticipation. Tyler had taught me that.

We chatted as we ate, our voices low, the candlelight bathing us in a warm glow. Alec behaved, eating every bite, but he couldn't take his eyes off my breasts, my arms, my face. I did my best to ignore him, but I couldn't take my eyes off him either. The way his scar pulled when he smiled, his tattoos peeking out of the top of his shirt, his strong hand wrapping around the wine glass delicately.

We polished off the entire bottle, and I was loose and a little giggly. Alec looked as good as I felt, and he still hadn't done more than touch my hand. His control was rivaling Tyler's.

After my last sip of wine, I got to my feet. "Time for dessert," I announced and leaned over Alec.

His eyes immediately became hooded and roamed my body. I kissed him, darting my tongue out to taste him. Then as he reached for me, I stood back up and walked to the kitchen, swinging my hips a little more than necessary. I could feel his gaze on my ass, the curve of my back. It made me feel so sexy.

Enjoying the feeling, I leaned down and pulled the honey tarts out of the oven, where Ethan had left them warming. I grabbed the fresh whipped cream from the fridge, plopped a dollop on each plate, and looked directly at Alec as I licked my thumb clean.

Desserts in hand, I sauntered over to him. He was leaning back in the chair, one arm resting on the table and fiddling with a napkin, gaze narrowed.

Suddenly the mood in the room wasn't so light and fun anymore. It was heavier, headier.

I put the plates down and sat in my spot. The fork cut through the tart as if it were air, and I dipped it in cream before bringing it to my mouth. It was sweet, the honey flavor delicate, and it melted in my mouth. I sighed, licked my lips, and had another bite.

The whole time Alec just watched me, still and silent. It was making my skin crawl in the darkest, most delicious way.

"Don't you want any dessert?" I finally asked when I couldn't take it any longer.

He rubbed his hand over his mouth, making a scratching sound against his stubble, then leaned his head on his fist. "Why don't you come over here and feed me some?"

That was an invitation I couldn't reject. With a smile, I got up and sat on his lap, my legs hanging off the side of his thighs. He was hard and not hiding it, but he wasn't moving or touching me yet. He still just sat there, watching me. I ground my ass into his erection as I leaned forward, scooped up a forkful of tart. I brought it to his mouth, and he opened for me, then wrapped his lips around the sweet treat as I pulled the fork back.

He swallowed and licked his lips. "Delicious."

His voice was as decadent as the dessert we were sharing.

I grabbed a bite for myself, then fed him another one. This time, I deliberately dripped some sticky sauce on his bottom lip. It slowly dripped down his chin as he swallowed, not making a move to lick it off. So, I did it for him.

His stubble was scratchy under my tongue as I licked up all the sweetness, then sucked his bottom lip into my mouth.

Finally, Alec moved. He gripped my wrist with one hand and reached the other around my waist to dip his finger in the honey sauce. Holding my arm out, he wiped it in the crook of my elbow, then brought it to his mouth and licked it off. The motion was beyond erotic, his lips on my arm sending tingles through my body straight to my core.

Alec growled and kissed me hard, and I moaned into his mouth, but just as suddenly he pulled away.

"Fuck this," he gritted out and got to his feet, holding me in his arms. He shoved things out of the way to set me on the edge of the table. A wine glass fell and shattered. We didn't pay it any attention. I'd planned to draw this out much, much longer, but as Alec made quick work of his belt, I found myself pulling the sheer material of my dress open, widening my legs. I needed him—now.

Alec shoved his pants and underwear down, and I pulled him closer by his shirt. He lined himself up at my entrance and pushed halfway in. With a moan, he pulled out again, then pushed in all the way. I clung to him and panted as he started moving in fast, frantic, desperate strokes.

He gripped my hair almost painfully, his other hand digging into my ass. I held on to the collar of his shirt, then wrapped an arm around his neck and threw my other hand out behind me for better balance. It landed in one of the plates, which I shoved away to plant my sticky hand on the table, not caring at all about the mess.

My climax was building, about to crash over me at any second. I chased it, grinding my hips forward harder, faster. Alec increased his intensity, and then he was crying out, throwing his head back, the tendons in his neck taut as he spilled inside me. I leaned forward and licked his neck as I kept rolling my hips, but he went still, his grip on my hips stopping me from moving against him.

I made a sound somewhere between a moan and a whimper. I was right there.

He looked at me, breathing hard, his eyes shining in the candlelight, and pulled out. "That's for teasing me."

He stepped back and pulled his pants up as my brain struggled to process the fact that he'd just denied me an orgasm. "What the fu—"

The word melted into a gasp as he leaned down and sucked on my nipple through the sheer fabric, making me arch my back. He gave the other one the same treatment, then looked up at me, smirking.

That asshole.

My brain cleared a little, and I remembered I was supposed to be in charge of this evening. I pushed him back and got to my feet. "I put all this effort into making a special evening for you, and that's how you repay me?" I tutted.

In answer, he grabbed my ass and pulled me flush against him. "I thought we were done with dinner."

"With dinner, yes." I removed his hands from my ass and led him toward the stairs.

"There's more?" He sounded delighted.

"There's always more, Alec," I said as I started climbing.

He stayed behind me, and when I glanced over my shoulder, I saw him staring at my ass.

Our bedroom was practically draped in candlelight. They covered every surface, but I went to the bathroom—which was also lit up with dozens of candles.

The tub was filled with steamy water. Josh had drawn it scalding hot before they left, so by now it would be a perfect temperature.

I turned to Alec and started undressing him. He let me unbutton his shirt and slide it down his arms. He stood still and silent as I removed his pants, underwear, socks, and shoes.

I stepped out of my heels, and he took my hands in his. I looked up into his face and froze. He was looking at me as intensely as ever, but there was something emotional and vulnerable in his gaze, something heavy.

I put my palm to his cheek and frowned.

"Why are you doing this for me?" he asked. "It's not my birthday or anything. It's just a Thursday night."

I smiled. "Because I don't need a special occasion to make you feel special. You guys do things for me every day. Whether it's Ethan making me my favorite food, Josh bringing me coffee when I'm working late, or Tyler knowing I'm in a bad mood before I do and being ready with hugs. And you . . . you've been taking care of me, protecting me, since before I even knew. You all make me feel so loved all the time. I want to take care of you too."

Finally, the heaviness lifted from Alec's eyes, and he blessed me with one of his rare, amazing smiles. I didn't ask what dark place his mind had gone to—I was satisfied that I'd pulled him from it.

"You're amazing, Evie. I'm lucky to have you. We all are." He kissed me reverently, his lips hovering over mine, the Light that flowed between us making me feel as if I were floating on Alec's devotion.

"I'm the lucky one," I said, then took his hand and tugged him toward the bath. "Now. Let me bathe you."

He raised his eyebrows and stepped into the tub. I pulled the stringy straps down my shoulders and let the light fabric cascade down my body before putting my hair up and following him in.

The water was perfect, warm against my skin and fragrant with bath milk and dried rose petals. I sighed and sat back, sinking in to my chin and closing my eyes as my legs tangled with Alec's in the water.

When I opened my eyes a few moments later, I was surprised and delighted to see him doing the same thing on the other end of the tub. His muscular arms were draped on the edges, his head thrown back.

I grabbed a washcloth and reached for his foot. His eyes sprang open, and he sat up, sloshing some water over the edge. "You don't have to do that."

"Just relax." I splashed his chest. "I want to."

"Fine." He sighed and sank back into the water.

I took my time with his glorious body. I wasn't really cleaning him—more like caressing him with the washcloth. Bathing him in my love and care.

Working from the feet up, I washed his legs one at a time, going extra slowly and deliberately up the insides of his thighs. I did his hands and arms, then dipped under the water to do his belly and torso, straddling him to reach. His hands started caressing my body under the water as I washed him, and once again, we were breathing hard, looking at each other through heavy-lidded eyes.

His hands were slick against my breasts, my shoulders, sliding down my back to grip my ass. I was going to burst into flames while soaking wet.

I focused on him instead, moving the washcloth down his chest, over his abs, and wrapping it around the one part of him I'd avoided so far. I dragged that washcloth over every hard, glorious inch of his arousal, making sure to pay some attention to his balls too.

"You're being very thorough," he whispered, his voice husky.

"Mmm," I hummed and gripped him tighter. "You're very dirty."

He chuckled, a low, deep sound that felt as if it reverberated through the water and all over me.

Before I could give in and slip myself onto him, chasing the release I so desperately wanted, I moved to sit behind him. I scrubbed his back, placing kisses to the scars on his shoulders and neck. He rubbed my ankles as I worked, then one of his hands went higher and higher up my leg until he was reaching behind his back. When he slid right between my thighs and buried two fingers inside me, I gasped and dug my fingers into his shoulders.

"You're soaking wet," he said, working his fingers inside me.

"Yeah, well . . ." I dropped the washcloth and leaned my forehead on the back of his head. "We are in a tub full of water."

With excruciating determination, I reached down and removed his hand from between my legs, then got out of the bath.

I dried off and let my hair down while Alec watched me from the tub. Holding out a warm fluffy towel, I gestured for him to get out. He stood up, and as his powerful legs stepped over the edge, water dripped down his body and glistened in the candlelight. I considered throwing all the towels out the window just so I could stand there and watch him dry off slowly.

But I shook my head and ran the towel over every inch of his body, chasing those water droplets all the way down.

"What now, precious?" he asked, smirking. I loved that he was letting me take the lead. I knew he could've batted my hand out of the way in the bath, maneuvered me to wherever he wanted me, and made me come apart in the water if he wanted to. And I would've let him. But I'd planned a whole night for him, and he was letting me see it through.

I took his hand and walked him to our bed. "Now you lie facedown while I have my way with you."

With another chuckle, he did as I instructed.

I grabbed the massage oil from a side table and straddled his hips. Starting at his neck and shoulders, I repeated what I'd done in the bath, caressing every inch of his glorious body right down to his feet. I massaged and rubbed, and Alec groaned from time to time, making me feel that warm rush of satisfaction that something I was doing was making him feel good.

When I was done with his back, I told him to flip onto his front and gave his arms and chest and all the rest of him the same treatment. Once again, I deliberately avoided his groin area—with my hands. It was impossible to ignore with my eyes. He was hard, and it was just sitting there, on his belly, begging to be licked.

I wiped the massage oil off my fingers and reached for the lube. I didn't need it. I was so turned on my thighs were slick, but I wasn't going to do that just yet.

Settling myself at Alec's side, I squeezed a bit of lube into my hand, grabbed his erection at the base, and coated it. I used both hands, stroking him up and down, twisting my hands lightly, changing up the pace. I was giving this one part of his body more attention than I had all the rest of him, really getting into it. He gripped the sheets on either side of his body and started to pant and writhe under me. It was beyond satisfying, and it was turning me on way more than expected, considering neither one of us was touching me.

"Eve," he panted and sat up. "Evie. I want to come inside you."

I slid my hands up his shaft one more time. It felt like warm silk over steel.

"Okay." I sighed and realized I was panting too, ready to have him inside me once again.

He pulled me on top of himself, but instead of letting me lower myself onto him, he jostled and maneuvered me until my thighs were on either side of his head. I barely had time to form a protest before he pulled my hips down and buried his face in my core.

I moaned and threw my head back, gripping the headboard so I wouldn't collapse and smother him. But it was impossible not to move, not to grind myself against his hot mouth, seeking more pleasure.

Alec gripped my ass with one hand and slid the other up my back to help hold me up. We'd been teasing and building for so long now that I felt the scorched edge of my climax coming over me within minutes. It was right there.

"Right there." I moaned, the filter between my mouth and my brain completely pulverized.

But just as I felt myself about to go soaring over the edge, another completely contrasting sensation washed through me, pulling me right back again.

Like the others, Alec had mastered every aspect of his ability. He didn't really have occasion to inflict pain on anyone much anymore, and he used his ability to take people's pain away much more frequently. But he'd also mastered another, more precise element of his talent—he'd figured out exactly where that fine line between pleasure and pain was. He said everyone's threshold was different, but he was so good at it that he could dig down and find exactly where it was. And since he wasn't using it with the intention to harm, he was able to use it on me. In fact, he'd used it on all of us at some point, taking our group sex sessions to some out-of-this-world places.

It was exactly what he was doing to me in that moment—overloading my senses with his ability, pumping just a smidgen more pain through my system than what would've made me come so hard I'd have nearly blacked out. Instead, it chased my orgasm away. Delicate, intense tendrils of pain floated through me in a way that was impossible to describe. There was no physical sensation comparable to what Alec could do to my body with his ability.

I groaned in frustration and smacked the top of his head. "What the fuck, Alec?"

He laughed, the sound literally reverberating through my over-sensitized core. Instead of an answer, he reeled his power in, then angled himself up and somehow managed to flip me onto my back in one smooth move, his hips settling between mine.

He kissed my neck and slowly slid his length inside me. "I love it when you get fired up like that," he whispered, his breath hot on my skin.

But I wasn't fired up anymore. He was inside me, and it felt so fucking good I couldn't have cared less about anything else.

"You're so fucked up," I managed to say as he started to slide in and out.

"So are you, precious," he panted, picking up his pace. "Don't pretend like you don't fucking love it."

His dirty words made me feel even more wild and free, but I remembered that I was supposed to be in charge. I shoved against his chest, and he propped himself up, frowning at me. I shoved him harder until he flopped onto his back. Judging by the amused smile, he'd let me do it.

I didn't care. I climbed on top of him and slid down his slick, hard length, raking my nails down his abs.

Balancing on his chest, with Alec's hands gripping my ass, my hips, my waist, my tits, I rode him hard. We grunted and groaned, staring each other down.

I could feel my climax building once again, but I was determined to push him over the edge first.

"Come inside me, Alec," I demanded. "Come in me, now."

His eyes widened slightly as his mouth fell open on a long moan, and he did exactly as he was told. I slammed down onto him, grinding my hips hard, getting the friction right where I needed it, feeling him deep, deep inside me. And then finally, finally I was coming.

I laughed through my moan as the pleasure crashed through me, so happy to finally fall over that edge, to jump off it, to run off it at full speed. This time, when Alec's pain zinged through me, it did exactly what I needed, heightening my orgasm and making me collapse onto his chest as I made raw, inhuman sounds.

Alec's arms wrapped around me, and we just lay there, breathing chest to chest for a long time. Eventually he tipped my chin up and kissed me, his lips impossibly soft against mine as he caressed my hair. He led me to the bathroom, and we cleaned up together before climbing into bed naked.

We left all the candles burning and cuddled up.

I was spent, and I knew Tyler would know exactly when they could come home, and Ethan would put all the flames out, and Josh would put anything that might spoil back in the fridge.

I was so fucking lucky to have them all.

I must've drifted off, but it didn't feel as if a long time had passed when I felt the bed dip behind me. I was facing Alec, my leg thrown over his, our fingers intertwined on the pillow between us.

The others were silent as they got into bed with us, but they'd obviously gotten the naked memo. A warm, lithe body pressed up against my back, and I smiled. Josh was already hard, his erection pressing into my ass. I didn't need to look over my shoulder to know Ethan was behind him. Right on cue, his big hand wrapped around us both and caressed my breasts.

Tyler reached from behind Alec and found his way to between my legs. Alec was still asleep, but he wouldn't be for long.

It was going to be one of those wild nights.

I'd be late to work tomorrow, but I didn't care. I'd give everything up just to be with them.

STRAWBERRY SEED

Author's note: This takes place several years after the end of Vivid Avowed, and after the events in the other bonus content.

I had to crawl for thirty miles to get to the edge of the giant bed when I woke up on Christmas morning. Some mornings the trek was so daunting I just rolled over and went back to sleep until one of the guys came to drag me out of bed—or my third backup alarm went off. But this morning I'd woken up when Ethan and Alec got up. I'd kept my eyes closed and my breathing even as Josh followed them not long after. I think Tyler knew I was awake, but after a kiss on the forehead, he left me to laze in bed for a bit longer too.

I didn't have lazing in mind though, and the trek to the edge of the bed wasn't so bad when I had a mission to complete—also my bladder was about to burst.

Despite the pressure between my legs, I still took the time to throw back the curtains over the massive balcony windows. It wasn't sunny, but it hadn't snowed yet either. The room filled with soft morning light. Snow was coming; I had smelled it in the air the previous night when Lucian and I sat on the patio off the kitchen. The occasional stiff drink after dinner had become a sort of ritual for us. We'd stare out at the dark yard, sip the smooth alcohol, and talk about Mom or the guys, or we'd just sit in silence.

I'd skipped the liquor the night before, citing an upset tummy, but now that I was finally alone, I let my mind go to the thing I'd been obsessing over and trying to ignore in equal measure for the past few days.

I felt . . . different. Not bad different or sick or anything like that. Something was just . . . not off exactly, but not like anything I'd felt before.

My bladder screamed in protest, and I rushed into the bathroom. No time like the present to either confirm or disprove my suspicion.

I was just going to treat this like a simple science experiment. Follow the instructions and observe the results. No need to get all up in my feelings about it, and certainly no need to get the guys involved unless the results were conclusive.

I had to lean on the sink and take a deep breath, squeezing my legs together to hold it in just a little longer. Once I was sure I wasn't about to pee myself, I opened the drawer under the sink and grabbed one of the countless boxes Ethan had stacked in there.

I ripped it open and dived for the toilet. There was no need to read the pamphlet—I'd memorized it long ago.

There wasn't much to it anyway.

A groan escaped as I finally let my bladder release, soaking the end of the pregnancy test. I put the cap back on it and set it on the counter. Then I thought, What if it's faulty? I forced my stream to stop and reached into the drawer again, awkwardly keeping my ass over the toilet seat as I grabbed another two tests. Three should do it.

I lined the tests up on the counter facedown, determined to ignore them, but it was impossible. I kept side-eyeing them as I brushed my teeth and washed my face and moisturized and brushed my hair. I never brushed my hair until after breakfast!

When all that was done, I had no idea how much time had passed, because I'd forgotten to set the timer. I never forgot steps in an experiment!

With a huff, I backed up against the wall and glared at the little plastic sticks. This was getting to me more than I realized.

The guys and I had talked about having babies over the years. I wasn't sure I wanted any for a long time, plus I wanted to focus on my academic career. But the more time that passed and the more we settled into life together, the more we talked about it, the more I realized I could do both. I loved having a family. I wanted more of that. Plus, there were five of us! It wasn't as if all the parenting would be on me. In fact, I'd made it clear I intended to go back to work as soon as humanly possible. I reserved the right to change my mind at any time, but I just couldn't see myself not doing science for any unspecified period of time.

It wasn't even remotely an issue. Ethan was ready to quit his job, close his three new restaurants, and be a full-time dad. That was how badly he wanted kids. But we'd figured out a better system. Ethan would hire a manager and work one day per week, taking the bulk of the baby-caring responsibility, and Josh would teach one less class and have at least one day at home with the baby. Alec and Ty were a bit less flexible, but we had plenty of support, and it wasn't as if we couldn't hire a nanny.

This was a lot of detail for a baby that didn't even exist yet, but the guys knew my mind needed to have all the information laid out. Even if it all changed the day the baby was born, I felt better having a plan.

So, about a year ago I went off birth control, and we decided to just see what happened. The very next day Ethan went out and bought a stupid amount of pregnancy tests. He checked them regularly and made sure to throw out the ones past their use-by date. I'd used a handful when my period had been late a few times, but I'd never felt like this before—this odd feeling in my body.

Deciding that it must've been more than five minutes already, I walked back to the counter and the pee sticks . . . and just stared at them, chewing my cheek.

What if I was pregnant? Was I really ready for this?

What if I wasn't? I was more bothered by that possibility than I'd expected. Shit, I really wanted a baby with those four fools who had my heart, body, and Light.

This was ridiculous, and I was wasting time. With a huff, I flipped the first test.

Eyes wide, I stared at it for a moment, then quickly flipped the other two. All three had the distinctive extra line—a clear indicator I was knocked up.

The door to the bathroom flew open, and Tyler burst into the room, breathing heavily, eyes wide. I shot up straight and turned to face him, for some reason hiding the pregnancy tests behind my back as if he'd caught me doing something naughty.

His eyes flicked between my face, my stomach, and the plastic sticks on the counter behind me, his face stuck somewhere between shocked and hopeful.

"Did you just run up three flights of stairs?" I asked. His breathing was heavy, and I leaned to the side, half expecting the others to follow him and come rushing into our bathroom too. But there was no one there.

"Did you just do three pregnancy tests?" Tyler asked as his face split into the biggest grin. He already knew I had, and he clearly already knew I was pregnant. We both knew that was why he'd come racing up the stairs.

Excitement bubbled up in my chest, and I couldn't help returning his smile.

"Holy shit!" He laughed.

"Why can't you ever just let me tell you things?" I grumbled. He always knew. My Light was coursing through him, through all of them, so steadily and constantly that Tyler's ability never failed to announce any relevant information before any of us could. He'd long given up pretending he didn't know things. There were no secrets between us anymore.

"Holy shit." He rubbed his hand over his mouth, then rushed forward to grab me and lift me up onto the counter. "Holy shit," he breathed and swallowed, his Adam's apple bobbing. His head was close to mine, his eyes fixed on my stomach as his thumbs rubbed the sides of it.

"You OK?" I asked gently, a bit of insecure nerves taking over my initial joy and excitement. With one hand at the nape of his neck, I brushed the messy bit of hair off his forehead.

He lifted his eyes to mine, the gray practically glowing. "I'm better than OK. We're going to have a baby. I couldn't be happier."

I smiled and released a breath. Despite how adamant they all were that they wanted this, I'd still had a momentary panic this news would not be received well. Completely irrational . . .

"Hey." Ty kissed my lips, so softly and gently I leaned toward him as he pulled back. "We want this. We all do. More than you know. Everything is going to be just fine. I've got you, baby. We all do."

"I love you so much," I whispered around the lump in my throat and pulled him in closer, wrapping my legs around his waist. He held me tightly and kissed me again. It started out as soft and loving as the last one, but it didn't take long for our tongues to get involved. The tender moment was turning into something more heated, needy.

Tyler pulled away first, panting once again. "Stop that," he chided. "I've already put a baby in you. Let's go tell the others."

I hopped off the counter and went into the walk-in to change. Once I had leggings and a white snowflake sweater on, I took Ty's hand.

"So now that the deed is done, there won't be any more sexytimes? I did not sign up for this. This was not in the baby-making terms and conditions," I complained, keeping my voice low as we started to head down the stairs.

"As if any of us could keep our hands off you for more than a few days." Ty chuckled, and we dropped the conversation. I didn't want the others overhearing it. I wanted to tell them properly.

In the kitchen, Tyler went straight to the espresso machine as I tried my best to keep a straight face. I didn't want to wait a second longer to tell them. If Ty knew, they should all know.

I was pretty sure Ethan and Alec had already gotten a workout in, but they'd changed into their Christmas PJs after. Ethan was at the stove, flipping pancakes, in bright red reindeer PJs. Alec was sitting at the island in a black

T-shirt and bottoms, talking to Josh, whose festive attire was closer to mine—plain bottoms and a sweater with Santa wearing sunglasses on it.

I stopped in the doorway to the kitchen for a second and just looked at them. My guys, my family, my Bond. I almost put my hand to my still-flat belly, feeling even more connected to them than ever, but Josh would surely notice that.

He looked over at me and smiled. "Morning, beautiful. Merry Christmas."

They all wished me a Merry Christmas, and Tyler gave me a meaningful look over the rim of his latte. I'd managed to convert them all to espresso, and now they were just as snobby about their coffee as I was. The several trips we'd taken to Australia and Europe over the years had opened their eyes to the wonders of truly good coffee.

I stepped farther into the room and cleared my throat. "Merry Christmas. I have something to tell you."

I sounded nervous even to my own ears. Three sets of suddenly worried eyes focused on me while Ty took a sip of his coffee, turning away from the others.

"You already know!" Josh pointed an accusing finger at him.

Ty held his hands up, keeping his mouth shut.

"So fucking unfair. I wanna be the first to know something," Ethan grumbled before flipping the last pancake onto a massive stack and turning off the stove.

"Evie." Alec's intense stare demanded my attention. Some things never changed. "What is it?"

"Well . . . uh . . ." Just spit it out, Evelyn. "I'm pregnant."

Silence and blank stares stretched on so long that I nearly walked forward to poke one of them to check if they were all right. Then Ethan whooped. He punched the air with his massive fist, throwing out a burst of fire. The fire evaporated before it could do any damage.

"I'm gonna be a daddy?" He laughed, his face lighting up brighter than the twenty-foot Christmas tree in the foyer. He ran at me, wrapped his arms around me, and spun me around, making me laugh. Once he set me back on my feet, he dropped to his knees and pressed a hand to my belly, his other hand resting on my hip.

I smiled and ran my hand through his soft black hair.

He stared at my stomach in awe and whispered: "Fruit of my loins."

I burst out laughing, as did Tyler and Josh. Alec was still sitting at the island, silent and staring, but before I could worry about him too much, Josh shoved Ethan out of the way and wrapped me up in one of his tight hugs. He rocked me from side to side, kissing my cheeks, my eyes, my nose, smiling in between, his eyes glassy.

"You don't know that." Tyler gently shoved Ethan as he got to his feet. "It could be any one of our loins that this fruit has come from."

A tiny gust of wind disturbed the hair at the back of my head, and I knew Josh had just fetched something from another part of the house with his ability. He leaned back to look at me, keeping one hand around my waist and holding up something between us with the other.

"Um . . . I hope you don't mind." He looked sheepish but excited as he handed me a small piece of cloth.

It was the tiniest little onesie I'd ever seen, and it was covered in little double helixes. My whole heart melted. In a little while, a tiny little human would be in that tiny little onesie. Our tiny little human. Our baby.

Holy shit, I'm going to be a mother!

Instead of letting my mind follow that spiral of anxiety, I made myself focus on this wonderful moment with my Bond.

"When did you get this?" I asked, my throat a little tight.

"Months ago." Josh shrugged. "I know nothing was certain, but I saw it and I couldn't help myself."

"I love it so much!" I wrapped my arms around him and gave him a big, lingering kiss, both of us smiling through it like fools.

When I pulled away from Josh, Tyler was standing on the opposite side of the island from Alec—who still hadn't moved or even blinked. Ty reached out a hand and snapped his fingers in front of Alec's face a few times.

Alec shook his head and frowned at Tyler before turning to look at me.

"You OK, Alec?" I asked, coming toward him.

"This house is massive," he said.

I frowned and shared a look with the others. "OK. Um, did you hear what I said about . . ." I gestured vaguely to my womb.

He glanced down at my belly, then got to his feet, running his hands over his buzzed hair. He hadn't worked for Melior Group in years, but he'd kept the short hair. I was glad—I liked how it prickled on my palm when I ran my hand over it.

"It's going to take forever to babyproof everything. I'd better start now." Alec rushed forward, heading past me.

I grabbed his arm with both hands. "Whoa there! Calm down."

It wasn't my grip on his arm so much as Ethan blocking his way that made Alec stop. I made him look at me, my hands on either side of his face. "What's going on in that thick head of yours? Did you change your mind? Do you not want . . ."

A baby. With me. Our baby.

Out of all of us, Alec and I had been the most reluctant to have kids. I hadn't been sure I wanted any, and Alec was convinced he wasn't father material. Ethan had wanted to be a dad since I could remember, and Josh and Tyler had started talking about it more and more the longer we built our life together.

Alec and I had come a long way—we all had—but every once in a while, I got insecure. His resistance and rejection at the beginning of our relationship had left scars, and sometimes they bled a little. I didn't want to question his commitment, but sometimes my stupid brain just went there anyway.

Finally, his beautiful ice-blue eyes sharpened, and his hands wrapped around my neck as his thumbs started to stroke my jaw. "Evie, put that out of your mind. I want this. I want you. I want whatever life throws at us. I'm just . . . what if we fuck this kid up? What if the world goes to shit, and we all die and—"

"Stop." I pulled his head down until our foreheads were touching. "I get it. I can't tell you how many horrific scenarios went through my head when I first realized. But there's five of us, and we're strong together. We're stable and full of love, and we're going to give this baby every possible chance at a happy life. There's no point worrying about things we can't control."

After a long moment he sighed and pulled me against him. I let him hold me for as long as he needed. This definitely wasn't the end of the conversation. Alec's fears would surely come up again, just as mine would, just as the other guys' surely would too. But we would deal with it together. Alec wasn't running away from me anymore, and that was all I could ask.

"All right! Pancakes!" Ethan clapped his hands together loudly. Alec finally let me go, and we all settled ourselves at the dining table.

"Did someone say pancakes?" Lucian wheeled himself into the room, wearing an old-fashioned sleep shirt, robe, and slippers, with a sleep cap on his head. He liked to read Dickens's A Christmas Carol every year and had taken the theme into his sleepwear. Josh had been joining him in the yearly reading since before we met, the two of them sharing their love of books through a Christmas tradition. Even though I wasn't much of a fiction reader, I'd joined in too. This year, even Tyler had sat with us for the past few nights as we read the classic in the formal living room with the fire roaring. Next year I planned to get a good audiobook version and rope Ethan into it too. Alec would join because he'd hate being left out. There was no making Alec do anything—I had to cajole him gently, let it be his own idea.

Lucian wheeled his chair into his usual spot at the head of the table and smiled at everyone. "Merry Christmas."

A chorus of joyous wishes rang out around the table, and we all got up to embrace the only father figure any of us had. We settled into our seats and dug into the fluffy, sweet breakfast treats, passing around the condiments and jugs of OJ.

"Christmas pancakes are the best," Josh said as he shoved a massive forkful of them into his mouth, a bit of maple syrup dripping down his full bottom lip.

"And they're celebration pancakes this year too. Double the yum!" Ethan was fully focused on serving himself his third helping and didn't even notice the rest of us had gone silent. I glared at him until he realized no one was saying anything and looked up, frowning. His eyes found my narrowed gaze, and he cringed. The other guys were silently eating their breakfast, avoiding Lucian's questioning looks.

"What am I missing here?" Lucian set his cutlery down and sat up straight. He may have retired from Melior Group, but he was still the smartest, most astute person I knew.

I gave him a smile. "I wasn't going to tell anyone else for a little while, but you do live here, so you'll probably figure it out anyway. I'm pregnant."

Lucian's eyes lit up, and the biggest smile I'd ever seen on the distinguished man's face appeared. "Wonderful news! Congratulations! All of you. Oh, this makes me so happy."

With the tension broken, everyone went back to being boisterous and giddy as Lucian hugged us all again.

I took a sip of juice, already missing my coffee, and gestured for everyone to calm down. "Seriously though, none of you can tell anyone just yet. I have no idea how far along I am. It can't be more than a few weeks. Eighty percent of miscarriages occur in the first trimester. So keep a lid on it." I pointed at them all around the table, and they all looked appropriately chastised.

"How do we find out how far along you are?" Alec asked.

"I'll need to book an appointment with a doctor." I smiled to myself. All four of them would want to come to every appointment—which was going to make for a spectacle.

"Of course." Josh nodded. "Only the best care for my little bun and my baby mama. But also . . ." He looked at Tyler and raised his eyebrows.

Ty smiled and leaned back in his chair. "You're five weeks and three days along, Eve."

Of course he knew!

Ethan whipped his phone out and tapped at it while shoveling more pancakes into his mouth. He swallowed, then turned the screen to us all. "At five weeks the embryo is the size of a strawberry seed. My little strawberry-boo," he cooed in the general direction of my belly.

Lucian had been quiet during this excitement, and when I turned to him, I found him watching me with a sad smile. I knew that look. I'd seen that smile countless times. He was thinking about my mom.

I reached a hand out, and he took it, squeezing my fingers firmly.

"She'd be so proud of you. So happy," he said, his eyes misty.

Immediately, my throat tightened, and my own eyes began to sting.

This bittersweet feeling had come rushing up at every major moment of my life over the years since I'd lost her.

The pain of not being able to share life with my mom was sharp, but it was dulled by Lucian every single time. He loved and missed her just as much as I did. Having him be a part of my life—having someone who knew her as well as I did, who knew what she'd be thinking and feeling—was comforting in a way I struggled to articulate. Joyce Maynard lived on in my heart and Lucian's—in these bittersweet moments we shared.

I cleared my throat past the lump and gave him a watery smile. "She would've screamed the house down with excitement."

We both laughed through the aching grief, wiping at our stray tears.

"She would've been an amazing grandma." Lucian chuckled.

"Hah!" I rolled my eyes. "Yes, but she would've been trouble. I have a feeling she would've spoiled this baby rotten—given it all the things I couldn't have growing up."

"We'll make sure our baby knows what an amazing woman her grandma was." Alec smiled, and the others nodded in agreement.

My heart swelled, feeling as if it were too big for my ribcage, ready to burst with all the love I had for these amazing men in my life.

Once we were all stuffed to bursting with pancakes, we moved into the living room and sat around the glowing Christmas tree. There were about a dozen trees in the house, professionally decorated and matching the other extravagant seasonal decorations. But the one in the family room we decorated ourselves, with old ornaments that had sentimental value, while Lucian got drunk on eggnog and told us inappropriate stories about our parents.

That was the tree we put all our gifts under, and that was the tree we made a massive mess around as we opened them all, taking our time to ooh and ahh and laugh and thank one another. It was nearly midday by the time we got our butts off the comfy couches.

Ethan started working on that evening's meal. He'd done much of the prep during the previous few days, but there was still a lot of work to do to feed our massive family. I'd offered to chop things, but the only person he'd allow close to his perfect Christmas feast was Aunt Olivia.

The rest of us tidied up the mess from the presents, set the table for dinner, and just hung out or read or chatted with Ethan while he cooked. It was the perfect, most relaxing Christmas.

Throughout the day all the guys had taken to placing their hands over my flat belly and smiling like goofs. I was setting out the last of the cutlery on the dining table when Tyler came up behind me and rubbed my stomach for the third time that day.

I rolled my eyes and had to hide the smile before turning around to face him. "You guys have to stop." I looked around him and raised my voice so the others would hear. "You all have to stop this obsession with my midriff before everyone gets here."

Their response was a series of noncommittal mumbles and avoidance of eye contact. I shook my head and used the sound of the doorbell as an excuse to walk out of the room for a few moments.

Aunt Olivia and Uncle Henry were the first to arrive around midafternoon. After tight hugs and warm Christmas wishes, Olivia planted herself in the kitchen next to Ethan, and Henry joined Lucian in the living room with a glass of brandy in hand.

About an hour later Charlie and Ed arrived, and I put out a cheese board.

"Don't fill up too much on the cheese and crackers!" Olivia called from the kitchen. "Leave room for this feast."

"I wouldn't worry about it, Auntie Olivia. Most of us haven't eaten since breakfast." Alec grinned at her and stuffed a massive piece of brie on a paper-thin cracker into his mouth. A chorus of agreement went up around the room. Everyone looked forward to Ethan's feasts.

"Mulled wine is ready." Ethan placed the steaming pot on a trivet on the island, and I jumped forward to grab the ladle.

"Who wants some?" I held the ladle up. I figured if I was the one serving it, no one would notice I wasn't drinking it. I freaking loved mulled wine.

"How's your family, Ed?" I asked and handed him a steaming glass.

"Good." He smiled as Charlie wrapped an arm around his shoulders. "We are leaving in two days to spend the New Year Eve with them."

"We're going to tell them the news in person," Charlie added.

"Any updates on that?" I asked.

"Not yet. But it's only been a few months," Charlie said, glancing at the mulled wine. He was almost as observant as Josh. I wondered briefly if I should just pour myself a glass and pretend to drink it.

"I hope we get a boy." Ed smiled wistfully. "Actually, no, I want a girl."

Charlie chuckled and shook his head. "He keeps doing this—swinging between wanting a boy and a girl—when he knows we'll be ecstatic with whatever child we have the privilege to raise."

Ed and Charlie had completed the lengthy process of applying to adopt and had been approved just a few months ago. Now they were waiting—a process that could take months, even years. Maybe they'd get a baby around the same time we got ours.

Before I could get choked up thinking about it, Dot and her family arrived, significantly increasing the level of noise and energy in the room.

Jamie and Nina had started school this year, and they looked adorable in their matching Christmas outfits. Marcus ran in and gave everyone a hug while Kyo carried Nina in on one arm, his free hand holding his phone to his ear. Running Melior Group was a demanding job, but he was always here for the important things, and Lucian was always ready to provide advice and support.

Marcus was weighed down by bags of gifts and the twins' stuff, which he dumped unceremoniously in a corner of the room.

Everyone gave them hugs and kisses hello, and I shoved a glass of mulled wine into Dot's hands as soon as she released me from her hug.

She chugged half of it down before taking a deep breath. "I love my kids, but fuck are they high maintenance sometimes. Even more than my boys."

"Hey! I heard that!" Marcus pointed at her from across the room, and Dot stuck her tongue out at him. Kyo was off the phone and handing Nina over to Grandpa Henry.

Dot turned to Charlie. "Juice me up."

"I saw you, like, two days ago. How did you—"

"Never mind!" Dot cut him off. "This is important."

Charlie rolled his eyes and swung his hand toward Dot's face, but she grabbed his wrist and leaned out of the way.

"I just put makeup on, you jerkface." She whacked him in the stomach with her free hand and held his hand in hers to get the Light she was demanding.

Dot was working as a vet in Bradford Hills. She specialized in complex cases—the ones other vets struggled to diagnose. Her ability gave her an edge.

"What's this about?" I asked.

Dot smiled innocently, which was always a bad thing. "Squiggles was trying to tell me something earlier today, but I just couldn't make it out. I'd drained myself last night getting the birds to sing the twins to sleep. They were too excited about Santa."

I narrowed my eyes.

Dot dropped Charlie's hand and smiled at me. A moment later Squiggles came running up and settled herself on Dot's shoulder.

I pointed a finger at them both. "That mouthy little hairy noodle better not be talking shit about me again."

Dot's eyes widened, and she stared at Squiggles for a moment before turning to me with a massive grin.

"Dot." I raised my brows and gave her my best reproachful tone.

My best friend squealed with excitement and started jumping up and down, sloshing her mulled wine. Ed took it from her and placed it gently on the counter.

I sighed. I hadn't even managed to keep it a secret for one full day. "Can I have no damn privacy in this family?"

Dot's antics had gotten everyone's attention, and they all answered loudly, and way more amused than they should have been: "No!"

Josh appeared next to me, his hand at the small of my back grounding and calming me. A warm hand wrapped around mine, and I found Alec on my other side. Suddenly my Bond were all standing with me, surrounding me with love and support.

"It's better if we tell them before Dot does," Tyler said, giving me an encouraging smile. Dot looked about ready to explode with the knowledge.

"OK, fine." I sighed but couldn't help smiling too. They were loud and pushy and sometimes had no boundaries, but these people were my family. They'd absorbed me into their orbit, and I'd be lying if I said I didn't like it. I nodded at Ethan, who looked as desperate to say something as Dot did.

"We're having a baby!" Ethan's booming voice filled the silent room as Josh placed a conspicuous hand over my belly.

Olivia started crying, pulling me into a massive hug, and the room burst into excited, joyous chatter as everyone hugged and congratulated us.

We settled around the massive dining table not long after, dish after glorious dish lining the length of it, and the noise in the room got a little higher as everyone passed the food around.

There was so much laughter and noise and love at that table. It was the complete opposite of what I'd grown up with, and for a while it had made me feel overwhelmed. It didn't anymore. This was exactly where I belonged—with my Bond and my family.

NOTE FROM THE AUTHOR

Thank you so much for reading The Evelyn Maynard Trilogy and all that bonus content! I really hope you enjoyed it and you'll consider leaving a review. As an indie author, reviews make a massive difference when it comes to my book reaching other readers. Even a sentence or two helps!

ACKNOWLEDGEMENTS

First and foremost, thank you to my readers. To every single person who's read Evelyn's story – whether you were one of the first ones, or you just found it recently – *thank you*. When I first hit publish on Variant Lost I didn't expect it to have anywhere near the kind of success it's had and is still having. Never in my wildest dreams did I think I could quit my day-job and be a full-time author within a *year* of publishing my first book, let alone a few *months*! I couldn't have done it without the love of my friends and family; without my husband John's unwavering belief in me; without my beta readers and my ARC team; without my talented editor and cover designer; without the incredible, strong women in this industry who have supported me. I could not have done it without all the readers brave enough to give my story a try. I'm living my dream and I will forever be thankful for that!

ABOUT THE AUTHOR

Kaydence Snow has lived all over the world but ended up settled in Melbourne, Australia. She lives near the beach with her husband and a beagle that has about as much attitude as her human.

She draws inspiration from her own overthinking, sometimes frightening imagination, and everything that makes life interesting – complicated relationships, unexpected twists, new experiences and good food and coffee. Life is not worth living without good food and coffee!

She believes sarcasm is the highest form of wit and has the vocabulary of a highly educated, well-read sailor. When she's not writing, thinking about writing, planning when she can write next, or reading other people's writing, she loves to travel and learn new things.

ALSO BY KAYDENCE SNOW

<u>The Evelyn Maynard Trilogy</u>
Variant Lost
Vital Found
Vivid Avowed

<u>Devilbend Dynasty</u>
Like You Care
Like You Hurt
Like You Should (coming 2021)
Like You Know (coming 2021)

<u>Standalones</u>
Just Be Her
It Started With A Sleigh